HENRY PORTER
Three Great Novels

Also by Henry Porter

Brandenburg

Henry Porter

Three Great Novels

Remembrance Day
A Spy's Life
Empire State

ORION

Remembrance Day Copyright © 1999 Henry Porter
A Spy's Life Copyright © 2001 Henry Porter
Empire State Copyright © 2003 Henry Porter

1   3 5 7 9 10 8 6 4 2

This omnibus edition first published in Great Britain in 2005 by Orion
an imprint of the Orion Publishing Group

A CIP catalogue record for this book is available
from the British Library

ISBN 0 75286 734 2

Typeset by Deltatype Ltd, Birkenhead, Merseyside

Printed and bound in Great Britain by
Clays Ltd, St Ives plc

The Orion Publishing Group Ltd
Orion House
5 Upper Saint Martin's Lane
London, WC2H 9EA

Contents

Remembrance Day

To my parents and brother

Author's Note

I would not have written this book without the help of Liz Elliot and Gilbert Adair, both of whom devoted much time to encouraging me. My editor, Jane Wood, and agent, Georgina Capel, are also owed debts of gratitude for having confidence in the book and – in the most delicate way possible – telling me where I was going wrong. I was lucky to meet Joseph I. Mulligan III, my tireless guide in Boston, and Kenny Young of the Ritz Carlton Hotel, Boston, whose conversation inspired a crucial idea in the plot. Professor Roy Anderson, Dr Alison Snape, Ed Ross, Manish Somani and Tom Standage were all generous with their expertise.

Finally, thanks to Riva Mantis who knows everything.

1

He knew where he had been standing. He knew what he had been thinking before that moment. He had been thinking that he'd like to speak to the girl in the short dress and tunic, a few yards from him on the pavement. She was swinging a small backpack against her thigh impatiently. She was waiting for someone too. He smiled at her but only managed a smirk, not the look of solidarity that he'd intended, which said, 'We've both been stood up.' She ignored him and moved towards the entrance of the tube station and made a great show of peering down the stairs. A breeze came up from the underground and lifted her dress. This seemed to annoy her. She slapped it down, brushing it as if it were covered in dust, then retreated out of the draught to stand by a curved glass recess at the front of an airline office.

Con Lindow remembered thinking that the evening was warm for October, like a late summer day in Boston. He strolled away to show that he was not trying to pick her up. He went twenty paces or so, then wheeled round back towards the station. There was a lull in the traffic and he began wondering why Eamonn was late, and exactly how they would spend the evening when he arrived. Eamonn had been vague on the phone. Said they'd have a few drinks and then go on to a Latin-American place somewhere north of Oxford Street. It hadn't sounded promising, but Lindow would be pleased to see him again. He imagined Eamonn shambling up from the tube station, a book and a newspaper under his arm, laughing ruefully at his lateness and then turning it so that Lindow would feel a prick for being so punctual. It was two years since their mother had been overwhelmed by cancer and taken before any of them had realised she was ill. That was the last time they had met. Lindow saw the funeral – Eamonn's wounded face in the procession of mourners that signifies a great Irish occasion.

A bus turned into Clarence Street and slowed to negotiate a traffic island. Lindow looked at it and idly wondered if his brother was on board. He guessed not because Eamonn had said he'd be coming straight from work by underground so he wouldn't have to worry about the traffic. He'd be there by seven fifteen for sure. He was definite about that, but you never knew. He might meet someone and forget the arrangement. No, Lindow reassured himself, he would come because they hadn't seen each other for so long, and it had been Eamonn who'd been pressing for them to get together. He'd be there soon enough. Lindow looked at the bus and glanced down at his watch. He remembered doing that.

It was seven thirty-five when the street exploded.

Lindow was lifted clean off his feet and hurled into a metal bollard, which smacked him on the back of his neck. He was knocked out, but only for a few seconds, and came to to find that his world had been extinguished. He couldn't see. He lay utterly still, hearing the sounds that fill the first moments after an explosion. Glass loosened by the shockwave was crashing around him, stabbing his legs, and somewhere along the street there was a terrifying roar, as if a furnace door had been opened. Alarms shrieked. People cried out with the awful recognition of what had happened to them. Lindow had one thought: he must shield himself from the glass still falling from the buildings above. He tried to move his right hand, but it was held by something heavy. He shifted a little and freed his left arm, which was locked behind his back in a half-nelson, then wrapped it across his face. But it wasn't his face. Then he understood. He hadn't been blinded at all, but something – some cloth – had fallen over his face and covered his eyes. He pulled at the material and found himself looking up. It was dark and the air was filled with smoke and dust. In the night sky quantities of paper flew on the thermals from the fire. He understood now that it had been a bomb and somehow knew it was the bus that had exploded, although he hadn't actually seen the explosion and couldn't see the bus because he was facing the other way. Then the pain came, coursing from the back of his skull to his forehead and down into his eyes. He squeezed them tight and felt his stomach heave. He was going to be sick. He had to get up, had to get away. He turned his head from the bollard and checked through an inventory of his senses. He wiggled his toes: they moved. He felt his chest gingerly with his fingertips, like a blind man reading Braille, and progressed down to his stomach and groin where there was a horrible sensation of dampness. He reached the belt of his trousers, and touched a viscous mess. Christ, he thought, the explosion had opened his stomach. He knew injuries like this confused the nervous system, knew that his brain would not make sense of the wounds for a few moments: people got out of car crashes with injuries like this, walked a few paces, then fell down dead. These would be his last conscious seconds. This was it – everything he so desperately wanted to do, the things that he thought only he could do, would never be accomplished. He readied himself for the final convulsions. Nothing came. Then he dabbed again at his stomach, probing a little deeper into the mess. There was no pain at all and – bafflingly – no wound either.

He heard a groan, a thick, guttural word he couldn't make out. It was a woman's voice. She had fallen across him, pinning his right side to the ground. Her tunic had flown up and covered his face, which was why he had the smell of perfume in his nostrils. Her head was very close to his, and very still.

'You hurt?' he said, and shifted his body so that she slid from him on to the stone and let out another groan.

'You hurt?' he repeated stupidly. He knew then that the blood pooled on his stomach was not his but the woman's, and that she must be very badly injured indeed.

He moved again, lifted his head and strained to look at her. It was the girl he had been watching by the tube entrance. He sat up, propping himself against the bollard, and with his right hand reached over to draw back the hair glued to her face. There was an earphone, which had come detached from the tape-player. He pulled away and looked at her face, saw a mass of blood on the right side with white flecks glinting in it. He thought he'd wipe it for her – then he understood that there was nothing behind the blood. No face. What he was seeing were her teeth, moving as the girl tried to cry out. Further down her body the dress was stained and shone wet in the light that still came from far inside the airline office. Beneath her ribcage was a very dark patch. He squirmed and tried to call out, but his voice had gone. He coughed and then shouted again, hoarsely. No one came.

He looked about him. Down the street, about seventy yards from where he lay, the bus was on fire. He could feel the heat on his face. Flames shot from the engine and heavy black smoke spilled from the windows. Between the billows of smoke he could make out a rupture along the flank of the bus. The rear of the vehicle had slewed round at the moment of explosion and mounted the traffic island in the centre of the road. Other cars had simply stopped in their tracks and a black cab, which had been following the bus, stood with its bonnet blown open and its front tyres on fire. Around the bus there were smaller fires. Wastebins and the plastic fittings of traffic-lights had ignited from the heat; bits of panelling, blown from the sides of the bus and now edged with ribbons of flame, lay in the road. He watched with astonishment as a figure ran towards the bus, vanished into the smoke at the front, then reappeared dragging something.

He couldn't remember how crowded the street had been before the bus came on the scene. He knew that a party of tourists had been filing through the stone arcade that straddled the pavement up to the corner where the bus was. Maybe they cleared it in time. He couldn't tell because of the curtain of smoke. Nearer to him – just beyond the station – what he had taken for a pile of rubbish moved. An arm emerged from the debris and waved in the smoke; a cyclist, whom Lindow had passed as he walked away from the girl minutes before, was standing up and straightening his helmet. Nearer still a man, whom Lindow recognised as the news vendor from outside the tube station, was crawling towards them. He stopped to rest on his elbows, looked down at his hands, then felt in his jacket for something.

Lindow shouted, 'Don't go any further, you'll cut yourself.' He was having difficulty finding his voice.

The man took no notice. He reached over to one of the bundles of newspapers and with a pocket knife slashed at the string that held it together, letting the newspapers sprawl over the pavement. Then, chucking the newspapers ahead of him, he made a path over the glass to where Lindow and the girl lay.

'Is she hurt bad?' he cried, as he shuffled towards them.

'Yes, I think so.' Lindow had cupped his right hand to hold her head so as to avoid touching her wounded face. The girl was moving in and out of consciousness, her jaw working in a slow, chewing motion.

'It's her head and stomach.'

'Oh, God, look at the state of her,' said the man, collapsing beside them. 'Where are the ambulances?'

Lindow saw the man's leg was sticking out at an odd angle just below the knee. He guessed it was dislocated, or that the tibia had been shattered. The man rolled over on his back. Then he did something extraordinary. He slid a hand inside his trousers and worked away at something, revolving his hips as he did so. Finally he shook his leg and it came off. It took Lindow several seconds to understand that this was an artificial limb.

The news vendor pushed himself up a little and looked down at his good leg. Lindow saw that the trousers had been shredded. There was a lot of blood.

'Jesus, I can't lose that one too. Bastard, bastard bomb!' he said, choking in a little tide of smoke that had crept to where they lay.

Minutes passed. No one came. But people were moving about, shouting for help and trying to find each other. Lindow decided that it was no use trying to move the girl. Better to sit there with her. He leaned back on the bollard and put his left hand down to give himself support. He felt something soft and warm in his palm. Without thinking, he picked it up. It was a bird, a starling that had fallen stone dead from its perch above them, killed instantly by the shockwave or a splinter of glass. As he dropped it on the pavement, a line he'd once read came to him. 'So easy and swift is the passage between life and death in wild nature.'

He wondered if the girl would make that passage. He looked at her again. She probably wouldn't. With her face like that, maybe it was better that she didn't.

Someone ran up to them. It was a cycle messenger, speaking into a radio strapped to him in a shoulder holster. He was radioing details of the injured and dying to his control.

'There are three here,' he shouted. 'Three, yes. That makes at least five seriously injured that I've seen. Yeah, they'll need blood . . . I'm looking at a woman. She's very badly hurt. And a man with a broken leg. Everyone's cut and bleeding. It's a fucking mess, I tell you.'

He said nothing to them and ran off across the street. Then a policewoman came and crouched between the news vendor and the girl. She was white-faced and on the edge of panic. She touched the girl's clotted hair with the back of her hand.

'Do you know her? What's her name?' she asked, her voice high and uneven.

'No,' replied Lindow.

'I don't know her name,' said the news vendor. 'But mine's Harry Ribb. Can someone phone my wife and say I'm all right? She'll know I'm here right in the middle of it when she sees the news. She knows where my stand is, see.'

The policewoman did not hear him. She said to Lindow, 'Stay here with her. Try to keep her conscious. Have you got something to cover her with? I've left my coat with a man over there.'

Lindow said that she could have his jacket. The policewoman held his shoulders as he leaned forward and helped him pull it off.

'You've got a nasty gash there,' she said, looking at the blood on his collar.

They placed his jacket over the girl. The policewoman got up and glanced at Lindow. Her lower lip was trembling. She turned her head away and sucked in air, frowning with effort. The sinews in her neck were working furiously. She was fighting to control herself. 'There's help coming,' she said, and hurried away with one hand clutching her belt to stop her night stick and radio flapping.

The alarms in the street seemed to have synchronised into a single pulse. Now that Lindow knew he wasn't badly hurt, he focused on the girl, leaned down and talked to her about anything that came into his head. He told her about Boston and the campus at MIT, about skiing in Vermont and how in the summer his laboratory became so hot that he had once opened one of the lab fridges and moved a desk into the doorway. He ran on, not knowing whether she heard any of it. At one stage she became totally still and he thought she had died. Then a fuel tank exploded down the street and he felt her stiffen. He bent down to her face and asked her name. A murmur came but he couldn't make out what she said. Harry Ribb looked up and drubbed a fist slowly on the pavement.

Some way behind them Lindow could hear the first ambulance make its way through the stalled traffic. He strained round to see it pull up in the middle of the road and two men get out. They ran over to a policeman, who gesticulated rapidly, showing them where the injured lay. Other people were staggering about the street now, all of them streaming with blood. Lindow shouted and waved to them, but they took no notice. At length one of the ambulancemen came to them, sliding and crunching on the scree of glass.

'You must help this woman!' demanded Lindow. 'She needs help now.'

The man ran a flashlight up and down the girl's body, then scribbled something on a clipboard. 'I'm sorry, sir. You're just going to have to bear with us. We're the first here, you see. We have to report back to Headquarters. Give them an idea of the scale of this thing.'

Lindow's temper snapped. 'Look, while you're making your goddam lists she could die. She's bleeding inside. Look at her. Look at her, man!'

'I hear you,' said the crewman coolly. 'But we have to do it this way. She'll be the first to be seen when the other crews arrive, I promise you that. They won't be long now. Stay here and keep her calm. It won't be long.'

He hurried away to another group where a woman was rocking over a body in the street, sending screams to the sky. Lindow was aware of a bright light tacking across the pavement. He looked round to his right to see a news cameraman who'd come from somewhere behind and was panning his camera from the wreck of the bus on to him and the girl.

'Get the fuck out of here!' Lindow screamed. 'Can't you see what's happened to her?'

He raised his arm to protect the girl's eyes from the camera's light. But he knew in an instant that the pictures could never be shown. The light spilled across her face and body and left nothing to the imagination. No station would use it because somewhere out there her parents would see it before they even knew she was hurt.

The light dimmed and the cameraman jerked back, unplugging himself from the eyepiece. 'I'm sorry,' he said, swinging the camera down from his shoulder. He walked away, shaking his head.

'Jackal – fucking jackal,' growled Harry, from the pavement.

Lindow decided that he must do something for the girl. They might wait all night before anyone came. He pushed himself against the bollard. His legs were stiff and cold, and they hurt like hell.

'Can you support her?' he said to Harry. 'I'm going to get help. She won't last otherwise.'

Harry moved around a little, dragging his artificial limb with him. Then Lindow eased the girl's weight slowly on to Harry's big belly. Her head flopped sideways. As Harry looked down at her, Lindow saw that his eyes had watered up and that tiny fragments of glass shrapnel glinted from the cuts in his forehead.

He stood up shakily and looked about. There were several ambulances now. A white Volvo estate car with a green flashing light had just pulled up at the front rank of emergency vehicles and was disgorging what he knew must be a medical team. The street had become cold. It was beginning to rain and the team were hurriedly putting on waterproofs. He tried to run to them but something stopped him. He looked down at his left leg and saw a piece of glass protruding from the outside of his thigh. Each time he put his leg forward the material of his corduroys snagged on it, causing it to work itself deeper into the wound. Without thinking, he reached down and pulled it from his leg like a thorn and flung it into the gutter. Then he ran to the Volvo.

'Are you a doctor?' he shouted, over the noise of the sirens and alarms.

'Yes,' the nearest man shouted back. 'Is it for you?'

'No, for a woman over here,' said Lindow. 'She's in a very bad state.'

The doctor saw Lindow's face in the flashing light and understood that he had to go. He told one of the nurses to accompany him and signalled to the others that they should follow with the ambulances moving up the street towards the bus and the victims lying on the opposite side.

'We shouldn't be here,' he said, as they clattered over the glass to Harry and the girl. 'The area isn't secured yet. The police say there could be other bombs. They don't know – no warnings.'

When they reached Harry, he was talking to the girl with a slow insistence about his garden and how the rain that was now falling had come too late to do any good. But there was always next year, he said, and he'd have another crack at the flower show, which he hadn't entered because of the drought.

The doctor handed Lindow a torch and told him to hold it high up so that he could see the girl as well as his bag. He was in his early thirties – Lindow's age, but with a heavier build, like a rugby player.

'Now let's have a look here, shall we?' He peered at her face then lifted Lindow's jacket to look at her stomach.

'What's her name?' he said, moving his head from side to side. 'Hold the torch over here, man. Here!' He pointed to the place with the finger of his surgical glove. Then he lifted the dress and got very close to the gash below her ribcage. 'What did you say her name was?'

The girl tried to speak.

'I think it's Kay,' said Harry. 'She was saying something like that just now.'

'Right, Kay. We're going to have you in hospital in no time at all. I want to examine you a little more and then I'm going to give you something to ease the pain. Okey-dokey? Good. You're going to be fine.' His expression said otherwise. 'Hold on there, Kay.'

A nurse arrived and set up a light, then a fragile stand on which she hung a container of fluid.

'We need to get a line into her,' said the doctor, 'and we'll give her a shot of morphine straight away.'

The nurse held a syringe up to the light, pressed the plunger until the liquid spurted out and gave it to the doctor. Still squatting, he manoeuvred to the girl's left side, felt for her buttock and rubbed it vigorously. He eased the syringe into the flesh and waited for a few seconds while it emptied. His eyes met Lindow's.

'What *do* they think they are doing?' he said quietly. 'What's she ever done?'

Almost immediately the girl relaxed and her head fell back into the crook of Harry's arm. Harry braced it with his free hand and looked away. He couldn't take the sight of her face.

The nurse inserted the drip of Hartman's blood substitute into the girl's right arm, then attached leads from the ECG to an area clear of laceration just above her right breast. The girl was breathing regularly, but the doctor looked worried. He leaned down close to her face. 'Kay, we're going to move you very soon. Hang on there.'

He stepped away and spoke to the nurse. 'Her liver may be pretty badly damaged. She's bleeding inside and there's a lot of glass in her. Get David Peretz on the phone and tell him I'm sending her to him. Explain her injuries. I'm going to get one of those ambulances.'

The nurse pulled the hood of her waterproof over her head and stood up. The rain was coming down hard now. Lindow shivered. She jabbed the number of the hospital on the mobile phone and put it to her ear inside the hood.

'Can you do this for me?' she shouted to Lindow. 'You don't need the number. Just keep pressing redial. I'll get these bandages on her.'

Lindow tried several times but failed to get through. 'I'm doing something wrong here,' he said. 'I can't seem to get a line.'

'There probably aren't any lines. The cell antennae will be blocked with people phoning to say they're okay, and calls from journalists. They keep the lines open and no one else can get on the network. It's always the same. We'll have to patch a message through the ambulance radio.' While she spoke, she ripped surgical pads from their wrappers and pressed them lightly to the girl's stomach and face. She unravelled a bandage around her head to hold one of the pads in place.

The doctor came running back with two ambulance crews, one for the girl and the other for Harry. Lindow wondered why they hadn't brought their vehicles up to the spot and then realised that they couldn't because of the certainty of punctures from the mass of glass.

Kay was lifted on to a stretcher and moved swiftly to an ambulance. The doctor and nurse went with her, he to use the radio and she to carry the bottle of fluid. The second ambulance crew began working on Harry, whose face was now covered in a mask. They wrapped his leg in a suction cast. As they prepared to carry him away, he pulled the mask from his face and told them drunkenly not to forget his artificial limb, which had been moved to one side by the crew and was now lying incongruously on the pavement. Lindow picked it up together with his own jacket and followed them to the ambulance.

Before climbing in to sit by Harry, he looked towards the wreck of the bus, which was crackling and steaming under the firemen's water jets. He hadn't seen them arrive – they must have approached from the other direction, but now five or six hoses arced over the bus and filled the street with a spray that was pooling in a great orange lake. The bus's superstructure had almost completely burned away, although odd bits of metal remained sticking up like antlers. The back of the vehicle had collapsed as the tyres burst and it squatted down, still burning, on the traffic island.

Lindow looked at his watch. It was eight thirty, near enough an hour since the bus had turned the corner into Clarence Street.

Commander Kenneth Foyle, head of the Metropolitan Police's Anti-terrorist Unit, had taken his first day off in nearly three weeks to watch the appearance of his daughter at a magistrates' court in the West Country. Along with thirteen others, she faced charges ranging from obstruction to criminal damage. Katherine Foyle was part of a group protesting against the building of an agricultural research centre. At dawn on the previous day the police, and security men employed by the local authority, had moved in on the camp around the new laboratories and Katherine had been hauled from the scene by two security guards. He knew this much because he had seen his daughter's picture in the following day's tabloids. He telephoned the Somerset police to discover that she had been charged with obstruction and threatening behaviour, and locked up overnight. Katherine! Threatening behaviour! He knew her better.

Foyle rang New Scotland Yard to tell his assistant, Graham Forbes, that he had family business to attend to and would not be in that day. He hadn't been any more explicit than that and hoped that no one at the Yard would recognise Katherine in the newspaper. Then he had dismissed his police driver and made the 150-mile journey to Somerset in his own car, reaching the court in time for Katherine's hearing. He asked if he could speak for his daughter, then assured the magistrates that she would not break the law again. The bench nodded in unison, not without some sympathy, and imposed a fifty-pound fine for each offence. Foyle paid by cheque on the way out of the court.

He minded about it all terribly, but driving back to Katherine's digs in Bristol he tried to avoid mention of the protest and her first night in police custody. He'd forgive Katherine anything because he held himself responsible for so much of her turbulent nature. There was a lot of him in her. When she was growing up, he had been away, running undercover operations for the Drugs Squad and then a succession of investigations into organised crime in the capital. But now that he had got where he wanted – heading SO 13 – his family seemed to have disintegrated around him. June had decided to make her own life: as Katherine was preparing to leave for Bristol University a year ago, his wife had told him over an anniversary dinner that she would now be spending much of her time away from home researching her doctoral thesis. When she was not bottom up in some desert burial ground, she'd be writing and lecturing at a university in the Midlands. She told him she'd finance herself with money left in her father's will, then added crisply that she was not ending their marriage but suspending it. Foyle didn't quite know what that meant. He was less certain in these matters than he was about police work and had decided to put up with the arrangement and get himself a housekeeper.

'Heard from Mum?' he asked Katherine.

'No, you?'

'Not for a while. When does she get back from Jordan?'

'Mid-November, or when it starts raining there.' Katherine looked out of her window at the bank of black cloud that smothered the last light in the west. A silence ensued while she picked at some mud on her jeans.

'Did you really threaten that police officer, Katherine?'

'Kate! I'm called Kate now, Dad. I just prefer it, if that's all right.'

'Okay, sorry ... *Kate*! Did you take a swing at him, like he said in court?'

'No, course not. I didn't touch him.'

'But you got your picture in the paper with those two officers.'

'I know, they showed it to us in the cells. I'm glad Mum didn't see it,' she said, looking conspiratorially at her father.

'It's not funny. You've got a criminal record now. That could count against you. It matters, Katherine ... Kate.'

She laughed. It didn't seem to worry her remotely.

'Tell me something,' said Foyle, 'what have you got against this agricultural centre, and why now, for goodness' sake? There's nothing growing at this time of year.'

'Dad, you know nothing about the subject – I mean, about the release of rogue genes into the natural world. It's very serious. They're sowing a new variety of genetically engineered winter cereal for next year's harvest. That's why we were there.'

Ten miles from Bristol they stopped at a steak house, where Foyle insisted that she have a proper meal because he thought she looked undernourished. He studied her as she read the menu. She had inherited his big-boned frame and dark looks, which came from his Cornish grandfather. But her hair was less wavy and happily she had not been endowed with his weathered complexion, nor his nose, which in profile looked a little like the old Duke of Wellington's. He also knew that she had taken on some of his mannerisms. June often remarked that they made the same quick, expressive movements with their hands.

After a glass of red wine, Katherine became chatty and asked him about work, something he never encouraged – partly because there was so much he couldn't talk about, but mostly because he didn't trust the company she kept. To his mind, the fringe that included road protesters, animal-rights activists and crop burners, of which Katherine was now apparently a member, were not too many degrees saner than the terrorists whose profiles filled his computers at New Scotland Yard.

'I hope you don't talk about my job to your friends,' he said.

'Course not, Dad. I'm not very likely to admit there's filth in the family.' She saw that he'd been stung. 'It's a joke, Dad. Seriously, how's it going?'

'It's not too bad, but we have to keep on our toes. I could show you faces of a hundred men – and women – who desire nothing more than to spray London commuters in the face with anthrax. And there's still plenty of potential in Ireland – the guns and explosives, the men. It's a way of life for some. It gave people a living and a sense of purpose.'

'Not unlike you, Dad,' she said, looking up slyly from her salad.

Foyle rose to the bait. 'The difference, if you really need me to spell it out, Kate,' he couldn't get used to the name, it made him feel as if he was talking to someone else, 'is that I'm appointed by a public body, and what we try to do is save lives and enforce the laws, which have been made by democratically elected representatives. And second, if it was all to stop suddenly, I'd be more than content to go back to catching your run-of-the-mill villain. I really miss the neatness of a straightforward murder.'

'Dad, don't be so serious. I was teasing.'

He smiled. They passed the rest of the meal talking about Katherine's hope of changing courses. She was fed up with drama and wanted to do law.

At eight p.m. Foyle glanced at his watch. He had to drop Katherine at her flat in Bristol then drive on to London. It would be three hours before he was home. He signalled for the bill to the three waitresses, who were talking over by the bar. They were engrossed and didn't notice him. He began to rise, at which point the woman who'd served them came over with apologies. 'I'm sorry, sir, they were just telling me about that bomb. It's terrible – when we thought that was all over.'

'What bomb?'

'The bomb that's gone off in London, sir. Some people are dead, they think. It was on a bus.'

'Where's the phone?' He cursed himself for not taking one of the office mobiles or a pager. Why hadn't he called in to the office? He dialled his assistant's direct line. Forbes picked up on the second ring and gave him the details. Foyle wrote hurriedly on the back of his cheque book, then asked the waitress to arrange a cab to take Katherine back to Bristol, paid the bill and gave Katherine a cheque for three hundred pounds.

She hugged him as he left. 'Dad. Thanks. Love you.'

Unaccountably Foyle blushed. He looked at her hard. 'Keep in touch, Katherine – and out of trouble.'

'Kate!' she said.

'Where do you come from, sir? You sound American.'

Lindow had given his name to the man in the hospital but didn't feel like answering the rest of the questions. He shifted sideways on the stretcher and collapsed his left arm over his face. The strip lighting of the emergency department at St Luke's hurt his eyes, and the back of his head was pounding. A little while before, he had felt faint and asked a nurse if he could lie down. Now he was grateful for the pillow.

'I've been in the States for a long time,' he said groggily. 'That's why I've got an accent.'

'So you're on holiday in London, sir?' his interrogator asked. He was a young man, but stout for his age, with fleshy cheeks and small, greedy eyes. His hair was damp and fell over his forehead in oily wet locks.

'No, no, I've come to work here. What do you need to know for?'

The man ignored him. 'So, if you're not American, where do you come from?'

'I'm Irish,' said Lindow.

The man looked down at him hungrily, as though he was some kind of quarry. Lindow sensed that he was waiting for him to expand, but he didn't feel like obliging him. Anyway, who the hell was he, asking these personal questions?

'So you're Irish and you're working here,' said the man. 'What do you do, sir?'

'I'm a molecular biologist. I've just come here to do research at Imperial College.'

'Genes and that sort of thing?'

'Yes, but it's a little more complicated than that,' said Lindow wearily.

'You're a researcher in genetics?'

Lindow began to explain that this wouldn't be strictly accurate and then stopped. 'Who are you, anyway? Why does the hospital need this sort of information now? Surely it can wait.'

'Oh, didn't I mention it?' said the man, straightening to go. 'Richard Abbott-Tring – *Evening Herald*.' He touched Lindow's hand with four chubby fingers. 'You've been most helpful, sir. Now, take it easy – you've been through a terrible ordeal.'

He departed with a hasty, self-important waddle. A clipboard that he had been holding behind him was now pressed to his chest.

Half an hour passed before Lindow was seen by a woman doctor. She peered into his eyes and examined the wound on his head. Then she kneaded his stomach with expert fingers and took a cursory look at the cuts on his legs.

'You've been very lucky,' she said, feeling the rest of his head. 'We'll X-ray this head of yours just to be on the safe side then get the cuts stitched and give you a painkiller. The nurse says you've been feeling faint, so I think it's best if we keep you in overnight. How are you feeling otherwise? Any shock?'

'I don't think so. Just tired.'

'That's understandable. You rest here and somebody'll be along shortly to take more details.'

He didn't rest. The noise and light of the emergency department reverberated in his head. He couldn't think straight, which was an unpleasant novelty. He struggled to order the last couple of hours in his mind, but all he could do was replay a stream of images from the street. After the bomb exploded he'd been plunged into a limbo, lodged between earth and hell. He remembered the brush-fire heat of the burning vehicles and the coldness of the paving stones. He remembered the smell of burning rubber and fuel, and before that a bitter odour, which he assumed was the explosives.

Yes, he'd been looking at his watch and waiting for Eamonn when the bomb had gone off, and then he'd been with Kay and Harry and the medical team had arrived and then Kay was taken away half dead. Now he was here in hospital and pretty much in one piece. Shaky, but nothing like that poor girl with her face. He couldn't stop seeing the moment when he'd lifted her hair that first time. God, he thought suddenly, where the hell was Eamonn? What had he been thinking of? He must get up and telephone him. He dropped his legs from the gurney.

A nurse came scurrying up to him. 'Not so fast, Mr Lindow, we're going to take you to X-ray now and then we'll deal with these cuts.' She held his head with both hands and peered at the gash. 'Goodness, you need this seen to, don't you? So pop your legs back up there and we'll wheel you in now.'

'Yes, but you don't understand. I must call my brother.' He was surprised at how loud and panicky he sounded.

'Look. I'll see if one of the girls on Reception can telephone him and let him know where you are. Then you can talk to him yourself a little later.'

Lindow fished in his wallet and gave her the piece of paper with Eamonn's number on it. She signalled to a porter to wheel him away. X-ray took a matter of minutes, then he was moved to have his cuts stitched and dressed. He watched with interest as his trousers were cut off by another nurse, leaving a patch of material that had dried into an open wound on his leg. While the material was being soaked off with warm water, the nurse who'd taken Eamonn's number returned with the piece of paper and said no one had answered. There was a machine on, and the woman had thought he'd prefer to leave the message himself so she'd hung up.

'There'll be a telephone upstairs in the ward,' she said brightly. 'You're being sent to the Liskeard wing. That's where the private rooms are so you'll have everything you need. Liskeard is the lap of luxury.'

Within a quarter of an hour he was lying in a private double room with a young black man, whose hands and right eye were bandaged. The ward sister said he had been thrown into a window by the explosion. He raised a bandage in greeting and introduced himself as Clovis Cox.

'Fuckin' mess this. Fuckin' mess!' said Cox, after mumbling to himself. 'Know what I mean? They got no fuckin' right.'

He turned his head through a complete right angle to look at Lindow with his left eye. 'You straight? You not a policeman, nor nothing?'

'No,' Lindow said. 'I'm not a policeman.'

'Not a policeman?'

'*No*, I said.'

Cox relaxed. 'Okay. Will you do somethin' for me? See the jacket over there? That's my jacket and in the linin' you'll find Charlie. Take the bag out and make me a line on this tray here. Then you throw the stuff out of the window.'

Lindow considered Cox's face. 'Is Charlie what I think it is?'

'You know, Charlie! Cocaine! Coke, powder, snow, blow. Get the bag and gimme some. I can't get into the linin' nor nothing with these.' He held up his hands for inspection like a heavyweight boxer before a fight.

'You mean you're going to snort that stuff without the slightest idea what other drugs are in your system?' asked Lindow.

'That's exactly what I'm going to do.'

'No.'

'Come on, man. It's pure stuff. I missed my connection tonight and there's no other use for it. See what I'm saying?'

'No.'

'Okay, okay. Just get the stuff and throw it away – out of the window. Now, please, man, I'm asking you. If the nurses find it, I'll be doing time again.' He gurgled a laugh.

Lindow thought for a moment. Without a word he got off the bed and went over to the jacket. He felt around the hem then retrieved the bag through the ripped inside pocket. Without looking at it, he opened the window and shook out the powder before letting the bag go in the draught gusting up the side of the building. As he closed the window, a nurse came in and asked what he was doing.

'Just getting some air, Nurse.' Lindow smiled at her. 'Do you have a phone I could use? I need to speak to my brother.'

As he left with her, Clovis Cox winked at him with his good eye.

He read Eamonn's number from the piece of paper, dialled, then heard a message. 'If that's you, Mary, we'll be at the Lancaster Arms until about eight thirty. Then we'll go to a restaurant called Sam Samosa's in Kellet Street. See you there. Anyone else who's calling, leave a message with your number.'

Lindow spoke into the telephone. 'Eamonn, it's Con. Had a bit of trouble with the bomb in the West End. Nothing to worry about. A few cuts and bruises, that's all. I'm in the Liskeard wing at St Luke's, but I'll be out tomorrow and I'll call you then. Hope you're having fun there. By the way, who the hell is Mary?'

He hung up. He wondered why Eamonn wasn't in. He'd probably gone to the pub, knowing he'd never find Con in the chaos of the West End. Perhaps he had met this Mary and was already lying in her arms. But surely even Eamonn was not capable of being so unconcerned. After all, they had arranged to meet right where the bomb had gone off. Lindow turned back down the corridor.

On the way, he stopped by the nurses' station where the television news was on. An agitated woman reporter was talking to a studio interviewer, brushing her hair aside and tripping over her words. She looked down at her notes. 'The latest figures we've been given are that seven people have lost their lives in this explosion and forty-five people have been injured, eleven of them seriously. Police say that no warning was received and that the bomb exploded on the bus as it was moving. In the light of the Irish Peace Agreement, they're not prepared to speculate about the origin of the bomb or which group planted it. Police say that as yet no organisation has claimed responsibility. It is understood that the Prime Minister has already spoken to the Irish premier and all sides of the Northern Ireland Assembly. All parties, including Sinn Fein, have agreed to await the outcome of the investigation.'

Lindow returned to the room where Cox lay asleep, propped up on the pillows. Some sandwiches had been left on a tray with a glass of orange juice. He drank the juice – an unchilled soup of vaguely citrus origin – then peeled back the bread of the sandwiches to inspect the tuna filling. He decided against them and climbed into bed. He switched off the reading light and lay in the dark with his eyes open. Tomorrow he'd go back to his new laboratory at Imperial: life would begin again and he'd resume his inquiries into the discreet messages transmitted between bacteria. The bomb would become yesterday's disorder and soon it would be folded up in the past like the other explosion – the one that rumbled, long ago, through an Irish summer dawn, blowing a crater in a church graveyard. He'd left that behind and he'd do the same this time.

His last thought before slipping into a fitful sleep was to wonder where the hell Eamonn was. Odd that he wasn't home by now, odd that he hadn't tried to contact the hospital. God, he hoped he was all right.

2

Lindow was in the street again, making love to the girl. He cradled her head as they rocked together; his hands were filled with bunches of her hair. He could smell the perfume rising from her and feel the undulating movement of her body. Then he slid from her, appalled. He looked down at the blood that swelled in her midriff, an unstoppable flow that came from the wound. There were other people in the street, standing just behind him. He heard them cluck with disapproval. He wanted to say that he hadn't done this thing, but then he couldn't be sure that he had not driven the wound into the girl. He began to hear other noises, noises that made him turn from her and concentrate hard. He left her in the cold wet street and groped towards the noises. Then he woke.

There was just one sound left in the hospital room – the whisper of a nurse's uniform, receding towards the door. Lindow opened his eyes as the door closed. He hadn't imagined it. Someone had been there because a smell of perfume – a clean, young scent – lingered in the room. He raised his head and looked over to the other bed. It had gone, and all trace of Clovis Cox with it. He concluded that his companion must have felt ill in the night and had called the nurse with the bell push. He'd find out in the morning. Then he sank back into sleep.

He woke again at 7 a.m. There were voices in the room, but he decided not to open his eyes. Two or three men were by the door and nearer to him was a woman. He smelt her scent again. It must be the nurse who had come in the middle of the night to wheel Cox away.

'He's still asleep,' she said. 'You can't talk to him until the doctor has seen him.'

The voices left the room. Lindow opened his eyes. 'What's going on?' he asked. 'Where's the guy who was in the next bed?'

The nurse didn't answer but busied herself straightening the bedclothes and moving away the bedside table.

'What's happening?'

'I'm sorry. I'm afraid I've been told not to talk to you. The doctor will be along shortly to look at your head.' Her manner was brisk and formal.

'Who are those men out there? Why are they here?'

She looked at him without smiling, and repeated that she couldn't talk to him. He lay back on the pillows with a rising sense of alarm. When the doctor came to see him a few minutes later, Lindow caught sight of a uniformed police officer in the doorway. Perhaps the other men were police officers too. That might explain why Cox had disappeared during the night – a drugs bust?

'Is this about Cox?' Lindow asked the doctor, as a light was shone into his eyes.

'No. I believe they want to talk to you.'

'What about?'

'About the bomb, I expect.' He paused to get Lindow's full attention. 'Your X-ray results were good. No sign of a fracture, or anything like that. Have you experienced any more dizziness?'

'No, it seems fine. My leg hurts a little, but that's all.'

'Good. Well, I expect you'll experience a little shakiness today, but that should be all. You ought to take things easy for a while and come back to us in ten days' time to have those stitches out of your head and leg. In the meantime I'll leave you with these.' He handed Lindow a bottle of pills. 'You may need them over the next few days. They're to stop your head hurting.'

The doctor was barely out of the room before two men came in. Beyond them stood an armed police officer.

'What do you want?' asked Lindow.

'Good morning, Mr Lindow. I take it you *are* Con Lindow – Constantine Lindow,' said the shorter of the two men abrasively. 'This is Detective Inspector Bostock and I'm Superintendent Simmonds. We want to talk to you about last night's explosion in Clarence Street.'

'I don't know much about it,' said Lindow. 'I saw the bus explode. That was all, but I'll tell you as much as I can.'

Simmonds smiled. 'We know you saw the bus explode, Mr Lindow. But what we don't know is what you were doing there at the time.'

'I was meeting my brother.'

'You can tell us all about that later. For the present you may consider yourself detained under Section 12 of the Prevention of Terrorism Act. You will be taken from here to a police station by Inspector Bostock and myself. Then we'll have our chat and you can tell us about your brother.'

Lindow gaped at them. 'What about my brother?'

Neither answered.

'You think *I* had something to do with it! For Chrissake, I don't blow people up.'

'Please get dressed as quickly as you can, Mr Lindow. The nurse has laid out some clothes for you. The trousers should be about the right size and she's sponged down your jacket and sweater.'

'This is absurd. I want a lawyer.'

'Not in the provisions of the Act. Please hurry, sir. We don't want to get caught up in the rush-hour traffic. As it is, it will be snarled up after last night.'

Dressing shakily, Lindow slipped the bottle of pills into his trouser pocket. Bostock took his arm and marched him along the corridor past the nurses' station to the service lift. There, another policeman with body armour and a machine-pistol waited, holding the doors open. They took the lift to the basement. As the doors opened, Bostock tightened his grip and pulled Lindow out into a corridor that was heavy with the smell of laundry and disinfectant. They reached a set of doors opening out on to a service yard. Four police vehicles were waiting there. Lindow was put in a van with Bostock and the armed policeman. The doors closed, someone banged on the van's roof and the convoy took off up a ramp to join the early morning traffic. Lindow could see a blue light flashing through the van's windscreen. There was no siren. He looked across at Bostock. 'You're making a big mistake here. I'll sue every one of you for this.'

Bostock leaned forward, swaying in and out of Lindow's face with the motion of the van. 'No, you won't. You won't sue anyone, you fucking terrorist cunt.'

The police vehicles crossed the river, passed through Parliament Square and headed up Birdcage Walk towards Hyde Park Corner. From there it was a matter of minutes to Paddington Green police station. Lindow was aware only of the car park as he was pulled from the van and hurried into a waiting area where he was regarded with indifference by two uniformed police officers. One of them held a white board on which was written in red felt-tip pen: 'Irish Suspect: Lindow.'

'Full name and address,' he demanded.

'I'm not saying anything until I have a lawyer. Not a thing. Do you hear me?'

'Under the provisions of the Prevention of Terrorism Act you are not entitled to see a solicitor for forty-eight hours,' said the officer.

'You mean I can't have a lawyer here?'

'Not for two days. Then, and only then, do you get legal representation, but that decision is taken with our advice. Now, get used to things here, Lindow. Full name and address!'

Lindow didn't answer.

'That's all right, Sergeant,' said Simmonds. 'He'll give us all we need. Won't you, Mr Lindow? Get him fingerprinted and photographed.'

Lindow stood against a wall, holding up a numbered board. The way he looked now – unwashed, unshaven, hair uncombed, crumpled shirt – he'd be convicted by any jury. There's another Irish suspect, they'd think. There's another murdering bastard sent here to blow our people apart and kill our children. But that was over now. What the hell were they doing arresting him just because he was Irish?

A uniformed officer with close-cropped hair took hold of his hands and scraped at his fingernails with a little instrument, dropping the dirt into a glass phial. He smelt of the night shift and, as he rolled Lindow's fingertips and palms in the ink, he looked up into his face and smiled.

'What was that business with my fingernails for?' Even as he asked, Lindow knew the answer. They were taking samples to be tested for explosives residues.

'Makes you nervous, does it? Well, you shouldn't play around with explosives. You people, you never think, do you?' the officer concluded, with mock exasperation. Then he demanded Lindow's watch, shoelaces and keys. He checked the trousers for a belt and put everything but the keys into a plastic bag and sealed it. He flipped the keys through the air to his sergeant.

Lindow was patting his pockets for his wallet. 'You've taken my wallet.'

'Yes, that's right,' said the policeman. 'It was removed by police officers at the hospital. You'll get it all back when you leave.'

At the far end of the corridor Simmonds, Bostock and three other plain-clothes officers stood in a huddle. The group dispersed as Lindow emerged to be led down the corridor. One of the policemen punched some numbers on a key-pad and they passed through a metal door. Bostock and Simmonds followed. The door shut with a hydraulic wheeze. Then they moved to a cell, where he was left with a man who introduced himself as the duty doctor. He checked Lindow's head and eyes, his back and arms.

'Look,' said Lindow, 'I was examined half an hour ago.'

'Yes, but this is to make sure you don't claim we gave you these,' the doctor said, thumbing the bruise on Lindow's bicep.

He left the cell and nodded to the policemen, who came in and took hold of Lindow. They marched him to an interview room where Simmonds and Bostock were waiting with another man, who sat some distance from the table and didn't look up when they entered.

Lindow was put in a chair opposite Simmonds. Bostock was sitting beside him. He had removed his jacket and sat stroking his brawny, fair-haired forearms.

'Right, Mr Lindow,' Simmonds began contemptuously.

'If you're going to be accurate,' said Lindow, 'it's Dr Lindow.'

Simmonds raised his eyebrows with theatrical admiration. 'So – Dr Lindow, when were you born?'

'November the fifteenth, 1965.'

'And you are a citizen of the Irish Republic?'

'Yes.'

'You still carry an Irish passport?'

'Yes.'

'And you were meeting your brother last night? What time would that have been?'

'Look, if I answer your questions, will you let me phone someone? I need to speak to my brother or my father. They'll be worried.'

Simmonds nodded. 'The sooner you answer our questions, the sooner we'll be finished with you.'

'I arranged to meet Eamonn at seven fifteen outside the tube station in Clarence Street. You can check with him. He said he was coming straight from work.'

'And did you?'

'What?'

'Go straight from work?'

'No, I went home first and changed.'

'Where is that exactly, Dr Lindow – your home?'

'You want the address?'

'Yes.'

Lindow thought for a moment. 'Flat two, forty-six Homer Road. It's in Notting Hill Gate – a rented place.'

There was a silence in the room. None of the officers made a move. Lindow searched their faces. They had desperately needed his address, but they didn't seem to be doing anything about it. Then he understood: someone was listening to this interview elsewhere. He looked up to a small dark glass bubble on the far wall. They were filming him too.

'That wasn't difficult, was it – giving your address?' said Simmonds eventually. 'Why didn't you give it to the hospital last night? The staff told us you gave your brother's telephone number and that was all.'

'I don't expect to be in the flat long. I'm looking for a place to buy, or somewhere to rent nearer Imperial College. I gave my brother's telephone number because I had it in my hand and I knew they'd be able to contact me through him when I moved. That's all there is to it. I suppose I could've given my direct line at Imperial, but it didn't occur to me and I'm not sure I can remember it.'

'So you went straight from your home to see your brother? Were you going to meet anyone else?'

'Yes, a woman was coming later – Mary someone. I'd never met her before.'

'This Mary, would that be Eamonn's girlfriend?'

'I don't know. Ask him.'

'Yes, we will . . . when we can,' said Simmonds. 'Now, tell me, what sort of work is it that you do, Dr Lindow?'

'I'm a molecular biologist.'

'Yes?' Simmonds revolved his hand for more information.

'I'm a researcher. If you need to know exactly, I'm researching what are called message chemicals. It's related to my original genetic studies.'

'And does this involve much laboratory work?'

'Naturally. It's mostly done in the laboratory.'

'So you come into contact with chemicals?'

Lindow saw where Simmonds was heading. 'If you think I've been making bombs in my laboratory, you're mad. Besides, I've barely been inside the place. I've only just got here – only just settled in.'

'From America? How long ago did you move?'

'Until three weeks ago I was working at MIT – that's the Massachusetts Institute of Technology. Imperial College made me an offer I couldn't turn down.'

'Are you telling me that you decided to leave a job in the States to come to London? Is that what they call the Irish brain drain?'

Bostock sniggered. Lindow ignored him. 'Nowadays, it's quite common for people to come from the US to Britain.'

'Was there another reason for your return. Was it part of a plan, Dr Lindow?'

'Of course not. It wasn't my idea to come back. They made me the offer out of the blue a year ago. There were negotiations to be completed about facilities, research funds, people. Check with Imperial, if you want. Check with Professor Sharma. That's Sethe Sharma.'

'You've quite an accent there. How long were you in the United States?'

'It's nearly fifteen years now.'

'And how many times have you been back to visit the Irish Republic in that time?'

'Four or five times. The last time was two years ago when I attended my mother's funeral.'

'But you kept in touch with your family there – kept in touch with Eamonn in London, kept in touch with the political situation in Ireland.' Simmonds was pushing now, leaning forward. Bostock had stopped scratching his arms.

'Of course I kept in touch with my family. But I don't know what you mean about the political situation. I know a little about the peace process – what I've read in the papers.'

'I mean "the struggle to throw off the British yoke".'

'I don't see it in those terms, certainly not now. There's a peace agreement, an assembly.'

'But you once did see it in those terms and you still share the views of your lot now?'

'I don't have a *lot*, if by that you mean the IRA. And, anyway, they abandoned their struggle a long time ago.'

'Still, you knew about them and their strategy, knew about the Real IRA.'

'Yes, I read about it in the Boston papers. There are a lot of Irish people there and the papers tend to cover the story well.' Lindow instantly regretted saying that.

'Yes, a big community of Irish folk, a big community that has sent money and guns to the IRA – some of those folk are still pouring money into the republican groups. They said they were griefstricken about the Omagh bomb, but they went on collecting, didn't they? You must have met many of those kind of people there. They're your people, aren't they? Did they urge you to come here and work for them? Who were your contacts in the Boston area?'

'I didn't have any *contacts*! I had friends and colleagues, but not contacts in the way you're using the word.'

'Did you have a girlfriend there? Some nice Irish-American lass?'

'No, I didn't.' Simmonds looked at him knowingly. 'I've had relationships in the past, but there's no one special at the moment.'

'No ties. That's always the best way, isn't it? Are you a homosexual by any chance, Dr Lindow?'

'No, I'm not, for God's sake. I just don't happen to have a girlfriend. My work consumes all my time.'

'Forgive me, Doctor, these are sometimes delicate matters.' He spoke with sarcastic formality.

'Look, I don't know what you want me to say. I was going to meet my brother last night and I was blown up. Then you haul me from my hospital bed, you bring me here against my will and you ask me if I'm gay. I mean – it's – it's – ridiculous. When are you going to let me speak to my family?'

Simmonds paused, which was evidently the signal for Bostock to take over. 'Where do you keep the explosives?' he asked.

'Oh, for God's sake!'

'In a garage? A warehouse? A safe house somewhere? Where do you keep them, Con?'

'I don't know what you're talking about.' Damn, that was always the phrase the guilty used. He'd have to watch what he was saying and how he was saying it. He eyed the new interrogator carefully.

'Who makes the bombs? Is it you who makes them? With all that technical expertise of yours, that shouldn't be a problem.'

'I don't make bombs. I study bacteria and human cells and a process called protein biosynthesis, but I don't suppose you'd know what that is.'

'No, I don't. But I'll tell you what I do know. I know I've got a bloody liar sitting in front of me – and a fucking terrorist to boot.'

Lindow didn't reply. It was useless. They weren't going to listen. They were going to lock him up. He'd have to be on his guard. Whatever they did to him, he wouldn't budge. He'd refuse to talk, refuse to give them anything – and then the time would come when they'd have to charge him or let him go. Until then he would retreat into himself, just as he had before when the RUC had questioned him about the explosion in Ireland. They had been rough. At times he'd thought they were going to kill him there and then, right in the interview room. But they hadn't and then one morning they'd let him go.

'I want a glass of water,' said Lindow. 'I haven't had anything to eat. I won't answer any more questions until you get me something to drink.'

That was the only way, Lindow thought. Fight back. Every small victory counts.

'Okay,' said Simmonds. 'I'll get you some tea. Milk and two?'

'No sugar.'

The tea arrived very soon, as if someone had known it would be called for. Lindow felt in his trouser pocket for the bottle of pills, which had eluded the policeman when he was being processed. He shook one into his hand under the table and was preparing to swallow it when Bostock reached over and grabbed his arm.

'What's this, then? Drugs as well? I just said tea. I didn't say we'd have a tea *and* drugs break, did I? I'll take those. Don't want any overdoses, do we, Dr fucking-Irish-cunt Lindow?' Bostock wrested the bottle from Lindow's hand.

'They're prescribed painkillers,' he protested. 'I was given them at the hospital for this.' He turned to show the back of his head to Simmonds.

'Very impressive,' said Bostock, 'but not half as impressive as Miss Gould's face, eh?'

'Miss Gould?'

'Yes, Kay Gould. Surely you remember her. The girl who was blown up in the bomb. They say you were with her. You must have seen her face – shredded by flying glass. Imagine being Kay Gould this morning, waking up with half her frigging face gone. Imagine that! Imagine that poor girl's life now. Months of plastic surgery. I mean, they're going to have to start rebuilding her face from scratch, aren't they? From the bone upwards, using skin from her arse and anywhere else they can find it. But it's not face skin, is it? Not the same – and she'll never be the same. No more nights out in the West End for Kay Gould, no candlelit dinners for Kay Gould. That's what you've done, Con. Destroyed a young girl's life. So now you're going to tell me what went wrong last night. You weren't aiming for the bus, were you? You were going to plant that bomb somewhere else, weren't you? What was the real target?'

'I'm not going to say anything. I have no comment. This is ludicrous!'

'No, it isn't. It's dead serious. You see, we can't ask anyone else about last night because the other suspect is unconscious. So it's you we have to ask, Con.'

Bostock looked at Simmonds. Something passed between them.

'What other suspect? What are you talking about?'

'The other bomber, you cunt! Eamonn, your brother – your accomplice.'

Bostock had moved round the table and was gripping Lindow's thigh just above the stitches. Lindow didn't feel the pain.

'What are you saying?'

'Oh, come on, now. You must've known Eamonn was on that bus. Blew himself up with the bomb, didn't he? Not dead – just unconscious. You see, we knew it was him when we found his wallet in his clothes early this morning. Then all we did was check through the casualty lists – and guess what we find? We find you in the same hospital. Another fucking Lindow, right under our noses. Wasn't that a coincidence, now?'

Lindow averted his eyes from Bostock's leering features and looked first at Simmonds, then at the other man who had been sitting silently at the back of the interview room. He knew it was true. 'Has Eamonn been hurt? Is that what you're telling me?'

Simmonds nodded.

'How badly? Tell me!'

Simmonds spoke. 'Eamonn was on the bus when it exploded. He's still alive, but he hasn't come round yet.'

Lindow lunged at Simmonds, but his mind clouded and the ground disappeared beneath him.

Foyle had risen early. Too early. He needed six hours' sleep and had had only three. It wasn't yet light, but from his kitchen window he could see his driver, Alex, waiting in the street in the unmarked green police Rover. He scribbled a note to the housekeeper about the shopping and the laundry, then left the house with little regret. He never minded leaving now.

'When are you going to move from Wimbledon, sir?' Alex asked gloomily, as Foyle sank into the back seat. 'The bridge is closed again so I'll have to take the long route.'

'Leave off, Alex, I'm not in the mood. Just get me there quick as you can.' He caught a petulant look from Alex in the driver's mirror and glowered back at him.

Foyle had got back to London by eleven fifteen on the previous evening, in time to see the bus still smouldering in Clarence Street. God, he hated bomb scenes – hated the smell and chaos and the sense of utter waste. But he had spent a long time there, tramping through the glass and water trying to envisage exactly what it had been like, asking himself why the bus exploded there. He found two explosives officers he knew who told him that the bomb had been placed on the lower deck at the rear of the bus. This was fortunate because it meant that the survivors were able to scramble down the stairs and leave by the exit at the front, although the doors had jammed for a few crucial seconds and the driver had had to use the emergency lever. He had dragged the injured from their seats, returning to the bus three times to bring people out. The two officers had estimated that twelve to fifteen pounds of explosive had been used, two or three times the amount usually deployed as the core of a car bomb. It had all the signs of a Semtex device which, because of its innate stability, was unlikely to have triggered itself unless given a severe shock. They thought the bomb was the work of a professional, and that, too, argued against self-detonation. As yet, little had been found in the wreckage and, as they had waited for teams of white-suited forensics officers to comb the street, they had both made the point that it didn't seem to add up. If someone wanted to cause serious damage in Clarence Street, it would have been easier to load a fertiliser bomb into a car and leave it in the street. That way much less Semtex would have been needed.

Since there was nothing Foyle could do in the middle of the night at New Scotland Yard, he called Forbes and told him he was going home. He knew that he would have to snatch as much sleep as he could. The next few days would be punishing. He got home at two a.m. and was soon in bed asleep. At five he was woken by a call from a detective constable in his department, who told him that two Irishmen, both named Lindow, might be involved. Both had been injured and subsequently taken to St Luke's. Eamonn Lindow was on the bus when it exploded. He had been badly hurt and was still unconscious. His brother, Constantine Lindow, was standing in the street near by when the bomb went off. He had suffered only minor injuries and would be well enough to be questioned that morning. Both brothers had been carrying ID. One had given his name freely at the hospital but when asked for his address had given his brother's telephone number. Police officers and forensics teams were already on their way to search Eamonn Lindow's flat in Peckham.

'Are you saying that one brother didn't know of the other's injury?' Foyle asked.

'Yes, sir. It seems he tried to call him from Casualty.'

'Has anyone informed him of his brother's condition?'

'No, sir.'

'Okay, keep it that way. Meanwhile, send my driver. I'll be ready in half an hour. Oh, by the way, did you get the address for the second suspect?'

'Not yet, sir, but we should have it soon.'

'Make it a priority.'

On the way to New Scotland Yard, Foyle considered what he had been told by the young officer and wrote a series of questions on a pad he kept in the car. When he arrived at the Yard he would rip the piece of paper from the pad and transfer the notes and questions into a big hardback accounting book that was laid out in columns. Foyle was convinced he had to guard against a disorganised streak in his character. Since his first murder inquiry twenty years before, when he had neglected a crucial piece of evidence at an early stage, he'd made it a rule to note down all the questions that had to be answered. He kept a smaller pad by his bed because his most creative period came in his first conscious moments of the day. These inspirational seconds had stopped about the time June left and nowadays he found he had to work harder at a problem.

He turned on the car reading light and wrote: 'If accidental detonation, what was intended target? If not, why blow up bus? Why *this* bus? Why large amount of explosives? Why both brothers at scene? Why carrying ID?' He then wrote, 'Who – Real IRA or other group?' and underlined the words so hard that the ballpoint broke through the paper.

He looked out of the window as the car crossed Wandsworth Common. The first overnight flights from America had turned over Essex and were now making their final approach to Heathrow, their lights dancing in the mauve-grey dawn. In a matter of minutes south London would be rudely dragged from sleep.

He returned to his notes and began to tease out the inconsistencies in what he knew so far. There had been no warning before the explosion and no admission of responsibility. It could be anyone – a renegade IRA group, the INLA, Ulster loyalists, Iraqis – bloody well anyone. And yet they were holding two Catholic Irishmen. But those were not grounds any longer. Besides, their behaviour didn't suggest that they were trying to conceal their presence. The ID on both of them gave the lie to that. So perhaps the bomb had gone off accidentally while being transferred from one brother to the other for use at a later date? But that didn't make sense either: if the slightly injured man had expected to take delivery of a bomb and an explosion occurred, the first person he would assume to have been hurt was the carrier – in other words, his brother. Moreover, the explosives section said they thought it was a professionally made bomb and was unlikely to have detonated by itself. He wrote again: 'Trigger mechanism? Origin of explosives? Background of brothers? Intelligence re R-IRA and OTHER groups.'

They were approaching Chelsea Bridge when Alex slowed down. 'Do you fancy some coffee and a sandwich from the cab stand, sir? It won't take more than a few minutes.'

'Good idea,' said Foyle, laying down the pad beside him.

Alex scampered over the road, holding his jacket together with one hand, and jumped the line of cab drivers who were waiting at the hatch. Foyle smiled as he saw him put up his hands in mock surrender and shout over their heads. He returned with a bacon sandwich and a Styrofoam beaker of coffee. 'A few late nights this week, I expect, sir?' he said. 'Unless those two were the ones that did it. But that seems too simple, doesn't it, sir? Too easy, if you know what I mean.'

'Yes, it does,' said Foyle, sinking his teeth into the sandwich. Alex had been on the beat himself once and had worked in various capacities for the Met for thirty-five years. As a driver, he picked up a good deal over the course of a day and acted as an information exchange between senior officers. Foyle had learned long ago not to talk detail with him, but it never deterred Alex, who'd already heard that a suspect was about to be lifted and taken to Paddington Green nick.

'Is that so?' said Foyle between mouthfuls. 'Promise to tell me when you've got the rest of the case sewn up.'

At the front entrance to New Scotland Yard, Foyle marched through the security barrier, took the lift to the eighth floor where the Anti-terrorist Unit was quartered, and presented himself impatiently at the security door where his credentials were checked. From there he moved swiftly to the general office, which acted as a kind of traffic control, communications post and secretariat for SO 13. Seven officers were there, including two women. Three were dressed shabbily and had obviously been on a surveillance operation. They had come in at the end of their shift to make their reports and hear about the Clarence Street explosion. The other four were manning computers and telephones.

'Forbes?' shouted Foyle. 'Where's Forbes?'

'He's just having a wash and shave, sir. He hasn't been home,' replied one of the women officers.

'Fine. Tell him I want him now. There'll be a briefing at seven thirty sharp. I want everyone there. I want reports on the suspects, their backgrounds, explosives and any intelligence we've got – the lot.'

He set off down the corridor towards his office, but before reaching it caught sight of two officers sitting with their door open. 'Kepple, Hardwood, what are you doing? Has anyone checked the cars in the area of the bomb? No? Right, well, let's start with the most inconspicuous models, blue or grey mid-range saloon cars, made from 1989 onwards. See if there were any parked in the vicinity of Clarence Street last night. Check the area around Eamonn Lindow's address. Ask about lock-ups in the area. And while you're about it, get me a plan of the bus route with a list of the places where the bus would have stopped before the explosion and where it would have gone on to. We also need to know the places where different bus routes intersect with ours. Got it?'

Foyle turned and saw Forbes standing by the open door of his office, tucking the excess material of a crisp white shirt into his waistband. 'There's something very reassuring about you, Graham,' said Foyle. 'How do you do it?'

'Army training, sir, as you well know, and a spare set of clothes in my locker.'

Foyle looked down at the gleam of Forbes's black shoes, shook his head and let out a whistle of admiration. 'What have you got for me?'

'I've set up the video next door. We've got some footage from the street. And there's a slim chance there may be something from the bus.'

'There was a camera on board?'

'Three. One at the back of the bus above the bomb, which was totally destroyed, but there were another two – one just in front of the stairway to the upper deck and another above the driver's head. The lab say it will be some time before they get the film. Possibly Friday. They have no idea what state it's in. There may be nothing at all.'

'Good. Let's see the other footage, shall we?'

Foyle threw his raincoat on to the sofa, skimmed his message book, placed his notes from the car journey under a glass paperweight and moved to the adjoining room where three officers stood waiting for him. He grunted a good morning.

The officer with the video remote control spoke first. 'This film comes from a camera belonging to Reeves and Cuddy, the store that occupies the building on the south side of Clarence Street, sir.'

'Which way was it pointing?' asked Foyle.

'It was positioned on the apex of the outer arch of the arcade, facing westwards. It was very close to the explosion, but was sheltered from the main force of the blast by the arches. We've got as much tape as we want up until that moment. The relevant material comes in the last fifteen minutes or so, but we'll be going over the rest again more thoroughly.'

The tape was played. At the bottom of the screen a digital clock gave the date and counted the minutes and seconds. It read 23.10 – 19:17:23. Foyle saw a smudged grey street scene that could have been anywhere in London, except that it was identified as CLAR ST at the top of the screen. On the left-hand side, about a third of the way up, he could make out the entrance to a tube station and a newspaper stand. People walked briskly in and out of the camera's field. Opposite the newspaper stand a cab pulled up and a man got out.

'That's one of the Lindows,' said Forbes, freezing the image. 'Inspector Bostock, who's at St Luke's now, identified him about twenty minutes ago. He says the jacket that Lindow has with him at the hospital is a match. There's a good shot of his face coming up.'

Foyle watched as the man walked a few paces to the tube station then withdrew to look into a shop window. A girl came on the scene. Other people passed. The lights of the oncoming traffic flared in the right of the camera's lens. A group of tourists emerged from the tube station, gathered round a tour leader and set off in the direction of the camera. It was 19:25. Three people ran to the tube entrance, a man chained his mountain bike to the railings on the left-hand corner of the screen and began fiddling with the rear wheel. Nothing happened for a minute or so. Lindow looked up and down the street then towards the tube station. It was obvious he was waiting for someone. He glanced at the girl who was standing by the entrance. Foyle noted how good her figure was and wondered if they'd talk, but then she moved away. Lindow kept watching her until her dress billowed upwards, then he averted his eyes and strolled in the direction of the camera. Now Foyle saw him clearly – a good-looking, slender man just under six feet tall. He wore trousers, not jeans, a V-neck sweater and an expensive-looking jacket. He paused, spun on his heels and walked back towards the tube station.

It was 19:35. Nothing moved in the camera's field. The street waited. The man looked to his right for a few seconds then down to his watch. That's when it happened. The picture shook, objects and people were propelled out of the top of the screen as it filled with a cloud of dense smoke. Foyle gasped. It reminded him of a film he'd once seen of an atomic test, which had been shot from a military bunker. There was the same ferocious blast wind. In Clarence Street the girl and Lindow had disappeared instantly, as if they'd been vaporised. Then the picture went blank.

'The cables from the camera were cut by falling masonry, sir,' said one of the officers. 'But it's a helluva picture up till then, sir.'

Foyle sat in silence for a few moments, his mind running through the evidence in the film. It told him several things about Lindow. The first was that he took care of his appearance. If he *was* a terrorist, he was a damned well-dressed one. More important, the man he'd seen wasn't acting at all suspiciously and hadn't tried to hide his face from the camera. This was in contrast to the usual behaviour of terrorist bombers, who were alert to the threat of security cameras and went about their business hooded and wearing sunglasses. Plainly, this man hadn't expected a bomb to go off. Furthermore, when he was taken to hospital it seemed that he had not even considered the possibility that his brother might have been one of the injured. This suggested to Foyle one of two things: innocence or a superb acting ability. But what did it say about the injured man?

Obviously, Eamonn Lindow hadn't planned to blow himself up. Perhaps he had stowed the bomb on the bus, setting a short time fuse in preparation for getting off at the next stop. But the danger of something going wrong was too great. A terrorist never took that sort of risk, not when even a basic alarm clock could be adapted to give him twelve hours to get away.

There was something else that Foyle noticed. Lindow spent most of the time with his back to the traffic, watching the entrance to the tube. Only once did he look at the road in the direction of the bus. Foyle was certain that he had been expecting his brother to come by underground.

'Where are the brothers now?' he asked.

'Eamonn Lindow is still unconscious, but Constantine – Con – is being processed at Paddington Green,' said Forbes, looking at his watch.

'What about the search of Eamonn's place?'

'Nothing yet – no lists of targets, no trace of any bomb manufacture, no signs of any operational paraphernalia. Just a lot of books and videos. They're going through them at the moment. An officer is coming back with a tape, but that's all.'

'What sort of tape?'

'An audio-cassette, sir. From Eamonn Lindow's answering-machine.' Foyle got up. 'Bring the video from the street to the briefing. I want them all to see it. I'll be along in a couple of minutes.'

He returned to his office, took a notebook from his desk and revised the questions he had asked himself in the car and added those that had just occurred to him. He reached for the phone to call Martin Scarratt, assistant commissioner in charge of Specialist Operations, whose duties included overall responsibility for counter-terrorism. Then he thought better of it. He'd prefer to conduct this particular briefing without Scarratt breathing down his neck. For one thing, the assistant commissioner always had fixed ideas about the way an inquiry ought to proceed; for another, his looming presence at the back of the room tended to inhibit the flow of ideas.

Foyle gathered the reports of the explosion from his desk and made his way along the green-tiled corridor to the briefing room where some forty officers had gathered. There was a low murmur when he entered – none of the usual banter. At one end of the room was a map of the Metropolitan area, a large white Nobo board, a screen that could be pulled down from the ceiling and a TV and video player. Foyle glanced out of the windows: they were coated with one-way reflective material and hung with Venetian blinds in the belief that the slats confused the vibrations that are picked up by bouncing a laser beam from a window.

The officers sat about in groups, more or less reflecting the different disciplines of the Anti-terrorist Unit – surveillance, computing, explosives, weapons, intelligence and records. Special Branch was there in force, as well as two forensics officers.

He went to a map of the Clarence Street area drawn on the board and spoke without preamble.

'We've had a bomb in Clarence Street – here.' He pointed to the map. 'It was detonated on a 147 bus travelling on a north–south route, between Peckham and Kilburn, at seven thirty-five p.m. last night. There were forty-seven casualties. Seven were killed immediately, three died overnight and twelve are in a serious condition. As you know, two of the injured are brothers. Constantine Lindow was standing outside the tube station – here – and was slightly hurt. We have film of him from a security camera trained up Clarence Street, away from the explosion. You'll see it at the end of the briefing.

'Then there's Eamonn Lindow, who was on the bus. We assume he was on the lower deck. His injuries tell us that the bomb exploded behind him, but we cannot as yet gauge how far behind him. He may have been dragged off by the driver, so we need to interview the driver at the earliest possible opportunity. We also need to pay particular attention to the people who were hurt on the bus and who are in a condition to talk to us, especially those sitting on the lower deck. Trace anyone who got on or off the 147 about forty-five minutes before the explosion – you'll need to talk to the press about that. Put out an appeal.

'This is a very serious incident indeed. But we can't assume anything. Now, Colin, if you'd like to tell us about this bomb, we'll move on to the intelligence reports and suspects.'

Foyle nodded at Inspector Colin Lafferty, the senior explosives officer of the Anti-terrorist Unit, who was standing at the side of the room. He was as tall as Foyle – well over six foot – but he moved with much greater agility, like a man who worked hard to keep himself fit. He'd told Foyle on more than one occasion that he owed his life not to his technical acumen, his safe-breaker's fingers, or his knowledge of timing mechanisms and explosives, but to his legs. If all else failed when he was dealing with a carload of explosives, he dropped everything and ran like hell. During his time as an ammunition technical officer in the Army he had acquired the name Legs. It had survived his transfer to the headquarters of the Met's bomb-disposal team near Cannon Row police station and was now so widely used that no one could remember his rank. That suited Lafferty just fine.

Lafferty made a sketch on the board of an oblong box then gave it a pair of wheels. At the lower right-hand corner of the vehicle he placed a cross. 'This is where the bomb was left – under the back row of seats, which probably means that at some time during the journey the bomber had occupied a seat in either of the two back rows on the near side of the vehicle. We believe that the device was contained in a canvas-type hold-all, something similar to a services kitbag, but of better-quality material. At that time in the evening such a bag wouldn't have remained unnoticed for very long. Sooner or later it would've been detected and the bomber must have known this. So, there are two possibilities. The first is that the bomb exploded and blew the pants off the bomber before he could get out. The second is that it was intentionally detonated – which must mean that Lindow isn't our man. There's no way of telling between the two possibilities because we haven't got a timing device yet. In fact, very little of that nature – circuitry, batteries, clocks or anything like that – survived the blast. What we do have are bits of the bag. Forensics will no doubt have things to say about that.'

Lafferty put his hands in his pockets and stepped towards the front row of officers. 'At first we thought the explosive used was a plaster gelatine, a very powerful high explosive that has a nitro-glycerine base. This might have accounted for an accidental detonation. But we're certain now that Semtex was used, about five or six kilograms – well over twelve pounds of the stuff. That's a lot more than it took to blow up the Grand Hotel in Brighton, which accounts for the considerable damage in Clarence Street. So this was a very compact, powerful bomb indeed. It's too soon to say what batch of Semtex it comes from, but the labs are working on the chemical traces that are placed in the material by the Czech manufacturers as a form of production date. This may help us with lines of supply and so forth.' He folded his arms. 'That's about all we've got so far.'

He looked at Foyle, then his audience, and waited for questions. None came.

Then Foyle called out, 'Intelligence, what do we have?' He knew there was nothing, but he asked nevertheless.

A detective sergeant from Special Branch, who was sitting at the back of the room, summarised the situation. There had been nothing to suggest that the Real IRA, or any other splinter group in Ireland, was planning an offensive. Sources in Dublin and Belfast were baffled. The men and women currently under surveillance by Special Branch could not have had anything to do with the explosion, and none had had any contact with either of the brothers. As to the Middle East, it was difficult to tell. Several groups were being watched in the London area, particularly one led by a Syrian named Emad. But these were thought to be involved in plotting explosions abroad.

'And what about the brothers?' asked Foyle. 'Let's hear about them, since they're the only thing we've got.'

'Yes, boss.' An eager young sergeant named Pennel stood up. 'They've both got a history. We've just had word that they were questioned in 1983 about an explosion in Northern Ireland, seven miles from the border. An arms and explosives cache blew up, killing two soldiers and wounding two others. The Lindow brothers were arrested by the RUC and given a going-over. Pictures from eighty-three have been wired and I've got some copies here.'

Pennel handed out the photostats of two young men, both with long hair and sideburns. They wore the fashion of the time. Big collars and tight-fitting sweaters. Eamonn Lindow, the older of the two, was thickerset than his brother and had a bruise to his left eye. Constantine was a good-looking young man with no sign of a beard, and light eyes that glanced away from the camera.

'At the times these were taken the brothers were twenty-four and seventeen years of age. This is Eamonn Cardell Lindow, born January the eleventh, 1959,' he said, holding up one of the photographs. 'He's the one injured on the bus. The other is Constantine Cardell Lindow, born November the fifteenth, 1965. Both were born in the Irish Republic and are Irish citizens, but they were brought up in Fermanagh in the North, where their father was a teacher. In 1986 the parents moved back to the Republic – Ballyhanna in Monaghan – after their mother came into some property. Marie Lindow is part of the Cardell family, an old republican clan, and is related to Jimmy Cardell, who was tried and convicted of killing an off-duty RUC constable in 1975. We don't know if the parents are still alive.'

Pennel stopped as the door opened and Assistant Commissioner Scarratt entered. He acknowledged Foyle, then turned towards Pennel. 'Don't mind me. Please continue.' A study of intelligent interest, thought Foyle.

'I was hoping someone could find you a chair, sir,' said Pennel helpfully. Foyle smiled. 'The circumstances of the incident in Droy cemetery', continued Pennel, 'are still a bit hazy. It seems Eamonn Lindow may have been watching the dump over a period of three and a half weeks. The place was also staked out by a group of soldiers who observed his comings and goings. They were hoping to pick up half the Fermanagh brigade of the IRA when the stuff was moved. It's not clear exactly what happened, but in the early hours of July the twelfth the cache blew up. Neither of the brothers was near the cemetery at the time, but they were taken in for questioning and held for thirty-six hours each. They weren't charged. Since then they've kept their noses clean. Some time in eighty-eight Eamonn Lindow moved to London and began working at a local library. We'll have someone round there when they open up this morning, but we've already talked to his neighbours. He's a quiet sort of fellow. Few visitors, goes out a lot.'

'We don't know what happened to Constantine – or Con, as he appears on his credit cards – except that he went to university in Dublin and then seems to have emigrated to the States. We'll check with the police and the FBI as soon as we can, and with the university authorities at MIT.'

'Well, we have two Irish suspects,' said Foyle, 'but it goes against everything we know about the intentions of the republican movement. These two could belong to one of the breakaway factions. Let's not make too many judgements at this stage. I want more information about this couple – friends, girlfriends, political affiliations, financial circumstances, bank accounts, who they talk to on the phone, how much contact they have had with each other and with people on both sides of the border in Ireland. I want a complete picture by the end of the day. Somebody should talk to the officer who investigated that explosion in 1983. He may know something that isn't in the reports.'

He looked around the room. An officer nodded to indicate that this was in hand.

'Have we got Con Lindow's address in London?' asked Foyle. 'Can we check through the credit-card companies? There must be something in his wallet.'

'No, sir,' replied Forbes. 'Everything refers back to addresses in America, which will be useful in itself because it'll give us a start there. But we expect to get his address here within the hour from the officers at Paddington Green.'

'Good, I want a forensics team ready to leave for Con Lindow's place as soon as we hear where it is. Now, what about the tape?' Foyle had seen a WPC hand something to Pennel, who stood up.

'This is the ansaphone message. It's been copied on to a standard-size tape so the quality may not be too good. There's a transcript coming.'

Pennel played the tape. First there was Eamonn's message, telling a girl called Mary to meet him at a pub called the Lancaster Arms. Then a woman came on the line. She was American and there was a smile in her voice. 'Hi, it's Mary. I guess I'll see you before you get this! You better be there, Lindow – byeee.'

There were two bleeps as callers hung up without speaking. Finally, there was Con Lindow's message. 'Eamonn, it's Con. Had a bit of trouble with the bomb in the West End. Nothing to worry about. A few cuts and bruises, that's all. I'm in the Liskeard wing at St Luke's, but I'll be out tomorrow and I'll call you then. Hope you're having fun there. By the way, who the hell is Mary?'

'That's what *I* want to know,' said Foyle. 'There may just be some kind of an American angle here.'

This was for Scarratt's consumption. Privately, Foyle was forming the opinion that Con Lindow was innocent, but he'd learned enough during the last year to know that it would be best to keep this to himself. The assistant commissioner's mind would already be resolutely closed to anything but the most obvious solution. Foyle imagined him preening at the press conference that would announce the detention of two men in connection with the Clarence Street bomb.

After the video from the street was shown, Foyle rattled off a stream of instructions and announced that there would be a briefing at five thirty that afternoon. Then he left the room, beckoning Lafferty to follow him.

'What do you think, Colin?' he asked Lafferty, once they were in his office.

'I'm not a detective.'

'I know that, but what do you think?'

'Well . . . I think it's odd, to say the least, that we've got what seems to be a very professional device, but two suspects who are rank amateurs.'

'Yes. But isn't it a possibility that this Con Lindow is an exceptionally cool customer and that he's putting on an act?'

'It's a possibility, I grant you. But it seems peculiar that he went to the hospital with those minor injuries and *then* agreed to stay overnight, risking detection and arrest. Terrorists don't do that – do they?'

Both men turned to see Scarratt standing in the doorway. 'Not disturbing you, am I, Commander?' He walked around the office, hands clasped behind him, looking at Foyle's pictures, which weren't the standard studies of police rugby teams, but watercolour landscapes. Scarratt sniffed and turned to Foyle. 'Well, that seems a very good start. I need hardly tell you we're looking for quick results on this one. With ten dead and that number of injuries the press isn't going to leave us alone. When can we expect charges, Commander?'

'When we've got a case, sir.' Foyle tried his damnedest to look co-operative.

'Come along now. You've got a case already. Two Irishmen known to the authorities placed at the scene of the bomb. You can't get luckier than that. It's plain to me that Con Lindow was a sleeper, sent to the United States of America to get himself a cover, while his brother dug himself in over here. What's the problem with that?'

'None, sir, except that I want to get the right people and we must consider the possibility that these two brothers are innocent. Unless I've been missing something, a peace agreement has been signed. They're all sitting down together behaving themselves.'

'Consider all possibilities. That is your job. But never forget the obvious, Commander. That would be a mistake.'

He left the room, flashing a swift, thin-lipped smile at Lafferty.

3

Three or four hours passed after Lindow was taken to the cells and examined again by the doctor. Without his watch, he didn't know exactly how long it was. The doctor gave him a tranquilliser and murmured that he should get some rest. Lindow looked at him incredulously, but tried to sleep after he'd left. Each time he dropped off he was woken by someone opening the metal observation hatch in the cell door, waiting for a minute then closing it with a ringing clank. They were keeping him awake. He lay on the bed with his knees raised so that they couldn't see his face, and looked up at the squares of bottle glass in the ceiling. He could just make out the daylight. If they kept him there, at least he'd be able to tell the difference between night and day. That was important. He had to hold on – keep track of time, not lose himself in worry about Eamonn. They wanted that.

They'd told him about Eamonn to throw him into a blind panic and then they'd put him in the cells to dwell on it. Soon they'd be thrusting statements in his face, demanding that he sign. He'd read something about that once – a woman from Belfast who signed a piece of paper after three days without sleep. She'd thought she was giving them a handwriting sample. Then they told her she'd confessed to being part of some plot or other. He would sign nothing. He'd say nothing until they let him speak to the hospital.

No sooner had he made these resolutions than he was overwhelmed by a sense of hopelessness and – more puzzling – guilt. What the hell did he have to be guilty about? He was as innocent as anyone else in the street last night, a bystander, like Harry Ribb and Kay Gould. He thought of her again and shuddered. If she'd got those injuries so far away from the bus, what would Eamonn look like? He was overwhelmed by a sudden cold certainty that the police weren't telling him everything. Eamonn was going to die. He wondered if his father and sister had any idea how bad he was. They must've heard by now. Tag would have taken a call from the hospital or opened the door to a sheepish young officer from the Garda. He hoped she would keep her head and stay in Ireland. If she came over

41

to England, she was bound to be arrested and held, like him, in a cell with no daylight to speak of and a bed that smelt of someone else's fear.

He looked around for something to distract him. There was nothing – just the aluminium toilet, the bed and the white prison-gloss walls, etched with graffiti beneath the last coat of paint. They wanted him to turn in on himself, to feel wretched and unwashed. But now he understood that, he'd be able to fight them. He'd fight like the last time, and he'd win again. He closed his eyes and tried to nap but within a few minutes the observation hatch was wrenched open. He peered round his knees. There was no face this time, just three fingers that twitched before drawing the plate back again.

He looked up at the daylight and thought of his father. If Eamonn died, it would destroy him. They were so alike in everything, right down to the same expressions of anxiety and pleasure; they had given the same sudden, downcast look when sensing disappointment in the only audience each of them had cared about, his mother. She had swooped on them with affection that could suddenly change into raging frustration. In her worst moments she had said outright that neither was quite man enough for her. Then they had slunk away, still hopelessly in her thrall. Father and son had bonded as victims of the same love, and when the cancer had sprung from her liver to kill her in a matter of weeks they had been equally stricken. Con never experienced the sharpness of grief, yet a void opened in his life and he was gripped by a puzzling sense of loss and also release.

The guilt returned like a stitch in his side. Fuck them! They wouldn't make him feel like this. He'd done nothing. 'I'm a doctor,' he muttered to himself, 'a doctor of science, a professional, legitimate person.' But the police didn't want to see that. They needed a terrorist bomber and he was it. He'd be held here for days. Then they'd bring him out, charge him and put him in prison. With each remorseless step the system would drench him in guilt. He'd become the shifty, banged-up Irish suspect.

Some time later the two uniformed policemen who had delivered him to the cell returned and beckoned him from the open door. One stood smiling and twirling a key in his hand.

'I want to phone the hospital where my brother is,' Lindow demanded.

They didn't respond, but came forward and hauled him to his feet.

'Don't want you falling down, do we, sir?' said one, taking hold of the waistband of his trousers and wrenching it upwards so his balls were crushed.

Lindow yelled, 'I can walk without your help.'

They pushed him into the bright light of the interview room, which made him shield his eyes for a second. Bostock and Simmonds were still there but Bostock's place at the table had been taken by a new officer, a man with a gaunt face and old-fashioned horn-rimmed spectacles.

'Sit down, please, Dr Lindow,' said the man, gesturing to the chair opposite him. He smiled, and the corners of his mouth turned downwards in a curious grimace.

Lindow eased himself into the chair, holding the material of his trousers away from the cut on his thigh. He wasn't much to look at, this officer. He was small and sat so that his back formed into a rounded hunch. He was also seedily dressed – knitted tie, checked shirt and dark grey suit that was shiny at the cuffs. His grey hair was plastered to his skull with some sort of lacquer.

Lindow studied the man's eyes, which were moving rapidly over a document, held up so that Lindow could not read it. He glanced to see what time it was on the man's watch, but it was hidden by a slightly frayed shirt cuff. That was one thing he could do for himself. He'd make sure he got the time before he left that room again.

'Good morning, Dr Lindow, I'm Superintendent Phipps,' the man began. 'Sam Phipps is my name. Now, perhaps we can get this over quickly. I know that you've had some distressing news.'

His manner was soothing, almost apologetic, like that of a bureaucrat commencing a wearisome formality that he knew would be trying yet which, none the less, was necessary. But in his behaviour there was also something hard: the deadly patience of a man who expected to be lied to.

'I don't care who you are or what you want from me. But I do know that you're holding me against my will and that these officers deliberately concealed information about my brother's condition. I won't answer your questions until I am allowed to speak to the hospital. I've done nothing to justify this treatment.'

Simmonds and Bostock smiled.

'I understand your concern, Dr Lindow,' returned Phipps, looking down at his papers. 'But you must try to see it from where we stand. Both you and Eamonn were in the vicinity of the bomb last night and this naturally gives rise to suspicion.'

'Why?'

'Because you have been questioned before, haven't you? That business at Droy cemetery in Ireland. I take it you know what I am referring to.'

Lindow wasn't surprised that they had found out about the cemetery. He could handle it. He'd say exactly the same as he had to the RUC Special Branch.

'We were nowhere near the place when the explosion happened,' he said. 'I told that to the police at the time. They accepted it. They let us go so they must have believed us.'

'Yes, they let you go and both of you went on to make fine careers for yourselves, particularly you. But it all looks too pat, if you don't mind my saying so. It looks to us as if you were working to a plan, a plan that involved your going to the United States of America and gaining a respectable cover while your brother, Eamonn, merged into the background here in London. During that time the developments in Ireland meant that you were cut off from the original cause. People who you believed were solid republicans joined the peace process so you sought out the hardliners associated with the Thirty-two County Sovereignty Movement. Then you returned to the British Isles and almost the moment you got to London a bomb went off. You must see that it doesn't look good – that it looks very much as if you were working to a plan.'

'Maybe that's the way you see things, but you're making a mistake. My brother and I are innocent.'

'As you say ... but let's go through these questions and see if you can demonstrate that you are indeed innocent in this matter, Dr Lindow.'

'I want to speak to the hospital. I want to call my father.'

'We'll see about that later. Perhaps it would help if Simmonds here gave you the latest bulletin from the hospital.' He turned to Simmonds, revealing to Lindow an oddly hooked nose. He could also see his eyes better. They were pale and watery and the lids were reddened as if afflicted by conjunctivitis.

Phipps dabbed his right eye as Simmonds referred to the back of an envelope and began to read. 'Your brother was operated on last night. He lost a lot of blood and suffered some burns to his back and legs. He will need further surgery, but the hospital say he is in a "comfortable condition".'

'I want to hear that from them myself, not from you. This is my brother we're talking about. I demand that you let me phone the hospital.'

'Yes, as I say, we'll see how things go,' said Phipps. 'Then you may be allowed to speak to the doctor. Now let's talk about you, Dr Lindow. Tell me about this episode at Droy church. Why did the police think you had anything to do with it?'

'I don't *know* why they thought we had anything to do with it. We were miles away when the explosion happened – at home in bed. There were some soldiers involved. I can't remember much about it now, but they wanted to prove that the soldiers hadn't set off the explosives by mistake. They arrested a lot of people – not just us, you know.'

'Yes. But they arrested you because you had both been seen at the churchyard on several occasions before the explosion.'

'We stopped there a couple of times on our way back from fishing. I don't think I even got out of the car. Both times Eamonn pulled over by the church and relieved himself. He liked stopping there – it was part of the crack. He drank a lot while we fished and by the time we got to the church he needed to stop.'

'Pure coincidence, then, that enough explosive material and weaponry was hidden there to keep the Irish Republican Army supplied for four or five years.'

'We didn't know that. We wouldn't have stopped the car there if we'd thought the place was crawling with British soldiers.'

'Yes, British soldiers. You say that as if you loathed the security forces. Is that right? Did you loathe the British presence? After all, they were only trying to protect people like you – law-abiding citizens.'

'No, I didn't hate the British, you're twisting what I said. Besides, all that stuff is over, isn't it?'

'But you *are* a republican?'

'Not in an active sense. I am a republican but I don't believe that anything except evil could come from the Real IRA, the IRA or from the loyalists, for that matter. All of them are detestable. Apart from that basic conviction, I don't give much thought to these things. Politics is not my interest.'

'But your mother is a republican, is she not – a fervent republican?'

'My mother died two years ago.'

'Ah, I'm sorry . . . but the fact remains that you were brought up in a fiercely republican household and that this hatred of the British was part of – how shall I put it? – the domestic culture in which you grew up.'

'That's not true. It *is* true that my mother was nationalist. I don't deny it, but there was no question of us imbibing it with her milk.' Lindow felt himself colouring. Phipps looked at him closely and seemed to murmur to himself with a private understanding.

'So, the RUC accepted this story of yours and you were allowed to go. Then the following October you went to Dublin to begin your studies. You became a biologist and graduated with a first-class degree. You began to specialise in an area of molecular biology and you were offered a post in America, which combined teaching and research. Is that more or less how things developed?'

'Yes.'

'While you were living in the United States, did you have much to do with your countrymen? Boston has a famously large Irish community, does it not? Did you perhaps see the Irish situation more clearly while you were there? Were you radicalised during those years?'

'One of the reasons I leaped at the chance to go to the States was because I found home oppressive.' He paused. 'I don't know how much you know about research – it leaves little time for anything else. It's very demanding and very competitive. I was part of a team working to identify chemicals that are used in the communication between cells. This was not just science, but big business. We were up against it because we knew that a group of scientists was working on the same problems on the West Coast. We were chasing patents, working all hours God gave us. I didn't have time to think of Ireland, let alone to be radicalised, as you put it. In fact I came to care about Ireland less and less. I expected to spend the rest of my life in the United States.'

'So why did you come to Britain? Was it the case that you were woken from your status as an IRA sleeper?' Phipps put the question as a harmless inquiry about Lindow's career, as though it was a matter of unsurprising possibility that, during all that time abroad, he might have been preparing himself to detonate bombs in central London.

'Look, for Chrissake,' Lindow exploded. He paused to collect himself. 'I explained it all this morning. I came because of the opportunities open to me here. Imperial College offered me a good salary and an excellent team of people to work with. I wanted my own set-up and they gave it to me.'

Phipps looked away to a corner of the room and revolved his tongue in his mouth. Lindow followed his gaze. He remembered being told by an American attorney that the best way of unsettling a too-confident witness on the stand was to turn away and look bored. Lindow waited for Phipps's eyes to return. He was determined to show the man that he could remain every bit as controlled as he was.

'Why are you smiling, Dr Lindow?'

'Oh, it was just something a lawyer friend told me about the art of cross-examination.'

'Yes, well, no doubt you will soon be able to make further acquaintance with the legal profession. But, to return to the matter in hand, you won't deny that you're a man of considerable ability, Dr Lindow? I mean, you are a person who works both theoretically and practically – you excel at both.'

'I don't know what you're driving at, but I guess I must be good at something – yes.'

'It's therefore within the bounds of possibility that a man like you could rig an arms dump so that it would explode. There would be no problem at all with that, would there?'

'In theory, I suppose, no, there wouldn't be. But if you're asking whether I rigged that particular booby trap, no, I didn't.'

'Which booby trap?'

'The one at Droy cemetery. That's presumably what you're talking about.'

Phipps was at him like a terrier. 'I didn't say there was a booby trap at Droy. You did – because you knew the dump was fitted with a device and that you made one or two adjustments so that it would blow up the soldiers who put it there. You've all but admitted to something which, until now, you've insisted you knew nothing about. Now we're getting somewhere, aren't we, Lindow? What were you doing in Clarence Street last night?'

'That's crazy and you know it. I did know that the police suspected that the dump had been rewired, or whatever, because they told me when they questioned me. So I knew you must be talking about Droy cemetery. And anyway, for the record, I'm not admitting to anything.'

'What were you doing in Clarence Street last night?'

'I went there to meet Eamonn. I've told you. I have told these gentlemen a dozen times that we were going for a drink, then a meal. That was all there was to it.'

'Who else were you going to meet?'

'Some friend of Eamonn's. Her name was Mary. I've never met her before.'

'Not even in the United States? Mary is, apparently, an American. You knew that.'

'No, I knew nothing about her.'

'So you were going to meet up and go for a meal. Are you sure about that? Weren't you in fact about to take delivery of the explosives in order to plant them at a predetermined target chosen by Eamonn? That's why you were meeting Eamonn, wasn't it? Eamonn was carrying the bomb, or at least the components of a bomb, and that's why he used the bus. He knew he could take it right across London without the slightest risk of being stopped.'

Lindow shook his head. 'No, no, no.'

Phipps ignored him. 'But when the bomb blew up, you knew that Eamonn would be hurt, if not killed ... By God, you kept your cool. I mean, all that business about ringing your brother from the hospital when you knew that he must have been dead – or damned near it ... You see, we know all about it. So it will be much better for you to come clean. Tell us what you both planned, Con. Tell us where Eamonn keeps the stuff. Tell us who else was involved. Was Mary part of it? Was she the link between the two of you? We need to know and put a stop to this mess. You saw what happened last night. You saw what an explosion of that force does to people.'

Then Phipps stopped, leaned over the table and spoke very quietly. 'Con, I know you did it. I know you're guilty. I've seen people like you before – a college lecturer just like you from Queen's University, Belfast. He thought I'd never tumble him. But I did because I could taste his guilt, just like I can yours.'

'That's ridiculous.'

Phipps shook his head. 'I know you, Con. I know about the murdering fanaticism that brought you here. I've been seeing it for twenty-five years now and I've learned to recognise the signs.'

'Believe what you like, but you must let me speak to the hospital.'

'Not until you start giving us what we want, Lindow. Not until you start facing up to what you have to tell us and what you did to those people last night.'

'I didn't do anything. You know it, I know it, and these people here know it. I DIDN'T DO ANYTHING.'

'We're not getting anywhere,' said Phipps, nodding to Bostock and folding his notes. 'Perhaps you need some time to reflect on the seriousness of your position.'

'I don't need any time. But I am begging you to let me phone the hospital. I must hear from them myself.'

'I am sorry. That won't be possible for the time being,' said Phipps. 'Right, take him away, please.'

Bostock knocked on the door. The two uniformed officers returned.

Lindow looked down quickly at Phipps's watch. It was four twenty p.m.

'Who did this?' Foyle demanded, holding the front page of the *Evening Herald* on which was emblazoned the words BOMBERS SNARED. 'I didn't authorise this. They've got the whole damned story – names, pictures. There's even a bloody interview with one of them. What the hell's been going on?'

'I don't know, sir,' said Forbes. 'I've had a word with the press department and they assure me that they didn't give out any of this material.' He proffered the single page of that morning's press release, which bore two deftly unspecific paragraphs saying that two men had been detained.

'Who's this Abbott-Tring?' Foyle asked, rapping the paper with the back of his hand. 'What kind of name is that? Is he a crime reporter?'

'No. Apparently they've never heard of him at the press department. It's significant that he didn't feel the need to check with them before running the story. That's because he knew it all. Must've been tipped off.'

'Where'd he get it from?'

Forbes shrugged.

Foyle put the paper down and planted a fist either side of the photograph of Con Lindow being marched from the hospital's service entrance. 'How did they get this?'

'The photographers were there all night. One of them must have spotted our vehicles at the service entrance and decided to wait and see what happened.'

Foyle picked up the paper and began to read.

One of the two Irish brothers who were taken into police custody after last night's West End bomb was interviewed by the *Evening Herald* before his arrest.

Con Lindow, a genetics engineer, who is the younger of the two men, spoke while waiting to be treated in St Luke's emergency department. He suffered minor cuts and bruises. His brother, Eamonn Lindow, who was on the bus when it exploded at 7.35 p.m. last night, is believed to be in a serious condition and is under guard in hospital.

Lindow described how he had just arrived from the United States to take up a job at Imperial College, London. Clearly shocked by his experience, he went on to talk about his work in genetics. At the time he was unaware that Eamonn was being treated in the same hospital for burns and blast wounds. It is understood that Eamonn Lindow, a librarian, was travelling on the bus when the bomb exploded in the early evening, killing 10 people and injuring 47.

Lindow was arrested early this morning by officers from New Scotland Yard's Anti-Terrorist Branch and taken to Paddington Green police station. He is being held under the Prevention of Terrorism Act. His brother remains under armed guard and is expected to be informed of his arrest when he regains consciousness.

Before anti-terrorist officers realised that the brothers were being treated at the same hospital, the *Herald* interviewed Lindow among the many injured at St Luke's. He told how he had spent the last decade living and working near Boston where there is a large Irish community recognised by American and British authorities as a major source of funding for republican hardliners.

A spokesperson for Imperial College confirmed that Dr Lindow had recently joined the college. She said: 'We cannot make any comment about last night's bomb. We are very sorry to hear that Dr Lindow was injured. He is a scientist of world standing and holds several patents for medically important proteins.'

Meanwhile Eamonn Lindow was thought to be still unconscious following surgery in the early hours of this morning. A hospital spokesman said that he was under guard and that Con Lindow had been discharged into police custody.

Earlier today the Metropolitan Police issued a short statement, which confirmed that they were interested in the two men and that one of these was being held. They appealed for witnesses who may have used the 147 bus last night to come forward

So far little is known of the brothers' background, except that they were both born in the Irish Republic and were brought up in Northern Ireland.

Foyle straightened up. The reporter had plainly got into the hospital the night before, but someone must have leaked the names for him to have made the connection between the suspect and the man he talked to in Casualty. The picture snatched by the paper's photographer in the morning must have confirmed that the person the reporter had interviewed was the suspect Lindow.

'Who's pushing this stuff?'

Forbes's eyes rolled to the ceiling.

'Upstairs? I wonder why. Anyway, whatever the reason, that smart-alec journalist had better watch it. If the Lindows turn out to be innocent, they'll both have excellent grounds to sue. I mean, "Bombers Snared" – you couldn't get less ambiguous.'

Privately he had an idea who might be briefing the press so hard that the editor had taken that sort of risk, but decided to keep it to himself.

Forbes flipped a sheet on his clipboard. 'I don't mean to hurry you, sir, but your meeting at the Cabinet Office is due to start in twenty-five minutes. Shall I get Sergeant Taylor to send for a car?'

'No, I'll walk. I need the exercise. What's it about? I mean, precisely what do they want to know?'

'Seems that the Cabinet Secretary has been asked by the Prime Minister to get together everyone involved in this inquiry. It replaces the Joint Intelligence Committee meeting, which is normally held today, and will include people from the current intelligence committees on Ireland and the Middle East. They're pooling all knowledge on this one for a quick assessment. The PM wants to be brought up to speed before his appearance on the television news tonight. He's due to meet the Irish premier and needs to know exactly what the position is. The unionists are getting hot under the collar, saying that the peace process has been blown apart by the republicans. No one can see a way out of it.'

'They don't normally ask us to meetings like this. Isn't the commissioner going?'

'No, sir. The official I spoke to said the Prime Minister wanted it from the horse's mouth. Assistant Commissioner Scarratt will also be there, along with representatives from MI5 and MI6. It will be chaired by the Cabinet Secretary, Sir Derek Crystal, who's reporting to the Prime Minister immediately afterwards. It should be interesting for you – it's *the* Whitehall powerhouse.'

Foyle rubbed his nose with a knuckle. 'Yes, well, it means that the five thirty briefing will have to be postponed. Make it six thirty. Okay.'

From New Scotland Yard Foyle walked through Queen Anne's Gate, leaving the fortress of the Home Office to his left. The weather had brightened and he decided to sit for a few minutes in St James's Park to gather his thoughts. He chose a bench under the drooping yellow leaves of a catalpa tree, picked a newspaper with thumb and forefinger from an adjacent bin, spread it on the bench and sat down carefully.

He was nervous about his appearance at the Cabinet Office. At this stage of the investigation, less than twenty-four hours after the explosion, he couldn't hope to provide anything but the haziest outline. What these people wanted from him was certainty, not doubts and conjecture. This he didn't possess, still less did he know the answers to the questions that had stacked up in his mind since watching the film of Con Lindow in

Clarence Street. He rose from the bench, walked to the gravel expanse of Horse Guards Parade then passed through the archway to turn right down Whitehall. His last thought before presenting himself at the security door of the Cabinet Office was that he should confine himself to the facts of the case and leave it at that. A detailed, neutral description – that was all they would get.

Foyle was ushered into a large room decorated in formal green and hung with portraits of long-deceased men of affairs. Twenty or so of their modern counterparts sat around a long mahogany table, helping themselves to coffee from two white Thermos jugs. Foyle noted that Scarratt was already there and had positioned himself at the far end of the room next to the director general of the security service, David Cantor. It was only the second time that he had seen the now legendary Whitehall operator and he watched closely as Cantor nodded at Scarratt with flattering interest. His face was well made and exuded a sense of polish and mild good humour. He smiled easily, the corners of his mouth spreading out, rather than upwards, to reveal a set of neat, even teeth. It was in the eyes that Foyle imagined he saw Cantor's strength of purpose. Hooded and grey, they seemed to perform a mute calculation, quite independently of the expressions that played about the lower part of his face.

'Ah, Commander,' said the man sitting at the centre of the table, whom Foyle recognised as Sir Derek Crystal. 'We'll get straight on with it, shall we? I expect you know most of the people here, but probably not Robin Teckman, the director of MI6, and Adam Durie, who runs the Joint Intelligence Committee.' He indicated a tall man by his side and a younger official opposite him. They looked up and nodded. For a moment Foyle had the idea that he was about to be examined by the membership committee of a grand gentlemen's club. There was a lull while Crystal sorted through his files and consulted another official. Nobody said anything to Foyle, so he sat looking at the portraits and feeling he ought to have something with him – some papers to show that he'd come prepared and knew what he was about. Then he looked round the table. Forbes was right. This was where the power lay, the arena in which MI5 had scored innumerable victories over the years, wresting primary responsibility for counter-terrorism in Northern Ireland from Special Branch and MI6, then moving into the Met's preserve of criminal intelligence, offering to integrate knowledge about surveillance and secret sources into the judicial process. Foyle had heard from Forbes, a keen observer of these things, how MI5 had consolidated its position by pointing out to a grateful Civil Service that the security of government computers was dangerously lax. In one move it gained access to all government data banks, including the police national computer. There wasn't a file that the people at Millbank could not read. Millbank was unquestioned and pre-eminent and now there were even suggestions that it would be shadowing certain Met operations in a drive against police corruption.

Sir Derek whispered a few words to the young man, then called the meeting to order with a businesslike smile. 'Perhaps you'd care to bring us up to date with your investigation, Commander.'

Foyle began with the basics: the positions of the bus and the Lindow brothers when the bomb went off. He described the way the bomb was contained in a canvas bag and how it had been carried on to the bus some time between six forty-five and seven thirty-five p.m. He said there were still a large number of unknowns. The police did not know whether the bomb had gone off of its own accord, or whether it had been intentionally detonated. No timer or trigger device had been found in the wreckage, and this was due to the damage caused by the large amount of explosive used. Debris was distributed over a wide area and it was difficult to distinguish between what might have been part of a bomb and what was not.

He moved on to the film from the security cameras showing Con Lindow, and told them how the younger brother had been interviewed twice that day but that nothing had come of it. Both the brothers' flats were being examined by forensics teams, but so far nothing had come of this either. Foyle presented it all in a scrupulous matter-of-fact tone. At each pause he stressed that the evidence could be read either way.

'But what do *you* think, Commander?' asked Sir Derek Crystal. 'An informed guess, if that's all you can manage. Are these two men members of a republican splinter group? Or are we dealing with some hitherto unappreciated menace from the loyalists, in which case these are clearly not your men? Is this a one-off, or are we in for a long campaign? I need your ideas on these questions.'

'It's difficult to say. There has been no admission of responsibility, but that is to be expected since it's been announced that we are holding two suspects. In these circumstances terrorist groups never confirm their men's involvement. Still, from an intelligence point of view, the attack was surprising. There may still be dormant active-service units here, which have become renegade, but there was no indication that they were about to start bombing London again. As to the loyalist solution – the idea that the protestant paramilitaries bombed the heart of the capital in the hope that the republicans would be blamed – well, there's nothing to suggest that they have been considering such a drastic step.'

'Are these the men who did it?' asked Sir Derek, the perpendicular cleft in his forehead deepening with impatience.

'To be candid,' said Foyle, looking up the table to Scarratt and Cantor, 'I am not yet convinced of it. If we accept that the explosion was an accident, and that they had planned to use the explosive material at a later stage, it's still difficult to know why both brothers were carrying identification. The IRA, like other terrorist organisations, has learned a lot in the last twenty years. We know that they have procedures and that one of these is to check that their people go out stripped of identity – of anything that helps us trace them. It means that if something does go wrong it gives the others time to escape. But, of course, other groups would have the same procedure.'

'But surely,' said David Cantor, from the other end of the table, 'we're not going to ignore the fact that one of these Irishmen had his rear blown off by the bomb and the other had just conveniently arrived in this country after a long period in Boston. These things *do* seem to add up.'

'Yes, on the face of it they're persuasive.' Foyle addressed his remarks solely to Cantor. 'Nevertheless, I believe we should keep an open mind.'

'Well, is there anyone else we suspect of blowing up Clarence Street?' asked Sir Derek.

'Not at present, sir, but—'

'Then we cannot rule out that this was a renegade IRA action. I take it, from what you are saying, that there will be no charges tonight.'

'Yes, sir. That's correct.'

'Will the police be applying to the Home Secretary for an extension of Lindow's detention under the Prevention of Terrorism Act?' asked Cantor.

'We have another twenty-four hours before that will be necessary, sir. But it is perfectly possible that we will. We may still have his brother to question,' said Foyle.

'And what state is he in?' asked Sir Derek.

'Not good. He's back on life-support this afternoon,' said Foyle.

Sir Derek made a note, then looked round the table with his eyebrows raised, inviting other contributions. Cantor darted to press home his point. 'I don't want to anticipate anything that you were planning to say, Sir Derek, but I think it would be useful for the Prime Minister to know that both these men have been interviewed before. Is that not the case, Commander? As I understand it, they were arrested in Ulster in connection with an explosion in a churchyard in the early eighties.' There was an implied question mark after the word 'churchyard', as if he couldn't quite remember the details. He looked for help from Scarratt, who obliged him with a nod.

'Yes,' said Foyle. 'There was an incident, but neither of these two men was charged. We're going over the papers from that time to gain a clearer picture of their involvement.'

'Our information is that Eamonn Lindow may be more than he seems,' Cantor continued. 'We have little in terms of hard evidence. As you will know, we've recently received much useful instruction from the police on the distinction between intelligence and evidence. I would place this firmly in the category of intelligence. But let me just say that Eamonn Lindow was not unknown to us. Before the ceasefire and the Stormont Agreement, he was mainstream IRA, a valued operator. After the settlement, many of the IRA's men here were stood down or simply receded into the woodwork. However, in his case there was a feeling that he was still effectively operational. We made it our business to find out what he was doing and we were watching him. After some months we concluded that he had been activated, but for what purpose eluded us. The important point is that our information adds to the significance of his presence on that bus and of his brother's at the scene. You may wish to keep an open mind, but I think you'll agree that we should not ignore what is staring us in the face.'

The room caught the note of menace in Cantor's voice. Foyle was beginning to feel a sense of doom when the head of MI6, Robin Teckman, leaned forward and spoke. His manner was deliberate and precise, each point emphasised by small sweeping motions of his right hand. Cantor's features remained impassive but Foyle noticed a concentrated look enter his eyes.

'Commander, I wonder if there is another point that we are ignoring here. This is not my area, but am I right in thinking that this bomb was unusually large? I believe it contained over twelve pounds of Semtex, whereas one or two pounds would have been easily enough to destroy the bus – enough to make the point, if you see what I mean.'

'You mean the size of the bomb has a bearing on the sort of target it was made for,' said Foyle, 'and therefore we might conclude that it was destined for another much larger target?'

'Yes, as you say, a larger target – a public building, a motorway flyover, an installation of some sort.' He removed his glasses to reveal two exceptionally large dark eyebrows, which had been masked by the frame. 'But there have been occasions when the opposite was true, when a large bomb was used to disguise the fact that the target was rather modest. There were two such devices used in Eastern Europe recently. These appeared to be aimed at a train and a large building, but were in fact targeted at specific individuals. In neither case did the relevant authorities appreciate that they were dealing with assassination devices. I mention this because if the bomb was not an accident, it may just conform to this pattern. We'll furnish your department with the relevant material by the end of the afternoon.'

Foyle thanked him.

'So I take it,' said Sir Derek, 'that I should tell the Prime Minister things are at an early stage, and that you will let us know if there are any developments, particularly if charges are to be made. Assistant Commissioner Scarratt, can I rely on you to liaise with my office? I don't have to stress how important this is in the current circumstances.' He paused and looked up with another bleak smile. 'If you'll forgive us, we just have a little more business to attend to. Thank you both for joining us.'

With that, Foyle and Scarratt were dismissed from the meeting.

Outside, Scarratt stood on the pavement looking at the traffic and slapping his black leather gloves against the palm of his hand. 'That, Commander, was a bloody disaster. We've got to get our act together on this one. We're in the front line, you know. Our performance is being scrutinised.' Then he turned to his car, swept off his cap and climbed into the back seat.

Foyle watched as he was driven off down Whitehall. Scarratt was an officious fool, but Foyle knew he was right: his performance had been woefully unconvincing. Still, the meeting had not been a complete waste of time. He walked slowly towards Parliament Square with Teckman's words playing through his mind. The more he thought about it, the odder Teckman's intervention seemed. It was plain that the director of MI6 was steering him, or at least trying to open the investigation to other possibilities.

It was just past six thirty when he arrived at New Scotland Yard. He went straight to the briefing room, where SO 13 and Special Branch officers were already assembled. He called for silence and asked Sergeant Pennel to read out what his team had learned about the Lindows' movements.

'I'll begin with Eamonn Lindow,' said Pennel. 'He left the library at five forty-five, which is his usual time, and walked to a pub with a colleague, where they had a pint. The colleague said he seemed relaxed until he realised that he was running late. She said that she told him the bus would be quicker because it would be going against the traffic flow into the West End. There were problems with the tube line and she was quite sure that she recommended the bus.'

'That's interesting. Was he carrying anything?'

'No. She was sure about that too.'

'What time was this?'

'She thinks it was about six forty-five. The pub is a ten-minute walk from the library. She reckons they were there for about half an hour.'

'And they didn't meet anyone else?'

'No.'

'When had they arranged to have a drink?'

'She said that it was a spur-of-the-moment thing to discuss some problem at the library. She suggested it.'

'Would Eamonn have had time to go back to his flat?'

'No, it's in the opposite direction, sir. And if he had, he would have travelled by another bus route into town. Of course, he may have picked up the bag along the route.'

'What about Con Lindow?'

'Much the same story, sir, except he seems to have gone back to his place to change before going out. The people at the university said that he had been wearing a suit when he left. There had been a meeting with a group from industry. He needed to make a good impression. But he wasn't in his flat long.'

'When did he leave Imperial College?'

'At five forty, sir. The department secretary remembers exactly because she wanted to leave early herself and felt she couldn't go before he did.'

'So what we are saying here is that there is nothing out of the ordinary in their behaviour?'

'That seems about right – yes.'

'Have we got anything on the woman they were going to meet – the woman on the message tape from Eamonn's flat?'

'Nobody at the library knew of her. Their impression was that Eamonn didn't have a girl. He never mentioned anyone. Apparently he has a lot of interests – poetry, old films, real ale – but nothing in the way of a permanent relationship.'

'So what do we have from the two flats?'

The officer in charge of the searches, Inspector Lockyer, rose and held up his thumb and index finger to form a zero.

'It's the same story, sir,' he said. 'Absolutely sweet FA. Both places clean as a bishop's bed. There's a lot of junk in Eamonn's flat, which we're going through. His clothing is being submitted to the standard tests for explosives and we're examining all the bed linen, soft furnishings, kitchen utensils but it doesn't look very hopeful. The brother's flat in Notting Hill is interesting. It's a service place on a short let. The sort of flat a wealthy businessman would rent for a couple of months. Not a lot of his personal possessions, apart from a few books connected with his work and his clothes. They're being tested too. There's a woman downstairs who looks after the place for the owners. Lindow told her he was looking for a bigger flat. He said he would move when he got his stuff out of storage. He had asked her to put out feelers and he was talking to estate agents. He didn't seem to want to buy, just rent.'

'How long's he been here?'

'Close to three weeks. The woman says that he's out most of the time. No sign of him ever cooking anything; goes early, returns late. No visitors that she knows of.'

'That ties in with the people at the university,' said Sergeant Pennel. 'They say he eats in the canteen and rarely leaves his office before nine p.m. The department secretary keeps his diary. She made two previous arrangements for him to see Eamonn, but they were cancelled.'

'Any reasons?'

'She remembers Dr Lindow saying that his brother had been ill.

Nothing serious. And then the second time he had to attend a welcoming party that had been sprung on him by his head of department.'

Foyle turned to Lockyer. 'You say his things are in storage. Any idea where that might be?'

'Yes, sir, we found the shipping forms. The container should be at Tilbury by the end of the week and they'll go into storage then.'

'Good, I want it searched as soon as it hits the dockside. Forbes, can you keep that in hand?'

Forbes nodded.

'Okay,' said Foyle, addressing the room. 'What we need to do this evening is to work on building up the profiles of these two fellows. I want to know everything about Eamonn Lindow. Millbank say they've had him under surveillance and that he seems to have republican connections. I'll get the relevant material from them this evening. We also need to trace anyone who knew Con Lindow in the United States. Start hitting the phones.'

'We already have, sir,' said Sergeant Pennel. Foyle smiled. Pennel had turned out well since he'd been brought in from a liaison job between Customs and Excise and the Drugs Squad. 'One of his referees for the new post was a Dr Peter Varrone. He also figures in Lindow's address book. We rang him earlier today and taped the interview. He had nothing but good things to say about Lindow. Said he was one of the smartest people to come his way in years. Lindow is the owner of patents that will make him a wealthy man. We're talking to other people in the address book. So far the picture we're getting is of a very dedicated person – brilliant in his field.'

'And what is that exactly?' asked Foyle.

'Originally he was involved in work on the human-genome project and then he moved on to studying bacteria and the way they communicate with each other. As I have had it explained to me, it's about the behaviour of human cells and bacteria. He dives in and out of different areas. Apparently he's smart enough to do that.'

'Good, we need more of that sort of thing. Find out where he lived. Talk to his friends, girlfriends, associates – I want to know about his political convictions and any contacts he had with Irish groups. Run it all past the FBI.'

The briefing continued with inconclusive reports from Irish intelligence and then routine updates from the Special Branch surveillance of other suspects. There were no obvious connections with the Lindows.

Foyle began to wrap up the briefing. 'While we'll be doing a lot of work on the Lindows tonight and tomorrow, I want you to try to think of this inquiry without them. Think what we would be doing if two Irishmen hadn't been handed to us on a plate. Where would we be looking? Who would we be talking to? It may turn out that the Lindows aren't our men, after all.' He turned to leave the room, then pulled up by the door. 'Oh, by the way ... we can't have any more coverage like this morning's. I don't want the press creating an atmosphere in which it becomes impossible for us to see our way through this thing. Just thought I'd mention it, although I'm certain none of it came from this department.'

Back in his office, Foyle found Sam Phipps waiting. 'What do you think, Sam? Guilty, or what?' He realised at once he should have known better with Phipps, who was famously noncommittal, particularly when in the middle of an interrogation – or examination, as he preferred to call it. In his view, interrogation smacked of beatings and intimidation.

'Hard to say,' he said morosely. 'It's difficult when one hasn't been in on it from the outset.'

Foyle knew that Phipps hated the fact that Simmonds and Bostock had been let loose on the first session with Lindow. Phipps liked to feel his way like a blind clock-maker working out the mechanism by touch and instinct. When he found a part he didn't understand, he never forced it, but left it alone until gradually the thing made sense to him. Only then would he allow himself to fit it tentatively into the whole.

'How long have I got?' he asked.

'Well, we can go for an extension until tomorrow afternoon, at which point we will have had him in custody for thirty-six hours. There won't be any problem with that. The Home Office will let us have him for the maximum seven-day period. Do you feel you're going to need that?'

Phipps sucked at his teeth. 'I'm not sure. Something's there, but I'm not certain whether it's relevant. It's that business in Northern Ireland. When I press him on it, he's easily rattled and becomes inconsistent. Yet when I ask him about last night and the circumstances that led him to come to Britain, I sense he's much more relaxed. I'll be in a better position to give you an opinion tomorrow morning.'

Phipps left. Foyle picked up the phone and asked to be put through to Peter Speerman, the deputy director of MI5. He knew Speerman, a thin, cautious bureaucrat with slightly sunken cheeks and an ill-disguised bald patch. They had met during Home Office sessions designed to increase co-operation between the police and the security service.

Speerman came on the line. 'Hello, Commander. Hope you're well. I've got some material for you.'

'Good. Is there anything in it?'

'The main point is that Eamonn Lindow has had some dealings with a character called Rudi MacMahon. You may have heard of him. He was a member of the IRA's army council. He went legitimate nine years ago and got himself elected as a Sinn Fein councillor. He has played a big part in the Stormont peace agreement. He's quite a player, and at root he's still a hard man. Lindow and MacMahon have met at least twice in the last five years. In fact, we have pictures of them talking in the street. They were at the same school.'

'You'll send the file over, then?'

'Certainly, and if there's anything else, please call me. We are here to help.'

Foyle hung up.

Later that evening Con Lindow was roused and taken from the cells. His eyes ached and his mouth tasted stale. Phipps did not look up when Lindow was put in the chair opposite him.

'Right, Dr Lindow. We need a few more answers from you. Then you can have a wash and shave.'

'You mean you're going to ask me to sign some damned stupid confession, then you'll let me have a wash. You know I'm innocent and you know that you're abusing my rights – my right to exercise, to sleep without being disturbed, to know the time of day, to take meals at the normal times, to telephone my family. And what about the right to visit my brother? You're abusing my rights, Phipps, and when I leave here I'll pursue every course open to me to expose you for what you are.'

Phipps looked up at him with the expression of a man waiting for a rain shower to pass. 'We have no further information about your brother. But we will let you know as soon as we do.'

'Then I will say nothing,' Lindow said, feeling his face flush.

'In which case we will have to take it that you have something to hide – and in these circumstances, Dr Lindow, a judge and jury are liable to draw an adverse inference from your silence. Even if you do get out of here, that silence may prompt the Home Secretary to make you the subject of an exclusion order – which, despite the advances of recent years, is still an option open to him. Now, just answer these few questions for us. Then we'll see about the other things. What do you know about a man named Rudi MacMahon?'

Christ, when the hell were they going to let up?

'I don't know anyone of that name.'

'Oh, come along. He's a friend of your brother's. They were school pals and they kept in touch.'

'Look, I can't answer for my brother. I don't know what he does. I'm here to answer questions about myself, not my brother.'

Lindow jumped as Phipps barked with surprising volume. 'Under section eleven of the Prevention of Terrorism Act you are required to answer questions about anyone we suspect of terrorism. If you withhold information you may be charged with a criminal offence. So please *do* answer our questions about your brother and MacMahon, Dr Lindow.'

'I don't know him. Eamonn never mentioned him to me.' Then he paused, remembering. 'Oh, of course, yes, I *do* know who you mean. Isn't he the Sinn Fein man? Yes, Eamonn was at school with him. But I've never met him and I'm sure Eamonn didn't keep in touch with him. They didn't like each other much.'

'It's very interesting you say that,' said Phipps. 'You referred to him as the "Sinn Fein man". Rudi MacMahon only became an official Sinn Fein candidate nine years ago. Before that he was the brigade leader in Fermanagh. How would you know that he was an official Sinn Fein candidate if you had not talked to your brother about him? By your own account you didn't keep abreast of the events in Northern Ireland so there's no other way you would know.'

Lindow sighed. 'Really, you are desperate, aren't you? I knew he was a Sinn Fein politician because I saw his picture some time ago in Boston. It was the St Patrick's Day parade and MacMahon was on the front of the local paper. I remember it because there were some stories about him getting a visa. The picture showed him holding up a little girl to the camera, like a politician would. At the time I wondered if the girl's parents had any idea about the things he had done in his life.' The room was hot and airless, and Phipps was so close to him that Lindow could smell his breath.

Phipps grimaced a smile. 'So MacMahon visited Boston. Did you happen to meet him while he was there, Dr Lindow?'

'No, of course not. I told you, I just saw his face in the paper. Nothing else.'

'But you agree that your brother was consorting with senior members of the IRA, men who posed as politicians but were still at the time deeply involved in the armed struggle. You agree that he was a friend of your brother's.'

'He was a contemporary of Eamonn's at school. That's all. You can't help who you're at school with. I mean, Eamonn and I ... we didn't know that he was definitely a Provisional.'

'Oh, please, Dr Lindow,' exhaled Phipps. 'You just said that you wondered if the girl's parents had any idea what Rudi MacMahon had done in his life – meaning, of course, that you wondered if they had any idea about the bombs and murders and beatings he was responsible for. That's what you said and everyone in this room heard it – I'll play it back on the tape for you, if you require. And yet now you say you didn't know he was a member of the IRA.'

'You know what I meant. I didn't know for certain. That's all I was saying. You have suspicions about people, but you don't know for sure.'

Lindow felt the fight draining from him and, in his head, he heard his voice rise in a panicky falsetto. Collect yourself, he thought. Lower your voice and cool it.

'Yes. We all have suspicions about people, don't we?' Phipps continued. 'For instance, I have my suspicions about you. I don't know exactly what happened last night, but my guess is that bomb was not primed to go off. Indeed, I think it likely that you were meeting your brother to take delivery of a consignment of Semtex, which would be used in several different devices that you were going to construct in your flat in Notting Hill. That would explain the unusually large amount of explosive in the suitcase. I'm right, aren't I? When you had finished your work, you'd leave the flat and bugger off back to America.'

'No, no, that's not right. Can't you see? What do I have to do to convince you, for Chrissake?'

'But then the Semtex blew up of its own accord, nearly killing Eamonn. Perhaps there was more in that suitcase than just Semtex – primer-charge material, detonators, batteries, tilt switches, timers. Who knows, a whole bomb-making kit? At any rate the case was subject to a sudden shock and the whole lot went up with a bloody great BANG.' Phipps crashed both fists down on the table. Lindow recoiled. 'You had a pretty good idea that Eamonn was injured but you knew that you had to pretend otherwise, which explains the pantomime at the hospital and all that acting in here today when you were told that Eamonn had been hurt.'

'No. None of this is true. You're wrong. You don't know how wrong you are. I am not a terrorist, for God's sake!'

'You're not listening properly, Lindow. We know what happened, so why not make a clean breast of it? Maybe we can fix something up. It'll be hard for us to prove that you had an intention to cause explosions and a good lawyer might even get you off altogether. Talk to me, Con. Tell me what Eamonn planned. Tell me where the rest of the explosives are hidden. Talk to me now, Con, then you can take your shower, have something to eat and get some kip ... Tomorrow you'll speak to the hospital and see a lawyer. We'll fix it. It'll be all right for you. You'll see.'

Phipps's face had tilted very close to the table. He was looking up into Lindow's eyes. Then he placed a hand on Lindow's shoulder and squeezed a little. Lindow felt the hand draw the tension from his neck. It made him yearn to sleep. He'd never felt so tired and he knew he was about to succumb to Phipps. He had to keep fighting him.

Minutes seemed to pass without anyone speaking. Then Phipps said, very quietly, 'You're going to talk to us properly now, aren't you? You all right, Con?'

'Yes, I am all right, thank you,' said Lindow, looking up to face the others. 'I won't bother with the shower, or any of the rest of it. I've done nothing. I am saying nothing more and I am going back to my cell. You can keep me here as long as you like, but I'm not confessing to something I haven't done.'

He got up, and before anyone could stop him, pinned Phipps's left arm to the table and snatched at the sleeve on his jacket to reveal his watch. It was eleven twenty p.m. Bostock leaped forward and cuffed him to the ground.

'That's enough,' shouted Phipps. 'Take him back to the cells and give him something to eat.'

4

'Can I give you some advice, Kenneth?'

Foyle had learned to be wary when Scarratt used his first name. Moreover, he knew the assistant commissioner had just returned from lunch at MI5's Millbank headquarters, a piece of intelligence gleaned by Forbes that morning.

'Yes, sir, if you like. I'd be happy to hear your thoughts on the case.'

'It's not so much the case, Commander, it's more your general approach. At this level you can't work in isolation. You must learn to see the bigger picture and understand the way the different parts interlock and depend on each other. We have to work with those different interests and take into account their requirements.'

'What are you saying, sir?' asked Foyle, although he was pretty sure what was coming.

'If you release Con Lindow, you will give out certain signals to those interests. To lock up a man and then let him go within a day or two looks as if we're not trying hard enough. It will tell the other agencies concerned that we do not respect the information and help that they have offered us over the past twenty-four hours. For instance, the director general of the security service has informed us that he knows of contacts between Eamonn Lindow and a well-known republican figure. It would be wrong to ignore that, Kenneth, very wrong indeed.' Scarratt took a turn around Foyle's office while waiting for his reply, then suddenly said, 'How's the family?'

Foyle raised his eyes to the ceiling. 'Away, sir.'

'Perhaps you should spend more time with them, when you can.' He was feeling the brush of his cropped hair.

'I saw my daughter on Tuesday.'

Scarratt swivelled round. 'Yes, I heard about that, Kenneth. Most unfortunate for you. Let's hope she stays out of trouble from now on. You don't want that sort of worry as well.'

Foyle had wondered how long it would be before Scarratt found out about Katherine. No doubt he had learned about it over lunch. MI5 kept files on various groups of troublemakers. Katherine's name must have been picked up on Tuesday.

'To return to this business about Lindow. It would be wrong – profoundly wrong – and impolitic not to hold him a little longer. You have to give Phipps more time with him, a day or two more and he'll have everything we need to know.'

'But on what grounds do I continue to hold him? Everything suggests that the brothers are innocent. The phone logs from both flats, their movements over the last two weeks, the forensic tests, their behaviour on the evening of the bomb – everything produces a negative reading. I can't hold a man without evidence. If there *is* more to him than meets the eye, he'll be just as useful to us on the outside. We're not going to get anything now.'

Scarratt's expression changed. 'Think about the man you're returning to the streets of this city, Commander. What if he gets away scot-free? Have you thought of that? You're on a fixed-term contract. I can't see it being renewed if you seek to defy the collective desire that Con Lindow's interrogation should be allowed to run its full course.'

So that was the threat: if Foyle didn't do the bidding of the 'collective', that is to say Scarratt's new friends at Millbank, he'd be out. Scarratt had been primed by Cantor or one of his creatures and plainly someone at Paddington Green was keeping him informed about the Lindow interrogation. It wouldn't be Phipps, who made no secret of his dislike of Scarratt. Maybe Simmonds or Bostock, or the spook who had been allowed in as part of his department's co-operation with the security service. At any rate, the fact that Millbank, Special Branch and his squad all knew that nothing had come from the interrogation was no bad thing. It helped his case to release Lindow.

Still, if a few more hours might placate Scarratt, it would be stupid to go against him and release Lindow now. He was on the point of agreeing to hold Lindow through the weekend when there was a rapid knock at the door and Forbes entered with his clipboard. 'Yes?' said Foyle.

'I am sorry to interrupt, sir. Eamonn Lindow's dead – died twenty minutes ago in surgery.'

Foyle looked at Scarratt. 'That changes things, doesn't it, sir? Has he been told yet, Forbes?'

'No, sir.'

'I think you'll agree', said Foyle, turning back to Scarratt, 'that it makes it difficult to hold him under these circumstances. We'll keep close to him. If you're right about him, he'll make a mistake and then we'll have him.'

Scarratt marched from the office without a word.

Foyle sat down. 'I want round-the-clock surveillance on Lindow. We mustn't lose track of him for a moment. I guess he'll fly home to Ireland some time next week with the body. It seems the natural thing to do. Ask the coroner's office to hurry along with the inquest and then brief the RUC and the Garda. We're going to need their help to watch him once he's out of the country. Right, I'm going to see Lindow to break the news.'

Forbes lingered in the doorway.

'Yes?' said Foyle.

'Well, I was wondering if it was strictly necessary – if it was advisable – for you to go to Paddington Green yourself. It might seem odd now.'

'Thank you, but I know what I'm doing,' Foyle snapped. Forbes should have known that Lindow was all he had got. He had to get close to him.

Forbes nodded.

Half an hour later Foyle was shown into the secure section of Paddington Green. He found Phipps in an ill-lit office looking at winter-holiday brochures. In the next-door room he could hear Simmonds and some others talking.

'Someone else's,' said Phipps drily, letting a brochure slip from his hands to the desk. 'But I could do with the break. What brings you here, Commander?'

'Eamonn Lindow's dead. I've come to tell his brother and after that I'm going to let him go, Sam. Have you had any more thoughts on him?'

'It's difficult to be precise at this stage. He's not one of your usual IRA nuts. I don't have a sense that he's acting and I'm sure he hasn't been trained to resist this kind of examination. I would have spotted it. As I said to you yesterday, there's an area I'm not happy about and that's the period in the eighties. He's all over the shop about that. But when it comes to the evening of the bomb, his story stands up. If you want a definite view, I really need more time.'

'I'm afraid that's not possible, Sam. But with Lindow out we might get something else. You never know.'

Phipps led Foyle down to the cells. On the way he told him that he'd kept Lindow locked up for the best part of the day because he thought the extension would be granted as a matter of course. That always did a lot to break a man's resistance and Phipps had kept him in the cells waiting for that moment. Except for a short time first thing that morning when he had been allowed to wash, and five minutes' statutory exercise, during which Lindow had been marched round the station car park handcuffed to an officer, he'd been in his cell for nearly sixteen hours.

They found him sitting on his bed with his head bowed. He didn't look up when they entered.

'Dr Lindow,' said Foyle, 'I am Commander Foyle. We are going to let you go in a little while, but first I'm afraid I have some bad news for you. It's about your brother, Eamonn.'

Lindow looked up slowly and searched his face. Foyle was impressed by the intelligence in his eyes.

'He died while undergoing surgery this morning. The injuries he sustained were very severe indeed. The hospital say that he never regained consciousness after the bomb.' He paused to let it sink in. 'Do you understand what I have said to you, Dr Lindow?'

Lindow nodded. Then he said flatly, 'I understand what you're saying ... Eamonn is dead.'

'I'm very sorry,' said Foyle, clasping his hands awkwardly in front of him. He hated this. He'd done it too many times before as a young officer. 'Believe me, Dr Lindow, I know how tough this is for you. I'm sorry that you've been held here at such a distressing time.'

Lindow opened his mouth, as if to cry out, but no sound came.

'Do you want to leave straight away or would you like to sit here for a while? There are just a few formalities to complete, then you'll be free to go.'

'Now!' said Lindow. 'I'd like to go now.'

A uniformed officer appeared with a sealed bag of Lindow's possessions and asked him to sign for them. Lindow checked through the bag.

'Where're my keys? They're not here.'

'They must be with us,' said Foyle. 'I'll get them to you this afternoon.'

'There's another set with the woman who looks after the place, but I'll need them tomorrow.'

Foyle led the way up out of the back of the station and towards his car, where Lindow stopped and looked up at the overcast sky. He blinked back tears and shook his head.

'I'm afraid they need you at the hospital to identify your brother's body,' said Foyle. 'Of course, there was identity on your brother and we're pretty certain it was him. Still, we would prefer it in these circumstances ... It isn't going to be easy for you. Would you like a cup of coffee beforehand? I'll take you to a place round the corner.'

Lindow inhaled deeply and shook his head. His tears had gone. 'What for? More questions? No. I've answered enough of your questions. I won't forget the way I've been treated here. Not once was I allowed to call the hospital about Eamonn. I'd have liked to have seen him before he died, or perhaps you don't understand that.'

'Yes, I understand very well, but you must see why we had to detain you. When so many people have lost their lives and been injured, we would have been failing in our duty not to talk to you. Ten people were killed. Now the toll is eleven – the largest count over here for years. We owe it to them to find the men who did this. I know it's been rough but I am afraid there simply wasn't an option. Look, why don't you let me run you to the hospital? It won't be any bother.'

Reluctantly Lindow climbed into the back of Foyle's car. Alex pulled into the traffic and began to retrace the route taken by the police van the day before. Foyle said that when they arrived at the hospital he'd better go in with him to ease the way.

'There was some publicity yesterday,' he said. 'Your picture was in the papers and they may wonder what you're doing out.'

'Are you saying that I may have a case against the press as well?' asked Lindow.

'In due course you may feel you have. I'm not a lawyer, but I would guess that you might want to press for some sort of retraction. We've no idea where they got it from. Only a short statement was released yesterday.' Foyle watched Lindow's reaction very carefully.

'But today you'll make another statement exonerating my brother and myself,' said Lindow.

'Yes, we'll make it clear that you have been released after helping with our inquiries.'

As they came to a halt in the jam around Marble Arch, Foyle examined Lindow properly for the first time. He was taller than he'd gauged from the security film and had finer features: a long aquiline nose, well-defined cheekbones and jaw, blue-grey eyes with lids that slanted down sharply at the corner. His light brown hair was thinning at the front, which exaggerated his brow. Foyle was struck by his composure. He did not look about him or fidget. His hands rested on his thighs, palms down, long thin fingers splayed out evenly. When he spoke, he did not turn to face Foyle. This wasn't a man who wasted energy on unnecessary movement. If he had something to hide, Foyle thought, it would take a long time to find it. And yet he also seemed open and human in his responses.

At the hospital Foyle took Lindow to the main reception, and told a receptionist there that they had come to identify his brother's body. While they waited Foyle gave Lindow his card and told him to expect that his flat and also his brother's place would look disturbed as they had both been searched. If there were any problems he wanted Lindow to call him.

Foyle shrugged his shoulders in apology then said goodbye, and went to a nearby phone to call Forbes. 'I have left him at the front desk of St Luke's. He's going to identify Eamonn Lindow's body. Tell them to pick him up as he leaves the hospital. He shouldn't be more than half an hour, unless he goes to Casualty and has his cuts dressed again. Impress upon the surveillance teams that they must not lose him. He's all we have at the moment . . . And, Forbes, get a press release sent out immediately saying that we've let him go.'

Lindow was shown to the mortuary by a man from the hospital administration, which had been warned by New Scotland Yard to expect him. At the back of his mind he knew that he was doing the wrong thing in seeing Eamonn's body. Eamonn had seen their mother in hospital after she died and he had written to Con to say the memory wasn't easily shaken from his mind. His lasting image of her was of her corpse.

In the long, tiled room a police officer was waiting with two other attendants, who looked on with sympathetic interest. Lindow was led to a spot in the centre of the room, where Eamonn's body lay on a trolley under a sheet. The administrator nodded to one of the attendants, who drew back the sheet.

'Is this your brother, sir? Is this Eamonn Lindow?' said the police officer quietly.

Lindow looked down at the body for several seconds. The only evidence of the monstrous trauma suffered by Eamonn was a large bruise that had coloured the skin on his jaw and neck a sickly ochre. But this wasn't the reason why he barely recognised him. Even in repose, Eamonn was never sombre. The gravity of his final expression seemed to have altered the whole structure of his face. Lindow had the uncomfortable impression that he was intruding on his brother, that he might wake suddenly and produce a vivid stream of invective, just as he had once when Lindow had barged into the bathroom and caught him sitting on the lavatory. He imagined his blue eyes flashing open. 'What are you about, Con? Can't a man get any rest without his brother sneaking up and peering at him like some sort of specimen in his laboratory?' He heard Eamonn drawing out each syllable for comic effect – 'spe-ci-men', he would have said.

Lindow held the side of the trolley. 'Sorry ... I haven't seen him for two years. What I mean to say is that he's changed.' He looked at Eamonn again. 'You see, he's lost weight and his hair has receded more. At first I didn't think it was him ... But it is ... Yes, this is my brother, Eamonn Lindow.'

'Thank you, sir. I am sorry,' said the policeman. 'Would you like a few moments here alone, sir? It's perfectly in order. We'll be outside.'

'No, that's all right.' He shook his head. He could feel himself losing control, but he knew that he couldn't – not in this place. He composed himself and turned to the policeman. 'Is that all you need?'

The officer nodded, then followed Lindow and the administrator out of the mortuary. At the door he asked for Lindow's telephone number so that the coroner's office could let him know about the inquest.

'Don't you have it already?' he asked.

'No, sir, I'm from the local police station, but I can get it from New Scotland Yard, if it's difficult for you now.'

'Isn't it on a list somewhere? I gave it to the people in Accident and Emergency Reception before.'

'Ah, yes, I didn't think of that. I'll get it from them, if you like.'

Lindow relented and gave him the number. Then he asked for

directions to the outpatients department. He wanted his stitches checked and dressed again. His leg was bothering him. The doctor gave him a local anaesthetic, removed another piece of glass that had come to the surface, then stitched the wound.

In less than half an hour Lindow left the hospital via the Casualty exit and walked down the ramp to hail a cab for Notting Hill. It was rush hour and the ride back to his flat was agonisingly slow. He longed for a bath and his bed. When he reached Homer Road he got out, felt for his keys, then, remembering that the police still had them, rang the bell of the ground-floor flat where he retrieved another set from the housekeeper. She looked at him suspiciously but wished him a good evening. Finally he dragged himself up the steps to the main entrance of the building and let himself in.

It was exactly forty-eight hours since he had been home. During that time the flat had been subject to a kind of hostile occupation. The carpets in all three rooms were curled up at the edges where they had been wrenched from the floor and, as he moved about, Lindow could feel the floorboards creak beneath him. They'd been pulled up then hastily nailed back. Everywhere there were signs of furious search and botched repair. The skirting-boards and panelling of the long window-seat in the sitting room appeared to have sprung free of their own accord. Most of the light fittings and electrical sockets were loose. The drawers in the bedroom had been rifled and upturned and the few books that he had kept out of storage thumbed then tossed aside. Even the back of the television lay broken on the floor. In the bedroom the ceiling of the fitted wardrobe was hanging down and the drawers from the unit inside piled high beside the bed, their contents heaped in a midden of clothes and linen. They'd been sure he wasn't coming back.

He went to the kitchen, where he found all the cooking utensils coated in fingerprint dust and smelling of a pungent chemical. He opened the fridge and withdrew a bottle of white wine. He poured a glass and drank it at a gulp, more from thirst than a need for alcohol. He poured another and returned to the sitting room where he pressed the flashing button on his answering-machine. There was a message from the letting agent whom he'd been due to meet the day before.

He picked up the phone and dialled his father in Ireland. Tag answered. Suddenly he found he couldn't speak. He was lost in the memory of the day that Eamonn had christened their little sister. She would follow them everywhere, never let them be alone, so he called her Tag Along. It was shortened to Tag and stuck. 'I'm sorry,' Lindow said eventually. 'I had to gather my thoughts.'

'Oh, Con! It's you. It's so good to hear you. We were worried sick. When did they let you go?'

'This afternoon ... Look, Tag, I've been to identify Eamonn in the hospital. That's why I didn't ring before.'

'Oh, God ... poor Con.'

Lindow heard her control a sob. Then she told him about their father who had had an attack of angina during the day and been given some pills and something to calm him down by the doctor. He was too upset to speak on the phone.

'I would come over to help,' she said, 'only Dad has taken it very bad. I can't leave him now.'

'It really isn't necessary. I can manage it all.' Lindow tried to soften his voice, but it was difficult because he was certain that someone would be listening. He had a lot to say to her, but it would have to keep until they saw each other.

'Tag, I don't want to talk now. Do you mind?'

'I know, we'll talk when you're here.'

'I don't know when that'll be. I'll phone the coroner tomorrow and see when they're prepared to release the body. Then I'll ring you and we'll talk about the arrangements.'

He rang off then dialled the number on Foyle's card. A woman answered and told him that the commander was in a meeting. He said he'd call back but would like to register a complaint now about the state of his home. He would be suing the police.

He didn't care much about the flat: it wasn't his place and he could easily settle the bill with the landlord. The money wasn't the point: the abuse of him and his home was. The next day he'd see a lawyer about his arrest. There was also the newspaper coverage to think about. He must get copies of Wednesday's papers.

The wine began to take effect. He walked unsteadily towards the bay window in the sitting room to let down the blinds. It was dark outside, but he could see two men sitting in a parked car across the road. The street lighting made the passenger's spectacles glint. A little way up the road was another car. A man wearing a motorcycle helmet was leaning down to the nearside window. They'd all be there the next morning, he was sure.

He pulled at the blind cords and began to strip off his clothes. Then he carried them into the kitchen and dumped them into the waste-bin. He'd never use the clothes he'd worn in prison again, nor the bloodied jacket that he'd used to cover the girl in the street.

He was hungry. He searched around for food and found some cheese crackers, a wedge of processed Cheddar and a packet of salami. Clutching the wine and the food, he padded into the bedroom, where he caught sight of himself in the full-length mirror. He stopped for a moment and regarded the white, bandaged figure framed under the light. While gazing at himself he munched a cracker and swilled it down with wine. He looked a full ten years older.

A few minutes later he had swept the mess from his bed and was asleep.

It was late. Foyle toyed with the idea of leaving New Scotland Yard for La Bourriche, a French bistro he'd taken to using once or twice a week because he'd become friendly with the owner, a woman named Carla Pryn. Their relationship had never quite developed into an affair, but Foyle had relied increasingly on her company after June left. He wanted to see her that evening but knew he needed to go over the files and reports that had accumulated on his desk during the day. Everything would have to be read again, absorbed, sifted and considered so that next morning he'd be able to supply new lines of attack and new inspiration, both of which were badly needed. Scarratt was on his back about Con Lindow and had formally requested that he set down his reasons for not using the full interrogation time provided under law. There was no doubt in his mind that Scarratt was preparing the ground to get rid of him, but Foyle was sure he couldn't move against him yet and he estimated that he had between ten days and a fortnight to produce some results.

He unlocked his hands from behind his head, rose and walked to the coffee and snack machines at the far end of the corridor. They'd been his idea, although – as the memo from Scarratt's office had pointed out – they needed to be stocked and serviced every day, which entailed a loss of police man hours. Each time the service man came he was accompanied by an officer to make sure there were no security implications. That was the phrase in Scarratt's memo: 'The coffee machine presents security implications for the department.' Foyle wrote back, facetiously telling him that the machines would be regularly swept for listening devices and checked for explosives. Scarratt solemnly replied that, after reviewing the matter, he would allow Foyle's department to keep its machines. In memory of his victory he patted the coffee vendor as it spewed a watery version of cappuccino.

Way down the corridor Foyle could hear keyboards at work and officers murmuring into phones. He returned to his desk and pulled over the folder sent that morning by Robin Teckman. It contained reports about two explosions, one in Prague and the other in Budapest, both apparently caused by portable devices. The Prague bomb had gone off at eight thirty in the morning of 10 December 1994 as a commuter train travelling from Konopiste in the south drew out of its last stop before the capital. The rear carriages had been blown off the track. Three people were killed, one of whom was a journalist named Jan Nosecky, who'd exposed the illegal export of arms from Russia to the Middle East through the Czech Republic. Nosecky had traced the individuals responsible for the trade through a number of shelf companies in the Czech Republic and their trading partners in the former Soviet Union. At first the local police refused to believe that such a large bomb had been deployed against one man. Besides, that day Nosecky had changed his routine by boarding a train. Nobody could possibly have known that his car would break down ten miles from the city and that he would have to resort to using the train on one of its innumerable stops northwards. At length they got round to examining his car and found that the fan-belt had been sawn part of the way through so that it would snap soon after the engine began to heat up. Somebody had wanted Jan Nosecky to take the train. But still, the police remained unconvinced and tried to persuade Nosecky's colleagues in the press that if someone had wanted to kill the journalist they had had only to fix a device to his car. Clearly they had access to it.

Foyle read on and noted that no timing or command device had been found in the debris of the carriages. It was a mystery as to how the bomb had been detonated. At one stage the Czech police had been tempted to view it as an accident, wondering for a time whether Nosecky had been carrying the explosives himself. Not until the Hungarian police researched the background of the victims in the Budapest bomb did the Czechs grasp that Jan Nosecky must have been the principal target in the train bombing.

On the face of it, the lunch-time bombing of the headquarters of the old state-enterprise organisation appeared to be a motiveless attack. The device had exploded in the foyer of the building, killing five people, on 9 March 1995. Among them was one Bela Namany, the chief executive of an agro-chemical company that traded with the Russians. It turned out that Namany had also been part of a smuggling operation and used his trucks to transport contraband cigarettes into the former Soviet Union and bring artefacts and drugs back to the West. At first it seemed he had been the victim of turf war between rival gangs in Budapest where bombing was considered the best way of eliminating a rival. But then the criminal intelligence branch of the Budapest police contacted the Czechs and they eventually concluded that Nosecky and Namany had separately offended some serious figures in the Russian Mafia, and that the same hitman had been hired to kill them. He'd used the ploy of deliberately killing more than one person to hide the nature of his contract.

The bombs themselves were remarkably similar, both in the amount and type of explosive used, as well as in the way they were disguised. Both were hidden in large sample cases, often used by travelling salesmen. The bomber had come and gone leaving not a trace of himself and no hint of how the bombs had been detonated at the right moment to kill their targets. The authorities in Budapest ruled out a timing device because it would have been impossible for the bomber to calculate the precise instant when the target would pass the case. The hitman must have seen Namany and detonated the bomb by remote control. The problem with this was that nothing like a radio receiver had survived the blast, although they had found some of Namany's personal belongings intact – a briefcase with a lap-top computer and a mobile phone, which, according to the injured receptionist, he'd used to make a call as he left the building. She knew that because she had handed him an urgent message as he passed, and he had acted on it immediately.

In the case of the train, the bomber was thought to have planted the device close to his target then alighted at the previous station. A short time fuse might have been used, but again it seemed more likely that the detonation was caused by a radio transmitter, probably an adapted model-aircraft control of the type utilised by terrorists from Bogotá to Belfast. But again, nothing was found – and none of the survivors could remember anything suspicious either. Even when they were shown a diagram that pinpointed their position in relation to where the bomber must have been, they remembered nothing unusual. That, Foyle noted, was the response they had got from passengers who used the 147 route on Tuesday evening. No one had seen a man getting on to the bus with a canvas bag between Peckham and the West End. Foyle made a note in his book to remind himself to get the copies of the film printed up and sent to the Hungarian and Czech police forces. There might just be a face that someone remembered. In return he would ask for the chemical analyses of the explosive used there – he was particularly interested in the batch of Semtex. It seemed improbable that the same stock was being used in London as in Prague and Budapest, but there might be an inference to be drawn about the bomber's supply line and his connections.

All of this, he admitted, was groping at the margins of the case. He reminded himself that he mustn't close his mind to any possibilities. The Lindows *might* have been involved, after all, and they were still the best thing that he had to go on. He must cast the net wider, but at the same time he should not appear to exclude the Lindows. To this end he'd ordered copies to be made of the papers that arrived by special courier from Thames House. They included the file on Eamonn Lindow, a much larger document than he had expected, which included photographs of Eamonn and Rudi MacMahon. The pictures had been taken on two different occasions and showed Eamonn talking animatedly with MacMahon in the street.

More interesting to Foyle were the reports from the mid-eighties that fleshed out the incident at Droy cemetery. The cache of arms and explosives was of crucial strategic importance to the Provisional IRA, but they'd never been aware that a small transmitter placed in one of the cases had allowed the shipment to be tracked by satellite on its meandering voyage from North Africa. The security forces knew exactly when the material was transferred from one ship to another in the Atlantic, 150 miles north of the Azores; where and when it was landed in the Republic; and how it had been transported over the border. The entire supply line run by the southern command of the IRA had been exposed by the electronic tracker: every stage of the journey had been lit up like a board in a railway signal box. The churchyard was put under surveillance by a team from a shadowy Army group called 14 Intelligence Company; the back-up was provided by a heavily armed special support unit from the RUC, which had set up base five miles away in a sewage-processing plant. The operation – codenamed CUDGEL – lasted four weeks, during which time there was little activity. At one stage the operation commander thought the Provisionals knew that the churchyard was being watched and considered removing the explosives and guns. Then Eamonn Lindow stumbled on the scene. He was sighted three times, although there was a lot that was ambiguous about his behaviour. He never entered the churchyard and only fleetingly looked over to the far side of the church where the cache was hidden in a large Victorian vault that housed the remains of an extinct line of flax merchants. All he did was pull up his car and relieve himself. When he was taken in by the RUC after the explosion he had seemed a rather hopeless character, too attached to his drink to be trusted with one of the IRA's largest ever consignments to have been brought into Ireland. The younger brother was reported as brighter and more resilient under questioning. But the RUC hadn't suspected him of having a role in the affair and had questioned him chiefly to get a better idea of Eamonn's movements and character.

The papers were vague as to why the dump had blown up. Foyle surmised that the IRA would certainly not have sacrificed their precious supplies to kill and injure four soldiers, so there was no question of them having booby-trapped the cemetery. Besides, the Provisionals appeared not to have known that the place was being watched. Something was missing. Foyle circled the passage in the report and made a note to call the RUC to ask how the explosion had come about.

He leafed through the folder again and stopped at the description of Eamonn Lindow's life in Peckham, a fairly humdrum existence led between the library and a first-floor flat in Jasmine Road. Still, MI5 had done considerable work on him, especially in the last year, when they were in receipt of exceptionally detailed information. There were minute records of his social life, the dates on which he attended the Yeats Society and a regular Irish folk-music evening in Croydon. The summary included the facts that Eamonn Lindow had been to confession at a nearby church three times during Lent and had occasionally attended a meeting of the local constituency Labour Party. Outwardly he did not fit well into the role of IRA master-bomber, or even intelligence officer. Foyle was intrigued by the profile, particularly at the effort mounted by

MI5 since the Stormont talks. He began to form a synthesis of two opposing solutions. What if Eamonn Lindow was, in fact, a republican sympathiser with IRA connections, but had not been responsible for this bomb? It seemed crazy, but it satisfied his doubts about the way the Lindows had behaved that night and it embraced MI5's surveillance and background material. What if Eamonn had been, in fact, the primary target?

Foyle had no idea why it seemed right to him. He must get more of a feel for Eamonn Lindow, and talk to his interrogators at the RUC. It was then that he remembered there were still some calls waiting to be returned. He pulled over his message book. There were six messages, three from Scarratt's office and three from outside the building. The press office had called with a request from the BBC for an interview; his housekeeper had passed on the depressing news that his washing-machine had broken down; and a Superintendent Blackett from the RUC had got in touch late that afternoon. The message said that he was on holiday in the north of England and asked Foyle to ring if he needed background on the Lindows. There was a mobile number.

Foyle thought he remembered the name but couldn't put a face to it. He looked at his watch. It was ten five p.m. – not too late to call. If Blackett didn't want to be disturbed, he'd have turned off his phone. He dialled the number and waited for the line to connect. Ten seconds passed. The number responded with a single ring, then it went dead. The connection was broken. Blackett must have switched off the phone when he heard it ring.

Foyle replaced the receiver. A long, dull crump sounded in the distance. He looked up in time to see his reflection vibrate in the windows of his office, then turned to find Forbes at the door. 'Is that what I think it is?'

'Yes, that's a bomb,' said Forbes.

Foyle snatched up the phone again. 'Put me through to the surveillance team outside Lindow's flat.' He waited for a few seconds then asked the voice on the mobile phone in Homer Street, 'Has he moved?'

'No. He's asleep,' came the reply. 'There's not a sound in the flat.'

He replaced the receiver. 'If that was a bomb, Lindow's not the bomber. Find out where it is and get a car for me.'

5

Kirsty Laing did not hear the bomb from her flat in Maida Vale, but ten minutes later there was a television news flash, saying that a device had exploded in Floodgate Street, to the north of the City of London. Then the deputy director, Peter Speerman, was on the phone, calling her back for an urgent meeting with the director general and relevant section heads. She was more than a little surprised to be included and spent the twenty-minute drive to Millbank wondering exactly why Speerman had summoned her. True, he had appointed himself her mentor and indeed her new position as head of government liaison had been largely won on the deputy director's recommendation, but it was difficult to see how she would be needed in the immediate aftermath of the bomb.

She steered the Golf hatchback into the deserted car park and hurried across the road to gate six at the rear of the building. As she took the short flight of steps to the night entrance, she noticed David Cantor's car sweep under the huge fortified door that protected the building's basement car park. Cantor sat in the front, wearing a dinner jacket, looking impassively ahead of him. A few minutes later he followed her into the special-conference area, a glass capsule set within a much larger room on the seventh floor. As she entered there were one or two looks of surprise. Angus Grove, in charge of D-Branch (counter-terrorism), cocked an eyebrow at Keith Craven-Elms, his counterpart at A-Branch (domestic surveillance). Then Rory Fuller, head of Domestic Terrorism, made an overly solicitous fuss about where she would sit, which caused Grove and Craven-Elms to smirk like schoolboys.

During the last eighteen months both had made overtures to her. In each case there was nothing so overt as a pass, but they'd enthused about her talent and indicated their availability over lunch. She had little difficulty in resisting them. Such manoeuvres were more about power and dominance than sexual attraction and, anyway, her interest lay elsewhere.

David Cantor coughed and ran his hands over the frosted-glass surface of the table, then looked expectantly at Speerman who took his cue.

'Scotland Yard have confirmed that a device went off at ten seven p.m.

It appears to have been placed in the foyer of a building named Black Lion Court, a medium-sized office block in Floodgate Street. About three-quarters of the block is leased by Interwaste, a company specialising in the disposal of hazardous material. At this stage there appears to be nothing to link it with the bomb on Tuesday, except that approximately the same amount of explosive appears to have been used. We will have reports from the Met's forensic team in the morning. They will be as anxious as we are to establish whether there are further connections to be made.'

'Yes, connections,' mused Cantor. 'What possible connections exist between a 147 bus and this unprepossessing building, I wonder? Has anyone got any ideas? Angus, Keith, what do you make of this?'

Angus Grove, the counter-terrorism specialist, answered first. 'There may be no connection between the two incidents. If it is our chap, he could be working through some sort of contract list, which would explain the disparity in the nature of the targets.'

This did not seem to satisfy Cantor, whose eyes flicked to Keith Craven-Elms, head of the 'watchers' section, who leaned forward and stared at his notes. 'Well, there's nothing to suggest that Interwaste is the kind of target that would appeal to the IRA or any of their lunatic subsets unless, of course, it's some kind of diversionary tactic. The report says that the bomb was placed inside the building, rather than in the street, which means that the bomber was aiming at Interwaste. That might argue for an ecological implication. If the explosive residues tie this with the first incident I would guess that we would have to look very closely at the motive for the Clarence Street bomb, because, of course, that has no ecological connotations, as far as we understand. I have to say that this doesn't look very Irish to me. Nor do I think it's a loyalist attempt to destroy the peace agreement. They'd make more of a job of it by blowing up a well-known target and admitting responsibility on the Real IRA's behalf.'

'What about these sightings your department has had?' said Cantor, placing his fingertips together and pressing the ends so that they went white. 'Have we made any progress on them?'

'We're still checking through Weegee's data from this evening, but as yet there's nothing. Floodgate Street is just outside the area covered by the cameras.'

Laing remembered learning about the Weegee project when Speerman undertook to give her a personal induction to the highest level of the security service by summarising the various technical innovations being used. Weegee consisted of a vast computer, in the basement of the building, linked to cameras positioned all over the West End and the City of London. Known officially as the Automatic Recognition and Tracking System, it was referred to by its acronym ARTS or the nickname Weegee, an obscure reference to the omnipresent New York crime photographer of the 1940s. Weegee was programmed to pick out a gallery of known faces from the crowds of pedestrians that thronged the centre of the capital. She recalled the vertiginous numbers involved. One camera working at forty frames per second produced nearly 3.5 million images a day. With thirty-five cameras operational, 120 million images had to be scanned and matched against the gallery of suspects in the computer's memory. Speerman had produced the statistics with a kind of pride, and Laing had taken care to remember them because she assumed that she would be called upon to defend Weegee to Whitehall when the inevitable civil-liberties fuss was kicked up in Parliament. For the present Weegee was still a secret.

While Rory Fuller reviewed the terrorist groups operating in Britain, Laing's gaze drifted briefly to her reflection in the glass of the special-conference room. She looked at herself dispassionately. Her hair was still its natural light brown and her skin was unlined – not bad for forty-three and a regular twelve-hour day. But when Fuller said something about 'our fellow', her mind snapped back to the proceedings around the table. It was a similar phrase to Grove's. And now it struck her as odd. Plainly the only suspect was under observation. How could they hope to be using Weegee to track a man whom they knew to be at his home in Notting Hill?

Fuller stopped talking as Cantor raised his hand. 'I assume we all know what is being discussed here,' he said, looking directly at Laing. His eyes were grey marble, unreadable and without passion. 'I assume that we know *who* we are talking about.'

The table was silent as the four men nodded in unison. Grove and Craven-Elms looked towards Laing and waited for her reaction. 'I'm sorry,' she said, 'but I'm not sure. Are we discussing Lindow or someone else?'

Cantor's eyes glinted with irritation. Laing knew she'd made a big error. At this level you had to find out things for yourself. Knowledge didn't just fall into your lap: you had to acquire it and make use of it. There were no training manuals. She could imagine what was going through the minds of Grove and Craven-Elms. No field experience, they'd say; not one of us, not one of the boys.

'Well,' said Cantor, 'I had assumed that Peter would have given you an outline of this matter by now. Can I take it that this will occur tomorrow, Peter? In the meantime we must step up our efforts to eliminate him from these two incidents. But I also want to know exactly what he has been doing these past few years, where he's been. No rumours. Hard facts – a complete chronology.'

Laing was reeling with the implications of what was being said. Who was 'our fellow'? And if, indeed, there was some other suspect, why hadn't the police been informed?

'I don't understand,' she blurted out. 'Who else can be involved, if not Con Lindow? Do we have a name?' Out of the corner of her eye she could see that Speerman was shifting uneasily in his chair.

Cantor's eyes returned to her. 'As I said, Peter will explain things to you tomorrow. But clearly the police can be expected to take the point that Con Lindow was not involved in tonight's incident because they have had him under observation since he was released this afternoon. So if the two bombs are linked forensically, this will serve to exonerate Lindow in the police's eyes. Thus they will be looking for other suspects.'

'What the director general is saying', said Rory Fuller, plucking the air with his forefinger and thumb, 'is that for the moment it would be helpful if the police continued to believe in at least a tangential involvement of the Lindow brothers. A legitimate suspicion hangs over them, and it is not difficult to imagine a scenario that ties them into this latest device. For instance, their colleagues in a renegade IRA unit might well have arranged for the explosion this evening in order to remove the blame from Con Lindow.'

'But why—' started Laing, before she was silenced by Cantor's hand.

'I think that is all that can be usefully said this evening,' he said. 'We'll await the outcome of the police investigations tomorrow. Peter, Keith, I wonder if we could have a word now. There's something I need to discuss with you.'

He rose and left the room, quickly followed by Peter Speerman and Keith Craven-Elms. Fuller and Grove swept up their papers and left also, saying goodnight to Laing with elaborate politeness.

She drove back to Maida Vale very slowly, wondering why on earth she had been involved in the meeting by Speerman when he knew she was not in full possession of the facts. As a result, she had made an absolute fool of herself and she didn't like it one bit, particularly as it had been in front of two enemies. But the offence to her self-esteem was quickly forgotten as she considered the alarming implication of the second, undisclosed suspect.

A voice came from Lindow's sitting room. He raised his head from the pillow and strained to hear. It was a man's voice and he was speaking rapidly. Someone was leaving a message on the ansaphone. He leaped from his bed, hopped into the grey light of the sitting room and lunged for the phone. The caller had gone.

Lindow cursed, then played back the message. 'Dr Lindow, this is Mr Lustig from the letting agency. My colleague Mr Robertson, with whom you were dealing last week, has found just the place you're looking for. I wonder if you'd be so kind as to give me a call between nine and ten this morning, or at the same time on Monday? The number is 08052 289476. Thanks.'

Lindow listened, wiping the sleep from his eyes. He looked at his watch. The hands stood at ten minutes to eight – too damned early to call. He shivered and ran back to bed. He would try Lustig in an hour or so. Better not oversleep.

He woke again at nine, called, but got no answer. He showered, dressed and phoned Professor Sharma, who told him to take as much time off as he needed. Then he called a civil-liberties group and asked their advice about a lawyer. The woman gave him the name of Casper Crisp & Co., a firm of young solicitors who specialised in civil-rights issues. They agreed immediately to act for him. They would get in touch with the coroner about the release of Eamonn's body and look into the possibility of a libel suit against the *Evening Herald*. They also said that they would help wind up Eamonn's affairs. The senior partner asked him to get copies of any insurance policies Eamonn held, the mortgage agreement on his home and, if possible, a will. Lindow was doubtful about finding any of these in Eamonn's flat. His brother, though organised in practically every department of his life, had never been strong on money.

Eventually he set off for Eamonn's, but first he went to Oxford Street to buy a new jacket.

Foyle strolled down Victoria Street towards Scotland Yard, carrying a bag containing a new shirt, socks and underwear that he had just bought at the Army and Navy Stores. Considering he had not been to bed for a full day he felt pretty well, unusually light-hearted.

Although no one had been injured by the bomb in Floodgate Street, there had been a hell of a mess when he reached the scene with Forbes twenty minutes after they heard the explosion. The force of the blast had ripped off the front of the building and deposited it in the street, crushing two vehicles. The windows of three residential tower blocks had been blown out and a car had been up-ended and tossed into the front of an electrical suppliers.

Foyle was intrigued by the nature of the target. Overnight, Sergeant Pennel had dug up some information about Interwaste and found that two years earlier the company, a subsidiary of a sprawling American combine called Fallon Group International, had been at the centre of controversy when it had been contracted to transport and dispose of thousands of gallons of chemical waste from Eastern Europe. The chemicals were moved by train through Poland and Germany, loaded on to ships and taken to a point in the Western Atlantic over the Milwaukee Deep and lowered into the trench. The operation had been accompanied by protests along the train's route through Germany and it seemed a distinct possibility that an extremist ecological group had now taken it into its head to blow up the anonymous little building where the disposal had been planned.

What did that say about the bomb on the bus? Almost nothing. In the early hours Foyle had instructed officers to return to the list of passengers and go through their backgrounds again to see if any of them was likely to have incurred the ire of such a group. He also had the bus route checked for other targets that might have attracted extremist eco-warriors. Nothing came of either search.

Foyle turned off Victoria Street, looked at his watch and hastened to the bank of lifts in New Scotland Yard. He had only twenty minutes before he was due at the Cabinet Office to update Sir Derek Crystal's committee. Once in his own office he pressed the speaker button on his phone and dialled the number that Superintendent Blackett had left the day before.

'It has not been possible to connect your call,' intoned the recorded voice. 'Please try again later.'

While taking off his shirt, Foyle called the operations desk.

'A few things, Nancy,' he said, recognising the voice of WPC Longmore. 'I've just tried to call Superintendent Blackett of the RUC on his mobile. He left a message with a number yesterday. See if you can track him down for me and arrange a time for us to talk later this morning. Can you also see that Con Lindow's flat keys are on my desk this afternoon – the ones that were taken from him at the hospital on Wednesday morning?'

He replaced the receiver and retreated behind a filing cabinet to remove his trousers and underwear. Forbes knocked and entered just as Foyle was pulling up the new pair of shorts.

'Sorry, sir, I'll come back in a little while,' he said.

'What the hell's so funny, Forbes? Something wrong with these boxers?'

'Well, to be honest, they look a little large, sir, and it seems odd to change in here.'

'Yes, well, I've got to be over at the Cabinet Office in a few minutes. Any news?'

'There's a match on the explosives, sir. Exactly the same batch.'

'Christ. That's interesting. What do you make of it?'

'For one thing it puts Lindow in the clear. But don't ask me who the hell is doing this. It doesn't add up.'

'No, it doesn't. But I'm not sure about Lindow. There's something nagging me and I cannot for the life of me work out what it is. I'm going to have a word with him this afternoon.'

He emerged from behind the cabinet, placed his laundry in a drawer, put on his jacket and swept up the folder that was waiting on his desk. 'Do not go naked into the conference chamber,' he said, clasping it to his chest.

By the time he arrived at the Cabinet Office, Scarratt was already speaking about the second bomb. Foyle nodded an apology to Sir Derek and settled into the same position he had occupied two days before. Scarratt concluded his outline and gestured to Foyle, saying, 'But I am certain Commander Foyle will be able to give you a clearer picture of what has been discovered overnight.'

'Yes,' said Sir Derek. 'Perhaps. What's the latest information, Commander? Were these devices planted by the same group?'

Foyle rose. Although it was not the practice in this committee to do so, he felt easier addressing it on his feet. 'Yes, they were. We've just had the tests back. The explosives residues match. We also know how and when the bomb was planted. At five fifteen p.m. yesterday afternoon a man telephoned Reception at Interwaste to say that he would be delivering two fire extinguishers. Fifteen minutes later he arrived with them and left them in the lobby. He called out to the receptionist – who also acts as the company's switchboard operator – that he would return early the next day to fit them. Then he was gone. The receptionist thought nothing of it until this morning when she heard that the building had been blown up. She remembers little about his appearance, apart from his overalls and cap. She detected no Irish accent, either on the phone or when he spoke to her in the lobby.

'In the four hours between the office closing and the explosion at a few minutes past ten p.m., the extinguishers lay undisturbed in their packing cases. The force of the explosion was considerable. Sixteen pounds of Semtex were packed into two nine-litre extinguishers and linked to a central firing mechanism.

'As for the implications this has for investigations into Tuesday's bomb, well, it's rather puzzling. As you know, Dr Lindow was released yesterday following his brother's death. We can account for his whereabouts for all last night and we know he made no significant telephone calls after his release. We are looking into the suggestion that Interwaste was blown up because of its work in dismantling a chemical plant in Eastern Europe. There have been no calls admitting responsibility and, as with the earlier explosion, there was no warning. We are at a loss to explain why these two incidents appear to be on one level consistent with each other but on another totally different.'

Sir Derek looked up at Foyle and removed his glasses. 'That doesn't really advance things much, does it, Commander? We have to know whether these bombs are being planted by an Irish group or whether we face some new threat. I don't have to tell you that things are very delicate politically. It won't take much more for Ulster to blow up again.'

Foyle opened his hands in a gesture of frustration and sat down. He watched as Sir Derek's gaze travelled the length of the table and settled on

Scarratt. 'Mr Scarratt, what are we to do in these circumstances?' boomed Sir Derek.

Scarratt opened his mouth to answer but was cut short by David Cantor's hand. 'These are very difficult matters to investigate, Sir Derek. I admit I couldn't see the wisdom of letting our only suspect go yesterday, but leaving that aside, it is my belief that the government should proceed on the basis that these two explosions were caused by an Irish group. Last night's attack may well have been designed to put us off the scent – in other words, to exonerate Con Lindow and his brother. We still believe that we are dealing with some kind of extremist republican element.'

Foyle made to object, but a look from Sir Derek silenced him.

'If this scenario of the rogue active-service unit were to be accepted,' continued Cantor, 'it would mean that the Prime Minister would be able to continue talking to Sinn Fein and the IRA – a head-on confrontation would be avoided. At the same time, we would look at these explosions entirely within the context of Irish terrorism and use all the methods built up over the last few years to track these men down. That is why it would be a distraction to cast around in search of an ecologically inspired terrorist group. There is no evidence whatsoever for that.'

Foyle saw that the room was beginning to relax and that Cantor had won over his audience. Sir Derek sat back in his chair and nodded to Adam Durie, head of the Joint Intelligence Committee, who then turned to the two men from the Northern Ireland Office and silently sought their reaction. Foyle reflected that intervention had been a virtuoso display of Cantor's skill, which satisfied everyone's immediate needs for a solution yet committed Cantor to nothing. There were no facts that he could challenge, nothing for him to disprove, so he remained silent.

'Very well,' said Sir Derek. 'I believe this will help matters over the weekend, but we cannot use it indefinitely. We must see an advance by next week. No doubt Scotland Yard and the security service will redouble their efforts to catch these people. Thank you all very much for coming.'

Sir Derek got up and moved past Foyle without looking at him. The other officials followed, the rear of the procession taken up by Scarratt and Cantor. As they neared him, Cantor squeezed Scarratt's upper arm, then slipped away. Foyle and Scarratt stood looking at each other while two junior civil servants scurried about the room clearing notepads left on the conference table.

'We need results, Commander,' Scarratt hissed. 'I'm meeting with the commissioner this afternoon. He will want to talk to you too, so please make yourself available.' He moved to the door. 'And, Commander, I would like to see your explanation in writing about the release of Lindow before that meeting takes place.'

Jasmine Road, Peckham, had known better times. The houses were large and set back from the street, a cut above the rows of dark artisans' cottages that Lindow had noticed, with a sinking feeling, on the train ride from Victoria Station. For the most part, though, they were shabby, the small front gardens untended and filled with rubbish. There were a few children playing in the street and a group of men leaning into the bonnet of a car, watching an individual in overalls pumping at a spanner in the engine.

Lindow found number fifty-six a little way up the street behind a large cherry tree, which had turned a mustard yellow. Much of the ground floor was hidden from view by an overgrown vine and a climbing rose, which reached up the façade of peeling plasterwork. He climbed five steps up to the front door and slipped into the lock the first of the three keys he had been given at the hospital. The hallway was surprisingly light and clean. There were plants, and mail had been stacked neatly on a polished side table. The entrance to his flat was on the first floor, a dark green door with two locks. Lindow hesitated before opening it, listening for any other sound in the house. He wondered if he should explain to Eamonn's neighbours who he was. But the house seemed empty. The only noise came from the children outside.

At first sight Eamonn's flat seemed undisturbed, but as Lindow looked closer he saw that it had been subject to exactly the same treatment as his own. This police team, however, had taken more care to restore what they had wrenched and stripped from the floors and walls. Lindow bent down, picked up half a dozen books that had been left in a pile on the floor, all volumes of Irish history, and replaced them on the shelf. As he did so he suddenly remembered his brother's surprising passion for order. When they were boys, Eamonn had spent all his time sorting and labelling boxes of fishing flies, cigarette cards, records – anything that could be subjected to different principles of classification. It had been his obsessive taxonomy that first stirred Lindow's interest in biology. Eamonn had once produced two trout from a wicker creel, one that he'd caught from a lake in the hills and another from a stream, and showed Lindow how they varied minutely in nearly every respect – colouring, shape of mouth, size of dorsal fin and tail. It was the first time he'd heard the word gene.

He walked around the flat, then poked about in the kitchen. It occurred to him that he should throw out the old food. He found a plastic bag and tipped the contents of Eamonn's vegetable tray into it, then emptied the fridge. Having left the bag outside the flat, he went to look in the bedroom. There was an old flat-topped partner's desk standing to the right of the window. Its leather surface had been ripped and he could see that it had been glued recently. He pulled open the right-hand drawer and found a folder of photographs, mostly snaps from family holidays in Donegal back in the early seventies. Eamonn wore long hair and looked sheepishly from under his eyebrows. Their father was brandishing a walking-stick. He looked at himself, aged eight, presenting a bucket of crabs to the camera.

Lindow picked up a small rucksack that was lying by the desk and put the folder of photographs in it. He found a letter he'd sent to Eamonn the year before their mother died. It was a quick, cold, casual letter. He grimaced and dropped it into the wastepaper bin. In the lowest left-hand drawer he found what he was looking for: a plastic file containing the papers relating to the ownership of the flat, the mortgage and Eamonn's life-insurance policy. There was also a clip of bank statements and a building society savings book, which revealed that Eamonn had £1,200 in his account. He put all the documents on top of the desk. Then he tried to push the drawer home. It was stuck. He pushed again, putting all his weight behind it, but the drawer wouldn't move. He crouched down to see if something was catching it underneath. He couldn't see anything. He looked inside the drawer to see if the bottom had come loose at the back. Again, there seemed to be nothing amiss. Finally he fetched a knife from the kitchen and slid it between the bottom of the drawer and the desk. By using it as a lever he was able to release the drawer inch by inch. At length he pulled it free and peered into the aperture. He could see that a panel of wood had sprung out from the side of the desk and trapped the drawer. As he tried to press it back into place, his hand felt something. A package was wedged behind the panel.

He pulled it out into the light to find that he was holding a thick brown envelope about the size of a paperback book. Inside was an American passport and a smaller envelope containing between forty and fifty hundred-dollar bills. He rose slowly to his feet and opened the passport. There was a picture of Eamonn, dressed in a dark suit jacket and a tie, looking much younger and slimmer. Lindow barely recognised him. Further on there were four US immigration stamps recording arrivals at Boston and Shannon where, Lindow remembered, it was possible to clear US immigration before boarding the flight. He flipped through the pages but found no other stamps. At the back a scrap of paper was lodged in the spine. He unfolded it and read, '– RHODES = 8 degrees – LIMERICK; 342 degrees – BELFAST. (Av Declination – 20 degrees) AXIOM DAY'. They were obviously compass bearings, but the relationship between Limerick, Belfast and the island of Rhodes escaped him. And what the hell did Axiom Day mean? This was all most unlike Eamonn, yet the deliberate handwriting was certainly his.

He replaced the piece of paper and returned to the front of the passport. Suddenly he sank back on the desk, winded. There was no mistaking it: the passport was held not in Eamonn's name but in *his*. For reasons that he couldn't possibly fathom, his brother had travelled four times to the States under the name Dr Constantine Cardell Lindow, born in Monaghan, Irish Republic, 1965.

*

Foyle crashed the telephone receiver down, breaking the plastic of the cradle. Lack of sleep was beginning to tell. Half an hour before, he had come close to resigning in a meeting with Sir Roy Urquhart, commissioner of the Metropolitan Police. Although Urquhart was clearly not yet prepared to go the whole way and fire him, a transfer from SO 13 seemed inevitable.

'What finally appears to be the problem, Commander,' Urquhart had said, at the end of the meeting, 'is that you have nothing else to go on. In the face of this onslaught from a highly organised terrorist group you have got *nothing* to offer – not even a theory. NOTHING! We will speak again next week. In the meantime, Assistant Commissioner Scarratt will use the weekend to carry out a complete review of the inquiry and your supervision of it, Commander.'

Foyle unplugged the phone set at the wall and stormed to the next-door office where, without a word to the three officers in the room, he dumped it in a bin and snatched up a spare set. On the way back to his office he met Forbes. 'I take it you've acquainted yourself with the latest developments,' he said, motioning his head to the ceiling.

'More or less, sir,' said Forbes regretfully.

'Yes, well, there's not much I can do. I saw it coming this morning. There's something about that man Cantor that makes my flesh crawl. For the life of me I can't see what he's up to, except that he's used Scarratt to get at the commissioner and have me thrown off this inquiry – and probably off the force. But for the moment I'm still here. What have you got for me?'

Forbes reeled off the results of investigations into the second bomb but trailed off when he saw that Foyle wasn't listening. 'I'm sure this can wait. Is there anything you want me to do, sir?'

'I want the keys to Lindow's flat. I asked for them to be put on my desk but they're not here. Oh, yes, there was something else. I was trying to get hold of Blackett at the RUC. Has anyone tracked him down?'

'Yes, they have. It's rather strange. He was always in Belfast, never on holiday – never in the north of England. And he doesn't have a mobile number either.'

Foyle looked down at his message book. 'Am I going mad? It's here, see for yourself.' He spun the book round to Forbes and busied himself plugging in the new phone set. Then he dialled the front desk and summoned WPC Nancy Longmore.

She arrived a few seconds after Foyle had replaced the receiver.

'Nancy, did you write this?'

She looked down at the message marked by Foyle's forefinger. 'Yes, sir. Superintendent Blackett phoned yesterday afternoon. He was anxious to see if there was any help he could give. He said he knew the Lindows and wanted to talk to you personally about their involvement.'

'But how come he's in Belfast, not in the north of England? And he doesn't own a mobile phone and, according to Inspector Forbes, who has spoken to him, he made no attempt to call me in the first place.' Foyle's irritation was aimed at the mystery, not Nancy Longmore, but she flushed none the less. Forbes coughed to tell Foyle that he was getting the thing out of proportion.

'It's not your fault, Nancy,' Foyle said evenly. 'Someone is playing silly buggers here. Get Blackett on the phone for me now and we'll see what the hell's going on.'

She retreated hastily. Within a few minutes Superintendent Blackett had been located in his Belfast office and was put through to Foyle's extension.

'What's this phantom message about? Inspector Forbes here tells me that you didn't ring me and yet I have a very specific message saying that you did. What's going on?'

'You tell me,' said the Ulsterman. 'All I can say is that I didn't call you. To be candid, it hadn't occurred to me to call you. But I've got all these messages here from you, so I'm very happy to help in any way I can.'

'Hold on!' said Foyle, tugging his ear. 'What messages have you got from me?'

'Well, I talked to your Inspector Forbes, and then there's this message to ring a mobile number. I've got it here now. I didn't get around to it because we've a lot on at the moment. I was going to give you a bell this evening when there was time to talk properly.' He repeated the number.

'I don't understand,' said Foyle. 'I never sent such a message and I don't recognise the number. No, hold on, it's the same number as I've got.' He paused and shook his head silently at Forbes. 'Well, since you're on, what do you know about Con and Eamonn Lindow?'

Blackett replied that he knew a lot about Droy cemetery because he had been involved with some of the undercover work and had had a hand in Operation CUDGEL. He remembered less about the brothers, although he recalled that under interrogation Con Lindow had been, as he put it, a canny young fellow. Foyle ended the conversation by saying that he was sorry for the confusion and that he would be in touch if he thought of anything else. He replaced the receiver and let his weight drop into the chair, causing the fake leather cushion to gasp under the impact. 'Well, what do you make of that?'

'About what?'

'About all these messages. It's a bit odd, isn't it? Blackett said he'd got a message to call me on the same number I was given. I mean, I never even thought of calling him.'

'It *is* odd, I agree. But don't take it the wrong way, sir, if I say that I think it's the least of our problems at the moment.'

'You're probably right. Can you see to it that I get those keys? I'm going to pay a visit to Lindow after the briefing. The surveillance team will need to inform me when he reaches home – if he does.'

6

Lindow slipped his hand inside the desk again and found that the panel could be pressed back and locked into place by a strip of wood that acted as a runner for the drawer. He moved the drawer in and out and saw that he could release the panel only when the drawer was pulled out to its maximum extent. Otherwise there was no hint of the tiny cavity hidden in the side of the desk. He reasoned that the catch must have come loose while the police were searching the desk and sprung out of its own accord when he opened the drawer. It was an ingenious design and he wondered who had made it. Eamonn certainly hadn't possessed that sort of skill. Then a more worrying thought occurred to him. What if the police had found the package and left it there for him to pick up? It'd be difficult to explain the fake passport in his name, even if it wasn't his photograph inside.

He jumped. A loud buzzing noise was coming from somewhere. Christ, the doorbell. He rammed the drawer shut and stuffed the package, with Eamonn's mortgage papers, into the bag, then went into the sitting room to pick up the entryphone.

'Can I come up?' asked a woman's voice. 'It's Mary Menihan – Eamonn's friend.'

He pressed the button to open the front door, walked out on to the landing and leaned over the stair rail.

'Hello,' said the voice. 'Is that Eamonn's brother?'

'Yes, it is.'

'Oh, good. I thought it was the damned police.'

'No, it's just me here. No police.' He watched the woman's head bob round the corner of the stairs.

She reached him, smiling, with her hand out. 'Hi. I'm Mary. I was a good friend of Eamonn's. Forgive me, I thought you'd come here after they let you go. I know it's kind of crass of me. It's just that I wanted to see you and had no idea how to get in touch. Look, tell me if it's a bad time.' She gazed at him with her head slightly cocked.

'No, no, no. Come in, please. Hi – Con Lindow.' He gave her his hand. They stood awkwardly in the doorway.

'The last time I came up those stairs, Eamonn met me here at the door with some lines of poetry. Do you know them? "From the going-down of the sun, I have dreamed that women laughing or timid or wild, in rustle of lace or silken stuff, climbed up my creaking stair. They had read all I had rhymed of that monstrous thing – returned and yet unrequited love."'

'Yeats,' said Lindow. 'I haven't heard it for twenty years.'

'Yep – Eamonn and Yeats,' said the woman, sighing. 'A lifelong love affair, wasn't it? He sent it to me on a postcard later. That's how I came to learn it by heart.'

Lindow looked at her. She was very striking: about five feet four inches, with thick dark hair worn short and brushed backwards. Her complexion was dark too, and when she smiled her mouth turned downwards and her eyes glistened with intelligent understanding. She held herself well, and even though she wasn't dressed for show – blue jeans, a grey V-neck sweater with a white shirt underneath and a short black leather jacket – he would certainly have noticed her in the street.

'I was just going through Eamonn's stuff,' he said, moving into the middle of the room and placing a hand on the back of the sofa. 'There's a lot to do. You never think of the bureaucratic side of death, do you? All the damned insurance and things. Look, would you like some coffee? I noticed there's some ground stuff in a jar – no milk, though.'

'I take it black anyway. Yes, I'd love some.'

'So, you're Mary and you're from the States,' Lindow called, from the kitchen.

'Yep. Half Irish, half Jewish and all American.' She wandered into the kitchen. 'It's strange us meeting here without Eamonn, isn't it? I'm truly very sorry for you. It was a terrible, terrible thing that happened to you – the police thinking that Eamonn and you had been planning it all along. It's crazy. I saw in the newspapers you'd been arrested. That must have been some ordeal when you knew Eamonn was so badly hurt.' She touched Lindow's arm. In his three weeks in London he had forgotten about Americans, how warm and natural they could be.

'At first they didn't tell me that Eamonn was injured,' he said. 'I didn't even know he was involved.'

'My God, that's awful.'

'Yes. It was. I still haven't got used to the idea of him being dead. It takes time.'

'But at least with the explosion last night, they can't possibly still suspect you.'

'That's what I'm hoping.'

'Hey! Why don't I make the coffee and you get on with what you were doing?'

'No, it's fine. I've found what I came for.'

'So what happens now?'

'The first thing is to take Eamonn back to Ireland. There'll be the funeral. Then I'm going back to work at Imperial. It'll be a relief to get back to it.'

'When will the funeral be held?'

'As early as possible, once the body has been released for burial. It will be good for my father to get it over with quickly – probably Tuesday or Wednesday.'

'Would you mind if I came?'

'Of course not. I can let you know all the details by phone. There are plenty of hotels near by so that won't be a problem.' He hesitated. 'Can I ask you something? Were you . . . ?'

'No I wasn't Eamonn's girl – "returned, but unrequited", I s'pose. He helped me through a rough time and we became very close. But you know how it is – that part of it didn't work out. I loved being with him, though. He was so interesting and well read,' she said, gesturing to the bookshelves with her mug of coffee.

They talked on for a little while, until Lindow said he should leave for his lawyer in South Kensington. Mary jumped up and suggested they travel together since she lived one stop from Kensington. He looked confused. He decided he wouldn't have time to replace the package in the compartment in the desk, and he certainly didn't want to do it while Mary was in the flat. He would take it to the solicitors instead and they could include the money in Eamonn's estate. He collected the bag from the bedroom then left the flat with her, locking both doors behind him and removing the rubbish to the bin outside.

It was just past three by the time they reached the station. Lindow noticed a tall man in his forties and a younger woman on the platform, watching the electronic display. It was something about the woman's body language that told him they weren't a couple. Between them was the discreet and almost imperceptible distance that a woman maintains before she's been to bed with a man. His gaze stayed with them for a few moments. The man noticed him looking, reached over to the woman and kissed her ear. As he did so she jerked back with a tiny recoil of surprise. They were police officers, Lindow was certain of it.

'He's left the brother's flat with a woman,' said Forbes, through Foyle's open door. 'They split up at Sloane Square and she walked to a house in Pimlico. We've got pictures, but Special Branch is already sure that she is Mary Menihan, the same Mary referred to on Eamonn Lindow's message tape. They're running a check on the owner and tenants of the Pimlico address.'

Foyle beckoned to Forbes to sit down, then fell into a brooding silence.

'That's interesting,' he said at length, 'because it tells us that neither of them minds if they're seen together. If they were members of an IRA cell they would be sure that we were following them – she'd have fled by now and he'd be keeping his head down.'

'Unless it's some kind of bluff.'

'That's hardly likely when you think of the risks involved. But you're right to keep on about Lindow. I'm becoming intrigued by him.' Foyle waved some papers in the air. 'I had these sent over from Blackett's office. I felt I owed him an explanation for this morning. In the end he was very helpful about the business at Droy cemetery.'

A look of mild exasperation passed over Forbes's usually composed features.

'I know you think I am becoming obsessive about it, but wait until you read this. It was a hell of a story at the time – Operation CUDGEL was a complete disaster. They had followed the supplies all the way from the mid-Atlantic by satellite. Then, somewhere in the Republic, the shipment was divided and part of the consignment was lost. The part that contained the tracking device ended up buried in a vault at the back of a disused country church at Droy in Fermanagh. The Army had rigged the dump so it would blow up the boys from the local IRA brigade when they came to collect it. Instead they blew themselves up, but in the oddest circumstances – nobody knows how it happened. The papers here refer to some sort of internal Army inquiry, but of course this has never been published. We don't even know the names of the men involved. All we do know is that the cache blew up after being visited three times by the Lindow brothers.'

'But we knew all this, sir,' said Forbes quietly. 'I can't see the relevance to what we're doing.'

'Don't you see that even if the sightings of the Lindow brothers had nothing to do with the explosion at Droy, a lot of people must have been left with the impression that they had?'

'So you're saying there is some sort of revenge motive?'

'Could be.'

Forbes looked down. 'It doesn't sound right to me, sir. Nobody kills ten innocent people and injures God knows how many others to get even with one person a decade and a half after the event.'

'Have a read of this, then,' said Foyle, chucking the MI6 file on the Prague and Budapest bombings across the desk. 'You'll see it's not such an outlandish theory.'

'Say your theory is right, sir. How do you then link in the explosion last night? We know that the same explosives were used and therefore must assume it's the same person – or persons – responsible for the manufacture and planting of the bombs.'

'I don't know how they're connected, but I'd like you to read this stuff over the weekend and see if any of your Army pals can help. I want the names of the soldiers involved in the original crew watching that arms cache. If you can't get them, see if Lafferty has any contacts from his time in Ulster. Try Blackett also.' Foyle stopped, ran his hand through his hair then leaned forward on to the desk. 'Have you got anything more on Floodgate Street? Anything turned up on Interwaste? Do we know how these devices are being let off?'

'Not much advance on any of those fronts. Lafferty's people will know more about the construction of the second device by this evening. There's one other thing I forgot to mention. The laboratory recovering the films from the bus has been in touch. It's taking longer than they expected. They hope to send the film by Monday.'

'Good, let's hope there's something on them.'

By the time Lindow tramped up Homer Road it was dark and the street lights wore orange haloes of moisture. It had turned cold – not the honest, harsh cold of a New England winter, which he liked in a way, but the cloying dampness of the British Isles. He stopped before mounting the steps to his front door and looked up and down the street. There didn't seem to be anyone watching him, but he was certain that they must be there, sitting in parked cars or in a rented room observing his flat. He didn't much care. He had left the envelope containing the passport and money at Casper Crisp and now felt less nervous. Jane Casper had placed it in the firm's safe, while telling him that Eamonn's body would be released for burial on Monday. She didn't ask about the envelope. Lindow said he would collect it after the weekend. As yet he had no idea what he was going to do with it. One option would be to hand it over to the police, but that would only risk further condemning Eamonn's reputation, and would almost certainly reinforce their suspicions of him.

But he'd kept the piece of paper from the passport because it intrigued him. It also worried him. He felt he'd stumbled on a nasty little secret, a secret that he'd rather not know about. After all, nobody hides that amount of money and a false passport innocently. He also felt hurt – abused. What had Eamonn been doing, assuming his identity like that?

Once in the flat he took the paper from his wallet and scrutinised it. Even without a compass or map to hand, he knew there was no obvious answer to it, for both bearings were northerly and he estimated that the island of Rhodes in the Aegean Sea would be at a south-easterly bearing of about 100 to 115 degrees from the two Irish cities. It was nonsensical. He returned it to his wallet, collapsed on the sofa and idled through a couple of scientific journals. Then he switched on the satellite sports channel and watched ten minutes of an ice-hockey game. But he couldn't keep his mind from turning over the discoveries he'd made. What the hell was Eamonn up to with all this cloak-and-dagger stuff? Why did a librarian need a fake passport and nearly five thousand dollars in cash?

For the second time that day he was disturbed from thinking about the package by a doorbell. It sounded right at the back of his head like a fire alarm and he shot up from his position on the couch. On the way down to the door he told himself that he had to get a grip.

A profile was cast by the street light on to the frosted glass of the door. He opened it to find the policeman who'd taken him to the hospital the day before – the big man with watchful eyes.

'Yes?' said Lindow, certain that he was going to be rearrested.

'Good evening, Dr Lindow,' said Foyle.

Lindow looked out into the street, left and right, then back to the policeman.

'It's just me. I'm here unofficially. Well, not quite. I came to return your keys.'

'Yesterday I'm sure you told me you were a commander,' said Lindow aggressively. 'Haven't you got constables to do that sort of thing for you?'

'Yes, I have. It's really an excuse. I wanted a few words with you. To be honest, I hoped you'd be able to help out.'

'Is this a formal interview, Commander Foyle? Should I consider myself to be helping police with their inquiries again, or are you trying to make up for the mess your officers made of this place?'

'Neither.'

'Then presumably I don't have to talk to you.'

'No, you don't,' said Foyle, his frustration beginning to show. 'But I'd be grateful if you'd spare a few moments, since I was the person who decided that you should be released. I may well pay for that decision with my job.'

'Are you serious? They still think I had something to do with the bombs? They must be crazy. I couldn't possibly have had anything to do with either of them.'

'All I'll say is this, Dr Lindow. It's in your interest as well as mine that we talk. I think you're involved in some way, although I don't believe you know how or why, but it has something to do with your brother. Maybe something to do with the past.'

Lindow studied Foyle. He was shrewder than he looked, and he thought he'd better find out exactly what he wanted. 'Look, my apartment's still a mess and I don't have much food or drink here. Do you mind if we do this in public? There's a wine bar round the corner that serves food.'

'Good idea.'

Lindow fetched his wallet and a jacket, then they left together in silence.

They were given a table in the corner of the bar, away from the heaving Friday-night crowd, and ordered straight away.

'What is it that you do, Dr Lindow?' asked Foyle, when the waitress had departed. 'No one in my department has quite pinned it down.'

'I came here to lead a project on bacteria. It is related to my work in the States, which was to do with the way that human cells communicate with each other by minute secretions of messenger chemicals. It's pretty dull stuff to the uninitiated.'

'Go on,' said Foyle, waving a knife covered in butter, his mouth already full of bread. 'I'm genuinely interested.'

Lindow was sceptical but continued. 'The difference between a bacterium cell and a human cell is that the bacterium cell doesn't have a nucleus. It's like a little bubble of genetic material. In a human cell the strands of DNA are mostly contained within a membrane at the centre of the cell. But the way both bacteria and human cells talk to each other is essentially the same. Bacteria send out messages that instruct other single-cell organisms to go and do things.'

'What things?'

'Well, to reproduce, to die, to defend themselves against viruses. In some cases they cluster together into little tree-like structures. In others they light up. I'll give you an example. There's a species of squid which hunts by night, but it can only do this because it's specially equipped with an organ that collects a particular type of bacteria in the sea. When the bacteria crowd into the organ they release a chemical which travels between them and causes the production of a protein in each cell that gives off a burst of light. So with the help of the bacteria the squid can see its prey. In return, the bacteria receive a safe, nourishing haven and are able to reproduce. Without each other, the squid and the bacteria would not do so well.'

'It makes you wonder how they got together in the first place. Which came first – the nocturnally feeding squid or the bacteria?'

'Both,' said Lindow. 'They adapted to each other gradually, natural selection causing the squid with better bacteria collectors to do better and pass on their particular characteristics to future generations.'

'But you're not researching squid, are you?' asked Foyle.

'No, I'm interested in tracking down other substances that bacteria use to talk to each other. They may be very useful to us, particularly in the control of disease.'

'And that's how you've made your money.'

'You *are* well informed! It's not as much as you'd think. I share in a few patents. That's all. I do okay,' said Lindow. 'What about you? Are you married – children?'

'Wife and daughter, both away on academic studies. My wife has taken up archaeology and is in the Middle East. My girl, Katherine, is at university, at the moment doing drama but she hopes to change to law.'

'So you live alone. That must be hard with your job.'

'No, it just means I work all the time.'

The wine and the first course arrived. Lindow poured the wine. 'After this week, I never thought I'd have dinner with a cop. I'm still not sure that I should be. The system here, which allows you to hold people without trial or without being charged, is completely wrong. Just because we're sitting here exchanging pleasantries doesn't mean that I've forgotten about it.'

Foyle shrugged. 'It'd be impossible to do my job without it. Remember, we're dealing with well-organised people, seriously bad people who don't mind killing mothers and children in the street.'

'Yes, I've heard the argument, but it doesn't make it any better when you've been in my position.' He paused and drank some wine. 'What do you want to talk about?'

'I want to know about Eamonn. Above all, I want to know if someone would go to those lengths to kill him. You see, there's evidence that he was involved with the IRA up until his death.'

'What evidence?'

'The first thing is this relationship with Rudi MacMahon. What was he doing mixing with someone like that? I've seen the surveillance photographs. There's no doubt about it. They were filmed in Ireland twice together, which probably means they met much more frequently.'

'Look, my brother wasn't a Provo. You didn't know him – he was incapable of hurting anybody.'

'But why did he see MacMahon? Did you know MacMahon was suspected of carrying out three or four assassinations in cold blood before he became a Sinn Fein politician? He was charged twice with murder but both times the witnesses simply faded away. He may be part of the peace process but this man is a very bad guy indeed. He has blood on his hands and none of the fine words of Stormont will wash it off. Why would your brother spend time with him if he wasn't somehow involved?'

'I can't tell you.'

'What about this business at Droy? Was he working for the IRA then?'

'No.'

'You seem very certain of that, but I believe you knew that the IRA got their hooks into Eamonn pretty early on and that Droy was the first job he did for them. You know, watching that cache of weapons and explosives.'

Lindow said nothing.

'That's what the security services think. They've been watching him in London. I've seen the file. They were convinced he was an important link man and they think he was part of a group continuing the armed struggle.'

'Your logic's all up the spout, Commander. On the one hand you say my brother was suspected of being a member of the IRA but on the other you suggest that he was a target of what looks very much like an IRA attack. That is almost the definition of a contradictory position. It seems to me that the police just change the story to fit each piece of evidence as it comes along.'

'Look,' said Foyle, 'I don't pretend to understand this thing, but it's in your best interests that I begin to. If I lose control over the inquiry, the first action my replacement will take is to rearrest you. They could come for you next week.'

'I'll be in Ireland for Eamonn's funeral.'

'Yes, but you won't stay. There's no future for you there.'

Lindow watched as Foyle ate his steak greedily, swilling it down with gulps of red wine. The policeman was boorish, but he was obviously good at his job and he possessed an agile mind. He had locked on to the one area that Lindow found it difficult to talk about. He couldn't be certain any longer about Eamonn, and he was aware that every time Foyle mentioned his brother it showed in his face.

'Tell me about Mary Menihan – sounds like a good Irish name,' said Foyle.

He knew he was being tested. 'I met her today, as you are no doubt aware. She was a friend of Eamonn's. She's American, from the East Coast, just south of Boston. She works here in publishing as a part-time editor. I'd guess she has money of her own because she only does a couple of days for the company and then some manuscript reading for another publishing house. She said Eamonn and she became friends after he'd helped her through a bad patch. That's all I know about her.'

'So you don't think she's got anything to do with all this?'

'No, I don't. She's a clever, good-looking, middle-class girl – frankly she was a cut above most of Eamonn's girlfriends. She's classy. Not the type to run around with Semtex in her purse.'

'What type is that?'

'Isn't that rather a dumb question? You know I know nothing about these things. It's just that this woman has other things going for her. Anyway, there's less Irish in her than you'd think by her name. Her mother is Jewish.'

'The IRA get their people from anywhere. Just because we've had this period of peace, it doesn't mean that the basic organisation isn't there and the more extreme people, the Real IRA, aren't still recruiting and setting up cells in Britain. By the way, these aren't your type of cells because they don't communicate with each other. In fact, they're the opposite. They have no knowledge of each other whatsoever. They just communicate with the lead man in the hierarchy in Ireland.'

'Oh, come on, Commander. You're not seriously suggesting that Eamonn was the link between a cell involving me and Mary and that we're under the direct control of Rudi MacMahon? That's fantasy-land.

For a start, MacMahon is part of the political process now. He's respectable. Wears a tie and kisses babies.'

'Maybe, but that theory looks good to my superiors. MacMahon may have been an old contact who was lost when the IRA started to talk.'

'Yes, but you don't believe their theory. Otherwise you wouldn't be sitting here with me. You know there's something else going on and you don't understand it.'

'Yes, and I have admitted that to you.'

'But what makes you think it?' Lindow was pleased to be driving the conversation at last. 'What else could be going on?'

'I shouldn't be talking to you about it, but I suppose, in these circumstances, I don't see why I shouldn't. There's not much to lose.' Foyle folded his napkin and began to probe his teeth with a toothpick that he'd taken from a pot in the centre of the table. Lindow waited for him to finish without saying anything.

Presently Foyle disposed of the toothpick and poured himself another glass of wine. 'To answer your question, I don't understand what's going on at all. There is a good reason for questioning you, but equally now there seem to be very good reasons for removing you and your brother from direct suspicion. And yet all the pressure from above has been to focus on you two. Possibly there's a political motive, I don't know. So much of it doesn't add up – the two targets this week are inconsistent in nearly every respect. The other thing is that the bombs are different from what we've seen before.'

'How?'

'They've got the same arrangements, explosive and detonator, but we don't know how they're being triggered. If we knew how they were being set off and we could prove that the bomb on the bus was triggered from a distance we'd be halfway to putting you and your brother in the clear. Look, this is sensitive stuff, I really shouldn't be talking about it. So I'd rather you keep it to yourself.'

'Why's it so difficult to work out how the bombs are being detonated? Your forensics people must have found clues at the scenes. Something must have shown up.'

'Nothing of that nature. Still, I don't expect you to help me with that. What I am asking you to do is to keep me informed of anything you discover about Eamonn which is relevant to this investigation. It may be painful, but in the long run it will be better. If you're going to Ireland, keep your eyes open. There may be some kind of republican presence at the funeral, which might tell us something, and I guess they may approach you.'

'I doubt it,' said Lindow. 'What would they want to say to me?'

'Who knows? But the main thing is that I've got your agreement to help me, if you can. That's right, isn't it?'

Lindow nodded. Foyle took out a card, wrote his home number on the back and gave it to him. 'If anything occurs to you over the weekend, call me. I don't have a cellphone but you can get hold of me at any time through my office.'

Foyle paid the bill and they made their way to his car. Foyle turned to Lindow. 'It's been good to talk to you, Dr Lindow.' He looked away up the street. 'You realise that you and I are like the squid and the bacteria at the bottom of the sea – we need each other.'

'Which of us is the bacteria?'

'I'm afraid it's got to be you,' said Foyle. 'I'm the one who needs to find his way in the dark.'

It was nearing midnight. Lindow did not go to bed immediately but returned to the sofa and flicked through the satellite channels – sport, soft porn and movies with bad plots. He ended up watching a programme about the history of telecommunications made for the Discovery Channel, but it held his interest for only a few minutes. He thought about Foyle's visit and wondered whether he should have told him about the things he'd found in Eamonn's flat. No, he had been right not to tell him. Despite Foyle's likeable nature and apparent openness, there wasn't anything to be gained from it, particularly if he was about to be kicked off the investigation. Better to keep it to himself. It did occur to him that Foyle might have known the package was there all along and was testing him, but somehow that didn't work. The contents would be too important to the investigation to be left there as bait on the off-chance that he would roll up and find them.

Eventually he turned in and fell into a deep, troubled sleep. He woke at five, then again at six, this time with a jolt that propelled him from the pillow. He'd been dreaming. He was in some kind of laboratory, but the equipment was unfamiliar. There were batteries and clocks and tangles of wire and telephones, lots of them from every age, like he'd seen in the TV programme. Now that he was awake he was quite certain he'd found the solution to one part of Foyle's problem. He knew how the two bombs had been detonated.

He got up and made himself coffee, fixing it in his mind. He left his flat and walked to the phone booth around the corner where he dialled the number written on the back of Foyle's card.

Foyle's voice came on the line, drugged with sleep. When he heard Lindow's name he said groggily, 'I'm sorry after all that I forgot to give you your keys last night.'

'I didn't ring about that. I've got a spare set now,' said Lindow, with impatience. 'Something occurred to me in the middle of the night. I think your bomber is using cellphones to trigger the explosions.'

At the end of the line Foyle was silent. Then he whispered, 'By God, I think you're right.'

His mind focused and he began to recall the report from MI6 about the Budapest bombing. Hadn't the victim received a phone message from the receptionist as he was leaving? Yes, and he'd pulled out his mobile phone and dialled a number. The call could easily have triggered the bomb that was lying, like the Floodgate Street device, in the foyer of the building. The explosion on the train near Prague could also have been set off by a phone call made by the bomber once he'd got off at the station. Lindow's theory certainly worked.

'Are you there?'

'Hold on. I'm thinking,' said Foyle.

Then he had a more chilling thought. No, it couldn't be! Foyle fumbled in his mind to get it absolutely straight. What had he been doing when that second bomb went off? Yes, he'd been trying to get hold of Blackett in the north of England – but Blackett hadn't been in the north of England. He had been in Belfast all the time. When he'd made the call on Thursday, the line went dead after the first ring. Then he had heard the bomb.

'Were any phone parts found in the bus?' asked Lindow, interrupting Foyle's train of thought. Foyle made an instant decision not to tell Lindow about the Blackett business.

'Yes.' He paused. 'I'm sure there were, but Forensic must've assumed they came from one of the passengers. Anyway, not much would be left if a mobile was attached to that amount of explosive. What in heaven's name made you think of this, anyway?'

'You remember I was explaining my work about the messages transmitted between cells by chemicals. Then you made a remark about the way IRA cells didn't communicate with each other. That, and a TV programme I watched about telephone technology, must have set my mind thinking about the relationships between different types of cells and the way they communicate with each other – or don't, as the case may be. One system of cells that do communicate with each other is the honeycomb network of the cellular phone system. When a phone call is made to a cellphone it is transmitted to anywhere in the cell from the antennae, which is the equivalent of the nucleus in a human cell. That's more or less an exact parallel to the way human cells work. Messages move from the centre to the outside. But when a call is made from the phone somewhere in the cell, the signal goes to the antennae at the centre, which is the opposite process.'

'Yes, yes,' said Foyle, anxious to stem Lindow's flow. 'Your theory only works if a phone can be connected up to a bomb. Are the electronics feasible?'

'I don't see why not. The phone would simply act as a switch – like a radio transmitter, an altimeter or a mercury tilt device.'

'You know an awful lot about this, Dr Lindow.'

'Oh, come on! This stuff is all common knowledge. It's posted in a hundred places on the Internet. Look, I'd hardly be telling you if I had anything to do with this, would I? Anyway, it's only a possibility.'

'Yes, but if it's true, the potential is terrifying. You could plant twenty bombs then set them off at will from anywhere in the world.'

'The battery life must be a factor.'

'Course,' said Foyle, 'if you're right it means a lot for you, doesn't it? For one thing it puts you both in the clear. Yet it also means that you've got to acknowledge that Eamonn was the target that night. The other casualties were incidental to that one aim. It means someone followed your brother on to that bus and placed that bomb right behind him. Who wanted to kill him so much that they were prepared to slaughter ten other people in the process?'

'I don't have any idea. Believe me, I'd tell you if I knew.'

'Right, I'll talk to you later today. Stay in touch and don't leave for Ireland without telling me. In the meanwhile, thanks. I believe you've helped us a great deal.'

Lindow hung up. He felt sick and deflated. Sooner or later he would have to tell Foyle about the envelope and what really happened in the churchyard.

7

A couple of hours after receiving Lindow's call, Foyle left his house with clothes for three days and drove to New Scotland Yard. By midday he'd assembled a small group of officers who were prepared to work through the weekend on the implications of Lindow's idea about telephone detonation. There were nine in the room when he outlined the theory, which he did without crediting the author because he wanted it to be given an unbiased hearing. Foyle's mood was upbeat, although he knew well that by the end of Monday he would probably have been relieved of his command. This was his last throw and he sensed that the nine officers perched around his room were pretty much trying to make it work for him.

They had little problem accepting Lindow's idea in principle. Lafferty nodded and said it had been only a matter of time before somebody thought of using the cellphone networks. Inspector Lockyer chimed in by reporting that tiny fragments of circuitry, consistent with the insides of a cellphone, had been found at the scenes of both explosions. There was no reason why these could not have been part of the devices.

Then Foyle told them about the call he had made on Thursday evening in response to a message left by Superintendent Blackett in Belfast and how it turned out that Blackett had also received a message to ring him. What was downright puzzling was that neither had phoned and yet both had been asked to call each other on the same number. It was possible that the bomber had set them up to ring each other, knowing that the first to make the call would detonate the bomb. It was just a second or two after he had dialled the number written in his message book that he had heard the explosion in Floodgate Street.

'Forbes will tell you. He was with me.' He glanced at Forbes, who was looking less than convinced. There was a silence. 'Yes, I know you all think I've lost it, but hear me out just this once because, if my suspicions are correct, it means that we're dealing with a very different type of terrorist altogether – someone who is playing with us, someone so confident that he's prepared to give us a massive clue like this and still know he's going to get away with it. If, for a moment, you accept the theory, several compelling questions present themselves. Why was Blackett linked with me in the bomber's little joke to get one of us to finish the work at Floodgate Street? Were we inadvertently responsible for detonating the Clarence Street bomb also? What point was the bomber making? Why was he making it?'

Foyle paused to look down at the notes in his book. Then he raised his head and revolved his index finger in the air as though he was conducting a very slow piece of music. 'You see, Blackett hasn't been chosen at random. There is a connection. In the early eighties Superintendent Blackett was one of the investigating officers after the explosion at Droy. He was the man who interviewed Eamonn and Con Lindow. If you draw this thing out, there are links between the two bombs, which go way beyond the similarity in design of the bomb and the batch of explosives. I'll show you what I mean.'

He turned to a board behind him and made two crosses, which he labelled 'Clarence Street' and 'Floodgate Street'. Then he drew a line downwards from 'Clarence Street' to a circle where he wrote 'Lindow'. He followed this with another line from 'Floodgate Street' to a circle in which he wrote 'Blackett/Foyle'.

'It's like this,' he said, sketching wildly between the two crosses and the two circles. 'We have a square in which everything is connected. We don't know the exact nature of all the relationships between these points, but there are hints. I believe there's a logical answer to this diagram and it's our job to solve the riddle before another bomb is exploded.'

'But this is all based on supposition, unproved theory,' said Lockyer, voicing the scepticism of the room. The forensics specialist had made it clear with a series of sideways glances to Lafferty that he doubted Foyle's sanity. 'I accept there's some good reasoning behind it, Commander, but you've no evidence for any of this whatsoever. Nothing.'

'Yes, you're right. I admit it. However, this theory at least explains the inconsistencies *and* the consistencies between the two bombs. Of course, if you've got a better idea about it all, I'm happy to give it a go.'

'There could be something in what you say,' said Lafferty. 'It's just that I feel uncomfortable when we're dealing with theories, not evidence.'

'Then we shall have to find that evidence,' said Foyle, 'and that is what I plan to do now.'

He divided the four junior officers into pairs: Kepple and Hardwood to go back over the Droy cemetery explosion and extract more records from the RUC, and Sergeant Pennel and WPC Tina Wei to research the cellular networks and the feasibility of cellphone detonation. Lockyer and Lafferty disappeared with their sergeants to review the forensic evidence gleaned from the two bomb scenes, while Forbes made himself useful, trying to find out the names of the Army officers involved in Operation CUDGEL.

The team did not meet again until early Monday morning, by which time Foyle's theory had established itself in each officer's mind as at least being feasible, although there was still no conclusive proof from either of the two bomb scenes. On another front, however, there was better news. The laboratory handling the film from the two remaining cameras on the bus had finally unpicked a two-hour tape from the forward-facing camera, situated halfway along the lower deck. The technicians had hoped to be able to take something from the camera above the driver's head, but everything had been lost when the electrical wiring in the cab caught fire.

On the inside of the salvaged spool they'd found a section of tape where the magnetic signal had not been melted. These fifteen and a half minutes from the beginning of the journey were in working order, except for a regular interruption lasting a second or two. The laboratory had transferred the film frame by frame to another tape and sent it round first thing on Monday. Forbes brought the envelope, still sealed, and gave it to Foyle as if it was a Christmas present.

They watched the film immediately. Eleven minutes passed during which the bus stopped five times. Then suddenly Eamonn Lindow appeared, clear as day, hurrying on to the bus with a book under his arm. He showed the driver a travel pass and moved through the camera's field, smiling, perhaps with the afterglow of the exchange with the driver or perhaps because he'd seen someone he recognised. There was a pause while an elderly woman paid her fare, and then two men got on. The first was using a walking-stick and took some time to haul himself up through the doors. He paid the driver and turned away from the camera to receive something from the man behind. It was obviously something heavy. At that point a party of four women crowded on board and the individual disappeared behind them. Because of the damage to the tape, the picture faded for a few seconds then returned in time to catch the man with the stick moving to the back of the bus.

'That's him,' murmured Foyle. 'That's got to be the bomber.'

He pressed the replay button then froze the image of the top of the man's head, but he had missed the moment he wanted. He moved it on a few frames, then back again and stopped the film on the man's face. Much of it was hidden, but beneath the cap you could make out the left eye, an ear and a very well-defined young jaw.

'Well, I think that's something, don't you?' Foyle was relieved at last to be dealing with some concrete evidence. 'The first thing that this film proves is that Eamonn Lindow carried nothing more than a book on to that bus. He could've been given the package later, but it seems unlikely since he was the one who was blown up. And look at his manner – all smiles, no concern in the world.'

'We should certainly trace that man with the stick,' said Forbes. 'I'm pretty certain that he's not among the people who've come forward and I know he wasn't among the victims. I wonder if any of those women remember him.'

'Right.' Foyle sprang from his chair. 'I think we're due at the briefing. Have the tape copied and stills made of the relevant frames, but first let's show it to the others.'

The film was played several times and the mood of SO 13 picked up. But when Foyle introduced the business of his phone call on the night of the Floodgate Street bomb, despairing glances were exchanged. The news that an inner group had been working over the weekend on this crackpot theory didn't help either. Foyle sensed the mood, and briskly asked Pennel to tell the briefing what he'd discovered about phone technology.

'In theory this might be an extremely useful method to a sophisticated terrorist. The maximum battery life of a standard phone can be as much as ninety to a hundred hours – nearly four days. Some advanced phones have as much as one week's standby time. The terrorist could plant his bomb, fly back to Libya or Belfast or wherever and then, at his leisure, phone the number. That's the first advantage. The second is that you can't jam the signal as was done in Ulster when the IRA used model-aircraft radio controls to detonate their culvert bombs. The security forces got on to the frequency and blocked it, at which point the Provisionals returned to using the old-fashioned command wire. But a phone cannot be jammed, unless you have the subscriber's number or you lay a curtain over a whole area. That's only been done a few times. We discovered that the Italians blacked out their parliament building to stop MPs using their phones during debates. That was a permanent arrangement. At short notice it would be difficult to screen off parts of London. You have six networks operating in Britain – four digital and two analog – and then there are several separate cells in central London with hundreds of local area networks, which are like micro-cells. You might be able to shut down one but you'd have to be sure that you'd got the right one. There are areas of overlap, which means a signal might still get through.

'The third advantage is that unless a phone is linked up to the GPS system – Global Positioning by Satellite – you cannot track a subscriber's phone even if it is switched on. Only when the subscriber makes a call can the set be traced because it sends out an individual code. However, in receive mode its signal to the cell antennae will not include an individual code. There's no way of telling which phones are switched on or where they are.' He looked across to Tina Wei, the Chinese detective with whom he'd been teamed up over the weekend. 'Is there anything I've forgotten?' he asked.

'No,' she said, 'except that there is another advantage and that is the sheer number of cellphones in circulation. There are about twelve million subscribers in Britain and the number increases annually by nearly half a million. Most of the phone companies insist on the production of proof of identity and address. But at least one doesn't, which means that any individual can buy a phone and a service on a credit or charge card that's held in a false name. There's also services in which you buy your talk-time in advance, so no references or credit cards are required. Once they're out there, there's no way of tracing these phones.'

'What about cloned phones?' asked Foyle. 'Is there any possibility that he is using them?'

'A cloned phone has no relevance in these circumstances,' replied Pennel. 'First of all you can only clone a phone by picking up a signal from an analog set and copying it. Of course, there'd be no point because the terrorist needs his bomb to have a unique number. If he has cloned a phone there will always be a risk that someone makes a call to the number while he is handling the bomb. Cloning is only useful to someone who wants to steal airtime – to make calls on the subscriber's bill. The purpose of a device attached to a bomb would be to receive calls only.'

After the briefing Foyle and Forbes adjourned as usual to Foyle's office. Foyle walked over to the window and looked down on Victoria Street. A few people were struggling along in the wind, which was wrenching their umbrellas from their hands.

'Jesus, what the hell do they want?' he said, crashing both hands down on the radiator casing. 'I gave them hard facts, direction and not a bad theory – all of which are advances on Friday evening – and yet the whole lot of them sat there nonplussed. What's going on, Forbes?'

'Well, you know how it is. If things aren't going well for us they get frustrated and they're beginning to wonder where the break's going to come from.'

'And what else are they saying?'

'They're wondering if you're going to be here next week.' Forbes looked down.

'Well, you can bloody well tell them I'm not going yet,' Foyle said, without conviction. 'This is my investigation and I'm going to complete it.'

After his call Lindow did not hear from Foyle and spent the weekend trying edgily to get back into his routine. But he couldn't settle to work. He went to a couple of movies and took solitary meals in his local Greek restaurant. Monday came as a relief. He started the day by calling Lustig, the letting agent. It was odd. The phone didn't respond at all. No message service – nothing.

He tried again, checking the number from his ansaphone, then rang Mary Menihan to tell her that the funeral had been fixed for Wednesday at eleven thirty a.m., which would mean that she would have to fly to Ireland on Tuesday. 'There's something else,' he said. 'I haven't asked my father yet, but I know he'll agree. Will you read something at the service?

A piece of Yeats, maybe, or something else that you know Eamonn would've liked.'

She thought for a moment. 'Yes, I'd be pleased to do that. I'll think of it as an honour – so long as your father likes the idea too.'

'He will,' said Lindow definitely. 'So, I'll see you tomorrow. Come over for a drink and meet what's left of the Lindows. It'll be just me, Tag and Dad.' He gave her the address and telephone number, and replaced the receiver, registering the pleasure he'd felt in talking to her.

It was nine thirty a.m. – two hours before the inquest opened on the victims of the Clarence Street explosion. He thought about Harry Ribb, who'd died of a heart attack after being sent home from the hospital on Saturday afternoon. His son had been quoted saying that it was the shock of the explosion, and the Sunday papers had no hesitation in including him in the toll.

Lindow decided not to go to the inquest and made a call from another phone box near his flat to ask the solicitors to represent him. Then he walked up to WH Smith on Notting Hill, where he selected some magazines and a child's geometry set, which he placed between the magazines as he approached the sales counter. He didn't know if he was being watched, but he certainly didn't want anyone to see him buy the instruments, nor did he want them to know what he planned to use them for. As the woman gave him his change, he asked her where the nearest library was. She told him there was one just off Kensington High Street.

He left and walked quickly along the pavement, trying to give no hint that he was looking for a taxi with its light on. It was still raining and there were few about. When one eventually came along he shot his arm into the street and climbed in. He pulled back the partition window, handed the driver a ten-pound note and asked him to drive to a large store in Oxford Street. He had a vague idea that it would be a good place to elude any pursuers he might have. The cab set off eastwards, passing the drenched landscape of Kensington Gardens. Lindow turned round a few times but stopped when he noticed the driver examining him in his mirror.

'Are you being followed?' the driver said, as they idled at some lights at Lancaster Gate.

'What makes you think that?'

'You keep looking out of the back. If you are being followed, there's an idea I've always wanted to try out. Do you want to give it a go?'

'Sure, why not?'

A little way down Oxford Street the driver took a left turn without indicating, then made another left so that they ended up in a car park attached to the back of a department store.

'I'll drive you in,' said the driver as he took a ticket at the barrier. 'Then you get yourself into the shop pronto and vanish. I'll wait in the car park a bit before leaving. That should do the trick for you.'

Lindow thanked him and gave him another ten-pound note. He entered the store through a door marked Furnishings and Kitchenware and moved through the more or less deserted floor to the escalators. He took a quick turn through Women's Fashion on the first floor then went down to the ground floor and left the store by one of the main exits. Out in Oxford Street, he hailed another cab and told the driver to take him to Kensington Library.

Once inside, he walked straight to the reference section, where he withdrew the largest atlas and opened it at the full map of Ireland. Realising he couldn't draw on it he made a colour copy on the library's machine and carried it back with the atlas to an unoccupied desk at the far end of the reading room. He then removed the protractor from its case and aligned it over the centre of the city of Belfast. To get a bearing of 342 degrees by using a schoolboy's protractor – not a compass – would be a simple matter of subtracting 18 degrees from the 90-degree vertical on the protractor. He made a mark at the edge of the protractor at 72 degrees, the equivalent on the compass of 342 degrees. He repeated the procedure for Limerick, but this time made the mark on the paper at 8 degrees, a little to the right of the vertical line on the protractor. Then he took out the ruler and traced the two bearings on to the photocopy. The lines intersected about 140 miles north of the coast of Ireland.

Lindow sat back and thought. Some way from him a woman with a shoulder-bag was browsing through the science and technology reference section. Then she went over to look at the set of the *Dictionary of National Biography*. He waited, making no secret of following her progress around the shelves. She knew he was watching her. Suddenly she looked at her watch and walked with haste to the entrance.

He returned to the copy of the map. Perhaps the bearings indicated the presence of a boat. It seemed unlikely. He was sure he was making a mistake with the figures, but he couldn't think how. Then he remembered that Eamonn's scrap of paper included another piece of information. He took it from his wallet and read the words 'Av Declination – 20 degrees'. This must have referred to the magnetic variation, the difference between magnetic and true north, which anyone using a map and compass in the field must allow for. There was no note in the atlas about the magnetic variation for Ireland, nor in any of the other atlases, so he asked at the desk where he could find out about declination for different parts of the world. The attractive woman librarian suggested he ring the Royal Geographical Society's map room and, with a smile, offered him the use of the library's telephone.

'Be my guest.' He noticed a glint in her eyes. 'It's library business, after all.'

The woman in the map room was equally helpful. She looked up an airline chart and came back on the line.

'No, no,' she said. 'Twenty degrees would be far too much. The declination for Belfast is eight and a half degrees west and for Limerick it's seven and a half. So to be accurate in Ireland you would need to set your compass at an average declination of eight degrees west of true north.'

'Is there anywhere in the world where the westerly declination is as much as twenty degrees?' asked Lindow.

'Oh, yes,' she said. 'From memory, I'd say parts of Canada and America have a twenty-degree declination.'

Lindow snapped his fingers, thanked her profusely and hurried back to the reference section, where he took down an atlas of North America. He ran his finger down the index. He knew there was another Belfast, some way up the coast from Boston, in the state of Maine. Was there another Limerick? His instinct was absolutely right. There was, and it was also in Maine. He turned to the map and found the tiny town of Limerick about twenty-five miles due west of Portland. He knew straight away that the two compass bearings would intersect somewhere in the north of the state. But he decided to be certain and wandered over to the library's large travel section where he scanned the shelves for anything on the east coast of America. He pulled down a large paperback called *Fifty Hikes in the Maine Mountains*, which confirmed in the introduction that 'Maine's declination varies from seventeen to twenty degrees, usually around twenty degrees for hikes in this book.'

He made a photocopy of the map of Maine from the atlas and traced out the bearings from Limerick. As he had predicted, the lines met in the north of the state, a little to the left of an area called the Allagash Wilderness. Lindow had heard of it, but knew nothing of the area; still less did he understand why Eamonn had pinpointed a spot that contained nothing but forests and lakes. However, he was certain he'd found the solution to the slip of paper. After all, it had been hidden in the passport that contained entry stamps for Boston, which was only a few hundred miles south. Something was there, something Eamonn had been anxious to keep secret. He wondered if he could learn anything from the dates of the entry stamps in Eamonn's fake passport.

He folded the copies of the two maps, placed them in his inside pocket and left the room with a nod of thanks to the pretty librarian. He couldn't help feeling a little exalted at his discovery.

Kirsty Laing nursed a large cappuccino and waited for Peter Speerman, who'd said he would drop by to give her the briefing. He had not found time on Friday and, when pressed by her, agreed to an early meeting on Monday. At nine o'clock. Speerman put his head round the door and gave her a conspiratorial smile. He was carrying a file under his arm and a National Trust mug, filled with strong tea.

'So, Kirsty, we must have our little chat.' His manner made Laing feel she was about to be told the facts of life. She sat back in her chair and waited.

'Some years ago we became involved with a man named Ian Rhodes – Major Ian Valentine Rhodes – one of the most remarkable soldiers ever to have served in the British Army. When he left in the late eighties the people at the top of the service believed he could be very useful to us. They were proved right. He was highly intelligent, and physically without parallel. There seemed to be nothing he couldn't do. He became attached to the service in an unofficial capacity and carried out a number of important tasks – on one occasion he single-handedly managed to release an informant from interrogation by the Provisionals that would have ended in certain death. He also undertook a number of missions abroad for us, which I won't enlarge on. Suffice to say they were all expedited with the minimum fuss and the maximum speed. But Rhodes came with problems that no one appreciated at the time. There was an imbalance – a nervous breakdown of some form, which was said to have been the delayed reaction to a skirmish in Ireland when his men were wiped out in an incident near the border. His trouble did not surface until the early nineties and he was hospitalised for treatment. When he recovered he went into business for himself, first as a contract agent to the private security firms that have sprung up in Victoria over the last ten years, then on his own behalf. We remained on reasonable terms with him and used him once or twice more, but it became clear that his own business took priority. Besides, there was no telling who else he was working for. Rhodes was an extremely capable individual, but he was also addicted to risk. There was evidence that he'd sold knowledge of our arrangements and *modus operandi* to the other side, by which I mean the IRA. This was before the first ceasefire. We weren't certain but we had our suspicions, and we knew the republicans were interested in doing business with him. Incidentally, so was every other terrorist group in the northern hemisphere. We began to think of Major Rhodes as someone whose movements it was prudent to track, which is why the watchers included him in the gallery of faces that Weegee was programmed to look out for.'

'And Weegee spotted him on the night of the first bomb.'

'*May* have spotted him.' He gave a matronly look of reproach. 'We're not absolutely certain it was him.'

'But surely we should have told the police.'

'That is not an option at the moment. When you read the file, I think you will agree about that.' Speerman picked up his mug. She felt him studying her.

'You're probably right, but surely the downside of sharing this information with the police is almost negligible. After all, the director general can't be held responsible for decisions taken by his predecessors. And if this man, who was never a member of the service anyway, caused the bombings, it would be only wise to bring in the police at the earliest possible opportunity.'

'It may come to that, but we would prefer to solve the problem using our own resources. That way our security is maintained and there's no danger of our association with Rhodes leaking to the press. But there may be a time when we need you to help explain this problem in certain government quarters, which is why I asked you to come along last week. That moment, however, has not yet arrived.' He slid the file across her desk and got up to leave. 'Return it to me before the end of this morning. It needs to go back into the safe. Oh, I hardly need tell you that no copies should be made.'

She read through the file and found that Speerman had covered most of the ground. The thing that absorbed her was the colour headshot of a man with a chiselled face and receding hairline, which was clipped to the inside of the file. At the bottom of the picture, time and date were recorded – 19.22:23.10. There were some other figures, which she presumed identified the camera and the subject's exact location on a grid of the street.

She examined the face. It wasn't possible to see the man's eyes, for he was glancing down to the right, but she had the strong impression that he was someone to be reckoned with. There was a composed, brutal intelligence about the face that Weegee had plucked from the street six days before. As she stared at the picture, she realised that she couldn't simply return it to Speerman's safe. It might never see the light of day. And, given the apparent determination of the service to save its own skin by pursuing Lindow, there was a very large principle at stake here. This was the moment she had always suspected would come. She argued with herself for some minutes, then got up and moved quickly to a small flat box by her filing cabinet – the scanner she used for copying newspaper clippings and documents on to her computer's memory. She placed the picture face down on the glass surface, closed the lid and set the machine to run. Some minutes later she brought up the picture on her screen. But instead of storing it in the computer, she printed off a copy. It was a laborious process but it meant that she had avoided having to use the photocopier down the corridor, which was too public and, anyway, was reputed to be fitted with a device that made a record of all copies taken. She examined the print, checking that the date/time line had been reproduced, then slipped it in a folder of old memos. Finally she deleted the file from her computer.

On the way back to Speerman's office to deliver the Rhodes file she kept reassuring herself that the picture would be used only if circumstances demanded. So, in a sense, she had not yet done anything against the service but was merely reserving the right to stand by a principle.

Speerman ushered her in, took the file and gestured to a chair. 'There's been an interesting development. Lindow's been acting very suspiciously this morning. He made an amateurish attempt to give us the slip in Oxford Street. Our people might have fallen for it had they not been lagging behind the police. Quite by chance they saw him run from a department store. I believe the police lost him some time before.'

'Perhaps he knew he was being followed and didn't like it.'

'Maybe, but then he went to a library and spent a long time in the reference section using the atlases. Obviously it had nothing to do with his work. He was observed making some sort of measurements by one of Keith's people, who couldn't get close to him. She thought he spotted her. Later we found out that he was making inquiries about magnetic declination with the Royal Geographical Society. We don't know what he was up to but the police have been informed. They will be none too happy, particularly as I gather that Foyle had more or less eliminated Lindow from his inquiry. This behaviour would suggest that he has something to hide.'

'Good,' she said. 'That sounds very promising indeed.'

Foyle read the MI5 report with a sense of mounting despair. The story of Lindow giving the police surveillance team the slip spread quickly through SO 13. Morale was not helped by the news that Millbank's watchers had kept in touch with their target and tailed Lindow to a library where they had observed him working on some maps. It was not clear what he had been doing, but the fact that he had used the ploy in Oxford Street so that he could be alone in the library was enough to convince practically every member of the Anti-terrorist Unit that Lindow was guilty. It was well known that terrorists used public libraries to research such things as targets, which was why Eamonn Lindow's job as a librarian had been regarded as being far less innocent than it seemed. In the mid-nineties, members of an IRA active-service unit had been observed thumbing through manuals on the national electricity grid. Lindow would not be the first bomber to curl up in the reference section with a good book.

Foyle knew now that his hours in the department were numbered. He chucked the report aside and asked Forbes with ill-concealed exasperation if Lindow had been located again.

'Yes, sir, we picked him up at his solicitor's office about an hour ago. We believe he has been settling his brother's affairs. The lawyer was at the inquest this morning and is apparently helping him with the arrangements for the transportation of Eamonn's body to Ireland.'

'Permission for burial has been given?'

'Yes, you said that you had no objections so I let the coroner's office know on Friday that it would be all right by us.'

'Do we know when he's going to Ireland?'

'It seems likely that he'll leave today or tomorrow morning.'

Foyle thought for a few moments.

'Should we have him arrested again?' Forbes asked.

'On what grounds? For giving our surveillance team the slip in Ladies' Hosiery?'

'On the grounds that he has been acting as if he has something to hide. That's reason enough, in these circumstances.'

'It would be pointless to arrest him,' said Foyle. 'He's not the man behind this. In fact, it was Lindow who gave me the idea about the telephones. It still seems the only workable solution we've got.'

Forbes raised an eyebrow. 'He gave you that idea? But don't you see that it helps his case if he can make us believe that someone outside that bus detonated the bomb? It's a very clever idea, but in his case it could be seen as self-serving.'

'Yes, that's what Lockyer said when I told him.'

'You told Lockyer? Lockyer and Scarratt are very tight. They're members of the same Lodge. It won't be long before Scarratt hears.'

'Oh, fuck,' said Foyle. 'Look, find out where Lindow is and let me know.'

At that moment Lindow was stepping out of a cab at Heathrow Airport. He had booked a flight to Dublin from Jane Casper's phone, having taken the passport and money from her safe. Instead of examining the US immigration stamps at the lawyers', he decided to wait until he got to Ireland where he'd have time to think through Eamonn's double life. He also wanted to ask Tag her opinion. She'd seen a lot of Eamonn over the last few years and would have a better notion of what he had been doing in the States. Tag had been the one member of his family to whom he had spoken regularly while he had been away. He had left Ireland while she was still young and had only properly come to know her two summers before when she stayed with him in Boston for three months, working at a restaurant on the waterfront. She had made a similar effort with Eamonn and visited him several times in London. They had got on well, although there were seventeen years between them, and Tag, like Lindow, had veered to the sciences, in her case chemistry.

Back at his flat, Lindow slipped the passport, money and the copies of the maps into the breast pocket of the suit he intended to wear for the funeral. Then he packed it, with clothes and some books, and left for the airport. All the arrangements had been made. The body was to be picked up by a firm of undertakers and would be flown to Dublin, there to be met by a hearse from Desmond Quorny, Ballyhanna's funeral director.

He had about an hour to wait at the airport, which didn't bother him. His mood was lightening somewhat at the thought of leaving London and spending some time at home. Over the weekend he'd resolved to put more effort into his family. That was what was in his mind when, on his way to the departure gate, he was approached by two men who asked if they could have a word. They assured him that he would not be delayed and that there was nothing to worry about. He followed them down a corridor to a suite of anonymous offices, without windows, where he was offered a chair and a cup of tea. 'Are you arresting me?' he asked.

'No, sir,' said one, a stout man with shiny hair. 'We're just interested in your travel plans. We thought you'd prefer it that we talk to you here, rather than when you're about to board the aircraft. Commander Foyle would like to have an idea of when you plan to return to the United Kingdom, sir.'

'I haven't decided yet,' said Lindow. 'I've been given compassionate leave by the university and it's possible that I'll choose to spend some time with my family. I may be away for a couple of weeks.'

'You can't be more specific than that?'

'No, I can't.'

'Are you travelling with your passport, sir?' asked the older man, a military type of about fifty.

'Yes, as a matter of fact I am, but that's out of habit. You don't need it to travel from Britain to Ireland.'

'That's right. Would you mind if I looked at it?'

Lindow felt inside his jacket and handed it to him. The man leafed through the passport while his companion studied Lindow.

'You see,' he said, still examining its pages, 'Commander Foyle wants to be certain of your return.'

'There's no question of me not coming back. Tell Commander Foyle that I'll be back by the first week of November, if not sooner. That's a promise. I've got a job to come back for.'

'Yes, well, just to be on the safe side, he wonders if you'd have a problem leaving this with us – to be collected on your return.' He presented it as a request, but Lindow had little doubt that the passport would be taken whichever way he answered.

'Have I got any option?'

'Not really, sir, unless you want to delay your departure and sort this out here in England. But if you're not planning to use it, there isn't any reason why you should mind, is there, sir?'

'That's not the point! The point is that you're taking my passport – an Irish passport – when you haven't any right to do so. I'm not under arrest.'

'You're very welcome to appeal against the decision, sir. As I say, this is a request made by Commander Foyle personally, in a spirit of trust. He hopes you will see it that way because he has already placed considerable trust in you.'

Lindow saw that it was no use arguing. He shrugged his shoulders and said that he would be willing to oblige the commander as long as he was guaranteed the return of the passport when he set foot back in England.

'That's understood,' said the other officer. 'If you hold on a moment there, sir, I'll go and get you a written receipt, which will enable you to collect your passport from New Scotland Yard when you come back.'

He disappeared for ten minutes, then returned waving a flimsy bit of paper, which he presented to Lindow with great ceremony. 'Thank you for being so understanding, Dr Lindow. We appreciate it, don't we?' he said, nudging his colleague.

'Oh, yes, we appreciate it, Dr Lindow. Now, have a good trip, sir.'

'Yes, sir. Have a good trip,' said the other.

Lindow left the Laurel and Hardy of the British Special Branch and made his way to the boarding-gate.

8

Lindow hired a car at Dublin airport and drove northwards. In the fading light, Ireland came flooding back – its louring skies and the sweet, earthy fumes of occasional peat fires.

He was reminded that Ireland was still a country where people walked because they had no means of transport. He picked up a couple of hitch-hikers, first a young boy lugging his schoolbooks home, then a middle-aged woman with her shopping. She got into the car and began talking about Irish politics and some scandal or other involving a minister and his mistress. He let her out at a crossroads where a telegraph pole was festooned with election posters. She said goodbye and strode away, muttering that each one of the faces that flapped in the breeze was exactly the same. He got out of the car, went over to the posters and examined them. She was wrong. The topmost poster showed Rudi MacMahon bursting from the Sinn Fein colours with a family-man grin. 'Vote MacMahon – A Better Chance for Peace', it declared.

He returned to the car and drove on to Ballyhanna, the market town ten miles south of the border where the Lindows had moved when his mother inherited some land and a comfortable house on the edge of the town. The White House, as it was still known, although painted a pale terracotta by Marie Lindow several years ago, was set back from the road at the end of a short gravel drive, which announced Lindow's arrival with a crunching sound that reverberated around the walls of the house.

As he pulled up the light over the front door came on and Tag bounded out to meet him. His father followed, stooped and smiling. 'Ah, that's good,' he said, gripping his son's arms. 'You look fine, Con. It's good to have you home.'

Lindow felt his eyes pricking with tears. He turned round abruptly, hauled his bags from the car, then walked to the front door between Tag and his father.

Not long afterwards they sat round the kitchen table eating a stew made by Tag and talking over the arrangements for the funeral – an agonising process for the old man, who fell into long silences during which he stared at the glass door of the wood-burner.

'The thing I don't understand, Con,' he said quietly, 'is why Eamonn? Why the bus with all those people on it? What's been gained by their deaths?'

Lindow and his sister looked at each other. Tag shook her head and placed a hand on her father's arm. Lindow waited a moment, then told them about Eamonn's friend, Mary, and how he'd asked her to read at the funeral. His father nodded to say that it would be fine, then he looked directly into his son's eyes with a kind of fierce bewilderment. 'I don't know what's been going on, Con.' He said it in a tone Lindow had never heard him use before. 'I don't understand it, but you must promise that you won't try to hide anything from me. You mustn't keep anything from me, Con. You must promise me that. Whatever it is, I want to have the truth. It's not knowing that is the painful thing. Just because we're to bury Eamonn on Wednesday doesn't mean that it's an end of it. I want to know everything. You understand that, Con?'

Lindow found himself unable to speak. He understood exactly what his father was saying, because he felt the same. 'I promise you, Dad,' he said. 'I'll tell you if I hear anything – promise.'

At that Gerard Lindow rose from the table and bade his children goodnight. As he left the kitchen to fetch his book from the living room he seemed to his son not so much older as smaller. Lindow and Tag waited until they heard the water running in the bathroom above before they began to speak again.

'Is there anything you're not telling us?' Tag asked.

'I was going to ask you the same thing. You saw him in London, Tag. You went over there and stayed with him. Was he doing something he shouldn't have been? Was he working for the IRA?'

'No, of course not. What makes you think that?' said Tag, with a flash of their mother's anger. 'You know Eamonn! Anyone could see that he wasn't a Provo. This is *our* brother we're talking about, Con, not one of those killers from Tyrone!'

'Yes, I know. I know, Tag,' he said, pacifying her with his hands. 'But there are things that I just can't explain. I mean, the police told me that the security services had been watching him for a long time. How do you explain that?'

'Because they still think every Irishman who sets foot on the mainland is a fucking terrorist. They don't see that it's all finished. The Provos will never go back to bombing.'

'But, Tag, Eamonn did have a secret.'

He got up, went to one of the bags in the hall then returned to the kitchen and placed the envelope on the table without saying anything. She picked it up and took out the passport and the money.

'I don't understand. This is an American passport!'

'Look at the name, Tag! It's my name, but Eamonn's picture. I found it at his flat on Friday, hidden in a desk with all that money. I'd have missed it if the damned drawer hadn't jammed.'

'But what's it mean?' she asked. 'What was he doing with this? Why was he using your name?'

Lindow shrugged his shoulders.

'So what does it mean?' she repeated.

'There was something else in the passport,' he said, placing the two photostats on the table and taking the slip of paper from his wallet. 'It took me some time to work out what it meant. The bearings from Limerick and Belfast appear to give you a position in Ireland, but if you draw them out on the map they meet each other in the Atlantic. The clue is the magnetic variation, which Eamonn put at twenty degrees. That's impossible in Ireland, but it isn't in Maine, USA, which has a town called Belfast and another called Limerick. Eamonn had obviously been up there but I don't know what for.'

Tag stared down at the maps while Lindow took the passport from her and looked silently at the US immigration stamps. At the end of the book there was one for 21 September that year – a little over a month before Eamonn was killed. He hadn't noticed it before, but it made complete sense. Eamonn had known he was leaving America to live in London so he had had to make use of his identity while he was still working at MIT. Why? What was so important to him there?

'He used this passport to travel to America four times in the last two years. Each time he landed in Boston. It doesn't say how long he stayed, but the point is that it ties in with the location in Maine, which is only a few hundred miles north of Boston – a stone's throw, in American terms. I was the perfect cover for him. What could be more normal than Lindow travelling from the British Isles to Boston where he worked at the Massachusetts Institute of Technology? Whatever Eamonn was doing, he was being damned cunning about it. You can see he lost weight before being photographed so he looked a little more like me. When I went to identify him, I noticed he'd got thinner.'

'Oh, don't say that. How could you?'

'I'm sorry, Tag. I just know there was something going on. When Dad asked me, I felt I couldn't explain it properly so I didn't try.'

'What are you going to do? Give it all to the police?'

'I considered that. But then I thought they'd use it against me. They already suspect me of complicity and you can just imagine what interpretation they would place on me finding this and not handing it over immediately. They'd probably use it to arrest me again. Have you any idea what it all means?'

'No. I was sure Eamonn had never been to the States. He never mentioned it, and you know that's the sort of thing he would talk about. For months we'd be hearing stories of his trip to the States.'

'Who did he see in London? Did you meet any of his friends?'

'Yes, a few men in the pub, but they were English. There wasn't anything odd about them. They talked football and films and made passes at me. Christ, they were just normal, harmless, boring Brits!'

'Did he ever mention Rudi MacMahon to you?'

'The Sinn Fein man?'

'The gunman.'

'No,' she said, flaring up again. 'He said nothing about Rudi MacMahon or any other terrorist – all right? For Christ's sake, it's as if you're talking about someone else, not Eamonn. What's going on with you, Con? It wasn't Eamonn's fault you were arrested.'

'You're right, it wasn't, but since I found the passport with all this money I've been turning it around in my head and I cannot think of an explanation that doesn't include the IRA. You know he had some kind of friendship – association, I don't know what you'd call it – with MacMahon. I want to find out what's been going on. But first we've got to get through this funeral.'

The next day passed uneventfully. Lindow walked into town to check the funeral arrangements with the priest, then retraced his steps down the high street to Desmond Quorny's Lounge Bar, next door to Quorny's Funeral Parlour. It was said in Ballyhanna that one half of Quorny's enterprise always kept the other supplied.

Quorny greeted Lindow with a little bow and ushered him away from the huddle of morning drinkers at the front of the bar. 'May I say how sorry I am for the great misfortune suffered by your family – and so soon after Mrs Lindow's passing away. It's a very tragic business to be sure, Dr Lindow. Very sad indeed.' He rubbed his hands together.

'Thank you,' said Lindow tersely, not wishing to encourage Quorny in his well-practised condolences. 'I came to see that everything would be all right for tomorrow.'

'Everything is in hand, Dr Lindow. The car will be outside the White House at half past nine, which will give us plenty of time to be at the church by ten. There'll be a good many people who wish to show their respects, given all the good friends Eamonn made here in Ballyhanna. He never forgot them when he was away in London. Some of them have offered to be pall-bearers and I've chosen six. In actual fact, they're mostly the lads I use when the family can't supply them.'

'It was my impression that Eamonn didn't come back that often.'

'Oh, no, that would be quite wrong, Dr Lindow. Your brother was still closely involved in the community here and popular too. He was many a time in this very bar, sitting at that table over there.' Quorny pointed to a table hidden by a screen at the back of the room. 'He liked to talk to his political friends there,' he added, with a knowing cock of one eyebrow.

'Political friends? Who were they?'

'Oh, I couldn't tell you who they were,' said Quorny shiftily. 'But I'm sure they'll all be along to pay their respects to Eamonn tomorrow.'

'But you must have some idea who they were. Were they nationalists?'

'I expect they might have been, sir, but I couldn't say for certain. I try to respect my customers' privacy.'

'Was Rudi MacMahon here with Eamonn?'

'I wouldn't know, sir. I wouldn't know who the gentlemen were, I'm sure.'

Lindow left the stale atmosphere of Quorny's and went to find Tag, who was arranging food for the mourners at the church hall.

Foyle took the call from the commissioner's office at one ten on Tuesday 30 October. He was required to see Urquhart at two thirty, at which hour, he had no doubt, the command of SO 13 would pass to Assistant Commissioner Martin Scarratt.

He put down the receiver gently. His anger had long evaporated and was replaced by an odd sense of liberation. He knew it wouldn't last but for the moment he enjoyed it. He settled down over the *Guardian* and consumed a chicken baguette, brought up from the Italian sandwich bar by Nancy Longmore. He rang Katherine – she was out – then Carla Pryn, to book a table at her restaurant in the evening. At least he'd be free to enjoy her company and maybe ... well, he'd see. He put the thought of her out of his mind.

Forbes walked in without knocking. Foyle motioned him to a chair.

'I'm being put to sleep at two thirty,' said Foyle, without emotion. 'By close of play Scarratt will be running things.'

'It's a great pity,' sighed Forbes. 'He won't be particularly pleased to have me on the team because I'm your man. So I imagine I'll be following you pretty soon, sir.'

'Nonsense, you're invaluable. Even Scarratt can't miss that.'

Foyle rose and stretched as if he was limbering up to take some exercise. He swung one arm in the air, then the other. 'It's all such a damned fuck-up. I feel I owe you some sort of apology, but for the life of me I'm not sure why. Perhaps I did become obsessive about linking the business in Ireland with all of this.' He swept a hand at a map of Inner London, on which the two explosions were marked with red stickers. 'The problem is, I can't believe I'm wrong. There's something in it, I'm sure of that. And the phone thing is looking even more feasible.'

'Oh, by the way,' said Forbes, changing the subject, 'I found out about that close-observation group involved in the Droy operation. Had a bite with a friend of mine at the Ministry. Somebody doesn't want us to know who was at Droy. They received specific instructions yesterday, but my friend had already written down the details so he gave them to me.

Anyway, he said that if we looked hard enough we'd find all the names on record somewhere – regimental newsletters, that sort of thing – so he didn't mind giving them to me.'

Foyle's interest picked up. 'Don't keep me waiting. What did you find out?'

'They're an *ad hoc* group of soldiers who came together for special jobs as a close-observation platoon. They'd done a couple in Ulster and some of them had served together in the Falklands War. There were six men in the group. The key figures were a young major called Ian Rhodes and his second in command Robert Lasseur.'

'Lasseur?'

'Yes,' replied Forbes. 'Seems he was brought up in Quebec, but he's a British national, his English mother having moved back after a divorce. The other men involved were Sergeant James Pascoe, Corporal Robert McGurk, Private Vincent Creech and Gunner Christy Calvert. McGurk and Creech were killed in the churchyard and Pascoe and Lasseur were injured. Pascoe lost his eyesight and Lasseur was badly scarred. Only Calvert and Rhodes were unharmed. None of the men is still in the Army. Calvert and Rhodes left quite soon after Droy – a couple of years or something like that.'

'So Droy finished all their careers. Do we know what happened to them afterwards?'

'There's very little on record, just gossip. But it seems that Lasseur left the country, Calvert went into personal protection and Pascoe lives up north on a disability pension. Nothing is known of Rhodes's whereabouts, or his occupation.'

'But at least it shouldn't be too difficult to trace Calvert and Pascoe. Might be worth someone having a word with them,' said Foyle.

'That rather depends on your meeting, doesn't it, sir?'

'Yes, I suppose it does, but in the meantime I'd like you to get someone started on it.'

Then Foyle went upstairs and waited outside the commissioner's office. Ten minutes later he was shown in. Scarratt and the commissioner were both in uniform. Foyle was not offered a seat.

'As you know, we have been concerned about the progress of your inquiry, Commander,' began the commissioner, 'and after a thorough review I've decided it would be best for you and the force if you relinquished your command of SO 13.'

He waited for Foyle's reaction, but nothing came.

'By my estimate you are owed three and a half weeks' holiday. I want you to take that leave starting from tomorrow and to return to work towards the end of November. Given the current circumstances, I do not think a return to SO 13 is either desirable or practical, so I'd like your thoughts on how you wish to develop your career. On reflection, you may feel that things have come to a natural end, in which eventuality we'll make the necessary arrangements.'

Foyle had heard all of it before in his imagination and knew exactly how this little speech would end, with the commissioner moderating his tone, which he did right on cue.

'For the moment, Commander, I want you to have a good break. Take some time for yourself and your wife, Kenneth. She's still abroad, isn't she?'

Foyle nodded.

'Why don't you go and see her? Surprise her.'

'I want to know why you're doing this, sir.'

'Oh, come on, man,' said the commissioner. 'The department's in a shambles and your judgement has been wide of the mark on practically every issue these past seven days. You let our only suspect go, then you deploy your department's resources investigating a theory, supplied by that very same suspect, for which there is not a shred of evidence. This is beginning to affect your men. I don't have to tell an officer with your exemplary record about the importance of morale in a department. Once a commanding officer has lost his men's confidence it rarely, if ever, returns. That's the stage we've reached with you. I'd be failing in my duty, failing in my responsibility to you too, Commander, if I did not take steps to resolve the situation.'

'What will you do, sir, if I turn out to be right about Lindow's innocence and if I'm right about the use of cellphones to set off these bombs?'

'We'll have to consider that, but I must deal with the situation as it stands today. What I have is a rudderless department, bogged down, demoralised, frustrated, failing. That's the only thing which concerns me now. I am certain, Commander, that you'll have valuable insights to offer Assistant Commissioner Scarratt and that he will be able to build on some of the work that you have already done. But to be brutally candid, Commander, I don't envisage that there's the slightest chance of you being right. I mean ... the idea that you were tricked by the bomber to ring a number connected to one of the devices is madness. Imagine the coverage in the newspapers if they heard about it.' He paused again, moved some paper on his desk, and said, 'I want you to hand over to Assistant Commissioner Scarratt formally tomorrow morning. You'll need time to go through things. Is that all right with you, Martin?'

'Yes, sir.' Scarratt turned to Foyle. 'We'll meet at midday tomorrow, or shortly afterwards.'

'And we'll talk in a month's time when you've thought things over,' said the commissioner.

He extended his hand in a gesture of farewell. It was then that Foyle realised that his career was over and that there would be no meeting in a month's time. He was out and he'd have to get used to it – get used to the idea of no longer being a police officer.

For him that was an unimaginable condition.

The following morning Foyle found Forbes waiting for him at the lift doors. The moment he saw his face he could see something was up.

'We've got another one,' Forbes said. 'Nothing certain yet. We've just had a report in a few minutes ago. There's a car with a suspicious package in it near King's Cross station. It's parked behind an office building on a piece of land due for development. Lafferty's on his way now. I've got a car waiting.'

They left immediately. The roads around King's Cross had seized up with the rush-hour traffic. In the back of the car, voice raised against the wail of sirens, Forbes filled him in. Earlier that morning a young policeman had become suspicious of a blue Audi estate, which had been parked in the same spot since Friday. He knew it hadn't been moved because leaves had collected along the bottom of the windscreen. His attention was drawn to a metallic suitcase, hidden under a rug in the back of the car. He made some inquiries about the car, which was found to belong to a Dr Richard Brett from Maidenhead. The Audi had not been reported stolen, but Dr Brett's daughter explained that her parents were away for a three-week holiday in Kenya and had left the vehicle in the long-stay car park at the airport.

'So whoever removed it knew it wouldn't be reported missing,' said Foyle.

'Yes, but that's not all. The officer noticed there were wires running from the case to the lighter socket.'

'A phone charger.'

'Exactly – and he got the desk sergeant to telephone the daughter again to find out if her father possessed a mobile phone and also whether he was likely to have left it on charge in the car. She replied that his mobile was sitting on his desk. She was looking at it as they spoke.'

'And the case?'

'As far as she knew, her father didn't own a case of that description.'

'Smart lad that constable, we ought to have him in the department.'

They came to a halt about two hundred yards from Euston Road. Foyle and Forbes got out and made for the spot where two Explosives Unit vans were parked. As they approached, Lafferty's face appeared from the back of the van. He hailed Foyle. 'You could be right about these bombs, Ken. The robot camera shows the package is connected to a telephone charger. That may be just acting as the supply but it could be attached to a phone in the case. We're going to get the barrow to break the rear window. If the bomb isn't hooked up to the car alarm we'll get it to stick its snout in and have a closer look.'

They went over to the second expo van. Foyle picked up a pair of binoculars and trained them on the Audi. He saw the robot edge to the right rear window behind the driver's seat, extend an arm and fire a punch at the glass. There was a barely audible phut as the window pulverised. The robot's arm extended further, allowing its sensors to sniff the air inside the car for explosives. At the same time a second low-light camera fixed to the end of the probe swept the interior of the car. The images and sniffer readings began to flow down a fibreoptic cable to a lap-top in the back of the van.

'There's definitely something in there,' said Lafferty, looking at a panel on the screen. 'Probably Semtex. If it was Co-op explosive we'd smell it from here.'

'What's Co-op?' asked Forbes.

'Nitrobenzine and sodium chlorate.' Lafferty was watching the screen intently. 'Smells like hell. The IRA used it to blow up a Co-op store in Belfast.'

Lafferty told the man operating the joystick controlling the robot to see if the camera could trace the exact route of the wire leading to the back of the vehicle. Nothing came up on the screen. The wire seemed to disappear into a crack just behind the rear seat.

'It could be a detonating cord,' Lafferty explained, 'which would transmit a detonating wave from the main charge in the suitcase to the bulk of the explosive in the boot. The stuff may be hidden in the spare-wheel well or under the rear seat.' He paused to concentrate on the screen. 'Still, my instinct tells me that the real business is confined to that suitcase and that there are no other explosives. We'll have to take a closer look.'

'Are you sure?' said Foyle. 'Can't you use the robot to blow it up?'

'Yes,' said Lafferty, looking down the alley. 'That thing's got every conceivable gadget – water disrupters, sidewinder shotguns, explosives sniffers. They say it can smell the difference between Pepsi and Coke. But that won't help us learn how these bombs are being made. We need to know how this guy is putting them together. My guess is that this device has malfunctioned in some way. We know it's been there for over five days, which means it was probably planted with that other bomb last week. If it's gone wrong it may be easier to deal with.' He paused, then said grimly, 'On the other hand he may have built in one or two surprises.'

They walked to the other van, where Lafferty checked a low trolley on which lay a portable X-ray machine, the metal pipe and explosive cartridge of another water disrupter, a roll of roofing lead and an attaché toolcase. He cut a dozen four-inch strips of insulating tape and hung them on the left-hand side of the trolley. Then he opened the tool case and ran his hands along the implements, an array of clamps, knives, electrical bypasses and tools adapted or fashioned by Lafferty during his time as an ammunition technical officer in Belfast.

He selected some wire-cutters and a pair of pliers, closed the case and put them on top. Then he turned to the uniformed officer from the Explosives Unit who stood holding the black body of a BBS-3 bomb suit. 'I still can't get used to these things,' he said. 'You can't move in them.'

The officer trussed Lafferty into the suit. When all the straps were secure, he picked up the pliers and wire-cutters and fixed each with a single piece of tape to Lafferty's left arm. Lafferty told Foyle that if he wanted to hear what was going on he should use one of the headsets over at the other van. Then he disappeared into the huge turret-like armoured helmet and made for the Audi, towing his trolley behind him. One of the expos explained to Foyle that Inspector Lafferty was moving slowly because he didn't want to be all sweated up inside the suit by the time he reached the car.

Foyle didn't need the explanation. Late one night over a tumbler of rare twelve-year-old malt, Lafferty had told him about the Long Walk from the police cordon to an Improvised Explosive Device. It was never more than 150 yards at most, but with each step taken, the expo would be calculating his chances of survival. He'd move from the maiming zone to the killing range, a place where a bomb suit afforded only a little more protection than a plastic mackintosh. And then he'd be right up close to the device, staring into the eyes of the beast and wondering about its electrical circuits. How much time did he have before the circuits closed and the detonator began to generate its lethal heat? Was there an anti-handling mechanism that would complete the circuit and trip the bomb ahead of the timer? Lafferty spoke as if each device had a personality, a crude projection of the bomber's own character. Some were easily understood, others sophisticated and devious. To Lafferty the business was very personal indeed, a test of his nerve and ingenuity against the terrorist's cunning. It was a game that was weighted in favour of the terrorist. While the expo risked everything, the bomber could never lose. Even when a device was defused he still chalked up a draw.

For what seemed like an age Lafferty, moving like a deep-sea diver, circled the car, bending down to peer inside at the roof. At length he spoke over the radio. 'It's no good,' he said. 'I think he's wired up the interior light to the bomb and I can't get at it without climbing through a window. I'm coming back to take this bloody suit off. Meantime, get the robot to break the front passenger window. Do you read? Front passenger window.'

Lafferty walked back to meet an officer, who helped him out of the suit and helmet and gave him a new earpiece. Visibly relieved, he jogged back to the car and hauled himself expertly through the newly broken window.

'Yes!' he said softly over the radio. 'The old trick: he's connected the detonator to the door light.'

The effect of the binoculars, combined with the sound of Lafferty's exertions over the headset, made Foyle feel that he was almost in the car with him. He saw Lafferty lift his arm and smash the light with one short well-aimed blow.

'Now for the main course,' Lafferty said, getting out of the driver's door and swinging round to open the door behind it. He pulled the rug from the suitcase and dropped it on the road with the sweeping motion of a matador. Then he squatted down and began to speak again. 'There are two holes bored in the case. At the hole nearest to me I've got what looks like the rubberised aerial of a mobile phone. Two wires exit the other hole, one to the light I've just smashed, and the second goes to the cigarette lighter. I won't touch them until I've X-rayed the case. I'm still pretty certain that the explosives are confined to the case. I can't see anything under the seat and there's no detonating cord going back to the boot.'

He stepped back into the road and removed the X-ray unit and the roll of lead from the trolley. He positioned the unit in the car, unrolled the lead and dropped behind it to lessen his exposure to the rays. A few seconds later he removed the machine. While he waited for the positive X-ray image to develop, he fashioned the lead into a crude three-sided shield then cut a square and placed it on the top.

'What's he doing?' asked Forbes, in Foyle's ear.

'He's making a screen so that a call can't get through to that phone,' replied Foyle, covering his microphone.

'That's right.' Lafferty had overheard. 'Ah, here's the X-ray. It's not as bad as I thought, but there's a shit-load of wiring in there. I'm going to cut the wire to the charger cable from the lighter.'

Lafferty was silent for a long while. The explosives officer standing next to Foyle exhaled. 'That wire may be connected to a relay – an electromagnetic switch – which means that when it's cut the power holding the switch open closes. The current goes straight to the detonator.'

Lafferty's voice came again. 'That's good. Now I'm going to try to open the case.'

Another long silence ensued while Lafferty placed his crude lead screen in the car and went to work on the case. At length he itemised the contents of the case over the radio. 'Three or four pounds of Semtex, a standard detonator, a cellphone and a video timer. The timer is a fall-back mechanism. If the phone doesn't receive a call, the video timer is here to make sure that the bomb detonates. The bad news is that the whole lot is still working on the phone's battery. The phone's display shows that it is fully charged. But it also shows that the reception is non-existent here. It's funny he didn't notice that.'

Another pause. 'Damn,' said Lafferty. 'What time is it? I can't turn my wrist to see my watch.'

One of the officers with a headset replied. 'It's eight fifty-five, sir.'

'I've got an hour then,' said Lafferty. 'This timer seems to be set for ten a.m. today, Wednesday October the thirty-first. Oh, Jesus. There's a tilt switch fixed to the bottom of the timer and it's wired into the detonator. I can't move it. So I'm going to confine my attention to the phone.

'Take this down carefully,' he continued. 'The back section of the phone has been cut away to expose the contacts of the ringer. Wires lead from the ringer to the detonator. When the ringer is activated by a call, it completes the circuit. By my count that makes four separate mechanisms connected up to the detonator – the phone, the doorlight, the timer and the mercury tilt switch. He certainly didn't want his little baby examined. Are you sure about the time? The display says it's nearly ten.'

'Yes, sir,' said the officer.

Foyle listened intently. Con Lindow's inspiration about the telephone had been spot on. What was especially interesting was that the bomber had done everything to ensure that the phone would not be retrieved. But something was stabbing at the back of his mind, a sharp anxiety that would not form into coherent thought.

He concentrated. The idea took shape and, as it did so, he rose and bellowed, 'Get out of there, Lafferty! It's going to blow! The clocks went back on Sunday!'

Forbes and the other police officers gaped at Foyle. Lafferty hadn't taken it in. 'For fuck's sake stop shouting in my ear,' he said.

'The clocks went back on Sunday!' repeated Foyle. 'The timer is on British Summer Time and is set for ten a.m. That means it's going to blow at nine a.m. You've got two minutes, Lafferty. Maybe less.'

'I'm coming. I'll bring this phone with me, though.'

'No!' shouted Foyle. 'Bring the card and get out of there!' He had remembered Pennel's lecture about cellphones. Every cellphone possessed a removable chip known as the subscriber identity module – or SIM card. This transmitted a unique number to the cell antennae when the phone was used. The card was the phone's brains. You could move it from one phone to another and transfer the subscriber number, and also the phone's memory. There was nothing you couldn't find out, once you got the SIM card.

'What card?' asked Lafferty.

'It's plastic, about two centimetres long with a serial number printed on the back. They're usually purple or yellow. It slides out. On the other side you'll find a printed circuit.'

'Got it.'

Foyle watched him turn from the car, dodge the trolley and run towards them with his arms outstretched. He reached the end of the alley and was crossing the road to the vans when the video timer switched on, causing current to flow into the detonator and fire the explosive charge. The Audi levitated and disintegrated in a violent white flash. The blast thundered up the alley, bringing a storm of bricks and metal fragments. Lafferty was flattened. The officers by the vans threw themselves on the ground, covering their heads against the flying debris. Then came a second roar as the scaffolding by the Audi collapsed in slow motion down the length of the alley, ripping masonry from the surrounding buildings and plunging it into the brew of smoke and dust below.

Foyle was the first on his feet. He shouted to Lafferty who had raised his face from the ground and was looking at Foyle with an odd, rueful expression. Together, they ran back to the cordon, where the other officers were picking themselves up.

'That', said Lafferty, 'was the exact same device used on the bus, give or take a few nasty surprises.'

'Have you still got that card?' asked Foyle.

He held it up. The sunlight streaming down the Marylebone Road glinted on the oval of gold circuitry. Foyle slipped it into his wallet, patted Lafferty roughly on the back and went to his car with Forbes.

Out of the corner of his eye, Lindow saw three men climb from a parked car and head towards the procession. He strained round from holding his father's arm, peering above the heads of the crowd to see if they joined the mourners. He couldn't be sure but he thought they had. He bent down to his father and Tag, and told them he was going back to check on something. Then he said to Mary Menihan, who was walking behind Tag, 'I think that bastard MacMahon's come. There're some TV people up at the church. I don't want them filming him here.'

He slipped from the procession and stood on a small rise at the side of the road, watching the faces pass. Most of the mourners were local, but there was also a big contingent from the North, which included a dozen or so Cardells – stout, wily people from his mother's family, who arrived outside the gates of the White House and waited for the hearse, shuffling and murmuring to each other in the early morning mist.

As the end of the procession approached, Lindow spotted Rudi MacMahon, flanked by two thickset men. He hadn't changed in twenty years: his hair was still dark and thick, there was no spare flesh on his face and very few lines. The only change Lindow noticed were the round gold-rimmed spectacles that MacMahon had acquired as a prop to his political legitimacy. He pushed into the crowd towards MacMahon, but one of the minders caught sight of him and placed himself squarely in the way before he could confront him.

'That's all right,' said MacMahon. 'This is Con Lindow, Eamonn's brother.'

'What the hell are you doing here?' Lindow demanded. The mourners around them looked at Lindow apprehensively. 'You're not taking over this funeral, do you hear? Eamonn wasn't one of yours. Now, please leave before I ask the Garda to remove you.'

'That's not possible,' said MacMahon, nodding at someone who had turned to see what was going on. 'Your brother was a friend of mine from school. I have as much right to be here as any of these folk.'

'You know damn well you're here to parade in front of the camera, not to mourn Eamonn.'

'Untrue.' MacMahon's eyes grew cold behind his glasses. 'I knew Eamonn for twenty-five years and I've come to pay my respects. That's all there is to it.'

The procession came to a halt as the coffin and first mourners passed through a pair of iron gates to file up the avenue of lime trees that led to the church.

'You knew him, all right, and you tried to use him,' said Lindow. 'If you'd any respect for Eamonn at all you wouldn't be here. Your presence means that the people in London will think that Eamonn was blown up by his own bomb. They'll believe that he was guilty – because you're here, making it look like every other fucking republican funeral.'

MacMahon's eyes narrowed and his lips formed into a slit. He kept his eyes fixed on the gates ahead and leaned very close to Lindow's face. 'The point', he said quietly, 'is that we know Eamonn didn't plant that bomb. That's why I'm here. And the people in London will know that *because* I am here. Do you understand what I'm saying, Con? We know Eamonn had nothing to do with it.'

They stood in silence, forced shoulder to shoulder by the crush of mourners. The slow toll of the church bell reverberated around the buildings either side of the churchyard. A stiff breeze came up from the direction of the town and whipped at the lime trees. Suddenly Lindow felt sickened by the contact with MacMahon. 'I don't want a killer at Eamonn's funeral,' he said, losing his temper. 'That's the bottom line, MacMahon. I don't want a killer here.' Then he grabbed hold of MacMahon's sleeve and tried to pull him to the edge of the crowd. Instantly the bodyguards were either side of Lindow, wrenching his arms downwards and holding them fast.

'That's okay,' said MacMahon calmly. He closed in on Lindow's face again. 'If I *was* a killer, Con, I wouldn't be the only one here with blood on his hands, would I now?'

Lindow recoiled as if he'd been slapped in the face, but he had no time to answer. Tag had struggled back through the gates and was snatching at his arm. 'Con, you're holding everything up,' she implored. 'For God's sake, leave him. Don't make a scene now.'

MacMahon withdrew, tugging the lapels of his jacket downwards. He walked through the gates and the mourners parted to let him through. Halfway up the avenue the cameramen switched on their lights and followed him to the church door.

'That'll be on every news programme tonight,' said Lindow. 'He's got what he wanted – a republican funeral.'

Tag took hold of him and didn't let go until they reached the front row of the pews where their father sat, looking mildly about him. A few minutes later the service began. Lindow's mind strayed to think about the night of the bomb and Kay Gould's injuries. His attention returned when Mary Menihan walked to the lectern to read 'The Second Coming' by Yeats. She stood for a moment and let her gaze travel over the congregation. Light streamed through the stained-glass window and fell across her, dappling her skin mauve and green. She recited the poem without referring to the book she held.

'"Things fall apart",' she said, her eyes moving to where MacMahon sat, ' "the centre cannot hold; mere anarchy is loosed upon the world. The blood-dimmed tide is loosed, and everywhere the ceremony of innocence is drowned. The best lack all conviction, while the worst are full of passionate intensity." '

Then Eamonn's coffin was borne a little way from the church to the cemetery and there lowered into the ground. A flight of rooks spilled from the trees as the priest began to speak. Lindow held his forehead and placed an arm on his father's shoulder. Tag wept, emitting short, girlish sobs. They left the graveside and moved slowly through the heavy autumn dew back to the church. Lindow noticed that MacMahon and his bodyguards were already making for their car, walking briskly down the avenue through the fallen leaves. One of the bodyguards stopped to answer his phone, placing a finger in one ear against the tolling of the church bell. Then he handed the phone to MacMahon. Lindow could just see MacMahon's features tighten as he answered. What the hell was going on?

9

After they'd escaped from the wake, they went back to the White House where Mary changed from a skirt into jeans, an old leather jacket, and wrapped a soft, green scarf around her neck. Lindow suggested they drive out into the countryside and take some air. They set off with no particular aim and drove through the empty border country, passing one or two sullen towns with their still-fortified police stations. Presently they came to an iron bridge, slung across a narrow part of Lough Erne. They parked and walked to the point at the centre of the bridge through which passed the border between North and South and looked out across the choppy expanse of the lake. The water was dark and streaked with rivulets of white foam.

'We used to come fishing here, Eamonn and I,' said Lindow, following her gaze. 'But it was only ever good in the spring, lousy for the rest of the season. See those frothy white trails on the surface? Eamonn always used to cast his fly near one of them. He said the fish waited for flies to get caught in the foam.' He paused, swamped by the memory. 'Christ, that seems a long time ago.'

Lindow felt that she was looking at him. Something had happened between them since they'd stood side by side at Eamonn's wake, both desperate to leave, but trapped by the excruciating solicitude of the mourners. They now had a kind of pact, he felt.

'What are those islands?' she said, pointing to the east. 'They look as if they had been put there.'

'They were,' replied Lindow. 'They're called crannogs. Some were built thousands of years ago. Each one supported three or four houses. Only the people who lived on the islands knew the route through the shallows to get out there.'

'So they didn't trust their neighbours in those days either.'

They walked along the side of the lake to a stand of Scots pines where a squat brick boathouse had fallen into ruin. Lindow explained that Eamonn and he used to moor up there, when the sun was too bright to fish, and drink themselves into a comfortable stupor, Eamonn's stories getting progressively wilder and more bizarre.

'You'll miss him, won't you?' Mary said.

'Yes,' said Lindow thoughtfully. 'I'll miss getting to know him again, which is what I sort of had at the back of my mind when I went to London. I'll miss finding out what the hell he's been doing these past ten years.'

'Didn't you ever talk?'

'Not much. I really wish we had now, wish I'd bothered to find out what was going on.'

'How do you mean?'

'There were things in his life that I don't understand. I can't explain them.'

'Things you disapprove of?'

'Maybe – I'm not sure. And that's the problem. I can't make a judgement because I don't understand them.'

'So, he's left you not knowing what to think of him. That *is* a problem for you. If you found out something that you didn't like, how would it affect your feelings towards him?'

'I can't say. You can never really know what goes into other people's decisions.'

'My, what an impeccable liberal you are! Do you know those lines from Swift?'

'Please go ahead,' said Lindow, gesturing with both hands. 'I'm endlessly impressed by your ability to remember verse.'

She looked out over the lake and spoke the lines. '"To guide his steps afford your kindest aid, and gently pity whom ye can't persuade. Leave to avenging heaven his stubborn will; For, O, remember he's your brother still."'

'Very good. But, of course, none of us believe in heaven any longer so we do our avenging down here.'

'You mean that you don't believe in heaven?'

'Nope. Do you?'

She shook her head.

Out of an old habit, and perhaps as an act of remembrance, Lindow heaped some pine cones together, broke a couple of fallen boughs into pieces and built a fire at the end of the dock. The resin in the cones made the fire flame quickly. They sat down with their legs swinging from the dock, mesmerised by the snapping of the fire and the slap of water against the old timbers.

He didn't hear them coming across the field from the lane that passed near the boathouse. Not until the last moment did Lindow turn to see five men bearing down on them, moving quickly and silently. One was holding a gun and coming straight for him.

The man placed the pistol against Lindow's ear and motioned him to get up. Mary was simply lifted to her feet by two of the others. Lindow saw the blood drain from her face.

'What do you want?' He heard his voice crack.

'A talk, that's all, so don't be getting yourself into a panic, Con,' said a short man in his sixties, who had followed the others up the old jetty. Lindow stared at him. He looked like any character you'd find on a racecourse – a small-brimmed trilby on the back of his head, dark green waterproof jacket, newspaper rolled up and stuffed in his pocket.

'A chat – that's all we want with you, Con.' The man came close. Lindow saw that the lid of his left eye drooped a little and that his cheeks were scrubbed shiny and patterned with burst veins. His eyes were full of purpose and he spoke with a soft Southern Irish accent.

'But if you want more than that we can certainly give it you, can't we, boys? Okay,' he said, gesturing with his chin, 'take her down there and keep her quiet until we've finished our business with the doctor.'

The two men pulled Mary away. She threw an imploring look over her shoulder but Lindow was concentrating on the man in front of him. He understood quickly that this was the most dangerous person he had ever met. This man would kill without the slightest qualm.

'It's a pleasant spot here to be sure. Wouldn't be bad for fishing, if you'd a mind to. No patience for the sport myself. So, Doctor, you heard about the bomb this morning. A nasty piece of work, by all accounts, and a professional job too.' He removed his hat and inspected the inside, revolving it in his hands and looking past Lindow at the lake.

Lindow didn't know how to answer. When they'd heard during the wake about the controlled explosion, the only thought that had occurred to him was that it would help to remove suspicion from him.

'Yes, I did, but I don't know any details.'

The men relaxed their grip on Lindow, but he could still feel the pistol pressed into his back under his left kidney.

'Sad business, your brother being killed. A good man was Eamonn. Carried the family's honour, there's no mistaking that.' He replaced his hat and looked at Lindow hard. 'How much did you know about your brother's work for us?'

'Nothing. I didn't know he worked for you,' said Lindow.

'Well, he did. He was never what you'd call an obvious candidate, but that was his advantage. No one suspected him, not until the end at any rate. I don't mind telling you that Eamonn was very important to us and we're going to miss him.' He paused to gauge the reaction he was having on Lindow. 'When he was killed he was looking for some men. They were people we once had business with. They went rotten on us and now they're giving us a bucketload of problems over in England. It's them that we think have been letting off these bombs in London. It's them that we

133

need to find before the whole thing blows up again. Do you follow me, Con?'

'Yes. I think so.'

'Good, because I'm going to take you into my confidence. Eamonn always said you had balls – said you didn't give an inch when you were taken in after that business at the churchyard. You know what I'm referring to? Good. I remembered that when we heard that you were held in London and I thought to myself, He won't give anything to the boys in blue. I was right, wasn't I? You told them nothing.'

'I didn't know anything to tell.'

'Ah, that's not true, is it, Con, my lad? You found something and you kept it to yourself. We both know that.'

'What makes you think so?'

'Come on, now. Stop fooling with me. You weren't shocked when I told you that Eamonn was working for us, were you? You knew he was doing something for us. You may be a clever fellow with every sort of degree in the world, but you're no actor. I'll tell you that for nothing.'

Lindow weighed up how much he should tell the man. Since talking to Tag, he'd decided that he would hand over the passport and the scrap of paper to Commander Foyle. The decision had come easily enough once he heard about the third bomb.

'So, tell me, what did you find at Eamonn's place? We know there was something there, but for obvious reasons we couldn't get at it ourselves. We knew that Eamonn had discovered something on his last trip to the States. But when we got into his place, the package was gone. The police didn't find it. We know that because they would be acting differently if they had. So we want it back. We want it all back because it's ours.'

'I don't know what you're talking about.'

The man jerked his head towards an old winch that stood about chest height on the dock. In an instant the two men holding Lindow bent him backwards against the teeth of the winding gear. They wrenched him backwards three times and slapped him about the face. He tried not to cry out, but failed when the cogs ate into his vertebrae.

'That's nothing to what we can do, is it, boys?' The man poked the embers of Lindow's fire with a stick. 'You may want to be a hero, but you're not the only one these boys can hurt.'

He turned round to face the boathouse and gave a short whistle. Two figures emerged from behind the building, one prodding the other forward with a gun. It was Tag. They came a little way up the dock, just out of earshot. She was gagged and blindfolded, and he could see that she was trembling.

'Don't fret yourself now, Con,' said the man. 'She's not been hurt. I brought her here to show you we can get to the lass any time we want. You follow me?'

He nodded.

'So about this package. What did you find in it?'

'Some money and a passport.'

'What did you do with it?'

'I left it in a safe in London – with my lawyers.' Lindow looked at him hard, hoping the lie did not show in his eyes.

'Did they know what was inside?'

'No, I didn't tell them. They didn't ask.'

'There wasn't anything else, nothing with some names written on it?'

'No, just the passport and money. The passport was in my name.'

'Does the name Rhodes mean anything to you? Or Lasseur? Have you ever heard those names, Con?'

He looked into the man's eyes. 'No, I've never heard those names.'

The man smiled and poked the fire again. 'Eamonn was on to them when he was killed. It had been a long-term interest of his, this character Rhodes. He knew what he was made of and we should've listened to him earlier. Now we need to pick up where Eamonn left off. That's where you come in. See, you're going to find them for us.'

'Why? How do you mean? I can't help you.'

'Nonsense, Con, you're the perfect fellow for the job. Eamonn told us where they were. They're in Maine, that's the state north of Boston. It won't be any problem for you to go over there. After all, we've been sending Eamonn over there under your name. Eamonn was always telling us how well connected you are. Our people over there don't have the sort of contacts we need for this. But you do. You've got plenty of influential friends and the like. He told us you know people in the FBI. Talk to them, find out where these two characters are hiding. You see, we're all on the same side now and we need to get to these men before they do any more harm.'

'Why don't you hand this information to the British police? They're desperate to find out who's responsible for the bombs.'

'You're a fine one to talk. You didn't tell them anything, did you?'

'No, but I don't know anyone in the FBI. I've never met anyone like that in my life.'

'Sure you do. What about that Varrone fellow?'

'How do you know about Varrone?' He was shocked they knew Varrone's name. 'He's a colleague – he's got nothing to do with the FBI.'

'You're forgetting Eamonn made it his business to find out who you knew. He had to learn about your life because he was pretending to be you when he was over there. One of the things he told us was that you had a friend who was an adviser of some sort.'

'But Varrone . . .' Lindow stopped. He looked over to his sister. The wind had got up and was fanning the embers of the fire. 'Look, if you let the women go, I'll talk to you. I'll do my best to help you.'

'Okay.' The man gave a smile that said nothing. 'I'll tell you what I'll do. If you agree to help us, I'll make sure they're safe at home by the time you get there later. That's as long as you co-operate with us, Con.'

'But what if I don't find Rhodes and Lasseur?'

'By Jesus, you've got a good memory there, Con,' said the man slyly. 'I just mention those names once and they're locked away in that memory of yours. A phenomenal brain is what you've got there, Con, a phenomenal brain to be sure.' He signalled to one of the men holding Lindow, a wiry young thug in a leather jacket. He seemed to know what he was meant to do for he jogged over to where Tag was being held, took her arm and led her towards the lane. When they were out of sight the man began speaking again. 'So are you going to do this thing for us?'

Lindow nodded.

'Okay, so you'll fly out to Boston tomorrow and telephone your friend Varrone. Mind not to tell him everything. Just say that you know it's a matter of life and death that you find these men. When you've found them, go to Melly's Bar in South Boston and ask for a man named P. J. McKenna. He's the fellow that runs the place. From the moment you give him the information you'll be off the hook. You'll never see or hear from us again, and your sister will be safe. Remember this, Con, you'll be handing us your brother's killers. We'll make amends for what happened to him and, if we're quick about it, we'll stop a lot of this mess in London. It's not doing anyone any good, least of all us.'

Lindow blinked at him. 'I don't understand any of this. I mean, the bombs are being planted in London so what makes you think these people are in the States?'

'Technology,' he said. 'Technology, that's the problem these days. Too much damned technology. Now, you've got the details right in your head, have you, Con?'

Con repeated the name of the man and his bar in South Boston.

'Good, because that's the only way you can contact us. There's one other thing. I don't want you blabbing your mouth off to the police. This business is between you and me. That's the way we'll keep it. Don't try and screw around with us, Con, because we can get to that young sister of yours any time we want.' He turned, keeping his eyes fixed on Con, adjusted his hat to the back of his head and walked back down the dock. 'So I'll be hearing from you in a few days,' he said.

A minute or two later, Lindow heard two cars start up and roar off down the lane. Then he was blindfolded and pushed across the field to a third vehicle. His head was forced down behind the driver's seat and a gun was pressed to his ear. Twenty minutes or so later, the car pulled up outside the White House, he was rolled out of the door and left sprawling in the driveway. He ripped off the blindfold to see his hire car parked a few feet away, and Tag and Mary running towards him.

'Don't tell Dad,' said Tag breathlessly, flinging her arms around Lindow. 'We said you wanted to take a longer walk. He doesn't know anything about it.'

The commissioner returned Foyle's call at three thirty that afternoon.

'Yes,' said the commissioner abruptly, 'I haven't got long, so please be brief, Commander.'

'In the light of this morning's discoveries, sir, I was wondering if you'd reconsider your decision to take me off the case. I was right about the mechanism behind these bombs and I believe I'm in a better position than anyone to develop this inquiry.'

'I'm sorry, Commander. That's out of the question. I appreciate that you introduced this new line, but I have to bear in mind that the theory came from Con Lindow. That's part of my overall concern about the way you were handling things. So, to give you a straight answer, no, I won't be reconsidering my decision.'

'But we are making a mistake, sir. We are making a profound mistake to think of this as an Irish problem. There's something else in it all, I know it.'

'I'm sorry, Commander, I don't have the time to discuss this now. We'll talk in a few weeks.'

When he'd hung up Foyle dialled Forbes and asked why the commissioner had been so unyielding. Forbes told him that there had been some new developments that pointed to Lindow's guilt. The SIM card taken from the bomb scene that morning had belonged to a telephone with the exact same number as one that had appeared three times on Con Lindow's phone log. Lindow had called on Friday morning and then twice again on Monday. All three calls had been made in the morning, during the rush hour.

'What? That's not possible,' said Foyle.

'To make matters worse, we've just got pictures of Eamonn Lindow's funeral this morning. There's one of Con Lindow talking to Rudi MacMahon. They're standing together in the funeral procession. It certainly doesn't look good. He's on record as saying that he didn't know MacMahon. That's what he told Phipps.'

'What do you think?'

'I think it looks very bad. The instant Lindow gets back here, Scarratt will have him locked up again. And this time they won't wait before charging him. It doesn't help you much, does it?'

'No. There's one other thing. You remember the girl Lindow looked after in the street after the bus explosion? What happened to her?'

'She's still alive. We tried to interview her but the hospital wouldn't allow it.'

'Do we know if Lindow actually helped her, or was that just something he told us?'

'I don't think we've established that one way or the other.'

'Have you got her name there?'

'Yes, she's called Kay Gould – single, twenty-six years of age. I don't think we ever found out what she does for a living. She's still in hospital. Why do you want to know?'

'Thought I'd see if she's able to talk,' said Foyle.

'Well,' Forbes sounded doubtful, 'I wouldn't say too much about that if I were you, sir. It's breaking every rule in the commissioner's book.'

'Thanks for the advice. Keep me in touch, eh?'

Foyle hung up and prowled about his sitting room. Everything pointed now to Lindow's guilt and, moreover, to his own colossal failure of judgement. Perhaps it was true that he wasn't fit to be a policeman any longer, which Scarratt had made brutally clear when Foyle returned to Scotland Yard after the King's Cross bomb. He'd found Scarratt sitting at his desk, leafing through his papers. 'You've brought it upon yourself, Commander. I tried to give you advice, but you wouldn't listen. You need to listen to people at this level. It's the first requirement.'

Since his unceremonious departure from New Scotland Yard a few minutes later, he'd gone over everything and concluded that he would not have acted in any other way. He'd made errors, certainly, and he regretted his feeble grasp of the higher politics at the Met but, on the essentials of the case, he had been sure of his instincts.

The news of these calls from Lindow's flat worried him. How could Lindow's behaviour be explained? He thought through the events of the last few days. The one point that Scarratt would not appreciate was that Lindow knew he was being watched and almost certainly suspected that his telephone was being tapped. That's why he had called from a phone box on Saturday. Foyle remembered hearing the sound of traffic in the background. If he had been going to detonate the bomb in King's Cross, he would hardly have used the phone in his flat. He must have made those calls innocently, thinking he was phoning someone else. That was it! Lindow had been tricked into making those calls, just as he had been on Thursday.

Foyle picked up his coat, felt inside the pockets for the three sets of keys he would need and left the house, slamming the door with unusual force. Half an hour later he produced his police warrant card at St Luke's Reception and was given directions to where Kay Gould lay in a private room. The sister in charge was reluctant to let Foyle see her, explaining that Kay had been on the brink of death when she was brought into the hospital and was still very weak. Foyle was on the point of leaving when a short dark man in an immaculately pressed white coat appeared in the corridor. After Foyle had shown his warrant card, he introduced himself as David Peretz, Kay Gould's specialist.

Foyle asked how she was doing.

'Remarkably well. She's got a lot stronger in the last thirty-six hours. I'm especially pleased with this case. She damn nearly didn't make it.'

'What about her face? I hear she was pretty badly cut.'

'Too soon to tell. But the damage was a lot less than we expected. She's a strong girl and she's doing a lot of the work herself. She's healing fast.'

'Is there any chance I could have a word with her?'

'Sorry, she's not up to it yet. Maybe at the end of the week. I'll have to see.'

'Did you operate on her when she was brought in after the bomb?'

'Yes.'

'How long was it before she got here?'

'Something over an hour, I'd say.'

'That would mean she was in the street with Lindow for nearly all that time.'

'Lindow ... was that the man you arrested?' Foyle nodded. 'Yes, apparently he looked after her pretty well. In fact, he contributed greatly to saving her life by insisting that she receive quick treatment.'

'So he stayed with Miss Gould all that time instead of making off?'

'Yes, and I believe he called on Sunday to see how she was doing.'

Foyle prepared to leave, but Peretz seemed eager to talk.

'We couldn't stop the haemorrhaging. At first I thought it was her liver, which wasted an awful lot of time. I was giving her blood by the gallon and she was slipping away from us, going into bleed-out. Then I found that her spleen had been punctured by a piece of glass and we stemmed the bleeding. It was touch-and-go for a couple of hours after that. She stopped breathing, her heart stopped, but each time we revived her. She just refused to give up.'

Foyle didn't have the stomach for extensive medical descriptions, but he was moved by the doctor's pride. 'Look,' he said, 'is there a phone I can use in private?'

Peretz showed him to an empty office and left him. Foyle closed the door, dialled international directory inquiries and asked for a listing in Ireland. Less than a minute later he was speaking to Con Lindow in Ballyhanna. 'We need to talk. Are you alone?'

'Yes, what about?'

'You heard that we had another bomb in London this morning.'

'Yes, but I don't know much about it.'

'Right, what you don't know is that it was wired to a telephone, as you predicted. We now have the number of that telephone. The problem is that the same number appears on the phone records for your flat.'

'What? I didn't make those calls. You must know that.'

'It doesn't matter whether I believe you any more. I'm no longer leading the investigation.'

'What happened?'

'I've been replaced by a man named Scarratt and am now enjoying a holiday, largely because I let you go. This business of your phone records simply makes everyone certain that I got you wrong.' He paused. 'Did I get you wrong, Con?'

'Of course you didn't.'

'Whatever. The important point is that you are now very likely to be arrested and charged with conspiracy to cause explosions. The case against you is very strong – overwhelming, I'd say.'

There was a silence. Then Lindow asked, 'When were the calls made?'

'On Friday and Monday during the morning rush hour, which leads them to suppose that you were aiming for the maximum number of casualties. Can you remember who else you telephoned after you were released?'

Lindow was silent, trying to recall. He told Foyle he'd phoned his sister on the evening of his release and the following morning he'd rung Imperial College, the lawyers and the police. 'Hold on. I remember now. I also phoned the agent after he left a message on my machine, saying that he'd found a flat for me. He rang early. I've got the number – hang on a minute.'

He returned and read out the number. It matched the one Foyle had been given by Forbes an hour before – 08052 289476.

'That's it! And you rang that number three times?'

'Yes, I think so. Yes, once on Friday and twice on Monday, nothing doing each time. I didn't keep trying because there was a lot to do before Eamonn's funeral. I decided to leave it until I got back.'

Foyle thought for a moment. 'If you're telling me the truth, the man who left that message on your machine is the bomber.'

'I *am* telling you the truth.'

'Did you wipe your messages before you left London?'

'No, I don't think so.'

'Right, I'm going round to your place. We'll need to talk later by phone. Will you be on this number?'

'Yes.'

Foyle had still got Lindow's keys. When he arrived outside the house he lingered in his car, watching the street for any movement. He looked up and saw that the windows of Lindow's first-floor flat were dark. He got out of his car and made for the front door.

Once inside he didn't switch on the lights, but groped his way to the kitchen where he opened the fridge. Just enough light spilled out to enable him to find the answering-machine in the sitting room. He pressed the playback button and listened.

There were a few messages that predated Lindow's arrest, then an estate agent named Robertson came on the line to ask why Lindow had failed to turn up for an appointment the day after the first explosion. He left a number, which Foyle noted down. The last message was from a Mr Lustig, who said he was Robertson's colleague and announced in a rapid voice that he'd found Lindow a flat. Lindow was instructed to ring a number between nine and ten that morning, or at the same time on Monday. Foyle knew, without checking, that the number given at the end of the message was the same one for the telephone hooked to the bomb in King's Cross.

The messages came to an end. Foyle pressed the eject button, removed the tape from the machine and placed it in his pocket. Then he closed the fridge door and left the flat.

Instead of returning to his car, he walked round the block to a telephone booth where he put a call through to the number in Ballyhanna. Lindow answered. 'Okay, I need you to find a phone outside the house and then to call me on this number. Can you do that?'

'Sure. Is it for the same reason that you didn't call me from my flat?'

'Yes.' Foyle gave him the number and hung up.

He waited for five minutes, watching a party of children dressed in Hallowe'en costumes, progressing up the street. The phone rang.

'You're right about the tape,' said Foyle. 'I've got it with me now and I want you to listen to it again.'

'Why didn't you play it over the phone to me from the flat?'

'The phone is tapped, as you appreciate, which is the reason I wanted to talk to you on a clean line. Look, I think we need to meet. There's a lot to discuss.'

'Yes.' Lindow paused. 'Have you heard of anyone called Rhodes or Lasseur?'

'Those were the names given to Forbes by his friend in the Ministry of Defence – the soldiers at Droy. Where the hell did you hear those names?'

'It's a long story. I was paid a visit this afternoon by some people, if you know what I mean. They mentioned them.'

'Have you heard of them before?'

'No, but Eamonn knew one of them. It's really too complicated to explain over the phone and I haven't got any more change. I'll tell you everything when we see each other.'

'You can't come to London. I'll have to come to you. I'll fly to Dublin and we'll meet in the airport. Can you get yourself down there this evening?'

Lindow said he could.

'Bring a suitcase. We'll need to spend some time on this. I'll see you in the main restaurant in the departures lounge. I should be there by nine thirty.'

Foyle rang off, then called Heathrow and booked himself on the seven thirty flight. He looked at his watch. He should just make it in the fifty minutes.

Lindow tramped back to the house and told his father that he had to leave, he had some urgent business in the States. He promised that he would be back as soon as possible to spend some time with him. Then he went to break the news to Tag, who was in the kitchen being calmed down by Mary. She was still pretty shaken. When he told her, she looked at him accusingly through her tears. Mary said nothing, but Lindow noticed her expression and her flickering eyes, which seemed to betray rapid processes of deduction.

Tag pleaded with him to stay, if only for their father's sake, although it was quite clear that she was fearful for herself as well. Mary intervened. 'If Con was worried about your safety, I'm certain he would stay here with you. Isn't that right, Con?'

'Of course. I can't say much at the moment, but it's best if I keep my head down for a few weeks before trying to go back to England. In fact, you'll be a lot safer if I'm in the States. This business I have there will sort things out for all of us.'

'What do you mean?' demanded Tag, both hands gripping the back of the kitchen chair. 'What can you sort out for us all? Are you working for the Provos? Is that what it's about? For God's sake, tell me.'

He took her in his arms. 'Believe me, I'm not working for anyone, Tag. I just can't say what I'm doing. There's no other way. I've got to go.'

He went upstairs to collect his things. Mary came into the room and touched his shoulder lightly. Lindow straightened from packing his bags to face her.

'Are you sure this is all right?' she asked.

'No, I am not.' Right now, he wished she wouldn't interfere.

'Then why are you going?'

'I've got to. They've threatened to hurt Tag.'

'Christ! Why?'

'I can't explain. It's too complicated.'

'Could you use some help on this? I've got family stuff to do over there anyway and two minds are better than one. You don't have to tell me what it is. I'll just be your bag-carrier, if you like.'

Without saying anything, he knelt to do up a suitcase. She touched his shoulder again and leaned down to kiss his cheek.

'And let me tell you,' she added. 'I really know Boston. I mean Boston Boston, not Harvard Boston.'

Lindow straightened again. 'Haven't you got to get back to London? Work and all that.'

'It can wait. I am freelance, remember?'

'Look, this could be dangerous – and, frankly, I haven't the first idea what I'm going to do.'

'But you'd like me to come along, right?'

'Sure . . . er, sure. If you want to and you've got the time, I'd like it a lot.' He was surprised at himself for having agreed so readily.

'Good. I'll stay here tonight and look after Tag and your dad, then I'll get a flight tomorrow from London.'

She gave him the name of a hotel in the centre of Boston and said she'd aim to get there late the next day. Then they went downstairs. Lindow hugged his father and sister, exchanged nods with Mary and climbed into his car.

Foyle found Lindow sitting in the Silver Lining restaurant with a cup of coffee. He walked over to him and sat down, placing a duty-free bag on the table.

'You look terrible,' said Lindow.

'You don't look so good yourself,' said Foyle. He produced a new tape-recorder from the bag and fitted it with batteries.

'Now, I want you to listen to this again very carefully and tell me if you recognise the voice.'

He inserted the microcassette from Lindow's answering-machine. The voice began in a flat London accent, but near the end of the message, when the man instructed Lindow to ring him between nine and ten on either Friday or Monday, it assumed a terse note of command. Foyle remarked on it.

'It could be anyone.' Lindow sounded despairing. 'The disturbing thing is that not only was this man trying to incriminate me, he must have known about my movements before the bomb in Clarence Street. He knew I was looking for a flat.'

'Yes, he may well have listened in to your calls last week.' Foyle noticed the restaurant was filling up. 'You know, I'd rather not talk here. What do you say we book into a couple of rooms in one of the hotels near the airport and discuss this over some food?'

Twenty minutes later they had checked into a large anonymous establishment decorated with garish lithographs of rural Ireland.

Foyle said that he'd put both rooms on his credit card and told Lindow to register as J. Peters.

'I don't want any kind of audit trail,' said Foyle. 'If I'm ever asked who J. Peters is, I will say it's my girlfriend and that, for appearances' sake, she likes to take a separate room.'

Lindow smiled and went off to deposit the bags in his room, while Foyle went straight to the restaurant and chose a table beside an oblong aquarium, where he sat down and watched a small black fish with whiskers position itself in a stream of oxygen.

When Lindow rejoined him he said, 'I read somewhere that you can only put fish from the same lake in the same tank. That way they don't kill each other. But if you put a strange fish in they kill it. I'm sure there's some kind of metaphor in that, but I don't know what.'

'There isn't. Things in nature just are. They don't have to have cute lessons for humanity.'

Foyle was surprised by his tone. 'You need food. I've ordered two steaks and some wine. That should set you up. Now, tell me what happened today.'

The wine arrived and Foyle listened to Lindow's account of the funeral and being snatched that afternoon. He pressed him for the exact words used by MacMahon and then for a description of the man by the lake.

'It seems likely that you had the pleasure of meeting Raymond H. McCreath – Chickpea McCreath. He's quite a legend. He gets his name from an incident back in the seventies when he replaced the lead shot in a twelve-bore cartridge with chickpeas. That way he could make one hell of a mess of someone's body but be sure not to kill them. He was one of the IRA's chief quartermasters but he was also an enforcer. When someone was misbehaving, skimming from IRA funds, he'd be brought in to sort them out. There was talk of him coming out of retirement to help the Sinn Fein leadership. If it was him, you can assume that he was working with Rudi MacMahon. MacMahon and McCreath are part of the IRA, which is an indication of your brother's loyalties. MacMahon is on the political side and McCreath has been deployed as the muscle. Anyone that looks like breaking away from the republican movement is paid a visit by Chickpea and his friends and is persuaded to toe the line. They have one chance. If the dissidents persist, they're beaten or killed.

'We received an intelligence briefing from Belfast a few weeks ago, which explained that McCreath had also been put in charge of retrieving IRA supplies that had fallen into the hands of the rebel republicans. It's not a pretty business. Several of the hard men from South Armagh have turned up dead. Others have been snuffed out in their beds. Very clean, very silent. Six months ago a woman in the border country woke up in the morning to find that her husband had been shot through the head with a silencer while she slept.'

'Jesus, my countrymen!'

'McCreath knows what sort of supplies are out there and, more important, where they're likely to be hidden. That's why they pulled him back. He's a real mystery man. The authorities have no idea what he looks like. The only picture of him was taken thirty years ago. He's never been arrested. In fact, the security forces almost wondered if he was a myth, like that old joke – Eamonn Wright.'

Lindow looked puzzled. 'Sorry?'

Foyle put down his glass. 'For years the police heard about a sniper called Eamonn Wright. He was killing British soldiers by the dozen. They could never track him down although everyone talked about him on the streets. Then eventually someone got the pun – aiming right.'

'That's sick,' said Lindow. 'So what you're saying is that the IRA believe the London bombs were the work of the rebel faction. Is that why Eamonn was killed?'

'No, it's not that easy. The bombs are too sophisticated. The Explosives Unit hadn't seen a device like the King's Cross bomb before. It was connected to a telephone, a timer and two anti-handling devices. The man who made it and then left that message on your machine intended that it would explode even if you never called.'

'But I did call. Why didn't it go off?'

'It's very simple. After the bomb was driven there, some scaffolding was erected on the adjacent building plot and clad with a mesh screen. This had the effect of blocking the signal from the cell antennae. The timer would have detonated the bomb this morning, but it was set on British Summer Time, so the disposal officer just had time to grab the important parts of the telephone before the whole thing went up. It was a very near thing.'

'So where does all this leave you?'

'A better question is, where does it leave you, Con? You see, I'm just a policeman now on enforced leave. I have no responsibility for this case at all. You, on the other hand, are in this thing right up to your neck. I'm here to help you and I want to, but you've got to help me, Con. Those names they mentioned to you this afternoon. You say that Eamonn knew them.'

'Only one of them.' Lindow dug inside the breast pocket of his jacket. 'I found this hidden in Eamonn's flat last Friday. You can see it's a fake US passport in my name. You will also see that Eamonn used it to travel to the US on four occasions. He was there in the last five weeks.'

Foyle examined the passport and picked up the paper that Lindow had placed in front of him.

'These are compass bearings. Originally I thought the word Rhodes referred to the place or a ship. Then I did some work with the atlases in the library.'

'That's what you were doing there.'

'So, I *was* being watched. I thought as much. That woman – was she yours?'

'No. She was the other lot – MI5.'

Lindow shrugged and produced the photostats of the maps of Ireland and the north-east coast of America.

Foyle pushed them back to Lindow's side of the table. 'Put those away. Just talk me through it.'

Lindow looked around. 'There's no one here, surely.'

'Nevertheless, I'd prefer you to talk me through it.'

'Well, the crucial point is that the bearings on the paper were taken from two towns in Maine, not in Ireland. Coincidentally they're called Belfast and Limerick. It was the magnetic variation that put me on to it. The one stated by Eamonn is too big for Ireland. Of course, I didn't know what Rhodes meant. Then this afternoon McCreath mentioned someone called Rhodes and I realised that Eamonn had left exact instructions on how to find him and, presumably, this other man, Lasseur.

'I nearly told them. Then I thought that if they were forcing me to find this man – which they are, because they're threatening my sister – at least I've got a head start. But they must have known Eamonn was on to something because they said that they'd tried to search his flat for a missing package. I assume the information is pretty new.'

'You can also assume', said Foyle, 'that they know you've got it and will be aware of your movements in the United States – that's if you go.' Foyle drained the bottle into Lindow's glass and ordered another. 'Do you know who Rhodes and Lasseur are?'

'No, I don't.'

'They're two former British Army officers. Both of them were at Droy when the cemetery blew up.'

Lindow was incredulous. 'Are you sure?'

'On Monday a colleague of mine acquired the names of the soldiers involved in the operation. Someone was trying to stop us which was interesting in itself but, leaving that aside, it means you've got a lot of explaining to do.'

Lindow's glass was poised at his lips. 'My head is beginning to spin with all this. Are you saying that two British soldiers blew up Eamonn, then tried to implicate me in revenge for something that happened in 1983? Why have they waited so long?'

'Who knows? But I can tell you now that you weren't the only one tricked into making a call. I was too. I didn't think anything of it until you came up with your theory about detonation by telephone. You see, Blackett had been asked to call the same mobile number as me.'

'Who's Blackett?'

'Blackett's the man who interrogated you and Eamonn after the Droy explosion.'

'But, as far as I remember, there were four or five police officers who questioned us. They worked in rotation.'

'Yes, but Blackett was the man in charge. The point is that neither of us had left a message for the other, but both of us received a message to call the same number. I was the one who called it first.'

Lindow slumped back in his chair. 'What's this guy about?'

'He's playing a game, a very subtle game, which may have something to do with Ireland. Or it may simply be the product of a deranged mind –

something on the lines of the Unabomber in the States. Still, it does seem to point to Ireland. With the exception of myself, the bombs have involved three people who were all connected with Droy – you and Eamonn were both suspects and Blackett was the investigating officer.'

'But where do you fit in? Why did he get you to make that call?'

'I was thinking about that on the plane. It's a kind of joke. He tricks the head of Scotland Yard's Anti-terrorist Unit into detonating a device that the hapless Commander Plod is then expected to investigate. Very neat, when you think about it.'

'So why haven't you told your colleagues?'

'As of midday today my services were no longer required. I am a non-person as far as the commissioner is concerned. And, besides, no one would believe me. But we're getting away from the main point here, aren't we? The line that runs through all these bombs is Droy. Rhodes was at Droy, you were at Droy, Eamonn was there and Blackett was the investigating officer. I need enlightening, Con.'

Foyle sensed that Lindow was wrestling with something. 'Yes, Con?'

'I wasn't there. I was nowhere near the place when it blew up. We just stopped there for Eamonn to take a piss.'

'Look, I'm not fucking around here,' said Foyle. 'I know you didn't cause any of this. But now you have to say what happened. Why has Rhodes come back? What made him flip?' He held Lindow's eyes with an intense glare, defying him to look the other way. 'You are the only person who can stop it all. The only person, do you hear?'

'I wasn't there,' Lindow repeated deliberately. 'I wasn't there.'

10

Lindow watched Foyle push back his chair, wipe his mouth vigorously and turn to look at the black catfish, which had come to rest on the side of the tank, its grey mouth suckered to the glass. 'For a clever fellow, Dr Lindow, you're one hell of a daft cunt.'

He said nothing.

'You don't see we're in this together,' Foyle said. He placed a finger on the glass by the catfish. 'Like I said before, we're two creatures at the bottom of the sea, trying to see their way. We need each other, but at present you need me much more than I need you. My career is strictly past tense, but you – you're up to your neck in trouble. The bomber won't be content to leave you be. He'll come after you. He's clever – cunning as hell – and he'll have you like he had Eamonn. Why you two is what I'm wondering. Tell me what he's got against you?'

'It's plain enough,' said Lindow, bridling at Foyle's manner. 'He believes that we were responsible for the explosion at Droy.'

'We – plural!' Foyle said the last word with such force that the other diners in the Kerry Carvery swivelled round to look at them. '"We" is not the word I'd use in this context. "I" is the word you're looking for, Con. You blew up that dump and killed all those soldiers and now the thing that you erased from your past has come back to besiege you. It's taken your brother's life and a good many others besides. There isn't any "we" about it, is there? It's all due to what you did seventeen years ago, and you won't even bloody well admit it to yourself. Why don't you say something? Come on, get it off your chest, man. If you tell me what happened I won't be able to do anything about it. It's all long gone. You won't be charged. It'll just be between you and me.'

'You've made your point,' said Lindow. 'Let me just say this. Droy was an accident.'

'That's it!'

'Yes. That's all there is to it.'

Lindow wasn't going to say any more. What Foyle did not know, could not know because Lindow had only just begun to see it himself, was that he had changed. The bomb, two days of interrogation, the wretchedness of Eamonn's funeral, the pummelling from the IRA and the vague but persistent guilt over Eamonn's death had come together to form a crude resolve.

He knew well that he had always let life come at him and that he used the gifts of his mind to avoid any sort of confrontation. It bothered him sometimes, and he'd once tried going to a shrink after his mother's death. The sessions had lasted only two or three months. Before he gave them up, the therapist had suggested that this lack of engagement stemmed from his mother's overpowering personality. He had simply dealt with everything else in his life the same way, deftly manipulating people to find the way of least resistance. 'Low-risk evasion strategies' was what she'd called them. She told him it was the reason he'd never fallen in love. Relationships involved too much exposure and threatened his cover.

Lindow hadn't liked what she'd said, but he conceded that the string of lab assistants and students who found their way to his bed had been selected precisely because they offered no risk and wanted little more than fleeting physical contact. The ones that had hoped for more – the girls who showed up once too often at his rambling apartment overlooking the Charles River – were quickly dumped.

As Foyle went on about the need to work together, Lindow was thinking not so much about what he should do, but about the rather astonishing fact that he was actually going to do *something*. He had no plan, no sense of how he'd get to the people who had killed Eamonn. But he'd make sure he found them and pass the information to the people who would put an end to them. It seemed unlikely that this would be the British authorities, who were lumbering several miles behind Foyle's understanding of the case. Much better to deal straight with the thugs he'd encountered that afternoon. In fact, he would do exactly as the man in the trilby had instructed. He'd make the connections and he'd try to locate the place where Rhodes was meant to be. At the same time, he'd keep the British on side in the hope that eventually he could resume his life in London. That was why he needed Foyle. He was out in the cold, but he'd be an excellent conduit if the trip to America did produce something. Foyle wanted to vindicate himself and would help.

He poured himself another glass of wine.

'So what're you going to do?' asked Foyle. 'Fly off to America then blunder about in the undergrowth of Maine? What then? It's not going to be easy for you to return to Britain, you know, not unless you want another few sessions with Phipps.'

'I'll see how things work out. I've got plenty of people I can stay with over there, and money isn't a problem.'

'Yes, but you can't just let things stand as they are. There has to be some sort of solution. Don't you see that?'

Lindow nodded slowly.

'Tell me about this girl, Mary Menihan. You mentioned she was with you when you were taken this afternoon. Was it her idea that you went for a walk? Did she suggest where you went?'

'No, to both questions. Why do you ask?'

'Just wondered. She seems to pop up at interesting times, that's all. I'm right in thinking that she called at Eamonn's flat when you found the package? How did she know that you were going to be there?'

'She said she guessed. Are you implying Mary has got something to do with all this?'

'You've got to admit it does look like that from the outside. She's from Boston and she was a friend of Eamonn's, which could mean that she was working with him. She may have turned up at the flat to retrieve a package the IRA knew was there. It fits perfectly.'

'Well, if she is, I'll find out soon enough. She's meeting me over there tomorrow.'

'Christ, she's sticking to you like a sheep tick. Be a good boy and don't take her to bed, Con.'

Lindow wondered about her reasons for staying in Britain. And Foyle was right – she had turned up at the flat. It was as if she didn't want to miss anything.

'I'll remember what you say.'

'Good,' said Foyle, 'because the Provos may just be using you.'

'How?'

'They probably know a lot more than you suspect. They could be sending you over there to draw the fire. They won't give a shit what happens to you.'

'But you're using me too, aren't you? You haven't told me to come back to Britain with you tomorrow because you think there's a slender chance of me finding out things that will put you back in your command.'

'Nah,' said Foyle dismissively. 'There's not much hope of that. The thing that drives me is that I want to find the man or men who did those things to your brother and Kay Gould – and the others. When you take away the intrigue of this affair, you're left with a lot of bodies and several people with their faces missing.'

Lindow thought of Eamonn in the hospital, the look of dumb resignation that had clouded his face for ever. Foyle was right. That's what it came down to: death and mutilation. And now he was following his brother, taking up the pursuit of Rhodes where Eamonn had left off.

Before they left the restaurant for their beds, Foyle gave Lindow his home number and told him he could also be reached through Inspector Graham Forbes at New Scotland Yard. Forbes, he said, was utterly trustworthy. Meanwhile, he would see what he could find out about Rhodes and Lasseur. 'I'll be off early in the morning, Con, so I won't see you. But stay in touch, and good luck.'

Lindow woke at nine, showered quickly and rang the airport to get a seat on the next plane to Boston. Then he took out Eamonn's false passport, examined the picture and raised it against himself in the mirror. Their faces were alike and his brother's weight loss helped, but Eamonn's hair was further receded, also wirier and darker. He put down the passport and went to the hotel shop, where he bought a pair of manicure scissors, a small tub of hair wax and a sachet of wash-out dye. He returned to his room, thinking that it was indeed a bizarre task to make himself look like Eamonn who had been trying to look like him. He gingerly removed the plaster from the back of his head, then cut the hair from his forehead back to the hairline. He rinsed a quarter of the dye into his hair, rubbed some wax on to his hands and ran them through his still-wet hair. While he waited for his hair to dry, he arranged for the hire car to be picked up from Departures at the airport, then called Peter Varrone's office voice-mail and left a message to say he was arriving that afternoon and would be staying at the Omni Parker Hotel in the centre of town. He used the office number because it was still the early hours in Boston and he didn't want to risk waking Varrone at home. An hour and a half later Lindow passed into the departures lounge without a hitch and boarded the plane to Boston.

The flight was only half full and he was able to stretch out. He drifted in and out of sleep, going over the conversations he'd had with Mary. He tried to remember exactly what she'd told him about her life. He had the impression that her father ran a business in the Boston area, that her parents were divorced and that she had money of her own, but he wasn't sure about any of it. In fact, the more he thought about it, the more certain he became that Mary had told him little about herself. She handled herself well in conversation, never gave much away and was always right up to the mark, coolly anticipating the other person's thoughts. Come to think of it, she'd been damned cool after their experience at the lake.

The plane was ahead of schedule at Boston, the first of the European flights to land that morning. The lines at US Immigration were short and moving quickly. Lindow found himself in front of a young officer. His eyes flicked between the passport and Lindow's face. The man turned and hit a few keys on his computer terminal. Satisfied, he held out the passport.

Lindow hurried away to collect his bags. He was soon outside in the sharp Boston air, making plumes with his breath and looking across Boston harbour to the towers of the city's business centre. They glinted in the flawless white wintry sunlight.

He took a cab and checked into the Omni Parker. No sooner had he set his bags down in his room than the telephone rang. Varrone's voice came on the line, smooth and reassuring. 'Couldn't keep away from us, huh?'

He muttered a reply.

'I'm working at home today, writing a briefing for the White House about quantum computing. The President wants a paper to read over the Thanksgiving holiday, would you believe? Why don't you come over and release me from this insufferable grind?'

Twenty minutes later Lindow pressed the entryphone beside a pair of discreet iron gates near the crest of Beacon Hill in the centre of Boston. From the outside, Varrone's home looked like a normal-sized townhouse, but he had also bought the properties either side and knocked them through to create two huge galleries on the first and second floors. Lindow had never asked his friend how much he was worth, but he'd seen figures in the press that referred to the sale of VBSS – Varrone Business Software and Systems – for a hundred and thirty million dollars. After the sale of his company he'd returned to teaching, writing and the activity he termed envisioning. When Lindow and Varrone had first met at a conference on 'The Future', Varrone had given a paper which held that what was imaginable, but technically unfeasible, in the present would determine the development of the future. The very act of imagining laid a trail into the future. Lindow had disagreed violently with the audience, saying that each new problem required lines of reasoning that would necessarily lead to solutions that no one could predict. They'd talked afterwards and hit it off, although Varrone was nearly twenty years older than Lindow.

The gates clicked open. Lindow made his way to the front door where Varrone appeared in his familiar working gear – plaid shirt, bulky blue cardigan, beige cords and sneakers. His eyes shone through a pair of heavy tortoiseshell spectacles and his hands quivered rapidly as if he was shaking water from them.

'My God, have you joined the music industry?' he asked, with a critical squint at Lindow's hair. 'What in the hell have you done to yourself? Come in and tell me about it.'

He led Lindow into a long kitchen where the cook was placing a dish of lasagne and a salad on the table. Varrone collected beer from the fridge and gestured to Lindow to sit down and help himself. 'What's going on?' he said, when they were both seated and the cook had departed silently through a side door. 'The London police called me after the bomb. It was big news on the TV. I was worried for you. They said your brother was injured and you'd been arrested. I told the guy they were being idiots. They didn't take a bit of notice. Are you still in trouble?'

'You could say that.'

'And the hair? It's awful.'

'I was trying to look like Eamonn looking like me. It's going to take a bit of time to explain.'

Lindow told his story, pausing only when his friend needed the order of events clarified. After an hour, Lindow reached the end of his tale and leaned forward to pour himself another beer. On the plane he had taken the decision not to tell Varrone what the IRA had said about him and the FBI. It wouldn't help.

Varrone sat, chin resting on his clasped hands. His expression was unusually solemn. 'There's one thing I don't understand. What do you hope to achieve by coming here and hightailing it up to the mountains with a compass? Even if you do find these guys, you're hardly equipped to deal with them. By what you say, they're professionals. You're not trained for this kind of work.'

'What else can I do? I can't go back to Britain because I'll be arrested. I can't stay in Ireland because it would endanger Tag's life. I had to come here, if only to make contact with their people and show that I'm doing what I can to find these guys. And there's Eamonn – I realise that I won't be free of this thing unless I do something to find Eamonn's killers. This is my responsibility. I owe Eamonn.'

'I understand that – really I do. But you're out of your depth with this thing. You're going to get yourself killed, Con. Aside from anything else, you'll be depriving mankind of a superb microbiologist. This isn't you! You can't handle it.'

'I've got to. That's the way it is.'

'Well, if you're bent on this thing, I'll help you. I'm going to put you in touch with a former student of mine, Frank Mundy. Frank works at the FBI here in Boston. He's a smart kid, one of the best students I ever had. He got himself a law degree then went into the Bureau. Go talk to him. There isn't anything he doesn't know about the Irish American community here. He was wired right into the Irish crews, as he likes to call them. I'm sure he'll be able to help you locate these guys.'

They went into Varrone's long sitting room where Lindow was left to inspect a fossil of an ichthyosaur, which Varrone had placed in the middle of the room on a raised slate platform. The beast was perfectly preserved. Its flippers worked at the rock and the long serrated bill was opening to snap at a prey that had vanished forty million years ago. It was as if it had been turned to stone in mid-stroke. He walked around the room, marvelling at Varrone's eclectic taste: four works on paper by Rothko, a sheet of calculations in Einstein's hand, a minute Leonardo sketch of a man levering a boulder, and a model of Watson and Crick's double helix.

The murmur of Varrone's voice came from behind the door and Lindow couldn't make out what he was saying. After about ten minutes, his head appeared in the doorway.

'He says he'll see you tomorrow. He's still on the phone. You can make the arrangement with him now.'

Lindow went into Varrone's workroom, a vast well-lit study with several screens and an enormous computer box. He picked up the phone and said hello.

'Hey, Dr Lindow, Frank Mundy here,' announced a vinegary Boston twang. 'The professor says you need advice. What you say we meet tomorrow outside my office at the JFK Building? You know it? Right. There's a memorial to the first transmission of sound by telephone there. Seems the appropriate place to meet, given the problems you've been having in London. See you there at ten tomorrow.'

Lindow hung up and joined Varrone in the sitting room.

'He's the perfect man for this,' said Varrone, letting himself down on to a sofa. 'I told him as much as I could – about the phones and Rhodes and Lasseur. He'd heard about Rhodes, but he wasn't sure about the other guy, so I guess he'll fix you up with some information. But he'll want something for himself. Tell him as much as you can. Leave out the stuff about you and the cemetery. He won't need that and, anyway, it's a long time ago. But don't spare any detail on the current stuff. That's what he'll want to hear about. I promised him it was going to be a two-way thing.'

'Thanks, Peter. You've been a good friend.'

'It's nothing. But, if you don't mind, I have to get back to work. I have to get this thing drafted by the end of the day and sent to the White House. Shall we do dinner tomorrow night?'

'Yes, if I'm still in Boston. Oh, by the way, I don't want anyone to know I'm here. That okay with you?'

Varrone nodded, got up and grasped Lindow by the shoulders. 'Look after yourself, Con, and use your brain. That way you'll get out of this thing alive. You'll call me after you've seen Frank, right?'

Lindow let himself out of the house and walked down to Charles Street where he hailed a cab to Harvard Square. On the flight he'd made a mental list of what he would need. The first thing that had occurred to him was a proper set of maps, and he knew he'd be able to find them in the Globe Corner Book Store, which lay just off Harvard Square. After browsing through the shelf devoted to Maine, he bought a guide published by the Appalachian Mountain Club that included lists of lodgings and hotels, a highway map of the state and the *Maine Atlas and Gazetteer*, which contained forbiddingly large areas of wilderness marked simply by the numbers of the state's geographic code. The next stop was a good hiking and mountaineering shop, for which he had to return across the Charles River to the centre of Boston. He found the store and bought a compass, a torch, a pair of lightweight hiking boots, an all-weather jacket and a small pair of binoculars. He paid by credit card.

By now, night was falling and the weather had closed in on the city, shrouding the top of the taller buildings with veils of mauve cloud. Lindow made his way back to the hotel and set out his equipment on the bed. He unfolded the highway map and scrutinised it under the bedside light. He'd be able to calculate where the two bearings crossed much more precisely in daylight, but he knew he'd be within a few miles of the location. With the scarcity of any kind of development up near the Allagash River, that would be all the accuracy needed. But what would he do when he got there? He had no plans to tackle Rhodes and Lasseur. Instead he'd hide out and watch the place. The one advantage he had was that they wouldn't be expecting him. Lindow folded the map and made a note on the hotel paper to remind himself to find the best camera store in Boston. Then he lay on the bed watching CNN. If the phone hadn't rung, he would have woken the next morning in his clothes.

'Con, I have a question for you.' It was Mary.

'Where are you?'

'In the lobby. This is my question. Are we going to economise on tonight, or what?'

'What do you mean?'

'Jesus, Con, you can be awful dumb sometimes. If we're going to spend the night together I don't want to waste two hundred dollars on another room.'

He was shocked – delighted. 'Very practical,' he said, smiling into the phone. 'And also very unromantic.'

'Try me.'

He gave her his room number and, in a very short time, Mary was beaming at his door and complaining that her plane from London had been carrying a basketball display team, each one of whom had made a pass at her.

She walked in and looked at Lindow's purchases. 'What's all this? Going hiking? You weren't going to leave your lover behind, were you?'

'You aren't my lover.'

'But I will be by the time you go hiking.'

Lindow put his arms around her and smelt her hair. She pulled her head back and made a face. 'What've you done to yourself? You look like—'

'Like someone in the record industry. I know.'

'No, it's more a kind of street-junkie look. The pallor is just the right side of dead.'

She touched his cheek with her fingertips. 'Dinner first,' she said. 'I need food now – never eat in the air. I'll show you a place down near the fish pier. It's full of scary Italian garbage collectors with pinkie rings.'

Lindow kissed her, brushing her lips tentatively with his. Then they left the room, content to delay the moment when they lay in each other's arms.

The restaurant was noisy and full, but Mary got a table by giving the proprietor a wickedly suggestive look. She told him later that her father did business with the man, who'd made a fortune developing the land around his restaurant and now ran it as a social accessory.

'So what's been going on?' she said accusingly, when they were seated. 'You've gone all mysterious since that thing at the lake yesterday. Shit, you know, I thought they were going to kill us.'

'I did too.' He resented being dragged back to reality.

'Are you going to do what they told you?'

'How do you know that they told me to do something?'

'It's obvious. You take off without a word of explanation and catch the first plane here. Tag told me you knew something. She wouldn't say what it was, except that Eamonn had left you something. And then those guys by the lake – the IRA – they told you something too, didn't they? They think the men letting off the bombs are here, right? And they've told you to find them, right? So you come here to find them and either deal with the problem yourself, though I can't imagine how you would do that, or tell someone else who will deal with the problem. But you're not sharing any of it with me, Con, because you don't trust me. Is that it?'

'No, I trust you. It's just that you don't need to know what I know.'

'So you *do* know who these guys are? You've got names, right?'

'What is this? An interrogation? Look, do we need to talk about this now? I've lived it every second of the past nine days and, frankly, I'd like a break.'

Mary leaned forward, placing her hands on top of Lindow's. 'It's just that I care about you, Con. I don't know how it's happened so soon, but you're important to me. I care what happens to you. And I worry that you think you can take on these people. They've killed your brother and they'll kill you too, if they get a chance.'

Lindow was embarrassed at the suddenness of her declaration. 'That's strange,' he said, looking down. 'Someone said that to me last night.'

'Well, it's true. How do you expect to do this thing on your own?'

'All I need to do is establish where they are – nothing else. I'm finding out as much as I can here, then I'll go to Maine and have a look around.'

'But it's not going to be that simple. This is serious stuff, Con, and you're an amateur.'

'And I suppose you're the pro?' He looked at her hard. He was now beginning to believe Foyle's warning about her. 'What's your interest in this, Mary? Are you here because of me, or something else?'

'I am here for you.'

'And ...?' He waved his fork. 'Who else? Are you working for someone?'

'Who, for Chrissakes? I'm a goddam book editor!'

'The Provisionals, for instance?'

'Fuck you, Con.' Her eyes flashed with temper. 'Fuck you.'

The meal ended quickly and in silence. They barely spoke on the way back to the hotel. Mary sat in the cab staring sullenly out of the window while Con was kept awake only by the motion of the cab bouncing over Boston's potholes. Once in the hotel room, they undressed without the slightest thought of making love. Mary showered, while Lindow collapsed into bed and straight away entered a clammy, restless sleep. An hour later he woke. Mary shifted beside him and raised her head from the pillow to peer at his face in the light that came from a crack in the curtains. He turned to her. She sat up and moved towards him. 'Don't do a thing,' she said. 'Just relax.'

She worked her way round to behind his head, lifted it and placed it in the cradle formed by her crossed legs. Lindow could feel the softness and abundant warmth of her lap. She began with his right arm, holding it up and gently working the joints, then rubbing the flesh and the muscles downwards towards his fingers where she locked her hands with his and kneaded his palm. She did the same with his left arm, taking care to avoid the weal on the biceps. He could feel the tension draining from him and gave himself completely to her touch. Then she moved her hands to his shoulders, pushing the skin up to the nape of his neck and using the base of her palms to massage the knots of muscle along the ridge of his shoulders. Her fingers splayed upwards into his hair, pausing to negotiate the scab at the back of his head, and then ran behind his ears and down to his Adam's apple. She lifted his head again, and revolved it in her hands.

After a little while she eased her legs sideways and lowered his head to the pillow. Lindow was still awake and aching for her touch. He hoped that she would not leave off yet and murmured something. She bent down to catch it. '*Acushla*,' he said again.

'What's that?' she whispered.

'It means darling in Gaelic.'

'*Acushla* – I like that.' She straddled his stomach and trickled her fingertips across his eyelids, down to his cheeks. He could feel the hair between her legs brush his stomach and her breasts graze over his chest, but he did not reach up.

Then he was asleep again.

Next morning Lindow woke to find Mary gone and a note on the pillow. 'Don't leave without me,' it ran. 'Seeing my dad – back by noon.'

There were a couple of hours yet before Lindow was due to meet Mundy so he breakfasted on some apricot juice and crackers from the minibar then unfolded the highway map of Maine. He'd need a larger ruler to work out the exact position from the bearings, but he could see that he'd have to aim for a point west of the Allagash Wilderness. He guessed it was about six or seven hours by car, perhaps more. Up in the north the roads became tracks and it would be slow going.

He left the hotel and walked the short distance to the windy plaza in front of City Hall. On his left was the John F. Kennedy Building, a twenty-two-storey block with a hundred-yard limb of low offices stretching out in its shadow. He took up position by the memorial at the front of the building and examined the bas-relief of the telephone, which looked like a small printing press. There was an inscription dedicated to the first transmission of sound by wire, in June 1875, from a building close to that spot.

'Hey there, Dr Lindow.' He turned round to see an exceptionally tall man in a long black overcoat advancing from the entrance of the building. He was in his mid-thirties with a vigorous brush of greying hair and alert, expressive blue eyes. He thrust his hand forward and gripped Lindow's. 'Special Agent Mundy – Frank Mundy. Pleased to meet you, Dr Lindow. Hey, you want some coffee? There's a Starbucks across the square.'

They sat on stools in the coffee-shop, looking out on the FBI building.

'I guess Peter told you that I'll be happy to help you, but that I want something in return. For a start, we want to know what's going on in London. Those bombs interested Washington a hell of a lot. The stuff about telephones hasn't been made public. It's the kind of gimmick that'll appeal to any number of our home-bred loony-tune militiamen. So, why don't you start by telling me about it?'

Lindow ran through everything that Foyle had told him about the wiring of the third bomb, then the circumstances of the previous explosions.

'So tell me about your brother,' said Mundy, reaching for a napkin. 'Why does this policeman – Foyle's his name, right? – why does he believe your brother was the target? A lot of people were killed on that bus.'

'It's complicated. The obvious reason is that Eamonn was working for the Provisionals. He knew who the bomber was and was killed before he could tell anyone.'

'And what's the un-obvious reason?'

'That it may have something to do with an explosion years ago near where we lived. We were both arrested and questioned afterwards. We weren't charged.'

'And it's been suggested to you that one of the guys at the scene of the explosion came back after all these years to take his revenge on Eamonn. And this guy's name is Rhodes and he's pitched up in Maine. Right?'

'Right.'

'Okay. So why are you here? If it *is* Rhodes, he's probably in London, not here. Why don't you tell all this to the British authorities?'

'For the reason that I can't go back to London because a lot of people think I'm the bomber. The other reason is that I had an ugly encounter with some people in Ireland a couple of days back – Provisionals. They made it plain that they'd hurt my sister unless I came over to look for Rhodes.'

'I'm missing something here. Why would they think you'd know how to find him? Like the professor says, you're a scientist, Dr Lindow. What would you know about this kind of work?'

'I don't pretend to know anything.'

'Yes, but you're leaving something out, aren't you, my friend? There's something you haven't told me.'

Lindow pulled out the passport and slid it towards Mundy, who flattened it open on the bar with his palm.

'I believe I'm looking at a federal offence here, Dr Lindow.' He wasn't smiling.

'I know, but it's the only thing I could do. The British are holding my passport. I had to use this to get here.'

Mundy continued to look at the passport. 'It's a pretty good job.'

'In the back of the passport I found this scrap of paper written by my brother.' Lindow reached for his wallet where he had slipped it behind an old MIT library card. He removed it and showed it to Mundy. 'These are two compass bearings from Belfast and Limerick. Originally I thought they were in Ireland, but they're not. They're in Maine. The magnetic variation or declination gives it away. Twenty degrees is far too large for Ireland. And here you see the name Rhodes and this odd phrase Axiom Day.'

'I know Belfast – it's on the coast,' said Mundy. 'But I haven't heard of Limerick.'

'It's in the south-west of the state, a very small town.'

'So the idea is that Rhodes, or his base or whatever, is at the place where these two bearings meet?'

'Yes.'

'Do you have any idea what Axiom Day means?'

'None at all.'

'There's another thing I don't understand,' said Mundy. 'If you had all this stuff, why didn't you hand it straight to the IRA, or the police? It would have gotten one of them off your case.'

'It was a question of timing,' said Lindow. 'I'd more or less decided to give it to Foyle at Scotland Yard. That's why I didn't tell the Provisionals about it by the lake. Then later that day I talked to Foyle in London. He told me that the number of the phone attached to the bomb corresponded with a number on my phone records. They still think that I tried to set off the bomb.'

'Jesus, what a fucking mess. Seems kind of rough on you, this whole thing.' Mundy paused to weigh up something in his head. The easy-going manner had disappeared. Lindow knew that he was being sized up and Mundy was not a person to cross. 'You're not bullshitting me, Dr

Lindow? I mean, I know you're a good friend of the professor's and all, but I can't afford to be screwed around by you. So don't even dream of fucking with me.'

'I wouldn't. I need your help. That's all.'

Mundy seemed to accept this, although his eyes did not lose their menace for a few seconds more.

'Okay, so here's the deal. I tell you what I know about Rhodes, so long as you guarantee to come back to me on what you find in Maine. If he *is* hiding up there, I want to know about it the moment you find him. Is that agreed, Dr Lindow?'

He nodded.

'This isn't my area now. If it was I'd have a couple of guys go up there with you. But it's just too damned complicated – I'd have to explain this thing to too many people. So you're on your own.' He paused again. 'We heard of Rhodes a long time back. We knew he came out of the military – some kind of special forces – and worked for both British intelligence agencies.'

'Is that right? That could explain why the British want to blame me and Eamonn. It might even explain why Foyle was taken off the case.'

Mundy nodded. 'Could be. In the early nineties he went off the radar screen, but then he comes back and broadens his client base and starts making real money. He may even have helped the IRA with some supplies.'

'You mean he worked for the security services *and* the IRA?'

'That's how we came to hear of him, because of our interest in the activities of home-grown Irish republicans. But he was a cut above the other gun-runners. He had a greater range. He could get anything anyone wanted out of the East – he built relationships right across the former communist-bloc countries. He even had some kind of outfit in Moscow. The overseas stuff was CIA business, but we kept tabs on him anyway because we were interested in the way he moved money around and because we got to hear that he was operating out of Canada. Believe me, a lot of bad people hang out in the land of the moose and the maple leaf. And your man Rhodes is a bad guy. It wasn't like he was just into supply, he actually went out and did some killing himself. No one screwed around with him. People always paid up.'

Lindow took out a pen and scribbled some notes on the corner of a newspaper. Mundy swept his hand across to knock the ballpoint from the paper's surface.

'You don't need to do that. I've got a printout here, which you can have later. Read it and then be sure to destroy it. I'm taking a big risk in giving it to you. But I owe the professor. He's helped out a huge amount with the work we're doing over there.'

'What's that?'

'We'll stick to the matter in hand, shall we? What you have to focus on, Dr Lindow, is that Rhodes and his partners are dangerous. Go up there like you're on a hiking trip, learn what you can. Then get the hell out of there and come back and tell me what you've found. I guess you've got some kind of Irish contact here. I won't embarrass you by asking who that is, but just be sure to tell me everything you tell them. Understood?'

'Understood,' said Lindow. 'Can I ask you another favour?'

'Try me,' said Mundy, draining his *caffe latte*.

'If I do find Rhodes, when the time comes would you be prepared to tell the British authorities that I've helped you?'

'I see no problem with that. Just tell me when.'

'I'll give you Foyle's number now. He'll confirm anything I've told you.'

Lindow copied the number on to the corner of the newspaper and gave it to Mundy in exchange for his card.

Mundy got up from his stool. 'So I'll be hearing from you.'

'Thanks.' Lindow rose. 'You were going to give me a printout too?'

'It's in your jacket pocket. Be careful now.' Lindow flipped a salute from his brow and slipped from the door with a predatory grin. He felt for the FBI file and transferred it to the inside of his jacket, before hurrying from the coffee shop. He had a lot to do.

First he went to a branch of the Bay State Bank, where the revenues from his protein work accrued each month from DahlTech on the West Coast. Lindow had wired $50,000 to an English bank a few months before, but the statement showed that the amount had already been made up by fresh deposits. He blinked at the total of $145,000, then arranged two payments to his credit-card companies and withdrew a further five thousand dollars.

On the way back to the hotel he bought a metal metre rule, a camera and low-light telephoto lens. He told the assistant in the camera shop that he planned to photograph wildlife in Maine and made him go over the operation of the lens and camera several times. Satisfied, he returned to the hotel with a dozen films and the camera equipment stowed in a small knapsack.

When he got into his room there was no sign of Mary, so he sat down at the table and began to read the outline of Rhodes's early life. He was born in Nairobi in 1952. He had been educated in England at two private schools, leaving the second at the age of seventeen. He joined the British Army in 1970 and was commissioned in 1972. His service record included periods in Northern Ireland, Borneo, Hong Kong, Belize, Norway and the South Atlantic. His expertise was listed as communications, ordnance disposal, languages, sabotage, undercover operations and surveillance.

It was at this point that the report became interesting, describing operations Rhodes had been connected with, his known associates and movements. Lindow skimmed the contents and decided to read it properly later. Right now he needed to check out of the hotel and hire himself a car. He packed his things, confining everything he'd need in Maine to one bag, and looked round the room. Then the phone rang. It was Mary.

'Con, I'm in the lobby,' she said brightly. 'When are you planning to leave?'

'Just about now.'

'Okay, so are you going to bring my bag down? I've hired a Jeep. It's outside.'

In moments during the morning he'd thought about Mary's behaviour during the night. It seemed to him that they were somehow still at odds. He had the impression that part of her operated independently from her corporeal self – as though she separated from her shadow and the shadow went off on its own business. He had his doubts about taking her. On the other hand, what could be more normal than a couple going on a break to Maine in the late fall?

'You there, Con?'

'Yes, I was just thinking. I'll come down now. I'll bring your bag.'

Fifteen minutes later Mary was driving them across the Tobin Bridge, going northwards to Route 95.

11

'Is this a bad time?' asked Speerman, from around Kirsty Laing's door.

'Not at all, do come in.' These visits of Speerman's were becoming a habit. It was his third in a week. 'How can I help?'

'I just wondered how you were thinking about things. There's no particular problem, but I've come to like our chats. They help clear my thoughts.' His face said otherwise. She knew there was a problem. Although she was out of the loop she had learned from a junior member of A-Branch that Lindow was now in Boston. The watchers had got a line into his credit-card account and had monitored transactions involving a car hire in Dublin, a travel-book shop in Cambridge, Massachusetts, a hotel in downtown Boston and a photographic shop that morning. All of this suggested to Laing that Lindow was acting with definite purpose and probably explained why he had been looking at maps in the reference library at the beginning of the week.

'Our friend Lindow is moving rather quickly,' said Speerman. 'I gather he's now in the United States – Boston.'

'Really, what's he doing there?'

'Difficult to know. Of course, he worked there until recently.' Speerman wanted to say more but she knew he needed to be helped.

'What's on your mind, Peter?'

'It's just that we believe Rhodes had some sort of set-up over there and it looks very much as though Lindow is on his trail. He's travelling north to Maine now.' Laing wondered how he knew this. The last credit-card transaction had been an hour or so ago at the photographic shop, which gave no clue about his movements.

'How does Lindow know about Rhodes?'

'Good question, Kirsty, which I am afraid I can't answer.'

'Maybe he learned about Rhodes from someone else?'

'We don't know. It's possible the IRA have given him some information this week. MacMahon was at the funeral and the two of them talked. We've got photographs.' He paused and looked at her with appreciation, his lips spreading into a rare smile. 'But tell me, Kirsty, what would you do in this situation?'

He was drawing her out. She had seen him use the technique before. He would appear genuinely in need of advice and then as soon as he had got what he wanted he would resume his official distance. She guessed he had learned it from David Cantor who famously let an issue unfold around him, allowing opposing sides to emerge, before revealing his own position. Speerman had told her nothing that she didn't already know, but here he was asking her to declare herself. She would play his game and say exactly what she thought.

'I believe we should come clean, as far as that's practical. The longer we continue to keep this to ourselves, the more people Rhodes will kill and the greater the potential scandal.'

'I wonder if that's true,' said Speerman. 'We think that the first bomb was aimed at Eamonn Lindow and the second and third bombs were both part of some sort of contract, issued by environmental extremists on the Continent.'

'I hadn't realised that was the case in King's Cross,' she said.

'It emerged last night that the building backing on to the alley was leased by an outfit called Worldwide Site Surveys, which acts as an agency for companies seeking to dispose of hazardous materials. There's a direct connection with the device at Interwaste. But the main point is that Rhodes may now have completed his work here. We know all three bombs were planted by last Friday morning. That's a week ago. He's probably long gone.'

'Yes, but it doesn't serve the cause of justice, does it? There *are* issues in this that are greater than simply what's good for the service.'

Speerman nodded solemnly.

She pressed home the point. 'Even looking at this solely in the context of our self-interest, we may be doing the wrong thing by keeping it to ourselves. Rhodes's involvement might emerge of its own accord – through Lindow's efforts, for instance.'

'What do you propose we should do?'

'I believe we must start preparing key people for the possibility that a former British Army officer is the bomber, playing up his long years of service in Northern Ireland and subsequent breakdown. We would distance ourselves from any involvement with Rhodes, and the MoD would be left fielding the questions about his service record. I could put the argument I've just made to the director general and persuade him that a change of overall strategy would leave the service less exposed.'

'Certainly not. He will already have thought of everything you suggest. We could review the situation on Monday, by which time there may be developments. If Lindow has genuinely good information about Rhodes and he finds him in the United States, other options will begin to open up for us.'

She nodded as if she saw the wisdom of the argument. 'Whatever you say.'

He sat in front of her for a few moments saying nothing, his mind evidently in turmoil. Then he got up with an oddly rueful expression. 'See you on Monday,' he said. 'We'll talk then.'

Even with his currently attentive mood Speerman could not be trusted, and she knew it had been risky to talk so openly about her views. Still, she was slightly ahead of his game. The day before she had been told that a Special Branch officer had seen Commander Kenneth Foyle leaving for Dublin. Put together with Lindow's presence in Dublin at the same time – established by the return of the car early on Thursday morning – it was worth rather more. Foyle's reason for going to Dublin could only have been to see Lindow. They must be working together. Lindow's sudden departure to Boston meant that they had much more information about Ian Rhodes than anyone in the service realised. She was sure there wasn't much time.

Foyle toiled up the last few flights of stairs in a near-derelict council block in Shoreditch. He had spent the previous twenty-four hours attempting to trace Lance Corporal Christy Calvert, one of the surviving members of the undercover squad at Droy, and had eventually got Forbes to access the police national computer. Since leaving the Army in 1991, Calvert had two convictions for assault and one for possession of ecstasy. He was now said to work as a bodyguard and club doorman in the West End. Police records gave his last known address as Aberavon House, Shoreditch, East London.

He reached the landing outside Flat 42C and knocked on the door. He heard a sound of voices inside the flat, then a man called out from close behind the door. Foyle explained that he was a police officer, seeking information. The locks were drawn back and the door opened to reveal a bare chest and tattooed arms. The face was still hidden.

'Mr Calvert – Mr Christy Calvert? I'm Commander Foyle. I wonder if I could ask you a few questions.'

The man stepped forward out of the shadows and looked down the stairwell. He had a compact physique that was still in reasonably good shape, but his face told another story. There was a graze on his left cheek, his nose was livid with tiny red pustules and his eyes shied from the light.

'You by yourself? What do you want at this time of day?'

'It's gone midday, Mr Calvert,' said Foyle, 'but I'll come back in an hour or two if you prefer.'

'I work nights. Only got to bed at six. But since you're here, you'd better come in. The place is in chaos, though.'

Foyle stepped into a fetid atmosphere that smelt of cooking fat and cigarettes. Calvert showed him into a sitting room with two armchairs facing a large TV. Sports magazines were strewn across the floor and several empty beer cans stood on the table. Calvert drew back the curtains before going to his bedroom to fetch a shirt. Through the open bedroom door Foyle could see the naked shoulders of a young man on the bed.

Calvert returned. 'I won't introduce you,' he said, sniffing and smoothing his bed-ruffled hair, ''cos I don't know his name. What can I do for you?'

'I want to know about an explosion in Ulster in July 1983. You remember? You were part of an observation patrol led by Major Ian Rhodes.'

'Yeah,' said Calvert, searching for something in his trouser pocket. 'You're talking about the churchyard.'

'Yes, the one at Droy. You were watching the place for two or three weeks before the cache exploded. Do you remember much about it?'

'Course I bloody remember it. My friends were killed by the fucking Paddies. Now the Paddies are taking tea at Number Ten – running around in suits, wearing green ribbons in their lapels, like they worked for some fucking charity. And look where I am – in this fucking shithole. Course I remember it. There isn't a day goes by without me thinking about those bastards.'

'Would you mind telling me what happened, I mean *exactly* what happened, at Droy?'

'Why do you want to know after all this time?'

Foyle watched Calvert tip a quantity of tobacco from a tin and begin to roll a cigarette. 'Because it may have a bearing on some recent terrorist actions here.'

'What, you mean the bombs last week? Nah, that wasn't the Micks. Too bloody clever for them.' He lit the cigarette and took a deep drag, causing his lungs to explode in a series of tight little coughs. When the fit was over, Foyle could hear the whisper of Calvert's chest from where he was sitting.

'Bronchitis,' said Calvert, dipping his ash into a beer can. 'So . . . Operation CUDGEL is what you want to know about. Well, we was there nearly three weeks. It seemed like years, but it was worth it because there was a charge fixed to the cache and we wanted to see it blow up when the Micks came to collect their stuff. Nothing too complicated, just a trip-wire that set off a five-second fuse down in the vault. We reckoned they'd be bringing the guns and explosives out when it blew up.'

'Do you remember which of you made the device?'

'Either Rhodes or Creech.' He paused. 'It might have been Lasseur. He was trained in sabotage.'

'What happened?'

'We saw this geezer a few times. Each time he gets out of his car and takes a leak. I had his dick in my sights twice – took all my training not to shoot it off. We didn't know if he was sussing the place out or if he just had a weak bladder. Then, after his last visit, someone came to the church at night. We heard him moving around but we couldn't see a fucking thing in the night scopes.'

'Can you show me where you were in relation to the church?' Foyle offered him a blank page of his notebook.

Calvert ignored it and placed his tobacco tin on the table to represent the church, then surrounded it with a ring of matches to show the graveyard wall. On the left of the tin he placed two cigarette papers to represent the road, then folded another paper to show a farm track that branched from the road and followed the line of the graveyard wall to the back of the church. 'The track was what made this the perfect place to hide the stuff,' said Calvert. 'They could unload and load without anyone seeing them from the road. There was an entrance to the graveyard at the back of the church. All very handy it was.'

'Where were you?'

'Four of us were in the trees up here.' He pointed a little to the right of the ring of matches. 'And there were a couple who covered the farm track. We were well dug in and we came and went through the woods without being seen.'

'And what happened on that night?'

'We heard someone in the churchyard. He must have made his way to the church on foot then sneaked along the inside of the wall. I remember thinking it was a fox or a badger. When you're dug in like that for a long time it's amazing how animals get used to you. Then one of the lads – I think it was Vince Creech – radioed that he'd seen a man. We thought that maybe he was checking out the place before the wagon came so we sat tight. Nothing happened for about ten minutes, except one of the lads said he saw a light from a torch. We waited and waited, and all the time the geezer was down there by the vault. Then the noise stopped and we realised he'd buggered off – vanished like a bleeding ghost, he did. Major Rhodes told four of us to see what this guy had been doing. Jimmy Pascoe and Bob McGurk moved in first from the woods, then Vince Creech and Lieutenant Lasseur left their positions near the farm track. Dawn was breaking and I saw all four of them in the churchyard. Then it went up, just like that. I couldn't hear for days. They found bits of Vince and Bob McGurk on the church roof.'

'What about the others?'

'It made a right mess of Pascoe's face. He was blinded too. The lieutenant was hurt down his left side – blast wounds on his face and neck. But when we saw the size of the crater, it was amazing anyone got out of there alive. They reckon there was a hundred pounds of Semtex in there. And that's saying nothing about the ammunition and mortar bombs.'

'Tell me about Major Rhodes.'

Calvert got up and went over to a side table, and poured himself a couple of inches of vodka. 'You want one?'

Foyle shook his head. 'No thanks.'

He returned to his chair and drank. 'Rhodes was a special kind of officer – not one of them public-school Ruperts. A real technician, a real pro. He'd done time with the signals, knew about codes and explosives, communications, sabotage, weapons, the bleeding lot. He had about a dozen languages and he could mimic anyone in the world. There wasn't anything he wouldn't do for his men. That's why he took the loss so bad – personal failure and all that. But he never showed it. And you know something? A few weeks later he was leading another op-react.'

'What's that?'

'It stands for Observation Post/React. Ambush, in your language. They had word that six Micks were planning to ram the gates of a police station with a JCB digger that was loaded up with a fertiliser bomb. So when they burst in with their digger they find Rhodes and five other soldiers. He killed two of the bastards, then went up to a third, who'd run out of ammunition, removed his glasses and shot him in the face. That wasn't the end of it. A couple of weeks later Jimmy Pascoe got this package in hospital – a pair of glasses and an unsigned postcard. Jimmy told me it freaked the nurses. They thought it was some kind of sick joke, see – him being blind and that. But Jimmy knew better. It was Rhodes saying he'd scored a Mick for him. That was the kind of man he was.'

'What happened to you all afterwards?'

'I went back to the regiment, lost touch with everyone. Then one day I saw Rhodes in the street. Must have been five, six years ago, anyway, some time after I'd left the Army. I called after him, but he never turned round. Then I heard on the grapevine, like, that he'd been in a home for nutters – lost his marbles big time. That explained why he didn't stop and have a word.'

'You said you heard it on the grapevine. Who do you know who knew Rhodes?'

'So it's the major you're interested in?'

'Maybe.'

'When I said the grapevine, I meant the security business. A lot of us went into security after the Army – bodyguards for the Sheikh of Araby, specialist driving, electronic surveillance, that sort of thing. It's all a load of crap to make the Arabs feel important, but it pays the bills. Anyway, I heard Rhodes was doing a bit of work for a company in Victoria. Cram Associates is the name, a cut above the agencies I was working for at the time, but they're in the same game which is how I come to hear about Rhodes going loop the loop.'

Foyle looked out of the window of Calvert's flat to the towers of

Canary Wharf and the Millennium Dome beyond. 'Tell me, Mr Calvert, did you ever hear who might have been responsible for the explosion at Droy church? Were you given any names of suspects?'

'We knew that the Paddy with the bladder problem was arrested with his brother. Can't remember the names, but we could've got them, if we'd wanted.'

Foyle rose and thanked Calvert. 'One other thing. Did you hear anything of Lieutenant Lasseur?'

'Not much. His face was in a terrible state. Burns, blast injuries. You know the score. He had a lot of surgery then left the Army – went back to Canada, I heard.'

Foyle thanked Calvert again, said goodbye and descended the thirty-odd flights of stairs to his car, where he called Forbes on his new cellphone and asked him about Cram Associates. Forbes said that the company was run by ex-intelligence people, but he wasn't sure of which variety. 'A lot of these companies sprang up in the early nineties,' he said. 'Cram is a pretty respectable consultancy – picks up work from the government and has a couple of retired permanent secretaries on the board. It's run by a man named Archie Cram.'

'How do you know all this?' Forbes never failed to surprise him.

'Actually I read it in the newspaper. There was an article in one of the Sunday business sections about the kidnap and ransom industry. Cram is "Mr K & R".'

Forbes looked up the number for him and they arranged to meet for a drink that evening.

Half an hour later Foyle presented himself at a basement in Buckingham Gate that had been gentrified by carriage lamps and potted bay trees. A young woman with an upper-class accent showed him into a conference room and gave him an information pack that outlined the careers of Cram's consultants. He glanced through the file and noted that most of them had intelligence backgrounds. Two specified M16 but the rest were vague, citing affiliations with various foreign agencies. He put down the folder and looked at a set of watercolours of the Middle East, hung on either side of the room.

'Interesting, aren't they?' said a voice behind him.

Foyle turned to see a tall man in a grey checked suit. He introduced himself as Archie Cram and offered Foyle a cold, tentative handshake.

'I picked them up in Cairo. They must've been done about the turn of the century. They're unsigned and I've never been able to establish who painted them.'

The man before Foyle had thinning, gingerish hair, a freckled complexion which had not fared well in the sun, and sharp brown eyes that darted in constant appraisal.

'So, how can I help you, Commander?'

'I'm looking into the background of a man named Ian Rhodes – Major Ian Rhodes. I believe you know him.'

'Yes, of course. I know him pretty well. He did some contracts for us after he left the Army.'

'What sort of contracts?'

'I take it you know what we do?'

'Yes. Kidnap and ransom, security, that sort of thing.'

'Then you'll know what Rhodes did for us. I can't give you many details because they're confidential. But let's say that he was a valued sub-contractor. Then, of course, he became ill.'

'What sort of illness was that?'

'Its immediate cause was some kind of virus picked up in the Far East. They never discovered what it was but it was obviously debilitating and eventually it triggered other problems – a nervous condition. It all happened just after he'd completed an assignment for us. Nothing very strenuous, compared to the things he was used to.'

'What sort of assignment? Can you give me details?'

'It involved negotiating the release of a hostage – an employee of one of our clients – held in Indonesia by a group of rebels. Rhodes managed to strike up a relationship with these people and he did an exchange.'

'What kind of exchange?'

'Weapons and ammunition for the hostage – this is all very confidential. We had nothing to do with it, but naturally we were pleased to get the hostage back for our client.'

'So he used the firm's money to supply the weapons.'

'No, no, no, not our money. He used the money made available in a bank account to pay the ransom – probably made a profit over the fee he was paid. But we saw no harm in that. You see, he was an exceptional operator and deserved all the perks he got.' Cram fixed Foyle with a look of suspicion. 'I wonder, Commander, would you mind telling me exactly what it is you want? Is this official business? Normally I'd expect someone less senior than you to be asking me these questions.'

'I'm looking into the circumstances of the recent bombing campaign in London.'

'Yes, but is this official business?'

'I'm continuing an investigation that began when the first bombs went off last week.'

'I see. So this is more in the nature of an unofficial visit. But tell me, why are you asking about Rhodes? He's hardly likely to be involved.'

'Why do you say that with such certainty?'

'Because, first and foremost, Ian Rhodes is a British soldier, and deep down his loyalties and values would prevent him from doing something like that. This is to say nothing of the lack of motive.'

'Yes, but you yourself said that he had some form of nervous breakdown. It may have unbalanced him for good.'

'No, I saw him afterwards and he was quite his old self.'

Foyle had the impression of watching an opening batsman, pushing away the ball with a series of expert defensive strokes. 'What about his background, his habits, his character? Can you help with any of that?'

'I don't think he made any secret of his background. His mother was Italian. I believe she was from Northern Italy and ended up with her parents in Ethiopia during the Italian occupation. His father was originally a railway engineer from Yorkshire who played quite a part in the Abyssinian campaign. That's how they met. After the war they went to Kenya and bought a farm. This would have been in the fifties, the time of the Mau Mau. The family farm was attacked while his parents were away in Nairobi, and he and his brother held off the Mau Mau from the roof with hunting rifles. A servant was killed in front of their eyes and then Rhodes's brother was shot before help arrived. I'm afraid I can't tell you much about his career in the Army, except that he was regarded as an extremely valuable asset, which is why we approached him. Then after his illness I gather he went into business for himself. Even had some kind of office in Moscow.'

'Doing what?'

'Well, some of the same areas of work as ourselves, but personally I never saw Rhodes as a natural businessman – not in the accepted sense. And such clients as he attracted were hardly corporate, if you know what I mean.' Cram looked at his watch to indicate that Foyle's consultation was over. 'Is there anything else you wanted to ask me?'

'Yes, do you have any idea where Rhodes might be?'

Cram shook his head. 'Absolutely none.'

'I've heard that he may have a base in the States. Is that at all possible?'

Cram shook his head again. 'I really couldn't tell you.'

Foyle left Cram Associates and walked back to his car, where he sat for a good ten minutes thinking. He had little doubt that Cram had held back in their interview and it wouldn't be long before word got out that he had been to see him. Still, it hadn't been an entirely wasted effort. With Calvert's information, a picture of Rhodes was emerging.

Fifty-odd miles north of Boston, Lindow and Mary Menihan passed into the corridor of land that allows New Hampshire to claim a portion of the Atlantic coastline. A little way on they came to the great wooded state of Maine. '"Welcome to Vacationland, home of the claw and the clam",' said Mary, reading a sign beside the highway. 'Con, you do realise that this state is something in excess of the size of Ireland? Perhaps it'd be a good time to tell me exactly where we're headed.'

He reached into one of the bags in the back of the Jeep and pulled out the map he'd used to plot the bearings from Belfast on the coast and from Limerick in the south. Then he ran his finger to a point in the north, thirty miles inside the border with Canada.

'My, what's all this?' She craned her neck to look at the map. 'Where did you get this navigational stuff?'

'Never you mind and keep your eyes on the road.' Lindow let his hand come to rest on her shoulder. There was no need to explain yet.

They travelled north for just under three hours, then took the road that branched westwards, outside the town of Bangor. Soon the land began to rise and the woods closed in on the road. Occasionally they glimpsed vistas stretching in tones of grey and brown into a baleful hinterland. They stopped once for coffee and doughnuts at a clapboard diner and stamped their feet in the car park. Mary peered gloomily over the take-out coffee and said there was snow in the air. Nonsense, he told her. It was fall. He pointed to the yellow leaves of the scrub beneath the trees and a maple that was still hung with vivid red tissues. As they stood, debating the point, a stocky little deer broke from the trees on the other side of the road, thought better of crossing and trotted back to merge into the cover. Lindow took the wheel and Mary sang desultorily, misting the passenger window with her breath. Each little town they passed through seemed overwhelmed by the woods and to peter out to a few scattered tin shacks, all dedicated to the storing of winter fuel and the repair of snowcats. There wasn't a settlement where men didn't seem to be tinkering with snowcats, oiling and firing up the engines and waving the clouds of exhaust from their faces.

'I told you so. Up here they can smell snow coming,' said Mary.

She took the wheel again because Lindow wanted to look at the large-scale atlas of Maine to gauge how far they'd be able to travel before nightfall, and also to find a place to stay. To the north they saw a huge grey cloud streaked with white that reared over Spencer Mountain like a skunk tail and made the land beneath a purply blue. He reckoned there wasn't much more than an hour's light left in the sky. But he wanted to reach the area of green on the map where Eamonn's lines met. He had the rough position, marked with a cross on one of the huge nameless rectangles numbered in the state's geographic code. There wasn't a settlement within twenty miles of the place.

'Look,' said Mary, 'this is crazy. We're not going to find anything in the dark. Besides, I'm not going to sleep in this. I want a bed and a shower and something to eat. It'll be much better if we get some sleep and start looking in the morning.'

Lindow reluctantly agreed and they made for a town on the edge of Moosehead Lake. There they were directed by a slow-talking garage hand to a hiking lodge with the Indian name of Piscataquis. The light was fading quickly as they climbed the mile or two out of town, but Lindow could just make out the shapes of seaplanes tethered to the shore and the unmistakable outline of a Dakota perched on two vast floats. The aircraft gave him an idea.

They arrived at Piscataquis Lodge, a squat wood and granite building, and were shown to a cabin decorated with old snowshoes and ancient skiing paraphernalia. The cabin was already too hot from a fire lit in expectation of weekend hikers turning up unannounced. Mary opened a window on to the night and leaned from the sill, listening to the pellets of ice rattling on the dry leaves of the forest floor as though someone was throwing handfuls of rice from the sky. She held out her hands to collect the grains of ice then turned and showed them triumphantly to Lindow. He inspected her hands and pronounced that it was hail, not snow, at which Mary shrieked a protest and threw it up into his face. He slipped his hands inside her jacket, held her for a moment and ran his lips down her neck, which caused her to wriggle in his arms and nip at his chin with her teeth. He reached up behind her to close the windows and shutters then drew her towards the fire and began to undress her, in the flickering light, kissing each newly exposed area of skin as he went. She tasted salty and her hair smelt of woodsmoke and scent. He crouched to pull her jeans to the floor. She stepped out of them. Her neat, olive-skinned body rose above him utterly naked.

'I had no idea how beautiful you were. I mean you *are* quite, quite beautiful.'

'You didn't notice last night?' She smiled down at him.

'That wasn't real. More like a dream. Anyway, I couldn't see you properly.'

She bent down, undid his belt and slipped her hand inside his trousers.

'For God's sake, undress, Con. I'm getting goose-bumps.'

She pushed him on to the bed and stripped the rest of his clothes off. She was strong and agile and, as she scrambled over him, he could feel the muscles working in her shoulders. Then she rolled to one side and guided him into her, fixing him with a playful myopic gaze. They moved for a long time in the firelight. At length Mary came with a series of small shudders. She smiled again and shifted so that her legs rested across his. She gripped his temples in the vice of her palms and brought him to a slow climax. 'Christ,' he said wonderingly.

Afterwards they lay for a while and Lindow moved down to place his head on the depression of her pelvis. Far out in the early evening a freight train pushed south along the Canadian–American Railroad, its horn sounding again and again across the lake and into the muffling firs.

Lindow raised his head from her belly to look at her. A glow of pleasure had settled on her face, but as the train thundered over a crossing below them, it seemed to shake her from her reverie. She abruptly disentangled herself from his body and sprang up, saying that she was hungry and needed a shower. Lindow clutched at the air as she went.

'Look, we have to have food and we're going to need some rest tonight,' she called from the shower.

He lay on the bed for a few minutes, feeling stung. Then he remembered the file on Rhodes, which Mundy had given him that morning. He fetched it from the bag and began reading it again. There was less to it than he had thought because Mundy had mistakenly printed out the file twice. He skimmed the details that he'd read earlier and moved on to the main body of the text.

Rhodes is regarded as a top-level operator by the British Army and intelligence services. Before resigning his commission in 1988, he was seconded to the Government Communications Headquarters at Cheltenham, England. Both foreign and domestic intelligence services unsuccessfully tried to recruit him. But for reasons unknown he remained an independent operator. In the latter part of the decade he undertook occasional assignments for MI5, the British domestic intelligence service. These were outside British sovereign territory and were connected with investigations into the supply of arms to terrorist organisations in Northern Ireland. It was on this basis that Rhodes came to the attention of the Bureau and other agencies in the United States.

Between 1990 and 1992 nothing was heard of Rhodes. In 1993 it was learned that Rhodes had moved his interests to Eastern Europe to deal in arms and other materials from the former Communist bloc. He has a relationship with at least one private security agency in London – Cram Associates. On behalf of Cram Associates, he was responsible for the negotiated release of Dr Lawrence Lloyd, a geologist employed by mineral concerns in Indonesia. It is believed that Rhodes supplied arms to gain the hostage's freedom.

His current status with the British security services is unclear due to the fact that, having traced and eliminated certain supply routes, Rhodes may have taken the opportunity to become a supplier himself to the Provisional IRA. Between 1994 and 1998, Rhodes made several visits to the US, which were confirmed by Central Intelligence sources in Europe. These trips were made under other names and their purpose is not known. It was believed that Rhodes was making his operations base somewhere in the United States.

He has been implicated in the assassination of two minor arms dealers. On March 11, 1997 Jimmy L. Marcuse was killed by a car bomb in Miami. Four months later on July 10, Patrick Lyne Jnr, an Irish-American businessman, was found dead in the Grange Hotel, Chicago. Marcuse and Lyne were business associates and may have dealt with Rhodes, although his whereabouts at the times of the murders was not established and in neither investigation was the subject questioned. As of this time, both cases remain unsolved. Rhodes has personal reserves of stamina, determination and technical expertise. Little is known about his political affiliations or his personal life. His only known associate is Robert Christian Lasseur. Born 1960, Quebec. Former British Army lieutenant. Height 5 feet 9 inches. 180 pounds. Distinguishing marks: heavily scarred on left cheek and shoulder area.

Known aliases: Rhodes is believed to travel under the name of Brian Carver, precision-tools salesman, born 1955, Leicestershire, England. He has also used the name Richard Saffarello, naturalized US citizen, born 1950, Padua, Italy.

Lindow sat on the bed and read the paper again. If Rhodes had worked for the security service and then started supplying the IRA, that would explain a lot – for one thing, why Eamonn was tracking him for the Provisionals. And it was also clear that Rhodes had all the necessary logistical and technical knowledge to mount his own bombing campaign in London. But why? Who for? Not the IRA – they wanted him found as much as anyone else.

Mary called out from the shower, 'Shall I leave this running for you, Con? Why don't you come in here with me?'

Lindow slipped the papers back into his jacket and went to the shower, where he found Mary looking absurdly youthful, her hair flattened and parted in the middle by the jet of water. He got in with her.

'What were you doing? You went awful silent for a while there.'

'I was wondering why you shot off the bed like a frightened virgin.' She kicked at him.

'Actually I was reading some stuff about our man. He sounds a pretty mean character.'

'Where were you reading about him?'

'In an FBI report.'

Mary cocked her head. 'I'm impressed. Where did you get it from?' 'The FBI.'

'Yes, but they don't just hand out files like tourist maps. You must know someone there.'

'I was put in touch with a guy. I saw him this morning. Agent Mundy, do you know him?'

'Why should I?' She left the shower, wrapped herself in one towel and took the other for her hair.

'No reason,' said Lindow, stepping under the jet and grimacing at the thought of a damp towel. 'It just occurred to me while I was reading that stuff about Rhodes that I don't know very much more about you.' He turned off the water and stood naked before her. 'You see, I'm in the odd position of imagining that I could fall in love with you, but also realising that I know nothing about you. May I have one of the towels?'

She gave him the one from her head before turning to get dressed. 'Let's go eat,' she said.

12

Peter Speerman waited for Cantor to speak. He noted that his face was a little paler than usual and that his eyes were quite drained of expression, moving only to evaluate what Speerman was telling him.

'I take it we're doing all we need to?'

'I think so. We've got the best part of five hundred people looking for Rhodes and there's been no trace of him. Nothing whatsoever. Weegee is being used to full capacity. A-Branch have been tapping into conventional street surveillance systems and London Underground's cameras. We have watches on every port.'

Cantor unclasped his hands and sat down. 'Assuming he did cause these explosions, I think we should conclude that he left the country after the last device. In fact, if we hadn't got the pictures from Weegee, I'd doubt he had ever been here.'

'Yes, but we do have them. And it looks as though Rhodes may be responsible.'

'I wouldn't put it as high as that.' He touched some papers on his desk with three manicured fingers of his right hand.

Speerman decided to wait again. The conversation with Kirsty Laing earlier had persuaded him that the initiative must be seized by the service before things ran out of control. What he needed most was a hint that Cantor had developed fallback positions in case the link with Rhodes was exposed. A hint was all he needed and Cantor would have his backing. He waited, but nothing came so he broke the silence himself.

'Have you been reading the reports of Lindow's movements in the US?'

'Yes, I've seen what Keith sent me.'

'It appears that he's gone north. We had a call from Brown Owl who said they'd hired a car and were driving somewhere in Maine.'

'Weegee, Brown Owl – for heaven's sake, who thinks of these names? Anyway, what did she have to say?'

'She believes that Lindow has been given information by the IRA that may lead him to Rhodes. As you know, both of them were snatched by McCreath's lot. It seems McCreath told Lindow to go to the States and threatened to harm his sister if he didn't. It's an improbable story, but she insists it's true. She also suspects that Lindow found something in his brother's flat, something the police missed. But she says he keeps his cards close to his chest. She's not sure when she's going to be able to get the information and call us again.'

'Menihan's her name, isn't it? What's she like?'

'Craven-Elms says she is extremely capable. We've had a relationship with her for nearly ten years. She was plugged into Eamonn Lindow for a while before his death, although not much came of her efforts. She is very patient and never loses control of a situation, which is how she managed to avoid being unmasked on a couple of occasions in the past. Keith says she'd be his first choice for a job like this.'

'Well, that's something. In the meantime the police investigation reveals not very much, I gather.'

'By that you mean the official police investigation,' said Speerman, causing Cantor's hands to seek each other's company on the top of his desk.

'Commander Foyle is proving rather tenacious. Earlier this evening I had a telephone call from Cram Associates – you remember Archie Cram? He said that Foyle was nosing round there this afternoon, asking about Rhodes's background. Cram didn't give him anything. Foyle asked whether Cram thought it possible that Rhodes was in America. This may indicate that Lindow and Foyle are working together, or have at least remained in touch. Why else would Foyle ask about America?'

'I'll have a word with the commissioner about Foyle's unofficial activity. If he persists, it might be possible to make use of that troublesome daughter of his. A little research into her life will produce many dividends, I'm certain of it.'

Cantor seemed satisfied with this and Speerman saw his attention move to the papers on his desk. He recognised this as an oblique dismissal, but he wasn't going to leave just yet. 'If Commander Foyle has anything serious about Rhodes,' he said, 'it's bound to come out. He had a lot of respect as a policeman. Just because he's been removed, it doesn't follow that he's lost all credibility among his colleagues.'

'Nevertheless,' said Cantor, with studied patience, 'it shouldn't be difficult for his superiors to ground him. I'll call the commissioner before I leave. Is there anything else?'

Speerman didn't reply immediately, but weighed up for the last time what he had been planning to say. 'I was wondering,' he began, 'how we're going to explain things if Foyle, Lindow or anyone else publicises the fact that Rhodes may've been involved. It would set things back ten years – a disaster for our relations with government, especially as half of them suspect us of keeping their files from the seventies. Might it not be prudent to admit the possibility of Rhodes's involvement and be seen to be instigating an investigation that features Rhodes as someone who has gone off the rails? Kirsty has made the point that we don't have to take responsibility for him. He wouldn't be the first British soldier to go over to the other side.'

Cantor looked up. A lethal stillness had passed into his face. 'I'm aware of Kirsty Laing's views but, Peter, I imagined you were more – how shall I say? – astute. Of course we can't have Rhodes in court, disclosing details of a highly sensitive nature. It would be unthinkable, even *in camera*.'

'Yes, but you can show that as director general you ended the service's involvement with Major Rhodes as soon as you took control – well, as near as damn it.'

'But that isn't quite true, Peter. The truth is that we have used him quite recently, more recently than you appreciate. You do understand what I'm saying to you?'

Speerman nodded. He understood perfectly. Cantor was making him complicit in the secret. He must have done the same thing with Craven-Elms, Grove, Fuller and even Brian Etheridge, the head of legal affairs, welding them into a defensive alliance around him. Speerman, however, instantly knew that he was going to have nothing to do with it. Cantor had kept him in the dark about the extent of Rhodes's work for the service and he wasn't going to accept retrospective responsibility simply to save him.

He gave no hint of his decision. 'We're already into the weekend,' he said brightly, looking out over London. 'Are you going away?'

'Yes, I shall be in Sussex, staying with some friends – shooting tomorrow.'

Speerman smiled at the idea of Cantor's social climbing. 'I have your mobile number if anything arises.'

'Good. Now, you do understand what I've just told you?'

'Perfectly.'

Cantor was already engrossed in his papers. Speerman withdrew.

Laing found Speerman sitting on a bench of dubious red velvet in the pub near where he lived. She thought he looked rather cowed. She wondered what had happened.

'How kind of you,' she said, looking at the two glasses of white wine. 'But if you don't mind, I'll have a gin and tonic. It is the weekend, after all.'

Speerman went off to get it and returned to sit down beside her so that both looked out on the thinning crowd of office workers.

'What did you want to say?' she asked.

'I've just had a word with the director general. He tells me that our involvement with the subject is more recent than we've been led to believe.'

'How recent?'

'Within the last two or three years, I'd guess, though he wasn't specific.'

Laing was genuinely surprised. The one thing she had not taken into her calculations was Cantor's direct involvement with Rhodes.

'The problem', he continued, 'is that we don't have much time. I feel certain that Foyle and Lindow are working together and that they're about to make significant discoveries. This afternoon I learned that Foyle had been to see a former colleague of ours. He was before your time, but perhaps you have heard of him – Archie Cram.'

In fact, she remembered Cram and knew that he had set up the supergrass deals in Ulster twenty or so years before.

'Actually he was with the service when I joined.'

'Well, Archie runs a small consultancy now, which used our friend once or twice. I believe he paid for his treatment after he suffered some kind of breakdown. He'd been working for him at the time and picked up a bug in the Far East, which apparently precipitated the collapse. The crucial point is that Foyle knows enough to have found Archie. Moreover, his line of questioning establishes that he knows there's an American connection. This bloody Foyle is a problem because we don't have the first idea of how much he knows. I mean, how the hell did he get on to Cram? Who else has he talked to?'

Laing understood now why Speerman was looking so damned rattled. Things were moving very quickly indeed. 'Then we've got to go and talk to him,' she said, 'and find out what he's up to.'

'Yes, but then we'd be committed to a course of action without knowing how Foyle will react. I've met him. He's like a buffalo – large and, once travelling in a particular direction, difficult to stop. The director general has some notion of getting at him through his daughter, who's been arrested for public disorder offences. But that seems to me to be surprisingly crude for him.'

'Tell me, have you met Brown Owl?' Laing had only heard about Mary Menihan from her source in A-Branch that evening. Normally she would have kept to herself the fact that she knew, but now it was important to learn how good Menihan was.

His eyes acknowledged the indiscretion. 'No, I haven't met her, but I gather she's first rate. As you probably know she effected a neat transfer when Eamonn Lindow was killed, effortlessly moving to watch the younger brother for us. Only in the last few weeks did she understand that Eamonn was acting as an intelligence officer. Originally we supposed that he was a superior form of quartermaster, or a scout. Then it became clear that he was one of their top men and that he was in charge of tracking down our friend. You see, the IRA had realised that Rhodes had killed two of their people in the States. This was a couple of years back and eventually they began to suspect him. They believed he might try to supply various Protestant groups, as well as themselves. There were any number of possibilities. But the main point is that these two fellows in the United States may have been eliminated at our instigation. That's something I did not appreciate until an hour or so ago.'

Laing emptied her glass and declared that she needed another drink, although what she really needed was time to absorb everything Speerman was telling her. As he went to the bar, she was struck by the terrible clumsiness of it all. She had always had a basic faith in the wisdom of the service, but it was vanishing by the second.

'You're saying that our friend killed two IRA arms suppliers then took over their business?' she whispered on his return.

'Yes, except by that time the peace process was so well advanced that the business was worthless.'

'Christ! This is a mess. So you think he planned to kill Eamonn? How did he know that Eamonn was on to him?'

'That's a fascinating question. Eamonn Lindow and our friend came across each other once before, in the early eighties, when Lindow was used to keep an eye on a supply dump. It was probably one of the first jobs he did for the Provisionals.'

'That was the thing at the churchyard?'

'Yes.'

'So you're saying that he knew Lindow's name and killed him, after all this time, as revenge?'

'It's possible, certainly. He would have had access to the names of the suspects and, given the circumstances of the explosion, he wasn't likely to forget them. Whether the bomb that killed Eamonn last week was intended as a revenge for Droy or as a horrendously wasteful way of eliminating a threat to his current operations we'll probably never know. Either way, the Droy explosion was the thing Foyle picked up on. By luck, intuition or investigative brilliance – I'm not sure which – he's stumbled on the right route through this particular thicket.'

'You know, Peter, I'm beginning to agree with the director general. This should never come out. It all seems so bloody amateurish.'

'You have a point.'

She knew he was on her side. 'Peter, the first thing we must do is find out how much they know. I'll speak to Foyle this weekend. The problem is going to be Brown Owl, who reports directly to Craven-Elms, which means that Cantor will get the information before us. We've got to talk to her directly. Do you remember from the credit-card records which hotel they used in Boston last night? They may return there.'

'It was a place called the Omni Parker.'

'I'll try to call her. I may have to explain a little of this to her. That'll be all right, won't it?'

'Be very circumspect.'

Kirsty Laing rose and put on her overcoat. Speerman remained seated. 'Aren't you leaving yet?'

'I'll finish this and go in a minute,' he said, gesturing to the untouched glass of wine.

Foyle lay slumped in front of his television set, watching a preview of Saturday sports fixtures and taking modest nips from a bottle of whisky. He could not have been less interested in football and rarely drank by himself. But he needed to stay awake and collect his thoughts, and he found that the cheery inanities of the two presenters acted as a kind of balm.

After seeing Cram he had driven out to Mayfield Manor, a private nursing home near Woking where Ian Rhodes had been treated for three months in 1993. Forbes had discovered this after talking to one of his contacts in the Ministry of Defence, who suggested that Rhodes might have been referred to Mayfield because of its reputation for the treatment of post-traumatic stress disorders. A lot of military personnel were sent there.

Foyle had seen the head psychiatrist, a courteous individual named Alexander Grocyn, who'd treated Rhodes. He confessed at the outset that Ian Rhodes had baffled him. He told Foyle how Rhodes had arrived by private ambulance early in 1993, swaddled in blankets and barely capable of walking. He did not speak or show any desire to communicate with those around him. 'In some senses,' said Grocyn, 'it was like a case of autism. He was obviously very run down physically. But you could not get through – he had shut down. Then after the first week he began to cry. I've seen it many times before and it's usually the symptom of great emotional or nervous exhaustion. At the time my feeling was that rest would probably be the best cure and, indeed, after the third week, Major Rhodes showed considerable improvement. We had several sessions together and it emerged that he had no private life whatsoever. It was quite extraordinary. There was no one he could talk to – no friends, no woman, no family to speak of, no intimate contact of any sort. One might have been tempted to read this as a sign of psychopathy, but that never struck me as being the right answer. He had none of the behavioural disorders associated with the psychopath's egocentricity. In fact, he possessed a rather acute insight into other people's motives, their hopes, loves, fears and so forth. In other words, his ego did not eclipse his understanding of the world. I suppose it was rather like talking to someone who had lost their sense of taste or smell. They fully appreciate that the sense exists in other people and understand why someone would go to a good restaurant or smell a bunch of roses, it's just that they cannot enjoy these experiences themselves. That is as near as I can describe his condition. There was something missing, but I could not say what it was.'

'How did you treat him?'

'I didn't treat him. I talked to him, yes, but I didn't treat him because I couldn't reach a clear assessment of his condition in my own mind. And, anyway, he made it plain that he didn't need my help. He would do whatever had to be done alone. That was the point – alone. I've met men like him, but never seen one quite so self-reliant, quite so alone. Clearly he felt strongly about things, but he was not prepared to share them with me.'

'Did he mention his childhood in Africa? Apparently he saw his brother shot in front of him.'

'Yes, he told me about it but I could not see that as being the root cause of his problems. He was matter-of-fact about it and talked easily about the loss of his brother. He made a kind of statement to me, which he had clearly formulated long before and which embraced the proper emotional responses, but did not betray any real signs of delayed trauma. I have to say that I took him at his word, although this, of course, is not the usual practice in my profession.'

'So what happened? How did he leave here?'

'He got better, and in the last few weeks took a great deal of exercise. By the time he left, which was in the early spring of that year, he looked fit and well, as normal as any of us. There's not much else to say apart from that.'

'And you felt there was no danger of him having another episode?'

'You can never tell. But my view was that this man had decided that he would not succumb to mental illness or nervous strain. He had analysed the problem and fought it. Some people can do that. It requires immense strength of character, but it's not impossible.'

When Foyle had returned to his home in Wimbledon he found the phone ringing. It was the commissioner, who was in his car on the way to an *Any Questions* radio discussion in which he was expecting to have to defend the Anti-terrorist Unit's performance. This hadn't helped Roy Urquhart's mood and he'd told Foyle that if he persisted in getting in the way he'd be dismissed from the force and his pension rights would be jeopardised. Later Foyle had turned on his radio to listen to the programme, in which Urquhart came in for some heavy criticism from the panel.

But now he waited for a call from Con Lindow. He looked at his watch. It was six thirty p.m. in the States: he still might phone. The football programme came to an end and Foyle allowed himself to be drawn into a French film which starred Stephane Audran and seemed to be set entirely in restaurants.

A few minutes past midnight his doorbell sounded. He hitched up his suit trousers and went to the door to find an attractive woman in a dark overcoat and scarf tied loosely around her neck. 'Commander Foyle?' she said. 'It's late, I know, but could we have a word?'

Foyle looked at her and wondered wildly if someone was trying to set him up. 'By all means,' he said. 'But who are you?'

'Would you mind if I didn't give you my name? I'd prefer that this conversation took place off the record. It'll be simpler for both of us.'

Foyle shrugged and showed her into the sitting room where Audran reclined in a silk slip, having moved swiftly from a restaurant to the bedroom.

'She's good, isn't she?' said the woman.

'Yes,' said Foyle, aiming the remote at Audran in mid-pout. 'What do you want to talk to me about?'

'The investigation into the recent explosions.'

'If you've information to give, you must approach New Scotland Yard. I'm no longer leading the investigation. Assistant Commissioner Scarratt will be happy to talk to you at any time.'

The woman sighed. 'Look, Commander. I am not trying to trap you. I know you've probably been warned off by the commissioner. I also know that if you continue getting under their feet they will seek to use your daughter as a means of acquiring your compliance.'

'Ah, I see,' said Foyle, 'you're from MI5. I should have guessed it. You might as well tell me your name now.'

'That won't be necessary. I'll say it again – I haven't come here to threaten you, merely to find out whether we can help each other. That's all. I mentioned Katherine because I believe they will attempt to embarrass you with an arrest, probably for drugs, so you should tell her to be careful for the next few weeks at least.'

'For the record, my daughter, Kate, does not use any form of drugs.' Foyle felt that he sounded less than confident.

'I'm sure. Look, we both know that your investigations have led you to a man named Archie Cram.'

'I assumed Cram might alert your lot. He told me very little and I know almost nothing else. I'm out of it, as you know.'

'You're underestimating yourself, Commander. I know you went to Dublin this week to see Con Lindow, and that subsequent to that meeting Dr Lindow left for the United States with information that he believes will lead him to the individual or individuals responsible for this campaign. You are collaborating with Dr Lindow and, far from being on the margins of this investigation, as you pretend, you are at the centre of it. I would guess you have a clearer understanding than anyone else at this moment.'

'So you want to know who I'm going to talk to. Well, to tell you the truth, I have no more leads. I've reached a dead end.'

The woman shook her head, then said, with an air of self-reproach,

'Perhaps I've mishandled this. Let me explain why I'm here. I care deeply for the service and I believe it has an invaluable role in modern government. This situation threatens everything. I can't pretend that my colleagues share my view, but I'm certain that the danger is real and immediate.'

Foyle's eyes rolled to the ceiling.

'No! Hear me out, Commander. This case is not simply a minor inconvenience to us. It's much more than that. It could destroy the important – and legitimate – work that we do, to say nothing of the advances we've made over the last few years within government. There are issues of justice in this, but I confess that I now believe there is a far bigger principle at stake, and that is the survival of my department as a credible force for good in this country. What I want to know is quite simply this. How close are you to the exposure of my department?'

'You mean you've come here off your own bat, without anyone knowing?' Foyle was incredulous.

'Yes, I've been utterly straight with you, Commander. I want to go away with an idea of the timescale involved.'

Foyle studied his visitor. It was just his luck to get saddled with some bluestocking spook at the very moment he expected Lindow to call. Still, she was attractive, in a formal way, and all this business about saving the honour of the service was too bizarre to be anything but true. The main point, though, was that she confirmed his suspicions that Millbank had a very special interest in Rhodes.

'Can I give you a drink?' An echo of Christy Calvert, he thought.

She shook her head. 'No, but I'd like to smoke, if that's all right?'

'Go ahead. I'd like to be able to help you,' he said. 'But my interest in this is solely about bringing the right man to court. Your people knew that Lindow was innocent and yet Cantor moved heaven and earth to get him charged – presumably to buy you time.'

'But there are still very good reasons for charging him,' said the woman. 'His phone records indicate that he made calls to the telephone connected to the last bomb.'

'My word, you are up-to-date. Nevertheless, we both appreciate that Lindow didn't make that call knowing he was dialling a suitcase full of Semtex. We both know that the bomber was playing a game. It's my belief that this character is unhinged, and I think these games he's been playing with the telephones indicate that he's got a taste for it and will explode more devices. We can explain the last two bombs, because they were clearly commissioned by some lunatic environmental group. But in each case he added his own twist. I believe – but I cannot prove – that the second bomb at the Interwaste building was detonated by a call I made. The same method was used with Lindow. He responded to a message from a letting agent.' Foyle paused. 'So, you'll forgive me if I do not put the reputation of MI5 high on my list of priorities at the moment. My aim is simply to stop this man creating the sort of carnage he did in Clarence Street.'

'Believe me, I understand,' said the woman. 'One of our people was badly injured.'

Foyle was shocked. 'Really! I didn't know that. What was he doing there?'

'I can't say. But I can tell you this. There is evidence of Rhodes's presence near Clarence Street that evening.'

'What sort of evidence?' demanded Foyle.

She gave him a look of regret. 'Again, I can't say. But I believe there is evidence, and you will need it because all you've got so far is a lot of hunches and instincts. There's nothing hard to connect Rhodes with the bombs.'

Foyle's eyes flicked to the message cassette from Lindow's answering-machine lying on the table. That was evidence, and in all probability the bomber had no idea that the connection had been made between his message to Lindow and the third bomb.

'I am prepared to help you,' she continued, 'but you've got to help me in exchange. You've got to tell me when you're getting close.'

'We'll see. But why can't you give it to me now, this evidence you have?'

'Because I don't have it in my possession.' He had a strong suspicion that she was lying. 'It's a well-guarded secret and at this stage I simply can't get it for you. But I will, at the right moment. Then I want you to give me an undertaking that it will only be used as supporting evidence. You won't produce it in court as primary evidence for the prosecution.'

'I can't agree to conditions until I see the evidence. Anyway, it's more likely that you'll get to Rhodes before I do. You must have the whole service working on this. I'm just one person.'

'Two,' she said.

'A former suspect and a discredited detective are hardly a match for MI5.' Foyle cocked his head sceptically at her.

She ignored the remark. 'You may need to get in touch with me. Here's my pager and telephone numbers.' She tore a page from the back of her diary.

'And your name?'

'You won't need my name with these numbers. They're all personal.'

Foyle got up and put the piece of paper on the table next to the message tape. The woman also rose and made for the front door where she turned to him. 'Thank you,' she said. 'I'd be grateful if you kept this private. It'll be in both our interests, I assure you.'

He watched her walk down the path until she was out of sight behind the laurel bushes at the end of his front garden.

*

As dawn broke Lindow got up and went in search of the lodge owner, who had promised the evening before to find them a plane and a pilot for the day. His only doubt had been about the weather. As Lindow walked from the cabin to the main building he looked through the trees towards the light in the east. The cloud cover seemed high enough, and although there was a wintry edge to the wind, it wasn't too strong.

He found the man making up the fire in the dining room. Without looking up or saying a word, he fished in his back pocket and gave Lindow the details of Lily Bay Aviation. Lindow called the number from a payphone at the reception desk and explained that he wanted the plane for a couple of hours to take some photographs of an area about fifty miles north of the town. The man at the other end of the line said the plane would be fuelled up and ready by eight thirty.

He returned to the cabin clutching two cups of coffee, one of which he set down beside Mary. She rolled her head on the pillow and laid a bare arm across the empty side of the bed. Then she withdrew it under the covers and moaned, 'Where've you been?'

'Never mind,' he said softly. 'There's some coffee for you on the table. I'm going to open the shutters? Is that all right?'

She didn't answer, but groped for the cup of coffee.

Lindow went to the table in front of the window and spread out the small-scale map of Maine. He wished that Eamonn had left a third compass bearing. Three would have made the triangulation pinpoint accurate. As it was, the best he could hope for was an accuracy of five to ten miles either way, which meant they might have to search an area of several hundred square miles. He noted the position of the intersection on the map, then transferred it, using his new ruler, to a page on the Maine atlas. He calculated that they would need to search between the longitudes of 69 degrees, 40 minutes and 69 degrees, 25 minutes and the latitudes of 46 degrees, 20 minutes and 46 degrees, 12 minutes.

While he worked, Mary got up. After showering she presented herself stunningly nude in the bathroom doorway. 'What are you doing?'

'Finding out where we're going today. You've got ten minutes to get dressed and have some breakfast before we go and find Lily Bay Aviation.'

She made a face at him. 'So you've got a plane?'

'Yep.' He turned to check the contents of his knapsack – notebook, pen, binoculars, camera, film and zoom lens. 'It's bound to be cold,' he said, examining the long-range lens. 'Take gloves and thick socks.'

'Con, quit bossing, will you? You're sounding like some kind of fucking instructor.'

He smiled, put on his jacket and shouldered the knapsack.

Fifteen minutes later they were driving down to the lake in the Jeep, Mary clutching her cup of coffee and a pastry she had lifted from the breakfast table. They found Lily Bay Aviation on the outskirts of town and pulled up outside a large corrugated-iron hangar, which sloped to the water's edge. Nearly a dozen seaplanes were tethered to a long pontoon. A man in his thirties with a weatherbeaten face came from a shed at the side of the hangar and introduced himself as Pete Tilsson, the proprietor and chief pilot of Lily Bay Aviation. He gave them each a muscular handshake. The wind whipped up from the lake, making his eyes water.

'Is the weather okay?' asked Lindow.

'As long as we don't go too far north it'll be fine.' Tilsson led them to a shed where they signed insurance forms and paid him three hundred dollars in cash. Then he turned to a wall map and eyed Lindow shrewdly.

'What is it that you're looking for?'

Lindow replied truthfully that his brother, who was now dead, had left him instructions to find a place north of Moosehead Lake where some friends of his lived. He added that it was his brother's last wish that he should find the place. By air seemed the best way. He showed Tilsson the atlas with the search area outlined in pencil.

'We're looking for somewhere that's well hidden, but probably consists of one or two buildings. I guess it'll be near a track, but that's all I can tell you.'

Tilsson looked doubtful. 'I know most of the folks up there. Can't think of too many places where I don't know the people. Still there may be some place and we'll stand more of chance of finding it with the leaves gone.'

He led them to a single-engine Cessna at the far end of the dock. He unclipped the wire that held the wing to the shore and two more that were attached to the starboard float. They all scrambled aboard and Tilsson started the motor, motioning Lindow to put on a pair of headphones. He mumbled something into the radio and steered the plane's nose out into the centre of the bay. When they were facing dead into the wind, he checked his gauges and looked along the wings one last time, then pulled back the throttle and sent the plane skidding across Moosehead Lake. A few seconds later the pounding on the floats ceased and the plane lifted clear of the waves, leaving the town behind the starboard wing.

They climbed for ten minutes, then levelled off at eight thousand feet. Out in the east, light shafted down from a sun they could not see and scores of lakes shone like slivers of silver foil. Ahead were huge black clouds, which trailed curtains of rain beneath them. Tilsson said they'd soon hit the bad weather. Lindow turned round to tell Mary who was staring from the window with a look of childlike wonder on her face. Quite suddenly hailstones began to crackle on the windscreen and roof of the cockpit. Tilsson pushed the throttle in, causing the plane to drop into a belt of cloud. A few minutes later they emerged into clear sky with the great northern woods spread out before them. Wisps of cloud hung in the forest as if clawed from the sky by the bare branches.

They passed over the Penobscot River and approached the search area. Lindow got out his binoculars and trained them along the roads and trails that snaked through the forests. They flew north, took a sharp turn westwards, leaving Allagash Mountain to their right, and looked down at the lumber roads that criss-crossed the wilderness. Tilsson turned south and later east, completing the first in a series of diminishing squares. They flew like this for forty-five minutes. Occasionally Lindow pointed down to a homestead, but each time Tilsson shook his head and shouted that he knew the people who lived there, or that it was used in the wintertime by skiers and snowcatters, or in summer by hikers.

They dropped down to two thousand feet and flew along a strip of water marked on the map as Black Finger Lake. Tilsson bellowed that he didn't know the lake well because the fishing was no good. On the south side there was a swamp, where hundreds of bleached pine trunks lay in the silt like bones. On the north side, the lake was bordered by a long shoulder of land that ended in a cliff. Behind that was an area of high ground, which sent out a ridge of rock that plummeted into the lake about a hundred yards along from the cliff. It was difficult to make out what lay between the two points because a squall had blown down from the high ground and was dumping rain along the shoreline, but as they passed the cliff Mary shouted that she had seen something – a roof by the water and a flash of wet metal glinting in the lee of the cliff. Lindow looked on the map. Nothing was shown, no trails or buildings. Tilsson flew down the lake then turned the plane to fly past the cliff again.

Now Lindow saw the buildings. There was a boathouse or hangar on the water, painted brown and dark green to blend into the terrain. A path led through the trees to a cabin, behind which was a barn and a parked vehicle. They passed over it a second time and saw a radio mast and a satellite dish. Lindow realised the place had been built to be almost completely hidden between the cliff and the ridge of rock. In fact, it could only be seen briefly from the air for a few seconds, or from a boat stationed directly in front of the cliff. Tilsson flew along the lake, losing altitude, and turned for a final pass at a few hundred feet. By this time Lindow had got out his camera and was aiming through the port window. He shot off five frames with the motor drive whirring before the buildings disappeared behind the ridge of rock.

'Wow!' said Tilsson. 'He's got a Beaver!'

'What?'

'He's got a DHC-2 Beaver – great little workhorse.' Tilsson pointed at the snub nose of a seaplane in the waterside hangar. 'Hey, you want me to put her down so you can take a closer look?'

Lindow shook his head. 'No, thanks. This must be the place,' he said, turning back to Mary. 'We'll come back in the Jeep.'

He asked Tilsson to fly north to see if there was a road that led to the buildings. They scoured the ground for several minutes before spotting a rough track that followed the shoulder of land, then disappeared into a narrow gorge, covered by pine trees. A few miles on they picked up the track where it climbed a hill to join a lumber road. Lindow looked at the map again. Nothing was marked, but he saw they'd be able to reach the lumber road via the main route to the Allagash Wilderness from the south. It shouldn't be more than an hour and a half's drive from Moosehead Lake. He signalled Tilsson to turn for home. With the wind behind them, they were soon approaching the town. They circled and for a moment the plane seemed to hang over the buildings before dropping down to the iron-grey surface of the lake, nearly clipping the trees along the shoreline.

They left Tilsson and went to buy food and a flask of coffee for the trip. Mary argued against leaving so quickly, saying that they should find out more about the people by the lake before crashing into a situation they knew nothing about. Someone was bound to have information about the place. After all, there was an aircraft that needed fuel and servicing; there were power lines running to the buildings. They would have to get gas for the vehicle that was parked by the lake.

But Lindow was adamant. If she wanted to stay behind that would be fine. Either way he was leaving. She said nothing more, but put on a pair of sunglasses and got behind the wheel.

About fifteen miles out of town the paved road ran into a wide dirt boulevard that was humped in the middle and strewn with bark. The sides had been eroded by storms, so Mary drove along the crown, swerving occasionally to miss the long coils of bark that had been shed from the lumber trucks. They saw no other cars, but passed two groups of hikers. At a place where the road dropped, giving them a rare view of the landscape, they stopped and hurriedly consumed a ham roll each and coffee. Lindow took a compass bearing from a mountain in the west, and then from Allagash Mountain, which lay hunched to the north. He estimated they'd need to go another twenty miles before they started looking for the trail to the lake.

'Con, are you sure you want to do this?'

'What choice do I have? All I need is the exact location, some pictures of the layout, maybe some shots of the people there. That ought to be enough.'

'You really think it's going to be that simple?'

He shrugged and got into the driver's seat.

They did not speak for the next half-hour. Then, as they drove through a long stretch of utterly featureless forest, she noticed an opening in the trees and shouted out. Lindow slammed on the brakes, causing the car to skid on the dirt. Thirty yards back a track joined the road at an acute angle.

'That's it.' Lindow swung the Jeep round. 'Let's go and have a look.'

It was clear that the track had been used recently. The grass between the two wheel ruts was brushed forward, and here and there was the imprint of tyres in the dirt. They moved gingerly down the hill, negotiating the pot-holes and the rivulets that ran across the track. Half a mile on, it levelled out and was smoothed with stone chippings. They passed several small ponds and a stretch of open land before the road began to rise again.

To their right, Lindow noticed a heavy electric cable running through the trees at a height of eight feet. Every so often there was a big loop of cable fastened to a post by a plastic belt.

'What do you think that's for?' he asked.

'It's to allow for falling trees and big animals. When the cable's hit, the loop springs free so it doesn't break.'

It was clear that they were reaching the high ground behind the cabin. They decided to continue on foot. Lindow ran the Jeep on to a piece of firm ground beneath some saplings and got out with his knapsack. He fitted the long lens to the body of the camera, then turned to the back of the Jeep to see Mary checking a pistol.

'What's that?'

'A nine-millimetre Glock – model seventeen.'

'I wasn't asking what model. I was asking what you're doing with a gun.'

'A girl's got to have some protection.'

'You know, Mary, I'd really like to know who you're working for. Book editors don't carry guns.'

'Book editors that are shit-scared carry guns.'

'I mean, where the hell did you get a thing like that? You didn't have it in Ireland.' His temper was beginning to show.

'No, I didn't have it Ireland, but that episode made me think I needed some protection if you were going to haul me into the wilderness with no more than a damned pocket knife.' He could see the subject was closed.

She pocketed the gun and set off through the trees to the left of the track. Lindow stood for a moment, suddenly wondering what on earth he was doing. He cursed himself, cursed Eamonn and the Provisionals, cursed Ireland and his mother's nationalism. What he wanted was normality – his books, his lab, his early morning espresso and the quiet daily purpose of scientific inquiry. He slammed the car door, locked it and trudged after Mary, resenting her impressive pace up the hill.

It was much further than they'd expected and by the time he caught her, he'd worked up a sweat. The hill had several false summits but eventually they broke out of the trees to an area of bald black rock that rose before them like the back of a whale. They saw the lake below and stood still. The place was utterly silent: there were no bird calls and the wind had dropped so that the boughs of the pines swayed only a little. They edged round the hill and the cliff came into view followed by part of the cabin roof. Mary crouched and waved him down, patting the air beside her. She whispered that they shouldn't talk because their voices would travel. Then she gestured to some dense brush that had taken root in the cracks of the rock and slid expertly on all fours into the cover. Lindow followed her in an awkward crab walk, moving sideways and holding the camera above him. Twenty feet on she stopped and pointed through a gap in the brushwood. The whole place was laid out before them. There were two cabins set at right angles and joined by a flat tin roof, under which were piled stacks of timber, a wood trellis, two snowcats, snowshoes, chain-saws, shovels, coils of rope and chain. Across the yard a large Ford truck had been moved out into the open. Down by the lake Lindow could make out the hangar. He focused the camera and took some photographs of the radio mast and satellite dish. Mary flinched at the noise of the automatic drive and hissed that he should use the manual wind-on. Then she took the binoculars from him and swept the yard, pausing on the truck. He watched her lips move, as she memorised the licence-plate.

Lindow was looking down when the patch of rock beside him suddenly sent up a shower of splinters. Then he heard the gunshot echoing in the trees, almost like a woodpecker. Mary rolled to her right, pulling the Glock from her pocket. Nothing happened; they could see no one. They searched each other's faces. Then they heard movement some way off to their right. Mary raised her head.

'Stand up,' said a man's voice. 'And come towards me. Please don't try to escape.'

13

The voice was English, very calm and with no hint of menace. Lindow looked stupidly around him, without the faintest idea where it was coming from. Mary jabbed her gun in the direction of their Jeep. He leaned back on the cold, wet rock to see the torso of a man about fifty feet away. The figure held an assault rifle to his shoulder and pointed to their position with his other hand. 'Get up and walk over here so that I can see you both – and don't move suddenly.'

'Look, we were just hiking through here,' said Mary, getting up slowly with the gun held behind her. 'We don't want any trouble. We'll leave.'

Lindow rose also. He could see the man properly now. He was wearing black work trousers, a dark green jacket and a ski mask.

'I was waiting for you,' he said casually. 'It was your plane that flew over here this morning, wasn't it? You saved me a lot of hanging about by coming so soon.'

They got to within twenty feet of him and stopped. Lindow wondered if this was Rhodes.

'Now, you with the gun,' said the man, facing Mary, 'put it on the ground and tell me what your name is.'

She placed the Glock on a carpet of pine needles and said her name was Mary Sheaffer.

'And you,' he said to Lindow, 'what's your name?'

'Richard Lithgow. What's yours?' said Lindow, searching the eyeslit of the ski mask.

The man ignored the question and waved his rifle towards a deer track, which curled round the hill down to the cabins. 'Go down there and no screwing around. You understand?'

'Look—' said Mary.

'Just do as I say.'

When they reached the yard, after sliding on their backsides and hands over an outcrop of rock that oozed water, he told them to go inside the far cabin and sit down on the floor. The place was larger and better lit than Lindow had expected. This was some kind of workshop. The other cabin must be where the man slept.

He ordered them to sit down back to back in the centre of the room. Lindow sat facing the window that overlooked the lake and aircraft hangar. Beneath the window was a long workbench with three lights angled over its surface. To the right of the bench some shelves held a radio scanner, a short-wave radio set and a TV screen, which was split into twelve small images of the surrounding forest. It was clear that the man had got all possible approaches to the cabin covered by cameras. In the bottom right-hand corner of the screen Lindow could see the milky image of their car. To the left were two views of the lumber road. He must have seen them pass the turning, go back and crawl down the track towards his cabin. He'd have known exactly which route they'd take through the woods. His eyes moved to the bench where there was a mass of equipment – circuit boards, a soldering iron, an ammeter, a rack of screwdrivers and many small electrical components still in their plastic wrappers. Everything was neatly ordered, marshalled for use.

'Yes, I saw you coming about forty-five minutes ago,' said the man, placing Mary's pistol on a table next to a computer. 'It's a very good little system. But it's rare that I see anyone. It's mostly animals and the odd deer-hunter from now on through the winter.' His tone was conversational. There was still no hint of menace.

He hit a key on the computer, which disengaged the screen-saver and brought up a menu. He waited, idly examining Mary's gun. Then he started typing with one hand. Lindow's eyes focused on the area below the workbench where trays containing electrical equipment were stacked. He recognised most of the components – five mobile phones, stripped of their casings, several different types of electrical switch, a digital display from a video-player and a number of electrical plugs, used by householders to turn on the lights when they're out.

One tray held an assortment of squat industrial batteries. Lying beside this was a plywood board, which might have been constructed by a schoolmaster to demonstrate a particular piece of circuitry. He concentrated on the panel. At the top of the board was a small plastic box, faced with a black concave mirror. Wires led from the box to a battery then to an electrical switch and on to what he assumed was a detonator. In an instant, he saw how it worked. The box was an infrared detector, of the type used in security systems to pick up the heat radiation of a human presence. Here it had been incorporated as a trip that caused a circuit to connect when someone approached – an ideal booby trap that relied on nothing more than the warmth of a living person.

The keys chattered for a little while, then they heard the dialling of a modem. Lindow could feel Mary straining to see what was going on, but he was concentrating on something else. He had just noticed a piece of yellow paper stuck to the side of the computer, on which was scrawled in large, untidy writing AXIOM DAY.

The man stopped typing and glanced up at the daylight in the window.

'Wind's getting up again,' he said. 'Hope we aren't going to have another storm. Nearly brought my dish and aerial down last time.'

Still staring out of the window, the man removed his jacket, tugged the ski mask from his head and turned to show his face to them. An area of puckered white scar tissue covered the left side of his face and ran down his neck to the line of his turtleneck sweater. The skin around his left eye was creased and shiny, like the permanent folds in a piece of parchment. Lindow put his age at no more than forty-eight. He was still youthful and it was obvious that he'd once been good-looking. His eyes were very blue and very still. His mouth smiled easily, but the scarred cheek did not rise with the other, giving him an odd lopsided look as he talked.

'Not very pretty, is it?' he said, challenging Lindow's gaze. 'But I've got used to it now. Causes me problems in the sun and in the cold. It's not as resilient as normal skin – hence the ski mask.'

The computer bleeped and the man returned to the screen. He read for a few seconds then turned to them. 'You have to tell me who you are,' he said, picking up the rifle. 'Are you with some kind of agency?'

'It's nothing like that,' said Lindow calmly. 'We're up here for the weekend. This place looked kind of interesting, so we thought we'd explore.'

'Yes,' said the man, his tone still even and civil. 'But why did you take pictures of my yard? Why did you fly over here three times this morning? And the lady here, does she usually go out hiking with a Glock in her pocket? This is hardly casual interest, is it? So let's stop pissing about. Tell me who you are.'

He came within a couple of paces of Lindow. He smiled, then without warning lifted the butt of his gun and brought it down on Lindow's collarbone. Lindow cried out and slumped over.

The man pulled Lindow up to a sitting position and felt inside his jacket. Finding nothing, he stepped back and poured the contents of the knapsack on to the floor. Eamonn's passport lay between the two maps. The man held it up to the light.

'It says here you're Dr Constantine Lindow.' He looked down at Lindow and smiled his crooked smile. 'But I don't think this is your photograph. So who are you – eh?' He delivered a well-aimed kick, which cut Lindow's ear open and sent him sprawling across the floor. He boiled with rage, but he stayed put and watched the blood dripping from the cut on his ear.

The man stepped across to Mary and squatted beside her, smiling solicitously. His left knee was behind her head. The barrel of the rifle pointed across the room at Lindow's stomach.

'Perhaps you'll tell me.' He grasped Mary's jaw and examined her face roughly.

'Leave her, for God's sake,' said Lindow. 'We came to find out why my brother Eamonn was killed in London. That's all there is to it. She was just a friend of his. She's got nothing to do with this. Let her go.'

'Tell me who you are then.'

'I *am* Con Lindow, as the passport says, but it's not my picture in the passport because it's a forgery. My brother had it done. He used my name and his own picture. I found it after he was killed.'

'Really?' said the man nastily. 'Now that's very interesting. Let me show you something.' He went over to a video-player, which sat beneath the CCTV screen on the shelves, selected a tape and shoved it into the mouth of the machine. He watched for a little while then stepped back with the remote. 'Pay attention to the right-hand picture. You will see a visitor of mine making his way through the woods, just as you have today.'

A figure appeared in one of the twelve sections of the screen. The man pressed a button so that it suddenly filled the entire TV screen. Lindow gaped. The figure stumbling up a hill was Eamonn. There followed several more shots from different cameras that culminated in a sequence which showed Eamonn running across the yard, looking through the window of the cabin for a few seconds and turning rapidly towards the lake. Then he vanished.

'He heard me coming in the plane, see. He must have legged it damned quick after that and he was lucky to get away without running into one of my little surprises.' He winked grotesquely at Mary and returned to her side.

Lindow knew that he had to engage him. 'Look,' he said reasonably, 'you don't have to hurt her. She doesn't know anything.'

The man took no notice. 'So, you see, you're not the first prat to blunder up here. That was your brother, wasn't it? And you've come up here looking for his killers. Am I right?'

'Not exactly,' Lindow began. 'I was intrigued by some instructions Eamonn left in the passport. They're still there, if you look in the back.'

Lindow saw Mary's eyes implore him not to say any more.

The man examined the scrap of paper and read out the bearings. 'Very neat,' he said at length. 'This device of using towns with Irish names – that's clever.' He paused and looked down at Lindow. 'So I take it that you know who Rhodes is?'

'No, I don't know who Rhodes is.' He noticed Mary's eyes fill with concentration. It was odd. Suddenly she didn't seem frightened.

'Rhodes was in charge of the operation when your brother blew up our little group at the church. I got away lightly with this.' He touched his cheek. 'A few months of plastic surgery and I was right as rain. The others weren't so lucky. You may know about it – two killed and another lost his sight. That's why Rhodes got your brother in the end. A point of honour for the op, you see. When we realised that it was your brother who was snooping on us, he became a priority.' He cleared his throat. He obviously hadn't spoken so much in a long time. 'The beauty of it was that he didn't know that someone had sold him out on his own side, someone in Real IRA or Pure IRA, or whatever they call themselves now. That's a joke isn't it – Pure IRA? You see, we had our contacts on that side of things. Rhodes had removed a couple of their people – maybe you know about that – and become their supplier. But then the whole thing shifted and it wasn't clear who was doing what to whom. Bloody funny, when you think about it. Then they found out what had happened here and decided to come back at us. But you know how it is, we had other business and we weren't about to get involved in some fucking war with the Micks. So Rhodes knew the way to sort it out was to get rid of Eamonn Lindow. He remembered the name. Odd name, Lindow. Where's it come from?' He threw the passport down with the rest of Lindow's possessions.

'I've never found out.'

Lindow knew for certain that they'd be killed. Why else would the man be telling him all this? It was then that he decided to give Mary a chance – maybe even himself as well. Her Glock was lying on the table by the computer. If he launched himself at the man's legs, he might just be able to give her time to grab the gun and fire off a round. She saw what he was thinking. Her eyes widened to signal a definite negative.

'And you don't have any idea what Axiom Day means?'

'No.'

'And you don't even know who I am?'

'No.' Lindow shook his head.

'You mean, you *really* don't know who I am? Bloody hell, you are a couple of amateurs, aren't you? Well, I see no harm in telling you. I'm Bob Lasseur – Lassa, as in fever – formerly a commissioned officer with Her Majesty's Royal Fusiliers.' The conversational tone had returned. He walked round the cabin, looking out of the windows. He was evidently enjoying himself. 'I'm inclined to believe the story that you've told me because, if you knew who I was and what Axiom Day meant, it wouldn't be just you two up here. The place would be flooded with FBI agents in body armour.'

He returned to the keyboard and began to type. This time Lindow could see more of what he was doing. After he'd composed the message, he stored it and ran a piece of software. The message flashed on the screen briefly then disappeared in a blur. He was encoding it. Finally the modem clicked and he dialled a number that he pulled down from the computer's telephone directory. Lindow knew he must be contacting Rhodes.

'We're going to have to wait,' said Lasseur. 'He's not responding.'

'Who are you trying to contact?'

'Rhodes. He's getting bad about returning messages. Still, it's under-standable. We're at the end of this thing. Partnership dissolving and all that. Money banked, leaving here, going our separate ways.' Lasseur looked distracted. 'I hate this business, you sneaking up here like this. It means I've got to do something about it.'

'No, you don't have to do anything about us,' said Mary quickly. 'If you're splitting up and leaving this place, it doesn't matter what we know.'

'Oh, but it does. It's been a very profitable partnership and all our operations have been run from this humble cabin. So we can't have the FBI crawling over the place looking for clues and working out what we've been doing or who for. No, I have to leave in my own time. This place has to be decommissioned properly, everything must be disposed of. It's going to take several flights to dump this lot in the surrounding scenery.' He gestured to the workbench. 'I don't want to be hurried.'

Lindow knew that they would be disposed of in exactly the same way. Lasseur would take them down to the hangar, shoot them and load them on to the Beaver. Then he'd weight their bodies and drop them over some distant lake. If he missed, it wouldn't matter much because there were plenty of hungry animals – bears and maybe even the odd wolf – that could be relied upon to distribute their remains through the woods. By the time spring arrived and the parties of hikers came up from Boston, there'd be nothing left of them. He had to act. Any second now, Rhodes would answer Lasseur's message with an instruction to kill them immediately.

He prepared himself by rising imperceptibly, drawing one knee to his chest and pushing himself up with his left hand. He moved his leg to get some leverage, while pretending to be concerned about his ear, dabbing at the blood with the cuff of his shirt.

He hoped Mary saw what he was doing.

'Would you mind telling me something?' she asked Lasseur, with the intelligent eagerness Lindow remembered from their first meeting. 'What is this thing – Axiom Day? What's it all mean?'

Lasseur leaned forward indulgently. His face passed into a band of light that was reflected through the window from the truck's windshield.

'That's not my business. That's Rhodes's affair. To be honest, I don't know what he's planning – I'm just the ordnance man on these things. I prepare. I make suggestions. I design equipment for the contracts. But I don't go out in the field. Too easily recognised, you see.' He brushed his cheek again.

Mary nodded sympathetically. 'Sounds like quite a lot of planning was needed.'

'Yes, it's going to be *his* statement – that's all I know about it. If there's one thing he can't stand it's disloyalty, a sell-out.'

'What do you mean – sell-out?'

'Ireland, of course. Talking to the Micks over the conference table, asking their opinions, doing deals with the bastards that killed our men, letting them out of prison. That's a sell-out in anyone's language.' He looked out of the window, seeking distraction. 'Wonderful light you get up here at this time of year.'

'Yes,' said Mary. 'Magnificent. I was thinking these forests must be very beautiful in the snow, very romantic.'

Lasseur smiled. 'Yes, it's certainly very impressive.'

Lindow let his right hand slip from his knee to rest on the floor alongside the other hand. Then he distributed his weight evenly between them, swung his bottom from the floor, bringing his legs into a sprinter's start, and aimed himself at Lasseur's chair. Mary flung herself forward also, moving fast and low across the dozen or so feet. But Lasseur was too far away for both of them. He sprang on to the balls of his feet, sending the chair hurtling backwards, and swung the stock of the rifle in a scything action at Lindow's neck. He raised it and jabbed a sharp blow to the back of Mary's head. Lindow rolled over clutching his jaw. Mary dropped at Lasseur's feet, unconscious.

Then he stepped back and aimed the rifle at Lindow. 'Get her over there,' he shouted, jerking the gun towards the workbench. 'Then both of you lie face down.'

Lindow's jaw raged with pain as he placed his arms under Mary's, locked his hands together over the top of her chest and hefted her back across the floor to the workbench. He was bleeding from two places now: there was a gash on his jaw where the metal on the rifle stock had cut into the skin, and his ear was still dripping copiously. The blood splattered on to Mary's unconscious face.

'Leave her there and get down beside her,' Lasseur commanded. He looked out of the window again, and ran his hand through his hair nervously.

Lindow laid Mary out and slid his hand down to feel her pulse. It was strong and regular.

'You shouldn't have tried that,' said Lasseur. 'I haven't decided what to do with you yet. You shouldn't have jumped me like that.'

Lindow could see that he was agitated. Lasseur was tough and very agile – there was no doubt about that – but he might not have the taste for the close-up kill. What else could explain his failure to shoot them there and then? He guessed – or, rather, prayed – that Lasseur had flinched from killing them, even in self-defence, because he couldn't. Then he reasoned that this was optimistic nonsense. Lasseur had probably been on countless operations in Ulster which required him to kill without hesitation. He wouldn't in the least mind shooting them. The only reason he hadn't was that he didn't want to mess up the cabin and then have the chore of dragging their bodies down to the lake.

But there was a hesitation. Something had stopped him. Perhaps it was Mary. As Lindow had dragged her across the room he'd seen the expression of awkward regret pass over Lasseur's face. He must try to bring her round, get her talking to Lasseur again and get him responding to her as he had before they'd rushed him. He drew the hair from her face with his left hand and blew on her cheek. Then he kneaded her shoulder. But she didn't come round. He thought of Kay Gould, lying beside him in Clarence Street.

Lasseur watched him. 'She'll come to soon enough.'

The computer bleeped. He sat down by the machine and laid the rifle across his lap. He leaned in to type a few commands and waited. Then he pulled his head from the screen, muttering, 'Have I done it? Course I haven't fucking done it! It's not that simple.'

Lindow shook Mary harder. 'Come on,' he whispered urgently. 'I need you now. Wake up, for Chrissake!'

At the other end of the room Lasseur had got up and was pacing around the computer. Then he suddenly announced, 'Rhodes says he expects I've already got rid of you. That's that. No need to discuss anything. It's all right for him. He's used to this kind of thing. I'm not.' He went to the screen and stabbed angrily at the keyboard.

Lindow glanced at the door and dismissed any idea of escape. There was no hope of making a run for it and, anyway, he'd have to leave Mary. He looked under the bench for a weapon. There was nothing. Then Lasseur marched over and pointed his rifle at them. Lindow forced himself to look up into his eyes. Lasseur must see his face – understand what he was about to do. 'Rhodes says he wants confirmation that you're dead. But I need time,' he said, with an eerie note of apology. 'I'm going to tell him you're dead. I've got to think about this.'

He strode back to the computer, typed a few words and encoded them. Then he stood, bent to the screen, waiting for a reply. Lindow thought furiously. There was nothing he could do. If he tried to tackle him again he'd make Lasseur's mind up for him. At that moment it seemed that Lasseur's anger was directed at Rhodes and that was good.

The computer bleeped again. Lasseur waited. Then he straightened up, frowning at the machine. 'What the fuck . . . ?'

He didn't finish. There was a flash. The console lifted into the air and sent a storm of glass and metal over the room. The blast hit Lasseur in the stomach, folding him like a leaf and throwing him into the wall on the other side of the cabin. Instinctively Lindow covered his head in one arm and wrapped the other round Mary. Then he looked up. The explosion had blown all the bulbs, but there was still some light coming from the windows. Lasseur was sitting crumpled against the wall looking aston-ished. A dark red patch had spread across his chest. A curious sputtering came from the remains of the computer. Ribbons of fire had sprung along the electric cables. Lindow jumped up and hauled Mary to a standing position. He hung her arm around his neck and dragged her at a trot through the door and out into the clean, turquoise dusk. As he laid her against the wheel of the truck she moaned. 'It's okay,' he said. 'There's been an explosion. We're going to be okay. He's badly injured. The computer blew up.'

She asked again what had happened. He said there wasn't time to explain and opened the door of Lasseur's truck to see if the keys were in the ignition. They were.

Then he heard a cry come from the cabin. Lindow rose from Mary's side and walked the few paces towards the door. Lasseur screamed again – a shriek that cracked his voice. Lindow went into the cabin and searched round for a light. The fire had moved to the wall socket and was edging along a shelf of papers and manuals.

'I'm coming.' He went over to Lasseur and found a switch above his head, which turned on a light in a corridor. He stood for a moment, looking at Lasseur. The blast had ripped the clothes from his chest and torn a hole in his stomach. His intestines were showing and, lower down, an organ had spilled out from the torn muscle. Lasseur wouldn't live much longer. Lindow squatted down beside him.

Lasseur's chest convulsed and a gobbet of blood showed at his mouth. 'I was going to kill you both. I'd made up my mind.' He sucked and revolved his tongue in his mouth, as if to rid himself of an unpleasant taste. 'Finish me with the gun. Finish me off, for Christ's sake. This is hell.'

Lindow said nothing and waited. Lasseur's pain seemed to ease and he began to speak in a hoarse whisper. 'The bastard wired the CD drive with a charge ... When I told him you were both dead, he sent me a message with a code that activated it ... and that fired the detonator ... That was my fucking trick – my idea. He must have put the stuff in there weeks ago. He knew he was going to kill me ... and I knew it too, but I thought I was safe while he was in England.' He paused and closed his eyes. Lindow noticed that the old scar tissue stood white in his face.

'That was damned clever,' he murmured. 'Damned clever, program-ming the computer so everything would be destroyed. He knew I'd be killed ... I'd have to be sitting there, decoding the message. He knew the charge would go straight for my head. But I wasn't sitting. That's why it got me in the stomach.' He swallowed several times.

'Don't talk.' Lindow rested a hand on Lasseur's shoulder. 'I'll see if I can find some water.'

'Listen to me,' whispered Lasseur. 'It's all here. Records – everything. I kept it all. Backed it up on Zip disks.'

'What're you saying?' asked Lindow, bending his ear to Lasseur's mouth.

'There's a loose floorboard . . . under the workbench. The disks are in there. They'll tell you everything.'

Lindow crawled under the belt of smoke to the workbench and tore at the trays, scattering the contents behind him. He worked his way under the bench and started thumping his fist along the floorboards. Near one of the legs he felt a panel move. He hit it again and the wood flipped up. He plunged his hand inside the cavity and felt a small plastic box. Inside there were six fat one-hundred-megabyte disks. He recognised the type at once: they were used to back up research data in his laboratory. He slipped them into his jacket pockets and ran back to Lasseur, coughing. The smoke was getting worse.

'Shoot me . . . I can't take this,' moaned Lasseur. Blood issued from his mouth with each word.

'What's Rhodes planning? Tell me what he's going to do.'

Lasseur didn't answer. Instead his eyes rolled in bewilderment.

Lindow stood up mechanically and fetched the assault rifle, which was lying a few feet away. The draught from the open door was fanning the flames. It would be only a matter of minutes before the cabin reached flashpoint. He held the rifle to the side of Lasseur's head. Lasseur felt the metal of the barrel on his skin, looked up and nodded.

'Don't!' shouted Mary, who was standing in the doorway.

Lindow hesitated, then looked down again. Lasseur's head had fallen to the left. His eyes were shut, but his last lopsided smile was still there. He was dead. Lindow threw the gun down and ran to the centre of the room where the contents of the knapsack lay in a pile. He scooped up the maps, camera and passport and ran outside, hooking his free arm round Mary in mid-stride. He pushed her into the truck, started the engine and tore from the yard. She was shaky and kept on asking him what had happened – how she had come to be lying out in the yard and why he went back into the cabin. Lindow didn't reply.

Only when they'd dumped Lasseur's truck and climbed into the Jeep, and were making their way up the track to the lumber road, did he begin to hurry through the sequence of events that had ended with the computer blowing. Once on the lumber road, he gripped the wheel to stop himself trembling, and spoke deliberately, as though to bring some order to the events of the last hour. He told her that Lasseur had used the phrase Axiom Day, and about the note on the side of the computer. He didn't mention the cache of disks under the floorboard because he'd grasped their value and, besides, it was obvious to him that Mary was a lot more than a book editor. The gun and the way she had handled herself in the past hour convinced him she'd been in situations like that before.

They reached the high point of the road where, earlier in the day, Lindow had taken bearings from the mountains. Mary looked back into the darkness and spotted a pool of orange some way off to the north-west. They got out and she made him bend down into the headlight so she could see the cuts on his jaw and ear. She wetted the sleeve of her shirt using their bottled mineral water and dabbed some of the blood away.

'Someone will see the fire,' said Lindow. 'They'll look into it tomorrow and it won't take long for Tilsson to make the connection. He'll tell the police about our trip this morning. I think it would be a lot better if we just left tonight.'

'You okay to drive? I still feel pretty rough.'

'I'm fine.' Lindow got back into the Jeep and they continued towards Moosehead, eating the remainder of the food and sipping the coffee, which the flask had kept warm.

'"Out there we walked quite friendly up to death—"'

'Are you all right?' Lindow worried about the blow to her head.

She repeated the line, '"Out there we walked quite friendly up to death, sat down and ate beside him, cool and bland – Pardoned his spilling mess tins in our hand, sniffed the green thick odour of his breath."' She paused. 'It comes from "The Next War" by Wilfred Owen. Did you know Owen was killed just a week before the Armistice was signed? That's tomorrow, the fourth of November. We should drink to him and celebrate our own survival.' He saw her lift her plastic cup in the light of the dashboard and shudder. 'Jesus . . .' she said.

'You're not a book editor, are you?'

'Yes, I am – and a few other things also.'

'What other things?'

'That's for another time, Con. We're alive. That's all that matters now.'

When they got back to the lodge they went straight to their cabin rather than walking through Reception. Lindow was particularly con-scious of his appearance and knew he needed to clean up before paying. In the cabin he removed his bloody shirt then sponged down his ear and jaw with warm water in front of the bathroom mirror. The cut on his ear turned out to be surprisingly small. The injury to his jaw was nastier.

Meanwhile, Mary scrutinised the lump on the back of her head by holding up a makeup mirror to it. She found a little of Lindow's blood on her shirt collar and pulled her sweater and shirt over the bruise with care. Lindow moved behind her, cupped her breasts in his hands and looked at her in the mirror. She turned in his arms. They kissed lightly, then greedily. 'I will tell you what I do,' she said, between kisses, 'but I can't yet. You must understand, Con.'

Lindow nodded in the knowledge that he hadn't been entirely open either. They began to make love urgently, slipping on the tiles of the bathroom floor before reaching the bed. There Mary straddled Lindow, climaxed quickly and slumped forward exhausted. She returned to the sitting position and rose to the point of disengagement, whereupon she lowered herself by degrees, looking down at him with an odd, distant expression.

Twenty minutes later they checked out of the lodge, telling the owner they were heading north, to Canada, an unlikely story at that time of the evening. But he seemed happy to accept it, particularly as Lindow offered to pay for the night they wouldn't be staying and added that they would certainly return when they were less busy.

They reached Boston six hours later at one thirty a.m. Mary had slept most of the way and, on arrival at the Omni Parker, was drowsily compliant to Lindow's suggestion that they should take separate rooms. The desk clerk handed her a slip of paper, saying that there had been several phone messages for her during the day. Mary read the message and tucked it into her jeans.

'What's that?' asked Lindow.

'Nothing. I told my father he could contact me here. I thought we'd be back sooner or later.' He suspected she was lying but said nothing.

Thirty-five minutes later he was sitting with Varrone relating the events of the past twenty-four hours.

'It's ingenious,' said Varrone, after Lindow had completed his account. 'This guy Rhodes obviously programmed the computer to think that a CD had been placed in the drive when it received a certain command. Thereafter it was a simple matter to wire the drive to a detonator and pack the box with plastic explosive. When the command came, hidden in one of their messages, the drive started and, boom, Lasseur gets it in the stomach. Let's have a look at these disks and see what they tell us about Rhodes.'

They went through to his workroom where he started searching the shelves for a Zip drive. At length he located an oblong blue box, about the size of a paperback, and plugged it into the back of one of his computers. He fed one of the disks into the external drive, which began to hum. An icon appeared on the blank screen, which he opened to reveal a series of numbered files. He clicked on one with his mouse and the screen filled with a patchwork of symbols and digits, as if someone had been hitting the keys and space bar at random.

'As I expected, it's encrypted. Know anything about modern cryptography, Con?' Varrone slipped another disk into the drive. 'We're going to need some serious computing power to read all this, particularly if these six disks have different codes.' He grunted as a new cyphertext appeared on the screen. 'From what you've told me, I think we ought to bring Mundy in on this now. I'll call him at home.'

'That's fine,' said Lindow, 'as long as I can be the first to take any relevant information back to the British authorities. In fact, I'd like to call Commander Foyle now.'

'Be my guest. There are several lines in the next room,' said Varrone, without looking up.

It was eight thirty a.m. in Britain when Foyle moved unhurriedly from the bathroom and picked up the phone by his bed. 'Yes,' he snapped. He was conscious of a certain opacity at the front of his head, the result of a bottle of Merlot shared with Carla Pryn over a late dinner at La Bourriche.

'It's Con Lindow. I know it's early.'

'Good heavens, don't worry about that,' said Foyle, wiping the shaving foam from his neck. 'I was hoping to hear from you. What's happening?'

'You're going to have to speak up. My hearing's not so good at the moment.'

'What's happening?' boomed Foyle.

'A lot,' said Lindow. 'There's so much I don't know where to start. The first thing I need to tell you is that Rhodes plans a further bombing. I don't know when or where, but he's got some kind of crazy operation called Axiom Day. You remember – that was the phrase I found in my brother's passport.'

'Yes, do you have any idea when?'

'No. Look, how do you want to handle this? I've got a lot to tell you. Do you want me to call when you're ready?'

'No, go ahead. I've got a pen and paper here.' Foyle settled himself on the bed and pulled the bedside table from the wall so that he could write more easily.

Lindow described the plane trip and told him how they'd spotted a cabin hidden in some rough terrain about thirty miles from the Canadian border. He related how they'd driven up there later in the day and were caught observing the place by a man whom they'd later learned was Lasseur.

'So, they're working together.'

'Were. Lasseur's dead. He was killed by an explosion today – actually yesterday. Rhodes had wired Lasseur's computer so it exploded on the receipt of a coded command.'

Foyle whistled. 'What? A kind of e-mail bomb?'

'Exactly.'

'Were you in the room?'

'Yes, he had us lying on the floor by that time so we were shielded from the blast.'

'Who's we – Mary?'

'Yes.'

'So, when the time comes, she can be a witness to everything you saw and heard in that cabin.'

'Yes, but not everything because he knocked her out when we tried to overpower him. But she definitely heard him talk about Rhodes. In fact, as I recall, she asked what Axiom Day was about. Lasseur told her that he only knew it was going to be Rhodes's statement, some kind of revenge on the British government for dealing with the IRA, letting prisoners go and so on. But there's something else. After I got Mary out of the cabin I heard Lasseur cry out. I went back. He had terrible injuries, but he was still alive. He knew Rhodes had caused the explosion and he knew he was dying. He told me that he'd backed up everything on some disks. All their messages, all the details of their plans – everything.'

'Good Lord. Have you got them?'

'Yes, but they're encrypted – it's going to take some time to decipher them. I don't know how long. I'm working on them now with Peter Varrone.'

'Tell him to keep all of this to himself. I don't want anyone to hear about these disks until we've got the whole picture and we can use the information to pin down this bastard. It's crucial that none of this comes out before we're absolutely ready – crucial for both of us. What about Mary? Does she know about the disks?'

'No, she was still unconscious while all this was happening. And I decided not to tell her about them.' He went silent.

'Con?'

'Sorry, I guess I'm pretty tired.'

'Well, I can't let you go yet, I'm afraid. It's too important.'

He then asked Lindow to imagine himself in the cabin and to describe everything he'd seen. Forty minutes later he had filled half a dozen pages of the notebook with a detailed inventory of the cabin and a record of what Lasseur had said about Rhodes and their operations. Towards the end of the conversation Foyle could feel Lindow's energy flagging. He was slurring some words and not finishing his sentences. 'Okay, Con. That's enough for the moment. There's a lot to do while we're waiting for those disks to be decoded. Where are you going to be in the next few hours?'

Lindow gave him Varrone's number.

'We'll talk later then. This is looking really good, Con. You've done marvellous work. Thank God you're safe.'

Foyle put down the phone gently, then stood up and clapped his hands together.

14

After talking to Foyle, Lindow stretched out in Varrone's sitting room and slept. Three hours later he was woken by the looming figure of Mundy, proffering a cup of coffee.

'We need you, Dr Lindow. Hey!' he exclaimed. 'You should have a real doctor take a look at that jaw.'

Lindow eased himself up and drank the coffee. Varrone came into focus, sitting on the arm of the sofa opposite. 'Thank you,' he said to Mundy. He rubbed the back of his head. 'God, I've come to hate mornings.'

'That's because you're young,' Varrone told him. 'Get to my age and you'll find mornings are accompanied by purpose rather than regret.'

'I'll look forward to that,' said Lindow sourly.

'Okay,' said Mundy. 'Let's cut to the chase here, Doctor. I need to know exactly the position of this cabin you were at yesterday. Can you point it out to me on this map here?'

Lindow peered down at a map on the coffee table and silently ran his finger north of Moosehead to a tiny strip of blue, marked Bl'k F'ger Lake. 'The cabin is on the north side of the lake. You'll find a track that branches at a sharp angle from the road here. It doesn't look promising but that's where you'll find it.'

'The wolf's lair, huh?' Mundy grinned and folded the map. 'You've certainly stirred things up, Doctor. Peter told me some of what happened yesterday. I'll go through that with you later. But at the moment I want to get some of our guys choppered up to Maine. There may be quite a lot we can recover from the cabin.'

Lindow nodded.

'We've had someone make discreet inquiries with the state police. They've received no reports of a fire, but at some stage they'll hear about it and then I guess this'll become a murder investigation. You and your friend, Miss . . . ?'

'Mary Menihan.'

'You and Miss Menihan are the only witnesses, so they'll want to interview you.'

'That'll have to wait,' Lindow said sharply. He didn't want Mundy taking over. 'What matters is the material on those disks. We need to get them decrypted, then I'll take the results to London.'

Before he could finish, Mundy had risen and was making for the door. 'Look, there's no problem here. All I want is to get this information to my people.'

'I was coming to the disks,' Varrone said, when Mundy was gone. 'They're interesting because I don't know what software they were generated in. Normally a file carries a tag to ensure that the computer recognises the type of software and responds accordingly. So the first thing I've done is to copy the header from one of the files and post it on an Internet site to see if anyone can help with the software identity. No replies yet. But we can start making some assumptions. Tell me what the set-up was – the way Lasseur sent his messages and what he did when he received them.' Varrone's hands shook. It irritated Lindow, but he checked himself, realising that his lack of sleep was the problem.

'Lasseur had a standard PC with the screen mounted on the box. There was a modem and that was about all. I think he had some sort of encryption software but I don't know whether he was using the Internet.'

'I wonder if he was using a secure modem too. It works on the same principle as a telephone scrambler and would add another layer of security. I think we may be dealing with something relatively simple here – a standard compression program, which can only be unlocked with a password consisting of an eight-character combination of letters and/or digits. People make their own choice, their mother-in-law's maiden name, a distant constellation – whatever takes their fancy. The method of compression, or the algorithm that encrypts the text, remains a secret held by the software company.'

'So in theory we could ask the software company,' said Lindow, pouring more coffee.

'Yes, but we don't know who they are – and, anyway, they're unlikely to help because it would invalidate their product if they gave it out to just anyone.'

'So what other routes are there?' asked Lindow, feeling fully awake now. 'Can we attack the password?'

'If there is a password, yes. But it's going to take huge amounts of computing time. We began to set up a relay of mainframe computers while you were asleep. I've called a few favours in, and having Frank around helps. The FBI carries weight in this area now.' Varrone paced the room, glancing across the roofs to Boston Common which, in the first light, had become a study in grey. 'We can start doing some work on the password now by pooling all the information we have on Rhodes and Lasseur, looking for areas in their backgrounds that would suggest a particular type of password.'

'That sounds damned hit-and-miss to me.'

Varrone ignored him. 'If we knew that either of these parties was religious, we could easily apply all eight-letter words in the Bible to the password, even eight-letter words that have slight spelling mistakes or where one letter is substituted by a number. For example, where the "I"s in "Divinity" are replaced by the number one. It follows that we can do this with a dictionary or any other reference book. Then it becomes a matter of time. But you can't be half right – either you get a match or you don't. The main problem now is that we can't do anything until we know what sort of software generated those files. Only then can we extract the encrypted password and start a brute-force attack.'

'You mean you can find the password in the file then feed it to the program? That doesn't seem to make sense.'

'No, the fact that you possess the password file doesn't mean that you're anywhere near compromising the encryption. Passwords are encrypted one way. There is no inverse route, you simply type in a word, the computer encrypts the word and waits for a match. If there is no match, the file stays in code. There's no way of pulling a password and reversing the encryption.'

'You know quite a lot about this, Peter.'

'A little. This is Frank's line of work now. He runs a cryptanalysis operation for the Bureau. I help him out with resources and contacts – sometimes ideas.'

'Look, there's something I need to say now. If you get anything out of those disks, it's crucial that I take the information back to London with me. If the wrong people get hold of the material it might easily be destroyed. There's official resistance to anything that links Rhodes to these bombs. That's why I'm here and why Foyle was removed from the investigation. To turn that situation around, I want to give Foyle complete access to the information before anyone else. What I'm saying is that Frank can't hand it on to MI5 or the police in some kind of act of fraternal co-operation.'

'Con, I know you've been through a lot, but cool it. There's no question of Frank jumping the gun. He's utterly straight – and, besides, his views on British law-enforcement agencies are not complimentary.' Varrone held a hand up. 'Hold on, I think I heard my e-mail come up.'

They rushed to his office and Varrone brought up the message. 'It's from some guy at Berkeley. Says the file is GenoType. Have you heard of it?'

'Yes, it's the software used by drug companies engaged in recombinant DNA technology – inventing drugs and vaccines from new combinations of genes, usually from different biological sources. In short, it means inserting a characteristic found in one organism into another.'

'Yes, yes, I'm familiar with these techniques, Con. What do we know about the software?'

'The point is that the combinations of genes have great value, so the data is stored in encrypted form to prevent theft, while the company applies for a patent and carries out more research. GenoType is a software that performs this task very quickly. But it's odd that Lasseur got hold of it. I wouldn't have thought he'd know where to find it. It's not exactly Windows.'

'It's not a problem with a software directory. He was probably just looking for an obscure encryption program. It's fast and relatively simple and, if used in conjunction with a secure modem, it would offer acceptable levels of privacy. Do you know anyone who uses it?'

'I guess I could find someone,' Lindow replied. 'But it's not going to be easy on the weekend – and, anyway, I doubt if they'd know much about the actual software.'

'True. I wonder if this individual here knows anything,' said Varrone, pointing to the e-mail still on his screen. 'I'll try him again.'

Varrone began typing a message. Lindow returned to the sitting room, helped himself to more coffee and took one of the pastries from a basket laid out by Varrone's cook.

Varrone joined him shortly. 'My Californian night owl is still awake. He's going to send me something in a few minutes.' No sooner had he finished speaking than a ping came from the computer mailbox next door.

The e-mail from California was quite specific. The password was to be found near the top of the encrypted file in a special cache. Varrone immediately located and isolated the code, then copied it into a separate file on his own system. He repeated the process with each disk, collecting six strands of code. Since there was no way of telling whether the passwords were the same he numbered the new files from one to six, and pencilled a number on the case of each corresponding disk.

'This man at Berkeley seems to know a lot about the software,' he said. 'I wonder if he's connected with the company that made it. I'll ask him later. But what we need now is to raise your friend Foyle and ask him to tell us everything he knows about the two men. I'll set up a conference call next door.'

In a few minutes Lindow, Varrone and Frank Mundy, who had returned from seeing off the helicopter mission, sat waiting for Foyle to answer his phone. At length Foyle came on. Lindow smiled. 'Hello, it's Con. We've made a little headway with these disks, but Peter Varrone, who's here with me, believes that you can help with your knowledge of Rhodes. I am also sitting here with Special Agent Frank Mundy from the FBI.'

'Is he trustworthy?'

'We're on a conference phone, Commander. This is Peter Varrone speaking. You can take my word for it that Mr Mundy has unimpeachable credentials.'

'Good.' Foyle betrayed no sign of embarrassment.

'Good morning, Commander,' said Mundy coolly, turning to a fresh page in his notebook.

'The position is this,' said Varrone. 'We have these files and possibly six passwords, which we'll need to break before decryption is possible. I have set up a relay of computers that can mount a brute-force attack, but it would be useful to narrow down the area of search. Anything you know might be helpful. We just don't know what it is.'

Foyle began with Rhodes's early years and went right through to his time as a freelance operator. Mundy wrote it all down. Lindow noticed him occasionally underlining words and phrases that might have been used. Nothing seemed to stand out and after nearly thirty minutes Foyle ran dry.

'Commander,' said Mundy, 'we shouldn't forget about the guy this end, Robert Lasseur. He was the desk man in this outfit. According to Con, he looked after the technical side of their operations, arranged supplies, kept the business records. It could be that he set the passwords.'

'I agree,' said Foyle. 'But Con met Lasseur.'

'I spent an hour in his company. The circumstances were not conducive to gaining a lot of information. But there were a couple of things I noticed. The first is that his designs incorporated devices normally associated with safety. In London they packed fire extinguishers with explosive. Up at the cabin I saw an arrangement that used an infrared detector from a burglar-alarm system. I'm certain that was a prototype booby trap. The other thing is the obsession with revenge. Lasseur mentioned Rhodes's final operation – this thing he called Axiom Day. He said something about the British government ignoring the sacrifice made by soldiers in Ulster – how the only people that were consulted were terrorists.'

'This ties in with what I've been hearing,' said Foyle. 'I'm going to have another word with Christy Calvert. He's the only other member of the Droy group still to be walking around. That's what I ought to be doing now, unless there's something else you need.'

The call ended and Mundy and Varrone went into a huddle around his computer to draw up a plan of action. Mundy already had a list of hackers and mainframe operators, who had been contacted by his office at the FBI that morning. Each one was now sent an e-mail with the encrypted passwords attached. He and Mundy divided the dictionary into eighteen sections, giving each operator one part. The Bible was divided into three sections and distributed between five large computers that used the UNIX operating system. Then Mundy got on the phone to his department and instructed a young programmer, who'd been hauled out of bed, to write the scripts that would search several smaller reference books, including a register of international radio-call signs and a history of twentieth-century military codewords. Mundy's hunch was that Rhodes and Lasseur had chosen words that had been used before in a military context.

Within two hours, some thirty people across the United States were engaged in the task of decrypting the six passwords. None had any idea of what the passwords would unlock – they just accepted Varrone's assertion that this might be a matter of life or death. He told them that when and if the situation allowed he'd make sure they all knew how important their contribution had been.

Mundy then left for his office to keep in touch with the team in Maine. Lindow grabbed a couple of hours' extra sleep, then also left, saying that he had to do something the other side of town. As he waited outside in the street for a cab, he wondered why he had kept to himself the knowledge that Eamonn had been caught on Lasseur's surveillance system. He had come close to telling Foyle during their first conversation, but had held back at the last moment. He wanted time to think about it. He hailed a cab and told the driver to take him to Kineally Street, the address of Melly's Bar, which he'd found in Varrone's Boston telephone directory.

The traffic was thin and the cab moved quickly from the city's financial district, through an area part wasteland and part hopeful regeneration, into Southey, the Irish enclave in South Boston, where the roads narrowed. They passed along several streets of identical clinker-built houses until they reached an intersection. On the far side stood Melly's Bar, a low, uninviting, red-brick block with grilles over the windows and a neon shamrock leaf advertising Budweiser beer.

It was late morning and the intersection was busy. Youths were hanging out by the local grocery store and bulky men stood about in groups, wrapped against the damp sea air that rolled up from Old Harbor. Lindow paid off the driver and entered Melly's, where a dead Saturday evening still lingered. A dozen drinkers were ranged along the bar, their upturned faces lit by the emerald green of a TV sportscast. He walked to the far end and spoke to the bartender, a young man with a stud in his ear and eyes that shifted resentfully between the action on the football field and Lindow. He ordered a beer and asked to speak to P. J. McKenna.

'Who are you?' asked the man.

'You're meant to say, "Who wants him?"' said Lindow, sliding Eamonn's passport across the bar. The man opened it then looked up. 'Are you McKenna?' asked Lindow.

The man nodded.

'My message concerns two men. One's called Rhodes, the other Lasseur. Lasseur is dead. Rhodes is presently in England. He's planning something big. The British authorities will shortly be made aware of this. They will learn that he is working on his own account.'

'And how did the other party come to be deceased?' asked the man, with a leer.

'He was killed by an explosion late yesterday afternoon. The FBI know about it and will contact the British police independently. The situation is now clarified. There is no longer any doubt about who's responsible for recent events in London. The authorities there will learn that it is Rhodes and no one else. Have you got that?'

The man nodded and started towards the TV set.

'I haven't finished, damn it.' Lindow's temper snapped and his hand moved to grip the bartender's sleeve. The man wheeled around, but something in Lindow's eyes made him lower his fist. 'You tell Chickpea, or whatever his damned name is, that my part of the deal has been completed. I expect him to leave me and my family alone now. He knows what my brother risked to help our friends. If he doesn't lay off, I will bring the entire force of the British security establishment down on him.' The last part was bullshit, but he saw that McKenna believed him. He turned and left the bar without looking back.

Outside, the street was still busy but there were no cabs in sight. Lindow swore for letting his go and began to walk in the direction of L Street. Then he spotted a cab coming from the west along Kineally Street. It slowed as it approached the intersection and, instead of crossing, came to a halt outside Melly's Bar. Somebody was about to get out. Lindow turned to run back and flag down the cab when it became free but then he saw a figure emerge, an attractive woman in a black jacket and scarf, who caused the knot of men on the other side of the street to turn their heads in unison. Lindow was seventy or eighty yards away, yet there was no mistaking Mary. He saw her bend down and say something to the driver, then enter Melly's Bar. She'd told the cab to wait.

He backed into a slight recess and watched the entrance to the bar, holding the collar of his jacket up to his face. No more than ten minutes elapsed before he saw her walk quickly from the door, look left and right, grimace at the group of men and climb into the cab. The driver did a U-turn and sped off westwards, with Mary sunk low in the back seat. She did not see Lindow.

He watched the cab disappear, blinking with anger. There was only one explanation for her sudden arrival at Melly's. She must be working for the IRA and using the same contact to send a message to them. Now everything made sense, like a problem that had been exposed to the correct formula. He'd half suspected her all along, but he cursed his stupidity none the less. It was so obvious. The IRA had used him to find the place where Rhodes and Lasseur ran their operations and they'd sent Mary along to keep track of him. They couldn't have done it without his help because they didn't possess the information that Eamonn had left. Yet they must have known that it existed. That's why Mary had come to the flat the day after he was released. But when she had found him there she had made up the bullshit story about hoping to catch him. Smart of her to ring the doorbell, instead of breaking in or using her own keys. She had turned it to her advantage and moved in on him, attending the funeral, going with him to the lake. She must have set him up. She knew that he'd be beaten and that Tag would be threatened in front of him. The whole point was to start him running, to make him use the information he'd got from Eamonn. It didn't matter that they didn't have it for themselves. As long as Mary was with him every second of the day, they'd know where he was.

And then there was the gun. Where does a book editor get a professional weapon like a Glock, if not from the back room of somewhere like Melly's Bar? That first morning in Boston she must have caught a cab out here, picked up the gun, then hired the Jeep and presented herself at the hotel with that cute smile. What an idiot he'd been, suspecting her all the time but never quite facing it. He'd been simple-minded about her from the start.

Then, as he tramped up the last rise before L Street, he began to think the situation wasn't so bad after all. For one thing, Mary must have confirmed his story about Lasseur to McKenna. The IRA would therefore know that he had told the truth. He had not wavered and they'd got everything they wanted from him or, at least, everything they could hope to get. So there was now no reason for them to continue to threaten Tag. That was the outcome and the only thing that had been hurt in all this was his pride. He could live with that, although in one way he knew that Mary was the best thing that had ever happened to him. Still, that was over now and he'd just have to live without it.

He walked on for a while, then spotted a bus going to the North End. He climbed aboard and, in a very short while, arrived at the hotel where he paid the bill and collected his things from his room.

Before he left he wondered if he should leave Mary a note. Part of him wanted to, but he couldn't think what to say.

Kirsty Laing tried all Sunday to get hold of Speerman, eventually raising him at six in the evening. He seemed mildly irritated to hear her voice.

'I hope you don't mind me ringing you at home,' she said, 'but I felt you would want to be kept abreast of things.'

Now it was her keeping him in touch, her telling him the score. It felt good to her.

'Yes?' he said.

'I had a long talk with Brown Owl earlier today. She and Lindow have been north and what they've found out is going to have grave implications for the service.'

'Does she know about Rhodes – about his past association with us?'

'Yes, she was in on it. Then Lasseur, who served with Rhodes in Northern Ireland, confirmed it. Before he was killed – I'll come to that later – he told Lindow that Rhodes was planning something big in London. That's the important point. A big operation that he called Axiom Day. God knows what it is, but she was definitely under the impression that it's imminent and well planned. So it makes Rhodes an absolute priority.'

'He already is.' Kirsty felt Speerman's manner stiffen at the other end. 'A huge proportion of the service's permanent staff of two thousand are in some way deployed to look for him.'

'And that means it will leak out eventually, however security conscious we are. But it isn't getting us anywhere, and all the time the service is being plunged deeper into the mire. Rhodes's name and our involvement with him are now bound to come out. The more we delay, the greater the risk to the general public. That's what matters now – not the politics, not the Millbank power games. It's the threat Rhodes poses to public safety. The wisest course must be to bring the police and the Home Office in on this. That way we distribute the responsibility.' She paused and took a breath for effect. 'If something goes wrong while this man is still at large and we haven't informed the police, we will take all the blame. All the blame, Peter, because our relationship with Rhodes is bound to come out. Foyle probably already knows what I know – maybe more.'

'You were going to tell me what happened in Maine,' said Speerman.

'Lasseur took both of them prisoner. It was clear he was planning to kill them because he talked openly about his and Rhodes's operations. He made no attempt to pretend otherwise. He told them that Rhodes and he were winding up their partnership. There was this one last unfinished piece of business to see to.'

'Then what happened?'

'Lasseur received some kind of coded message from Rhodes and his computer blew up. Brown Owl didn't see any of this. She was knocked out by Lasseur when they tried to disarm him. Lasseur died later. I gather the cabin was destroyed in the fire caused by the explosion.'

'Completely destroyed?'

'She said they saw the cabin still burning twenty miles away.'

'That's something, at least. But I take your point that the Americans are likely to comb through the place.'

'Yes. We must assume that Lindow has already told the FBI. Apparently a friend put him in touch and they showed him their file on Rhodes.'

'Is there no honour in our community these days?' Pompous fool, thought Kirsty. 'Tell me how the computer blew up. They don't just explode of their own accord.'

She knew he was stalling her, but she was prepared to humour him. 'The computer had been programmed to act on a hidden code – I believe it's called a TSR, terminator stays resident, a very apt description in this case. It triggered the explosion when a signal was received through the modem. Look, Peter, there's a TSR in this affair. The whole thing is ready to blow up. Are you with me or not?'

'Of course, of course,' he said.

'Does that mean yes?'

'Apart from a few minor reservations, yes.'

'Then you'll come with me to the Home Secretary tomorrow morning. It will greatly help to have you there because your rank will add weight. But, to be frank, what's going to happen is going to happen, whether you come or not.'

'Do Craven-Elms and Fuller know about the developments in the States?' he asked.

Kirsty understood that Speerman wasn't just playing for time now: he was assessing the risk involved. If the watchers section and Domestic Terrorism had heard from Brown Owl, it would only be a short time before Cantor was informed. All the advantage would be lost and the director's defence would begin in earnest. She knew enough about Cantor to appreciate that in a fight for his survival there was nothing he wouldn't do.

'I don't know whether she has made her report yet.' She kept her voice neutral. 'She could wait until tomorrow, or she might already have been in touch. My purpose in talking to her was not to persuade her to follow a particular course. It was to find out what the situation was.'

This was a direct lie. She had pleaded with Mary Menihan not to call Craven-Elms before eight a.m., East Coast time, on the following day. That meant no one would know about the events of the weekend before one p.m. in Britain. She lied because she saw no reason to make it simple for Speerman. He had to show that he wasn't merely looking after himself.

'Kirsty,' he said, in the mandarin manner that was beginning to get on her nerves, 'I'd like to sleep on this. You understand it's a very big step going straight to the Home Secretary. As far as I know, it's never been done before.'

'We've never been in such a mess before.'

'Yes, but the disloyalty entailed is very great and needs to be carefully considered.'

'Then hold your nose, Peter. When you've reached your decision you know where to contact me tomorrow.'

She realised she was on her own. Speerman hadn't even asked for the time of the appointment. He had no intention of going with her.

'Foyle's pulled it off, Con,' said Varrone, flying down the stairs. 'He's found the needle in a billion haystacks.'

Lindow put his bags down in the hallway. 'He's got all six passwords?'

'No, just two, but it was brilliant work. He interviewed a guy named Calvert, who was in the original group of soldiers, and got him to talk about Army slang and the nicknames they used for each other.' Varrone referred to a yellow legal pad. 'Two of the original group, Vincent Creech and Robert McGurk, are dead. Creech was called Muffhound or Lunchbox. Muffhound was too many letters so I tried Lunchbox, and bingo – we hit the jackpot. The encryption matched perfectly. Without Foyle's information we'd never have got it. Lunchbox is not in Webster's dictionary, so we might never have found it. By the way, why in hell would anyone be called Lunchbox?'

Lindow smiled. 'It's slang for the male genitalia, specifically in the context of athletics when the guy's shorts leave little to the imagination. They suggest a package containing lunch ... Forget it.'

'Damn British humour. But if that's obscure, listen to this one. McGurk was called Disney. You've got to use a Scotch accent to hear the joke – he *diz nay* work. It rhymes. "Robert McGurk diz nay work" – see?'

Varrone's Scots accent was poor, but Lindow got the point.

'So,' continued Varrone, 'I tried Disney with every possible combination of letters and numbers. Eventually I came up with DISNEYWK. And, hey presto, we got ourselves a fully decrypted file.'

'That's incredible,' said Lindow. 'So what's on the files?'

'I haven't opened them. You risked your life to get them, so I thought you'd like to be the first to read what's there.'

'Thanks.'

'But, before you do, I want you to look at something else for me.' They began to walk up the curved staircase. Varrone put a paternal arm round Lindow's shoulder. 'We didn't have any success in this brute-force attack, so a couple of hours ago I e-mailed the guy in California. Somehow I guessed he'd be waiting for me, and I was right. He was still awake. So I asked him outright whether he wrote the software. He wasn't going to answer that, but I pressed him and he sent me an intriguing little puzzle. I'm certain this guy wrote the program, but he's trying not to give too much away. Maybe he's a little scared. He wants to help, but can't.'

They reached the workroom. 'You know next to nothing about cryptology – right?'

'Not much.' Lindow bridled. However much he admired Varrone, the assumption that Varrone knew more than he did about any given subject grated with him.

'Well, in certain government-endorsed cryptosystems there are rumoured to be "trap-doors" – weaknesses that have been built into the program so that law-enforcement agencies can access the vast flow of digital traffic without using brute-force attacks. The idea is the cryptanalyst drops in on a particular communication, performs a rapid decryption using the trap-door, then moves on. It's a way of keeping an eye on a lot of different stuff – money-laundering operations, that sort of thing. I can't say whether these official trap-doors exist, but it wouldn't surprise me. Now, the point is that a lot of software writers out there have had the same idea. They write the program and build in a trap-door without their company ever knowing. Mostly they're just having a little fun, showing off to their peer group. Other times it's got a more sinister purpose. They include their own personal key to unlock the encryption so that at some future date they can rip off whatever's been encoded in that software. Let's say this guy out on the West Coast wrote the program and built in a trap-door that only he knows is there. It'd mean that he could read any file stored in the program – and if that happened to be research data on some new kind of disease-resistant potato or an all-purpose flu vaccine, or whatever, he would be in possession of something of real value. He could steal what he wanted without anyone suspecting, right?'

Lindow nodded.

'Say this guy has made a trap-door,' continued Varrone, 'but he can't say what it is, either because he'd be liable to a suit from the software company or he'd be laying himself open to criminal prosecution. He wants to help and he understands the urgency of the situation, but he just can't do it.' He picked up a printout of the e-mail. 'I know you want to read these files, but absorb this for a moment and see what you think. Let it marinate, Con, let it sink in and see if you can come up with anything.'

Lindow looked at the e-mail. There were two separate blocks of numbers, each arranged in two rows.

$$3\ 2\ 2\ 7\ 7\ 5$$
$$5\ 7\ 7\ 2\ 2\ 3$$

$$2\ 2\ 3\ 5\ 7\ 7$$
$$7\ 7\ 5\ 3\ 2\ 2$$

'It doesn't mean anything to me,' he said, 'except that both blocks can be read either way – they're symmetrically arranged and the groups are combinations of the first four prime numbers.'

'Yes, but there must be something else to them. I've got a couple of kids from the math department seeing if they can spot any special properties. Anyway, let's have a look at the files.'

Lindow folded the printout of the numbers and put it in his wallet.

Varrone typed in LUNCHBOX with a flourish. The screen filled with several dozen icons, each representing a separate document.

He clicked on an icon at the top left of the screen. It opened and they began to read.

Lake to Scalper: Collection of supplies underway by Shrodinger. Rendezvous at Pizek due sth of Pilszen 23.00 hours / 23. 3. Casmar Brath has sent $US 20K for payment to usual destination.

Scalper to Lake: Nothing doing. He didn't show. Is this man reliable? I've taken contract so cannot disappoint. Sincerely hope he produces necessary goods by Monday (26.3). Will wait for him at previous rendezvous. No fuck-ups this time. Has transfer gone through? $US60K sent to BA no 3476/78949276 acc 2. Confirm receipt.

Scalper to Lake: Supplies received and stored. Will move in due course. Two CCs needed in name of Richard K. Holmes. Expedite without delay.

Scalper to Lake: Closure. Contract completed. Final payment routed through Korean Bank. Should be in Melbourne (Account 42751684/04SZ). Retrieve asap. Parties satisfied. More contracts on offer – one v. hazardous with price tag of US$150K. Negotiate up by 50K – two-thirds to be deposited in Georgia State Agro on acceptance. Information needed on cellphone set-up in Hungary. CCs not here yet. Get a grip.

Varrone frowned. 'Foyle told me that Scalper is Rhodes's nickname. Lake presumably refers to Lasseur. Does the rest mean anything to you?'

'Yes,' said Lindow, feeling a rare, nervous excitement. 'It could be very important. There were two explosions in Eastern Europe which were thought to be terrorist actions but turned out to be assassinations, each aimed at one individual. A cellphone was used in both cases. That's why the last lines are important. They might be crucial in linking Rhodes with the technique used in London.'

Varrone began to print out the documents so that Lindow could read them on paper. In all there were forty-one documents in the LUNCHBOX disk. Most were brief, telegraphic communications between Rhodes and Lasseur, conducted in the commercial language of a shipping agent. The pattern seemed to be that Rhodes would go out and find the business while Lasseur was left to arrange the details and delivery of any special equipment needed. Their field of operations extended through Eastern Europe and Turkey. Occasionally Scalper's rovings would take him back to the British Isles, though for what purpose was unclear. He occasionally made terse remarks about England – 'Fucking bad weather. Dripping noses and crap food. Leave Saturday,' was one that made Lindow smile. But, in general, a hectoring note pervaded Scalper's communications – he was a martinet, endlessly complaining that equipment wasn't good enough, or that it had arrived late. By contrast, Lasseur seemed amenable and compliant, making suggestions rather than issuing instructions. Both showed an acute interest in the financial side of the operations. One document appeared to be a kind of profit-and-loss account. After expenses, money held in fourteen different bank accounts totalled US$367,000. On receipt of this information, Rhodes had apparently queried the division of spoils, arguing that a one-third/two-thirds split was unjust. He claimed that a one-quarter/three-quarters division better reflected the effort he put into the 'marketing and sales operation'. Lasseur agreed without complaint and transferred Rhodes's share ($275,250) to a bank in Buenos Aires, routed through Antigua. He attached a warning that Rhodes should lose no time in distributing the funds to other bank accounts or investing in securities.

Lindow read the forty or so sheets again, trying to work out a chronology. The messages were undated, but it was possible to place them in a rough sequence by using internal evidence. Judging from Rhodes's movements and the amount of business transacted, the period covered by the LUNCHBOX disk might be anything up to two years.

The DISNEYWK disk was altogether less interesting, but Lindow knew that what seemed dull to the casual eye might prove exceptionally interesting to Foyle. In one message Lasseur described taking delivery of the plane and the arrangements made for a regular fuel stop over the Canadian border. He had had a bad winter, with an emergency generator breaking down and constant problems with the plane's ignition system. Evidence that the pair had accumulated a great deal of money was shown in the figure of US$747,000 that appeared in a message to Rhodes, which didn't satisfy him: he repeated in several different messages that they needed to put the business on a firmer footing, and rely less on one-off contracts. Lindow assumed that these were 'hits'. At any rate, it was clear that Lasseur had taken this to heart. There were records of the companies he had set up, the names of lawyers and banks that had been used and a list of company names, with the ostensible trading purpose entered alongside each one. Lakeside Electronics operated out of Chicago and was a retailer of electrical components. Ridgeway Hyde Inc was based in Alabama and had interests in British Columbia. Dix Metal Salvage, operating in Philadelphia, specialised in the recycling of valuable alloys. Invoice numbers were listed, along with payment receipts, bank statements, consignment numbers, the dates of their arrival and dispatch. In some cases, the original paperwork appeared on the screen, copied into the computer's memory by a portable scanner.

Lasseur had undeniable talents as an accountant and bookkeeper. Lindow imagined him out there in the wilderness, diligently constructing the network of cover operations and bank accounts, then moving to the workbench to design some new device for Rhodes. He was a kind of

Jeeves, the terrorist's gentleman who anticipated his master's every need and was locked into service by the unalterable fact of that scarred face.

Then a couple of lines in one of Rhodes's messages caught Lindow's attention. He read them again.

Have agreed to take on two jobs in US for Millbank boys. Will not make us rich, but may provide opportunities in the future for bigger deals. Also good to keep up contacts with Millbank. Jobs do not require special equipment. Will need to collect papers and CCs in name of R. C. Cannon within two–three weeks from friends in Baltimore.

'I may have something really important here,' Lindow told Varrone, who was also engrossed in a mass of messages. 'I'm going to call Foyle. Did you tell him that the nicknames got us into two of the files?'

'Christ, I forgot.' Varrone slapped his head.

'It doesn't matter – I'll tell him.'

Foyle answered on the second ring.

'We've got the Crown Jewels – or whatever the equivalent is in police terminology. Two of the nicknames worked as passwords. The two dead men from Droy, LUNCHBOX and DISNEY.'

'That's marvellous. What's in the files?'

'Pretty much everything – a complete and detailed record of all their activities. Well, not all because there are still four disks to unlock. We're missing four out of six passwords.'

'Give me a summary of what you've got so far.'

'Rhodes seems to have had some contact with the security service, and quite recently – there are references to Millbank and the Millbank boys. You used that phrase. Millbank is MI5, right?'

'Yes, it is. This is exactly what I needed. Well done.'

'You did it with the nicknames.'

'What else have you got? Any mention of Axiom?'

'No, but there's a lot of detail – bank accounts, cover operations, supply lines, messages between Rhodes and Lasseur. And there's the other four disks still to come.' Lindow became aware of Foyle talking to someone in the background. 'Did you hear that?'

'Yes, yes. We've just been discussing when you should come back. I think we need you back here as soon as possible – by tomorrow morning. Meantime can you fax everything you've got to me at home?' He gave the fax number from June Foyle's machine.

'Yep, that's okay. I'll come tonight. I expect I'll have to catch the shuttle from Boston to New York and get the last flight from JFK.'

'Let me know which airline and I'll pick you up first thing in the morning. That should avoid any problems you might have with that duff passport of yours. Oh, by the way, have you got any cash?'

'Yes, a lot.'

'Then pay for your ticket with it, just in case someone's looking at your credit-card transactions.'

Lindow put the phone down. 'He wants me to go tonight. What shall we do about the rest of it?'

'Nobody's been in touch, so I guess we'll have to chip at it through the week. You never know, the kids working with the number blocks may come up with something, or we could get lucky with the computer search – there are a lot of people out there working on this problem. I'll copy the disks on to my system and make some more copies to be on the safe side. You should take the original set, plus a printout. And you've got that copy of the e-mail with the number blocks.'

Lindow nodded. 'Should we give this to Frank Mundy now?'

'Sure. Give him everything now, just so long as he agrees not to release it to the Brits before you get to London. You can make a trade so he tells you what they find up in the cabin. Sounds to me as if you're going to need everything you can lay your hands on to catch this guy.'

Lindow called all the airlines and eventually got a reservation on the overnight flight from New York to London. Then he prepared to leave the house. He put the e-mail from the West Coast in his pocket, then slipped the disks and printout into his hand luggage. Varrone saw him off at his gate. Lindow was not usually demonstrative, but now he was overwhelmed with gratitude and clasped Varrone to his chest. 'You've been a real friend, Peter. I thank you from the bottom of my heart.'

Varrone looked more than a little taken aback, and as Lindow climbed into the cab he noticed the other man's hands go into their water-shaking spasm.

15

By the time the first sheets from Boston began to unfurl from the fax, six people were gathered in Kenneth Foyle's living room. A little over an hour earlier he'd summoned Graham Forbes, Sergeant Pennel, WPC Nancy Longmore and Detective Constable Kepple. With varying degrees of reluctance and scepticism, they made their way to Wimbledon, bearing the lap-top computers and mobile phones he'd urged them to bring. Finally Katherine Foyle burst through the front door of the family home, having been told by her father a little earlier in the day to come from Bristol to help with some urgent typing. The expressions of Stephen Pennel and Jim Kepple lightened somewhat with the appearance of Foyle's striking offspring.

He handed each of them a drink, then told them of the extraordinary developments in the States. He took the story at a gallop, without bothering to deploy his usual layers of supporting detail. For this was no theory – not even a wild version of the facts – but the truth. Con Lindow had located the hideout of two former British Army officers. One of them, Lieutenant Robert Lasseur, who was now dead, had admitted to Lindow that his old Army colleague, Ian Valentine Rhodes, was responsible for the three explosions. The first had been designed specifically to kill Eamonn Lindow, who was a senior member of the IRA's intelligence section. The other two were contract bombs. Rhodes was believed to be planning another spectacular attack, codenamed Axiom Day.

Foyle set up one of the lap-tops and continued his story. 'By last week it was plain that Rhodes had no further use for Lasseur. Their partnership was at an end so he arranged for Lasseur's death by sending a signal to a computer that had been primed to blow up.' Foyle made a key stroke on the lap-top. 'In other words, he e-mailed the command to the bomb. Lasseur died soon afterwards from injuries to his stomach. This happened last night about ten.' He paused and straightened from the computer. The expressions around the room were grave. Katherine looked at her father with new eyes. 'That's the sort of man we're dealing with. He is probably the most dangerous assassin at large in the world today. Rhodes is resourceful, cunning, highly trained and imaginative. So far he's made fools of us. But now we have an advantage. We know that he is planning a dramatic outrage in Britain. But more important is that, unknown to Rhodes, Lasseur kept computer records of their dealings. Before he died he was able to tell Con Lindow where six encrypted disks were concealed. Lindow took them from Lasseur's base in Maine and they are presently being decrypted in Boston.'

Right on cue, Lindow's call came through, telling Foyle that two disks had yielded their secrets and that there were vague references to MI5. While they spoke, the first file from the LUNCHBOX disk shuddered out of the fax machine.

'That was Lindow,' said Foyle, turning from the phone to look down at the fax. 'There is another aspect to this, which I have known about since Friday evening and which is now established in these files. Ian Rhodes worked for the security service, which in part accounts for the difficulty we've had investigating this case. The files will show the extent of their association. These details must remain secret, which is why I have chosen each of you to help me sort through the evidence that will come from Boston over the next few hours. I know I can rely on you not to talk about what you read tonight. So, let's get to it.'

Katherine suggested that she make copies of the fax at the late-night grocery around the corner. She set up a run between Foyle's house and the shop, which was persuaded to stay open by the production of Pennel's warrant card. At length each person had a complete set of the seventy-eight-page fax. Then the group assembled around Foyle's dining table and began sifting through the files and separating the information into three broad categories: operating methods, evidence of past crimes and intelligence about future actions.

There was little of the last category but plenty of the first two. After an order of pizzas had been delivered and consumed, Katherine and Nancy Longmore began to type up the first coherent accounts of the activities of Rhodes and Lasseur. Katherine's document consisted of several tables: a roll-call of contacts referred to in the communications between Rhodes and Lasseur, a list of banks and account numbers mentioned, and a roster of suppliers who furnished them with explosives, timers, detonators and other equipment. To this Graham Forbes added a rough chronology that he'd distilled from Lasseur's electronic correspondence with various banks. Their patterns of business, the way they'd cultivated their client list and Rhodes's remarkable operating range were all suddenly brought into focus.

Nancy Longmore's draft co-ordinated all references to Rhodes's use of explosives and the clues about the way he planned and researched his jobs. There was evidence of the meticulous care he took to equip himself with a new identity for each operation and important hints about the way they marketed themselves on the Internet. Each observation was cross-referenced with a page number from the original fax so that when the members of SO 13 came to read the papers next morning, as Foyle fully intended, they would be able to get a quick grasp of the new information.

At two thirty a.m they broke for coffee, made by Katherine. As she brought the tray into the sitting room, the phone rang. Foyle answered a call from a friend of his daughter in Bristol. She listened, then replaced the handset. 'We've just been raided by the police.' She was looking at her father aghast. 'The drugs squad in Bristol. They only searched my room. Nowhere else. Just my room!'

Foyle laid an arm on her shoulder. 'Don't worry. I was expecting it, which is half the reason I wanted you up here.' Everyone except Forbes looked baffled. 'It's fine. Just someone's fun and games. Now we've got all this I'm afraid they're going to have to call it a day.'

He sat down again at the head of the dining table and momentarily considered the strangeness of the situation. Four of the people in the room had not reached thirty. Only Forbes and himself had seen their fortieth year. And yet it fell to this group to unravel one of the greatest scandals in British public life, a very great secret, which in a matter of hours would hurtle through Whitehall.

He drained his coffee and started to write a complete review of the case, leading off with the evidence that had come from America and describing how it fitted with the results of his own informal inquiries. Then came the revelation of Rhodes's past association with MI5, which he stated as a matter of unassailable fact, backing it up with three further references to the security service that had been found in the decrypted files. Foyle cited the payment of nine thousand dollars received by one bank, and placed this against Rhodes's report of 'closure'. The word closure appeared many times, and in most cases it meant that a person had been executed. This was the probable outcome of Rhodes's meeting with two American citizens who had supplied arms to the IRA. There was good reason to believe that members of the security service were aware of Rhodes's involvement in these deaths. They were also fully aware of his presence in Britain and of his possible involvement with the bombings. The motives were clear to the security service, yet they had withheld this evidence.

He moved on to the danger now presented by Rhodes, who was evidently planning an attack in the near future, probably in London. The events in the USA suggested that he intended Axiom, as he called it, to be a final horrific gesture. When the remaining files were decoded there might be more to go on, but Lasseur had told Lindow that he knew only that it was to be Rhodes's 'statement'. Plainly the two had not discussed Axiom.

The review ran over seven pages and ended by recommending an immediate concentration of police and MI5 resources in the hunt for Ian Rhodes; a publicity campaign in which the country was made aware of Rhodes's appearance, using pictures from Army files; a survey of the cellphone networks in London and other major cities that would determine the ability to shut down particular networks at short notice; a news black-out on the events in the USA so that Lindow's survival and the existence of the disks remained secret; and a thorough psychological profile of Rhodes, to be undertaken immediately. Foyle had many more minor recommendations, but that would do for the present.

By now it was four thirty a.m. Foyle checked what he had written, then asked Forbes to go through it.

'It's very powerful and persuasive,' Forbes concluded. 'The only point I'd argue with is where you say that MI5 intentionally suppressed evidence.'

'I was paid a visit late on Friday evening by a curious woman who refused to give me her name. She was plainly from Millbank, though I'm certain she came on her own behalf. She was concerned about what Lindow might discover in the United States and asked me to let her know when I was close to exposing Rhodes. She said that she wanted to avoid meltdown in the security service – that wasn't her phrase but it was what she meant. She gave me a bloody lecture about the good work that would be lost to the nation if the service was discredited. But the important point, apart from her inadvertently confirming practically everything I suspected, was that Millbank had gathered evidence that Rhodes was in the vicinity of the first bomb.'

'What was she up to?'

'It was all very bizarre, but I believe she was genuinely concerned about the ability of the service to operate if all this came out.'

Forbes thought for a moment. 'I'd take it out if I were you. It's the only part that isn't backed by hard evidence. It means that you've got a card you can play later.'

Foyle deleted the sentences. Then he signed and dated the paper as it juddered from the printer and placed it in a large brown envelope with a copy of the original and the two memoranda typed up by Katherine and Nancy Longmore.

'Right, this is what happens now.' He rose from his place at the table to address his little team. 'You leave all the copies of the decrypted files and your notes with Graham Forbes. When you see these papers again, you may notice certain deletions. For instance, the references to the security service may disappear. This is for a good reason. I am not in the business of revelation for its own sake. I simply want this investigation to get under way as soon as possible. No purpose will be served by their humiliation. The fact that they will shortly understand the extent of our knowledge will be enough for us to get what we want. Our job is to catch this lunatic, not act as some kind of government ombudsman. So I want an assurance from each one of you that nothing will pass your lips on the subject of Rhodes or Millbank. This is very important. The second point is that you must keep Lindow out of all discussions until you hear otherwise. Is that all understood?'

The group nodded in unison.

'Okay. Pennel, Kepple and I are going to Heathrow to collect Lindow, who'll be arriving in a couple of hours' time.' He held up the envelope. 'Inspector Forbes will deliver this to Sir Derek Crystal at the Cabinet Office. Graham, if he isn't available, find out where Adam Durie is and give it to him. Don't take no for an answer. Say it's a matter of national security and make sure you stay there until it's been read. Then tell them I'm coming in with the chief witness. I should be at the Cabinet Office by eight thirty a.m. Nancy, I want you to go into the department as normal and dream up ways of explaining the absence of Forbes, Kepple and Pennel. Not a word about anything, mind. Just lie through your teeth.' He stretched, raising his arms like the Angel of the North. 'So I'll see you all in a few hours.'

Lindow tried to sleep on the flight from New York, but couldn't keep his mind still. The last few days had merged into one long day that was still nowhere near ending, and now his body was so high on adrenaline that he simply couldn't rest. It was as if he had become trapped in the action of a clumsy dream sequence, in which, as part observer and part player, he stumbled through a series of ultra-vivid setpieces.

An hour out from Heathrow breakfast was served. Lindow drank his coffee and pondered the e-mail from Varrone's Californian night owl, the man they were sure had designed the GenoType software. His neighbour, a middle-aged Englishwoman with a leathery tan and spectacles on a gold chain, let her curiosity get the better of her. 'Do you mind me asking what in heaven's name that is?' she said, wafting a heavy scent towards Lindow. 'You've been staring at it for half an hour now.'

'It's a palindrome,' Lindow told her, without thinking. 'You know – when something reads the same forwards as it does backwards. It's like one of those phrases "Madam, I'm Adam" or "Live not on evil".'

'But why?' she persisted.

'It's part of a scientific problem I'm working on.'

'Oh, I see,' she said, no wiser, and returned to her breakfast.

Lindow looked at the numbers again.

$$3\ 2\ 2\ 7\ 7\ 5$$
$$5\ 7\ 7\ 2\ 2\ 3$$

$$2\ 2\ 3\ 5\ 7\ 7$$
$$7\ 7\ 5\ 3\ 2\ 2$$

The blocks were all palindromes. There were only four elements to each block – the numbers 2, 3, 5 and 7. They were prime numbers, but maybe that wasn't important. Palindromes occurred somewhere else in nature along the sequences of DNA. He borrowed a small gold diary pencil from his neighbour and wrote:

$$A = 2$$
$$C = 3$$
$$G = 5$$
$$T = 7$$

Then, using this key, he matched the numbers to letters which he wrote above and below the rows of numbers.

```
C A A T T G
3 2 2 7 7 5
5 7 7 2 2 3
G T T A A C

A A C G T T
2 2 3 5 7 7
7 7 5 3 2 2
T T G C A A
```

He studied it for a while, trying to seize hold of the thing that was flitting about in his memory.

Then the seat-belt sign came on. Within a few minutes the 747 had slipped from the darkness and lined up over the illuminated circuit boards of London, heading for Heathrow. They landed and taxied to the terminal. But there was a problem. The captain asked everyone to remain seated until a party had boarded the plane and made an inspection. Lindow looked towards the front of the plane to club class. Several businessmen, who had grabbed their coats and luggage, were being told firmly to sit down. A lot of interest was being directed at the three men making their way through the cabin. Eventually Lindow saw the unmistakable bulk of Kenneth Foyle.

'Ah, here he is,' boomed Foyle. 'I'm afraid we must ask you to come with us, sir.'

Lindow blushed, climbed over his neighbour and searched for his bags in the overhead locker.

'Just point them out to us,' said Foyle formally. 'We'll bring them for you.'

They left the plane and walked to Immigration. 'I'm sorry about this.' Foyle broke into a smile. 'Bloody Special Branch started kicking up, so I pulled rank and told them it was a matter of national importance that I make an arrest. Now, give me your passport. Pennel is going to put some handcuffs on you for the benefit of Immigration and HM Customs. Just look guilty.'

Foyle flashed the passport and his identity at one of the duty officers, who waved them through. There was no sign of anyone at Customs and they walked briskly out of the terminal to the car, where Pennel released Lindow from the handcuffs.

Forty minutes later they reached Whitehall. The time was eight five a.m. Foyle told Lindow that the papers had been delivered to Sir Derek Crystal's office earlier that morning. He should have digested them by now. They were shown into a small anteroom by a bustling young man. Lindow noticed the flicker of alarm that entered his small blue eyes as he stared at Lindow's hiking boots, which still bore the traces of dirt from a hillside in Maine.

Foyle must have noticed it too. 'Is there some kind of problem?' he asked.

'No, no!'

'Good. This gentleman hasn't been to bed for at least two days. So perhaps Her Majesty's Government might see its way to providing a pot of coffee.'

The young man retreated, saying he'd see what he could do.

'You look bloody rough, Con,' said Foyle. 'How did you get that bruise on your jaw – Lasseur?'

'Yes, but it's not a problem.'

'What about Mary? Where's she?'

'That's another story. I guess she must be still in Boston. We haven't seen each other since yesterday.'

Foyle frowned quizzically.

Outside in the corridor they heard secretaries and civil servants arriving for work. The door opened and Sir Derek Crystal entered, looking worried. The cleft in his forehead was long and deep.

Foyle introduced Lindow, then Forbes.

'This is an extremely serious, not to say complex, situation,' said Sir Derek, closing the door behind him. 'I've sent a copy of your remarkable document to Number Ten for the Prime Minister's immediate attention. I'd like you to come to my office. We can discuss it there.'

Lindow and Foyle followed him, while Forbes made his excuses and slipped away. As they passed along the corridors, Lindow attracted one or two strange looks but took no notice. He was still pursuing the train of thought that had come to him on the plane.

They reached Sir Derek's office, a large, airy room that overlooked Horse Guards Parade and St James's Park. Sir Derek gestured to a tray of coffee and biscuits.

'When I started reading this document I expected that there would be much that was unreliable or lacked evidence. But I find I cannot argue with your evidence, your logic or your conclusions. It is clear that this man Rhodes has got to be found as a matter of national urgency. It is also clear that there has been a grave attempt to divert the proper course of this investigation. That's why we owe you both a debt of gratitude. That should be said before anything else.'

Lindow hardly noticed his remarks. He knew he had approached the threshold of a solution. He had the sensation that something was fixing itself in his mind, like a photograph in a developing tray. He pulled out his wallet and unfolded the number blocks to stare at them once more. 'I think I've got it,' he said slowly. 'In fact I'm certain I have. Do you mind if I use your phone?'

Sir Derek looked at Foyle. 'What have you got, Dr Lindow?' he said.

'I think I know how we can unlock those other four disks. Can I use your phone?'

He was on his feet and requesting the dialling code before Sir Derek had time to nod. He dialled Boston and waited, looking at Foyle. 'There may be another way into the disks without using passwords.' He began speaking into the phone. 'Peter, it's Con here, I think I know what those numbers are. They're recognition sites. Hold on a moment. I'm with some people here – do you mind if they listen in on this?'

Sir Derek moved to his desk and pressed a button. Lindow put the receiver down and continued talking. 'Have those kids had any luck with the number blocks?'

'No,' said Varrone. 'I'd heard nothing by the time I went to bed a couple of hours ago.'

'There's a good reason for that. It's not a math problem – well not strictly. What I think he has given us are recognition sites. You can think of them as gateways, or docking points, which appear periodically along human DNA. In most cases the enzyme recognises the gateway because it is a palindrome – the base pairs of DNA read the same way forwards as backwards.'

'Where does that get us? We've got numbers, not letters.'

'The guy in California expects us to replace the numbers with letters. All we have to do is substitute the numbers 2, 3, 5 and 7 with the letters A, C, G and T which, as you know, stand for the chemicals that make up DNA – adenine, cytosine, guanine and thymine. We don't know yet which letters substitute which numbers, but you understand the general principle?'

'Yes, I'm there.'

'Good.' Lindow darted an encouraging smile at Foyle and Sir Derek, who both looked mystified. 'The man who wrote that software obviously knew something about genetics. When he built his trap-door in the software's encryption system he used the idea of these gateways. A basic one would be A C G T T G C A. There are others which involve ten letters. Each palindrome attracts an enzyme, produced by a particular bacteria. That is the crucial point. Are you with me?'

'Yes,' said Varrone, his voice rising in the still air of Sir Derek's office. 'You think the first part of the decryption is based on these gateways and the second part utilises the chemical make-up of the enzyme which enters via the gateway.'

'Exactly, exactly,' said Lindow. 'If we can work out which numbers should be replaced by A, C, G and T, it will be simply a matter of looking up the recognition site in the standard reference books.'

'Then we'll know which bugs it attracts.'

'Yes, yes.'

'I'll make a start now. Where're you going to be?'

'I don't know – I'll call you in a couple of hours.' Lindow hung up.

He looked up at Foyle and Sir Derek and saw they were still struggling. He reached across the desk for a piece of paper then drew a diagram.

ACGTCG
GCTGCA   <   Protein sequence of enzyme

TGCAAG
GAACGT   <   Protein sequence of enzyme

'On the left,' he said, 'there are two blocks of letters. These are the gateways I've been talking about. Sequences like these occur along the three billion units of human DNA and they're special because they attract the enzymes made by certain bacteria. What we have to do is work out which gateways we have been given. That will tell us which enzymes they attract. Then we feed the whole lot to the encrypted software.'

'When you say "feed", what do you mean?' asked Foyle.

'We'll input the blocks of letters on the left here. This will alert the program that another set of letters is about to be presented.'

'I'm not sure I understand,' said Foyle.

'Look, it's simple,' said Lindow with a flash of impatience. 'We're building a gateway in each encrypted disk, through which we're going to pour hundreds of letters. Then the file will simply unscramble itself.'

'Good, I'm glad you think it's so promising. Now,' Sir Derek turned to Foyle, 'what I have to tell you, Commander, is that the Prime Minister has already decided that you will be reinstated at SO 13 – that is to say, your enforced leave has ended as from this moment. The commissioner is being informed by the Home Secretary, who I gather had some hint of this affair. Early this morning he had a meeting with a high-ranking officer in the security service. She gave him an outline of the affair that you have told us about in your briefing, although her version was naturally nothing like as detailed and included none of the intelligence from the United States.'

Foyle smiled.

'You were aware of this dissent in the security service, Commander?'

'Yes, I had a curious approach from a woman on Friday evening. She wanted to know how close I was getting to Rhodes.'

'Well, it was undoubtedly the same person who talked to the Home Secretary. It was admirably principled of her – and timely, too, because it meant that the Prime Minister had confirmation of the main allegations in your briefing without having to instigate an investigation. That means that we can move now. At eleven thirty there will be a full meeting of the Joint Intelligence Committee, which you will address. It would be helpful if you were to play down the connection between Rhodes and the security service. Everyone in the room will guess or know anyway. Our purpose must now be to move forward in a united effort to apprehend Rhodes.'

'Does this mean there won't be any sort of inquiry into their behaviour?' asked Foyle. 'I mean, it amounts to a criminal conspiracy, to say nothing of the commission of criminal acts on foreign soil.'

'Yes, yes, Commander, I have already indicated that the Prime Minister takes this very seriously indeed, and you can be assured that action will follow. But, as I say, we must put this aside until Rhodes is behind bars. MI5 is still a formidable intelligence service, and over the coming days you will need its resources.' He paused. 'However, I would say that, given your unequalled understanding of the case, it would be wise for them to comply with your wishes and offer you every assistance.'

'I'll believe it when I see it.'

'By mid-morning there will be no doubt in their minds as to who's running this investigation,' he said, rising and buttoning his jacket. 'So, we'll meet in a couple of hours, Commander. Dr Lindow, it has been a great pleasure. Thank you for all your efforts.'

They left the building and passed into Whitehall. 'That was our moment of triumph, believe it or not,' said Foyle, waving to Pennel, who was parked a little way up the street. 'It never gets better than that, so don't hold your breath for the victory parade. Look, I'm afraid I'm going to need your help on these final disks. I hope you won't mind coming with me now.'

Lindow nodded. He was anxious to get to another screen.

'I have some more bad news,' Foyle continued. 'We're going to have to keep you under guard in a hotel. I can't risk Rhodes hearing that you're still alive. He knows your telephone number. It follows that he also knows your address.'

The moment Speerman entered Cantor's office he knew something had gone terribly wrong. Keith Craven-Elms and Angus Grove were there, both looking appalled.

'Why haven't we heard from Brown Owl?' Cantor demanded, in an accusatory hiss. 'Where the hell's her report? You told me she was glued to Lindow – he couldn't move without us knowing about it. But now he's miraculously back in Britain along with a complete record of Rhodes's activities. Did she know about these disks? If so, why did she not inform us? Where is she? Keith?'

'We thought she was out of contact. There was no way of getting hold of her over the weekend. She was with Lindow all the time and wasn't expected to make contact until this morning.'

'Well, find her, damn it. You must all realise how important she is to us now.'

Speerman immediately saw Cantor's escape route. He was going to use Brown Owl's assignment to show that the security service, far from wishing to suppress information about Rhodes, was active in his pursuit. That Lindow had suddenly returned to Britain with information he'd kept from Brown Owl could not – and should not – be used to discredit the service's motives.

The case would take some building, but it was not beyond Cantor. His survival would now depend on two things: the extent to which the security service was implicated by the disks and his ability to demonstrate that MI5 had no knowledge of Rhodes's presence in London during the bombings. The second would be easy enough: the secret film taken by one of Weegee's cameras two weeks ago had almost certainly hit the incinerator, although there were probably some stills hanging around. The disks were a bigger problem. He would have to find out exactly what was on them and prepare his defence accordingly. Speerman concluded that the odds were marginally in Cantor's favour. While Rhodes was free, there was no question of any action being taken against him and that meant there was everything to fight for.

The meeting broke up with the director general urging Grove to use every contact he possessed to acquire a copy of Lindow's disks.

Kirsty Laing was sitting in her office running through the conversation she'd had over breakfast with the Home Secretary when Speerman entered.

'Well, it's broken. The Prime Minister and the Home Secretary have spoken to the director general already. Lindow has brought some important material back from that place in Maine, some computer disks, apparently. These enabled Foyle to produce a briefing overnight, which was delivered to the Cabinet Secretary this morning.'

'Really?' Kirsty Laing licked cappuccino froth from her finger.

'It means that your plan to talk to the Home Secretary has been overtaken by events. The cat is very much out of the bag. The government knows everything they need to know and you don't have a lever any longer.'

'I see.' She tried to look anxious. 'Well, that's that, then. As you know, I've only been concerned that we don't put our interest before the public's safety. Clearly that will not be allowed to happen now.'

'A small piece of advice, Kirsty.' Speerman's manner made her think that 'threat' would have been a better word. 'Don't put money on the director general going. If I were you, I'd do everything in my power to secure the information on those disks.'

'I'll do whatever I can.'

Speerman departed abruptly. Laing saw exactly the way he was playing it. If Cantor fell, Speerman would be sufficiently remote from the involvement with Rhodes to be considered his natural successor. If, on the other hand, Cantor survived, Speerman's loyalty during the crisis could never be doubted.

She looked out of her window on to the car park below and allowed herself a smile. The timing was perfect. The appearance of Lindow had occurred at exactly the right moment. Everything would be blamed on him and no one in the service would have the slightest idea about her *tête-à-tête* with the Home Secretary.

She picked up the phone and dialled the number of the new hotel, the one to which Brown Owl had moved instead of flying straight back to London.

'I'm going, I'm going,' said Scarratt petulantly as Foyle opened the door. Foyle knew that the assistant commissioner had only received the news of his reinstatement a few minutes earlier, but he wanted him out straight away.

'Where're my pictures?' he demanded, looking at the bare walls.

'They're down there, by the filing cabinet,' said Scarratt. 'I found them distracting. Everything else should be as you left it.'

'Good.'

'I wish someone would tell me what's going on.' Scarratt gathered a dozen files into his arms. 'This is no way to conduct a proper investigation.'

'You're quite right. We've lost a week because of you and your friends down at Millbank. Now, if you don't mind, I've got a lot to do.'

Scarratt tucked the files under his arm and marched stiffly from the office.

'Bloody fool,' murmured Foyle, bending down to pick up one of his watercolours.

Lindow was put in the adjacent room, where Foyle's video and TV were kept – the very place in which Foyle had first set eyes on him, caught in the murky footage from the Clarence Street security camera. Pennel came in bearing a computer, connected it to a phone line, then left him to his own devices.

Half an hour later, having gone through his plans with Forbes, Foyle walked to the briefing room to address his staff. The room was packed and humming. He moved to the front, nodding to one or two of the officers, then waited for the talk to die down. He was guilty, perhaps, of waiting just a bit longer than he needed. He coughed once. 'As I was saying,' he began.

The room exploded with laughter. Foyle waved for silence.

'Thank you,' he said, the brief smile vanishing quickly. 'As I was saying . . . a week ago, we have a serious problem with a terrorist bomber. We now know his name to be Ian Valentine Rhodes. He has planted three devices in London already and information brought from America last night indicates that he's planning at least one further attack. I believe we have very little time. But we've got an advantage – we now know a great deal more about Rhodes than he suspects. Even he is unaware that the information now in our possession exists, and we must keep it that way. Two disks from a computer at his American base were decrypted last night and they provide us with remarkable insights into his working methods, his contacts and his psychological state. The remaining files will, I hope, be unscrambled today.'

Foyle signalled to an officer at the back of the room, who dimmed the lights and turned on a projector. The screen behind Foyle was filled with a picture of a young soldier in regimental uniform with a cap tucked formally under his arm. He possessed a cautious smile and small dark eyes that gave nothing away. His blond, possibly light red, hair showed the beginnings of baldness.

'This is Rhodes aged twenty-two,' said Foyle. 'The photograph was supplied by the MoD this morning, as were these shots.'

The room was silent as three further photographs were flashed on the screen in quick sequence. In the first two Rhodes wore the same neutral smile. The last picture showed a group of four soldiers in fatigues, carrying a selection of unorthodox weapons. Rhodes was second from the right, the only member of the group without a beret. His left thumb was tucked into his belt, his right hand supported an Armalite rifle. Strapped across his body was the belt of another weapon that looked like a long-barrelled sniper's rifle. A tuft of hair glinted in the slanting sun. Rhodes didn't smile along with the others.

'This was taken in the late summer of 1982 for a military publication. Rhodes was about thirty. He had just returned from the Falklands – or, rather, Argentina,' said Foyle. 'At the time the SAS and Fourteen Intelligence Company, of which Rhodes was a member, were very active in Northern Ireland. This picture shows four of the six members of the close observation post at Droy cemetery. On the right of Rhodes is Christy Calvert, who is still alive and is available to help us – I've spoken to him twice but he needs exhaustive interviewing. The two on the left are

Sergeant Jimmy Pascoe and Robert McGurk – "Disney", as he was called by his mates. Pascoe was blinded at Droy, McGurk was killed. Pascoe is probably in some kind of home. We need to trace him and interview him today.

'These pictures will be released to the press in due course. But I want them circulated to police and ports first, also to second-hand car dealers and every phone shop in the Metropolitan area. Then we'll hit the press. But we need to think about this carefully. If Rhodes sees his face in the evening paper, he won't hang around for people to recognise him on the TV news later that evening. The first scent of trouble and he'll be off. So we need maximum simultaneous coverage. Inspector Forbes will handle the release strategy and is setting up the free telephone lines.'

In fact, Forbes was already handling a number of issues connected with the MoD's picture file. Copies of the photographs had been sent for computer analysis to see if Rhodes's face could be matched to any of those that had appeared fleetingly in the salvaged video from the bus. He had also arranged for a computer graphics firm in Soho, which specialised in image manipulation, to age Rhodes's face. His hair would be thinned and receded, the skin under his eyes darkened a little, the line of the jaw and neck slightly altered. Then the result would be released to the press with the original picture.

Foyle spoke without pause for fifty minutes. Even the seen-it-all-before brigade at the back of the room had to admit that, in five days of enforced leave, he had produced an incredible amount of material. Foyle took the narrative from Rhodes's childhood in Kenya, and his beating off the Mau Mau with a hunting rifle, through the disastrous undercover operation at Droy and his nervous collapse to his subsequent emergence as an assassin, arms dealer and terrorist with a beady eye for profit and loss. There was also the trajectory described by the life of Eamonn Lindow, the deceptively amiable elder brother of Con Lindow, who had moved to London after the Droy affair to become a librarian and one of the IRA's most successful intelligence operatives.

Eventually their paths had collided. Eamonn had been deployed by the IRA to track down Rhodes, but Rhodes had heard somehow of his assignment and struck first, killing Eamonn with a bomb that was intended to look like an IRA action. The next two devices had also seemed, on the surface, consistent with an IRA attack, although they were probably the result of a contract. That was part of Rhodes's illusionism: he enjoyed making one thing appear to be another. Thus a fire-extinguisher left at Interwaste became a bomb; a burglar alarm, as Lindow had reported from Maine, was converted to a trigger device; and a seemingly innocent phone message became the instruction that would kill and maim scores of people. That's why Rhodes had ignored the risk of leaving a recording of his voice on Lindow's ansaphone. He was arrogant enough to assume that he could get away with the joke. As a result, said Foyle, holding up the microcassette from Lindow's flat, they could now put a voice as well as a face to the name Ian Valentine Rhodes. The recording would be released to the media once Christy Calvert had confirmed that the voice belonged to Rhodes.

Foyle said little about the role of the security service, only mentioning in an aside, which few in the room seemed to pick up, that Rhodes was briefly considered as material for the service. No formal arrangement had been reached, though he may have done some odd bits of work in the past. It was hardly the whole truth, but it wasn't a lie either. He congratulated himself that he had at last found some political nous. He caught the eye of Forbes, who'd just walked into the briefing, and smiled.

Foyle moved back a pace or two towards the image of Rhodes on the wall and gazed up. The light from the projector was in his eyes as he turned to his audience. He shifted sideways to avoid it. 'We see the whole picture now,' he said. 'We understand how it all fits together. We've got a suspect. We've got evidence coming out of our ears. We can build a case and present it in court tomorrow to prove who killed those people in Clarence Street. What remains is the man-hunt. Everything must be focused on the capture of this man, whom we know to be planning a final, dreadful act of terrorism – the thing he refers to as Axiom.' He paused and looked grimly down at his audience. There was not a sound from them.

'So,' he continued, 'only two questions remain about Ian Rhodes. Where is he and what the hell is he planning? Ladies and gentlemen, we have very little time.'

Foyle returned to his office and looked into the adjoining room to find Con Lindow asleep, chin down, hands folded across his chest like a dead man. He closed the door and hurried out of New Scotland Yard for the Cabinet Office. He decided to walk, but instead of going through St James's Park he took the shorter route along Tothill Street through Parliament Square and Whitehall.

As with the first meeting, nearly a fortnight before, he had no papers. There was really no need: he possessed the answers to all the questions that would come his way – except, of course, those concerning the whereabouts and intentions of Ian Valentine Rhodes.

16

Lindow snapped awake with the first shake of Pennel's hand.

'You've got a call, sir.' Pennel noted Lindow's pallor. 'From FBI headquarters in Boston. Agent Mundy is on the line. Says to tell you that he's with Varrone. They've got some letter combinations for you and he wants to know how to send them.'

Lindow sighed. 'You must have an e-mail address – why not use that?'

'As long as that's all right with you, sir.' Pennel hesitated. 'I wonder . . . could you speak to him anyway? The commander wants to know what was found up at that place in Maine. He'll probably tell you more, seeing as you were there.'

Lindow watched as Pennel cradled the phone and had the call put through, while simultaneously logging on to his computer. 'Here you are,' he said, handing him the phone. 'I'll write the e-mail address down here while you're talking.'

'Hey, Lindow.' Mundy's voice grated in his ear, not helping an incipient headache. 'Christ, you must have the stamina of a horse. Look, Peter's had some success with those number blocks. He's pretty sure your instinct is right and that each of the numbers represents letters in the genetic alphabet. I'll talk to you in a second about what's going on up at the cabin.'

'Tell me now, if you want.'

'Well, nobody saw the fire, that's the first thing, so there hasn't been any kind of publicity. We'll keep it that way for as long as we can. There was every kind of nasty waiting in the woods – anti-personnel mines, booby traps. It was a miracle you weren't blown up before you got to the cabin. You were lucky to get out of there alive.' So was Eamonn, thought Lindow. 'So we have to move pretty slow. I'll hand you over to Peter and we'll talk later. Is this Commander Foyle's direct line?'

Without thinking, Lindow replied that it was. Then Varrone came on the line and told him the letters A, C, G and T could be 2, 3, 5 and 7. Lindow retrieved the crumpled e-mail from his wallet and wrote out the message again, substituting letters for numbers.

GAATTC

CTTAAG

AAGCTT

TTCGAA

Lindow's mind focused. He was almost certain that he knew the first configuration. There was an aptness and beauty about it. 'I think the first group is the recognition site for an enzyme isolated from a nasty bacteria named *E. coli*,' he said.

'The food-poisoning bug?'

'Yeah,' said Lindow. 'But it's not the bug we're interested in. It's the enzyme produced by the bug and this is the DNA sequence that it cleaves to – the gateway.'

'I think I'm with you.'

'What's important is that we have the first part of the lock. We need to identify the second sequence and make a couple of calls to find out the amino acid sequence. I believe we're nearly home and dry, Peter. I've got the disks here. I can load them on to the computer in front of me, and then we can work in parallel. I'll call you when I've identified the second recognition site. Then it'll be a matter of minutes before we find the key.'

As he approached the Cabinet Office, Foyle slowed his pace. He wanted to arrive a minute or two later than the others. Perhaps he was guilty of relishing the moment a little too much. He strolled past a couple of policemen and a man loading a ladder on to a van, took a deep breath and walked inside.

The room was a good deal fuller than it had been for the two previous meetings. He guessed between twenty and thirty faces turned towards him as he entered. The commissioner of the Metropolitan Police walked over with the Home Secretary and effected a quick introduction, then took the opportunity himself to shake Foyle's hand. Adam Durie, the head of the Joint Intelligence Committee, looked up from a conversation with Derek Crystal and nodded. Robin Teckman, the chief of MI6, did likewise, although with more understanding in his expression. Foyle's eyes moved round the room as the table came to order. At the far end was David Cantor, seemingly engrossed in some documents. He alone remained apparently unaware of Foyle's entrance.

Sir Derek began, 'You know most of us, Commander. We've been joined by Giles Levington and Sarah Turville from the Northern Ireland Office, Ann Cumber from Number Ten and Linus Tabor from the MoD. Before you start I thought I'd offer a general view of the situation so we know exactly how we stand and we don't waste your time.

'It is clear that we know we are dealing with a homebred terrorist who is, for his own reasons, bent on destroying the Ulster Accord and all that the people of Northern Ireland voted for. He believes he is vindicating the actions of the British security forces in Ulster over the last twenty years. All sides now understand that this man is a maverick, rather than belonging to any of the loyalist or republican factions. Most of you know that the advances in the case have been made by Dr Lindow and Commander Foyle here. We are also receiving help in this area from personal contacts of Dr Lindow's. The FBI is aware of the situation and we can expect news of the events in Maine to reach the highest American circles within the day. I mention this ahead of what Commander Foyle has to say because we must assume that this knowledge will soon leak to other countries, in particular the Irish Republic, which has close connections with the staff of the White House. So, Commander, tell us how you see things.'

Foyle began to speak about the disks and the manner of the decryption. As with his own staff, he made no mention of the relationship between Rhodes and MI5. He assumed that most people in the room had an inkling of it anyway. He outlined the severity and urgency of the problem facing them all. He had their complete attention. Occasionally one or other of the officials around the table made a note or glanced meaningfully at a colleague, but they didn't interrupt. Foyle was aware of the commissioner looking on with an attitude that suggested headmasterly pride. He forbore to smile.

'The first step must be to strengthen the security arrangements for all big public occasions over the next few weeks.' He paused. 'Even though all the Northern Ireland parties will be made aware that this man is a maverick, and almost certainly mad, there could be no more devastating way of harming the Peace Accord than by repeating the IRA's action at Enniskillen on the eighth of November 1987. Given this man's hostility to the current situation in Northern Ireland, and to the Army in general, we shouldn't rule it out. We have a crisis, ladies and gentlemen, and I'm here with a wish list of what I need from you.'

He bent down and took a sip of water.

'First, I want the Ministry of Defence to make available to my department all the files concerning Rhodes's career, no matter how secret. We are especially interested in this man's mental state so any psychologist's report would also be appreciated. Second, my officers will have to acquaint themselves thoroughly with the sort of training Rhodes has received. We want to know how he will react in certain situations – his escape strategies, his knowledge of anti-surveillance techniques, his training in urban warfare and so forth.' The defence official wrote rapidly as he spoke. 'The best possible option would be for you to let us have a couple of your people from the SAS regiment at Hereford, probably instructors. I want them on hand from this afternoon to tell me what sorts of things will be going through his head once he knows we're closing in. For the moment that's all the help that we require from the military.

I'm anxious that this remains a police operation to the end because this man's motives and his methods are acutely interesting to us. We need to know what he's done and what he's planning. If my thinking changes, I will of course let you know.'

Foyle turned to the Home Secretary. 'From the Home Office and the Department of Trade and Industry we need permission to switch off the cellular phone networks in any part of the country at a moment's notice. As we know, sir, Rhodes uses cellphones to detonate his bombs. There are twelve million phone sets in circulation and, frankly, we are unlikely to pinpoint the numbers he plans to use – although we will be trying. So circumstances may arise in which we know about a particular device but cannot get to it in time. We need both departments to approach the five big companies and tell them this must be done. We will then agree a procedure for rapid shut-down with them.'

The Home Secretary nodded and signalled to an official.

'Moving to our own efforts, we plan to co-operate closely with the security service on this investigation. Given the misunderstandings of the past few weeks – the overlaps of effort and the information that has slipped between us – this is essential. I believe we should open a direct line of communication, placing officers in each other's buildings.' He looked at Cantor, who gazed at him unblinkingly. 'The communication will be two-way. So there won't be any confusion in either camp about what we're both doing.' Foyle's tone was almost placid, but nobody in the room mistook what had just happened. He'd challenged the director general of the security service and was now telling him exactly how things would be in the future.

He inhaled deeply and folded his hands on the conference table. 'That, for the moment, ladies and gentlemen, is all I have to say. I will keep you informed as things develop. If there is anything you want to know over the coming days, please don't hesitate to contact me.'

There was a murmur from the far end of the room. Cantor was leaning forward in his chair, poised to speak. All eyes turned to him.

'I wonder, Commander,' he began, smoothing the papers in front of him, 'when you're going to share the results of Dr Lindow's expedition. You see, we have a fair interest in those disks – almost as if we'd brought them back ourselves. You may not know this, but we were also on Rhodes's trail. Our operative accompanied Dr Lindow at every stage of his journey, having already monitored the activities of his brother Eamonn for us. So you will understand that we're most anxious to see the results of that investment of time. Indeed, I'm bound to say that we're a little surprised, in this new era of co-operation, that you haven't yet chosen to show them to us. Could I now therefore formally request sight of the material, both decrypted and still-encrypted disks? We have our own expert cryptologists, and I'm certain we'll be able to make some headway with them.'

His eyes moved between Foyle and the commissioner. Urquhart looked uneasy. Nobody in the room imagined that Cantor would come out of his corner fighting so effectively. If the security service had been after Rhodes all the time, it certainly put a better complexion on their behaviour.

'Dr Lindow and I were aware that Mary Menihan was working for someone,' said Foyle. 'He believed that it might be the security service or the IRA – he didn't know which. In any event, he was unwilling to disclose the existence of the disks to Miss Menihan and this, I am also bound to say, turned out to be exactly the right decision because the information contained in them is very sensitive.' He let that last sentiment hang in the air, then continued. 'However, once we have all the disks decrypted, we'll be happy to let you – and anyone in this room – have copies of the material.'

There was neither concession nor belligerence in Foyle's expression, just a trace of admiration. He knew Cantor wanted the disks badly, but more urgent was his need to put on record that the security service had been actively pursuing Rhodes. He'd done this with his usual efficiency and the seed of doubt had now been successfully sown around the table. He might well extricate himself yet.

At that moment Foyle was aware of the muffled ring of a mobile phone. He looked round and realised it was his own. He apologised to Sir Derek, took it from his pocket and answered the call. It was Pennel.

'Sorry to bother you,' he said. 'Thought you'd want to know the disks have been decrypted. They look pretty good to me.'

'Right,' said Foyle softly. 'I'll be back in a few minutes.'

He returned it to his pocket. 'Unless there's anything else, sir,' he said to Sir Derek, 'I think I should be going. The last four disks have been successfully decrypted and apparently contain very useful information.'

Lindow had loaded Pennel's computer with the encrypted disks then phoned Professor Sethe Sharma at Imperial College. He found Sharma in his usual vague form and barely aware that Lindow was still absent from his department. Sharma identified the second group of letters as the recognition site for the enzyme produced by *Haemophilus influenzae*, a bacteria that causes pneumonia, ear infections and meningitis. He hung up, saying that he would e-mail the amino acid sequences for both enzymes produced by *E. coli* and *Haemophilus influenzae*. Ten minutes later the e-mail came with two attachments from a database named Swissprotein, which included the sequences of amino acids. Lindow printed it out. On the left of the long columns of letters he wrote the original palindromes.

E. coli

(Recognition site
or gateway)   (Enzyme sequence)

	SNKKQSNRLT	EQHKLSQGVI	GIFGDYAKAH	DLAVGEVSKL	VKKALSNEYP	QLSFRYRDSI
G A A T T C	KKTEINEALK	KIDPDLGGTL	FVSNSSIKPD	GGIVEVKDDY	GEWRVVLVAE	AKHQGKDIIN
	IRNGLLVGKR	GDQDLMAAGN	AIERSHKNIS	EIANFMLSES	HFPYVLFLEG	SNFLTENISI
C T T A A G	TRPDGRVVNL	EYNSGILNRL	DRLTAANYGM	PINSNLCINK	FVNHKDKSIM	LQAASIYTQG
	DGREWDSKIM	FEIMFDISTT	SLRVLGRDLF	EQLTSK		

Haemophilus influenzae

(Recognition site
or gateway)   (Enzyme sequence)

	MKKSALEKLL	SLIENLTNQE	FKQATNSLIS	FIYKLNRNEV	IELVRSIGIL	PEAIKPSSTQ
A A G C T T	EKLFSKAGDI	VLAKAFQLLN	LNSKPLEQRG	NAGDVIALSK	EFNYGLVADA	KSFRLSRTAK
	NQKDFKVKAL	SEWREDKDYA	VLTAPFFQYP	TKSQIFKQS	LDENVLLFSW	EHLAILLQLD
T T C G A A	LEETNIFSFE	QLWNFPKKQS	KKTSVSDAEN	NFMRDFNKYF	MDLFKIDKDT	LNQLLQKEIN
	FIEERSLIEK	EYWKKQINII	KNFTREEAIE	ALLKDINMSS	KIETIDSFIK	GIKSNDRLYL

'All we have to do now is type this lot in.'

'May I make a suggestion?' said Pennel, who had grasped the principles of the decryption far quicker than Foyle or Sir Derek. 'Why don't you try it out with one of the files that have already been decrypted? Use the encrypted version to see if it works.'

Lindow agreed. He loaded the encrypted form of the LUNCHBOX disk and typed in the first palindrome followed laboriously by the sequence of 300-odd letters that he had got from Professor Sharma. He repeated the process for the second palindrome. On the last keystroke the screen clouded in a blizzard of characters.

'Christ,' said Lindow, 'the damned thing's destroyed itself. Call Varrone and tell him we've got the right letter combinations but that, if they're not entered in the correct order, the file self-destructs. I'll make copies so we can try a different sequence.'

He thought for a moment, then entered the original palindromes because something told him it would make more sense to fit the gateways before introducing the stream of letters denoting the amino acid sequences. After typing furiously for a few minutes he waited. Nothing happened. The computer seemed to be mulling it over. Suddenly a page of plain text appeared on the screen.

Lindow yelped. 'I've got it. It's going to work.'

Within ten minutes he had repeated the procedure and all four disks were decrypted and stored on the computer's hard disk.

Pennel rushed off to find a printer for the computer and to tell Forbes. Meanwhile Lindow, hardly less jubilant, tried to make sense of the material. The first three disks contained 194 separate documents, some only a few words long. The last disk was a rambling and intermittent journal, started twenty months before by Lasseur when the cabin had been apparently cut off from the outside world by an ice storm. Lindow skimmed the journal, which was written in an odd, staccato style, but soon realised that Lasseur's existential crises offered little of immediate interest. He moved on to the other disks, scrolling through the documents at random and occasionally dipping in to read. There was enough to fill several books, an immense amount of fresh detail that would be invaluable to Foyle. It was just as Lindow was beginning to feel that he really had pulled off something and that he might now have made a real contribution to the arrest of Eamonn's killer when his eye latched almost subconsciously on to his own name. He read from the beginning of the message.

> Money not here. Also need det cord from usual supplier. Other supplies arrived on time. Quaid says a man named Lindow is being used by the Paddies to find me. Will trace him and deal with him before attempting German contract.

Lindow shuddered, then went back through the documents to see if there were any other mentions of Eamonn. In one message he recognised the name of Jimmy Marcuse, the businessman suspected by the FBI of selling arms to the IRA, who had been killed in a car bomb in Miami. There was a message from Rhodes, which reported setting up a business meeting with Marcuse, after which he had followed him to a parking lot where he found Marcuse's reserved space. It was a simple matter to return and attach a device to the car. Next came Patrick Lyne, another name that 'interests our friends in London', and which Lindow remembered from the FBI's file. Lyne died in his bed in a hotel room. Rhodes did not say how, but the result was that a full payment came from London – and Rhodes stepped into the vacuum left by the two men's deaths.

The laconic style of the messages often made the thread hard to follow, but Lindow worked out that a man referred to as J. Quaid was the IRA's North American scout. He'd bought from Marcuse and Lyne. Rhodes reported making contact with Quaid, whose confidence he gained with one or two small deals. But these 'stuck in my craw'. If he was going to sell to anyone in Ireland, it would be to the 'Prods'. A deal followed through unstated avenues. Lasseur and Rhodes banked thirty thousand pounds as a result of the connection. Then came the message that had caught Lindow's eye. He read on.

> Scalper to Lake: Remember Lindows? Not a name I will forget. They were the Mick brothers arrested after Droy OP. They weren't charged. RUC fuck-up by a man named Blackett.

> Lake to Scalper: Of course. Lindow may have been up here two weeks ago. Caught someone on CCTV. Further inquiries established that a Dr

Lindow of MIT stayed local. Checked with MIT switchboard, which has a Dr Lindow. Are both brothers involved or one using other's cover? One must have our location.

Scalper to Lake: News here bad. Everyone crawling to kiss Irish arse. Killers all gone free. AXIOM, my special goodbye, will remind them what it was really about. Final arrangements made. Traced Eamonn Lindow to S. London. Will effect closure when time is right.

Scalper to Lake: Breakfasted with friend Lindow a table away. Reads the *Guardian.* Phone tap in place and heard from his own lips about the arrival of brother here – moved last week from Boston to London. Possible both in on this thing. Could bag two Micks with one shot. Closure this week/early next. Then German contract closure and AXIOM. Money not in bank here yet. What are you playing at? J. Miles on bread line.

Scalper to Lake: Lindow's account closed. Brother arrested – not bad result for the veterans of Droy. Tomorrow German contract closure. Tell them. Then AXIOM. Money arrived. You must leave within two weeks. Leave nothing there.

Lake to Scalper: May take more than two weeks. Much to dismantle and dispose of. Final accounts squared. Your share routed to agreed destinations.

Scalper to Lake: Let me know soonest about arrangements at lake. Need to hear moment you're through. Doctor has been released. That's twice he's got away. Not a third time. Got his address/number. Will deal with him in time.

Lindow sank back in his chair, shocked by the bald description of Eamonn's death, but oddly unaffected by the revelation that Rhodes knew where he lived. There was no longer any point in concealing Eamonn's presence in Maine.

Foyle burst through the door and gripped Lindow's shoulders. 'Con, you have performed a miracle. What's the material like? Is it good?'

He leaned over Lindow and read what was on the screen. 'Is it all this detailed?'

Lindow explained that there was one disk that contained a journal, but that the rest seemed full of valuable operational information.

'Excellent! Forbes, we'll print one copy of this and then divide it between yourself, Kepple, Longmore and Pennel – the old team. Mark up the passages concerning MI5. Aside from that we're only interested in material that will lead us to Rhodes – look for names he might be using, patterns of behaviour, any place-names, associates. Once you've weeded it for mentions of Millbank you can distribute it throughout the department. Again, the same conditions pertain. Not a word of this must leave the floor. No chats with the press. Nothing to go to other departments in the building.'

'Why are you removing the stuff about MI5?' asked Lindow, when Forbes had left to round up the others.

'Because there's no point in detonating a ruddy great mine under them now. We need them and there'll be time enough for that later.'

'Yes, but—'

'But nothing,' said Foyle. 'Why don't you start reading these disks? Go through the one with the journal – you'll probably make the most sense of it. Just say the moment you want to go. We'll get a room across the road in the St James's Hotel.'

Pennel arrived with the printer, followed by the other members of the reading team. Foyle left to tour the department, moving from one office to another, harrying and chivvying, pulling suggestions from the air and convening impromptu meetings. He appointed two officers to liaise with the FBI over the investigation at the cabin and told them to get an inventory of everything that had survived the fire. The most urgent task was to extract the records for the telephone in the cabin, which he knew would yield the numbers most recently dialled from Lasseur's computer. Then it would be a simple matter of using the reverse directory held by every police station to find the addresses used by Rhodes.

Foyle had formed the definite opinion that the capital would be exposed to the maximum danger that weekend. However, he'd arranged for security to be stepped up immediately on all targets, especially public figures. Every uniformed policeman was now searching for the face that looked out of the Ministry of Defence photograph with such disturbing self-possession. The picture was being distributed to all outlying police stations in the Metropolitan area with an instruction from the commissioner himself that the individual should not be approached and that under no circumstances was the media to be informed. The release of the pictures to the media would go ahead on the following afternoon. In the meantime, Foyle reckoned that Rhodes would be unaware of the desperate efforts to find him. He was exposed to a window of vulnerability and Foyle wanted to keep it that way. With the help of Frank Mundy in Boston, a story was released through the international news agencies about a fire in Maine. The bulletin stated that three bodies had been recovered, one of which was found to be carrying a British passport. This also made it into the evening paper, appearing under the headline BRITISH BACKPACKERS DIE IN MYSTERY FIRE, and was featured on the mid-afternoon radio news with the detail that the campers were burned beyond recognition and that two of them had died in each other's arms – a lurid touch added by Mundy.

Some eighty police officers were sent out with the photograph to cover the sources that so often provided information about terrorists. London car auctioneers were visited and the managers of storage units and warehouses were asked to stay on site until they had been shown the photograph. Local police stations were requested as a matter of urgency to work through the lists of rented garages or lock-ups that each police station keeps for such an occasion. Foyle wanted to hear about any unusual activity or recent lets to a well-spoken Englishman with thinning sandy hair.

A separate team telephoned estate agents specialising in short-term lets above a certain value. Foyle felt sure that Rhodes had chosen an upmarket property. Perhaps he was posing as a respectable businessman who needed easy access to the motorway network and, of course, to Gatwick and Heathrow airports. He drew a crescent stretching from Bexley to the east of London, to Slough in the west, and told the team to check all the estate agents within that arc. One officer doubted whether it would be possible before the deadline of four p.m. the next day.

'Contact all the head offices,' Foyle said roughly. 'Get the home numbers for their managers. Then start phoning them. Don't stop until you've finished.'

He placed his greatest hopes in the operation to contact the hundred or so dealers in Central London who sold or hired out mobile phones. Here, the police had a distinct advantage. Rhodes still had no idea that his use of cellphones to detonate the bombs had been tumbled. In each case he would be confident that the bombs had pulverised their secret on detonation. He would not know what had happened to the King's Cross device – from which Legs Lafferty had torn the SIM card.

The tiny plastic chip had enabled the police to discover where and when the phone had been purchased. Two months before, a Mr Keith N. Stephen had bought the set and network service from a shop in Holborn. He had paid £30.99 for the Japanese-made set with a 100-hour battery life and a further £130 for the service. He had settled the account using an American Express card, which turned out to have a billing address in Philadelphia.

First thing that morning two police officers had returned to the store and asked the manager and assistants if they could identify the man in the picture. Nobody remembered seeing him. Still, there was a lot to be learned from the purchase. Stephen had taken care to choose the network service that asked least about the financial state of its new customers. A credit card and an address were all the company required. Naturally the address given by Stephen was false, but there was no reason for this to be discovered. The credit card was debited with the charges each month – and, anyway, the phone had not been used to make calls. This was not a rare occurrence, the manager explained. Tens of thousands of cellphones remained operationally virgin because they were mislaid or were forgotten while their owners were abroad.

Foyle surmised that Rhodes was likely to follow a pattern of buying the same model of phone and signing up with the same undemanding network. It narrowed the field considerably. The phone companies were asked to run through their records and provide lists of all the people who had bought similar combinations of phone and service in the last six months.

It was too much to hope that Stephen had used his credit card again, but Foyle was sure that there would be other significant information on the card's expenditure records. He assumed that the card company would have been contacted in his absence, but found that no action had been taken.

'You mean this vital line was ignored?' he shouted incredulously, at a young inspector named Aylmer.

'Yes, sir, it must have slipped through the net during the handover to Mr Scarratt.'

'Incredible,' said Foyle. 'Lafferty risked his bloody neck to get that information.'

Aylmer busied himself in getting a fax of the expenditure record, which was confined in all but one case to the United States. At the bottom of the list Keith N. Stephen was listed as buying fuel at a motorway service area north of Milton Keynes on 19 September.

'Phone the garage,' said Foyle. 'Ask them if they keep security video from that far back. If they do, find out what time Stephen was there. That will be in their cash records for the day. Then wind back the video to the time of his visit. We're looking for the registration number of the car he was using that day.'

By early afternoon the reading group had reported back to Foyle. As Lindow had said, there was a vast amount of detail, and all of it useful in proving the case against Rhodes. But the journal was almost without value. Lindow had skimmed it and concluded that Lasseur's character didn't improve with scrutiny. There were flashes of paranoia and the whole document reeked of self-pity. On one page he would speak of his finer feelings and on the next he described using a small charge to blow up a moose that had come to the lake for water.

The most useful discoveries concerned the new identities that Lasseur had recently put together for Rhodes. There were another four, including J. Miles which appeared in the passage about the Lindows. Documents and credit cards had also been issued in the names of Jeremy Edward Capon, an insurance executive, and John Larson and Edward Lydd-Taylor, both described as company directors.

'Have it distributed to everyone,' said Foyle, handing the paper back to

Forbes, 'particularly the officers chasing up estate agents and phone dealerships. If this continues, we'll have the bastard before the day's out.'

'You might just be right about that,' said Forbes, sliding another piece of paper across Foyle's desk. 'I found this a couple of minutes ago. There's an account been opened for Miles by Lasseur at one of the high-street banks, which has the branch address of Crossways. Here's the sort code number. It won't take a moment to identify the bank.'

'Good,' said Foyle, levitating from his chair and seizing Lindow. 'Now, Con,' he said, steering him towards the door, 'I want you to go and get some sleep. You're booked in across the road. You'll be under guard. I'm afraid that, for the time being, there's no going back to your flat or your department at Imperial. By now Rhodes may believe you're burned to a crisp, but I don't want any mistakes.'

Lindow smiled at him weakly.

Only when the vivid blooms of Bonfire Night burst in the sky did Foyle register that night had passed from daylight into darkness. During a brief moment in his office, alone with a cup of coffee, he looked out of his window at the displays and thought of the archetypal terrorist, Guy Fawkes, and his end, now being celebrated in the burning of effigies all over London. He remembered the letter from King James authorising the torture of the Catholic hero. The phrases had stuck in his mind after he had used them in a lecture on anti-terrorist operations at the police training college. 'The gentler tortures are to be first used unto him and so by degrees proceeding to the worst – and so God speed your good work.'

God speed your good work. He put it from his mind and surveyed the chaos of his desk. Then he thought of Katherine and phoned Peter Speerman at MI5.

'I was hoping you were still there. It's about my daughter. Last night her place was raided by the police in Bristol, who were acting on a tip-off that she was in possession of a large amount of drugs.'

'What's that got to do with me?'

'Let's put it this way,' said Foyle. 'If my daughter is harassed in any way over the coming weeks, with or without your encouragement, I will simply brief the crime correspondent of the *Guardian* with some of the choicer extracts from these disks. In fact, I'm seeing him for lunch at Simpson's next week.'

Speerman attempted to interrupt.

'No, Mr Speerman, listen to me. I'm certain that there was an operation to plant drugs on her, and that if she had not been with me at the time she would now be facing a charge for possession. Any more crap like that, and I'll have the whole lot of you hanged from Lambeth Bridge. Is that understood? Good. Then go and see to it, Mr Speerman.'

He hung up and phoned Katherine. 'Okay, you can go back to Bristol now. Look, Katherine—'

'Kate!'

'Oh, for God's sake, then, *Kate*, I wanted to thank you for your help last night. Truly, you were brilliant. I was really proud of the way you worked. But remember it's all very hush-hush. Not a word to your lunatic friends.'

'You sure I'm not going to be raided again?'

'Yes, that's in hand. There won't be any problem. When this is over let's go and do something, eh? You, me and Mum?'

'Yes, that would be great.'

He hung up and turned to see Forbes at the door.

'The men from Hereford are here, sir. Where should I put them?'

'How many of them are there?'

'Just two. They're instructors with the Regiment. Do you want to speak to them now?'

'Show them in.'

A short, wiry soldier in his late forties came in, followed by a younger version of the first, who was also wearing trainers and an anorak.

'What we want to know', said Foyle, without waiting for them to introduce themselves, 'is what sort of training our man's received and what he's going to do when he knows we're on to him.'

The older of the two men spoke. 'I understand we're dealing with Ian Rhodes. As it happens, I've met him. He was never in the Regiment, but we were on the same exercise in Norway years ago. He's a tough nut, no doubt about it. To answer your question, there isn't a course that he didn't qualify on. He knows the job and he's very good at it too. Is he working with anyone else?'

'Not now,' said Foyle. 'He had someone in America – a fixer. But he's dead. Rhodes killed him.'

'So he's by himself. That won't be a problem for him. Probably prefers working that way.'

'Yes, but what's he thinking? Where will he hide?'

'Two questions there,' said the older man. 'One, if he's planning some kind of operation for the near future, it'll be well under way by now. He won't stay to watch the fun. He'll be gone. Two, he's probably got several bolt-holes. He'll use them in rotation. Maybe another place where he hides his supplies. That way he's never caught short. Have you got any dates on this? Any likely targets?'

'No, our only information is that he is planning a big operation, which he has code-named Axiom Day. Could be anything.'

'What makes you think he's definitely planning something?'

'We've got hard information from the States. Before his partner died, he told someone about Axiom and said it was imminent.'

'Then I'm certain he will already have planted the explosives,' said the older officer. The younger man nodded in agreement. 'It stands to reason. If he isn't a complete head case, he's not going to hang about.'

Foyle felt depressed. 'All right. What if we do find him? Are we going to be able to take him in?'

The younger man gave a brief smile. 'No, sir. There won't be a moment when he doesn't believe there's some way of getting out of the situation. He'll fight, and then he'll move very quickly to a pre-planned escape route. I'm not talking about you catching him in the street now. Let's imagine you've got him in a house and he's surrounded and the situation looks hopeless. He'll still be thinking he can get away. He'll go for it.'

'How dangerous is he?' asked Foyle.

'If he's got the weapons and the circumstances are right – lethal,' said the younger man, who spoke with a slight Scottish accent. 'He could start using grenades. You see, he's not a terrorist, sir. He's a professional and he's been trained in exfiltration techniques – trained to think himself out of these situations. That's the point you've got to remember. He won't give up. He'll go for it and he'll kill a good number of people, if he has to.'

'I'm getting the message. The long and short of it is that I'm unlikely to be able to bring this man to justice. Is that what you're saying? We're going to have to kill or disable him?'

The two men nodded in unison.

'Thanks for the advice,' said Foyle wryly, signalling to Forbes, who had been looking increasingly amazed through the exchange. 'I'd be grateful if you could be on hand over the next couple of days. Various officers may want to talk to you. Please help them as much as you can. Forbes will find you desks and telephones.'

Forbes left with the two men, then returned with his head cocked sideways and his eyes raised to the ceiling. 'I've put Bill and Ben, the killer men, in the briefing room, sir,' he said. 'Perhaps we should go home and leave the whole thing to them.'

'I know what you mean. Where do they get these people? A few hundred years ago they'd be breaking men on the rack. By the way, is there any news from the shrinks? I want the psychological profile as soon as possible.'

Forbes said that it would be ready in the morning.

At ten fifty-five p.m. the first break came. A woman police sergeant, recently transferred from Criminal Intelligence, had been sent to south-west London to visit the district offices of several large estate agents. She had interviewed most of the employees involved in letting properties. By seven p.m. only one company, Romney-Brand, remained, a small outfit run by two partners in Kingston upon Thames. She had traced the home address of one of the partners and waited until she arrived back from an evening out. The agent immediately recognised Rhodes – or, as she knew him, Mr Capon. In August she'd let him a property, at £470 per week, just outside Kingston. She knew the address by heart as she'd had Ash View in Palmer Road on her books for six months before Mr Capon came along.

A surveillance unit was dispatched to stake out the house, a detached thirties villa hidden behind a screen of *leylandii* trees. The local police were asked to keep a low profile while a second team of thirty-five plain-clothes officers spread through the area at a half-mile distance from the house. By twelve fifteen a.m. Foyle was satisfied that they had the place covered.

Five hours passed. No movement or light was spotted in the house. It was clear that it was empty. Foyle said he was going to snatch an hour or two's sleep and left instructions that he should be woken at the first sign of any activity. He dozed a little, but spent most of the time agonising about whether he should order the house to be searched. At six a.m. he woke and authorised the insertion of small microphones but then remembered the booby traps Lindow had described seeing in Maine. The men were called back before they reached the house.

Just before first light, a red Nissan saloon emerged from one of the winding suburban streets that led to Palmer Road. The surveillance team assumed that it was a local man going to work, but the Nissan slowed as it approached the house and turned into the drive. The car stopped and idled on the gravel driveway for no more than ten seconds, its lights flooding across the lawn. Then it calmly reversed out of the drive and returned the way it had come, moving without haste into the maze of suburban streets. The ring of mobile units was ordered to stop and apprehend the driver, but the car vanished.

A few minutes later Foyle spoke to the head of the surveillance unit from the operations room. 'What happened?'

'He must have seen the footprints on the lawn. There's a heavy dew this morning. The officer with the listening equipment left some pretty obvious tracks.'

'Damn,' said Foyle quietly. 'Did he see anything else? Was he aware the place was being watched?'

'I can't be sure, but I don't think so, sir.'

'Look, I want you to stay there. Don't approach the house again. He may have rigged it with explosives.'

He hung up. 'Damn! Damn! Damn! We could've had him.'

'They got the car's number, sir,' said a woman officer on the operations desk. 'It's registered to John Larson of number thirteen, The Maltings, Sutton. The previous owner was a Mr Craig Meon of Leatherhead, Surrey.'

'Get both checked out. Nothing obvious with the address. The odds are that it doesn't exist. Trace Mr Meon and find out when and where he sold his car. Now, remind me where we are with the bank. We know it's a NatWest branch in Croydon. Any more news on that? Have we interviewed the manager?'

'Not yet, sir,' said another officer on the desk. 'He's due back from holiday today. But we do know that the account was opened in the name of Jonathan Kemp Miles in June, with an initial sum of three thousand pounds. There were references from two banks in the US. A further fifteen grand was deposited in early October. A little under ten was withdrawn immediately, but no one remembers what Mr Miles looked like. They've been going through the bank's video overnight.'

'Good,' said Foyle. 'That reminds me. What about the motorway service station at Milton Keynes? Any joy with the video recording for the day he filled up his car?'

'No, sir, the film was destroyed last week. They only keep records for six or seven weeks. We just missed it.'

Foyle looked at his watch. It was eight a.m., Tuesday 6 November. He left to get some breakfast in the canteen. As he went, he called over his shoulder to Forbes, 'Today's the day when we put this bastard behind bars.'

'The position this morning is this,' said Speerman. 'Our man over there has copies of all the material from the disks. There's nothing that connects us to the subject. However, he suspects that the material may have been edited.'

Speerman was standing in his own office, speaking to Cantor on the phone, which was why he was being guarded. He waited for a response from the other end but nothing came, so he continued, 'Apparently they just missed him near Kingston upon Thames. They've found a house they believe he's using, but he seems to have been scared off. They've got a registration number and some promising leads from the disks. I'd say they're getting very close.'

'Yes, it does sound like that,' said Cantor slowly. 'I think we must open up one or two lines of communication elsewhere. I'll be in within the hour.'

There was a click as the director general hung up. Speerman stood with the receiver in his hand, wondering what was in Cantor's mind. It was all very well to use Brown Owl's intelligence reports on the Lindow brothers to prove that the service had been pursuing Rhodes, but the situation would change dramatically if Rhodes was arrested and started talking. So the 'other option' that Cantor had spoken of a fortnight before was now his only possible course: Rhodes would have to be killed before he could talk.

Speerman replaced the receiver gently and took a turn round his office.

He knew that he must act immediately. He had either to throw in his lot with Cantor and risk his entire career to save Cantor's, or he must oppose the elimination of Rhodes. That could be ugly and dangerous. There would be no third way. Cantor would make sure of that by informing him of the arrangement in advance so that he would not be able to protest his innocence.

Speerman left his office and made his way to Kirsty Laing's. She was sure to be there by now.

Laing looked up without pleasure from a file as Speerman entered. 'After you said our discussions had been overtaken by events I did not imagine you'd be back so soon.' She did not invite him to sit down.

Speerman looked pained, as if he had been the victim of a terrible misunderstanding. 'I've come to value your directness, Kirsty. It's a great asset in a situation like this. You're right, everything has changed – and I wanted to take the opportunity of talking things over with you before we're pitched headlong into the day. It promises to be an unusually gruelling one.'

'What's on your mind?'

'Well, actually I was wondering what was on yours. I think it's fair to say that we both share the view that the service should not put its interests before the safety of the public. But, in a way, that concern is no longer relevant. By the end of the day Rhodes's name will be known in every household in Britain. The public will be alerted to the danger he presents. At the same time, the threat he poses to the service is far greater than it was before. If he's arrested, he may well expose our association. How would you feel about that?'

'I'd be extremely concerned.'

'Then would you mind if I asked you how far you'd be prepared to go to protect the service?'

She thought for a long time. 'What you're asking me is whether I would support action to eliminate the threat to us. I'd have to think very carefully about it, but my instinctive response is that I would not.'

He searched her face. 'Why?'

'It's simple – and perhaps it seems ridiculously pious, Peter. But I'll say it anyway. If we don't stand for justice and the rule of law, we are nothing. We simply become another corrupt, suspicious bureaucracy motivated by self-interest.'

'Yes, I see,' he said. 'You've been most helpful. Forgive me for dropping in on you like this again. I just wanted your take on things.'

He slipped away, leaving Kirsty Laing with considerably more knowledge of the situation than she had possessed ten minutes before.

She didn't need to think what to do next. She unlocked her filing cabinet and removed a scanned version of the Rhodes surveillance photograph from a folder marked the 'Security Service and Public Perception'. She folded the paper into four, slid it into the box of tampons in her handbag then left the building by the main entrance.

Foyle's call to the FBI headquarters in Boston went through at nine thirty a.m. Without ceremony he began to pump one of Mundy's colleagues about the phone line from the cabin.

'The trouble we're having here, sir, is that the phone company hasn't got any kind of record,' said the man.

'But that can't be,' protested Foyle, running his hand through his hair. 'We know he used one.'

'Yeah, that's right,' said the voice, which was less than a hundred per cent alert.

'But there must be some kind of phone cable running up to the cabin.'

'No, sir, and there's nothing inside. It's pretty much burned out. There's no way to fix a phone to the cable and get the number that way.'

'Why don't you get the phone company and ask them to run a search of the subscribers in that area and see which of them has recently been making a lot of calls to Britain?'

'We've tried that too. Nothing showed up.'

'Well, let me know if you get anything on this. I can't stress the urgency too much.'

Foyle slammed down the phone and marched off to the operations room, where he commandeered a large board and wrote the names of the five aliases Rhodes had used recently, and beside each the use to which he had put them. Keith N. Stephen had bought petrol at Milton Keynes and was in possession of at least one credit card. J. Miles banked at the NatWest, Croydon. Jeremy Edward Capon had rented a house in Kingston upon Thames, and John Larson owned a red Nissan. The police had not yet heard anything of Edward Lydd-Taylor, but Foyle had no doubt that they would by the end of the day.

Earlier on, a promising lead had been produced by two detectives who'd traced the previous owner of the red Nissan. He told them that he'd sold his car through Albion car auctions. They visited the auctioneers on the south side of Wandsworth Bridge. The owner looked up the Nissan in his records and found that it had been knocked down for £1,950 on 23 September and sold to a man named Larson. They showed him a picture of Rhodes. He remembered the face. The man had been several times to the Monday-evening auctions. After he bought the Nissan he came back again. He seemed to be looking for another car with special features.

The auctioneer went back over the records for the last six auctions. Then he recalled a grey Vauxhall van with thirty-five thousand miles on the clock, a decent little motor which he'd thought might do for a friend of his. It went for too much, though. The man in the picture had paid over four grand for it. The auctioneer said he seemed a fussy sort of bloke. He'd checked the tax disc several times and inquired about spare parts. He wanted to know where he could get hold of a set of bulbs for all the van's lights.

This piece of information was of particular interest to Foyle. Terrorists and other criminals, who wanted to avoid attracting the attention of the police by committing a minor traffic offence, such as driving with a faulty brake-light, paid exemplary attention to a car's roadworthiness. They also took care to see that the tax disc was up to date.

The auctioneer found the car entered for sale on the page for Monday 15 October, noting that it was taxed until August the following year and had been sold for £4,150. Then he remembered it wasn't Larson who had bought the car. According to his records, the new owner was a Mr J. Capon.

The detectives took the registration number.

A couple of minutes later the number was checked with the Driver and Vehicle Licensing Authority at Swansea. The car's owner was indeed registered as J. Capon of 13 The Maltings, Sutton.

Foyle was wrong about the address: 13 The Maltings did exist, after all, and it was now being watched by undercover officers. The signs weren't promising, however. An officer posing as a postman had been to the door of the small terraced house. One look through the window had told him that the place was unoccupied. Foyle concluded that Rhodes must be using it as a postbox and probably no longer needed to go there. Nevertheless, the house was kept under surveillance.

A distinct South London bias was emerging. Foyle traced a line between Croydon, where Rhodes banked, and the two addresses in the south-western outskirts of the capital. Somewhere along that corridor he believed there'd be another house, and also, possibly, a lock-up or a garage, even an old barn where Rhodes could work undisturbed on his devices.

At ten thirty a.m. Foyle held a briefing, in which he instructed his staff to go through the larger data banks searching for any of the five names. He was convinced that, sooner or later, another clue would turn up. Somewhere there'd be a card billing address for one of the names, another car-registration number, a passport application or a parking permit issued by one of London's boroughs.

He left the briefing before it was over and rang the commissioner to give him an update before they attended the meeting at the Cabinet Office.

'Have you any idea yet what Axiom Day means?' asked the commissioner. Foyle guessed that this would be the only thing that interested Sir Derek Crystal's committee.

'No, sir. Not as yet. But I have high hopes of catching this man. We're within a whisker.'

They went in separate cars to the meeting. Foyle grabbed the disks from the locked drawer in his desk then told Nancy Longmore to accompany him so that he could arrange the next few hours in his diary.

When he got to Whitehall he found fewer officials than there had been the day before, but Robin Teckman, Adam Durie and David Cantor were all there. Cantor was displaying a new composure, directing confident smiles around the table.

At breakneck speed Foyle took them through the previous twenty-four hours, ending with the discoveries about the cars and the two addresses. He played down the failure of his officers to arrest or even follow the driver of the red Nissan, saying that his men had been only just in place when the car appeared.

'What are your hopes for today?' asked Sir Derek. 'If this man isn't caught soon, we really are going to have to think about making some changes to the weekend. What's your view?'

'I'm confident we'll catch him, sir.'

'Not on this morning's form,' shot Cantor. In an instant Foyle realised that the director general's people must have been listening to the radio traffic between New Scotland Yard and the surveillance teams. 'I understand that there were no members of the Tactical Firearms Unit at the house. If there had been, this affair might well be at an end.'

Foyle took a deep breath, aware that his temper was about to snap. 'With respect, sir, in just under forty hours, we've taken this investigation from a standing start to the point where we know all the addresses he uses, the cars, the aliases and the bank accounts he holds. We will get our man, I assure you.'

'But you haven't yet, and that is the problem, Commander. Not only is he still at large, but you may have lost the element of surprise, in which case he is likely to bring his plans forward. And if I may say so, I think you're slightly underestimating the time your officers were outside that house in Kingston. How are we to know that mistakes like last night's will not be repeated?'

Foyle let the question pass with a philosophical shrug. He turned to Sir Derek and asked if there was anything else, as he'd like to get back to the Yard. The Cabinet Secretary's eyes traversed the table.

Cantor spoke again. 'Could we establish the media policy? When do you plan to release the story to the press?'

'We haven't yet decided, sir. I hope to be talking over the decision with the commissioner this afternoon. But we will keep you informed.'

Foyle rose with the rest of the table, but instead of leaving, waited for Robin Teckman to reach him. 'I wonder if I could have a word,' he said.

'Certainly,' said the director of MI6. 'Let's find a quiet spot, shall we?'

They went to the anteroom where Foyle had waited with Lindow.

'It's rather a shot in the dark,' Foyle said. 'We have had difficulty tracing the number from which Lasseur made his calls in the US. We need it to work out which number he was calling most frequently in the UK.' He pulled the disks from his pocket and handed them to Teckman. 'These are the original disks that Con Lindow brought from Maine. They contain the encrypted and decrypted versions of the files, most of which are messages sent by the standard phone lines across the Atlantic via a scrambling device. Lasseur and Rhodes had belt-and-braces security – the messages were encrypted by GenoType software, then scrambled by a modem.' He paused, conscious of Teckman's shrewd eyes.

'I don't want to put you on the spot about the work of GCHQ, sir. But it occurred to me that if GCHQ made a habit of recording such traffic it might be possible to find a match between the material on the disk and the signals picked up out of the air. Do you see what I mean?'

'If, indeed, there was such a practice,' replied Teckman, 'yes, it might, in theory, be possible, although it would be essential to know the dates and the times of the transmissions. It would also be essential to know the type of scrambler being used.'

Foyle handed him a four-page analysis of the disks. 'We've narrowed down a few recent messages on the disks to within about twelve hours. And I think in an hour or so I might be able to get you the type of modem they used.'

'Then it may be possible. I must say I think it's ingenious of you, Commander. We'll talk when you've got some news about the modem.'

Foyle knew perfectly well that MI6 wouldn't confine itself to matching the signals. They'd read everything on the disks, including the details of Cantor's involvement in operations on foreign soil – which, of course, was the ferociously guarded territory of MI6.

He returned to his office with a number of decisions under his belt. He phoned the commissioner to tell him that he was going to postpone the media campaign until the next day. While he spoke, he glanced through the psychologists' report on his desk and saw that it told him nothing new. He already knew the stuff about Rhodes's traumatic childhood and his exaggerated feelings of responsibility, so he told Forbes to get rid of the two men who'd prepared the report.

Then Frank Mundy was called in Boston. 'Have you got anything on the phone line?'

'No, it's a goddam mystery,' rasped Mundy. 'Things weren't helped by an early snowstorm up there yesterday. The area is totally shut down.'

'Okay. I've two favours to ask you, Frank. The first is that we need to use our combined brains to work out what Axiom Day means. I didn't want to call Varrone at this hour, but I wonder if you could have a word and see if he can't put his mind to it. We may be overlooking something in the word itself – another code. The second thing is that we need to know the type of modem attached to Lasseur's computer.'

'Sure thing. We've got that information right here.'

Mundy returned and told Foyle that parts of an IRE Model HS Remote Encryptor had been found in the cabin. Its lead was still plugged into the back of the wreckage of Lasseur's computer.

Foyle thanked him and called the headquarters of MI6 with the information.

Then he phoned Lindow at the St James's Hotel and said he was coming over to take a shower and a nap. He had a feeling that he wouldn't see a bed again for at least another twenty-four hours.

'Okay,' said Lindow. 'What do I do with my guards?'

'Take them on an improving tour of the National Gallery for a couple of hours, and while you're there you can be thinking about Axiom Day. We need to know what it means, Con. I'm sure you'll come up with something.'

At three p.m. Kirsty Laing found a pretext for dropping into Peter Speerman's office.

Speerman's secretary, a large woman with a permanently anxious expression, informed her that the deputy director wasn't in. Prompted by Laing's concern, she spilled out her worries. 'He left me a note saying he'd gone with his wife to the clinic this morning. Then he telephoned to say he wouldn't be in at all. Said he was going to the Wallace Collection then out to lunch. Well, when the director heard that he was very cross. Told me himself to send someone round to the gallery and find Mr Speerman. But they'd left. I do hope everything's all right. It's really most unlike him to take off like that – specially when there's such an important meeting on.'

Laing agreed that it was indeed most unlike the deputy director.

She returned to her own office, where two or three casual inquiries established that a meeting involving the heads of Counter-terrorism, Domestic Terrorism and Domestic Surveillance had begun in the director general's suite at two p.m. and was still in progress. She smiled at the idea of Peter Speerman skulking among the displays of Sèvres porcelain to avoid Cantor. She put him from her mind and thought about the evening ahead, and the restaurant she should choose for her first meeting with Brown Owl.

17

'You'd better get back here quick, sir. Things are warming up.' It was Forbes on the mobile. Foyle dragged himself from a profound sleep and forced himself upright. 'We've got one sighting of the Nissan in the area south of Croydon, which ties in with some information from a shop manageress in Croydon itself.'

'I'll be there in a few minutes.' He bathed his face, hurried fifty yards from the hotel to New Scotland Yard and went straight to the operations room.

Forbes came towards him, speaking rapidly. 'The car was spotted by a policeman on the beat in Banstead. He didn't get a clear look at the driver, but he knew that we were after the car. He made a note of the number then checked with his station. It looks as though Rhodes has got a place somewhere in that area and that he wasn't just passing through. Ten minutes ago we interviewed a woman in Croydon who manages a shop called the Personal Phone Company. She met Rhodes four weeks ago. He didn't buy a phone but he spent a lot of time in the shop asking about various phone services. The point is, this woman took a fancy to our friend. She remembered him and noticed him a couple more times in the area, once in the street in Croydon and once waiting at a set of traffic-lights. The sightings were within a few miles of each other over a period of a fortnight. The local police are looking for the Vauxhall and the Nissan now.'

'Tell me about the phone shop. What did he want to buy?'

'She said he was interested in a mobile with a 165-hour stand-by time – that's almost a week. He wanted to connect this phone to the pay-as-you-go service. You pay up front now for talk-time, no questions asked.'

'So we can't trace the telephones.'

'When we do find him we're going to have to consider shutting down all the cellphone networks in the Croydon area, although of course it wouldn't stop him making a call via a conventional line. And if he's moving about in a car that's not going to bloody well work. I can talk to the phone companies anyway, sir.'

'Do that. I'm going to have a word with the commissioner. Meantime, get Dick Cubbit from Tactical Firearms up here. I have a feeling we're going to need the services of SO 19 tonight. Explain the situation to him – especially about those phones.'

Foyle went back to his office to call the commissioner, but before he could pick up the handset his phone rang.

It was Robin Teckman. 'You were right, Commander. Unusual traffic of coded signals was noted. Our people have just made a match between one of the items on the disks and some archive material at Cheltenham. They located the subscriber's number for you. It's 01737 5544744.'

'Thank you,' said Foyle, scribbling it down. 'Thank you a thousand times. I believe you've cracked it for us.'

He hung up and rushed to the operations room, where he almost forcibly removed a detective constable from a computer with access to the reverse directory. He keyed in the telephone number. Within seconds the name and address of the subscriber was on the screen: G. Castermayne, Pope's Farm House, Upton Pond Road, Nr Caterham, Surrey. He scribbled the address, checked it and straightened up.

'Pay attention, everyone,' he said, moving to a map of the Metropolitan area. 'We have an address a few miles south of Croydon.'

'Where from?' asked Forbes.

'That's between me and my clairvoyant. Who've we got down in Croydon?'

'About thirty officers at present.'

'This place can't be more than a ten-minute drive.' He handed Forbes the paper with the address on it. 'I want a unit to recce this house. They're not to approach it or do anything that gives rise to suspicion. Tell them to drive by slowly, get the lie of the land and look out for signs of life. Meanwhile, get some maps of the area up on the screen. And get hold of the local police. See if anyone knows anything about the property.' As he spoke, officers peeled away and picked up telephones.

Foyle continued to work through the list he'd been assembling in his mind over the previous twenty-four hours. 'Get hold of all the cellphone companies and give them the exact location of this house. I want one person here – Inspector Aylmer – to co-ordinate a shut-down of the cells in the immediate area. This is not to happen until I give the word. But all four digital and the two analog services must go down at the same time. Give this bastard an opportunity and he'll take it. Also we need at least one helicopter on stand-by, maybe two. It's rush hour, and the traffic won't ease for another hour and a bit. I want an aerial surveillance team deployed on this job, but no flying over the house yet. I'll be in my office for the next ten minutes. Let me know the moment we hear anything from the officers outside the house.'

Foyle returned to his office, and phoned the commissioner with the news.

'I'll come back to you,' Urquhart said. 'The Home Secretary will want to be informed.'

Fifteen minutes passed.

Then a sergeant in the car that had been sent to cruise past Pope's Farm House rang into New Scotland Yard from a phone box, explaining that he didn't want to use a radio in the vicinity of the house in case Rhodes had a scanner. The property stood in a swathe of countryside just outside the Greater London area. There were no signs of life that he could make out from the road. Foyle pondered this information while the sergeant remained on the line.

He turned to the officer holding the phone. 'Okay, tell him to stay put. Get the other units discreetly covering all the exits to the farm. Then have the local police prepare to put up road-blocks at a distance of half a mile on all roads leading to the farm. And tell the sergeant that he can use the radio. I'm not having this operation run from a bloody phone box. If he's worried about a scanner, he can refer to the farm as "the Factory" and Rhodes as "Mandy".'

As Foyle spoke, he became aware that the commissioner had entered the operations room. He turned to see him beckoning.

'What's your thinking, Kenneth?' Urquhart asked, when they were in the corridor.

'It depends if he's there. But he must have a phone, which will complicate things.'

'So he's doubly dangerous. Not only is he likely to shoot my officers, he can also arrange for bombs to explode in the capital, or anywhere else, for that matter.'

Foyle could see the way the conversation was going.

'I've been talking to the Home Secretary. It's his opinion, and also the Prime Minister's, that the Regiment should be used.'

'The arrest record of the SAS is not good, sir. Rhodes will almost certainly be killed and we need him. God knows what else he's already deployed.'

'Yes, but I have to weigh that against almost certain loss of life in the force.'

'I appreciate what you're saying, sir, but we have to move quickly. The SAS is in Hereford. It's going to take a couple of hours at least to get them from Hereford to Croydon.'

'They're already here in force, Kenneth. There's a team at Chelsea Barracks ready to take off as soon as they receive word. They came up last night with the advisers who have been here.'

'So, the decision was made yesterday.'

'No, but we thought it best to be on the safe side. You, above all people, appreciate how dangerous this man is.'

'Who's going to be running this operation?'

'You are, but when the time comes you'll consult with Major Jackson, who's in command of the SAS team. You'll need to work closely with him.'

There was a knock at Foyle's door. Forbes came in. 'Someone's been seen in the house. A man moving about on the ground floor. They don't know if it's Rhodes.'

Foyle wheeled round to face Forbes. 'Get the road-blocks up at a good distance from the farm. No flashing lights, no sirens. Just shut down the area quietly.' Pennel, who had been standing behind Forbes, went off to make the arrangements.

'What about the cellphone networks?' Foyle continued to Forbes. 'Are they ready to help us?'

'Richard Aylmer says that they hope to effect a blackout of the area, but it's going to be difficult. They're reluctant to blank out whole areas of the country for long periods. They need a time.'

'We will give it to them, but tell them they've damned well got to comply.'

The commissioner started towards the door. 'I'll leave you to it, then. Good luck, Kenneth. Let's hope we get our man.'

'I'm sure we will,' said Foyle quietly, to the commissioner's retreating back.

'What's going on?' asked Forbes, puzzled by his tone.

'What's going on? I'll tell you. The Home Secretary has taken the view that the SAS should be used rather than SO 19. I don't have to explain to you what that means. It means one dead body and no answers.'

'Can't you say that to them?'

'I'd be wasting my time. The Prime Minister was involved in the decision. The SAS have been standing by at Chelsea since yesterday so everyone's known that they would be used as soon as we found him.' He reached to a peg on the side of his bookcase and took down a dark blue raincoat, a pair of racing binoculars and a large-brimmed waterproof hat. 'In fact, I wouldn't be at all surprised if Cantor has had something to do with this. The last thing he wants is Rhodes alive.'

'Hasn't he been discredited by everything that's come out of the disks?'

'No, not really.' Foyle tugged at the mackintosh belt. 'It's embarrassing for MI5, yes, but there's no evidence that they impeded our investigation. The civil servants, the politicians – they already know that it's a dirty job and they'd prefer to forget the whole thing.' He braced himself. 'Let's get on with it, shall we?'

He looked at his watch – seven thirty-five p.m. Two weeks to the minute since a number 147 bus had turned into Clarence Street and seemingly blown up of its own accord.

Fifteen minutes later Foyle took off for some playing fields a couple of miles west of Pope's Farm House. He knew that teams from the forensics and explosives sections of the Anti-terrorist Unit were following by road, a route having been cleared through the thinning rush-hour traffic. He had ordered similar teams to make for Sutton and Kingston upon Thames.

Kirsty Laing rose from her chair and turned as Brown Owl was shown to the table in the Aphrodite Taverna. They shook hands and sat down. Brown Owl bent to stow a bulging leather shoulder-bag under the banquette, then glanced round the restaurant, giving each table a quick, professional appraisal.

Habits of survival, thought Laing. 'They're mostly tourists,' she said. 'Except the man over there with the escort.'

'How do you know she's an escort?'

'Because he's too awful for any woman to consider without being paid for it. He won't hear us – he's too busy negotiating her price for the rest of the evening. Mary – I can call you that? – what would you like to drink?'

'I'll have some retsina and a large bottle of water.'

The waiter came over, full of effusive charm, but then retreated rapidly to fetch the wine when the faces of the women failed to light up.

'I've ordered *mezze*,' said Laing. 'I hope that's all right. I thought it'd be simpler – it's very good here.'

Mary Menihan took a radish from the bowl of crudités and dipped it in salt. 'So, what exactly do you need from me now?' she asked, taking the first bite from the radish. 'I delayed calling in when you explained the situation to me and I guess I'm in the shit for that. What more do you want?'

'That won't be a problem,' said Laing. 'They're obsessed with Rhodes. They've got a man holed up in an address somewhere in the south. They think it's him.'

Mary Menihan arched her eyebrows. 'No kidding. How did they come by the information so quick?'

'I'm not certain – I'm out of the loop. But obviously the disks had a lot to do with it.'

'Yes.' Mary took another radish. 'It was extremely uncute of Con not to mention what he found. Made me look such an asshole with Craven-Elms. Anyway, it doesn't matter now – in fact, I'm glad the whole damned thing is over.'

Laing watched her guest closely, trying to ignore her beauty and gauge how Mary Menihan would react to her proposal.

'You probably don't fully appreciate how your work with Eamonn Lindow and your efforts over the last two weeks with his brother will help them. It means they can make out that you were on Rhodes's case all that time – that you were using the Lindows to get to Rhodes.'

'Yes, you said that on the phone. And it's true.'

'It's true, but they only wanted to silence him. Did anyone tell you to kill him if you got the chance?'

'Not in so many words, but they couldn't have seriously imagined that I'd do it. I've had some training – self-defence, and I know how to use a gun – but I'm not up to that kind of stuff.'

'But that doesn't invalidate the point. They obstructed the police investigation by suppressing everything they knew about Rhodes. You agree on that?'

'So?'

'So, it meant that they – we – exposed the public to a terrible danger.'

'You said all this before. What's new?'

'Well, there's a principle at stake. And I want you to help me fight for it.'

Mary's eyes widened. 'When did anyone talk about principles in this line of work? I mean, please, be real, Kirsty.' She said it with gentle mockery, her eyes glinting with a smile that caused Laing to lose concentration for a moment.

'It's just part of the game,' continued Mary. 'I happen to have got sick of the game and I plan to leave, as I told you. That's because the game doesn't change. It can't.'

'How long have you been with us, Mary?'

'On and off, ten years this fall.'

'And you were recruited how?'

'I thought everyone knew this story.' She looked out of the restaurant windows at the rain pounding the cars in the street. 'I was the lover of a man named Devlin – Richie Devlin. He was a bastard, but I didn't know that until some people came and told me what he did when he was away from me . . . the beatings, the killings, the torture of young men. They asked me to keep them informed about his friends and tell them about his movements. It was simple stuff. It didn't cause me any problem, once I knew what Richie did to his victims. Hell, I was living with a psychopath. It was the ultimate deception and I was happy to do something to get back at him. I endured it for that reason.'

'And this was in Ireland?'

'We met when I was doing my master's at Harvard. Then we moved to Ireland. That's when they came to see me. Two years later he was shot by the UVF. No one knew for sure who did it but that's what the police said. He was at a pay-phone ten miles south of the border. Anyway, this kind of worked for me. I was the grieving girlfriend and it established my credentials with the republicans. They trusted me and because I was American – or that's what they thought – it didn't seem odd that I moved back and forth and held down a publishing job in London. In fact, it suited them.'

'But you *are* American, aren't you?'

'Kind of. My father was Irish, although he was a British citizen. My mother was Jewish American, originally from Hungary. My parents didn't exchange a word for twenty years. My father died – oh – fourteen years back. Never got to know him properly.'

'What happened after Devlin was killed?'

'It was very casual – I never pushed it. I built a circle of friends in Ireland and became accepted. Occasionally they asked me to run a message to a guy in London, bring some money over, nothing big. Each time I told Craven-Elms what was going on and that's how things developed.'

'And you met Eamonn Lindow through these friends in Ireland?'

'No, we had to work harder on that. I put myself in his way. When he found we knew people in common he relaxed. We became friends on a certain level, but I never saw the real Eamonn, the other Eamonn, because he was too damned good at his job. He never gave a hint of what he was doing for the IRA. He was really something – so secretive.'

'What about his brother? How do you feel about him?'

Mary looked away but Laing caught a flash of hurt passing through her eyes. 'I liked him. But the way he took off . . .'

'Tell me something. To all intents and purposes you're an American. You look American, you sound it. Why're you working for us? This isn't your fight. In fact, most Americans sympathise with the republicans, particularly the ones with Irish blood like yourself.'

Menihan toyed with a cube of grilled cheese. 'Okay. It's like this. I was appalled – shocked – by the things that Devlin did. You know, he liked to kill people in front of their wives and girlfriends. He made them beg, then killed them anyway. And I slept with this guy every night because they needed me to stay with him. I used to lie there, trying to understand how he did these things, why he did these things. Eventually I just took a decision that I was prepared to do anything to stop him – stop men like that because they weren't in the game for an ideal. They liked the killing. They did it, no matter what effect it had, no matter who it hurt, no matter what it did to the children.' She stopped speaking as more dishes of *mezze* arrived. 'And you know something? Devlin and Rhodes, they're exactly the same people. They were just on different sides.'

'So that's why you were in touch with the republicans while you were over in the States?'

'Sure, Craven-Elms knew all about it. We had to move very fast, make it up as we went along because it all developed so quickly. Actually, that side of the last few days didn't work so badly.'

'What did the IRA want you to do? Did they want you to kill Rhodes?'

'No, they've got more sense. They just told me to find out what Con knew and how he knew it. I guess they were going to make their own arrangements. But you've got to understand there was no way I could get out of any of this. It was a shitty position – no back-up, no support, no contact with anyone. Just some garage hand in Boston who supplied the gun.'

'You must've had your hands full, watching the same man for opposing sides.'

'You could say that. And I had to go along with it all and play the dim companion. Never again, I tell you, never! But Con's a helluva sweet man, and pretty smart too.' She drank some wine. 'Look, we've got off the point here. How do you want me to help you?'

'I want you to back my story that we knew two weeks ago that Rhodes was responsible for the bombs. You're the one person who can testify to that.'

'What's the point?'

'I told you, it's the principle of the thing.'

'But you say they're about to arrest Rhodes. What does it matter now? It's just about over – unless he gets away. Then, if he does, they just put his face all over the papers and he won't be able to move.'

'It matters that we were using a paid assassin.'

Menihan frowned incredulously. 'Everyone uses paid assassins, for Chrissakes!'

'The British don't – generally.'

'Give me a break. What was the SAS doing in Ulster? You know about the executions.'

'They were defensive actions, not executions.'

'Defensive actions that wound up as executions. Every one of those IRA gunmen died from a shot to the head, usually a bullet from a Browning handgun, as I recall. Doesn't make such a mess. But you know what? They could never find a hole in the balaclavas that the gunmen wore. And why was that? It was because the SAS soldiers removed the balaclava, took a good look at the guy, finished him off then replaced the balaclava. That wasn't terribly bright, was it?'

'You're talking like a Provisional, Mary.'

'And that's part of the problem. This thing has got to me so I can empathise with both sides. But I belong to neither. That's why I was good at it, but that's why it's also time to go. I'm tired of other people's arguments, of all the bullshit. I have to find my own argument.'

She broke off to look at a party of large, beery German tourists making a commotion at a table near the door. One of the men saw her looking and waved her over with a plump hand. Mary stared at him until he turned away. 'Tell me,' she asked Kirsty, 'you've got an angle on this, haven't you? You want to go higher, maybe right to the top. Am I right?'

'I want the service to be something else. I know this is going to sound sanctimonious to you, but I believe intelligence work has a valuable role to play in a democracy. It's there to serve the system, not deceive it. We're licensed to operate in secrecy, but when we abuse that secrecy we betray a profound trust.'

'Do you really believe that, or is it just the pitch?'

'Both. I want you to help me.'

'Oh, what the hell! I'll help you if I can. I'm leaving anyway, not that I even had a permanent job with you. What do you need me to say?'

'Tell me the facts of the last two weeks. I won't say where I got them. I'll certainly never let Craven-Elms know. I'd just like to be in a position to set things right.'

'Okay.' Mary smiled and waved the empty retsina bottle at the waiter. 'I'm all yours.'

Foyle landed on the rain-sodden playing fields a few minutes after three Army Lynx helicopters had disgorged a dozen SAS troopers and six military technicians, who were now heaving a large crate from one of the aircraft to the tailgate of a Land-Rover.

Foyle hurried from underneath the rotors of the helicopter to where a sergeant from SO 13 stood by a car. As they moved off, the sergeant gave him the latest news. A man – possibly Rhodes – had been spotted moving around in one of the rooms upstairs: lights were on and curtains had been drawn on the ground floor. The house was completely surrounded, but police activity had been kept to a minimum. An operations centre had been set up in a church hall about two miles from the house – the mobile communications vehicle was on its way. The sergeant asked if Foyle wanted to go straight to the church hall.

'No, I'd prefer a look at the place myself,' he replied. 'Just tell the officers who are watching the farm.'

They passed along several narrow lanes bordered by high hedges, and climbed a hill to a wooded chalk plateau where Pope's Farm House stood. Foyle could see why Rhodes had chosen the place. The suburbs of London were only a few miles away, yet here, in this surprisingly rural spot, there would be no problem with prying neighbours. The three or four tracks that led to the farmhouse meant he could slip in and out of the property by a different route each time. And there was another advantage, which Foyle had noted as the helicopter came in to land: Pope's Farm House was no more than ten minutes' drive from Reigate Hill interchange on the M25 motorway.

Foyle told the sergeant to slow down as they reached the main entrance where a sign read 'No Salesmen'. It was difficult to make out much through the streaming windows but it was immediately obvious that Rhodes would see a car approaching from a long way off.

They made a wide arc through the lanes so as not to pass the house twice and arrived at the church hall, a long brick building painted cream.

Inside, the one bleak chamber echoed with the sound of soldiers working the actions of their machine-guns. Maps and a crude layout of the house were spread out on a horseshoe of three trestle tables, in the middle of which stood a large uniformed superintendent fussing about which way the maps should face. Foyle remembered the man from his days in the Drugs Squad, a nit-picker who saw any spark of talent in his juniors as a rebuke to his own prestige.

He shook hands with him and said curtly that the tables should be placed in a block in the centre of the room and the plan of the house should be fixed to the end wall for the briefing. The current outline was nowhere near good enough. Foyle insisted that rooms on both floors had to be identified on separate plans, and that the passages, doorways and exits from the house should also be marked. When the superintendent tried to talk strategy, Foyle told him to concentrate on keeping the roads clear, fobbing off the media and putting the local fire service and hospital on an unspecified alert.

A young man in a one-piece black battle-suit detached himself from a group of soldiers and walked over to Foyle.

'Major Jackson,' he said, in a soft public-school accent. He was in his mid-thirties with keen eyes and the pinched look of the fitness fanatic. 'I may be able to help you with the layout of the house.' He gestured to the crate that had been unloaded outside and was just visible through the door of the church hall.

'What's that?' asked Foyle.

He followed Jackson into the car park to find a round object, which looked like a hybrid of an extractor fan and a flying saucer, standing on three supports. The machine measured about three and a half feet across and consisted of a circular fuselage with two rigid rotors fixed in the centre, one above the other. A couple of cameras were mounted at diametric positions on the outside of the fuselage.

'We call it a doughnut – it's a pilotless Sikorsky. It'll recce the farmhouse for us and send back pictures. It's fitted with conventional and infrared cameras that can be linked up to a light machine-gun. But we prefer to rely on our own skills in that department.' He smiled humourlessly.

'I'll bet,' said Foyle. This was Rhodes fifteen years ago.

The major ignored him. 'Once the cameras have been checked, she's ready to go. She'll stay airborne for two and a half hours so we can take a good long peep through those windows.'

'What about the noise?'

'Virtually silent, and in this weather he won't hear a thing. We'll send her off in a few minutes, if that's all right with you, sir. Meantime I suggest I get some of my men round the house.'

'Not yet. We'll have a briefing first. Major, perhaps this is a good moment to get things straight. I want an arrest out of this, not a body. Have I got your clear understanding on that?'

The major nodded. 'Of course.'

'Good, so we're going to take things quietly and make a judgement about the best time to move. I would guess the early hours of tomorrow morning. But we'll see. For the moment the primary objective is not to give the slightest hint of our presence. If you can guarantee that he won't hear that machine, prepare to launch it.'

He went back into the hall to find Pennel, who had produced four locals who knew the layout of the house. As they spoke, the information was added to the ground- and first-floor plans that were being drawn up. A retired farm-worker gave a detailed account of the out-buildings to the south of the house and a large barn in the west. When one of Foyle's officers produced an aerial photograph of the area that had been hanging in the local pub, the old man was able to point out two paths that ran from the back of the barn down a wooded hill to the west.

Jackson joined Foyle as this information was placed in red marker on the large-scale map. 'If he gets out of there, it's not going to be easy to find him, particularly if he's on foot. He knows how to hide himself and he's easily as good as my men.'

Foyle was thinking the same. They had to pray that nothing would alert Rhodes before he went to bed. That way they stood a reasonable chance of taking him without bloodshed. But he had to be on the safe side. He picked up the phone to Forbes, who was still at New Scotland Yard.

'I want thirty officers from Tactical Firearms down here within the hour. In fact, get as many as you can rustle up. Tell Urquhart that because of the topography here we're going to have difficulty in covering every avenue of escape. Make it clear that they will be used as back-up only. Then get yourself down here. I need someone to organise things.'

'I'll hitch a ride with the commissioner. He's been on the phone every bloody minute and now he's threatening to join you.'

'Oh, Christ.' Foyle hung up and returned to the map of the farm.

An hour sped past, during which Foyle listened to Jackson and the SAS sergeant thrash out a plan of attack. Three of their men had already been inserted into the grounds and were reporting back over their radios. As yet they had no positive sighting of Rhodes, but they confirmed that someone was moving about the house. Shadows had been seen on the downstairs curtains. Foyle told Jackson to keep his men outside a fifty-yard radius and to watch for booby traps. Then he went to the end of the hall and called for attention. 'We have a man in a house. We do not yet know that this is Rhodes, but it's been confirmed that the place was let to an individual named Edward Lydd-Taylor, an alias we know he has used. We're pretty sure it is him. Our main concern is that he does not leave the property. At present we plan to move in at three a.m., by which time we hope he will be asleep. We may be forced to change this, according to what's going on in there. At the same time as we move on the farmhouse, officers will break into the properties that Rhodes has been using in Kingston and Sutton.'

He placed a finger on the elevation of Pope's Farm House. 'Major Jackson's men will go in at two points. Four men will move with assault ladders to the north side and break in through this first-floor window. Three will go through the front door. The remaining members of his team will position themselves around the house to cover all the exits. Beyond them we will have a ring of armed police officers and road-blocks, which are already in place. There are tracker dogs and a surveillance helicopter on stand-by.' He turned to face the room, which now included Forbes, who had slipped through the far door. Foyle looked past him and through the door to see two Army Range Rovers pull up outside. He waited for the noise to die down.

'The difficulty we face is that Rhodes may have rigged up all sorts of surprises to foil this kind of operation. Given what we know about him, we should work on the assumption that there will be various booby traps and, if he has warning of the attack, he may well try to use a cellphone to set off devices. The phone companies have agreed to effect a blackout of the area for an hour starting at two thirty a.m., but remember, this house has a commanding position and it's possible that a signal will get through to a distant beacon. It is imperative that Rhodes is not allowed to use a phone. Just because this appears to be an isolated property, don't be deluded that we have isolated the target. There may be many more lives at stake than we imagine.' He paused and looked at Jackson, who nodded. 'However, I stress that what we want out of this operation is an arrest. Rhodes is infinitely more valuable to us alive than dead. Tomorrow I want him in an interview room, not on a slab. Just in case any of you have doubts, remember this. On September the fifteenth 1984 Patrick Magee checked into the Grand Hotel in Brighton. On September the seventeenth he planted twenty pounds of high explosive in room 629. The detonator was wired into a video timer. The device was primed for a full twenty-six days before it exploded under Mrs Thatcher and the rest of her government.

'Right, that's it for the moment. There'll be another briefing in an hour or so, by which time we'll know more about what's going on in that house. Two of Major Jackson's men are preparing to move forward and insert microphones into the house. It's going to be risky, but we believe it's crucial to know what's going on in there. Oh, by the way, we shall continue to refer to the farm as "the Factory" and Rhodes as "Mandy". The signal to go will be the word Sundowner.'

The meeting dispersed. Foyle walked over to Forbes. 'So, you managed to leave the commissioner behind?'

'Yes, I told him he'd have a long wait before anything happened. He's coming later.'

Foyle's eyes drifted to the remaining members of the SAS team, who were bent over the map, listening to Jackson. They were in full gear with assault hoods and masks dangling from their arms. Most of them carried Heckler and Koch 9-mm machine-guns, which were fitted with torches and infrared sights. From their belts hung a variety of sidearms, ammunition clips and G.60 stun grenades. One of them was carrying a shotgun with a clip of cartridges attached to the barrel.

Foyle sniffed. 'Somebody's going to be injured once this lot move in. We'll need a couple of ambulances, also a fire appliance. In the event of anything going wrong, the ambulances should approach the house from the north, the fire appliance from the west. But I don't want them racing round the countryside before we're ready, so get them to report here before they go to their positions.'

At ten thirty p.m. Foyle sanctioned the launch of the flying camera, which lifted into the darkness with a low, frantic whurr. The craft found its mark quickly but there was some difficulty in keeping it steady in the wind, and the camera wasn't focusing properly. He left the technician's side and went over to listen to the radio contact with one of Jackson's men. A microphone had been inserted through a French window on the east of the house. They were waiting to establish where Rhodes was before trying to place another device in the ventilator of the kitchen window. The first was transmitting well and, with the aid of a booster in the field, was sending a clear signal to the headphones of the SAS backup man.

Foyle heard the man operating the Sikorsky call out, 'I've got him. He's upstairs.'

He tore over and saw an illuminated window dance on the screen.

'Can't you steady it?'

'I could bring her down out of the wind, but I don't want the fuselage to catch the light from that window. He might just see us.'

The operator moved the joystick forward a fraction, and then used the keyboard of a lap-top to extend the Sikorsky's camera to maximum zoom. As the craft drew nearer to the house, Foyle saw a man move slowly across the room, pass the bedroom window and leave through a door.

'Oh, Christ,' he murmured.

'What, sir?' asked the operator.

'Nothing. Keep the craft in its present position.' He beckoned to Forbes. 'We've got a problem. I want you to keep it to yourself. There are a couple of bags on the bed. Looks like he's going somewhere. Get Pennel to check the airlines for all the aliases he's been using. And find a car for me.'

He went over to Jackson, who was holding a hand to an earpiece and staring down intently. 'You'd better listen to this, sir,' said Jackson quietly. 'It's one of my men on the south side of the house. He says a light's been switched on outside.'

Foyle picked up some headphones. 'Mandy's coming out,' said the voice. 'No. He's in the garage. There must be a connecting door to the house. There's a car – looks like a family estate. He's in the car. Fuck, he's going. No. Hold on. He's moved the car out of the garage. He's parked and he's got out. It's him, no doubt about that. Now he's gone back into the house.'

'I think we'd better get down there,' Jackson told Foyle. Then he spoke to his men. 'You lot, join the others in the vehicles. I don't think we're going to need the ladders but take them anyway. I want two men on the deck of each vehicle. I'll be out in a moment.'

'He can't be going yet. He's got to pick up some bags in the house. So you may have some time, Major.'

'Right,' said Jackson, 'but we'd better get down there just in case. One team will take the western approach. I'll be with the other vehicle at the head of the main drive in the north. You can refer to us as Blue and Red teams respectively. That's Red coming from the west and Blue from the north.'

'It still leaves the track to the east,' said Foyle.

'The men on the ground will cover that.'

'Okay, but you'll wait for my order to deploy.'

Jackson grimaced and went outside to the Range Rovers.

Foyle picked up the headphones again. He could hear a man's breathing. 'I've got a better view now. I can see that he's moved a bike out of the garage – a trail bike. The back of the car is open. He could be going to put the bike in the car.'

Foyle heard Jackson's voice. 'Okay. We'll be coming on the track from the west and the drive from the north. You three position yourselves on the eastern road. Did you read that, base?'

'Who the hell is base?' demanded Foyle.

One of the technicians looked up to him. 'He's talking to Hereford, sir. They'll be listening to everything. Standard procedure on an operation like this.'

'Jesus Christ.' He looked over to Forbes, who was watching the pictures from the Sikorsky. 'Can you see anything?'

'Not much. He's turned on a light downstairs – that's all. God knows what he's doing.'

Foyle felt that the operation was slipping from his hands. He called his officers together for a rapid briefing. 'Rhodes looks like he's going to do a runner. We need to alert the armed officers now. If he does start moving and he gets away from the house, we'll need to know immediately which route he's taking. The surveillance helicopter should be ready for immediate take-off. The ambulances are to move only when they hear the word. I will be in the car with Forbes and Kepple on the lane that runs past the easterly side of the farmhouse. We'll pick up one of the armed officers on the way and park fifty yards from the entrance. Sergeant, you'll be responsible for keeping me informed about what's happening in the house. Anything seen by that camera, I want to hear about it. Right, I think we'd better be going.'

'What about the phone companies?' asked Forbes. 'Can we get a shut-down of the network in time?'

'Get Aylmer to push for an immediate shut-down.'

Foyle went outside and walked over to the two matt black Range Rovers, each of which was fitted with a platform and a huge, looped radio antenna. He leaned in to Jackson's window. 'Don't go in until I give the command. You've got that?'

The major nodded. The two Range Rovers sped off to take up their positions to the west and north of Pope's Farm House. Foyle drove to one of the road-blocks where a group of armed officers was being deployed. He recognised a marksman called Silk, who carried an automatic weapon and a side-arm, and told him to get into the car. He drove on up the hill to Pope's Farm House, stopped the car by a gap in the hedge and trained his binoculars across the fields. He could see very little. The rain was coming down hard and the windows were misting up.

Pennel's voice was on the radio. 'Commander, he's booked on a flight to Bangkok under the name of Larson. It leaves Gatwick in just under three hours' time. There's a stop-over at Frankfurt.'

'What about the phone companies?'

'Nothing doing. Trying but they can't achieve a total shut-down in the time.'

'Did you hear all that, Major?' said Foyle.

'Yes.' The voice was lazy and relaxed. Foyle heard the sound of the Range Rover's engine straining, as though someone was labouring the clutch. 'We've got to go soon, Commander. Otherwise this bird is going to fly.'

Another voice came on the radio. It was the soldier outside the farmhouse, who was being patched through to Foyle by the mobile control centre at the village hall. 'He's in the garage again. I think he's doing something with the bike. He's bending down.'

Foyle picked up the handset. 'Ask him if he's brought his bags out of the house.'

No answer came. Either the soldier couldn't see, or he didn't think it was important. The silence from the SAS made Foyle nervous. He drummed his fingers on the steering-wheel, convinced that something was happening without his knowledge.

'Look, I want to see what's going on.' He started the car and crept forward to the gateway of the eastern drive without using his lights. He got out and leaned on the roof to look through the binoculars. Despite the rain, the murky orange glow of London's lights was evident in the northern sky. He swept the binoculars down to the house, then back again up to the top of the main drive. Suddenly he saw something moving against the skyline – an unlit vehicle was making its way steadily down towards the house.

'What the . . .? It's bloody Jackson. He's going in now.' He knew exactly what must be in Jackson's mind. Once the soldier had told him that Rhodes was in the garage, Jackson had decided to push his luck and approach the house from the blind side. In this weather he could be pretty sure that Rhodes wouldn't hear. Foyle switched the binoculars to the light coming from the garage. There were some bushes in the way so he had to move a few paces to the right. He saw the car and the silhouette of the bike against the garage light. There was no sign of Rhodes.

'Christ, he's gone. Forbes, warn Jackson that Rhodes has left the garage. He's in the house, in which case he may hear them coming.'

It was too late. Jackson was shouting, 'SUNDOWNER! GO, GO, GO!' Foyle saw the beams from the second Range Rover stab through the trees at the back of the house. There was just time for him to curse before the explosions came – three distinct flashes that pulsed across his vision. He dived down beside the car as the blasts rumbled through the landscape. A couple of seconds passed, then Forbes, Kepple and Silk sprang from the car, shouting. Foyle took no notice. He straightened up and looked towards the farm. There had been three explosions, he knew that – one at the back of the house, another right in front of him and a third where Jackson's vehicle had been. He raised his binoculars. A twister of white smoke was being ripped by wind from the spot to reveal the burning wreck of the Range Rover.

'He mined all the fucking approaches to the house,' Foyle shouted to Forbes. 'He mined the fucking roads!'

He threw himself in the car. The others followed. All hell was breaking loose on the radio. No one knew what was going on or where Rhodes was. Foyle shouted Jackson's name several times. There was no answer. He called Pennel. 'Alert the outer ring that Rhodes is on the move. Get the helicopter over to the farm now.'

He rammed the car into gear and steered down the track towards the house.

'What are you going to do?' asked Forbes.

'We're going to find out what the hell's happening. Those men will need help.'

'You think that's wise?' Forbes shouted.

Foyle took no notice. The wheels of the police saloon were spinning in two deep ruts made by farm vehicles. He wrestled with the steering-wheel and managed to push the car up the grass bank, where it gained some traction. About sixty yards from the house the track ended in a steaming crater made by one of the explosions. There was no way through to the yard. Foyle got out and beckoned Silk forward with him. They struggled around the crater by clinging to the boughs of a blackthorn hedge and walked on. The house was dark now and the lights in the garage had been extinguished.

'He's gone,' whispered Forbes, who had followed them. 'He must have left on foot.'

They waited and watched. Then, as the wind died in the branches of the hedge, they became aware of a man's groans. Forbes plunged through a patch of dead grass to a ditch where the sound was coming from. Foyle and Silk got down to watch the yard ahead of them.

'There's a man injured here,' Forbes called out. 'One of the soldiers.'

'How badly?' hissed Foyle.

'He says he can hang on. Leg injuries.'

'Then bring his gun.'

Forbes slithered back across the grass and crouched down beside them with the gun.

'You know how to use that weapon, Graham?'

'I've used one before in the Army.'

'Right, if you see him, aim low.'

Above them, on the main drive to the house, the wrecked Range Rover had caught light properly, causing a strange popping noise. Silk said it was the ammunition exploding. Foyle waved his hand to shut him up. A noise was coming from the woods behind the house – an angry whine that went first one way, then the other. Suddenly there was a stutter of gunfire and a liquid stream of tracer bullets arced over the yard in front of the house.

'He must have been waiting to make a break for it but they've cut him off in the woods. He may come this way.'

'I can't see a damned thing,' Forbes shouted.

Foyle glanced round and saw the lights of a surveillance helicopter closing on them from the east. The noise of the engine was borne away from them by the wind and they could barely hear it until it was directly above the crater, whereupon a column of light sprang from its belly and swept up the track. He turned back to the house and at that moment saw the bike burst into the yard. The rider ran straight into the beam of the light.

Forbes and Silk opened fire. The rider skidded to his left and lost the bike, which slewed across the gravel in a flurry of sparks. The man was down. He was hit and lying on the ground. Foyle waved and shouted for them to stop shooting. The man had struggled up and was standing in the light, making not the slightest attempt to escape. Foyle whipped up his binoculars. It was Rhodes. He let them drop and started forward at a jog, his drenched mackintosh flapping in the downdraught from the helicopter. Forbes and Silk followed. There wasn't more than forty yards to cover before they reached Rhodes.

But now he was moving too, dragging himself towards the house.

'Stay there!' Foyle yelled, over the noise of the helicopter, which was hovering five hundred feet above the yard.

Rhodes was holding something in his hand which he had taken from his pocket. Foyle could see it wasn't a gun. What the hell was it? A thick, slow-moving incredulity clogged his mind. Then he understood. He stopped and held his arms out to prevent Forbes and Silk running forward. Rhodes was lifting a phone to his face. He was speaking. He was talking to someone and he was smiling.

'Get down!' shouted Foyle. 'Get down!'

They flung themselves into the mud. Nothing happened. Foyle lifted his head and watched with one eye, as Rhodes lowered the phone and looked out towards them. Then Pope's Farm House seemed to inflate and its windows flashed orange like the eyes of a Hallowe'en pumpkin. The blast penetrated every part of Foyle's being and as the storm of bricks rained down on him, he clawed and ate into the mud, praying for his life. His legs jerked involuntarily to his chest and he felt his lungs let out a single gasp of terror. A long way outside him he heard the explosion thunder into the world. He looked up. The house had disappeared in a billowing taffeta of smoke and dust.

Rhodes had, quite simply, vanished.

18

'I don't know what it is about you, Kenneth,' said the commissioner, looking with exasperation at Foyle, who was slumped in the chair facing his desk. 'You've always got to go against the grain. You've pulled off this investigation against insuperable odds and, I have to admit, at times without my full support, but you still have to kick up some damnable fuss. Others would enjoy this triumph – and deservedly so – but you, Commander, you want to start an investigation into the SAS's behaviour.'

Foyle let the speech wash over him.

'For goodness' sake, man, forget this nonsense. They lost two men and three others are badly injured in hospital. If it makes it any easier, I'll tell you formally now. This isn't going to stick. There'll be no investigation because the Army discharged its duty with courage and honour, and so did you.'

'Yes, but they went before the order was given. Had they waited, we might well have been able to take Rhodes without the loss of life.'

'Oh, come on, Commander. Rhodes was about to escape. We all know that. No one had any choice in the matter.'

'But someone was giving orders to the SAS independently of me and those orders were to kill him, come what may. Rhodes is dead and there can be no embarrassing investigation into the director general of the security service. He will escape scot-free.'

'These are not matters for you, Commander.'

'But they do concern us. Because the security service suppressed information that would have enabled us to track down Rhodes earlier. Their actions had a direct bearing on the conduct of our investigation.'

The commissioner looked at him with despair. 'Foyle, you're a bloody pain in the neck. This is going nowhere, do you understand me? You can't prosecute the security service. Look, the Prime Minister's office has already called to congratulate us on your work. Next week he plans to thank you personally. It doesn't get any better than that for a policeman. Now go and get some sleep. You look dreadful.'

Foyle was not leaving just yet. 'There's a lot to do, sir. We still don't know what Axiom Day means. We don't know what Rhodes was planning. I have to work on the assumption that if he was flying out last night, he must have completed all the preparations for Axiom Day.'

The commissioner shifted uncomfortably, but Foyle saw he had accepted the logic.

'What's emerged overnight?' he asked eventually.

'It's clear he used the place at Kingston to make the devices. There are a lot of high-explosive residues in the garage. The van at the farmhouse was barely touched by the explosions and this, too, carries evidence of Semtex. There was nothing at the flat in Sutton. He used the place as a postal address.'

'What about bomb-making equipment?'

'Nothing so far. He must've got rid of it all, or deployed it in other devices.'

'What about the other car?'

'Forensic are going over every inch of it now. He was working to a very careful schedule. We think he disposed of the Nissan some time yesterday and planned to destroy the van on his way to the airport last night. There was a computer in the front. He'd already been at the hard drive with a hammer and blow-torch.'

'Any news about the people who contracted him to plant the two other devices?'

'Not as yet,' said Foyle. 'MI6 are using the information from Lasseur's disks to trace the origin of the payments made to Rhodes and Lasseur. They're certain that the bombs were inspired and paid for by a Continental group, but until they trace the banking route there won't be any proof. I believe they're working with the German authorities on the problem. We're not yet sure what the legal situation will be. I mean, it's thought that these people are linked up on the Net – they're based in different jurisdictions, they don't know each other.'

Urquhart looked at his watch, smiled and moved to his door. 'You've done well. You were very fortunate to be unhurt but you must take things quietly for a few days. An explosion like that at such close quarters does something to a person – it's a shock to the system. In the meantime I accept what you say about the need to be alert and I agree we should keep the heightened security arrangements in place. But, Commander, let's forget about taking on the SAS and the security service.'

Foyle got up stiffly and left.

With a day's growth of beard and a mud-splattered suit that had been worn for over forty-eight hours, Foyle knew he made a far from impressive sight as he trudged back to his office. Ordinarily he would have gone home to change, but he was determined to remain in his office until that evening. There was, indeed, a lot to be done.

He entered his department, where things were quieter than usual. The mood of celebration that had momentarily spread among his officers when news of Rhodes's death came through had evaporated when it was learned that two soldiers had lost their lives.

Foyle went to his office and shut the door behind him. On his desk were the final editions of the morning newspapers, each with its own ecstatic, garbled version of the events at the farmhouse, which were variously presented as a 'Dramatic SAS Raid', 'Raging Gun Battle' and 'Master Bomber Gunned Down At Farm'. One tabloid described Rhodes in his final moments drawing a gun and being mown down by 'masked SAS siege-busters'. At least he knew how the MoD was going to spin the story. Still, it was probably better that the newspapers didn't dwell on why Rhodes had a telephone in his hand.

He swept the newspapers into his bin and sat down to think of the problem he now faced, which was acutely more challenging than finding Rhodes. He'd have to go back through the evidence, searching for clues about Axiom Day. Everything that was known about Rhodes's psychological state, his methodical planning and his use of surprise had to be sifted and weighed again. Lasseur's disks, which had been only skimmed for clues about Rhodes's whereabouts, had to be exposed to a much deeper analysis. And then there was the physical evidence, the things Rhodes had left behind, which contained meanings that Foyle couldn't guess at – the van, the bike, the houses he had used. Every choice he'd made was a clue.

The task made him feel weak, but it had to be faced for there was one overwhelmingly important fact. Rhodes had remained in the Metropolitan area for a full twelve days after planting his last device. Then he'd packed for good, cleaned everything meticulously and arranged his departure. That had a meaning – it had vast significance – and it puzzled Foyle that no one else could see it. Even Urquhart, a fine detective in his time, had had to be pushed into recognising its importance.

Foyle's mind ran over the last twelve hours, scrutinising his own actions. He was furious with himself for allowing the SAS to take control. It was damned naïve of him to imagine they'd help him effect an arrest. Rhodes was always going to be killed. MI5 had seen to that, although he could only guess at the way the argument for his execution had been sinuously elaborated through many intermediaries so that when it reached the top, death was the only available wisdom. Another victory for Cantor's powers of suggestion by proxy.

He kept on returning to the scene outside the farmhouse. He saw Rhodes in the shaft of light, his left arm hanging limp, dragging his wounded leg towards the house. By then he knew there was nothing he could have done to stop him issuing the one-word command to the cellphone. No one had foreseen the use of the voice-recognition technology. One word – that was all that was needed to prompt the speed dial to send out a call that triggered the explosions as Jackson's men surrounded him. Another word and another number must have been reserved for the bomb that detonated in the house.

When his burned and crushed body was removed from the rubble the police could not even be sure that it was Rhodes. But Foyle knew for certain. Only Rhodes was capable of such deliberate violence against himself. As he looked down on the hideous remains, he had had the sharp impression that Rhodes had beaten him. There was nothing he could discover from him now: the investigation had suffered a final act of sabotage.

Angrily Foyle booted a desk drawer shut and stood up. But this wasn't the moment for self-pity. He had to go on and find out what Rhodes had intended. One thing he realised now was how Rhodes had planned to dispose of all the evidence at the house: he would simply have dialled the same number from abroad so that the house suddenly and mysteriously blew apart. Meanwhile, the properties in Kingston and Sutton would yield nothing to hurt him and eventually the leases would have lapsed.

The grey Vauxhall van was a different matter. It was plain that Rhodes had planned to destroy it on the way to the airport then continue his journey on the bike. That was why he had been leaving earlier than was necessary. But there was something about the van that had stuck in Foyle's mind. The light from the fire had caught the side of it and shown up areas where some adhesive had been applied to the metal indicating that the van may recently have carried a sign. This was odd because he was certain that the van had been bought without any distinguishing marks. In all aspects – age, model and colour – the Vauxhall was perfectly inconspicuous. Rhodes must have added the sign to give him cover on one of the jobs. It wasn't much, but it would get Foyle started again.

He picked up the phone. 'Nancy, find me some officers. I need something checked.'

When they arrived a few minutes later Foyle spilled out his instructions. 'Get Forensic to look at areas on the side of the van. I want to know how recent those marks are. It looks as if someone has tried to wipe off the remains of glue. Find all the sign-writers in South London and ask them if they've worked recently on a grey Vauxhall van. I want to know the exact date and also the details of the lettering. Two of you go to Floodgate Street and show the picture of the van around. See if anyone remembers it from the afternoon of October the twenty-fifth. Now, off you go.'

He called Nancy Longmore again. 'Where's Inspector Forbes?'

'Just got in. He's on his way to you now. By the way, sir, it's no longer inspector. He's been made chief inspector. The promotion came through yesterday. It's on your desk, sir.'

Forbes came in looking drawn.

'This is marvellous news,' said Foyle. 'My heartiest congratulations.' He raised his eyebrows. 'What's up, Chief Inspector?'

'Nothing – just lack of sleep, I expect.'

'We had a rough time of it last night, Graham. Everyone did.'

Forbes nodded.

'But we're not out of the woods yet. I'm convinced there's one big device somewhere out there. That's what he's been doing all this time.'

Forbes looked unenthusiastic.

'Tell you what,' said Foyle, revolving his chair to look out of the window. 'Let's go and have a bite to eat. We'll talk it through.'

Before leaving, he phoned Nancy Longmore once more. 'Can you find Dr Lindow? He must have checked out of the hotel this morning. He may be at Imperial College by now. Ask him when he's free for a chat.'

Kirsty Laing looked around her office before leaving, conscious that she might not see it again. She had little choice. There had been a meeting in the director general's suite that morning, a rally for his supporters of which there were now many. During the past two days one or two had questioned his wisdom, tactically placing tokens of doubt on the table as the wheel spun, but few had seriously worried about his ability to survive the Rhodes problem. With Rhodes dead, all that was forgotten. David Cantor had survived and a flush of confidence now lit his cheeks.

The relief was not expressed explicitly. Her colleagues were never so crass. But she saw it in the body language of the department heads, heard it in the eager questions about future policy, all of them encoded with signals of fealty. She also noted how few people looked at her during the meeting and that no one spoke to her on the way out. Even Speerman did not once glance up at her. That was an important sign in a room of cowards. Her opposition had been subliminally noted and soon it would be acknowledged openly. She was finished, as far as they were concerned.

On leaving the building, she walked first to a friend's flat where she collected the photograph she'd left there two days before. Then she went to a call-box and rang Mary Menihan.

'Is it all right still?' she asked. 'I won't use it if you tell me not to.'

'Yes,' said Mary, sounding altogether more optimistic than she had been at dinner. 'Go ahead. I've sent my letter of resignation round by messenger to Craven-Elms. Actually, it's not so much a resignation as a withdrawal because I'm not employed by them. Anyway, I've withdrawn on a matter of principle.'

'Do you want me to deliver any message to Lindow through Commander Foyle, or are you going to contact him yourself?'

'I don't know. I feel we should talk, but I'm not sure whether either of us is ready.'

'Fine, I'll leave it to you then. Be seeing you.'

'Yes, I'd like that.'

Fifteen minutes later she was shown up to SO 13's offices after the front desk at New Scotland Yard had phoned ahead to Foyle's office. Foyle came to meet her at the security door. 'I assumed it would be you,' he said. 'Are you going to tell me your name this time?'

'Kirsty Laing,' she said, smiling. 'We have some unfinished business, Commander.'

They went to his office where, without a word, she placed the dated picture of Rhodes on Foyle's desk.

Foyle looked up at her. 'What is it? I know it's Rhodes, but where's it come from?'

'I told you we had proof that Ian Rhodes had been sighted in the area of the bomb on October the twenty-third. As you see, the picture is dated and timed. It comes from our visual-recognition system. We call it Weegee. That photograph of Rhodes was in our possession within a few hours of the explosion in Clarence Street. We knew Rhodes was in the vicinity and we knew that he had been taking an interest in Eamonn Lindow. This information was suppressed because of our association. The picture is on file and was also lodged in the computer's memory, although that may have been erased in the last few days.'

Then she drew Mary's two-page statement from an envelope. 'You don't have to rely on my word or, indeed, on the evidence of the photograph. This is Mary Menihan's recollection of what she was told by senior figures in the service. She confirms that she had been instructed to prevent information reaching you from Con Lindow in the United States. Fortunately Dr Lindow did not tell her about the disks, but if he had she'd have done her utmost to stop you seeing them.'

'Why are you giving this to me?'

'If you have no use for the material, I will make sure that the Home Secretary sees it. But I'd rather not take that route again.'

'You misunderstand me, Ms Laing. I understand its value, but why are you doing this?'

'Because I don't want them to get away with it. Last night's operation stinks. You can't be happy about it. I mean, it creates a huge problem for you, doesn't it? Ian Rhodes didn't hang around Croydon to be shot by the SAS. He stayed for a reason.'

'I agree, but I've had great difficulty persuading anyone else to think like that.'

'So, you'll use this as you see fit, but I believe there's enough here for you to make a serious case against my lords and masters. This can't be ignored. Will you let me know when you plan to use it? You've got my number from last time, haven't you?'

'Yes, but I will also need to speak to Mary Menihan. This is going to drop you both in it and I think I should talk to her beforehand.'

'Certainly, but you don't have to be too specific in this. I accept that I'll come in for some flak, but the very existence of the photograph should be enough to do the trick. If possible, I'd like to keep Mary out of it. She's an exceptionally brave woman. She spent years working under cover in the IRA, and she's been put under immense pressure over the last fortnight – nothing that she couldn't handle, but I would hate to see her suffer in any way.'

'I understand. Does Lindow know about Mary – about her role?'

'Not the whole story, but I think you should give him some idea of her position. They were close. It'd be a shame if they weren't reconciled after all this.'

'I never thought to hear a senior member of MI5 play Cupid.'

'Didn't anyone tell you that's what we do? Undercover Match-making and Covert Reconciliation is our speciality.' She gave him a smile and turned to the door. 'I wish you luck, Commander . . . and you can wish me some too.'

'I do, Ms Laing,' he said. 'I do.'

At four p.m. Foyle gave a press conference in which he selectively set the record straight. He would not speculate on Rhodes's motives or state of mind and he referred all questions about the man's past and the SAS operation of the previous evening to the Ministry of Defence. He then made an appeal, asking the public to come forward with information about Rhodes. The police were still anxious to trace his movements over the last month and wanted to hear from anyone who had seen him buying electrical equipment. He didn't enlarge on this or refer directly to telephones, but he did say that certain equipment remained unaccounted for and that there was an outside chance that Rhodes had been planning another outrage when he was killed. Finally, he paid tribute to the unspecified help given by members of the public, by which he meant Con Lindow. Only one or two reporters noticed that the standard pleasantries about co-operation with the security service were missing.

He hurried out of the press room and back to his office, where he made calls to Frank Mundy and Peter Varrone to thank them, and also to plead for more help, insisting that the disks and the cabin might yet offer up clues about Axiom. Varrone sounded distracted, but said that he would put his mind to it. Mundy was altogether more enthusiastic and told Foyle that the mystery of Lasseur's telephone line had finally been solved.

'We made the bad assumption that he was using an ordinary phone line,' he said. 'Then yesterday, when the ice began to melt, we traced a line leading up to a hilltop and found a specially adapted cellphone positioned in direct line of sight to the phone company's antenna. The cabin was wired into three separate installations, which allowed the guy to make calls through three different routes. Consequently no pattern of calls showed up for a particular number – kind of brilliant. We've got a list of the numbers called, but I guess that's not as urgent as it was.'

Foyle thanked him again and hung up.

It was nearing six p.m. and the light had faded from Foyle's window without him noticing. He dragged himself to the second briefing of the day. The first had been a desultory affair, but now he had a clearer idea of the way he would direct the rest of the inquiry. His conversation with Mundy had reinforced his instinct that cellphones still lay at the heart of the investigation. He increased the number of officers visiting phone stores and spread the net wider to take in the Home Counties. He assigned another dozen officers to track down the remainder of the explosives. Finally he detailed six officers under Aylmer to sift through all the evidence and come up with a list of possible targets.

The last information that he was to remember from the day was that the glue on the van was, indeed, only one or two days old. And he was right: the van had been auctioned without markings. But by now his reserves of stamina were giving out. He jerked in his chair, having almost drifted off. Forbes came forward with a piece of paper as if to give him an urgent message.

'You must get some rest,' he said, touching Foyle's shoulder.

Foyle slurred a protest but did not resist. As Forbes guided him to the door, a faint ripple of applause spread through the ranks of the Anti-terrorist Unit.

Next day he woke at ten thirty a.m. feeling no better. He remembered that June had been there when he'd got in the night before. She was standing in the hallway, holding her unopened mail. She brushed his cheek with the back of her fingers, kissed him and ran him a bath. She barely said a word, but he recalled that she looked different. She'd lost quite a lot of weight and she seemed to have slipped from middle age back into her thirties.

It hadn't been a hallucination. He could hear the radio from the kitchen now. He got up for a pee. When he returned, she was in the bedroom with a cup of tea. He sat sipping it on the side of the bed.

'How have you been?' she asked brightly.

'Work.' It was his condition, not his occupation.

'Have you got to go in today?'

Foyle nodded. 'What time did you get back?' The atmosphere was strained, as it always was when they'd been apart for any length of time. Their marriage worked on regular, if not prolonged, contact. Once they were away from each other they lost the habits of concession.

'Six thirty, yesterday evening. Have you really got to go in? I hoped we'd be able to talk.'

Foyle caught the note in her voice and examined her face. 'What about?'

'About us, Ken. About us. This isn't a good time. I know you're very busy – I saw you on the news last night.' She paused. 'Look, I think we ought to try a separation.'

'We just have,' he said. 'Nearly three months.'

'Yes, but this is different.'

He looked at her, knowing what she was going to say. The loss of weight, the bloom of happiness in her face, had already told him that she'd fallen for someone.

'I'm in love.'

'Oh, Christ. That's all I need. Who with?'

'It's hit me so suddenly, I don't know what to make of it. I don't feel any less love for you. I don't respect you less. It's just that I need time to work it out. I've lost my bearings.'

'Who with?' He was angry now, but with himself – for not seeing the way things were going, for not taking steps to stop it.

'Dr Hussan.'

'The archaeologist – the man you introduced me to?'

'Yes, but things only developed in the last few weeks. I wasn't looking for it, Ken. It's just that you're so ... so involved with your work. I thought I needed to find something for myself when Katherine went away. Then, when this happened, I realised what I'd been missing – affection, companionship. God, if only you knew how lonely I've been with you, Ken. Your work is a mistress and I can't compete.'

Foyle drank his tea, reflecting that every scene from every marriage was played out in the same bloody stupid language, each person uttering commonplaces with the conviction that they'd never been said before. 'Have you told Katherine?'

'No, I thought we both ought to do that. We could go down to see her on Saturday and explain things – you know.'

'No, I don't know. What things?'

'Well, that it's not just me running off. There's a history to this. I want her to understand that we've had some difficulties and that we're going to try living apart for a while and that it's not necessarily a permanent arrangement.'

'She won't believe that. And nor do I, come to think of it.'

'But I do,' said June, levelling him a look of resolution. 'I'm working things out. I just wasn't going to do that thing of not telling you. I wanted to be straight.'

'So you're sleeping with him.'

'Yes,' she said defiantly. 'We have slept together.'

'Then it is bloody well over. That's it.'

'Oh, for God's sake, don't be such a child, Ken.'

The phone rang. 'Leave it,' he said.

She reached to the side of the bed and answered it. 'It's Graham Forbes.'

'Not now,' said Foyle.

'Come on, don't be stupid, Ken. It may be important.' She handed him the phone.

'Yes,' he snapped.

'Bad moment? I'm sorry. I thought you'd want to know there's a meeting at the Cabinet Office at twelve thirty. Do you want me to make your excuses? I'm sure they'll understand.'

'No, I'll be there. Can you get a car sent? Thanks.'

She took the receiver from him and replaced it.

'I *do* have to go,' he said.

'I'm used to it.' She got up from the bed with a sigh. 'We'll talk about this over the weekend.'

'You're not going to be here tonight?'

'No, it's better that way. I'll stay with some friends.'

'You mean Hussan.'

'No. He's not even in the country. Look, we'll see each other on Saturday and drive down to Katherine. They must at least let you have the weekend off.'

She went downstairs. Foyle bathed and shaved, without being aware of what he was doing.

June's matter-of-fact briefing on the state of their marriage did not metabolise in Foyle's emotions until an hour or so later when his car was creeping along the Chelsea Embankment. He suddenly remembered Dr Hussan's ingratiating smile and slammed the *Daily Telegraph* down on the back seat. The sound startled Alex, who looked in the mirror and proclaimed defensively that there was nothing he could do about the traffic.

They reached New Scotland Yard a quarter of an hour later, which gave Foyle just twenty minutes to collect himself and make some calls. He closed the door of his office and dialled the number in Pimlico that Kirsty Laing had given him the day before. There was no answer from Mary Menihan's phone. Then he phoned Con Lindow, who picked up on the second ring. 'How're you fixed today, Con?'

'Busy,' said Lindow.

'Tonight?'

'No good. I've got a work thing.'

They agreed to meet the following evening.

Then Foyle unlocked his bottom drawer, took out the photograph and statement that Laing had given him the day before and slipped them in his inside pocket. As yet he did not know how he would use them, but if Cantor came back at him again he would certainly consider it.

When Foyle arrived at the Cabinet Office he found that he was the appendix to another meeting about the proliferation of biological weapons. Sir Derek looked up and swept off his glasses when he entered and sat down at his usual place. 'Welcome, Commander Foyle. I learn from the commissioner that you have some outstanding anxieties, which is why I've asked you here this morning. But first I think it appropriate that we should convey our thanks to you. The deaths of two soldiers were tragic but our sorrow should not let us obscure the debt we owe you.' He smiled at Foyle, and, with a glance round the table, prompted the others to follow suit. 'Now, what is it you have to tell us, Commander?'

While Sir Derek spoke, Foyle focused on a point a little to the left of Cantor at the far end of the table. It was already plain to him that there were no rifts in the room and that the position of the director general of the security service was not remotely threatened. No doubt he had lost some ground in the Whitehall battleground. Perhaps he'd even received a ticking-off from the Prime Minister. The payments to Rhodes for the elimination of two arms dealers would certainly be frowned upon, but they weren't grounds enough to sack him, particularly as Cantor had so adroitly made the case that Rhodes had been the target of their investigation all along. Nothing would change. Cantor had returned to his old silky form and was looking as imperturbably in control as he had the first day Foyle set eyes on him.

Foyle rose. 'Thank you, sir. In return I'd like to pay tribute to the invaluable help we received from MI6 in tracing Rhodes. Without it, I believe we might still be looking for him.'

Robin Teckman gave a nod of appreciation.

'But I take little satisfaction from the operation on Tuesday. Instead of a live suspect, we've got a body in the mortuary and a question we can't answer. The question is this. Why did he stay here nearly a fortnight beyond the time he could have left? We simply don't have a satisfactory explanation. Yet we do know that the phrase Axiom Day had great significance for him. Everything we've learned about this man leads me to believe that he was preparing to leave the country having already executed his plans. We could be months or hours away from a devastating attack, which he timed to occur after he had gone. We've got a stack of evidence that hasn't yet suggested an answer to this problem, but we're looking in the right direction, tracking his movements over the last few weeks, which is easier now that his appearance and the aliases he used are public knowledge. More important is the identification of targets – the targets that would attract Rhodes's peculiar form of homicidal narcissism, which is the way one of the psychologists described it. Of course, as soon as we have anything on this we'll make it available to you. The problem, gentlemen, is that we're not only dealing with an exceptionally clever maniac, but also a dead one.' He sat down.

'The commissioner intimated that these were your worries,' said Sir Derek. He looked at David Cantor. 'What's your assessment of the situation? Is it as forbidding as Commander Foyle's?'

Foyle could no longer contain himself at the idea of Cantor being asked his view, and emitted a growl of disbelief.

'I couldn't be more at odds with it. We have no intelligence whatsoever to support the commander's statement.'

'I wasn't talking about intelligence,' Foyle fired back. 'I was talking about evidence – the solid fact that there are telephone sets not yet accounted for, explosives not found, motives still unidentified.'

'These surely aren't facts in the accepted meaning of the word,' replied Cantor. 'They're simply gaps in your knowledge, which is hardly the same thing. There are many acceptable explanations for his delayed departure, one being that any assassin or terrorist worth his salt does not flee the country once a bomb has gone off. He lies low for a few days then makes a move without hurry. We know that Rhodes used this time to tidy things up, making sure that he left as little behind as possible.' Cantor's tone eased to a conciliatory note. 'I'm certain, however, that Commander Foyle is right to keep us on our toes – that is the policeman's duty – but we should not allow him to persuade us that Rhodes is capable of operating from beyond the grave. As we've learned this morning, there are many other threats to the security of this country. These, unfortunately, are a clear and present danger. As the commander pointed out, Rhodes is dead.'

He ended with a small, self-satisfied smile. That was the thing that made Foyle rise to his feet again. He fixed Cantor with a cold stare, checked his temper, then began to speak. 'You'll forgive me, sir,' he said slowly, to Sir Derek, 'if I don't pay too much attention to what the director general has to say on matters of security. He knows very well that for an entire fortnight he did everything in his power to prevent the name of Rhodes entering the police investigation. Not only that, he pressed for Dr Lindow's continued detention, arguing that he was guilty. You were all here when he made that case. In fact, he was so persuasive that I remember almost agreeing with him myself. But all the while he knew Rhodes was in the vicinity of the first explosion and that he was probably responsible for subsequent bombings.'

'You're straying into areas of defamation, Commander. You have no proof of that.'

'But I do, you see,' said Foyle, producing the picture from his breast pocket and unfolding it. 'This photograph of Ian Rhodes is one of half a dozen copies made on the night of October the twenty-third by technicians at Millbank. It was distributed among the senior staff at a meeting that evening, a few hours after the bomb exploded.'

He held it up to the room, which was by now electrified with interest. Adam Durie and Robin Teckman rose from their seats to get a better look at the photograph. 'Although it is timed and dated to that evening, this picture was never offered to us as a possible lead. You can imagine for yourselves where we'd be today if we had been able to begin our hunt for Rhodes on that Wednesday. We might have prevented two further explosions and there would have been no question of Rhodes carrying out his Axiom threat – whereas now, of course, I believe there is still that possibility, even though he is dead.'

Cantor stood up too, his fingers splayed out on the surface of the table. 'These are operational matters, Commander. You have no business with that photograph, which I hasten to add is classified intelligence material.'

'Wrong, sir! It's evidence, and you suppressed it because of your association with Ian Rhodes.'

The blood had drained from Cantor's face and a lock of hair had fallen across his forehead. 'It is on record that the security service has been pursuing this man for many months. Naturally we had his picture on file and clearly we would have pulled it from our system on the night of the bomb. That's what the date and time indicate – the time the file was retrieved from our system.'

'Good try,' said Foyle. 'I might have believed you, but for three details, each of which I'm sure will comply with your scrupulous definition of a fact. First, this picture comes from the Weegee secret surveillance system that automatically recognises and tracks a suspect in a crowded street. Some of the people around this table will know about your tailor-made system, which is officially known as ARTS. This photograph was taken within a few minutes of the Clarence Street bomb – that's what the date/time line indicates. You knew Rhodes was close enough to be implicated and that it was probable he had just alighted from the bus, having carried the bomb on board and stowed it behind Eamonn Lindow's seat. Second, I have two witnesses who'll say that your senior staff suspected Rhodes's involvement and were intent on hiding this from the police. There's a statement in my pocket to that effect, and I'm in a position to take another at any time I choose. Third, I have here a recording of Rhodes's voice. This message tape was retrieved from Dr Lindow's flat in Notting Hill.' He placed the tape on the table in front of him. 'On it you can hear Rhodes pretending to be a letting agent and instructing Dr Lindow to call a number in connection with his search for a flat. The number turned out to be connected to the King's Cross bomb. It was Rhodes's way of incriminating Lindow. Now, this is the point, gentlemen. MI5 were monitoring Dr Lindow's calls. Mr Cantor's people knew about this call and yet they said nothing when the police released the number to them. In other words, there was a deliberate suppression of the evidence.'

Sir Derek tried to cut him short with a motion of the hand, but Foyle's voice had risen. 'What this amounts to, sir, is that you and your colleagues are liable to charges under Section 18 of the Prevention of Terrorism Act (Temporary Provisions), which specifically makes it an offence to withhold information, knowing or believing that it might be material in the detection of a terrorist.'

'That's enough.' Sir Derek made himself heard. 'You've made your point, Commander. I'm not having this committee turned into a court. I'm certain the security service has adequate explanations for all this. In the meantime, I take your point that there is still a certain level of threat and will advise accordingly. That'll be all. Thank you.'

Foyle was aware of the clock ticking on the mantelpiece. He'd never noticed it before, but that was because the room had never been so silent. He glanced round the tableau of shocked expressions. Sir Derek had buried himself in his papers; Adam Durie held his brow with one hand and shook his head; and the man from the Northern Ireland Office had spotted an interesting insect on the ceiling. Only Robin Teckman looked unembarrassed. He sat, examining Cantor, with his right index finger pressed to his lips. As Foyle turned to the door, Teckman removed his glasses and gave him another nod.

By the time he reached the main entrance to the Cabinet Office, Foyle realised he'd gone too far. He would be deemed guilty of inappropriate behaviour, however obvious Cantor's crimes. It was a question of table manners in Whitehall. Assassins were permitted, as long as they held their knives properly.

Outside, the car was nowhere to be seen so he began to walk. As he reached Parliament Square, he thought of the photograph in his pocket and reminded himself to find out where it had been taken. He was sure Laing had told him and he'd forgotten. But there were a thousand other things to remember. For that moment Foyle forgot them. He marched into the wind, which blew across Parliament Square like a sea breeze, soft and damp with the promise of more rain. It made him feel better – a lot better.

Friday 9 November began early for Peter Speerman. He couldn't sleep, so he rose before dawn and went for a walk with his wife's dachshund, an animal he heartily detested but which threatened to wake up the house if it was left behind.

He had a vague but piercing sense of anxiety as he trudged through the empty streets towards Kensington Gardens with the damned dog winding its lead round every possible obstacle. He knew things had gone badly wrong at the Cabinet Office the day before, but was unable to find out what had happened. This in itself was worrying, for it meant that he had been left out of things. All Cantor would say on his return was that a grave breach of security had been committed. Circumstances led him to believe that Kirsty Laing was the source and that she would be suspended, pending further investigations. Cantor made it plain that he held Speerman responsible for Laing's advancement and thus her treachery.

'Well, find out what she's been doing,' he snapped, in answer to Speerman's protestations, before dismissing him from the room with a flick of his hand.

He had tried to find Laing, but she was out of the office and her home phone number was permanently engaged. No one knew where she was, although a lot of people were eager to speak to her. Rory Fuller and then Angus Grove rang him, each in a state of blind fury.

'Why should I know where she is?' he replied defensively to Grove.

'Because that fucking frigid dyke bureaucrat is your creature, Peter. You made her and now she's doing her damnedest to destroy the service and all of us with it.'

Speerman was particularly worried that he had no clear idea of what Laing had done, but he certainly wasn't going to ask Grove or Fuller. It was disturbing that he'd apparently read so much the wrong way. From the moment Rhodes was killed, Cantor had appeared to become fireproof again. The revelations from the disks had been swept under the carpet in the general jubilation and Cantor had smoothed any remaining doubts about the service's behaviour by arguing that it was sometimes regrettably necessary to get close to an individual like Rhodes. That was the very essence of intelligence work.

But now everything had changed. What the hell had happened? Why hadn't she involved him? And what had she got that was so devastating for Cantor?

He walked on past Kensington Church Street, towards the gardens, thinking back over the meetings of that week. It had been his suggestion to get Kirsty involved. Despite her seniority, he remembered regretting it. She seemed utterly out of her depth. She didn't even know enough to keep quiet when Rhodes was discussed. Cantor had been angry and told him to bring her up to speed. Oh, Christ! That was it. He'd given her the file with the picture of Rhodes – the dated picture of Rhodes. Laing had squirrelled it away then dropped it in the lap of Foyle or someone at the Home Office.

Speerman had to find out for sure. He dragged the dog to the nearest call-box, and dialled Laing's number. The number rang.

'Ah, Peter,' she said, without surprise.

'What's happened, Kirsty? Everyone was looking for you yesterday. Where the hell were you?'

'At the Home Office.'

'At the Home Office? Why?'

'I can't speak on the phone.'

'Can we see each other?' He knew he sounded desperate. 'Look, I'm out walking the dog. Why don't we have a cup of coffee somewhere?'

'Can't this wait?'

'No, it can't. I want to know what's going on. Everything's in such a state of confusion.'

'I've got a car picking me up in half an hour. We'll meet at eight in the Pret à Manger near Marble Arch tube.'

Speerman hurried home, propelled the dachshund through the door and hailed a cab to Marble Arch. Laing was already there, standing at one of the shelf tables along the window. She looked taller to him, and altogether more tailored and polished. He didn't bother buying coffee for himself, but perched on a stool beside her.

'Good morning,' he said, trying to strike a note of conspiratorial bonhomie. 'I hope you're going to tell me what's been going on.'

Laing put down her coffee and studied him. 'In due course. But I'm glad of this chance to talk. I want you to stay on, Peter, but not as deputy director. Andreas Guthrie from D-Branch has agreed to be my deputy. Meanwhile I want you to develop a new role, with special responsibilities for government liaison. After this, we're going to need to win back people's confidence and you are by far the best person for that. But it will mean taking a slightly higher profile. I want you to be our public face, Peter. In relation to me I see you assuming the position of special counsellor.'

'I don't understand,' he stammered.

Laing smiled. 'Oh! I am sorry. I had assumed David Cantor would have told you by now. He resigned yesterday evening – or, rather, he decided that he was taking early retirement. It was for the best. It'll be announced to the press next week, but naturally the news will be circulated at Millbank today. So, if that's all, I've rather a lot to do. There are going to be some changes, Peter. We need to start behaving like a responsible department.'

She drained the last of her cappuccino. 'Oh, I nearly forgot. How's Mrs Speerman? I take it she's better.'

'Eh ... ? Oh, yes, of course, she's fine now. Well ... I suppose ... I suppose I should say congratulations.'

'Thank you, Peter. I know I can look forward to receiving your full support.'

19

All Friday Foyle struggled to keep SO 13 focused on the case, but there was little for his officers to bite on. No trace had been found of Rhodes's explosives and it was proving impossible to identify cellphones he might have bought. Foyle insisted again and again, as much for his own benefit as anyone else's, that the body lying in the mortuary in Croydon still presented a very real threat. By now the commissioner had accepted this and agreed to increase security for the two parades over the weekend. Barely an officer in southern England would be allowed off for Remembrance Day and the City police were already running heightened security checks along the route of the Lord Mayor's Parade, monitoring the cars, passing through the ring of steel and searching empty buildings.

After Foyle's eruption in the Cabinet Office, relations with the top floor had again cooled dramatically. In the early afternoon he'd been summoned to the commissioner's office to be told of Cantor's departure and then given a dressing-down by Urquhart. Foyle played doggo, as the commissioner paced in front of him, and thought of June and their visit to Bristol the next day – a trip that filled him with much greater dread than Urquhart could inspire. Eventually he was dismissed, having assured the commissioner that the information about Cantor's obstruction would have reached the Home Secretary and Prime Minister by at least one other route that he knew of.

Later in the afternoon, Sergeant Pennel entered Foyle's office bearing a small wooden crate. 'You've got a fan, sir. Feels like a bottle to me.'

'Well, don't shake it, man. What drink improves with shaking?'

'A martini, sir. By the way, Con Lindow's on his way up.'

'Ask him to make his statement about the business in Maine before I see him. The FBI need to calm down the local police force.'

'What about Miss Menihan? Couldn't we wait and do them together?'

'No, she's not due until after seven. You get Dr Lindow's under way and then show him in here. It shouldn't take more than an hour. And, Pennel, don't tell either of them that the other is here. Is that understood?'

The sergeant nodded and left Foyle to open the crate. Inside lay a magnum of champagne, with a note that read, 'Here's to a new era of co-operation. Yours, with best wishes and thanks, K. L.'

Foyle smiled – chiefly because the bottle was chilled.

Three thousand miles away another law-enforcement officer, Special Agent Ralph Cartergue, scrambled to the bald, windswept summit of a nameless hill in Maine. The hike from the cabin, only a mile away as the crow flies, had taken him through half a dozen small bogs and numerous thickets of scrub on the leeward side of the hill. The trip wasn't necessary, but Cartergue welcomed the air and he wanted to see one of the telephone installations for himself. The other two had been located and dismantled earlier in the week.

At the top of the hill the cable he'd been following broke out of some thornbushes and ran across the rock to a small wooden construction about the size of a bedside cabinet. On the top was a solar panel, which he realised acted as the backup supply in case of power failure. Beside it was fixed a four-foot plastic-coated antenna. He walked round, peering through cracks in the wood. The box was plainly designed to be mistaken for an automatic weather station of the type used to transmit data from inaccessible locations. Cartergue gave it a thorough check for booby traps, then broke open the side with a long hunting knife.

Inside, the phone was set in a cradle of polystyrene insulation. It was still switched on. Without disturbing the wires that sprouted from the back, he peered more closely at it. The phone's display indicated there had been several unanswered calls. Cartergue was familiar with the model, so he went through the steps to recover the numbers. Each time, the display showed INT'L, meaning that the calls were from abroad and the numbers were not registered by the phone set. However, it did tell him the date and time of each call. The first had been made at 7.01 a.m. on Wednesday 7 November and the others had followed on the hour, at 8.01 a.m. and 9.01 a.m. and so on throughout the morning.

Having noted down the times, he radioed to his colleagues at the cabin and asked them to retrieve the numbers from the phone company's computer. He took some pictures of the inside and outside of the box, then removed the wires from the back of the phone, cut the copper strip leading to the outside aerial and placed the phone in his pocket.

By the time he reached the cabin the phone company had responded to the FBI's request. The same London number had called Lasseur three times. Cartergue was intrigued. By Wednesday morning Lasseur had been dead for over three days while his partner had been killed some time during the night before. So who had made the calls from London? It might have been a misdial – perhaps a fax machine stubbornly redialling the wrong number. But, in that circumstance, the calls would have been made and logged in quick succession, not at hourly intervals. What else could explain the precise timing of the calls? It probably meant nothing, but he'd ask Mundy when they next spoke.

Lindow finished giving his statement to Pennel and was taken to Foyle's office where other members of Foyle's Sunday squad – Forbes, Kepple, Longmore and Hardwood – had assembled for the opening of the champagne.

Foyle popped the cork inexpertly, filled the odd collection of glasses that had been scavenged by Nancy Longmore and proposed a toast. 'We drink first to Con Lindow – the most valuable and co-operative suspect this department has ever had the good fortune to detain. Also to Graham Forbes, who, as you all know, has won promotion this week. This is to all of you.' He lifted his glass to his lips. 'Sterling work, ladies and gentlemen, sterling work.'

There was an embarrassed pause. Foyle shuffled his feet and took some more champagne, swilling it briefly in his cheeks. 'But we're not home and dry yet. Rhodes is still with us – I'm sure of it.'

The remark extinguished the tentative mood of celebration and soon the three junior officers made their excuses, leaving Lindow, Forbes and Foyle standing in an awkward frieze.

'You must be relieved to be back at work,' Foyle mumbled to Lindow.

'Yes, it's surprising how quickly you lose the habits of the mind.'

There was another pause. Foyle looked down at his desk, then glanced at Forbes with a cocked eyebrow.

Forbes took the hint. 'Well, I think I'll leave you to it. I need to remind myself what my wife looks like.'

When he had gone, Foyle helped them both to more champagne then crashed down on the sofa. Lindow took the chair opposite.

'So you didn't get the arrest you wanted,' began Lindow.

'You can say that again. I was naïve – bloody naïve. And now I'm left with this unnerving mystery. What the hell did Axiom Day mean to Rhodes? Am I missing something here, Con? I don't suppose you've come up with anything?'

'Nothing. I'm no good at word games. But surely there's only a limited number of targets he could pick to make his big gesture?'

'Yes, we've got it all covered – Parliament, the Cabinet, the main ministries, prestige buildings and the Royal Family. You name it and it's covered.'

They talked on. Lindow drank a good deal more than he meant to, which was why he didn't notice the acute watchfulness enter the policeman's expression. But Foyle was also busy masking his attention with a succession of expansive gestures.

Then he struck.

'So . . . are you going to tell me now, Con?'

'Tell you what?'

'Are you going to tell me what happened at the churchyard in Droy? I mean, what really happened.'

Lindow threw himself back in the chair and looked away. 'So that's what this is about,' he said indignantly.

'You don't have to tell me, of course. But I'd like to know because everything leads back to Droy. It set you all on different courses. Each of you, Rhodes, Lasseur, Eamonn and yourself. You all dispersed from that incident with your lives changed for ever. Then, years later, fate contrives to bring you together again. And now you are the only one who is still alive.'

Lindow revolved the glass in his hand and watched the centrifuge of bubbles. Without looking up, he began to speak.

'At first I didn't suspect anything, but Eamonn kept on stopping by that church. I knew there had to be a reason why he was taking the longer route home every time. Then a couple of things happened. I saw Eamonn sitting in a parked car with Rudi MacMahon. They'd hated each other at school but there they were in that car like the best of friends. I didn't understand it. A few days later I heard my mother and Eamonn talking. They didn't know I was in the house. She was going on about MacMahon and how Eamonn was helping him. She was saying that it was a fine and brave thing he was doing and that his forebears would be proud of him. Well, that meant only one thing – she'd got him working for the Provos. You see, he'd had years of that crap about his sacred duty and he just didn't have the will to resist her. So, if you're looking for culprits, one of them is Ma.

'Anyway, we went fishing one more time and we had a row. I asked him outright what he was doing at the church. I said I knew he was watching something for MacMahon. I said I thought the police would be interested to hear about it. He denied it all, but it was obvious he was lying. So I decided to find out for myself. I was worried for him, you see. I felt I had to protect him because only I knew the pressure he was under from our mother. I knew he'd got himself in too far and wouldn't be able to handle the Provos. At any rate, that's what I thought then. Little did I know . . .

'I had a small bike at the time, a Honda. The night after our argument I left home about two or three in the morning and set off for the church. I didn't know what I was going to do. If I found something in the churchyard, I thought I might tell the RUC by using the informer's line, or maybe just confront Eamonn with it. I didn't want to get him into trouble.'

Lindow paused. Foyle knew enough not to prompt him. He waited in silence, fascinated by Lindow's sudden lapse into a pure Northern Irish accent. Phipps had noticed the same thing in the interrogation.

'About three miles from the church I left the Honda and went across the fields on foot. I'd put on some waterproof trousers. I was worried because they made a rustle when I walked. I got to the church and waited on the other side of the lane, watching. I thought someone might be there, but of course I didn't think of the Army.

'It was dead quiet. I s'pose I was a bit scared – being in a cemetery at night and all that. I was also kind of excited. You know how it is when you're that age. Anyway, I slipped over the road and crawled along the inside of the cemetery wall. There was a lot of dew on the ground so I was glad of the trousers. I got to the spot that Eamonn had shown so much interest in and turned on this little flashlight. It was like a pen – we used it to tie on fishing flies when it got too dark to see. I put it between my teeth and groped around a bit. I was very close to the ground, which is how I came to notice that some earth round the top of a vault had been disturbed. People had been working there, but you could only have seen it when you were right down on the ground, like I was.

'I knew that I'd found something. I should've left the cemetery then but I didn't. I wanted to know for sure. I felt around the top of the vault some more and realised that turf had been laid over some wooden planking. It was an old door. I pulled the turf aside and lifted the end of the door a few inches, jacking it up with a brick so I could feel under the wood. About halfway along, in the middle, I touched a piece of wire hanging from a metal eye, which had been screwed into the underside of the door. One end was fastened to something below in the vault. The other end ran through the eye and was tied round a big iron shackle.'

He paused and looked round Foyle's office, then his eyes returned to Foyle. 'If you lend me your tie, I'll show you how it worked.' Foyle undid his tie and handed it to Lindow, who then made a knot in one end.

'When the door was lifted the wire ran free until the shackle snagged in the eye.' He tugged the tie so that the knot jammed in a hole made by his thumb and forefinger. 'At that point, anyone lifting the door away from the entrance would be pulling directly on the other end of the wire down in the vault, which must have been fixed to detonator and charge. It was a cunning arrangement because the few feet of free wire meant you wouldn't feel any resistance until the door was clear of the opening. I suppose it could have been attached to a hand grenade, in which case there would have been a longer delay.

'I hadn't any idea that it was a booby trap. I unscrewed the eye and laid it with the wire and shackle out on the ground. The other end of the wire was still attached down in the vault. I lifted the door a few inches and pointed the torch into the vault. There was a lot of stuff down there. Most of it was covered, but I saw these gun muzzles poking out of some sacking. It looked as though mice had eaten away at the sacking. There was a strange smell down there too – like engine oil or something. I still remember it now.

'So I knew exactly what Eamonn'd been doing. I just lay there, shocked to pieces. I couldn't think what I was going to do. Then, suddenly, there was this damned noise over my head – very close. It was an owl swooping down into the churchyard. I panicked and just took to my heels back along the wall, leaving everything sticking out of the vault. I don't know how they set it off, but it must have acted as a trip-wire when they went to check it.'

'What happened next?' asked Foyle.

'I was about half a mile from home when the explosion came. They said people twenty miles away heard it. My problem was I had to get in the house, undress and pretend I'd been woken by the noise. It wasn't long before the police came and arrested us. Someone must have noted down Eamonn's car number when we stopped there. As they were taking us away one of the policemen put his hand on the engine of the bike. Before I had time to think of an excuse, Eamonn told them that he'd been out with a girlfriend. That was a joke. Eamonn didn't have girlfriends. Anyway, they rang her and it checked out. You see, he'd got a permanent alibi fixed up. There was an agreement that if the police called she'd say that he had been there for the night. He was in a lot deeper than I ever knew.'

'Did you know how the dump exploded?'

'No, they never told me and I only got to working it out in the cells. At first I couldn't believe they'd set off their own damned booby trap. They must have known someone'd been down there.'

'They did,' said Foyle. 'They were waiting to see what you were going to do. Then you vanished and four of them went to look and, as you say, one of them must have tripped or pulled on the wire. Did you ever tell Eamonn what happened? He must've suspected you'd been up to something when he told the lie about the bike.'

'He never so much as mentioned the bike. But I did tell him – a couple of years ago when Ma died. We had a long talk about things, my mother, what she stood for – the damned cause and all that. It came up then.'

'What did he say?'

'Not much, but he suspected I'd been fooling around in the churchyard. He said it was all in the past and it had been a lesson to him because he might have lost me in the explosion. He told me he never had anything else to do with MacMahon after that, which wasn't true. They must've kept in touch all those years. Now I find it hard to know what to think. I mean, when we talked after my mother's funeral, he told me he was glad that I'd got out of it – gone away. He was proud of me and all that. I believed him, and still do, even though he used my identity, what I had become in the States, to help the IRA.'

The phone rang. Foyle ignored it and poured more champagne. 'Why didn't you tell anyone else?'

'With my mother's background? You can't be serious! She took us on civil-rights marches from the year dot. We were a "republican" family, with a cousin that'd killed a policeman. There's no way anyone would've listened to my story and believed it. I would have been accused of rigging the arms cache myself and killing those soldiers. Then what? Twenty years in the Maze? That's why I didn't tell them the truth. That's why I didn't tell Phipps.'

'He got a pretty fair idea about it. He felt it still preyed on your mind. Does it?'

'Look, I know those men died because of me. But I didn't put the booby trap there. They did. They wanted to kill – not me. I wanted to help Eamonn, that's all.'

The two men were silent. Foyle felt secretly elated by Lindow's account. He'd already guessed most of the details, but he'd been determined to hear the whole truth from Lindow himself. If asked why he'd pressed him now, he would have put it down to curiosity, the thing that made him a good detective. Yet at a deeper level he knew he was driven by the more powerful need for vindication.

'So you think Rhodes was changed by what happened at the cemetery?' asked Lindow, fingering the bruise on his jaw.

'No. He was on his way to the person he became long before that. His brother was killed in front of him when he was a child – that must've had a vast effect. But a hell of a lot of it was in the blood. His old man was a loner and a real bastard, by all accounts. So you can't blame yourself for what Rhodes became. And the interesting thing is that I don't believe he had any notion of finding your brother and killing him when this whole thing started. He was an opportunist, and when he discovered Eamonn was working for the IRA in London he decided to settle the old score. Then you arrived and he thought he'd have some fun setting you up.'

'But he couldn't have known I was here. Eamonn and I hadn't seen each other.'

'Yes, that puzzled me too. Then I realised he must've tapped your brother's phone. It's easy to attach a caller display unit to the line. He would've known exactly who was calling Eamonn without having to monitor the phone. After that, it was no trouble finding you. He bugged your phone. That's how he knew you were looking for a flat and why he left a message, pretending to be an estate agent.'

'What was the point?'

'I don't know if there was one, except he got you to make the call to the phone connected to the bomb. If something went wrong with the device on the bomb and it didn't explode, it would lead back to you. I suppose he also appreciated that the cellphone companies can recover the position of a mobile user on any single call. That might have given us an idea of his movements. So by getting you and me to make the calls, he put himself at one remove. Course, he could have dialled the bombs from a phone-box, but it wouldn't have been so much fun.'

'But why you? Why did he get you to make the call?'

'It wasn't just me. Remember, he left a similar message with Blackett. He must have laughed at the idea of both of us dialling that number. Why me? My name is in the papers the whole time and, as I said, the idea of having the head of the Anti-terrorist Unit detonate a bomb must have been irresistible. This prankster aspect is what worries me now. There are any number of scenarios that Rhodes might have dreamed up that work after his death, although I appreciate he didn't expect to die. For example, he could use the classified-advertisement section of a newspaper. All he'd need to do is place a suitably enticing advertisement with a phone number to appear days – maybe weeks – later and the timer would be set. Whatever happened to him, wherever he was, he'd know that on the day the paper was published some sucker would respond to the ad and dial the number that would detonate a bomb. That's why I don't think this is over. But where do I look? How do I find this thing? Apart from shutting down the cellphone networks for the next month, there's absolutely bugger all I can do. Rhodes didn't leave much behind him.'

Foyle heaved himself out of the sofa and went to the window, where he looked down at the traffic streaming along Victoria Street.

'It could be anywhere. We could be sitting on it, for all I know. Frankly, I haven't the first idea what I should be doing, and that really worries me.'

'Then why are you going away tomorrow? Pennel told me you were going down to the West Country. Couldn't you put the trip off for a few days?'

'I've got to go. My wife has left me, or is in the process of leaving me – I'm not sure which – and I've agreed to go and see Katherine with her to explain things. There's a point when you've got to put the job second and I've reached it. If I don't go, it will be a clear signal to June that I don't care – to say nothing of hurting Katherine's feelings. And I do care very much about both of them, Con. Of course, if we had something more to go on then I could persuade June to let it wait. But there's nothing. Not a damned thing.'

The phone rang again. Foyle picked it up. 'Yes . . . fine. That'll be okay.'

He hung up and looked at Lindow. 'I want to thank you for telling me about Droy. I know it was difficult and, in case you're interested, I don't hold you responsible for any of this. It's just that you bloody well should've told me before – I'd have believed you, you know.'

Lindow shrugged sceptically, put down his glass and rose to go.

'You can't leave yet,' said Foyle, his expression brightening. 'I've got a surprise for you.'

The door opened and Pennel came in, followed by Mary Menihan.

Con involuntarily started towards her, then something stopped him, a notion that he might be rebuffed.

'Leave me in Boston, would you, Con Lindow?' she said, coming into the room, her hand outstretched to meet Foyle's.

When they had introduced themselves, she turned back to Lindow. 'Sneaky old Con. Didn't tell me anything, did you?' Her eyes danced over his face mischievously.

'That makes two of us,' said Lindow humourlessly.

'Don't be so pompous, Con.' She laughed. 'I was only kidding.'

'We were just having a drink,' said Foyle, anxious to head off any kind of scene. 'Perhaps you'd like to join us?'

'Certainly. But then I've got a dinner engagement – I take it you're free, Con?'

Lindow found himself smiling. She looked wonderful – hair glistening like a crow's wing, eyes liquid and warm. Lindow knew he'd never desire anyone more completely. Mary Menihan was it: the thing he'd never dared to look for.

'Good,' she said, reading his slightly dazed expression as acceptance. 'There's a great Lebanese restaurant near my place. We'll go there and confess to each other. Is that okay with you, Doctor?'

Lindow nodded. 'More than okay.'

They got up to leave Foyle's office half an hour later, during which time Lindow came to realise he was seeing the real Mary for the first time. She began by asking Foyle about the steps that had directed the police to Pope's Farm House. Her questions tumbled out in quick, logical succession, until she pinned Foyle down on the way the match had been achieved between the information on the disks and calls from a number in Croydon. No one else had thought to ask him exactly how he had got the telephone number that led to Pope's Farm House, but within a few minutes Mary had prised the information from him. Lindow saw that the commander was taken aback and, having himself just surrendered to Foyle's interrogation skills, enjoyed the spectacle of the big policeman struggling to return Mary's baseline volleys.

As they left, Mary shook the policeman's hand with a kind of coquettish modesty. Lindow thought she looked very slight beside him. Then Foyle remembered something, and removed a brown envelope from his desk. 'This is yours.'

'What's that?'

'The statement you made for a friend of ours.'

'I shan't be needing it any longer. I've left all that. Listen, why don't you just destroy it?'

Outside New Scotland Yard, Mary said she'd prefer to walk so they made their way across Parliament Square towards Victoria Tower Gardens. They bent their heads to the wind as they went, grabbing at each other as they slipped on the pavement of wet leaves. In the gardens a bonfire smouldered, which filled the air with a smell of burned humus. At the point near Lambeth Bridge where the gardens tapered, they stopped and looked down at the river.

'You know that piece by Auden?' Mary asked. Without waiting for a reply, she began to recite:

> And down by the brimming river
> I heard a lover sing
> Under an arch of the railway:
> 'Love has no ending.
> I'll love you, dear, I'll love you
> Till China and Africa meet,
> And the river jumps over the mountain
> And the salmon sing in the street—

She broke off. 'I don't remember the rest, except there's something about loving your neighbour's crooked heart.' She squeezed his arm with both her hands and darted a girlish kiss to his cheek. 'Will you love my crooked heart, Con?'

'Yes, if you stop quoting goddam English poetry at me.' He looked down again and shuddered at the thought of the river's waters.

They walked on past Millbank and the Tate Gallery, then cut up into Pimlico to find Mary's restaurant, a discreet place with booths separated by panels of intricate latticework. Mary told him all about what she'd done for the security service, running messages between Ireland and England, and how, when sitting on the floor in Lasseur's cabin, she had sworn she'd leave the business, if she got out alive. 'I lost my nerve a while back,' she said, her eyes swivelling from Lindow across the room to a party of thickset Arabs, wearing big rings and horizontally striped ties. 'At first I kind of got a kick out of playing dumb yet knowing all the moves. Then I got sick of having to watch myself, having to watch everything I said – the long, long lie that became a kind of parallel life.' She sighed. 'One time in Dublin, about three or four years ago, I was taken for a drink by a republican named Jerry Crane – only it wasn't a drink. Before I knew it, this guy had driven me out of the city to some kind of trailer-park. It was like a vacation place by the sea. There were three other men there. Do you know what the IRA call them? A nut squad. That's because they nut people – kill them. They interrogated me all goddam night. It was like a security vetting. There was one man who said nothing. He sat a little way away from the others, playing with this pointed piece of wood. He kept on working at it with a knife then holding it up to the light. I got a pretty good idea what he'd do with that wood if I started to forget my story. He was the one they'd let loose on me if my story cracked. And these people aren't stupid. They're really smart and cunning and I knew they'd get to me soon enough. So I feigned outrage and told them I'd inform the people at the American Embassy about their treatment of me. They weren't sure enough of their ground to go the whole way and start hurting me because then they'd have to finish the job. And they couldn't do that because I'd made sure that people knew I was with Jerry Crane. So I ranted on about my friendship with the ambassador. They knew it might be true, because their people had seen me at an embassy reception in Dublin. So finally they apologised and let me go. That arsehole Jerry drove me back to the city, giving me a whole lot of bull about security. You want to know something? I threw up for a straight two days after that night.'

'So they didn't have anything to go on – no evidence against you?'

'Nothing. I was involved with them and they thought they'd better check me out. But that wasn't the only thing. There's a certain type of man that gets a thrill out of a woman's terror.'

She looked at him and a shudder rose through her shoulders. He touched her chin and held it until the warmth returned to her eyes.

'It's okay.' She kissed the palm of his hand. 'God, I want you. You see, I'm not a heroine. I spent a lot of the last ten years scared shitless.'

'You were pretty cool at the cabin and before that at the lake. Or was that a set-up? Did you plan it all with them?'

'Christ, no. I had an idea that something would happen. They were just so damned desperate about the bombs. I didn't plan it and I didn't know they were going to use your sister. What could I do? I couldn't blow my own cover. I had to wait to see what they wanted you to do. Then I was locked into the crazy attempt to find Rhodes.'

She put down her napkin, slipped round the table and placed her hand on Lindow's thigh. She kissed his neck and squirmed beside him.

'We have to go now – I need you,' she said.

'Before that I want to know one thing. Did you know that Eamonn had been to Maine? Was that why MI5 put so much effort into having Eamonn watched by you?'

'No, it wasn't like that. I had no idea where he had been. You see, we didn't know much. We knew Eamonn was important and even after the peace accord was signed we got the feeling he was still very active. Craven-Elms told me to search his place and for this I needed to get closer to him and find out where he would hide things.'

'Would you have slept with him?'

She looked at him and he saw something happen behind her eyes. 'Yes.'

'Jesus!' He threw down his napkin.

'Oh, Con, it's over now. I've quit. And you're all I want. I implore you to believe me.'

He said nothing but signalled for the bill. 'It's okay,' he said, as he gave the waiter his credit card. 'I guessed as much. All I can say is that he would have been lucky to have you.'

Mary led him the few hundred yards back to her flat, a sparsely decorated place on two floors, much of which was given over to neatly stacked piles of manuscripts. They rushed to her bed, as though running out of the rain, and there Lindow began to make love to her. This time she submitted, smiling as he ran his lips over her body, leaving a snail-trail of dampness that made her shiver and giggle. Then they joined together and moved slowly, noiselessly, in the half-lit room. When it was over she held his head with greedy hands and kissed him hotly.

Lindow rolled on to his back and looked up through the skylight at the clouds tearing over the city catching the orange light from below. 'Do you feel like sleeping yet?'

'Yes,' she said softly. 'We've got all tomorrow and then the day after that and the day after that and the day after that. It's endless.'

He pulled the covers up around them.

'Let's get a dog,' she said. 'We need a dog in our life.'

And they slept.

Later, Lindow returned to the churchyard at Droy. He was crawling between the gravestones on his belly, slithering like an eel across the damp, damp dew. Someone was with him, but he didn't know who. He reached the opening of the vault and peered down into the chamber. Eamonn was stretched out on the sacking, Mary curled up beside him, her hands tucked under her cheek. Both were quite, quite asleep and, however much he shouted, they couldn't be woken. Then Foyle came and dragged Lindow away through the damp, damp grass. An owl swooped down upon them.

Foyle left London with his wife at one thirty p.m., having satisfied himself that the Lord Mayor's Parade had passed off without incident. The journey was spent discussing exactly what they would tell Katherine, who had already sensed that something was wrong when June called her the day before. Foyle watched his wife from the corner of his eye as he drove past Heathrow and out into Berkshire. There was a lightness in her manner, a kind of youthful flippancy he found difficult to deal with. He could remember seeing her like this only once before – when they'd just been married. It was obvious that she was in love with the Arab bone-hunter, as he thought of Dr Hussan, and that his marriage was over. He said this gently, arguing that they should be completely straight with Katherine. If there was no chance of them staying together, they shouldn't offer hope. Now it was June who refused to accept the inevitable, and during the two-and-a-half-hour journey she repeated over and over that all she needed was time to work things out. Eventually Foyle retreated into himself, occasionally murmuring a response, but for the most part he thought about the Rhodes investigation and wondered what he'd missed. What did Axiom Day mean?

Lindow and Mary rose late and drifted out to breakfast at a coffee-house in Sloane Square. Mary clung to his arm as they walked, teasing him that he had an almost English fear of showing affection in public. He denied it furiously, then wrapped his right arm around her shoulder and looked ahead of them self-consciously.

In the coffee shop she held up a huge cup of *caffe latte* and looked over it with a glint in her eye. 'Our problem is that we don't have a history, you and I. We don't know anyone in common, we don't have anything in common. I mean you're a scientist and I'm a book editor.'

'And a spy.'

'I'm a book editor and former spy,' she corrected. 'Look, the point is that we've never done anything together, never been to a movie or a play or a gallery together. We've never bought anything together, never looked around old shops together, never fought over a newspaper, argued about politics, read the same book. I mean, we're like strangers. So what I want to know, Constantine Lindow, is how are we expected to stay married?'

Most of her face remained obscured by the cup, but he saw her eyebrows arch with expectation and a serious look enter her eyes.

'Are you joking, or what? I never know with you. I mean, this is serious stuff, Mary. I mean serious.'

'Answer my question,' she demanded. 'How're we meant to stay married?'

'Before we decided to get married,' he said, now smiling broadly, 'we would have to put ourselves through a kind of rapid induction, just to make sure we had something in common. I suppose we'd try to do it all very quickly – go to a lot of movies, plays, galleries, antique shops, football matches.'

'No sports,' she said. 'I don't watch sports.'

'Okay, no sports. But we'd do all these things in rapid succession and see if we were compatible.'

'So, what are we waiting for? It's just two weeks and one day since we met. But I want you. I want to become the dull wife of a dull scientist and get a dull little dog. That's what I want, Con. It's all I want.'

'So this *is* a proposal?'

She sipped again, then glanced away shyly. 'Kind of.'

Con put his hand out and turned her face to his. 'Is it okay if I give you my answer at the end of the day, when we've been through our cultural initiation? But there's one condition – you have to stop quoting poetry at me.'

'That's a big sacrifice. I'll work on it.'

They left the coffee-house and went shopping, an occupation that Lindow heartily loathed. She bought a short black overcoat and insisted that he buy two dark shirts in the same store. He went along with the suggestion, anxious to show they had some of the same taste, though he disliked them. Then they wandered through London, diving into bookshops, trailing through antique markets and talking.

Eventually, in the late afternoon, they reached Imperial College, where he showed her a mass spectrometer and then a gallery containing some false-colour images of resistant bacteria strains. He told her how the genes of a certain strain of a bacterium called *Staphylococcus aureus* produced a protein that shielded it against antibiotics.

'Will it wipe us all out?' she asked.

'Not yet. But it's poised and, with a few modifications in its genetic code, it might.'

Night had fallen by the time they left the college and took a cab to the Gate cinema in Notting Hill, a favourite place of Mary's because she said the people hanging around outside always reminded her of movie lines in the States. They watched an obscure art-house film, which bored both of them, but neither said anything. Then they ate at an Indian restaurant and snapped poppadoms together. Towards the end of the evening she suggested that they stay at Lindow's flat because she'd never been there. 'You may live like a pig and I couldn't endure that.'

In less than twenty minutes Lindow unlocked the door to his flat in Homer Road.

'Hey, look,' said Mary. 'You've got a message. Your machine is flashing.'

'No tape,' said Lindow. 'Foyle took the message cassette and I haven't replaced it. It means that people hear the greeting tape but don't know that they're not being recorded.'

'Yes, but you can dial the recall service and find out who called you.'

Lindow dialled the four-digit number, feeling that Mary was being a little bossy. 'No number.' He put down the phone and took her in his arms.

'I guess it's safe,' she said slyly. 'No one's watching.'

'Does the state of my establishment meet with my lady's exacting standards?'

'Yep, just about.'

'Good. Would she like to hear my answer to the question she put to me this morning?'

'Yep.'

'It's yes. I guess we could make it together, even with a dull little dog.'

They fell into Lindow's ill-sprung double bed and made love easily, as if they'd known each other for years. Mary went to asleep in Lindow's arms, her breasts against his chest. He could feel the beat of her heart and remembered what *acushla* meant literally in Gaelic – pulse.

A clock chimed in the distance and 10 November became 11 November. Remembrance Day.

A little after eight a.m. Lindow received a telephone call. He woke as the bell ceased to sound and a voice spoke into the ansaphone.

'Con, are you there? This is important. Answer your goddam phone, for God's sake. I know what Axiom means. Pick up for God's sake. Damn you, Con.'

He recognised Varrone's voice, sprang from the bed and ran to the sitting room. He dived for the phone but Varrone had gone.

It must be important if he was calling from Boston in the middle of the night. He dialled Varrone's number and got the answer-machine. 'I'm away for a couple of days. Leave a message and I'll get back to you.'

He must be at the beach-house, thought Con. He looked up Varrone's weekend number in his address book, dialled and got another ansaphone. This time Varrone's voice told the caller to leave a message or try his Boston number. Lindow left a message saying that he was in London and waiting for Varrone to call.

Twenty minutes later the phone rang again. Lindow got there in time.

'Peter! Is that you?'

'Where've you been?' Varrone sounded irritated. 'I left three messages for you. Don't you return calls any more?'

'The ansaphone isn't working. No message-tape. Hey, it's late for you,' said Lindow, looking at his watch. It was three thirty a.m. in Boston.

'I'm in Seattle for the quantum computing conference. It's only half past midnight here. I came out here with Frank. Look, this is important. I believe I've figured out what Axiom Day means. It's a kind of acronym, which is why we couldn't crack it with normal decryption programs. You said this guy Rhodes was half Italian, right? He had an Italian mother, right? So this is the way I think it works. The A means 'At' in Italian, the X and the I stand for eleven in Roman numerals, the O stands for *ora*, which means hour in Italian, and the M stands for *mese*, which means month in Italian.'

'So?' said Lindow.

'You don't see it, do you? With the word "day" it precisely describes today's date. As near as damn it, it means "at the eleventh hour of the eleventh day of the eleventh month" – the day the Armistice was signed in 1918, Veterans' Day in the States and Remembrance Day over there.'

Lindow scribbled Axiom Day on the pad by the phone, spacing the letters out. Then he saw how it worked. 'I'll call Foyle,' he said.

'I already tried that earlier. He isn't at his home number.'

'Yes, I remember him saying he was going away,' said Lindow.

'I also spoke to New Scotland Yard a couple of hours back. I tried to explain it to a duty officer but he thought I was a lunatic. He didn't understand what the hell I was talking about.'

'Okay, I'll call them now. We'll talk later.'

Lindow hung up without saying goodbye, then cursed that he hadn't taken Varrone's number in Seattle.

He dialled New Scotland Yard and was put through to the duty officer at the Anti-terrorist Unit. A laconic, know-it-all voice came on the line. Yes, said the police officer, someone had spoken to Dr Varrone and he'd left a note for the commander that explained Dr Varrone's observations. The commander was due in, but he couldn't say when and he didn't know Foyle's mobile number.

Lindow saw he was getting nowhere and left a message for Foyle to call him urgently. Then he tried Foyle's home number and let the phone ring for a couple of minutes. Foyle must be in Bristol still.

Just as he got back into bed the phone rang again. He hopped into the living room and snatched up the receiver.

'Commander?' he said.

'No, it's me again,' said Varrone. 'What's with you? You hung up before I finished. Look, Mundy's just got in from dinner. He's got some information from a man up at the cabin. It may be nothing but they have faxed it to New Scotland Yard. He says a London number has been dialling one of Lasseur's phones in Maine. The number called several times on Wednesday morning, each time at a minute past the hour, one call an hour. The crucial point is that by Wednesday your friend Rhodes was dead. Mundy's man traced it through the phone company to London.'

'Could be a misdial.'

'Sure, that's what Mundy thinks. Here's the number. It's 0171 701 7972. You should have someone check it out.'

Lindow wrote it down on the notepad beside the words 'Axiom Day'. He thanked Varrone, then dialled New Scotland Yard. The officer still had no idea where the commander was and assured Lindow, in a heavily condescending manner, that he would pass on his message.

It was twenty to one on the west coast of the United States and eight forty a.m. in London. Lindow returned to bed, clutching the piece of paper he'd written on, and slipped in beside Mary's warm, curled-up body. She stirred and drew his arm around her.

'You're cold,' she said.

'Sorry.'

He kissed her on the nape of her neck. He would wait half an hour, then try Foyle again at New Scotland Yard.

*

Foyle had intended to leave Bristol the previous evening, but the way things turned out it had not been possible. Katherine had taken the news of the impending separation badly and set about trying to reconcile them over dinner, pointing out that neither could live with anyone else. Foyle had waited for June to say something about her new interest, as she referred to her lover, but she hadn't. This he had dared to read as a good sign. He decided to leave it as late as possible before driving back, but by the end of dinner he knew he'd drunk too much and he checked into a small hotel near Katherine's flat. June stayed with Katherine.

Now he was making good time and was able to stop for a much-needed cup of coffee at a service area. He reached London by nine twenty a.m. but then got caught on Chelsea Embankment behind a convoy of coaches, carrying British Legion veterans to Whitehall. Eventually he lost patience and pulled out of the line of coaches, waving his warrant card through the window at the traffic police.

It was nine forty-five by the time he arrived at New Scotland Yard and parked his car in a side-street. As he stepped out he looked up. The sky was sombre and a steady wind tugged the still-green leaves of the plane trees. To the east he could see two police helicopters hovering over Horse Guards Parade, where thousands of veterans, wearing their campaign medals, bowler hats and old service berets, would now be assembling. Foyle thought of his own father, a paratrooper and Arnhem veteran who, in the last weeks of his life, suddenly attended the parade, having resolutely refused to think or talk about the war for thirty years. Foyle had been one of the uniformed officers lining the route and had caught sight of him marching along, chin thrust out and eyes watering with pride. He saw him only once more. Two weeks later he was dead of a heart attack.

He hesitated for a moment to catch the sound of the bagpipers and buglers practising a few hundred yards away in the Wellington Barracks. Then he hurried across the street to the main entrance and took the lift up to his department. It didn't matter that he'd missed the briefing as he had no direct responsibility for the security operation and, anyway, he was familiar with the arrangements – the numbers of officers from the Tactical Firearms Unit on the rooftops overlooking Whitehall, the increased force of plain-clothes officers mingling with the crowds, and the position of Bomb Squad Range Rovers. Lafferty had put most of his explosives officers into the Westminster area, and, on the way, Foyle had seen some probing man-hole covers and unscrewing the service plates of the traffic signals and street-lights along the southern end of Victoria Street. Below ground other officers would be wading through sewage ducts, checking every recess for unusual devices.

SO 13 was practically deserted, most of its officers having been drafted into the security operation. Foyle found Pennel in the corridor outside his office, clutching a folder containing overnight messages, one or two faxes, the latest copy of the security briefing and some outstanding reports from officers involved in the Rhodes investigation. Pennel said that Chief Inspector Forbes had intended to look through it, but he had been called into the operations room. Foyle said that was fine. He would join Forbes there and go through it himself while waiting for the parade to get under way.

He went into his office to dial Katherine's number in Bristol and asked how things were going. She was guarded. Foyle could hear June in the background talking to one of Katherine's flatmates. He made a point of sending his love to her and said he would call Katherine later.

It was nine fifty-nine a.m.

Lindow had entered another deep sleep and it was not until twenty minutes past nine that he was woken by Mary.

'Shit. What's the time?' he said, reaching for his watch.

'Was someone calling earlier?' she asked.

'Look, it's late. I've got to try Foyle.'

'Who called?' she persisted.

'Peter Varrone – you know, my friend from Boston. He's got a theory about the meaning of Axiom Day. He thinks it's code for today's date.'

'Yes?' she said, interested. 'How did he figure that?'

'It's not exact,' he said, 'but it's convincing.' He swung his legs from the bed and pulled his arm out from under her to hold the piece of notepaper in front of her. 'Here, see how it works.'

'That's neat,' she said. 'It's like a crossword answer.' She propped herself up and scrutinised the paper again, pulling her head back to focus on it. 'Con, why have you got Eamonn's number written down here?'

'It's not Eamonn's number. Varrone just gave it to me. The FBI retrieved it from one of the phone sets at the lake. Apparently that number rang one of Lasseur's phones several times on Wednesday morning.'

Mary shot upright and took the paper from Con's hand. 'No, you don't understand, Con. This *is* Eamonn's number. I know it by heart. Don't you know your own brother's number?'

'No. I only called him there a couple of times. Are you sure?'

'Tell me exactly what Varrone told you.'

'He told me that when one of the phone installations had been checked in Maine it was found that a number had been calling Lasseur. He said the number had rung several times on Wednesday morning, a minute past the hour each time. They traced the number and it turned out to be this one. I'll check it in my book.'

'He said Wednesday, right?'

'Yes, by which time Rhodes was dead.' He went into the sitting room and returned with the book. 'Jesus, you're right.'

'What's it mean, Con?'

'I don't know but I think the fact that those calls were made on Wednesday is really significant.'

'Why?'

'Because Rhodes had a schedule. By Wednesday morning – that's to say Wednesday morning East Coast time – he would have been in the Far East. Perhaps he programmed the computer to send a coded message to Lasseur's computer, once he was safely out of the way.'

'He'd already done that. We saw what happened to Lasseur.'

'Yes, but perhaps these were fail-safe calls, programmed into a computer well before we went to Maine.' He paused and momentarily absorbed the beauty of her body on the bed. 'Look, we'd better get dressed. I'll find us some coffee.'

By the time Lindow returned with two cups of Nescafé she had pulled on her jeans and sweater and was drying her face. As he searched around for his own clothes, his mind tore at the problem.

'The fail-safe must have been the original plan for killing Lasseur and destroying everything that was important in the cabin. Then he decided Lasseur was becoming a liability. You remember how strung out he was? Rhodes must have sensed that and decided to get rid of him right then. Once he thought we'd been killed, he had no further use for him and sent the message that detonated the explosives in Lasseur's computer.'

'But that doesn't make sense,' she protested. 'Why would he program the computer to make those calls when he knew Lasseur was already dead?'

'I don't know, but I think we should go over there and take a look. I've got to use the bathroom. You try Foyle and tell him we're going over there.'

She dashed into the sitting room. As Lindow urinated, he heard her shouting at someone at New Scotland Yard.

'Well, find him now! Tell him we'll be at fifty-six Jasmine Road, Peckham. That's fifty-six! Yes! Say we're going there now. It's important. Say we'll call him on the way. Our names? I told you, for Chrissake – Mary Menihan, Con Lindow.'

She slammed down the receiver and came back into the bedroom.

'They're not even sure he's in the building. They're going to get a message to him. Christ knows how long that'll take.'

Lindow snatched up his jacket, felt for his wallet and took Eamonn's keys from a bowl near the telephone.

As they left the flat he glanced at his watch. It was nine fifty-five a.m. Another ten minutes passed before they found a cab.

20

Foyle stood in the operations room with a folder under his arm, sipping at a Styrofoam beaker and skim-reading an account of the death of Ian Rhodes in one of the Sunday papers. Towards the end of the two-page spread there were vague references to David Cantor's expected retirement, which were phrased in such a way as to imply that the director general was being blamed for the failure to capture Rhodes. A sidebar devoted to Rhodes's mental state was particularly well sourced and included information from the psychological profiles, drawn up for Foyle at the beginning of the week. This and the material on Rhodes's childhood could only have come from the police or the Home Office – probably the latter since the Home Secretary emerged from the main article with a greatly enhanced reputation for decisiveness.

Foyle sat down and concentrated on the magnified image of Rhodes. The eyes gave nothing away, but prompted a dull anxiety to move in his stomach. There was no sense in obsessing about Rhodes, he thought. He was an unreadable blank, an aberration. He glanced from the paper to the banks of television monitors. Each screen showed evidence of the huge police presence. He watched a feed from a helicopter, positioned high above the Cenotaph, then another from a military camera, which showed the final inspections of the bands in front of the Guards. A third camera was trained along the first storey of the Foreign and Commonwealth Office where the blue drapery of the royal balconies was trembling in the wind.

From street level to rooftops, scores of cameras panned, zoomed and observed as Whitehall readied itself to honour the Glorious Dead, the 1,694,999 men and women from Britain and the colonies who lost their lives in two world wars. Foyle reasoned with himself that the operation being played out on the screens in front of him was impressive, a perfectly timed piece of choreography that allowed for more or less every conceivable eventuality. Even some of the phone networks had been shut down for the morning, although it was impossible to screen off an area in the heart of London where scores of small repeaters enabled signals to penetrate every nook and cranny of the street layout.

He drained the beaker, feeling the jip of the caffeine, and looked again at a monitor showing the faces of the people moving through one of the checks in the south. They smiled with good-natured deference as police officers frisked them and handed out service sheets. Soon the pavements, which stretched the two hundred yards from Parliament Square to the Cenotaph, would swell and the thoroughfare itself would fill with ranks of servicemen, military bands and clerics, making an odd, curiously human pageant of British life. Before the hour was up, the Prime Minister, members of the Cabinet, the leaders of the main political parties, three or four ex-prime ministers, the chiefs of the General Staff and up to fifty-three high commissioners would file from the Foreign Office and form up around Sir Edwin Lutyens's austere Portland stone monument. Finally the parade would be called to attention and the Queen and three princes, encumbered like turn-of-the-century generals with great-coats and ceremonial swords, would move stiffly to their position north of the Cenotaph. The service would begin, a moment of national homage to the fallen, in which the entire establishment stood clustered within a few square yards, more vulnerable than at any other time of the year.

Foyle folded the image of Rhodes into four and placed the newspaper deliberately on the floor against the leg of his chair.

'Everything seems to be going pretty well, like clockwork.' It was Forbes who had come up behind him.

'Yes, for the moment it is. But I'll be happier when this damn parade is over.' Foyle thought of Remembrance Sunday in Enniskillen when the IRA had killed eleven people.

Forbes drifted back to the desk where he'd been sitting.

Left alone, Foyle opened the folder of messages and read through the security schedule for the morning. For a few minutes he concentrated on a diagram giving the exact position of each VIP during the service. Overleaf was a chart showing the protection arrangements before and after the ceremony. He moved on through the folder and paused at a report from Sevenoaks Police, which had been faxed over that morning by an officer named Andrew Gresham who was leading the investigation into the murder of one James Hallwell. Foyle assumed that there had been some sort of error but on the first page of the report was a yellow sticker, indicating that Gresham had called that morning to make sure that the report would reach him. He read the first sheet, which described the unremarkable slaying of a small-time drugs dealer, then he flipped through the remaining two sheets. On the third Gresham had circled a passage concerning a grey Vauxhall van and written, 'Could this be your man's vehicle?'

A grey Vauxhall van had been seen in Hallwell's workshop the previous week. Sevenoaks Police had no record of the registration number of the van but they were anxious to trace the owner. Foyle went back to the beginning of the report and began to read carefully. James Hallwell had been murdered the previous weekend. At first an overdose had been suspected. The body was found slumped on an old car seat in the workshop and a syringe, containing a mixture of heroin and cocaine, was lying by his right hand. Gresham noticed that this didn't tally with the nicotine stains on the victim's left index finger. He confirmed that Hallwell was left-handed and, after finding no other needle marks on the body, concluded that Hallwell had not administered the dose himself. A search of the premises gave no clue as to why he had been murdered, but it did turn up some vinyl strips from which letters had been individually peeled and, according to a neighbour living opposite the workshop, applied to either side of the van. There were eight strips, which had been output from different machines – an indication, perhaps, that the owner of the van had something to hide. Using the remains of the vinyl strips Gresham worked out that the van bore the words 'Jefferton Brothers 24-hour CCTV Repair and Service'. There was no trace of any such firm in the area.

Foyle sat back in his chair, furiously trying to make the connections that he knew were waiting for him. Then he realised there was more to it than just the van. According to Gresham's report, at the time of his death Hallwell was working on a special job, which he had not wanted to discuss with friends or his neighbour opposite. All anyone knew was that it involved the production of aluminium boxes. Filings and shavings consistent with this were found on the floor of the workshop and almost certainly indicated that he had just finished the work at the time of his death. There was no sign of these boxes, but by measuring the gaps in two vices, Gresham had estimated that the boxes were between eight and ten inches wide.

Foyle's mind was on the point of crystallising a conclusion when an ashen-faced Sergeant Pennel burst into the operations room.

'This is important, sir. There was a message last night – several, in fact – from Peter Varrone. The overnight man wrote it down for you on the system, but didn't print it out at the end of his shift. Varrone's cracked Axiom Day. He thinks it means November the eleventh. It's code for "at the eleventh hour of the eleventh day of the eleventh month".'

'For God's sake, slow down, Sergeant,' snapped Foyle. 'Tell me what Varrone said – exactly.'

The operations room had fallen silent and some of the officers had swivelled their chairs. Pennel explained how the word Axiom could be read as an acronym. Added to the word Day, it was a clear indication that Rhodes had been planning something for Remembrance Day. He went on to say Miss Menihan had phoned. 'Her message wasn't clear but the officer who spoke to her said she was desperate to get in touch with you.

She and Lindow are on their way to Eamonn Lindow's address in Peckham.'

Foyle was silent for a moment. His eyes went to a large clock on the wall. It was ten twenty-seven a.m. The second hand was moving with incredible speed around the clock face.

'Get me Kirsty Laing on the phone now,' he shouted to Forbes. 'And the minute Menihan or Lindow phone, put them through to me. Get some officers to Eamonn Lindow's address in Peckham. Find out what the hell's happening. I want Lafferty up here.'

The superintendent in charge of the operations room came over. 'What's going on?'

'Wait there, and I'll tell you what to do.'

Foyle had guessed right. Kirsty Laing was in her office. 'Tell me where that first photograph of Rhodes was taken,' he demanded. 'You know, the one you gave me. Where was it taken?'

She hesitated. 'In Whitehall, I think.'

'You've got Weegee operating there the whole time?'

'Yes, why?'

'Find out if there were any more sightings. Get your people to work out exactly where he was in the first photograph. There's very little time.' He gave her his extension number and hung up.

'We've got a problem,' he said to the superintendent. 'There may be a device in Whitehall.'

'There can't be,' the officer protested. 'Every square inch of the street and buildings has been searched. And not just once, several times.'

'Believe me – I'm serious. We've got to evacuate Whitehall immediately. There could be more than one bomb.'

'What evidence have you got? I can't abort the whole damned thing without some convincing evidence that there's a device down there.'

Foyle had no time to reply. He was suddenly aware that the commissioner and Martin Scarratt had entered the operations room. One of the officers on the main operations desk must have alerted them.

'What's happening here?' asked Urquhart.

'The commander says there may be a device in Whitehall, sir.'

'What reason do you have for believing that, Commander?'

Foyle was silenced. What reason did he have? Apart from Varrone's solution to the phrase Axiom Day and some circumstantial evidence concerning the activities of a small-time crook in Sevenoaks, there wasn't much to go on – nothing firm, nothing that was going to convince the commissioner. He hastily explained the inquiry into the murder of James Hallwell, pointing to the ringed passages in Gresham's report. Then he moved to MI5's surveillance photographs, saying there was evidence that Rhodes had been in Whitehall on 23 October.

Urquhart looked at him despairingly.

'Yes, but where are these bombs?' he said. 'Who's going to set them off? I mean, we've got to have more than this, Foyle.'

Lindow and Mary's cab was stuck behind a line of vehicles, waiting at some emergency gas repairs, near Clapham Common. They looked ahead of them nervously.

'Jesus,' he said, clapping his forehead. 'I know what it all means.'

'What?' asked Mary.

'Those calls came from a computer in Eamonn's flat. Rhodes must have set it up there. He must have programmed it to call Lasseur's number and send the message to explode his computer and kill him.'

'We've been over this,' said Mary. 'It doesn't make sense to program a computer after he knew that Lasseur was already dead.'

'No – that's the point. He'd already set it up in Eamonn's place. He probably did it some time before last weekend. But he kept all the same software – and the same code – on a lap-top he carried around with him. We know he had more than one base, why not more than one computer? Do you see? It means that he probably sent the coded message to kill Lasseur from his lap-top, although the other computer at Eamonn's had already been primed to do the same on Wednesday morning.'

'So what're you saying?'

'What I'm saying is there's a computer hooked up in Eamonn's flat that was programmed to send the message on Wednesday after Rhodes had left the country. It kept on calling the number that morning – right? If it was capable of sending a stream of calls to a telephone in the US on Wednesday, it's capable of performing the same task in London today. Mary, it's still sitting there and it's operational.'

'God, I hope you're not right.' She looked out at the traffic in front of them, swore and slipped from the back seat to perch on one of the fold-downs behind the driver.

'Can you get us out of this jam?' she said to the driver, proffering a twenty-pound note through the partition window. 'It could be a matter of life and death.'

'Certainly, madam.' He took the money.

They swung round out of the line of traffic, went back up the road they'd been waiting in and dived into some side-streets, which took them through Brixton. Mary looked down through the partition. 'Hey, is that cellphone working? Can I borrow it for another twenty?' She snapped her fingers at Lindow for the money.

'For another twenty I'll tap-dance on the roof,' said the driver. 'How long do you need it for?'

'About an hour. Can I make a call now?'

The driver passed the phone over his shoulder. As the cab stopped to join the flow of traffic going up Denmark Hill, Mary dialled New Scotland Yard and handed it to Lindow.

'It's Lindow, sir,' said Pennel. 'He's on a mobile.'

Foyle took the phone. 'Con, where are you?'

'I'm with Mary. We're five minutes from Eamonn's flat – maybe less. I believe there's a computer there which is primed to send out signals. Did you talk to Varrone?'

'No, but I got a message. I know about Axiom. What did you say about a computer?' Foyle heard the engine of the cab revving. Lindow's voice rose over the noise.

'One of Lasseur's phones recorded several calls received from Eamonn's number the day after Rhodes was killed. The FBI traced the calls. Mundy faxed you last night. You should have had the information by now. The point is that the computer was most likely programmed to make the call to Lasseur after Rhodes had left England. Do you see? He set up a system to dial Lasseur's number about midday our time, in advance. That was when he originally planned to kill him. Then we arrived and he decided to do it immediately, but the other computer was still set to send out the signal. If it can do that on Wednesday, it can do it today at eleven o'clock.'

'Now listen to me very carefully,' said Foyle. 'I don't want you blundering into the flat. I'm sending officers and I'll be in direct contact with them. The Explosives Unit are on their way too. Now, I'm going to put you on a speaker. I want you to keep this line open and tell me where you are at every stage. You are not to go in. If you're right about this computer, the place is likely to be booby-trapped. Do you understand, Con? You're breaking up, Con? Con? Can you hear me?'

The line went dead. Foyle brought his fist down on the desk. Then Forbes shouted that Kirsty Laing was on the line. Foyle reached over to another phone, picked up the receiver and pressed the button next to the flashing light.

'Yes.'

'He was at the northern end of the street, about fifty yards south of the Whitehall Theatre,' she said, without preliminaries. 'And there was an unconfirmed sighting this week – on Monday. The picture wasn't good and there'd been several false alarms.'

'Where was he then?'

'In Whitehall again, lower down, near Parliament Square. We weren't sure it was him. It might've been a camera repairman. The man was in white overalls and was driving a grey van. He was carrying out some repairs.'

'Christ! Oh, Christ!' Foyle turned to the room and met Forbes's eyes. 'You say a grey van?'

'Yes.'

Foyle dropped the phone. 'It's in a bloody camera!' he shouted at the commissioner, who was at the other end of the room talking to Scarratt. 'The bomb's in a security camera. It's got to be. That's his pattern – turning a safety device into a bomb. That's what he was doing in Sevenoaks – building something which looks like a camera. Sir, you've got to stop the ceremony.'

Urquhart nodded. 'Right. Evacuate immediately! Get the place cleared and the damned royals out of Whitehall now and all the rest of them – the Cabinet and diplomats. Now! By God, I hope you're not right, Foyle.'

Foyle didn't reply. For some reason, his eyes came to rest on a big jolly-faced woman with an ample bosom, who was standing directly in the line of the street-level cameras. She dabbed at an eye as she watched the massed bands strike up 'Men of Harlech'.

At the bottom of the screen a digital display recorded the time as ten hours, forty minutes and twenty-four seconds.

Apart from a disconsolate young man plodding back from the newsagent's with a carton of milk and the newspapers, Jasmine Road was deserted. A flock of pigeons pecked furiously at some breadcrumbs under the watchful eye of a cat, sitting on a wall about twenty feet away.

Lindow and Mary got out of the cab and stood in the road. It was beginning to spot with rain.

He dialled Foyle and was put through almost immediately. 'We're outside the flat now,' he said. 'There's no sign of any policemen. What should we do?'

'Hang on. They should be there any moment. Let me give you my extension number in case you get cut off.'

He wrote it down then looked up at the building. Nothing had changed, except that the vines had shed a few more leaves, exposing the cracked plaster. There was no sign of life in any of the windows and the curtains were still drawn in the ground-floor flat.

Mary walked the few steps to the garden wall and looked up, then returned to Lindow's side, hands thrust forward in the pockets of the coat they'd bought together. 'Where're the police?' she demanded.

'God knows.' Lindow looked up and down the road.

'Give me the keys. I'm going to take a look.'

Lindow was listening to the voices coming over the phone from the operations room. 'Hey, shut up for a second, will you? Something's going on. I think they've stopped the parade.'

Mary pointed to her watch. 'Have you seen the time, Con? We've got to see what's in there.'

Foyle heard her. 'Don't let her go, Con.'

'They say we've got to wait,' Lindow said to Mary sharply. 'So just stay here, will you?'

The cab driver chimed in, 'So what do you want me to do? My meter's going here. I'll have to charge you waiting time, as well.'

Neither of them took any notice.

Within six minutes of the evacuation order being given, three suspect cameras had been identified in Whitehall by police marksmen, using binoculars and rifle scopes. The helicopter spotted a further two in the side-streets leading down to Victoria Embankment. All five devices were fixed at a height of about fifteen feet by means of brackets bolted to the masonry walls of the buildings. Inspector Lafferty, who had been rushed the few hundred yards from the corner of Parliament Square to New Scotland Yard in a police Range Rover, estimated that the two-feet-long camera housings might contain as much as twelve pounds of explosives each – enough to bring down the sides of the buildings. Pointing to a map of the area, he addressed the commissioner and a knot of senior officers gathered round Foyle.

'These boxes are almost certainly packed with nails and bolts, which will act like shrapnel. They're probably timed to go off in a relay, the devices nearest the Cenotaph exploding first, followed by the ones in the side-streets. They'll catch the people escaping from the first explosions.'

'And there's no hope of disarming them?' said the commissioner.

'Not in the quarter of an hour we believe is available. We're examining one of them in Whitehall – here.' He tapped the map at a point on the south-east side of the street. 'There's no way we can lift our equipment up to the boxes, and we certainly can't tackle five at once. There may be all sorts of anti-handling devices attached to them.'

The head of Tactical Firearms suggested that it might be possible for his officers to shoot off the rubberised antennae that could be seen protruding from at least two of the silver casings. But Lafferty dismissed the idea, saying that a stray bullet might detonate the explosives. Then he left the group to radio the men who were examining one of the devices from a window on the east side of the street.

'The only sensible course is to get the people out of the area as soon as possible,' said Urquhart. 'How're we doing on the Royal Family?'

The operations-room superintendent replied that the balcony outside Room 238 in the Foreign Office was being cleared at that moment and the remaining members of the Royal Family, the Prime Minister, members of the Cabinet, diplomats and chiefs of the Defence Staff were being rushed from the area. The main problem was the vast number of people still in Whitehall.

In unison the group turned to the screens. To the north of the Cenotaph well over a thousand veterans, a good number of them blind or in wheelchairs, were mustered in the centre of Whitehall, ready for the march-past. On either side crowds were held back by crush barriers. The obvious escape routes lay to the west, through the arch to Horse Guards Parade or over the open ground in front of the Ministry of Defence. The latter route, however, would bring them too close to the suspected device in the east. And in the north there was another device, with a blast range that meant the street to Trafalgar Square was effectively cut off. The only solution was to send them back through the arch.

An order was sent out to turn the veterans back and funnel them through to Horse Guards Parade, but the monitors showed that the police on the ground were having difficulty communicating this to the leaders of the various sections, particularly those in the middle of the mass of servicemen patiently waiting for the service to begin.

To the south the only solution was to get the people out into the centre of the street and down to the square. That would remove them from the immediate killing zone. But things were already going badly wrong. Gaps had not been made in the crush barriers and people were either attempting to climb over them or pressing back along the pavements towards the security gates at the southern end of the street. On both sides monitors showed the police trying to pull the high wire fences aside to release the pressure of the crowd.

But the chaos was not yet universal. In some places along Whitehall, the crowds seemed unaware of the danger. What they did notice, however, was that it was beginning to rain. Umbrellas appeared, which meant that people's view was obscured and for a few seconds longer they remained ignorant of what was going on. But word was spreading quickly along the pavements. Soon the umbrellas were dancing as the crowds shifted first one way, then the other. As they realised that they were trapped between the buildings and the barriers, their eyes widened and their mouths opened. Waves of panic and disbelief rippled across their faces.

In the midst of the calamity there were some bizarre sights. Without orders, many of the servicemen seemed unwilling to break the formations around the Cenotaph. The twelve ranks of the massed bands were still intact, and detachments from the Household Cavalry and Welsh Guards stood at ease demonstrating either bone-headed stupidity or a suicidal sangfroid.

Others were quicker to react. An officer from the Green Jackets regiment could be seen organising his men to move aside the crush barriers and herd the crowd towards Parliament Square. Beside him, a BBC cameraman was filming, and around the street nine other crews relayed the unfolding scenes to the world.

The commissioner grasped the situation quickly and barked a stream of orders to the officers in front of the monitors. Most of them repeated the instructions already radioed to the ground, but the controllers went ahead and reissued them nevertheless. It was clear that response time was slowing as every minute passed. What had been an exemplary reflex between the command of the operations room and response on the ground had atrophied.

Foyle listened with one ear, but the majority of his attention was devoted to the speaker-phone over which he could hear Lindow and Mary Menihan talking in the street outside Eamonn's flat. He looked at the clock. It was ten forty-seven and there was still no sign of police in Jasmine Road.

Then Lafferty was at his side. 'We know what's in them. One of my officers has been lowered on a rope out of the window. You can see him on the far monitor over there. He's just unclipped the lid of the device on the south-east side. He's telling us there's a cartload of explosives in there. The detonator is hooked up to a telephone and has anti-handling circuits. It's a wonder he got the damned top off without blowing himself up.'

'Power supply?' asked Foyle.

'Batteries,' replied Lafferty.

'There's got to be a command device in Eamonn Lindow's flat. Are your people anywhere near there?'

'About five to seven minutes away, I'd guess, maybe more.'

Foyle looked at his watch and shouted across the room. 'Pennel, anything from the networks? We need the area shut down now.'

Pennel was gesturing as he spoke into his phone and did not reply immediately. 'They're doing their best, but there's still a chance a call will get through. We always knew that it was going to be impossible to seal off the whole area.'

'Well, tell them to do everything they can,' Foyle bellowed. 'Thousands of people are still out there.' Then he turned to the speaker-phone. 'You still there, Con? What's your brother's phone number? We need to have it cut off immediately.'

Lindow told him. This time he didn't have to think about it.

Mary looked at her watch again. 'Give me the goddam keys, for Chrissake. There's twelve minutes left. We've got to find out what's in there. Come on. I'm going in.'

'Don't let her go,' barked Foyle in Lindow's ear.

'You can't,' said Lindow. 'Stay here.'

She plunged her hand in his jacket pocket and pulled out the ring of keys. Lindow was holding the phone in his right hand and tried to snatch at her with his left. But she was too quick, escaping from his grasp and bounding up the steps.

'She's going,' he yelled to Foyle. 'She's got the keys. I'm going after her.'

He glanced from Mary to the cab driver, then back at Mary. 'I'm coming too.' He lowered the phone to silence Foyle's protests.

'Hold on there!' said the driver, getting out of the cab. 'How do I know you're not going to run off?'

Lindow turned to see Mary open the door. She glanced back at him and disappeared inside. He started forward, but his right foot slipped sideways on the damp, greasy pavement. He recovered his balance and tore up the steps after her.

'No,' cried Foyle several times, but his voice was lost in Lindow's clenched fist.

He pounded through the empty hallway and up the stairs. Mary reached the corner of the landing and grabbed at the banister to pull herself up the six stairs to Eamonn's door. Lindow was halfway up the first flight when she inserted a key into the top lock, then tried the lower one, pushing at the door with her knee. He saw the blur of Mary's form and her dark hair flying as she vanished through the doorway.

'Ma—!' he shouted, but the rest was lost in the blast.

Before he fell, he saw a flash and something being propelled out of the disintegrating door frame. Then he was slammed backwards by the shockwave. His face smashed into the dado rail and he was thrown down the stairs in a storm of splintered wood and brickwork. He came to rest at the bottom of the stairs. The house roared as if in the grip of some demonic possession. All around him was the soot-fall of plasterwork and the sound of breaking glass. He opened his eyes. The flash was imprinted on his retina. He blinked and blinked to rid himself of it. He knew he was cut somewhere on his face. Blood streamed backwards into his hair from a gash just above his right eye.

Some time later – how long he didn't know – he heard the tiny muffled voice in his fist. He had kept hold of the phone and, miraculously, the line was still open. Foyle was there. 'Con? Con! Con, are you all right?'

'There's been a bomb,' he whispered, and then the terrible knowledge of what had happened formed itself into words. 'Mary's hurt. Get someone here fast.'

He shifted on to his side and swung his legs backwards so that he could get up, and began to drag himself up the stairs. It was very dark and the stairway was dense with ugly black smoke. He climbed to the first landing, where he could see better. The explosion had blown the glass from the windows and smoke was pouring out into the street. Way off, there were voices. People screaming. Below, the cab driver was shouting through the front door.

Then he saw Mary's crumpled body curled up against the wall. He leaped up the remaining stairs and pulled the debris from her. There was blood everywhere. The wall was sprayed with tiny droplets.

'Con,' she groaned. 'Is that you? I can't see.'

'You've been blinded by the flash,' he said. 'It won't last. You're going to be okay.' He concentrated on her face, on her eyes, because he dared not look down at her injuries. He knew the full force of the blast must have driven up into her abdomen and thighs.

'Don't lie. I know I'm not.' Her voice was a whisper, fading.

'Yes, you are,' he said. He drew the hair from her face and smiled at her. 'Hold on there, my love. For God's sake, hold on.'

He glanced inside the flat. He couldn't see much, except that some of the furnishings had caught light and were producing an almost liquid smoke that was flowing down through the hole in the floor. The charge must have been set four or five feet inside the door, he thought. It had blown right through to the flat below, splintering the joists into matchsticks. An electricity cable was fizzing and a water-pipe had been blown apart. Somewhere there was the sound of a cistern filling.

He knew he must move Mary. In a few minutes the building would be burning. He placed the phone on the floor beside her head, shifted from his knees to a crouching position and slipped his left arm under her shoulder.

'You're going to be fine, my love, I promise.' He touched her cheek with the fingertips of his free hand and smiled again. She looked up at him.

'You were right. I can see now.' She smiled faintly then her eyes settled on something behind him. Lindow looked up.

'What is it?' he asked, and then he understood.

'No, you can't do that! No! ... Mary! ... No!'

He gripped her by the shoulders, as if to stop her falling asleep and shouted her name over and over again, but she was light in his hands – empty and limp. He looked down at her wounds for the first time and sank back, appalled. Nothing could be done for her. She'd had enough. She'd taken flight from her bloodied, ripped-up body and left him with it. He let her down to the floor gently, a part of him feeling a terrible repugnance – not for Mary, but for the ordinary human frailty that had taken her. It was death that made him recoil.

Then he heard Foyle's voice. Still looking at her face, he slowly lifted the phone to his ear.

Until the explosion in Peckham, all attention in the operations room had been focused on some juddering pictures from a video camera, held from the window above the bomb nearest to the Cenotaph. The explosives officer who had lowered himself on a rope could be seen attempting to unscrew the antenna from the phone without disturbing the anti-handling circuitry.

Then Foyle's cry to Lindow had thundered around the room, stopping everyone in mid-sentence. Officers rose from their screens and looked over to him. Others pulled their headsets aside, straining to hear the speaker of Foyle's phone.

'They're not going in!' Lafferty shouted with alarm. 'He's bound to have rigged something up.'

The words were barely out of his mouth when the unmistakable noise of the blast tore through the speaker. The line crackled and then seemed to fade, but it came back again. There was a roar and a sound of clattering, followed by a dreadful silence. Foyle thought both of them must have been killed. He rose from his chair, shouting their names into the speaker. Then he broke off, wild-eyed, to demand where the explosives team were. Eamonn's flat was the priority. Whitehall would never be cleared in time and the fate of all those people was now controlled by a device – a very well-protected device – in 56 Jasmine Road.

'Has that phone been cut off yet?' he shouted to the room. 'Get that damned phone cut off.' He turned to Lafferty. 'How was that set off?'

'It must've been wired into a burglar alarm – a movement or a heat sensor. There are any number of ways. Christ knows what else is in there.'

Then Lindow's voice, hoarse and uncomprehending, came over the speaker. They heard him climb the stairs and find Mary. He was coughing a lot but from the way he was talking to her they knew she was badly hurt. She began to speak but her voice was weak and seemed to grow distant. A few seconds later came Lindow's cry of agony.

Foyle winced and shook his head. He looked at the clock. There were only seven minutes left. He shot a glance at Lafferty and the commissioner. The commissioner nodded. They couldn't wait any longer. They had to tell Lindow to go into the flat and find the command device.

'Con, Con – answer me! Is anyone with you?'

'No ... there's no one here,' came the reply. 'Mary's gone.'

'Hold on, lad, we're going to get people to you. But now we have to find out what's in there. Can you do that for us? Are you up for it? There's no time.' Foyle was now very calm. Lindow mumbled something. Foyle repeated the question.

'Yes,' replied Lindow more clearly. 'I'm here. I'll do it.'

'Good, I've got the head of the Explosives Unit with me – Colin Lafferty. Colin's going to talk you through the next few minutes. Tell him exactly what you see. Okay? I'm here too.'

Lindow got up. He felt nauseous and had the sense of floating in unreality. He straightened himself, flicking blood from his cut eyebrow to the wall, and waggled a finger in each ear to stop the ringing.

Foyle was talking to him, but there were also noises downstairs – other voices, other cries. Someone had been hurt in the flat below. A man had ventured halfway up the stairs and was calling to him.

'Are you police?' shouted Lindow.

'No . . . they're coming,' replied the man.

'Then stay back – it's dangerous.'

He turned to go into his brother's home, holding the phone to his left ear.

'Where are you?' asked Foyle.

'I'm going in now. There's a lot of smoke.' As he spoke he edged around the hole in the floor, testing the floorboards with one foot to check they'd take his weight. He picked up a rug and beat at the fire on the upturned sofa. The flames disappeared quickly. He looked around. The place was unrecognisable. The TV set had been shattered and hurled into the bookcase. Books had tumbled to the floor and were covered in chunks of plaster. Every pane of glass in the flat was broken and the curtains were torn and catching on the jagged edges of glass as they flapped in the wind.

'What am I looking for?' he shouted.

'The telephone line,' said Lafferty calmly. 'The number is being taken out of service. But let's start with it anyway.'

Lindow searched the room, coughing up plaster dust from his lungs as he went. He found a telephone and traced the lead to a socket on the wall. He kicked aside the debris and bent down. 'There's no wire,' he said. 'The telephone is plugged in, but there's no wire leading from the socket.'

'He must've laid it somewhere else,' said Lafferty. 'Can you look outside the window? There should be some kind of junction box. Follow the wires from that.'

Lindow threw up the shattered window and scanned the wall. A crowd of onlookers had gathered in the street.

'Is anyone hurt up there?' a man shouted.

He took no notice. He leaned down and examined a small square of unweathered paint just below the window. He reported this to Lafferty.

'It means he moved the junction box too. We need to know why. You're going to have to look for it. He's probably put it at the back of the house.'

Lindow began hunting along the skirting-boards, pulling bits of furniture aside. The sofa was beginning to flame up again, but he ignored it and stumbled towards the kitchen to take a quick look around and then to lean out of the window.

'Got it. There's a box outside the kitchen window at the back. It's out of reach – a lot of wires are coming from it. More than one line.'

'He may have wired in the telephones from the other flats,' said Lafferty. 'It means we have to find the device. A call may still get through.'

'What are you doing now?' asked Foyle.

'I'm moving to the bedroom. One wire leads to the bedroom window. Hold on, something's different. The desk's been moved.'

He looked hard and tried to remember the room as he'd left it. The desk that had contained the secret compartment had been shifted a few feet towards the window.

He bent down to look at the skirting-board behind it. Then he heard two things. First Foyle's voice came rasping through the handset. 'British Telecom have confirmed that they have cut the telephone.'

'Shut up!' said Lindow. He strained to hear and recognised the hum of a computer.

'It's in the desk,' he shouted.

'Where?' said Lafferty.

'One of the drawers.'

'Which drawer? It's very important you tell me before doing anything.'

Lindow put his ear to the desk. 'It's the middle drawer.'

'Don't open it. Take out the drawer above. You may be able to see from there.'

Lindow already knew that the desk had no partitions between the drawers. He removed the drawer above and found himself looking through the gap to a folded lap-top computer and a confusion of wires.

'I've got it,' he said. 'It's here in front of me.'

'What do you see?'

'There are a lot of wires. Two or three are coming from the direction of the junction box. Then there are another two that are attached to copper strips at the side. One strip is fixed to the body of the desk, the other is on the drawer itself. They're about an inch apart.'

'That's the booby trap. If you pull open the drawer, you'll connect up the circuit and it'll blow. Somewhere in there will be a detonator and a charge.'

'I think it's under the computer. It seems to be resting on something ...' Lindow broke off as his lungs choked on the dense smoke. 'It's resting on something about the size of a book,' he said.

'What's happening with the computer?' Lafferty demanded. 'You've got to open it up and find out what it's doing.'

'Hold on, I can see the power supply. Should I unplug it?'

'No!' said Lafferty. 'That'll be rigged too. Find out what the computer's doing.'

'Okay! Okay!' said Lindow. His eyes were streaming from the smoke. 'I've got to put the phone down for a moment.'

He wiped his eyes, then worked his hand into the drawer. He slipped the catch on the front of the computer so that he could ease the screen up. He grabbed the phone from the top of the desk.

'There are six numbers on the screen,' he shouted. 'It's preparing to dial out.'

He heard Foyle yell to the operators, 'Tell everyone on the ground to take cover.'

Then Lindow remembered Droy and the booby trap and how a simple tug had sent the whole lot up.

He put the phone in his pocket, rushed to Eamonn's wardrobe, flung the door open and saw what he was looking for. He grabbed a clump of ties that were hanging on a rail inside the door and started furiously knotting them together. When he had a length of four, he ran to the desk and fastened one end to the handle of the middle drawer. He went back to add ties to the other end. He was out of the bedroom when he tied his sixth knot.

He took the phone from his pocket and shouted, 'I'm going to deal with this fucker once and for all.'

He tugged at the rope of ties. Nothing happened. One of the knots was snagging on the bedroom-door frame. As he manoeuvred into a line of sight with the desk to free the knot, he heard the rapid music of the modem dialling out. He yanked again, and as he did so he turned his back to the bedroom and rolled towards the floor. The drawer shot forward, causing the copper contacts to meet for a split second and send a current to the detonator. The detonator fired a shockwave through the block of Semtex, shattering its fragile chemical bonds and setting off a rapid expansion of gases, which moved from the bedroom with satanic fury, throwing everything before them at the speed of sound.

Lindow had not hit the floor before the blast reached him and blotted out his consciousness.

Forty-five seconds later, the firemen and police officers who had arrived outside fifty-six Jasmine Road just before the explosion picked themselves up from the pavement and made for the building. They'd been told that a man was in there, but they didn't rate his chances of survival. Two firemen with breathing apparatus went in first, followed by the policemen who wouldn't heed their warnings about the smoke. On the landing outside the flat they found the woman. One officer knelt down, confirmed that she was dead and prepared to drag her body from the stairway. The firemen plunged on into the flat, feeling ahead of them in the smoke with axe handles. They found the man at the front of the sitting room, just under the window. He was lying on his back on a pile of books. They wiped the plaster dust from his face and felt for a pulse. It was good and strong. They took hold of him by the arms and legs, lifted him up and bore him from the building, leaving the tattered pages of what had once been Eamonn Lindow's library of Irish history to the flames.

Epilogue

Lindow waited in his wheelchair for Foyle at the hospital reception. A nurse fussed round him. His left arm was in plaster from the wrist to the elbow, and his left eye and cheek were covered with a cushion of bandages. He had been told that he might lose the sight of that eye and that he would need plastic surgery to his cheek. That was why the doctors had been reluctant to allow him out so soon. But Lindow had been adamant and he had phoned Foyle the day before to ask for a lift to his flat so that he could change for the funeral.

When Foyle appeared at Reception, Lindow climbed out of the wheelchair and greeted him in a low, cracked voice. Foyle touched his shoulder, took hold of his right arm and led him down some steps to where Alex was waiting in the car with the engine running. He moved slowly: the lacerations to his legs and torso were nowhere near healed and the two cracked ribs on his right side hurt as he inhaled the cold, sharp air.

Foyle helped him into the back seat then got in beside Alex.

'You know what day ... ?' said Lindow. He cleared his voice. 'You know what day it is today?'

'What do you mean?' asked Foyle gently.

'It's my damned birthday. Course, I'd forgotten. Tag just called to remind me. She was planning to come over, but she can't leave my father. He's not well.'

'I'm sorry to hear that,' said Foyle, turning in his seat to face Lindow. 'I don't know what to say – I mean, about your birthday.' He turned back and stabbed at the window button with irritation. 'For Pete's sake, Alex, why do you keep the car so damned hot? I can barely breathe in here.'

Alex gave Lindow a look of uncomplaining resignation.

'Okay, let's be off. We haven't got all bloody day,' said Foyle.

Outside Lindow's flat a lone press photographer was waiting. Since Sunday the newspapers had not ceased writing about Mary and Lindow. The shot of him being escorted from the hospital three weeks before had been used over and over again. To his regret no one had unearthed any photographs of Mary, which served only to increase the interest in the

329

'mystery MI5 heroine' who had given her life to save the people in Whitehall.

As Foyle's car drew up, the photographer raised his camera and advanced towards them. Foyle leaped out, put his hands up to the camera, then wrapped a huge arm around the photographer's shoulder and led him away down the street. After a few moments of forlorn resistance, the photographer packed his things into the boot of a car and left.

'I gave him the address of a church in South London,' Foyle said, on his return. 'That should keep him well away from Chiswick this morning.'

Nobody had been in the flat since Sunday. It was as though they had only just left. The bed was unmade and Mary's coffee cup still stood where she had left it by the phone. The green scarf she had worn by the lake in Ireland, and which she had taken off when she bought her new coat, was hanging on the back of the chair. Con folded it with his good hand and lifted it to his face.

'You know that you two are national heroes,' said Foyle, looking slightly embarrassed. 'That isn't going to go away, I'm afraid. They've been trying everything to get a shot of you together. They've even asked the security service for their file pictures of Mary.'

'Have they got any?' asked Lindow, with interest. 'I'd like one.'

'I don't know. I can find out for you.'

Lindow changed slowly into the suit he had worn for Eamonn's funeral, which had travelled with him to America and back, crushed in one of his bags.

'It doesn't look very good, does it?' he said, as Foyle draped the jacket round his shoulders.

'It's fine,' said Foyle. 'I find creases tend to fall out once you've worn it a bit.'

The mist was lifting off the Thames as they drove westwards, and by the time they reached the little church on the outskirts of London the sun had broken through the autumn haze. There were several official cars outside the church and a number of police and security service personnel, but no press. Before they climbed out, Foyle explained that, at the request of Mary's mother, the funeral had been arranged by the security service. The vicar, an MI5 man from the Cold War era who had been ordained ten years before, had found a plot for Mary in the churchyard and waived the usual requirements about the deceased being a parishioner.

'I thought her mother was Jewish,' said Lindow to Foyle, as Alex helped him out of the car. 'And what about her father?'

'Her father died a long time ago,' said Foyle. 'Didn't she tell you?'

'No, there was a lot she didn't have time to tell me.'

'You're right about her mother. Apparently she is Jewish but she felt that Mary tended towards Christian beliefs.'

'She didn't have beliefs,' said Lindow. 'Not of that sort, anyway.'

Inside the church Mary's coffin lay covered in flowers on a low catafalque. Lindow could not bring himself to acknowledge its presence and passed to the front pew, looking fixedly beyond to the altar. A short middle-aged woman in a dark blue coat and pill-box hat turned when he entered the pew and smiled at him with Mary's eyes. Foyle introduced her as Mrs Jessie Harkovitz – Mary's mother – then indicated a tall woman named Laing and mumbled that she was the new director general of the security service. Across the aisle Lindow recognised only Stephen Pennel and the Cabinet Secretary, Sir Derek Crystal, who, Foyle explained, was representing the Prime Minister. He whispered the names of Peter Speerman, Keith Craven-Elms, Adam Durie, Angus Grove, Rory Fuller, saying that most of them were Mary's colleagues. They meant nothing to Lindow.

The service began with an address by the vicar, a slight man with tufted grey sideburns brushed back over the top of his ears. As he spoke he looked down at Lindow and Mary's mother. For most of the proceedings Lindow was numb. He listened, as though from a great distance, to the lesson read by Sir Derek Crystal who also made a short address about Mary's bravery and her long service in the fight against terrorism. Lindow remembered her reading Yeats at Eamonn's funeral and thought, with a stab of grief, that it was probably the moment he had fallen in love with her.

There was another reading, this time from Kirsty Laing, and then a hymn, during which Foyle's voice reverberated around the church. But by this time Lindow had removed himself altogether, returning only to wonder about the couple who had arrived late and were now sitting at the back of the church. His bandages did not allow him to see them properly.

Then Mary's coffin was taken from the church. Lindow and Mrs Harkovitz followed the pall-bearers into the graveyard, where small patches of frost lay in the shadows of the old gravestones. As Mary was lowered into the ground the priest's words registered with Lindow. 'For as much as it hath pleased Almighty God of his great mercy to take unto himself the soul of our dear sister here departed we therefore commit her body to the ground; earth to earth, ashes to ashes, dust to dust ...'

Lindow stepped forward and laid a bunch of flowers, handed to him by Foyle, which bore a card inscribed with the word *acushla*. In due course, he would have it cut into Mary's headstone.

The mourners stood for a little while, each lost in thought. Foyle held his hands clasped in front of him and considered the terrible aptness that the train of events which had begun in a churchyard so many years before should now reach its conclusion in another graveyard.

As they turned and moved away from the graveside, Lindow saw the couple who had arrived late and now stood at a little distance on the gravel path. Like him, the woman wore bandages over her face. It was evident that she needed the support of the man beside her. One or two MI5 people went up to exchange words with her, then Kirsty Laing walked over, touched her arm and asked how she was. The woman acknowledged them all with nods, but her gaze did not leave Lindow. She seemed familiar, but he couldn't think why.

'Oh, yes, Con,' said Foyle, composing himself and guiding Lindow towards the couple. 'You never met properly, did you? This is Kay Gould, the woman you helped in Clarence Street. You remember?'

'Yes . . . of course I remember,' said Lindow hesitantly. He offered her his good hand. 'But why are you here?'

'Because I worked with Mary,' she said.

A Spy's Life

For Liz, with Love

Acknowledgements

I owe a debt of gratitude to many people who helped me during the preparation of this novel. I would particularly like to thank my editor, Jane Wood, and my agent, Georgina Capel, both of whom provided encouragement and contributed much to *A Spy's Life*, and also Pamela Merritt, who read the manuscript and made many suggestions.

There were countless individuals in the USA, the Czech Republic and the Former Republic of Yugoslavia who took time to explain how things were and are. Some would prefer not to be named here, however, I want to mention Mila Rádová and Hasan Nuhanovic for giving me special understanding of the Czech Republic and Yugoslavia. In Prague, I received matchless assistance from one individual who was closely involved in the events which form part of my story. He knows who he is. I hope he knows how grateful I am for his hospitality and insight.

At the United Nations Headquarters in New York I encountered patience and generosity among officials who described the complexities and procedures of their organisation. Others gave me invaluable access to the building.

In matters of aviation I am indebted to three pilots – Philip Waterer, Mark Seymour and Phil Bachelor – the US National Transportation Safety Board and Sharl Stamford Kraus Ph.D., the author of *Aircraft Safety: Accident Investigations, Analyses, and Applications* (McGraw–Hill), a fascinating and rather terrifying book.

As far as my medical researches go, I would like to acknowledge debts to the journalists on BBC Radio Four's *Science Now* programme, who made available their material on Locked-in Syndrome, and to Dr Caroline Miller who helped me understand a small but crucial detail concerning inheritance.

As always, friends have been very helpful. My thanks go to Lucy Heller, Shameen Bhatia, Xan Smiley, Lucy Nichols, David Campbell and Janine di Giovanni, all of whom gave me support and ideas.

HP
London, 2001

1

The East River

A lip of ice protruded from the bank just in front of his face. It was no more than three feet away and he could see it with absolute clarity in the light that was coming from behind him. He contemplated the ice through the mist of his breath, noticing the lines that ran around its edge like tree rings. He understood they were formed when the tide lapped its underside, adding a little to the surface, then receded, leaving it hanging over the mud. He was groggy, but his powers of reason were working. That was good.

Harland moved his head a little and listened. There was a ringing inside his ears but he could hear the slap of the water and the agitated clicking of dead reeds somewhere off to his left. Beyond these there was a commotion – sirens and the noise of a helicopter.

The light didn't allow him to see how he was trapped, but he felt something heavy pinning him down from behind and he knew that his legs were bent backwards because the muscles in his groin and on the tops of his thighs were burning with pain. The rest of him was numb. He reckoned he must have been there for some time.

He pulled at his arms which had been plunged vertically into the mud. The movement caused his face to fall forward nearer the mud and his nostrils to fill with the smell of the sea. The tide! He could see that the water had risen a little in the time since he had become conscious. The tide would come in and cover his face. He had to get free – shift the weight that was holding him down. But he felt weak and dazed and there was nothing for him to push against to hold his face away from the mud. He groped behind him and felt the seat. Jesus, he was still strapped into his seat! He ran his right hand up and down searching for the seat belt and found it stretched tight across the top of his chest. That explained the pain in the area of his heart. Eventually he located the buckle, flipped its tongue with his thumb and sagged forward into the mud.

337

It was going to be okay. He'd be able to shift the seat, or wriggle from underneath it. A little more purchase was all that was needed. But that wasn't going to be easy. Exerting the slightest pressure made him sink closer to the water. He knew that the mud had absorbed the force of his impact and had saved his life, but now he cursed it.

He began to prod and grope beneath the mud. After several minutes he touched something solid, an old plank of wood. It was slippery, but it did not move when he gripped it with both hands and then pushed upwards with all his strength, bringing his legs awkwardly into play. Nothing happened. He slumped down again and inhaled the odour of decay. He had to concentrate on controlling his breath, which was coming in shallow puffs.

As he waited, the breeze peppered his face with grains of ice and he realised for the first time how cold it was. He breathed deeply, right into his stomach, and tightened his grip beneath the mud. He was going to do it. He was going to lift the damned seat because he hadn't survived the crash to be drowned in six inches of the East River.

He pushed again and this time felt the right side of the seat lift slightly. He threw his bottom up and with a desperate writhing motion managed to free first one leg, then the other, and roll over into the sea water. The cold made him gasp. He lunged upwards, knocking the lip of ice, which broke off with a chink, dug his fingers into the bank and pulled himself to a kneeling position. The mud sucked at his shins. He saw the seat now and a tangle of metal and torn plastic attached to the back of it. He looked up and across to Manhattan, ranged along the skyline like a miniature tiara. He realised that he was seeing it through a gauze of tiny ice particles floating on the breeze. But there was something else – the insides of his eyelids seemed to be imprinted with a golden light that flared every time he blinked. And there was a new sensation in his head, halfway between pain and sound.

Shielding his face from the wind, Harland turned and peered towards La Guardia. It was difficult to make out exactly what was happening against the background of the airport's lights. There appeared to be two fires that were being fed by plumes of foam from the emergency vehicles. The nearest was a few hundred yards away. The lights shot across a long horizontal shadow, which Harland took to be some form of dyke, to play across the mudflats and skim the sea. He wondered how the wreckage of the UN plane had ended up so far from him. Maybe it had kept travelling after breaking up; or perhaps there'd been a collision which would explain why he could see two fires. But that didn't match his memory of the moments as they approached the runway. He had felt no impact, just the shocking lurch to the right that came as he turned from trying to see the lights of Riker's Island to Alan Griswald's face. That was all he knew before a terrible force took hold of him and obliterated everything in his mind.

He climbed on to the bank, shook the worst of the mud from his legs and rubbed his calves and thighs to get the circulation back. The bank which he had taken for part of the shoreline turned out to be a tiny island of a few square feet. Despite the frost, the ground crumbled easily and when he moved, clods of soil and dead vegetation slipped into the water. He peered down into the darkness to see how far he would have to wade to get to the shore, his mind fumbling to make sense of his situation. He had to think about the depth of the water and the possibility of sinking into the mud and getting stuck. And he had to remember the tide because he wasn't in any state to swim, not even a short distance in the currents which he knew hurtled through the East River. There was also the ferocious cold. It was already way below freezing and the wind-chill was getting to him, sapping energy from his legs. He might die of exposure before they found him.

Where was the helicopter he'd heard? Why the hell weren't they looking? They must've worked out that the plane had broken up and there would be casualties out here in the tide. But the runway was raised quite a height above the mudflats and he knew that would mean they wouldn't spot anything by chance. They would have to be looking – they would have to know people were out here.

He looked out over the water to see if any rescue boats had been launched. No lights, no sound – nothing. He searched the dark around him and then as his eyes moved across the sea towards the Bronx he caught sight of something about forty feet away. It was a piece of wreckage – another aircraft seat, he was sure. A little closer to him was an oblong object bobbing in the water – perhaps a door. A cry rose up in him and he bellowed, 'Over here, help! Over here.'

He told himself not to be so damned stupid. No one could hear him above the wind. He cautioned himself to keep a tighter control of his fear. He must conserve his energy.

But then it struck him that someone might be out there and that they could be trapped. He looked again and thought he saw a foot projecting from the end of the seat. Without thinking more about it, he lowered himself into the water and gingerly tested the depth. The mud shelved away to the right but ahead of him it appeared to be level and, although his feet sank into the mud with each step, it was just possible to wade.

He moved slowly out into the open where the breeze was skimming foam from the tops of the waves. The headlights of a truck had manoeuvred in the distance and sent a beam across the water to pick out part of the seat. He was about halfway there and he could see that the seat was tipped backwards and was propped against a stack of tufted soil. Around him was a lot of other wreckage, knocking about in the waves. He grabbed a long plastic panel and felt the rest of the way. When he reached the seat he called out once then took a step sideways to see better and prodded it with the panel. The seat fell sideways and a body slumped into a patch of light.

He knew he was looking at Alan Griswald, although most of his face had gone and part of the neck and shoulder had been torn away. He must have been killed instantly. Poor bastard: one moment draining a tumbler of scotch, the next he was out here, mangled and ruptured and dead.

Harland felt dreadfully cold. A shudder welled up in his back and ran through his entire body. He had been stupid to get so wet because it reduced his options. Before he might have waited, but now he was so cold he had no choice but to wade back past the little island and strike out towards the lights of the emergency vehicles and to what he hoped was the shore. At the same time he realised that his strength was going and – more alarming – he could feel the increased drag of the tide plucking at his legs.

He turned to go, then stopped and listened intently to a new noise. He cupped his hand to his ear. It was a muffled sound – muffled but insistent – and it was coming from Griswald's body. Suddenly he understood: it was a cellphone. Griswald had kept his phone switched on and now it was ringing. He waded through the water, ran his hands over the body and felt the phone inside his breast pocket. He thrust his hand inside Griswald's jacket, steeling himself against the blood and pulp of his chest, and pulled out the phone and something else – a wallet. He was about to throw it away when something told him it would be needed for identification. He slipped it into his hip pocket.

The phone was still ringing. He stabbed at the keypad and brought it to his cheek.

'Hello.'

'Al?' came a woman's voice. She was a long way off and the wind was making it difficult to hear, but he thought he recognised the voice.

'Look,' stumbled Harland.

'Who is this?' demanded the woman.

Harland grimaced to himself. 'Look, Alan can't take your call.'

'Who is this speaking? Where's Alan?' The panic in her voice was rising. 'Why have you got my husband's phone?'

Harland saw nothing for it but to hang up. Sally Griswald would learn soon enough. He held the phone in front of him and dialled his own direct line at the UN building.

'Marika?'

'This is she.' The voice was brisk – troubled.

'Marika, I need you to listen very carefully.'

'Oh, my God! Mr Harland? You don't know what's happened. It's terrible. The plane's crashed at La Guardia. The flight from Washington. All those people. We just got the news a few minutes ago.'

'I was on the flight.'

'What are you saying? I can't hear you.'

'I was on the flight. I'm okay. But I need you to tell them where I am.'

'I don't understand. It's not on your schedule—'

'Listen, for God's sake, Marika.' He was shouting and he knew he was terrifying the life out of her. 'I was on the flight. And now I'm stranded in the East River. You've got to tell them where to find me.'

'Oh, my God . . .'

'Tell them I'm in a direct line between the northeast runway and Riker's Island. The tide's coming in fast and I need them to get here quickly. Marika, now don't hang up! Keep the line open . . . Marika?'

Another voice came on the line. 'Bobby, it's Nils Langstrom.'

'Thank God,' said Harland. Langstrom had a cool head. 'I was on the flight that crashed. I'm stranded in the East River. I guess I'm about one hundred and fifty, maybe two hundred yards from the runway on a line with Riker's Island. I'm in the water and I'm going to try and get myself back on dry land. They'll see some wreckage from the plane. I'll wait there. But tell them they've got to move quickly. There may be other people out here.'

'Got it. I'll make sure they understand where you are.'

'I've got to hang up now and get to the island.'

'Don't take any risks . . .'

Harland pressed the 'off' key and clamped the phone between his teeth. He ignored the taste of blood on the phone and looked up to get his bearings. It wasn't easy. Wading out to where Griswald lay had been fine because the light from behind him had shown him the way. Going back was a different matter. Beneath the distant beam from the truck everything was pitch black. He picked up the plastic panel, which he had kept wedged between his legs, and set off, jabbing at the water ahead of him. All around him was the excited rippling of a tide in full flood.

Part of him remained aloof from the situation, a dispassionate observer, registering the difficulty he had pulling his legs out of the mud, noticing the shortness of his breath, the lifelessness in his arms, the fatigue clouding the front of his brain and tempting his eyes to close. The cold was beyond anything he'd experienced. It was robbing him of his will, making his thoughts sloppy and his movements clumsy.

This part of Harland, the remote, calculating part, recognised that he had only a very short time.

It was beginning to snow. Big snowflakes were streaming across his vision making a little vortex along the line of the headlight beam. He put his head down and worked his shoulders to take several quick strides. The water had reached halfway up his thighs when he put his left leg down, found nothing and toppled sideways into the current. His lungs contracted with shock, expelling the air with a succession of hollow shouts, the first of which caused him to let go of the phone in his mouth. Then, as he flailed in the water like a child learning to swim, he lost his grip on the panel. He knew his only chance now was to make it back to the point where he could stand, but the current was very strong and his power to resist it had gone. His lungs wouldn't keep the air down and he was swallowing water. He tilted his head back and stretched out his arms, his brain grasping at half a memory of a training session he'd endured long ago in Poole Harbour. He was floating, allowing the current to take him and to twirl him around like a piece of flotsam. He was aware of looking up at the snow. The light seemed to be growing fainter and the snow was getting denser. His terror was being edged out by blankness and submission. One thought kept moving through him: this is it, I'm going to die; this is it, I'm going to die.

And then his foot hit something and the current spun him round so that his bottom grazed the mud. He had been washed up on another bank. He reached his hands out backwards and clawed awkwardly at the mud, trying to get his head above the water. He found some roots just below the surface. With the last reserve of energy he turned and brought himself to all fours and choked the water out. He stayed there heaving and gulping in the terrible cold for what seemed like several minutes. Then he looked up and squinted through the sea water that was still stinging his eyes. There was no sign of anyone. They weren't looking for him.

He listened. A seabird called out in the dark and again he heard the rasp and click of reeds nearby. He had to think. He had to think, dammit. But his mind was moving so slowly. He'd crawl into the reeds where the mud would be firm because of the roots and he would drag himself to his feet and stand so that they would see him. That's what he'd do. He would get up and wait there and not give in to the cold. Someone would come. He knew it. Marika and Langstrom must have made them understand where he was. He inched towards the clump of reeds where a mess of snow and sea foam had collected, grabbed on to a handful of stalks and hauled himself towards them. He rose to his feet and stood, swaying like a drunk.

A few moments later he heard the helicopter's roar, turned and saw a light coming towards him. He raised both arms and held them high until it was hovering in front of him and throwing up a whirlwind of snow and dead reeds. Next he saw several bent figures emerge from a cloud of snow and foam and rush towards him. They carried lights and a stretcher. He felt himself stagger on his feet, topple backwards and then lurch forwards into their arms.

2
The Missing

Sister Rafael was rather proud of her patient in Room 132. Since the British UN official had been brought in early on the previous evening, she had seen the TV film of him standing out in the East River with his arms raised like he was defying death. It was a miracle that he hadn't been killed with the others. The TV news had said twenty people from the two aircraft had died, and now their bodies were lying in a temporary morgue at the airport, most of them burned beyond recognition. It made her shudder to think of so many people's grief, especially now, before the holidays. She felt his wrist and touched his forehead with the back of her left hand. There was no sign of fever and his pulse was normal.

She peered at him in the sliver of morning light that was coming through the blinds. He was a big man and she guessed he was naturally strong. When he was brought in they'd needed three people to lift him to put on the Heibler vest so his temperature could be stabilised. His face interested her because it had none of the weak, fleshy appearance she associated with the British. The jaw was well defined, like his dark eyebrows which ran horizontally until they plunged down at the ends. His hair was a lighter brown and was cut short so you could see where it had receded on his forehead. She felt there was an openness in his features, except in the mouth, which even in medicated repose was clamped shut. Tension showed itself elsewhere – in the long furrows that ran from his cheekbone nearly down to his jaw, in the crow's-feet at the corner of his eyes and the single cleft at the centre of his brow. His eye sockets were blackened by fatigue.

She wondered what expression his eyes held when they were open and what his voice sounded like and whether he was married. There was no wedding ring on his finger and when his sister called from London to speak with Doctor Isaacson, she had not mentioned a partner or any family. Of one thing she was sure. Mr Harland was important. Twice that morning a woman had called from the Secretary-General's office to ask about his condition. She had instructions to pass on his concern and to let them know when the doctor said it would be okay to talk to him. Everyone wanted to talk to him – the TV and the accident investigators, and the Secretary-General was even threatening to come visit in the hospital. People understood that this man's escape was extraordinary. That's why the picture from the TV film was blown up in all the papers and why they were still playing it on the news bulletins. She could see him in her mind's eye, standing there, feet slightly apart, his arms raised outwards in an almost religious attitude.

She moved to the window and parted the blind to look down into the dazzling snow light. Four or five news crews were still there, waiting in the sunshine to hear about her patient. Then she returned to the bedside and gave the face a last glance before leaving the room. He would sleep for a while yet.

Late on the third morning after the crash, Harland woke as a breakfast tray was brought to him. He felt alert but also curiously light-headed. In snatches of wakefulness during the past forty-eight hours, he had struggled to make sense of the events that had brought him to a hospital bed. Drowsily he watched a report on TV and got more or less all he needed – the casualty figures, the shocked reaction in the UN headquarters, the approximate circumstances of the crash and the mildly unnerving fact that he had been picked up by a helicopter that was carrying a TV crew who had filmed the rescue. It had taken a few seconds before he recognised the absurd, panicky figure, gesticulating like a maniac out on the shoreline. He had pressed the remote and had almost immediately fallen asleep.

Now he was hungry and set about the eggs and toasted bagel with relish, his mind returning to the crash. There was a lot he didn't understand, chiefly how he and Griswald had been thrown out of the fuselage and landed so far from the line of the wreckage path. He thought of finding Alan Griswald's body and hearing the telephone ringing in the dark and then speaking to Sally Griswald. He remembered her from years ago when the Griswalds were doing the rounds of East European embassies. He could see her now, a small, bubbling natural blonde from the Midwest who never took anything very seriously, least of all her husband's work as the CIA Station Chief. She was a breath of fresh air in the otherwise self-consciously discreet gatherings of spies and embassy staff. The Griswalds had two small boys then. They were now at college. Griswald had talked about them on the plane. They were home for the Christmas holidays and he was going to take ten days with them.

The door opened and the woman who had introduced herself the day before as Sister Rafael came in, followed by the doctor, who looked him over quickly and pronounced himself satisfied with Harland's recovery.

'Anything we should know about your medical history?' he asked. 'You have had one or two operations – appendectomy and . . . er?' He pointed below Harland's midrift to his groin.

'That was a long time ago.'

'And it's what I think it was?'

'Yes, but I've been clear for a dozen years or more now.'

'Diagnosed early then?'

'Yes,' he said with finality. He didn't particularly want to discuss it in front of the nurse.

'And these scars on your wrists and chest. Nothing that should concern me?'

'No.'

'What were they caused by?'

'An accident,' said Harland, with a discouraging look.

Isaacson nodded, a trace of doubt showing in his eyes. He told him how his body temperature had crashed below the eighty-eight-degree mark and that it had been touch and go for an hour after he was brought in. An incubator had been used to warm him on Tuesday evening. He had spent the first night on a supply of slightly heated, moist oxygen. Now all he needed to do was to concentrate on building his strength with rest and a high calorie intake. He warned that there were bound to be some after-effects. He would feel weak for some time and his muscles would continue to ache for a few days. There might also be problems of delayed shock. If he felt unusually depressed or listless in the coming weeks, he should seek trauma counselling. It was important that he should not try to deal with the experience by himself, but talk it out with a professional. Harland nodded obediently, although the idea was absurd to him. He had talked only once in his life – to an elderly woman in North London. He'd found it exceptionally hard to be precise about the effects of torture.

Isaacson noticed his expression. 'How would you feel about speaking with the crash investigators? I mean, about the facts of the crash – what you remember about the airplane journey? They're very anxious to speak with you.'

Harland agreed and after another cursory check, Isaacson left. Half an hour later, two men were shown in with great ceremony by the nurse. They introduced themselves as Murray Clark from the National Transportation Safety Board and Special Agent Frank Ollins of the FBI.

Harland slipped his legs from the bed and indicated to the nurse that he would like the robe hanging near the door.

'Are you okay about this, Mr Harland?' asked Murray Clark. 'We can do it later.'

'I'm fine,' he said. 'Wish I'd shaved and washed before you came.' He nodded to the nurse who left, almost regretfully. He stood up and looked at them. Clark was short and a little overweight and looked as though he had been plucked straight out of a college laboratory. Agent Ollins was in his mid-thirties and was crisply dressed in a blue suit and white shirt. He had a steady gaze and seemed more purposeful than Clark. They both carried heavy anoraks and had mud on their shoes.

They sat down either side of the little table at the end of his bed.

'Why are you involved?' Harland asked Agent Ollins. 'This isn't a criminal investigation, surely.'

'Too soon to say what this case is about,' Ollins replied equably. 'We're hoping that you will be able to help with that. There were a lot of important people on board and we need to cover all the angles. Mr Clark here is going to find out what went wrong with your plane. We take over if we think some party or parties intentionally caused that malfunction to occur.'

'Fortunate about the cellphone,' said Clark brightly. 'You might still be out there if you hadn't found it. We hear you suffered quite badly from exposure – it's good to see you doing so well already, sir.'

He turned on a small tape recorder and asked Harland to take them through the flight, remembering anything that might be of use to them.

He told them how he had finished his work in Rockville, Maryland, and had gone to Washington National Airport, thinking that he had missed the ride offered to him by Alan Griswald. He explained that he had met Griswald the week before in Holland. They had travelled to Washington on consecutive days and had hoped to meet up in DC as well as fly together to New York. Both knew they were too busy and the arrangement was vague. However, he had bumped into Griswald at the airport which was how he came to be on the plane.

Harland said that there were some other UN people with him, people who had been at meetings at Congress. They were travelling together but there was some diplomatic nicety which meant that this was not an official delegation from the UN to Congress. Griswald seemed to know some, but not all of them. He remembered there were two or three young women in the party.

'How did you know Mr Griswald?' asked Ollins.

'We worked on the same diplomatic circuit back in the eighties.'

'Right – you were diplomats.'

'Yes,' said Harland. 'We were diplomats in Europe. Griswald was in Germany and Austria for a long time, with a spell in the Middle East. We served in some of the same places. I saw a lot of him and his wife in those days.' He paused and took some coffee. 'Do you want some of this? I'm sure I can get a fresh jug.'

They shook their heads.

'Were you both in the Middle East?'

'No, just Griswald.'

'So tell us about the flight.'

'We left pretty soon after we met and we flew up to New York without any trouble. About twenty minutes out of La Guardia, I went to the lavatory and noticed that the cabin had grown very cold. As I was about to take a pee, the lights went out. So I went back into the cabin which was pitch black. Then we were struck by some turbulence which was uncomfortable but not severe. I think the pilot came on and told us to fasten our seat belts.'

'Did the captain say anything else at this time?' asked Clark, making a note.

'Maybe. I didn't pay much attention. We could see the lights of New York below us and we weren't especially worried.'

'What else do you recall?'

He said there wasn't much he could add. He remembered Griswald turning on his laptop to use the light of the screen. As he spoke, Griswald's face came back to him, lit by a blue-grey aura, smiling at the thought of one of his sons returning from college. Griswald lifted the computer and they struggled to fold away the table in the dark, and then looked down at the Bronx. Harland saw the white rooftops in his mind, the grid of little streets and the scrawl of new tyre tracks in the snow. Griswald made some remark about the weather.

'Did the lights return before landing?' asked Clark.

'No.'

'Can you remember anything else unusual, sir? What about the sound of the engines? Any significant increase in engine power while you were experiencing the turbulence? Do you recall a change of note in the engine noise as the plane came in?'

'I'm not sure – maybe just before the impact. I was looking out towards Riker's Island on the left of the plane and Alan Griswald said something which I didn't hear. I turned back to face him. Then, bang! I don't remember much else.'

'Let me get this straight,' said Clark. 'You were looking out at Riker's from the left of the plane? The first question is this: could you see Riker's Island?'

'I could see an orange glow which I assumed were the lights from the prison.'

'But surely you mean you were looking out to your right, not left.'

'No, I was in a rear-facing seat, across the table from Alan Griswald.'

'Ah, I see. I guess that's one of the reasons you're here. Being at the back of the plane and facing backwards meant that you avoided the whole force of the impact. Tell me, was anything about the approach unusual?'

'No.'

'You didn't think that the plane was unusually low?'

'No, I didn't. Have you any theories yet?'

'Right now, we're considering a number of possibilities. The flight data recorder and the voice recorder were recovered on Wednesday; both are being analysed at our headquarters in Washington. We'll get the results at the weekend.'

Ollins plucked a piece of fluff from his suit, looked up at the ceiling and began speaking.

'As yet we don't know why the plane crashed, Mr Harland. None of the theories about icing, wind-shear, poor visibility or a freak collision with Santa's reindeers comes anywhere near to explaining it. How could this aircraft, flown by a pilot with over ten thousand flying hours, come in without any reported problems and just nose-dive into the runway?'

Harland got up from the edge of the bed, walked a few paces and worked his bare toes up and down to get rid of the prickly sensation in his feet. They watched him.

'Nobody has told me what actually happened,' he said, looking at Clark. 'I mean, I still don't see how the other plane was involved. Surely it was nowhere near where we came in?'

Ollins exchanged a look with Clark, as if asking his permission.

'It's simple,' he said. 'Your plane comes in too low, banks right and clips the light tower with the starboard wing. An explosion occurs in the fuel tank, debris flies back, tears into the cabin at the rear and loosens the spars supporting the starboard engine. The engines have already been put into maximum thrust because the pilot realises he needs altitude. All three engines are full on. The Falcon climbs momentarily, comes down, rolls through ninety degrees, banks right and hits more light towers with incredible force. The fuselage sustains more damage and the starboard engine becomes detached and is thrown forward for a considerable distance. It hits the wing of a Learjet waiting to take off. The Learjet explodes and catches fire, killing all seven passengers and the pilot. Meanwhile the Falcon is ploughing a trench at a thirty-degree angle from the runway towards the Learjet. Then your plane also catches fire.'

'Jesus,' exhaled Harland. 'How on earth did I get out?'

'Some time at an early stage in this sequence,' replied Ollins, 'the seat anchors in your section of the Falcon break free and you are propelled out of the fuselage and land in the soft terrain at the edge of the East River.' He paused and gave a bleak smile. 'The chances of anyone surviving this crash without injury must be one in fifty billion, Mr Harland. People don't get breaks like that too often. I think you'll realise that when you see the wreckage.'

'You want me to see the wreckage?'

'Not so much the wreckage, but I would like to take you over the crash scene and have you look at a reconstruction we've set up there.'

348

Harland sat down on the bed. Clark asked if he wanted them to leave. But Ollins was clearly disinclined to go just yet.

'There are a few more questions I want to ask you before we leave,' he said. 'It's important that I have your attention for just a few more minutes, Mr Harland. One of the things we need to do in this investigation is to construct profiles of all the passengers and crew. We need to know a little more about your life also.'

A part of Harland went on guard. 'What do you want to know?'

'First off, tell me about your work, sir. You're doing a special report for the Secretary-General's office. Is that right?'

'That makes it sound more important than it is. I'm looking into the ownership of the supplies of fresh water in Asia and Eastern Europe.'

Ollins looked puzzled. 'Please explain.'

'One of the big problems facing the developing world – in fact, the entire planet – is the shortage of fresh water. There are too many people and the major fresh-water resources, chiefly lakes and aquifers, are being drained at a very fast rate. The reduction in some of the bigger lakes, like the Aral Sea, is showing up on satellite photographs. Others, like Lake Baikal, which contains about a fifth of the world's fresh-water supply, are being polluted by industry – a big paper mill in that instance. What this means is that fresh water is becoming a very scarce and valuable commodity. The Secretary-General wants to know who owns what. He believes that it's going to become an important issue. He wants a briefing as much as anything else.'

Ollins listened to this impatiently. 'But this wasn't always your line,' he said rather too quickly.

Harland realised that Ollins had already talked to people at the UN.

'You probably know that I've done a lot of things. Banking for a short time when I was young, British Foreign Service, Red Cross for ten years. I started out as an engineer – that's what I studied at Cambridge and that's how I can find my way around this subject.'

'That's a lot of different careers to cram into one life. You're only in your late forties?'

'Forty-nine.'

'The Foreign Service – that's the diplomatic service, right?'

'Yes, I just said that I knew Griswald in the diplomatic service.'

'Were you hired by the UN to do this report?'

'Not specifically. I came to advise about rapid relief programmes. Three years later, I'm still here. I'll be ready to report in six or seven weeks. Then we'll see what happens.'

'And you were visiting Rockville in connection with this report?'

'Yes, there're a couple of companies down there that have large water interests. I'm trying to assess their current holdings and the extent of their ambitions.'

'A kind of investigation, then?'

'In the loosest sense, yes. It's a case of tracking down who owns what.'

'So you could make some enemies in this line of work?'

'Not really, most of the material that interests me is in the public record – somewhere. It's just a question of finding it and, as I say, establishing the plans of some of the big multi-nationals.'

He could see that Ollins was tiring of this line of questioning. He'd give it ten minutes, then make an excuse to get rid of them both.

'So tell me a little more about the flight. Did you talk to anyone besides Mr Griswald?'

'I said hello to Chris Lahmer and André Bloch. There were a few other faces I recognised – a man from UNHCR but I forget his name.'

'Philippe Maas?'

'Yes, that's right. They were all sitting near each other. I assumed they'd been at the same meetings in Washington.'

'So you can only put names to three or four people on the plane?'

'Yes, I suppose that's right. Is that important?'

'Well, it's like this. We have one unidentified body – a man. And we're not even sure that we have the right toll yet, because we could have lost people in the water. It took a while to find you and it's conceivable that other victims were washed out into the ocean.'

'But surely there was a passenger list – a manifest of some sort?'

'No. There should have been. But this was a private flight that didn't cross any national borders so it was forgotten, I guess.'

'Yes, but this man must have been missed by his relatives.'

'That's what we thought. But we've had no calls. The problem is that pretty much everything was burned. A few personal possessions escaped the fire – thrown out of the plane with you and Mr Griswald – and we are working on those. We may retrieve more material and there is the possibility of identifying bodies by dental records, jewellery and other possessions. It's going to be a long operation. But you're right, it is kind of strange that we haven't gotten a call.'

All this time, Clark remained silent, occasionally checking that his tape was going round, but otherwise studying Harland benevolently.

'What does that suggest to you, Mr Harland?' continued Ollins.

'I don't know – possibly no one knew he was on the plane. Maybe he was a foreign national who would not be missed immediately by his family. But presumably if he was on the UN plane, he was connected to the UN in some way and someone – a secretary or a department head or people at one of the national missions – would notice his absence?'

'Exactly the same thoughts occurred to us. It is odd. But look at it this way. If you'd been killed it might have been some time before anyone made the connection between the crash and your disappearance. Might've been a few days before anyone went back over your schedule and made some inquiries in Maryland and then put it all together. That's why we need very accurate descriptions of the people you saw on board. Then maybe we can start to work out who he was. I want you to think about them all and make some notes for me. I also want you to go over the journey again and record anything out of the ordinary – the smallest detail may be of crucial importance to this investigation, as Mr Clark here will tell you. Think of the passengers, Mr Harland – what they were carrying, where they sat, who they talked to. Think about the behaviour of the crew, what the captain said to the passengers – everything. I know it may be painful for you at this time, but I'm telling you, we need some help here. We'll talk again tomorrow and maybe you'll feel strong enough to come out to the airport and look over the model of the plane we have out there.'

He looked to Clark who nodded and turned off his tape recorder. Both gave him cards with cellphone numbers. They took his number and address in Brooklyn.

'Call us when you want to come out to the airport,' said Ollins from the door with a brief, wintry smile. 'And hey, don't forget to bring those notes you're going to make for me.'

With a sudden inward start, Harland realised that he had lost nearly three days. He phoned his sister, Harriet, in London and discussed staying with her family for Christmas. At the back of his mind he wondered how he was going to get on another plane so soon. But he was also certain that he did not want to spend the holiday in New York. Most of the UN would be shut down, with a lot of people returning to their home countries for a full fortnight. He said he would let her know in the next day or so. Then he talked to his office and told Marika what he would need in the way of clothes from his apartment. He asked her to get a new cellphone. His had been destroyed along with his briefcase.

After lunch he slid down into the bed and watched the sun descend behind a pearl grey shroud. It reminded him of the light over the Fens in England and the enormous cold skies of his youth. Harland tended to avoid introspection, but he knew there was now a before and an after in his life, divided by the few minutes when he was taken by the current and was certain he was going to die. He looked into himself without sentiment or fear and understood that his fortune at surviving might come with a penalty, an essential loss of confidence perhaps, like he'd suffered before when he was brought to another hospital bed, beaten so badly that the nurses at first hid their eyes from the sight of his injuries. That had taken a long time to get over, but he had managed it and he would this time too.

He closed his eyes and thought of Griswald and the party of people standing a little way off in the airport. It was a pretty typical UN crowd, with their cellphones and laptops. All of them good people, bubbling with brave initiatives, yet each in varying degrees mistaking furious animation for achievement. He tried to hold the scene in his mind. There were two or three groups of people, waiting to catch the minibus out to the UN plane. A few went outside the terminal building to smoke. The others stood in twos and threes inside. Something wasn't quite right about the way he was remembering it; something was tripping him up. His mind's eye moved across the groups, trying to pick up information. The young men both with computer cases. The woman in a long, black coat. Lahmer's anorak with a fur-trimmed hood. A lot was missing.

He'd give some thought to it later. Now he would sleep. He drifted off, this time thinking not about the flatlands of his boyhood, but an empty square in a hilltop town in central Italy. The unbidden image haunted him only rarely these days.

Next day he woke early. Having nothing else to do, he went to get a pen and paper from the duty nurse down the hall. He was moving more easily now. The bruises across his back and chest were still causing stabbing pains when he breathed deeply, but his legs were less stiff and the mysterious neuralgic patches on his stomach and thighs, which had woken him in the first nights after the crash, had gone. He cadged some coffee and returned to his room.

Dawn was breaking with a mustardy smear in the west. He sat down on the bed and noticed a small black bag. Marika must have dropped by with his things the previous evening. Inside there was a note from her, some of his own clothes, three hundred dollars in advance expenses, a new phone and a set of keys to his apartment. He smiled at her efficiency. He swung his legs onto the bed, and settled back on the pillows to write an account of the flight. He found he wasn't able to add much to what he'd told Clark and Ollins until he sketched a plan of the interior of the cabin and placed some names in the little oblong grid of seats. He marked himself and Griswald facing each other in the two rearmost seats on the starboard side. He knew that André Bloch was a little forward from him and that he had sat down opposite one of the women. On the other side of the aisle to him, on the port side, was Chris Lahmer. Before they took off, he recalled that Bloch leaned across the aisle to show Lahmer something. They were laughing with the man from UNHCR – Philippe Maas – which meant he must have been facing Lahmer.

It was difficult to say what people were wearing, and even more so to recall what they had carried on board, something which was obviously of interest to Ollins. One of the passengers, maybe one of the younger men who had sat up front, had carried a suitcase on board. He remembered there was a fuss from the flight attendant about stowing it. He wrote it all down as dispassionately as he could and annotated a diagram of the seating with the names of the passengers that he could remember.

He focused again and again on the scene, trying to glean more detail. The sensation of the first impact came back to him, the terrifying lurch to the right which threw him against the cabin wall. He saw Griswald's face again, contorting in a flash from the window. He held that image in his head and then let the paper slip from his lap and the pen drop to the floor.

The young man left the hotel on Tenth Avenue and 23rd Street early in the morning. His body was still on European time and he couldn't sleep. He bent his head to the wind and trudged to breakfast at the café he'd used a couple of times since arriving. It wasn't much of a place but it suited him fine because it was cheap and he had to watch his cash supply. There was also a table by the window which provided a good view of the intersection and the hotel entrance. He doubted very much that he had been spotted, but it was as well to be on the lookout.

He ordered from the waitress, a tired little brunette with too much eye make-up and an accommodating manner who seemed to be there at all hours. She was the other reason he liked the café. As she took down his order he thought how remarkably pretty she was – an exquisite pale face and beautifully shaped mouth that twitched nervously into a smile as she spoke.

When she had gone, he laid out the newspaper cutting which he had brought from England and examined the photographs of the sole survivor of the plane crash. The picture was given prime position on the front page, hardly surprising, given the starkness and drama of the image. That was what had caught his attention; what had held it was the inset of a small portrait of Robert Cope Harland which had been released by the UN following the crash. He realised at once that he had found the man he was looking for, which was why he'd packed a rucksack and had got on the plane within six hours of picking up the newspaper.

The waitress returned with the food and he laid the newspaper clipping aside. She made some comment about the picture and the crash and then asked where he was from. He told her Sweden. Was he on vacation? 'Something like that,' he said. He read the nametag on her breast – Shashanna – and remarked that he had never heard of anyone called that before. She said that she believed her father had made it up. Then she complimented him on his English and told him that he looked like he belonged in the city. That pleased him because he took pride in his ability to merge. She went away, darting a look over her shoulder.

He was calm, unusually so considering what he expected to happen in the next few days. He felt pretty pleased with himself, having obtained Harland's address so easily. He wondered if they were usually so lax. After all it had been a simple matter to go to the UN as a tourist, buy the current United Nations handbook and look up a suitably impressive name, in this case the one belonging to the Assistant Secretary-General for External Affairs, a Dr Erika Moss Klein. Posing as her assistant, he called Robert Harland's office and told them that the Assistant Secretary-General needed the address before the weekend. He said there was a package that had to be urgently delivered that evening. The woman, by now a little flustered but also charmed by his manner, gave it to him without a second thought.

Now all that remained was to decide on the approach. That was going to take a lot of thought. The actual words with which he was going to break this astonishing news had so far eluded him. He had made the speech several times in his head since seeing the newspaper photograph – it was all he thought about on the plane trip – but each version seemed hopelessly melodramatic and artificial. Thank God he had remembered to bring the identity cards with him. If all else failed they would surely persuade him that he wasn't a crank.

He went over to a pile of newspapers on the counter and selected the news section of the *New York Times*. He wanted to see if there was anything more about the crash. The day before, the paper had said Harland was still in hospital but was expected to be well enough to leave by the weekend. As he flipped through the paper, he wondered if he should leave it a couple of days before going over to Brooklyn. No, he thought, he would try that day.

There was nothing more in the paper and he put it down. Shashanna took this as a signal that he was available for a chat. She offered him more coffee and asked his name. 'Lars,' he replied, thinking how much he disliked it. But Lars Edberg was the name on his Swedish passport and he had to live with it for the time being. There was no reason to tell this girl his real name.

'What do you do, Lars?' she said, perching on the side of the chair opposite him.

'I'm in the music business.' That wasn't strictly true, but it had been. 'I'm part of an outfit that publishes original music on the Net. In a way I guess it's an anti-music business.'

'Do you have a girl in London?'

'Yes, I do,' he said. He thought of Felicity – Flick – who was ten years older than him and ran a successful flower business. She had picked him up in a bar, given him a place to live and asked no questions about his past.

'Does that mean we can't go to the movies tonight, Lars?'

'I guess it does.'

The rejection registered in her eyes. He put his hand on the table not

far from hers. 'I have a lot on, Shashanna. Another time and we would go
to the movies. But ...'

She silenced him with her hand.

'That's okay,' she said and rose from the chair.

He didn't want to mess about with this girl and he had no time, but
that wasn't the point. The problem was the thing that he carried inside
him, the heaviness of heart – the guilt – which, far from dissipating over
the years, had grown and now occupied much of his being. Flick had
somehow discerned this and devised a way of living which meant that this
unspoken secret did not dominate their relationship. He was sure she
knew that it was there.

3

Griswald's Music

As the car neared La Guardia, Harland remembered that he'd left the notes and diagram that he'd made for Frank Ollins back at the hospital. It wouldn't matter. He could arrange for them to be faxed later when he returned to collect his things and to receive a final check-up.

The car dropped him off at the old marine terminal building. Harland was directed to a hangar that was plastered with temporary signs, warning that entry was restricted to the FBI and Federal Aviation Authority and Safety Board personnel. He rang the bell labelled VISITORS and looked across the black water of Bowery Bay towards the end of the runway where the UN flight had crashed. A medium-sized jetliner was landing, its wings visibly seesawing over the last hundred yards of its flight. Harland grimly watched for the puff of smoke from the wheels as it touched down. Then he turned to find Ollins scrutinising him from the doorway.

'When you've seen what's in here,' he said, gesturing behind him, 'you realise what a helluva miracle it is that they don't crash more often.'

Ollins led him into the vast cold space of the hangar in the middle of which lay the remains of the Falcon jet, crudely assembled into the configuration of an aircraft. The temporary lights erected around it gave the wreckage a stark, fossilised look. 'See what I mean?' said Ollins matter-of-factly. 'It doesn't take long to reduce several million dollars' worth of sophisticated machinery to this. Just a matter of seconds.'

Harland said nothing. He was watching the accident investigators move round the plane. Each piece of wreckage was numbered with spray paint and here and there ribbons and tags were fixed to the twisted metal. Almost nothing of the plane's original white and red livery remained, except on the tailplane and one of the three engines. The cockpit was unrecognisable, as was the starboard wing, although a light was visible on its leading edge. The fuselage was crumpled like an old beer can. The dull, inky-coloured metal reminded him of the clinker produced by the boiler in his childhood home.

'What are they doing?' he asked Ollins.

'Determining the precise sequence of events at impact, looking for clues, selecting pieces of the wreckage for further analysis – that kind of thing. A lot will go away for further testing. Clark would tell you better than I can.' He stopped. A hint of disdain passed across his face. 'But Clark and his people already believe they've got this investigation tied up like a Christmas gift with a fancy bow on top.'

'And you don't?'

Ollins gave him the thin professional smile that Harland remembered often seeing in his colleagues back in Century House in London. It was an expression that came with knowledge and enforced silence.

'The Safety Board no longer believes there's a need for criminal investigation,' Ollins said. 'But I can't hide from you the fact that there are unresolved issues here.'

So brisk and confident when he appeared in his hospital room, Special Agent Ollins was now weighed down, fatigued. Harland knew that look too.

They walked around the wreckage in silence. Harland was struck by how small the plane seemed, and also by the smell, which contained several elements – burnt plastic, aviation fuel and a scorched, rusty aroma.

When he had seen enough, Ollins led him up a flight of open stairs and into an office where a ten-foot model of the plane was set out on a large board. The top of the fuselage had been cut away to reveal the inside of the cabin. It was clear that the model was being used as an aid to thought rather than any kind of scientific measurement. Around it were tags and arrows leading to the seats. His name and Griswald's were attached to the two facing seats at the rear of the model. The labels for Maas, Lahmer and Bloch were beside the plane, as were the ones for the three women on the plane – Elsa Meinertzhagen, Courtney Moore and Noala Shimon. Three other labels were named Male: A, Male: B and Male: C. There were also red markers which apparently indicated baggage that had been identified as belonging to one or other of the victims. Ollins told him that most of the bags had been incinerated, but here and there were clues that enabled identification.

'Have you got the names for males A, B and C?'

'A and B have been identified as Roger Clemence and James Gleeson. Mr Gleeson had served the UN in Iraq and was subsequently attached to various observer missions run by the Security Council. Clemence was a lawyer from New Zealand who worked in Africa – Sierra Leone, Rwanda.'

'What about C?'

'We've got no further with him. He's a complete mystery.' Ollins went over to a coffee pot, gestured to Harland who shook his head, and poured himself a cup. 'Why don't you take that chair, Mr Harland, and talk me through the people that you saw at Washington National Airport last Tuesday afternoon – the people who boarded the plane with you? Did you bring your notes?'

'I'm sorry, I stupidly left them at the hospital.'

'That really is a pity,' said Ollins curtly.

'I can get them later,' said Harland. 'I'll fax—'

Ollins put his hand up. 'Could you wait a second?' He leant back and tapped on the window of the adjacent room with a key. 'You people need to hear this.' Four men came in. Each nodded to Harland and found a perch. They had all brought notepads with them.

Harland was puzzled by the FBI's behaviour. If the Safety Board was satisfied that the accident was not the result of sabotage, why was Ollins working under the assumption that it was? Ollins nodded and Harland took them through what he could remember of the meeting at the airport and the minibus ride to the plane. He could now definitely say that Bloch and Lahmer and one of the women were in a huddle inside the terminal and that outside another woman was smoking with Philippe Maas. A third woman, with dark hair cut in a bob, was talking to two men that he didn't recognise. He could not be sure until he saw some photographs. Standing apart from all these was a man in his early thirties – good-looking, obviously fit and with a standoffish manner.

'That's C,' Ollins cut in. 'The woman with the dark hair was Courtney Moore, which means she was talking to Clemence and Gleeson. Can you remember what any of them was carrying, Mr Harland?'

'Most of them had small pieces of luggage – overnight bags and work bags. Alan Griswald and I both had larger cases – we'd been travelling for longer.' He thought about boarding the minibus. He and Griswald had had to stow their suitcases at the back while the others had held them on their laps. 'The man you call C had a large shoulder bag and placed it on top of Griswald's stuff. I think he may have been carrying something else – a smaller bag perhaps.'

'When you got to the airport,' said Ollins, rolling the cup between the palms of his hands, 'you expected to be taking the shuttle. Then you came across Mr Griswald. Who saw whom first?'

'I think I spotted Al.'

'Who was he talking to?'

Harland thought for a moment. 'He was with C. They were standing together, but not talking.'

Ollins looked around the ring of FBI agents to make sure they had understood the significance of this.

'And he didn't introduce you to him?'

'Nor to anyone else, although I'm not sure how many people he knew on the plane.'

'So where did C sit on the plane?'

Harland went to the model. 'Here at the front. One of the women, a blonde of about thirty-five, sat opposite him. She had been looking him over at the airport.'

'That's Elsa Meinertzhagen ... And his baggage would have been placed in the hold with the bigger pieces?'

'No, I think there was some trouble stowing it in the hold. He brought it into the cabin and the flight attendant dealt with it.'

'And he didn't talk to Griswald during the flight?'

'Nope, I was with Griswald the whole time, except when I went to the toilet.'

'That was what – ten, fifteen minutes short of La Guardia?'

'Yes, about that.'

'The lights were extinguished and you returned to your seat. You say you noticed the heating system was malfunctioning at that time. It was cold in the cabin, right?'

'Yes.'

Silence descended on the group as Ollins mulled this over. They all looked tired. The room held the sour atmosphere of long and unrewarded labour.

'Do you want me to try and place people on this model?' asked Harland.

'Sure,' said Ollins, 'and then we'll go out to the crash site. They're switching the landing runway and delaying all take-offs for a half-hour. I need you to try to trace your movements out there.'

Harland went through the cabin placing labels by the seats. He wasn't sure about Male A and Male B and he couldn't remember which of the women had been sitting across the aisle from him. But Ollins appeared to have lost interest and was anxious to get out on the runway. A call was made to the air traffic control tower and in a few minutes they got clearance to drive out to the far end of the runway.

On the way, Ollins laconically indicated the positions where the main parts of the fuselage had come to rest and the Learjet had been hit. All the wreckage had been cleared away and on the spot where the tarmac had been damaged by the Learjet explosion a new surface had already been laid. They moved up the runway, beside the huge blackened scrape which marked the wreckage path of the Falcon. The distances seemed much shorter in daylight and when they got out of the Cherokee Jeep, Harland was astonished how close he had been to the side of the dyke. Now he understood why he hadn't been seen. The main beam from the fire trucks, although appearing to illuminate his surroundings, must have overshot him. He could see that he'd been about twenty feet below the level of the runway.

He walked to the edge of the dyke with Ollins and looked down. Out on the mudflats were several men wearing Day-Glo jackets, sweeping the surface with metal detectors. Two other men were in a rubber inflatable. One punted up the little rivulets while the other operated two probes. The tide was still low. Marker buoys floated on slack lines in the water and flag-sticks protruded from the mud. There was a fair amount of ice about and for a moment Harland's eyes settled on a brittle white shelf which projected over the mud.

'That's where we located the cockpit voice and flight data recorders,' said Ollins, pointing to the furthest flag. 'They were carried in the tail section which is why they were thrown out along this line.' He made a sweeping gesture with his hand. 'Over there is where we found Mr Griswald's body. And right over there is where the chopper picked you up. It's a long way between the two points. How'd you get there, Mr Harland?'

Harland was finding this harder than he'd expected. He stared down at the tufts of grass and the little streams that snaked through the mud. It all looked harmless enough now, but down there in the dark and with the tide rushing in, he had been damned certain that he was going to lose his life. He thought of Al Griswald's body propped up grotesquely in his seat and the freezing water swirling round his chest and sucking at his legs.

'Mr Harland!' shouted Ollins over the roar of a plane that had just landed on the other runway. 'What happened? How did you get there?'

'Swam,' he shouted back.

'That's a hundred yards or more. You were swimming out into the East River?'

'I was being swept out there – I was taken by the current.'

'And the phone?' asked Ollins, leaning into Harland's face and shouting over the noise of the plane that was now manoeuvring towards the terminal. 'Can you say where you were when you dropped the phone?'

Harland looked down at the place where Griswald's body had been and worked out that he had waded in a line that was parallel to the runway. With the tide being so low now, it was difficult to pinpoint the spot where he'd dropped down into the water and let go of the phone, but he hazarded a guess that it was where the mud shelved down sharply into a gully. At high tide it would be way out of his depth and he could see that what was a trickle of water would become a channel for the tide flowing from the west. Ollins produced a radio from his pocket and guided his beachcombers to the area. A voice came back to tell him that they had already searched there several times. The phone had probably been taken out on the tide. It could be anywhere.

'Why's the phone so important to you?'

'We're just researching as much as we can about all the victims.'

It occurred to Harland that they would want it to see who Griswald had been calling.

Ollins looked out towards Riker's Island and then turned to him. 'I have to ask you this: did you take anything from Alan Griswald's body?'

'No,' said Harland, mystified. 'I thought I was about to lose my life. I wasn't in the business of ripping off the dead.'

'Nothing?'

'No.'

Ollins looked at him intently. The wind made his hair stand up vertically in a crest. 'Were you ... er ... involved with Mr Griswald in any way? I mean his business at the War Crimes Tribunal. You had nothing to do with that?'

'My work is much less glamorous, if I can put it that way. I barely knew what Al was doing and I expect you've found out that he was an exceptionally discreet person.'

'Yes, that's what the agency said. You're sure that you didn't take anything? It could be important.'

'Why are you asking this?'

Ollins didn't answer. He turned towards the car and said, 'Let's get out of the cold, Mr Harland.'

They climbed in. 'Clark says the two black boxes have been retrieved,' said Harland. 'Surely they will tell you all you need to know about the plane? As I understand it, they record everything that happened during the flight. They're very sophisticated these days.'

Ollins started the engine distractedly and executed a lazy turn towards the Marine Terminal, steering the car with just a couple of fingers. 'You're right. The data recorders are very good – a near-perfect record of that flight. Mr Clark and his colleagues at the NTSB think they've got enough evidence to say what happened to your plane. But I find I want to know more than they can answer.'

He drove in silence to the hangar where he deposited Harland by the cab that would take him back to the hospital. 'We'll be in touch,' he said, moving off. 'And don't forget to fax me those notes you made. The number is on the card I gave you.'

At the hospital, Harland ate lunch and dozed for a short time before receiving a final examination. While waiting for the cab from Queen's Limousine Service to arrive he got his few possessions together. As he cleared out the drawer of the bedside table he found a black wallet. It was bulkier than his own but, like his, the leather was distorted from being immersed and then dried out. He opened it and found Griswald's credit cards.

Slowly he remembered how the wallet came to be there. At the moment of trying to answer Griswald's phone he had slipped it into his pocket and forgotten about it. The hospital staff must have dried it out with the rest of his clothes and placed it with his own wallet in the drawer. He looked again and found pictures of the Griswald children. The photos had suffered from the water, as had the receipts and the cover of a mini-disc which was in one of the wallet's compartments. Harland pulled it out and saw that it was a compilation of work by Brahms, Chopin and Mendelssohn. This surprised him since Griswald was famously hostile to any music which did not involve saxophones and trumpets. He looked at the disc then returned it with the box to the wallet, at the same time remembering the many evenings he had spent with Griswald – more from friendship than shared enthusiasm – searching out increasingly arcane jazz haunts in West Berlin.

He put the wallet with the rest of his things, reminding himself to tell Ollins about it, and went to find out what had happened to the cab. Sister Rafael made a call and a few minutes later put her head round the door to say that the car was on its way, but that there was another call waiting – a Mr Walter Vigo from England.

Vigo! What the hell did he want? He hadn't seen Vigo for at least a decade. On the day he left MI6 for good in 1990, Vigo had come to him and offered a limp hand of regret together with the assurance that their masters would take Harland back if he found he could not make a go of things outside. They both knew this was impossible.

Harland picked up the phone.

'Bobby,' said the voice. 'It's Walter here. How are you? I was phoning to say how concerned we've all been to hear about your ordeal.'

We, thought Harland. Who the hell is *we*? A great crowd of well-wishers at the new headquarters of SIS, unable to think of anything but their ex-colleague's health?

'Thank you,' he said. 'It's good of you to call. Where are you ringing from? It's nine p.m. in London and it's Saturday – you can't be at work.'

'I'm here in New York. Davina wanted to do some Christmas shopping and see a show or two. I took a few days off and came along with her. I'm pleased to say that our flight was rather less eventful than yours.'

Harland remembered that Davina Vigo was wealthy. She had the kind of background – Vigo's euphemism for money – that enabled Vigo to treat his government salary almost as loose change. They lived in a large house in Holland Park and were always nipping off for weekends in Italy or Switzerland. People wondered why he hadn't left the service when his wife inherited in the mid-eighties, but that was to misunderstand Walter Vigo and his profound commitment to the profession. He liked intelligence work and was prodigiously good at it. Harland knew he was pretty near the top of the service now.

'How long are you staying in New York?'

'Until Monday – just a short trip. I was wondering if you'd like me to visit you. I'd do a lot to get out of the play Davina has fixed for this evening. If I came late this afternoon, I could reasonably excuse myself for the whole evening.'

'They're letting me go home,' Harland said. 'I'm waiting for a car to pick me up now.'

'Really! That is good news. Then what are you doing this evening? Can't be much fun going back to an empty flat in Brooklyn.'

How uncharacteristic of Vigo to make a mistake like that, thought Harland. Vigo could only know he lived in Brooklyn if he had been making inquiries about him. Harland was not in the phone book and, though he never made any secret of it, few people knew where he lived.

'How do you know it's empty?' asked Harland, smiling to himself.

Vigo laughed. 'I admit to the assumption, unwarranted perhaps, that your personal life is in its usual state of disarray. Otherwise I imagine that someone would be collecting you and that you wouldn't be waiting for a car.'

A fast recovery, thought Harland. Maybe he wasn't losing his touch after all.

'But forgive me, if I'm wrong,' said Vigo. 'Look – it would be lovely to see you. Why don't we have an early dinner? Shall we say Noonan's Steakhouse at seven? It's at Lexington and forty-eighth Street. I'll book – it's on me.'

Harland was about to decline, but then thought that an evening by himself was precisely what he did not need. He was feeling rested and, besides, he was curious to know what Vigo wanted. He'd bet his life that there was a very specific reason for the call. Walter Vigo always had a purpose, even if at first he did not declare it.

4

Philosopher Spy

Harland was late at Noonan's, arriving at twenty past seven. As he waited to check the old blue overcoat he was using as a substitute for the one lost in the crash, he looked around the restaurant and decided it was an odd place for Vigo to choose: a phoney club atmosphere; hearty back-slapping men, and women with the expensive, caramelised look of over-decorated pâtisserie. No, Noonan's was not at all Vigo's natural habitat.

The maître d' gestured to a booth in the far corner of the restaurant and told him that Mr Vigo had been there for some time. He found Vigo tucked into the booth, with his back to the rest of the diners. The fingers of one hand rested on the stem of a vodka martini, while the other held down the pages of a Sotheby's auction catalogue.

He rose as Harland approached and proffered his hand. 'Bobby, what a pleasure to see you – and looking so well too. Slide in there and let's get you a drink.' He examined Harland in the light of the lamp over the table. 'Let me look at you. Gracious, there's not a scratch on you. You're a bloody miracle and a famous miracle at that. I suppose you know that every daily newspaper in the world published the picture of your rescue.'

'I'm beginning to appreciate that,' said Harland regretfully.

'You're going to become one of those icons of photography, an exquisitely comic fate for an ex-spy, don't you think?' He paused to irradiate Harland with a smile. 'Now, what are you going to have to drink, Bobby – champagne?'

Harland accepted and reminded himself to guard against Vigo's we're-all-in-it-together bonhomie.

Vigo clapped his catalogue shut and held it up for Harland to see. 'Incunabula!' he proclaimed. 'Isn't that a marvellous word? It refers to all books printed before 1501 – just a few years after Caxton's press.'

'Yes, Walter, I think I knew that.'

'But do you know what it means in Latin? I learned the other day that

364

incunabula are swaddling clothes – I suppose it's the idea of the very first stage in any given development.'

Vigo hadn't lost his pedagogical style. And physically he hadn't changed much either, although Harland knew that he must have passed his fiftieth birthday. He had the same polished skin, the same prominent, fleshy nose and slightly popping eyes. Even his hair, a unique mass of tight curls that bunched at his collar like the improbable locks of a wig, seemed as thick and vigorous as it had been when Vigo had come to lecture Harland's SIS intake at the Fort training school on Euro-communism. But he had gained weight around the shoulders and chest, and his face had thickened at the jaw, which added to his appearance of substance. A stranger might have taken him for a professional connois-seur, an art dealer or wine merchant. But there was nothing refined about Walter Vigo, nothing ponderous or precious about him. He could mix it with the best and, when circumstances required, was capable of demonic application. As he sat beaming across from Harland, he seemed more than ever to project a massive and protuberant cleverness.

Harland's champagne arrived. Vigo ceremoniously raised his own glass. 'Here's to your survival, Bobby. Good health.' He drained the martini, never letting his eyes leave Harland's. 'From what I hear, it was a remarkable feat. You were half-dead when they got to you.'

'I was lucky, the others weren't. It's as simple as that.'

'Yes, but surviving in those conditions. That took some guts – not that there was ever any question about your personal courage, Bobby. We know that. We know what you did in Germany and Czechoslovakia. And I hear you've been in some pretty tight situations since you left us.'

'As I say, I was lucky.'

'I suppose in one sense you were. I mean happening upon that phone. What an extraordinary piece of fortune that was. And you knew the man whose phone it was.'

'Yes, it was Alan Griswald's.'

Vigo was certainly on top of things. Almost none of this had been released to the press. Harland realised that the information would have been quickly picked up by the SIS contingent at the UK mission who had any number of friends in the UN.

'Ah yes, of course. Alan Griswald. Now we've come across him before, haven't we?'

Harland wasn't going to help. 'Have you, Walter? I wasn't aware of that.'

'Yes, where did we meet Mr Griswald before?'

'He was in Europe – Vienna and Berlin. Also in the Middle East.'

'Oh yes, Alan Griswald. CIA to his boots, a good soldier, a good solid Cold War warrior. I remember him. He had a wife ... um?'

'Sally.'

'Yes, Sally. Poor woman. Of course there were many other casualties, but it means a great deal more when you know someone. Griswald retired from the Agency. What did he go on to do? Was he involved with the UN?'

'He was working for the War Crimes Tribunal. I saw him in The Hague last week. I was there for the World Water Convention. We bumped into each other outside the convention centre and then both of us walked slap-bang into Guy Cushing – you remember the man in the Far East Controllerate who had the money problem? Pushed out because of his debts and the gambling thing?'

'Of course,' Vigo said unenthusiastically. 'Yes, Cushing.'

'Guy works for the UN chemical weapons agency in The Hague. We all had dinner that evening in the old town – a place near the Palace. Griswald didn't say much about what he was doing because Guy was there. He said that he had been engaged in some follow-up work for the Tribunal. I didn't know what that meant. He said he was going to Washington and we loosely arranged to hook up because I was going to be in Rockville, which is no distance from DC. That's how I came to be on the plane.'

'Yes, I heard that from someone.' He signalled for another martini. 'Any idea whether he was going to see his former employers at Langley, Virginia? That's not far from DC either.'

'No,' said Harland, now certain that this was not a friendly fixture. He thought suddenly and rather guiltily of Griswald's wallet. Griswald had gone on about some big breakthrough he had made and on the cab journey to the restaurant Harland distinctly remembered how he had patted his breast pocket and said that he had found everything he needed for a hell of a case. 'One day,' he had said, 'I'll tell you the whole goddam frigging story and you, Bob, will be especially interested.' That was the trouble with the last few days, Harland thought. He was so bloody vague; things were coming back to him, but very slowly.

'So, then you flew back on the UN plane to New York,' continued Vigo gently. 'Had you seen each other in Washington?'

'No, in the end it wasn't possible.'

'But you had arranged to fly back together on the UN plane.'

'Not really. Vigo told me the time of the departure and said where they'd be. I thought I had missed it by a long time, but then I found them in the airport and took the ride.'

'Anyone else on the plane that I'd know?'

'I don't think so, but they haven't all been identified.'

'How many remain unidentified?'

'One – a man.'

'Odd, that. I mean you would think he would have been missed by now. What did the investigators say to you? They've been to see you?'

'Yes, I've seen them twice. I went out to the airport today – went over the crash scene.'

'Did they have any ideas about this individual?'

'Not that they told me.'

The maître d' appeared at their booth. Harland ordered soft-shell crab and lamb chops, Vigo lobster bisque and blinis of almas caviar – the roe of an albino beluga sturgeon. Vigo told the man to bring the wine they had discussed before Harland arrived.

'How's your sister?' he asked, suddenly snapping a bread stick. 'You knew Harriet was at Oxford with my wife, Davina. Davina always says that she was far and away the most able of her generation at LMH. What's she doing now?'

'She's married to Robin Bosey, the advertising man. You may have heard of White Bosey Cane. That's his agency.'

'Oh yes, I know exactly who you mean: always in the papers; designs his own clothes, works for the Labour Party.' A flicker of disdain swept through Vigo's eyes. 'And she's happy with *Robin*?'

'I think so. She does some financial consultancy, but brings up the children mostly. She had three, the last one four years ago.'

'Seems an awful waste of such a good mind – I mean Harriet sitting at home and being married to a man like Bosey. You're frightfully close, aren't you? I believe she was a great support when you had that terrible year. What with Louise leaving and your getting ill, it must have been an extremely difficult period for you, Bobby. That's all all right now?' Harland nodded and smiled at Vigo's parenthetic concern for his health.

'What a year that was, eh?' mused Vigo. 'Stumps drawn on the great game. Enemies and friends wearing the same suits and driving the same cars and suddenly we had to look very hard indeed to understand the new patterns of play. It was unsettling, and yet deeply stimulating at the same time. The people who suggested that the twentieth century ended in those months are absolutely right. Look at what else happened – the technical revolution and the leap to globalisation. It took some time, I have to confess, for us to get the point that digital information was infinitely more fluid than the information that's written down on a piece of paper, placed in a file and locked up in a steel vault. Secrets developed wings of their own. Things that had been stationary became fleet of foot; those that were solid and impenetrable became porous. Secrecy was no longer an absolute condition, but something that was measured in degrees.' He stopped to taste the wine that the maître d' had brought, nodded and waited as it was poured. Harland picked up his glass, reflecting on the fact that he'd need the drink to get through the evening. 'But, of course,' continued Vigo, 'what was our weakness was everybody's weakness. There were new lines of attack, new pathways to explore and new friends to be made. You've missed a lot, Bobby. It's been challenging for the old lags who've clung on.'

Vigo had certainly clung on. Harland had heard the details from a colleague who was brushed aside in his ascent. Vigo had served for a brief period in Washington. In 1995 he had manoeuvred to take over the newly formed Controllerate responsible for the Middle East and Africa. Five years later he had become Controller, Central and Eastern Europe. Recently he had got an even grander position which required a special title which no one could remember, but which seemed to incorporate security and public affairs.

'But you've done very well for yourself, Walter. I hear you're a great power in the land. You must be going for the top job?'

'No, no. I am sure that won't come my way. Robin Teckman may be asked to stay on for three more years, which means that his successor will be chosen from the generation below me. Tim Lapthorne or Miles Morsehead are the obvious candidates. I'm content with my lot and there's much to do in the years that remain to me in the Service.'

Harland remembered Lapthorne and Morsehead, two bright stars of the early eighties' intakes. Morsehead was the obvious choice. From an early moment in his career he had managed to seem bold and reassuring at the same time.

'You're sounding like a politician, Walter,' he said.

Vigo ignored the remark. The food arrived and he set about drawing up the bisque to his lips in a fluent scooping motion. 'Of course,' he said eventually, 'you would have gone a long way up the ladder yourself, Bobby, if you hadn't bailed out. You've got what it takes – intelligence, imagination, discipline, charm. You were good at winning people's confidence, a very light touch with the most difficult of characters. Remember that Russian diplomat in Turkey you persuaded to drive over the border with a chunk of the new Soviet armour welded into his car engine? What was his name?'

'Tishkov – Avi Tishkov.'

He paused and glanced around the restaurant with an air of someone experiencing public transport for the first time.

'Why did you go?' he said emphatically. 'Why? There was no need, surely? We would've made certain you had time to recover properly. You were marked for the top, Bobby.'

Harland opened his hands in a gesture of appeal. 'When you've had a brush with cancer, you think through your life and see it in a different light. It's a terrible cliché, but it's true. I decided to do something else. That was all. What I didn't appreciate at the time was that Louise was thinking along the same lines.'

'Yes, discipline,' mused Vigo, failing to follow the trail about Louise's departure. 'That really is your foremost quality. You never gave in to what

I would guess was an essentially turbulent nature. It was that tension between impulse and control that made you a good agent. You watched yourself as carefully as anyone else. You became a philosopher, a thinker, because that way you would survive. I admired you for that thoughtfulness and the way the habit of weighing things extended into your work. Yet I have to say that I feared what would happen if you let go of the reins. That would be the end of the philosopher spy, I was always sure of that, the end of the man who talked Descartes to some poor Polish trade official and induced him to donate all his country's economic information to our data bank.'

Harland saw that the nature of the conversation had changed entirely. He had the impression of a very large ship edging towards its berth.

'What's this about, Walter?' he asked. 'Is there something you want to know?'

Vigo looked up from the nearly drained bowl, his eyes glittering with purpose. Harland was momentarily fascinated by the size and sensuality of his face. He remembered how someone in Century House had found a picture of a ceremonial mask from a Pacific island in one of the Sunday supplements and had pointed out that it looked exactly like Walter Vigo. For a short while afterwards he was called the Love Mask.

'Oh yes, Bobby. There's a lot I want to know. I want to know who was on that plane and what Griswald was taking with him to Washington. And, more particularly, I want to know whether your relationship with Griswald holds any significance. I ask myself, can it be that you really just happened upon each other in The Hague and had dinner at the Toison D'Or? Or was it that you two had some business there and in Washington? I want to know whether your presence is important on the flight, or whether it is simply Alan Griswald I should concern myself with. Yes, I would like to know the answers to these questions. Can you help?'

'Not really, Walter,' said Harland. 'By the way, I didn't mention the Toison D'Or. How did you know?'

'I assumed it. The Golden Fleece is the only place there.'

Smooth, thought Harland, but unconvincing. 'I have had no professional dealings with Griswald whatsoever for more than a dozen years,' he said. 'I liked him and that's why I was sitting with him on the plane. Indeed, that's why I was on the plane. There's nothing sinister about it.'

Vigo sat motionless with his hands splayed on the table while the plates were removed.

'I'm right in thinking that you and Griswald knew each other very well once,' he said, when the waiter had gone. 'You worked together in the eighties and you were both involved in that operation after the Wall came down – the operation to lift the Stasi files in East Berlin. God, what an excitement that was! And with good reason. Those files were matchless.

369

They contained everything we could have wished to know about the East Germans and their intelligence service – absolutely everything.'

He paused, as if to catch hold of the fading memory, eyes to the ceiling, hands stroking the tablecloth. 'Yes . . . they were handed over in a villa in Berlin – Karlshorst – but not to you, not to the CIA, but astonishingly to the KGB. Then Griswald's pals in Moscow station obtained them for an exceedingly large sum of money. I recall your excellent report, describing Alan Griswald's pivotal role in the coup, and outlining what those files would mean to West German society and to us – the understanding of the Stasi's strategy, the highly placed agents who'd been working for the East, to say nothing of their ingenious trade-craft. They *were* good, weren't they?'

'Yes, I suppose they were, but it all seems so long ago. The world's moved on, as you say yourself.'

Vigo was not easily diverted.

'But then you and Griswald overreached yourselves and went south, to Czechoslovakia, on an extremely dubious fishing expedition to seize the files of the State Security Service in Prague. That was an occasion when you may have been driven by impulse rather than reason, I fear. But we were all carried along by your enthusiasm. Bobby Harland, the magician of the East European Controllerate, was going to bring home the bacon – everything we wanted to know about the StB. Your argument was so alluringly pitched. If I remember rightly, you pointed out that we couldn't know what would happen in Eastern Europe. It might all be a flash in the pan, you said, so we'd better move quickly. We knew it was blue-chip intelligence, the real stuff, and we all desperately wanted it.

'Everyone liked the idea,' said Harland, knowing he was sounding defensive.

'Oh yes, I know your plan was cleared by the Head of Soviet Ops and the Security Branch Officer – who incidentally had no business sanctioning such a harebrained scheme. Operational security! There was no operational security and everyone knew it. You didn't know the set-up in Prague and our people there were extremely doubtful about the contacts you and Griswald had conjured from nowhere. But you insisted that cash would open the right doors and, well, I suppose we were all guilty of greed, weren't we? A matter of days and you were arrested and beaten so badly you couldn't walk. If The Bird and Macy Harp hadn't got you out I doubt whether you would be alive today.'

Harland suddenly saw the loping figure of Cuth Avocet, known to all as The Bird, and his equally improbable partner, Macy Harp. Both MI6-trained, they'd turned freelance and during the Cold War went behind the Iron Curtain to sort out problems which were underplayed as 'situations' in the argot of the great game.

'How long were you in that Austrian hospital – five, six weeks? It all still puzzles me. I felt there was more to it than met the eye. Worth further thought some day, I said to myself, because it seemed to me that they were expecting you. You weren't held in a standard prison, were you? Some bloody house on the outskirts of the city.'

He stopped to let the waiter set down the second course, then looked down at his caviar with an expression of regret, perhaps caused by the thought that he would not be able to devote his full attention to it.

Harland fought to put the image from his mind, the image of the room where he had been held for all those days and beaten senseless. But he didn't succeed. He saw The Bird stepping into the doorway and saying, 'Hello, old lad. Time to be on our way, don't you think?' And then The Bird had freed him from the leather restraints and virtually carried him out of the deserted villa. On the way they passed two guards who had been dispatched by him. And then they found Macy Harp waiting patiently in the street behind the wheel of an old but very fast BMW, and they had driven like the blazes to the Austrian border, where The Bird had squared things with the Czech border guards. There had been others involved in the operation, but he never knew their names, and when at length he visited The Bird and Macy to thank them, they had been stubbornly mysterious about how they had found him and who else had helped. It was part of their service, they said, and they had been well paid for it. However, they would prefer not to discuss the matter any more.

Vigo was watching him now.

'Was it the beating, Bobby? Was that what finally turned you against the Service? I know it must have been a terrible experience, but it's not as though you went into some quieter line of business afterwards. I mean, Kurdistan in the early nineties, followed by Tajikistan and where else? Azerbaijan, Chechnya? Not a sheltered life, by any means. To tell you the truth, it always looked to me as if you were going out of your way to find danger. I used to ask myself why that might be.' He paused to let the thought hang in the air. 'In another man I would hazard that such compulsion was an indication of guilt.'

Harland looked at him mildly. 'Not guilt, Walter, just a change of interest. The reason I went to those places was that I could speak Russian. As you can imagine, the Red Cross didn't have too many Russian speakers in those days. And, you know something? We did some good in those places, which is what I liked about the job.'

Vigo returned a knowing smile and then sighed. 'But let's just go back to the matter in hand, if you wouldn't mind – this thing you had with Griswald, this association, this alliance. He must have given you a hint of what he was doing. You see, we know he was bringing something to New York of great value. When I saw you were on the same flight I said to myself that this information might be the sort that Griswald would share with an old and reliable friend such as Bobby Harland.'

'The answer is no. I really haven't the first idea what he was up to. I guessed that it was important – in fact, he said so. But really I can't tell you any more than that.'

'But I have a steer that you did indeed know about it all.'

Harland remembered Guy Cushing in The Hague and wondered whether Vigo had prevailed upon him to bump into Griswald and find out what he could at the Toison D'Or. Harland was certainly not put off by the nauseous look that came into Vigo's expression when he first mentioned Cushing. It was quite possible that Cushing had been keeping an eye on Griswald for some time. He must owe Vigo all sorts of favours after his unceremonious expulsion from the Service, which was said at the time to be a lenient punishment. Yes, he would owe Vigo, and Vigo would have pressed for repayment. That was Vigo's way.

'Walter, you asked me why I left the Service. It was partly to stop wasting my life on this sort of crap. Let me be clear about this. Griswald and I collaborated at one time and I really was genuinely fond of him, but our lives developed in different directions. The steer you have is a bad one.'

Vigo said nothing.

'The other thing you're forgetting,' Harland continued, 'is that the crash appears to have been an accident, which stands to reason. If you were to sabotage a plane, you would arrange for it to blow up at twenty-eight thousand feet, not at fifty feet as it was coming in to land.' He pulled his napkin from his lap and began to work his way out of the booth. 'Walter, I can't give you the answers to your questions because they're too damned silly.'

'There's no need to leave, Bobby,' said Vigo, holding up both hands. 'Please do stay. I'll explain as much as I can. You see, we believe that Griswald had benefited from an unusual source.'

'What kind of source?'

'I'm not at liberty to say, but I can tell you that the source is random in focus and sometimes oddly juvenile. We are anxious to learn a little more about the source and so naturally I came to you, believing that perhaps Griswald had told you about it.'

Harland felt his temper rising. 'Look, I had absolutely no connection with Griswald. He wouldn't tell me what he was doing. You must understand that. Why don't you ask this bloody source?'

Vigo considered this while adding sour cream and caviar to the mound of chopped egg on one of the blinis. When he had finished, he picked up the pancake, squeezed the sides gently and placed it in his mouth. Silence ensued. Then he spoke. 'I can't talk to this source because at present it's anonymous.'

'Look, somewhere along the line there's a physical entity who you can grab by the throat and demand he tells you what he's talking about.'

'In this case we can't. Things aren't nearly as simple as they used to be and this is a very delicate, not to say dangerous, situation.'

'Are you getting this all off the Web? Some crackpot intelligence site?'

'No, it's rather more specialised information – designed for the trade only, I suspect. I believe Griswald was in receipt of a bespoke service, if I may call it that.'

The trade only! Bespoke service! He wished Vigo would stop talking like a fucking butler. He looked at him and wondered vaguely if he had any concept of life outside the Secret Intelligence Service.

'But this source is some kind of friendly voice?' ventured Harland.

'I couldn't say.'

'Then what the hell are you talking about?'

'I can see you're sceptical about all this, but I assure you that we believe it to be important.'

'Yes, I'm sceptical, but I was also thinking that it's a long time since I've had a conversation like this when I haven't the first idea what is being said to me.'

'Oh, come on, Bobby, you do yourself a disservice. As you well know, you are rather good at all this. Don't tell me you've been converted by the happy-clappy folk at the UN, because I won't believe you.'

'For fuck's sake,' Harland snapped. 'Out there, there are vast problems of poverty and with the environment. These problems are getting worse and they need people to think about them. When it comes down to it, the intelligence community – as it is laughably called – does damn all to help.'

Vigo sat back to examine Harland with ironic amusement, his eyes popping with superiority and malice.

'I see the philosopher spy is in the grip of a moral imperative – or is it a categorical imperative? I am never sure. However, before you get too carried away, let me just point out that a great number of people at the UN belong to the community you so despise. No less than a fifth of every national mission at the UN is devoted to the unlovely practice of your former trade. They're ferreting around, snooping, poking, prying, stealing, poncing and generally doing their level best to find out what each other is up to. They may wear national costumes and talk humanitarianism while queuing at the vegetarian counter in the UN cafeteria, but let me tell you that a good many of them are spies, and pretty second-rate spies at that.'

Harland drank some wine and decided not to reply. Time to go.

'Look, Walter, I'm not much company. I wish I could help you about Griswald, but I can't. And now I really do think that I should go to bed. I'm still feeling pretty done in.'

He got up.

Vigo looked disappointed. 'Yes, of course. I quite understand, Bobby. It's been a pleasure to see you. I hope you haven't minded our talk. You can probably see that it's important to me. I hope also that you'll understand if I have to call on you again.' He composed himself and smiled. 'What are you doing for Christmas? Going back to dear old England or staying here?'

'No plans yet.'

'Well, keep in touch. And Bobby, all of what we've talked about aside, I'm really very pleased to see you alive.'

Harland shrugged and thanked him for the meal. He went to collect his coat at the front desk. The girl at the coat check had some trouble finding it. As he waited he cast a look back at Vigo in the booth. His hands were just visible, leafing through the catalogue of incunabula. Then a man appeared, perhaps from a table on the opposite side of the restaurant, and went over to say something to him. Vigo did not raise his head to look at the man.

Harland walked down 48th Street towards the East River, relieved to be out of Vigo's oppressive company and also a little angry with himself for allowing Vigo to nettle him. He was sure that the stuff about Prague, dropped like an iron bar into the conversation, was there to menace him. Of course, Vigo didn't know anything about Prague, but he must have had suspicions at the time which he had resurrected now to use as a lever. Well, he could forget it! There was no way he was going to succumb to a clumsy threat like that.

Try as he might, he couldn't stop turning over the conversation in his mind. What was it Griswald knew that Vigo was so desperate to get hold of? It had occurred to Harland beforehand that the mini-disc might just carry something, if only because the choice of music was patently not Griswald's. The next day he would take it to Sally and ask her if she thought it had any special significance. He would also see if she knew what her husband was working on. The Griswalds had an unusually close relationship and he was sure that Al kept few secrets from her.

But what about Vigo? What the hell were his motives? On reflection, Harland felt he'd almost been sitting with someone who was playing Vigo, rather than Vigo himself. The humour and effortless speed of mind had been replaced by a pantomime version of the original – an indication perhaps of his desperation. There was no doubt that the problem was consuming all Vigo's considerable resources because he was well informed about the crash. Maybe he had a line into the FBI? But it was more likely he was getting this stuff from someone in the UN, someone who was being kept informed of the progress of the investigation.

Harland turned right at Second Avenue and kept walking simply for the pleasure of the bracing night air and the glittering vistas of midtown Manhattan. His mind was clearing and with that came a burst of optimism, which had been waiting to break out since he left the hospital. He had survived, dammit, and that was all that mattered. He stopped at a

Korean deli and bought himself a small container of freshly squeezed orange juice to clear his mouth of the thick, musty taste of the wine. He undid the top as he waited for the store assistant to change his twenty-dollar bill and swilled the juice in his mouth before swallowing it. Then something occurred in a deep part of his consciousness. An old nerve ending tingled which made him look round through the doorway and catch sight of a man on the other side of Second Avenue. He had stopped and was fiddling with one of the newspaper vending machines that are on every corner in midtown. Harland understood that he had been followed from the restaurant. He took his change and lingered to the side of the doorway, waiting for a cab with an illuminated sign to draw up to the lights. The man threw one or two glances his way, then withdrew a newspaper from the machine and ostentatiously started leafing through it.

Bloody amateur, thought Harland as he walked smartly from the doorway and flagged down a cab. What the hell did Vigo think he was playing at, sending his idiot footpads to follow him?

5

The Wooden Hat

The young man waited to catch sight of Harland outside the Flynt Building in Brooklyn Heights for much of the day. But the wind was blowing straight off the East River and several times he had been driven inside by the cold, first to find refuge in a bar and then in the cinema on Henry Street. After the movie, he decided to find out whether Harland was expected back that day. He talked to the surly Russian porter at the Flynt and discovered he'd missed him. Harland had returned from hospital and gone out again. At 10 p.m. the young man returned to his post behind some recycling bins across the street from the building. He would give it an hour and if Harland didn't show he'd go back to the hotel.

Ten minutes later a cab drew up and a man in a long overcoat got out and walked slowly to the building's entrance, patting his pockets for keys. As he reached the door, he paused and shot a glance quickly up and down the empty street. It was then that he caught sight of the man's face. Although he was thirty yards away and the light was not good in that part of the street, he was certain that the tall, slightly stooping figure was Robert Harland. But now that the moment had arrived, he found his mind tripping over itself in an effort to choose the right words. Hell, he'd had enough time to think of what he was going to say, but he couldn't find a coherent sentence in his being. And so he watched while Harland pulled the door open and passed into the lobby.

He was just pondering how long he should wait before asking the porter to call up to Harland's apartment when another cab coasted to a halt at the end of the street and two men got out. Instinctively he withdrew further into the shadows behind the bins. He saw one of the men jog a little way down the street, stop and hold up his hand to shield his eyes from the light of the street lamp. He seemed to be interested in the cab which had dropped Harland off, and was only now moving away.

After a few seconds the man retreated and disappeared with his companion into Henry Street.

Harland could never enter the Flynt Building without marvelling at his good fortune in landing the apartment when the previous tenant left for Rome. He made for the elevator, raising a hand cheerily to the young Russian who served as the weekend doorman. Boris grunted something but did not look up from the mini TV balanced in his lap.

When he unlocked the door of his apartment he would sometimes go in without turning on the lights, take a drink from the fridge and look at the view for a few minutes. The room was large and airy, and all along one side was an uninterrupted view across the East River to Wall Street and the World Trade Center. But now he flicked the switch because the answerphone light was blinking. He pushed the play button and heard the machine announce in its hesitant, half-feminine voice, 'You have . . . five . . . new messages.' The first caller hung up without speaking. The next three were well-wishers from the UN, and then came Harriet, again insisting that he should spend Christmas in London.

As he listened to her, his eyes ran over his desk. Something was wrong. The letters he'd picked up from the mailbox that afternoon had been placed in a different order. And the bill from the electricity company, which he'd left on top of his laptop so he wouldn't forget to pay it, had been moved to the side and turned over. Also, the lid of the computer was fractionally open. He knew he had left it shut tight.

He looked round the apartment. Nothing else seemed to have been disturbed. He went back to the computer and turned it on. All the files on his water report were in order and appeared not to have been tampered with. His e-mail, however, had been downloaded from the Internet provider and read. Some sixteen messages that he had not seen before were displayed in the inbox. None was in the bold type that indicated an unopened message.

His first thought was that Vigo had arranged for the search, knowing he was safely at dinner with him. His hand rose to feel the lump of Griswald's wallet in his jacket and the hard edge of the disc's cover. That was the only thing Vigo could want unless he was convinced that Harland's laptop contained some clue to Griswald's secret. Still, it didn't seem quite right to him. A professional team from SIS would have stolen into the apartment and gone through his things without leaving a trace. They certainly would not have made the mistake of opening his e-mail and then leaving the computer open and in sleep mode.

He left the apartment and went down to the lobby where he found Boris who was leaning back in his chair, distractedly pulling a strand of gum from his mouth.

'Did I have any callers when I was out, Boris?'

'World and fucking wife try reaching you,' he said without turning round. 'Too many people looking for you come here.'

'Too many people? What do you mean – the media?'

'Many people. Not media.'

'Well, who then?'

Boris's sallow features looked up at Harland. 'Two men from UN. I show them apartment.'

'What! Which men from the UN?'

'They have ID and documentations. They take nothing. I check.'

'You mean you let some strangers into my apartment.'

'They have documentations; they have ID.' Boris stood up and thrust his hands out with the exaggerated innocence of a footballer caught fouling. 'Like the woman she come yesterday.'

'Which woman?'

'The woman who take clothes to hospital.'

'Yes, that was my secretary who you gave a spare set of keys to. But who were these men? What did they look like?'

'One tall with grey hair, like Bill Clinton. Other man, younger. They stay in five minutes. I wait outside door. Then they go.'

'This isn't bloody Russia, Boris. You don't have to do what everyone tells you just because they flash an identity card at you. Why didn't you say something when I came in just now?'

'You deen aks me.'

Harland briefly marvelled at Boris's mastery of street idiom.

'How on earth was I supposed to know that you had let a couple of complete strangers into my apartment? I think we're going to have to talk to the building manager about this, Boris.' He turned to the lift.

'You deen aks me about kid neither!'

'What kid, for heaven's sake?'

'A man like my age – maybe more young. He speak Russian and English like me. Smart kid. He say he come back later.'

'What did he look like?'

'Tall like you, Mr Harland. He wears big jacket and hat – like this.' Boris clamped his hands over his head.

'A woollen hat?'

'Yes, a wooden hat,' said Boris triumphantly.

'Did he say what he wanted?'

'He say he see you when you come back.'

'Fine, call me if he appears. But don't let him come up to the apartment. Have you got that?'

The moment Harland closed the apartment door behind him, the buzzer went. Boris was on the other end, now evidently anxious to help.

'Kid with wooden hat is in street. I see him now. He come in building

. . . No . . . He stand outside door. Now go away.' The commentary trailed off.

'I'll come down.'

He got downstairs to find Boris lurking at the side of the front door. Without bothering to hide himself, Harland peered through the glass and saw the figure across the street.

'Are you sure it's the same man?'

'Yes,' said Boris definitely. 'I tell him fucking get lost?'

'No, let's see what he wants.' Harland opened the door and saw the man more clearly. He had moved into the light of the street lamp and was looking in his direction, stamping his feet in the cold. Harland moved out into the wind and called out.

'What do you want?'

The figure made a hopeless gesture with his hands and seemed to smile, although it was difficult to tell in the dark. Then he started across the empty street.

'Do you need something?' Harland shouted again.

'Is that Mr Harland?' called the man. 'Yes, I would like to talk to you for a few moments.'

Boris had moved to stand behind him, apparently expecting trouble.

'He looks okay,' said Harland. 'Why don't you go back inside, Boris? You can call the police if there's a problem.' But Boris wasn't in any hurry to leave.

The man came up to them wearing a rather odd, eager smile. Harland gauged he was in his mid to late twenties. He had a thin, fairly handsome face and a sparse growth of stubble on his chin. He wore a padded ski jacket, black denims and tan-coloured boots. A dark blue woollen hat was shoved tight over his head and around his neck was wrapped a bulky olive green and black scarf.

'Mr Harland?' he said, still smiling.

'Yes. What do you want?'

'To talk to you. I have some things to say – important things.'

Harland registered an educated foreign accent and a pair of light brown eyes, which were perhaps a little troubled – or at least hesitant.

'What things?'

'It's quite difficult to explain.' He was now standing about three feet from Harland. The wind whipped the steam of his breath from his lips.

'What's this about?' said Harland impatiently. 'I'm not standing out here all bloody night.'

The man opened his jacket and rather deliberately slid his hand inside, which caused Boris to shift his position at the door. The young man held up his other hand and said to him in fluent Russian, 'There's nothing to be worried about. I am a friend.' Harland noted that the accent was again faultless.

He pulled out a wallet and withdrew a card which he shielded from the few flakes of sleet that were being borne down the street by the wind. 'I wanted to show you this.'

Harland took it and held it up to the light. It was an Italian identity card, frayed at the edges and discoloured. A picture of a young woman was rippled with the impression of an official stamp. He looked closely. There was no mistaking her. The name on the card confirmed his fears. EVA HOURESH was printed in capital letters and below the photo and in a different type face were the words 'Design Student'. The card was dated 1975.

Harland felt his stomach churn. But he did not react – he could not react, because he was certain that Vigo must have put the boy up to it. He wondered wildly whether the encounter was being observed. Was he being filmed? He glanced to the darkened windows of the apartment opposite and then to a blue van which stood under the line of gingko trees on the other side of the street.

'You don't recognise her?' said the young man, who had removed his hat and now stood looking rather crestfallen. His eyes were watering and his face was pinched with cold. 'Then I will show you these.' He took out two further cards and presented one to Harland. 'They have different names. I will tell you why in a moment.'

Harland examined the first one, a membership card for the Communist Party of Czechoslovakia, dated 1980. Eva Houresh appeared as Irina Rath. No occupation was given. Her hair was shorter and her face was a little older. If anything, she looked more attractive. The photographer had caught the expression of mockery that he remembered so well. Her eyes looked boldly at the lens and her lips seemed about to part in a smile.

The last card was party membership for 1988 and had belonged to Irina Kochalyin. The photograph was almost identical to the one taken eight years before. The card was in better condition and everything seemed in good order – the stamp, the serial number and regulations appeared authentic. Harland concluded that the outfit in SIS that had undoubtedly produced the cards had done a pretty good job. But how had they obtained the pictures of Eva? That worried him a lot.

He handed the cards back. 'I don't know why you think I should be interested in these.'

The boy looked confused. 'I thought you would recognise this woman.'

'I am sorry. I haven't the first idea who she is.'

'You must do! You must remember her! This is the woman that you knew as Eva Houresh! Her real name is Irina Rath and her married name was Kochalyin.'

Harland shook his head. 'I'm sorry, I think you must have got the wrong man.'

'But you are Robert Harland, are you not? I saw a photograph of you in the newspapers after the accident and I knew it was you. I knew you were the Robert Harland I wanted to find.'

Harland was watching him closely. He was obviously bright and he spoke excellent English, but he was no professional. There was too much raw emotion playing in his face. No one but a very talented actor could fake the oscillation of hope and embarrassment in his eyes. Still, Harland wasn't willing to take him on faith yet – not by any means.

'Look, I'm sorry,' he said, 'but I'm afraid you're very much mistaken if you think I know this woman. I wish I could be of some help to you. But there it is, I can't.'

He nodded to Boris who opened the door and went in. Then he turned towards the door himself.

'I don't need help,' said the boy indignantly. 'I came because I believe you are the man that this woman loved.'

'Well, I'm sorry,' Harland said with a finality that would deter most. 'You've got the wrong person.'

The boy continued, 'If you are that man, I need to tell you something very important.'

Harland kept walking because he knew he didn't want to hear any more. There were things in the boy's manner which had made him feel uneasy, and when a certain look had flared in his eyes, a very troubling doubt crept into his consciousness.

'Mr Harland, please,' he said more urgently. He came forward a few steps and caught him at the door. 'I think you are lying when you say that you didn't recognise her. I tell you this – she is my mother. If you are the person that loved her when she was a young woman . . .' He looked down and then up into Harland's face with urgency. 'If you are that person it is very possible that you are my father. In fact, I believe it is certain.'

Harland was speechless.

'I know where you met, you see. I know you went to a town called Orvieto in Italy and that you had to keep your affair secret because she was Czech and you were working for British Intelligence. I know about Cleopatra's Needle.' He suddenly seemed to lose momentum and stammered, 'I – I did not want to tell you in this way.'

Only Eva knew about Cleopatra's Needle – the place where they had arranged to meet in London but hadn't, for what reason Harland never knew because that was the last he had heard of Eva Kouresh. Still, the point remained that nobody else could know about it. It was conceivable that Eva had been traced by Vigo and had told him how she had failed to turn up – and about everything else, no doubt. But why would Vigo bother with this nearly thirty years later? What would be the point? He struggled to fit it into the conversation he had had with Vigo and tried to work out his motives. Nothing came to him.

'What do you mean by coming here with this tale?' he demanded.

'Maybe you should seek some kind of medical help because I can tell you that this idea you have is a dangerous fantasy.' He stopped. 'Is there something else you want. You want money?'

The young man shrugged and looked down at his feet again. 'I want nothing from you. Nothing at all.' He emitted a short ironic laugh. 'That's the odd thing. Now that I have told you, I don't want anything from you.' He paused as if remembering something then put his hand out with a disarming smile. 'I'm sorry I haven't introduced myself. My name is Rath – I am Tomas Rath.'

'You may find this amusing. I don't. Now, please would you leave.'

Harland knew he was playing for time. There was no reason why Tomas couldn't be Eva Houresh's son, that much he was prepared to concede. In fact, it had occurred to him the moment he saw the first identity card which showed Eva exactly as she was when he met her in Rome. The boy looked like her. His colouring was right, particularly the lightness of his eyes and the fine dark hair. And though he hated to admit it, he had much of Eva's manner. The photographs had stirred his memory and moments that he had not recalled for decades were flashing into his mind. He saw Eva, turning from some frescos in Orvieto to argue about their meaning. He could be Eva's child, certainly, but it didn't follow that he was his son. There was nothing of himself in the boy. Nothing whatsoever: not a cell, not a look, not a hair, not a gesture. This was not his son.

6
The Boy's Story

'Who put you up to this?' Harland asked. 'Is this some kind of stunt? Is Walter Vigo responsible for you coming here?'

Tomas shook his head, confusion clouding his face. 'I have never heard of this Vigo. No one knows I'm here. I came from London when I saw your picture. I didn't tell anybody that I was planning to do this. It was an impulse when I saw your photograph.'

'How did you know where to find me? I'm not listed in the telephone book.'

The boy told him how he had got the address from the UN. When Harland questioned him closely about whom he had spoken to, he produced the name of the Assistant Secretary-General. It sounded unlikely that he'd be able to bluff the address out of them. On the other hand, it was perfectly possible that one of the people on his floor had taken the caller on trust.

He opened the door and gestured Tomas inside.

'You wait here,' he said. 'I'm going to get a coat. Then we're going somewhere to talk and you will tell me what the hell is behind all this.'

It would have been much easier to take Tomas up to his apartment but Harland wanted to have the conversation in a public place. There was something about him that was desperate and uneasy. Besides, there seemed every possibility that his apartment had been fitted with eavesdropping devices by the people who had broken in. As he collected his coat he made a mental note to search the place later on.

When he returned Tomas had put his hat on and was sitting quietly on the polished bench near the door under Boris's suspicious gaze. Harland thought he looked like any of the thousands of young men on New York's streets.

They walked a few blocks to a restaurant where there was a bar at the front. It was late on a cold Saturday night and the place was pretty full, but they found a good table by the window at the rear of the bar area. Harland ordered a couple of beers from the waiter and told Tomas to sit down.

'Right,' he said abruptly, 'tell me your date of birth.'

Tomas was not going to be hurried. He unwound his scarf then took his jacket off to reveal a charcoal grey and navy plaid shirt. He folded the scarf deliberately and put it on the chair next to Harland, together with his gloves and hat. He looked around, wiped the condensation from the window with a serviette and peered into the street.

'Are you quite ready?' Harland said.

'I was born on the fifteenth of November 1975,' said Tomas evenly. The colour was returning to his cheeks.

'Where?'

'In Prague.'

'What age was your mother when you were born?'

'She was was twenty-two on the twelfth of October that year.'

The dates were just about right, thought Harland.

'And where does your mother live now?'

'Outside Prague, but we moved around a lot when I was kid.'

'Your mother is married?'

'She married a Russian citizen, but they are divorced now.'

'And she lives in the Czech Republic?'

'Yes.'

'And you? Where do you live?'

'I was living in Stockholm where I worked. Now I live in London for a while. Maybe I will move soon.'

There was a good deal that was unconvincing about the boy: while he had become more confident in his attitude to Harland, there was also an edginess in his manner. His eyes kept darting to a mirror behind Harland.

'I can tell you about my mother if you want,' he said. 'Ask me some questions.'

Harland thought for something else to ask him. 'Does she have any distinguishing marks?'

'Yes, on the nape of her neck, below the hairline – a patch of dark brown skin.'

He remembered the moment when he'd made the discovery of her oval-shaped birthmark in bed. They had fled, for that was what it seemed to both of them, to Orvieto in the dead of winter. It was early in 1975, when they had known each other just five months. They needed time together, both being too young for the pressure of their professions. They had stayed there for four nights in an ancient hotel's best suite. The town was empty, standing still and cold about them as though it had been struck by the plague, without a soul, it seemed, to hear the ceaseless tolling of the bell towers. It was quite simple: for those four days they had merged into each other. He was closer to her than he had ever been to another human being in his life. But it was just a few weeks before he had had to return to London to complete his training. By then there were no secrets between them. He knew what she really was – an agent working for the StB, the Czech Security Service. Her language skills and considerable beauty had been deployed in Rome, initially against the Czech dissidents who were running a propaganda operation there, and then with a view to compromising diplomats at the American and British embassies. She told Harland that he had been singled out as an inexperienced SIS officer who would be susceptible to her charms. She told him everything, but she never gave him her real name because she was too frightened. They had got something on her. He never knew what it was. Then they had parted on Rome station one morning. Harland thought back to the scene. At the time it had felt like an amputation.

'So how did your mother meet the man that you think is me?'

'It was in a bar. You were introduced by an American diplomat my mother knew. You were his regular tennis partner, she said. You went out with a big crowd of people that same evening. You talked about the books you had been reading. It was a great evening for her – very exciting, being in Rome with Westerners and drinking and laughing. A big change from the life she had known in Czechoslovakia. Even though she was working for the State Security Service, she said it was one of the most carefree evenings of her life. She said that afterwards you strolled through the city for most of the night. It was late summer – the month of August or September – and you walked until you found a café at dawn in a market near the French embassy. You had to catch a taxi and go straight to work. See, Mr Harland, I do know about it.'

Harland ordered another beer for himself, the boy not yet having touched his, and asked the waitress if she could find him a cigarette. She delved under her apron and shook a Marlboro from a crush pack. Tomas lit it from a matchbook on the table and sat back with a smile.

'I did not imagine you as smoker,' he said.

Harland ignored the remark. 'Who gave you the idea of approaching me?'

'Nobody,' said Tomas earnestly. He leaned forward to place his elbows on the table. 'You think I make all this up. How can you believe that?'

'You tell me. I mean, you walk up to me in the street like some kind of professional stalker, announce that you are my son and expect me to greet you with open arms. So what am I supposed to do now? Change my will? Put the family silver in your name – eh? You can't seriously expect me to believe all this?'

'I know about Cleopatra's Needle,' he said. 'That will prove I'm speaking the truth. No one but you and my mother knew about that.'

'You mentioned it before,' said Harland indifferently. 'So why don't you tell me about it?'

'My mother said you had a joke that she was Cleopatra because you believed that your love for her would destroy you. There was some dark humour there, she said. A few weeks after you left Rome she rang you and said that she was in London. You arranged to meet that evening at Cleopatra's Needle by the River Thames because you did not want to risk being seen with her. She understood this. It was very difficult for you – she knew that. She said she remembered it very well. It was a beautiful day in spring. She found the rendezvous place and then she walked by the river and did some thinking. She had a big problem which she was planning to tell you about but then she decided that she could not tell you. That is right, isn't it? She did not come and you never saw her again. You never learned why she had come to London.'

He waited but Harland didn't say anything.

'So here my story becomes less romantic, although you are not to blame because she believes that you really did love her. When she talked to you on the phone she did not explain that she was going to have an abortion? No, of course not. She would not do that.'

The word dropped to the pit of Harland's stomach.

'As you will appreciate,' continued Tomas, 'that kind of thing was then an impossibility in Rome. She made some excuse to leave Rome because she was desperate to tell you her news. I think some part of her believed that you could make everything right. Yet she knew that she was caught in a trap. She had two choices – get rid of the child or have the child back home in Czechoslovakia. If she did the first she might be able to see you a few more times, but you were in London and she was in Rome and it wasn't easy. Some time during that day in London she made the decision to have the child and that was why she did not come to you. She could not bear to tell you that her decision meant she had to go back to Prague and that would mean she would never see you again. The choice she made is why I am here. I am that child, Mr Harland, and, incredible though it may seem to you, I am your son.' He picked up his beer and drained it in one, evidently relieved at having unburdened himself.

Even if he had wanted to, Harland could not react. He had no idea what he should feel or how he should deal with this boy. The only emotion he was aware of was annoyance. These were his secrets, his history that this boy was spilling out, telling him more than he had ever known about his own life. He was angry and appalled. The fact was that it had never occurred to him that Eva might have been pregnant. He'd thought of everything else, but not that. When she didn't appear he had been in despair, and so caught up in his own sense of loss that he didn't think it through at all. For weeks afterwards he called her number in Rome. He phoned people who might know where she had gone, but no one had any idea. Then he flew to Rome one weekend and searched for her in their old haunts. Eva Houresh had simply vanished and left Harland feeling jilted and exposed.

He was so distraught when he returned to London that he took a friend into his confidence, a good sort named Jimmy Kinloch who was in his SIS intake. Jimmy told him that he was well out of it – a relationship like that could ruin a man's career and get him into a lot more trouble besides. And so Harland had forgotten Eva, at least he had stopped tormenting himself by thinking of her, which was an altogether different thing from forgetting her. What he did was to relinquish her, although some part of her was still in him.

'Tell me why your mother had to return to Czechoslovakia. Why couldn't she defect? If, as you say, she was pregnant, she could have defected and had the baby in the West. She would have been looked after.'

'It is obvious. If you'd listened to her, you would have known that she could not leave because of her mother – Hanna. Hanna was why she went back. She is still alive today. Do you know her story?'

Harland dimly recalled that Eva's mother had been in a concentration camp. He nodded to the boy to tell the story.

'In 1945 my grandmother, Hanna Rath, was found in Terezin. The place is called Theresienstadt in German. The Nazis made it the holding camp for the Jews of Bohemia and Moravia. She was nine years old and the last member of her family alive. All of them had been sent to Auschwitz on the transports but she managed to survive. Terezin was full of Jews helping each other. But without protection of any kind – no family, no friends – it was very hard for her. Somehow she escaped the transports. She has told me that she memorised the names of other children in the latest groups to arrive at Terezin and learned where they came from. That way she could pretend to be part of the new shipment. She also had a hiding place which she went to when the transports were being assembled for the death camps. Sometimes she stayed there for a day at a time, with just a little water. She told me that she imagined herself to be invisible and even today she says she has the power not to be noticed. She can walk down a street and not be seen. Can you believe that, Mr Harland?'

Harland nodded. He had met such people in his old trade. They were called ghosts.

'When Terezin was liberated by the Russians in May '45, she was found at the gates of the castle. She was the first to receive treatment from the Soviet army doctors. Later in the summer of 1945 she was taken to an orphanage near Prague. She was one of just three thousand survivors of Terezin. Ninety thousand had disappeared into the camps, but this little girl had survived. She was alive yet she was never able to reclaim her family's property. The home and the business were gone. She could not say what her family owned and anyway she did not know where the proof of that ownership lay. She couldn't even prove who she was because there was no one left from her town who could identify her. No one – not a teacher, a doctor, a friend or one single member of her family – was alive to say who she was. They were all gone. She was left with a name – Hanna Rath – and that was all.

'And so she stayed in the orphanage. Then at sixteen she became pregnant – that was with my mother. There was some kind of scandal. She would not say who the father was. She had to leave. But Hanna was very smart. She got work and she raised my mother in a room in Prague with almost nothing – just the two of them together. That is the story of the woman you fell in love with in Rome. Maybe you did not know it all?'

'You didn't explain why your mother had to return to Prague,' observed Harland, apparently unimpressed. Inwardly his heart churned at the thought of Eva.

'That is simple. She could not leave her mother there. Remember what it was like at that time – the "Normalisation" after the Prague Spring. It would have been unthinkable for my mother to defect to the West and leave Hanna to face the authorities. Everything in her life depended on her keeping in favour with the authorities – her job, her home. As it was, she had very little. My mother could not do that to the woman who had made so many sacrifices for her.' He stopped and looked at Harland intently for a moment, then turned to signal to the waitress for another beer. 'I have told you my story. What more can I do to persuade you? I guess there is a DNA test which would prove it to you. But that would be humiliating and there is no point because – you must understand this, Mr Harland – I do not claim anything from you. I do not want anything from you.'

'So let me ask you again, Tomas, why have you come? You could probably have traced me before now.'

'I have known this story for only a little time. Before, I thought someone else was my father – the man she married. And I didn't know where you lived. There are many Harlands in the London telephone directory. Besides, I have had my own concerns.'

'What do you mean by that?'

'I don't want to talk about them now,' he replied, with an oddly grave expression. He looked away. 'Maybe I'll tell you some day, Mr Harland.'

'Look, forget the Mr Harland, will you? Use my first name if you must call me anything.'

'I think I prefer Mr Harland until things change between us.'

'As you wish.' Harland put down his glass. He acknowledged to himself that he was affected by the directness of Tomas's manner.

'Do you go to London?' asked Tomas, apparently composing himself.

'Yes, sometimes. I have a sister who lives in London, but I haven't spent much time there over the last ten years.'

'Will you be visiting your sister for Christmas?'

'Probably. I haven't decided yet.'

'If you go, we could see each other. My girlfriend is in London and I will leave her number with you, together with my own number. If you feel you want to see me again, you may call me.' He paused. 'I know you don't believe my story now. But maybe you could after a time.'

'Maybe, but I would like to speak to your mother.'

Tomas shook his head.

'You do see your mother?'

He shook his head again. 'No. I have not seen her for some time. Look, it's difficult to explain, Mr Harland. There are many things you don't know. And it is perhaps better that I do not tell you everything at once.'

'What do you mean?'

'I cannot say.'

'But you won't mind if I take her number?'

'No, but she will be angry that I've told you. She doesn't know I have come here.'

'Well, I'd like to speak to her about this. You can understand that.'

Tomas shrugged and for the next few minutes there was a silence between them. Harland studied him as he shifted his chair to make room for a couple of young women who had planted themselves with a great fuss at the next table and were unbundling in the warmth. There were a few sideways looks and some giggling, which Tomas returned with an offer of help to one of the girls who was coquettishly struggling to remove her jacket. He had something and it was working on these two girls, thought Harland.

Suddenly he felt incredibly tired. When he closed his eyes the golden light which he had noticed after the crash was flaring in front of him. He got up and indicated that he was going to the lavatory at the back of the restaurant.

Facing the urinal, he put his hand to the wall to steady himself, and thought about the young Eva. He tried to imagine how she would look now – dumpy and probably gone to seed, he thought. Still, he would have to call her as soon as possible because it was now imperative that he establish whether the boy was telling the truth. If this turned out to be an elaborate hoax inspired by Vigo, he would have to prepare his defence and work out what was behind it all. But it seemed unlikely because preparing Tomas's story and the fake identity cards, complete with the actual pictures of Eva, would have taken longer than the few days since the crash.

Harland's thoughts were disturbed by a man coming in and entering one of the cubicles behind him. He zipped himself up and turned to rinse his face in the basin. He needed to pull himself together and concentrate because there was a lot more he wanted to ask this Tomas character – a lot more.

When he returned to the bar he instantly noticed that Tomas's chair was empty and the pile of cold-weather kit had gone. He glanced at the door and caught sight of him at the tail of a group of six or seven people who were leaving. Tomas gesticulated in a diving motion with both hands towards the two girls. Then he put his right hand to his forehead in a salute which flipped up into a wave. Harland went to the table. One of the girls looked up.

'Hey, your son had to go. He left this for you.'

'What do you mean, my son?' he said, seizing the scrap of paper she held out.

'Oh, I'm sorry,' said the woman. 'We just kind of assumed you were related.' Her companion worked the gum in her mouth and nodded.

There were two numbers on the paper. One was for a cellphone; the other had a central London prefix. 'Ask for Lars Edberg', said the note.

Lars Edberg, thought Harland. Why was Tomas using an alias? There was no number for Eva.

'Did he say why he had to go?' Harland said, looking down at the two puzzled faces.

'No,' said the gum-chewer. 'He was looking out onto the street and then he turned back and just kind of got up and left. He gave us the note and said you'd understand.'

Harland tossed down a twenty and worked his way through the tables towards the door. Out on the street there was no sign of Tomas. He hurried back to the intersection at the top of the hill and caught sight of a figure running down Clinton Street. Whoever it was, he was moving very fast, then he dodged to the right and disappeared from sight behind a truck. Tomas Rath had vanished.

7

The Pulse

Next day, as Harland moved from a rotten night's sleep to a blank New York Sunday, he recognised that part of him wanted to accept the boy's story. But he consciously decided to suspend judgement and concentrate on the immediate mystery of what Griswald had been carrying with him.

Three hours later he stepped down from a train bound for Canada on to the platform of a small station some fifty miles north of New York. He waited there, looking across the sweep of the Hudson River towards the Catskills, and thought about Griswald. This part of the Hudson valley, Griswald once told him, had been settled by Germans, some of them Griswald's ancestors. It reminded them of the Rhine and their homeland which accounted for the names of the local towns – Rhinebeck, Rhinecliff, Staatsburg.

Sally Griswald's old station-wagon swept into the car park. She got out, looking much as he remembered her a dozen years before, and gave him a bereft, wordless hug. Then, taking his hands, she drew back and looked at him with a staunch smile. At length she said, 'If there was one man that Al would have wanted to survive while he was taken, it would have been you, Bob. Believe me, it is a consolation at this time to know that. There were very few people that Al admired and liked as much as you.'

Harland felt her loss with a sudden, useless clarity.

They drove to a large white clapboard house, set behind some conifers in two or three acres of frost-scorched lawn. Griswald's boys, Eric and Sam, were waiting to greet them. They stood in the hallway, pretending to remember Harland from the past, sheepishly concealing their grief. They were unmistakably Griswald's progeny – big and friendly with Al's shrewdness lurking in their expressions.

She led him through to the kitchen where a pot of coffee was already laid out with some cups, and food was in the oven. They all sat down. The boys looked at him expectantly as if he was about to produce some news or insight.

'So it was you who answered the phone out there,' said Sally, shaking her head. 'How terrible for you to deal with that. I want you to know I totally understand why – you know – why you hung up. I'm glad you did ... in a way. It gave me quite a chill to learn that you were out there with Al and that I was speaking to you at that awful moment.'

'Your call saved my life, Sally,' said Harland. 'They didn't know we were out there. I'm sure I wouldn't have lived if you hadn't rung at that moment.'

'It was lucky Dad kept the phone on,' said Eric, the elder boy. 'He should have had it switched off.'

'True,' said Harland.

'But if you hadn't been going to help him, you'd never have heard it,' chimed in Sam.

Over lunch they talked of old times in Europe, stories which fleetingly brought Alan Griswald to life in the minds around the table. Sally had to explain the circumstances of each of the stories to the boys – who the characters were and the politics of the embassy at the time. Harland filled in a few details, which briefly made her face light up. He let the conversation take its own course and only at the end of lunch did he begin to ask how Griswald had come to work at the War Crimes Tribunal.

She told him that he had left the CIA in 1994 and gone as an observer to the Balkans for the War Studies Forum in Washington which put out reports on Western policy. He hadn't much liked the writing aspect of the job but he had become fascinated by the civil war in Bosnia and convinced that the West's policy hovered disastrously between inadequate help and criminal hindrance. They had been worried about money and she had found it a struggle for most of the nineties when Al had been travelling for the Forum. But she understood that he was obsessed with the failure of the West to capture the people responsible for the crimes that he knew about in Bosnia. For him there was a lot of unfinished business in the Balkans and she supported his determination to see some kind of justice done. Eventually he was suggested to the War Crimes Tribunal and created a job for himself, applying the skills he'd learned in the CIA to hunting war criminals – all the espionage stuff that she didn't have to explain to Harland.

In the early nineties she moved into the house that Griswald had been left, partly to save money, but more to give the boys a base in the States. Al continued to commute to Europe. He kept his work out of the home but sometimes she asked him things and he answered her straight. About a month before, on his last visit home, they had been out to dinner in Rhinebeck and he had talked about the cases he was working on. He had told her about five or six men who had been responsible for the massacres in Bosnia at the end of the war. She couldn't remember the details but he did say that there was another case which he had just begun which might prove to be very important. He hoped to be able to complete the investigation and then he would think about finding a job which would allow him to stay in the States.

'You don't know any more about this last case?' asked Harland.

'No, why do you ask?'

He would have to take this gently, he thought. Sally was as quick as her husband and he didn't want to alarm her.

'Well, there is an awful lot of interest in what Al may or may not have been carrying with him to New York.'

'From whom?'

'From the FBI, which is investigating the crash as a matter of routine, and, rather curiously, from my old lot.'

'British Intelligence? Why would they be interested?' Her eyes narrowed. 'Are you saying something else, Bob? Are you saying there was something sinister about the crash? I know the media was speculating, but that was just loose talk – wasn't it?'

'As far as I know, the crash was an accident. The Safety Board are going to announce their findings, and they apparently believe it was an accident.'

'Right, so what is it you're saying?'

Harland hesitated and looked at Eric and Sam, and the image of Tomas Rath flashed into his mind. He remembered Griswald's pride in his boys and he fleetingly wondered what it was like to have a son. Then he pulled from his pocket the wallet that he had kept with him since leaving hospital.

'I know this may seem odd, but I took this from Al's body when I answered the phone. I can't absolutely recall what was in my mind, but I suppose I wanted to make sure there was some identification. Yesterday, I remembered he said he was carrying some crucial evidence.' He placed the wallet on the other side of the table.

Confronted with something so close to her husband's extinction, Sally Griswald had put her hands up to her face and was looking at the wallet with horrified fascination. She picked it up and felt the hard, desiccated surface of the leather with her fingertips.

She said nothing as she went through the contents. Eventually he took the mini-disc out and handed it to Eric who shook his head.

'This isn't Dad's music,' he said. 'There are four hundred records in the den and not one piece of music was composed before 1920. You know he was a jazz fanatic?'

Harland nodded. 'Famously so.'

'Have you played it?' asked Sam.

'No, I only remembered that I had the wallet yesterday. Anyway, I don't have a player for these things. Do you?'

Sam said he had one, picked up the disc and got up to fetch it. Eric went to join him, and Sally and Harland were left looking at each other.

Harland broke the silence. 'Is there someone at The Hague I can talk to discreetly about the investigations that Al was working on – a secretary, an assistant?'

'Yes, her name is Sara Hezemanns. She was Al's secretary but I'm not sure how much she will be able to tell you. You know how cagey Al was.' She wrote the name and Griswald's old office number on the kitchen pad.

'And what about this person he was travelling with?'

'On the plane? I don't believe he was with anyone, apart from you.'

Harland didn't press the point. 'And in Washington was there a hotel he stayed at regularly?'

'Yes, he went to the Fillmore Hotel on Tenth Street – he knows the manager there. He had some kind of deal.'

'He knew the manager?'

'Yes, but I forget his name.'

'Do you have any idea what he was doing in Washington?'

'Well, I guess he went to Langley. I know the Agency helped him with stuff like aerial pictures and radio intercepts. He visited there often because he was anxious to get these guys in Yugoslavia prosecuted.' She paused and glanced away, focusing on a pot of parsley on the window. 'We haven't got Al back yet. His body, I mean. That really hurts. It's ironic because Al said one of the things that obsessed those people in Bosnia was that they never found the bodies of their loved ones. They couldn't bear for them to be not buried properly. Did you know that?'

Harland shook his head.

'He told me it was a big thing for them,' she said, 'and I really begin to understand that now. It matters.'

The boys came back with the disc player and a portable speaker. 'I listened to some of this upstairs,' he said. 'Nothing strange about it, except Beethoven and Chopin was definitely not Dad's taste.'

They listened to the disc. Then Harland realised that the music playing was different to what was described on the disc cover, which listed highlights of orchestral works by Brahms, Chopin and Mendelssohn. What was playing now was the second movement of the Archduke trio by Beethoven. He picked up the cover and examined it.

'I noticed that too,' said Eric. 'This is the wrong cover for the disc.'

Before the next piece there was a sustained tapping – something between a Geiger counter and a door creaking open. The noise lasted five minutes more and was followed by the first bars of a Chopin nocturne. They listened to see if the noise returned, but heard nothing. Then Eric suggested that he could make a tape of the noise and slow it down. Both of them went off together, relieved to have something to do.

They returned ten minutes later, bearing Eric's recording equipment and arguing like young teenagers.

'It's code,' said Eric definitely.

'How would *you* know?'

'I just do. Listen.'

Eric played the tape he'd made, slowing it as much as he could on his equipment. There did seem to be a definite structure to the sound, almost like a pulse. As they listened, they realised that the individual taps consisted of many different elements. 'If we could bring this down real slow, I think we'd find something there.'

'Maybe I could find someone to do that,' said Harland. 'Would you like me to?' Sally nodded. 'I'll take the original disc, then, and the slowed recording if that's okay.'

'I've got a copy,' said Eric, 'so if you lose it you'll know where to come.'

'Good. Look, I'm not going to mention this to anyone. Let's keep it between ourselves. If there is something here, I certainly don't want anyone thinking that you've got it.'

Soon afterwards, Sally drove him to the station. They waited in the car park until the train was about to arrive. 'Bob,' she said, staring ahead of her, 'find out if something's been going on – you know what I mean. Find out for my sake and Al's – he would want that.'

Harland promised he'd do everything he could.

He got to the UN late in the afternoon as the setting sun washed a pink light over the west side of the great monolith. There were still a few tourists about but the restricted areas were deserted. He was glad. He wanted to work in quiet and avoid the fuss which would certainly accompany his return to work on Monday.

He unlocked his office, noted the two-weeks' worth of mail and sat down at his desk to think. He got the number of the Fillmore Hotel in Washington, dialled and asked to speak to the manager, saying that he was a friend and colleague of Alan Griswald's. At length a wary English voice came on the line. Harland explained that he was making some inquiries for the UN about Griswald's expenditure prior to his death. Just tying up some loose ends, was the way he put it. If this worried the manager, he was welcome to call him back on the main UN switchboard. Harland heard the voice relax.

'You can never be too careful,' said the manager.

Harland smiled at the motto of British caution and continued in a flat bureaucratic voice. 'We're dealing with the expenses incurred on his last trip. In the circumstances, we are concerned that they are fully reimbursed. I believe Mr Griswald was travelling with another gentleman who was also on United Nations business.'

'And you're doing this on a Sunday?' said the man.

'It's the Christmas rush. We need to make sure that his family is reimbursed before the holidays.' He grimaced at the lameness of his explanation and continued. 'The trouble is that we cannot immediately lay our hands on the name of the second party. Would that be something you have in your records?'

He heard the manager ask reception to look up the previous week's bookings. While he waited, the manager told him how he had met Alan Griswald some fifteen years before when he was deputy manager at the Jefferson Hotel. The death was indeed a tragedy, he said. Harland detected just the slightest strain of campness in his manner.

A voice sounded on the distant intercom. Two rooms were booked for two nights and paid for by Mr Griswald. Harland jerked his fist in front of him.

'The name of the other gentleman does not appear on the account,' said the manager, repeating what he had heard, 'but it does on the registration card. It is Luc Bézier, a French citizen apparently. No home address is given.'

'Anything else?'

'No. No passport number, no vehicle registration or contact number. Just the name Bézier.'

'Were there any additional charges to the bill – telephone calls? Meals?'

The manager replied that there were some other items. In a very short while Harland had persuaded him to fax copies of the bill and the registration cards. Five minutes later they slipped noiselessly from the machine by Marika's desk. He found what he was looking for halfway down on the second sheet of the bill – a telephone number recorded by the hotel's switchboard which began with the country code for France. There were two calls to the same number on successive afternoons, lasting seven and fourteen minutes respectively. Harland bet himself a cigarette that Luc Bézier was calling his wife or girlfriend.

He checked the number with International Information and found that it came from the Carcassonne area. It was nearing five – too late to ring. Besides, he wanted to know if the person who would answer the phone in France had been informed of Bézier's death. It seemed quite possible that they did not know, although they surely must have begun to suspect that something was amiss when the regular calls abruptly stopped after Monday. They would have started making inquiries, perhaps contacting Griswald's office in The Hague or the French embassy in Washington, and sooner or later someone would have suggested that Luc Bézier had been on the flight with Griswald.

Harland now felt sure that the FBI must have gone back over

Griswald's journey and stumbled on Bézier's name. Ollins had been so interested in the fact that he had seen the compact-looking foreigner with Griswald at the airport that he must have traced the hotel booking and then, in all probability, located his name on a passenger list from France over the previous weekend. It would have taken one further call to acquire Bézier's passport details from the US Immigration Service. And that meant Ollins knew as much as he needed about Luc Bézier. So why hadn't he included Bézier in the final toll? Was that the reason for his shiftiness out at the airport? Had he been prevailed upon to keep Bézier's name secret, or was he doing it for reasons of his own?

Harland rang Sally Griswald and asked if she had heard of Bézier. The name meant nothing to her. Al had not mentioned that he was dealing with anyone from France. Harland was about to ring off when she told him that she had been going through Griswald's recent mail and had found a sheaf of interview transcripts that had been expressed from his office in The Hague after he left. She had only skimmed them but thought they might be interesting. She would send the pages to his fax.

He made two further calls, the first to his sister, Harriet, to say that he would be in London for Christmas. Then he dialled the mobile number which Tomas Rath had left him. He assumed the phone was on a European service and so didn't expect an answer, nor was there one. He composed himself for the message service. 'This is Robert Harland,' he said evenly. 'I will be in London next week, so we can continue our conversation of last night. I hope that nothing is wrong. You departed in quite a hurry.' He finished by leaving his new mobile number and Harriet's home number and told him not to call before Tuesday.

He kicked his legs off the desk and went over to the fax to see if the documents had come. The engaged light was on. He waited while the cover sheet and the first of thirty-two numbered pages dropped into the tray. He read part of an interview with a Bosnian Muslim named Selma Simic. It didn't seem particularly important so he went off to the kitchen area to make himself some tea.

The floor was silent, except for the gentle background hum of the empty building. Most of the offices around him were dark. He made his tea, thinking about the order of phone calls he would place to Europe in the early hours of the morning, then returned towards his office.

As he stepped through the partition by Marika's desk he was aware of a rush of air to his left. He saw nothing, but felt a powerful blow to the ribs on his left side which hit the disc and glanced upwards to his Adam's apple. At the same time another force assailed him from behind. Two blows to the back of the neck, a jab to the kidneys, followed by a kick to the small of the back. Harland doubled up and threw himself backwards with all his might, flinging the tea, which astonishingly he still held, towards his left. A man cried out and lunged at him, but missed. Harland encountered the bulk of a second man whom he managed to propel with a crash into the partition on the other side of the corridor. He heard a gasp behind him but the fellow was strong and was soon up on his feet. Harland whistled round, aimed two punches to the stomach and brought his knee up to the man's chin. He fell. Then he felt a stunning blow to his head and knew nothing more.

8

Wake-Vortex

He came round with a flashlight in his eyes. Two men were standing over him. His office was very cold and he could hear the wind tearing at some papers on the window-sill. He lifted his head from the floor. A voice told him to stay still. Everything was going to be okay; an ambulance was on its way. Harland took no notice. He raised his head again and pushed the light away.

There was a chemical taste on his tongue and at the back of his throat. He moved a little more. His head hurt and his ribs and back were throbbing with new bruises. He rolled on to his side and pushed himself up to face two UN security guards who were crouching in front of him. He looked round, vaguely wondering why the window was open, and realised that he was some distance from where he had fallen. He had been out in the corridor and now he was beside his desk and there was a hell of a mess and the window was open.

'How are you feeling?' asked one of the guards, trying to get a clear look at his eyes.

'I'm okay.' In fact, he felt nauseous and irritable. 'Look, will someone bloody well close that window?'

'We can't,' said the other guard. 'It's jammed open – it's broken.'

Harland sat for a few minutes, consciously trying to still his stomach. Then he wiped his nose with the back of his hand, cleared his throat and looked up at the guards.

'What happened?'

'Jim found you five minutes ago,' said one. 'He reckons he must have disturbed them when he came out of the elevator.'

Harland now recognised the taste in his mouth as cocaine. It was making him a lot sharper than he might normally feel after being hit over the head. He turned to the window and focused on the vibrating slats of the Venetian blind. Now he understood why the window was open. They

399

were going to tip him out of it and make it look as though he had been on a cocaine binge and jumped. His single thought about this astonishingly crude plan was that Walter Vigo had nothing to do with it. Whatever the deficiencies and moral laxity of his former colleagues at Vauxhall Cross, they rarely behaved like gangsters.

'Did they take anything?' asked the guard called Jim.

Harland got up shakily and held on to the desk. Then he felt for the tape and disc in his breast pocket. They'd gone. 'I had some loose cash,' he said. 'Several hundred dollars – it's been taken.'

'They took your wallet?'

'The cash was in my pocket. My wallet was in my coat over there on the back of the door. Can you check for me?'

While one of the guards went over to check the coat, Harland scanned his desk. The copy of the hotel bill was still there and a glance at the fax machine told him that Sally Griswald's documents had arrived undisturbed. So, whoever had jumped him was simply interested in the disc and the tape. He thought of the copy that Eric Griswald had kept for himself and wondered if the Griswalds were in any danger. However, he was sure that he had not been followed out to the Hudson valley that day because he had taken the usual dry-cleaning precautions before leaving Penn Station, which had included loudly asking for a ticket to Trenton, New Jersey. Besides, he was absolutely certain no one else had got off the train at his stop. So for the moment he guessed Sally and her boys were okay.

'Sir, the wallet's here in your coat,' said the guard.

He picked up the hotel bill and went to collect Sally's fax, ignoring the entreaties of the guards. Once he had checked that all thirty-two pages were there, he sat down in Marika's chair and asked for a glass of water.

The hospital had tried to keep him overnight for observation, but Harland had been at his most hostile with the young doctor and had eventually just walked out and gone home. The next day he felt as well as could be expected with a bruise across the back of his head, which a paramedic had ventured was the colour and size of a small aubergine. He had no doubt that somebody had been about to kill him, and that frightened him a great deal. But in another way it intrigued him and put him on his mettle. Old juices were beginning to flow.

He left his apartment at eight, having packed for a week, and took a cab to the UN building. When he arrived, he found his office had been tidied up and the window fitted with new locks. Marika was there and gave him a gushing welcome which involved a long hug. Harland had never quite got used to the American embrace and didn't know when to let go. Eventually he was released from her ample chest and allowed to make his phone calls. She said nothing about the strip of plaster at the back of his head, possibly because she assumed it was a result of the crash.

The first call was to Sara Hezemanns, Griswald's assistant in The Hague, who immediately insisted that she check his credentials with Sally Griswald.

Five minutes later she called him back and listened while he explained that he was interested in Alan Griswald's last investigation.

'It was the one involving a French contact.'

'I'm sorry I cannot help you with this,' she said warily. 'It is all confidential.'

'But you know the identity of the Frenchman and you knew he was on the plane with Griswald?'

She said nothing.

'Am I right in thinking that his name is Luc Bézier?'

Still no answer.

'Do you know whether he had any family in France – someone I could phone and ask what this is about?'

'I know nothing about him. He came to Mr Griswald out of the blue. Just rang up and asked to meet him. I was the first person he talked to which is how I know his name. Mr Griswald said very little about it afterwards and that is all I can tell you.'

'Have you been asked not to talk about this?'

'Look, Mr Harland, you must understand that much of the work we do here is very secret. I am not allowed to talk about current investigations with outsiders.' She was speaking very quietly now. Harland guessed that someone had come into her office.

'I'm going to ask you some questions and you can answer with yes or no, okay?'

'Yes.'

'Did this case involve the killings in north-eastern Bosnia in 1995? Is that what he was investigating?'

'Yes ... and ... also no.'

'Have you tried to contact Monsieur Bézier's relatives in France?'

'No.'

'So you don't know whether they have been told?'

'No.'

'Has anyone from the War Crimes Tribunal discussed the death of Mr Griswald and Monsieur Bézier?'

'Yes.'

'Who, the Chief Prosecutor? The Chief Investigating Officers?'

'Yes ... yes.'

'Did they suspect the plane was sabotaged?'

'No, I don't think so.'

'I have some documents which were sent to Alan Griswald's home by your office last week. Sally Griswald let me have them. They appear to be interview transcripts from 1995 and 1996. Are they relevant to the last case that Alan Griswald was investigating?'

'Maybe.'

Harland remembered Griswald's painstaking approach to any problem, the marshalling of every possible scrap of intelligence.

'Was he going to read them in the hope of finding something which may have been overlooked in the past?'

'Yes,' she said. He could hear she was pleased that he had guessed right and he knew she really wanted to talk to him.

'Perhaps it would be better for me to read these documents thoroughly, then ring you later?'

'Yes, that's a good idea.'

'Some time in the evening your time, say eight o'clock today, or tomorrow?'

'Yes,' she said, and abruptly hung up.

Harland looked at the number Bézier had rung from Washington and weighed up whether to dial it now or wait until he had talked to Sara Hezemanns again. A little reluctantly, he decided that it was better not to blunder in.

His next concern was the disc. Clearly the theft was significant, but he didn't want to alarm Sally Griswald, so when he rang he simply told her that the disc and tape had been stolen overnight from his office. He omitted all mention of the attack. Even so, it worried her that Eric had made a copy and she said that she felt threatened by its presence in her home. Harland suggested that it would be possible for them to send the recording by attachment to his e-mail address, or to express it to Harriet's home. He gave her both addresses, after fending off several more inquiries about the theft. For the next hour or so he sat, closeted in his office, thinking and making little diagrams. They resembled electrical circuit boards, with each component related to the other. Where Harland was unsure, which was often, he put a dotted line to indicate the tentative or unproven nature of the connection. He spent a good deal of time standing at the window looking at the gradations of blue in the distance of Long Island. Every so often he would dart back to his desk to add a few more lines or another box to the diagram. None of what he produced was very satisfactory because there could be no single interpretation to such random events – yet – but he was coming to grips with the problem, and when Marika brought him some coffee he was at least clearer in his mind about the nature of his task.

She set the cup down and looked over his shoulder with unconcealed interest. Harland asked her to book him on to the six o'clock flight to London and chase up the expenses from a trip in early November. At this, Marika clapped her hand to her forehead and said that she had quite forgotten to tell him about the press conference on the crash that was due to start on the third floor. Maybe he would like to go? Yes, thought Harland, he wanted very much to hear what the Safety Board was going to say about the crash.

He loitered a little distance from the conference room, mingling with a large group that had just emerged from the Security Council, and waited for the press briefing to get under way. Then he realised that he didn't have to go in. Behind him was a monitor showing the proceedings. He could see Frank Ollins from the FBI and Murray Clark from the Safety Board on either side of Martin Dowl, one of the UN press officers.

Clark, looking rather larger than normal against the background of UN blue, had just risen and was taking the reporters through the procedure that followed the retrieval of the two black boxes. He said that the preliminary findings of the Safety Board meant that sabotage had been ruled out.

'This was an accident,' he said. Then he looked up and repeated the word 'accident'.

He reached behind him for some display boards which he held away from his audience of journalists. 'We now know that the Canadian Government Falcon 900, on loan to the United Nations, was subjected to exceptional turbulence caused by the preceding USAir flight that landed at La Guardia eighty seconds prior to the crash. This disturbance is called wake-vortex and it is associated with large airplanes, particularly the Boeing 757 which has a wing-flap design that generates a powerful vortex of air. This can force a following airplane into an unrecoverable loss of control. In this accident the preceding airplane was a Boeing 767 which is capable of creating the same type of hazard, although there are fewer recorded incidents involving 767s.'

Clark spun one of the boards round his fingertips to show a diagram of two planes on the same flight path, three nautical miles apart. The camera zoomed in and Harland could see that behind each wing was drawn a spiral.

'These are the vortices,' said Clark, pointing with his knuckle. 'At their core the airspeed may be as much as ninety knots. They can linger for a minute and a half after the plane has passed. Eventually they dissipate or move away. Some descend to the ground before dissipation and bounce right back up into the path of a following aircraft. And that is one of the big problems with this invisible phenomenon. The velocity at the core of the vortices is so powerful that it can affect a big plane like a McDonnell Douglas 88 – which is about three times the weight of a Falcon.' He turned to his audience. 'For your information that comes in at around twenty-two thousand pounds.'

He let this sink in then set off again. 'There used to be five or six serious incidents a year due to this phenomenon. There are fewer today because the Federal Aviation Authority and the National Safety Transportation Board have stipulated minimum distances between landing aircraft. These recommendations and the latest data on vortex incidents are printed in the *Airman's Information Manual*, which is readily available to all pilots.'

He turned another board which showed how the vortex had hit the ground and then risen to a height of 120 feet, where it encountered the Falcon.

'It's hard to estimate the speed and lifespan of a vortex because it varies according to wind gradient and strength. However, we believe that a bouncing vortex intersected with the path of the Falcon at the threshold of the runway. The pilot experienced an uncommanded ninety-degree roll and pitch. He had no time to regain control and the aircraft continued in a right motion until the starboard wing appears to have collided with a light tower. There's evidence from the flight data recorder that the pilot applied a full left deflection of the rudder and aileron, but could not bring the aircraft under control in time. The pilot had only a fraction of a second to react. All the indications are that he did the best he could to respond to the situation.'

Clark paused to take a sip of water which allowed a journalist from the *New York Times* to throw in a question. 'The speed of reaction does not entirely release the pilot from blame,' he said. 'Your diagram shows that he was close enough to the Boeing to expose his airplane to these vortices. Was this his fault or Air Traffic Control's?'

Martin Dowl lumbered into action. He evidently knew the reporter. 'Mr Parsons, we will take questions at the end of this conference.'

Clark leaned forward and said he didn't mind answering because it was important for the pilot's family. 'Our feeling is that he was well within the safety margin and he had little reason to believe the conditions were conducive to wake-vortex. No warning had been given by Air Traffic Control. This means that aircraft landing on the same runway during the hour prior to the crash had experienced nothing like the catastrophic vortex that he encountered.'

A woman's voice asked about the casualty list.

'We're coming to that now,' said Dowl testily. He picked up a prepared statement, which he began to read with the gravity of a judge. Harland listened intently, waiting for the official toll. But Dowl was taking his time, first describing the business of the UN officials on board, which turned out to be an informal briefing of Congress on the resources needed for peace-keeping operations, then touching on the reason for Canada's loan of the plane for the Secretary-General's forthcoming tour of South American capitals. He concluded with a passage about the Secretary-General's great sorrow at the death of twelve dedicated professionals in the service of the United Nations.

So, thought Harland, the corpse known as Male C was as good as dumped in the East River. Luc Bézier was never on the plane.

Dowl put the statement down. Then the camera focused on Parsons who had stood up and was asking another question. 'All through last week we were told that thirteen UN people had been killed on the plane. Now you're saying only twelve were killed. How could anyone make a mistake like that?'

Dowl took off his glasses and nodded to Clark, who began speaking with laboured patience. 'Sir, you have to understand the conditions at a crash scene where there has been a violent impact and wreckage is spread over an area of several hundred yards, where the body of the plane has been burned in a fire with temperatures reaching thousands of degrees. These conditions do not aid the recovery of bodies. I am afraid mistakes do occur.'

'But surely,' Parsons shot back, 'there was some kind of passenger list you could check against?'

'Not in this case,' said Clark, making it plain with a look to Dowl that this was one for him.

'Nothing?' said the reporter, transferring his gaze from the right of the platform to Dowl at the centre.

'No,' said Dowl. 'The aircraft was returning to New York anyway. The UN personnel were making use of it as an economy measure. It will not escape your attention that many of the people on that plane had been at Congress arguing for the payment of late contributions to the UN budget.'

'So you didn't know who was on that plane. How can we be sure that you haven't made a mistake? There could still be people unaccounted for. Isn't that right?'

Dowl shook his head. 'No, that's not possible.'

'And you're saying that the next flight would have carried the Secretary-General. When was that trip scheduled for, Mr Dowl?'

'Last Friday. He was due to visit Colombia with members of the Economic and Social Council.'

'And the trip didn't go ahead?'

'That's correct.'

'Colombia, that's a dangerous spot. This must have occurred to the accident investigators and the FBI. I mean, if this crash wasn't caused by wake-vortex, you would have to look for another cause, wouldn't you? Have you ruled out any tampering with the plane's systems?'

'That's a hypothetical issue because the NTSB has established wake-vortex as the cause of this accident.'

'If I'm not mistaken,' returned the reporter, 'the only hypothesising going on around here is Mr Clark's. However convincing the theory appears to be, it is still only a theory – a hypothesis.'

Clark interrupted Dowl with a raised hand. 'Sir, we are certain that this accident was caused by wake-vortex. It's more than hypothesis – all the flight and cockpit data comply with the pattern of previous incidents. Since 1983 seventy serious incidents have been minutely studied, and that's just in the United States. During a ten-year period in Britain five hundred and fifteen incidents – not accidents – were reported at London's Heathrow alone. We know what we're talking about here. This is a well-documented and well-understood phenomenon.'

'Plainly not a well-avoided one,' said Parsons, and, before anyone had time to react, he added, 'If the Falcon was too close to the Boeing, someone must be to blame, Mr Clark.'

'The wake separation distance was satisfactory. We're looking at all the meteorological data of the time to see if the vortex was capable of an abnormal lifespan. These findings will be included in the final report. But I stress that we are not saying that the investigation is closed.'

'That's exactly right,' chimed in Dowl. 'This conference is an exercise to keep you, the media, abreast of the preliminary conclusions.'

Harland had heard all he needed.

9

The Quantum Foe

He returned to his office to find Marika with arms imperiously folded across her chest, remonstrating with a man who was fiddling with the fax machine. She gestured Harland into his own office and said sternly, 'Why didn't you tell me what happened here last night?'

He shrugged. 'I didn't want to worry you. I just had some money taken, that's all. And I've got a bit of a bruise.'

'But you were mugged! Here, in the United Nations! It's terrible. Everyone is shocked that such a thing could happen to you after last week.'

'Well, there it is. I was a little shaken up, but I'm okay now. I'm looking forward to going away for a bit of peace. By the way, how did you hear about it?'

'One of the guards who found you came by. Asked if there was anything else missing. I said nothing except the fax roll. Somebody stole the damned fax roll. Can you believe that?'

'What do you mean?' He knew perfectly well what she meant and instantly realised the significance of the theft. The imaging film, which passed through the machine between two rolls, much like an old-fashioned camera, contained a complete record of the faxes he had received the previous night. All someone would need to do to retrieve the documents was to place the film, page by page, in a photocopier. It was as simple as holding an old piece of carbon paper up to the light – in fact simpler because each section of the imaging film was used just once.

Harland hid his reaction. 'Someone on this floor must've taken it when their machine ran out.'

This didn't satisfy Marika, but she had something else on her mind. The Secretary-General's office had called down. There was a brief gap in Benjamin Jaidi's schedule just after two, and he wanted to see Harland.

He arrived outside the Secretary-General's suite of offices a little ahead of time, and walked up and down the corridor looking at the framed pencil sketches of the UN buildings. Suddenly he was aware of the guard at the end of the corridor stiffening in his chair. He glanced to his left and found the Secretary-General standing almost next to him.

'It's a good trick,' he said, 'I learned it when I was a boy. The man who taught it to me said the secret of sneaking up on someone is to imagine that you are leaving half yourself behind. I am sure he was pulling my leg, but it seems to work, doesn't it?'

Harland looked down into the garnet-black eyes of Benjamin Jaidi. He had met him five or six times before and had always been struck by the man's eerily fluid presence. Diplomat, crusader, politician and seducer of despots, Jaidi inhabited many roles, but would only agree with the job description of a predecessor who said that a Secretary-General was like a secular Pope. There was something in that, but it didn't embrace the illusionist's craft that the neat, inscrutable little man practised in his every waking moment. Harland thought of him as a modern, dark-skinned Merlin. He was without obvious origins. He spoke with an unplaceable lilt, which someone once described as dockside sing-song, and his looks might have come from anywhere – the Middle East, Africa, India, even South America. In fact he was born in Zanzibar, was schooled in European universities and had spent most of his working life in the United States.

He took Harland by the elbow and walked him slowly back to his offices pouring out charm and concern for his ordeal. With Jaidi you felt immersed in sympathy.

They sat down in a sofa with their backs to the view.

'I must say, that looks a nasty injury on your head. Is that the result of the crash?' He paused. 'Or did you receive it last night?'

So Jaidi knew.

'Last night, but it looks much worse than it feels.'

'Yes, you certainly seem to have been in the wars, Mr Harland. You must look after yourself in future.'

'Yes.'

'So,' said Jaidi, clasping his hands over his crossed knees, 'Alan Griswald was a friend of yours?'

'Yes, a good friend.'

'Did you know he was coming to see me with information which he would only convey to me in person?'

'I had some idea. Would you mind if I asked what it was about?'

'It concerned his work in The Hague for the International War Crimes Tribunal, but I can't tell you more because I don't know.' He paused. 'Do you think this crash was an accident as they are saying?'

Harland weighed his reply. 'Well, I just watched the press briefing downstairs and the Safety Board's findings seem feasible enough. There's no evidence of sabotage.'

'Yes, wake-vortex is certainly a convincing explanation,' said Jaidi ruminatively. 'I haven't heard of such a thing before. But let me ask you what you really think, Mr Harland.'

'I think there are very good reasons to suspect that it was sabotage. Someone didn't want Alan Griswald to talk to you.'

'But you're right – there's no proof. It's disturbing that such a thing could happen – so many good people killed and yet there's no evidence of a crime. It makes one feel powerless and angry.'

'Yes, it does.'

Jaidi sat in silence with a queer expression on his face. Through an open door beyond him, Harland could see the business of the Secretary-General's office in full flow, but Jaidi seemed in no hurry. 'I haven't had any lunch. Shall we see if we can get some tea? I think we need tea and cookies, don't you?'

He sprang to his feet and went through the open door.

Quite soon afterwards a very tall, Scandinavian-looking woman brought in a tray. Jaidi took a plate of biscuits and began to talk while steadily munching through them.

'I think we both know more than we are admitting, Mr Harland. Can I make that assumption without offending you?'

Harland nodded and wondered what the hell was coming next.

'You see, I've learned that you know about Monsieur Bézier and that you've made inquiries about the work being carried out by your friend Griswald.' He saw that Harland was about to interrupt and put up his hand. 'Please, let me finish. I understand that you may be upset by this, but I've had to acquaint myself with the facts as fully as I can. I am facing – or rather we are facing – a very difficult time. I think we have to embrace each other and share what we know.'

'What are you saying, sir?' asked Harland, tired of Jaidi's opaque formality.

'That we have a common purpose and we need to acknowledge it.'

'No, before that, about Bézier. How have you acquainted yourself with the facts?'

Jaidi sighed and bowed his head a little.

'Are you saying it was one of your people who took the fax roll from my office? And the break-in at my apartment, the attack last night? I can't believe it. Are you saying these were at your instigation?'

'I knew this would be difficult.' Jaidi sighed again. 'Yes, I plead guilty on two counts. Let me explain. It seemed to us, by which I mean Mr Ollins of the FBI and Sean Kennedy, the head of security here, that you might have taken something from Alan Griswald's body. We suspected that you knew what he was bringing me because you were friends. Old friends, I gather. There *was* something, wasn't there? But then last night it was stolen from you. Mr Kennedy wondered what else you knew and went to your office and found the fax roll. I'm afraid that he also arranged for a search of your apartment over the weekend, though he did tell me that he and his colleague were let in by a porter. So it was not strictly a break-in.'

'That doesn't make it any better, sir,' said Harland sharply. 'They read my private correspondence.'

'Yes, I agree, it's inexcusable, but up until this morning we weren't sure where you stood. Then it became clear that you were as interested as we were in finding out what had happened to the plane and what Griswald was doing. Those actions spoke well of your motives. But now you must tell me what you took from Griswald's body.'

Harland told him about Griswald's wallet and how he had found it on Saturday afternoon and then about listening to the disc and the pulse of sound which he suspected was some sort of code. He left out his visit to the Griswald family.

'And you no longer have that disc?'

'No, it was taken last night.'

'Yes, we thought something like that had occurred. It was a pity you didn't tell Ollins in the first place, wasn't it?'

'I didn't realise until Saturday afternoon that I had it. By that time I was beginning to think that Ollins was not being entirely straight. That impression was pretty much confirmed by the press conference this morning when there was no mention of the Frenchman.' He paused. 'Look, sir, can I ask you why you are so keen to conceal Bézier's presence on the plane? Sooner or later, someone is going to have to admit that he was killed with the others.'

'Yes, that's true. The answer is that Ollins and Kennedy, who I should mention used to be colleagues, wanted time to find out about Bézier. It's also important that the people who are trying to prevent me learning about Griswald's evidence do not know that Bézier was on the plane.'

'But if this was sabotage, surely Bézier was one of the targets.'

'Not necessarily. It's my conviction – no, my instinct – that Griswald was the lone target. I don't think they knew about Bézier. The important thing is that we learn how he fits in.'

'You keep on saying *they*. Who are *they*?'

'Are you familiar with quantum theory?'

'Yes,' said Harland doubtfully.

'Because that is what Alan Griswald mentioned in the one conversation that I had with him. He said he was dealing with a suspect who was like a quantum entity.'

'What on earth did he mean?'

'I'm not sure, but in the quantum world, as I understand it, very small entities can be a wave and a particle at the same time. They can also be in different places at the same time. This defies common sense.'

'Yes,' said Harland, dimly recalling a physics lecture at Cambridge, 'that's to do with the Uncertainty Principle. As one manifestation becomes definite, the other recedes and becomes hazy. The point is that you can never be sure of the hazy state.'

'Exactly! Griswald said he had managed to focus on one aspect of this individual which concerns a crime in the Balkans but he was hazily aware of this individual's other roles and his influence, which may even have penetrated the War Crimes Tribunal. He said it was almost inconceivable how this individual had multiplied his identities to operate on so many different levels. That's why he used the quantum analogy and why he was coming to me. The War Crimes Tribunal is, as you know, a UN-sponsored operation. He wanted to know that he had my support before he began to pursue this matter in earnest. Obviously he did not gain that support because next week Griswald will be buried along with all the others who died in the crash.'

'So you're sure that it was sabotage.'

'No, I'm not. I can only say that it's likely because this is not my forte. I rely on people like Sean Kennedy to keep an eye on things and he has his friends, but in the world of espionage we are babes in the wood.'

'Espionage? What has this got to do with espionage?'

'Didn't I mention that? Alan Griswald told me on the phone that the man he was investigating had important relationships with several intelligence services. I'm afraid I didn't ask which intelligence services because I thought we would be able to discuss it in person.'

'So what do you intend to do, sir?'

Jaidi paused and aimed a boyish smile at him.

'Well' – he took another biscuit – 'I was hoping that you would help. Your report on the water resources must be nearly complete. Is that right?'

Harland nodded.

'I was going to propose an extension of that contract, during which you'll find out who Alan Griswald was investigating. I believe things will follow on from there. Get that evidence and the people who caused the crash will not have won.'

'But,' protested Harland, 'even if I was to consider this, you're being wildly optimistic about my chances of success.'

'You underestimate yourself, Mr Harland. You're already doing what I am formally asking you to do.'

'Yes, but . . .'

'But what?'

'I have no authority.'

'You have my authority. You will be my personal representative, which still carries a little weight in some places. You will have a letter that states you are my representative and requests the cooperation of the government of any member state or agency thereof that you believe can help in your inquiries. This should be used only as a last resort because I would prefer that our arrangement remains *sub rosa.* You will learn far more that way. Shall we say an extension of current terms for six months? Afterwards you can deliver the water ownership report to me. Of course, in the long run that is the more important issue, but I'm afraid this is the more pressing one.'

Harland couldn't see a way out of it. Besides, he had already promised Sally Griswald that he would do much of what Jaidi was asking of him.

'Suppose I agree to this, how will it operate? Do you want regular reports?'

'You can call me any time, but you will liaise with Sean Kennedy. I suggest you go and see him now. He's aware of the proposal I'm making to you and has your letter of authority.'

'Okay, but I've got my doubts whether I'll find out anything for you.'

'Naturally you do.' Jaidi stood up. The interview was clearly over. Harland rose also and followed him into the corridor. 'I don't know how to say this,' Jaidi said, putting his hand out to shake Harland's, 'but it looks like this story is making its way to you. Call it what you will – destiny or just plain bad luck – but events seem to be reaching out to you, Harland. Much better that you go forward and meet them, don't you think? We'll be in touch after Christmas.' With a fleeting smile he turned and slipped back into his office.

Harland looked at his watch. It was three o'clock – nine in Europe. He knew he had missed speaking to Sara Hezemanns; he would have to call the next day. Realising he now had little time before having to leave for JFK, he hurried off to find Sean Kennedy's office in one of the backwaters of the third floor.

Boris was right. Kennedy had a distinctly Clintonian hairstyle, a bouffant of wire wool, obviously kept in place by a daily application of lacquer. Harland noticed a slight sheen as he stepped forward to greet him with a handshake that was meant to be eloquent of Kennedy's no-nonsense masculinity.

'I knew you'd agree to the Secretary-General's proposal,' he said. 'Hell, this is the guy who persuaded a room full of Balkan mass murderers to demonstrate their national dances.'

Harland was already sure that he didn't like Kennedy. 'Has anyone spoken to Bézier's number in France?' he asked abruptly.

'No.'

'You mean his relatives haven't been informed?'

'No, not as yet.'

'Well, who's going to do that?'

'I thought we could discuss that now.'

'You mean you want me to do it?'

'Well, if you're going to be working on this thing, it would be for the best.'

Harland thought for a moment, then picked up the phone to Marika. 'Cancel my flight to London. I want the first available plane to Toulouse in France.'

'How do you know it's Toulouse?' asked Kennedy.

'I checked the number. It's from the Carcassonne area. Toulouse is the best airport at this time of year.'

'Right.'

'I'm going to call whoever is on that phone number this afternoon. Then I want some back-up. Whatever is available in the way of insurance or hardship allowance must go to these people. And I want someone to call and explain these benefits as soon as I have been to see them. That must happen before Christmas.'

'Yes, I'm sure that's possible. I'll talk to the relevant department.'

'Next, I want a complete run-down of Griswald's cases from the War Crimes Tribunal – all his past investigations. I'll also need an idea of the set-up at the War Crimes Tribunal – the structure and personalities. You can send both these to my e-mail address. Naturally, you will not give them any idea why this material is needed. They are bound to suspect something, but nobody should know I'm working on this.'

Kennedy nodded. 'Pity about the disc,' he said, trying to regain the upper hand.

'Yes, it is,' said Harland tersely. He wasn't going to tell Kennedy there was a copy. 'Now, can you talk to Ollins and tell him that we are all in this together. He needs to share any information he gets. And I will do likewise. Tell him I will call him in the next few days. I have his numbers. Now all I want from you is the letter of authority from the Secretary-General and the fax roll that you took from my office this morning, plus any copies you have made.'

A few minutes later, Harland was back in his own office. He shut the door and thought for a long time about what he was going to say. Then he picked up the phone and dialled the number in France.

10

Two Officers

The phone rang for a full minute before a woman answered. Harland asked whether he was speaking to Madame Bézier.

'No,' replied the woman, suspiciously. 'There is no Madame Bézier. This is Colonel Bézier's residence.'

'Colonel Bézier?'

'Yes, Colonel Bertrand Bézier.'

'Not Luc Bézier?'

'No!' said the woman, a little crossly. 'He does not live here. He is a grown man. He lives in Paris.'

'I see,' said Harland, now understanding that Colonel Bézier must be his father. 'I am ringing from the United States. I think I should talk to the Colonel.'

'Impossible. He is a sick man. He cannot be disturbed.'

'It's very important. It concerns Luc Bézier. Madame, is Luc Bézier his son?'

'Yes, Capitaine Bézier is his son.'

'I see. This is going to be very difficult, Madame. I think I will have to explain this to you. Can I ask who you are?'

'Madame Clergues. I am the Colonel's nurse and housekeeper.'

'I see. I have some very bad news.' He paused for a fraction of a second. 'I believe that Luc Bézier was involved in a plane crash last week on Tuesday.'

There was a gasp at the other end. 'Is this a joke?'

He explained who he was and told her about the crash, and after a little while she seemed to accept that he was telling the truth. 'It will kill him,' she kept on repeating. 'It will kill him. He is very frail.'

Harland told her that he was prepared to break the news himself, if she could wait until he arrived in France the following day. On the whole she said she thought that it would be better if the Colonel heard it from someone he knew. She had been with him for two years. She would tell him in the morning in the presence of his doctor, who was visiting anyway and would be on hand if the Colonel suffered a collapse. They agreed that Harland should arrive in the afternoon and speak with the Colonel, having first telephoned her from the airport.

Harland didn't ring off straight away but gently prompted the woman to tell him about Luc Bézier. It seemed that the Béziers were an old military family. During the Napoleonic wars, one of Luc's ancestors had served in the Imperial guard and fought at Waterloo. Luc had refused to use his father's contacts and had joined the French Foreign Legion, later transferring to the Parachute Regiment. He had left the military two years before and gone to work in Paris.

Harland rung off. He had been wrong about Bézier's calls to a wife or girlfriend. No cigarette.

He did not drink for fear of worsening the surges of pain from the back of his head. A whisky or two might have done something to dull his newly acquired knowledge of how quickly a plane is reduced to charred scrap, but he went on board sober, and as he dropped into the aisle seat he was aware of two things: the illusion of reliability about him and the slight tremor in his right hand. He knew he had to distract himself fast because he realised that the faith – or whatever he had left out on the East River – had indeed completely deserted him.

He took out the transcripts and began to read. There were six interviews, all typed in single spacing. The first four were personal accounts of women whose menfolk had disappeared from a place in Eastern Bosnia called Kukuva, one of the 'safe havens' overrun during the Serb offensive in the summer of 1995. The last two were men who had apparently escaped execution and fled together through the hills to the Bosnian front line.

He picked up where he had left off in the account of Selma Simic. She was a dentist's assistant who lived with her husband and two boys in the town, which she described as a neighbourly place where everyone knew and helped each other. On a July evening her husband had taken her two boys, aged twelve and fourteen, into the hills overlooking the town. Knowing that she did not possess the stamina for what would be a gruelling march to Muslim territory, she had stayed behind with the older women and helped the mothers who were nursing babies.

The Serbs arrived early the next day, many of them reeking of plum brandy. The women were rounded up in the town square and questioned about their men, most of whom had taken flight in the previous twenty-four hours. By now the sun was beating down on the square and the women implored the soldiers to give them water and to allow the young children to rest in the shade. Selma Simic had been one of the women who had gone forward and talked to an officer. He told her and a friend that they could fetch water from a nearby bar. Inside she found a dozen Serb soldiers resting up. They let the women make four trips with a bucket and ladle, and then without a word they barred their way out.

The soldiers took turns with them, at first casually, as if they had nothing better to do. There was a TV on and some of them watched a news bulletin while the rape was in progress. Simic and her friend refused to cry out because they didn't want to alarm people outside, especially the children. This enraged the men and drove them to more barbarous acts; they seemed to want to hear the women cry out. But still they refused. Selma remarked to the tribunal investigator that she endured by concentrating on some flies that were milling round a piece of food on the floor.

When eventually the soldiers had done with them they were thrown out into the square. The soldiers, she noted, were apparently sickened by their own behaviour, as though Selma and her friend had somehow encouraged them. At that moment, she felt they would be killed. But the men sloped away. They rejoined the group in the square and found that most of the younger women had been taken away and given similar treatment. One woman suffered a miscarriage and another died after an assault which Selma could not bring herself to describe to the interviewer.

The day wore on and eventually a bus drew up in the square. Fifty-eight people were pushed on board. Many of the older women were suffering from heat exhaustion and the children were hysterical. Before the bus set off, the women saw some of the older men who had remained in the town driven out of their hiding places at gunpoint. They stared at the ground and would not look up when the women called out to them. Selma Simic saw her neighbour, a widower of sixty-five who grew roses and carved wooden ornaments in his spare time. She could tell by the expression of terror in his eyes that he knew he was going to be killed, even though the Serbs insisted that they would be reunited after the men had been interrogated about terrorist activities. She said that among the group of men there were two boys a little younger than her sons. In all, there were forty-six men and boys. Not one of them was ever seen again.

As the bus departed, the women believed they were going to be killed and sent up a terrible cry. But instead they were taken on a meandering journey westwards, which included several stops while the Serbs debated which route to send them. At one crossroads they sat for nearly two hours watching columns of men and armour moving forward in the dusk for the assault on the Muslim stronghold to the north. During this time they caught sight of an infamous Serb general whose face they'd seen often on television. He was unmistakable, a huge, sweating man with a wide, red face and a beer drinker's stomach. She was shocked at seeing the author of the evil all around them standing so near. His voice carried across the road to the open windows of the bus and the women could hear his commands barked at a radio. These were interspersed with remarks about women and what he was going to eat that night.

At that time she did not know about the slaughter that would occur over the next few days. But thinking back on it, she could not get over the fact that he was talking about food and drink at the very moment that he must have been planning the operation to murder thousands of people. She told the interviewer that she could never rid herself of the image of him standing there in the sweltering summer evening. He perplexed and appalled her at the same time. He was not part of the universe she knew.

The other three women had equally harrowing stories of being separated from their men, terrorised and raped. The rawness of the experiences made Harland read them with more than an eye for possible leads in Griswald's investigation. He had seen plenty of similar things along the southern borders of Russia, but nowhere had he witnessed the pointless violence that they described. These women had been brutalised by their neighbours, men who lived a few kilometres away and who visited their towns; by mountain boys who had once brought their livestock to Kukuva market and who had given vent to their darkest desires and fears.

He read the testimonies of the two men, a tractor mechanic named Orovic and a school sports teacher who was identified by his initials DS. They had been captured a day later and sent to the killing fields on separate buses. There they were forced to watch from the windows as a dozen men at a time were taken from the bus, lined up in the doorway of a derelict barn and shot. The men had prayed, begged with the soldiers and even tried to bargain for their lives, offering their savings of Deutschmarks. Only a few went to their deaths cursing their killers.

Orovic's turn came early in the afternoon. When the shots rang out he fell backwards into the pile of bodies unhurt and lay there absolutely motionless, as more and more bodies were heaped on to him. During a lull in the slaughter, some time towards the end of the afternoon, Orovic had been aware of the general's presence at the mouth of the barn. He also knew his face well. Some kind of inspection was obviously taking place. The general had come to make sure the bodies were going to be properly disposed of and that his men had enough ammunition and would complete their quota of killing the next day. He heard him say that there were several hundred men being kept in a hall a few kilometres down the road. As the voices receded, Orovic squinted his eyes open and saw the general strutting away, talking to another man. They turned and threw a final contemptuous look towards the barn before getting into a vehicle and driving off.

Later, after darkness had fallen, Orovic heard a whispering in the dark. It was the teacher, DS, who had been winged on the shoulder but was otherwise unhurt. They waited until the early hours of the next day, then they extricated themselves from the mound of bloody corpses and from the terrible smell that already filled the barn, and escaped through some loose panels at the back of the building. Several shots rang out when the soldiers heard them running across the gravel road. The two men plunged into some dense undergrowth on the other side and began snaking their way up the hill. Four days later they staggered over the Bosnian front line, suffering badly from blisters, hunger and dehydration.

As he read DS's evidence, which was nearly identical to the mechanic's, something began to fall into place for Harland. What linked all six people was the evidence of the general at the scene. But that could not be the point of interest for Griswald because the general was already the subject of an indictment for genocide from the War Crimes Tribunal. They had quite enough evidence of his involvement. Harland went back to the end of Simic's account, to the part where she described seeing the general on the roadside.

'There was a man with him,' she said, 'in a brand new uniform. I could not see his rank. All men in camouflage look the same. But this man was somebody of importance. You could see that by the way the general took care to consult him. I don't remember much of what they were saying now. We were too frightened to remember. But I am sure the man was a foreigner, not Serb. He had an accent and he could not speak the language well. A few times they had difficulty understanding each other and the general would slap the man on the back heartily. The general was anxious to please him, you could tell that.'

The investigator had prompted her to give a fuller description of the general's companion.

'He was shorter than the general,' she had replied. 'He was the same age – late forties, maybe early fifties. He was a dark man with a small face and a well-shaped nose and mouth. He might have been quite good-looking in his youth. The general was excited and pumped up with nervous energy, but this man did not move much. He was very composed.'

Harland realised that buried in each account was a mention of this man. All the women had noted his presence in passing and he had been seen by the two survivors of the massacre at the barn. The sports teacher had got a much clearer view than the mechanic because he had fallen to the side of the door and was able to watch undetected through a crack between the planks of wood. He said the man walked with quick short steps. He also heard a foreign accent.

Harland was sure that this character was the person Griswald was investigating. He supposed that hundreds, maybe thousands, of interviews had been combed for evidence of his presence in Eastern Bosnia during the final Serb push before the Dayton Peace Accord. The witnesses' statements which placed him at the scene of the massacre with the general were obviously of crucial importance in building a case against the man, whose identity Griswald must have known. But what did this all mean in the greater scheme of things? Why was Griswald being more secretive than perhaps he would have been about any of the other war criminals pursued by the tribunal?

Harland folded the transcripts and put them in his jacket pocket. For the rest of the trip he entered a shallow sleep. He awoke as the plane touched down at Toulouse in the dark, feeling dreadful. He bought himself breakfast and arranged for a hire car. Before leaving he called Madame Clergues to say that he was on his way.

Tomas Rath had slipped into Heathrow on a twin-engine turbo-prop from Reykjavik, having the day before flown from New York to Iceland in the hope that the route would make him a fraction less conspicuous. As he waited in the EU line for immigration control at Heathrow he turned on his cellphone and listened for his messages. To his surprise he heard Robert Harland's deliberate voice suggesting they see each other when he got to London that day. He noted down the numbers that Harland had left him and snapped the phone closed. That was really great news, he thought.

On the way into London he tried calling Flick a couple of times. He wanted to tell her about Harland, to say that his impulsive visit to New York had paid off. But he couldn't reach her. He supposed that she was at Covent Garden market because she often did the run to pick up the day's order herself. Tomas usually went with her. It was part of their life together and he loved setting off in the van, listening to Flick's collection of 'adrenalin rock', arriving at the huge flower hall just south of the Thames where he breakfasted on coffee and a bacon sandwich while Flick put together the order. His job – the lifting and loading – came later, so for the best part of an hour he watched her move between the stalls, haggling and flirting with the wholesalers. One morning a couple of weeks back he had caught sight of her in a shaft of light and his heart turned over. He knew then that he was falling in love.

He reached Belsize Park tube station and went through a complicated procedure which involved doubling back on the Northern Line to Camden Town, whereupon he left the station and walked to Flick's flat in Hazlitt Grove, South Hampstead. When he got there, it struck him as odd that her dark blue van was still parked outside her flat. By this time she was usually either at the shop in Hampstead or at the market. He unlocked the front door of the house and found a note on the doormat. It was signed 'Pete', who was the manager at the shop. The note, dated and timed the previous day, asked if anything was the matter.

With a sense of dread, Tomas climbed the stairs. On the first landing he waited and listened. No sound came from the floor above – another sign that things were not right. If Flick was there, she'd have music on. He continued up the last two flights, taking care to avoid the creaking floorboards, and arrived at the door. Standing under the skylight he pressed his ear to the door. He could wait no longer. He thrust the key into the lock and pushed the door open.

He found Flick lying naked in a foetal position on her bed. Her legs and arms were bound. She had been killed with a bullet in the head. There was blood on the wall and on a pillow which had been used to muffle the shot. Tomas dropped to his knees beside the bed and touched her hands, which had been yanked down to meet the twine around her ankles. He knew that she had suffered terribly. He saw marks on her arms, breasts and thighs – cigarette burns and welts that had risen into livid bruises before she died. In the corner of his mind he had already taken in that the place had been turned over and that they hadn't found anything. There was nothing to find.

He brushed her face with his hand. She was utterly cold. He let out a cry, not of self-pity, but of remorse. They had tortured her to find out where he was and they had tried to make her tell them what she knew about his activities. But Flick knew nothing. She'd never asked and he had never told her. This was it – the retribution he'd been expecting. At that moment he would have given his own life never to have met her. But she had smiled at him across that bar, walked over and sat down beside him. He should have done something to put her off, but he'd let her take him home to share her quirky, beautiful, decent life. And now she was dead. Dead because of him.

He sat there for some time, tortured by self-loathing. This was the end for him too. There was nowhere for him to go. He could not bring Flick's terrible fate on anyone else. Now he had to finish the job. He would let everything go – everything.

He rose and left the flat in a trance. On the first landing he stopped, unscrewed two locks, lifted the sash cord window and climbed out on to the narrow brick column which had been added to buttress the wall at the back of the house. Once he had got his balance he leaned over and pulled the window shut, then let himself drop three feet into a gully which was formed by the pitched roof of a Victorian extension. He edged along to a point where he knew the roof would take his weight and shinned up to a dormer window that faced the back garden. He reached the window and wrenched up a flap of roofing lead that concealed a small cavity. He groped inside with one hand, found the package wrapped in several plastic bags and slipped it into the big pocket inside his jacket.

When he had first moved in with Flick and was looking for somewhere to conceal the package, he had discovered that he could not take the route back to the landing window because the climb up to the buttress from the lower roof was too difficult. At the time he thought it was an advantage because it might deter others from venturing out there. Once he had got the package, he scrambled to the other side of the roof, let himself down to the top of a garden wall and into a paved area where refuse bins were kept. Within a few seconds he had left the premises and was walking down Hazlitt Grove – where to, he did not know.

Harland drove south towards the Pyrenees in bright sunlight. He made good progress and arrived at the small château on the bank of a river an hour ahead of time. He waited at the end of an avenue of lime trees until he saw a man leave in a Renault car, then drove up to the house and parked in front of the door. An attractive woman in her forties hurried out to meet him and introduced herself as Madame Clergues. Harland held out his UN identity card, but she didn't take it.

When told about his son two hours earlier, Colonel Bézier had said that he already knew. Something had told him that the silence from the United States boded bad news. Madame Clergues said he knew inside that Luc was gone and that this firm intuition accounted for his frail state in the last week. She asked Harland not to cause him undue torment.

He was shown into a conservatory where an old vine had run riot. Bunches of shrivelled grapes hung from the glass roof and dead leaves had gathered under the table. Colonel Bézier was seated in a green wickerwork chair with a tartan shawl thrown round his shoulders. He gazed through the open doors across some pasture to a line of poplar trees, beyond which lay the river. Beside him was a table with several bottles of pills, a book, *Le Monde*, mineral water, glasses and an old Lalique lamp. Harland saw that he spent nearly all his time there. A few seconds after he entered, the Colonel turned and threw a hand out in the direction of a chair where he intended Harland should sit.

He looked much younger than Harland expected – no more than mid-sixties. Except for his white pallor, there was not much of the invalid in his face. He had a strong jaw and cheekbones and close-cropped, dark grey hair. He examined Harland for a moment with watery, dark eyes, then wearily asked him to tell him as much as he knew about his son's death.

In rather mechanical French, Harland told him about the crash and his subsequent discoveries about Griswald and Luc Bézier's business in New York. He left little out because he understood that the Colonel needed to hear everything. He even told him about the disc and the transcripts. Throughout, the sick man nodded, as though Harland was confirming things that he had suspected for himself all along. Eventually he said he had heard enough and methodically took out a pack of Gauloises, lit a cigarette and held out the pack. Harland declined although his hand had involuntarily jerked forward.

'Good,' said the Colonel flatly. 'These things have put me in this chair.' He let out a thin stream of smoke from his closed lips. 'You know that my boy was a hero? Not the sort of hero you read about in the papers because he was on specialist operations. Four medals and too many commendations to count. That was Luc. That was my son.' He paused. 'I knew from the start that the business in the Balkans was a catastrophe. Those people massacre each other every fifty years. They're barbarians. The rest of Europe should have nothing to do with them. We French understood this, but the Americans and NATO, they had to get involved. Let them stew in their own hatred, is what I said. But Luc went because he could not pass up a challenge. He excelled at his job, you see. You know that he learned Serbo-Croat in a matter of months so he could speak like one of those damned peasants?'

Harland shook his head and smiled. 'What exactly was he doing there, sir?'

'He was running an undercover squad. They were trying to seize the war criminals. His work was like my own early service in Algeria. Most of it was surveillance, but they captured one or two of the bastards – just cow hands, nobody important. They shot a couple more, although my son said several of these men developed the habit of travelling with children in their cars, so it wasn't easy for the army. His longest job involved the man named Lipnik. Big Cat, they called him. For this operation, Luc's team had to go beyond the area where the French UN troops patrolled in Bosnia, right into Serbia. They watched him for about two weeks. They got to know his habits and routines although he was very discreet. The plan, I believe, was to snatch this Lipnik at a restaurant where they knew he was going to dine early one evening. Luc told me about it in detail. You'll see why in a moment.

'They knew they'd got the right man because the Americans had traced his phone and intercepted a conversation with Lipnik making an arrangement to be at the restaurant. Luc was doubtful about spotting their target, let alone being able to seize him and spirit him away without a fight. Their plan was to pretend to be Serb security agents who had been sent to protect him against an assassination attempt. It gave them the perfect excuse for hustling the man out of the place and into a car.'

'Sounds as though it might have worked,' said Harland.

'Well, they never found out,' said the Colonel emphatically.

Harland was worried that he was becoming too agitated. He wondered whether his son's death had sunk in properly.

'What happened then, sir?' he asked quietly.

'They saw him arrive at the front of the hotel. There were no guards in evidence – just a driver. To their amazement, Lipnik chose a table at the front of the restaurant overlooking the street. He and his guest were visible to the whole team. Luc got the vehicles into position and waited for a wedding party to pass inside. Then he gave the order to move in, but at that moment two men appeared from the throng of wedding guests and began shooting. The men at the table were killed instantly – quite an irony, considering the cover story Luc's team had made for themselves. In the confusion that followed, one of Luc's men went into the restaurant to check that Lipnik was dead. It was a terrible scene – complete carnage, apparently. Those men were dead all right – they were unrecognisable.'

'When was this?'

'Late '96 or early '97, I'm not certain.'

Colonel Bézier's gaze left Harland and drifted over the meadow in front of them. The sun had come out again to light the few brilliant yellow leaves that clung to the poplars and dance on the barely rippled water beyond. He fumbled for another cigarette. Harland understood that the Colonel was going to smoke as much as he liked now. There was no point in minding his health. They sat in silence for a long time before the Colonel shook a small hand-bell. A maid arrived. He ordered a cognac and cocked his eyebrow interrogatively at Harland. Harland said that he was driving.

'But that was not the end of the story,' he said. 'A little time afterwards Luc left the army. He'd had enough and he was interested in making some money and settling down. Sensible boy. He went into the art business. It sounds odd for an ex-soldier, particularly of Luc's calibre, but he had a very good eye and he was ready to learn. He made a success of it because he applied himself. He'd been with a gallery for about two years last summer when he was sent to Vienna on business. He was walking in the street right outside a hotel when he ran slap-bang into Lipnik who was getting out of a car. This was only two or three months ago – about three years after the shooting in Serbia. But Luc was certain that it was the same man. Remember, Monsieur, that he'd studied his target minutely – he knew his mannerisms, his walk, everything. It was Big Cat! He was walking around, breathing like you and me – like you, at any rate.'

'Who is Lipnik? Do you know his first name?'

'A moment, Monsieur,' he said irritably. 'Let me finish. Naturally, Luc did his best to make some inquiries about the man he'd seen and eventually he told a friend in the State Intelligence Service. They took no action. But it was obvious to him that the whole thing had been a set-up – the shooting had been planned for the benefit of his team who, of course, had been made the unwitting accomplices to yet another crime in the Balkans. Two men were killed that day, remember, shot to pieces so no one would take a close look and ask whether one of them was indeed Lipnik. There was enough circumstantial evidence for the identification to go unquestioned. The restaurant booking, the fact that several people had seen Lipnik enter the establishment and the things they found on his body must have convinced them that this was indeed Lipnik. But it wasn't. The man was a double, somebody who was persuaded to act like Big Cat for an afternoon and got killed for his trouble.'

'But the tracing of the phone?'

'All part of the plan,' said the Colonel decisively. 'Luc realised that the whole thing had been a set-up. The phone was the lure that drew in Luc's team.'

'But surely they didn't suspect that the Americans were in on this.'

'Who knows, Monsieur, who collaborated with whom? It could be that they were really hearing Lipnik's voice on that phone and they had been genuinely fooled like we were.' He stopped and put his hand down to a tortoiseshell cat that had wandered in from the garden and was twirling round an oxygen cylinder propped against his chair. 'Or it might equally be the case that the whole thing had been American-inspired right from the start. Luc said there was no way of telling. About four weeks ago he was down here for some hunting and he asked my advice. I said if you feel strongly that you are right about this man and he has got away with something, then you should go to the War Crimes Tribunal. Let them handle it. This is how he met your friend Mr Griswald. And this is why he's dead.'

Harland was silent for a moment. 'To be frank, sir, I can't see why Griswald took your son along with him. He had all the information he needed. There was no reason why he shouldn't pursue his lead alone.'

'That might be correct if the Tribunal was immune to pressure from the United States and Britain and France. Apparently Monsieur Griswald did believe that. He felt Luc could persuade them of the importance of pursuing this matter.'

'Can I ask you again who Lipnik is?'

'Having heard the beginning of the story, I asked Luc to keep me up to date with developments. I was interested and it gave me something to think about sitting in this damned chair. Monsieur Griswald believed that Lipnik was not his real name from the start. It was a *nom de guerre*, used during his time dealing with the Serbs at the time of the war. He smuggled arms and ammunition and traded secrets with them and he acquired an identity to do that.'

'Did your son know what nationality he was? Did Griswald have any idea?'

'They thought he was Russian. That was their belief, but I cannot tell you why. They knew they were dealing with someone *comme Protée.*' Harland asked what he meant. The Colonel said someone who could assume different forms like the sea god Proteus. 'They believed he had several different identities – and lives to go with them.'

'Even so, supplying arms and selling secrets is not an indictable offence,' said Harland, now certain that he had been right about

Griswald's purpose in gathering together the witness statements from 1995.

'The point is that they knew from other sources that Lipnik was involved with the implementation of the massacre. They knew that way back and they knew what he looked like. Otherwise they would not have sent Luc's team in. The question is, was Luc being used? He suspected that he had been. That's all I can say.'

Harland could see the Colonel was getting tired, and he said that he ought to leave. But before he could get up, Madame Clergues brought the phone to the Colonel and asked if he was up to talking to a person from the United Nations in New York about arrangements for the shipping of Luc Bézier's remains. He looked at Harland with an expression of great sadness, then shook his head.

'Will you deal with this please, Béatrice,' he said.

His voice had grown weak and his eyes were closing for longer periods each time he blinked. Harland rose and touched his hand.

'Thank you, Colonel. I think I should leave now.' He had planned to say something encouraging about continuing the investigation, but words failed him. He wished the Colonel well and thanked him for his time.

At that moment the Colonel propelled himself forward and clutched Harland's hand.

'As you can see, Monsieur, I will not live long. I am the last of the Bézier family now. We have served France for two hundred years and we have lived on this land for generations. All that was extinguished when my son was killed. If you can do anything to avenge his death and set things right, please remember that, Monsieur Harland.'

11
The Crèche

By the time he reached Heathrow, Harland was exhausted. He had taken a short nap on the plane from Toulouse but it had only made him feel worse. As he waited in a line of jaded businessmen on their way home for Christmas, he switched on his phone and called Harriet to let her know that he would be with her by nine. She told him that Robin was hosting his office party and he wouldn't be there until late.

A few seconds after he had hung up, his phone rang. He put his bags down and answered. It was Tomas.

'Mr Harland? Where are you?' He was shouting against the noise of traffic.

'I'm in London. Where are you?'

'In London too. I need to speak with you. It's very important. Something has happened.'

'Look, I've just arrived at the airport. It's a bit difficult now. Let's talk later.'

Tomas wasn't listening. 'My friend has been killed. She has been killed – murdered.'

Harland stepped out of earshot of the queue. 'Murdered? What are you talking about, for Christ's sake? Who's been murdered? Which friend?'

'Felicity – Flick. She has been killed . . . She was in the apartment when I got back. They shot her and tortured her.'

'Have you told the police?'

'No, I cannot. I left her there.'

Harland gave him Harriet's address in St John's Wood and told him to go there immediately. He made him repeat the address then phoned Harriet to explain that a young man was about to arrive and that he would be in some distress. He'd explain when he got there.

He had missed his place in the queue and other passengers from another flight were now in front of him. Furiously wondering what the

426

hell Tomas's call meant, he rejoined the line and moved slowly forward to the immigration desk where an official in an ill-fitting blazer was taking rather longer than usual to inspect the passports. Two men were looking over his shoulder and glancing along the queue. One of them appeared to focus on Harland and said something to his companion. As he approached the desk, one of them came forward, a thickset man with wiry black hair and ruddy Celtic cheeks.

'Mr Harland,' he said, 'my name is Griffiths.'

'Yes,' Harland said crossly. 'What do you want?'

'Would you come with us, sir? Mr Vigo wants a word. There's a car waiting outside. We'll have your luggage brought on, if you'll give my colleague here the baggage receipts.' A third man had appeared from nowhere and put out his hand.

'But what does Vigo want?'

'I'd rather not discuss it here, if you wouldn't mind. Mr Vigo wanted to talk to you this evening. It's nothing to worry about. He says it won't take long.'

Harland wondered how they knew to meet the flight from Toulouse, then realised that SIS would have had no difficulty in finding out about his departure from the US and would have then contacted the airline to alert them when he was on the London-bound plane. There seemed nothing else for it because he knew perfectly well that they could force him to go with them. He put the baggage receipt into the man's hand.

He was driven to a four-storey office block in West London, somewhere between Hammersmith and Earls Court. The car turned into a side street and passed a sign which announced FM AGRO PRODUCTS: NO DELIVERIES and then into a garage area where several cars were parked. A door closed automatically behind them.

Harland realised he was in The Crèche, an almost mythical establishment among MI6 staff, which periodically changed location but always served the same purpose. It was where MI6 conducted its initial interrogations and where various suspects and defectors were placed on ice in conditions of quasi-arrest. He had taken it for granted that all the dreary outposts of the service had been subsumed into the spanking new headquarters at Vauxhall Cross. Plainly not. This one still possessed the atmosphere of the Secret Intelligence Service that he had joined – the down-at-heel drudgery and suspicion of the Cold War. There was a feeling of impermanence about the building, as if its occupants were prepared to leave at a moment's notice.

He was led into a room where there was a small conference table, several chairs and a functional sofa at each end of the room. They asked him to sit down and told him he wouldn't have long to wait. Then they left, closing and locking the door behind them. He could hear voices recede in the corridor. He reckoned he had a very short time. He took out his cellphone and pressed redial. Harriet answered.

'Bobby, where the hell are you?'

'Listen, I want you to call the UN in New York. Get on to the Secretary-General's office. Make it clear that you are phoning on my behalf. Tell them that the British government is attempting to hold me without charges. It's got something to do with the affair that the Secretary-General has asked me to look into.'

'Where are you?'

'I'm in a building belonging to SIS – in West London somewhere. A former colleague – Walter Vigo – had me picked up at the airport just after we spoke. Get the Secretary-General's people to phone the duty desk at the Foreign Office and kick up a stink. Tell whoever you speak to that I'm working on the Secretary-General's personal instructions. Got that? Good.'

While he was speaking he used his free hand to transfer the interview transcripts, which had been uncomfortably rolled up in his breast pocket, to the front of his trousers. The moment he hung up, he slid the phone's battery off, extracted the SIM card and placed it into the fold of material on the underside of his shirt collar. Then he opened his wallet and removed the bits of paper, on which he had written various numbers, and tucked them into the slit of a little coin pocket just beneath his waistband. None of these measures would be remotely effective if he was searched, but he hoped they weren't going to take things that far.

There was a murmur outside the door. Griffiths entered with two other men. They did not introduce themselves, neither did they smile or give any other sign of greeting.

As they sat down opposite him, he leaned forward, placed his hands on the table and said, 'Where's Vigo?'

'Mr Vigo will be along at some stage, I expect,' one of them said. He was in his fifties, dapperly dressed in a Windsor check suit, a cream shirt and a red tie which was embroidered with tiny fishing flies. Old MI5, thought Harland, no doubt brought up from some Home Counties village for the occasion.

'He'd better be. As far as I'm concerned, I'm here to talk to Vigo. I make it plain now that when I wish to leave, I will. If you attempt to prevent me from doing so, you will be breaking the law and, furthermore, you will find yourselves explaining your actions to the Foreign Secretary and the head of the Joint Intelligence Committee.'

'Yes,' replied the man quietly. 'We'll see how things go, shall we?'

The other man was vaguely familiar to Harland. He was heavier than his companion and wore large square-framed spectacles, behind which lay rather dead eyes. His mouth closed in an unattractive pout and he was less fastidious in his appearance – a sagging charcoal grey suit, a coffee stain on the cuff of his white shirt and a tie which showed its lining. Harland took him for a bit of a thug, an observation which helped him to remember his name. It was Blanchard – Derek Blanchard – and he had seen him in the eighties at meetings about the Soviet efforts to infiltrate the Campaign for Nuclear Disarmament. Blanchard was also MI5. Not top flight by any means and within five or six years of retirement, Harland guessed.

'I know your name,' he said to Blanchard, then looked at the other man. 'But what's yours?'

'Rivers,' he said. 'Anthony Rivers. Shall we proceed? This is not what I would call a normal interview, Mr Harland. We find we have very little to ask you, except in order to satisfy our curiosity about your motives. So I will come straight to the point. We know categorically that you have betrayed your country and are in contravention of the Official Secrets Act. Between 1975 and 1990 you worked under the code name *Lamplighter* for the StB, which I don't have to tell you was the Czechoslovak Security and Intelligence Service.'

Harland said nothing. He had been prepared for this moment and knew exactly how he was going to handle it. But why had it come now? And why had these two time-servers been fielded for the interrogation? He had the impression that this operation did not have the full weight of SIS behind it. There was something cobbled together about the whole thing.

Rivers produced a file from the chair beside him and opened it.

'You are Robert Cope Harland. After standard interviews and enhanced positive vetting procedures you were accepted as a trainee for SIS. At your first interview you were required to read and sign the Official Secrets Act.' Without looking up he flashed some papers, each of which bore Harland's signature, and continued speaking. 'Having completed your initial training in London and Portsmouth you were sent in 1974 for your first operational experience. This was intended as a purely observational role, a period of learning at the front, if you like. In those days it was customary to throw people in at the deep end a little earlier than we do today. You performed your duties with moderate flair and became involved in the operation to determine the extent of Eastern Bloc influence in a number of international institutions. We were also at that time concerned with the communist action against dissident groups that were based in Rome, principally those involved in the dissemination of anti-Czechoslovak propaganda following the Prague Spring. Is this all correct?'

Harland nodded wearily.

'At some point in your tour of duty in Rome – we believe it to be September or October of 1974 – you were introduced to a woman whom you discovered was an agent working for the StB. She was living in Rome under the name of Eva Houresh and her code name was *Lapis*. You initiated an affair with *Lapis*, knowing that she was a member of a hostile foreign intelligence service. Is that correct?'

Harland did not react. Rivers waited a second or two longer and pursed his lips, as if to indicate that he had had the misfortune to face many liars across an official table and Harland was no different.

'You returned to London and took up a number of posts, working in East European Controllerate. You joined the Intelligence Branch and worked in Berlin, Vienna and – briefly – in the embassy in the Soviet Union. You also spent short periods in the Middle East – the Lebanon and Turkey. I do not need to rehearse the details of your career; we all know it well enough. Suffice to say that you were approached by a man named Josef Kapek, an agent for the StB who was attached to the trade mission in London. He showed you a photograph of yourself in bed with *Lapis* which was taken in 1975. This we believe was in 1980, by which time you were regarded by your colleagues as reliable, even promising material.' He unclipped a photograph of Kapek taken in the street and showed it to Harland. This time he searched Harland's face for reaction. When he got none he gave a bleak, knowing smile and returned it to the file.

'Kapek threatened to send this item to the head of your department, together with details of the woman's background. In consequence you agreed to his request to supply biographical sketches of the people you worked with in Century House and various embassies. He also revealed that there was a tape recording in existence. He told you that Eva Houresh is heard admitting to you her role in the StB and that you in turn reveal your own status in SIS.'

He paused. Rivers held up a cellophane envelope and withdrew a photograph with some flourish. It showed Harland and Eva making love, well, at least lying in bed together. Both faces were clearly visible. Harland didn't look at the picture closely. He remembered the image well enough, although he'd never been sure exactly where it was taken. He did notice, however, that the print was new, which was interesting because it might indicate that Rivers's dossier had only recently been assembled. He wondered whether they would produce even newer pictures of him speaking to Tomas Rath in New York. Was the boy part of this too? Was he an attempt to ascertain for certain his relationship with Eva Houresh? If that was so, what could possibly explain his call an hour before? Harland found no answers, but deep down he was convinced that Rivers and Blanchard were, despite their self-assuredness, somehow uncertain of what they were doing. He returned to focus on Rivers.

'Over the ten years between 1980 and 1990 you are known to have cooperated with Kapek and his associate Milos Hense, a diplomat working in the Czechoslovak embassy in Vienna. Contacts in this period between you and Kapek and his intermediary were frequent and helped to build incremental understanding in the StB of Western signals and human intelligence. There is every reason to conclude that in your role as *Lamplighter* you served the KGB in the same way.

'In May 1981, for example, you reported to Hense on your part in Operation Stormdrain, an exercise in feeding the KGB a number of false impressions about the defence capabilities of Britain and her allies. Two years later you confirmed the identities of foreign journalists in Poland who were members of Western intelligence agencies. There are numerous documented examples of your disclosure of Western efforts to penetrate political institutions among Warsaw Pact member states. One particular instance that catches the eye is your contact with Kapek in Ankara, Turkey in 1987 during which you alerted the Czechs to the presence of a woman named Ana Tollund in the Secretariat of the Praesidium. Ana Tollund was subsequently tried and executed as an American agent. I do not have to explain to you that her death was the direct result of the information you gave Kapek.'

For several minutes longer, Rivers continued to read out a litany of betrayal. Harland sat back in his chair taking care to cover the slight bulge in his trousers with his jacket. He remembered a word that Griswald used when confronted with weak material. 'Scuttlebuck,' he would say. 'It's all damn scuttlebuck, Bob.' The dossier was exactly what Harland would expect from an investigation that drew on secondary sources, not his original file in the StB archives. And they could never get hold of that because Alan Griswald had burned it in front of him in 1990 – a late Christmas present, he called it.

Even if by some fluke there was a copy of the StB file, Harland had always known that he would be able to defend himself against allegations of spying for the East. In every instance he could demonstrate that he fed them misleading information or intelligence, which he was certain had already reached them from other sources. As to Ana Tollund, he knew Kapek had simply cited her as a source because he was anxious to claim a part of what was deemed to be a famous StB coup against the West. Kapek was a lousy, gullible second-rater. When he didn't know something he made it up. Harland could account for everything – every sleight of hand, dodge and manoeuvre which enabled him to keep the Czechs at arm's length while at the same time maintaining loyalty to SIS.

He concluded that Rivers's dossier had been assembled from brief references to him in other files. He'd always known that he was bound to appear in Kapek's own file, in Eva's and in a few others. Destroying his own file hadn't eliminated the problem, but it made it a lot less acute. It was obvious now that SIS had gained access to the StB archive, which he knew still existed in Prague, with orders to get as much as they could on him and as quickly as possible. The photograph must have been located in Eva's file or some other part of the archive. Its existence was embarrassing and Harland had dreaded it being found. But now the moment had arrived he knew he could handle it.

'There you have it,' Rivers concluded after a few more sentences. 'The A to Z of your betrayal.'

Harland paused, then allowed a smile to spread across his face.

'I suppose you expect me to roll over now and throw myself on your mercy. But, of course, you know this is all crap. For a start, not one of those accusations is backed up by independent evidence gathered by SIS or the Security Service. I don't deny that I was enticed into an affair – a young man's mistake that I regretted for its lack of professionalism, rather than any threat it posed. But I can show that instead of leading me to betray the service, I used it to our advantage. I even told Jimmy Kinloch at the time, so you can see it wasn't any big secret.'

Blanchard let out an exasperated wheeze, but Harland continued, holding Rivers's eyes.

'What you have there is a lot of gossip from a couple of bottom-feeders who were desperate to impress their masters. They had to produce fortnightly reports and because they were mediocrities they filled them with bollocks. We all knew that and moreover we used that need for a constant supply of information against them. Walter Vigo even knew about Kapek. It was he who told me how and when to use him and I distinctly remember filing reports of my contact with both Kapek and Hense, which doubtless you have got tucked away somewhere. Men like Kapek were the interface of the time. It was how we engaged the enemy. We used them while they thought they were using us.'

'Yes, but few of our people were stupid enough to have their pictures taken with a known agent,' said Rivers, rallying to regain control over the proceedings. 'You compromised yourself and then your loyalty, Harland. I don't think you have grasped the seriousness of your situation. You are facing a very lengthy jail sentence.'

Harland regarded him with a combination of wonder and disdain. 'Oh, for goodness' sake! Any public prosecutor would laugh at this pile of shit. Where are the covert pictures of my meetings with Kapek and Hense, eh? Where are the copies of bank statements showing that I received payments? Where's evidence of my ideological conviction? The men and women that I have suborned in the course of working for the Czechs? The transcripts of telephone conversations? The grainy pictures of dead letter boxes?' Harland stopped and looked at Blanchard and Rivers in turn. 'You don't have a thing, except a lot of fantasy scraped from the bottom of a few files in Prague. I doubt whether you can even prove that Kapek and Hense exist.'

Blanchard blew air from one cheek into the other and revolved his wedding ring with a thumb and one chubby finger.

'Oh, I assure you we have all we need,' said Rivers. 'We can produce Josef Kapek and Milos Hense any time we choose. You are forgetting that when Vasily Mitrokhin's archive was smuggled out of the Soviet Union to the West, it was taken as evidence of de facto guilt. We wouldn't have any problem gaining a conviction, Harland.'

'The Mitrokhin material led to no prosecutions – a bit of cheap sensationalism in the newspapers, that's all.'

'But those people weren't serving SIS officers. It's an entirely different matter to unearth evidence of this behaviour in a member of SIS. We know everything, you see, and frankly we are unable to ignore such a serious crime. We even know that you attempted to destroy your own files during or after the Velvet Revolution.'

'For heaven's sake, I was in hospital. I'd been beaten up by the Czechs – the very people you say I was working for! Doesn't that strike you as utterly illogical? I mean, why would they beat me up if I had been serving them all those years? Did it not occur to you that I was held and tortured for the very reason that I had misled them? Tortured, you understand. How many SIS officers go through that?' He was shouting now. 'Almost immediately after being freed I received treatment for cancer – surgery and chemotherapy. So you see I was hardly in a condition to run around chasing bloody files. By the way, how do you think that's going to look in court?'

'We know about your problems, Harland,' said Blanchard. 'But the fact remains that you did try to destroy the evidence. Luckily, you didn't get everything.'

'Well, if you're so bloody confident, why don't you have me arrested and charged?'

'In due course, we will. You may take that as a certainty,' said Blanchard.

Harland rose. 'I'm going to leave, this is getting ridiculous.'

'I am afraid that won't be possible,' said Rivers, also getting up. 'We will speak in the morning when I'm sure you will view your situation more sensibly. What we want from you is a statement, an admission of your role with StB. Then we will decide what to do with you. But we do need this from you, Harland, and I would advise you to cooperate as fully as you can.'

Blanchard by now had pushed his chair back and was making for the door.

Harland's temper snapped.

'You keep me here one moment longer and tomorrow you will be answering for your actions to the Foreign Secretary and the head of the Joint Intelligence Committee. I'm not pissing around. I have an authority from the Secretary-General which effectively makes me his personal ambassador. That means you hold me here at your peril.'

'Oh, in what capacity do you represent the Secretary-General?' asked Blanchard with laboured sarcasm. 'The investigation of the world's sewage treatment plants? The distribution of electrical appliances in the developing nations? Do you have proof of your role, or must we take your word on it?'

'Just accept that it exists.' Harland wasn't going to give him the letter yet. Much better for them to get a call from Jaidi's office. He prayed Harriet had got through.

'We will see you in the morning, Mr Harland,' said Rivers, opening the door. 'In the meantime, I recommend that you think very carefully about your position.'

Harland sat down. A minute or two later, the two men who had picked him up at the airport came in and told him to follow them. They showed him into what looked like an army barracks bedroom a few doors along the corridor where Griffiths asked for his personal possessions. Harland handed him his wallet, passport and phone and said he had nothing else. Griffiths seemed to accept this.

He looked around the room. There was a small window, high above the bed, a table, a chair and a reading lamp. He supposed it had once been a storeroom. On the walls regular indentations indicated that shelves had risen from floor to ceiling. The room smelt as though it had been sluiced down with cleaning fluid.

He sat down in the cold, stale air and unscrewed the top of a bottle of mineral water, left on the table together with some sandwiches. He poured the contents into a paper cup, peeled the wrapper from the sandwiches, and consumed them automatically. When he'd finished he lowered himself on to the bed and shifted to his side. There was no pillow and his head was still sensitive to the touch. He wondered about Tomas's call. Was he all part of some ludicrously Byzantine plan of Vigo's? If he had been, they surely would have produced Tomas in some shape in the general slew of allegations. The fact that they hadn't mentioned him made his story a lot more believable. Then quite suddenly his mind switched off. He shut his eyes and fell asleep.

At about six in the morning he was aware of the door opening. It caught him in the very deepest sleep and a few moments passed before he realised that Vigo was standing in the doorway. He rubbed his eyes as Vigo moved into the room and switched on the table lamp, angling it in Harland's direction. Harland swore.

'For Christ's sake, turn that off. What the hell are you playing at?'

Vigo nudged the lamp so that the light bounced off the wall and threw an aura around him. He sat down and stretched out a leg.

So, Vigo had come to hear his confession: Vigo, the cardinal confessor. 'I imagine that you've been contacted by the UN,' said Harland.

He didn't reply.

'You know bloody well that you can't keep me here. That stuff your stooges from Five threw at me was grotesque. Not a word of it will stand up in court.'

'A matter of opinion, Bobby, a matter of opinion.' Vigo sighed to underline the gravity of Harland's situation. 'You know, I always had my suspicions. There was something too good about you. You were too anxious to please, too controlled. I knew that wasn't your character. I knew that there had to be a reason for this façade. And that reason, of course, was guilt.'

Harland propped himself up.

'What's eating you, Walter? I don't want to trespass on your problems, but all this does seem rather panicky and amateurish for you. I mean, for Christ's sake, we all talked to those termites from the East, so why on earth are you hounding me now? What's got into you all of a sudden?'

'Because you're a traitor – a traitor who's squared his conscience with a lot of sanctimonious nonsense about working for the international community. That's why.' He stopped and looked despairingly at Harland. 'Do you know about the poetess Sappho? Perhaps I can tell you about her. You see, none of Sappho's poems has survived. There are just fragments of poems which were used in the teaching of grammar. So we have some sense of Sappho's genius and we know from contemporary accounts that she existed, but we do not have her work. That's more or less how I think of your case, Bobby. There's now only fragmentary evidence of your activities, but from those fragments we can deduce a great deal about your importance as an agent for the StB.'

Harland got up and straightened his jacket.

'Sit down. I haven't finished yet.' The tone was surprisingly harsh. For the first time it occurred to him that Vigo would have no compunction about killing someone. Wet jobs were what the Soviets used to call assassinations. Vigo wasn't above resorting to a wet job, he thought. But that wasn't the point now. Vigo wanted something, something that he believed Harland had inherited from, or shared with, Griswald.

And then Vigo confirmed everything Harland was thinking.

'Unless I see some sign of cooperation, Bobby, you are going to be put away. At the very least your career will be ruined. My own belief is that higher authorities will deem your crimes to be so serious and so persistent that there is no other course but to prosecute you.'

'I've told you, I am not in a position to give you anything.'

'Of course you are. Why would the Secretary-General ask you to investigate the crash if he wasn't certain there was something to investigate – i.e. that you possessed some special knowledge? What is that knowledge, Bobby? Why you? What qualifies you? The only possible knowledge that you could have must derive from Griswald. Griswald, the man who accompanied you to Prague in '89; the man you travelled with to New York; the man who was taking his big secret to the United Nations. It all goes back to Griswald, doesn't it?'

Harland listened, fascinated by the movements of Vigo's face in the shadows. 'You're losing your touch, Walter. From what you say, I gather the Secretary-General *has* called the Foreign Office. Judging by the hour of your appearance here, I guess he must have talked to the Foreign Secretary. That means you've been told to release me pretty damned sharp.' He paused. 'So, Walter, if you don't mind, I'm going to get the hell out of here.'

He moved to the open door. Vigo put up a hand.

'You've got absolutely no idea what you're dealing with, Bobby – no idea at all.' He shifted in his chair, then turned his face up to Harland. 'As to this investigation into your activities, don't for one minute think that it's over. Your head's in the noose and we're not going to let go of the rope.'

Harland left him sitting in the room and walked towards some light spilling into the corridor from an office. A man he hadn't seen before handed him his things. 'Order me a cab,' Harland demanded, 'and put it on your account.'

Harriet had waited up all night for him. It was seven o'clock when he was dropped outside her house in St John's Wood, a large neo-Georgian affair which Harriet called nouveau-Georgian. He saw her through the window, as he crossed a gravel drive which had been silenced by frost. She was asleep over the kitchen table with her head resting on folded arms. He stretched over a well-barbered box hedge and knocked gently on the window with his knuckle. She awoke, dragged herself up from the table, and gave him a despairing smile.

Their closeness was surprising: there were eight years between them and they were different in practically every way. Where Harland was tall, dark and concise in his movements, she was short, fair and animated. Harriet positively leaked energy. While his face, as he had been told often enough by Louise, gave little away, hers flickered with change, sometimes settling into a look of intense, happy concentration. She smiled when she was thinking hardest, which was perhaps why so few saw her coming. She would listen with that smile, her eyes oscillating ever so fractionally as she processed information at a ridiculous speed. And then she would dispatch her opponent with a few lines of deft logic, her expression becoming, if anything, sweeter.

She unbolted the double door and reached up to Harland to kiss his cheek.

'Bobby,' she said. 'You have to stop this. I cannot take the endless anxiety surrounding your travel arrangements. You can't seem to get off a plane like a normal person. First this terrible crash and now bloody

Walter Vigo is marching you off to secret locations. God, I remember him! He married Davina Cummings. What a pompous creep! I don't suppose he's improved with age. Still, I gather by your appearance that the call did the trick. They seemed pretty concerned when I explained the situation.'

'Yes, thanks, Hal. Did the boy turn up?'

'No, he didn't. Who the hell is he anyway? What's this all about?'

'It's a long story. Wouldn't you rather hear it all tomorrow – I mean later?'

'No, I can't stand the suspense any longer. I've waited up all night and now I want some explanation.'

'But it's Christmas Eve, haven't you got things to do?'

'Not now, I haven't. And anyway everything is done: presents bought and wrapped; meals prepared; husband overdosed on champagne and flirtation. Look, Bobby, I want to know what's been happening to you. I haven't seen you for five months, for goodness' sake. And if it hadn't been for some providence of which you're entirely deserving, my darling brother, I might never have seen you again. So you have to tell me everything now. Please, I can't wait.'

They went into the kitchen. Harriet made tea and slapped some ham and cheese between a couple of pieces of bread and put them into a children's sandwich toaster shaped like frog. Harland told her everything and the familiar tremor entered her eyes as she snatched at the story. When he told her about Tomas she gasped and put her hands to her mouth to suppress a giggle.

'I know this is all very serious, Bobby. But you've got to see it's funny. I mean, it's like *Twelfth Night*. Lost love, people being washed up on foreign shores, relations appearing out of the blue. "What country, friend, is this? This is Illyria, lady." That's where you are Bobby – Illyria.'

12

A Christmas Party

After calling Harland, Tomas decided not to wait for him at the address. Instead, he checked into a small tourist hotel in Bayswater where the Lebanese on the front desk seemed to be glad enough of the business and didn't ask him for an ID. A rowdy couple next door might have kept him awake, if he'd wanted to sleep, but he had a lot to do, preparing the two small computers and encoding them with information. As he worked, he wondered furiously how he had been traced to Flick's home. It was baffling. There was no question of him ever using the telephones at her apartment and he'd never so much as touched her laptop. That side of things was watertight. He'd always made sure that he was absolutely untraceable. Yet something must have led them there – a mistake in the past six months which had been seized upon very recently and resulted in Flick's death. His body convulsed with a shudder as he saw her again all trussed up and broken. He had thought of calling the police after he'd left, but realised that the manager of the shop was already concerned and that she would be found soon enough. He stopped working and slumped in the chair, thinking back over the past few months. Then it came to him. It must have been the parcel from Mortz.

Mortz was his contact in Stockholm – a friend, though they had never actually spoken or met. Well, perhaps they had once in a bar in Stockholm two years before, but neither of them was sure and he couldn't put a face to Mortz, neither had he the slightest idea of his identity, his job or his age. Mortz could have been a college professor or a computer freak. Tomas inclined to the former because there was something thoughtful and restrained about his communications – a seriousness of purpose, for want of a better expression. They were very different, he could tell that, and yet they'd become friends, companions in arms, partners in the big project. He often wondered why Mortz showed such zeal for their work, and once he asked him about his motives in a rather

438

cautious e-mail. Mortz did not reply. For a week there was silence and then he came back with new information from one of the half-dozen or so disenchanted intelligence people he'd cultivated over the Net. Things were back to normal.

Tomas composed new short bursts of information. That was his side of things. All the infiltration channels had been dreamed up by him. He started by using the phone-in programmes that are the standard fillers of airtime in radio stations the world over and during the calls played a tape of the condensed, coded message. He finessed his procedure by attacking the broadcasting computer systems with a benign virus – a vehicle which carried the messages. It was surprisingly easy – like a mosquito biting a sedated elephant. The stations, about thirty in all, were never aware of what was going on, but Mortz and he were certain that the messages were reaching their targets, causing acute discomfort and alarm in various intelligence services.

Mortz's idea was to reveal how the agencies of five or six Western powers, which were notionally on good terms, were using their resources to spy on each other. It was, he said in one of his oblique missives, a very wasteful hypocrisy. That was the nearest he came to articulating any motive.

Tomas had to admit that he had been caught up by his own ingenuity almost as much as he relished the revenge. The information which arrived in the package – the very last means of communication that anyone would suspect – gave him a great deal more to play with. It was like an archive of their operation but there was also much that was new in the package, much that concerned him personally.

It arrived one day back in September. Mortz had told him to expect something addressed to Mr J. Fengel. There was no flat number on the parcel so it had been delivered to the house and just left on the table in the hallway. Tomas reckoned that the only way anyone would know to go to that house was if Mortz had kept a record of the address. And that meant one thing: Mortz had been tumbled and somebody had gone through his things and found it. He reckoned this must have happened within the last ten days because he'd received a couple of messages from Mortz on the Sunday before he left London for New York. Yet since then two e-mails had gone unanswered. The question was, how had they found Mortz? How had they located a man whose whereabouts Tomas didn't even know?

Both of them had always understood there were risks, especially for Tomas because his role involved using the phone system. In fact, there had been a problem nine months before when an Internet café he'd used in Stockholm just once was inexplicably raided. That was when he decided to leave for Britain and lie low for a while. Then quite by chance he'd come across the perfect way of using the phones without being detected, and Mortz and he had started up again. He'd encoded the photograph he'd kept all these years with a new algorithm and let the virus vehicle loose on a small radio station in Germany.

Tomas imagined the picture being passed up an intelligence hierarchy and landing in someone's in-tray and their having to work out who were the people in the picture and why the photograph had been published in this unconventional manner. They would take it seriously because they appreciated what else had come to them in this way. There was a hint of this in the feedback Mortz got from his sources. Some of the agencies would be baffled by the photograph; others, like the British and Americans, would have no difficulty in identifying the man in the foreground. They wouldn't, of course, recognise Tomas who stood to the side of the main subject, but he hadn't censored the image as a matter of honour – as a matter of admission, he told himself. Not long after Mortz had said he had used the photograph again. He exchanged it for more valuable information with a former CIA agent – new material on the practices of the CIA and National Security Agency. Tomas had sent a second photograph to Mortz in coded form which they were planning to use at some stage, although Mortz had already exchanged this for information too.

He worked through most of the night, his mind dodging between incidents in his past, to Flick and to Robert Harland. He was almost feverish with thought and yet he was aware of a manic clarity of purpose. He had little time. He knew they must be very close to finding him. They'd tracked him down to Flick's place, forced her to give them the name he was using and almost certainly learned that he had left for the States. Perhaps that's why they weren't watching the house when he returned? Or was it because Flick's body lay inside? Maybe they assumed he'd fled for good and were now looking for him in the States.

He thought of the bar in Brooklyn where he'd talked to Harland. Jesus, what a terrible misjudgement that had been! How could he expect Harland to believe his story? Harland was a suspicious, unyielding person, not at all how his mother had described him. But it was seeing that other man in the reflection of the mirror which he thought of now. The same character who'd got out of the car at the end of Harland's street and shown such interest in the building had walked straight into the bar. It couldn't have been a coincidence. That's why he'd left immediately, even though he knew it would only confirm Harland's suspicions about him. He had caught something in Harland's voice when he spoke to him on the phone that night. He barely reacted to what he was saying. He had just given his sister's address and told him that he would be there. That was not what he needed now. He would go tomorrow and tell Harland how he had found Flick and force him to understand that he wasn't making any of this up.

At about five in the morning Tomas completed his work and ran through a few procedures to make sure the two small computers were working properly. Then he left the hotel, telling the night porter that he couldn't sleep and needed a walk. He knew very little about this part of London but he was certain of finding what he wanted and within a few minutes he noticed the familiar oblong shape by a wall at the end of the street. He decided it was in too prominent a position so moved on and came to a quiet road of large, private houses where he found another slightly bigger cabinet.

People pass these waist-high boxes every day in London without knowing what they contain. Indeed Tomas hadn't noticed them until he saw a telephone engineer open one up near Flick's flat. The man explained they were officially known as Primary Connection Points – the first stop on the way to the exchange for an area's telephones. Tomas instantly realised that it would be possible to utilise the lines inside if he could open the cabinet. While talking to the engineer, he had discreetly jerked out the universal key that was lodged in the door and put it in his pocket. Thereafter he had used the boxes whenever he wanted, connecting his computer at random to one of the lines for a few minutes. It meant he could send the coded messages virtually undetected.

Now he worked fast. He opened the box, placed the computer on top of the panels of wiring, so that it was pretty much hidden, and connected it to several different telephone lines. That way the computer would use a different phone line each time it automatically dialled out. He knew that by the time anyone happened upon the irregular wiring, the messages would be sent, the battery spent and the information on the drive wiped.

He repeated the procedure a few streets away with the second computer and then returned to the hotel, feeling exhausted and cold.

Harland slept until eleven o'clock, then rose and checked the messages on his cellphone. There was still no word from Tomas, but when he got downstairs Harriet showed him a report in the *Daily Telegraph* on the murder of a thirty-five-year-old flower shop owner from Hampstead named Felicity MacKinlay. She had been discovered in her flat by the manager of her shop. She had been bound, gagged and tortured before being shot through the head at close range, said the police. The officer leading the investigation believed there might have been some sexual implication for the murder but he did not rule out other motives.

He was anxious to interview a man named Lars Edberg, a Swede in his mid-twenties who had returned to Britain at about the time of her death. A surprisingly sketchy description of Edberg was given and the manager was quoted as saying that he knew very little about Edberg and only saw him when he sometimes dropped flowers off in the morning. The Swedish authorities revealed that Edberg must have been travelling on forged documents. No passport had been issued to a Lars Edberg in the last five years, not to a man in this age bracket at any rate.

Harland put the paper down without saying anything.

'Do you think he did it?' asked Harriet.

'No,' said Harland. 'I told you he called me last night. I don't think he would've done that if he was guilty.'

'Unless he wanted help and somewhere to hide.'

'Could be, but I don't think this lad is capable of it. You can make your own mind up if he comes here.'

'Well, it will certainly make a change to have a fugitive from justice for Christmas lunch.'

The noise of Harriet's three children reminded Harland that he needed to buy Christmas presents and he ordered a cab to go to Regent Street. As he crossed the driveway, Harriet flung open the kitchen window.

'Call your friends in the States – you know, Griswald's widow – and tell her not to use your e-mail address. Vigo's people must have copied everything on your computer last night. You can set up another address from here.'

Harland phoned immediately he caught a cab. Sally recognised his voice and said that her son would send the material – she used that neutral word rather deliberately, he thought – when Harland got in touch with a new address. She told him that Griswald would be buried in a few days' time and that there would be a memorial service early in the spring. She hoped he would come.

After he'd hung up he ran through the conversation and realised that she had not used his name. There was also something constrained in her manner. He supposed that she might simply be depressed at the prospect of facing Christmas without Al. But it was possible that there was another reason. Perhaps someone had been in contact with her, someone who wanted to know the precise nature of Alan Griswald's last investigation, and, being no slouch in these matters, Sally had suspected that her phone was no longer entirely secure.

In Regent Street Christmas crowds had already thinned, leaving a rump of male shoppers desperate to buy presents in the few hours that remained. He quickly acquired a cashmere sweater for Harriet in the Burlington Arcade, then bought a couple of biographies of entrepreneurs for his brother-in-law at Hatchards. It was outside the bookshop that he noticed two men hanging back in the street – a fellow in his thirties hovering near a phone box and a man in a parka who was looking in the window of an airline outlet on the other side of Piccadilly. What was interesting about both, apart from a marked lack of urgency, was that neither of them carried shopping bags. By the time Harland had reached Regent Street, he was certain he was being followed by a surveillance team.

Quite suddenly, as if he had just remembered something, he plunged into a clothes store named Cavet and Bristol, which was still quite crowded, and took the stairs to the outfitting department on the first floor. Then he immediately turned right into the lift and descended to ground level where, as he expected, he found the parka hood hesitating at the bottom of the stairs. Showing no concern, Harland strolled to a table where some ties were displayed and selected a couple. He took them over to the counter and proffered them to an Indian woman who was bent over a stocktaking form.

Without changing his expression, he informed her that he'd just seen the man with the parka place two lightweight pullovers under his jacket. For good measure, he added that he suspected the woman thumbing her way along a rail of men's casual wear was working with him. Harland had spotted her when he entered the shop and just now, as he'd turned from the tie counter, he had asked himself what woman shops for her man with only a few hours to go to Christmas?

The assistant picked up the phone and in a very short time the man and woman were being accompanied by security guards to a back office. The man protested, wrenching his arms free of the security guards. But they caught hold of them more firmly and led him away. Harland nodded a smile of seasonal goodwill to the assistant and slipped away, somehow failing to hear her plea that he should stay and make a statement about what he had seen.

He soon completed the rest of his purchases and caught a cab back to St John's Wood. A palpable stillness was settling over the city as the first carols from the service at King's College, Cambridge came from the cab driver's radio. Harland thought of his father and a Christmas Eve twenty years ago when they went together to midnight mass in a big echoing church that rose above the Fens, half a mile from the family home. He could just hear the carol he particularly remembered from that service above the noise of the cab's diesel engine. He looked out on the emptying streets and wondered where Tomas was.

He arrived back to find his brother-in-law supervising the placing of presents beneath a perfectly decorated Christmas tree. He was dressed in a long collarless black tunic and slippers embroidered with his initials. He greeted Harland with a handshake that involved a brief semi-hug. Harland remembered that Robin had taken to bestowing this on practically anyone who came within range, as a declaration of his openness and modernity. Robin made the children sit down and listen to what was a condensed version of the crash. When Harland finished, he jumped up and gave him another brief hug.

'It's good to have you with us,' he said, silencing Harland's youngest nephew, Conrad, who wanted to know how many dead bodies he'd seen.

The news that Harriet had forgotten to tell him was that fifty people –

locals, as Robin put it – would descend on the house at six-thirty for Robin's traditional Christmas Eve drinks party. Harland went off and set up a new e-mail address in Harriet's little office, sent it to Sally Griswald's address, then made himself useful, setting out glasses and lugging cases of drink into the kitchen.

At the appointed hour several couples arrived at once, one or two of them having been dropped off by chauffeurs. The party very soon reached critical mass and for a time Harland avoided making conversation by handing drinks round, although this was unnecessary since a couple of waiters had appeared from nowhere and the children were already scurrying between guests with opened bottles of champagne. Eventually he was snared by Robin who introduced him to a couple named Lambton.

'He's the celebrity of the evening – the only survivor of the La Guardia crash. You'll have seen his photograph in the papers last week. We're very lucky and pleased to have him with us.'

The woman, a psychologist of some sort, goggled at him and, after listening to an even shorter account of the crash, urged Harland to find some counselling. The man looked on indulgently while his wife got closer and closer to Harland. When she drew breath, Lambton told him that he was in property and often visited New York. Could Harland advise him where to stay? He was tired of The Pierre and wanted somewhere younger and fresher.

'To take his girlfriends to,' chipped in his wife, with a high nervous laugh.

Harland's eyes drifted across the room to a pretty woman in her early forties who was talking to Harriet. At that moment Harriet revolved and beckoned furiously, which allowed Harland to excuse himself from the Lambtons.

'This is Anne White,' she said when he reached them, 'now divorced from one of Robin's partners. Anne has been telling me that she's going to dinner with Luke Hammick and his wife, around the corner, but that they are coming here first. Guess who else they're having to dinner this evening?'

Harland shrugged good-naturedly.

'Davina and Walter Vigo. And even better news is that the Hammicks are proposing to bring the Vigos here beforehand for a quick drink. You and Walter will be able to catch up on old times.'

Anne White looked on with interest, trying to fathom the underlined nature of Harriet's delivery.

Harland muttered, 'Don't worry, Hal, he can't come.'

'Oh, but you're quite wrong,' she said brightly. 'In fact, they're here now.' She left with a whispered, 'Bloody brass neck.'

Harland turned and saw a couple in the doorway being greeted by

Robin who was bobbing furiously. Beyond them he could see Walter Vigo in the hall talking to one of the children. The sight struck him as bizarre. Children weren't part of Vigo's universe. Indeed, Walter Vigo at a Christmas party seemed an odd idea. Vigo looked up and caught sight of Harland and, without changing his expression, nodded imperceptibly. Harland turned back to Anne White.

'So you're a spy,' she said with a challenging smile.

Harland shook his head.

'You must be if you work with Walter Vigo. Everyone knows he's something important in the Foreign Office, which means spook in any language.'

'I don't work with Walter Vigo,' he said. 'I look at water pipes for a living.'

She continued with one or two more flirtatious sallies. Harland smiled down at her and parried a little.

Soon the children were lined up in front of the Christmas tree with two friends and required to sing a carol. Robin stood, hands clasped in front of him in frozen applause. When they had finished he turned to his guests with a wide grin, which Harland guessed had concluded many advertising presentations, and wished everyone a happy Christmas. He coughed once and added, 'We are also much relieved this year to have Bobby, Harriet's peripatetic brother, staying with us. As some of you may know, Bobby only last week escaped a terrible air crash in New York. He was the sole survivor and, as you can see, has managed to make the journey here to be with his family for Christmas. Bobby, we thank providence for your survival.'

Harland smiled and thanked Robin, although he heartily wished him dead.

Anne, who had been watching him, said, 'You're wondering why on earth your brilliant sister married him, aren't you?' She paused to take a drag on a thin cigarette. 'The answer is that he isn't threatened by her. Of course he's completely ludicrous in every way, but he's also very kind.'

'Yes,' said Harland.

'You know she's made an awful lot of money while looking after those kids, don't you?'

'No, I didn't.' He was genuinely interested.

'She's been trading on the stock market. Made her own little investment fund with various people's savings, although I don't think she actually took control of the money. That would be deeply on the wrong side of the law. Robin tells me she made two hundred thou' last year. Clever ole sis, huh?'

'Yes, clever ole sis,' said Harland. He watched Harriet weave towards Davina Vigo – who was plainly unaware of any difficulty – and thought glumly how little he knew of his sister.

445

Once or twice he could feel the weight of Vigo's gaze but turned to find him looking away into the middle distance. His presence didn't quite create a stir but everyone in the room was aware of him, even if most had not the slightest idea who or what he was.

The party swelled so that it became difficult to move in Harriet's sitting room and many guests spilled into a large conservatory area – the sort of sunroom that the English build without knowing what it should be used for. By now Harland and Anne had been joined by a lawyer with a blotchy skin named Deakin, who was clearly struck by Anne. Harland took a back seat in the conversation and wondered what precisely Vigo wanted. What was he afraid of? When he'd told Harriet the whole story she despaired of finding a unified theory of everything, as she put it. Sometimes, she said, you had to accept that things were simply unrelated.

Suddenly Harland became aware of Vigo moving in the side of his vision. He turned to find him making his way through the crowd, his mouth wearing a friendly smile, although his eyes told a different story. Anne made a tactful withdrawal, steering Deakin away into what he took for promising intimacy.

'Yes, Walter?' said Harland with quiet hostility. 'Have you come to apologise for that crap last night?'

'No. I just wanted to explain that this was sprung on us when we got to the Hammicks. I really had no option but to come.'

'But now you're here, you're quite happy to case the joint. I assume you already have this house watched.'

'Believe what you like Bobby, but I can assure you that's not true.'

Harland was aware of someone calling his name above the noise of the party. He looked round to see one of the waiters heading towards him after being given directions from Mr Lambton. At the same moment he saw Harriet with an alert expression making her way from another point in the room. The waiter got to him first.

'Mr Harland? There's a gentleman to see you. He's at the door. Says he won't come in.'

Vigo's eyes settled with interest on the waiter. Harriet arrived.

'Is there something wrong?'

'No, madam, there's a young gentleman to see Mr Harland. He's at the front door.'

'Oh,' said Harriet, without looking at Harland. 'That must be the Smithsons' boy, Jim. He's just left the LSE and I told them you might be able to get him something at the UN. Why don't you go and ask him in for a drink, Bobby?' She placed a hand on Vigo's forearm. 'Davina's just been telling me how you took her for a surprise weekend in New York. I wish Robin would think of things like that.'

Yes, Harland thought as he left them, a surprise visit arranged instantly Vigo heard about the crash. That meant that Vigo wasn't on official

446

business? He threw a glance in their direction as he reached the hall and saw that Harriet had shepherded three or four people into a group round Vigo, trapping him in the conservatory. She meanwhile had detached herself and by the look on her face was planning to follow him.

Tomas was waiting for him in a recess by the front door which acted as a cloakroom. He was plainly overawed by the size of the house.

'Jesus,' said Harland, 'you look terrible. Where have you been? Why didn't you come before now?'

'I stayed in a hotel. I had work to do.'

'Work! Look, this friend of yours – Felicity MacKinlay. You know the police are looking for you?'

'Mr Harland, I did not do this thing. You must believe me.'

'Yes I do. But you must talk to them.'

Tomas produced his crestfallen look.

'You don't understand. That's impossible. This is too complicated, too dangerous.'

'What's too complicated, for Christ's sake? You have to start talking, Tomas. Enough of this damned mystery. Why the hell did you leave that bar in New York?' Harland could hear himself. He sounded very much like a father.

Several people passed on their way out and threw rather puzzled looks in Tomas's direction. Harriet came into the hall, closed the door behind her guests and turned towards Harland.

'Look, you can't stay there. Walter Vigo is about to come out any moment.'

'Who is Walter Vigo?' Tomas asked both of them.

'He is a former colleague of Robert's and I don't want him to see you here, particularly with all that was in the papers this morning. You can go upstairs if you like and wait there until the party is over.'

Tomas picked up his bag. Then something seemed to occur to him.

'Mr Vigo is in the intelligence field, as you were?'

'Yes,' said Harland hastily. 'My sister is right. Why don't you go upstairs?'

'I don't think I should remain here with him in the house. I will come back. No, I will call your phone and tell you where to meet me.'

'Give it an hour,' said Harland. 'Do you need any money?'

'No,' said Tomas with a brief, shy smile to Harriet, who simply shook her head. 'I have money, Mr Harland.'

'Ah, there you are,' came a voice behind them. It was Davina Vigo and the Hammicks with Walter Vigo bringing up the rear. Harland saw him look over his wife's shoulder with interest at Tomas disappearing through the front door. But his view was blocked by Harriet reaching up to kiss his wife and then each of the Hammicks.

'What a lovely party,' said Davina. 'You must come to supper very soon in the New Year. I will get Walter to look at his diary.'

Harland and Vigo exchanged looks. The Hammicks and Vigos made for a Mercedes which had pulled into the gravel crescent at the sign of Davina Vigo waving a small purse through the open door. There was no sign of Tomas.

Harriet closed the door behind them, swivelled her eyes and blew out her cheeks.

'Why does he call you Mr Harland? Aren't you on better terms than that yet?'

Harland exhaled. 'He refuses to use any other name until I accept him totally. But I've only spent a couple of hours with him. How am I meant to react?'

'Well, I think you had better get used to him calling you something else. Bobby, he couldn't be anyone else's child. He's a dead ringer for you when you were that age – all gangly and intense. There's no question about it. He's yours.'

13

Cleopatra's Needle

Harland's phone rang at 9.45 p.m. but it wasn't Tomas. Instead, he heard some paper being shuffled and then the voice of Agent Frank Ollins.

'Ah, Mr Harland. I'm glad I've tracked you down. Is this a bad moment?'

'Could be better,' replied Harland.

'It won't take long, sir. There are just a few more questions I want to ask you about the period immediately before the crash.'

Harland slapped his forehead with annoyance. The last thing he wanted to do was block up his line. He was sure this could wait.

'Okay,' he said, 'but I may have to interrupt you. I'm expecting an important call.'

'At this hour? It's nearly Christmas Day with you, right?' said Ollins sceptically. 'Look, I want to take you through the last part of the flight. Can I remind you of the account you have given us so far?' He paused. 'Fifteen minutes out of La Guardia you get up out of your seat to go to the bathroom. Is that correct?'

'Yes.'

'At that moment the cabin lights are extinguished and you return to your seat?'

'Yes.'

'Then you notice that the heating in the cabin seems to be malfunctioning – it's gotten damned cold.'

'That's right,' said Harland wearily.

'The lights did not return before the crash?'

'No, they didn't. Look, is this relevant? I mean, does it have any bearing on the crash?'

'Hold on there, Mr Harland. This is important. We need to take this slowly. To answer your question – no, the lighting and heating systems are not directly relevant. We can see at what point they failed on the flight

449

data recorder and there appears to be nothing to connect those two failures with the eventual destruction of the airplane. Does that answer your question?' He paused. 'Now, as I recall it, you said that as you were coming in to land, Mr Griswald held up his laptop computer and used the light from the screen to see what he was doing. You mentioned you could see his face in the light of the computer. It's here in the transcript of your first talk with me and Clark last week.'

'Yes, I remember that well.'

'In what way did he hold the computer up?'

Harland tried to remember.

'I think he held it up several times but I don't know what you mean by what way.'

'I mean, how did he hold it to maximise the light coming from the screen?'

'Well, at least once he held it up to see his seat belt and then I think he held it up several times to see how the table was folded away and to gather his possessions together. Are you suggesting that the computer being on might have interfered with the aircraft's systems?'

'I'd rather you let me ask the questions. But no, I'm not. Let me go over this again. First, did he hold the computer up as though he had simply raised it from the table, i.e. with the keyboard still horizontal?'

'I'm not sure, it was dark. It wasn't easy to see.'

'Is it possible that Mr Griswald turned the computer and held it like a book so that the hinge was vertical, that is to say that the screen and keyboard were also in the vertical plane? It would make more sense if you were using the light from the screen to see what you were doing, would it not, Mr Harland?'

'Yes, it's entirely possible that he held it that way. I guess he must have done so at some stage.'

Harland saw Griswald holding the computer, a cumbersome affair which he realised was protected by a special cladding.

'And he was holding it out in front of him, not to the side of his body or above his head?'

Harland sensed that he was on a speakerphone. There was the noise of someone moving beyond Ollins's voice. 'Yes, I'd say he held it out in front of him for a time although he must have moved it around a little to see what he was doing.'

'And you're sure about that?'

'As sure as I can be.'

'Thank you.'

'Can I ask what this is about?'

'We're just looking into every aspect of the crash – testing a few theories, that's all. Happy holidays, Mr Harland.'

'Wait a moment! I thought we had an agreement to share information through Kennedy at the UN. Can you tell me a little more?'

'I don't know what you're referring to. But if there was such an arrangement, that would surely take in your visit to the South of France yesterday. I don't remember you calling me about that, although what you learned may have a direct bearing on this crash.'

'Okay, what about a trade?'

'I'll think about that while I'm eating my Christmas cake.'

Harland tried another tack. 'Did you find the computer?'

There was silence while Ollins mulled this over. 'Well, I'll give you this one for free. Yes, we found the computer on the other side of the runway.'

'Was it burned?'

'No.'

'So you've learned what's on it.'

'No, the hard drive's all knocked to shit.'

This stumped Harland. What was the point of all these questions about the computer if it neither represented a threat to the plane's electronic systems nor provided any useful information about Griswald's activities?

'But you still think the computer is important?'

'Could be. We're just going over everything here, winding down for a day's R and R.' He paused. 'Oh, there was one other thing. Can you confirm that you removed the cellphone from Mr Griswald's breast pocket? You imply this in the transcript but do not actually state it.'

'Yes, it was in his inside pocket.'

'Would that be the right or the left breast pocket?'

'His right.'

'That makes sense. Mr Griswald was a left-hander. I guess he'd tend to favour the right-hand inside pocket.'

Just then Harland was alerted to an incoming call on his line by a series of beeps. 'Look, I've got to go.'

'That's okay. I still got plenty to do here. We'll talk after Christmas.' With that he hung up and Tomas's call came through automatically.

'Mr Harland?'

'Yes. Tomas,' he said, 'would you just accept that I accept that everything you've told me about your birth is true – okay? So call me something else. Right, where are you now? I'll come and meet you.'

'Be careful not to be followed. It was foolish of me to come to your sister's house. I was worried they were watching it.'

'Well, don't worry. The party was exceptionally good cover – a lot of people coming and going.' Then Harland thought about what the boy had just said. He couldn't possibly know about Vigo's people following him. 'Tomas, who do you think could be watching you?'

'The same people who tortured and killed Flick. The people who will kill me, if they find me.'

'Who are they? Why in heaven's name would anyone want to kill you?'

'It's a long story. I will tell you everything later. I will be at Cleopatra's Needle in half an hour. You haven't forgotten where it is?' he asked, and hung up after Harland said he knew precisely where it was.

He put the phone in his pocket and thought back twenty-five years and wondered whether he was on the point of understanding everything.

He went and found Harriet who was looking after a few stragglers at the party. He took her aside and whispered. Harriet smiled and briskly announced to the group that she was going to take her brother to midnight mass and would therefore be happy to drop off anyone who needed a ride home. Even the most determined couldn't fail to shift after her unambiguous hint.

It was Harland's particular request that Harriet should not bring her RV round to the front of the house, so they all had to file through the kitchen to the garage. He took the middle of one of the rear seats, having insisted that the love-struck Deakin sit in the front. As the garage door opened and the car moved out into the drive, he slid right down into his seat so there was no chance of him being spotted leaving the house.

After four stops they were left alone in the car. Harriet said she was sure she hadn't been followed, but to be on the safe side he told her to turn into the entrance of a large mansion block which was obscured from the road by a hedge. Harland opened the door and hopped out while the car was still moving. He waited a little time after Harriet had disappeared and then headed in the direction of Baker Street tube station.

He arrived at Victoria Embankment just before eleven o'clock and left the tube station by the north exit. Some way off he could hear the rumble of music from one of the clubs in the bowels of Charing Cross station. He walked quickly to a run of short railings on the right of the street and, placing his hand on the top, vaulted over into Embankment Gardens. Nothing much had changed in the twenty-five years since he'd last been there – the layout of the gardens was more or less the same and the gates which led onto the embankment had not been changed. He knew they were easily scaled. He moved quickly to the south side where he waited for a while. He could just make out Cleopatra's Needle from where he stood behind the gates, but he would have to get closer to see if Tomas had arrived.

He questioned why he was being so careful – after all, no one could possibly know where they intended to meet. Maybe, he thought, this tension was prompted by memories of when he'd come as a young man with a mixture of hope and dread to meet Eva. He'd taken ridiculous precautions not to be followed that day, applying the skills recently acquired during training at the Fort and, no doubt, looking rather foolish.

All the business of doubling back on himself and popping in and out of pubs had caused him to be late. And when he got there Eva was nowhere to be seen. He'd waited and waited, then circled the area until nightfall. She never came. He obsessed about being late, although it had only been a matter of fifteen minutes – twenty at the most – and he imagined that she thought she'd been stood up. He expected her to call him later. But not a word came.

Grasping the spikes at the top of the gate, he climbed up the railing until he could place both feet on the top bar, and let himself down the other side. The gates stood back from the main boundary of Embankment Gardens so he could drop down without being seen. He glanced towards the obelisk and then back down the embankment to Hungerford Bridge, where two policemen stood drinking coffee by their car. The traffic was very light and there was almost no one about. He waited while his eyes ran over the scene. Then he made his move across the road and walked sharply along the river wall, noticing that the tide was low. The wind carried a faint smell of mud to his nostrils and his mind flipped back to the East River.

As he approached the first of the pair of huge bronze sphinxes that guard Cleopatra's Needle, he realised he'd forgotten nothing about the place. He found himself recalling its history – the hazardous journey across the Bay of Biscay when six men lost their lives; how the scars and pockmarks around one of the sphinxes had been left to commemorate the very first air raid by German aeroplanes on London in 1917; and the fact that the granite obelisk had been carved nearly one and a half thousand years before Cleopatra was born. Myth attributed the obelisk to Cleopatra although it was doubtful whether she had even laid eyes on it, unless she had happened to see it raised at Alexandria, a few years before Christ's birth and her own death. But Harland dwelled on that myth and as his search for Eva went on he had gradually merged Eva and Cleopatra into a single, mythic nemesis.

'Age cannot wither her,' he murmured to himself as he touched the flank of the sphinx, 'nor custom stale her infinite variety . . . She makes hungry where most she satisfies: for vilest things become themselves in her.'

He knew too much about the damned needle and it reminded him of the obsessed, cocksure young intelligence officer who thought he had all the answers.

He walked round the end of the sphinx to look over a short flight of steps, to the wide stone platform that projects from the line of the embankment into the Thames. There was no sign of Tomas so he moved past the obelisk to the second sphinx, whereupon he stopped and peered again. Nothing. He looked up and down the road as a shoal of seven or eight cars was released by the traffic lights a little further to the east, and then mounted the steps that led to the platform. He found him hidden, sitting on a ledge directly beneath the monument. He called out to him but Tomas didn't turn. He had his hands over a pair of earphones and he was staring down the river towards Waterloo Bridge and the illuminated cupola of St Paul's Cathedral.

Harland moved in front of him and placed a hand on his shoulder. He noticed that the stone was covered with a thin film of mud so he sat down beside Tomas and lifted his feet to the ledge. He was about to say something but was silenced by the view. He had never imagined London could be so still. Even the city's permanent background hum of traffic had faded with the approach of Christmas Day.

'So,' he said, 'what are we going to do about all this?'

Tomas looked at him. He was shaking a little and his face was pinched with cold, like the first time Harland saw him.

'What if my mother had come here that day? Would I have been born, I wonder? Would I have grown up with you as my father? Would I have lived in London? Would Flick be alive today? I was thinking about those things.'

Harland opened his hands in a gesture of helplessness.

'I don't know the answers to all that,' he said. 'But I'm certain that you should now tell me everything you've held back from me. Then we can decide what we're going to do about them. Maybe we should call your mother and get things straightened out.'

'I have not talked to my mother in two years.'

'Why not?'

'Because she deceived me about my father, because I could not talk to her about the things I had seen and done – things that I cannot talk to you about, Mr Harland.'

'Call me Bobby, for heaven's sake. I'd find it a lot easier.'

'Bobby,' he said bleakly.

'Spit it out,' said Harland gently. 'Sooner or later you're going to have to talk to the police and tell them what you know about Flick's killers. Otherwise, they're going to think you had something to do with it.'

'Well, I did. I did cause her death, just like I caused the death of the man in Bosnia.'

'Bosnia? Why the hell are you talking about Bosnia?' His mind was flooded with all kinds of connections, but he wasn't going to push things. He told himself to allow Tomas to speak in his own time.

It had begun to spot with rain. Tomas got up, walked to the parapet and turned to Harland. He was about twenty feet away and reduced almost to a silhouette by the three floodlights that were ranged along the top of the parapet to light the obelisk. Harland watched the raindrops fizz on the floodlights and waited for his son to speak.

'It all begins here,' said Tomas, throwing out his hands. 'Everything in my life begins here. Tell me, is there somewhere like that in your life, Bobby, some very significant place?'

'Yes,' said Harland after a while. 'Here.'

'How strange that is.' There was a hint of a smile in his voice.

Suddenly his hand jerked upwards and he staggered forward. Then his body folded like a hinge at the abdomen and he was pushed back with a terrible force. Harland's mind took in two further shots. One hit the middle floodlight and caused it to explode; the second cracked into the parapet about a foot from where Tomas's head had come to rest. He flung himself forward to Tomas's body. Another shot came and ricocheted with a long whine between the parapet and the obelisk. He looked at Tomas and in an instant knew he was dead.

He scuttled back crab fashion to the steps which on his side were ten deep, as against the six on the other. He edged into the shadow of the obelisk and peeped over the top step. A flash in the shrubbery across the road told him the gunman's position. But he didn't register the sound of the shot, just the burst of mud and stone some fifteen feet behind him. He looked again. There was a slight disturbance in the bushes. The gunman was leaving. Maybe he was coming after him.

He crawled back to Tomas and looked down into his lifeless face. There was a mass of blood pooled by a wound in his throat and he appeared to have been hit in the stomach also. Harland felt the uninjured side of his neck where there wasn't a trace of a pulse. So he picked up a hand and fumbled beneath the cuff of Tomas's jacket. There was something, a very faint flicker of life, although he wasn't sure whether he was feeling his own racing pulse.

He looked up again and saw a movement. Someone was running across the road. Maybe there were two of them. He crouched down again and made for the gap in an iron railing which allowed access to a steep flight of steps running down to the river. He could see in the light from the street that their surface had been greased to a treacherous finish by the tide. He lunged to his left, found the handrail and plummeted down the steps, slipping and falling, but never quite losing his grip on the handrail.

He had some notion that he would be able to escape along the sandbank which was showing at the edge of the water into the shadow of the embankment wall. But that idea ended with the snapping fire of a different type of gun behind him and a sudden, livid pain in his shoulder. His hand instinctively released the handrail and he fell forward, somehow managing to propel his weight around the corner of the massive Victorian stone buttress and into utter dark.

He was convulsed with pain, but he was certain his wound wasn't serious. For one thing he could still clench and unclench the fist of his right hand. He hugged the wet stone, clinging to the crevices with his fingernails, and waited for his breath to subside. He strained to work out what was going on thirty feet above him, but the groans of an old pleasure boat buffeting against the wooden piles nearby made it impossible to hear. He waited. There was a brief sound of a siren and the squeal of tyres. More gunfire. Then right behind him there came a sloshing noise and a voice croaked in the dark, 'Hey, you! What's happening up there?'

He swung round to find a dim torch a couple of feet from his head and beneath it a very old face, much of it covered by a grey beard. The torch appeared to be part of some kind of headgear because every time the face moved the torch did. Harland was aware of a fretful pair of eyes looking at him.

'Get that light off,' he said under his breath, 'unless you want to get killed.'

A hand reached up and switched off the torch. 'What's going on up top?'

'Someone's been seriously injured – my son. Who the hell are you?'

'Saint George,' said the figure, apparently unconcerned by the news. 'Cyril St George – mudlark. This is my patch. Been here twenty-two years. Before that in Southampton – under the old pier there. Maybe you know it.'

Harland didn't reply. He realised that the old man must work the riverbank at low tide for coins.

'Can you get me out of here?' he said. 'I've been hit.'

'Not for a few minutes, I can't. Wait for the tide, because sure as eggs is eggs it won't wait for you.' He switched the lamp on and looked at a watch pinned to one of his many outer garments. 'Five minutes or so and we should be all right. Good conditions this evening. Couldn't miss a tide like tonight's.'

They waited without speaking, the old man's breath rasping in Harland's ear.

'Right, let's be having you,' he whispered, and took hold of Harland's left hand and placed it on the hem of some very coarse material. 'Don't lose your grip and follow me. If I take off into the current, don't be afeared. I know what I'm doing down here – I should do after all these years.' He coughed a laugh.

They set off and edged along the wall immediately below the obelisk in about a foot of water, then turned right so they were wading across the current.

Harland wondered why the old man didn't carry some sort of stick but he seemed to know his way. They moved out of the shadow of the wall into a part of the riverbank where there was more light. In the shallower areas he could see a number of weighted traffic cones which he guessed the old man had appropriated to serve as markers when the tide was not fully out.

'Nobody can see you down here,' he said. 'You think they can, but they can't. Don't you go straying now.'

They stopped while Cyril St George caught his breath.

'Guns!' he said with contempt. 'I find a lot of guns in here. They throw them in the river after they done their shooting and they 'spect them to stay put. But the tide brings them to me and I take 'em straight to the police. It's not just guns I find down here. Saint George knows where to look, see, and he finds rings and jewellery and very many ancient artefacts. And I see bodies. The suicides and murder victims all come past my bank.'

Harland could barely take this in. His shoulder was burning and it required all his concentration to stand still in the water without crying out. They set off again, tacking slowly towards a pontoon which was moored about a hundred feet ahead of them. The water was getting deeper and Harland felt the combined strength of the outgoing tide and the flow of the river. The tugging and sucking at his legs took him back to the East River and he wondered whether this time the water would win. Twenty feet from the pontoon the old man stopped.

'You're on your own now, son. It'll go over my waders if I carry on. I'll wait down here until the coast is clear, then take the steps.'

Harland edged round the old man and went ahead, struggling to control himself. He was certain that at any moment he would put his foot down and find nothing and be swept away. Such was his fear that he had difficulty in committing himself to each step, but the old man urged him on until he was within a few yards of the pontoon. He made out a metal ladder fixed to the end but saw that the pontoon was rising and falling with the swell of the river. He realised he would have to time his launch so as to catch the bottom rung before it rose out of reach. He watched the pontoon and tried to accustom himself to its motion, all the while hearing the sounds of the water reverberating in its huge buoyancy tanks. As the ladder reached the zenith of its climb, he dived forward praying that he'd meet it on its way down. A few desperate strokes and he caught the rung with his good hand just as his legs were being dragged under the pontoon. The whole structure reared upwards with the next wave, pulling him out of the water like a bottle cork. A few seconds later and he had clambered up the ladder and was sprawling on the deck of the pontoon.

'Go on my son,' came the voice behind him.

Now the only thought in Harland's mind was for Tomas. He ran the length of the pontoon, climbed the gangway to the bank and scaled the padlocked gates at the end. He couldn't see any movement around the obelisk, but a police car was slewed across the carriageway on the far side of the road. Its blue light was flashing and both doors were open. Only when he reached Cleopatra's Needle did he see the bodies of the two policemen lying in the road. A car had just pulled up behind their vehicle and the driver was standing in the road speaking into his mobile. Harland shouted that there was another badly injured person on his side of the road, then leapt over the steps. Tomas was where he had left him. He knelt down and felt for the pulse again. He'd been right. There *was* something. A flicker of life.

He ripped off his own shirt, bunched some of the material together and held it against the neck wound with his right hand. At that point he realised that he himself had bled profusely. While he pressed the bandage home, he felt his own back with his free hand and located a shallow gouge aross his shoulder blade to the upper arm. He returned his fingers to Tomas's wrist, willing the pulse to continue.

They operated on Tomas for six hours, extracting a bullet from his stomach without much difficulty and patching the wound where a second had passed clean through his shoulder. But the greater proportion of that time was spent on a delicate procedure to remove a bullet lodged in his brain stem, the area at the base of the brain which leads to the spinal cord. The shot had been deflected off a metal clasp on Tomas's jacket and passed through his throat into his brain.

While Harland was being treated one of the surgeons came to see him to explain what they were doing. She said it was touch and go because Tomas had lost a lot of blood. At this Harland suddenly jerked up from the bed he was lying on. He'd remembered his own blood group which he had inherited from his father. Rhesus-null was one of the rarest in the world and the point about it – as he had discovered before his cancer operation – was that it clashed with O negative, which was used as a match-all in emergency operations. He told the woman that this might be a possibility. She looked at him strangely, then phoned through to the operating theatre.

As Christmas Day dawned, Tomas was placed in intensive care. The surgeon returned together with a distinguished-looking man in his fifties, who the nurses had informed Harland was Philip Smith-Canon, a leading neurosurgeon. The specialist introduced himself and asked Harland if he'd like some coffee in a nearby office.

'So I gather from the blood group of the patient that you're next of kin.'

Harland shook his head.

'I will be tracing his mother in the Czech Republic. It would be better if you regard her as his next of kin.'

Smith-Canon looked puzzled, but decided to ignore it.

'I ask because there are likely to be some difficult decisions to take over the next ten days or so. The patient is in an extremely serious condition and even if he survives the immediate threat to his life from this bullet and pulmonary infections, he is likely to face severe disability.'

'What do you mean exactly?'

'If you were to press me, I'd say it's probable that he will suffer total paralysis and lose the ability to communicate. I'm sorry to be so blunt but I cannot hide that the prognosis is very poor. This kind of injury is the equivalent of a brain-stem stroke or a serious tumour in that region of the brain. Whatever the etiology, that is to say the cause, we can predict the outcome with a relatively small margin of error. He's still at considerable risk, of course, but he's young and strong which may mean he'll live to regain consciousness.'

His voice softened. 'Mr Harland, he will wake to experience quadriplegia, mutism and facial paralysis, which may include the ability to blink. This is only half of it. There'll be numerous smaller symptoms, respiratory problems, altered breathing patterns, involuntary movements of the face, incontinence of bladder and bowel. You understand what I'm saying? We're talking about a state of extreme privation, fear and discomfort. But inside he will be aware of what's going on and able to think normally.'

'There's never any chance of better recovery than that?'

'Not in my experience. The trauma suffered in his brain stem was very considerable and although he may not experience all the symptoms I describe, essentially my prognosis is right.'

'I see. But you knew this when you were operating to remove the bullet.'

'Not until we were well into the operation. But you have put your finger on something we must talk about and that's the question of resuscitation. There may be occasions over the next week or so when we will be faced with the decision of whether or not to continue to treat him. Often in these cases the patient is susceptible to pneumonia. That may be regarded – with the proper management – as a way out.' He paused and drank some coffee. Then he looked at Harland with genuine sympathy. 'I believe you to be his father, Mr Harland. I won't hazard at the reasons for your wish to hide this fact, but the blood group match is almost irrefutable evidence. There are questions which cannot be dodged. If your son lives there are enormous problems to be faced concerning specialised treatments and care. No person in this condition can live without round-the-clock attention.'

Harland thought for a moment.

'Look, as you have guessed, I am his father. I have known this for less than a week. The circumstances are extremely difficult to ...' His voice faded. He felt almost drugged.

'How long is it since you've had a decent night's sleep, Mr Harland?'

'I can't think. Three days?'

'I suggest that you get some sleep soon.'

'Let me just finish. I was going to say that I cannot tell you why anyone

459

would wish to kill Tomas, but I suspect that there is a very evil man behind this shooting and the death of Tomas's girlfriend. It will help me greatly if you do not reveal that Tomas is my son.'

'You are asking me to lie?'

'No. If the police ask you, I would not want to prevent you from telling the truth. It's just that I don't believe that the police will ask you. After all, they have no reason to interview you.'

Smith-Canon nodded.

'Very well, I agree, and I will tell Susan Armitage, who came out with me just now, to do the same. But we will still need a next of kin to consult over the next few days. What of his mother?'

'I will try to trace her in the Czech Republic. But it's going to be difficult. She has changed her name several times.'

'I see,' said Smith-Canon.

'If I leave the country, I will put you in touch with my sister who will be able to get in touch with me wherever I am. Her name is Harriet Bosey.'

'Right, shall we agree on this, then – that your son remains here until he is out of immediate danger? I will then arrange for him to be transferred to my hospital and we will begin to assess the situation.'

Harland gave him his telephone numbers and dragged himself out of the chair. His arm still hurt like hell but the pain had faded as he learned of the true nature of Tomas's condition. He walked back down the hallway, away from the operating theatres, to where he knew the police would be waiting for him.

14

The Bitter Madeleine

Harland told two officers about the shooting and his escape along the riverbank. They said that one of the policemen had been killed, the other would recover but there was a likelihood of his not being able to walk again. After twenty minutes he began to feel faint. They called a doctor, who said he must have immediate rest, and he was driven to Harriet's house where two police guards were posted outside.

He slept until six-thirty that evening when Harriet woke him with a concise version of what had plainly been an elaborate Christmas lunch, which she brought to him on a tray. She didn't need to ask what had happened because she had learned all she wanted from the police guards to whom she had given lunch in the kitchen. There was also a detailed report on the evening news that made much of the tragedy of the young constable's death on Christmas Eve. Harland was sure there would be a lot more coverage. It would only be a matter of time before his name was released and someone linked him with the La Guardia crash. Then there was the connection to be made between the death of a young florist in a North London flat and the shooting of her boyfriend.

Robin joined them, stealing into the room with a stage tiptoe. He seemed genuinely horrified by the account of Harland's conversation with the surgeon and said that he would do anything to help with Tomas's care. All bills would be taken care of. Harriet touched him on the hand and smiled. In that instant Harland saw why their marriage worked.

'One thing bothers me,' she said, turning back to her brother. 'How did they trace you to the embankment? They must have followed you from here, I suppose.'

'No,' said Harland emphatically. 'They would have shot him outside the house, no matter how many people were around. They were obviously desperate to kill him.'

'Then they must have waited for you to join him before the shooting. After all, they'd tried to do away with you in New York.'

'That assumes a lot of things, the first of which was that they knew that it was me at Cleopatra's Needle. The second point is that they didn't make any real attempt to shoot me once I fled down those steps.'

'Not half, they didn't,' said Robin, looking at the bandage on his shoulder.

'No, I mean it. These were professional killers. If it had mattered to them, they would have gone after me.'

'But they saw or heard the police coming and made their getaway,' said Robin. 'So they couldn't chase after you.'

'No, that doesn't quite work either. The first shots were fired by a relatively quiet sniper's rifle. Only when they came across the road did they use a machine gun, which could be heard. That's what drew the attention of the police car. You see, I didn't hear its siren until I was on the riverbank.'

'What's all this add up to, then?' asked Robin.

'Bobby thinks that they haven't made the connection between him and Tomas,' said Harriet, 'or at any rate that they didn't identify him last night. That's right, isn't it, Bobby?'

'Yes.'

'But why didn't they shoot before you arrived?' said Harriet, then she clapped her hands and answered her own question. 'Because they had only just got there themselves! And that's interesting, Bobby, because although they had only just arrived they knew enough about the meeting to position themselves across the road in that park. Right? And that can mean only one thing: they'd listened to the phone call that Tomas made to you. So, if we assume that they didn't know who he was calling – and we've already agreed that there are good reasons to suppose that – it means they must have been monitoring his cellphone. They knew his number – that's the only solution.'

'You could be right,' said Harland. 'And it would have been a simple matter to extract that number from his girlfriend, or even from some sort of record they found in the flat – a phone bill perhaps.'

Robin had sat down on the end of the bed. 'But doesn't it require considerable resources to do a thing like that? I mean, intercepting a particular mobile number needs a lot of sophisticated equipment. That's the sort of operation GCHQ goes in for – you know, collaring underworld barons in Marbella.'

'Yes, you're right, you do need pretty comprehensive equipment,' said Harland slowly, and he thought of Luc Bézier and the phone-tracking operation that had lured the French special forces team to a hotel in the Balkans.

'Well, perhaps you should point all this out to the police,' said Robin,

pleased with his contribution. 'They're downstairs – two rather senior
detectives. That's why I came up. I can tell them to go away if you want.
After the last week and a bit, you've got every excuse to take a night's rest
without being bothered.'

Harland said he would be down in a few minutes. When Robin had
gone, Harriet helped him to put his shirt on.

'You're not going to tell them any of this,' she said.

'Of course not, Hal.'

'And you aren't going to let them know that Tomas is your son.'

'No, but they may work that out for themselves. And if the police
don't, I'm sure Vigo will. He won't have forgotten seeing a young man
disappearing out of the door. And since he's already claiming I spied for
the Czechs and that I had an affair with Eva Houresh, it may not take him
long to work out who Tomas is.'

'Which will make the allegations about your past much more difficult
to deny.'

Harland nodded silently.

'What a terrible mess this is, Bobby.'

He went downstairs and found the two officers waiting in the sitting
room. A short man with alert eyes and a brisk manner swivelled on his
heels and gave his name as Commander Maurice Lighthorn. The other, a
rather jaundiced fellow with watery eyes and a moustache, introduced
himself as Chief Inspector Roger Navratt. Harland sat down but the
officers remained standing.

'How are you feeling, sir?' asked Lighthorn.

'Better, now I've had some sleep.'

'And the injury. How's that doing? Much pain?'

'No, but they expect it to heal quickly – it's a surface wound.'

'In that case, we were wondering if you felt up to accompanying us to
the station.'

'Are you arresting me?'

'No, sir, but we do need your help and there's a lot to go through in a
case like this. It will be easier at the station.'

Harland agreed to go, although both Robin and Harriet tried to
persuade Lighthorn to wait until the next day.

Lighthorn listened, unmoved. 'I don't mean to be rude, madam, but
this is a very serious incident and we have reason to believe that there is a
link to another murder. Two people are dead, two very seriously injured.
In my book, these circumstances require an urgent response.'

They drove to West End Central station where business was slow. A
few uniformed officers sat dejectedly waiting for the end of their shifts.
Lighthorn explained that the investigation was being carried out at New
Scotland Yard, but that they hadn't acquired all the space they needed yet.

Lighthorn's appearance galvanised things and they were quickly shown into one of the station's interview rooms.

Coffee was produced. Navratt switched the interview tape recorder on and formally identified all those in the room.

'Mr Harland,' Lighthorn began after Navratt nodded, 'we have your account of the shooting which will form part of your statement in due course. What I want to do now is to ask you about your relationship with the man known as Lars Edberg. Can I start by asking how long you've known him?'

'I met him for the first time in New York last week.'

'In what circumstances?'

'Well, we had a few drinks in the bar around the corner from where I live in Brooklyn.'

'Did you meet there?'

'No, we got talking in the street outside my apartment and I offered him a drink.'

'Just like that?'

'More or less. He seemed a friendly young man – very bright and good company.'

'And you had no knowledge of him before that moment.'

'No, I had not set eyes on him or heard his name before that evening.'

'But you seem to have forged a strong relationship in that short time. Would you mind if I asked you the nature of that relationship? You will agree that it's unusual of a man of your age to strike up a conversation with somebody of Mr Edberg's age.'

'As I say, he was interesting.'

'And there was – how shall I put it – no sexual motive?'

Harland shook his head. 'No, nothing like that.'

'However, you were in contact this week after your return to this country.'

'Yes.'

'Were you aware at any stage that Lars Edberg was travelling on a false passport? No Swedish passport has been issued to a man named Lars Edberg.'

'Only when I read it in the papers yesterday.'

'Did Mr Edberg tell you about the murder of the woman he had been living with – Felicity MacKinlay?'

'Yes, in a phone call two nights ago.'

'Can you describe his state of mind at that time, Mr Harland?'

'It was a very short call and I didn't have a chance to ask much about it. But I would say that he was extremely upset. I gave him my sister's address and told him to go there.'

'And did he?'

'Not that evening.'

'When did you next hear from him?'

'Last night when he turned up at my sister's. It was difficult, though. There was a party on so we agreed to meet later.'

'Last night – Christmas Eve,' said Lighthorn significantly. 'That means that when you saw him you were fully aware that the police were looking for him. Because you yourself have just said that you read in the morning papers that Edberg was travelling under a false name. So the question is this: why didn't you phone the police then, Mr Harland? He was, after all, a major suspect.'

'I wanted to find out what was going on. In fact, I told him when I saw him by the river that sooner or later he would have to explain himself.'

'Still, it was a pity – some would put it a lot stronger – that you didn't phone the police at that stage. It would almost certainly have saved three people from being shot – four if we include your own injury, sir.'

'Look, I knew that he couldn't have had anything to do with the murder. I also knew he was frightened.'

Lighthorn's eyes darted to Harland's.

'Are you telling me that from one casual encounter you gained the certainty that this man could not have committed murder? You *do* know this woman was very brutally tortured before she was killed – tortured, sexually assaulted and executed.'

'I didn't know the exact details,' he said.

'But you read enough in the newspapers to know that her death was extremely ugly. Yet you still went to the Embankment to meet this Edberg – a man who you knew to be travelling on a fake passport, who was wanted by the police. That would suggest a very cavalier attitude to your own safety, unless you knew what Edberg was running from. Is that the truth of it? Did Mr Edberg tell you something in New York?'

'No, all I knew was that he believed someone was trying to kill him.'

'Why?' Again the eyes scanned Harland's face.

'He made veiled references to the danger he was in, but he did not specify what that danger was.'

Lighthorn seemed to digest this. In another context Harland would probably have admired his technique. He was clear-headed and possessed an unswerving instinct for the truth. But there was also something of the martinet in him.

'The reason I'm asking you these questions is not because we suspect Mr Edberg. We have ruled him out in the murder inquiry for the very good reason that we know he returned to this country about twenty-four hours after Miss MacKinlay was murdered. A baggage tag on the case that he left in her flat gave us the information on the flights he took. And we have since found the day and time of his departure to New York from another airline. What is significant is that the people who work at Felicity MacKinlay's flower shop told us that Edberg had said he would help with a large delivery of Christmas trees that day. Then without notice he left. What this suggests is that he left in a hurry and went to the States for a particular purpose. Do you know what that was?'

Harland shrugged.

'Come along, Mr Harland. You're an intelligent man – you must have asked him what all this was about?'

'I did, and he was about to tell me when he was shot.'

'Yes, by what appears to be a professional hit man. This was no casual drive-by shooting. This was the work of a top-notch pro who'd been hired to track down this young man. In the process he tortured and executed a young woman, murdered a police constable and crippled another.' There was genuine anger, genuine indignation in Lighthorn's manner.

The door opened and a young plainclothes policeman came in and whispered something to Lighthorn. Navratt looked at Harland, as if to deter him from listening in. Lighthorn left for five minutes then returned with an envelope which he placed on the table.

'In these circumstances,' said Lighthorn slowly, 'where a man has been shot at a secret meeting, it is often the case that one of the parties in that meeting has arranged the shooting.'

'What?' said Harland contemptuously. 'Are you suggesting that I arranged for the gunman to be there?'

'It's possible.'

'Then why on earth would they shoot me? And, second, why would I return to To—' He said the first syllable of Tomas's name, stumbled and said the name Lars. 'Why would I go back and wait for the police to come?'

Harland was sure Lighthorn had noticed the stumble, although he didn't pursue it.

'That's precisely the point I wanted you to make for me. Why in heaven's name did you go back to the scene of the shooting? I mean, you told the officers in the hospital how you fell down the steps at Cleopatra's Needle, and how you came across this character St George and then made good your escape. Remember, at this stage you were certain the young man was dead. You also told my officer that you felt for vital signs and there were none. So, I ask again, why would you return to the scene when it presented such obvious dangers? You were certain that Edberg was dead. Surely the most sensible course would have been to run in the opposite direction and find a phone box. Instead you returned to the monument.'

'Well, I wasn't sure he was dead. So I went back to check. By that time I'd heard the siren and —'

'And a lot more gunfire,' interrupted Lighthorn. 'That's what you told my officers.'

'Yes, and a lot more gunfire. So what are you suggesting?'

'I'm suggesting that your relationship with this young man was very important to you, important enough for you to race back along the embankment to be with him. Important enough for you to remain outside the operating theatre for an entire night, while you yourself must have been in some pain and suffering from your ordeal in the river.' He paused to pick up the envelope. 'I wonder if you would take a look at this, Mr Harland. It's a copy of the *Daily Telegraph* from last week.' He unfolded the paper and laid it on the table. 'It was found in Miss MacKinlay's flat in her recycling bin. As you can see, there's a large part of the front page missing. One of our officers decided to find out what had been cut out of this newspaper. He contacted the *Daily Telegraph* library a little while ago – fortunately they are publishing tomorrow – and found that it was the picture of your rescue in the La Guardia air crash last week.' He let this sink in. 'I remember the picture myself. You certainly have been through a lot this last week, Mr Harland. If you think about it, Mr Edberg must have cut this picture out of the paper before you say you met him. How do you explain this action?'

'I can't.'

'Is that all you've got to say? I mean, it's clear that this newspaper photograph acted as the prompt for Mr Edberg. Within hours of seeing it he was on a flight to New York, in all probability clutching this cutting – there is no sign of it in the flat.'

'Well, we did talk about the crash. He showed tremendous interest in it. Maybe that's why he stopped me in the street. He did mention that he had seen the picture.'

'Ah, but you're missing the point. This newspaper picture was the inspiration for Edberg's dash to New York. He plainly went to speak to you, showing, incidentally, the same devotion that you were later to show on the riverbank to him. This means he must have known where to find you.' He glanced at Navratt with just a hint of triumph for he knew that this must all be news to Harland. 'I've already had one of our officers check with International Inquiries and it appears that you are not listed in Brooklyn. Answer me this: how would he find you unless he knew where you lived? If he knew where you lived, it's a reasonable assumption that you had met before last week.'

'All I can say,' said Harland, 'is that I never saw him before that night, or spoke to him, or had any type of contact with him. I don't have the first idea how he traced me, although a determined person would not find it difficult to extract the number out of the United Nations.'

Lighthorn looked at him steadily.

'You're asking me to believe that this chap with a foreign accent appears out of the blue at your home and starts talking to you about a crash that you were in and you invite him for a drink, without having any idea who he is or where he comes from? It doesn't make sense. It's clear to me that Edberg went to New York for the purpose of seeing you. During that visit I believe he gave you information crucial to the understanding of Miss MacKinlay's murder and to the shooting at the Embankment. I want to know what that was. I'm not pissing about here. We're looking for a man – or men – who callously gunned down two police officers and murdered a young woman. Those men may still be in the country. I believe that you may even be aware of their identity.'

'That's ridiculous. How could I possibly know them?' He leaned forward in his seat and couldn't help grimacing as the bandage on his shoulder shifted. 'I've told you what I know.'

'Then you give me no option but to hold you here. You may consider yourself under arrest, Mr Harland.'

'On what grounds?'

'On the grounds that we suspect you of an arrestable offence, namely involvement in the murder of PC Jeffrey Gibbon and shooting of PC Clive Low and the man known to us as Lars Edberg. I believe that you're withholding information which would help us make arrests, Mr Harland. I hope that over the course of the next few hours you will realise that your only option is to be completely frank with me.'

'But you don't believe any of this! You're making it up to keep me here and force me into giving you information I don't possess – that I couldn't possess. I have a statutory right to see a solicitor. I take it that you aren't going to ignore that too.' He noticed his hand was shaking and he knew his voice was somehow thinning.

'By all means make a telephone call,' said Lighthorn evenly. 'I will see you later.' With that he swept up the newspaper cutting and walked out of the room, leaving Navratt fumbling with the tape recorder.

He made the call to Harriet. She hurriedly told him that Robin had already been in touch with a solicitor named Leo Costigan who was standing by. She told him that she'd phoned the hospital and that the boy was still in a coma. They were doubtful whether he would ever wake.

Harland was taken to the cells. Several drunks and homeless men were there, who'd got themselves arrested in order to spend Christmas night in the warmth. There was a faint odour of urine in the corridor. Suddenly Harland experienced the stirring of blind panic. He reasoned to himself as he was led to the cell that he had already spent a night pretty much in custody and that he hadn't suffered unduly. But he found he couldn't control the fear and had to ask the policeman to wait for a few moments before locking him up. He said he felt faint.

'You ought to have thought of that before you dried up on Commander Lighthorn,' he said, and steered Harland into a cell. The door was shut and locked. He heard the policeman walk back down the corridor.

He tried to get a grip on his horror by sourcing it. What was it? Where did the panic come from? Of course! It was the smell of urine, the stench that had brought him round the first night in the villa in Prague. It was a smell he detested. He'd known it was his smell and that he must have pissed his pants while unconscious. And that was just at the beginning. There were many days more of him lying in his own filth, being woken up with a bucket of cold water and hauled into a room where a terrible intimacy was begun between him and his nameless torturer. For most of the time he was blindfolded and could not see who was in the room. But he learned by the echoes and the scuffling and the sniggering to count the number of men. Sometimes three or four; other times, just one. The man who spoke to him in the dark with that soft, cracked smoker's voice, and went over and over the past, insisting on more and more detail and, when Harland couldn't supply it, accusing him of lying and telling him he would be punished. Lying? About what? Things Harland didn't know. Things he couldn't know about because he simply hadn't been told, wasn't involved in this or that operation, or was somewhere else at the time.

He had worked Harland with a dedication that was senseless because all about them – although Harland didn't know to what extent – Eastern Europe was rising up against the communist regimes. Yet in the dilapidated villa and its fetid cellars remained a corner of Stalinist Russia. Seventy years of oppression and cruelty was channelled by the torturer into Harland's nerve endings.

It was the intimacy that Harland could not stand. Each day would start with the man hurting him. Then there would be talk, the offer of water or sometimes coffee, and the torturer would pass the time of day with him, discussing such bizarre topics as boar hunting in the Carpathians or the plum brandy to be had in Yugoslavia. He affected to be a man of the world, a man of taste with many high standards. Nothing was ever good enough for this connoisseur. As he talked, he tempted Harland into a man-to-man intimacy, in which Harland was required to give his opinion on the coldness of English women, the myth of French passion, the superiority of Russian hockey players and slovenliness of the Poles, the Turks and the gypsies, all of whom the man loathed heartily.

There was no question of Harland not responding because it would only advance the moment when the man hurt him again. His sole strategy was to delay being hurt. For the longer he put him off, the longer he would survive and the greater the chance of his being rescued. So he talked to the man, gave his all to the discussion. That involved relating to him, reacting genuinely to what he was saying, as though he was having a normal conversation and was not bound in a chair or stretched across a table, stinking of his own urine. It took all his energy to find ways of delaying that moment. But, of course, the torturer knew what he was up to. He let it be known – quite subtly – that he interpreted these ingenious diversions of Harland's as a peculiar confirmation of his own power: only he could drive this Englishman to argue that a salmon caught on a fly rather than a spinner tasted better, while that Englishman's body cried out from five hours of being bound on the stone floor.

As the day wore on the Russian would rib him about each red herring, like a parent indulging a child who is trying to avoid its bedtime. Then quite suddenly he would turn on Harland. It was back to business, he would say. He would start with his questions about an operation that Harland had never heard of or a piece of intelligence which had been fed up the line and had proved inaccurate. Why? Who? When? What motive? Harland was being called to account for everything he'd done, indeed for the entire Western intelligence effort over the past fifteen years. That was perhaps the only hint the man gave that he understood what had happened when the Berlin Wall fell. His world was over and now he was conducting a final inquiry. An inquisition. But it was also plain that he was exacting revenge. For what? The collapse of the communist system? The superiority of Harland's side? The end of his power and prospects?

Harland pathetically attempted to make a stab at the right solution and work it into a reassuring message during the conversation, but never to any avail. Sometimes the man would break into song or speak some impromptu doggerel, which wove Harland's observation into rhyme. Harland knew the man was watching his expression and he tried – oh, so very desperately – to hide his revulsion.

Before the man started hurting him again with the electrodes or the hot iron or the belts and clubs and needles, he would get very close to Harland, squatting or sometimes even lying on the floor beside him, and Harland would smell his breath and his aftershave and sense the slight aroma of a leather coat or a woollen jersey. Not once did he see the man's face for he always made sure that Harland was bound and blindfolded before he entered the room. He had seen the others though, the thugs who were called upon to beat him up, or do the lifting when the torturer wanted Harland stretched across a barrel or hung from a beam in the cellar. Even though he never laid eyes on him, he knew this man.

The truth was that he had succumbed. The terrifying, faceless presence had got to him. In his rare conscious moments in his cell he reasoned to himself that he was only trying to survive, but he understood that he had put himself in the position of the supplicant. Like a lover almost, he was dependent on the torturer's approval, alert to his whims and moods, desperate to please, but always knowing that in the end he would be hurt. It was intimacy of a truly demonic kind and it had left Harland with a peculiar terror. To him closeness was torture, except possibly in his relationship with Harriet. Somehow that had survived.

These memories ran unchecked through Harland's mind for the first time in the decade since he had taken a cab to a quiet North London street and talked to a very good woman about his torture. She had set up a discreet outfit for victims of torture like himself and he had gone on a doctor's recommendation, almost with the sense that he had something to confess. Torture, he was surprised to learn, had left him with a sense of guilt, just as severe bereavement can cause feelings of shame. The damage done is so great and particular that the mind can only express itself through one or other of the more common human emotions. He had returned many times to the woman who just listened and allowed him to voice the most dreadful thoughts. After six months or so he picked himself up and found himself a job. He never saw her again and never mentioned it to himself again, at least not in a way that would resurrect the images that played in his blindfolded mind all those years ago.

He thought of that woman now. She was the very antithesis of his torturer which was why it had been strangely difficult for him to talk to her on the terms and with the intimacy that he'd used in the villa. He had explained the irony and she had nodded and said she understood. He kept her face before him as he lay on the bed in the police cell and watched his hands shaking from what seemed like a very great distance indeed.

He noted that his detachment had come back again, the same part of him that had coolly advised that he was about to die in the East River. But now there was another message, an odd phrase that repeated itself in his head. 'Blank out. Blank out. Blank out.' He wanted blankness and the end of his terror.

Some time later that night he was aware of the cell door opening. In the doorway stood a man in a silvery blue suit who was rhythmically brushing the stubble on the top of his head. Harland scrutinised him with ultra clarity. A short man, a bustling man, carrying a briefcase, an overcoat and small black astrakhan hat.

'This won't do at all,' said the man several times. 'Look at him, for heaven's sake. When was he last checked?'

He knelt down by Harland's side. 'My name is Leo Costigan. I'm your solicitor. I'm going to get you out of here as soon as possible. These bastards will pay for this.'

Harland took in the ashen face of the constable who had locked him up.

'Mr Harland?' said the lawyer, shaking Harland's good shoulder. 'Mr Harland!' Then he turned to the policeman. 'This man is in shock. Don't just stand there. Get a doctor, you idiot!'

The policeman ran down the corridor.

'It's going to be okay. You're going to be okay, Mr Harland. Can you hear me? I'm your lawyer, Leo Costigan.'

He stopped speaking and put a hand to Harland's forehead and stroked it. For some reason Harland could not reply.

The officer returned with a uniformed sergeant and Navratt, whose rheumy-eyed indifference had been replaced by a look of pure panic.

'It is plain that this man has suffered a nervous collapse while in your care,' said Costigan. 'I do not want him moved until the doctor has assessed his condition. You can all see that he has been allowed to wet himself and that his hands are shaking. He is unable to focus and cannot react. You lot are looking at the end of your careers. I don't suppose any of you were aware that this man is the personal representative of the Secretary-General of the United Nations?' He looked up at the three policemen. 'No, I didn't think so.'

Harland smiled inwardly. Costigan was doing a grand job. Harriet had been right about him – a good chap, a little terrier.

It was strange how he tried to talk but nothing happened. He was dimly reminded of the effect of a computer virus: the words seemed to move very slowly to the front of his mind and then disintegrate before his eyes. Still, inside he knew he was okay. He had come through and he was intact. He just needed sleep. That was all.

15

Two Halves of a Dollar Bill

For the next few days no one was allowed to bother Harland. A visit from the family doctor confirmed the police doctor's view that he'd suffered a delayed reaction from the twin traumas of the air crash and the shooting. His problems had been compounded by lack of sleep. Harland went along with the diagnosis, but he knew very well that the shock to his system predated both these events by a long time. He was prescribed sleeping pills and a course of what the doctor described as mood improvers. He ignored the second bottle and instead buried himself in a biography of an aviation pioneer and watched old films on television with Harriet's children.

There was also a visit from Leo Costigan, who told him that the police had no intention of pursuing the case against him. He was pressing for an inquiry and had already made representation with the Police Complaints Authority. Harland asked him to inquire about Lars Edberg's possessions. Since Edberg was alive, he had every right to them. More important, a clue to his interests might be in that bag: the sort of music that might help wake him from the coma. Harland mentioned this because it had occurred to him that there was a lot in the bag that might eventually fall into Vigo's hands, in particular Eva's old ID cards. Costigan said he would do what he could but was doubtful since the bag would almost certainly be regarded by the police as relevant to Tomas's identity.

By Monday evening he began to feel himself again. He lay on a couch in the conservatory thinking how he was going to find Eva. It wouldn't be easy, especially as Tomas had never given him any hint of her whereabouts or the name she was using. If he was to go to the Czech Republic, he would have to think very carefully about his departure and then his means of search. Suddenly he thought of Cuth Avocet – The Bird – and Macy Harp. He couldn't think of anyone who knew Prague better. He'd put money on the fact that The Bird still resided at a pleasant flint farmhouse between Lambourne and Newbury, where his wife ran a stud farm. And if The Bird was still there, Macy Harp would not be far away.

Late next morning Harland asked Robin if he could spend some time at his office. He said he felt like getting out of the house and he needed to make some phone calls. They drove together in Robin's Alvis to the White Bosey Cane building, just off Charlotte Street. Robin went into a large, sparse office where there was an exercise machine and a flat-screen TV, leaving Harland in the care of a whey-faced woman in her twenties named Cary who looked as though she suffered from multiple allergies. He explained that he wanted a private office, a phone and an Internet connection. She had no difficulty in finding somewhere since most of the agency had taken the week off. That was just what Harland needed – space to himself and the certainty that no one would be listening to his calls.

He took out some notes he'd made the night before. The first name on it was Sara Hezemanns', Griswald's assistant in The Hague. He dialled her direct line and got through straight away.

'Are you alone?' he asked her.

'Yes, there are many people on holidays,' she said. 'Why did you not call before? I waited two evenings last week.' She sounded put out and slightly disappointed, which Harland took as a good sign because it meant she wanted to talk.

'I'm sorry, I was never near a phone at the right moment. But, believe me, I really do need to speak to you about Alan's last investigation.' He paused to read his notes. 'Tell me – did we discuss Luc Bézier?'

'We touched on him.'

'I have since read all the papers you sent to Mr Griswald. It's obvious that the man mentioned as being present in Bosnia in July 1995 was the subject of Alan's interest. He is not identified in any of the witness statements but I assume he is the individual that Bézier's group had been sent to Serbia to kidnap. That means he was under an indictment from the War Crimes Tribunal. Is that right?'

'Yes.'

'I understand from Colonel Bertrand Bézier, that's Luc Bézier's father, who I visited in France last week, that his name was Lipnik. I don't have a first name.'

'His name is Viktor Lipnik and, yes, it is true that he was the subject of a secret indictment. We believed it would be better if he did not know he was being investigated.'

'But he did know about the indictment.'

'Probably.'

'And that was all that was dropped when he was reported to have been killed. You see, Luc Bézier was the witness to the shooting at the hotel. I assume the report was filed to SFOR – that's the NATO commanders in

Bosnia – that he'd seen Lipnik killed. I also assume there was no further investigation.' He stopped and briefly imagined Sara Hezemanns – an earnest, bespectacled blonde with an unswerving sense of mission. 'Look, Sara – can I call you that?'

'Of course.'

'Sara, I must tell you that I do have authority to pursue this matter on behalf of the UN. But I should also warn you that you may feel that my questions compromise your loyalties. If that is the case, just say you can't answer. Please don't hide things from me.'

'Go ahead,' she said.

'I suspect that Alan Griswald was working towards a second indictment of Viktor Lipnik, but that he was coming up against some resistance. People were either too sceptical about him still being alive or were motivated to obstruct Alan. If I read his actions right, he was gathering conclusive evidence that Lipnik was still alive, proof that no one could rebut?'

'Rebut?'

'Proof that no one could reject.'

'Oh, he had this proof,' she said. 'He was taking it to Washington and New York to show people. Luc Bézier was his proof. Monsieur Bézier saw Lipnik in Vienna.'

'Yes, I know, but what was the other proof?'

'This is difficult.'

'Why?'

'Because I'm not sure ... At first everything was fine and Mr Griswald was given permission to find out what he could about Lipnik. Then he was told there were diplomatic interests involved.' She gave the phrase an ironic edge. 'He knew what that meant. This came from high up. Mr Griswald believed it originated in NATO headquarters or the UN – maybe his own country. He wasn't sure. He was very upset because he knew for sure that Viktor Lipnik had taken another identity and that he was a killer.'

'What was the proof?'

'I don't know. It came to him a few weeks ago. Maybe by e-mail. I am not sure. But not to his office here.'

'So it might have been sent to his laptop?'

'I think so.'

'You don't know what it contained?'

'No. Mr Griswald called them two halves of a dollar bill.'

'What did he mean by that?'

'At first I did not understand, but when I thought about it, I realised that the first piece of information was worthless without the second. Like two halves of a dollar. Only when you have the second half can you stick it together and spend it.'

'And these came at different times and Alan stuck them together?'

'I don't know.' She paused. 'I think Mr Griswald gave something to get the second. He talked about it vaguely with me. The morality of it. He hinted things. He said there was a higher purpose, though he had misgivings about what he was doing. There was a negotiation and he decided to give the source what he wanted. After that he got the second piece of information.'

Harland digested this. 'And they were in code, these e-mails?'

'How did you know?'

'It's difficult to explain. Not everything was destroyed in the crash.'

'But I think you are making a mistake, Mr Harland. I believe there was one e-mail only. He received the second piece of information personally. You see, he went on a trip to the East three weeks ago. No one knew where he was. He did not tell me. He did not claim for the expenses. He said nothing about it.'

All along Harland was thinking about the mini-disc. He was certain it contained the proof that Griswald was planning to show to Jaidi because he must have had everything he needed with him on the plane. Also he remembered Griswald tapping his pocket and saying how he would tell Harland one day because it would be particularly interesting to him.

Then something else occurred to him. Griswald and Bézier had spent two nights in Washington. That could mean that they were seeing someone else with the evidence. Washington was close to the CIA at Langley, Virginia, and also the National Security Agency's base at Fort Meade in Maryland. He might have been visiting either, perhaps gathering some confirmation for his material. He asked Sara Hezemanns what she thought.

'That's simple. He was seeing Professor Norman Reeve of the War and Peace Studies Forum. He used to work there, I believe.'

'But he wasn't just paying a courtesy visit?'

'No, he went to get some photographs that Professor Reeve had acquired.'

'Of what?'

'They were aerial photographs of a place in Bosnia. That's all I know. There were many taken during the civil war and also during the Kosovo war.'

'What did they show?'

'I cannot tell you. Mr Griswald was hoping to find something. But he did not explain this to me.' Harland made a note to find Reeve's number.

'You implied that there had been some discussion about Alan's death on the aeroplane. What were people saying?'

'There was nothing definite. When he died, some of his work was given to other people, although most of it only he could do.'

'Did they believe the plane had been sabotaged because it was carrying Griswald and Bézier?'

'Some people speculated. But no one knew about Bézier.'

'They knew about the other stuff, though – this proof he was carrying?'

'Yes, people did understand that he had something important.'

'Has the case been given to anyone else to follow up?'

'No, the case was never reopened. So as far as we are concerned it was simply a private theory of Mr Griswald's.'

He said goodbye to Sara Hezemanns, promising to let her know what he found out. Then he sat pondering Griswald's negotiation for the second piece of information. He knew that Griswald had given something of great value to his source, something, perhaps, that he had learned in the past with the CIA. Griswald wasn't in the habit of sharing his thoughts with those around him. For him to have talked to Sara must have meant that he was troubled by what he was doing. Was that why Vigo was so intensely interested in Griswald's activities? Did that explain Guy Cushing bumping into them in The Hague?

He looked at the desk clock and decided to call Sally Griswald even though it was only 7.30 a.m. on the East Coast.

She picked up immediately.

'Can you talk?' asked Harland, hoping she would recognise his voice.

'Yes,' she said straight away. 'I just wondered last week whether we had a problem. Perhaps it's best to be on the safe side.'

'Yes, concerning that material, it is.' He paused. 'Sally, do you remember a one-legged man on the circuit in Germany and Austria? He wasn't on our side of the business. The commercial end of things. Al made up a song about him. If you do remember his name, don't say it.'

Sally Griswald laughed. 'Yes, I believe I do recall the name.'

'Good, I've set up a hotmail address in his name. Could you have the material sent to that address in the next hour?'

'I'll get it done straight away.'

'There's one other thing. Is it possible that Al was seeing his old employer in DC? Not the CIA, but a later employer?'

'Yes, they were big buddies. Al respected him and often asked for his advice. Do you have his name?'

'Yes,' said Harland. 'Can I get his number from information?'

'Shouldn't be a problem, but let me know if you can't. He's worth talking to. I should have thought of that before.'

'I'll call him today,' he said, then hung up.

For the next hour or so he checked the in-box of the hotmail account he had set up in the name of Tony Widdershins. Eventually a message arrived with two very large attachments. The message from Eric Griswald explained that he and a friend had had a stab at decoding the pulse, but it hadn't yielded to the various algorithms that they had applied. The two attachments consisted of the original sound and a diagram, which Eric pointed out showed the patterns involved. Harland copied the two attachments.

Then he called Norman Reeve in Washington and, after listening to a detailed message about his movements, eventually located him in Florida.

As Reeve talked, Harland vaguely remembered reading something about him in one of the foreign affairs journals – an Austrian Jew with an anglicised name who'd survived the camps and had set up the War and Peace Studies Forum in the sixties. Reeve was cautious. There were no pictures, he said. He had not seen Griswald for over eighteen months.

'What did you think about the plane crash?' asked Harland. 'Weren't you in any way suspicious, knowing what Alan was investigating?'

'There is always conjecture with these things,' said Reeve. 'What I deal with is facts, Mr Harland.'

'If I was to provide you with some facts, would you help me?'

'That would assume that I was in a position to help. But I'm not in a position to help, whatever you tell me.'

'Can I put it this way, sir,' said Harland. 'If you knew of a Nazi war criminal who'd got himself another identity and escaped justice, wouldn't you feel that it was your duty to expose the man?'

Reeve snapped back at him. 'Don't you lecture me about the Holocaust, Mr Harland.'

'All I am saying is that Alan Griswald's final investigation was exactly that. He was trying to expose someone who faked his own death and escaped prosecution for terrible crimes.'

'You are obviously very inexperienced in these matters, Mr Harland. I accept that your motives may be honourable. But you just cannot telephone in the middle of my vacation and expect me to help when I have never heard of you and have no knowledge of your credentials.'

'What should I do to prove myself?'

'Again, this supposes that I have something to offer.'

'Yes, but the plane may have been sabotaged. I was on that plane, Professor Reeve, and I survived. Alan Griswald was a good friend of mine and I want to make sure his work does not go to waste. So I'm asking you again about those pictures. I gather they were aerial photographs taken in 1995, either by satellite or U2 spy plane. Alan believed they would establish some part of his argument.'

There was silence at the other end. 'You say you were on the plane with Mr Griswald?'

'Yes, and Luc Bézier and a number of other innocent people who were killed. This is to say nothing of the people on the other jet or the four people who were shot in London last week – two of them are dead. It's just possible that the man that Griswald was investigating is responsible for these deaths and shootings.' Harland knew he was on thin ice but it seemed to give Reeve some pause.

The professor sighed. Harland fancied he could hear him sit down and shift the telephone. He began speaking.

'Of course, there were many pictures taken by the US military during the Bosnian war and, no doubt, by other agencies too. A few have already been used to establish that major crimes did take place. They pinpointed the location of the crimes, of course, not the individuals involved, although this could be inferred by other knowledge.'

'Telephone intercepts, wireless traffic.'

'Yes, and eye-witness accounts that tally with the events picked up from the air.'

'So they can conclusively prove something happened on a particular date?'

'No, they prove that there was military activity in the area of a crime and that maybe some earth-moving took place contemporaneously. But they do not prove a crime.'

Harland thought for a moment and then had an inspiration.

'Is it possible that Griswald was investigating a crime which has so far gone undetected or ignored?'

'You would have to ask the War Crimes Tribunal about that,' said Reeve, returning to a defensive note.

'They won't tell me. Griswald's casebook has all but been abandoned. I understand that they viewed his latest investigation with scepticism, or that it may have been obstructed in some way. These are the things that Benjamin Jaidi has asked me to investigate and that's why I'm asking for your help. I'm sorry, perhaps I should have mentioned that before now.'

From the murmurs and exhalations at the other end of the line, Harland could tell that he had piqued his interest. Then the professor said abruptly, 'You say the Secretary-General has asked you to look into this. What precisely? The crash? Mr Griswald's investigation? The War Crimes Tribunal's behaviour? Which?'

'All those things and one or two other matters also. There's another aspect to this that I don't understand. Viktor Lipnik – if he exists – receives some special protection.'

'A veritable one-man crime commission, Mr Harland. I hope you're up to it.'

'So do I. Tell me what you need from me.'

'A date and a target area and I'll see if we can help.'

'But surely you know the date? Griswald would have told you.'

'He did tell me. But I never saw Mr Griswald before he went to New York. We had an appointment and I know he waited in Washington, but I was too ill. I'm down here recovering from pneumonia.' He paused and wheezed a cough as if to underline this. 'A date, Mr Harland. Give me a date and we'll do business.' With that the line went dead. The old buzzard was testing him. He wondered if Sally could bring any influence to bear. Maybe even Jaidi could phone him.

His eyes moved down the list and settled on Frank Ollins's name. But this set off an alarm at the back of his mind. He had increasingly begun to think that the protection that Viktor Lipnik received must have been provided by the Americans. Maybe the British were also involved. That would account for Vigo's manoeuvrings. Added to this was the probability that Tomas had been tracked by some exceptionally sophisticated equipment which only the major powers possessed. Britain and America were the big listeners and, of course, the Americans would have been the people tracking Lipnik's phone in Serbia before he was 'assassinated'. To talk to a member of the FBI in these circumstances required lunatic trust and cunning.

He dialled the mobile number and caught Frank Ollins in his car on the way to work. He sounded chipper and rested.

'I was just wondering how things were progressing,' said Harland.

'They're doing fine, thank you.' From the tone it was also clear that Ollins wasn't going to volunteer anything.

'I wondered,' said Harland nonchalantly, 'what you meant by those questions last week? This business of how Alan Griswald held his computer just before we landed. What did you mean by that? What relevance does it have?'

'Look, I have a feeling that you haven't played straight with me, Harland.'

'Oh, why?'

'The more I thought about the people who attacked you in the UN building, the more I got to thinking that you had something that they wanted. I guess they probably took it from you too. Is that correct?'

'The answer to that depends on your position, Ollins. We don't know each other well. This affair gets more complicated by the minute and, frankly, I can't afford to talk to someone who is going to share what I have with too many people.'

'So you didn't lose everything that night in the UN?' Harland said nothing. 'Okay, so are you suggesting a trade?'

'That depends on what you have and what your position is.'

'My position is this: we're certain your plane was brought down, but as yet the Safety Board are out of the loop and it has not been disclosed to the public because it has terrifying implications. So, I want to find the people who did this. We are working on the same side.'

Harland decided to make the leap. 'Well, inadvertently I didn't tell you everything I knew.'

'Ah,' said Ollins. 'Would you mind waiting while I stop the car? I don't want to miss this.' There was a pause. 'Okay, what did you *inadvertently* forget to tell me?'

Harland explained about the wallet and how he had discovered after leaving the hospital that it contained a music disc encoded with some kind of message between the tracks of the music.

'That's certainly interesting, and since we are working on the same side, I'll tell you something that you'll keep under your hat. We found the phone that you took from Griswald's pocket and we got to reviving those little circuit boards in the phone, which incidentally is a WAP, and you know what we found? We found a stored e-mail message of precisely one hundred and eighty digits in length. That also is encrypted.'

'Then we may have two halves of a dollar bill,' said Harland. 'I've learned that Griswald's investigation received two separate messages which only work together. I happen to have the bigger half but it's worthless without yours.'

'So we're going to make a trade, aren't we? What do you say we send these two pieces of information by e-mail to each other at nine o'clock my time – two yours?'

Harland said that seemed fine. He gave the Widdershins address and wrote down Ollins's.

Then something occurred to Ollins. 'What happens if you decode this material before I do? You're going to send it to me, right?'

'If that's a reciprocal arrangement, yes.'

Ollins agreed, but Harland wasn't ready to hang up quite yet. 'What about those questions you were asking me? What did you mean? Obviously they had something to do with the phone because you asked whether it had been shielded by the computer.'

'Now, that one isn't for free.'

'But you think that this is part of the solution as to how the plane went haywire in the last seconds of the flight?'

'It's not the cause, it's a symptom. And that's all I am prepared to say. Be seeing you.'

Ten minutes later the strand of code arrived. Harland had not the first idea what to do with it and felt rather deflated. The three calls he'd made that morning had each brought him hard intelligence, but not understanding. Codes were all very well, but his interest and faith in that side of intelligence work had always been slight. They distracted from the human issues of motive and betrayal. But he did have Griswald's secret and he had to find a way of decrypting it. His only idea was to see if The Bird knew anyone who could tackle it.

In the next hour Harland made a few more calls, the first to Philip Smith-Canon, Tomas's neurologist, whom he arranged to meet later in the afternoon. Then he put in a call to the Secretary-General's office and left a message requesting that someone, preferably Jaidi himself, prevail on Reeve to help him. Lastly he got hold of The Bird, who had been riding out on The Ridgeway.

Cuth listened with undimmed enthusiasm, but said the only hope of their being able to meet in the next twenty-four hours was if Harland was prepared to travel to Cheltenham for the New Year's Eve race meeting the next day. Cuth had a part share in a horse which stood a better than average chance in the 2.35. Macy was in the syndicate and would be there also. They would look in at the Arkle Bar in the members' enclosure periodically throughout the afternoon. Harland explained a few of the things he wanted to talk about in an oblique fashion and mentioned that he wanted something decrypted. Cuth told him to bring all the material. Then he inquired as to what sort of company he'd been keeping over the last few days. Harland understood that he was asking whether he was being watched. He replied that he had seen quite a few old friends since arriving in London.

'I see,' said The Bird. 'Well, let's keep this to ourselves. A private drink at the races, eh?' Harland smiled. It would be good to see both of them again.

The Neurological Unit to which Tomas had been transferred was contained in an unpromising red-brick hospital in Bloomsbury. Harland arrived there as it was getting dark. The lights shone out on a deserted pavement; there was very little sign of activity. A building in a coma, thought Harland.

He knew perfectly well that he should have summoned the energy over the weekend to visit Tomas, but the analogy with his own terror of imprisonment and pain was too close for him.

Dr Smith-Canon appeared soon after Harland announced himself at the reception and insisted they go straight away to Tomas's room. He said progress was good, considering the severity of his injuries, but Harland should prepare himself to see Tomas – it was an unsettling sight at first.

He was led into a soft-lit room. A nurse rose from a chair, clutching a magazine to her breast. She looked from Smith-Canon to Tomas and back again and said there had been no change in his condition. The doctor nodded and, sensing Harland's hesitation, guided him by the elbow to the side of the bed.

Tomas's upper body was raised at an angle of thirty degrees. His head was encased in a helm of bandages and elsewhere there were pads and dressings which marked the places where the bullets had entered. A tracheotomy collar had been fitted to his neck to allow him to breathe. Tubes ran to his nose and mouth and from under the covers to his stomach. The machines beside and behind the head of the bed hissed and sucked and occasionally gasped in a rhythm of their own.

Smith-Canon said Tomas needed constant attention at this stage. For instance, it was necessary to prevent the tracheotomy tube from becoming blocked by mucus. But Harland's attention was distracted by the air in the room which was warm and moist and overlaid by a brisk, medical odour.

Smith-Canon took hold of Tomas's right hand and felt the pulse. Then he bent over his face and shone a torch into an eye which he held open by pulling the eyelid upwards with his fingertips. Harland saw the light glance through a very small, expressionless pupil. The doctor let the eyelid drop and turned to Harland.

'I'm afraid there's no sign of consciousness but that can be deceptive: often a patient will creep towards consciousness and although he appears to be dead to the world he can be fully aware of his surroundings.'

He talked Harland through the equipment around Tomas's bed, explaining that he would have the tracheotomy for many months yet, probably for all his life. For the moment he was being fed by a tube which went straight into his stomach, but this might have to be changed over time because of the risk of the patient aspirating regurgitated food. Arrangements had been made to cope with the bowel and bladder, and these too would need to be reviewed.

Harland looked at his son's face. It wasn't quite vacant. There was definitely a look of his mother, and in the crease of his forehead he read an expression of frozen apprehension. He wondered whether this would be lifelong, but he didn't ask the doctor. He was too overwhelmed by the sense that Tomas, whatever his problems, had been effectively snatched from him just as he had come to accept him as his son.

The doctor looked at Harland sympathetically.

'I know, it's all rather unpleasant. But it's best that you're fully aware of the situation. He's going to need an awful lot of care, and there are many hurdles along the way which I can explain to you in a moment. But first I'd like you to do something for me. I want you to sit and talk to him. I think it would perhaps be best if you did this alone.'

He nodded to the nurse with a smile. When she had left, he said, 'I believe it's time we started using his real name. Of course I shall maintain his file and records in the name of Lars Edberg, but if we continue to address him as Lars, he may simply fail to recognise it. On the other hand, his real name is bound to mean something to him. The same may apply to use of the English language. I don't know how well he spoke English, but even if he was a fluent speaker, I believe his birth language would be better. His mother – have you had any luck tracing her?'

Harland shook his head.

'Well, it's imperative that she's found. When he comes round, his understanding will be not impaired, but he won't be able to communicate the slightest wish. It's an extremely frightening experience and can rapidly lead to depression. This is often expressed by the patients locking themselves in further by refusing to attempt to communicate – it's the only thing they can control. But there are several ways for him to communicate – for instance the use of an eyelid, or the vertical movement of a pupil. Locked-in patients can also be trained to alter the activity in their brain so that they can move a cursor on a computer screen.' He paused and glanced at Tomas. 'But this is all a little way down the road yet. The main aim now is to get him awake. So would you sit here for a few moments and talk about things that would mean something to him?'

Harland was aware that the very last thing he wanted was to be left alone with Tomas's lifeless form. In some way he was repelled by what he saw and that filled him with guilt.

'I know it will be awkward at first,' said Smith-Canon. 'But open your heart to him. Talk about things that mean a lot to you. The nurse will be just outside if you need assistance and when you've finished she'll know where to find you. Then we'll have a chat.' He smiled and departed.

Harland moved to the chair at the head of the bed and sat for a few moments, wondering how the hell to start. He cursed himself that he had asked Tomas so very little about his life.

'Tomas? I hope you can hear me. The doctor says that you may be able to even though you're in a very deep sleep.' He stopped, leaned forward to the boy's head and fought the fleeting fear of intimacy. His mind went back to the villa in Prague. How odd it was that now he spoke quietly into a person's ear, a person who could not interrupt, object or walk away. 'It's difficult for me to know what to say because I realise I was far too wary when we met for the first time. I asked you nothing about yourself ... nothing about you ... and so I don't know much about your life. If you can hear this, I'd like you to know how much I regret my attitude. I also want you to understand that I accept you as my son.' He faltered for a moment. His eyes came to rest on Tomas's hands. The fingers were long and delicate, almost like a woman's. He was shocked that he had not noticed them before.

He started again. 'Perhaps you'd like to hear how I met your mother. I know her as Eva, but she has a real name, which you know and I don't. I was a young man – younger than you are now – and on my first posting abroad. It was actually more of a training session with a little work thrown in. It wasn't difficult and I had a lot of time to get to know Rome and make friends. You know how we met because you told me about it. Your mother has remembered it more or less right. We were in a restaurant and I sat next to her and by the end of the evening I was lost to her. It's impossible to talk about these things without sounding like an idiot. But I was smitten. From then on we spent a lot of time together, but because we were both working in intelligence we had to keep our relationship secret. In the end we found it was easier to leave Rome at the weekends. We stayed in some pretty run-down places. One time we went to Ancona, a resort on the Adriatic, for a couple of days. That was a happy time. We could just see the Dalmatian coast from our bedroom window. The Romans used to call it Illyria. We promised each other that one day we'd go there together. Some promise. I suppose we both knew neither of us would be able to keep it.' He paused. 'God, I wish I was better at this. I feel I'm failing you again. Perhaps the doctor is right that you would respond better to Czech. That's why I'm going to try to trace your mother and bring her here. That's what I'm going to be doing over the next few days so I won't be able to come and see you. But when I get back I will come and we can work out a lot of things.'

At that moment Tomas's head jerked backwards, and his entire body seemed to be racked by an electric current. His arms flew into the air, his fingers splayed in fright. One leg kicked out, the other folded towards his stomach. Harland watched horrified as the muscles and veins just beneath the tracheotomy collar bulged and Tomas's face went puce. Then all four extremities began a slow rhythmic motion. Harland leapt up, tipping the chair over, and called out.

'He's waking. He's moving. He's coming to.' Before the words were out the nurse was through the door and pushing him aside. She snatched a syringe on a tray nearby, held it up to the light then injected Tomas in the buttock. The movement in the legs and arms began to subside and his head slipped back to the pillow.

'Why aren't his eyes open?' asked Harland. He turned and saw Smith-Canon.

'That was an involuntary spasm,' he said quietly. 'He'll be all right in a few moments. It's one of the problems with locked-in syndrome, though it usually occurs when the patient is conscious. I think we ought to leave Nurse Roberts here to deal with this. Everything will be fine in a few minutes.'

They went to Smith-Canon's room and sat on a small sofa. Harland felt exhausted.

'This kind of episode can be avoided once we get used to the patient,' said Smith-Canon. 'In each case we have to learn about the kind of things which set off a spasm. Sometimes it's associated with breathing difficulties or the use of a tracheotomy, other times with problems in the bowel.' He sensed Harland didn't want to hear. 'Okay, I can see you've had enough for one day.'

'Yes,' said Harland absently.

'Look, I'm not quite sure how to put this. But I had a visit over the weekend from a man called Walter Vigo. I must say I didn't much take to him.'

'Yes, I know him. What did he want?'

'It wasn't easy to say. He was rather an oblique fellow, if you know what I mean. He wouldn't tell me what he did precisely, but he did stress that he was dealing with an urgent matter of national security. He was interested in Tomas's identity and wondered if I had any clue about it. He asked if I had been contacted by any relations. And he was particularly interested in his condition – whether he was likely to die and what the future held if he lived.'

'What did you say?'

'I told him that it was confidential information and that it was none of his business. However, I thought you ought to know. Clearly it has some bearing on the things you were telling me the other day. I think he thought that Tomas was going to be out of action and that he was no longer of much concern to him.'

'Thanks for that. Walter Vigo is a senior member of MI6. I'm not sure where they stand on all this. But you're right, his interest does have a bearing on what we were talking about.'

'Yes, I thought as much. Look, there's one other thing.' He opened the drawer of his desk. 'Bearing in mind your caution about revealing your son's identity, I decided not to hand this in to the police.' He placed a light Terylene wallet on the table. 'This was in your son's jacket. Actually, I believe it was in the lining. At any rate they missed it. I think it contains a lot that will help you.'

Harland opened it and found a smaller leather card-holder which held Eva's three identity cards and a couple of credit cards in the name of Edberg. There was some money – ten fifty-pound notes and a couple of hundred-dollar bills. 'Thank you. I can't hide the fact that I'm extremely relieved that you didn't give these to Vigo or the police. It might have proved very difficult for me to trace his mother without them.'

'Yes, I could see that. But you are, after all, his next of kin and I couldn't imagine that the police would have a better use for it.'

Harland rose to leave.

'I hope you find her, Mr Harland. It's very important for the boy.'

'I will. And thanks again.'

16

A Day at the Races

Harland caught the 10.30 Race Special from Paddington and arrived in time for the first race. But he did not see any sign of Macy Harp or The Bird until the middle of the afternoon. He hung about, watching the crowd – an untroubled mix of gentry, spivs and local farmers.

Before the 2.35 race he made his way through a wide tunnel which ran under the stands towards the paddock in the hope of spotting them. He felt a tug at his arm. It was Macy Harp who had darted from a doorway in the tunnel. 'This way,' he said with a conspiratorial smile. 'The Bird's got a private box. None of yer hoi polloi for Cuthbert Avocet these days.'

Macy hadn't changed a bit – a roguish red face, dancing eyes and quick, furtive manner.

They found The Bird positioned at the front of the box with his binoculars trained on the crowd below. Without removing them, he flapped a hand in Harland's direction and said, 'Bobby, grab yourself a drink. I recommend a whisky mac on a day like this.'

After a few moments he swivelled round and stood up. 'Good grief, Bobby, you look dreadful. Is that what aid work does for a man?'

'And a few other things too,' said Harland.

'So I gather. There's a good view from up here. We've been watching you plod hither and thither. We felt we ought to make sure that you hadn't been followed here. There're one or two suspicious characters down there but I think your coat tails are clean.'

'They should be, after the palaver I went through leaving my sister's house in London.'

'Good,' said The Bird, with an encouraging smile. 'And I know you too well to ask whether you called from a safe phone yesterday.'

Macy planted a drink in one of Harland's hands and a large chunk of fruitcake in the other. 'Get that down you, laddie. It's Veronica Harp's renowned Christmas cake.'

They both picked up their binoculars and turned to the racecourse. 'Ours is the blue and maroon colours,' said Cuth. 'Maltese cross on a blue background. Can't miss her. She's a gorgeous animal but doesn't usually pull her finger out in the cold.'

Harland tried to show an interest in the fortunes of Manse Lady but was distracted by the realisation that both The Bird and Macy were extremely well turned out – tailored tweed suits, and, in Macy's case, a coat with chocolate brown velvet collar and expensive brogues polished to a military shine. Harland hadn't heard much of them in the last ten years but he knew that they'd extended their freelance interests in Eastern Europe into a number of enterprises that made use of their contacts behind the old Iron Curtain. They'd been into caviar, lumber, truck parts, aluminium, engineering tools – the lot.

The field laboured home with Manse Lady struggling up the hill to take third place. The Bird and Macy shouted a great deal, but to no effect.

'Damned jockey,' said The Bird. 'Thinks we're paying him to go on a nature ramble.'

Macy snapped his binocular case shut.

They had another drink and Harland began to feel the warmth of the whisky mac in his feet.

'You two seemed to have done well for yourselves,' he said. 'Business is good, I gather.'

'Can't complain,' said Macy, stroking a patch of blond stubble on his chin. 'Can we?'

'As you know, Bobby,' Cuth added, 'nature always smiled on us, now fate has joined her.'

They looked and spoke like a pair of amateurs, thought Harland, yet in their field they were unmatched. They were both in shape and The Bird in particular would still present a formidable challenge to anyone unwise enough to take him on.

'So, we hear you've been having quite a time of it,' said Macy. 'What's up?'

'Where do you want me to start?'

'Well, let's get something sorted out first,' said The Bird. 'You said you would bring something for us – some encrypted material. We have a friend on the course who might care to take a look at it now.'

'Really! How on earth did you fix that up?'

'We didn't. He's always here. Horse fanatic. Works at GCHQ and sometimes moonlights by operating the photo-finish camera. Good sort – listens to telephone conversations for a living and can decipher practically anything – except, of course, a racecard. But steady as a brass bedstead otherwise. Won't talk.'

'So where do I find him?'

'You don't. Macy will take it to him now. I told him that he was likely to need a computer. Is that right?'

Harland handed Macy the two discs, one containing the material from Ollins, the other from Sally Griswald's e-mail. He explained they were a pair and that they only worked in tandem.

'Now,' said The Bird, 'tell me what's been going on. I know that you've been shot at and that you've been in an air crash and I gather you were jumped by some heathens in the UN building. What else?'

'You're well informed. How did you know about the UN thing?'

'Word gets about. Look, why don't you tell me the whole bloody lot? The rest of the card's not up to much so we've got plenty of time.'

As Harland spoke, Cuth listened closely, his resourceful eyes darting from Harland's face to a hamper where he picked at the fruitcake. When Harland showed him Eva's identity cards he held each one up to the light, sniffed it and flexed it. Then he handed them back and returned to his chair to rock on the back two legs, his hands clasped round the back of his head. Harland talked for half an hour. He brought the story to a close with a description of Tomas's condition, and explained that he urgently needed to find Eva.

The Bird lifted a slender cigarette case from an inside pocket.

'Hell, Bobby, you're a dark horse. I knew you had some Czech connections, but I didn't realise you had a bloody family there.' He laughed, then his face grew serious. 'Vigo's interest puzzles me. I can't believe he's really concerned about you boffing some Czech teenager back in the Dark Ages. Did you give the Czechs anything?'

'Nothing of value. The odd bit that I knew they already had. I worked it to our advantage – you know how it was.'

'Yes, but you weren't always so canny. They turned the tables on you in 1990 and went at you hammer and tongs, didn't they, old boy? You looked a terrible mess, I can tell you. And that meant someone was pretty upset with you. What did you do to them?'

'I made the point to Vigo's friends from the Security Service, who are meant to be investigating me. They were hardly likely to beat up a major communist intelligence asset.'

'Yes,' Cuth persisted, 'but you didn't quite answer my question about what you might have done to them. I mean, the Czechs weren't into that kind of thing. They slung people into prison and roughed them up a little, sure – but torture wasn't their style.'

'I have no sense of having done anything to them. I imagined they were going to ransom me, then they started interrogating me about something I couldn't have known.' He paused, aware of The Bird's gaze. 'The Russians were capable of this thing. The man in the villa was Russian.'

'And, of course, you just mentioned that the fellow who was present at the massacres in Bosnia was also Russian. Are we talking about the same man?'

'Obviously I considered that because Griswald said I'd be particularly interested when he nailed this fellow Lipnik.'

'But still, it doesn't explain the motive, does it? I mean the savagery of it.' He rubbed his thighs vigorously and poured them each another glass of whisky mac. 'I wish Macy were here. He's good at this sort of thing. But anyway, let's just talk about Griswald for a moment. So, Griswald fixes up this business in Berlin which eventually results in the KGB selling the East Germans' archives to the Americans. Then you two go off to Prague with the idea of snaffling the Czech files too. You blow into town. You find the place is seething with revolutionary fervour and commence negotiations. Is that about right?'

Harland nodded.

'How much money did you take?'

'Fifty thousand dollars as a down payment. Half supplied by the Americans and half by us.'

'And who were your contacts in Prague?'

'They were Griswald's. I didn't want to use the man I had dealt with over the years. Too untrustworthy, too low down the pecking order.'

'And you didn't see this Eva woman?'

'No, not since '75.'

'So what happened?'

'Al went off to meet his contact and the next thing I know the place we were staying at was raided and I was under arrest. I spent the first night in StB headquarters, where they didn't seem to know what to do with me. Then I was handed over to this other lot. They took me to the villa.'

'Who knew where you were?'

'As far as we knew, not many, apart from our people that end and a few in Century House.'

'And Griswald – what happened to him?'

'He never got close to doing the deal. In fact, they took the money and left him high and dry. The Americans were pretty good about it, but Century House were not so understanding. Still, they did pay for you two to get me out.'

The Bird smiled. 'I think the terms of our agreement with Alan Griswald permit me to say categorically that Century House did not commission us. Now that he's dead, I can tell you that Griswald paid for the operation. There were a lot of expenses but we returned some of the money to him – having taken our standard fee, of course. I expect you can guess what he did with the rest of the money.'

Harland thought for a moment. 'I should have thought of it before. He used it to buy the StB file on me.'

'He certainly was a friend to you, Bobby, which makes his death all the more sad. Let's think about those files for a second. If Vigo's little helpers can ferret round those archives, there's no earthly reason why you shouldn't. That's surely your best bet, to trace Eva through her various changes of identity. At the same time you might also usefully learn who Vigo's people are.' He stopped and let the chair return to its four legs. 'You know, I think we may be able to swing this for you. But it'll take time.'

The door opened and Macy appeared, followed by a stout woman in a blue housecoat who was holding the nozzle of a vacuum cleaner.

'We maybe ought to make a move in the next ten minutes or so,' he said. 'They want to clean the box.' The woman muttered something and left them.

'I have just been hearing about Bobby's troubles. They'll make what little hair you've got stand on end. By the way, what's our Nissen hut genius have to say about Bobby's codes?'

'He's rather agitated – to put it mildly.'

'Couldn't he do anything with them?'

'No, there was no difficulty. What's bothering him is the type of code used. He wouldn't say more than that. Apparently it's the same encryption used to leak damaging information about agency operations in Europe. Everyone – the British, Americans, Germans, French and even the saintly Dutch – is affected. He wants to know where it came from. Apparently it's a priority of GCHQ at the moment to find the source of this stuff.'

'What's the code say?'

'Nothing.'

'What do you mean, nothing?'

'It's a photograph – a video still. A man in a uniform on the side of a mountain.'

The Bird's gaze flicked to Harland. 'Friend Lipnik, I imagine. But I bet it's more than just a bloody holiday snap. Griswald wouldn't have taken the trouble to have kept the codes separate otherwise. Can we see it?'

'No. As I say, he's agitated. He suggested we meet at a pub about fifteen miles away just off the Oxford road – the Queen's Head. Says he'll see all three of us there in an hour.'

'He wants to see Bobby?'

'It seems so.'

As they left, The Bird muttered, 'Puts the bloody air crash into a new light, doesn't it?'

They set off in Cuth's Range Rover. He mentioned that a pub on New Year's Eve didn't seem ideal for a quiet meeting, but when they pulled up at the Queen's Head, an old coaching inn in a lonely spot, high on the Cotswolds, it was obvious from the empty car park that there would be little revelry to contend with.

Macy vanished into the pub to find their man. Harland and The Bird waited in the car, watching the rain turn to sleet until he appeared at the front door and waved them in.

'I've got some drinks coming. Our chap's in the back.'

They found him lodged in a tall wooden settle by the embers of a log fire. Harland had expected a desk man in his mid-fifties, a bureaucrat on the glide path to retirement. But a much younger man turned to greet them with a reluctant smile. He was in his early forties and had an alert, rather academic face. He sat with an anorak still zipped up, legs crossed, swinging one walking shoe towards the fire. On the table was a tin of tobacco and a cigarette rolling machine.

There were no introductions. Macy brought the drinks over.

'I've been telling them you're worried about this material,' said Macy quietly. 'You want to explain the problem?'

'Not really,' said the man disagreeably, beginning to feed tobacco into a cigarette paper. He looked up at Harland. 'Where did you get it from?'

'A friend.'

'And how did this friend come by it?'

'I'm not certain. I think he got it from a friend or two friends. What difference does it make?'

'Your disc contains a family of codes that are associated with one of the biggest intelligence disasters of the post-communist era. That's all.'

Harland remembered Vigo's conversation in New York when he had referred to an unusual source of intelligence that he insisted Griswald had access to. He had laboured the point and then refused to give Harland any detail.

'This is not really concerned with all that,' said Harland. 'I'm more interested in the picture Macy says you've found stored in the code. It may help with an investigation that this friend is no longer able to complete.'

'Believe me, the issue is not your damned photograph. Tell me, what form did the code come to you in?'

'One half came as sound, the other as a one-hundred-and-eighty-digit message.'

'Exactly,' said the man. 'Sound. And that's where your problem is.'

'Come on, loosen up,' said Macy. 'This is a friend of ours. Tell him what he needs to know.'

The man put down his pint glass.

'Look, this is not a question of favours, or what I owe you, or who the fuck your friend is. This is as serious as you can get.' He paused to light the roll-up. 'About ten months ago, maybe longer – no one is sure – our counterparts in Israel noticed that a number of radio and TV stations were subject to sustained bursts of interference. It sounded like the static caused by a prolonged electrical storm, and yet it was clear that this sound wasn't being caused by atmospheric conditions. They investigated and saw they were dealing with a set of elaborate, yet fairly unchallenging, codes. It seemed to be the work of a talented outsider who was getting his kicks from devising a series of puzzles, knowing that the only people who would possibly investigate his sounds would be professional listeners. Some of these codes were pretty ingenious. For instance, one was based on the Periodic Table and used the relationship between the symbols of the elements and the atomic numbers. Another was constructed on the position of the English Premier League on a particular Saturday last October.'

He took a draught of beer.

'The whole thing was seen as a kind of game, this individual bunging his messages into the ether using the unsuspecting services of about thirty different radio stations. Everyone in Europe has probably heard this noise at some stage over the last year, but only a very few were in a position to understand it. No one had any idea where it came from but it was obvious that whoever was doing this had developed a virus to penetrate the phone systems of practically every broadcasting station. There's a lot of insecure equipment in a studio and somehow this joker had worked out a way of getting his hidden messages into the programmes.

'Then just as he'd got everyone's attention the messages became a lot more serious. He started talking about this and that operation – highly embarrassing for those agencies involved. He'd obviously tapped some good sources of information – people in the business who were feeding him. It was clear that a lot of his stuff was coming from renegade intelligence officers who may have used the Net to talk to him. Some of the information looked very much like the material being posted on the Net by known dissenters and troublemakers. He named agents, especially in the economic sector. For instance, a woman in the German finance ministry who was passing information to the French. There was no pattern to the messages in as much as they didn't favour one country over the other, but they did concentrate on corrupt deals, on high-level bribery and that kind of thing.

'Anyway, to cut a long story short, tracking down this individual or individuals became a priority in all the big Western agencies. They wanted to close him down big time. That wish increased when it was revealed in alarming detail how the Americans and British were supposed to be using their resources to gather intelligence on European business competitors. He was particularly accurate about the activities of the NSA at Bad Aibling.'

'Remind me what's there,' said Harland.

'At Bad Aibling the Americans can hear a man's teeth chattering in the Ukraine. It's a listening post, about fifty miles south of Munich, a very big one which employs a fair slice of the eleven thousand US intelligence personnel still in Germany.'

'I see. He's offended everyone – but why?'

'With respect, I don't think you see at all. The discs you brought to me use some of the same codes. They're pretty basic but I'm sure this stuff hasn't been seen before. It's new to me, anyway, which means there's a direct line back through the friend who gave you this material to the individual who's doing this. You may hold a key to the identity of the source and that makes it rather important.'

The Bird looked at Harland. 'That rather puts things in a new light. But perhaps they already know the identity.'

'That's not my area,' said the man. 'All I know is what I hear and what we filter from the air. But I do know there was a brief interruption of these messages about three weeks ago. We wondered if they had been closed down. There were a lot of people whose Christmas would be made if this fellow was deposited in a frozen river. But they started up again about a week later. Every bloody carol concert broadcast in Eastern Europe was interrupted by this interference.'

'Can I look at the picture you've got?'

'There are two. I found the second while waiting for you to arrive. But I'd rather do this somewhere else. I don't want some colleague of mine blundering in here on a New Year's Eve pub crawl.'

They went outside and got into the Range Rover. The man from GCHQ unfolded a slender laptop which had been concealed in his anorak and pressed a key.

'I'll show you the second photograph first.'

A picture of a middle-aged man appeared instantly. He was standing by a wicker table. His jacket was folded on the arm of a chair and there was a swimming pool in the background. On the table was a tray of drinks, a newspaper and some documents. The man was holding some papers and appeared to be speaking. Clearly he wasn't aware of the camera.

Harland craned forward from the back seat to get a better look at the screen. The man was conventionally dressed – a businessman, still wearing a tie at the poolside. He was of average height and build, with a large head that was slightly out of proportion with his body. There was a dip at the front of his trousers to allow for the beginnings of a paunch, but otherwise he looked in reasonable shape. His eyes were in shade and it was difficult to read any expression in them.

Now Harland grasped the significance of the photograph. The folded newspaper might be German, but more important was that the front page would be dated. If this was Lipnik, it would prove he was alive after the supposed assassination. Enlarging the picture might also yield information from the documents – names, dates and the type of business he was engaged in.

494

'I'll give you the discs so you can take a closer look at this later.' The
man clearly wanted to be on his way. 'But I'll show you the other one
quickly.'

The machine hesitated before producing the second image from its
memory. It unfolded from the top of the screen, first with a couple of
inches of clear summer sky that lit up the interior of the Range Rover,
then the top of some distant hills over which were traces of cloud. Then
the whole picture materialised and Harland found himself looking at the
same man, this time in khaki fatigues. He was standing in the foreground
of a group of soldiers. They were gazing down into what appeared to be a
ravine, for at the bottom of the picture was a very dark area, in shadow.
The man was in sunlight, and despite the slightly liquid quality of the
video, it was possible to make out a good deal about him. He wore a
peaked cap and had his thumbs tucked into a canvas belt, from which
hung a holstered pistol. He looked slimmer. Harland thought there were
a few years between the two pictures.

He glanced over the rest of the scene and then his eyes settled on one
of the soldiers. He didn't have time to know whether it was the angle of
the head or the slightly diffident way the soldier stood back from the
others that had attracted his attention. All he knew was that he was
looking at Tomas. Tomas standing on a mountainside in the punishing
summer heat of the Balkans. Tomas with a war criminal. Tomas in the
uniform of a Serb soldier.

Harland began to breathe again and sat back a little. He could still see
the screen through the gap between the front seats.

'Any way of bringing this up a touch?' asked The Bird.

The man muttered something and worked the keyboard for a few
seconds. He turned the screen to face them.

'Yes, I thought so.' The Bird pointed with the nail of his little finger to
the shaded part at the bottom of the picture. 'See here? I think you'll find
those are bodies. You can just see the light on a leg here and over here
there's someone lying on their side. I suppose they may've been chucked
off the top into a pit. Who knows, but I think what we're looking at is the
site of the massacre. Wouldn't you agree, Bobby?'

Harland nodded. 'Yes, I think you're right.'

17
New Year's Eve

At eight-thirty that evening Harland was dropped off at Oxford Station by The Bird and Macy Harp. On the short ride from the pub, The Bird had filled Macy in with an expert summary of Harland's story. For them the story was a matter of professional curiosity – but only that. He imagined them happily chewing it over on the way back to Berkshire where their wives now prepared a New Year's Eve party. He wondered if their horsy neighbours had any idea what The Bird and Macy got up to when not running around the country in well-tailored tweed suits. As they pulled away, The Bird told him they would be in touch as soon as they'd found a reliable guide in the Czech Republic.

The trains were running infrequently, but at length a cross-country service pulled in. Harland boarded an empty first-class carriage and sank back in the seat, now alone with the knowledge of Tomas's presence at the scene of the massacre. Later he would look at the photograph again and enlarge it to see if the Bird had been mistaken about the shapes at the bottom of the picture. Broken branches or boulders in a stream might be the explanation. Whatever he found, he could not ignore the fact that Tomas was in the company of Viktor Lipnik, a suspected war criminal.

Dead tired, Harland tried to frame his thoughts unemotionally. The photograph did at least have the virtue of clarifying things. The process of reconciling two streams of events was over. There was a whole to consider now. And everything, as he had tired of telling people, sprang from Griswald. It was odd. As he learned more and more of Griswald's activities he seemed to lose the ability to bring to mind his face. Alan Griswald had become an abstract component in the mystery. That was all.

The important gain of the day was the information that the Americans and the British were exercised about the release of secrets about their spying activities against European powers. The probability was that Griswald had exchanged these secrets – easily gathered by someone in his position – for evidence that proved that Viktor Lipnik, far from being interred in a Balkan graveyard, was very much alive and prosperously in business. Whatever he hoped about Tomas's presence in the video still, he also knew that it was unlikely that Griswald had taken all that trouble to acquire the picture if it did not prove Viktor Lipnik's involvement in a war crime on a certain date. Christ, yes! There was a date on that video still. Harland had been so absorbed by the image that he had not taken it on board. At least it would prove useful in persuading Professor Reeve to provide the satellite images.

But how far was he prepared to pursue that line? After all, what was the point? Griswald was dead. Tomas lay in hospital unlikely ever to speak or move again. Others had been killed or crippled. Was it time to drop the whole business? For a full minute he thought of throwing the discs from the train window.

It wasn't that simple, though. The discs weren't the cause of the deaths and maimings, and getting rid of them wouldn't quiet Vigo, settle scores with Viktor Lipnik or bring Tomas out of his coma. The pictures existed as an ineluctable fact. He turned and caught sight of his reflection in the train window. A haggard, middle-aged man stared back at him. He thought of his younger self – the first-class degree, the fond expressions of tutors who recognised promise, the absolute confidence, the ease of entry. The memory of himself for some reason brought back the image of Tomas on the mountainside in army fatigues, shrinking from the edge of the gorge – or was it perhaps a hurriedly excavated burial pit? If that image was a record of a massacre it meant that Tomas was a witness and that would certainly explain why he had been tracked down by a team of killers.

'Or would it?' Harland asked aloud to the empty carriage.

Tomas knew that he was alive. He had known that for some time. There were things that came to him from the world outside him – smells, noises and the lights and shadows which passed across his closed eyelids. But the pain inside his head and the clamour of discomfort from distant sites all over his body was too much for him and he had retreated back down the stairway. It was strange how he thought of it as a stairway. He could see it and feel it and as he got closer to the top there were certain things that he noticed about the stairway. The walls were cold to the touch and there was rope fixed to the side which he clung on to for dear life. He was never quite sure how he went back down again, whether he took it carefully, minding not to fall, or whether he just somehow arrived at the bottom where there was no light, no feeling – just dreams. He was content down there, though he only knew this once he had begun the journey up again and realised what he was leaving and what lay at the top. That was why he could never quite bring himself to leave the stairway for good. At the top he knew he would find himself, which was to say his body and his mind would be joined again and become aware of each other. Then Tomas Rath would live and act and do as other people did, but he didn't want that yet.

The clarity of these thoughts surprised him because he had been aware of a certain fogginess of late, quite separate from the pain that periodically surged in his centre and blotted everything out. He was thinking better and he'd quite consciously recognised that once he reached the top there were decisions to be taken. The nature of these evaded him for the moment, but he understood that they were there and that they would crowd in on him very soon.

He heard a woman's voice and he decided he would open his eyes and see who it was. He felt little pain at the moment – a hot, sticky feeling on his back and buttocks, tenderness in his neck and shoulders and a gentle throb in his head. But nothing he couldn't deal with.

He waited as the voice got louder. Someone was talking to him because they were using his name – Tomas. And they were speaking in English. That was inconvenient, but he'd handle it. He began to open his eyes and noticed only one was opening, and that it was pretty much blinded by the light. He blinked a few times so that gradually he became accustomed to the glare. Just then, it struck him that he was having terrible difficulty in breathing. There was a hissing noise in his ear and his heart was pounding as if he had just taken some exercise. The real pain now was in his throat. Not the agony of before, but a raw, scorched dryness like a very bad infection. He also had the sense that something was obstructing his airway. It was thirst. He had never known thirst which hurt. He tried to swallow to get some saliva down there but his throat wouldn't allow it.

He realised that a new note had entered the voice to his left and that the woman was probably speaking to someone else. But he couldn't listen because he was concentrating very hard on trying to move his head. He'd never had to think about how to do this before and now, quite inexplicably, he'd forgotten. But he *did* need to remember because he wanted water and he would have to get up and find that water or at least tell the woman, who was now talking to him in an odd, soothing manner, that he needed water above all else. Above all else, do you hear? He knew he was speaking. He was sure of it, but he could not hear the words. And then he understood that there were so many things in his mouth that he couldn't possibly speak. He would have to take them out in order to speak and to drink the water.

So he told his hand to grapple with the things they had shoved in his mouth and were causing him to experience that raspy, parched feeling at the back of his throat. Which hand he used didn't much matter – either would do. But nothing happened. He wanted to look to see if he still had hands. He thought he could feel them. But when you can't look down and they don't respond to your command, it's not easy to know whether you still have them.

Suddenly his other eye opened, and, although it took some time to get used to the light and he had to blink a bit, he was soon able to look ahead of him. There was a light on the ceiling and at the end of his bed he saw a man and two women. He was in a hospital. He looked down to see where his hands had got to but found that they weren't quite in his field of vision. He would move his head and check on them. That would be simple now he was fully awake. He moved, or rather gave the instruction to move his head but nothing happened. Again he wondered how he'd forgotten something so basic. Maybe they'd given him some drugs to keep him still.

He looked up ahead of him and a thought came to him that a preferable existence was to be had down the stairway, where at least he wouldn't experience this raging thirst and his limbs would move according to his wishes. But the man was saying something to him. He must be a doctor. He spoke very slowly and very insistently, as if he was stupid. Just because he was temporarily unable to move, it didn't mean he was a moron.

'Tomas,' he said, 'Tomas. That's your name, isn't it? We're pleased to have you with us again. You've been unconscious for nearly a week. You've been in a coma.'

'Is he responding?' asked another woman's voice. 'His eyelids may just be fluttering as part of the aftershock.'

'For goodness' sake, Claire,' said the doctor, *sotto voce*. It was impossible to miss the impatience. 'If you haven't got anything better to say, do please shut up.'

Tomas could see the woman. She wore glasses. Straight black hair. Pretty but severe face. Quite sexy. He hoped he wasn't making a fool of himself in front of her. He must look absurd lying there.

'Your head probably hurts a bit,' continued the doctor, 'and that's because we took a bullet out of it on Christmas Day. You probably don't remember much of what happened, but you were shot and the bullet went up through your throat into the bottom of your head. Still, we managed to get it out pretty cleanly and you're healing very well. In fact, you're making excellent progress, Tomas.'

He drew breath heavily and came closer. 'The thing is, Tomas, you're going to feel a bit unwell for some time yet. Part of the effects of an operation like this is to render you paralysed.' He paused to let the words of this sentence sink in. All Tomas knew was that he was translating everything into Czech. The word *parolyzovany* repeated itself in his mind.

'You won't be able to move much for a while. That's a good thing in a way because it gives your injuries a chance to heal, but in other ways it's going to be very inconvenient and frustrating for you. But you can rest assured that we will be working very hard for you, pulling together to make things a bit more comfortable for you.' He paused again and put his face directly in front of Tomas's. It was difficult for Tomas to focus so close because his eyes now seemed to be bobbing up and down. He wanted to move his head back just to get a proper look at the man.

'I believe you're all there, Tomas. That's terribly good news. Really, I couldn't be more pleased. Well done, you.'

Well done, me? thought Tomas. How very English to say that. All I've done is walk up a stairway.

The woman came round to the doctor's side of the bed. Tomas saw a nametag on her breast and he could smell her scent.

'I'm not sure,' said the woman. 'He doesn't look as if he has taken in much of what you've been saying.' She appeared to be a doctor too.

'Oh yes he has,' said the man confidently. 'I know it.' He gave Tomas's hand a tiny squeeze. 'And I know he can feel that too. You're fully aware of what's going on around you, aren't you, old thing?' He paused again. 'So I thought I would tell you a little about what we're going to do. For quite a while we will be feeding you through these tubes here and helping you breathe with this machine which you can probably hear to your left. For that reason we've made a very small hole in the front of your throat to allow the air to pass into your body without something getting in the way. That may feel a bit uncomfortable and a bit strange until you get used to it.'

Now Tomas was registering what he had been saying, not the stuff about tubes, but about guesswork. Did they mean that he wasn't going to be able to communicate the smallest wish to them and that they would therefore have to guess his needs? How would they know that his throat was parched and his arse was sore and his side ached with a mysterious dull pain which reminded him of acute constipation? How could they possibly know these things? And how long would this state of total dependence last? When was he going to get better? He wanted to know the answer to that question most of all. There was an open-ended quality to the doctor's statements that made him uneasy. If he was going to be like this for months, he wished they would tell him.

He tuned again into what the doctor was saying.

'At the moment our first priority is to establish a way that you can use to communicate your needs. We want to be able to ask you questions such as – Would you like a different channel on your TV? And for you to be able to give us the answer yes or no. That can be done with your eyelids, which I'm optimistic that you'll be able to control.

'Now . . . I understand that you are a Czech speaker, but that you also speak English pretty well. Mr Harland, who you know, has told me that he will visit the Czech Republic at the earliest possible opportunity to contact your mother. He will bring her here and you'll be able to hear your native language. Of course, I have every hope that we will be able to work out this code in English. That'll make it much easier for us to get through the next three months or so.'

Three months, thought Tomas. He could just do three months – as long as there was going to be an end and he'd be able to move. Then he thought of his mother. Her lovely, dark, elliptical face came to him. The eyes that smiled and said nothing; the gaiety that defied confrontation; the conversation that left so many infuriating gaps – how would she cope with this? How would he?

His mind clouded with despair. He no longer had a choice in these things: if she came, he couldn't very well walk away.

God, he wished he could remember what had happened. He remembered he had been with Harland and that they were by a river. For some reason he was feeling optimistic. Harland had said something conciliatory to him. He had accepted him. Tomas was aware of his mind stalling in certain areas. Yes, he had been shot. The doctor said so, though he couldn't remember when it had actually happened. Was it after they'd been at the river? He remembered Flick. Flick was dead. He saw her bedroom and her body curled up on the bed. Had he imagined that? No, he hadn't because that's why he'd run and found himself in that little hotel room doing the final work. He noticed that his mind was vibrating so that it was difficult to hold on to a single thought: he would be thinking of Flick then his mother would come to mind; he would remember what Harland had said to him and then a big house full of people would appear.

He stopped scurrying between these images. Someone was laughing. He listened. Incredibly the noise seemed to be coming from his own mouth. The mouth which could not speak or drink or breathe by itself was now laughing. But there was nothing funny: he wasn't responding to a joke made by the doctor and he certainly hadn't been thinking of anything humorous. Yet his belly pulsated, his eyes were closing and the noise struggled past the tubes and hole in his throat to fill the room with a desperate, mirthless gurgle. Suddenly it stopped and Tomas realised – or rather suspected – that his face was frozen in a terrifying rictus because the doctor peered at him and he saw the horror and the pity in his eyes.

The female doctor asked her colleague something quietly. Tomas heard him pooh-pooh her suggestion, then he picked up the phrase 'involuntary motor activity', whose meaning he couldn't quite pin down because he was having trouble with words.

A terrible thought began to creep into his mind, a suggestion that this paralysis was not the side effect of drugs but was a permanent condition. Perhaps he would never again walk over to a basin and get himself a glass of water, never feel the weather on his face, touch a woman's breast, make himself heard, take a piss without someone holding his dick or plugging him with a tube. For some time now he'd been aware of the smell in the room and now he realised that it was his own smell. Would he have to live with that? With the leaking of catheters and bags? With the heat and accumulating sweat of his own body?

Panic flooded his head. He could hear his heart beating very fast and something had happened to his breathing. First there was a total cessation so that he was fighting to get air into his lungs, then he could feel himself take tiny short gasps of air. He heard the doctors say something and the next thing he knew was that he was looking at his arms and legs, which had reared up in front of him and, in the case of his arms, were moving up and down as though he were conducting a very slow piece of music. The cramp at the back of his calves and in the top of his thighs was excruciating. But the one thought at the back of Tomas's mind was that he still possessed movement. This sudden reflex was evidence that he would eventually be able to tell his body what to do.

He felt the jab of the needle in his buttock and then saw his limbs fall back to the bed. The nurse who had administered the injection gave his legs some help by easing them down and placing the cover over them. But he didn't want that. He was too hot and he wanted to tell her to leave him alone and let him make his own decision about the cover.

The shot had an immediate effect. He was calmer and the doctor was talking again, but not to him. He was explaining something to the woman whose scent he longed for. He waited, wondering what would happen next. It occurred to him that he wasn't just a prisoner of his body but that it had declared a kind of independence and it was going to do anything it pleased, except serve its master. Was this the future? He had a superstitious sense that he had been occupied by a being that was going to force him to laugh and cry and gesticulate at inappropriate moments simply for the cruel pleasure of it.

He felt drowsy and began to slip towards sleep, knowing that he would never find himself at the bottom of the stairway again.

Harland arrived at Harriet's house, too weary to care much about who might be watching his movements. Near the end of the train journey from Oxford it had occurred to him that Tomas's presence in one of the pictures had prevented him from seeing them for their true worth. Far from being a kind of curse, they endowed their keeper with a certain power.

He installed himself in Harriet's office at the top of the house and fed the disc into her computer. He looked at the picture of the mountainside first, isolating and enlarging the portion that contained Tomas. There was no doubt about it. Tomas was standing there with an oddly vacant expression, one foot lifting to the right, in the process of turning away. As far as Harland could tell, he was not armed.

He began to trawl the rest of the image for clues and information. He had been right about the date. It appeared over a patch of white rock that made it easy to miss. The events recorded had taken place at 2.15 p.m. on 15.7.95. That was probably all he needed to elicit the satellite pictures from Professor Reeve. He noted down the date and time, momentarily wondering whether the type of rock in the foreground was limestone. That might be a clue to the place. He moved over to the other side of the picture, framed the dark area at the bottom left-hand corner and instructed the computer to fill the screen with it. His first impression was of a detail in one of those mediaeval studies of the Day of Judgement – the souls of the damned cast into hell. There were five or six bodies lying there in the shadows. All of them appeared to be men. A glint of machinery caught his eye also, a crescent of metal, possibly the blade of a piece of earth-moving equipment.

Time and place were obviously important to Griswald's investigation and he realised that the mountains at the top of the screen might establish an approximate position. He flipped back to the whole image. There was a V-shaped nick in the furthest range which consisted of one fairly prominent peak. That might be identified if the direction of the camera was known. Yes, because a clue to this lay in the time that the image was made – a little over two hours past midday. That time seemed to tally with the amount of light in the picture and the shortness of the shadows. More crucial, however, was his observation that the shadows ran away from the lens, which meant that whoever had been filming the scene had his back directly to the sun.

Harland closed his eyes to assemble his little knowledge of using the sun as an aid to orientation. At midday a shadow cast by a vertical object would give a reading for north since the sun was in the south. As the afternoon wore on the shadows would swing to the right and, using the principle of the sundial, it would be possible to gauge the time and also to get a bearing between zero and ninety degrees. The further the sun went west, the more the shadows would veer to the east and a bearing of ninety degrees. He remembered that the season had to be taken into account in such a calculation but since the picture was dated to just over three weeks after the summer solstice of 21 June, he assumed that variation would not be great.

He was unsure of his geometry and decided to make a copy of the picture on Harriet's printer. Then he began to trace a series of lines fanning out from a point in the middle of the bottom of the frame. It was all very hit and miss, but after borrowing a protractor from his nephew's geometry case he estimated that the shadows were pointed at a bearing of between 20 and 25 degrees. That put the V-shaped incision in the range at a bearing of 15 degrees and the large peak at a few degrees east of due north – say 355 degrees. If he could get the profile of the mountain range identified, he'd be able to mark out a rough area where the massacre had taken place. And that process might be refined by estimating the distance between the camera and the mountain range – not, perhaps, a problem for a surveyor – and the safe assumption that this spot was probably close to a road or track because of the inconvenience involved in moving a bulldozer over a lot of rough terrain.

He called up the other picture and squared off sections that he wanted to examine more closely. The screen filled with the still life of the table – a German-language newspaper dated 29 May 1998, the tray of drinks which included a bottle of Pernod, Martini, whisky of an identifiable brand and various mixers. Harland focused on the papers in front of the drinks tray. They were in German and appeared to be some kind of report. The type was too small to read from the screen, but he picked up a couple of signatures at the bottom of one sheet and with greater magnification these could be deciphered.

He went back to the whole frame and tried to see what else might lie there. Way off in the background were two men in dark suits, standing with their hands clasped in front of them in the manner of silent heavies the world over. The landscape was rolling rather than mountainous, and it was possible to make out pastures and clumps of pine trees. It could be anywhere, thought Harland. There was countryside like this all over the Balkans and Central Europe but, given the newspaper, he'd bet on Austria or Germany.

Finally he addressed Viktor Lipnik, enlarging him to fill the whole screen. The three-quarter view gave him much more sense of Lipnik than the profile in the first picture. He had a rather long face with a nose that was slightly hooked at the end, a feature enhanced by the angle of his rather thin nostrils. His hair was straight and dark – perhaps dyed? – and he had a light beard which was only visible above his lip. All things considered it was not an unpleasant face.

Harland stared at the whole picture. He was aware of something speaking to him. It wasn't the sense of Eastern European style in the sheen of his suit, the angle of the shirt collar, the Windsor-knotted tie. Nor was it the suspicion that Viktor Lipnik had invested in cosmetic surgery, evidenced by a vertical scar in front of one of his ears. It was his Rolex watch – exactly the same chunky symbol of wealth that he'd been surprised to see on Tomas's arm in the first picture. He knew that Tomas had not worn it on the occasions that they met.

He printed two fresh copies of the pictures and two sets of the details he had examined, and placed them in envelopes. As he dialled Frank Ollins's mobile number, he let his eyes play over the photograph. As usual Ollins picked up immediately.

'Did you find anything in that material?' asked Harland.

'Not yet.' Ollins was unfazed by Harland's lack of greeting. 'The people who were looking at it haven't come back to me.'

'Which people were dealing with it? You see, some might regard this material as poison and its bearer as a national security risk.'

'Whoever you're talking about isn't going to get his hands on it. This is an FBI investigation into a very serious crime. We won't swerve from the completion of this inquiry, I can promise you that.' Harland was taken aback by this rather formal statement. Perhaps Ollins was speaking for the benefit of others.

'Good,' said Harland, thinking of that audience. 'Of course, anyone interested in suppressing this evidence would need to know that it's possible to place the information on the Web or to give it to newspapers. At this time of year they're always short of news.'

'So what did you find?'

'Two pictures of a man named Lipnik, who was indicted as a war criminal before he was killed off in an elaborately staged assassination. The pictures prove that Lipnik is alive and that he took part in a massacre of some scale. This man was the subject of Griswald's last inquiry and must be regarded as a suspect in the Falcon's crash.'

'What are you going to do with the pictures?'

'Send them to the Secretary-General's office.'

'Not before you give them to me as per our agreement, right?'

This was entirely within Harland's plan, but he wanted Ollins to know that he was doing him a favour.

'Why don't you tell me a bit more about the crash? What did you mean by the questions you asked me?'

'I'm sorry,' said Ollins resolutely. 'I can't say more.'

'Well, tell me whether you'll be keeping the Secretary-General informed on developments.'

There was a pause.

'Yes,' said Ollins. 'Look, to get back to our agreement. We said that whoever decoded the material first would send it to the other. That's what you agreed. Are you welching?'

'No, I'll send it in an attachment this evening using the same procedure as before.' Harland sounded reluctant but he knew that he was only too happy to pass the pictures to the FBI. The pictures represented power, but it was not the kind of power that needed to be hoarded.

They said goodbye, exchanging a sardonic New Year's greeting.

The next call was to Jaidi's office, which was still manned. He told the woman on the other end that he would be sending a two-page memorandum to the Secretary-General and that he would need a fax number or e-mail address that would ensure Jaidi read it the next morning. He stressed the need for utter secrecy and speed. She gave him a fax number in Davos, Switzerland where Jaidi had improbably holed up for a few days with his Swedish-born wife and child.

He slowly replaced the phone, already in the act of composition. But his thoughts were interrupted by Harriet telling him that there were just ten minutes to go before midnight. They were opening champagne.

Harland got downstairs to find Robin sprawled almost horizontal, his long legs stretched in front of him. He smiled comfortably at Harland.

'So what've you been up to, Bobby? Haven't really had a chance to ask since you vanished from my office yesterday.'

Harriet looked on edge, as though she guessed he'd discovered something important.

'Oh, this and that,' he said, as pleasantly as he could. Whatever Robin's deficiencies of intellect, he was certainly a good host. He deserved politeness. The strokes of Big Ben came. They embraced, Harland enduring a longer than usual hug from his brother-in-law.

The phone went. It was Philip Smith-Canon breaking the news that Tomas had emerged from his coma. He had been awake for twenty-five minutes. He was very weak and there were problems with muscle spasm. They would be working on this in the next few days.

Harland hung up and told them.

'Well, that's some good news to start the year off with,' said Robin.

'I wouldn't be so sure,' said Harriet.

18
Vigo's Map

After a while Harriet and Robin went upstairs. Harland returned to the little office to begin a memorandum for Jaidi. It was a laconic affair which, if anything, underplayed the sabotage theory, although he did mention that the FBI had made unspecified discoveries concerning the electronics systems of the plane. The rest concerned the pictures of Lipnik whom he assumed was the man that Jaidi referred to as the 'quantum enemy'. He asked the Secretary-General to expand on his phrase for, as far as he knew, Lipnik had only one other identity – the one assumed after the staged assassination. He gave a hint or two about the evidence to be gleaned from a close examination of both pictures. He ended the note by saying that he was continuing his inquiries in Eastern Europe. He signed off in the hope that they would speak soon. He sent the e-mail with the photographs in an attachment, knowing that Jaidi would not concern himself with the identity of the young soldier in the background of the earlier picture.

As he was clearing up and preparing to go to bed, Harriet slipped into the office and perched, in an ancient woollen dressing-gown, on the desk beside him. Her face was scrubbed clean of make-up and glistened with moisturiser.

'Okay,' she said in a bad American accent, 'quit stalling on me. What've you got?'

'A lot,' he said glumly, and withdrew one of the prints from the envelope and handed it to her. 'That was taken in Bosnia. It's the scene of a massacre. You can see Tomas in the background.'

Harriet let out a gasp. 'God! How on earth did you get this?'

'Griswald was carrying it on the plane. His interest was in the man in the foreground. That has to be Lipnik.'

'So everything does connect. What are you going to do now?'

'I'm going to go to Prague to try to trace Tomas's mother. It's essential

507

that she's found to help communicate with him. But she must also be able to explain how he came to be in Bosnia when he was just twenty years old.'

'Who have you showed these pictures to?'

'So far the FBI and Jaidi. Both within the last hour or so.'

'I see.' She paused. 'Lipnik could reasonably assume that they were no longer in existence. After all, they took the mini-disc from you in the UN and wouldn't have expected you to have copied it. But that doesn't explain why Tomas was hunted down like that. It can't have been because he was witness to that thing in Bosnia because they would have found him before. So why now? What's the connection?'

'Maybe Tomas knew Lipnik was alive.' Harland didn't sound very convincing to himself. He went on to tell her about his afternoon with the man from GCHQ.

'So the connection could be something to do with these codes.'

'Maybe.'

'So that means you're still much in danger?'

'I think not. But who knows? I haven't got to the bottom of this thing.'

'And you're going to Prague.'

This came out like an accusation. She knew about the last time, not the details of course, but she saw him in hospital only a few days after The Bird and Macy had delivered him there. She sighed heavily and rubbed her hands together. There were tears of anger and frustration in her eyes. Harland started to say that he had to go.

'Oh, for Christ's sake, don't you think that you've run out of lives, Bobby? I mean, let's face it, you came back from the police station the other night in a terrible state. I know what caused it. So do you. You had a flashback. And now you're going back to Prague. What do you think will happen? Surely you can trace this woman and simply telephone her?'

'It's not that easy. I'll need to look at some old files there.'

She pressed her hands together and interlocked her fingers. 'You're a bastard to cause me so much worry. I hope you know that.'

He said nothing.

'I mean it, Bobby. You're a bastard.'

'I'm sorry.' He shifted in his chair. 'I really am sorry. But I'm stuck in the middle of this thing. I can't go back. I have to go forward.'

'Well ... you'll need the things I've been holding for you. I always knew they'd be useful one day.'

She pushed him gently out of the way with her forearm, knelt down to the bottom drawer of a cupboard and pulled out a red petty-cash box.

'You remember you had me keep everything up to date when you were with SIS?' She looked at him despairingly. 'You know – your covers! You got me to maintain these bloody false identities and make sure there was activity in your accounts while you were away.'

Of course Harland remembered. From the moment he entered Century House on the Intelligence Officer's New Entry Course, he was taught how to build and maintain cover. In his time at SIS he had five or six. Each cover usually – but not always – included a false passport, a driving licence, a cheque guarantee card and one or two credit cards. It was drummed into them from the very first that these identities must have 'hinterland', by which it was meant a life that could be inferred from membership cards, receipts in the name of the cover, letters and so forth. It was advisable to have an ACA – an Alias Cover Address – where correspondence could be sent and someone would vouch for you if inquiries were made.

Harland was allocated a man in Wimbledon, a retired SIS officer who had settled down with a Dutch widow ten years his junior. His name was Jeavons. For a time the relationship worked well: Harland gained invaluable tips on trade-craft.

But it was a laborious business, keeping Jeavons sweet and making sure that there was enough convincing 'wallet litter' for the identities he used. Towards the end of Harland's time at SIS, Jeavons lost interest and his wife took over the running of Harland's affairs. But then Mrs Jeavons started to invent reasons for Harland to visit her, usually when her husband was out. It was plain that he had to go to bed with her, or move cover address. He opted for the latter and asked Harriet to manage things while he found someone new. It wasn't ideal but she had married and got a new name and as ever had inexhaustible energy.

By this time he had two main covers – Charles Suarez, a construction engineer from the British community in Buenos Aires, and Tristan O'Donnell, a salesman from County Cork. Both possessed false passports from the country of origin, arranged by SIS in the days when these things were less closely monitored. His colleagues who had been issued documentation by the passport office in Petty France were required to lodge them at Century House when they were not being used. But nobody seemed to mind the abuse of a foreign passport and Harland had been allowed to keep his.

Into Harriet's safekeeping also went the two bank accounts, one held at Coutts in the Strand and the other at the Royal Bank of Scotland in Victoria Street. Over the years, Harland had achieved a degree of realistic churn in the two accounts, using them occasionally to bank money of his own or pay off his and Louise's household bills. From these two accounts were also paid magazine subscriptions, video library fees, annual donations to Amnesty International, Shelter and The Salmon and Trout Association. In the days when he needed the services of O'Donnell and Charles Suarez he used in spare moments to write off job applications in either name so that he would have recent letters addressed to him to keep in a briefcase.

In the late autumn of 1989, when Harland travelled as an 'illegal' to Prague, he went without the protection of his own diplomatic passport and instead became Charles Suarez. This had been his own decision because he didn't want his name turning up on an immigration or customs list when he crossed from East Germany to Czechoslovakia. With his arrest, the usefulness of Charles Suarez and his carefully nurtured interests and ambitions ended. In fact, he never again saw the passport or the briefcase containing his reply from a construction firm in Reading. When he resigned from the service a few months later, nobody thought to ask him about any other identities he had cultivated alongside Suarez's.

Harriet unlocked the box with a key she took from the desk, and fished inside. There were bank statements, a driving licence, a video card and membership to a club in Mayfair called the Regency Rooms.

'Hal,' he said, 'the passport must be out of date. It's a decade or more since I looked at this stuff.'

'Nope,' she said, pulling a pristine EU passport from a brown envelope. 'In a bored moment I applied for a new one to see what would happen and they sent this back without batting an eyelid. Anyway, I somehow didn't want Tris to turn his toes up quite yet. Look, there's you.' She showed him the picture. 'Not bad. You gave me a whole strip of photos for visas. Don't you remember?'

Harland did vaguely remember. 'And I suppose the driving licence is current and clean?'

'What did you expect?'

He picked up some bank statements and looked at a recent sheet for 1999. His eyes settled on a column in the right. 'Hal! This was in credit twenty-five thousand pounds last year. Where did this come from?'

'That's why I didn't want Tris to die,' she said with a giggle. 'He's been quite a success on the stock market. In fact Tris is currently in the black to the tune of forty-one thousand pounds.' She handed him the latest bank statement.

'Jesus, is this your money?'

'Yes, it's all completely legitimate. I just wanted to keep certain transactions separate. Tris has two credit cards – banks kept on offering him gold, platinum and what have you, so he accepted. Last winter he paid for us all to go to Antigua, first class.' She handed him all the papers. 'It's all completely kosher. If you have to go to Prague again, you can go as Tristan O'Donnell.'

'You know Prague's a different place now.' He moved to touch the top of her hand but withdrew at the last moment. 'They're members of NATO. They're officially part of the West. The Czechs are a civilised people and all anybody wants to do is buy Gap and eat McDonald's.'

'Semi-West! I read the papers. Half the corruption scandals in East

Europe are traced back to Prague and Budapest. Look, I just don't want you to be hurt – that's all.' She looked at him with an utterly vulnerable expression. He muttered some reassurance but knew he was pushing her away.

She rose from crouching over the petty-cash box. 'When this is over, you really ought to talk things through with a sensible shrink. You don't seem to be aware of what's going on outside you much. You seem to experience fear, but have no idea about danger, no concept of risk. You used not to be like that, you know. You were more balanced.'

'You're probably right.'

'I am.'

'I've been thinking about Vigo,' he said, shifting his position on the chair. 'How bloody odd it is that he's just gone off the radar. He went to see Tomas's doctor and asked about him. Then nothing. What's that suggest to you?'

'That he no longer needs to pressurise you, that he's found out what he wanted.'

'How would a visit to the hospital satisfy that, unless Vigo was somehow aware of the hunt for Tomas and was keen to learn whether he was effectively silenced as a witness? I think I'll pay Walter a visit. You know those people who brought him here for the party – the Hammicks? Do you think you could persuade them to give you Davina's home address?'

'We don't have to ask them. Davina Cummings is bound to be in the LMH Annual, even if only to let all her contemporaries know what a wonderful life she's enjoying.'

She reached up to a shelf at the far end of the room and withdrew a slender ring binder. 'Here she is: "Davina Cummings – brackets Vigo – twenty-three, Kensington Hill Square, London W11". Funny, I thought they lived in Chelsea. Still, the book is last year's so it ought to be right.'

Harland made a note of the address. 'There's one other thing,' he said. 'I'll be away for three or four days. Can you go and tell Tomas where I am and what I'm doing? He must be pretty terrified and I'm sure it would be good for him to see a friendly face. You'd better talk to the doctor beforehand. Tomas may not know how bad his condition is.'

'Of course. After all, he is my nephew.'

He rose early and took one of the Bosey cars to Kensington Hill Square in Holland Park. The day was cold and hazy and the sun had not yet dispersed the mist in the side streets. He parked outside number fifteen and counted the doorways to twenty-three, an averagely plush residence for the area with two conical bay trees at the entrance. Although the terrace was set back from the line of the road behind a run of nineteenth-century railings, it was possible to see the doorway to the house.

He decided to make his move at eight o'clock and spent the next fifteen minutes running through the questions he had for Vigo, and intermittently musing on the price of a house in the square. Two and a bit million pounds, he thought. Davina Vigo certainly had 'background'.

A little before eight a black London taxi passed his car and pulled up outside number twenty-three. Harland sunk a little lower in his seat and watched two men get out. As one turned to pay the driver Harland recognised his main interrogator at the Crèche, Anthony Rivers. The other was Derek Blanchard, the unlovely MI5 man. They appeared to be expected because they were let in immediately. A few minutes later a dark blue Mondeo saloon drew up and a further three men got out and went into the house. He was sure one of these was Griffiths, the thickset Celt who had approached him at the airport. And the parka? That must have been the same individual who'd followed him in Regent Street.

He waited for an hour, watching the windows for signs of activity. The more he thought about it, the more this breakfast meeting, held on a public holiday at the home of a senior member of SIS, seemed decidedly unofficial. He remembered that at the Crèche it had struck him he was being questioned by a couple of retreads. And there was a distinctly weekend feel to the others – the men who staffed the Crèche and had followed him so blatantly the next day. A proper surveillance operation would have used scores of men and women and however much he went through his dry-cleaning procedures it would have been virtually impossible for him to shake them off.

So Vigo was making do with limited resources, a group of individuals who came from intelligence backgrounds but who were no longer employed by MI5 or MI6 – people like Guy Cushing, who owed him. The purpose of this personal crusade baffled Harland. But plainly Vigo was at odds with his colleagues at Vauxhall Cross, and that knowledge gave Harland a lot more leverage than he had possessed when he set out that morning.

His thoughts were interrupted by a cab drawing up outside number twenty-three. Blanchard and Rivers reappeared and got in. The other three men followed them through the open door and, without looking back, climbed into the Mondeo and departed. Then a man and woman, who must have arrived some time before the others, left together. For a moment Harland wondered whether he should follow one of the vehicles, but realised that he stood to learn much more by catching Vigo off guard.

He waited ten minutes so that Vigo wouldn't suspect he had seen his visitors, then approached the laurel-green front door and rang the bell. A few moments elapsed before Vigo's voice sounded on the intercom.

'It's Bobby Harland, Walter. I thought we could have a talk.'

'It's not a terribly convenient moment, Bobby,' came the voice, unruffled.

A SPY'S LIFE

'You'll change your mind when you hear what I have to say.'

The entry-phone went dead and the door opened a few seconds later.

Harland noticed his clothes first: suit trousers and a tie – a silk job with a plump knot. 'Off to work on New Year's Day, Walter? You must have a lot on.'

Vigo regarded him with wary interest.

'Can I come in?'

'If it can't wait, yes. But I do indeed have a lot on.'

He led Harland to the far end of the hall and into a small room lined with wire-mesh fronted bookcases and antique maps. All three windows were secured by impressive metal trelliswork. The floor consisted of old black and white tiles and above the carved eighteenth-century fireplace hung a bulbous convex mirror. On a Jefferson reading lectern lay a couple of closed volumes. The room had the air and silence of a scholar's retreat.

'So this is where you keep your incunabula?'

'Such that I possess,' Vigo replied tartly.

'It's a very soothing room. It makes me think that I should have paid more attention to where I live and what I surround myself with. I admire you for it, Walter. It's important in your job to maintain a balance. Do you still trot off to the London Library for an afternoon's reading?'

'Not as much as I'd like,' said Vigo. He was waiting for Harland to get to the point.

'I've come to talk to you about Alan Griswald,' said Harland. 'You know you were interested to find out what he was carrying. Well, I have the information with me.'

Vigo cocked an eyebrow.

Harland withdrew the envelope and selected the print of Lipnik by the swimming pool. 'This is Viktor Lipnik, an indicted war criminal who is believed to have been killed. Griswald knew he was alive. The picture was hidden in a code, which, I suspect, was your interest.'

Vigo looked at the photograph like someone who has been called upon to admire a child's painting.

'Well ... thank you, Bobby. That's most helpful of you.'

He took out the second image and showed it to Vigo, having carefully placed his thumb over Tomas's head. 'And this one is of Lipnik at the site of a massacre in Bosnia. Enhancement of the bottom left-hand corner shows several bodies. As you can see, it's dated to the period of the Srebrenica massacres in north-east Bosnia.'

Vigo put his hands in his pockets. 'It's good of you to show me these. No doubt you've forwarded your find to the relevant parties.'

'The UN and to the FBI as well. They're looking into the sabotage of the plane's electronics systems. Viktor Lipnik is therefore the chief suspect in the investigation.'

513

Vigo emitted a ruminative sound. 'Yes, I imagine that must be the case.'

'Walter, I don't seem to be getting a reaction here.'

'What did you expect?'

'For a start, an explanation for the investigation of my past by you.'

'That must be perfectly obvious, Bobby,' he said evenly. 'You are suspected of having committed serious offences against your country. In due course the authorities will decide what to do with you. It's out of my hands. I am not an officer of the law.'

Harland looked down and noted the impressions left in the seats of the two sofas by Vigo's recent visitors. He sat down and brushed his hand over the fabric.

'That's all bollocks, Walter. The only thing the authorities knew about the charade the other night at the Crèche was the call they got from the Secretary-General's office. I bet you had to do some fast talking to explain *that* to Robin Teckman and the Foreign Secretary. No doubt, they were rather bemused by the call, but I imagine you wriggled out of it. You knew you had to let me go and to pack the place up. You see, I know that wasn't the Crèche, Walter. You just borrowed some bloody building to give me a working over.'

Vigo removed his hands from his pockets and walked to one of the antique maps on the wall where he paused in rapt contemplation of a sketchy coastline of northern Europe.

'And if the Crèche was a fake,' continued Harland, 'Blanchard, Rivers, Griffiths and the others were operating outside the law, and – I'm certain – without the knowledge of the Director of SIS. What is interesting about this is why you have bothered with this elaborate charade. Clearly you aren't interested in the photographs of Lipnik because nothing as basic as evidence of an appalling crime motivates you. I remember you saying that Griswald had benefited from an unusual source to obtain his evidence. So it must have been the means of communication that interested you and the possibility that Griswald had exchanged something for those images. Am I right?'

Vigo remained immobile, then gestured to the map.

'You know, it's thought likely that this very map appears in the background of one of Vermeer's paintings, which is as good as saying that he owned it. There's no proof, of course, but it certainly is pleasing to have touched something that he handled. And that's the point. But if an expert were to come along and prove categorically that the story was myth, the map's charm would be drastically reduced.' He turned and studied Harland. 'It's the same with the snapshots of this man, Bobby. Your faith in them derives entirely from their recovery from the plane crash, about which, incidentally, you persistently lied to me. But leaving that aside, you have imbued them with a special significance, ignoring the counsel of your more rational self which must have suggested that these photographs could not be crucial evidence against a war criminal, whether alive or dead. For instance, the scene showing him in uniform could equally be interpreted as the excavation of a mass grave. An officer orders his troops to uncover the evidence of another army's crimes. How about that for an alternative caption?'

If only Vigo knew how that interpretation tempted him.

'There is the date on the image,' he replied, 'and the witness statements which put this man at the scene of the cleansing operation.'

'Very vague and circumstantial, rather like the provenance of my map. But look, Bobby, why are you concerning yourself with Bosnia? It all happened so long ago. There have always been massacres in the Balkans and there always will be; the people are intractable and murderous by nature. They won't change, no matter how much aid and intervention is advocated by the do-gooders at the UN.'

Harland had had enough of Vigo's diversion.

'This is not about Bosnia, Walter. It's about the release of intelligence secrets through the broadcast media in Eastern Europe. I know about the code and the way it's being used against the major intelligence agencies. The reason you were keen to get your hands on these pictures was that you thought they would lead you back to the original source. But that doesn't alter the fact that these pictures are valuable evidence and – much more important – they were probably the motive behind the crash.'

'Believe what you like, but I really must be getting on. Is that all you wanted to say?'

'Of course not. But I am surprised that you take the destruction of two aircraft and the loss of twenty lives so lightly. What I came here for is an assurance that your band of part-timers will not meddle in my affairs or obstruct my inquiry any longer.'

'Oh, that's another matter entirely, Bobby.'

'Well, it's one that you had better sort out, Walter, because you, Rivers and Blanchard were not acting in any official capacity and I'm quite certain that Robin Teckman would be interested to hear how you have been abusing your position. And what about Miles Morsehead and Tim Lapthorne, your two contenders for the top job at SIS? You deny your ambitions, but I know you too well. You want the power and the standard-issue knighthood. I'm sure they'd like to hear about all this.'

Vigo spun round from another excursion along the coastline of seventeenth-century Holland. His face was distorted with temper.

'You seem to have been unhinged by your experience in the police station. A nervous breakdown, they said. Wet your pants, carried from the cell blubbering.' His tone softened, not with sympathy but menace. 'Let me make it utterly plain that I am in a position to destroy you, Bobby. Those files from Prague produced grade A material: the real thing.

You were a bloody spy for the communists. You're bang to rights. In these circumstances you would be well advised to shut up and keep your head down. But if you persist in making wild allegations, these discoveries may well find their way into the press and then prosecution will be inevitable. You know how the press never lets go of a thing like this and you can imagine the fun they'll have with the pictures of the comely Czech seductress. And the recent dramas in your life – a plane crash, shootings, the torture and execution of a flower girl? It's meat and drink to those people.'

Harland cut him off. 'Still, your colleagues will be very interested to learn about your little group. Its mere existence will lead them to suppose that you are conspiring against them and the interests of SIS.' He stopped, placed his fingertips together and levelled his gaze at Vigo to tell the lie. 'You see, every one of them was filmed coming into this house this morning. Blanchard, Griffiths, Rivers – the lot. I can't name all of them, but I'm sure it won't take Sir Robin long. Naturally you will attempt to slide out of this one by giving them a lecture about provenance and the interpretation of images. You will perhaps explain that this is the early-morning meeting of the Incunabula Society, a seance of amateur cryptographers, a confessional meeting of the local AA chapter. The story will be ingenious, I'm sure. But they won't believe you and moreover they're unlikely to pursue the crazy allegations that you subsequently make about my past.'

Vigo sat down. He was at least going to deal, thought Harland.

'Why have you come here?' His voice showed no sign of anxiety. 'You're a clever man, Bobby, but it seems to me that everything you do betrays your guilt. Is that all it is – guilt? Or is there something you really want?'

'The links – I want the links, Walter. How does Viktor Lipnik tie in with this coded material? What does he have to do with the shooting of Lars Edberg? Why did you make inquiries at the hospital to find out about his condition?' Harland knew some of the answers but he wanted to see Vigo's reaction.

Vigo placed his hands on his knees and leaned forward.

'Lars Edberg,' he mused. 'I must say I'm touched by your devotion to him. It really is a fascinating aspect to this whole thing. I fancied I saw him at your sister's place on the evening of the shooting, but maybe I was mistaken. Possibly it was some friend of your sister's? Who knows? Who cares? You see, I no longer have the time to ponder your unlikely trysts beside the Thames. My interest has moved on from you, Bobby, which is why I would like you to leave now.' He stopped and looked away. 'I imagine you're still at your sister's place.' Another pause. 'Davina is right – Harriet has very special qualities. You can tell that instantly.'

His massive head turned back to face Harland. In the sunlight which now flooded through the lancet window, Harland noticed that the rims of his eyes were red and that the lower eyelids were drooping a little. It occurred to him for the first time that Vigo was under considerable strain. 'It would be regrettable if she became mixed up in this.'

'You're threatening me, Walter,' Harland said with surprise. 'You're saying that if I send that film to Teckman you cannot be responsible for my sister's safety. I won't tolerate that. If anything happens to her or her family, I will kill you. It is as simple as that.' He felt angry and foolish in the same moment.

They rose together and looked at each other.

'I will say one thing to you, Bobby. Let this go. You have no idea what you're dealing with. If you persist, you will endanger other people's lives.'

Harland heard a woman's voice call out from the stairs.

'That's Davina,' said Vigo. 'I think you'd better leave now, don't you?' At that moment Davina glided into the room. 'Bobby was just going,' he said to his wife's surprised expression.

Harland nodded awkwardly and brushed past her to the front door. Even as he closed the door behind him he knew that he had made a bad mistake in coming.

517

19
Bohemia

The O'Donnell passport carried Harland into the arrivals hall of Prague airport without a hitch. The Bird had told him to look out for a driver with one of two names displayed on a board. If the name was Blucher, Harland was to walk past the man and catch a cab to the Intercontinental Hotel where he should await further instructions. If he saw the name Schmidt, he was to make himself known and the driver would take him to the meeting place.

Harland immediately spotted a young man by a coffee stand in a worn sheepskin jacket. He was holding a board, but the name was hidden by his hand. As Harland approached, the man raised the board up to display the name Schmidt, smiled imperceptibly and led him to the car park. Outside it was damp and snow lay on the ground. Harland noticed a metallic smell in the air that he associated with the uninhibited mining and smelting of the old Eastern Europe.

In a short time they were heading along the Vltava River. He tried to get his bearings. At the back of his mind he was orienting himself so that he knew the direction of an area named Dejvice where he was held the first night of his arrest in the StB building. The date was Friday, 17 November 1989, a propitious but bloody day which came to mark the beginning of the Velvet Revolution. Harland didn't learn the importance of the events he witnessed until long afterwards.

Harland looked out across the river to the Old Town Hall and remembered Griswald going off to meet his contact. There had been little for Harland to do so he had spent much of the day sightseeing in the Old Town. As the day wore on it became obvious that something was brewing. Every so often he would come across furtive groups of students passing leaflets to each other, then melting away into side streets as the plainclothes security police arrived. A young woman in a white knitted hat had pressed a flyer into his hand, announcing a march in memory of

Jan Opletal, a student who'd been killed by the Nazis a little over fifty years before. They talked for a short time. Harland said that it seemed downright perverse that while the world held its breath to see whether the East German uprising would spread to Czechoslovakia, the students were preparing to commemorate an obscure martyr of the Nazi era. She replied that it was a symbolic protest against the regime. In the two decades since the Russian invasion and the collapse of the Prague Spring, it had become second nature to the Czechs to make their protests metaphorically – at one remove.

Harland was much more alert to the movement of security forces than the students and, as dusk gathered that afternoon, he noticed the discreet arrival of troops dressed in khaki and red berets. It transpired that these were members of the Division for Special Purposes, an anti-terrorist group that had been infiltrated into the city to set a trap. A few hours later they would wade into the students, causing hundreds of casualties. When the fleeing students banged on the doors along Narodni Street to be let in, their fellow Czechs were too frightened to open up.

He had been tempted to stay and see what happened, but he decided to make himself scarce and returned to the ill-lit room where he and Griswald had camped out for a day and a night. Five StB men and three uniformed policemen were waiting for him. They were convinced that he had been sent by foreign powers to ferment revolution on the streets. The leaflet in his pocket about that evening's demonstration didn't help his denial. He was taken to StB headquarters and questioned. The next morning, as open dissent began to break out among all classes and professions in Prague, and Václav Havel hurried back from his retreat at Hradecek to lead the revolution, Harland was handed over to three men who took him to a villa. Time rushed forward for the Czechs but for Harland it went into reverse – back to the Stalinist purges.

All of that was very near the surface now. Harland made a conscious effort to think of something else.

The driver took a sharp right, away from the sweep of the Vltava, and rattled down a cobbled side street. As they waited at some lights, he turned round and handed Harland a monochrome tourist map of Prague Castle. Harland unfolded the map and examined it, remembering that before he was arrested he had planned to come up to the ancient citadel which overlooks Prague. In the second courtyard he found a red circle marking an object in the centre, which the key told him was a fountain.

They tore up the final few hundred yards to a deserted square in front of the castle. There the snow streamed across the headlights almost horizontally. Harland paid off the driver who responded by making a shooing motion with his hands to indicate that he should go through the gateway in front of the castle. It was bitterly cold. He passed between two sentries who did not seem to notice him and stole into the great, dark precincts of the castle. The fountain was ahead of him in the first courtyard, but not a soul was to be seen. Some way off he heard the stamp of more guards marching to their watch. He walked gingerly across new snow and passed under a second archway to find he had run slap-bang up against the west front of St Vitus's Cathedral. The façade rose up before him with the effect of a photographic negative, the snow picking out the details of the carvings. He looked up for a moment, then retraced his steps back to the fountain, followed by three guards in blue greatcoats and high fur collars who had appeared from the direction of the Old Royal Palace. From nowhere a tall figure had materialised by the fountain and was tracing a circle in the snow with his feet, as he talked animatedly on a phone. He raised a hand in acknowledgement of Harland and finished the conversation.

In an educated accent reminiscent of Tomas's, he said, 'You are Macy Harp's friend? Harland?'

'Yes.' Harland took in the gaunt, slightly hunched giant. He wore an ancient brown leather coat which rose up his back and sagged at the front. Under this was a suit and badly knotted tie. His dark hair was lank and long, parted at the side in a style that had been fixed in the seventies.

'I am Zikmund. Mr Harp is a friend of mine also. We have to wait a little so we should welcome the New Year with some beer – no?'

'Zikmund?'

'Zikmund Myslbek.'

They walked to a Skoda outside the castle and Zikmund folded himself into the driver's seat. Ten minutes later they were in a nameless bar full of smoke and the smell of beer. Zikmund gestured to a door at the back that turned out to be the entrance to a cavernous pool hall, at the end of which was a stage.

'No band this evening,' said Zikmund apologetically. 'The fun was last night.'

They sat down. Beers were brought, and two horseshoe frankfurters coated in mustard. Harland looked at his companion in the light. He guessed he was in his mid-fifties. His face had once been very striking, but now his cheeks were sunken and his skin was grey from work and cigarettes. He was evidently a prodigious smoker and forked the frankfurter into his mouth while a cigarette smouldered in his left hand.

They drank in silence for a while, Zikmund eyeing up a voluptuously built woman who was packed into jeans and a blouse and teetered on high heels. Without taking his eyes from her, he said suddenly, 'I am sorry for what happened to you here in Prague, Mr Harland.'

'Macy filled you in,' said Harland. 'Do you mind me asking how you know him?'

'Not at all. We met back in the seventies when he was working for your people.' Harland remembered that Macy and The Bird had briefly had legitimate jobs with SIS. 'I passed on the work of dissidents that could not be published here to Macy. He took them to the West.'

'And what do you do now?'

'I used to be deputy director of the new intelligence services for the Czech Republic.'

Harland couldn't conceal his surprise. Zikmund smiled again. 'We had an excellent chief after the revolution. I was his deputy when we set up the new service. Here we have one service that combines domestic and foreign work.'

'So what do you do now?'

'I do jobs here and there and get to sleep till noon when I want.'

Harland looked at Zikmund with new eyes.

'What did you train in?'

'Architecture. I was an architect but I could not have a job under the Communist regime. So I translated for a living and I cooked.'

'You cooked!'

'Yes, I cooked and I wrote a couple of cookery books – traditional Bohemian recipes and my own. Cooking became a passion for us after the Prague Spring. The Czechs hibernated. We each lit a fire inside and kept warm and waited for another spring to come. We made love, we talked to people we trusted and we cooked. Cookery was a good business to be in – more cookery books were sold than any other type of book in the seventies.' He paused. 'So, about this woman. Macy told me about her but none of the names mean anything to me. If she lived in Prague, I am sure I would know her. Still, a lot of those people who worked for the StB in the old regime keep their heads down now.'

Harland showed him the three cards – Eva Houresh's student ID of 1975 and the Communist party membership cards for Irina Rath from 1980 and Irina Kochalyin from 1988.

The last one appeared to mean something to Zikmund. He looked at all three again and seemed to be about to say something, then thought better of it.

'Are we to assume that her maiden name was Irina Rath?'

'Yes. Her son is named Rath and I know that Eva was not her real name.'

'But she is not in any phone book in the Czech Republic. I looked today.'

'But you have access to the old files?'

'Unofficial access,' said Zikmund, with a smile. 'I hear that this woman was once regarded as important. Her file is kept away from the others. We will have to wait until my contact calls me.'

'Tell me,' said Harland, 'do you know if anyone from the British SIS has recently had access to the archive?'

Zikmund looked longingly at the buttocks of the girl in stiletto heels who was stretching over the pool table for a difficult shot.

'This lady here, she is the girlfriend of one of the big Russian mafia bosses when he is in town. She is an athlete. She throws the discus for Czech Republic. A mighty woman, no?' He looked at Harland. 'Yes, they were here two weeks ago. I do not know what they were looking for. They spent a short time here and they didn't get to see any of the special files. Very few do.'

Harland explained that they must have seen something of Eva's file because they'd obtained pictures of her from the early years.

'Maybe something, but not all. We will hear later. My friend will be able to tell you what they saw.'

They drank for a further hour. Harland found himself warming to the Czech's lack of ceremony. Secrecy for him was plainly a matter of occasional expedience, not a religious faith. He said something on these lines when he leaned over and grasped Harland's shoulder.

'Tell me why you English believe espionage is like gardening.'

Harland said he didn't know what he meant.

'Listen to the language used in intelligence work – you *cultivate* contacts, you *plant* listening devices or *bugs*, you have *moles* and you *weed* documents. Why is this so?'

'I don't know. But I think the mole was invented by a novelist.'

At half past midnight Zikmund received a call and they left, this time for a much longer drive to the southern outskirts of the city. Eventually they pulled up outside a building with an anonymous brick façade and got out. Zikmund pressed the bell at the only door and spoke into an entry-phone. There was a buzz and then a clunk as the action of a heavy electronic lock worked. They passed into a short corridor and repeated the procedure at a second door, which opened inwards into a long, cool space lit by fluorescent strips. Harland realised that the StB archive was housed in what had once been a refrigerated warehouse. A sprinkler system had been installed and rows of shelves stretched to the end of the building, but its original use was evident from the rails, chains and lifting gear that still hung from the ceiling. To one side was a long metal table with half a dozen reading lights, and beyond this four construction site offices joined together to provide desk space for the staff.

'Here the guilt of a nation is stored,' said Zikmund quietly. 'Every betrayal, small or large, of fifteen million people is in these shelves: every whisper of the neighbourhood informant, every dirty little compromise made by the ordinary man trying to keep his head above water. Every single squalid word is here, kept under lock and key. Very few of our people have seen inside this building.'

'Did you ever read your own file?' Harland now saw that the space was much greater than he had thought and that the archives ran off into the distance where the lights had not been turned on. He also spotted some sort of safe, way off in the distance.

Zikmund nodded slowly.

'It was the first thing I did when I got my job. One of the worst decisions I ever made. I discovered too much about the people I thought I trusted. I tried to put what I knew behind me, but it was difficult to forget that a friend I had known since architectural school had kept tabs on me for the authorities. Every conversation we had had was noted. It was for this reason that he found himself a very good job and that I was never permitted to work as an architect. I do not see him.'

A man issued from the office and approached them. He looked at Harland over a pair of glasses and started speaking rapidly in Czech. Zikmund translated.

'He says he has found the file you are looking for but that it only goes up to the early eighties. This he did not give to the two gentlemen who were here before Christmas. He says they were interested in seeing your file, but although there are cross-references to your name, it appears to have gone missing. He did not like the men who came. He says they were arrogant and he didn't oblige them too much. They took copies of some pictures from the Intelligence Operations Section. But they didn't get much information.'

'Would he mind also showing me the files that he gave them?' asked Harland.

The man appeared to understand. He handed Harland a green folder and pointed to the desk, then set off to the far end of the building.

'I must sit here with you,' said Zikmund. 'I'm responsible for you.'

Harland turned on a reading light and opened the file. 'I'm glad you're here because this is all in Czech.'

With little sense of expectation or dread, Harland began to sift through the pages of Eva's file, inspecting each entry then handing it to Zikmund for translation. Her full name turned out to include Eva. She was Irina Eva Rath, the only daughter of Hanna Rath. She was born in 1952 in Prague and attended school and university in the city, passing out top of her languages course in 1970. Zikmund remarked that it was unusual for someone to leave university so early and that she must have possessed a lot of natural talent. Copies of her grades in English and German were included, which confirmed this.

There was a long section devoted to her mother's circumstances and what her neighbours said about her and her daughter. They appeared to have kept to themselves, although mother and daughter were known to be active supporters of the regime and both possessed Communist party membership. The mother was on several local committees and was thought to be a willing, though unproductive, informant. When she left university, Irina Rath was recruited into the StB and trained. No details of this were given but it was mentioned that she operated under the code name *Lapis*. 'She was plainly very promising material,' said Zikmund, 'and attractive too. I understand what you saw in her, Mr Harland.' He picked up the black and white study of *Lapis* that had slipped from a cellophane envelope.

Harland had been looking at it too. It was odd: he felt none of the excitement that he'd experienced when Tomas first showed him the identity cards in New York.

Zikmund read on in silence, which made Harland impatient. He pressed him to say what he had found.

'Everything about Rome is here. It seems you were not her first conquest. There was an American named Morris who helped the StB at Nato – he was Drew Morris, a naval attaché, aged thirty.' That was news to Harland. Zikmund flipped a couple of pages. 'Her controller is this man who is referred to as K.'

'What else does it say?'

'This document has been *weeded*.' He looked up and winked. 'There are two pages missing. You see, you appear at the bottom of this page and then there is no mention of you again. Also a name has been erased here and here.' He held up the paper to show how words had been razored out of the typescript and replaced with tiny strips of paper which had been stuck over the back of the sheet. 'This must have happened before the revolution. Nobody would bother now. Nor would they get access to the files.' He stopped and looked again. 'From the sense of these pages I guess they have cut out mentions of the man known as K. But they have missed one or two, especially at the end. Do you know who K is, Mr Harland?'

'It could be Josef Kapek – but somehow I doubt it. Kapek was one of my contacts after 1980. He worked in the Czechoslovak Trade Mission in London and would be in no position to control *Lapis*. Besides, he was very low grade. He drank a lot and in the time I knew him, which was about ten years, he never gained a single piece of useful intelligence. A dunderhead.'

'Dunderhead,' repeated Zikmund, relishing the word. 'Then we look for another Mister K. But, still, Kapek tells us something, does he not? It means that you were being handled through the StB, not the KGB. That gives me an idea about K.'

'What idea?'

'All in good time. Tell me, did you help these dunderheads, or were you leading them up the *garden path*? Did you give them much genuine information?' Zikmund contemplated him over narrow spectacle frames.

'No. I gave them things that would mislead or stuff they already knew. You're familiar with the nonsense of intelligence work: you know what I'm talking about. Look, why don't you read the file from beginning to end? I feel I'd get a better idea of it then.'

Zikmund began in a reluctant monotone. There was a lot of operational detail – the record of their being followed in Rome and to Ancona, but not Orvieto. The conversations they had about his exact role at the British embassy in Rome were also described. There wasn't much that surprised or shocked Harland. In Orvieto she had given him an account of everything that she could remember telling them. There were a few other notes. One stated that *Lapis* ceased all operational work in 1988 and that for five years before that she had served as a translator and code expert, occasionally on attachment to the service of a friendly power. 'That means KGB,' said Zikmund.

They looked through the file again. The librarian brought two much thicker folders from the dark interior of the archive before returning to the cabin where he put his feet up to doze.

'He makes no money and he came out as a favour to me tonight,' said Zikmund, looking at the librarian over his shoulder. 'Give him something when we leave. Foreign currency will do.'

Harland nodded.

They started with Hense's file, the smaller of the two, and found four mentions of Harland, including an overblown account of a cup of coffee they'd shared in Vienna. Harland could see how the details from Hense's reports of the time had been woven into the case presented by Rivers. Operation Stormdrain, the disinformation campaign about Britain's military preparedness, had been worked up into a great scoop by Hense, although when they talked about it, they both knew the whole thing had long since ceased to have any significance. In all, five encounters with agent *Lamplighter* were recorded.

Kapek's was a much fuller account. The handling of *Lamplighter* appeared to be a major part of his career and he devoted much space to the analysis of Harland's character, which hinted at sexual promiscuity, a fondness for drink, his debts and a predisposition to melancholy. Zikmund read a passage which described a meeting in an art gallery when Harland was the worse for wear.

'I never met that little toe-rag in an art gallery,' said Harland, nettled by the slur.

'Toe-rag. I like that word too.'

Kapek had been careful not to overdo the character assassination. The conclusion his masters were meant to draw was that while *Lamplighter* suffered the symptoms of general cultural degeneracy, his information was still valuable. A couple of times he went out of his way to say that Harland had told him how he loathed Milos Hense.

'This guy wanted to keep you to himself and remain in London,' commented Zikmund.

Harland was aware that something was tugging at his mind. Suddenly it came to him. Kapek had shown him a copy of the picture of them in bed, but he had never actually produced the tape. He had mentioned it, of course, with a sly little smile, which was meant to keep Harland on side, even though he was being threatened. But he had never actually played it or even shown him a cassette. Harland had taken it for a bluff and ignored it. However, the important thing was that no tape was mentioned in any of the three files. That meant that Vigo had another source – but a source who was wrong.

They went through the papers for a second time. Then Zikmund produced a hip flask, popped a tiny cup from its top and filled it to the brim with liquid. Harland shook his head at the proffered cup.

'What's your theory about K?' he asked.

'Mister K, Mister K. You are aware there is another K in this story. It's Kochalyin. The name on your girlfriend's last identity card.'

'It was her married name. I know she's no longer married. Does it mean anything to you?'

'You see there was a man named Kochalyin – Oleg Kochalyin. He was KGB-active in Prague during the seventies. Not much is known about him, except that he was in the Soviet embassy here during the first years of the Normalisation. If this is the same man, it would explain the ambiguity that is suggested by *Lapis* working for the KGB while Hense and Kapek served the StB. Kochalyin was acting as a link between the two agencies.'

'But you say he was here in the seventies. Eva does not appear to have married until well into the eighties.'

'There are many things which would explain that. She might have been slow in changing her name. But the point is that when we came to set up the present service there was a lot of house-cleaning to do. We had to make sure that the people we employed had no connection with the StB and that they weren't tainted by corruption. It was in this time that we came across a former KGB agent. He was known as Peter and he was responsible for the Peter Organisation, which was notionally a new enterprise set up to trade with the West. It seemed to be based in Budapest, but we came to realise that it was based wherever this man Peter was. It possessed no office, no records, no accounts, no staff. Peter was the oil king. That means that he defrauded the state of millions in revenue.

'In Hungary the fraud relied on the difference between the import duty on heating oil and diesel oil, which are virtually the same chemically. The Hungarians placed a dye in the heating oil so that it could not be resold as diesel. What the Peter Organisation did was to import tons of heating oil and remove the red dye with sulphuric acid. Another chemical cleansed the acid from the oil. A similar scam was used here in the Czech Republic. We soon understood that Peter was behind this and that the entire fraud was being run by ex-KGB people and their contacts in the intelligence services of Czechoslovakia, Poland, Hungary and Romania.'

'And Yugoslavia?' Harland cut in.

'Of course. Where there was an alliance between the KGB and the local intelligence service, Peter set up business. They were smart people and a lot quicker to realise the benefits of capitalism than the ordinary man. Within a year after the revolution they had a grip on the four main sources of illegal revenue – the sale of arms, illegal immigration into Western Europe, the drug routes and prostitution. The scams to avoid tax in different territories were the beginning of all this. The important thing was that these KGB people were used to dealing in strategic terms, thinking of the Warsaw Pact countries as one entity. Borders meant nothing to them. It took them little time to discover how to use the global banking system to hide and clean their money.'

'And you think Peter and Oleg Kochalyin are the same person.'

'He was one of our main suspects. But we never got any proof. Maybe they have now. I will ask.'

Harland showed him the picture of Lipnik by the pool.

'This is the man I'm interested in. Do you think this could also be Peter – Kochalyin?'

'He means nothing to me. I'll take a copy of the picture to show an old friend of mine. He may know him.'

There was one last file which had not been withdrawn by Vigo's researchers because – of course – there was no reason for them to look into *Lapis*'s background. It was the slender dossier devoted to Hanna Rath. It gave a few personal details, but mainly dwelt on her exemplary service to the Communist party at district level, in particular her appearance at thinly attended meetings to hear the wishes and initiatives of the Praesidium. A note dated 1985 recorded that she had moved from Prague to a village in the area known as Jizerské Hory. Zikmund jotted down the address.

'She's old now, but she may be there still,' he said.

Her daughter was mentioned several times but there was no cross-reference which would lead to the *Lapis* file in the Intelligence Section. However, a recommendation, underlined in red ball-point, directed the interested reader to a section where newspaper cuttings were stored. Zikmund was for leaving it, but Harland insisted they dig out the relevant file.

The envelope contained just one clipping – a yellow newspaper picture and caption in Russian from 25 August 1968. It showed a woman posing with Russian soldiers who were squatting in front of a tank. In one hand she held out a wicker basket, from which protruded a loaf of bread and a bottle; in the other was a plate of sausage and sliced meat. The headline over the picture read LOYAL CZECH WORKERS WELCOME SOVIET SAVIOURS.

The extended caption described how Hanna Rath had given food and drink to the young Russian tank crew whose job it was to defend the Czechs from a Western-inspired coup. Harland read out the quotation from the tank captain at the end of the piece.

'We are honoured by the reaction of the ordinary Czech worker to our presence here. This was just one of many acts of gratitude that we have experienced,' said O.M. Kochalyin, tank captain.'

'Mr K!' exclaimed Zikmund.

'Yes,' said Harland, 'and maybe Mr Lipnik also.'

He unfolded the print of Lipnik again and placed it by the head of the young man who crouched in the middle of the tank crew with his helmet tucked under one arm.

Zikmund swore in Czech.

Harland said nothing: he didn't need to. The eyes were the same. The angle of the nostrils was right. The way O.M. Kochalyin held his chin had not changed in thirty years.

They put the files back into order in silence then tapped on the cabin door to wake the librarian. Harland held out one file slightly open for him so that he would notice the fifty-dollar bill lying inside.

'That was good of you,' said Zikmund as they left the building.

'Cheap at the price,' replied Harland.

20

The Blink of an Eye

It was the fly that made Tomas finally understand his situation. Somehow it had got into his room the day before and worked its way over every exposed surface of his body. He felt it on his face, on his ear, on his hands and arm. For a full day the trickling, cold sensation of the fly's legs drove him mad. And it was very smart, this fly. When a nurse was near, the fly would disappear for a while. He imagined it hid in the machinery until the coast was clear. Then it returned to complete its minute survey of his body. He wondered if it was going to lay eggs on him, eggs which would hatch into maggots in the warm atmosphere and begin to feed on him. He told himself that this would be impossible, but he became obsessed by the possibility that the nurses would miss the crucial part of his skin when they were washing him and allow the eggs to survive.

Eventually the fly disappeared of its own accord. But being at its mercy had in some way made him understand that he had lost all movement and that this was for ever. The doctor of course had been extremely vague, but in the three brief consultations – his word – that they'd had, Tomas had listened hard for any mentions of time. There were none.

He realised also that as well as movement he had been robbed of day and night. There was no natural light in his room, no darkness. Always the same gentle, pinky-orange glow greeted him when he awoke. There were no meals either; no clocks that he could see; or any pattern in the staff changes to give him a clue about the time of day. Whenever he opened his eyes a nurse was beside his bed or busying herself in the room, monitoring the various machines and pumps, emptying things, washing him and changing his position. He'd quickly become used to each nurse and familiar with their mannerisms and degrees of thoroughness.

His favourite was Nurse Roberts. She had a gentle manner and was unafraid of his condition. The others all in some slight way communi-cated their horror. One talked in a loud, distancing voice – like a teacher instructing a classroom of kids. Another fussed, endlessly redoing the chores that were part of her duty. A third, a large girl with a pink complexion, would occasionally stop and look at him – not as a nurse, but as a gawping bystander. This one had no imagination: she couldn't grasp that beyond all the tubes and the sighing machinery and the wildly gesticulating limbs, he was sitting quietly inside, as capable of being hurt as the next man. He disliked this woman. She had no more empathy than a suet dumpling. He called her the Dumpling.

Nurse Roberts disliked her too. He could tell that by the note in her voice when she talked to the Dumpling. It was formal and firm. Every time the Dumpling tried to prolong the conversation or make some remark about his condition or the abilities of the other staff, Nurse Roberts cut her off.

What was it about Nurse Roberts? Well, she smelled nice and she took care over her appearance. She was quick to read the expression in his eyes and would in this way consult him about the position he preferred or a change of television channel. They had a secret too.

Sometimes she would tell him about her evening out or something she'd read in the papers. What she had to say about these things was always clear and to the point. She would look at him as she spoke and she understood that he would rather listen to her than the damned TV.

At times there were more people in his room than he would have liked. He wanted to tell some of them to get out. After all, it was his room. But at least he could guess the time of day by the visit of the two doctors – the man who had introduced himself as Philip and the sexy woman in her thirties whom the doctor addressed as Claire. They came twice a day, in Philip's case sometimes more. Claire was cold and rather dogmatic, Philip a bit of an old buffer who didn't listen much to his colleagues.

These observations of the people in his new life absorbed him for only a little of the endless day-nights in the room. The pain in his head regularly built in a screaming crescendo then subsided but never completely disappeared. Sometimes he saw lights when his eyes were closed. They reminded him of the patterns he discovered he could make as a small boy when he rubbed his eyes very hard. They were brighter now and pulsed with the pain in his head. He was fascinated by them and imagined that they were somehow the manifestation of frustrated neurons firing in his brain.

He had made a list of his problems so he could decide which was the worst thing he had to put up with each day. Today it was his breathing and the pain in his right lung. It felt thick and congested and sometimes there was a stabbing pain in his ribs. If the machines were switched off, he was sure he would hear a rattle in his lung. Yesterday it was the heat of the bedclothes and the soreness on his back and buttocks. If only he could have moved to where there was a little fresh air. If only someone had thought to position a fan to cool his body.

Yesterday was the day of incredible thirst and dryness. He couldn't think of it now because it had caused him so much torment. Torment. That was the word he had been trying to find. Not a word he had given much thought to before. But it was exactly the right word. He was being tormented by his condition and the surprises it sprang on him. He would be lying there, trying to calm himself and suddenly he'd be crying, or a steady buzzing and tinkling would start up in his ear, or he'd be going into the upside-down-crab position with his heart pounding in his head and muscles burning. The point was that he couldn't let the pain out – he couldn't wince or cry out or clench his fists. He was locked in with the pain.

His condition kept him on his toes all right. And although his thoughts were on the whole quiet and controlled, there were periods of screaming red panic when his mind made no sense at all. It gave him very little time for the kind of thinking that he needed to do.

Yet he had arrived at a conclusion. He wanted to die. It was not a difficult decision in the circumstances and he was sure that he would be able to make himself understood with the blink of an eye. Already he had gained some control so that when Nurse Roberts asked him a question, he replied with a single blink for a yes, or double-blink for no. That was their secret. The Dumpling had tried this technique and breathed fumes of cooking fat and halitosis at him and he had not replied because he didn't want to encourage her. Besides, it gave him a feeling that he could at least control whom he communicated with. It was one of the very few things that was left to him, and even though it sometimes caused him to suffer when he didn't reply, he nurtured this tiny degree of independence.

The doctor was back again and the Dumpling was scurrying about trying to impress him with her efficiency, making nauseating purrs and coos as she went.

'Hello Tomas,' he said. 'Treating you well, are they? Good. I have someone here who wants to see you.' He stopped and told the Dumpling that she should take her break now. When she had gone he said, 'Her name is Harriet and she is your father's sister. I have mentioned before that your father has taken me into his confidence, but I wasn't sure whether you had understood me. However, Nurse Roberts tells me that you are fully aware of everything that is being said to you and that you understand English.' Some secret, thought Tomas. 'That's very good news. Anyway, I believe your father is at this moment in Prague, getting in touch with your mother. His sister thought she would pop in and see you while he was away. I think you'll find her very refreshing company.'

Tomas was not at all happy at the idea of meeting someone who didn't know him. It was stupid to feel so self-conscious, but it *was* different seeing a person from the outside world. He prayed that his body would behave for the next few minutes and he cautioned himself not to let anything stressful float into his mind because those were the thoughts which seemed to set off his spasms.

The woman came in and showed her face at the end of the bed. It was a pleasant, animated face.

'Hi,' she said. 'I'm Bobby's sister. My name is Harriet. I saw you fleetingly a week or so ago, but I'm sure you don't remember me.'

He did remember her, but couldn't think where he'd seen her. His first thought was that she did not look at all like her brother.

He waited. He was the victim of conversation now. People came in and they talked at him and he had to listen. Sometimes he wished he couldn't understand. But his English had come back and, in fact, he was thinking in English most of the time. He believed his dreams were still in Czech, though.

She began to speak quietly and not in a rush, which most people did to fill the silence and cover their embarrassment. She looked at him directly in the eye also, which was a good sign. Only Nurse Roberts did that properly.

'I know Bobby will have told you nothing about himself so I thought you might like to hear a bit about him.' She paused. 'He's always been like that – not saying much about himself, but he's got a lot worse in middle age. He spends too much time by himself. He travels an awful lot and I suppose he's got out of the habit of talking to people properly. He's good at what he does and he's very persuasive and charming when he wants something. But it's such a pity that he doesn't let people see more of himself in other ways. You know, he can be really funny. Hardly anyone ever sees that side.'

This is exactly what he wanted – a story, the story of his father's life. Harriet moved to the chair that the Dumpling had just left and sat down. She leaned over to touch his hand and then decided to perch on the side of the bed.

'I hope you don't mind,' she said with a laugh. 'It's just a lot easier to see you.' Harriet was fearless, but she was not overpowering. She continued speaking, stopping to allow the ventilation that occurs naturally in a conversation. That was considerate because his brain didn't move as fast as it used to and sometimes he needed a moment or two to catch up. She was smart too: she anticipated what he wanted to ask her. Just as he was thinking that he would like to know something about Harland's background, she began to tell him.

'There's eight years' difference between us, so for a lot of my childhood Bobby was away. You see, our mother died quite early so having him home was just perfect. My father, whose name was Douglas, was a scholar – he lectured and wrote about theology. He used to go off to Cambridge

University to do a spell of lecturing and he'd bring Bobby back with him for the weekend or, better still, the long vacation. Then things brightened up. My father started smiling again and we were a family. You see, we all missed my mother dreadfully.' She paused. 'She died in a road accident a few miles from our house. I don't remember much, except a terribly sombre atmosphere settling over our lives. And there wasn't any escape because we lived in a desolate and flat part of England, called the Fens. Things stay put in the Fens. Nothing shifts or moves on its own and that was the case with our grief. It stayed. My father never really got over my mother's death and died at quite an early age himself. I was twenty then and Bobby was twenty-eight. I suppose it brought us together. We've been pretty close for most of the time since then.'

She looked away. Tomas felt this was because of her own sadness and regrets and that it had nothing to do with him. She was behaving naturally and he felt complimented.

She continued in this vein for some while, telling him how her brother had given up the idea of doing physics and changed to an engineering course, a sign of his practicality as well as his basic modesty. He was much brighter than he ever believed, she said. Perhaps that's why he had gone into intelligence work. It had seemed to their father a waste of his talent and decency.

Harriet talked to him about meeting Eva.

'Was her name Eva? He thinks she has another name.' She looked into his eyes. 'I wish you could talk to me, Tomas. I really do. We shall have to work out a way of you communicating with me. The nurse says that you sometimes use your eyelid. Is that right?'

Tomas blinked once.

'That means yes?'

Tomas blinked again.

'And twice for no?'

Another blink.

'Now that I know, I promise I won't plague you with questions – not everything has a yes or a no answer. But can I ask if she's called Eva?'

Tomas blinked once and then blinked twice more rapidly.

'A yes and a no. Perhaps Eva is part of her name?'

Tomas blinked once.

'I see – she used her second name. Your mother was a big thing in his life. I don't imagine he has told you how important she was. I'm only just beginning to understand that when he stopped seeing her, a part of him closed down. I don't know the details. Maybe you do, but it obviously had something to do with your arrival.' She looked hard into his eyes. It was not a gaze you flinched from. 'How strange life is. Having a son is the one thing that might make Bobby connect with the world. Your coming to him has affected him deeply but I'm not sure he appreciates this yet. Was he very suspicious when you first met?' She smiled and waited.

A blink.

'I thought so.' She smiled again. 'That's typical. But you must forgive him. He's been through a lot. Do you want to hear more?'

A blink.

'Not tired?'

He lied with two blinks.

'Good. I'm going to tell you a little about him which will make you understand him a lot better.'

Tomas listened as she began to speak about his father's trip to Prague in 1989. She said he was badly treated – badly hurt. Tomas wondered what that meant exactly. Then he had become seriously ill. He had sorted this out, but she was sure that the effects of the beating had stayed with him.

Tomas was aware that he was suddenly having difficulty breathing. The machine pumped air into his body, but his body didn't seem to want it. And in some remote part of him – his legs? – there was a new tingling which was something between the sensation of a skin warming up after being exposed to extreme cold and a nettle rash. He made a conscious effort to divert his thoughts to the boy of fourteen that he had been during the Velvet Revolution.

He pulled the images from his memory and forced himself to concentrate on all their details. He saw the train ride to Prague. 'It was the first week. They had heard about the police attacking students in the city because way up in the mountains where they spent most of their time they could receive German TV. It was odd: his mother was usually so cautious and wary of the authorities. But a few days after that news she took him out of school and bought two train tickets to Prague. The day after they arrived – a Thursday – they went to Wenceslas Square to join the crowds. It was bitterly cold – the first day of winter. They waited from the middle of the morning to late evening. His mother was flushed and kept on plucking his arm and hugging him, which was a little embarrassing.

'Remember this, Tomas,' she had said, holding his face between her gloved hands, 'you're watching history being made. Promise me that you will never forget this.'

And he had remembered that day, mostly because of the aura that surrounded her. She had never been so alive, so passionate, so moved. It was as if she'd been pretending to be another person all those years.

In the following days the gatherings in Wenceslas Square had swelled. They went without fail each morning and stayed until the evening, buying food from the street vendors who materialised along the fringes of the crowds. At times he found it boring, listening to speeches over a poor public-address system. But eventually he understood that the crowds were holding vigil until the moment when freedom had been irrevocably seized. He was fascinated by his mother during those days. Strangers in the crowd would latch on to her, drawn by her infectious optimism. Everything she was thinking was expressed in her face and that gave it a new beauty. He would never forget those days in Wenceslas Square.

He was better now. The distraction had done the trick. He returned to Harriet.

'Can I ask you a question?' she asked.

He felt tired but he blinked once.

'Well – I think you have just given me your answer. So, I'm going to go now. I'll be back tomorrow, if you like.' She paused and examined his face. Then she touched his cheek just above the stubble line. 'I have left some music which I know you like. I got the police to tell me what was in your bag. They wouldn't give me the original CDs, so my husband's secretary spent the morning getting duplicates.'

He said thank you, which he hoped she would realise was three blinks.

'There is one other thing,' she said, getting up from the bed. 'I have done some research about your condition on the Web. There are quite a few devices which will enable you to communicate more easily. Most will allow you to send e-mail. I'm going to talk to the doctor and see which he thinks will be the best for you. It's really important that you're able to say what you want.'

He blinked once and closed his eyes.

After dropping Harland off at a small hotel by the Old Customs Yard in the centre of the city, Zikmund did not return for a full twenty-four hours. He phoned mid-morning to say that it would take him all day to do some essential research. He would tell him about it that evening or the next day.

The city was choked with fog and few people were about. Harland spent a listless time walking around and reading in coffee shops. In the early afternoon he returned to his functional suite of rooms with a paperback of Dickens's *The Old Curiosity Shop*, which he'd bought at an English bookshop near the hotel. He read for a little while, opened some wine and looked out at the day congealing to dusk.

With a leaden certainty, he knew that nearly everything had fallen into place. Kochalyin was Lipnik. Kochalyin had also been Eva's husband. This explained how Tomas had come to be in Bosnia and why he'd been traced to London and shot. Kochalyin had ordered the death of his stepson and the torture and death of a young girl of whom he knew nothing. As for the plane crash, that too must have been Kochalyin's work, although the precise mechanism that caused the plane to swerve into the lighting towers as it came into land was only known to the FBI. He had pretty much everything he needed to make the full report to Jaidi.

At ten that evening he answered the phone to The Bird.

'Friend Zikmund gave me your number. Are you finding him helpful?'

'Yes, very,' said Harland. 'Why're you calling me?'

'Because there've been a lot of developments which are going to take the heat off you.'

'How?'

'It seems our country and western disc jockey got back to work yesterday to find a great fuss.' Harland remembered the old crack about GCHQ – it's in the country and west of London. 'Every spare man, woman and child with a gift for cryptography and other dark arts was deployed on tracing the source of these coded signals. Since Christmas there has been a burst of the stuff and the first few days of this week there was an awful lot of activity. The Americans and our lot at GCHQ were fairly hopping and decided they had to close this thing down once and for all. Macy heard from another source that they had wired up several of the radio stations used by these jokers in the past and started to trace all the incoming calls.'

'That's a big operation.'

'Yes. But it wasn't as though they hadn't thought of it before. Apparently these characters had some kind of routing system in Stockholm. Stockholm's full of Internet wizards, it seems. They bust a place last year and then just last month they pinned down the routing system and worked out who the sources were. A troublemaker named Mortz met a sticky end, I gather. God knows who killed him, but he was dead and things went quiet which is all anyone cared about. Then all hell blew up when the radio stations started pumping out more of this stuff during Christmas week. Again, they thought they had solved the problem – I don't know how they thought this, but they did. However, the coded signals kept coming. And guess what?'

'Just tell me, Cuth.'

'They traced this last batch of calls to London – to about a dozen numbers being used in rotation in the Bayswater area. With their usual towering incompetence, our former colleagues set about watching every house where one of these calls had come from. They assumed there was some kind of cell operating in the area – people running from house to house with a laptop. But this particular spot in London happens to be an area of high Arab ownership and Arabs do not spend the winter in damp old London. Most of the houses were empty and there was no sign of any activity. Then some bright spark realised that the telephone exchange must have been interfered with. They found two computers at different points in local junction boxes. Crisis over. Everybody goes home for tea and crumpets and hearty congratulations from the secret brotherhood flood in. Only problem is that they never find the bloke or blokes who were responsible. Still, the disc jockey tells me that there hasn't been a bleep out of any of the radio stations for thirty-six hours or more.'

'So whoever left these computers in the exchange boxes is free. He could be anywhere?'

'From St Bart's to St Petersburg.'

Or a neurological unit in central London, thought Harland. There was no other explanation. That was why they'd killed the young girl and pursued Tomas, using every possible tracking device. He wondered whether Vigo was part of the operation. Why else would he have gone to the hospital and cross-examined the doctor about Tomas's condition, unless he wanted to make sure that Tomas was effectively out of action? And once he knew this he had told Harland that his interest had moved on. Of course it had. He already knew that it was simply a matter of finding the devices that were sending out the coded messages. That's why he no longer needed Harland. But this supposed that Vigo knew of Harland's real connection with Tomas, and there was no reason to believe that because Vigo would have used it. Moreover he had approached Harland in New York before he knew of Tomas's existence. Something was still missing in the Grand Theory of Everything.

'Are you there?'

'Sorry, I was just thinking about Vigo's angle in all this. I can't work it out.'

'Well, you can be sure it has something to do with his own interest. He never stirs without a percentage of the action.' The Bird coughed. 'Look, I gather Macy and Ziggers have been on the blower all day. I'll let Zikmund give you the SP when he sees you. I'll only balls it up if I try to tell you.' Harland remembered that Cuth always deferred to Macy's intelligence-gathering skills and business sense.

'But surely you can tell me roughly what they've been discussing?'

'Friend Oleg – the man you discovered in the photo library.'

'Ah, I see.'

'Good hunting. I think things should be fairly quiet from now on. Come and see us when you get back.'

Harland hung up and sat for a while in the echoing, brightly lit sitting room of his suite. He noticed a couple of cigarettes that had been left by the cleaner in an ashtray, presumably dropped by a previous guest. He took one and went to the window where he lit up with a book of matches. He pulled the window open and looked down on the damp, cobbled street. A violin was being played in the apartment block opposite. The sound filled Harland with a deep melancholy. He was glad that he would not have to spend too much longer in this city.

21
Eva

The next day they set off early from the hotel in a hire car, which Zikmund conjured at a cheap rate from one of his contacts at the airport. He explained that he wasn't sure that his own car would go all the way to Jizerské Hory.

As they passed through the western outskirts of the city, Harland asked about the conversation with Macy Harp. Zikmund turned to him, his yellowish-grey complexion not improved by the morning light.

'Yes, I talked to Macy. I also talked to the FBI here. Did you know they have a bureau in Prague? How things change, eh?'

'What did they say?'

'The FBI clammed up when I started asking questions about Kochalyin. They said they weren't investigating anyone of that name. But that's not true. Macy told me he'd heard about the investigation of a particular bank account in London through which a very great sum of money has passed to New York. Macy would know about this because he does business here and all over Eastern Europe. There's this one bank account in the name of Driver. Driver is a Russian who took his wife's name when he married. She's an executive in the Illinois State Metal Bank which is why they didn't look so closely at the money going through his account. Eight billion dollars – maybe more – passed through and fanned out into a hundred different directions, mostly as payments to overseas companies. The operation was pretty hard to pin down because some money went the other way as camouflage. But the East–West flow was larger.'

'And this was Kochalyin's money?'

'Yes, certainly,' he said, flicking a cigarette out of the car window. 'But it's only one account and the FBI – though they do not confirm this – know there are a lot more involved.'

'Macy told you that?'

'Yes.'

'What's this add up to? Every Russian mafioso launders money through the Western banking system. There's nothing new in that.'

Zikmund looked mildly irritated. 'Listen, I'm giving you background, Mr Harland. You may need it. The point is that Mister K has become so powerful that Western governments rely on him for certain services. He negotiates contracts between East and West. He brokers information. He buys people off. He fixes elections. He makes sure there is just one bribe on a deal. That bribe goes to him, then he sees that the contract is completed on time. That's an important guarantee to have if you build a dam in Turkey or a power plant in Slovakia. Business will pay a lot of money for that.'

'You're saying he's so useful that Western governments ignore the money laundering?'

'Yes, but you're missing the point. Mister K is a very fluid, very adaptable man. He is nowhere and everywhere. He does not have a base, no single home, no single office, no single citizenship. He inhabits many different identities and owns many different businesses. He can control everything from a computer screen. Nobody has to see him for a deal to be completed. He is like a wisp of smoke and when a situation goes bad for him, like his interests in Yugoslavia, he becomes someone else. It's like that process – what is the word when a maggot changes into a cocoon and then a butterfly?'

'It's not a maggot, it's a caterpillar, and the process is called metamorphosis.'

'Metamorphosis – like the Kafka story. How could I forget? But there have been many more stages than with a butterfly. They are without limit but there is always some type of maggot at the end.'

'Do you get all this from Macy?'

'No, just the information about the Driver account. The rest came from my colleagues in the service here.'

'When you talk about the business in Yugoslavia, you mean his part in the war crime?'

'Yes – partly. There was a reason that it became necessary to have Lipnik assassinated. He had also been involved in taking money from the Serbs. At the beginning of the war the Serbs froze all private savings and took over the National Reserve – the part that was left in Belgrade. A lot of money was taken out of the country in the next three years. It went to Cyprus and then most of it disappeared. He was offering to launder money for the Serbs using the traditional import–export routes. But he took a very fat commission. He stole most of it. So in '97 the Serbs ordered him to be killed.'

Which led to the plan of the staged assassination, thought Harland. Settling Lipnik's account with the Serbs and the War Crimes Tribunal in one burst of gunfire.

'But he still has business in the Balkan states. My former colleagues are researching the illegal immigration that goes across the Czech Republic. The European Union requires us to do this. They know that the main routes being run from Ukraine and Romania go through Yugoslavia and Bosnia and Croatia. They suspect that Mister K is behind those too.' He paused to light up again. 'He's no idiot, this man. The Serb leaders imprisoned themselves in their own country. They cannot leave because of the indictments from the War Crimes Tribunal. K has done as much as them yet he can move anywhere at any time. He's outplayed them all. You know why I am telling you this?'

'Yes, you're warning me. You're saying that the proof that Lipnik and Kochalyin are the same person and the evidence that he is alive is a very dangerous possession.'

'Right, because you don't know of the alliances this man has made in the West. There are many who want to keep him alive and free to carry out their business for them. And you are about to contact the woman who was his wife. She may still be on friendly terms with him. Her home may be watched. They must know about you.'

'You're probably right. But this man tried to have her only child killed so they can't be on particularly good terms.'

'You are not listening to me. This is a very risky plan you have and I want you to think about how you are going to contact this woman. Remember, she worked for the StB. She was a spy for the Communists. She may not be reliable.'

Harland said nothing. He opened the window to get some fresh air. A few minutes later Zikmund motioned ahead of them.

'This place here is where the Warsaw Pact troops gathered before the Soviets ordered them to go into Prague in the summer of '68.'

Harland looked out at a featureless grey plain.

'And I want you to notice the road sign along here.'

'Why?'

'If I remember this road right, you will see, Mr Harland.' Harland noticed now that there was always an ironic edge when Zikmund addressed him formally.

A few miles on they passed a sign which directed drivers north, to a town twenty-five kilometres away. Its name was Lipnik.

'You see, this guy carries things from the past right through his life. He must have been here in August 1968 and he used the name in one of his false identities. Remember that, when you see this woman – he carries things through his life.'

They took another hour to reach the Giant Mountains and begin the climb to Jizerské Hory. Zikmund explained that the area had been cleansed of Germans at the end of the Second World War on the orders of the Allied powers. The property was given to the Czechs or seized by the government.

They pulled up in a village square and Zikmund went off to ask for directions. Harland got out and wandered into a nearby churchyard. Every headstone bore a German name. Along the street behind him the faded paint of German store signs was still visible.

It was odd then that Zikmund managed to find one of the few Germans whose forebears had not been tossed back into Saxony. He was a thin, bearded blond with a weather-beaten face, who had just tramped up the village street, prodding his way with a stave through the rutted snow. Two sheepdogs crouched and trembled in the snow as he stopped and answered Zikmund's questions. He spoke in broken Czech at first but then fell into German when he realised that Zikmund and Harland could understand him better. Yes, he knew old Mrs Rath. She was a good sort – she spoke German well. He used to deliver wood to her and she in turn allowed him to graze his sheep on her pastures in summer. She'd lived here fifteen years back, and her daughter and grandson had moved in with her for a period. They left about ten years ago. He had an idea that they were in Karlsbad in western Bohemia. He said the postman might be able to supply them with an address.

For the next hour they chased a post van from village to village. Eventually they caught up with him at a bridge and he gave them the address in Karlsbad.

'So we have learned something about the Rath women,' said Zikmund as they set off on the long drive. 'They are not poor. That German fellow said they had come into money. So perhaps Mister K has been generous to his womenfolk.'

An hour passed as they descended from the mountains and headed west across another flat expanse of landscape. They spoke little. At some stage Harland became aware that Zikmund was looking in his wing mirror more than seemed necessary, given that the road was free of traffic. He scrutinised the mirror on his side for a few minutes but saw nothing and sank back in his seat.

'Who knows you are here? asked Zikmund accusingly.

'No one but Macy, The Bird and my sister.'

'Someone else does. They follow, then they don't follow; then they follow. A car, maybe two. I'm not sure. But they are behind us, Mr Harland. I know it.'

Harland turned in his seat. The road behind them was still empty.

A few miles on, Zikmund pulled the car into a turning, then reversed at great speed on to a piece of ground that was hidden by a disused barn. He climbed out and peered round the barn. Harland did likewise.

'I was right, we do have a companion,' he said. 'This is the car.'

The blue Saab had to slow down before taking the bend in front of them and they were able to see that it contained two men. The car appeared to be in no hurry, but Zikmund was agitated. He took out a mobile phone, speed-dialled a number and began to speak slowly, enunciating the Saab's registration which he'd scrawled with his finger in the grime on the rear window.

'I called an old colleague,' he said, lowering the phone. 'He will arrange for the police to stop the car in the next town and inspect it for faults. That should delay them. We will take the road south so if there is anyone still following us they will think we are going back to Prague.'

They waited for ten minutes before driving on. The landscape became a smoky blue and then for a brief period the setting sun appeared in the west. Zikmund said that even with the detour they would make Karlsbad by eight that evening.

'You know something?' he said, after another period of silence. 'I've been thinking of Ostend.'

'Ostend? In Belgium? Why?'

'It's a very interesting place. There are a lot of planes at Ostend and those planes often leave Ostend with no cargo. They fly to Burgas in Bulgaria where they pick up their cargo. Do you know what that cargo is? Military supplies. And then the planes leave for their destinations in Asia and Africa – sometimes South America. It has been the route for most clandestine arms traffic in the last seven years.'

'Ostend?'

'It's near Nato headquarters. Many of the illegal arms shipments are made with Nato's blessing because they are destined for the armies and militias that Nato supports. Kochalyin is very big in the arms trade and his contacts in Burgas are excellent. Is it possible that Nato owes him a favour or two?'

'You're forgetting something,' said Harland. 'During the Bosnian civil war, Nato was trying to stop arms shipments from the East into Yugoslavia. That's how Kochalyin got his foot in the door with the Serbs, by supplying them with arms and fuel. So he was never Nato's best friend.'

'Yes, but things change! Nobody cares about Bosnia anymore! Maybe NATO needed his help in making shipments to other parts of the world – you understand what I am saying? So they arranged to fake his death and then tried to prevent your friend investigating it.'

'What's Ostend got to do with this?'

'One of the enterprises that we know Mister K has an interest in is an air freight business in Ostend. Two modified Boeings and a few smaller cargo planes that will go anywhere if the price is right.'

It was certainly a better theory than Harland had supposed at the beginning of Zikmund's little speech. He had always known that the phone-tracking operation which led Bézier's soldiers to the hotel must have involved some cooperation from Nato to pinpoint Lipnik's location and pass it to the French. The same influence that had staged his death could also be brought to bear on the War Crimes Tribunal, which was wholly reliant on Nato for the enforcement of the indictments. This wouldn't mean the corruption of the tribunal, merely a firm prod here and there to suggest that Alan Griswald's evidence didn't amount to much and that the tribunal could spend its time more profitably.

Harland straightened in his seat and groped for the cigarettes and lighter on the dashboard. Zikmund flashed him a saturnine grin in the glow of the instruments and told him to make sure his belt was fastened. The speedometer rose to 120 kph, then beyond.

'Is this necessary?'

Zikmund didn't reply. They took a turning on to a smaller road and moved at breakneck speed for about ten miles. Then Zikmund pulled over into a deserted depot, manoeuvred behind a rusting petrol tanker and switched off the engine and headlights. They waited. Three or four minutes later a car passed by travelling fast.

'Well, it wasn't the Saab,' said Harland.

'No, it wasn't. We'll go back to the main route and continue to make periodic diversions.'

Harland's mind returned to Kochalyin – anything rather than think about Eva and how he'd break the news to her. He thought about the code. Clearly the code's significance was twofold. In the wider context, it had become a matter of urgency for the intelligence organisations to stifle the random exposé of their operations. This was reason enough for the five or six big agencies to combine in tracing the source of the transmissions, which had been quickly achieved with the discovery of the two computers in London. So, in that respect, Cuth was right: the heat was off.

For Kochalyin, the interest in the code was acute because it revealed that Lipnik, the war criminal, was alive. Harland thought back to his conversation with Sara Hezemanns. She had said that Alan Griswald received the crucial part of his evidence after a visit to the East. That trip must have been to Stockholm. Because the images were hidden in the same code as the transmissions, it was reasonable to assume that they were either being prepared for broadcast or had already been used. Either way, it didn't much matter. The important point was that whoever killed Mortz must have learned that Griswald was in possession of the pictures. Plans were laid to destroy Griswald and the evidence. That left the only other member of the code-making syndicate to deal with. A week later Tomas was effectively silenced by the sniper's bullet.

Harland now dwelt on his son's motives. The more he thought about them, the more heroic they seemed to be. For in using the pictures, Tomas must have understood that he had signed his own death warrant.

Kochalyin would know they could only have come from him. But why had Tomas released the video still which showed him with Kochalyin on the mountainside? Was it a kind of admission to the world of his guilt – a shriving of his sin? Or was he sending a discreet signature to Kochalyin? He must have appreciated that he would eventually be found and killed. It was at that point that the astonishing coincidence occurred. Tomas saw his picture in the newspapers and decided to risk going to New York. He knew he had very little time and he wanted to meet his real father.

Harland no longer needed to ask himself about Vigo. From the outset his only purpose had been to find out whether anything had survived the plane crash. All his actions were generated by the belief that Harland had retrieved the information or was somehow in league with Griswald and the code-makers. The cursory search of the files in Prague, the phoney Crèche and the clumsy deployment of the surveillance teams were eloquent of Vigo's agenda. Everything was designed to press Harland into giving him the evidence. That could only mean that he was working for Kochalyin.

Zikmund gestured to some lights in the hills above the road. 'Welcome to Karlsbad', they said. He pulled out the hip flask and raised it in the direction of the town. 'Let us drink to Karlovy Vary – as we call this city – and to the success of your meeting.' He passed the slivovitz to Harland who drank a silent toast. Then he remembered something Tomas had said in their last conversation. A man in Bosnia had been killed because of him. How could he have forgotten that?

The apartment building was not difficult to find. They drove past it quickly, then returned on the other side of the street to make a more leisurely inspection. The corner block had been built at the turn of the last century and was lavishly covered in art nouveau detail. Along the upper storeys ran metalwork balustrades which vaulted outwards in a series of balconies, each of which was supported by a pair of muscular hermaphrodite giants. At the corner of the building was a turret-like structure that rose high above the roof and was capped by a small cupola.

'Money,' said Zikmund, glancing upwards at the shuttered windows. 'These people are rich.'

They checked into a small hotel nearby, having left the car in a public car park some distance away. They asked for a room overlooking the street so that they could see the apartment building. A tree stood in the line of sight, but they could just see the entrance from the corner of the room. Harland suggested that one of them should remain in the room and watch the building, while the other took a closer look.

Zikmund left and did not reappear until the early hours. He came back slightly high and bubbling over with information gleaned from a cleaner, a neighbour and a bartender. The Raths had moved to the building about ten years before, the old lady having been advised by her doctors that the hot springs of Karlsbad would do her arthritis good. The younger woman – who *was* known as Irina – taught yoga. But this was not because she needed the money: the Raths were well off. As far as Zikmund could tell, the building wasn't being watched.

'Did anyone mention Tomas?'

'No one could remember a kid living there or visiting the Rath women, but this is an apartment building: people come and go without being noticed.'

From a supermarket bag he produced a royal blue jacket bearing a logo on the chest and back.

'This belongs to the company that services the elevator. The last inspector left this behind. The cleaner kept it in his storeroom and I bought it from him for fifty US. Wear it when you go tomorrow.'

They took turns to watch the building. Harland's shift ran to dawn. At eight he shook Zikmund awake and told him he was going. He put the jacket under one arm and a dark plastic folder used to hold the hotel stationery under the other. The folder would pass as an inspector's clipboard, he thought.

Ten minutes later Harland walked past the doorman in the apartment building and motioned to the elevator with a grunt. He got in and pressed the buttons for all five floors, in case the concierge was taking sufficient interest to notice where he got out. Flat seven was on the second floor, opposite the entrance to the lift. He moved to the double-door entrance and listened for any sign of life with his hand hovering by the bell. There was no sound. He rang, and after a short pause a woman's voice came. She seemed to be asking a question. Harland said hello in English, which struck him as stupid, but it had the desired effect. He heard two bolts being drawn and the turn of a key. Suddenly he was looking at Eva.

She had changed little since the picture was taken for the last identity card. If anything, she had lost some weight. She was slightly flushed and her forehead was beaded with sweat. Her clothes – a black leotard top and baggy red pantaloons – also suggested that she had been exercising.

She was frowning slightly, trying to reconcile the English greeting and the jacket. She said something in Czech.

'Eva,' said Harland, looking at her steadily. 'It's Bobby Harland. It's me, Bobby.'

Her hands rose to her cheeks and her mouth opened slightly. But no words came out. Then three distinct emotions passed rapidly through her eyes – doubt, fear and pleasure. She took a step backwards. 'Bobby? Bobby Harland? My God, it *is* you.' She hesitated, then smiled.

The same perfect English, Harland thought, the same lilt in the voice, the same light brown eyes.

'I'm sorry to come like this,' he said. 'I should have phoned, but I felt it was better I came in person.'

'How did you find us? Why are you here?' She looked him up and down again. Her eyes came to rest on the logo of the jacket.

'Is it all right if I come in? I need to speak to you.'

An elderly woman's voice called out from the corridor to his right. She used the name Irina.

'I'm sorry, I forgot that you don't call yourself Eva. I can't get used to Irina.' He said it pleasantly but Eva looked at him as if he was accusing her of something. This was not going to be at all easy.

Eva's mother appeared in the light that was flooding into the apartment. She was the type of small, well-dressed old lady you see in tearooms all over Middle Europe. She held a metal walking stick and moved with difficulty. Harland nodded at her and briefly looked past her into the apartment. It was large and comfortably furnished. The dark parquet floors were covered in expensive rugs.

The two women spoke to each other in Czech. Eva's eyes never left Harland's face.

'My mother asks the same question that I did. Why are you here?'

Harland waited for a moment. He had planned what he was to say.

'It would be better if I came in.'

Eva stepped aside and motioned him through a second pair of double doors to a sitting-room filled with scent from a large bunch of lilies. Eva moved to her mother's side, arms folded.

'Does your mother know who I am?'

'Yes, she knows who you are.'

'It's about Tomas,' he said.

'You've heard from Tomas?' There was a proprietorial edge in her voice which seemed to say, 'You have no right to talk about my son.'

'Yes, he came to see me in New York. He told me I was his father.'

'Where is he now?' she demanded.

'In London.' The old lady touched her daughter's arm. Eva's eyes betrayed relief.

'But ...' Harland was appalled at what he was about to say, appalled also at the arc of fate that had brought him there to say it. 'But he is ill. He's in hospital. That's why I'm here, to tell you.'

'Ill?' she demanded. 'How? How ill is my son? What do you mean ill?'

'Please,' he implored, 'I think you will need to sit down. Your mother will need to sit down.'

Neither moved.

'Tell me why he is in hospital,' she said defiantly, as though he might be making up the story.

'He was shot.' The words were barely out before she had flown at him and slapped his face. She recoiled for a split second and then lunged again, beating his head and shoulders with her fists. Harland did not flinch. Eventually she fell back, head in hands, towards her mother's arms.

'Tell her what happened to Tomas,' said Hanna Rath in perfect English.

Harland exhaled. 'It is a very complicated story, but it ended with the shooting last week. I was with him when it happened. I'm afraid Tomas was hit several times.'

'But he is alive, yes?' said Eva, brushing back her hair. Her eyes blazed. There were no tears.

'Yes, he's alive, but he's not well. I have brought the doctor's phone number. You can talk to him and find out Tomas's latest condition. He was improving when I left England.' He waited. 'It's still only seven in the morning there, but we can call my sister, Harriet. She will know how he is.'

'Who shot him? Who shot Tomas?'

'They haven't caught anyone.' He had decided beforehand that he would leave out Kochalyin and Tomas's involvement with the transmissions. That was too much for her to deal with. He stood in silence for a moment. 'Look, do you want me to go? I can come back later.'

Eva moved to the window and looked out. Harland heard her saying something to herself in Czech – or perhaps it was to her mother because Hanna moved to the next room, to a kitchen and dining area. Eva now had her head down. Her shoulders were shaking with grief.

'Why didn't you come before?' she said through her tears.

'Because I didn't know where you lived.'

'But Tomas knows. Tomas has the phone numbers—' She searched Harland's face again. 'Why didn't Tomas tell you?' Harland shook his head helplessly.

'Because he couldn't tell you,' she said at length.

Harland moved two paces towards her, reaching out. But he stopped when he saw her recoil.

'He was in a coma,' he said. 'As I left England I heard news that he'd come out of it. Eva – they had to remove a bullet from the base of his brain. He may be permanently disabled.'

Harland saw Hanna looking through the door, horrified. It was as if both women had been scalded.

'I will go to London,' Eva said. 'I must go to London to see him. I will leave today.' She cast about the room, evidently trying to collect herself and think about the arrangements.

'I'll come with you,' said Harland. 'I'll take you to the hospital.'

Hanna came back into the room and motioned him to sit down.

'You will now tell us why Tomas was shot.'

'How much do you know about Tomas's activities in the last year?'

'Activities is a sinister-sounding word,' she said. 'It suggests something not legal. Tomas is a good boy. He needed to get away. He had his problems and we were content to let him work them out by himself. My daughter and Tomas have not spoken for some time. But we knew he was in Stockholm and that he had put his talents to good use there.'

'Do you mind me asking why you had not spoken to him?'

Hanna looked over to her daughter. Harland waited, but neither said anything.

'Well, it doesn't matter. I can tell you that he left Stockholm and moved to London. He had a girlfriend there.'

'We did not know that but, as you say, it doesn't matter now. All that matters is that my daughter sees him.'

'No,' said Eva from the window. 'I want to know everything. I have to hear the worse things now.'

Harland could not help noticing her beauty.

'How much do you really need to hear now?'

'Everything.'

Harland had no intention of telling her everything.

'Look, this is going to be very distressing. Why don't you take it one step at a time. We'll get the flights to Britain and we can talk on the way.'

'No!' she shouted. 'Tell me everything now.'

'Tell her,' said Hanna.

'Tell me, Bobby.' It was the first time she had addressed him by his first name.

'Well . . .' He paused and inhaled. 'I think there are very good reasons to believe that Oleg Kochalyin was responsible for the shooting.'

'That's impossible,' said Eva contemptuously.

Hanna studied Harland.

'Why do you say these things? Oleg would not hurt Tomas. They were close. For most of his life, Tomas knew Oleg as his father, and he was a good father to him. They saw each other after my daughter's divorce.'

'When was the divorce?'

'Nineteen eighty-eight,' said the old lady. 'It was amicable. Oleg took care of us. Irina and he still have an affection for each other, you see. This iş why you are wrong.'

Harland wasn't going to pursue it.

'Look, I think you need time by yourselves. This is a terrible thing to happen. You will want to discuss what you're going to do without me being here. I'll go back to the hotel and wait to hear from you.' He pulled a sheet of notepaper from the folder that he'd been carrying and placed it on the coffee table. 'The telephone and room number is on this.'

He left the building. It occurred to him that he had eaten little in the last twenty-four hours, so he decided to find breakfast before returning to the hotel. He also wanted time to gather his thoughts before talking to Zikmund. Seeing Eva again had thrown him, though he barely dwelled on this because to do so would be to put his desire above her distress. He felt deeply for her, and it didn't matter that she had been cold and suspicious with him. That was natural. He knew he'd been the same with Tomas.

Half an hour later he went back to the hotel. As he climbed the narrow stairs to the third floor two men brushed past him. He thought nothing about it until he reached his room and found the door unlocked. He called out, then pushed the door open.

Zikmund was lying in bed in much the same position as he had left him a couple of hours before. He had been shot in the head.

22
Escape

His first instinct was to leave the room immediately. The two men were bound to return once they realised that they'd passed an elevator inspector on the stairs of a hotel that possessed no elevator. But Harland was held to the spot. He looked down at the two small-calibre bullet wounds about two inches apart at Zikmund's temple and reflected bitterly on the waste. He had come to like the man, his decency and humour, and felt he owed it to him to stay and see that his body was treated with respect. But he couldn't.

He looked around the room. The contents of his bag had been tipped on to the floor. He swept everything back, knowing that there was nothing to reveal his false identity, and slung it over his shoulder. He felt in Zikmund's jacket pockets and removed the keys to the hire car. Then he left, without looking at Zikmund again, and hurried downstairs. He was still wearing the jacket that had saved his life when he sprinted across the road and burst through the entrance of Eva's building. The doorman, by now suspicious of his comings and goings, shouted something after him. Harland took no notice and bounded up the stairs to the second floor. Eva opened the door to his hammering and stared blankly at him. She had changed out of the exercise gear and now wore black trousers and a grey rollneck sweater. She looked composed – remote. He pushed past her, slamming the door behind him.

'The man who helped me find you has just been murdered. His body is in the hotel room over the street. He was asleep in bed when they shot him at close range with a silencer. The killing was ordered by the same man who shot Tomas.'

Eva looked at him and then at her mother who was still sitting in the same place on one of the sofas.

The lack of reaction annoyed him.

'Did you hear me? Kochalyin has killed again.'

The old lady was the first to speak.

'You have no proof, Mr Harland, that Oleg is responsible for the death of your friend.'

'No, I don't, but I do possess proof that he is a psychopathic murderer. It's the same proof that your son – our son – released to the War Crimes Tribunal in The Hague. This proof is so dangerous to Kochalyin that he has been prepared to cause the death of twenty-three people to suppress it. That figure includes a young woman named Felicity – Tomas's girlfriend. She was tortured to betray his whereabouts, then executed, like my friend. This toll includes many people who had never heard of Oleg Kochalyin – the passengers of two planes in New York, one of which he sabotaged. Then there was a young policeman in London who was mown down on the same evening as Tomas. His companion, by the way, is disabled for life.' He paused for breath. 'And Tomas? I'll be brutally frank about his prospects. Tomas will never move again. He will not speak again. He will never feed himself again. He is a prisoner of his own body.'

He reached into the inside pocket of his jacket. 'And the proof, that it was worth inflicting so much pain for? It's these pictures of Oleg Kochalyin, also known as the war criminal Viktor Lipnik.' He unfolded the print of the video still and placed it on the coffee table. 'This shows Kochalyin supervising the burial of victims of a mass execution in Bosnia. As you can see, Tomas is in the background. It's clear that he was made to witness this disgusting event when he was not yet twenty years old – by a man who you apparently regarded as the perfect father figure.' He looked down at Hanna. 'Forgive me,' he said harshly, 'that wasn't quite how you put it, but it's clear that from the moment you welcomed Kochalyin into Prague in 1968 with that basket of food, you have never ceased to trust him. I don't know whether you knew his true nature, but you must have had some idea when Tomas came back from his little trip in 1995.'

'We did know something had happened,' said Hanna. 'But he would not tell us about it.' She was shaken.

'And you didn't press him?' Harland demanded. He turned to Eva. 'What did you think you were doing?' he said, jabbing at the photograph. 'How did you let Kochalyin take him to Bosnia?'

Eva shook her head. She looked as if she couldn't take any more.

Her mother spoke. 'You don't understand. Tomas had a drug problem. Heroin. Oleg paid for the clinic in Austria where he was taken off the drugs. Oleg was attached to the boy and Tomas listened to him. When he said he would take him on business to Belgrade, we thought it would be good for Tomas. We knew he was going into Yugoslavia, but we thought it was Belgrade.'

'And he told you nothing afterwards. No hint?'

She lowered her eyes.

'Did you know that your KGB friend was supplying weapons and fuel to the Yugoslavs? Did you know he was laundering their money and stealing a good bit on the way?' He threw his arms out wide, indicating the room. 'Eva, for Christ's sake, where do you think all this comes from?'

'My name is Irina.'

'Not to me, it isn't.'

The old lady looked at her daughter. 'Tomas *did* say he had seen something terrible and we did think he had come back a very changed person. He would not talk.' She looked up at Harland. 'But you know he still went to see Oleg long after these events.'

'That's because he was gathering as much evidence as he could against Kochalyin,' said Harland. He placed the second picture on the table. 'This was taken on or after the twenty-ninth of May 1998 – probably by Tomas. It proves that Kochalyin – that is to say Lipnik – was alive after the staged assassination in Bosnia. Tomas certainly knew what he was doing. This photograph is in many ways more important than the first one.'

Both women looked at the picture.

Harland waited, then said, 'When did you tell him about me?'

'Two years ago,' Eva said, without raising her head.

'And he reacted by breaking off relations with you – is that right?'

She hesitated.

'We didn't see him, but he wrote to say that he had made a new life in Stockholm. He told me he'd done well and made some money for himself from an Internet company. He said he needed to get his life straightened out. He didn't send his address and I didn't try to find him.' She paused and moved to her mother's side. 'Of course we were anxious for him, Bobby, but what could we do? I knew he needed time to himself to sort out his problems. All I cared about was that he wasn't using drugs again.'

Harland watched her, partly absorbed by her face, and partly wondering at the compromises she'd made in marrying Kochalyin. Maybe they weren't compromises. Perhaps that was what she had wanted all along.

'I understand you've had your problems,' he said.

'Do you have children?' she asked abruptly. 'I mean other children. No? Well, how could you know about these things?'

'Well, maybe that's true, but I do know our son is lying in hospital and that I'm going back to Britain. You can come with me, or you can go separately. Either way, I'm leaving now.' He picked up the photographs. 'These have made me a marked man. And it's only a matter of time before Zikmund's body is discovered and descriptions of me are provided by the hotel staff.'

The phone rang. Eva moved to answer it but changed her mind.

'It's on the machine,' she said. The bell continued to sound. She cocked her head as it stopped and a recorded message played. A man spoke in

Czech – a gravelly, controlled voice that did not hesitate. After a few short sentences he hung up without giving a name.

Eva looked at him to see if Harland had guessed.

He had. 'That was Kochalyin. What did he want?'

'He asks me to call him. There's something he wants to talk to me about. It's not important.'

'But he didn't leave a number, did he? That means you must be in regular contact.'

'I have a number where I can get him when I need to.'

'How often is that?'

She shrugged.

'A few times a year. A message is passed on and he calls me back.'

'And what do you talk about?'

'Nothing – financial arrangements. He has bills to pay for us.'

'And?'

'And he has sometimes made attempts to find Tomas. I didn't ask him to, but he has done this anyway. He says he does it to – how do you say? – to put my mind at rest.'

'And he calls to find out if you've heard from him?'

She nodded.

'Well, I'm sure he was very concerned,' said Harland. 'But fortunately Tomas hid himself well. He got himself another identity. He has been living under the name Lars Edberg.'

Eva let out a weary, wry laugh.

'What?' It was at that precise moment when he became aware of something reaching deep inside him and snatching at his guts.

'The family trait,' she said. 'We've all pretended to be other people.'

Harland didn't respond. Now he knew what it was. That voice on the answering machine – he'd heard it before. It was in the villa. On the first day they'd tied him to a chair and left him blindfolded in the old air of the cellar. He was there for an hour or more in complete darkness and silence. And he'd thought he was alone, which is why he let out the sighs and self-recriminations that a person only voices when he knows he is by himself and facing death. Then the man spoke – the cracked smoker's voice he'd just heard. He was shockingly close and Harland had instantly understood that he'd been there, sitting beside him the entire time, watching his fear.

There was no conversation during that first session. But there was pain, a sudden, swift statement of the man's power. The first blow was to his groin. There were many more. He thought perhaps that it was a club or baseball bat, but it might just as easily have been the toe-cap of a heavy boot.

In some ways Harland was not surprised. All along he had wondered about the connection between the Russian in the villa and the elusive

Kochalyin. He looked at Eva. Did she know about this? And what about the old lady who had made the first contact with the young tank officer, who had brought him into her home and practically offered her daughter up to him?

'How did you get here?' asked Eva.

'By car. We were followed. They know the car. They're probably watching it. But I have the keys and if there's no other way to leave I will try to use it.'

'Were you registered under your own name at the hotel?'

'No. Zikmund took the room in his name and showed his ID. They didn't see mine.'

'But the people who killed him must know who you are.'

'Of course. And they know I came to see you, which is why you just got that call. It is also probably true that they would very much prefer it if you didn't learn about the evidence against him. You must know a lot about Kochalyin's background which he would hate to see combined with the material I have. Everything you know will add to the case against him – for example, the dates of his business trip with Tomas in 1995. Soon, Eva, there'll be a point when Oleg Kochalyin will have to decide what to do about you. It may be that this man is still obsessed with you.' He paused, sat down on the arm of a sofa and removed the inspector's jacket. 'But how long is that likely to last now? It has only just occurred to me that while you didn't know what had happened to Tomas, you were no threat. But now he suspects that you've learned about the shooting and the reasons for it and about the other barbarities, he will come to see you as a danger to him.'

'He never will see her like that,' said Hanna.

'You seem very confident.'

'I am. She is the only person that man has ever loved. He could not harm her.'

Harland wondered how much the old lady had pushed Eva's relationship.

'Don't be too certain,' he said to her. 'He attempted to kill the boy and you yourself told me how fond he was of him.'

Eva squeezed her temples and rubbed her face.

'We'll leave now,' she said, looking at the floor. 'I already have my bag packed.'

She spoke a few words in Czech to her mother, then picked up the phone and dialled. This time she spoke in German, saying without preamble that she was returning the call of fifteen minutes before. She informed the person that she was going out to give a class at the Thermal Sanatorium and to do some shopping. She would be back in the early afternoon, although she'd be on her cellphone in the meantime.

She went to get her bag and began to assemble a few more things for the journey – a book, her purse, passport, a cellphone and an envelope of money, which she took from a desk.

'You know that Tomas was probably traced by Kochalyin because he was using a cellphone,' he said. 'All he needs to do is to ring you to get a fix on your position.'

Eva thought for a second.

'We will need it,' she said firmly.

Having rung down and told the doorman to order a cab for her, Eva led Harland to the first-floor landing and through a metal door. They took a spiral staircase to the ground floor where there was a boiler room and service area. Another metal door opened on to a shabby little street at the back of the building, piled with dirty snow. She looked left and right, then bolted across the street. Harland followed, carrying both bags. At the first turning on the right she held her keys in the air. Harland saw the side lights of the dark green BMW blink ahead of him. She got in and started the engine before he had managed to sling the bags on the back seat.

'Now, get my phone out,' she said, scanning the street ahead of them, 'and also one of the credit cards in my purse.'

As they moved off, Eva wedged the phone between her ear and shoulder and asked for the British Airways number in Prague. Then she made another call. Realising she was booking flights on the afternoon service to Heathrow, he felt for his passport and held it open for her. She nodded to him as she spelled out Tristan O'Donnell's name. Harland had an idea what she was doing, but didn't say anything.

They left the side street and moved sedately towards the eastern fringes of the town. The traffic began to thin out. When they reached the open road Eva glanced in the mirror and put her foot down. For twenty minutes they drove at a remorseless speed, the needle of the speedometer never dipping below 140 kph. On the open stretches they moved at 180 kph. In a patch of forest they slowed down and took a turning left into a range of hills.

'Where did you learn to drive like this?' he shouted, as she accelerated round a corner to take the one-in-ten gradient.

'Russia. I was on a course there once.'

He'd ask her about that later.

'You think we're being followed? There's nothing behind us.'

'I hope they believe we're going to Prague – they will have got someone checking the flight bookings. But my instinct says they're not going to leave this to chance. They'll try to follow.' She paused. 'I guess they missed us on our last turning, but if they're smart they'll pick us up on the road to the north. It depends how quickly we can make it.'

She said there was a map in the pocket of his door and that he should start working out routes through northern Bohemia into Germany. She was planning to drive through Teplice and Usti. At each stage she wanted him to give an alternative route to cut through the mountains.

They passed through a forest of bare oak and beech, then dropped down to a plain, where they joined the road that would take them to the border. Harland was reminded of another trip in a BMW tearing through the Czech landscape to a border crossing. He had lain folded up in the back seat. Macy was at the wheel; The Bird was up front, but reached back and kept a hand on his shoulder for a lot of the journey. They thought they were being followed, but they were armed to the hilt and there was no question of them being stopped.

On the outskirts of a town called Chumotuv, Harland and Eva entered a region known as the Black Triangle. All about them were tar-black scars of lignite mines and chimney-stacks pouring out thick, sulphurous smoke. Each town was a monochrome study of Communist functional-ism – soulless prefab blocks drenched in pollution; factories of fantastical scale and filth. Everything was blackened – the piles of snow, the surface water, the road signs. Through it all the people moved as shadows. The towns looked as if they were still being run by Communist party bosses.

The country passed by in a toxic blur. At a place called Most, they halted for petrol. As Harland filled the tank, he gazed absent-mindedly across the road at an abandoned building. A prostitute dressed as a rodeo girl lifted a leg in the doorway in half-hearted enticement. Another joined her at the window and pouted. It was then that he noticed the blue Saab flash by. From the payment booth, Eva saw him duck and waited for a few seconds before returning to the car.

'Was it the silver Mercedes?' she asked.

'What Mercedes? This was a Saab.'

'I think there's a Mercedes also – German number plates.'

They didn't see either car again until Usti, where the Saab fell in a few cars behind them at some lights. They jumped the lights and lost it but Eva said she didn't think they'd shake it off for good. Five miles down the road they came to Decin, the last big town before the border. She turned into a desolate housing estate. A few hundred metres on she apparently found what she was looking for – four young toughs, three in skinhead uniform, loitering outside a bar. She got out and talked to them, gesturing and smiling. At first they looked wary, but she won them over within a few minutes. She returned with two, who sheepishly nodded to Harland, climbed in the back of the car and put the bags on their laps.

'What the hell are we doing?' asked Harland.

'I think it's better if we take the train. These boys are going to have a night out in Prague. I've promised them a hundred dollars. They weren't going to accept until I said it would be dangerous.'

As they prepared to get out at the station, Harland noticed Eva take her phone from the side pocket of her bag and slip it into the tray beneath the dashboard. That was smart of her: she was leaving it for the young men to use so they'd lay a false trail.

An hour and a half later the local train pulled into Dresden. They got out and separated. Harland went and bought two tickets to Amsterdam via Berlin and Cologne. At all three cities they would have the option to get off the train and take a plane to London. Having established that the train left in thirty-five minutes, he made for the spot where they had agreed to meet. Before he got there he was aware of her at his side in the crowd.

'I think they're here,' she said, looking in front of them. 'There's a train leaving for Warsaw in ten minutes. We'll meet on it.' She forged ahead of him and vanished towards the station's main exit.

Harland turned and walked quickly in the other direction and boarded the train waiting at the nearest platform – an express bound for Munich. He moved along two carriages and became stuck in the middle of a third. Behind and in front of him were passengers sorting out their seats and stowing luggage. He pushed back past a group of soldiers to the door. But this too was blocked. Then he realised that the door on the track side of the train would be just as easy. He opened it, dropped down to the rails and ran across to the other side where he scrambled up. He made the Warsaw express with thirty seconds to spare. There was no sign of Eva.

He gave up looking for her and sat at a table with two young German priests. About half an hour later she appeared and said she had a compartment to herself at the front of the train. She had bought two tickets to Warsaw where they could make a connection which would take them back to Berlin. He nodded to the priests and followed her to the compartment, on the way passing a ticket inspector with whom Eva was clearly already on good terms. They sat down opposite each other.

Now that they were alone, a rather odd formality settled over them. Eva tried reading her book but let her gaze drift to the unbearably bleak countryside. Their eyes fastened on the same village churches and impenetrable pine forests. Soon dusk snuffed out the landscape and they were looking at each other's reflections.

'I saw you on television,' she said suddenly. Her tone was matter-of-fact. 'I saw you on television in 1989.'

'I wasn't on television in 1989,' he said. 'I was still working for SIS. Serving officers don't go on television. It's one of the things they taught us.'

She didn't smile. 'But you were on television. That's how I knew you were in Prague. That's why I took Tomas to Prague and stayed in my mother's old flat. I thought I'd see you again in the streets. I must have been crazy.'

'How do you mean, you saw me on television?'

'It's true. I did. You remember how it started with the soldiers beating them up?'

He nodded.

'There was a German camera crew in Prague secretly filming in the streets all that day. They were waiting for something to happen like it did in the GDR. About four days afterwards, the film was smuggled out and shown on German TV, which we could receive where we lived. I knew it was you. I recognised your walk first. You were going away from the camera and then you stopped and someone gave you something. Your face looked directly at the camera for a few seconds, though you didn't know it was there. You were talking to a young woman, then you turned away. Bobby, I know it was you. You were near the end of Vaclavské Namesti – Wenceslas Square – by Narodni Street. That was where the police attacked the students. Why were you there?'

'Because of you,' he said simply.

'You were looking for me?' She was puzzled.

'No, I was there *because* of you. I was trying to eliminate my records of contact with the StB. Look, I don't have to explain this, surely. You knew about the photograph of us in bed. They threatened to send that other material to SIS. I had to get those files before the regime collapsed.'

'What are you talking about? There was no photograph.'

He contemplated her and wished he had a cigarette. 'The whole thing was rigged. I think it must have been at the hotel we went to near Campo dei Fiore. But I'm not sure, except I know it wasn't Orvieto.'

'You must believe me, Bobby. I never cooperated in such a plan.'

'Well, it doesn't matter now,' he said. 'But that was one of the things I was trying to get before everything collapsed in your country.'

'How could you hope to do such a thing?'

'The Stasi files were taken from East Germany at that time. The KGB ended up selling them in Moscow.'

'Yes, but these things were protected in Czech.'

'Less so, actually. My companion had a contact. We went to Prague to make a down-payment.'

She absorbed this and looked away. 'Do you know who your contact was?'

'It was my friend's. I was representing the British side of things. But he'd let me in on the deal because we were old associates. The Americans were going to bear most of the financial weight of the transaction, although we were going to get equal access to the files.'

'And did you get anything?'

'A little, but not enough to eliminate all trace of me.'

She was sailing very close to the subject of his detention and torture. That might be expected of someone who didn't know about it, but equally of a person pretending ignorance.

'Believe me, Bobby. I did not know of the photograph. I wouldn't have allowed it to happen.'

'Oh, for fuck's sake! What about the naval attaché? You compromised him before you met me in exactly the same way. You slept with him, right? Drew Morris was his name and he was forced to pass secrets to the StB – another victory for K.'

She looked appalled. 'How did you find out these things?'

'I finally saw the files. Zikmund got me in this week. I traced you through your mother's file.'

He could see her calculating what else he might know. The crease in her forehead had knotted and she wore the glazed, neutral expression that he remembered she used to hide her thoughts. A lot of him was still fascinated by her face; even in the unforgiving light of the compartment it was extraordinarily vital. For the first time he noticed half a dozen freckles on and beside her nose which were in fact tiny moles. Smile lines showed on either side of her mouth and she had one or two strands of iron grey in her hair. She was very beautiful, but for him now it was an entirely objective beauty.

'You know everything, then.'

'No, your file was remarkably slender. Kochalyin had long ago made sure that there was very little there.'

'But you have to believe me. I didn't know about the camera or the photograph.'

'It doesn't matter now.'

'No, this is the truth and it's important you accept it.'

Harland glanced at her reflection in the window.

'Why didn't you tell me that you were pregnant?'

'Because I knew you wouldn't be able to do anything. I had no choice: if I had defected, my mother would have been punished. That's why I didn't see you.'

'Yes, your mother – your mother has played a big part in all this,' he said acidly. 'Did you know there's a picture of her in the archive from '68, giving Oleg Kochalyin and his crew a basket of food? It was used in the Soviet papers. That act changed our entire lives. There is just one thing I don't understand. Was Kochalyin in the KGB then, or did he go back to the Soviet Union and train?'

'You want to know about all that?' she said, matching his vehemence. 'It is very simple. Oleg was undercover KGB in the army. They were worried that the troops would not do what was necessary. Oleg, who had been in the army before the KGB, was put in as tank captain to make sure there would be no sympathy for the Czech people, that there would be no weakening of resolve among the troops. When the tanks were ordered into Prague, they had no food. Did you know that? The great Soviet military machine forgot to give its army provisions. By the third or fourth day those soldiers were desperate. They hadn't eaten and they were out of water. It was very hot that August and they couldn't leave their tanks to find provisions. Anyway, the Czechs were not going to give them help.'

'But your mother did and then a Soviet army photographer happened by to capture the scene for the Russian newspapers.'

'It wasn't like that. This tank crew was outside our apartment for a day. They were suffering and so she gave them food. When the Russians heard about this they sent a photographer and they staged the scene again. Of course she was against the invasion – everyone was. But she gave them food because once a Russian soldier had saved her life. Did Tomas tell you she survived the camp at Terezin – Theresienstadt?'

Harland nodded impatiently.

'When the camp was liberated by the Russians a tank captain in General Rybalko's Third Guard Tank Corps found her. That night he looked after her – he gave her water and small amounts of food because she could only take a little. She was very, very weak and on the point of death. Maybe she reminded him of his own child – she never knew why he took so much care of her. But she says that kindness – the relief at finding kindness in the world again – was what saved her. It gave her hope. Do you understand? And then all those years later she saw a tank crew who needed exactly what that officer had given her – food, water, kindness. You see she saw them as people and she knew in her heart that she had a debt of honour and that was far more important to her than the issue of the invasion. It was a personal obligation. And for that act she paid greatly. We both did. We were hounded from the neighbourhood. People did not speak to us. They spat at us in the street. They called us Russian whores.' She paused and smoothed down the cover of her book. 'So, you see, not everything is as simple as it appears.'

'How did Kochalyin keep in touch?'

'Oleg stayed in Prague. He was working full time on the Normalisation programme and overseeing work with the StB. He was stationed in Prague permanently. I don't know how my mother found him, but she did and that was a good thing because the new regime was beginning to move against the Jews again. Those few Jews that remained in Czechoslovakia after the war were accused of anti-state and anti-socialist activities – a Zionist conspiracy. Oleg gave her protection. He found us another apartment and he got her a new job.'

Eva paused.

'People in the West don't understand now how difficult it was. She depended on him. When she came out of Terezin she didn't have one living relation in the world. So, you see, if I had defected in 1975, she would have lost everything for the second time in her life. I had to go back, Bobby, and I couldn't tell you why.'

Harland wondered if Hanna Rath had been Kochalyin's lover before he transferred his attentions to her daughter. Had he been waiting all that time for Eva? Had Hanna pushed the match to keep her protection?

'And you?' he asked quietly. 'When were you thrown into the bargain?'

She looked away. 'You're very cruel. I don't remember you being like that.'

He persisted. 'When did you become his lover? Before or after me?'

Her eyes darkened.

'After you. We needed to survive. I was pregnant, for God's sake!'

'So you had Tomas and resumed work for the StB, or was it the KGB? What did you do? You said you went on a driving course in Russia. That sounds like you were being prepared for some type of active service. What were you doing? Wet jobs? Courier work? I want the whole story.'

'You have no right to my story, Bobby. You were my lover twenty-eight years ago. That's all.'

'And the father of your child.'

'Biologically – yes. But that doesn't give you any kind of moral authority. Who are you to judge the decisions I was forced to take? They were very difficult and I made the best of my life after I took them. As for you, you didn't have any of these responsibilities, did you? You just continued your career in the British Secret Service.'

There was no longer even a pretence of politeness.

'Let me remind you of a couple of things,' said Harland coldly. 'You were living with a KGB butcher and a sadist. However much you averted your eyes, you must have known what he was. Second, you were serving a regime, the entire purpose of which was to suppress the Czechs and Slovaks – your people. So when it comes to morality, even I may have the edge on you.'

'You spied for that regime,' she said. 'What does that make you?'

He looked at her with a new understanding. 'How did you know what I did?'

'You just told me.'

'I didn't say anything about that. I said that they just threatened to send the material to my superiors. I didn't tell you how I reacted.'

At that moment a door opened and an officer from the Polish border police asked for their passports.

'You are both travelling to Warsaw, sir?'

'Yes,' replied Harland. 'A business trip – one or two days.'

He examined the passport again.

'This passport was issued three years ago. The photograph is much older, no? You are more young in the photograph, Mr O'Donnell.'

Harland smiled ruefully and coughed.

'Vanity, I'm afraid. I liked that picture.'

The man seemed to accept this and turned to Eva.

'Have a pleasant journey,' he said.

23

A Halt in Poland

They remained in silence for half an hour. Harland wished he had something to read because his eyes kept returning to Eva's rigidly averted features. She knew more than she'd let on – he was sure of that. But he didn't want to have it out with her now.

Quite suddenly the train slammed on its brakes. Eva got up and angled her head to look forward out of the window. Harland went into the passage and opened a window on the right side of the train. They turned to each other. Eva left the compartment and hurried back to the doors at the end of the carriage. She wrenched open the windows on both sides of the train and peered up the line.

'There's a station about a kilometre in front of us,' she said.

Harland went to join her and leaned out of the window. The wind hummed in the electric cables overhead. He could just make out a row of white lights ahead of them and off to his right one or two clusters of orange lights that he supposed were villages. There was nothing obviously wrong, but he knew from the German travel schedule, issued with the tickets, that the *expresowych* wasn't due to stop until they reached Wroclaw in half an hour's time. What lay ahead was little more than a halt for local trains. He thrust his head out of the window and squinted. Now two or three pairs of lights were scything through the darkness towards the station. The first pair stopped and were extinguished. Harland turned round to tell Eva to fetch the bags, but she'd already done so and was looking out of the opposite window. They waited.

The train began to ease forward, the wheels groaning with inertia. They travelled a further hundred yards but without picking up much speed. It was obvious they were going to coast into the station ahead of them for an unscheduled stop. He went through the possibilities. The engine might be malfunctioning; the line ahead of them could be blocked; or the railway was suffering from a routine delay. But it did seem odd that the cars had turned up at that exact moment.

'What do you think?' he shouted over to Eva.

Without saying anything, she tried the door handle and found the automatic locking system was on. 'Can you get out of this window?' she said.

She put the bag over her shoulder, gathered up a short blue duffel coat and swung one leg up in a balletic arc so that it rested in the top of the window. 'Like this,' she said.

'That's all very well,' said Harland, 'but don't you think it would be better to get out this side where there's no track?'

'It was for demonstration purposes,' she said with a sarcastic grimace. 'Perhaps we should stay on the train. You don't look in very good shape, Bobby.'

He poked his head out again. There were figures on the platform ahead of them. 'No, I think we should leave. We can catch another train at the station or thumb a ride.'

'In this weather? I don't think so,' she said.

She went first and with very little effort wriggled her legs through the window and then turned round so she could lower herself to a step below the door. She held the window with one hand and worked the handle of the door from the outside. It opened a fraction. She smiled up at him, then dropped from the train, squatted for a fraction of a second and rolled into the darkness, like an expert parachutist.

Harland opened the door, grasped the vertical hand-rail and felt for the step below. Then he leaned back and slammed the door shut. The hand-rail allowed him to crouch down within two or three feet of the ground. He found he could hang there quite comfortably with his bag over his shoulder and so he decided to get nearer the station before launching himself into the dark. About two hundred and fifty yards from the end of the platform the train's brakes began to grind again. He shifted his bag from his shoulder and leapt, hugging it with both hands. His jump was not as neat as Eva's. He misjudged the distance and hit a mound of snow which sent him sprawling into a frozen ditch. He picked himself up, brushed the snow off and looked round to see Eva jogging towards him, taking care to keep out of the light thrown from the carriages.

She made her way to his side. The last coach passed and left them bathed in the glow from two red tail-lights. As the train juddered to a halt so that only the engine and the first coach reached the platform, four figures moved from the covered section of the station and boarded. Harland thought he saw uniforms.

'What's going on?' Eva said.

'I think they're police.' It was clear to him that the train had been ordered to slow down so that it wouldn't arrive at the station before the cars did. But it didn't make sense. Anyone who wanted to avoid them would simply jump down beside the track, as they had done.

They moved forward fifty yards to a piece of ground covered in rusting oil drums and concrete sleepers. Magnetic tape from a discarded cassette was caught in the branches of a stunted thorn bush and shimmered like Christmas streamers. They squatted behind the bush and waited. Harland was aware of two policemen moving towards them along the track. They were sweeping the snow with the beam of a torch, looking for footprints. They reached the last carriage and stopped. A man's voice called out to them from the other side of the train, where the same operation was apparently in progress. Then both men looked up as a head appeared at the door of the last carriage. They exchanged a few words during which Harland registered a note of dejection. Eva bent to Harland's ear and whispered that she'd heard that they had searched the train and found nothing.

The train eased forward with the police officers following and peering to see if anyone was hiding under the carriages. It drew level with the platform and stopped, whereupon the roof and the gaps between the carriages were searched. Eventually all the police officers assembled on the platform. There was a good deal of shrugging and gesturing and stamping of feet. Harland knew they'd given up on what was a hopelessly flawed plan. He rose a little, peered over the bush then edged round it and began to make his way towards the platform. Eva hissed at him to stay back, but he took no notice. She swore and scuttled after him, her blue duffel coat rasping over the surface of the frosted snow.

There was an officer in the middle of the group who turned from his men to someone hidden in the shadows. A lot of toing and froing ensued and now passengers were leaning out of the windows demanding to know why they were being delayed. A rail official came up and gesticulated, and then the man from the frontier police who had checked their passports joined in, insisting that the rail authorities hold the train at the station. He's been well paid, thought Harland.

'They're going to have to let it go,' said Eva.

'Well, let's go with it.'

'Get on again?'

'We can't stay here,' he hissed. 'No cars, no roads – nothing. There's bugger all here.'

Without consulting her further, he crouched down and slipped over the tracks into the shadows on the other side of the train. Eva followed so quietly that for a few seconds Harland didn't know that she had joined him. She moved very close to him and stood, looking up at the door of the last carriage, her shoulders rising silently.

His plan was to step up and open the door as the train began to move off. But he saw the lights of another train approaching rapidly from the opposite direction and decided to make his move when it passed them. The murmur which preceded the express grew to a roar. It thundered through the station dragging a cloud of ice particles in its slipstream. Harland jumped up and wrenched the door handle downwards, but it wouldn't shift. He thought it might be frozen and reached up again to hammer it up with his fist. Nothing.

Just at that moment the wheels protested and moved a few inches on the track, paused then moved some more.

'Fuck! Fuck! Fuck!' Harland spat out the words.

Eva glanced at him and gestured with her head to the right. She dropped back behind the last carriage and jogged beneath the tail-lights. He followed because he didn't want to be left standing like an idiot in the middle of the tracks. There was about a carriage distance between them and the end of the platform. Just as the last few feet of the carriage passed the platform, he understood what she planned. She crouched and flipped herself over the rail and landed in the blackness under the concrete lip of the platform. The projection offered about two feet of shelter but much more shadow. A second later Harland dived too, but made a hash of it. The strap of his bag got snagged on a bolt that held the rail to a sleeper and he was forced to let go and roll over the bag. Eva's hand darted forward, released the strap and pulled the bag towards her. The train had travelled almost the length of the platform before they settled themselves under the concrete lip, knees clasped tightly to their chests.

Suddenly there was quiet. Most of the voices receded into the station buildings. But the sound remained of two or three pairs of footsteps moving randomly above. One pair came close to the edge about ten feet to the left of where they were huddled. The person seemed to be standing there in contemplation. Harland looked at Eva. She had put her finger to her nose and was lifting her head. He understood she'd picked up the scent of his heavy cologne.

Then came the voice, the voice of Oleg Kochalyin in the stillness of the deserted station. Eva flinched. Harland put his hand up to her mouth.

'We'll leave,' Kochalyin said in Russian. 'They're not here. Get the engine started.' There was no reply, just the scurrying of a pair of feet hastening to carry out an order.

He stood there for a few moments longer. Then he was gone and after a minute there was the cough of an ignition, followed by the whine of a helicopter engine. Harland realised that Kochalyin must have arrived at the station some time before the police. There was no mystery in this. It wouldn't have been difficult for him to work out which train they had taken from Dresden. The problem must have been to galvanise the Polish authorities to stop the train and have it searched. He wondered what story he'd used to persuade them to do this.

The noise of the engine reached a pitch behind the station buildings and then the helicopter lifted into the air with a sudden roar. It paused over the station and shot off westwards down the track.

'What do we do now?' asked Eva, shivering.

'It's still early. We'll get on the next train, whichever way it's going.'

Most of the lights on the platform were turned off and they were able to move away from beside the track. An hour later a slow service going east pulled in and they boarded for the next station down the line where they changed to a faster train to Warsaw. Late that night they boarded an overnight service for Poznań and Berlin. A bribe of fifty dollars bought them the last free couchette. Before they left, Harland found a phone and put a call through to The Bird to tell him that Zikmund Myslbek had been killed that morning. The Bird already knew but wanted to hear the details. He said that Macy was extremely upset: he'd known Zikmund for over twenty years. Then Harland phoned Harriet to say that he was on his way back with Eva. She was cautious on the phone and said that the patient had had one or two unexpected visitors, but he was doing well. Harland bombarded her with questions but she refused to answer.

He returned to the couchette to find Eva sitting on the lower of two bunks scrubbing her trousers with a nailbrush. She didn't look up.

'How is he?' she asked.

'She says he's doing well – improving.'

'Nothing more than that?'

'No, she couldn't talk.'

She turned her head up. The closeness that had come so naturally when they were relying on each other a few hours before had evaporated.

'I think you have to explain all this to me,' she said.

Harland waited.

'And you too – you have to tell me about Kochalyin and what you were doing in Prague in November '89.'

She looked puzzled.

'I don't know what you mean.'

'Well, let's have something to eat and and we can talk.'

They went to the restaurant car and ordered as the train left the station – soup, lamb and potatoes, and a bottle of rough red wine.

Harland drained a glass.

'You say I don't have a right to know your story. I disagree because the entire course of my life was affected by our ... our meeting in Rome.'

'Mine too was changed,' she said sharply. 'I bore the child – remember!'

'Well, at any rate I'd very much like to know about your relationship with Kochalyin, especially after your divorce. I want some answers first, then I'll tell you why.'

'It's simple. I had to marry him because that was the only way we could survive. I told you that no one understands those days. Looking back now, we know that it all ended in '89, but in the early eighties communism looked as though it would last for centuries. The system seemed impregnable and we had to make arrangements accordingly. Oleg was my arrangement.'

'He was obsessed with you?'

'Yes, I suppose you could say that.'

'And he was your mother's lover before?'

She looked at him defiantly.

'I will tell you my story, not hers.'

'If you needed him, why did you divorce in '88?'

'These things are difficult.' A look of pain swept through her face.

'Was it the sex?'

'You're so crude, Bobby. Of course it was the sex. I could not love him. He knew about you and he blamed you for my failure to respond to him.'

'But you kept on good terms with him?'

'Oleg is not a normal man. He never knew his parents. They died soon after the war. He was an orphan and he plunged himself into our little family. He recognised certain things in my mother – her lack of parents for one – and in his weird, obsessive way he decided to become the man in our household. He spent much time away and so it was bearable. You ask about the sex. I will tell you. There was none – at least there was no conventional sex.'

'He was sadistic?'

'It's not so simple. Yes, he had those tendencies. He was abnormal – tormented.'

'Did he beat you?' Harland didn't want to know but something made him ask.

'Bobby, you aren't going to understand this. This man was distorted. He showed affection to me and my mother and Tomas, the only time perhaps in his life. But I could not return it. And when he understood that that exchange wasn't going to happen, he found gratification in other ways. There was a darkness in him. I don't know how I can express it any other way.'

'Humiliation?'

'Yes.' She was embarrassed.

'But I don't understand why he remained in touch with you after your divorce. It's been nearly fourteen years. And for all that time he kept you in some style.'

She looked at him coldly.

'Because I know him. I know his secrets; I know him like no one else can. I hold part of him. It was important for a man like Oleg, who is so much a mystery to himself, to feel that someone knew him.'

'And Tomas?'

'That was part of Oleg's idea of himself as a father. We did not have children – there was no chance of that. But Oleg wanted to give Tomas what he did not have himself. It mattered to him that Tomas did not have a father. It was one of the very few normal parts of him. That was another reason why he kept in touch with us after the divorce.'

'And did you tell him that I was in Prague that November?'

'No, why would I do that?' She paused. 'Bobby, I wanted to see you. Why would I tell Oleg? Besides, I did not know where he was. He was obsessed with keeping his movements secret. That was the way he lived. He phoned us, or made arrangements through an intermediary. Why do you ask about that time in 1989? What does it matter now?'

He smiled weakly. 'Were you working for the StB then?'

'No, I worked until 1988. This was not active service, as you said before. I never served as an illegal after Rome.'

'Why the training in Russia?'

'I had been suggested for a job with a high-security clearance and the Russians wanted to test me. So I was sent on this training course which at the same time was a type of examination of my trustworthiness.'

'In what field was this new job?'

'Signals Intelligence.'

'Ah!' exclaimed Harland. 'Code-breaking – that makes sense.'

She looked at him strangely.

'And you were based in Prague for this?'

'Yes – after training I got clearance and worked in Prague.'

'Tell me about the operation.'

Her brow knotted. The habit of secrecy dies hard, thought Harland. He poured her some more wine.

'We were concerned with acquiring cipher material from the Western embassies in Prague. We were breaking their codes and for this we needed cipher material.'

'But the Soviets ran the Sigint operation in the Eastern Bloc,' said Harland. 'All the friendly agencies, like the StB, fed into a central pool. As far as I remember, this was all part of the KGB's Sixteenth Directorate. Surely you didn't attend the training school of cryptanalysts as well?'

'No, I was trained at Moscow Centre. The training school was for Russians only. They thought it was secret, but we knew about it.'

'So you returned to Prague with this new skill of yours. Was Kochalyin a part of this set-up?'

She shook her head.

'But he would have had access to your material?'

'Yes,' she said.

'So you were working with him right up to your divorce?'

'Not directly.'

'Tell me, what success did you have?' This was interesting simply from a historical point of view to Harland. He recalled that the Americans and

British were absolutely certain that the signals traffic wasn't being read by the KGB, particularly after the leaps in computer-generated cryptography in the eighties.

'We could read everything,' she said simply. 'Everything!'

'The British and American traffic?'

'Everything. We had been working on this for many years. Your people . . . your people were lax in many areas. There was a man in the US embassy. He fell for one of our agents. He never knew how much she stole.'

'So you were reading all the communications by '89?'

'Yes, we knew what your embassy was saying to the British Foreign Office.' She paused. 'We tapped the line from the telex centre to the encryption machine.'

So they had got all the telegrams. That must have been how Kochalyin had learned of his and Griswald's plan. Before they had set out from Berlin there had been furious exchanges between Prague and London, the embassy staff insisting that the plan to open negotiations for the StB files was fraught with danger. Three or four cables arrived saying that under no circumstances should it go ahead. What response these elicited from Century House, Harland never learned, but he knew they would almost certainly have told the embassy that the operation was off. But anyone with the slightest notion about these things or the way that SIS worked would have concluded that the operation was most definitely on. After that it would have been a simple matter to trace their entry into the country. And when Griswald started putting feelers out, well, there was no hope of them going undetected by Kochalyin.

They sat in silence for a long time. Harland was considering whether to tell her what had happened after that.

'I met your friend at that time,' he said. 'I encountered Kochalyin.'

She looked startled.

He exhaled heavily and drank some wine. 'I was . . . I was held by the StB then handed over to Kochalyin. But only this morning did I know for sure that it was him. I never once saw his face. I knew he was a Russian and one or two of the men with him were Russians. All I knew was his voice – the same voice that I heard leave a message on your machine this morning. I was absolutely certain at the station when we heard him again this evening.'

'I don't understand. Why did you never see his face?'

'I was blindfolded.' He paused, his eyes settling on a man at the far end of the restaurant car. 'It was a clever observation of yours when you said Kochalyin is a mystery to himself. I can understand that. But there again, we all live our lives like that. Our histories are hidden from us. For all these years I had no idea why I was taken by him. I only understood today what it was all about. I . . . he . . . he was taking revenge on me for you.'

'He hurt you?'

'Yes. I never understood the pointlessness of what he did – the attention to detail of inflicting pain. But now I do. He was taking revenge for you. He was taking revenge for that photograph of you and me in bed – the picture you say you knew nothing about.'

Her hands had risen to her mouth.

'And I imagine that the same motive was behind his taking Tomas to Bosnia. He wanted to contaminate him. He wanted to destroy him because he was my child, not his. There is no other explanation for what he did. You see Eva, he knew what was going to happen in eastern Bosnia that summer. He supplied the weapons and ammunition – the fuel. Kochalyin knew all along what he was doing.

'I've been thinking about those pictures I showed you and I've come to recognise that Tomas didn't just witness the massacre – he took part in it. Just before he was shot he said he'd killed a man. I ignored it at the time Tomas was in hospital fighting for his life and forgot about what he'd said. But they wouldn't have let him see it without involving him – that was their way.'

He continued to look away from her although he felt the heat of her gaze.

'That's what they did in Bosnia. There are stories about the civilian bus drivers who were used to drive the Muslim men to the killing grounds. Each one was made to kill a man. That way they could never act as witnesses without admitting their own crime. I'm sure they wouldn't have let Tomas see the things that he did without involving him in it. They would've made sure he understood that it was either him or the man kneeling in front of him.'

'He could have told me,' she said helplessly.

His eyes returned to her. 'No, he saw where you lived. He knew how much money Kochalyin had put into your apartment. He knew he was paying your bills, paying for your life. And he knew you were indebted to Kochalyin for the drug treatment. He thought you wouldn't believe him, which meant he had to deal with this guilt by himself. That's why he left.'

'Yes, but he knew I and Oleg were no longer—'

'Were no longer what?' At that moment it dawned on Harland that Kochalyin had kept in touch long after the divorce for a very good reason. There must have been some residual sexual relationship – some service that only Eva could provide.

'When did it end, Eva? Or is it still a going concern? Is that what you mean by knowing his secrets, knowing him in a way that nobody else can know him? Jesus, Eva, what the hell do you two do together?'

He waited for her response. Nothing came.

'Well,' he continued, 'it certainly explains why Tomas had to get the hell out of your life, and I suppose that's why you never tried to contact me.'

She had lowered her head.

'You're right. There was something. But not now. Tomas knew that.'

'The thing I don't understand,' said Harland, 'is how your mother let this happen. She must have had a very shrewd idea what Kochalyin was about, even as a young man.'

'For God's sake, Bobby, you're so remorseless. Can't we stop talking about this?'

Harland pushed the plate of lamb to the side.

'The answer is, no, I can't leave this alone. You above all people know how this man has possessed our lives – yours, mine, Tomas's and countless others. He has infected us, Eva, he has used us, used you – he's a bloody aberration. He must be stopped. That's why I need to find out everything I can about him to nail him once and for all. It's not just Tomas I'm doing this for. It's for Griswald, for the people on the two planes. Those crimes in Bosnia extend right to the present.' He paused. 'You know, when I mentioned the plane crash this morning, you didn't bat an eyelid. You didn't ask about it. Perhaps you're no longer affected by these things. Just think of what he did, this man you've lived off for a quarter of a century. Two planes – twenty people wiped out like that. Good, innocent people, who were doing their unremarkable best in a bewildering world. People who worked for a living. They earned their keep, Eva. They didn't lie on their backs being fucked to get their money. They had families and friends and loved ones. Then nothing. And you know what? He still didn't destroy the evidence which Tomas gave to my friend. You see, I didn't tell you the final irony in all this. I was on that plane. I was with the investigator who was about to reveal that Viktor Lipnik was Kochalyin. I was the sole survivor. In fact, that was how Tomas found me. He saw my picture in the papers.'

'A photograph again,' she said.

'Yes, a photograph again,' he said, without interest. Some part of him didn't care any longer.

'How did you get out?'

'Luck and a rear-facing seat.'

It was past midnight. He had said all he could. He paid the bill and they went back to their couchette. He waited in the corridor while Eva got ready for bed then entered to find that she had taken the top bunk and turned off her reading light. They said nothing. He lay down in his clothes and listened to the carriage wheels keeping time on the track. Twenty minutes later he gave up trying to sleep and went back to the restaurant car where an understanding waiter gave him a tumbler of whisky.

He sat nursing the drink for several hours as the black void of Middle Europe slid by.

Tomas was having difficulty with the name. Was it Lyhorn or Lithethorn? Or was there a hard sound in the middle of the name? He tried out variations in his head. He wanted to test the sound in his mouth, to bring his tongue down from behind the upper teeth to form the hard, explosive 't'. That was the thing about language, he realised. So much of it relied on the little womb of the mouth where the words were made and born. Now he no longer had the use of his mouth in this way he found difficulty in remembering the new words that came to him.

When the doctor addressed the man for the fourth time, Tomas decided it was Lighthorn with a hard 't' sound in the middle – Commander Lighthorn, evidently a policeman who had come to ask him questions. They had learned he was able to respond with his eyelid. But they didn't know about the equipment Harriet had obtained from another hospital. He'd been working with it all day, but Nurse Roberts had removed it a few minutes before their arrival. She said that the software was going to be checked and then leaned over him and gave him a conspiratorial wink.

Besides the doctor, three men were in the room now. There was the crisply dressed, unsmiling Lighthorn, a man called Navratt – no difficulty with that name – and a third character who was carrying a case that Tomas glimpsed as they came in. The atmosphere was tense. Smith-Canon wasn't bothering to hide his hostility and Lighthorn's companions plainly had their doubts about being there. He could see that Navratt was appalled by the sight of him and the man with the case was doing everything he could not to look down. However, Lighthorn's eyes fastened on him with a look of unfeeling appraisal. He moved to the side of the bed.

'So, the doctors tell me you are out of any immediate danger and that you have been feeling better. I've been wanting to speak to you since the shooting because I believe you can help us, Lars.' He paused. 'The first thing I have to tell you is that I know that you have another name. I'm quite sure that you are not Lars Edberg, and I've begun to doubt whether you are even Swedish.'

He peered at Tomas's face for a reaction.

'I have read that with your condition it is sometimes possible for the patient to use his or her eyelid to communicate. Dr Smith-Canon concedes you may be able to do this. You are lucky, he says, to be able to blink. So perhaps you could blink once to show me that you have understood what I've been saying?'

Was this man stupid? thought Tomas. He had few things left, but he'd still got the right to silence.

'Just blink once,' said Lighthorn. 'I know you can do it – a bright lad like you.'

'Look, this isn't on,' said Smith-Canon fiercely. 'I told you that it might be possible, not that he definitely possessed the ability. Please treat my patient with respect. There will be none of your bullying here.'

'I'm not bullying the patient, sir. I'm asking for cooperation in a very serious inquiry. Two of our police officers were shot and this man's girlfriend was brutally murdered because of him.' He returned to look at Tomas. 'That's true, isn't it? She was murdered because of you. I expect you have a fair idea who killed her, which means that you know who was responsible for the events on Christmas Eve. Look, Lars, I know you were up to your neck in something. We took fingerprints from the flat and the same set of prints have subsequently been found on a piece of equipment – two pieces of equipment, to be precise.'

Two, thought Tomas. They'd found both computers. He wondered how much had got out before they'd shut them down.

'I'm seeing something in your eye which says you know exactly what I'm talking about. Of course, you have much more idea about what was on those two machines than I do. Highly classified material, as I understand it. I believe those machines were set in operation by you on or before the evening you were shot. We're here to tie those machines to you, Lars, and to work out how they fit into this story, which brings me to the man you were with. The mysterious Mr Harland.' He stopped and put his face closer to Tomas's. 'Robert Harland has gone missing. He just vanished into thin air on New Year's Day and we haven't heard from him since. I believe he told you where he was going. It's a great pity that you can't tell me because I very much want to see Mr Harland again.'

Tomas stared at the wall that he had been looking at since he came round and wondered if Harland had traced his mother.

'I don't understand where Mr Harland fits into all this,' continued Lighthorn. 'I know that you went specifically to see him in New York because you cut out his picture from the newspaper coverage of the crash at La Guardia airport. But why? What caused you to drop everything that day and fly to America? Perhaps it had something to do with the information on those computers.'

'This is ridiculous,' Smith-Canon interrupted. 'Have you any idea how taxing this is for a person in his condition?'

'Well, what am I supposed to do?' asked Lighthorn quietly. 'I believe he knows exactly what I'm saying and can answer my questions.'

'But you're not asking questions,' protested the doctor. 'You're telling him things which you know will distress him. I'm sorry, I can't allow it.'

'Doctor, I understand your concern for this patient, but has it occurred to you that he cannot decide whether he wants to help us until he has the full facts, which is what I'm trying to give him now?'

'There's no knowing what he understands.'

Tomas listened as from the room next door. It was odd how people talked in front of him nowadays.

'But, Doctor, in your office just now you said that it was likely that Mr Edberg had no cognitive impairment. That was the phrase you used. I didn't dream it up. So he can understand everything I say to him. You can't go back on that.'

'Yes, and a victim of a heart attack has no cognitive impairment,' said Smith-Canon, 'but you wouldn't treat him in this way. This man had a bullet removed from his brain less than two weeks ago. And I don't have to explain to you that there are few more distressing conditions than the one he is in now.'

This silenced Lighthorn for a few seconds. 'You won't object if we take his fingerprints?'

The doctor sighed. Tomas assumed that he had nodded his consent. It was outrageous but there was absolutely nothing he could do, and before he knew what was happening the man with the case had grasped his right hand and was rolling each finger in turn along an ink-pad and then planting it on a strip of paper. The operation took some time. Tomas decided to remove himself and think about the things he had learned that day on Harriet's equipment.

It was quite a simple idea. A screen was placed in front of his head, while electrodes were attached to his forehead and behind his ears. Before Harriet and the technician even explained, he understood that the machine would measure the electrical activity in his brain. By simply thinking he could move a light point up the screen to hit a group of letters. At first it had been rather difficult to grasp the idea that he could actually move something in the outside world, but gradually he got used to charging his mind with thought and then emptying it when he wanted the light ball to drift to the bottom of the screen. He repeated the procedure, gradually eliminating all but the letter that he wanted. The program was designed to second-guess the operator with a version of a spell check. The letter T appearing at a certain stage in a word might mean that an H followed. There was some difficulty because the program was written for English speakers and his English spelling was not good. Also he had to get used to retaining in his mind the word that he wanted to spell out, at the same time as alternately filling and emptying his brain. Still, the first sessions had been successful and the technician Harriet had brought with her said he was the quickest beginner he had yet seen. Harriet clapped when he wrote his first message, 'hi thnk u email?'

There was a long way to go, but he was already thinking of short cuts. If only he could have a brief conversation with the technician, he'd be able to suggest ways of improving the software.

He returned to what was going on around him. The police officer had taken his fingerprints and was now apologetically wiping the ink from his hands with cotton wool and cleaning spirit. Lighthorn appeared at the other side of his bed and scrutinised him.

'Of course!' he said. 'It's been staring me in the face all along. I couldn't think what it was. Now I see the resemblance plain as day. You're Harland's son, aren't you?'

The doctor coughed.

24

History Lessons

They boarded the ferry from Calais to Dover late on Sunday night. A problem with the weather in the English Channel meant they did not set out until five the next morning by which time the gale had swept through leaving a nasty swell. Harland had called Macy Harp from France the night before to ask if he knew a safe place for them to stay in London. He said he would arrange for them to be picked up at Dover and taken to a place Harland knew well, but which no one else would think of.

Harland slept a little on the ferry then went out on the upper deck for some fresh air. Eva joined him on the soaking decks with two cups of coffee. They had said little to each other since the previous evening but now she seemed to want to talk.

'It's nearly twenty-eight years since I was in Britain,' she said. 'Do you like it here?'

'It's good to come home to. But I prefer to live abroad.'

'Was your wife English? You haven't mentioned her. You *were* married, weren't you?' He noticed her face and hair were beaded with droplets of spray.

'For nearly ten years. We divorced in 1991, although she had moved out before that. She was American – a banker. Louise Brinkley was her name. We met when I did a few months in one of the merchant banks after university and later hooked up and got married.'

She looked at him with curiosity. 'And no children. Why?'

'I was abroad a lot. Louise had a good job and she didn't want to be left at home with no money and looking after children. We said we would leave it until later.'

'Did you tell her what happened to you in Prague?'

He didn't answer. He remembered now that Walter Vigo had given her a bare outline. Louise liked Vigo and thought of him as the respectable side of espionage. She wanted the Vigos' kind of life and couldn't

576

understand why Harland hadn't got it for her. By the time he returned to England, Louise had gone. She never came to see him in hospital in Vienna, but he suspected that this was because Vigo had been vague about the extent of his injuries.

'So you kept it to yourself.' She paused and shook her head. 'What was she like?'

'Restless, outspoken, mobile, ambitious, attractive.' Harland thought of her constant anxiety. She always looked as if she thought she was missing something. 'She lives on the West Coast somewhere now. We haven't seen each other for ten years.'

'And did she call you after the crash?'

'She wouldn't have known where to find me.'

'Tomas did.'

'Yes, he was very determined.' He thought for a moment. Somehow they were on neutral territory – they could talk. 'Tell me about him.'

'You saw him.'

'Only twice.'

She looked out to sea.

'He's a solitary person, like you. For a period his teachers at school were worried that he was withdrawn because he took no part in group activities. In a communist country this kind of individualism was considered a dangerous sign. But he did well at his lessons and he wasn't badly behaved. Later I decided that it was better for him to go to a country school and let him find his level without being watched too much.'

'What did he study? What were his strengths?'

'Math and languages. But when he was a small boy he was fascinated with stories and history. He liked the Middle Ages – anything to do with knights and wars and the crusades.'

'You mean they dared to teach the proto-imperialist campaigns of the crusaders in a communist school?'

'He read about it,' she said impatiently. 'At thirteen he started showing incredible abilities, particularly in mathematics. He won all the school prizes and then a place at university. They said he possessed great intelligence – one of the best minds of his generation. The problem was that he could do everything so well. He left university early and went into music. He made friends for the first time and because he'd had so little practice he chose the wrong people. That is when the drug problem started. There was a girl – his first girlfriend. She introduced him to drugs. He was picked up by the police in a flat in Prague. Oleg got him released and paid for the rehabilitation.'

'Why did you tell him about me?'

'It was simple: he knew he wasn't Oleg's son. If what you say about Bosnia is true, then he had good reason to question that.'

'But he was in Bosnia a long time before you told him – what was he doing in that time?'

'He came back to Prague and became involved with computers. He understood what the Internet meant ahead of most people in Eastern Europe. He did programming and set up some sites concerned with music.' She paused. 'And he did some work for Oleg. I don't know exactly what kind of work – it was technical.'

'He was seeing Kochalyin regularly all that time?'

'Yes, before he went away.'

'And you don't know what he was doing for him?'

'No.'

'What was he like during this period? Your mother said that he was changed when he came back in 1995. How?'

She looked up at the cliffs to their right. 'He was hardened – more withdrawn than usual and he lost his temper. He never did that before. I found out he was seeing a therapist in Prague, but he didn't tell me this. I discovered a medical bill in his pocket. It was this doctor who suggested that he should ask me about his father.'

The sea was a good deal rougher on the British side of the Channel. There was an announcement that the ferry would have to lie off Dover until conditions improved. They passed an unpleasant few hours riding the waves with the boat's prow pointed into a north-westerly of renewed vigour. It wasn't until late into the afternoon that they finally disembarked and were picked up by Macy's driver.

Harland knew where he was immediately they passed the Imperial War Museum in south London. He looked out of the darkened windows of the Mercedes. The café was still there, the barber's shop and newsagent were unchanged along Kennington Road. The driver, a rather sullen ex-military type, said nothing. They had turned right into Westminster Bridge Road and passed Lambeth North tube station before Harland managed to stammer a question about their eventual destination.

'We're stopping just now, sir,' said the driver.

'But this is Century House, the old headquarters of . . .' His voice trailed off.

'Mr Harp told me to bring you here, sir.'

Century House, even when it was built in the early sixties, was an unremarkable complex consisting of a block of twenty storeys, a wing which rose just four storeys and a block which joined the two together. That had gone, together with the petrol station, once manned by SIS employees, in the forecourt between the two buildings. But the main part of the building was still there, tarted up with chrome, wire and glass and a light-coloured brick cladding on the first few storeys. A sign invited interest in a unique conversion with apartments of one, two and three bedrooms with panoramic views.

They were dropped at a new entrance, away from the old security door which Harland had passed through for the first time in 1973. Eva hadn't any idea where they were and didn't ask. All she wanted was to get to the hospital.

'Before you go,' he said, 'we need to fix somewhere for you to stay tonight.'

They took the lift to the twentieth-floor penthouse and were greeted by The Bird, who had changed from his country tweeds to the camouflage of an executive.

'Always knew we'd rise to the top of this building somehow, but didn't think I'd have to buy it.'

'You bought the building?'

'No, just a couple of floors. I saw them up for sale last year and couldn't resist it. We do most of our business from here now. Frightfully central.'

He introduced himself to Eva who seemed unimpressed. Harland lifted his shoulders in apology to The Bird as they walked into what once had been the Director of SIS's office. He couldn't help but smile at the arrangement at the end of the room – a small partner desk with an old anglepoise lamp, flanked by a shabby sofa and an armchair. It was as if Ally Simmonds, the director of SIS when The Bird and Harland joined, had just got up and left the room.

'That's our Simmonds shrine. It's Macy's idea of a joke, though, of course, none of our foreign clients get it and it really has become too laborious to explain. I think he should have dressed it better with an old copy of *Horse & Hound*, a pair of ornithologist's binoculars – brackets unused close brackets – a white shirt, ready for formal evenings, a raincoat and a copy of the Moscow telephone book.'

Harland ignored Eva's rather contemptuous expression and peered through the door where there were five people working at computers.

'That's our staff,' said The Bird proudly. 'They're the core of the trading operation. God knows where we'd be without them. Recognise any of them? They all did a spell in the old firm.'

Harland shook his head. For a few moments he saw something else. Century House twenty years before, a secretary walking down a corridor with a cup of coffee passing a board on which were pinned notices concerning fire drill, the procedures to be followed at the end of the day, particularly in regard to the return of files to the safe, flat-sharing opportunities and the odd newspaper cutting – selected for some elusive irony. And off this corridor, which was much the same on any floor in Century House, were offices that owed their allegiance to one of the five controllerates – Western Hemisphere, Central and Eastern Europe, Middle East, Far East and Africa.

It was all remarkably normal, like the premises of a shipping company, perhaps, or an insurance office. To the initiated there were subtle variations of dress, character type and idiosyncrasy between the controllerates, but an outsider – of which, of course, there were none – walking through Century House would not have detected these differences. All he would have noticed would have been a series of nondescript rooms in which people worked over one or two files with remarkably little else on their desks. True, there were pot plants, mascots, pictures of loved ones, telephones and typewriters, but accumulations of paper were a rare sight. And, of course, there were no computers, it having been established by a team from GCHQ that the early models leaked enough radiation for someone to read a file from across the street.

Harland saw everything in the old secret capsule – the dirty magnolia wall paint, the tiled carpeting, the metal windows that didn't close properly and were plugged with tissue paper to stop the draughts, the secret servants – the inscrutable, the flirtatious, the drab, the reliable, the nervous and the new young Turks, straining for an effortlessness that fooled nobody.

The Bird touched him on the shoulder.

'Perhaps you should explain to your friend where you are.'

'Later. It's not important. We need to get over to the hospital. Got any ideas about accommodation tonight?'

'Well, there are bedrooms here. Should be as safe as anywhere else. I can give you keys. There's a chap who looks after these two floors – he's on site the whole time – and you have a driver who is handy in any situation. It's up to you.'

Harland looked at Eva. She shrugged a yes.

The Bird showed them to some rooms at the far end of the apartment. Eva stayed behind to wash and change, saying she wanted to look her best. Harland knew she was composing herself. Earlier, as they pitched and rolled off Dover, he had gently described the room that Tomas was in and the overwhelming amount of medical equipment and care needed to keep him alive. He also told her about the spasms and the sudden fits of meaningless sobbing and laughing. He did this because, since seeing her for the first time in Karlsbad, he'd noticed she possessed a curious ability to cut out and not take on the implications of a problem. That was presumably how she dealt with Kochalyin. But he wanted her to understand how bad Tomas was so that she could conceal her shock when she saw him. He tried to explain this but she accused him of taking a sadistic pleasure in telling her. The truce of the Channel was very short-lived.

While waiting for her, he borrowed a phone from The Bird and set about making some calls.

He found Harriet in the hospital with Tomas, which was convenient because it meant she could tell him that Eva was about to arrive. He asked how Tomas was.

'Good,' she said. 'You'll be impressed, but somehow I don't think he's going to stick around for long. I just have a feeling.'

Then he dialled Special Agent Frank Ollins. He would have liked more time to talk with him but he was in a hurry.

Ollins took longer than usual to answer.

'I wondered how things were going,' said Harland, without saying who he was. 'It's a few days since we spoke.'

Ollins cleared his throat.

'I've been hearing some bad things about you,' he said flatly. 'I don't know if they're true or not, but either way these allegations make it very hard for me to cooperate with you.'

'What did you hear?'

'That you are under investigation for spying for the Iron Curtain countries during the eighties and that the case against you is watertight.'

'Where did you get this from?'

'It came down the line – the British have warned the US authorities about you. There's a lot of disquiet over the way you hid that material from the plane. People aren't happy about either your relationship with Griswald or the fact that these pictures were encrypted with the same code that has been causing our folks a big pain in the arse over in Europe.'

'And what do you think, Frank? You met me. Do you think I was a communist spy?'

'It's not relevant what I think. All I have to go on is the fact that you lied about what you found on Mr Griswald's body and that everyone tells me to stay clear of you.'

'The UN too?'

'I haven't spoken to them.'

'But you can at least tell me about the crash investigation.'

'I can tell you nothing.'

'Are you still investigating the possibility of electronic sabotage?'

'That was always your assumption. I did not state that as a fact.'

'You near as dammit did,' protested Harland.

'If you want to know anything about the crash, please address your questions to Mr Clark at the Safety Board or their spokesperson.'

'Does that mean that you are no longer investigating for sabotage?'

'It means this conversation is over. I'm going on vacation tomorrow and I need to get my stuff ready. It's been nice speaking to you.' He hung up without letting Harland say any more.

It was obvious that Vigo had been spreading his poison. But why? He himself had said that his interest had moved on from the pictures. Yes, that could be true in one sense. The pictures didn't matter much because they had presumably been broadcast in the same way as the other secrets. Now the much greater danger to Vigo's interest was the possibility that Kochalyin would be fingered as the leading suspect in the sabotage of the UN plane. That being so, he had pointed out the danger to the Americans and had besmirched Harland to make sure that no one would take him seriously. Harland wondered if he had pulled off the same deft footwork at the UN.

Before ringing Jaidi's office he put in a call to Professor Norman Reeve, the head of the War and Peace Studies Forum in Washington.

Reeve answered with an impatient 'Yes?'

'Sir, this is Robert Harland from the UN. I want you to listen to two pieces of information. First, I have the date you requested. It is the fifteenth of July 1995. If you have any satellite or U2 material from that date I would be most grateful. The photograph I have was taken at quarter past two in the afternoon, but anything immediately before that could be useful.'

'And the second thing?' said Reeve rudely.

'This is harder to explain because I'm not certain exactly what's going on. But I believe that there is some kind of international effort to have the plane crash written down as an accident. I suspect an alliance of intelligence agencies is responsible for this – the same people who have used the services of a war criminal known as Viktor Lipnik. In fact he is a Russian named Oleg Kochalyin.'

'I see,' said Reeve. 'Let me ask you how certain you are of what you've told me.'

'I can only say that I will be making exactly these points in a report to the UN Secretary-General. This is a complex matter, Professor, and there's a considerable effort to obstruct my inquiries, but at the core there is a war criminal and war crimes and I know that this will concern you.'

'Mr Harland,' he said wearily, 'I have asked you not to lecture me before, so please do not try and influence my decision with these trite points.'

'I'll do anything I can to influence your decision, sir. I asked the Secretary-General's office to contact you and persuade you to help me. Did they get in touch?'

'Yes, but what they had to say was of no interest to me.'

'Well, what can I do then?'

'Nothing – tell me about the photograph you have in your possession.'

Harland explained that there were internal clues about the location in the photograph. Using aerial surveillance pictures as well, it might be possible to pinpoint the site and mount some kind of investigation.

Despite the original indictment, there could be no prosecution of Kochalyin without evidence that the murders had taken place. Harland added that some of the witness statements Griswald had been working on at the time of his death concerned a village called Kukuva, where some sixty male Muslims had gone missing at the time. The picture might be of their grave.

'It seems to me,' said Reeve after a short period of rumination, 'that you have an awful big tree to climb, Mr Harland.'

'Yes, but I have a witness – someone who can testify that Lipnik and Kochalyin are the same person and saw the massacre.'

'Then why can't he tell you where the site is?'

'We're working on that.'

Reeve said he would see what he could do in the next twenty-four hours. He gave Harland his e-mail address and hung up.

Eva appeared as he was about to dial the UN. He decided to leave it until later. There was still plenty of time left in the American working day.

Tomas was getting better at separating his mental activity into two streams – the hot lava thought, which he needed to propel the light point on the screen, and the articulation of what he wanted to say. Today most of the time had been spent working the machine for the technician so that he could make the adjustments that would allow Tomas to hook up to the Internet, open, write and send an e-mail file, and shut down the computer by himself. The procedure was quite complicated but the programmer was quick to interpret Tomas's thoughts and had some good ideas himself. The only problem was that he couldn't live with the electrodes permanently attached to his head. He still had to rely on someone to put them in position and turn on the machine.

Harriet had been in the room for most of the time. She suggested that an eye-gaze machine – a video camera which tracked the movements of a pupil – could be used in conjunction with what was called the brain-computer interface. That way he could look at a particular spot and activate the computer.

He was impatient for these adjustments to be made because he knew he was fading. He felt wiped out all the time, which surprised him because he had not expended any energy on movement. He had thought perhaps that it was the drugs but now suspected that this inert body was running on very low reserves.

He was just thinking that he would have a sleep when Harriet answered her phone to Harland. Then she told him what he had already guessed. Harland and his mother were on their way to the hospital. Jesus, that was the very last thing he wanted now. Although he knew the meeting would require nothing from him – no reaction, no remorse, no apology – he still felt he ought to consider his attitude as though he was going to have to talk and explain things. God, it was going to be strange to see his parents in the same room for the first time.

He needed time to prepare. But he needed a lot else besides – to fill his lungs with the fresh air of a winter's day, a glass of red wine or a beer, the sensation of a woman's hair – Flick's hair – in his fingers, sex, a cup of coffee and newspaper, live music and a landscape. He wanted the sense of distance in front of him, to let his eyes travel over the fields and forests, taking in the extraordinary beauty of the world before he left it. It was odd because all his adult life he had tended towards music and the patterns of mathematics. That was the bent of his brain, but now he thought only visually and spent his time summoning places in his imagination, remembering the smallest details of bars he used to go to in Prague, a friend's apartment or the walks they used to take in the mountains – he and his mother and his grandmother, tramping through woods, the village below them like that picture by Breughel. What was it called? Ah, yes, *The Hunters in the Snow.* He missed snow and wanted badly to scoop some up in his hands, compress it and touch his lips with it.

He decided he would doze before they came. As he drifted off, he heard Harriet and the technician moving the equipment to one side, then felt her detach the electrodes from his head. She squeezed his hand and left.

25

Disasters of War

Harland knew that the hospital would be watched, probably by Vigo's people. But there was also a good chance that the same men who had put a bullet in Tomas's head would be deployed to end Eva's life.

She was agitating to leave, wringing a scarf in her hands and glancing about as she had done in her apartment in Karlsbad. But he insisted he make a call to Philip Smith-Canon before they left. He got through and asked the doctor whether there was another way into the hospital. He replied that there was a staff entrance but it was just as public, then he said he would send someone to meet them a couple of streets away at a pub called the Lamb and Falcon. It would be a young woman called Nurse Roberts. She would bring a white coat and the essentials of a nurse's uniform. That way they could pass unnoticed through the staff entrance.

It was then that Smith-Canon dropped the news that the police had been to the hospital to take Tomas's fingerprints. They had made a connection between Tomas, the flat where the murdered girl was discovered and two computers found in London. But the more important point was that the policeman had noted Tomas's resemblance to Harland and said out loud that he thought Tomas was probably Harland's son.

They took their leave of The Bird, who said that he would be away for the night on unavoidable business, and set off through the damp early evening to Bloomsbury. On the way Harland thought about Vigo. It would be only a matter of time before Vigo heard about this. But if he had been working for Kochalyin he would surely have known who Tomas was all along. From all his actions, it was clear that Vigo hadn't known. Harland was sure that there was something he didn't understand, another level of the affair of which he had only the slightest intimation.

They arrived at the pub and found a nurse whom Harland recognised from his first visit to the neurological unit. She handed them a

Sainsbury's supermarket bag which contained the coat and uniform. They put them on and the nurse led them back to the hospital. On the way she told them that Tomas had mastered a new piece of equipment which allowed him to write messages.

They passed through some iron gates and up a short flight of stairs to the staff entrance. Harriet was waiting for them outside the room on the second floor.

'He's pretty tired,' she said, smiling at Eva and taking her hand briefly. 'The doctor is with him. He said you should go straight in.'

Harland ushered Eva in, saying that he would join them later. He knew she would want to be alone with him.

Harriet took him for a cup of coffee down the corridor.

'How is he?' he asked.

'Weak – his lungs aren't very good.'

'What about the police?'

'Well, there's nothing they can do, is there? He won't respond to their questions and they can't lock up someone who's already in a prison.'

'So they don't know he can communicate.'

'They suspect it, but they've no idea that he can use this new equipment. He's really impressive, you know.'

'Eva says he has a very good mind – starred student and all that.'

Harriet looked at him with a significant arch in one eyebrow. 'And? What's it like, seeing her again?'

'She's not at all as I expected. Not at all. There're parts I recognise. But she's changed a lot.' He told her the story about Kochalyin. He took it at a gallop, throwing out shorthand observations about Eva's life and what he regarded as her eerie detachment. When he told her that Kochalyin was the torturer she touched him on the shoulder. For some reason he winced. He explained how Kochalyin's focus had shifted from Tomas to Eva who now represented a far greater danger to him.

'But you also,' she said quickly. 'You're still his major threat.'

'Which is why I'm going to write the entire report tonight. Most of it's in the bag. Once it's delivered, there's nothing he can do.'

'And Vigo? Where's he in all this?'

He felt himself smiling although he wasn't sure why.

'I wonder how many times we've asked that in the last three weeks,' he said. 'I'm almost at the point where I shall go and see him, hand him a copy of the report and say fuck you.'

'Are you putting him in it?'

'Not by name, because I don't have the evidence. I know that the intelligence services were all desperate to close down Tomas's operation and that they used Kochalyin to do this. But the UN will probably view this as simply a question of these different countries protecting their interests. Anyway, I haven't been able to make the leap to tie Vigo in with the plot to release Kochalyin from his obligations at the War Crimes Tribunal. And I have no evidence whatsoever about the crash because my one contact in the FBI has gone cold on me. So, it's down to the war crime.'

'What about Eva? Can she help with any of this?'

'Yes, I imagine with the background. Tomas can. He saw the massacre. He can make a statement about the murders. That'll be an important addition to the stuff that Griswald was marshalling. The next step will be to find the site of the massacre. I have high hopes of that.'

His sleep had not taken him to some pleasant scene from his childhood, but to a hot mountainside where the noise of insects was deafening and his mind was clouded with fear and incredulity. How odd it was that now his eyes had fastened on to a tree with curiously black bark and limp grey leaves which he hadn't registered at the time. Now he could see it as if it were in front of him.

He knew she was in the room – he had heard the door. He opened his eyes and saw her beside him. She looked down at him as if she was waiting for a reaction. She wore the same perplexed expression she greeted him with when he returned from his classes and wouldn't tell her what his day had been like. He wished he could give her that reaction now – the smile and peck on the cheek that he'd always eventually conceded.

He saw she was shocked. She hadn't grasped that he would be *completely* paralysed. Her eyes moved frantically around the room alighting on each piece of equipment. She was trying to work out what they all did. She touched his arm and his forehead, but her eyes were still darting about the tubes and monitors. He knew he looked like some kind of installation, and he was aware that he was making one of his uncontrolled grimaces because he could see the horror in her face. It wasn't like her to be afraid.

He blinked a hello at her. This seemed to encourage her and she began speaking, jumping from one subject to the next without finishing her sentences. He wished she would relax and tell him how Harland had traced her and what she thought of him after all these years. Was she angry with him for going to find his father?

He waited. He had already learned that people calmed down after a while. Sooner or later they became aware that they were sounding stupid or hysterical. Then something else happened, to do with the lack of emotional feedback. They began to speak almost as if they were alone. He became a kind of bathroom mirror, a confessional.

His mother stopped and sighed. She picked up his left hand and drew it to her.

'Forgive me, Tomas, I'm in shock. I find this very, very distressing. I can't ... don't know what I'm saying. Forgive me for everything. God, how did we get here? When you went away, Tomas, I was so hurt. But I understood why you had to go and find your own life, away from me and Nana. She has missed you too. With her past, it mattered a lot that a third of her entire family had vanished. But we read your e-mails and we knew you would come back to us one day.'

She looked at him. Her eyes had softened; the fear was beginning to go. 'Did Bobby tell you who did this to you?'

At last a direct question, he thought. He blinked once, meaning that he knew who had done it to him.

'What else did he tell you?'

Wrong sort of question. He refused to blink in the hope that she would realise he was only capable of giving a yes or a no answer.

'I'm sorry.' She had understood. 'Did he tell you anything else?'

He blinked once, though it seemed to him that he had more to tell Harland.

'What did you feel? Did you like him?'

He blinked once.

'He told me what happened in Bosnia. Is it true?'

One blink.

'Oh, God, how could I have failed you like this?'

This was not a question he could answer in any circumstance, but especially now. Anyway she hadn't failed him. The truth was that he knew what Oleg was like – but when he was a teenager he had found him glamorous, a challenge, a rule-breaker.

Minutes passed during which she started several sentences, then smothered them. 'He said that you were forced to kill someone,' she said eventually. 'Is that true?'

One blink.

She hid her face and murmured something into her hands.

'And he put you here,' she said, dropping her hands. Tears were running down her cheeks. He had seen her cry only a few times. 'Do you want me to tell you everything?'

One blink.

She sniffed and composed herself.

'You remember how we went to Prague in '89? You know I took you out of school. I wanted you to experience this great moment because I knew you'd remember it for the rest of your life. What I didn't tell you then is that I had caught sight of Bobby Harland on television. It was fifteen years since I had seen him, but he'd changed very little. I recognised him immediately. Bobby was in Prague. I cannot tell you how happy it made me. I thought we were bound to find him. How crazy can you get? I was right, though – he was in Prague. But by the time we got there he was already under arrest. Then Oleg got hold of him. I don't know how he found him. Oleg always knew who he was and that you were Bobby's child. He was insanely jealous – you remember how he could be? He hurt Bobby very badly during that time. That's why I should have suspected that something would happen when you went to Belgrade with him.'

How he wished he could stop her. She was rushing over things. He wanted to know what Oleg had done to Harland. That was important – couldn't she see it was a pattern? How had Harland escaped? What had happened to him after that? Did she know at the time what Oleg had done? Why didn't she find him then if she had been so damned keen to see him again? Tomorrow he'd put some questions on the screen for her and beg her to take things more slowly and to think of the things he would want to know.

'Bobby says that all this time you have been using your knowledge of Oleg to get back at him. Is that right?'

He blinked.

'And that you published pictures of him to help the War Crimes Tribunal?'

One blink.

She gave him a quick, ironic smile. She seemed to be about to tell him something, but he suddenly felt drained again. He thought of himself as diminished by the equipment around him – a lump of flesh in the middle of the rhythmic iteration of the machines. He couldn't keep up with them. He closed his eyes and sank into sleep, much quicker than usual.

A nurse came and told Harland that Eva was sitting with Tomas while he slept. He went in once to give her a cup of coffee and a sandwich. She thanked him but did not look up. He left because he felt she wanted to be alone with Tomas. His one impression of Tomas was that he was paler than before and a little thinner.

He spent much of the evening alone in the waiting area. Harriet had gone to fetch him fresh clothes, a laptop, a telephone, the War Crimes Tribunal interviews and copies of the two coded images. He would need most of these things in order to start work on his report later that evening.

At just past 10 p.m. Smith-Canon appeared in the corridor with Eva. She looked drawn and smiled nervously at Harland, shy perhaps of showing her grief to him.

Sensing that he should take his chance while he could, Smith-Canon had come back from a dinner engagement to talk to them. He took them to his office, produced glasses and made them each a weak whisky and soda. Harland thanked him for all he had done, particularly for keeping Tomas's identity secret. It had bought them valuable time, he said.

There was a pause. Harland knew Smith-Canon was wondering how to approach Eva.

'Your son is a very resourceful young man. I've never seen anyone learn this brain-computer technology so fast. He must have extraordinary powers of focus – also a tremendous mental agility, I would imagine. Is that right, Mrs Rath?' She nodded.

Harland was grateful to him for talking about Tomas's qualities in the present, not in the past.

'I'm glad you're here because we really have to discuss some difficult issues. Unfortunately we can't leave them because a patient like Tomas may be struck down by an infection very rapidly indeed.' He paused and drank some whisky. 'A couple of days ago I explained the exact position to him. It was hard for him to bear this information by himself, with only myself and Mrs Bosey in the room, but I knew he'd probably already arrived at a fairly accurate conclusion about his prospects. I told him about the risks of infection, chiefly of the respiratory and urinary systems. The former is far more dangerous and I felt I needed to establish his views on cardiopulmonary resuscitation in the case of a life-threatening infection developing. If resuscitation – what we call CPR – is not wished for by the patient it is important for us to know that beforehand. Your views count too and I can give as much advice as you need. But the point is that Tomas has made his wishes utterly clear. This morning he wrote that he did not want resuscitation. I have a copy of his message here.' He handed Eva a sheet of paper. She looked at it for a moment and passed it to Harland.

There was just one line. 'I want natural death – not unnatural life – Tomas Rath.'

'Of course,' Smith-Canon continued, 'he can revise his view. He can change his mind every day if he wants – in fact every hour is fine by me. It's his life, after all. Still, I thought you should know his thinking because you probably want to discuss it between yourselves and talk it over with him.'

Eva was looking down at her hands. 'Is he in pain, Doctor?'

'A fair amount of discomfort – yes. He suffers from spasms and these are very painful. The business of catheters and tracheotomy tubes is also unpleasant and there are numerous minor complaints which make life wretched for him. His head appears to have mended very well but I believe he is suffering from some pretty nasty headaches. Of course, there are some things which may improve as the tissue in his brain heals. We have noticed that the response of his eyelids has got much better and he has more lateral movement in his eyes than he possessed when he first came out of the coma. But I must emphasise that I think the chances of him regaining substantial movement are very slim indeed.' He stopped and puckered his chin.

'I'm very sorry, Mrs Rath. I hate to have to tell you these things. I am also very, very sorry that this should have happened to a clever young man like your son.' Harland saw that Eva was touched by his solicitousness. 'So' – he gulped the rest of his whisky – 'we shall have another talk soon, no doubt. Meanwhile, you must come and go as you please.'

As they neared Century House, Eva turned round to him in the back seat and said quietly, 'Bobby, whatever you need me to do, I will do it – anything.' She held his eyes for several seconds after saying this. He understood. They were on the same side now.

They took the lift to the top floor and were greeted by a young man in jeans and a heavy pullover who introduced himself as Jim, the caretaker. He said he would be a floor below them. His job was to keep watch on the two floors through the night, so if they needed anything they only had to ring down. He'd be up whatever the hour.

Harland settled himself at a long glass table with a view over Waterloo station and the Houses of Parliament and opened up the laptop. Eva sat down in a rectangular leather chair and contemplated him, one arm supporting the other and two fingers pressed to her temple.

'You're going to write this report?'

'Yes,' he said, without looking up. 'I need to get it off tomorrow. The sooner they have it, the less exposed we are.'

'You have had no sleep for two days.'

He looked up. 'I've slept a little, but I work best like this. Besides, I've always been able to concentrate in this building.' He tapped the side of his head. 'I'm sorry, I didn't tell you. This is the old headquarters of MI6. I worked on the sixth floor in the eighties – not such a good view as from here.'

She looked perplexed. 'But why are we here?'

'Because Cuth Avocet also used to work here and he thought it would be amusing to base his business in the building when it was converted. He says it's the one place nobody would look for us.'

She was unimpressed. 'That's a very British thing to do. Why does everything have to be *amusing* to you?'

'It doesn't – it's just a whim of his. That's all. It doesn't mean anything.'

She seemed unconvinced. She rose to find herself a drink. By the time she'd opened a bottle of red wine and returned to him with a glass, he had started an outline of the report.

'You don't show anything, do you, Bobby? You're sealed up like an old building that's dangerous for people to enter.'

He didn't reply but turned from the screen and looked at her.

'You feel things,' she continued, 'but you don't express them. I know you feel badly for Tomas – that's why you came to find me. But you haven't said anything about what you feel and you don't choose to acknowledge what others feel.'

Of course she was right. Louise had been right too. Harriet was right. Everyone was bloody well right.

'Look, a lot of time is wasted with people's pity for themselves. By writing this report I can at least affect something. I can begin to settle things with Kochalyin – and it won't be just for me.'

'Did he do this to you – did he cripple your empathy?'

'You speak as if it was some kind of physical organ,' he said sharply. 'If you must know, he didn't damage my *empathy*, as you put it.'

'See, look at you pushing me away. You don't like to talk about these things. Perhaps it's not your lack of empathy. Perhaps it's your inability to trust other people.'

'And where did you learn this sensitivity of yours – in bed with a war criminal?'

She was stung and turned away.

He softened his tone.

'Look, you're probably right about my faults – but you're not telling me anything I haven't been told before. Just now I need to focus on this. That's all there is to it.'

She sat down, stared at the view, then levelled her gaze at him.

'I hope it will be all right if I stay here,' she said quietly. 'I don't want to be alone.'

He didn't hear this. He had already started the first sentence of the report, which reminded Jaidi of the terms of his brief. He was eager to put everything on record because, apart from his letter of authority, no paper had passed between them.

By 5 a.m. he'd finished a draft. Most of it had come easily but there was a problem with the section concerning the massacre. He needed to be more accurate about the site and explain the origin of the two pictures. He also had to have Tomas's statement.

He got up and arranged the blue duffel over Eva's curled-up form on the sofa. He stood and watched her for a moment, feeling the pity he had failed to express earlier. Then he slumped down on the sofa opposite her.

Tomas started making his statement at eleven that morning. Harriet was in the room with him. He took a short nap, then continued with Harland by his side until about two in the afternoon. At Eva's suggestion they had taken turns to be with him because she knew he found it harder to concentrate with them all there. No one looked at what was on the screen until he had finished. Then Harriet printed it out.

Harland sat down and read the single sheet of paper. In a glance he knew that it was exactly what he needed.

i am tomas rath – a czech citizen – on 15 7 95 i was in bosnia with oleg kochalyin – aka viktor lipnik – and witnessed a massacre – this was arranged by kochalyin and serb army – we followed four serb trucks into the hills – they contained 70 muslim men and boys – when we arrived we heard first shots – i did not know about this until i saw bodies – the hands of victims were tied behind them – i helped a man who fell from truck – because i did this they kept him to last and i was made to shoot him – i killed this man – they said they would shoot me if i did not kill him – i am guilty of murder – i wish to say sorry for what i did – oleg kochalyin is my step-father – i have given two photos to tribunal – one of him in austria which proves he was not killed – the other photo of massacre was filmed by serb soldier – i took the film later – I testify this is all true – t rath.

Tomas was exhausted from the effort of writing but he could not sleep. He watched Harland as he read the statement, then his mother and Harriet. He felt an enormous shame. Taking so long over each letter and each word had meant that he'd dwelled on the scene for the best part of four hours. Yet he hadn't possessed the stamina to hit the thousands of letters it would have taken to express how he'd been trapped into witnessing the massacre.

Oleg had told him there was some action on the hill. They got into the army vehicle with the smirking Serb soldiers and drove the two kilometres up a narrow, unmade road. It was a long climb. The soldiers passed a bottle of plum brandy around. When they came to a halt, Tomas saw the men in the trucks ahead of them and it had dawned on him what kind of action Oleg had been referring to. The prisoners were terrified. They knew there was no escape because even if they jumped from the trucks and made a run for it, the hill was bare and offered no cover but scrub. The Serbs enjoyed their fear and toyed with a few of the Muslims, pretending to let them go, then shooting them.

They were taken out in small groups, lined up along a flat wall of rock and shot. Some begged for their lives, but most were so shocked they couldn't speak and faced their death with a leaden, drained resignation. Literally, their blood ran from their faces and they began to stare, almost as if death had entered them before the bullets. Tomas couldn't believe what he was seeing, the way the soldiers casually executed them. Oleg helped with a special, silent glee, standing with a younger Serb officer shooting his pistol. Tomas had started to edge away. His arms were free and he could run and he thought Oleg would stop them shooting at him. But as he slid round a truck a middle-aged man was rifle-butted out of the back of it and fell sprawling on to the stones. He was cut on the side of his forehead and instinctively Tomas went to help him, picking him up from the road and examining the wound. The bewilderment in the man's eyes was something Tomas would never forget. The man couldn't reconcile this simple act of human concern with what he knew was happening fifty metres away.

The Serbs saw an opportunity for some fun. They pretended to the man that he had been saved by Tomas, and he was allowed to stand on the other side of the road so that he could be taken back to his village. He stood convulsed by grief as his friends and relations were killed. At the end of the slaughter the Serb officer, a man in his thirties with narrow eyes and a vicious temper, marched over, pulled out a pistol and gave it to Tomas. Then he held his own pistol against Tomas's temple and ordered him to kill the man. Tomas refused. Oleg came over and barked at him.

'Don't think I will save you. It is him or you. If you don't kill him you will both be shot.'

He laughed as if he had made a joke and Tomas pulled the trigger. There was nothing else for it. A simple calculation – one death against two.

It was some days before he could think straight again but when he emerged from his shock he decided on two actions: he would eventually admit his own crime to whichever authority would deal with it and he would act as a witness to the massacre and Oleg Kochalyin's part in it. That was why he had remained in touch with Oleg after the return from Bosnia and why he went along with the fantasy that Yugoslavia had been little more than a hunting trip – a chance for two men to bond. Kochalyin had tested him, slyly referring to the events to see his reaction. Tomas had smiled knowingly, as if the whole thing had been an escapade. Over the months and years of this revolting pretence he'd got everything he needed. He had the evidence of Oleg's rapidly expanding operation and the enormous numbers of people who were corrupted by him. He came to understand that the man he had known all his life was not an individual but a force of evil. That was melodramatic, but there was no other way to describe it.

There was a heavy silence in the room. They had all read the statement. Harland coughed, came over to him, put his hand on the unbandaged part of his shoulder and said, 'You had no other choice. This is not your crime, it's his. Any court in the world would agree on that. The main point is that the statement is very helpful and perfectly written – well done.' He squeezed him gently and smiled.

His mother and Harriet added their congratulations. He wasn't fooled; he still knew he was guilty.

'Tomas is on the Internet now,' said Harriet brightly. 'The man came to fix it all this morning. He's got an e-mail address which he can open up by himself.'

'In which case you will need my address,' said Harland. 'Shall I put it in your contact list?'

Tomas blinked.

While he tapped at the keyboard, he said, 'I have been writing the report to recommend the opening of the investigation into what happened. I need a location for the massacre. Does Kukuva mean anything to you? It's a village in the Serb part of Bosnia with a Muslim population.'

Two blinks.

'It was a long shot anyway. Do you have any clear idea where you were on that day?'

Two blinks.

'I thought not. Still, we may be able to do it another way. I got some maps this morning from Stanfords and I've drawn over them so that we can use them together.'

He left the computer and rummaged in a plastic bag.

'But first,' he said, 'I need to go over the photograph with you. Can you face it?'

A blink.

He produced the video still. It was the first time Tomas had seen it for a few months.

'At some stage we will need to include this in your statement and then have both notarised, which means a lawyer comes in here to see you swear that the statement is true and that the photograph was taken at the time of the events you describe.' He paused, swivelled the computer screen so that it was a couple of feet in front of Tomas's face and rested the picture against the screen.

'It struck me that there are one or two clues in the photograph that can help us. For instance, we know that the man holding the camera was pointing more or less north because of the time the film was made and the shadows on the ground. That means the massacre took place about forty kilometres south of that mountain range – maybe a little more. I'm not sure. If we can identify these mountains on the map, we can start plotting a corridor in which the site must lie.' Harland ducked down then bobbed up again. 'Right, here's the map I've prepared.' He folded it and propped it against the screen. His mother came round to stand beside Harland. They looked natural together, he thought.

He saw that Harland had drawn a grid over eastern Bosnia. It extended from the Drina River in the east to Sarajevo in the west, and from Foca in the south to Tuzla in the north. The vertical scale was numbered from one to twenty, while the lateral one was labelled A to O.

Harland had got a pencil out and was running it up the map, stopping at each line and turning to Tomas for a reaction. This was no good. Harland's hand was getting in the way and Tomas needed longer to think about where they went. The trouble was that they had dodged hither and thither with the Serb troops.

'He can't see the map,' his mother said, with an impatience that he knew well. 'Why don't you let him look, then call out the numbers and letters?'

Harland nodded.

Tomas was beginning to remember. They'd crossed the Drina River and had gone north to Visegrad, where they camped out the first night. They muddled on in the same direction after that. Then for two days Oleg had gone off and left him with a Serb detachment in a deserted village. He returned on the morning of 15 July. That was the day of the massacre and they had travelled west which would mean they had been somewhere north-west of Visegrad. He found the town on the map and blinked, indicating that he was ready. Harland failed to notice.

'I think he's ready,' said Harriet from the other side of the bed.

Harland began moving the pencil up the map. At each line he turned to look at Tomas's eyes. Instead of blinking no at each turn, he waited until the pencil reached lines 7, 8 and 9 when he blinked once each time. They repeated the procedure moving west to east. This time Tomas blinked once for the letters H, I, J and K.

Harland snatched up the map and squinted at the area.

'That means that the mountains in the video film are probably the Javornik group. What's brilliant is that you've picked the area that includes Kukuva.' He pointed to a speck on the map. 'I believe that's where these people came from and that's important because the authorities will be able to trace their relatives and look for DNA matches. Well done, it's really good to have pulled that off.'

Tomas thought it was probably the first time he'd seen Harland smile properly.

26
A Letter to Tomas

The next two days passed with little incident. There was no sign of Vigo, and no hint either that they'd been traced by Kochalyin's people.

Harland busied himself with the report, inserting the pictures and captions into the text, together with a map. He pressed Tomas to add a little more to his statement about Kochalyin's trip to Belgrade and eastern Bosnia and his recollections of the people Kochalyin had dealings with, particularly the infamous Serb general who'd featured in two of Griswald's witness statements. He also asked Eva to swear an affidavit about her relationship with Kochalyin which she did in front of the solicitor Leo Costigan. The resulting text gave a lot more weight to the section dealing with Kochalyin's background and his business dealings in Eastern Europe. She outlined his career in the First Chief Directorate of the KGB (Foreign Intelligence), his period with the Sixteenth Directorate (Communications, Interception and SIGINT) and his roaming brief in Czechoslovakia and Hungary during the eighties, which fell under the auspices of the First Chief Directorate, Department 11 (Liaison with Socialist countries). She showed how this last shadowy role had developed into a criminal career during the first months of the liberation.

To Harland's surprise, her recall was clear and exact, particularly about his business dealings. For instance she knew a lot about the tax fraud involving heating oil and commercial diesel as well as about the shipments made by Corniche-HDS Aviation, Kochalyin's company in Belgium. After she made her statement she glanced at Harland with an expression of defiant innocence, a look which alerted him to a secret.

He was anxious to send the report, but felt he needed more on the air crash. As he redrafted this section, he thought it might be worth tracking down Murray Clark in the US. Clark was the proponent of the wake-vortex theory, but he might at least be able to provide some explanation for Ollins's odd line of questioning. Besides, it seemed unlikely that Vigo

597

had blackened Harland's name with Clark's outfit, the NTSB, as he had with the FBI.

It was also worth bringing Tomas into this. Everyone agreed he was benefiting from involvement. Tomas had applied himself to his own statement and also to Eva's which he corrected here and there, adding dates. There was another sign of improvement. The nurses said that he was spending a lot of time using the computer, apparently following Internet trails and reading for his own pleasure. No one knew what he was doing because Eva had insisted the computer should be his private domain, unless he specified that messages were to be read. That seemed right to Harland.

One thing had stuck in his mind. Eva had said that Tomas helped Kochalyin on some technical matters during the period after Bosnia. He had asked about this again and she'd looked blank. Rather than trying to explain it to Tomas in person, he decided to send him an e-mail. This would allow him to digest the problem at leisure.

'My dear Tomas,' he wrote, 'I may see you before you read this, but I wanted to say now that despite all the terrors and tragedy of the past weeks, nothing in my life has meant quite so much as the discovery that you are my son. Thank you for having the courage to find me. I regret my initial reaction when you did find me and I hope to make it up to you.' He added a reassurance, again pointing out that Tomas's guilt about the killing in Bosnia was misplaced.

He was aware of a certain stiffness in his style, but he went on to ask if Tomas would apply his mind to the air crash. One of the things he understood about his son was that he possessed exceptional reasoning skills as well as being technically adept. Harland described exactly what had happened before and after the crash then went on to describe the mystifying call from Ollins on Christmas Eve. Why was Ollins so interested in the phone and the angle at which Griswald had held the computer in the last moments before the plane dropped from the sky? These two details seemed to concern Ollins more than what might be contained in the phone's memory and the computer's hard drive. That was surely significant.

He re-read the message, feeling that he was maybe asking a little too much of his son, but then sent it anyway. It was important that he say the first part.

Since he was on-line, he decided to look up the NTSB site to see if anything had been added to Murray Clark's preliminary finding that the Falcon jet had fallen victim to a powerful wake-vortex. There was nothing more so, before trying to track down Clark, he read through some other incidents involving wake-vortex so that he could talk knowledgeably to Clark. He found an accident synopsis concerning a Cessna Citation jet that had crashed in December 1992 after following a Boeing 757 into Billings Logan International Airport, Montana.

In this case the smaller Citation had been flying below the path of the Boeing and the separation distance between the two aircraft had been less than three nautical miles. Forty seconds before the plane encountered the vortex and went into a roll the pilot was heard to say, 'Gee, we almost ran over a seven fifty-seven.'

Harland made a note to ask about the separation distance. He seemed to remember that the Falcon had been about eighty seconds behind the Boeing 767. It had stuck in his mind because it seemed such a short time. What did that mean in terms of distance? In the Montana crash the Cessna had been seventy-four seconds behind the Boeing and had begun to roll at a distance of 2.78 nautical miles. So it seemed to Harland that the Falcon might just have been in the danger zone, under three nautical miles from the Boeing.

A few minutes later, his eye was caught by some general notes on wake-vortices. He read that the wing designs of the Boeing 747, 757 and 767 all left unbroken trailing edges from the fuselage to the ailerons. This was what caused the vortex to form. But wind conditions had to be right. Firstly, the wind speed had to be very low. A vortex which lasted over eighty-five seconds could only be generated in a wind of less than five knots. A wind of between five and ten knots cut the life expectancy of the vortex to under thirty-five seconds. He thought back to his struggle in the East River and instantly realised that the wind had been much stronger than ten knots.

He remembered looking up at the Manhattan skyline in the distance and feeling the ice particles against his face. The sea was choppy. The waves lapped against the mound of soil where Griswald's seat had come to rest.

He read on and found that the wind direction was also crucially important. A vortex usually lingered longest in a cross-wind that tended to increase the rotational energy. If the wind was against the rotational direction of the vortex it would radically reduce its life.

He closed the site and took Clark's card from his wallet. He dialled and heard the helpful but slightly self-important voice of Murray Clark answer.

'What can I do for you?' he said. Harland smiled. Unlike Ollins, Clark had not been got at.

'I don't want to bother you. It's just that the Secretary-General has asked me to find out how things are going along – on a purely informal basis, you understand.'

'I don't have much more to add to what is already in the public domain.'

'Can I ask you some questions? They're pretty basic.'

599

'Shoot. I have some time,' said Clark.

'The Secretary-General has a theory that the plane might have been low on fuel and he wonders if that has been considered in the investigation.'

Clark sighed. Harland could almost hear the word *idiot*.

'No,' said Clark. 'We've ruled out that possibility. The plane refuelled in DC. The extent of the fire indicates that it was carrying plenty of fuel.'

'What about pilot fatigue? Apparently there's been some concern at the Federal Aviation Authority that pilots are flying when they're exhausted. There was a crash a couple of years back when the pilot was practically asleep at the controls.'

'No, no. The pilot of your plane was well rested. A medical exam two months back shows he enjoyed good health. And his safety record was impeccable.'

'So it's got to be the ... what do you call it?'

'Wake-vortex. Yes, that is our thinking.'

'The planes were too close, then?'

'Not necessarily,' said Clark. Harland could tell his mind was elsewhere.

'The separation distance for the two aircraft was, what? Eighty seconds? What does that mean in distance?'

'A little over three nautical miles.'

'So normally that would be in the safety margin?'

'Yes,' said Clark, more alert now having noticed the change of gear in Harland's questions.

'What was the wind speed at the time?'

'Why are you asking these questions, Mr Harland? It sounds to me as if you have an agenda.'

'It is not my agenda, it's the agenda of the Secretary-General and the Security Council.' He added the 'Security Council' without a murmur from his conscience.

'I thought this was an off-the-record conversation.'

'It is. And I will have an off-the-record conversation with the Secretary-General when we've finished speaking.' Damn, thought Harland. That was stupid. There was no point trying to intimidate the man.

'I'm sorry,' said Clark formally. 'I feel I should seek advice before commenting on these matters to you.'

'Oh, forgive me. I'm sorry. I was getting carried away. I don't want to compromise your professional standards.' He waited.

'As it's you asking, Mr Harland,' said Clark at last, 'perhaps I should help if I can. But this *is* background?'

'Surely.'

'What is it you want to know exactly?'

'Just the wind speed,' he said innocently, then added, 'And the wind direction.'

'Let me see, the wind speed was between fifteen and twenty knots, gusting twenty-five to thirty.'

'And the wind direction?'

'South-westerly, as I recall. Yes, that would be it, south-westerly.'

Harland had what he wanted. He burned to get off the phone but rather than alert Clark, he thought of something else to ask.

'When will you make your final report?'

'Any day now.'

'Thank you so much. I'd better not waste any more of your time.'

He knew that it hadn't been a particularly subtle interrogation, but that didn't matter now. The wind speed was far in excess of the necessary conditions for wake-vortex, and the wind direction was completely wrong. He would check with a map, but he was certain that the landing runway pointed southwest – that's why the Manhattan skyline was way off to the right when he first struggled out of his seat. The plane had landed near enough smack into the wind and there could have been no side wind to give the vortex extra life.

The theory, then, was a fraud, but maybe the NTSB was not consciously guilty. It was possible that the readings from the flight data recorder so perfectly mimicked the action of a plane in the grip of a vortex that the board had opted for the only reasonable explanation – wind speed and wind direction notwithstanding.

He added a couple of paragraphs on the crash and then phoned Jaidi's office. Eventually a superior-sounding assistant came on the line and warned Harland that the Secretary-General wouldn't be able to read it for at least five days. Harland protested, to no avail.

He hung up, reminding himself that Jaidi was probably working with at least three of the governments who'd helped protect Kochalyin. These days the international agenda shifted with each revolution of the planet – an air crash that had seemed so tragic and puzzling a few weeks before was now of only minor historical interest. No one was waiting for his report. Indeed they'd probably prefer that it hadn't been written. And even if the great master of mobility and inclusion did read it, Harland had to face the fact that there was little hope of anything being done about Kochalyin. He would adapt and avoid and survive because he knew the global attention span diminished by the day.

But there were still one or two things he could do to hurt Kochalyin. He copied the report into another e-mail file and sent it to Professor Norman Reeve's address. Then he thought of the journalist at the press conference in the UN. Parsons was his name: he worked for the *New York Times*. If he delivered the report to him with background on Tomas's operation to expose SIS and CIA operations in Europe, it would, he was sure, make a hell of a newspaper story.

So he wasn't beaten yet. Not by any means.

*

Tomas had had a couple of good days – just two nasty spasms. The big problem now was the dreams – the dreams about movement. Some mischievous part of his subconscious had decided that he should only dream about the things he used to do. Last night he was cross-country skiing as he'd done in the mountains as a boy. He could feel the sweat on his face in the cold air as he pushed himself, arms and legs working to maximum exertion. He could see the winter landscape in every detail and taste the hot, sweet red wine that he shared with his mother at the end of each trip. He dreamed about walking, running and touching things, and each time his subconscious articulated the exact pleasure that he would never again enjoy.

He looked out of the window at his new view. A faint print of the half-moon was just visible in the late afternoon sky. Across the square, lights were being switched on in the offices and a woman had opened a window and was now leaning out to smoke. In the premature twilight of the square a figure in a bulky overcoat was standing beneath a cherry tree on which were still hanging a few vivid orange leaves. Tomas had gazed at the cherry often since his bed had been moved.

His attention returned to the room. His mother had come in and was saying an overly polite goodbye to Harriet. She smiled at him and briskly attached the electrodes to his head, switched on the computer and manoeuvred the screen towards him, blocking out most of the square.

He urged his mind to fill with hot thought and with little difficulty pushed the floating white light to hit the new e-mail icon. There was one message on his new server. He read the first paragraph, and smiled inwardly, then moved on to Harland's description of the moments before the flight. It certainly was an intriguing problem. He would enjoy working on it later.

27

Strange Meeting

Harland left Century House by the underground car park and walked eastwards through the dismal quiet of a public housing estate. He'd told Cuth's driver to stay with Eva, who between spells with Tomas was looking for an apartment near the hospital to rent for a few weeks. They were beginning to feel they were getting in the way at Century House.

A few minutes later he left the housing estate to cross a main road stalled with traffic, and merged with the crowds of commuters at Waterloo station. It was then that he sensed he was being followed, but this time by a more expert team. He stopped on the main concourse of the station, bought an evening newspaper and took the escalator down to the Underground, returning to the concourse on the upward escalator. He didn't spot anyone, but he felt the familiar weight at the back of his neck. He wondered whether they had picked him up at Century House, or later.

He paid for an all-zones travel card and for the next hour or so hopped on and off a dozen trains. Then he began to notice that the watchers were no longer bothering to hide themselves. As he travelled round the loop of the Circle Line he realised that there were now five individuals stuck to him. Every move he made they followed. Eventually he confronted a tall man in his mid-thirties who was carrying a knapsack, and asked what the hell he thought he was doing. The passengers around them looked on with the disengaged interest of London commuters. The man didn't reply but simply smiled back at Harland as though he was some kind of lunatic. At Victoria he got off and made his way to the street exit. As he fed his ticket into the automatic gate another man, in suit and tie, approached him.

'What the fuck do you want?' Harland demanded.

'Mr Vigo would like a word.'

'What for? To play charades in some clapped-out building?'

'No, sir. He suggests you meet in a place you know.'

'Where?'

'Carlton House Terrace.'

'Then why all this fucking around?'

'We were looking for an appropriate moment, sir.'

'Bollocks you were.'

'There's a car outside. We can be there in a few minutes.'

'I've been through this before. I'll go by cab, if you don't mind. Number three Carlton House Terrace, right?'

The man nodded.

Twenty minutes later his cab pulled up outside the familiar porch in St James's. Nearly thirty years before Harland had been there, invited by a man who called himself Fletcher. There had been three interviews in all and at the final session Fletcher had asked him to sign the Official Secrets Act, at which point his induction into MI6 had begun.

It was obvious that Vigo wanted to give Harland an unambiguous signal, firstly to demonstrate that he couldn't move in London without being followed and, more important, that he, Vigo, was no longer running a crew of irregulars. He had access both to a full surveillance team and official SIS premises.

Harland was shown into the grand but sparsely furnished room where he had once sat across from Mr Fletcher and his two silent colleagues on a warm spring afternoon. Vigo came in almost immediately.

'Hello, Bobby. It's good of you to take the time. I wanted to have a talk in what are rather changed circumstances.'

'Which are?' Harland noticed that the look of bustling confidence had returned to Vigo's expression.

'We met under rather difficult circumstances last time. We didn't perhaps have the kind of discussion that we needed to have. I accept this was my fault and I'd like the chance to clear things up now. That's all.'

'What do you want to clear up, Walter?'

'Any false impression you might have received.'

Harland laughed.

'I want to persuade you we have been working on the same side all along, Bobby.'

'No Walter, that doesn't work. You work for Kochalyin. I work for the UN, which despite its faults is still a force for good. You work for a man who has killed countless numbers of people.'

'I do wish you would stop being so dramatic, Bobby. What you say is simply not true.'

'You expect me to believe that after you tried to threaten me with an Official Secrets charge; after your band of occasionals chased me round London; after my son – yes, I know you must know he's my son – was tracked down using special equipment at GCHQ to locate his telephone?

Walter, you're in this up to your neck and just because Tomas is no longer a threat to your grubby arrangements, don't think that I or the UN have any intention of hushing things up.'

Vigo sat with his hands across his stomach and produced a look of elaborate sympathy, which also included elements of pity, indulgence and disdain.

'That is in part why Robin has asked me to see you.'

He had dropped the name of the sainted chief of SIS, the untarnished Sir Robin Teckman. That meant something too. Harland sighed.

'Okay, Walter, spit it out. What's been going on? Some kind of battle at SIS in which, no doubt, you have triumphed?'

'You know I'm not at liberty to discuss these things.'

'But the answer is yes, isn't it? That's what you're trying to tell me in your sly little way with all this – the crack surveillance troops, tea and cakes at Carlton House Terrace and using Teckman's name. What happened to Miles Morsehead and Tim Lapthorne, eh? Taken early retirement; fixed up with undemanding posts in the oil industry?'

Vigo said nothing.

'So,' said Harland, 'all that crap over Christmas was part of some SIS mud fight. You had your own pantomime season, Walter, mustering your little army and playing spies. You do know we're dealing with a war criminal? It's no more complicated than that – a very sadistic man who has killed an awful lot of people. You know that Oleg Kochalyin was the man who did me over in '89?' Harland looked at him hard. 'Yes, you bloody well did know. And you knew the reason behind it, didn't you?'

'I guessed at both, Bobby. I had no definite knowledge, certainly not enough to inform you that these were certain facts.'

'Did you know that Tomas was my son?'

'No, and we had no idea he was responsible for the transmissions.'

'That's rubbish. You knew. You must have known. That's why GCHQ helped track the signal from his phone.'

'You're wrong, Bobby, and you'd be well advised to keep such idiocies to yourself.'

'Then how on earth did they find him on the Embankment?'

'They followed him from your sister's house. When he arrived early, they realised he was waiting for someone – a contact. That turned out to be you, which is why they opened fire when you arrived. We would have tried to give you protection but you managed to give my team the slip, and of course we didn't know what he looked like so he was able to leave your sister's house without being spotted by us.'

'But why didn't they kill me at the river? Why haven't they tried to kill me since?'

'I think they have. We heard about Zikmund Myslbek's death. We know that your journey after that was pretty fraught. In fact in many ways it's surprising that you made it back here. As far as the shooting at the Embankment goes, I think it's fair to say they thought you had been hit and were floating down the river. Anyway, by that time I gather the two unfortunate constables had arrived on the scene and the gunmen had to make good their escape. Believe me, we really were trying to protect you.'

'Crap,' snapped Harland. 'You were using me. You thought I knew a lot more about those coded transmissions than I did and you were using me as a bait.' He thought for a few moments. Vigo watched him working it out. 'But you had limited resources because someone in SIS was telling Kochalyin what was going on. That's why you were working with your little band of trusties. In fact I'd guess that a considerable faction was embroiled with Kochalyin in one way or another. But then the baffling part of it for you and everyone else was why the messages kept on being transmitted. You couldn't work it out, could you? You knew I wasn't responsible and you knew Lars Edberg was in hospital on life support.

'It was at that point your *interest* moved on. The Lipnik pictures were old hat. You couldn't give a fuck about them because they only represented a tiny fraction of what Mortz and Tomas had put together. You were obsessed with a far greater threat and also a far greater prize. The threat was to your beloved service which was hurting from the sheer amount of detail that Tomas published – the eavesdropping operations against your competitors in Europe, the undermining of contract negotiations, the men and women hired to leak economic plans. And let's not forget the planes that left Ostend, collected their cargo of arms in Burgas and flew on to supply the nasty little wars in Africa. You couldn't afford for any more to come out – nor could the Americans, or the Dutch or the French or the Germans or the bleeding Belgians. So you had to stop it, and on the morning I paid my visit to your house, you knew you were within an ace of doing so. That's what that meeting was about: you were briefing your band of trusties after the latest batch of transmissions.'

Vigo tried to demur, but saw the look in Harland's eye and backed off.

'What a race that must have been,' continued Harland. 'Your lot against the official SIS team. And you won the prize. While they were watching the houses in Bayswater, you or one of your friends had the bright idea of searching the telephone junction boxes. That meant you got the computers with all their information and you could use it to nail the competition for the role of successor to Robin Teckman.'

'That's quite enough,' said Vigo. 'There are things that you don't understand and never will.'

'Oh, I'm nowhere near finished, Walter. You may think that you have arranged this meeting to silence me. But let me just tell you that I have all the cards. At the press of a key everything I know about this affair will go to the press and that means the government will be asking questions, which is hardly going to be conducive to your candidature. So if I were you, I'd sit tight and shut up.'

'Bobby, there's no point in this – really,' said Vigo. 'You don't have the whole picture.' He cocked his head to the sound of opening car doors outside. 'Look, I think we're about to be joined. I hope you will be able to listen to what is said to you.'

'No, it's you that has to do the listening ...' His voiced trailed off because Vigo had got up.

'Would you just hold on a second,' he said irritably as he left the room.

Harland paced around the mahogany table for a few minutes. Then the door opened and Vigo came in followed by the gaunt, polished figure of Sir Robin Teckman. He sat down and smiled pleasantly at Harland.

'Walter's filled me in on your position ...'

'Yes, I'm sure he has,' said Harland curtly. He liked and respected Teckman from his time with him in the East European Controllerate, but he wasn't going to be sweet-talked into silence. 'I was saying that there are outstanding matters to discuss. Kochalyin's crimes can't all be swept away. There's a massacre to consider in Bosnia, the plane crash that I was involved in and the killings and shootings in London. Just because you've sorted out your internal difficulties, it doesn't mean that we can forget what Kochalyin is responsible for.'

'And what did you have in mind, Bobby? How do you believe we should pursue these matters?' The eager, helpful smile had not faded.

'Firstly Britain should instigate the reopening of proceedings in The Hague. It's clear that we were involved in helping him fake the assassination in the first place.'

'That's not true,' said Teckman evenly. 'We believe another foreign power was responsible, probably the French, who kept their lines open to the Serbs all through the Bosnian civil war and the Kosovo conflict, as you probably know.'

'Why would they do that?' asked Harland.

'We believe it was some kind of deal involving an aero-industry contract. I cannot be more specific, I'm afraid, because we don't know. However, I suspect he furnished the crucial contacts which resulted in an order. They obliged by fixing up the drama in the hotel and putting their own troops on the job to act as witnesses.'

'If we weren't involved in that business there'll be no embarrassment at all to the British government.'

'Bobby, in the hope that you understand the spirit in which I make these remarks, I'm going to be open with you. Kochalyin has caused us considerable problems, principally because different parts of the service were engaged with different manifestations of him. It wasn't until Walter started pulling it all together two years ago that we understood that we were dealing with one man. I think the same can be said of a number of

different agencies which have been equally compromised and embarrassed by these illegal transmissions. Tell me, have you learned anything
about the motives of your boy and this fellow Mortz? Clearly the boy held
a deep grievance against his step-father, and Mortz was a clever trouble
maker from radical seventies stock. Put together they were a devastating
combination. The motive puzzles me however. You see, the lad must have
got very close to Kochalyin to have been able to gain the information he
used. Was this premeditated – what was the trigger? What caused this
resentment?'

That was something they didn't know and Harland wasn't going to
enlighten them. 'He hated Oleg Kochalyin because of his treatment of his
mother. That's obvious. But I haven't exactly had the chance to question
him. He's frail and cannot speak.'

'But I understood he was capable of some rudimentary communication.'

'Occasionally, but he's not up to being questioned about this. His
doctor says that he is prone to infections and needs to be kept quiet.'

'I see,' said Teckman.

'The point,' said Harland, 'is that I have a duty to report on all these
matters to the UN Secretary-General. It's not just the massacre in Bosnia,
but the air crash in New York. There's every reason to believe it was the
work of Kochalyin.'

'What evidence do you have?' asked Teckman, in the manner of a tutor
drawing out a pupil.

'I believe the plane was brought down by an electronic device – a virus
maybe. I might have been able to pursue this further if Walter hadn't
warned the FBI against talking to me, but I know that the crash wasn't
caused by wake-vortex. The evidence of wind speed, wind direction and
distance between the two landing aircraft at the time make a vortex
virtually impossible.'

'Maybe what you say about the vortex phenomenon is true, but I don't
think it quite justifies the claim that the plane was sabotaged. There could
be said to be rather a gap between the two.'

Again there was no hint of a challenge. Harland could see that he was
being manipulated into a position where he would be forced to concede
he had little definite proof and therefore had no reason to take further
action.

'Well, I've raised this in my preliminary report,' he said, a little
defiantly.

A glint of concentration entered the Director's eyes. 'You have already
sent this to the Secretary-General?'

'Yes, although there's much to add.'

'And what do you envisage the Secretary-General doing with your
report?'

'I imagine he'll use the evidence to reopen the case into Kochalyin's activities in 1995 and maybe there are some lessons to be learned about the way powerful states employed this man.'

'And there again, he may do nothing,' said Teckman.

'That's up to him. It's his report – he commissioned it. But I will urge an investigation into the war crimes. By the way, you know there's evidence that Kochalyin was present at more than one massacre.'

Teckman exhaled and looked at Vigo. 'Naturally, Bobby, we're concerned that this report of yours doesn't fall into the wrong hands. It would be quite awkward for it to appear in the media in its unformed state.'

'You want me to wait until I've got more?'

'No, of course not. This is very dangerous material and it contributes to the sense that our institutions are degenerate. We want to build public confidence, not destroy it. I think that Walter and I have demonstrated to you that we rooted out the difficulty we were having and that these things can be addressed, without worrying everyone. That takes courage, you know. Look, I understand why you see this as something of a personal crusade – who could blame you after what happened in Prague and after what has been done to your boy? But I also want you to remember you are still a citizen of this country and that you signed the Official Secrets Act. If there is any publicity about this I think it would be damaging to the national interest in ways that you have perhaps not foreseen.'

Harland rose from his chair and shook the tension from his shoulders. Also, he wanted to show that he did not feel constrained in their company.

'In what ways will it be damaging?' he asked.

'With your background, you must understand that relations between countries are not a simple affair. Two states may be friends on one level, but competitors, even enemies, on another. For example, on drug-trafficking we are at one and there is a high degree of co-operation between states, but when it comes to crucial defence contracts or tenders to build a dam in Turkey each state pursues its own interests. The public finds this very hard to understand – but it's a system that works, after a fashion. When something like this gets into the open it tends to colour the entire relationship for a very long period. Politicians get hold of it and inflate the issue for their own purposes, which needless to say is not the common interest.'

'But there *is* a principle here,' said Harland. 'We know the identity of a war criminal who has also committed countless other crimes. What possible harm comes from putting him in the dock to answer for what he's done?'

'That assumes you can lay hands on the man. But let's accept that you effect this miraculous arrest, what then? Kochalyin appears at The Hague and, seeing that he is bound to be sentenced to a long term in jail, decides he has nothing to lose by telling the story of the last dozen years. You don't imagine the Americans are going to allow that to happen, do you? Or the French or the Germans? They have all used him in one way or another.'

'To say nothing of the British.'

'To say nothing of the British,' repeated Teckman, with a brief patrician smile. 'It just isn't going to happen, Bobby. And that's all there is to it.'

'Then what will happen?'

'Well, nothing immediately, but let me assure you that Kochalyin will not be able to continue operating as he has been. There are too many people who know what he did in his various roles. That is in large part thanks to your son. So, sooner rather than later, he will arrive at a messy end, in which case you can hardly be less than satisfied.'

'There's some kind of contract on him?'

'Good heavens, no. His time will come – that's all I'm saying. He's been exposed. People have made the connections; they know what he has done. For instance, Walter was telling me that he's stolen an awful lot of money. That does enrage people, you know.'

'But you don't believe there is any case to answer in Bosnia?'

Teckman looked pained. 'Of course I do, Bobby. Of course I do. Please remember how much effort the British have put into capturing these people. No country has a better record of apprehending indicted war criminals than we do. None!'

Harland sat down again and looked at each of them in turn.

'I'm sorry, I can't wear this. The world may work like this, but it used not to. There were once ideas of right and wrong, however crude. We presumed to claim that we were on the right side because all of us knew of the evil of the regimes in the East. That was our motivating faith, however ragged and abused in execution. But now . . .'

'Now we have to make much harder choices,' said Vigo quietly. 'Robin is right. We can't have your report floating about and giving people the wrong impression.'

'The odd thing about it all,' said Harland, still looking at Teckman, 'is that there is almost nothing in my report about the transmissions. Do you know why that is? It's because I don't know much about them. I suspect that you caught a good deal before it was released from those two computers, in which I case I will never know. Tomas is hardly in a position to tell me.' Neither Teckman nor Vigo showed any reaction. 'So,' he continued, 'my report chiefly concerns the air crash and the war crime. As I told you, it has already been delivered to the Secretary-General. There's nothing you can do.'

Vigo cleared his throat. 'I think what Sir Robin wants is an assurance that you will not add to this report and that you will not seek to have the current draft distributed.'

Harland said nothing. He imagined a plan was already in place to persuade Jaidi to bury the report in exchange for some diplomatic favour. All they needed now was to ensure his silence.

'We all want to leave this room with a clean sheet,' said Teckman. 'Without acrimony or misunderstanding.' He paused. 'You see, we're working on the same side, Bobby, even if in the past there has been some doubt about that. You know what I'm referring to.'

Harland understood very well that he was being threatened again. A release of his report might not be followed by a charge, but certainly a campaign in the press to destroy him. He'd seen what had happened to younger members of SIS who had broken ranks recently and he knew that his former employers would not hesitate to use the material they had on his 'Prague connection'.

'Are we working on the same side, Bobby?' asked Teckman, with an interrogative lift of his eyebrows.

Harland was about to shake his head.

'I believe we are, perhaps more so than you appreciate.' Teckman nodded to Vigo who rose and left the room, closing the door behind him.

No more than thirty seconds later Vigo came in and waited by the door. Someone was hesitating outside. Harland leaned over and saw Eva standing anxiously in the light of the corridor.

'You see, we really are on the same side,' said Teckman.

28
The Final Work

There was only one thought in Harland's mind.

'How long?' he demanded icily. 'How long have you worked for them?'

Her eyes moved from Vigo to Teckman, whom she clearly hadn't seen before. He put out his hand and motioned her to a chair.

'Three years.'

It all made sense to Harland. Now he understood why she had remained Kochalyin's lover and how she'd been able to supply so much detail for his report to Jaidi.

'And you knew this, Walter? You knew who she was?'

Vigo nodded. 'Needs must, I'm afraid,' he said sombrely. 'We had to get the information on Kochalyin. You know how it is, Bobby.'

'You bastard, Walter.'

'But,' said Vigo, raising a hand to deflect the insult, 'Irina here will confirm that we had no idea that she was *Lapis* until late last year. We simply knew her as Kochalyin's former wife. We needed to build a picture of this man – his character, his habits, his business dealings. We needed to piece his different existences together. Irina helped us a great deal and we are very grateful to her. You may not believe this, but not once was your name mentioned. You see, you weren't in the picture until you got on that plane in Washington.'

'It's true, Bobby,' implored Eva. 'They didn't know about us until last month. They didn't know about Tomas – why would I tell them? I was just helping them with Oleg – that was all. Why would I discuss who Tomas's father really was? Tomas had his own life. And you? You were in the past.'

Harland sat down. 'Did you help them with information from the files?'

'No,' she said. 'He didn't tell me anything about you. Why would he?'

Vigo nodded in agreement.

'But why didn't you mention this arrangement before? We were travelling for nearly three days together. When we got to Century House, what happened then? You knew that Walter and I must have worked in that very building together. Surely that jogged your memory.'

'You didn't tell me where we were. You didn't mention the history of the building until after I'd seen Tomas. I didn't even know that you knew Walter. How could I? He didn't say anything to me and nor did you.'

'The penalties of discretion,' chipped in Teckman, who had sat down in his original place at the table. 'It's all true, Bobby. I have to say I was nearly as dumbfounded as you are when Walter unravelled this whole conundrum for me the other day. It does, however, rather underline my point about us all being on the same side. Everyone has been working against Oleg Kochalyin.'

Harland was watching Eva. For a fraction of a second she stared at him, her pupils dilating with significance.

'There's one thing that doesn't ring true to me,' said Harland. 'When Tomas was shot, why didn't you tell her, Walter? You could have called her.'

'Because at that stage we hadn't made the connection between Irina and Tomas and you. The police were late in telling us about the newspaper they'd found in his flat – the one with your picture removed. And by that time, you have to remember, we were desperate to find the source of the transmissions. So the real identity of Lars Edberg wasn't a priority. We knew he must have had something to do with the transmissions, yet they were continuing after he had been shot. As you can imagine, Bobby, at that moment our sole aim was to stop the transmissions. Later, when we had located the source, I had the police take his fingerprints and we were able to make a match between those in the flat, the computers and Lars Edberg.'

Teckman took over the narrative. 'By that stage we had begun to sift through the information that Irina here had given us. We were comparing it with some of the things we'd seen in the transmissions. Suffice it to say there was an overlap. The information came from the same route. That was when Walter put all the pieces in place.'

'At what stage exactly did you know that Tomas was our son?'

'Some time in the middle of last week.'

'By which time I'd left for Prague.'

'Yes. We knew you would break the news to Irina and bring her back here.'

'And you were following us?'

'We have limited resources in the Czech Republic,' said Teckman. 'We caught up with you in Karlsbad and followed you to Dresden. Then we lost you. There was some confusion at the station. We were worried because our two men knew Kochalyin's people were following you too.'

'And here?' asked Harland belligerently. 'Here in Britain?'

'We've had you covered the whole time,' replied Teckman. 'The fact that Cuth Avocet put you up in the old building greatly aided us.'

'And the phones? Have you been tapping our calls?'

'No,' said Teckman. 'Our chief concern has been to see if Kochalyin would follow you here, in which case we would certainly have had a word with him.' He gave a bleak, deadly smile. 'His people are here, but he hasn't graced us with his presence, which doesn't surprise me in the least. It's far too dangerous. The reason you are still alive, I suspect, is because Walter has had you watched since The Bird's driver picked you up on the Kent coast. As to the phones, no, we haven't been listening. Besides, with the Harp-Avocet operation in full flow every day it would be difficult to pinpoint the calls.'

A flat lie, thought Harland. They were bound to have tapped into the phone lines. It explained why they had approached him now. They must have read every word of his report to Jaidi – they'd been forced to make their move and had produced Eva in a desperate attempt to stop him adding anything. He must also assume that they knew about the calls he'd made to Clark, the websites he'd visited while reading up on wake-vortex and the contents of his e-mails to Tomas and to Professor Norman Reeve.

'And The Bird and Macy? Were they in on all this?'

'We informed them this afternoon that you were in danger and that we were shadowing your movements,' said Vigo. 'They had suspected something. Their driver spotted a couple of our fellows in the course of the week.'

Teckman was winding a strand of cotton round a loose button on his jacket. Harland knew the distraction meant the head of SIS was concentrating very hard on his responses.

He would react accordingly. 'So it seems you've got us pretty much trussed up,' he said with a hint of resignation in his voice.

'I wouldn't put it like that,' said Teckman amenably. He looked up from the button. 'We just don't want any more killings on our patch. We want this business with Kochalyin to take its natural course, and I do promise you that it *will* take its natural course. That's why I've been anxious to point out that we're advancing on a unified front.'

'So what do we do now?'

'You carry on as you have been, while we watch your back for you. I don't know how long this business will go on, but at some stage we will know when to make alternative arrangements for your safety. It will be clear to Kochalyin that he can no longer rely on Irina. After Tomas was shot he must have known that this would eventually happen, although of course he well appreciated that she didn't know where Tomas was and moreover she was unlikely to hear of the shooting for some time. So clearly Irina is a priority target for him but he also knows she will be well protected. My guess is that he will make a move later on, once he has settled other accounts. He will seek to eliminate her and possibly her mother. Oh, by the way, Irina, I should mention that we've found Hanna the accommodation I was talking about in Switzerland.'

He paused and placed his hands together on the table.

'So, to conclude, for the moment I think you should remain in Century House, where we can keep a close eye on you. You should continue to visit your son in hospital, where we can also make sure you are undisturbed.' He looked at Harland. 'In the meantime, I would very much like your assurance that you will not add to the report. What you have already said on this affair surely discharges your obligations. I don't want any gestures, Bobby, no desperate resolve. Just keep a low profile. Is that understood?'

Harland gave a brief nod. There was no mistaking the instruction, and there was little point in letting the Director know that he had no intention of obeying it.

'So I think that wraps up our business,' said Teckman, clasping his knees and pushing up from the chair. 'We'll be in touch. If you need anything, you can phone Walter.' He moved to the door. 'I'm glad we've had this talk. I can't tell you how important it is to know we're working on the same side.'

Tomas hadn't seen his mother leave because he was dozing. He had worked steadily for two hours and then fallen asleep while she was with him. When he awoke, he noticed a very sharp pain which sprang from beneath his ribs every five or six breaths. He would have liked to have held his breath to see if the pain still came, but the machine took the option away. It commanded his lungs to inflate at regular intervals. He was forced to breathe – whether he wanted to or not.

There was another feeling that he hadn't encountered before, a general enervation which, on thinking about it, he likened to his body being drained of blood. This thought came from his paranoia. He was haunted by the idea that he was being kept alive for medical experimentation, involuntary blood transfusions, even organ donation. How could he tell whether he still had both kidneys? Did they have plans for his eyes – his heart, his liver? And his hands? Would the doctors take his hands from him and sew them on to someone's arms, fusing the nerves to another man's impulses? Or why not a woman's? Flick always said his hands were delicately made. They were sensitive, she said – artistic. She didn't know they were a killer's hands.

Nothing like this had gone through his mind when he was being taken off heroin. The sweats and arthritic fever of cold turkey were a picnic compared to this. Now, once his mind had got hold of a thought it seemed to take pleasure in supplying innumerable permutations of a particular horror. He had become fixated on what he regarded as the certain distribution of his body parts. Perhaps the intended recipients had already been matched with him and were waiting in beds around the hospital, longing for him to die and give them new life.

He sank a little more into himself. The pain was getting worse. Was this it? Was his heart giving notice of expiration?

He opened his eyes again and saw that the white ball light was quivering in front of him. The computer was on and the electrodes were still conveying the blistering heat of his panic to the screen, making the light bob like a fishing float. He decided to continue with his work. Practically everything had been completed because his mother had very quickly grasped how to help him. It had given him a thrill working with her and for a few moments that afternoon he had forgotten where he was – and how he was.

He logged off to still the ball of light and struggled to put some thought to the problem his father had set him in the morning. There wasn't much to go on – the lights and heating in the plane had failed, then a little time later the plane had crashed. This might indicate a virus at work, but it would be a pretty crude one to knock out the lights needlessly. Maybe he was barking up the wrong tree. Perhaps the lights going out was only relevant in as much as it had forced Griswald to open up his computer and use the glow from the screen to see what he was doing. They had asked about the angle of the computer and where Griswald had held it in relation to the phone in his right-hand pocket. What could be the point of that?

He let his mind drift, hoping that something would occur to him. Five minutes later a glimmer of a solution came to him, but just at that moment he was racked with a particularly violent pain in his chest. The nurse hadn't noticed and neither had she bothered to ask how he was. He wished she'd give him something.

He thought again. That was it! The reason they wanted to know how the laptop had been held was because they believed it had shielded the phone. They wanted to know how it still came to be functioning in Griswald's pocket after the crash. Shielded from what? Not the impact of the crash, surely? Then he realised what the investigators were being so cautious about. He had heard of such things and, more important, he knew that Kochalyin was familiar with the device.

As he tried to remember exactly what was involved, the pain returned and filled his chest. He was sure that he was running a fever, his eyes were stinging. There was a clamminess – hot and cold in the same moment. He knew this was the beginning of the end. He'd be going down that stairway and not coming back.

But he wasn't going yet. He still had things to do. He rallied himself. Yes! He remembered. Back in '97 – or was it '98? – Oleg had seen a man from a weapons research establishment in the Ukraine. God knows how he knew about the place – probably something to do with his past. The man came to him to explain the technology and, later that week, Oleg had sounded Tomas out about the production of such a device because he knew he was interested in radio frequencies. Tomas had been genuinely intrigued by the simplicity of the device.

He summoned all his will and laboriously went through the process of an Internet search. He read for over an hour then copied the relevant parts into an e-mail and addressed it to Harland. A second copy he placed on his hard disk for use later. Harland was right, he thought. It had been a logical problem and he was glad he had been able to crack it for him.

The pain was still with him and the fever was taking hold, but he had to get this one other thing out of the way. He prepared to concentrate for the last time that evening and visited his personal archive – a virtual locker which he had set up after Mortz sent him the package – and began selecting the coded information. Most of it had been used before, but there were one or two items that hadn't. He placed them in five separate files, attached the virus that his mother and he had worked up over the last couple of days, and began making calls to the numbers his mother had pinned to the laptop for him. Half an hour later everything had been sent.

But that wasn't quite the end of his work. He went back to the archive and withdrew everything – coded and uncoded material – and placed it on the old Czech website he had set up five or six years before – www.rt.robota.cz. For good measure he added the material he'd found for Harland.

29
DNR

'So that's all of it?' he asked. 'No more surprises?'

She shook her head, took two rapid puffs from a cigarette and inexpertly tried to stub it out.

'No,' she said. 'There are no more surprises, Bobby.'

She was sitting on the sofa with her legs folded under her. Harland had taken himself to the north window and was looking out towards the Houses of Parliament. They'd been through it all: how Vigo made contact with her; how he met her once in Hanover and how she subsequently communicated what she learned of Kochalyin's affairs through e-mail. It all seemed an extremely unlikely story.

He left the window and went to the fridge. There were a couple of bottles of white wine in the door. He withdrew the Chablis, pulled the cork and poured two glasses. He raised his glass to The Bird for putting it there and handed her the other glass.

'Vigo put up quite a case for my arrest and prosecution,' he said conversationally.

'I had nothing to do with that. I knew nothing about them going into the archive in Prague.'

'You know, seeing that picture of us made me feel very old.'

'You haven't changed much, Bobby. A little heavier and not so much hair. But you're the same man.'

'I ache all the time,' he said, smiling. 'I feel my age and I look it. But you, you've kept in terrific shape. It must be the bloody yoga.'

She returned his smile.

'Did you ever see the picture?'

'No, of course not. You have to believe me. I had nothing to do with that. But I knew that it existed, of course, because Oleg told me about it.'

'I do believe you.'

'Nor the tape recording. I would never have done that to you, Bobby – set you up like that.'

He looked at her hard. She was very beautiful. He believed her. 'I know that too. You see, there was never a tape of us talking. Kapek threatened me with it, but that was just bluff – something he pulled out of the hat on the spur of the moment and then boasted about in his report to Kochalyin. Maybe he told him personally. I don't know.'

'There was no tape recording?'

'No, just the picture of us.'

'I must have misunderstood.'

'Yes, you probably did. But your mentioning the tape is interesting because it indicates that at some stage Vigo and his friends were told there was one.'

'I didn't tell them.'

'I wonder where they got the idea?'

'I don't know.' She seemed genuinely perplexed.

'Who told you there was a tape – Kochalyin?'

'I can't remember – I have believed this for years. Oleg wasn't concerned with the operation in Rome. But he had access to the information. So maybe it was him. Why are you interested?'

'Because it means one of two things.' He put his glass down on the table and sat down opposite her. 'One solution is that they had another source to help compile the dossier about me before Christmas. But who could have helped them in that short time? Not Kochalyin, for obvious reasons. Not Kapek because he knew there was no tape, and anyway no one knows where he is, and not you because Vigo didn't want to alert you to the fact that he was putting something together on me. Of course, there is another solution. Perhaps they already knew about the supposed tape. Perhaps they already had it on file and dug it out for the interview with me. You see what I'm saying?'

'No, I don't.' She searched his face.

'Originally I thought it was you. I thought you had worked for Vigo in the eighties.'

She shook her head. 'No, Bobby. I wish I had in many ways. It was what my heart wanted. But I couldn't have risked Tomas and my mother so I stayed loyal.'

'Yes, that was my reasoning. Besides, like every other intelligence organisation, the StB had firewalls between different departments. There was no way a code breaker like you would have had knowledge of how Kapek was handling me. And vice versa of course. Only a few individuals had total access and saw the whole picture. So whoever told them about the tape was either directly responsible for Kapek or was very high up. Kapek was Czech and so one presumes he reported to a senior StB man.

Perhaps this individual was SIS's informant, but my inclination is that it was someone else.'

'But why are you interested in this now? It has nothing to do with the present.'

'But it does. There is one person who had access to everything the StB was doing – Kochalyin. He also told you that there was a tape, repeating Kapek's little myth. Perhaps he didn't know that there wasn't a tape. After all you said he had nothing to do with the operation in Rome. So maybe he just took Kapek's word for it. The important thing was that this was never committed to Kapek's file which means that SIS could only have got this information from Kapek or Kochalyin.'

'You're saying that Oleg was working for SIS? That's too incredible.' She paused and groped for another cigarette. 'Aren't you placing too much significance on the tape and the fact that it wasn't mentioned in Kapek's file?'

'Yes, perhaps,' he said. 'But there's something else. Over the last few days I've been thinking about Ana Tollund. She worked in the Secretariat of the Praesidium. She was a quiet little mouse of a person by all accounts, but she fed the West vital intelligence for twenty years after the Prague Spring. She was very good – subtle, courageous and discriminating in what she passed on to her handlers. Then in '88 she was caught, tried and executed. I heard about her a little time before her arrest, but I knew nothing in detail about the case and I certainly didn't say anything to Kapek about her. However, when I was questioned before Christmas, they accused me of tipping off the Czechs about Tollund. That was Kapek making it up to boost his own importance after the event. But somehow this was passed back to SIS. It could only have been Kochalyin.'

'Why weren't you accused then, if she was so important?'

'Because they knew that I had no access to the information about Ana Tollund. They knew I couldn't know but they kept what Kochalyin had told them on file nevertheless. Everything, you see, is noted down and kept.'

'But you have no evidence that it was Oleg.'

'No, and I never will have. On the other hand, we know that subsequent to the Velvet Revolution Kochalyin had a relationship with SIS. And we know one of his prime motivations is money. Does it not seem likely that he was on the SIS payroll *before* the revolution? He'd have been an incredibly valuable asset to them and when the collapse of the régime came they would have been very willing to extend the association. More than a few favours went his way, I bet.'

She drank some wine and absorbed this.

'It's true,' she said, 'that he always had money. Nothing would stop him selling information if he thought he could get away with it. Maybe you're right, but you will never know. Perhaps you have become a little obsessed with this. Maybe you should stop thinking about the past, Bobby.'

'Possibly,' he said. 'But it is my past. Ever since I talked to Tomas in New York I realised how damned little I knew about my own life. You said something on the train about a person's history being hidden from them. I want to know my history.'

'But there's something more to this for you, isn't there? You think that Kochalyin learned from your colleagues about your plan to buy the intelligence archives. You're thinking that they told him you were coming?'

'Right,' he said. 'That's exactly what I believe. I had a theory about his interception of the coded traffic between here and the embassy, but it seems much more likely that his handlers here sounded him out about the plan. And that was all he needed. He knew exactly where to find me and he could do what he liked without anyone hearing about it in London.'

'Do you think they guessed?'

'That's an interesting point. I think Vigo had his suspicions. He may even have been responsible for alerting Kochalyin in the first place, but I doubt that he intended what happened.' He stopped. 'I'll tell you one thing, though. Kochalyin saved my life.'

'How do you mean?'

'Oleg Kochalyin saved my life. When the swelling in my groin didn't go down, the doctors investigated and discovered I had cancer in one testicle. They got it just in time.'

Her mouth opened in surprise. 'Are you serious?'

'No doubt about it. I didn't suspect anything was wrong. If Kochalyin hadn't done me the favour of whacking me in the balls on the first occasion that we met, I'd probably be dead now.'

She winced. 'Are you all right now?'

'Not a sign since. They did a good job. Everything is okay in that department.'

A silence ensued, both of them lost in their own thoughts. Harland got up and walked to the window again. It was odd that he should end up in Century House with Eva and the ghosts of old suspicions.

'You gave me a look when we were with Teckman and Vigo,' he said from the window. 'You were saying something to me. What was that about?'

She smiled. 'You'll see. You have a very clever son, Bobby. He's like you. He thinks everything through until he finds the solution.' She looked up at the ceiling then quite suddenly her composure collapsed. Her head sank to her chest and her shoulders convulsed with a sob. She began to run her hands distractedly through her hair as her shoulders continued to heave. 'I cannot believe what has happened to my beautiful son. It's my fault.'

Harland moved to her side, put his hands on her shoulders and held her. 'It's not your fault,' he whispered. 'You must understand that.'

She tried to speak but couldn't get the words out. He drew her to him and stroked her head with his right hand.

'He's going to die,' she said. 'I know he's going to die. He told me he wanted to die. Bobby, I don't know how I'll live without him being alive. It mattered when I didn't see him for all that time, but at least I knew he was alive.'

'Have you thought that he might have left you because he knew he was going to do something dangerous and he didn't want to get you involved?' he asked quietly.

'That's kind of you. But, no, he left because he couldn't tolerate me seeing Oleg. If only I'd told him what I was doing.'

'But you have now,' said Harland, knowing she must have shed the whole story during the long hours by his bed.

'Yes. Oh, Bobby, I can't bear what has happened to him. I cannot live with the thought of him like that. I know it's better for him to die, but ...' She sank into herself, falling forward on to her thighs. Harland stroked her back, feeling inadequate to the task of comforting her. The intimacy of shared grief, he now discovered, was as difficult as the intimacy of love. He sat looking ahead at the empty, darkened suite of offices which lay beyond the living quarters, wondering why he'd never recovered that part of himself.

At length Eva sat up a little and dried her eyes. She had the glazed look of someone whose mind is utterly elsewhere. For a time she looked out of the window, her head nodding gently as her thoughts raced. Then she stretched for the bottle of wine on the other side of the table. Harland leaned forward, retrieved it for her and filled her glass. She thanked him and stretched again, this time going for the packet of cigarettes. As she did so her hair fell from the back of her neck and he caught sight of the oval of dark skin just beneath the hairline, the birthmark he'd kissed a hundred times during the long night in Orvieto. It seemed then to be the essence of her – the mark of her uniqueness. He leaned forward and kissed her neck as she came back to the sitting position. It was an impulse. He didn't think before doing it and for a fraction of a second afterwards he expected her to whip round in horror. She said something which he didn't hear and turned to face him, smiling weakly.

'I remember you doing that before.'

'In Orvieto,' he said.

'Orvieto.'

He bent down to rest his face at the back of her head and kissed the birthmark many times again. And he murmured the thing that had been formed in complete sentences somewhere in his mind, waited to be voiced for over a quarter of a century.

'I love you, Eva. I've always loved you. I never stopped loving. I cannot stop.'

She turned her face again to him. 'It's strange of you to go on calling me Eva. I like it.'

'*Eva*,' he insisted. 'I love you, *Eva*.' He was surprised. He wasn't watching himself. He had dropped his guard.

She held his face between her fingers as if trying to steady it and looked at him. Her eyes were desperate.

'You have to . . .' she stammered. 'You must . . .'

'Help you?' he asked. 'Of course I'll help you. You know I will.'

'He's going to die very soon,' she said, quietly and matter-of-factly.

In his former life – five minutes before – Harland would have sought to reassure her by saying that there was a chance that Tomas might recover some of his movement – it was after all a gunshot wound, not a stroke. He would have talked about Tomas building his strength and finding ways of living with his condition. But now Harland had bridged the void that existed between them, or, more accurately, between himself and the rest of humanity, he didn't say any of this. Instead he said exactly what was in his mind.

'When he dies, I will help you in every way I can. I will never leave you. I am here. Nothing else matters to me.'

She kissed him, first with gratitude and relief, then with passion. Her hands fell from his cheeks to the base of his neck and she pulled herself to him, lifting her legs to the sofa and moving against him. He held her close, feeling the softness of her breasts against his chest and the firmness of her arms and shoulders in his hands. Her lightness surprised him, as it had done when they were young. He marvelled at her and fell to her neck, then kissed her on her mouth, on her eyes, on her cheeks.

The scent of her awoke memories in Harland which were not exclusively erotic. He could hear the tolling of the clock tower near the hotel in Orvieto and smell the wood smoke that filled the town on winter evenings. There were inexplicable noises in the hotel. The wooden ceilings shifted and groaned in disapproval. Corridors creaked outside their door and the shutters on the windows juddered in the wind. He remembered her lying on the coarse linen sheets, twisted to an incredible degree at the abdomen so that her legs turned away from him but her torso remained flat on the plane of the bed. He remembered the miraculous curve of her hips – good child-bearing hips, he had said in a silly way, running his hand up the rise of her pelvis and down the slope of her leg and then back again, feeling the resistance of minute hairs on his fingertips.

At some stage in the long night of their weekend together, he had broken free of her and thrown open the windows and shutters and gazed down on the huge deserted square in front of the cathedral. The sight of this silenced operatic set – the illuminated façade of the mediaeval church, a cat slipping into the shadows at a low furtive run, the eddies of a few leaves in the recesses of the buildings around the square – had stayed with him in a clear, dream-like still, as if this moment had been the only time that he had seen the physical world as it really was. There was a ghostliness in the square and it prompted in him an equal joy and fear that they were the only people left alive in the town.

He had returned shivering to her warmth and laid his head on her stomach. She turned her legs and pushed herself up from the bed to watch him as his mouth drifted towards the line of her hair and down between her legs where he parted her flesh with his tongue. From the corner of his eye he could see her gazing at him with an intensely serious expression. Her hand suddenly reached down to press his lips closer to her and she came with a shudder, her head falling silently backwards so that he could only see the alabaster shaft of her throat. Quite some time afterwards she produced a gasp and her head dropped forwards on to him and she smothered him in kisses and brushed her hair across his body. In the early stages of their affair, during the collisions in the hotels of Rome, Harland, who was used to the milk-and-water sex of the English, had been taken aback by the ferocity of her attention. Eva gave, but also took with equal passion, and when at last she had exacted what she needed she lay back on the bed with utter lack of modesty. He was amazed at the whiteness of her body and its strength.

The sequence in Orvieto – moving from the window to taste her body and watching her strain backwards – he had played over and over in his head, partly because it brought her to life like no other memory, but also because it was the only order of events he could remember from the entire weekend. By that stage they must have told each other everything. He often thought of the taverna where they had sat and she had taken hold of one hand and sternly made him listen. But there was no real order in his mind to the three days because apart from that couple of hours in the restaurant they'd ruthlessly shut out the world and greedily merged into each other.

Then as now. They stayed in the half-light feeling as young and awed by their delight as they had twenty-eight years before. Their joy was limitless and engrossing. But there were few words between them. He mostly kept his eyes shut to sense her the better, and in the rare moments he opened them he saw hers were closed too.

Some time in the middle of the night they made their way into her bedroom and sprawled on the bed where he struggled with her remaining clothes. Her head flopped lazily from one side to the other as he removed her bra and drew the white shirt from her arms. He stopped for a moment and absorbed her beauty, feeling less self-conscious than he could ever remember being. She looked drugged with expectation.

As he kicked off his shoes and removed his own clothes, she began to weave about him, nipping at him with her teeth, clawing him gently, holding him to her to find the tightest fit. She didn't need to tell him that she loved him or that she had often replayed the way they made love in her mind because everything was as it had been, only more urgent, more serious.

He watched her moving to a climax, lifting her head from the bed and opening her eyes with a look of surprise.

About an hour later the phone in the sitting-room began to ring. Harland awoke and wondered furiously what time it was. He groped for his watch but found he'd left it in the other room and decided not to answer. But the phone went on ringing and after a couple of minutes, by which time he was fully awake, he dragged himself out of bed and went to pick it up.

'Mr Harland. This is Professor Reeve. I have the information you wanted.'

'Yes,' said Harland, and cleared his throat.

'Well? Do you want it?' demanded Reeve. 'After you sent me the report, I went to considerable trouble to get this information for you.'

'No, no – of course I want it, sir. Let me just get a pen.' He reached for his coat pocket. 'Right, I'm with you now.'

'From the information that you gave me,' said Reeve briskly, 'my contact was able to identify the likely location of the massacre site. So write this down – the position is forty degrees and two minutes north, nineteen degrees and thirteen minutes east. Computer models of the local topography confirm that the picture you sent me was taken by someone facing the mountains of the Javor and Javornik ranges. The profile of the mountains that you can see is about twenty-five kilometres north-west of the site.'

'Thank you,' said Harland, groping for the maps he had used with Tomas in the hospital. 'It'll be useful to be able to pinpoint the place in the report.' He paused, opened the map and quickly ran his finger to a spot not far from the road that meandered through the mountains.

'Are you there?' said Reeve, who had been explaining that his contact was a CIA target-spotter who was familiar with the terrain in the Balkans.

'I'm with you,' he said hastily. 'I was just glancing at the map and wondering whether it would be possible to learn if the grave was known to the authorities in The Hague.'

'You don't have to bother,' snapped Reeve. 'I've already checked on the data base we have. This site is new to us and will be to the people at The Hague. It was what Mr Griswald was undoubtedly working to expose.'

'Well, I'm most grateful to you. My heartfelt thanks, Professor.'

'But I haven't finished. I rang now because this site has suffered some disturbance in the last twenty-four hours. My contact has been doing some research into this area with the usual resources at his disposal. And he noticed in yesterday's pictures, which are exceptionally clear, that there was earth-moving equipment in the area. There is a two-hour gap between the first set which shows the equipment moving up a road toward the site and the second set which reveals the vehicles gathered round the site.'

'The evidence is being destroyed,' said Harland. 'He's digging up the bodies.'

'Precisely. With the harsh weather in those mountains at this time of year, it's unlikely that anyone would countenance carrying out large-scale construction work. The cold wouldn't allow it. So that is the only conclusion to draw. Someone should get some photographs of what's happening on the ground. But they'll need to get there during daylight tomorrow. It won't take long for those people to dig up and distribute the remains around the hills and then it will be a very difficult task indeed to prove that anything happened at that place.'

'I take your point,' said Harland

'So, I leave it with you,' he said. 'Good hunting, Mr Harland. I'll send you yesterday's images. You'll need them to find the exact spot. Let me know what happens.' He hung up without saying goodbye.

Harland thought of going back to bed but then he began to look at the map. He could fly to Sarajevo, hire a car and be there by early afternoon. All he would need to buy was a camera – maybe a video recorder too.

It was just five o'clock so he made some tea and returned to Eva who was lying on her side, sound asleep. He sipped the tea while his eyes moved over her face.

Harland's ears pricked up. Someone was moving on their floor. He put the tea down, crept to the door and peered through. The figure stopped and looked at the open map. As he moved against the glow of London in the window, Harland recognised The Bird's profile. He called out softly so as not to wake Eva.

'Hello, old chap. Sorry to wake you so early.'

'You didn't. What's going on?'

'Only the entire security establishment frothing at the mouth, but don't let it worry you. I'm sure it's all in a day's work for you.'

'What *are* you talking about?'

'Radio stations across Europe are spewing out the code again – just one code this time, and the whole bloody lot is being blasted out at the rate of knots. Vigo is named – so too Brother Morsehead and Friend Lapthorne. Did you know they were tied up with Oleg Kochalyin from way back?'

Harland nodded. 'I guessed.'

'But you didn't know that innocent-looking little fucker Morsehead was on his payroll. Apparently Morsehead used to pay Kochalyin. Come the revolution, Kochalyin paid Morsehead. It's the end for him and his ambitions.'

'Who's been translating this stuff for you?'

'The man you met after the races. The first broadcast came on the dot of midnight. Cheltenham went haywire. He was called in to trace it. Bobby, they're sure it's coming from London. Though they haven't got the exact spot yet. I've told him to keep me posted.'

'And you came to check it wasn't us?'

'It did occur to me that you'd rigged up some system here while you were canoodling away with the Bohemian Temptress.'

'Well, it isn't me.'

'What about her?'

'I don't know. She's asleep. I can wake her if you're worried.'

'Leave her,' said The Bird, looking down at the map. 'What's this all about?'

Harland told him about Reeve's call and his decision to leave for Sarajevo that day.

'So you're still pursuing this thing?'

'Yes. In all the fuss everyone forgets that there's a fucking war criminal walking about doing exactly as he pleases.'

'Why don't you let it drop, Bobby? This man is pure poison. You know that better than anyone. You'll just get yourself killed if you go.'

'It's obvious, Cuth. Oleg Kochalyin has affected every part of my life. I want to see him nailed. I'm going to get pictures of that place if it's the last thing I do.'

'It will be,' said The Bird. He examined Harland again. 'Are you sure the transmissions aren't your work, Bobby?'

'Yes.'

'Then who the hell is responsible?'

There was a noise in the passage leading from the bedroom. Eva appeared, wrapped in a towel. She looked at them in turn.

'I know what you're talking about. The answer is Tomas. I gave him help, but he did most of it himself. I told you, Bobby, he's very clever. It took incredible willpower to do what he has done in the last two days.'

'But how?' asked Harland. 'How could he possibly do it from his hospital bed?'

She sat down on the arm of the sofa. 'He had stored everything in an electronic archive. The only thing he needed was the virus – but the codes and everything were there, waiting to be used. He learned to use that machine and we worked from there.' She looked at her watch. 'There'll be another one soon. I believe he intends this to be his memorial.'

'I'll say,' said The Bird, missing the point. 'People aren't going to forget this in a long time. The only mercy is that Fleet Street's finest can't read it on the bloody Internet.'

Eva looked down at the map. 'Are you going there, Bobby?' she said.

'Yes, I've just had a call from Washington. The satellite pictures yesterday picked up some activity at the site.'

She was about to say something when the phone rang. The Bird answered and handed it to Harland. A duty sister from the hospital was on the line. Tomas had contracted a case of double pneumonia and was running a high temperature. She said they should get there as soon as possible.

The Bird drove them there in fifteen minutes flat and went inside with them because, as he pointed out, the danger from Kochalyin was now very great indeed. In Tomas's room they were made to wear surgical masks. There were two nurses, each watching different monitors, and a woman doctor standing by his head. As Harland passed the end of the bed he saw the initials 'DNR' – Do Not Resuscitate – written along the top of his medical notes.

Eva made room for herself and sat by his bed, one hand touching his head, the other holding his hand. The nurses kept throwing glances in Eva's direction, trying to gauge her reaction. The respirator groaned and clicked with its usual rhythm, but from Tomas there came a new noise, a rattle, almost a bubbling sound, from his chest, which the doctor said had been drained but was already refilling with liquid. Harland looked down at his son's wasted limbs and then at the little knot of concentration in his forehead.

'He's exhausted,' said the doctor. 'His reserves are very low indeed.' This was aimed at Eva – a warning that she should expect the worst. 'The infection took hold late last night. We gave him some powerful antibiotics. But he was obviously in great pain and we have relieved that with diamorphine. The problem is that his defences are down, plus his stomach is reacting badly to the antibiotics.'

Eva took no notice. Her eyes were fastened on the clear plastic mask over his mouth and nose. Harland touched her on the shoulder and said he was going out. He went to find The Bird, who had made himself comfortable by a coffee machine and was absorbed in a nursing journal. He looked up and smiled sympathetically.

'It's not good news, is it?'

'No,' said Harland leadenly, 'I'm afraid it isn't.'

'Terrible for you, old chap. I'm dreadfully sorry for you both.'

'Thank you,' said Harland, for no reason thinking back to the Embankment and the sudden shocking grief he'd experienced while waiting for the ambulances to arrive.

'Well, at least you won't be able to hare off to the bloody Balkans,' he said. 'No good can come of that.'

'Yes, but it means that the evidence that Griswald and Tomas wanted to make public will be destroyed. Their work – their sacrifice – will be wasted. That does matter, Cuth.'

The Bird considered this. 'Look at it this way. They both did a lot to expose the links between Kochalyin and our former colleagues. There's going to be a dreadful stink when this gets into the system.'

'Yes, I suppose so, but it doesn't do anything to get Kochalyin.'

'But what on earth can you do? Running off to some godforsaken mountainside in Bosnia with your Sureshot camera is not going to help.'

Harland didn't argue.

Half an hour later, Dr Smith-Canon appeared and said he wanted to speak to Harland and Eva. It wouldn't take long, but it was important. They went into his office.

'I'm not going to beat around the bush with you both,' he said. 'The situation is very serious. We might just be able to save him but it's going to take everything we've got and even then we won't know how long he'll last.'

Eva nodded dully.

He waited. 'You do understand what I'm saying?'

She nodded again.

'We have your son's wishes on record. You believe those are still his wishes?'

Without speaking she turned to the door. Smith-Canon searched Harland's face for clarification. He nodded and followed Eva back to Tomas's room. She settled by Tomas's side again, and Harland stood behind her, holding her shoulder.

Tomas could feel very little. There was some small part of him that was making decisions and taking things in and communicating these things to the centre of his being. It was like a voice on a bad telephone line, becoming fainter. He knew that he was fading with it. What more was there to say? He was going and soon he would not be having these conversations with himself.

It wasn't like this the first time. He had no sense of the definite surroundings of the coma. There was no stairway, no damp walls, and no warm place at the bottom where he could rest. But his mind was full of something – tiny firings of light and flickers of memory. They didn't added up to much and he was tired of them.

One more time. He would open his eyes one more time and see who was there. It was difficult but he managed it, and when he focused he saw that his mother was very close to him. She looked so distraught that he almost didn't recognise her. He saw Harland too, leaning forward into his field of vision. They were standing together – mother and father. That was good.

She spoke in Czech, which was a relief: he couldn't handle anything else. She was saying how much she loved him and she wanted him to fight and struggle and beat the illness so they could go home together. She said she knew he could do it. He smiled to himself. She used to say that when he was small – she knew he could do it. But this time he couldn't. He'd done his best and he was going to have a sleep.

He closed his eyes. Then there was noise in the room. Raised, angry voices. He felt the bed move. What was going on? He couldn't be bothered to find out. No, he was tired and he was going to have a sleep.

The commotion started in the corridor. Harland heard Smith-Canon and The Bird's voice rebuking someone. There were other voices. He didn't turn towards the door because he knew the moment was near. Tomas had opened his eyes and gazed at Eva with pinprick pupils, then shut them with a flutter. The monitor on the other side of the bed had been showing an increasingly irregular heart beat.

A few seconds later the noise spilled into the room. Harland whipped round to see Vigo still in his overcoat march towards the computer stand which had been pushed against the wall. Smith-Canon came in followed by two other men who he realised must be Special Branch officers.

'Do you hear me?' hissed Smith-Canon, snatching at Vigo's sleeve. 'My patient is dying! You have no right to be here. You must leave now.'

Vigo's face was set with purpose.

'This won't take long. We just need the machine. That's all.'

Harland leapt up, pushing the bed away from him, and placed himself between Vigo and the computer.

'Get the hell out of my son's room, Walter.'

The other men forced their way past him and began unplugging the computer and detaching the electrodes which still dangled from the stand. Harland swung round to them.

'Have you no sense of what you're doing?' he demanded.

Harland glanced at the monitor beside Tomas, then at Smith-Canon who had moved forward and stood shaking his head by the bedside. Eva lifted Tomas's hand to her cheek, closed her eyes and silently fell forward on to his chest.

In that moment it occurred to Harland that Tomas had not left him, but had simply withdrawn to a distant level of existence. It seemed possible that a body which had been all but lifeless for the past few weeks might still harbour a trace of him and that he'd make himself known as miraculously as he had done before. As if he had read these thoughts, Smith-Canon leaned over and turned the respirator off. The noise of the machine subsided and the gentle rise of Tomas's rib cage stopped. Harland moved to Eva's side and touched her lightly on her back, then felt Tomas's arm. It was already cold. He had gone.

Vigo hesitated a few seconds longer, then nodded to the men who had picked up the computer and its leads.

'I take it you have some kind of authority to do that,' said The Bird with deceptive mildness from the door.

'The Official Secrets Act,' replied Vigo, and left.

30
Flight

An hour passed during which a startlingly bright day broke outside and the sounds of the city going to work reached their ears.

The room itself was silent and heavy with Eva's grief. Harland stayed with her for about half an hour but guessed she'd want to be alone with Tomas. He slipped out to find Smith-Canon and thank him for all he had done. On the way back to the room, he was approached from behind by one of the two Special Branch officers who had been waiting a little way down the corridor. The officer, a young man with sunken cheeks and a blond moustache, informed him that he and Eva should consider themselves under arrest.

Harland looked at him with disbelief.

'If I were you,' he said, 'I'd make sure that I had that instruction from the very highest level, because one word from me, and the whole of this business goes to the press. Now fuck off.'

'We have our orders, sir.'

'Nevertheless,' said Harland fiercely, 'you tell them that any discussions we have will be on our own terms. And during that meeting Mrs Rath will be treated with the respect due someone who has just lost their only child.'

With that he turned and went back into the room. Eva looked up. Evidently she'd heard something of the exchange.

'Don't worry,' he said. 'They're not going to bother you.'

'What now?' she asked at length.

'We must make arrangements,' he said quietly, looking down at Tomas. 'I guess we take his body back to your country.'

'Yes,' she said, 'but what are you going to do?'

'I'm going to Bosnia to get pictures of the site. It's now or never. Everything will be gone by tomorrow.' He stopped. 'I feel I ought to stay with you but . . .'

She shook her head. 'No, Bobby, you should go.'

'I'll only be away a couple of days.' He looked into her face. Her eyes were bewildered and shocked.

Half an hour later they left the hospital with the Special Branch officers. Notions of arrest had apparently been suspended – at least temporarily. They were led through a maze of passages near Admiralty Arch at the top of The Mall and into a large room, surrounded with a dado of Victorian ceramic tiles and hung with paintings of naval battles. A band of sunlight fell from the window across the centre of the room and heated the floor polish, giving the air a faint odour of resin and leather and a sense that the room was left over from an era of gaslights and plumed helmets. An odd place for Vigo to choose, thought Harland.

He sat with three other men in a crescent beside a conference table covered with a blanket of green felt to protect its surface. Harland guessed that two of them were from MI5 and he assumed the third was either from the Foreign Office or was a colleague of Vigo's from MI6.

Vigo motioned them to two chairs and then pulled his own slightly nearer the table.

'We all know what we are here for,' he said, without looking up. 'We're here to establish exactly what other allegations are going to be made in these transmissions.'

Harland coughed. 'But surely you have everything you need in the computer that you seized in the hospital.'

'The computer had a number of concealed files that destroyed themselves when they were opened.' His eyes had risen from a blank notepad and were levelled at Eva. 'Tomas had learned something since we last took his computer away from him. Or perhaps that was your work, Irina? He plainly could not have done all this without your help. We also fully understand that the additional information which has been released in the last nine hours must have come from you. So, it is our urgent purpose to learn what else is going to come out. The Government needs to respond to this mess.'

Eva shook her head. 'It was my son's work,' she said simply.

'You must have helped him in the hospital?'

'Why are you so hot under the collar, Walter?' said Harland, seeking to draw the fire. 'All the material has been used before.'

Vigo leaned forward so that his shoulders and chest merged into one uniformly grey bulk. 'I don't think either of you quite understands the gravity of your position.'

'Nor you yours,' Harland shot back.

One of the two men that Harland had pegged as MI5 sighed. He had been studying Harland closely, as if watching for adverse character traits in a psychometric test.

'I mean it,' Harland insisted. 'For once your systematic hypocrisy has been exposed – spying on allies, using a war criminal to transport arms while paying lip service to his arrest and prosecution. It's going to come out.'

'We understand you were threatening to give this to the press,' said the Foreign Office type.

'Yes, when one of your police officers said he was there to arrest us. But as you know, I have had no access to the transmissions. I still have only a vague idea of their exact nature. So I'm hardly in a position to publicise it, am I?'

'However, Irina, you are,' said Vigo. 'Did you make copies of what Tomas has been putting out?'

She shook her head.

Vigo looked sceptical and returned to Harland.

'But the fact that you were prepared to make the threat underlines our fears. Only yesterday we had your word that your report would be taken no further and that its circulation would be limited to those who already have it. You appear to have abandoned that undertaking.'

This was all said with moderation, but Harland had no illusions about Vigo's intention. He was making the case for his colleagues, pointing up Harland's unreliability, his hot-headedness.

'You forget,' he said in an equally measured tone, 'that I am a servant of the United Nations. I work for the Secretary-General. I cannot therefore be subject to the interest of one state above all others. Of course this affair is embarrassing for you, but the fact remains that a man who had been indicted by the War Crimes Tribunal for Former Yugoslavia was working for you and the Americans. As a permanent member of the Security Council, Britain signed the resolution to establish the tribunal and is legally obliged to support its work. The same goes for the US. But both countries have done the opposite. Whoever set up Kochalyin's assassination in Bosnia is no longer of any real interest. What is relevant, however, is that Kochalyin relied on you from the winter of '96, '97 onwards. I accept that you were not responsible for this, Walter, but that's too bad. You're carrying the can for the flexible morals of your friends.'

'You have no proof that he has been used by either us or the Americans,' Vigo stated.

'Perhaps no direct proof, but if the facts were laid out about the crash and the faked assassination, together with all the other material – the pictures and so forth – then I'm sure people would draw the right conclusions.'

Harland had realised a while back that what they were worried about was the potential alchemy between his report and Tomas's transmissions. If the coded material ever reached the public domain, it would be denied by all concerned as a work of fantasy. But a UN report, commissioned by

Jaidi, which supported some of the allegations, would lend credibility to the rest.

Vigo's attention flicked back to Eva.

'Of course, this is not quite the issue of high principle that you claim it to be – is it?'

She didn't respond.

'Irina, we know your son was involved in the murder of those Muslims – he admits it in the coded material of last night and he has apparently given the same statement to Harland.'

'How do you know that?' asked Harland, alert to the possibility that his e-mails had been read.

'Because he included it at the end of the last transmission and said as much. Was this his last word?'

'Yes,' Eva said. 'He was taking responsibility for his actions before he died. But it was not his fault. They forced him to kill that man.'

'As indeed he makes plain in his little account of the incident,' said Vigo with indifference. 'Was it his way of signing off? I mean, was this how he planned to finish the entire transmission?'

She looked up and nodded slowly. 'Yes, there's nothing more.'

'Good,' said Vigo. 'Then we know what we're dealing with and can plan our response. As to the report, I take it that your assurance of yesterday still stands?'

Harland didn't answer because he was puzzled by the sudden fading of Vigo's concern.

'Let me remind you,' Vigo continued, 'that you agreed not to distribute it further and that you would not add to it. I hope you're clear that you will both feel the full force of the state if you go against your word. So do I have your assurance?'

Harland shrugged. 'If that means you will leave Eva and me alone, then yes.'

'Our business here this morning is therefore concluded,' said Vigo. 'You may now leave. We don't expect to be in touch again, unless we learn that you've broken your agreement.'

Harland knew perfectly well that their business was nowhere near concluded. For Vigo, closure would only be achieved when he and his report had been neutralised.

They left the room and after retracing their route back through the dismal corridors, they broke into the sunlight of The Mall. He put his arm round her shoulder.

'I think we should go and sort things out at the hospital.'

'Yes, then you will go to Bosnia. I'll come with you.'

'You want to?'

'Yes,' she said. She had understood what the meeting had been about all right.

Later, at Century House, they were met by The Bird who had piled some anoraks and boots by the entrance to the lift. He greeted them with a cavalier look dancing in his eyes.

'You've missed the flight to Vienna which connects to Sarajevo this afternoon,' he said. 'There's no point going to Zagreb because there isn't a connection to Sarajevo until tomorrow. So I've made other arrangements. A charter firm we use is sending a plane to Athens tomorrow to pick up a party of shippers. They're happy to send the plane to Sarajevo *en route*. But there are three conditions: you pay for the landing charges and a tank of fuel, you give the driver a steaming great tip, and you take me along for the ride.' He searched their faces for a reaction. 'I know some people in Sarajevo.'

'When did you ever go to Sarajevo?'

'Never, but one meets people hither and thither. I gather it's crawling with chaps pretending to their wives they're reconstructing Bosnia when all they're doing is banging Balkan beauties.'

'I know the type.'

'You are the type,' said The Bird, looking down at the mound of clothes and boots. 'Okay? Right, let's shift this kit down to the car. We've got to be at Blackbush airport in under an hour. Oh, by the way, I've got a good digital camera so you don't have to bother with that.'

'How much is this all going to cost?' said Harland, when Eva went to get her things.

'No more than three thou' – we'll sort it out when the invoices come in.'

'Thanks for organising it – thanks for everything, Cuth.'

'Think nothing of it. I want to get this fucker as much as you do.' He paused. 'Terrible shame about your lad.'

'Yes.' Harland paused. 'Cuth, you understand that Vigo will have us followed to the airport and he will get the flight plan within a few minutes of us taking off. He'll know where we're going and it won't take him long to work out that you fixed this all up. Are you sure you want him on your back?'

'Fuck him. Too slippery by half is Brother Walter. I didn't like the way he descended on that hospital one bit.'

Harland collected a few clothes, a phone, his map and the computer he'd need in order to download the images from Norman Reeve. Ten minutes later, Cuth's Range Rover exited the underground car park and sped out of London towards Blackbush. A dark red Ford, a motorcycle and a blue Nissan tracked their progress but were left behind when they drove through the aerodrome gates. Well before anyone had time to prevent them from leaving, the Gulfstream had taken off.

Almost subconsciously Harland settled himself in the rearmost seat of the little jet opposite Eva.

If he hadn't been so concerned for her he would certainly have been thinking about the risks of travelling on another plane. Once they were airborne, he snapped off his seat belt and leaned forward to hold both of Eva's hands between his. She smiled weakly, but her eyes quickly turned away, down to the English countryside lit golden in the early-afternoon sun. He knew she didn't want to talk.

Harland closed his own eyes to think about the task ahead, but within a short time he had fallen asleep. He was awoken by a hand on his shoulder.

'We've got less than hour.' The Bird was looking down at him. 'We need a plan of attack.'

Harland glanced out of the window to see the Alps ahead of them. A feather of vapour was trembling on the Gulfstream's wingtip.

'What information about this place do you have?' asked The Bird. 'Should we try to get as near as we can tonight, or wait until tomorrow?'

Harland showed him the position on his map.

'That's got to be an hour or two hours' drive from Sarajevo. It'll be dark long before we get there. Have you got the latest pictures of the site?'

'Blast,' said Harland, rubbing his eyes. 'I meant to log on before I left and collect my e-mail. I forgot.'

'That's all right. There's a phone socket by your elbow. You can log on through the plane's communications system.'

Harland downloaded his mail.

There were three messages – two from Norman Reeve with attachments and a third from an address he didn't recognise. The first included the picture from the day before, which showed the vehicles as little more than specks on the hillside. Harland made out some rocks and a road that had been cleared to the position of the four vehicles. The second picture was greatly magnified and had obviously been taken later in the day. It showed two trucks, a digger and a long loader. In the middle of the photograph was a black scrape where the snow and rocks had been removed by the digger. Around it were the marks of caterpillar tracks.

The Bird peered down at the screen from over Harland's shoulder. 'Could be anything,' he said. 'They might be making a reservoir.'

'At this time of year? Besides it's near the top of the hill. You can see from the light and shade. Who makes a reservoir at the top of a hill where there's no catchment area?'

He closed the picture and pulled up the second e-mail. Reeve had written: 'This was taken at 11 GMT, noon local time. Hope you bring home the bacon, Mr Harland – NR.' He opened the attachment. The trucks had changed their position, but the digger and loader were in more or less the same spot. They had been joined by a fifth vehicle, a smaller green jeep or pick-up. Harland squinted at the screen so that he could see the dots which made up the picture. He was sure the shape of the scar on the mountainside had not grown. He wondered: are those tiny strokes of shadow people?

He turned the laptop round to Eva. 'We may be in time. Nothing seems to have happened today.'

She looked at it doubtfully. 'I wonder if he knows this can be seen,' she said quietly.

'Well, they're lucky to have got the shots,' said The Bird. 'They've been having a lot of snow. We'd better get ourselves a bloody good vehicle if we're going to get up there.'

Harland had been on the point of saying something, but the thought left him. 'Any ideas where we can get that?'

The Bird said he had, but it would take the evening. They talked on for a while until the pilot shouted through the open door that they were twenty-five minutes from landing at Sarajevo. The Bird sat down on the other side of the aisle and fiddled with his seat belt. Harland scrolled through his inbox and found the third e-mail which came from an AOL address that meant nothing to him. It took him a few moments to see that it was from Tomas because the message was only signed T after the heading, 'Crash solution'. He realised that it had been sent just a few hours before his death. It was probably the last act of his life.

He decided to say nothing to Eva and began to read. It was clear that the material had been copied from various websites because of the different formats and typefaces used. All the quotations concerned high-powered microwave weapons and a new, cheap variant called a Transient Electromagnetic Device, which produced a devastating spike of energy. Harland glanced over a diagram showing a tube wrapped in copper wire and packed with high explosive at one end. It seemed that the detonation of the explosive sent a shockwave down the tube, generating a pulse of electromagnetic energy in the coils of wire. This issued at great speed from the nozzle of the tube and tore through every electrical circuit in its path.

Harland immediately realised the implication. A portable version of this weapon must have been set up along the shoreline of the East River and fired at the Falcon jet as it rushed across the water to land. The electrical circuits in the plane would have been instantly fried, causing a catastrophic loss of control which in every way mimicked the effect of a wake-vortex.

Suddenly he understood the meaning of Ollins's questions. The failure of the lights on the Falcon was only significant in as much as Griswald had held up his computer to use the screen's light to see what he was doing. When the pulse of energy struck the plane, the protective cladding of the laptop shielded the computer's circuits and – crucially for Harland – the phone in Griswald's pocket.

His respect for Ollins had taken a quantum leap. It was damned smart of him to have worked it out. But it was even smarter, not to say heroic, of Tomas to spend his last hours, paralysed and choked with fluid, battling through the problem.

The pilot announced they were beginning their descent and would be landing in fifteen minutes.

'I can't believe it,' said Harland, overcome with emotion. 'This e-mail is from Tomas. He's found out why the plane crashed in New York. It's incredible. He did it from his bed and sent this last night. What's more, the FBI reached the same conclusion long before he did. They knew it was sabotage and they've kept it quiet.'

Eva and The Bird listened intently as he explained the theory in quick clear sentences.

'Why would the FBI have covered this up?' asked The Bird. 'What was in it for them?'

'Who knows? I suppose they might not want to publicise the potential of this weapon. It would scare the shit out of a hell of a lot of prospective passengers. But perhaps we're looking at a cover-up involving all the major intelligence agencies of the United States and Britain. God knows!'

'Are you saying the US helped bring down that plane?'

'Not necessarily. Maybe Frank Ollins got to the bottom of the investigation and someone told him to forget the whole thing and go along with another theory involving the wake from the jet that had just landed. I don't know who pulled the levers and I don't know their reasons for doing it. But it certainly seems like a cover-up.'

'It would need careful planning,' said Eva quickly. 'They would have to know the likely times of departure and arrival and the runway that was going to be used. A lot could change at the last moment.'

'Yes, that's true. But remember Kochalyin owns an aviation company. Hell, he's used it to transport arms all round the world. Taking one of these devices into the States wouldn't prove very difficult. More important is that the people who work for Corniche-HDS Aviation must know a thing or two about listening into communications between a pilot and the control tower.'

'Christ, I wish you'd saved this until later,' said The Bird. 'It's giving me the bloody jitters.'

This made Harland suddenly concentrate.

'What was that you said just now?' he demanded of Eva.

'What do you mean?'

'About the satellite pictures. You wondered whether Kochalyin knew he could be seen.' What were you thinking?'

'It occurred to me that Oleg appreciates what can be photographed from a satellite. Everyone knows that the graves around Srebrenica were picked up by US satellites and spy planes. I remember seeing the pictures in the newspaper.'

'So what would be a better way of gaining our attention and luring us out here than digging up that grave?' asked Harland.

'It's a bit late to have that thought now,' said The Bird, shifting in his seat.

'And why hasn't there been any further digging today?' Harland persisted. 'Maybe he had done enough to gain our attention and ordered the work to stop.'

'But he would have to be sure that *you* knew about the excavation,' said Eva.

At that moment the pilot dimmed the cabin lights: the plane was on its final approach. They had banked sharp right and were coasting along the side of a mountain. Harland could see houses, each with one or two lights shining in the prolonged dusk of a snowy landscape. On the starboard side he glimpsed the city of Sarajevo sprawling in the bowl of the valley. He heard the whine from the landing gear being lowered.

He unbuckled and rushed forward to the cockpit. 'I can't explain this now,' he shouted at the back of the pilot's head, 'but it's just possible some kind of device will be fired at us which will knock out all your electrical circuits. Can you land without them?'

The co-pilot turned round and shifted his headset. He plainly thought Harland mad.

'Can you land it without any electronics? Because that's what you may have to do.'

'Take a seat, sir,' said the pilot calmly. 'We're very close now.'

Harland looked ahead of them and saw the lights of the runway approaching.

'Two thousand feet,' said the co-pilot.

The radio sounded and the pilot moved the flaps down. Harland heard the engines throttling back.

'Fifteen hundred feet,' intoned the co-pilot. 'One thousand. We're fully configured for landing, sir. Please sit down while we pop her on the deck.'

Harland reeled back through the cabin, knowing that it was now too late for him to avert the disaster. He dropped into the seat beside Eva and fastened his belt.

And then the miracle happened. They touched down – so quietly that it took a few moments for Harland to realise they were on the ground. The jet skated past a checkered military control tower and began to slow down as it headed towards the end of the runway.

'Welcome to Sarajevo,' said the captain with pointed calm. 'The local time is ten minutes past five. It's a clear evening. The temperature is minus seven degrees centigrade, nineteen degrees Fahrenheit. Wind-chill factor is high. Wrap up warm and have an enjoyable stay. We're aiming for a fast turnaround to get on our way to Athens, so I'd be grateful if you could leave the aircraft quickly.'

From sheer nervous energy, Harland had already flipped off the seat belt, risen and put on his anorak.

'Bloody hell, Bobby,' said The Bird. 'I'll think twice before getting on a plane with you again.'

Harland felt slightly foolish.

'I'm sorry,' he said. 'I thought he'd planned the whole thing so he would take the plane out when we came in.'

The aircraft came to a halt at the end of the runway. Eva got up.

'There's a truck in our way,' said the captain. 'It's going to lead us into the terminal. We'll just be a few minutes so you may as well make yourselves comfortable.'

Eva bent down and peered out of the window between their seats on to the uninviting wasteland of the airfield. Suddenly she recoiled back into Harland who was also looking out.

'Down!' she cried.

Harland had seen the flare of orange a hundred yards away, out to their right. But he hadn't reacted as quickly as Eva and only when the rocket hit the tailplane on the starboard side did he understand what had happened.

The pilot was also quicker to grasp the situation. He increased the power in the engines and the plane lurched forwards, sending his three passengers hurtling backwards.

The plane surged over the edge of the concrete runway and began to head across the snow towards the terminal building. The engines were kicking up a storm of ice crystals that were being whipped forward by the wind in rhythmic billows.

Harland struggled to his feet and threw himself towards the cockpit.

'What the hell're you doing?' he shouted over the noise of the engines.

'Trying to get away from him. There's no one out here who's going to help us.'

Harland looked out of the side of the cockpit across the deserted airfield to the small terminal building. Nothing moved. Ahead of them was a truck, on the back of which stood two men. One jerked something to his shoulder. The rocket fired and passed just to the left of the cockpit. The pilot whistled in relief. Harland instinctively ducked.

He felt a tug on his arm. He turned to see Eva, pulling at his jacket. The Bird had both hands on the lever of the port door and was preparing to jerk it upwards. Harland lunged to snatch his and Eva's bags and turned to see The Bird wrenching the door inwards and then pushing it against the cabin wall.

The deafening scream of the engines entered the cabin with a blast of cold air. The Bird gripped Eva, but she signalled for him to go first. He jumped and she followed. Harland dropped out of the door shortly afterwards and crashed to the ground in a kneeling position. In the blinking light coming from the plane's belly he saw The Bird helping Eva to her feet. The plane had gone about thirty feet from him. At that point a third rocket hit it on the starboard side of the fuselage. Before the explosion ripped through the fuel tank on the far wing, a lone figure dropped out of the door.

The plane continued for a fraction of a second longer, then seemed to pause before shuddering and collapsing away from them. At that the second fuel tank exploded with much greater force and blew the fuselage apart. Harland got up and ran to where the man had fallen and recognised the co-pilot. He was lying in the snow. He called out that he'd hurt his leg and wasn't sure if he could walk. Harland could already feel the intense heat of the flames through his clothing. He took hold of the man's shoulders and hefted him upwards so he could drag him across the snow. The Bird rushed over to help him. Together they carried the co-pilot to a concrete block where they laid him on the ground and propped his head against the concrete.

Harland bent down with his hands on his knees, heaving from the effort.

'Better you don't tell them we got out. Play dumb. Say you don't know who else got out. It's very important. Can you do that?'

The man nodded groggily.

'It's just for twenty-four hours,' said Harland. 'Then you can get your memory back.' He straightened and turned to The Bird and Eva. 'Right, let's find a way out so we're not seen.'

They ran towards the perimeter fence, away from the jet and the truck. Two military fire tenders had emerged from the terminal area and were lumbering towards the plane. From the centre of the airfield came a pair of military vehicles, bumping over the ruts in the snow.

Harland reached the fence first and looked back. The truck had vanished into the dark of the airfield in the east. He indicated that they should make for the terminal which was about 300 yards away. They passed a padlocked fence, then a single-engine Cessna whose wings were tethered to the ground, and continued along the fence until they were fifty yards from the concrete apron in front of the terminal building. All hell had broken loose. Troops had disgorged from the building and were rushing to their vehicles, while what seemed to be the entire staff of the airport were milling about, watching the fire.

No one noticed Harland approach and look through one of the windows. The terminal was a rudimentary affair, in fact little more than a large warehouse with its guts on display. Heating and wiring ducts were in the process of being installed and the customs and immigration posts looked more like ticket booths. Neither was manned.

He turned and waved the others forward. They walked smartly through the door and past the immigration post and in no time at all found themselves in a deserted car park on the other side of the building. Because the last of the commercial flights had landed there were no cabs to be found. They stamped their feet in the cold and searched each other's faces.

'You're a member of the UN staff,' exclaimed The Bird, eyeing a row of white four-wheel drives, each emblazoned with a UN crest. 'And you are on an important mission for the Secretary-General.'

They moved quickly along the line of cars until they came to an Isuzu with its sidelights on and the keys still hanging from the steering column. The driver had obviously left in a hurry to see what was happening on the airfield. They got in without a second thought and drove sedately from the compound into a desolate, ill-lit boulevard flanked by burned-out buildings.

They found a hotel in a street named Kulovića in the old part of the city and parked the Isuzu in a covered area at the rear, tipping the attendant more than his month's salary to watch the car overnight. They checked into the hotel but avoided having to leave their passports at the desk when The Bird deftly palmed another large tip to the young manager.

Half an hour later they all went to a restaurant near to the hotel where they ate from a menu of home comforts aimed at Western aid workers. As they walked the few yards back to the hotel, The Bird abruptly announced he was going to see someone and strode off down the street, hands thrust into a dark green jacket, scenting the wind like a lurcher.

Strung out and exhausted, Harland and Eva went to their room, where Eva went straight to bed. Harland drew back the curtains and looked down on a confusion of dwellings and terraces and arrested construction. Ahead of him was a pockmarked minaret lit by a single arc light. He thought unsentimentally about the trajectory that had brought him to this strange, persecuted little city, and the two spies who had danced a distant quadrille down the years – Walter Vigo and Oleg Kochalyin.

He went through the steps in his mind. The first involved his own ensnarement in Rome. But Kochalyin, the instigator if not quite the architect of this embarrassment – for that was all it was – had himself been lured by SIS to sell the secrets of the East. There followed the collapse of the Communist system. Kochalyin lured members of SIS into arrangements which began as convenient exchanges of information in a world which SIS was struggling to make sense of, and ended in the total corruption of at least one individual – Miles Morsehead. In response, Vigo had hired Eva to find out as much as she could about each new incarnation of Oleg Kochalyin.

At that point they were even, but then came Vigo's move against his colleagues, a superb piece of footwork which eliminated Kochalyin's allies in SIS and left Vigo the uncontested heir, the saviour of the service.

Harland knew, however, that any ideas of pattern in all this were simply false. Everything was temporary and fluid. The moment it suited Vigo and Kochalyin they would join hands in a fleeting partnership. They had done so before and there was nothing to stop them doing it again.

That brought him back to the question that had hovered over their little party at the restaurant. How had Kochalyin learned of their imminent arrival at Sarajevo airport? Had he lured them using the bait of satellite pictures, or was someone in London keeping him informed?

He turned from the window, gazed at Eva for a few chilly seconds, and slipped into bed beside her.

They slept in each other's arms. At some point during the night, a bell rang out in the city of victims. They stirred and made love, almost in their sleep.

31

A Nameless Mountain

Eva was in the shower and Harland already dressed when he heard a knock at the door. The Bird looked strained. The skin around his eyes was taut and his optimistic manner had vanished.

'We should leave soon,' he said quietly. 'Let's try and get out of the city by six-thirty.'

He was holding a tray with bread rolls and a jug of white coffee that he had spirited from the hotel kitchen with the night manager's aid.

'Come on in,' said Harland.

Outside there was a steady dripping from the gutters and the lights were haloed with moisture. A thaw was setting in.

Harland downed a cup of coffee in a few gulps and looked at The Bird.

'What's up?' he asked. 'Where'd you go last night?'

'To a bar the manager told me about. It's where the diplomatic people hang out in the Old Town. I found a chap there who does the security for the British residents. I had a feeling I'd bump into somebody. Macy and I have been trying to get this fellow to work for us.'

Again Harland wondered dimly about the exact nature of Harp-Avocet's business.

'What did you find out?' he asked.

'That the attack on our plane is the only thing anyone's talking about. All the men involved are dead and it goes without saying that the pilot was killed. The good news is that we weren't seen at the airport.'

'That's something. What about the car?'

'No mention of it. I gather that vehicles are nicked here then sold back to the dear old UN bit by bit as spare parts. Premature recycling, they call it.'

'What's eating you, Cuth?' asked Harland, focusing on The Bird's manner again.

'The same thing as you, Bobby, the same thing as you. Who the fuck told them we were coming?'

'Maybe nobody did. Maybe it was a set-up from the start,' said Harland. 'Maybe the business out there in the mountains is all designed to draw us here so we can be finished off. Maybe it was fixed from the very moment Reeve sent me those satellite pictures. After all, he got them from the CIA – the Americans are just as compromised by this affair as our lot and just as hot under the collar. They don't want my report circulated any more than Vigo does because it will add weight to Tomas's allegations.' He paused and thought. 'The alternative theory is a phone tap at Century House. I'm pretty sure that Vigo has been kept up to speed with my calls and e-mails which means he knows exactly what Reeve has been sending me. He knows I've learned the exact location of the site, and it wouldn't take a genius to pass our intention, together with the time of departure, to a man that half SIS have been talking to for the last twenty years.'

The Bird's eyes narrowed. 'Vigo's a cunt, but is he that much of a cunt?'

'He's desperate. They all are.'

'Yes, but it would have been a lot cleaner if they'd let you get out to the mountains before bumping you off. I mean, what the hell was the point of that mess at the airport last night?'

Harland didn't answer and instead poured more coffee.

Eva emerged from the bathroom, still drying her hair.

'It's simple,' she said, without looking up. 'We know that Oleg wants us dead and we know that would suit the British SIS. They both have equal motive. Therefore it's possible they are both trying to kill us – separately or together.'

'So the rocket attack was organised by Vigo?' said Harland. 'Is that what you're saying?'

'And made to appear like some kind of terrorist incident,' said The Bird.

'It's possible,' she said.

Harland thought again.

'Look, we'll work on the assumption of maximum jeopardy, which means that we take it for granted that both parties want us out of the way. In those circumstances it's sensible that only one of us goes – me. I will take pictures and if necessary bring back bones and then we'll get the site officially excavated – or at least guarded until they can get a team there.'

The Bird shook his head.

'Very noble, Bobby, but it's not on. Leave Eva if you want, but I'm coming. Besides, I've already fixed up a sort of driver-cum-guide. He only goes if I go.' He produced the keys of the Isuzu from his pocket and waved them in front of Harland to underline the strength of his position.

'We will all go,' said Eva.

Ibro stood waiting for them in the lobby, chatting to the night manager. His proportions revised the known limits of the human body. He was short – no more than 5' 2" – with a torso of near unimaginable breadth and strength. Harland saw that he had no neck to speak of and that he was compelled to hold his arms out at forty-five degrees because of the size of his chest muscles and biceps. His head poked out from the upturned collar of an old US airman's jacket. He smiled as they arrived in the lobby and wiped crumbs of pastry from a black chin.

'This is Ibro,' said The Bird, as though they were old friends. 'He speaks a little English and a lot of German.' They all shook hands. 'You are meeting quite a legend – one of the heroes of the siege of Sarajevo. He tells me he used to re-aim cannons by lifting their tow bars. Then he became the prime minister's personal bodyguard and now he's the hotel driver.'

They set out at six-twenty and travelled eastwards along the Miljacka River. Ibro pointed out sites on the way – the shelled-out National Library and a cemetery on the hill where some comrades were buried.

'*Weil Ich war,*' he recited, '*wie ihr wart und ihr werdet sein, wie ich.*'

'Come again,' said The Bird, trying to disentangle the German words from a thick Balkan accent.

'For I have been what you are now, and you will be what I am now,' said Eva. 'It's an inscription from a gravestone – a message from the dead to the living.'

'*Memento mori,*' murmured Harland.

Climbing out of the city, they passed a line of civil-war trenches, then a truck halt called Café Dayton, at which point they plunged into a tunnel that led them to the Republika Srpska – the Serb part of Bosnia. Dawn was breaking in the east. They were now moving through a softer, more rural landscape with well-tended smallholdings. The houses and barns along the way were no longer burned out. Nothing stirred.

They skirted the unremarkable town of Pale, the Bosnian Serb capital where the mass executions of 1995 were planned, and headed for the barren regions in the east. The road surface was broken and streaming with rivulets of snow melt. At a place called Rogatica they swung north, into the mountains. Harland began to feel they were getting near and once or twice he thought he glimpsed the range from the video still. They stopped the car in a wild, lonely place overlooking a valley and examined the map and satellite images again. Harland estimated they were five kilometres from the place where a road branched left and would take them to the site.

'What do we know about this place?' said The Bird.

'Not much. There's a small gorge at the top, which was the actual place of the massacre. A track leads past it and down the other side of the mountain. It's large enough to take trucks and a sizeable loader.' For a moment there was silence while The Bird pored over the map with Ibro, who at length gave his opinion that the road had been built as a short cut and that it would descend near a settlement on the other side of the mountain.

They continued on their way in silence until they reached a wooded area where they began to see clods of soil on the tarmac. Here and there they noticed evidence of the mud stuck to the snow banks either side of the road. Eva asked Ibro what the weather had been like over the last two days. He replied that temperatures had not risen above freezing for the past thirty-six hours.

Harland knew what she was thinking. The heavy frost explained why there was no change in the satellite pictures. They hadn't been able to work the ground.

They rounded a bend and came to the track exactly at the moment Harland expected. It was obvious from the marks on the road that the trucks had descended from the mountain, bringing the mixture of snow and soil with them. Ibro stopped, peered upwards and shook his head. The track was churned up and there were wheel ruts which would be too deep for the light Isuzu. They agreed to split up. Harland and Eva would climb the track, while The Bird and Ibro would drive round the mountain and look for another way up. If they failed to meet at the top they would rendezvous at this place in two hours' time.

As Harland opened his door, The Bird jumped out of the front seat and came round to meet him. He handed him a camera and then from his jacket pocket produced a Glock pistol which he placed firmly in Harland's hand. He gave a black CZ75 to Eva, remarking that it was appropriately a Czech-made weapon. It seemed Ibro came with a small arsenal of handguns.

They set off up the track, all the while seeking signs that trucks had passed that morning. They guessed not, since it was only just past eight-fifteen. Gradually the surface became firmer and they were able to make good progress. The mountain range in the distance came into view and they could see the track snake up the incline then skirt left of a rounded summit. They walked on. The landscape was very still. The only noise came from a pair of large ravens cavorting lazily in the updraft from the valley.

At the top there was a longer hike than they'd expected. They paused for breath and looked out across the grey and white mountain scenery. Eva touched him on the face with the back of a gloved hand and they continued on their way. Fifteen minutes on, the track climbed sharply for about fifty yards then took a sudden turning to the left by a large protrusion of rock. They found themselves on a plateau bordered by two walls of rock that rose twenty feet above them. The place looked like an old quarry and it had the acoustics of a natural auditorium. Every sound they made reverberated around them.

Their eyes traversed the scene. In front was a turning place where a battered truck stood, leaking oil on to the snow. It was obvious its wheels had become locked in the freezing slush. Beyond this was a large digger with its arm resting on the ground. A lot of tracks were visible in the snow, but no other sign of the vehicles shown in the aerial photographs. To their left the land shelved gently to form a depression, at the head of which was an opening in the earth. From this fanned caterpillar tracks of the digger.

Harland scanned the treeless slope to their right and wondered about the squat shepherd's hut that hugged an outcrop of rock about two hundred yards up. He saw that the track led across the plateau and plunged down on the north side of the mountain. Here the snow was untouched by vehicles.

Eva muttered something about the place having a bad air. Harland didn't reply. He was listening intently to the mountains and he wanted to make utterly sure they weren't being observed. His eyes swept the whole scene again, taking in possible hiding places and routes of escape.

Eva inhaled. Visibly steeling herself, she went forward to the excavated area.

She bent down, grasped hold of something and heaved backwards. He went to help her and saw that large conifer boughs had been laid across the opening in the ground. They worked together to pull them away without getting down into the pit or letting their eyes stray to the earth. Soon they could no longer avoid it. The sun had surfaced in the east and threw a cold light into the pit.

What they saw was unmistakable. Eva drew back a few feet and looked down. Many remains were down there but only in a few cases was the natural configuration of a skeleton intact. The digger had worked against the general orientation of the bodies. The teeth on the end of the bucket had clawed across them laterally, mixing up the bones and leaving sets of long striations across the ground. Harland counted the remains of about twenty people, but realised that the grave was much deeper than he had originally thought. Bodies had been piled on top of each other. When the massacre was over they had filled the hole with rubble and junk with the result that before reaching the bodies, the excavator had had to remove a layer that included chunks of road tarmac, a car door, old tyres, a fridge and a buckled bed frame.

He got out his camera and began taking pictures, half his mind knowing that the camera would act as a barrier between him and the horror. He aimed the camera at the digger and the truck, taking care to include the registration plates. He stopped. Eva had sunk to her knees at the grave's edge. Her face wore an expression of measureless pity. He moved to her side and saw what she was looking at. At the side of the pit was the skeleton of a child – a small boy, judging by the shorts and faded red T-shirt still visible. His hands were tied behind his back with wire. His skull was averted to the left, the mouth open. A little distance away was the complete skeleton of a man.

'Was that his father?' she asked simply.

Harland took two more pictures but he was no longer able to distance himself from the scene. His eyes welled with tears of outrage and horror. He thought of the heat of that day, the certainty in each man and child's mind that the soldiers were going to do this monstrous thing. He thought of Tomas and the stumbling, tearful old man who was tricked into believing he was going to be saved. The casualness and cruelty of the act struck him as though he were witnessing it at that very moment. He thought of the jeering soldiers and wondered how they might remember that day and whether it haunted them as it had Tomas.

He was determined that nothing should be lost. He walked around the grave, shooting from every angle, climbed into the bucket of the digger and focused on some bone residues. He took pictures of the far wall of rock where the men had been executed and the bullets had chipped at the surface, of the shell casings that had been exposed by the movement of the digger and glinted on the ground. He made studies of how the wrists of the victims were bound with fence wire, of the crumpled shoes, of a green and red checked shirt and a belt buckle, which might subsequently be used to identify the victims. Then he walked over to the truck and let down the tailgate, to be confronted by half a skull lying on a mass of earth and bone fragments. He photographed this from close up, from above and from a distance.

He dropped down to Eva, overpowered by a sense of shame – shame for Tomas, shame for himself, shame for all men. It was by far the worst thing he had ever seen. Eva looked at him and shook her head slowly. After a little while he said they ought to be going because it wouldn't be long before the men would arrive to finish the job. He needed to get back to Sarajevo with the pictures before all trace of the massacre had vanished.

She turned her face to him again. An act of commemoration was needed, she said. They must do something to recognise Tomas's part in what had happened there. She did not use the words massacre or slaughter or war crime. What they were looking at didn't have a word, but they both knew that it was the result of an incomprehensible hatred, just as evident in the treatment of the remains. Eva muttered that the people in the grave were no less loved now than they had been on the day they were killed. Harland hadn't thought about it like that, and he realised how much she was feeling the loss of Tomas. He shook his head, not knowing whether it should be an act of commemoration or atonement.

At that moment they heard a loud report from the northern side of the mountain, not a gunshot but an explosion which sent two ravens wheeling into the air below them. They ran over to look down and saw the Isuzu on its side in flames about four hundred yards from them. The Bird and Ibro were nowhere to be seen. Harland took a few strides in the snow and then stopped, realising the car must have hit a mine. The road had been mined to protect the site from the curious but there wasn't time to communicate this thought to Eva. He turned to see her gesturing up the hill to several figures who had issued from the stone hut and were now moving with difficulty through the snow down to the car.

Harland and Eva bent down and withdrew to the digger. Harland guessed the men had been sent to watch the site until the weather changed and work could begin again. They must have overslept or got bored – at any rate they hadn't thought to look down to the plateau.

From where he stood he couldn't see the car, but a little later the men, some of them dressed in old combat fatigues, reappeared, hauling Ibro along a bank of snow above the road. Their voices carried up the slope and it became obvious that they were moving directly towards them. Half of him wanted to run back down the way they'd come. But he couldn't leave Ibro and The Bird. Without saying anything, they slipped back along the wall of rock, at the end of which they found a good hiding place in a crevice, behind some pine saplings. But it wouldn't take two. He pushed Eva down and told her not to move, then scuttled around the top of the pit and down the other line of rock. He groped his way down to a point where the outcrop fell away into a void. He grasped hold of a narrow tree trunk and used it to swing round into a gap between two slabs. Below him was a drop of thirty feet.

Harland heard the voices come closer. A young man in a ski hat and leggings appeared and immediately noticed that the branches had been removed from the pit. He jogged to the edge, peered down and then shouted to the others. Two more came and finally a fourth man, dragging Ibro by the collar of his jacket. Harland saw he was cut on his head and bleeding from his right leg. He was prodded to the top of the pit and forced to kneel with his hands behind his head, whereupon they began questioning him. Much of it was abuse, but after a bit Harland recognised one or two of the words because of their similarity in Russian. He understood they were asking him who else had been in the car. Ibro looked up at his interrogators with silent contempt, for which he received several kicks and blows. At length they tipped him into the pit and told him to lie face down by a mangled skeleton. That gave them great amusement.

Harland waited with his face hugging the cold surface of the rock. If he moved a little he could just see where he'd left Eva. He prayed she wouldn't do anything rash or betray her presence.

Suddenly the young man in the ski hat aimed his automatic weapon into the air and fired off a burst. Harland turned to see one of the pair of ravens crumple in mid-flight and fall to the ground. This seemed to upset two of his companions and they shouted and jabbed at him with their guns. A row ensued, but died as quickly as it had flared. It occurred to him that these men must have been in the paramilitary squad that had taken part in the massacre. They were being used to oversee the work because they could be relied upon to keep quiet. It was their crime as much as Kochalyin's.

He became aware of the sound of a truck, grinding and labouring up the final stages of the track. A few seconds later it came into view, throwing up a jet of mud from its back wheels. It pulled up and another man in fatigues got out. The new arrival sauntered over to the pit to inspect Ibro and hurl a few insults his way. The others called him back. Cigarettes and a bottle of liquor were handed around and they fell to laughing and needling each other. It was the familiar, easy companionship of any group of men out on a job.

One of the five moved up to a flat piece of ground above the main plateau and pulled out a cellphone. He was obviously having difficulty getting a good signal and he paced around trying to find the best spot. Once or twice Harland thought he might be in danger of being spotted, but the man was too absorbed to notice him. After about ten minutes he shouted to the others and slid down the bank to rejoin them.

Harland was extremely cold. The muscles that had been torn in the top of his thigh after the air crash at La Guardia were playing up again. He rubbed his leg, clenched and unclenched his hands and worked his toes inside his boots. Then he looked at his gun, slipped the safety catch down towards the double action trigger and tried to estimate the number of rounds in the clip. He stared at the blotches of pale blue lichen on the rocks and padded the cleft in front of him with damp leaves so that he could look through without chafing his face. Occasionally he glanced over to where Eva was, but saw no movement.

He was now certain that The Bird must have been killed in the explosion, which meant their only option was to sit tight and wait until the men had finished their work that evening. Why the hell didn't they get on with it? What were they waiting for, these cowherds and mountain men?

Another fifteen minutes passed. Harland pricked up his ears. He thought he'd picked up a faint throbbing in the air. Yes, it was the beat of a helicopter coming in from the north. He searched the sky and saw a Sikorsky rise above the wall of rock where Eva was hidden and curl up to the plateau. For a moment it hovered directly above him and he feared he would be spotted. He glanced over at Eva and saw a hand grasp a sapling to prevent it from being blown over in the downdraft. A leg of tan corduroy, however, was exposed for a few seconds. He raised the Glock and darted a look towards the trucks. The Serbs were shielding their eyes from the whirlwind of snow and grit. Thank God. They hadn't noticed her.

The helicopter swung into the wind, and landed with its pointed snout slightly raised at the place where one of the men had used his phone. He remembered the rosette-shaped swirl in that exact same spot on the satellite picture. The helicopter had visited this place before.

In the corner of his eye he saw a movement. Ibro was using the distraction of the helicopter to haul himself down the pit on his belly. His shoulders were doing all the work; his right leg made no movement at all. The young man who had first noticed the disturbance of the branches caught sight of him and whipped round to spray the ground ahead of him with a well-aimed burst of automatic fire. The ricochets zinged into the rocks around Harland. Ibro's head slumped down. His arms remained crooked in a push-up position. Harland was pretty sure he hadn't been hit.

The helicopter's rotor slowed with a whine and the blades began to droop towards the ground. Eventually the engine was shut down and the cabin doors opened. A smell of aviation fuel reached his nostrils. He didn't dare to look up because he thought any movement would be seen from the helicopter. So he just held on, his right cheek pressed to the rock, watching the clouds out of his left eye and trying to ignore the insistent nagging of a bladder that had not been emptied since Sarajevo.

Harland picked up the murmur of respectful greetings. He lifted his head a fraction and saw that three men had got out of the helicopter, while the pilot remained at the controls. They had moved down the bank to the plateau and been led to the far side where they stood, looking down the side of the mountain. He could not see their faces but it was plain that an explanation was being given by the man who had made the telephone calls. He seemed anxious to please and there was much gesturing in the direction of the Isuzu.

Harland worked his head between the crack and looked out. The group had moved in his direction and spread out to reveal a figure standing squarely by the grave's edge. He wore a dark grey overcoat and a black cap with ear flaps. His gloved hands were clasped in front of him as he contemplated the prone figure of Ibro.

Oleg Kochalyin was shorter than Harland had imagined, but he possessed a palpable presence. To Harland, now lying in excruciating discomfort, he completed the dismal fear of the old quarry, a fear that penetrated his being and made him weak and nauseous. He moved his eye from the crack and for a few seconds consciously stilled his panic.

Then he glanced up and saw that the darkened sky, which he had somehow attributed to Kochalyin's arrival, was in fact caused by a bank of low cloud that had snuffed out the sun and shrouded in mist the summit of the mountain.

He looked back at the group. Kochalyin had not moved and, as far as he could tell, had said nothing. He just stood taking everything in, his eyes flicking about him. He pointed to the branches pulled from the grave by Harland and Eva and asked something in Russian. The men did their best to follow what he was saying, then struggled to explain their failure to find out who had moved the branches. They looked at each other and fell silent. Suddenly, from above them, there was a noise which seemed to roll down the hill. It was a loud phut rather than a bang, followed by a more impressive rumble. Something had blown up inside the hut. The men shouted. He speculated that one of them had left the cooking gas on when they rushed to investigate the landmine explosion. At any rate, a fire had taken hold quickly and smoke was streaming from the door and one tiny window. Three of the men set off to rescue their possessions, paying no heed to the voices that ordered them to stay. Ultimately, thought Harland, these mountain men did exactly what they pleased.

He watched for a few seconds longer, wondering if the explosion could possibly have been contrived by The Bird. But there was no sign of anyone up there and he returned to peer through the crack in the rocks. Now something was happening. He shifted his head in the crack and saw two men drop into the grave and seize Ibro by his arms. They dragged him to the top of the grave where he was questioned again, this time by Kochalyin. Each time he refused to answer he was struck in the kidneys or stomach with a rifle butt, blows which would have felled and crippled a weaker man. Harland couldn't watch. The pain was too familiar to him. Several times he was on the point of leaping up and firing off as many rounds as he could, but that would do nothing to save Ibro and would almost certainly jeopardise Eva.

He lay there feeling wretched and powerless, as if the blows were raining on him. And then a strange thing happened with his bladder. Some deep physiological memory stirred in him and he was beginning to piss, just as he had when Kochalyin, having kept him in some agonising position for hours, began to really hurt him. He flattened his back to the rock, withdrew his penis and let himself go. When it was over he shuddered, zipped himself up and looked through the crack. It was okay: they hadn't seen.

He felt better now, more capable of thinking about what to do. Kochalyin made a swift movement with his hand and now Ibro was being dragged to the side of the pit. He cried out as one of them kicked his injured leg. Harland thought he was being taken to the digger. He had to see what was going on. He flashed his head up and took one mental snapshot of the scene. Ibro was being bound by a chain so that his arms were pinioned to his side. They were knotting the chain and looping it around his neck. Harland knew what would follow. The digger's engine coughed and a plume of exhaust showed in the sky. He darted another look and saw that the chain had been attached to the bucket. The arm was rising. There was a clank as the bucket righted itself in the air and took up the slack in the chain. They were going to hang Ibro if he didn't answer their questions.

This he would not stand for. He slipped the camera from the jacket pocket and aimed it over the rocks, silently shooting off three frames. He checked the images on the camera's screen. Kochalyin was clearly visible in all three – as were the date and time. Then he put the camera in his glove and wedged the package in the rocks. Some day soon someone would find it and think to look in the camera's memory. It was a slight chance perhaps, but his report was out there, complete with accurate coordinates. If he disappeared, someone would come looking here, he was sure.

He drew his gun, rose to a kneeling position and aimed. The only face turned in his direction was Ibro's. So he scrambled over the rocks and began walking, holding the gun out in front of him at Kochalyin's back. What was going through his mind were the words of the instructor at the Fort – aim low and let the evil bastard inside you do the rest. He was perfectly calm and utterly focused on killing Kochalyin. He knew he would be killed too, but that now meant little to him as long as Kochalyin went as well. He glanced up at the helicopter, expecting to see the pilot, but there was no one sitting in the cockpit. Still no one turned round. And that, he realised, was because the digger's engine was revving and the hydraulics along the shaft of the arm were squealing for lack of grease. Besides this, the men were engrossed in what was happening to Ibro. The bucket lifted with a jerk, the chain strained and then pulled Ibro into the air. Harland saw his face going puce. He reached the end of the pit and was forty feet from the digger when he stopped, placed the gun on his left arm, and aimed. Only then did he see Eva walking towards them from the rock. She was calling out in Russian.

'Enough, Oleg! Enough!'

Her appearance seemed to surprise the men. They shifted and looked embarrassed. They didn't raise their guns to her because she walked to them with her hands empty. Kochalyin turned to face her. He nodded to the man operating the digger. The arm dropped and Ibro crumpled to the ground, gasping for breath. Eva bent down and loosened the chain around his neck. No one moved to stop her.

'Enough of this,' she said, straightening up. 'This killing, this torture – this shame.'

Then one or two of the men caught sight of Harland and levelled their weapons at him. Kochalyin turned and took him in with an unsurprised nod. But that was not what froze Harland's blood. It was the face of the man standing next to Kochalyin. The obliging features of Macy Harp had also turned to gaze at him.

Kochalyin saw his expression and smiled.

'Not everything is as it seems, Mr Harland,' he said.

Harland couldn't take it in. Macy! Macy Harp, who'd rescued him with The Bird from the villa in Prague – from Kochalyin's clutches. Macy, the busy little fixer with the plausible, county manner. What the hell was he doing with Kochalyin? He struggled to make sense of it. Christ, he thought, was The Bird in on this too? Had they been working for Kochalyin all along?

Kochalyin was speaking again, very quietly so that Harland had to move a few paces forward to hear. Now every weapon was levelled at his head. He kept his aim, but he couldn't fire without hitting Eva and Kochalyin knew that.

'This man is the true killer of Tomas,' Kochalyin was saying. 'Tomas was like my own son, Irina. You knew that. I paid for his treatment. Whatever our disagreements, I couldn't have him killed. Harland was the only one who knew where he was. Ask yourself, Irina, is it more likely that I was working with them to kill Tomas, or that Harland was? He is still their spy. He led them to Tomas because he was the only person who could.'

Harland could hardly believe what he was hearing. He spat out a denial. Kochalyin took no notice.

'I was trying to find him,' he continued, 'but Harland got there first. He set up the hit by the river. If you don't believe me, ask this gentleman here. His name is Mr Harp. He knows the truth because he worked with Harland. He knows what sort of man he is.'

Macy produced an accommodating smile.

'I'm afraid it is true,' he said in English. 'Mr Harland was employed to hunt down Tomas and then Mr Kochalyin here. He is here to kill your ex-husband.'

As this was being said, Kochalyin moved a few feet towards Harland.

'This man has some crazy ideas in his head. He says I tortured him back in Prague. It is a condition he has – a mental condition. But even if you ask him now, he will tell you that he has never seen me before. And if you ask Mr Harp, who rescued him with his associate, Mr Avocet, he will tell you also that he did not see me there.' Macy obliged with a nod. 'Why would I want to torture this man, anyway? You maybe did not know that I was working for British Intelligence?' He paused. 'Yes, I, Oleg Kochalyin, worked for the overthrow of that corrupt Communist system. I saw what was going on around us. Everyone did. These were dangerous times, Irina. Naturally, I could not speak of what I was doing, but ask yourself –

why would I celebrate the end of those bad days by torturing him? Why would I do that? It doesn't make sense at all.'

Kochalyin had adopted the rhetorical style he'd used on Harland, the probing interlocutor before administering the electrodes. Harland noticed his appearance with detached interest – a waxy skin, dyed eyebrows, an exceptionally cruel nose, a yellowish sickly colour to the whites of his eyes and pupils that yielded nothing. He noted the expensive but poor taste of his clothes and the flash of gold between his glove and the sleeve of his overcoat, the watch that he had first seen in the video still. Kochalyin was the picture of small-time crookedness, nothing more impressive than that. But what raised him above average evil was his sense of command.

He glanced at Eva and saw a flicker of doubt in her eyes. And then, as if to match Kochalyin's surreal challenge to the truth, the mist rolled down the mountain and in a very short time smothered the old quarry, isolating them from the rest of the world. The helicopter, the trucks and even the pit were blotted out. Harland noticed Macy looking around, and the man who was clearly Kochalyin's bodyguard shifted a little and glanced up at the mountain.

'You surely don't believe this, Eva?' Harland demanded. 'This is a pack of lies. You know it is.'

Kochalyin smiled.

'You call her Eva when her name is Irina? See how crazy this man has become. Look at him. He is shaking.'

It was true. He was trembling, but that was because he had lain in the cold for so long.

Eva turned to Kochalyin with a look of interest.

'Then, Oleg, why are you here? Why were you going to kill this man?'

'Oh, this man is nothing. We knew Harland was here and we wanted to find out who else was in the car. I have to protect myself, you know. Anyway, he would not have been killed.'

If she believes that, thought Harland, she's lost her mind.

'But why are you here, Oleg? If you are as innocent as you say, why have you come here?'

'To protect the reputation of the boy I loved. I admit I have paid these men to destroy the evidence. They were all here that day and they got carried away. They're crude folk, as you can see, and Tomas was caught up with the excitement. There was nothing I could do. I wasn't even here when they started killing these people. It was a bad business, for sure, but Tomas was not responsible for his actions and I did not want his memory to be tainted by this.' He gestured to the grave. Then he turned towards Ibro. 'I have no intention of killing him, although he came here to kill me. They found many weapons in the car.'

'And the attack on the aircraft last night – did you do that?'

He shook his head convincingly.

'Of course not. It must have been your friends in British Intelligence, Irina. They are your friends. Yes, I knew about your work for them. It hurt me at first that you would do such a thing to me. But then I let it go because I realised that we were all born to treachery. All of us at some stage have been Mr Walter Vigo's friend.' He smiled magnanimously at her and then winked at Macy, who returned a rueful look.

'You aren't going to believe this crap?' said Harland. 'He's not here clearing up some youthful indiscretion of Tomas's. He's been forced to dig up these bodies because the world knows about the slaughter that took place here. He will do anything to hide his actions. He sabotaged the UN plane. He had Tomas's girlfriend tortured and killed. His men murdered Zikmund Myslbek. There's nothing he won't do to hide the proof.'

'See what I mean, Irina,' said Kochalyin with a dismissive sweep of his hand. 'He has lost his mind. He believes that everything that is wrong with the world is the fault of Oleg Kochalyin. Does that seem likely? I do not have to listen to this. I could have him killed this very second, but I let him continue because I want you to see the man for what he really is. He is the murderer of your son. Tell him to put that gun away before someone gets hurt.'

Eva walked to Harland and put her hand out. As she did so, Harland thought he saw her light brown eyes pulse with a secret intent. She stood in front of him for a few seconds, shaking her head. He wondered furiously what she was going to do. Then Macy Harp, who was nearest to them, stepped forward and with both hands pushed the Glock upwards and wrested it from Harland's grip. He moved away, casually inspecting the weapon.

'Good,' said Kochalyin, his eyes playing over the scene with a deadly satisfaction. 'So it must be for you to decide what should be done with this man, the killer of your son.'

Now Harland understood why Kochalyin had been making his grotesque argument. He wanted to watch Eva kill him. That would be the ultimate revenge against their love – the payback for Eva's betrayal. He felt the resignation and blankness settle in him, as it had in the East River when he thought he was going to die. Although he'd seen that look in her eye, he didn't trust it. The bond she had with Kochalyin could not be doubted – it was evident in her every gesture. As that was the case, he really didn't mind dying. Now his life seemed nothing more than a series of calamitous misjudgements. Hell, he hadn't even seen Macy for what he was.

Eva seemed to have reached a decision. Kochalyin looked at her expectantly. She glanced round the group of men, then moved over to the young man with the automatic weapon. Kochalyin nodded to him. Somewhat reluctantly, he slipped the strap from his shoulder and showed

Eva the safety catch. Harland didn't understand. He knew very well that she had her own gun.

Then she made her way back to Harland, motioning to the two men who had moved either side of him, to take him to the pit. The mesmerising look was still in her eyes, but now Harland was convinced that all it held was hatred.

'Don't you see, Eva?' he pleaded in English. 'He wants you to kill me. Then he will tell you he made the whole lot up and have you killed too. It's his revenge for you loving me – the final rape of your life by this man.' His voice had grown dull.

One of the men cuffed his ear with the barrel, then each of them took hold of his arms and frogmarched him to the edge of the pit. At the edge Harland stumbled and fell into the unspeakable grime. He pushed himself up and wiped the filth from his face. Except for Macy, who had somehow indicated his distaste for the execution and had withdrawn, the group of men moved as one nearer to the pit, Kochalyin and his bodyguard at the centre. Kochalyin nodded.

Harland looked up at Eva as she aimed the weapon at him. 'You were wrong, Bobby,' she said. 'I never loved you. I only ever loved one man.'

'Don't do this,' he said. 'For yourself – do not do this.' His voice trailed off and he looked up into the mist, certain that he was about to die. He glimpsed something in the periphery of his vision, an indistinct shape darting in the mist between the trucks. He turned to look at Eva. He blinked once.

There was a shout, followed by a prolonged burst of automatic gunfire that raked the ground around the men. In that moment Harland's mind registered Macy Harp diving to the snow with his gun and Eva whipping round to open fire on the men above her.

Harland was so stupefied by the sudden turn of events that he simply stood gaping at The Bird, who had emerged from the shelter of the trucks and was now advancing steadily, sweeping the area in front of him with his machine gun. Some of the men had turned to face him, but they were now being fired on from three directions and not one managed to raise his weapon. In rapid succession each crumpled and fell.

Harland blinked again. It was over.

Kochalyin had dropped to his knees at the grave's edge, right in front of him. His face did not betray the puzzlement which is said to fill the expressions of those who have been shot, but Harland did see a final look of anger in his lifeless eyes.

And that was all he noticed for several minutes. His breath, emotion and thought simply seemed to have vacated his body. When eventually he found his voice, he stammered, 'What the ... what the hell was Macy doing with Kochalyin? Why was he on the helicopter for Christ's sake?'

The Bird glanced over to Macy and Eva, who had gone to help Ibro.

'Our Macy's a shifty little fucker,' he said, without a flicker of humour, offering his arm to Harland so that he could haul himself out of the pit. 'When Zikmund Myslbek was killed in Karlsbad, Macy was damned annoyed. You see, they went back a long way and they were good pals and all that. Macy wasn't about to let the murder of his friend go unpunished. He decided to find out about this character Kochalyin and we agreed that the only way that could be achieved was if Macy went to Kochalyin with information about you two. It turns out we had business interests in some of the same areas and, to cut a long story short, Macy and Mister K found they had a lot in common. They talked the same language, you see. Macy then tapped the phones in Century House for him. After that there was no question of him not trusting Macy. That was his *big* mistake.'

'And you knew about this?' Harland asked incredulously. 'You knew that Macy was feeding him everything?'

'Yep, which is why I stuck to you two like a tart on Easter Sunday. When Kochalyin made his move, Macy was going to tip me off. I knew he was with him, but I had no idea he'd be on his bloody chopper. I could hardly believe it when I saw him get out.'

'And where the hell were you? You didn't go with Ibro in the car, did you?'

'No. I thought it was best to stay with you two, so I followed you up the track at a distance, then made myself scarce.'

'And the hut? Did you do that?'

'Yes, an old trick. I gather it was a local favourite in the war. You place a lighted candle in the highest part of the building – in this case a beam by the chimney – turn on the gas and walk away. Being heavier than air, the gas takes a while to rise to the flame, by which time the whole place is full of the stuff. I learned the trick from Ibro. I believe it was used in the ethnic cleansing operations. Anyway, it certainly distracted those chaps for a bit.' He nodded in the direction of the hut. 'Two of 'em are unconscious. The other one got trapped inside,' he said absently.

They considered waiting for the helicopter pilot to recover from the blow delivered earlier by The Bird to his head, but decided he wouldn't be fit to fly them to Sarajevo. So they carried Ibro to the second truck and loaded him into the passenger seat. The Bird took the wheel and, once Harland had retrieved the camera from its hiding place in the rocks, Eva, Macy and he climbed into the back.

Harland wiped his hands of dirt and looked into Eva's eyes. 'You had me fooled back there,' he said. 'I really thought you were going to shoot me.'

'For a moment I thought so too,' Macy commented with a glimmer of a smile. 'Then I realised she must have had her own gun but was angling to get the better weapon from one of the men. Bloody clever to pull that off and then get you down into the shelter of the grave.'

They both waited for her to say something. But the engine roared and The Bird started the laborious business of turning the truck, pitching them forward then back to the tailgate with a series of jolts.

Eventually she shouted, 'You must have known I wasn't going to kill you. Didn't you see it in my eyes?'

'Not this time,' said Harland grimly.

He glanced at the pit and the grotesque figure of Oleg Kochalyin. His arms were limp by his sides and his head lolled a little to the right, causing his black cap to sit at a rather jaunty angle. It was as if some unseen hand had forced him to kneel and was now holding his body in penitence for the scores, maybe hundreds, who lay in that unquiet grave. Around him sprawled the men who had carried out the massacre – the perpetrators of a long-neglected barbarity. Justice had been served, Harland reflected, albeit crudely.

They began the descent to the road and dropped out of the mist. As they swayed with the motion of the truck, they fixed their gazes on the hills to the west, away from the shame of this nameless mountain. Out of the corner of his eye, Harland caught sight of a lone raven circling the crags below them, searching for its mate.

Empire State

For Graydon Carter

Acknowledgements

Thanks are due first to my agent, Georgina Capel, who showed great faith in this book from the start, and also to Jane Wood, my editor, who tirelessly made suggestions and gave me encouragement during its writing. She was helped by Sophie Hutton-Squire. It would be difficult to overestimate their contribution, or that of Puffer Merritt, who read and corrected the first draft with her usual enthusiasm and generosity.

The idea for *Empire State* came to me on a fishing trip organised by Mark Clarfelt in June 2002. So I thank him for the happy accident that set off a train of thought, and also Stephen Lewis, Matthew Fort, Tom Fort, Jeremy Paxman and Padraic Fallon who unwittingly nurtured the plot during the course of a very idle afternoon by the river. My friend David Rose introduced me to Hadith literature, Roger Alton made many clever suggestions, Lucy Nichols helped with occasional research and Aimee Bell gave me the 1949 first edition of E.B. White's hymn to New York, *Here is New York*, which contains some inspirational thoughts used here.

During the research of a book of this nature there are many who help but cannot be thanked by name. I was particularly grateful to a man who, at some risk to himself, arranged a tour of the Egyptian prison system, and then found the island where part of this book is set. My contact in Albania was also invaluable. He shed light on his mysterious homeland and gave me insights into the history and workings of the intelligence service.

Empire State is a work of fiction – no secrets are betrayed here – but there is some authentic detail which has been gathered from numerous sources. Without them I would flounder. In parts of the book I drew from actual incidents. There *was* an al-Qaeda cell in Albania. Five suspects were arrested in a CIA-backed operation and flown to Egypt where they were tortured before being tried. Two were subsequently executed. I have also used part of a story of a group of migrant workers who were gunned down by the Macedonian security forces on March 2, 2002. At the time, it was alleged they were terrorists, planning an attack on the US and UK embassies in the Macedonian capital, Skopje, a claim which the United States government was unusually forthright in rejecting.

Finally, I would like to thank my wife, Liz Elliot. Throughout the writing of this book, as with the others, she has been the source of much support and good judgement.

Part One

1

The passenger known as Cazuto arrived in the Immigration Hall of Terminal Three, Heathrow, in the early afternoon, carrying a raincoat and a small shoulder bag. He joined one of the lines in the non-European Union section. Looking mildly about him, the American registered the two uniformed policemen with Heckler and Koch machine guns on the far side of the immigration desk, and then a group of men who were clearly searching the lines of travellers about to enter the United Kingdom on that stupefyingly cold day in May.

Larry Cazuto, in reality Vice-Admiral Ralph Norquist, guessed they were looking for him and noted the urgency on their faces. This interested him because they could not have known which flight he was on. His schedule was kept secret even from his wife and secretary, who knew only that he would be in Europe for a time, not on what day he was travelling or that he would be seeing the British Prime Minister and his intelligence chiefs.

The President's special counsel on security matters decided that he would not at that moment make himself known. Instead he did what comes easily to a middle-aged man with a paunch and a slight academic stoop – he merged with the crowd and turned his benevolent gaze to the line forming behind him. He glanced upwards to the security cameras but none was trained on him and it was clear they weren't sweeping the surge of travellers in the Immigration Hall. In front of him, a woman in her late forties – rich-looking and attractive in a brash way – was struggling to change her phone from an American to a European service while keeping hold of several pieces of hand luggage. He leaned into her vision to ask if he could be of assistance, and as she replied she dropped the open passport clamped in her teeth. He picked it up and returned it to her, noticing the semi-circular impression of lipstick on one of its pages. 'You've given yourself a visa stamp,' he said pleasantly.

The woman smiled. As she took the passport, one of the bamboo handles of a large tapestry bag escaped her grip and the contents tumbled to the floor. He crouched down and helped her again. As she swept everything back into the bag with the speed of a croupier, he examined her and wondered whether he imagined the intent that pulsed briefly in her eye. She got up, thanking him profusely and they went together to the desk, where he made a point of looking over her shoulder to see if the name in her passport matched the initials on the silver cigarette lighter that he'd retrieved from the floor. This was second nature to him and it struck him as odd, and almost certainly significant, that they did not tally, not even the first name and initial.

By now the men on the other side of the barrier had spotted him. Norquist recognised one of them; the knobbly faced Peter Chambers, a senior bureaucrat from MI5 whom he'd met eighteen months before.

'I'm afraid we've got an emergency, Admiral,' said Chambers. 'We're going to escort you into London.' He gestured to a man who had come up behind him. 'This is Sergeant Llewellyn from the Metropolitan Police Special Branch. He will . . .'

Before Chambers could say any more, Norquist held two fingers to his chest then jabbed them in the direction of the woman, who was now headed down the escalator to the Baggage Hall, her bags hooked over her shoulders and the little gold-coloured mobile raised to her ear. 'Can you check her out? Her passport says her name is Raffaella Klein but she has the initials E.R. on her cigarette lighter. She seemed to be making a point by dropping everything. This may help,' he said, slipping Chambers a chip of plastic the woman had failed to pick up and which he'd palmed as a matter of course. It was the SIM card for her US phone service and it would tell them everything they needed to know.

'We'll get right on to it,' said Chambers. He beckoned to a lean, casually dressed man who had been hanging behind the two armed police officers and gave him the card. 'Get Customs to search her and then keep her under observation.' He turned back. 'Now, if you don't mind, sir, we're in a bit of a hurry. Your luggage has been taken directly to the car. I'll explain everything once we're on our way. We really *must* go, sir.'

'If you've got the baggage it means you know the name I was travelling under.'

'That's rather the point, sir. Your security has been compromised.'

They made for a door at the side of the hall, which opened from the inside as they approached, and passed along a corridor of mostly empty offices. Here two policemen in anoraks and fatigue trousers joined them, so a party of more than a dozen descended three flights of a metal stairway, causing it to vibrate with a dull ring. At the bottom the corridor turned right and led to a fire exit where a security officer was on hand with a swipe card. He signalled to a surveillance camera above and operated the lock, throwing both doors outwards. The fumes of aviation fuel and the noise of taxiing aircraft filled the corridor. Rain slanted through the door. Norquist began to put on his raincoat, but Llewellyn took it from him and passed it, together with Norquist's bag, to one of the policemen behind. He waved the two uniformed police out to a line of four cars just visible off to the right.

'We're having to make this up as we go along,' said Chambers. 'We've had very little notice.'

Norquist shrugged. 'Right,' he said.

They waited a few more moments until a voice came over Llewellyn's radio. The rest of the men bunched round Norquist and they spilled from the door in a security rush, holding his head down until he was in the back of a black Jaguar. Chambers climbed in beside him; Llewellyn got in the front. The rest of the men divided between a dark green Range Rover, a Ford saloon and a BMW which brought up the rear.

'What's going on?' asked Norquist.

'We understand they are going to make an attempt in or around the terminal. I'm afraid this arrangement is far from ideal. We'd have preferred to use a helicopter to get you into town. We may yet have you picked up on the way, but the main thing is to get you away from public areas of the airport now.'

Norquist nodded patiently as if being told of some further minor delay in his schedule. The plane had already stopped for two hours at Reykjavik with a computer fault.

'We think it's a big operation. No details though,' continued Chambers, giving him a significant look which was to say that he couldn't talk in front of the driver and Llewellyn.

The cars moved off, weaving under the piers of Terminal Three. They had to slow for aircraft manoeuvring in and out of the gates and occasional service vehicles that blocked the route across the concrete apron. The squall that had blown in from the south-west didn't help their progress either, and several times the Jaguar hesitated, either from poor visibility or disorientation in the sprawling tentacles of the airport. After a few minutes they cleared Terminal Two and set off at speed over the open ground between the take-off and landing runways, towards the vast hangars on the east side of the airport. They were held up once by a yellow airport car to allow a 747 to be towed across their path from the service hangars. Instead of taking the exit by the British Midland hangar off to their right, they moved towards the head of the runway a few hundred yards away, close to the eight aircraft waiting to take off. Rain and exhaust from the engines blurred the landscape and they had to slow to look for the exit. Someone spotted a policeman on a motorbike waving in the distance.

Llewellyn yelled into his radio over the noise of the engines. 'Route Three. Is that understood? Route Three.' He sat back as the cars started forward and said under his breath, 'Let's hope this works.'

A little over a mile away a man held a Bresse Optic telescope to his right eye and scrutinised the procession of vehicles with twenty times magnification. The few plane spotters that had remained with him through the rain and poor light on the observation terrace of Terminal Two also trained their binoculars and telescopes to the head of the southern runway – or, as they referred to it, Runway 27 right. But when the four cars veered off through the grass margins of the airfield towards the emergency gate in the perimeter fence, their interest returned to the line of Boeings, followed by two Russian-made aircraft – a Tupolev Tu-154 and a Yakovlev Yak-42 – which by chance landed seventy seconds apart on the northern runway – 27 or left.

The men on the observation terrace mostly carried telephones. Some even held hand-radios with which they chatted to fellow enthusiasts around the airport. So it was perfectly natural for the man with the Bresse Optic to turn away from the noise of a taxiing Tunisair flight, to gaze across Heathrow's roofscape of air-conditioning ducts and radio masts and dial a pre-set number on his phone. Muffled in their anorak hoods, absorbed in the comings and goings of the jets, fiddling with their Thermos flasks and packets of sandwiches, the plane spotters paid scant attention to what he said about the cars leaving the airport and turning right towards the A30.

A surveillance operation of an entirely different kind had just ended in the Terminal Three Departure Lounge when a mixed team consisting of an Arabic speaker from MI6 named Isis Herrick, three officers from MI5 and four members of the police Special Branch were pulled off the observation of Youssef Rahe, an Arab bookseller. They were told by New Scotland Yard and MI5 headquarters at Thames House that an important American had just arrived in the terminal and that the highest possible priority was being accorded to moving him from the airport to Whitehall. The Prime Minister's armoured Jaguar, being driven back from Cardiff to London without its usual passenger, had been diverted to Heathrow. Through her earpiece Herrick then heard that the four undercover policemen with her were being summarily removed from the mixed surveillance team and would be armed with handguns in a room near the Immigration Hall.

Herrick and her three slightly dour colleagues from MI5 – Campbell, Beck and Fisher – went off to have coffee, Beck caustically remarking that the Special Branch officers had taken with them the keys and parking receipts for two of the three cars. As they sat, they were informed that the few Special Branch officers permanently stationed at Heathrow had also reported to the Immigration Hall. She realised this meant that Youssef Rahe would leave Britain unobserved, except by the security cameras. It was no great disaster. As an anonymous voice pointed out from MI5 headquarters, Rahe, a minor intellectual figure in London's North African community, represented no threat to the aircraft whatsoever. He and his baggage had already been thoroughly searched and he was, after all, travelling on an Arab airline to an Arab country. Once he got to Kuwait, the cooperative members of the local intelligence service, al-Mukhabarat, would watch him and log any contacts he made.

Still, Rahe's hasty departure from the Pan Arab Library in Bayswater had interested Herrick because there was no warning of his trip. He travelled little, spending most of his days seated at the desk in the front of the store, glasses dangling on a chain, testily answering customers' questions or consulting his computer. He was not a key figure by any means: they weren't even sure if he had connections with Islamist groups. However, during the sweep of Arab communities in Britain the name of the bookshop had come up, and it had been learned from the FBI that a suspect arrested in Canada had visited it while in London.

Herrick had been assigned to the operation for a few days. She had taken the first appointment at the hairdresser that lay diagonally across from the Pan Arab Library. She arrived just before it opened at 9.45 a.m. and by ten she was in position at the seat nearest the window where the mirror allowed her a clear view of 119 Forsythe Street, an unusual nineteenth-century building, Italianate, a cut above its neighbours.

Rahe usually appeared in the shop just after ten, having left his family in the flat above, and unlocked the door from the inside to a sluggish morning trade. The plan was for her to drop into the bookshop in this slack period, look around for a while and engage Rahe in conversation on the pretext of needing to practise her Arabic. Despite Rahe's unfriendly manner, she'd learned that he appeared to have an eye for English women. The watchers monitoring his visitors from the street and from a room in a flat opposite had noticed he stared longingly at the fair women passing his shop and that he became more helpful on the rare occasions they went in.

'You never know,' said the officer running the surveillance, 'he might take you to dinner. There are one or two very good Leb restaurants in the area where you can order in Arabic and then you can charm him.'

Herrick watched for signs of Rahe in the mirror, but nothing happened until 10.35 a.m. when she saw him step out into the street with a small suitcase and what looked like a folder of travel documents. He was dressed nattily – bright tie, dark grey flannel trousers, olive green jacket and shoes with a showy buckle at the side. A few moments later a minicab pulled up and, after patting his right breast pocket to check his passport in the gesture of nervous travellers the world over, Rahe climbed into the back.

Herrick got up, removed her gown and shook out her almost-dry hair. She reached for her black leather jacket, and announced she'd just remembered she had a meeting. By the time she was outside and calling the other members of the team on her mobile, they had already phoned the cab company and learned that Rahe was on his way to Heathrow. A search for his name on the airline computers began.

Three surveillance vehicles followed the cab along Goldhawk Road and the M4 to the drop-off point for Terminal Three departures. Rahe got out, entered the building then walked out. This he did a total of three times without checking the notice boards for the 2.15 p.m. flight to Kuwait on which they had now established he was booked. At length he seemed to settle something for himself and walked purposefully to the Heathrow chapel near Terminal Two, where he sat in the Garden of Remembrance reading a newspaper and occasionally checking his watch. Herrick thought he seemed unsure rather than nervous, and wondered whether he was expecting to meet someone. But after half an hour he suddenly got up and hurried over to the check-in area, where he waited behind about half a dozen passengers. He did not speak to anyone or, as far as they could tell, use his phone.

Still, his behaviour was considered suspicious and when he got to the security checks he was asked to step into a room and submit to a thorough search involving sensors being run over his clothes and shoes. His suitcase was examined intensively and scrapings of plastic were taken from the handle and sides and tested for explosives. Everything was found to be in order and Rahe was sent on his way. It was at this moment, as he wandered off towards the duty free shops, his dignity visibly ruffled, that the order came from New Scotland Yard that Special Branch officers watching Rahe should instantly drop what they were doing and report to Peter Chambers in the Immigration Hall.

Herrick had grown slightly impatient listening to Campbell, Beck and Fisher discuss the events of the morning in the usual oblique code. Thames House had made the connection between Rahe's presence in Heathrow and the arrival of the American but had concluded that it was nothing more than coincidence. Besides, a few minutes before the American had been located in Immigration, Rahe's distinctive olive green jacket was seen on the security cameras, making its way to the gate where he duly presented his passport again and boarded the Kuwaiti airliner.

As she was about to suggest they all return to London, Campbell, Beck and Fisher were summoned to the Baggage Hall to observe a woman named Raffaella Klein and follow her from the airport. They left immediately, now intrigued by the flow of commands from London.

Herrick, alone with her coffee and free of the in-house banter of her MI5 colleagues, began to think about Rahe's behaviour. It just didn't seem right that this unimpressive North African had suddenly departed for the Middle East. She wondered if he had a rendezvous on the plane – the best possible place for a long, unobserved talk, as long as you fixed the seating. She drained the coffee and experienced a random flash of memory: fishing with her father in Scotland, making the last cast of the day without hope of a pull on the line. What the hell, she had nothing else to do. She'd go to the security room and see what she could find out about the people on the Kuwait flight with Youssef Rahe.

Fifteen minutes later she was sitting at a desk with the passenger manifest of Kuwaiti Airlines KU102 on a screen and noting down the names of the people seated in Rahe's immediate vicinity at the back of the plane. Around her were three men from Heathrow security who had kept tabs on Rahe by the airport CCTV system as he moved through the terminal to his departure gate. She asked them to print off the complete manifest from the computer, then let her eyes drift to the screen immediately in front of the supervisor, who had compiled a medley of clips showing Rahe as he progressed through the airport. He appeared in the check-in area at 12.30 p.m., a few minutes after the flight opened. At no stage did he talk to anyone or make any sign to a fellow passenger. The cameras then picked him up just after he had been searched and followed him to the duty free shop where he paid for two bottles of Johnny Walker Black Label whisky with cash. Ten minutes later he was seen buying a newspaper, then he crossed the field of another camera and entered a coffee bar. After this he vanished for a period of about twenty minutes, although the supervisor insisted that with a few hours they could piece together his movements for the whole period. As things were, they could be sure that Rahe had got on the plane. He ran the final film and Herrick watched Rahe approach the desk, swap the duty free bag and his little suitcase from his left to his right hand and show his boarding card and passport.

She put her hands to her mouth, aware that her mind was tripping over something. 'That's not the same man,' she said, without consciously understanding what had produced such certainty. 'That's not bloody Rahe!' Vehemence made her voice rise.

'Right gate,' said the controller, yawning. 'And the jacket – I doubt there're two jackets like that on the planet, let alone in this airport.'

'It's the same jacket,' she snapped, banging the desk with her hand. 'But it's not him. Rahe is right-handed. When he gave his passport to the woman at check-in he took it from the left breast pocket with his right hand. Here he's using his left hand to take the boarding card out of his right pocket,' she said, jabbing at the screen. 'Look! He changed the bags over so he could do that. Even from behind you can see they're different – this man's got a narrower head, a longer neck. He's thinning at the crown.'

The supervisor leaned into the screen. 'Maybe you're right. But the angle's not too clever up there. We had to shift our cameras because of work on the cabling ducts for the visual recognition system. It's a shame we don't have a head-on shot of him there.' He knew she was right.

'I've been following Youssef Rahe all bloody morning and that's not him.'

They went back over the footage of Rahe in duty free, and noted how he walked away from the camera with short paces in which his feet veered outwards as they came down. The man who had just boarded KU102 walked with a definite roll and his arms worked more as he went along. There was a further, clinching anomaly. As Rahe waited in duty free he looked at his watch several times, thrusting his wrist out of his sleeve and revolving the gold strap which hung loose like a bracelet on his wrist. The man at the boarding gate appeared not to be wearing a watch, at least not one that could be seen below the sleeve of his jacket, nor as his left hand reached up and plucked the passport and boarding card from his inside pocket. Admittedly, they were seeing him from above and behind, but there was no doubt that while Herrick caught a flash of shirt cuff in this movement she could not see a watch.

She didn't need any further confirmation. She dialled the direct line to the operations room at the Security Services. 'Youssef Rahe didn't get on his plane. There was a stand-in. Rahe may be your problem.'

Route Three took the convoy of cars from the north perimeter road westwards towards Terminal Four along a canyon formed by tall leylandii bushes and noise barriers at the edge of the airport. They travelled at 80 mph with the Range Rover sitting within a few feet of the Jaguar's offside rear bumper. One false move by the Prime Minister's driver, Jim Needpath, and there would certainly be an accident, but he had worked with the protection officer in the Range Rover before. Out in front, five police outriders leapfrogged each other and raced past the convoy of cars to hold up traffic at every intersection. As they came to the roundabout near Terminal Four, they turned left and doubled back along the A30 towards London, the plan being to cross over to the M4 motorway by a dual carriageway and make their way to central London using the fast lane reserved for buses and taxis.

Inside the Jaguar, Chambers was on the radio, demanding to know why there was no sign of the police helicopter that was going to act as a pathfinder into central London. The sardonic reply came back that it was generally considered poor aviation practice to place a surveillance aircraft in the main flight path into Heathrow. At this Norquist smiled and looked out at the dismal housing estate rushing by – people walking with their heads bowed to the rain, a pair of cyclists struggling along in cagoules and an Indian woman sheltering her kid in the folds of her sari. He wondered briefly how the Brits managed to keep their sense of humour in this climate.

The outriders shepherded the motorcade smoothly through the roundabout under the M4 before the four cars rose on a slip road to join the motorway. Two motorcyclists stayed just in front of the Jaguar while the other three formed a chevron to snowplough the traffic out of the fast lane with their sirens and lights. At this point the helicopter appeared and hovered for a second or two at about 1,000, feet before spinning round to join the flow of traffic eastwards. Llewellyn was patched through to the pilot and told him that he needed an exact description of the traffic conditions ahead, and a warning about vehicles parked on the hard shoulder and on or under bridges.

The road was unusually clear and they covered the four-mile stretch quickly, with the pilot giving regular snatches of laconic commentary. Suddenly an interested note entered his voice and he told them he was going to take a look at a white lorry that had pulled up about a mile in front of them at the beginning of the elevated section. As they rounded a bend they saw the truck with the helicopter positioned above it. Llewellyn told the drivers to reduce their speed and then sent the three motorcycles on to investigate.

'What do you see?' he asked the pilot.

'There's just one man in there,' came the reply. 'I'm taking her down a bit. He looks Asian, but I can't be sure. He's not responding to anything we do. He looks a bit freaked.'

They saw the helicopter descend on the left of the motorway.

'Hold on,' said the pilot, 'the lorry's moving. No. He's stopped again. He's put the vehicle across both lanes. You might just squeeze behind him or in front of him, as the cars are doing, but there's not much room either way.'

'That's not an option,' said Llewellyn. It was fast occurring to him that there were very few options. If they tried to pass the lorry and a device was detonated inside, it would certainly blow them all into the next world. And they could not cross the central reservation to the westbound carriageway or mount the bank to their left, which was fringed with dense hawthorn trees. Reversing up the hard shoulder to the service station a mile or so back was the only way left to them, unless the lorry moved of its own accord.

By now the Jaguar and its escort had slowed to 35 mph. The traffic that had been held up behind the lorry had all slipped through the gap and a stretch of about 800 yards of open road lay ahead of them. The two remaining police outriders had dropped back to prevent anyone overtaking the convoy.

'Shit,' said Llewellyn. 'This is a fucking mess.'

'If you can keep this part of the motorway clear,' said Chambers, 'you could bring the chopper down and we can hitch a ride.'

'Let's do that,' said Norquist, his voice moving from compliance to command.

The pilot heard this in the cacophony that was now reaching him from central control, but he had other things on his mind. 'You've got two vans approaching from behind – a red Transit and a dark blue Toyota. They're about half a mile along the bus lane and closing fast. I'll come down and get you, but the wind isn't good for this kind of thing and you've got to do something about those vehicles.'

Llewellyn told the drivers of the two unmarked escort vehicles to fall back and prepare to block the vans, forcing them off the road if necessary. He knew the conversation was being heard in New Scotland Yard and he told them very deliberately to open fire if they judged it to be the only way of stopping the two vans. He was now convinced that an attempt on Norquist's life was in progress and he said as much to New Scotland Yard, adding that it wasn't effing well going to happen on his watch.

The Jaguar and Range Rover shot forward over the next seventy yards then coasted along the hard shoulder, reducing their speed to almost walking pace. Jim Needpath's eyes moved from his wing mirror to the lorry, every part of his being jangling with the imperative to take flight, to bolt from the situation and save his passengers. In front of them they saw the driver of the truck jump down from the cab, run the few yards to the side of the deserted carriageway and scramble up a bank towards the breaking wave of hawthorn blossom. Two of the three police motorcyclists brought their machines to a halt just before a narrow rail bridge over the motorway, kicked them back on their stands and set off in pursuit of the driver. The third drove up to the truck, circled it and accelerated away shouting in his helmet microphone that a liquid was seeping onto the road from the side of the truck. The vehicle was an Iveco diesel but the liquid smelled like petrol.

The helicopter pilot took matters into his own hands and decided to land on the motorway. The aircraft swooped over the rail bridge and flew at a height of a hundred feet towards the Jaguar, throwing up a storm of spray in its wake. At the exact moment that he lifted his nose and settled the aircraft onto the tarmac, the red Transit burst along the hard shoulder followed by the police BMW. The driver of the Range Rover saw what was happening, slammed his vehicle into reverse and went to meet the van, colliding with it a second or two later.

Needpath didn't wait any longer. He shot the Jaguar forward to the helicopter, pulling the car round with a handbrake turn so that Norquist's side was protected from whatever was going on behind them, which was not at all clear because of the roar of the engine and the swirling clouds of spindrift. Llewellyn and Chambers got out, dragged Norquist from his seat and pushed him towards the helicopter, ducking under the rotor blades. They were halfway there when the Toyota van appeared through the mist and hit the Jaguar on its flank, just behind Jim Needpath's seat, and caused it to spin round. The Ford saloon carrying four Special Branch police officers was not far behind, but it slewed to a halt without hitting either car and disgorged at least three of the policemen, who began to shoot at the van. The same thing had occurred on the hard shoulder after the Range Rover launched itself backwards into the red Transit van.

Llewellyn and Chambers didn't wait to witness the battle on the motorway. As they lifted Norquist through the door of the helicopter, a shot glanced off the hard perspex in front of the pilot. Chambers had just scrambled in behind Norquist when the helicopter rose, tipped forward and roared away.

They climbed to 1,000 feet before the co-pilot turned round to check that his passengers were strapped in and saw blood was coming from a wound in Norquist's neck.

He was already unconscious.

2

On a grassy bank running down to a swollen stream about ten miles from the Albanian border, a man dozed in the morning light. The sun had not yet risen above the hill in front of him so the ground and his bedding were still wet. For some time he had been aware of his travelling companions moving around him, packing and rolling up the sheets which they'd hung between the bushes to give shelter. They coughed and grumbled to each other, mostly in languages he didn't understand. But the sounds of the camp breaking in the early morning were familiar – men stiff from a night in the open, wondering how they found themselves without bed, food or a good woman.

Someone was prodding the campfire into life. At first he didn't understand why: they'd eaten the last of the food the night before – dried lamb and a broth made from chicken bones – and he knew there was no coffee or tea. Then he smelled the mint and remembered they'd gathered it in a ditch the night before. They'd made mint tea and now one of them was beside him, nudging the back of his hand with a warm tin cup. He opened an eye to see a grin of chipped teeth, spreading in an unwashed, slightly pock-marked face: the youngest of the three Kurds, an amiable character who was always jollying the others on. He said in English, 'Drink, mister, for your health.'

The party began to move off down the bank towards the track, but he still couldn't bring himself to jump up and follow. The delicious memory of his dream was still fresh and part of him didn't want to leave it behind. He watched shafts of light moving over the hill to catch the top of a tree nearby. A tiny bird, one that he had never seen before, was flitting to and from a vine that had become detached from the tree. Each time it arrived to perch on the twig, it bobbed up and down, checking the area for predators before diving into the shade of the vine to feed its young. He realised the bird must have been there all night, within a few yards of the fire and the men under the shelters, and he marvelled at its nerve and discretion.

At length the sunlight fell on the ground above him and he shook himself from his reverie, stood up and stretched. He had only a few possessions and it didn't take long for him to bundle them up and tie them together with the belt that he'd kept with him these past six years. As he made his way down the bank, slipping on the damp grass, the men's voices were brought to him on a soft, warm wind. It would be a good day, he thought. Yes, they were due some luck after all that had happened to them. Maybe they would find a way of crossing the border into Greece without being arrested and treated like dirt.

In the past he might have prayed to Allah. Now it did not even occur to him. After so long in the holy war the Western part of him was reasserting itself. He was leaving the wilderness and the barbarity behind and he was taking back his old name – Karim Khan – and with it the hope of finding the young medical student, who drank alcohol and loved and charmed but who was no less in awe of the Prophet because of these activities. Belief had not deserted him, but faith in sacrifice had gone, along with the *nomme de guerre* – Mujahad, or soldier of Islam – and just now he would rely on himself and not God's will.

He climbed down on to the track and noticed the bunches of twigs that had collected in the ruts along the road, borne there by the rainwater of the day before. Beetles were feeding on insects drowned in the storm. The pulverised rock in the road's surface sparkled with chips of quartz. Everything seemed beautiful and in its place that morning, and he felt a surge of optimism. He shuddered at the words that had taken him to war: 'Allah has conferred on those who fight with their wealth and their lives a higher rank than those who stay at home.'

No more of that. No more slaughter. No more chaos.

But whatever he thought, he was still the veteran campaigner and his ability to march on an empty stomach was undiminished. Soon the stragglers of the group ahead came into view. As always it was his two fellow Pakistanis at the rear. Both were very thin and clearly at the end of their resources. Nine months the two had been on the road. Having started from a mountain village in Northern Pakistan they had crossed to Iran and walked to the Turkish border. Most of their money had gone when a con man promised them flights and a visa to Greece, but they kept enough to get them to Bulgaria. Ahead of them went the Turk, Mehmet, and the Arabs, a Jordanian called Mumim, and a Palestinian from Lebanon who gave his name as Jasur. Out in front were the three Kurds – the young man who had given him mint tea, his uncle and a friend from his uncle's village. They had the promise of work in Athens and had only been travelling for a matter of weeks. They were the freshest of the party and it was clear they felt themselves out of place in this group of migrants, harried from one country to another and sometimes reduced to eating leaves and grubs to survive.

High in the pastures above them Khan noticed one or two locals moving about with their beasts. Cow-bells sounded with an unmusical clank across the valley. He was glad his party was not walking bunched up together because that always made people suspicious. In this country, where Muslims were so feared, they had to keep their wits about them. The men with dark skin – the two Pakistanis and the Jordanian, who had African blood in him – had to be especially careful. Not for the first time, he was grateful for his own light colouring, which family tradition held came from Alexander the Great's soldiers. Some part of him registered that he should feel at home here in Macedonia.

As he was having these thoughts he noticed the Kurds hesitate. He stopped and put his hand up to the sun and tried to see through the shimmer of heat already coming off the road. They had seen something in front of them. One had dropped his bed-roll and knapsack and spread his arms in surrender. He was showing that they weren't carrying weapons. His companions turned round to consult the others, or maybe to warn them.

Khan saw a figure moving in the clump of bushes on the left of the road. He was wearing a uniform that was exactly the same colour and tone as the shaded vegetation. A wisp of smoke came from behind him – a campfire – and beyond that tarpaulins had been stretched across the lower boughs of the trees. On the other side of the road, parked up in a cutting, were a truck and two covered jeeps.

The Kurds didn't seem to know what to do. One of them began to retrace his steps. He was gesticulating, shooing the rest of the party back up the way they had come. More soldiers moved from the shade onto the yellow strip of road; they swaggered and almost dragged their weapons along the ground. Khan recognised the type – soft, untested, conscript bullies. He had seen them before in the Balkans and he knew exactly what was going to happen next.

One of the soldiers, probably the first man to move from cover, raised his gun waist high, fired and brought down the retreating man. The other two Kurds turned back in disbelief to the soldiers, raising their hands. They dropped to their knees to beg for their lives but were killed the instant they touched the ground. One slumped forward; the other keeled over in slow motion.

With the first shot the remainder of the party had taken to their heels. The two Arabs and the Turk ran straight up towards Khan, but the Pakistanis had thrown away their possessions and dived for the bushes. The soldiers were galvanised. They ran across the road, climbed into their jeeps and, with great swirls of dust, turned the vehicles and tore up the valley towards the three men still on the road. Unlike the first shots that had killed the Kurds, the fusillade of gunfire that came from the lead jeep echoed around the hills. The Turk was hit in the leg but limped on. One of the Arabs stopped and tried to drag him to safety, but the soldiers were upon them in a second and both men were mown down. Khan moved to the side of the road into shade. He watched the jeep pull up and the soldiers unleash a volley of shots into the corpses. The other jeep had stopped a little further back so that the Pakistanis could be hunted down. Shortly afterwards Khan heard another crackle of shots. A man cried out. Then a lone shot – the *coup de grâce* – snapped through the woods.

Khan shouted at the Palestinian who was now about a hundred yards away. He knew their only chance was to head off into the trees above them. He yelled and yelled at the man as if willing him to win a race. Khan had been in such situations before and, judging by the way Jasur was bent double and zigzagging the final few yards towards him, it wasn't the first time he'd been under fire either. Together they slipped through a gap in the bushes and began to climb. The undergrowth was still wet from the storm and the soil gave way easily under their feet, but in a few minutes they got above the road and saw that both jeeps had pulled up below them. They heard shouting and a few shots were loosed off into the trees, but it was obvious the soldiers were unwilling to go in after them just yet. A truck arrived and they saw a man get out, an officer shouting at the top of his voice. He was clearly organising a sweep of the hillside.

Khan watched for a few seconds longer, steadying Jasur by holding his shoulder. He looked up the slope and decided that rather than crashing on through the wood and giving away their position, they should stay where they were. He explained in a mixture of Arabic and English, then pushed his still uncomprehending companion into the undergrowth and covered him with saplings wrenched from the loose soil. He went to find his own hiding spot about twenty paces up the hill and dug himself in, efficiently covering his legs with dirt and pulling boughs across him to hide the disturbance. Once in place, he hissed a few words of encouragement down to Jasur just as he had done a few years before when waiting in an ambush with a group of novice Mujahadin, all of them quaking in their boots.

For about fifteen minutes he heard no noise from either the road or the woods around them, but gradually the sound reached him of the soldiers slashing at the undergrowth and calling out to each other. He fastened his gaze on the bushes where Jasur was hidden, hoping that the Palestinian's nerve would hold when the soldiers passed by. He wriggled a little and felt in his back pocket for the knife he'd picked up in Turkey. He placed it in his mouth then swept the dirt back over his chest and arms and sank into the forest floor.

The soldiers were close to them now. He estimated that one was about thirty yards above him while another, who was moving much more slowly, would eventually pass between him and Jasur. He held his breath and waited. Suddenly the uniform appeared a few yards from him. The man stopped, unzipped himself, thrust his pelvis forward and started pissing. The stream of urine glittered in the light filtering through the trees. As he neared the end he shouted up the hill to his friend, a crude joke bellowed to the forest.

Khan decided to launch himself the moment the soldier turned away. Just then, the saplings which had so artfully concealed Jasur erupted, and his head and torso appeared. The soldier was caught unawares. He turned and yelled out a single syllable of surprise. But instead of firing he struggled to zip himself up and seemed to have difficulty getting hold of the automatic which he had swung round on his back while he urinated.

He must have heard Khan behind him, the movement of earth and rush of air, but he showed no sign of it as the weight of his body was pulled back onto the knife. His shaven head came back and his eyes met Khan's with a strange awkwardness, an embarrassment at the sudden intimacy with the man covered in dirt, not understanding that the first blow of the knife had neither punctured his heart nor severed his spinal cord, and that there would be no second blow. Khan let him sag to the ground and in an instant removed his water bottle, gun, and ammunition clips. He wagged his finger at the soldier and put it to his own lips. The soldier looked up terrified, but managed a nod.

Jasur came to his side and crouched down. They were hidden from the soldier above them who had started to call out to his companions, repeating one name. Alarm rang in his voice, which communicated itself up and down the line of soldiers and they all started calling out. Khan darted another look at the soldier and jabbed the gun at him in a way that couldn't be misunderstood. They turned and began to climb, moving around the main thickets so as to make as little noise as possible.

A minute or two passed then all hell broke loose. The soldiers discovered their wounded companion and started up the hill, firing shots into the trees above them. The old maxim of mountain warfare came back to Khan – flight is always better than fight. Long-practised at fleeing into the mountains, he quickened his pace and blocked his mind to the pain that would come with the exertion. They went straight up for a hundred and fifty yards but soon Jasur was begging him to slow down. He had given his all in the sprint up the road. Khan put an arm round him and felt his skinny frame heaving and his heart racing. There was virtually no muscle or fat on him. He tucked his hand under Jasur's armpit and started to haul him up the hill, the Palestinian's breath wheezing in his ear. They went another fifty yards and scrambled over some rocks. Ahead of them the trees thinned out to the pastures where he had seen the cattle herds. Beyond these he remembered the rocky crags that he'd noticed in shadow when he was lying in the field. It meant they were steep, but it didn't follow that they were impassable.

He turned round. Jasur, who had fallen to his knees, was silently coughing phlegm onto the rock. His eyes and nose were streaming and his skin had become grey. The medic in Khan guessed these were not tears but some kind of allergic reaction, probably caused by pollen or the leaves he'd been covered with, but when he took hold of his head and looked into his eyes, his diagnosis changed. Jasur was having an asthma attack and showed every sign of heart strain. Khan rolled him onto his back and started to give him mouth to mouth resuscitation, then pressed down rhythmically on his chest a dozen times. The Palestinian coughed again and began to breathe more easily, but his eyes showed that he knew exactly what was happening and Khan thought he'd probably experienced an attack like this before. He put his hand to the man's pulse – more regular now – and lifted his head to give him some water from the soldier's bottle. At that moment they heard the soldiers making their way up the hill. He dragged Jasur back across the rocks so he was out of view and then snaked forward on his stomach to look over the edge. There were four of them and further down the slope came another trio, but they had no appetite for the climb and were stopping every few feet to mop their brows and curse.

He tried the safety catch of the AK47, made sure that the magazine would come away when he needed it to, then lay flat on the rocks with his face resting on the polished wooden stock. As he waited his thoughts slipped back to the first moment of the day and he realised dully that whatever his dreams and hopes for the future, this was the way his life was cast. His fate was to be covered in grime and sweat, waiting in ambush with a murderous old gun in his hand.

Behind him Jasur uttered a dramatic series of gurgles and retches. Khan was worried for his companion but could not risk turning now. He nudged him gently on the shoulder with his boot and that seemed to quieten him. For one moment he thought the change in direction of the soldiers' voices meant they had given up, or taken a path off to the left, but suddenly he heard them directly below him. He pulled himself forward and raised his arms so that the gun was angled downwards over the edge of the rock. After the initial burst he bobbed up and saw that he'd hit some of the first group in the legs. They fell backwards without even knowing where he was. One recovered and fired in the direction of the rocks, a long way wide of the mark. Khan sneaked another look and squeezed the trigger. This sent them tumbling from their cover down the slope. They don't mind killing unarmed men in the open, he thought, but they've got no taste for real battle. He fired, changed clips and fired some more. Now there was no sign of them, although he heard one yelping like a lost puppy in the woods.

He turned and wriggled back to Jasur, lying against the rock, facing away from him. He touched him on the shoulder and said they ought to be going. Could he make it? He shook him and, feeling no life, rolled the Palestinian over.

His skin was ashen, saliva foamed at his mouth and his eyes stared without meaning at the tiny red spiders that circled on the rock surface in front of him. Khan was shocked. Bewildered. He pushed himself to his knees and shrugged, thinking that he should – no, he must – find out who this man was and one day let his family know what had become of him. He felt all over the body and eventually located a little pouch hanging from a string inside Jasur's trousers. He flipped it open and saw some folded documents, one or two pictures, a printed prayer and an identity card. He would look at them properly later. Now he had to leave and hope that the Macedonians would bury the Palestinian.

He got up, and without looking down the hill, jogged off into the next clump of trees and made for the crags above.

3

Herrick put down the evening paper. It reported that Vice Admiral Norquist had not recovered consciousness before expiring at 5.30 a.m. this morning, May 15. He had died from heart failure during an operation to remove the bullet that had lodged in his spine. The President of the United States issued a statement saying that the assassination of his friend and mentor was a deep personal blow to him and his family, but more than this, it was another strike against America and all good Americans should mourn his sacrifice.

Thinking that the report was less than complete, Herrick turned to her desk and the FBI watch list, a summary of essential information on every known Muslim terrorist. She found this easier to use than the British version because of its layout and concision. From left to right appear the first names of the suspect or wanted felon, followed by his aliases, date of birth, US social security number (if any), place of birth, address, phone number and email. The far right column gives a unique identity number for the suspect and, in the middle of the page, there is a column headed Function. This column is left blank in the version of the list circulated daily at 8.00 a.m. EST to banks and airlines, and copied into their computer systems so that any transaction made by one of the individuals triggers an alert. But in the thirty-four-page document lying in front of her, the FBI logged trades against the names of some of the 524 men – computer expert (trained engineer), weapons and explosive expert, strategist/trainer, banker, facilitator and communications specialist. Most were guesses and the addresses and email accounts had long been abandoned, but the list fixed the last known position of suspects and in one or two cases hinted that they were anchored to a cover, like Youssef Rahe, although his name did not appear.

She flipped through the list once more, making notes and adding to a chart she'd begun on a large sheet of drawing paper bought from a shop in Victoria that afternoon. A series of names plus lines and arrows and several brief sentences were written in her neat hand. She knew the diagram didn't add up to much, but she found it a useful way of working through a problem, putting a thought down, discarding it and moving on. On her desk were two packets of sandwiches, a piece of fruit cake wrapped in cellophane, a bottle of water, a banana and a bar of chocolate – not a feast considering the quantities of food she put away during periods of concentration. She ate one of the sandwiches distractedly and turned to the papers propped against her computer screen and on the floor around her feet. These were printouts of web pages showing the landing and take-off times for planes that passed through Terminal Three the day before – a timetable that varied considerably from the published schedules, she noted.

She didn't expect to prove anything conclusively; it would be enough to show that Rahe's disappearance was important, though he clearly had no role in the shooting of Norquist. She now knew for certain that he had not got off KU102 in Kuwait. Half an hour before, a clear head-shot had arrived of the man travelling on Rahe's passport, taken in Kuwait City airport before the individual flew on to the United Arab Emirates. By this time he had disposed of Rahe's clothes and adopted the local white jellabah. However, the Kuwaiti Intelligence service, al-Mukhabarat, were certain it was the stand-in.

She emailed the picture to Heathrow security and asked them to go through CCTV film to see if he'd come from London or arrived on another flight. Her belief was that he'd flown into Heathrow that morning, which was why she was trying to match possible suspects' names with passengers who had ended up in Terminal Three, a forlorn task if ever there was one. Still, she liked the solitary purpose of working late and was buoyed by the idea that while the rest of the Secret Intelligence Service was absorbed by muffled agony over the killing of Norquist, she was at least making some positive steps to unravel the events at the airport.

As she talked on the phone to a security officer named George, she looked out of the window and into the streams of traffic moving along the north bank of the Thames. Her focus drew nearer, to her reflection in the window, which she examined without reproof or anxiety. She looked good for thirty-two, although the lights made her appear haggard and – God – she *had* to get some new clothes!

George still had nothing for her. She put the phone down and went back to the watch list, thinking that Manila was the perfect place for the stand-in to embark. Just then she noticed a movement behind the glass panel in the office wall and saw Richard Spelling, deputy head of MI6, and his sidekick, Harry Cecil.

Before she had time to compose herself or her desk, Spelling was inside the door. 'Mr Cecil here says you've got something good.'

'That would be a bit premature of Mr Cecil,' she said, smiling at Cecil without affection.

'Well, you must have something if you've been asking favours of our friends in Kuwait City.'

'I was checking on the man who took Rahe's place on the Kuwait flight. As you know, I told Thames House yesterday afternoon, but I think they're rather tied up at the moment and nobody has got back to me about it. So I thought I'd do some ground work.' This was weak. She knew she was going way beyond her role of walk-on part in the surveillance of Rahe.

Spelling sat down on the other side of her desk and indicated to Cecil that he was dismissed. 'I'll say the Security Services are tied up!' he said.

Herrick cautioned herself not to say too much. She nodded.

'It doesn't get much worse than the President's special envoy being killed before his meeting with the Prime Minister. I mean, how bad does that make us look?' He gave her a despairing look and then exhaled heavily, which caused his lips to vibrate. She didn't like Spelling, his punchy name-dropping manner or the managerial style that someone had described as exultant decisiveness. Around the building it was said that his intelligence was sharp rather than deep and that he had none of the incorruptibility, shrewdness or ease of the outgoing Chief, Sir Robin Teckman. Spelling had won the appointment as a moderniser. There was much talk of horizontal management structures and the flow of ideas between different levels, but the evidence pointed to the opposite leaning. He was a hierarchical bureaucrat pretending to be a general.

'What do you make of it?' he asked. 'The shooting, I mean.'

'Well, I've been pretty busy today. I haven't had time to catch up with the people I was working with yesterday.'

'Yes, yes, but you have a view. You must wonder.'

'Yes, I wonder why Admiral Norquist was on a scheduled flight and there was no security prepared and ready to meet him. It all seems a bit slapdash.'

'And further down the time line...?'

Time line was a typical Spelling phrase. 'You mean later on – when the shooting occurred?' She put it as neutrally as possible. 'It looks pretty confused.'

'Yes, it was certainly that.'

She remained silent. It was still his call.

'And you don't have any theories about where that bullet came from?'

'Nothing apart from what I've read. I imagine they'll know if they retrieved it from his body.'

'Oh, I don't think that will happen.'

'So there *was* an exit wound. I didn't notice that mentioned in the papers. They said it was lodged in his spine.'

'They tend not to publish too much of that sort of thing – it's distressing for the family.'

'I see,' she said, understanding that there would be no official revision of the story. Norquist had been 'assassinated' in an operation involving a pair of young men, traced by the registration of one of the vans to the Pakistani communities in the Midlands, and the truck driver, who was also believed to be of Asian origin. With the two men dead and the driver still missing after an escape through the undergrowth along the railway embankment, the British media happily accepted the theory of a carefully coordinated plan. The enthusiasm for this account had not been dampened by the fact that no detonator had been found attached to the drums of petrol on the lorry.

His eyes scanned her desk. He reached forward and turned one of the Terminal Three schedules towards him. 'Now, tell me what you're doing here, Isis.'

'I'm trying to see what Rahe's likely destination was yesterday.'

'Any ID on the man who took his place?'

'Not yet.'

'Could you write a side of theory backed up by a few facts? The Chief's very interested in what happened out at Heathrow.'

She hesitated. 'You want a report on this? It's all very preliminary . . .'

'By tomorrow then. If you need help, Sarre and Dolph are around. Tell them this is for me and the Chief.' He made for the door, but before he reached it, stopped. 'And in your report, leave out all mention of the shooting. Just focus on the contemporaneous events at Heathrow. That's what interests us.'

Herrick went back to the airline schedules. Out of seventy-two flights to land between 5.55 a.m. and 1.45 p.m., fifty-one had come from the United States or Canada, which she excluded for the moment because of the heightened airport security and emigration watches in North America. The remaining twenty-one flights came from places such as Abu Dhabi, Dhaka, Johannesburg, Beirut and Tehran, cities where controls were far less stringent. She guessed that most of the aircraft were wide-bodied jets, carrying an average of two hundred passengers, which meant that around four thousand people had landed at Heathrow that morning. It would be an enormous task to search all the flights for a man matching the picture, and to establish what had happened to Rahe.

She founded Philip Sarre in the library, leafing through some material on Uzbekistan, which he informed her was now his speciality. 'If you go to Langley, you find whole rooms of Uzbek specialists; here it's me in my coffee break.'

Sarre always maintained that he had been brainwashed by MI6 and was actually meant to be in Cambridge watching particle acceleration experiments. His friend Andy Dolph was equally improbable. The son of an independent bookie, he had come to MI6 via the City of London and a banking job in the Gulf States where he had allowed himself to be recruited to relieve the boredom. Sarre reported that Dolph was across the river in a pub waiting for him and an Africa specialist named Joe Lapping. Sarre said he'd extract both men and bring them to Heathrow.

An hour later Herrick and the three men were crowded into the security room at Terminal Three having arranged for two of the technical people to stay as long as they were needed. Their first break came after 1.00 a.m. Dolph had been going over the film from the gates of two flights that landed consecutively from Bangkok at 9.15 and 9.40 a.m. when he saw the man who had taken Rahe's place walk off the second flight. Wearing a dark red jacket, a bright tie with hibiscus motif, grey trousers and black shoes, he was among the last passengers to leave the plane. This told them that he had probably been seated at the back of the Thai International Airways 747. The airline's records showed that one of the rearmost seats had been occupied by an Indonesian national named Nabil Hamzi, who they later found was travelling on to Copenhagen at 11.40 a.m. from Terminal Three.

Herrick gasped. 'Rahe didn't check in until past midday,' she said.

'So?' said Sarre.

'Don't be a fucking idiot,' said Dolph. 'It means that Rahe couldn't have made the Copenhagen flight. And that means there wasn't a straight swap between Rahe and Hamzi.'

'There had to be a third man, at least,' said Sarre.

'By George, he's got it,' said Dolph, pinching Sarre's cheek.

'And the third man must have arrived in the airport before eleven to give him time to change clothes, tickets and passports with Hamzi and get himself to the Copenhagen departure gate.'

They crowded round a screen to watch film of flight SK 502 to Copenhagen boarding and with little surprise saw a man in a red jacket, hibiscus tie and grey trousers waiting to present his boarding card and passport. It was neither Rahe nor Hamzi but another individual who was the same height and build and who was also in his mid-to-late thirties. After a couple of hours they found this man on footage from one of the long corridors leading to the departure gates. Then, working back through recordings made by a series of cameras, they traced him to a flight from Vancouver. This worried Herrick – it had implications for the other North American airlines. Still, there was no way of pairing the face with a seat number and therefore a name, because they couldn't work out at what stage he'd left the aircraft. However, Dolph realised that there was probably a pattern.

'Look,' he said. 'These guys aren't going to be travelling with baggage in the hold. And they are all likely to be booked on connecting flights out of Heathrow on the afternoon of the fourteenth. So all we have to do is go through the manifest of the Vancouver flight and match the two criteria.'

This produced the name Manis Subhi, who was travelling on a Philippine passport and had left London for Beirut four hours after landing.

Herrick wondered out loud whether she should let Spelling know the provisional results.

'No, let's tie this thing up, darling,' said Dolph. 'Present them with a fucking bunch of roses in the morning. Let's follow the trail until it ends.'

Sarre reminded them that they hadn't yet discovered the eventual destination of Rahe.

'Maybe it's not so important,' said Herrick. 'Perhaps he was just one element in a serial identity switch involving many people.'

'A daisy chain,' said Dolph.

'Yes, just because we spotted that Rahe didn't get on the right plane, it doesn't mean he's the crucial figure. He unwittingly let us in on the secret – that's all.'

'He loaned out his identity?' said Dolph.

'Could be. The whole point must be to shuffle a lot of key figures at once, and they can do that here in Terminal Three.'

'Because it's like the General Assembly of the United Nations,' said Dolph.

'No, because departing and arriving passengers mingle on their way to and from the gates. Also, passports are barely inspected when passengers are boarding – the airline just matches the name on the passport with the name on the boarding card.'

They watched film of the Middle Eastern airlines flight to Beirut, recorded by a camera close to the desk, and duly noted that Manis Subhi had been replaced by another, obviously taller man who, other than wearing the red jacket, hardly bothered to impersonate him. He also carried a bag that Subhi had not had with him. Then by chance, when the technician made an error and fast-forwarded the film instead of rewinding it, they spotted Rahe in a dark suit carrying a camera bag. This meant that Rahe had left for Beirut with another man involved in the operation.

It was now 5.00 a.m. and Herrick had seen all she needed. She asked the technicians to splice together the film of each man onto a single videotape. Then she borrowed a security pass and a radio and walked into the terminal building. There was a surprising amount of activity in the public areas – maintenance men fiddling with cable ducts, gangs of cleaners moving slowly with their machines like ruminants, and one or two passengers waiting for the first flights out. After half an hour, having tramped the best part of a couple of miles, she found what she was looking for.

Discreetly tucked into a bend was a men's lavatory, the entrance completely hidden from CCTV cameras. She went in and found a cleaner wiping down the basins. The name on his identity tag read Omar Ahsanullah and by the look of him she guessed he was Bangladeshi. The washroom was relatively small and consisted of six cubicles, a row of urinals, four basins and a locked storeroom.

She nodded to the man, then went out and radioed Dolph in the security room. She wanted him to watch as she walked down the corridor so that he'd see the exact moment she disappeared from view on the cameras. They found there was a blind spot of about fifty feet either side of the entrance. Although they were unable to watch the washroom's entrance, she realised they would be able to go back over the film for the two nearest cameras and get all they needed: anyone making their way to the men's toilet would have to pass under them. Dolph said he would try to verify her theory by checking the film for these two cameras from 12.30 until 2.00 p.m. to see if Rahe showed.

The sight of the cleaners reminded her that there must have been a man on duty in the lavatory when the men were swapping their clothes and possessions. She went back in. The cleaner explained that there were two shifts, one that started at 5.30 a.m. and finished at 2.30 p.m., another that ended at 11.30 p.m. It was possible to do a double shift, and those with many relatives back home often needed the extra money. As he spoke, she suddenly saw the drudgery and fatigue in his eyes and she remarked that it must be a hard life.

He stopped polishing the mirror and replied that yes, it was tiring, but he was in the West and his children would get a good education. He was lucky. He paused, then told her if he was looking unduly sad that day it was because a friend, a fellow Bangladeshi, had died in a fire. His wife, two children and his mother had also died. Herrick remembered hearing about the blaze in Heston on the radio news the day before. It was being investigated as a hate crime. She said how sorry she was.

The man continued to talk about his friend in a distracted way and then as an after-thought mentioned that he had been a cleaner at Heathrow too. He had been working there on the day he died, the fourteenth.

'Here?' asked Herrick, now very alert. 'In this washroom?'

The man said that he was on this floor on Tuesday because they had both worked double shifts that day. But he couldn't be sure that he was working in this exact toilet.

'I am sorry about your loss,' she said. 'Is it possible for you to give me his name?'

'Ahmad Ahktar,' said the man.

She said goodbye. As she was about to leave the washroom she noticed a sign propped under the basins. She bent down and turned it, almost knowing that it would read 'Out of service'.

By the time she got back to the control room, they had found Rahe on the film taken near the lavatory. More important, they had got him in both sets of clothing and were able to see which man he had changed with. Dolph and Lapping had started cross-referencing the information they had gathered with names on the FBI and British watch lists. It was an inexact process but they had seven faces to play with. Dolph made an impressive case that two of them belonged to an Indonesian cell. He told them he'd lay odds on it.

Herrick had other things on her mind. It was obvious that the timing of this operation was subject to flights arriving late or being diverted. They must have built flexibility into the schedule so that if one man was delayed, there was still someone for him to switch identities with. That probably meant there were one or two floaters, men who at the beginning of the day were prepared to be sent anywhere. These would have to be European citizens with clean passports who could board a plane bound for Barcelona or Copenhagen and enter the country without raising suspicion. She thought of Rahe, a British citizen, sitting in the Garden of Remembrance. Although they hadn't seen him use his phone, he must have received a text message or phone call to tell him when he was due to swap.

Some of the detail could wait, but they were getting a picture of an impressive operation. To put as many as a dozen people into Heathrow from all over the world, with passports that were stamped with the correct visas, and then to achieve what was in effect a relay switch, required miraculous scheduling skills. Whoever was controlling the switches would need to speak to each man the moment he arrived, which was why, she now realised, three suspects had been filmed talking on their mobiles just after disembarkation. The controller would also have to ensure that the men didn't all arrive in the washroom at the same time. An early flight might leave a man loitering in the corridors, drawing attention to himself, so a premature arrival would have to be taken out of circulation, perhaps hidden in the locked storage cupboard, until the moment his pair arrived and he could be sent on his way.

There was one more question she needed to answer before returning to London and writing the report for Spelling, which she now rather relished.

She went down to Arrivals, bought a cup of coffee and stationed herself under the flight displays. Heathrow was now open for business. Four flights were expected in the next quarter of an hour and already the roped-off exit from Customs was fringed with small welcoming parties.

She noticed that the chauffeurs and company drivers seemed to know instinctively when planes had landed and the passengers would start to clear Customs. Often the drivers appeared from the car park exit with just a few seconds to spare. She asked a lugubrious man clutching a sign and sipping coffee how they managed it. 'Trick of the trade,' he said, blowing across the cup. 'The top deck of the car park for this terminal has the best view of the airport. When you see your aircraft landing you drive down to the lower floor and then you know you've got another half hour or so to wait. It makes a difference if you're doing this three times a week.'

'What about when it's busy?' she asked.

'At peak you've got about forty to fifty minutes,' he replied.

Herrick could have gone back to the control room, satisfied that she'd tied up all the loose ends of the operation, but the obsessive part of her nature told her there was always more to be had by seeing something for yourself. A few minutes later she was standing in the open on the top level of the car park with a little huddle of plane spotters. She watched for a while, briefly marvelling that men stirred so early in the day to jot down the details of very ordinary-looking Jumbo jets, then caught the eye of a man with an untidy growth of beard and asked him if this was always the best place to see the aircraft.

'Not always,' he replied without removing his eyes from a jet taxiing in to the terminal. 'They change the runways at three in the afternoon on the dot. Whichever one is being used for take-off becomes the landing runway. Then we go across to Terminal Two and watch from the proper viewing terrace.'

She was about to ask him whether he had seen anyone acting unusually the day before last, but thought better of it. That was a detail. Special Branch could deal with it later.

She walked out of earshot of the plane spotters towards the centre of the near-empty car park and dialled the duty officer at Vauxhall Cross.

It was 6.45 a.m. Isis noticed she was very hungry.

4

Silence. No word from the Chief's office; not the merest hint that her report had been discussed at the Joint Intelligence Committee, which Herrick knew was meeting four times a day in the wake of the death of Norquist. Even the people in anti-terrorism, who had been known to make the odd, oblique compliment, said nothing. Dolph, Sarre and Lapping shrugged and went back to their work. Dolph said, 'Fuck 'em, Isis. Next time we'll stay in the pub.' Sarre pondered the behaviour and came up with the phrase 'institutional autism', then went off to look at a map of Uzbekistan.

Herrick was not as easily resigned. She didn't understand why there was not an immediate operation to trace the men who had darted into the glare of Heathrow's security system and dispersed into the dark. Anyone could see these men had been imported into Europe for a specific purpose, a particular act of terrorism. But the trail was growing colder by the minute.

This just confirmed her belief that the parts of the Secret Intelligence Service were more decent and reasonable than its sum. She trusted colleagues individually, but rarely the collective, which she regarded by turns as needlessly calculating, merciless and plain stupid.

This had been her view since the Intelligence Officers' New Entry Course when, like the others in her class of a dozen, she was sent abroad on what was presented as an actual mission. A cover story was provided, fake credentials, a task and a deadline. Everything seemed straightforward, but during the trip the trainees were arrested by the local counter intelligence service, held and questioned, the object being to test their powers of resistance and resourcefulness.

The test is never pleasant but Herrick knew that, like most female entrants, she had received especially severe treatment. She was detained by the German police and members of the BFD for a week, during which she was questioned for long stretches at night, roughed up and deprived of sleep, food and water. The particular harshness perhaps had something further to do with the fact that she had followed her father into MI6. No daddy's girls in the Service, not unless they could stand having a chair broken over their back by a border-line psychopath.

Every reason to take the Cairo posting offered to her a couple of weeks earlier and get out of Vauxhall Cross. Egypt was one of the few Arab countries where she could use her language and work without having to remember at every step she was a woman. Besides, the cover job in the embassy as political counsellor would not be too difficult to master alongside the business of spying.

She shook herself – she had work to do – and returned with little enthusiasm to the investigation of Liechtenstein trusts being used to move Saudi money to extremist clerics and mosques around Europe – a worthwhile job perhaps, although it seemed pedestrian after her night at Heathrow.

Khan had kept going through the first day and, having taken care to memorise the shape of the landscape ahead of him, walked through the night, too. By the following morning he reckoned he had put a good distance between himself and the security forces. He decided to rest up in the shade. But down in the valleys he saw much more activity than would normally be expected in the pursuit of one fugitive. He realised they couldn't let him leave the country with his knowledge of the massacre of innocent men. He lay low until the early evening and set off again in the warm twilight, eventually coming across a village in the mountains where some kind of celebration was in full swing. A small dance floor had been erected; strings of lights had been hung between its four corners and a band was playing. He guessed it was some kind of religious feast or a wedding.

He had gone for two days without food, sucking leaves and grass and eking out the water in the soldier's canteen. But he made himself wait a good half-hour, watching a group of houses that could be approached under cover of a wall that ran down from a ridge not far from where he lay. He set off, moving cautiously, at every step of the way looking back to see his best escape route. He entered two houses but in the dark couldn't find anything to eat. He came to a third and felt his way to the kitchen, where he found a loaf of bread, half a jar of nuts, some dried beef, cheese and olives. He wrapped them in a piece of damp cloth that had covered the bread.

An ancient voice croaked from the room next door, making him freeze. He put his head round the door-frame and saw an old woman sitting in a chair, bathed in red light from an illuminated religious icon. Her head moved from side to side and she was slashing at the air with a stick. He realised that she must be blind. He crept over to her, gently laid his hand on hers and with the other stroked her brow to reassure her. Her skin was very wrinkled and cool to the touch and momentarily he had the impression that she had woken from the dead. He caught sight of a bottle of Metaxa brandy and a glass, which had been placed out of her reach. He poured an inch or so, put the glass in her hand and helped her lift it to her lips. Her wailing suddenly stopped and she murmured something which sounded like a blessing. Placing the bottle in his piece of cloth, he left the house by the front door.

A couple of dogs pursued him along the wall and he was forced to sacrifice some of the meat, which he hacked off with his knife and chucked at them. Then he melted into the rocks and scrub, making for the place where he had left his belongings. He ate a little of the cheese and bread to give him energy, but it was another hour before he found some rocks where he could make a fire that wouldn't be seen from below, or indeed from any other direction. He prepared a sandwich, eating it slowly so as not to give himself indigestion, and washed it down with some brandy mixed with a little water. It was his first alcohol in seven years and he knew himself well enough to watch his consumption.

He did not stamp out the fire straight away, but moved some flat stones into the flames then settled down near the light to look through the Palestinian's pouch of documents. There were a number of identity cards with different names. The most frequent name used was Jasur al-Jahez and all the cards included pictures of the dead Palestinian. He noticed that many were out of date, but felt sure that somewhere among the mostly Arabic documentation an address would be found. When he'd had them translated he would write to Jasur's relatives and tell them what had happened. The death of the man who'd fought so hard to live had stayed with him all day and, as with his men in Afghanistan, he felt a keen responsibility to the relatives who had been left behind.

Some time later, he pulled the stones from the fire and placed them in a line, digging them in so their tops were flush with the surface of the ground. Then he swept the embers away, buried them and laid his bed-roll where the fire had been and along the line of warm stones. It was a trick he'd learned during his first winter in Afghanistan. Going to sleep by a fire was less efficient than lying on ground that had been heated for several hours. With rocks placed in a line under your body you stayed warm all night, or at least warm enough to go to sleep.

Next day he woke at dawn and packed his things quickly. He was about 700 feet above the village and a good mile away as the crow flies. A slight haze hung over the mountains. When he moved to look down he noticed that an army truck had pulled up in the main square of the village and a knot of figures were gathered round it. It could mean nothing; on the other hand, there was every possibility that the old lady had reported him and the missing food had lent credibility to her story. He moved off without a second glance and decided on the tactics he'd used the first day, of marching further than anyone thought possible. But it was already quite hot and the one thing he hadn't thought to do while in the village was replenish his water supply. He would have to save the cup or two that remained in the canister.

Half an hour later a helicopter appeared and circled the ground immediately above the village. He saw troops moving up the mountainside. They were much fitter and faster than the soldiers who had hunted him two days before and he estimated that if he stayed where he was they would reach him in under an hour. However, it would be suicide not to pick his route carefully while the helicopter was so close.

He waited under some bushes, remembering what a Stinger missile launched from a man's shoulder could do to a chopper. As soon as it shifted, he sprinted into a plantation of pines and moved rapidly up the slope, running with the gun in one hand and the sack of possessions tied round his back with the gun strap. He reached some open ground and decided to make for a long shelf of rock about a hundred yards ahead.

Something must have attracted the pilot's attention. The machine dipped and slewed across the mountainside towards him. Khan dived under a clump of bushes to his right, rolled onto his back and pushed the muzzle of the gun through the foliage, briefly aiming it at the tail rotor as it came into view. Instead of settling over the bushes the helicopter passed him. He wiped the sweat that was trickling from his brow and took a sip of water from the canister. He could see very little, but from the rhythmic thud he judged the helicopter was in a steady hover high over a position about a thousand yards to the north of him.

He pulled the shirt-sleeve across his face again, dabbed his eyes and took in the pinpoint clarity of the day. The sun had burned away the haze and was heating the ground so that the air was filled with the smell of herbs.

His eyes returned to the skyline above the shelf. One or two scrawny mountain sheep had appeared and were looking over the ten-foot drop. They were joined by the rest of the flock, obviously scared by the helicopter. With one sudden movement they cascaded over the edge, many of them landing legs akimbo or on their sides. They struggled up and stampeded past him like a river in spate, down towards the pine trees. They were followed by a pair of dogs and a shepherd boy who stood on the edge of the shelf, waved a stick and shouted. Khan noticed that he had a blanket tied across his chest and was carrying a good many pans and bottles that made almost as much din as the sheep bells. As the boy scrambled down, a corner of the sack-cloth came loose and neat bunches of herbs tumbled out. He dropped the sack and ran on after the sheep without noticing Khan's boots protruding from beneath the bushes.

The helicopter's engine was producing a more laboured note. He saw it pop into view above, climb rapidly and drop away to his left. He caught another noise – the unmistakable sound of automatic weapons firing and a heavy machine gun, or even a cannon.

He scrambled up to the rock and put his head above the parapet. About two hundred yards away he saw a group of men moving into the open from an old stone shelter. They didn't seem to be in the least concerned about the presence of the helicopter sitting above a cliff some distance away, and were moving without haste up the scree towards a cleft in the mountains. Several packhorses or mules followed them.

He realised these must be the insurgents he'd heard about from the Bulgarian truck driver who had brought them all the way from Eastern Turkey and left them near the town of Tetovo, West of Skopje. It was a long way from the agreed drop-off point and they had missed their connection, so the driver had got out a road map and showed them that they were south of the place where the borders of Macedonia, Kosovo and Albania meet. He told them there was a lot of trouble because the men from the north crossed into Macedonian territory and stirred up trouble with the local Albanian population. He had been forced to change his route countless times by the Macedonian patrols. Khan had only half-believed him, but here were the men he had spoken about and they might well provide a means of getting over the border.

Shading his eyes from the light, he peered down the mountain to look for the soldiers. At first there was no sign of them but then he noticed that the sheep which had scattered into the pine plantation were now bolting from cover. He saw a figure flash across a patch of light and realised that the soldiers were nearly in range. They would reach him in minutes. He had a choice. He could try to conceal himself but risk being discovered, or he could warn the men above him about the size of the approaching force. He opted for the latter, and jumped up, letting off a burst in the air to gain their attention, then loosed a full magazine into the trees without hope or desire of hitting the soldiers. They rose to the bait and returned his fire and so announced their presence. He turned and raced across the plateau towards the men, shouting and waving, praying they understood he was one of them; at least that he had earned an audience.

This performance brought them to a halt and even now they seemed to have time to exchange looks and rest their hands on each other's shoulders and point at the man tearing across the bare plateau. He reached them almost incapable of speech, but gestured down the mountain and said the word soldier in as many languages as came to mind. The men stared back at him. They were all quite short with dusty hair and faces. Beneath the grime was two or three days of stubble and without exception a look of undisguised suspicion. One of them gestured he should fall in behind the column and then they moved off again. A hundred feet up, Khan saw why they were so confident. Hidden behind a wall of boulders was a heavy six-barrelled American machine gun, known as a Six-pak. As soon as they passed the gun, a young man of no more than eighteen years, with eyebrows that met in the middle of his face and the solemn concentration of the truly insane, opened fire, strafing the ground immediately in front of the rock shelf and kicking up an impressive spray of pebbles and dust. Still firing, he swung the weapon in an arc towards the helicopter and pumped rounds in its direction, causing the pilot to rise and feint to the left. He kept up intermittent bursts until the men and mules passed through the opening of the rock, at which point he gathered up the gun and ammunition belts and ran to join them.

'Albania,' said the man who was evidently their leader. 'This Albania. Albania is shit. And you? Who you are?'

'Mujahadin,' replied Khan, thinking that this was his only recognisable credential, but at the same time regretting that he had resorted to his past. His name was Karim Khan now.

'Mujahadin is shit also,' said the man.

5

It seemed to Herrick that life continued with bright, feverish simplicity. The Saturday papers learned that Norquist had been travelling in the Prime Minister's car and concluded that the events of May 14 could only be read as an attempt on the Prime Minister's life. No one seemed to take any notice of the reports in the *International Herald Tribune* that asked how the terrorists knew Norquist's travel plans when his own secretary hadn't been told. It also questioned the nature of the information that the British had been acting on. Was it a tip-off or the result of secret surveillance? The most important issue, said a columnist from the *Herald Tribune*, was how the Pakistani assassins mistook the President's old ally for the British Prime Minister. The two men could not be more dissimilar, even in the reportedly wild conditions on the M4 that day.

After finishing the papers, Herrick did a couple of hours impatient shopping, which produced two new suits, a pair of blue jeans and a white shirt. She dumped the clothes without looking at them again at her house in West Kensington and returned to Heathrow, this time on an entirely unofficial basis. What had hardened in her mind was the absolute need to link the identity switch with the operation against Norquist. But the contrast between the care and timing of the switch and the haphazard nature of the hit, which had apparently only succeeded because of a stray police bullet, suggested that different minds were behind them – unless the disparity had been planned.

At Heathrow, she went to the viewing terrace and began asking the plane spotters tucked away in a shelter whether they had seen anyone acting unusually in the last week or so. They were unsurprised by the question because the police, for which she read Special Branch, had already been to talk to them and they had provided a description of a man in his late thirties. He had Mediterranean looks, was overweight by twenty or so pounds and spoke fluent English with an Arab accent. His knowledge of aircraft was good but he seemed a lot more interested in the carriers than their planes. Referring to their notes from May 14, one or two were able to place him in the context of planes arriving and leaving and claimed to remember him making a remark about two Russian planes. No one could remember seeing him after that day.

She took the description to the incident room at Hounslow police station, where she had arranged to meet a Chief Superintendent Lovett who was leading the investigation into the fire at the home of the washroom attendant. The policeman was cagey but eventually agreed that the washroom attendant Ahmad Ahktar had associated with a man who more or less fitted this description. He had made contact at the mosque in central London which Ahmad had attended when his work allowed him. They were treating the case as multiple murder because the injuries on Ahmad's head and back could not have been sustained by the roof collapsing. There was another, more telling clue: the youngest child was found to have high levels of Tamazepam in her body. The remains of the other members of the family were being tested and there was some hope of retrieving enough tissue for analysis.

Herrick had all she needed. The Ahktar family had been murdered to stop Ahmad talking about the identity switch and it was possible that the man who had watched the planes come in was responsible for this. But the important fact was that her line of inquiry had already been followed by Special Branch. They had made the connection between the man on the viewing terrace and the fire in Heston. In other words, someone was acting on the memo and the medley of CCTV clips she had sent.

Late that afternoon, she called Dolph and arranged dinner in a room above a pub in Notting Hill. Dolph arrived late and for a time they talked about 'the office' in neutral terms and drank some cocktails of Dolph's invention.

'They're holding their breath, Isis,' he said, 'waiting for something to happen – or not to happen. The whole bloody place's on edge. You can feel it.'

Herrick murmured that she thought something was already happening, but that they were being kept out of it. Dolph didn't pick up on this.

'They're constipated,' he said, 'bent double with it. They need a fucking good dump.'

Herrick grimaced. 'You're a barbarian.'

'You can't deny there's something weird about it.' He paused and looked across the room of mostly young diners. 'Look at this lot,' he said. 'There's not a person in this room who earns less than we do – and that's including the waiters. What do we do it for?'

'Vanity?' she offered.

Dolph turned back. 'That's why I like you, Isis. You get it all. Do you think this weird mood in the office has anything to do with the Chief going?'

'Might have.'

'Oh come off it. Talk, for Christ's sake. I want to know what you think.'

She smiled. 'I am talking, but this isn't the best place for it.'

Dolph eyed the waitress and then let his gaze fall on Herrick. 'Okay, tell me about you. What happened to the man in your life – the academic?'

She shrugged. Daniel Brewer, outwardly a soft-hearted academic, had turned out to be an incipient drunk, a clever Cornish working-class boy prone to bouts of despair and unreason. 'He found someone who listened better than I did. And he didn't like our business – the vanishing act, the secrecy. He felt excluded.'

'You told him what you did?'

'No, but he guessed. That was part of the original attraction, I think.'

'What about your father? Did he like him?'

'Didn't say.'

Dolph ordered some wine. 'Did you know I went to your father's lectures? My intake was the last to get the Munroe Herrick treatment. He was very impressive. Believe me, I'd never have survived all that crap in the Balkans if it hadn't been for him.'

'Yes – he had stopped by the time I was taken on.'

Dolph regarded her sympathetically with his handsome, dissolute face. As he was choosing the wine she had noticed his expression suddenly betray the very sharp intelligence which lay behind the façade of effortlessness. 'I often think about you,' he said. 'I wonder what's going on with you.'

She shrugged. 'Nothing Dolph, just bloody work. I'm considering taking the Cairo job.'

'You should have some fun.'

She revolved her eyes in an arc, knowing what was coming next. 'Yes, I should,' she said. 'Which is why I'm going to take Cairo.' She smiled a full stop.

He laid his hand on hers. 'Look, this is embarrassing. But I'm really fond of you, Isis. Really, I mean, I think you're the one.'

'And I'm fond of you too. But I am not going to sleep with you.' She let his hand remain for a while then gently removed it.

'Pity,' he said morosely. 'Are you sure?'

She nodded.

'You'll miss the pillow talk that keeps the girls coming back.'

She shrugged. 'It's hardly an inviting prospect, Dolph – the idea that I would be one in a bus queue of women listening to your ravings.'

'God, you're so fucking prim. Perhaps we should do it now – I mean the pillow talk.'

'If you can do it discreetly.'

'Loosen up, Isis. That's the point of pillow talk.' He drank a glass of wine and smiled at the restaurant. 'Your friend, the man in the bookshop, was doing interesting things with his PC.'

Herrick set down her glass and looked at Dolph's black eyes dancing. 'Can you talk about this *now*?'

'Of course. He has a novel line in screensavers. Actually it's one screensaver – an aquarium with fish swimming across it. You know the kind of thing.'

She nodded.

'Only, his aquarium is different, you see. It's got a little timer in it that ticks away and then releases information.'

'There was a message hidden in the image?'

'Not quite. What happens is this. He logs on in the morning and automatically downloads the same screensaver – same bloody guppies, same bloody eels, same bloody octopus with the smiley face. Then half an hour later, maybe an hour, maybe two hours later – the interval changes according to the day of the week – he clicks on one of the guppies and a message is sent from the screensaver to a pre-prepared file on his hard drive. You only have a few minutes to read it before it disintegrates.'

'Where'd you get this?'

'Friend of mine – a bloke I play poker with in the office. Good guy. Crap at cards though.'

'Why'd he give it to you?' She lowered her voice. 'This is sensitive stuff.'

'He owed me a couple of bob from a game. I told him he had to tell me something interesting to stop me breaking his legs.' He saw Herrick's brow furrow. 'Look, I'm joking. Don't be so fucking serious.'

'What else did you find out?'

'This and that.'

She gave him a look of exasperation.

'Try me,' he said.

'Okay, so why was Norquist here?'

'Cabling – they're going to lay high capacity cables under the Atlantic so the Americans can get more of the stuff they already don't have time to read. It's as simple as that. '

'But why was the Prime Minister involved? That's all a bit nuts and bolts for him, isn't it?'

'Strategic matters also, I hear. That is to say, what are we going to do about the Europeans?' Dolph lit a cigarette and offered her a drag which she declined. 'We'd be good together, Isis. Really, we'd be fucking wonderful because we get each other.'

She shook her head. 'So this screensaver works like a virus?'

'Not quite. It's more targeted than a virus. For one thing it doesn't reproduce itself, and for another it's got a very short life span. If the correct procedure isn't followed at the right moment the message disappears. And here's the beauty of it. If the screensaver is intercepted, all you get is fish. Nothing else. It doesn't work unless you've got the software that goes with it – the male plug and the female socket, if you see what I mean.'

'Yes.'

'Good pillow talk, no?'

She nodded. 'What do you think it means?'

'That Rahe was a shit-load more important than we thought he was.' Dolph looked out on the muddy evening sky. 'The men at the airport, why do you think they were all dressed like Senegalese lottery winners? What was that about?'

'Reverse camouflage,' said Herrick quietly. 'The more noticeable your clothes, the less people look at your face. It's the opposite effect to the one you achieve, Dolph.'

He ignored the remark. 'Like having a parrot on your shoulder?'

'Yes. Can I ask something else?'

'You have my full attention.' He began to fold his napkin.

'Do you think the two things were connected at Heathrow?'

'Of course they were. I quote you the product law of probabilities. 'When two independent events occur simultaneously their combined probability is equal to the product of their individual probabilities of occurrence.' That means it was bloody unlikely that the two events were unconnected. They were *syzygial* – yoked, paired, conjoined, coupled – like we should be.'

He finished the origami with the napkin and balanced it on his shoulder.

'What's that?' she asked.

'A parrot – so you won't notice what I look like.'

706

6

The silence ended with a single dramatic sentence. 'Youssef Rahe was ours.' Richard Spelling said it with studied understatement. 'He was our man.' He folded his arms and looked at her over a pair of slender reading glasses.

Herrick was not totally surprised. She had been at the point of articulating Rahe's double role for herself, but hadn't gone the whole way because of the surveillance operation. Why had they put all that effort into watching a man who was already working for them?

'Was?' she said.

'Yes. His body was found in the boot of a car near the Lebanese border with Syria. He had been very badly treated and finished off with a shot to the head which, without going into detail, made him practically unrecognisable. As well as this, the car had been set alight. However, we are absolutely certain it is Rahe.'

'I see,' she said. 'Was he killed by the second man on the Beirut flight?'

'We're not sure. We suspect he had something to do with it but there were others involved.'

She asked herself why they were telling her this. Not out of any sense of obligation, that was for sure. She had been summoned to the high table and was being told an intimate secret for a reason. She looked around the room and wondered what they wanted from her, apart from silence. The constituent parts of this late-night gathering were altogether odd. Colin Guthrie, head of the joint MI5-MI6 Anti-Terrorism controllerate, well, you would expect him to be there, but not Skeoch Cummings and Keith Manners from the Joint Intelligence Committee. The JIC provided intelligence assessments for the Prime Minister and the Cabinet and wasn't responsible for making or implementing policy, yet here they were, comfortably ensconced in the inner sanctum of the intelligence executive. And why Christine Selvey, the deputy director of Security and Public Affairs? What the fuck was she doing there, with her powdery skin and brittle, bouffant hair which Dolph had described as 'South coast landlady with a passion for china dogs and young actresses'?

There was one other man there and his presence baffled her most. As

707

she entered he had risen, turned and offered her a soft, cool hand and asked after her father, a pleasantry which seemed out of place and was calculated, she thought, to wrong-foot her in some way. Walter Vigo, the former Head of Security and Public Affairs. Isis knew perfectly well that her father would have nothing to do with him. Why was Vigo there and not the Chief? What did Vigo's presence mean six weeks before the handover from Sir Robin Teckman to Spelling? Vigo was the outcast, the defrocked prelate who'd been exposed by a former SIS man, Robert Harland, for his connections with a gun runner and war criminal named Lipnik. She'd got some of the story from her father, who had trained both Vigo and Harland at different times during the Intelligence Officers' New Entry Course. Vigo had escaped prosecution because he was in a position to make life seriously unpleasant for the entire Service. Instead he had been declared a pariah, with Teckman forbidding all contact with him and the members of Mercator, the security consultancy he ran in tandem with an antique book dealing business called Incunabula Inc.

There was silence. She was expected to ask a question. 'If he was ours, why was he under surveillance?'

'Our relationship was a very, very secret matter,' Spelling replied. 'We shared his product, but not his identity with anyone. Only four people knew that he worked for us. Those were his conditions when Walter Vigo came across him two years ago and we abided by them.'

Vigo stirred to give Spelling a nod of gratitude.

'The surveillance was to give him credibility?' persisted Herrick. 'Was that why we laid it in on with a trowel?'

Spelling whipped off his glasses and folded them in his left hand. There was something unpractised and self-conscious in the gesture. 'Yes, he was worried he'd been tumbled.'

'Can I ask whether you knew about the operation at Terminal Three in advance?'

He shook his head. 'No. No, we don't think even he knew what was happening, though he had told us in the morning that he was going to a meeting with some important people. We were hoping for big game. But we had no notion of the switch you spotted and that means he didn't have any idea what was to happen at Terminal Three. We now think he believed he was being observed by them at Heathrow and was worried about making a call to us. No doubt he hoped we were there watching him too and we were, which is how you noticed what had happened. We realised he was in trouble when you called in, but by this time things were unravelling, and it's fair to say we lost sight of what was important. A few hours later he contacted us from a room in the Playlands Hotel in Beirut. They said the meeting would take place in the next few days and that he should stay put until they got in touch with him. Very shortly after making that call he vanished. We didn't have time to get anyone over to the hotel.'

Guthrie coughed and said, 'All of which underlines the thesis implied in your report on the events of May the fourteenth, that the alert over the President's man was a . . .'

'A strategic diversion,' offered Vigo, with his eyes closed.

'To achieve several things,' said Guthrie, 'among which was enticement of Rahe out of the country.'

'Can I ask you if the information about the hit on Norquist came from Rahe's computer?'

Vigo shot her a look of interest.

'What do you know about Rahe's computer?' asked Spelling sharply.

'I assumed that if he was working for us you must have had access to any information that came to him via his PC. After all, he barely left that shop and we had his phone covered so I imagined it was simply a matter of interception somewhere along the line.' This was feeble but she had to protect Andy Dolph. 'I'm simply asking if the information about the possible hit on Norquist came from Rahe, by whatever means. From the outside that seems to be the important point.'

'There was an oblique reference to it amongst the usual blazing rhetoric,' said Guthrie. 'But this was released after he left for Heathrow. Another source confirmed in some detail what was to happen.'

Spelling moved to take control. 'We believe he was unmasked during WAYFARER. As most of you are aware, this was the operation to track a hundred-odd kilos of sulphur and two hundred of acetone from Rotterdam to Harwich and then on to a factory in Birmingham. They must have examined their security arrangements after that and come up with Rahe's name. He was involved in some of the shipping arrangements.

'The important thing is that Rahe was tortured very badly indeed. He will have told them everything he knew about us before he died, which owing to Walter's deft handling was kept to a minimum. Still, he wouldn't have failed to learn quite a bit during the course of the twenty-odd months he was working for us, if only from the questions we asked him. And we must assume certain techniques are now in the hands of the terrorists.'

There was a pause. Vigo had listened to this expectantly, as though waiting to make a bid at an auction, but he said nothing. Christine Selvey seemed to be readying herself for something – a straightening of the back, a pluck at the front of her Sunday blouse.

'We heard you were out at Heathrow yesterday,' said Guthrie in what was clearly a planned intervention. 'What were you doing there?'

'Trying to tie up some loose ends for my own satisfaction. I wondered if the murder of the lavatory attendant and his family had anything to do with the man who was seen watching aircraft landing from the public viewing terrace. You see I hadn't heard from—'

'Yes, well, no more blundering around like that,' said Spelling fiercely. 'This is a very delicate situation and we can't afford the local police or anyone else putting it all together and feeding the theory to the media. Nobody – I repeat *nobody* – must know that we appreciate the real significance of the events at Heathrow.'

Given that she'd spotted what was really significant that day, Herrick didn't much feel like the gesture of submission that was called for, but she apologised nonetheless, saying that it was often difficult for someone at her level to see the whole picture.

'There is one thing,' she said, levelling her gaze at Spelling. 'Won't our discovery of Rahe's body in Beirut mean they expect us to go back over his movements at Heathrow? After all, he was meant to be in Kuwait or the Gulf States, not the Lebanon, and that might very well lead us to check which plane he boarded and so go over the film.'

'It's a good point,' said Vigo. 'I'd like to know the answer to that one.'

Spelling shook his head. 'We didn't move the body. His wife doesn't know he's dead and I'm afraid we're going to leave things that way. She must believe he's alive in order for our operation to go ahead. And they must believe we've lost him. It will be essential to the safety of the people we're going to put in the field over the next few days.' He cleared his throat. 'As you know, the Chief has asked me to oversee the setting up of RAPTOR, the name of our response to the events of May the fourteenth. You will hear in the next few days what your part will be – the arrangements are being finalised at the moment – but I wanted to speak to you this evening because everyone involved must understand that this is an exclusively transatlantic operation. We are going to work very closely with the Americans on this, but not with the Europeans.'

'International cooperation in the war against terrorism is still at a very early stage of development. Everyone pitches in and there have been some notable achievements in the sharing of information, but we're a long way from full co-operation. You'll remember Djamel Beghal, one of the men who was planning to blow up the US Embassy in Paris. He was arrested on his way back from Afghanistan and began to talk, providing valuable names and addresses, top grade material in fact. The counter-intelligence services of France, Spain, Belgium and Holland ran a joint surveillance operation in their individual territories to watch the cell at work. But then details were leaked to the French press, with the result that most of the network escaped. One or two were arrested, but there wasn't enough evidence to put them away for any length of time. In our opinion it was a serious loss not to be able to observe and watch these people's MO, the way they moved their money, communicated, planned, provided themselves with false papers and the supplies necessary for the large-scale attacks that they need to keep their movement alive. That's something we're not going to allow to happen again. Owing to your excellent work at Heathrow – a superb piece of intelligence gathering – we are now in a position to watch eleven individuals who are currently under surveillance as they merge into their new covers. We and the Americans plan to observe these men and get a fix on the person running the European networks. We know next to nothing about him, but believe him to be in Europe.'

'The same man who planned May fourteen,' she said. It now seemed more like fact than opinion.

'Possibly – certainly a very ambitious mind was deployed that day, someone who sees an operation as a means of achieving several things at once. It was daring and well thought-out to pull off an assassination of that order while shuffling his men around Europe.'

'But surely—' she began.

'If you wouldn't mind.' Spelling gave a tight smile that indicated he wouldn't suffer the interruption. 'I should have mentioned that tests have been carried out and there's no doubt that the bullet came from the machine pistol in the first van. Abdul Muid was the assassin. I gather that will be the finding of the inquest that opens tomorrow. It will also make plain the pattern that the two men – Muid and Jamil Siddiqi – were pulled from our midst to perform these acts of terrorism. Neither of their backgrounds suggests training by al-Qaeda in any formal sense, which I think is an interesting aspect · that the Security Services will want to explore. There is still no trace of the lorry driver, which perhaps indicates that he was an integral part of the plot, rather than someone who was caught up in the incident.'

Skeoch Cummings nodded. Guthrie brushed the end of his nose twice while Vigo looked into the distance with an expression that suggested he had not even heard what was being said.

Fine, she thought, they're running with that fiction. The possibility that a British bullet had killed Norquist was not going to be contemplated, which obviously suited both sides. The Americans knew what had happened, but when it came to their closest allies they were capable of miraculous forbearance. After all, they had absorbed the blow of Israeli warplanes attacking and sinking the USS *Liberty* spy ship in the Six Day War without any public comment whatsoever. Norquist had already been buried at the Arlington National Cemetery with full military honours. His widow had received the folded Stars and Stripes from the President himself and not a word of official complaint had been made. Not in public, at any rate.

But it was another matter in private, she thought. The White House must have used Norquist's death to maximise the US position. They would have received something in exchange and it was likely to be the contents of her report passed up to Number Ten through the Joint Intelligence Committee. She imagined a telephone conversation between the White House and Number Ten during which the President insisted that the US be involved as an equal partner in the pursuit of the live cell. That meant the continental intelligence services would be kept in the dark.

Now she understood why Teckman was not there. The Chief had either lost the battle to keep the Europeans involved, or was standing back waiting for his successor to make a hash of things while he was still in control. Whatever the tactic, it was his absence that gave the meeting its furtive air. This, and Vigo. Spelling may have been in the chair but it was Vigo's return that established a new era of transatlantic exclusivity.

Spelling put on his glasses again and read something from the paper in front of him. Then he looked up, as if to address the whole room, and began to outline RAPTOR. Each of the eleven men so far identified and tracked would be allotted an entire team that would remain permanently on that individual's case. In effect the teams would mimic the classic cell structure of terrorist organisations, shadowing the suspects and bedding in around them with an equal regard for cover and security. Herrick would be in one of those teams, and those involved would be expected to drop everything for the operation. That requirement had had some influence on the personnel being chosen: men and women with families would take roles where they could be inserted and removed without rippling the surface. Both the CIA and MI6 would call on the services of retired intelligence officers used to long-term surveillance operations, who would bring the field skills that were perhaps lacking in some of the younger generation.

'This is about close surveillance of an exceptionally discreet order,' he said, splaying his fingers on the table. 'It may go on for months, even years, because that is the timescale the terrorists work with. We will have to match their stamina and patience. Every step of the way will be monitored by us here and the Americans at Langley and Fort Mead. The risk assessment for the entire operation will be provided by the staff of the Joint Intelligence Committee, which will report three times a week. The Americans have agreed to abide by their recommendations though I stress that these reports will not define policy. The JIC will simply gauge the degree of menace presented by these men at any given moment. The Americans will naturally take their own view of how things are progressing and have insisted that each surveillance team has access to armed back-up. That means they can move against a target and arrest him if the situation requires. And so can we.'

Spelling's confident presentation of the battle plan didn't fool anyone. If the Americans and British, already welded together in an exclusive eavesdropping treaty known as Echelon, were to start killing or seizing suspects on European soil, untold damage would be done to an already shaky Western alliance. The resentment would last for years. This was to say nothing of the risk – or in Herrick's mind, the certainty – of one or other European agency catching on and, out of justified concern or sheer bloodymindedness, pre-empting the situation by arresting the suspect and causing the others to flee. She also knew that the terrorists were nothing if not close students of Western intelligence tradecraft, and that the mastermind who had planned the switch at Heathrow would be the kind of man who had set up tripwires to give early warning of just such an operation. Sooner or later, someone would stumble across one.

Everyone got this. Equally, they understood they were just at the start of RAPTOR. As time went on, the situation would change; the grand scheme would be buffeted by chance and circumstance. They were going along with it because during an operation the policy makers – in this case a none too bright President and a Prime Minister with attention deficit problems – would become dependent on those who implemented their plan. All of which meant there were great opportunities for the secret servants: advancement, increase in influence and, in Vigo's case, rehabilitation.

But why show *her* the secret mechanism? The answer, of course, was that she had made the breakthrough, put it all together, so Spelling had been forced to include her. But why not Dolph, Sarre and Lapping? Simple. She had written the two-page report and then followed it up with her own inquiries at Heathrow. She understood the total operation on May 14 but had not spoken about it to them. That's what distinguished her and that's why Spelling had to get her on-side.

Spelling moved his papers together and looked around the table. 'I think we've just about covered everything. Isis, have you any questions? You will of course be briefed over the coming week. In the meantime, I suggest you take some leave, say two days. We'll see you on Wednesday. You'll receive instructions tomorrow about time and place.'

'There's one thing,' she said. 'I want to get clear in my mind why we're excluding the European agencies as a matter of course.'

'Because that's what our political masters have decided,' replied Spelling crisply. 'And that is what the Chief agreed with the Prime Minister and Foreign Secretary this morning at Chequers.'

The invocation of all these authorities seemed weak, apparently even to Vigo, whom she was now sure owed his place in the secret deliberations to something more than his recruitment of Youssef Rahe. He shut his eyes with a hint of exasperation, and Herrick had the odd sensation that it didn't matter whether they were open or closed, Vigo still watched.

She was dismissed a few minutes later and left convinced that she'd already blown it by raising the business about the Europeans. It was crass of her, especially as she now understood that the sole point of the meeting had been to test her reliability, to see if she was fit for the game only the adults played.

She went to her desk, picked up her bag and left a note saying she would be out for a couple of days and if there were any problems to call Guthrie or Spelling. She saw a few people – the shades that always haunted Vauxhall Cross at night – but there was no sign of Dolph, Sarre or Lapping, whom she knew would be regarded somehow as her co-conspirators. They would be seen too, but she didn't think they'd get the full treatment with Madame Selvey, Walter Vigo and the inscrutable pair from the JIC.

She left the building, collecting the cell phone that always had to be checked in at the front entrance. As she walked out into the dreary no man's land of the Albert Embankment she noticed that she had a text message. 'Drnk tonite any time – Dolph.'

She replied. 'No thanx. Dead tired.'

7

Khan expected the Albanians to descend into the valley once they crossed over from Macedonia, but they marched on into the mountains taking increasingly untravelled, treacherous paths that caused the six mules to stop every so often, snort and shake themselves as if to adjust their loads. After the first exchange with the head man who had given his name as Vajgelis, they said little to Khan and seemed bent on covering as much ground as possible before the middle of the day. A couple of the youths tagged along behind, apparently speculating about him and his bundle of possessions, which they occasionally poked with their sticks. He turned round and grinned at them, but the only response was a surly lift of the chin to tell him to keep his eyes on the way ahead.

When the sun was at its highest they stopped in the shade of some pine trees and squatted to eat a little cold meat and onion stew, produced from tall canteens. They offered it to him saying, 'Conlek, eat Conlek.' In return he offered them food stolen from the Macedonian kitchen, and then asked for water. They gave it to him gracelessly and now seemed to be making jokes at his expense. He smiled, nodded and thanked them. He remembered what they had said in Bosnia, the tales of savagery and endless slaughter amongst their Muslim cousins in Albania. For nearly thirty years the country had been the world's only official atheist state and under Enver Hoxha the people had happily pulled down their mosques or turned them into cinemas and warehouses. The civilised Bosnians shuddered at the godless barbarity of what had happened under the Marxists. But there again, he thought, he'd seen plenty of that kind of thing in Afghanistan without doing anything: the destruction of monuments; the execution of a whimpering boy who'd been caught listening to a music tape. He'd seen it and, willingly or not, he'd been part of it.

After eating, the Albanians dispersed through the woods to sleep, leaving a couple of men to guard the mules. Khan lay back where he had been sitting on a carpet of pine needles and, hugging his gun and pack into his stomach, told himself that he must snatch the rest while he could. He closed his eyes in the songless, dry forest and fell asleep thinking that he would now have to make his way to Italy rather than Greece. They were a more tolerant people.

In what seemed a very short time he was woken by someone tugging at his gun. The muzzle of a pistol was drawn across his cheek. He looked up. The two young men who'd trailed him during the morning were crouching either side of him.

'Come Mujahadin. Good. Come.' Standing above them was Zek, one of the mule guards, who placed his boot on the AK47 while one of the younger men pulled it gently from Khan's grasp. The third, who had been holding the pistol to his face, withdrew it.

'Okay. Mujahadin. Come.' Zek, who was a wiry man of about twenty-five, motioned for them to hurry. Khan got up and shook himself free of their grasp. He didn't know what they wanted, but since they had tossed his gun away he had to go with them. They walked to a hollow, about fifty yards from where the others were sleeping, and he was prodded roughly down the slope. Khan thought he knew what they were going to do. What they planned to do afterwards was anyone's guess – shoot him and say he had started the fight, or simply throw him down the ravine they had skirted a few minutes before entering the forest? He raised both hands and made as if to welcome the idea by reaching out to touch Zek's shoulder.

Zek told the two younger men to hold Khan over the tree, and started unbuckling himself to reveal a rank pair of undershorts. With an interested glance Khan again tried to show that he was more than happy about the situation and indeed enjoyed the prospect of indulging them. He even made to undo his own trousers. But they turned him and forced his head down violently on the tree trunk. The smell of resin and forest mould reached his nostrils. He glanced under the young man's arm and saw the guard behind readying himself. Lust had drained all meaning from his expression and he hissed for his two accomplices to hurry. Khan placed his feet squarely apart, to appear cooperative, and wiggled with a little coo of excitement. The young man holding the gun to his head sniggered, relaxed his grip and swapped hands to free himself to help yank Khan's trousers down. This was the opening Khan had waited for. He slipped from under his captor's arm and jabbed his left elbow back twice into his face, grabbing the barrel of the pistol and sending him to the ground. The completion of the movement brought him face to face with Zek, whose expression flooded with consternation. He smiled awkwardly just before Khan butted him once in the forehead, then knocked him cold with a second blow from his forehead delivered as he grabbed the man's shoulders and held him.

He spun round, but there was no need to attack the third boy, who had jumped away, raising his hands with a sly smile as if to say the whole thing had been a bit of harmless horseplay. Khan arranged his clothing and walked to the top of the hollow where he found Vajgelis contemplating the scene. He held Khan's AK47 under his arm, his hands tucked into the waistband of his chocolate brown corduroys.

'These men shit,' he said, his chin jutting with contempt. 'These men, they fuck pigs. I sorry for these hospitality. These men . . .' Words failed him, he shook his head and held out the machine gun for Khan, at the same time reaching for the pistol that Khan had taken from the young man. As Vajgelis took hold of it, he snatched the machine gun back from Khan's grasp. 'You walk with me now, Mujahadin.'

A minute or two later the two injured men staggered up from the hollow with blood over their faces. Zek's nose was split and ballooning. They went to Vajgelis and Khan understood they were pleading to be allowed to kill him, but the request met with a tirade of abuse from Vajgelis, who tweaked Zek's ear and cuffed the younger man around the head.

A few minutes later they set off, Vajgelis at the head of the column and Khan just behind him with two older men now appointed as his minders. For four or five hours they walked along the parched tracks. As the sun sank behind the mountains they came to a lumber road littered with bark. The mules were tethered to the trees where they hung their heads and steamed and stamped their hooves. The men stood around smoking and glancing down the mountain.

Shortly, Khan saw truck lights slash through the trees and heard it grinding up towards them with many changes of gear. The men began to loosen the straps on the mules, but were told to stop by Vajgelis. He ordered them into the middle of the track with their guns showing. The truck appeared a few minutes later and pulled up. About a dozen men, all armed to the teeth, scrambled down from the back and flashed torches across the faces of the men in the road. Vajgelis moved forward. Recognising the driver of the truck, he signalled for the mules to be brought up and unloaded.

Long before this moment Khan had suspected that Vajgelis's band was involved in drug smuggling, not insurgency, and as the first tightly filled sacks were deposited at the tailgate of the truck, he wasn't in the least surprised to see the driver slit one open with a knife and taste the contents. Each time a mule was unloaded he sampled at random.

The time came for departure and the men from both sides lined up to face each other. Vajgelis pointed to a man in the line opposite and beckoned him across the track. Khan realised they were exchanging hostages. Now it was the driver's turn. Vajgelis moved closer to Khan, laid an arm round his shoulder and moved him back out of range of the truck lights. The trick worked perfectly. The driver walked over to them, placed his hand on Khan's other shoulder and steered him to the truck. Vajgelis laughed and murmured, 'Mujahadin is shit also.'

Khan was thrown in the back and nobody took much notice of him as the truck made its way down the mountain and then bumped across a flat plain to the coast. A couple of hours later, the truck suddenly turned off the road, careered down a rutted track and juddered to a halt. The men tumbled out, unloaded the sacks and bore them off to a jetty where a powerboat was tethered. Khan could make out its shape in the dark and he heard the engine's exhaust spluttering in the gentle swell.

They set off back up the mountains and after a couple more hours came to a small, almost derelict village. They pulled up in some kind of farmyard or compound. Cats darted from the lights of the truck and some dogs barked. Here the remnants of an old agricultural living were jumbled with the trophies of drug trafficking. There were animal stalls, a collapsed cart and a hay-rick, but also a large satellite dish and a pair of identical black SUVs chained by the fenders to a metal post. Khan was stiff from the ride and moved gingerly into the light. When the men saw his face for the first time there was a sudden uproar, and he was pulled from one man to another, spat upon, kicked and rifle-butted. There was no doubt in Khan's mind that these were his last moments on earth. But their anger subsided and the driver who had picked him from Vajgelis' group walked up and looked him over, muttering imprecations under his breath and asking questions. All Khan could do was smile idiotically and shake his head saying, 'English? I speak English only.'

'No ingleesh,' said the driver. 'No ingleesh.'

He was taken to one of the stalls and tied to a beam, while they made a cursory search of his possessions. At length someone was fetched from a neighbouring village to interpret. He was a mild, emaciated man in middle age, wearing mittens and a scarf wrapped around his head though the night was warm. He introduced himself to Khan as Mr Skender. He had once been a waiter in London, he said, but returned to his village after developing tuberculosis. To Khan he looked very sick indeed.

'I have to hear some things from you,' said Skender, rubbing the circulation into his hands and wiping a runny nose. He gestured to the driver. 'Mr Berisha wants to know why you are working with Vajgelis. Tell Mr Berisha who you are.'

Khan gave his name and said that he had come overland from Pakistan, looking for work in the West. All the time looking directly at Berisha, he said he was from a high-born family but that he was without money. He had rich friends in the United States – one who was like a brother to him. This man would reward handsomely anyone who helped him now, in a way that was beyond Mr Berisha's dreams. He added that they should take no notice of his present appearance.

Skender gave a brief translation to the driver, who called for a table and chairs. More lights were brought. Berisha sat down and poured some *konjak* for Skender and himself.

'Mr Berisha thinks you are terrorist,' said Skender.

'Then tell Mr Berisha that I'm not a terrorist,' said Khan. 'All I want is to find work and continue my medical studies.'

'You are a doctor?' asked Skender doubtfully.

'I studied medicine in London and I plan to return there to continue.'

At the end of the translation Berisha stroked his chin and growled a few sentences.

'Mr Berisha wants to know why a doctor, an *educated* man, is in the mountains with Vajgelis? He is a very dangerous man, this Vajgelis. You are fortunate to be alive. He trusts only his own people.'

Khan told him about the killings on the road, his flight from the Macedonian security forces and how he'd met Vajgelis' group on the border. Berisha sat with his lower lip hanging and his foxy little eyes darting around Khan, as if this would somehow prise out his secret. Skender explained that Berisha was a very clever man: Khan's presence there was like a philosophical problem to him. He might be a Muslim terrorist, or he could be a Macedonian agent who'd been sent to infiltrate the network and report back to the authorities. Maybe he was a plant from the Vajgelis clan to see if his part of the network could be taken over. The very thought of this prompted Berisha to get up and prowl around the stable stabbing at his imagined foes in the dark.

'Mr Berisha wishes you to know that he is strong and will not tolerate a challenge to his authority in this part of the mountains from Vajgelis. He will cut Mr Vajgelis' testicles and feed them to his dogs. He wishes you to tell this to Vajgelis if you are allowed to live long enough to see him again.'

To emphasise this point, Berisha opened a door and allowed two fighting dogs to bound into the stable and sniff around Khan's feet.

Skender went rigid. 'Mr Berisha will discover the truth of your mission if he has to rip your testicles off with his own teeth.'

'I can see that Mr Berisha is a man of standing,' said Khan, making sure that he did not give the dogs the slightest provocation. 'But tell him I could not be a plant because he chose me. Mr Berisha walked to the line and chose me himself. Vajgelis could not have engineered that.'

'Mr Berisha believes he was tricked by Vajgelis to think you are important to him,' said Skender with a note of sympathy entering his voice. 'He says you are worthless. Now he is having to pay money for his cousin who is with Vajgelis and that makes Mr Berisha very angry. He says he may kill you now because you are a worthless piece of shit. Forgive me, Mr Khan, this is Mr Berisha's words, not mine.'

'But it is obvious that I am worth more alive than dead.'

Skender tried to translate this but was suddenly silenced by a dusty cough that rose from the depths of his lungs and convulsed his whole body. At one point Khan thought he'd pass out from lack of oxygen but

Skender eventually managed to recover and drank a little of the *konjak*. Then he wiped his eyes and nose with his shirt-sleeve, throwing Khan a glance of terrible resignation.

'You should see a doctor.'

Skender shook his head and inhaled gently so as not to aggravate his lungs again.

'Tell Mr Berisha that I will only talk to him if he pays for your medical help.'

'I cannot tell him this,' Skender looked shocked. 'You do not bargain with Mr Berisha. Mr Berisha is the boss here.'

The driver made them go back over the ground they'd covered while he finished the bottle. Then his head began to droop. He got up, ejected the dogs and announced that he would decide what to do in the morning. In the meantime both Khan and Skender would sleep in the stable under guard. Skender seemed to have expected this and, without complaint, lay down on a rough blanket and wrapped the free side around him. Khan was cut down and his possessions thrown at his feet. He pulled them into some order but instead of laying out his bed-roll, he propped himself up and tried to block out the smell of drains that seeped from under the wall. Any fears he had about falling into too deep a sleep soon vanished with the sounds that came from the house, the unmistakable noise of a woman being beaten and taken by force.

Khan looked over to Skender who raised his hands above him hopelessly. 'In what neighbourhood in London you were living?' he asked by way of distracting them from the murderous noises next door.

Khan replied that he had shared an apartment in Camden Town with some students.

'I am living in Hoxton,' Skender said. ' There was I happy.' His cough began again, with a more rasping note.

Khan listened for a while then reached down to the bottom of his trousers and silently made a little opening in the seam. From the cavity in the material he withdrew a roll of money slightly thicker than a cigarette. He got up, crab-walked over to Skender and placed the four twenty dollar bills – half of what he had left – in the palm of his hand. 'This will buy you a visit to a doctor and some medication. It seems that I may not need it now.'

Skender shook his head but his hand closed around the money. 'Thank you, Mister Khan.'

'I want you to do something for me in exchange. Do you have a pen?'

He produced a stub of pencil from his pocket and handed it to Khan, who quickly wrote a message on one of the three remaining postcards.

'I want you to send this to America by airmail. If I am killed, please write separately to the address and tell them how and where I died. You understand? Tell him what is happening to me.'

Skender took the postcard and slipped it into his clothing. Khan scuttled back to his bundle to await his chance to escape, reflecting that he had never been in as wretched and menacing a place. Berisha was, he thought, probably mad. He felt that anything could happen to a human being who came into Berisha's orbit. For a time he listened to a young woman's voice alternately wailing and remonstrating until the volume of the TV was turned up and a soccer game drowned her words.

Next thing he knew it was daylight. He woke to see Berisha sitting not far from him, holding a cup. He was dressed in sports kit – trainers with a gold Nike flash and an outlandish American football jacket with a dragon emblazoned up one side. Beside him stood Skender and two men in uniform.

'Mr Berisha has made decision,' said Skender apologetically. 'You must go with these men from police.'

Isis Herrick was met at Newcastle station by her father, who had bought himself a new car, a replacement for the dark blue Humber Super Snipe that had met with an unspecified end a month before. The Armstrong Siddeley Sapphire was older and less sedate. Herrick eyed it with little enthusiasm, but the journey to Hopelaw village fifteen miles over the Scottish border passed without incident and the car did seem to make her father happy. As they climbed through the moorland, upholstered in the soft green of new bracken, her spirits lifted and she told him that she was coming round to the Siddeley.

They didn't talk properly until after lunch, when they took a walk up to Hopelaw Camp, an iron-age fort above the house. They reached a flat rock pitted with ancient cup and ring carvings and sat down. The discussion was new for them: they had never spoken about her job, let alone discussed individual operations, and she thought they would find it awkward. But he listened to her acutely, gazing south, his eyes watering slightly in the breeze, occasionally pressing her for detail.

'When your mother died,' he said, 'I thought the best thing I could do was to keep you out of this business. But it wasn't my choice, was it? You did what you wanted and you never asked my advice.' He searched her face. 'But at least you're doing so now.'

He picked up a field snail's striped shell and examined it carefully. She knew it might appear in one of the paintings her father had been producing on and off since he was required to find himself a convincing cover during World War II in the Pyrenees. Herricks were now more sought after than ever; they fetched thousands of dollars in America and on the continent, although his work was generally disdained by art critics for the simple reason that they missed the point of minutely recorded still lifes. One said that they were just 'quotations' from nature.

He peered at the shell again. 'It's the surface of things that's usually important. Most people don't understand that everything is staring them in the face. They just have to look a little harder than they are accustomed to. Here, have a squint at this.' He handed her the shell and a magnifying glass. 'You'll see that there's a yellowish varnish that's been worn away in some parts by the sun, and beneath that there are little ripples made as the snail secretes the substances that make the shell. From the top you can see the black stripe achieves a more or less perfect spiral, yet there are flaws in the design that remind you of the miracle of its creation. Here you have all you need to know about the snail, but it's remarkable how few people are willing to spend time looking closely at anything.'

She had heard the lecture before. She handed the shell back to him. 'It's lovely. But what do you think about this operation?'

The old man looked across the hills, and she wondered whether she should be bothering him with it. 'Intelligence work contradicts my view about the surface of things,' he said, 'I think your operation is probably destined to failure because of that.'

'How?'

'Because you can't get an idea what these people are planning from simply watching them. Before the attacks on America in 2001, I understand various security agencies had those characters in their sights. The cell in Germany was under surveillance and I believe someone in the FBI had noticed that they were taking flying lessons. They were looking but they didn't see.'

'That was a failure of the system – people not putting it together with other data.'

'Data! How I do hate that word.'

'You know what I mean, Dad – intelligence. They weren't analysing it properly.'

'The only way to deal with these bastards is to penetrate their organisation and that's going to take a long time, unless you're lucky enough to have one of them drop into your lap. None of it's going to mean much until you've got the man on the inside telling you what's going to happen.'

She told him about the murder of Youssef Rahe.

'That's a bad sign,' he said. 'It means they know you tried and are now aware of the process which led him to become your man, the recruitment and so on.'

'Yes, he was tortured.'

'But not by the characters who have flown into Europe for their big party. Some other part of their organisation determined that he was working for you and got hold of him.' He coughed and felt for a pipe that wasn't in his pocket. He had given up tobacco four months before. 'In that case I think this is a very dangerous affair. These people have already proved exceptionally adept at carrying on their business while being observed. I'd take the view that there's very little useful intelligence to be had from watching them. Arrest the whole lot and throw them into jail on whatever charges keep them in there longest – or worse.'

'You mean kill them?'

'Yes, these men have no fear of suicide. They've moved to a certain level. You can't reason with men like that or seduce them from the cause because self-interest in the normal sense has been rejected.' He paused and raised his eyebrows. 'And Teckman is apparently out of the picture?'

She nodded.

'And that bloody little tick Vigo is back – astonishing!'

'Yes.'

'Well, I doubt the Chief is really out of it. Just lying doggo, waiting to make his move.'

'Against his successor?'

'Let's hope so. Spelling is all mouth and no trousers. Complete phoney.'

She smiled. Her father's forceful opinions meant that he had never stood a chance of rising in the Service, although the operations he conducted against the KGB along the Iron Curtain for twenty-five years were textbook studies, celebrated for their panache and cunning. He had once summarised it thus: 'They relied on my judgement to keep myself and others alive in the field, but when I got back to London I was expected to let others think for me. I couldn't get used to it.'

'What about the operation itself,' she asked. 'Any advice for me?'

'You know it all, Isis. Probably more than I do. The first thing you must realise is that these men know they're in enemy territory. They're like we were during the war. We couldn't trust anybody in France and these holy warriors will suspect everyone they come in contact with. They will have had training in anti-surveillance techniques, so don't fall into any dry cleaning traps. If they're taking a particular route every day they'll get used to the sights along that route and will know what is normal. They will also build in a couple of observation spots along the way so they'll be able to tell when they're being followed. Apply all the same rules if cars are involved, only more strictly.'

She nodded. She knew most of it but there was no stopping him now.

'What you need to do is to learn the place thoroughly before you start the watch. There wasn't a street I didn't know in Stockholm or Vienna during the Fifties. I could have been a tour guide in Istanbul. This is very important: you can't just go to a foreign town and blend into the scenery without knowing the place like the back of your hand. Take care with your clothes, too. Study what the women wear locally. There're always slight variations of fashion between towns on the continent. A particular shop may be popular and you will need to get one or two items from there. If you need cover, a job to help you get close to your target, choose this very, very carefully. It's important to keep your flexibility, so don't rush into his local café and get yourself work as a waitress on the grounds that he visits the place twice a week. You won't learn anything that way and you'll tie yourself up. Other opportunities will present themselves.'

He stopped and examined her with fierce compassion. 'Isis, you know these men aren't playing things the way we used to. If we were spotted it often didn't matter. It was part of the game of cat and mouse. But these men are utterly ruthless – they butcher air stewardesses without the slightest qualm; they think nothing of killing thousands of people one fine morning. They're different from what we had to face – much, much more dangerous. But remember, you're different too. You're one of the few people who know the full extent of the operation against them. If you fall into their hands, they may work out that you have a lot to tell them and that is not an enviable position to be in.' He put up his hand to stop her interrupting. 'Of course I know there will be others with you, but from what I gather your people are nothing like as good at field craft as we were. Not interested in the detail, no preparation. You'll have to watch your colleagues as closely as you do your own behaviour. I don't want some berk from Vauxhall Cross on the phone telling me you've been killed, do you hear? You've got to use your own judgement.'

He slapped his hand against his thigh and then rubbed his knee. 'It's not much fun, this business of getting old. I've lost the feeling in my legs sitting here. I'm going to have to move.'

She helped him up. They stood on the Cup and Ring Rock and he looked at her, his rigid grey hair standing up in the wind, his eyes misted by limitless affection. 'You know I can't help seeing your mother in you. It's twenty-four years since she died, but there hasn't been a day I didn't think about her. And now I see you so close to the age she was when she died, well . . . I fear for you, Isis.' He stopped and looked apologetically down at her. 'It's an old fellow's panic, I know. But I think I've reason enough to be worried.'

'Come on, Dad. I may look like Mum but inside I'm all you – hard and practical.'

'You're going to have to be very hard and very practical,' he said, almost angrily. 'Don't lose your concentration for a moment.'

They took the longer route back to Hopelaw House, stopping along the way for her father to pluck things from the hedgerows and scrape pieces of moss from the trees. 'I mean to go on to some studies of lichen,' he said, 'and the moths that pretend to be lichen. They're getting rarer and that's because their camouflage is only good for one set of circumstances. The lichen disappears with all this pollution and the moth is left sticking out like a sore thumb. So, end of moth. It's a point to remember. Your cover should be adaptable.'

'Dad! I've been trained.'

'Yes, you have,' he said as though to scold.

They tramped back to Hopelaw House and her father disappeared into his study where the bits and pieces he had collected on the walk were interred in cotton wool. Then he emerged clutching a felt envelope.

'Found this the other day,' he said. 'Thought you ought to have it. Mislaid it for years.'

She undid the package and found inside a photograph frame and a small black and white picture of herself and her mother, bent double with laughter in the sunlight of an afternoon long ago.

8

Khan was beaten casually and inexpertly as a natural part of detention. Perversely the treatment gave him hope. As he sat, shackled to a chair in the first-floor interview room, hearing the sound of children playing in a sunny courtyard below, he reasoned that if the police had thought him important, they'd have made sure that they could hand him over to higher authorities without a cut lip, swollen eye and bruised ribs.

The police captain, a man named Nemim, had departed. Khan sat respectfully and passively, hoping to look cowed. The hot afternoon passed slowly. A lone policeman sat in a chair tilted against the wall. An old 303 rifle lay in his lap. Khan thought that he might be able to overpower him, if he could persuade them to remove his manacles – perhaps for prayer – and climb down from the window into the courtyard. But where to after that? He didn't have the strength to run. He had caught sight of his reflection in the police van's mirror on the way in and hardly recognised the haggard face staring back. He looked condemned, just like the two poor Pakistanis on the road. It would be better to sit this out; get some food in him, sleep, make a plan.

This discussion with himself ended when Captain Nemim came back with a sheaf of papers and an open notebook. A look of animated curiosity had entered his expression. Khan realised that Nemim now saw him as an opportunity, a gift to an officer who could speak English and harboured ambitions way above his present tenure as the chief in a mountain station.

'So, Mister Khan, or is it Mister Jasur? What do we call you?'

'Khan – Mister Khan.'

'Then why you are carrying these documentations belonging to Mister Jasur?'

'Mister Jasur died when we were chased by Macedonian security forces. I took his possessions so I could tell his family when I reached safety.'

'Ah yes, the terrorist party executed by the Macedonians. You were with them?'

'Yes, and so was Jasur. But we were not terrorists. You have to believe

726

me. He was a Palestinian. A refugee. He died of a heart attack while we were escaping.'

'Of course we Albanians are used to these stories about terrorists. To the Macedonians and Greeks we are all terrorists and we do not believe what they tell us. But the Macedonian army say there were eight terrorists on the road.'

'That's right. We were just looking for work. We wanted to go to Greece. Those men with me were all innocent. None of them was carrying a weapon.'

'But, Mister Khan, you are not understanding what I am saying to you. Maybe you do this on purpose – not understanding me?'

'No, no. I am trying to understand what you want.'

'They say there were seven terrorists and one other who escaped after he was cutting the Macedonian with knife.'

'Yes, that's right. That was me. I stabbed him and took his gun.'

'Look at these photographs. Mister Khan.' Captain Nemim flourished a newspaper and showed him a photograph of a mortuary in Skopje. Seven bodies were lined up and at their feet lay an assortment of automatic weapons, pistols and grenade launchers. Khan recognised the men – the Kurdish trio, the Pakistanis and the rest of them, laid out like trophies with their killers standing behind them.

'They weren't carrying these weapons,' he said.

'We know that,' said Nemim. 'This weapons used by the Macedonian security forces. But you make not to understand me again. I am not stupid man, Mister Khan. You see? Which is the Palestinian gentleman please?'

Khan peered at the picture. 'He's not here. They must have left him on the hill. Maybe they didn't find him.'

'But you say seven men were killed. There are seven bodies here but where is Mister Jasur?'

'Hold on,' said Khan, adding up the members of the party again.

'Maybe he was ghost. Maybe this Jasur has flown away.' Nemim seemed pleased with his sarcasm and looked to the junior officer who had come into the room, as if to say this is how it is done; you are watching a master at work, a man who is going far.

'But the soldier I injured with the knife knew there were two of us who escaped. He would have reported this to his senior officer. There were nine people in our group.'

'No, this is what they say. The Macedonians like to boast about this murders so there is no reason for them to lie. They say seven men were killed and one escaped. That is you. There is no other man.'

'But they saw the other man . . .'

Nemim shook his head. 'There was no other man.'

There followed a hurried exchange with the junior officer during which

Nemim's eyes never strayed from Khan's. Then the junior left and Nemim folded his hands on the table with a look of satisfaction.

'You know we weren't terrorists,' said Khan. 'You said yourself that these weapons belong to the Macedonians. So why are you holding me here?'

'It is necessary for us to know who you are. I have spoken to Mr Vajgelis.' He nodded several times to signal that this was the first of many trump cards. 'Mr Vajgelis says you are fighter. He saw you attack the security forces with a machine gun and then you were wounding his men with your head and arm like this.' He threw his elbow backwards and did a head butting action. 'He say you are professional Mujahadin. And you tell him you are Mujahadin. You are saying this to Mr Vajgelis. That is why he gives you to Mr Berisha and Mr Berisha gives you to me. They are good men.'

Khan's shoulders sagged, as much out of fatigue as frustration. 'Good men?' he said. 'What are they taking to the coast – peanuts and Coca Cola? These are good men in your country, Captain Nemim? No, they are drug smugglers. If these are good Albanians, I pity your country.'

Nemim leaned forward and hit him hard with the back of his hand on both sides of his face. 'Who are you?' he shouted. 'What are you doing here in our country?'

A rotten taste spread in Khan's mouth, which at first he imagined was some physical manifestation of his fear, but then he realised that the blow on the left side of his face must have burst an abscess. It was months since he'd cleaned his teeth properly and he had been aware of a swelling on his gum. In Afghanistan he had periodically developed these infections, lancing them himself and treating them by washing his mouth out frequently with salt water. He supposed the bacteria had never cleared properly and in time built up to form another abscess. But this gush of decay in his mouth was something else entirely and he was disgusted – by this taste and also, now he came to think about it, the stench that rose from every part of his body and seemed to fill the room.

'I will tell you about myself, Captain, but I must wash. I need to do this, sir. You can hit me as much as you like, but I will talk better if I am allowed to do this. For our religion I should wash before I pray this evening.'

The Captain considered this for a few seconds then gave some instructions to a policeman standing outside the door. Khan was taken to a tiny chipped basin at the back of the building under which was a large container of water. He took the block of soap and for ten minutes washed all over his body. He cleaned his mouth once again and then dried himself with part of his shirt.

He sat down now opposite Nemim determined to bring some reason to the interview. 'I told Vajgelis I was a Mujahadin fighter because I wanted him to accept me,' he began. 'I wanted to escape and I needed his help so I shouted out the first thing that came into my head. The reason I hurt his men was because three of them tried to assault me. You know what I mean. Any honourable man would have done the same.'

'Before this, where you come from?'

'Bulgaria, Turkey, Iran.'

'With all these men?'

'No, we came together in Turkey. Then we went by truck to Bulgaria, but were cheated many times. Our money was stolen by men who promised to take us to Greece by boat. There was no boat.'

'You say you are Karim Khan – not Jasur . . .' he checked the notes and the identity card he had in front of him. 'Not Jasur al-Jahez. Or Jasur Faisal or Jasur Bahaji. The man with many names. You are not him.'

'No, I am Karim Khan.'

'How can I believe this?'

'Because it is the truth. Look at the picture of him. He is younger than I am and he is different. Look at him. Jasur has curly hair. I have straight hair.' He touched his damp head.

Nemim shrugged, then moved on to examine the photograph in Khan's passport. 'Why you are not black like Pakistani man? You are like an Arab man, I think. You are Palestinian terrorist, no? You are Mister Jasur?' He held one or two of the passport's pages to the bulb above them, which had attracted a swirl of small black flies. His brow furrowed. Then he brought it down on the table and began to scrape at the page that included Khan's details and photograph.

'This passport is changed – here.' He held it out to reveal the spot where the expiry date had been altered. 'And here the paper. Where is the paper? Why no paper here?'

The page had been razored out by the man in Quetta who'd suggested that an entry stamp for Afghanistan at the tail end of 1996 was enough to put him in jail. The same man had changed the date, quite expertly, Khan had thought, but he had to admit that the passport was barely tested. He had crossed from Pakistan to Iran along the Siahan range without being stopped by a border patrol, and the man on the Turkish border with Iran had not looked beyond the twenty dollar note folded in the front.

Nemim flipped through the passport again and came to a page containing a British visa.

'So you go to London City in nineteen ninety-one?'

'Yes, that was my second visa. I was studying to be a doctor. I was at school in London before then.'

The policeman looked at him sceptically. Khan had the odd thought that perhaps he had dreamed his past; everything before Bosnia and Afghanistan had been a kind of fantasy to protect him from things he had done and seen. Nemim was talking but he didn't hear properly and asked the policeman to repeat himself.

'This British visa is dated. This makes your passport thirteen years old,' he said. 'No passport can be that old. This passport is dead.'

He closed it and swept the notebook and Jasur's documents up from the table. 'We understand you. We know who you are. You are international terrorist,' he said. He got up abruptly and marched from the room.

Two hours later Khan was shaken awake. He saw the bread, cheese and water that had been set in front of him while he slept. He snatched at it but managed to eat only a little before being taken from the room. Outside the police station quite a crowd was waiting, in the middle of which was a TV crew. Khan stood in the glare of the lights, feeling shrunken and exposed. Nemim was enjoying the moment, although he did not seem to know whether to present his captive as the heroic survivor of Macedonian brutality or a dangerous terrorist, and allowed for both options in his manner.

The media opportunity ended, but instead of being taken back into the police station, Khan was placed in a van and borne off into the night.

9

At 7.00 a.m. Isis Herrick arrived with her bag at the gentrified mews house – French shutters, geraniums, carriage lamps – not far from the American Embassy in Grosvenor Square. The door was opened by an American carrying a machine pistol. He explained – a little apologetically – that the house was part of the embassy and she was now on US soil. Then he showed her to a room where two men stood listening to Walter Vigo, installed in a revolving leather chair with a cup of coffee and the *Wall Street Journal* draped like a napkin over his lap. Vigo was in his element – the nexus of the 'special relationship'.

'Ah,' he exclaimed, tipping the paper to the floor. 'Here's the brains responsible for RAPTOR.' He introduced her to the two men. 'This is Jim Collins and Nathan Lyne from the CIA's Directorate of Intelligence. Both these gentlemen were with the Directorate of Operations and have experience in the field so they know the problems and pitfalls of an operation as complicated and wide-ranging as this. Jim is one of the people in charge of things out at Northolt and Nathan is running your desk.' He stopped for the Americans to murmur hello and give Isis firm handshakes.

'Northolt?' she said.

'Yes, we've moved the operation out there. I think you'll be very impressed with what you're going to see. We expect you to spend a week or two there before a transfer to the field but, as you'll appreciate, things are and will remain very fluid. I hope, by the way, you won't mind the accommodation, but it seems simpler and more secure if we're not all being ferried to and from the Bunker in minibuses.'

'The Bunker,' she said, surprised. 'Are we confined to barracks?'

'No,' interjected Collins, a stout man with a pinkish complexion and a brush of fine blond hair. 'But we're trying to keep this as tight as possible, at least for the time being. There are not too many great restaurants in the area, but you're welcome to leave for R&R when you need. It's more a question of not having large numbers of American spook-types filling up the trattoria in Mayfair. Besides, the facility under Northolt has a great deal of space and there's plenty of room for solitude. There's even a restaurant and a gym.'

Collins nodded to Nathan Lyne, who rose and moved to sit on the sofa beside her. Tall, with a slow, understated manner, Nathan Lyne haemorrhaged high caste Yankee confidence, which she later learned was the result of Harvard law school and a short period with a Washington law firm.

'You're the only person we've brought on the team who doesn't need the introduction so I'll cut to the chase,' he said. 'We now have eleven suspects under surveillance. All of them passed through Heathrow on May fourteen and as far as we know at the present time, they are all lilywhites. No record of any misdemeanour and only tenuous Islamist affiliations. Certainly no training in Afghanistan. We're making some progress on who they are and we have names for some of them.'

'We've split the suspects into three groupings – Parana, Northern and Southern. The Parana group has a homogeneity of its own and it's the one we've had most success with. Your work at the airport allowed us to trace three of the eleven suspects to the Shi'ite community in the tri-border region of Brazil, Argentina and Paraguay. The river that flows through the area is named the Parana. There's a strong Lebanese contingent in the area that has links to the Hizbollah organisation and its many business interests in Lebanon. The three men appeared to have been sheltered rather than trained in the towns and ranches, sitting out the worldwide hunt for terrorists and establishing unblemished credentials for themselves. A successful operation to penetrate the community by us put names to the stills from the Heathrow security film. These guys had the smell of North Africa about them, though no one was certain about their exact nationalities. Anyway, eventually the trail led to a man named Lasenne Hadaya, a former officer in the Algerian security forces who was reported to have undergone a religious conversion after seeing a sign written in a desert rock.

'Hadaya led to a man named Furquan, with whom he had had contact in Rome. Finally we nailed the identity of the third man, a Moroccan engineer and part-time college professor named Ramzi Zaman. By the way, we had help with all this from the North African intell' services but they have no idea exactly what we're doing. Anyway, these three guys vanished in the late nineties, having lived quietly in Italy's large North African community and worked in various menial jobs that were way below each man's capabilities.'

Without asking Herrick, Collins placed a cup of coffee in her hand. She nodded gratefully.

'So, these men wind up in Western Europe. Hadaya is in Paris, Furquan in Stuttgart and the Moroccan, Zaman, is in Toulouse. Each was received by a bunch of North African helpers, who prepared for their arrival by arranging work, accommodation, cars and all kinds of local permits and passes.'

Lyne continued for another half hour talking without pause. The Northern group consisted of five men, two in Copenhagen, one in Stockholm and two who had come to rest in Britain after flitting around Europe on May 14 and 15. They were working on the suspects in Scandinavia and were now sure that they included an Indonesian national called Badi'al Hamzi who had once been a science teacher in Jakarta. The Syrian in Denmark and the Egyptian in Sweden were unknown quantities. The two suspects in Britain were a Pakistani and a Turk. Lyne said neither of these gentlemen could break wind without MI5 and Special Branch watchers knowing about it.

'In fact they had an astonishing piece of good fortune yesterday. The Turkish fellow, Mafouz Esmet, was taken ill on the street, outside a tube station in East London. One of the female officers with the Security Services called for help and then went with the guy to hospital. He was suffering from appendicitis and had an operation last evening. She's going to visit with him tomorrow, and you know what, this could be a very important break for us.

'Okay, so now we come to my specialty – the Southern group. These three men landed in Rome, Sarajevo and Budapest. For a time we lost one of the guys in Budapest but then we got another lucky break. An agent with the FBI's outfit in Budapest, which is mostly devoted to the Russian Mafia's activities, was travelling on a bus and just happened to see the very man whose picture he was carrying in his breast pocket. He trailed him to a poor part of town where the guy is living with a couple of Yemenis. This rang bells and again we had all three members of the Southern group checked out against descriptions of men who served in Afghanistan. But Pakistan's Inter-Service Intelligence couldn't find a match for any of them. Besides, these men don't really look the part. They're out of condition and spend a lot of time eating, drinking and smoking. They're not clean-living Muslims, that's for sure.' Lyne put his hands together and turned to look at her with radiant American purpose. 'So, basically, your job will be to chase up everything you can on these three guys. You speak Arabic, I hear. There's going to be a lot of reading to be done. You'll live and breathe these men for as long as you're with us.'

'Questions, Isis?' said Vigo, in a tone that implied he didn't expect any.

'Yes, do we have any idea about their plans? I know it's early. But are there any suspicious shipments being made? Have they been observed looking at potential targets? Do we have any communications intercepts?'

'As yet we don't have the vaguest notion what they plan,' said Collins. 'They haven't been talking to each other and there's no movement of anything like your WAYFARER. Chemicals and stuff – nothing like that.

There's a general feeling among the surveillance teams that the suspects are in a period of stasis, a kind of hibernation.'

'Aestivation,' said Herrick.

'Come again?' said Lyne.

'The summer equivalent of hibernation,' said Vigo, not disguising his irritation.

'Perhaps I should say something about how RAPTOR is set up,' said Collins. 'We've split the operation between surveillance and investigation. The surveillance teams on the ground – there are about thirty officers in each team – report to a desk dedicated to each suspect, which is manned twenty-four seven. Once the subject is moving, his route is plotted on an electronic map so everyone knows where he is. The field officer in charge of each surveillance consults the desk on questions of strategy and security. When there's a problem with implications for the entire operation the issue is settled by RAPTOR control, which consists of myself, Walter here and a representative of the National Security Agency. Beyond that there is a level of analysis and risk assessment reporting to our respective governments.' Collins smiled weakly, as if he had made a poor joke.

'There should be a lot of interaction between the two sides so anyone working on the investigation desks, like you, will have real time access to surveillance, all the communication traffic between the watchers, photographs and film, when they are available. Equally, we want to feed the material you're finding out to the surveillance teams as soon as you get it.'

'Can I ask a little about the surveillance? How many of our people are involved?'

'You know a few of them,' said Vigo. 'Andy Dolph, Philip Sarre and Joe Lapping are all involved on the ground, as you would expect. You will know many others too, but as we've made clear, this is a very closed and secret order. We've had to choose personnel who do not have past associations with the cities we're covering, except in the case of Sarajevo where we felt it would be better to have people who've got Balkan experience. That's why Dolph is there.'

Herrick could feel herself bridling and hoped it wasn't showing. Dolph deserved a place in any surveillance operation: he was sharp and versatile. Sarre was at best mediocre and Lapping downright feeble. She remembered what Dolph said about Lapping after they'd been on a job together. 'He needs help crossing the road, that Lapping. You've got a better chance of going undercover with Liberace.'

Vigo saw what she was thinking. 'There's no room for personal competition on this team,' he said firmly. 'It's all for one and one for all right from the top. Believe me, those people in the field will need to be rotated and your turn will come. But we thought you would appreciate a period experiencing the whole operation beforehand. After all, it's your baby, Isis. None of us would be here were it not for you.'

She made appreciative noises.

On the way to the car that would take them to the outskirts of West London, she saw Collins murmur to Lyne, 'Brittle, but cute.'

'And a fair lip-reader too,' she said, before climbing into the Chevrolet. 'Though not in Arabic.'

The Bunker was part of the Nato command centre at Hillingdon and sat directly under an airfield where there were one or two military and private aircraft. At first glance she thought of a trading floor built for decades of nuclear winter. Two constellations of circular desks spread out across the vast space, almost like molecular diagrams. RAPTOR's full complement was never seen because of the shift system but at present she reckoned there were about 130 officers from three US agencies, the FBI, CIA and NSA, and the British counterparts, MI5, MI6 and GCHQ. Lyne explained that the surveillance operations were handled to the right of central aisle. To the left were the investigation and intelligence desks, three modules per terrorist group. They walked towards a vast notice board which featured the faces of the eleven suspects. Every known detail had been summarised and added next to the name. Lyne said the board was more reassuring than helpful. He was equally dry about the tracking operation in which the suspects' positions were marked at any time of the day or night on one of the electronic city maps. A touch of a key would give an officer a record of an individual's movements over the entire course of the operation and, if desired, the program would helpfully point out his favourite routes, where he met contacts, even the bars where he took coffee in the morning. All of this had been subject to furious but so far fruitless scrutiny, he said.

RAPTOR was still experiencing teething problems. Technicians were crawling about the floor, adjusting screens or hooking cables across the ceiling. NSA programmers struggled with two large mainframes that lived in their own special environment way off in the distance. There was a good deal of noise above, and someone from a surveillance desk would occasionally call out that one of the suspects was on the move. 'Number Two going walkabout, number Six in transit.'

Raised from this activity was a control box with glass sides where Vigo, Collins and the man from the NSA, a Colonel John Franklin Plume, worked. Vigo had already taken his seat and removed his jacket to reveal a pair of vermilion braces. In front of him was a large screen, split to accept several different feeds at once from secret surveillance cameras. Above the aisle was a much larger screen that could be seen by everyone. The screen was being tested and flashes of blue TV lightning probed the recesses of the cavernous space above them.

735

They went over to the investigation and intelligence desks. Lyne introduced her to his group, then to the 'Wallflowers', a team of twenty eager young American research assistants whose work stations were ranged along the concrete wall of the Bunker. 'These are the slaves of the investigation desks,' he said, giving a managerial shoulder rub to one of them. 'Our Stakhanovites.'

She looked down at the desk. Each Wallflower was on the internet. Their work stations were choked with boxes of files and copies of every conceivable reference book. Herrick read some of the titles – *Gulf Maritime Conventions, Ancestry and the Tribes of Saudi Arabia, The Dictionary of Muslim Names.*

'That's about it,' said Lyne. 'Coffee, food, exercise machines, massage, laundry, sleeping arrangements: you can find them for yourself.'

She nodded, impressed.

'This is America mobilising,' he said.

'Right,' she said, and sat down at Southern Group Three.

It soon became clear to Herrick that every second of the day, RAPTOR was producing a vast amount of information which in turn spawned endless new investigative possibilities. Field officers were being sent to check out the most casual contacts made by the suspects while a lot of work was being done on the helpers who had eased the men into their hiding places. A separate data bank was dedicated to this information as it constantly threw up possible links and cross-references in the back-grounds of people and organisations across Europe. Already, interesting connections had been made – men who had attended the same university or were from the same Middle Eastern tribal grouping; clerics who had visited mosques in Stuttgart and Toulouse; businesses belonging to the fixers which had arrangements with cities where suspects were present; the use of the same banks or hawala agents to transfer money.

The range of activity was bewildering. The hackers based in Crypto City at Fort Meade were penetrating the defences of every relevant public agency, including in a few instances the computer records of European intelligence services. Vast amounts of data were sucked up and flung unedited in the direction of London, where the systems people had breakdowns trying to absorb the flow of information and make sensible arrangements for its analysis. Added to this was the work of the Special Collection Service, a joint unit run by the CIA and NSA, based in Beltsville, Maryland. Known simply as 'Collection' it had sent a substantial proportion of its staff to Europe to eavesdrop on the suspects and their helpers. A similar outfit run by MI6 and GCHQ was also on the ground, erecting eavesdropping antennae disguised as TV aerials and dishes, and attaching devices to the suspects' phone lines. But circum-spection was called for because a few of the helpers and two of the suspects were seen carrying out anti-surveillance routines while on the street. This meant they would also be alert to the possibility of electronic eavesdropping and might have access to the equipment to detect it. Electronic surveillance added another swollen tributary to the flow of intelligence that the Bunker attempted to process each day.

The British and American service chiefs let it be known they were already exceptionally pleased with the detail being gathered and sifted – they were already far in advance of their previous understanding of terrorist methods and planning, and most importantly there had been no breach in security.

'In due course,' said Spelling in a rallying speech at the end of Isis' second daily briefing in the Bunker, 'these networks of sleeper cells and enablers will be lit up like an air traffic control board. We will know the routes, the timing, the intention of these people before they know themselves. This is a very great step in the war against terrorism.' Beside him were Barbara Markham, Director of MI5, and Walter Vigo.

The Americans had all fallen in love with Vigo. They said he knew what it was like to be at the sharp end. Herrick observed that he often wandered over to the investigation desks and chatted to Lyne. On Friday evening he had made a crucial suggestion. The Rome suspect had disappeared for two days after losing the surveillance at the city's northern rail terminal.

'Have a look at the Muslim student groups in Perugia,' said Vigo. 'There's a foreign university there and our chum may be in contact with the radical groups around the Italian university.'

This advice turned out to be spot on, and two Arabic-speaking Americans were sent to the Umbrian town to sign up for Italian language courses. After this, Vigo made a point of coming over to them at least once a day. He would pull up a chair and sit with his hands folded across his Anderson and Sheppard suit to attend to detailed questions about the beliefs of the Wahabis or the transfer of gold through the Gulf States. His manner was that of a concerned PhD supervisor. The vibration of sophisticated menace Isis felt in the late-night meeting with Spelling a week before had been replaced by an almost amiable focus.

Her misgivings about Vigo and the operation receded at equal pace mostly because of the pressure of work. Lyne was demanding and insisted that every avenue was investigated thoroughly. He nagged them constantly to remember the two central questions: what were the eleven planning and when were they going to move?

Lyne knew which buttons to push. When he wanted a favour out of the embassy in Riyadh he dashed off a cable and routed it through the State Department, marking it for the attention of several diplomats, even though he knew they couldn't read it because of the special encryption used by RAPTOR. What mattered was that America's spies knew their performance was being watched by the highest levels of government in Washington. On scrambled phone lines to CIA stations all over the Middle East, Lyne harried officers to make that last call. Late one night Herrick heard him organising funds to bribe an official in the Qatar immigration service. It was four in the morning in Qatar but he ordered the station chief round to the man's house and told him to email copies of the passport applications to the Bunker by morning Middle Eastern time.

Herrick pushed the British embassy officials in a similar fashion, though most of the MI6 officers working undercover in British embassies already sensed the urgency of the situation, even if they did not know precisely what was going on.

It was Herrick's conversation with Guy Laytham, the MI6 man in Oman, that produced a crucial breakthrough. Laytham remembered a reception early in the spring when a director of one of the country's bigger banks had pointedly asked him about the funding of rebuilding programmes in Sarajevo. The question struck Laytham as odd because he hadn't served in the Balkans and was unfamiliar with the levels of corruption. The banker said he was worried about a client's money that was being sent to a Muslim charity he had not heard of, through the Central Bank of Bosnia CK. Could Laytham make inquiries about the bank and the charity? Thinking about the conversation later, Laytham realised that his contact was not asking him to check out the bank and charity; he was telling him that one or both were involved in something that would interest him.

Herrick hung up and arranged to speak to Dolph in Sarajevo. Dolph, no slouch when it came to Middle Eastern banking practices, said he welcomed the distraction since the RAPTOR team was tripping over itself in Bosnia. The local suspect was only a little more active than a pregnant sloth, he said.

Fifteen minutes later he came back to her.

'How about sending a second donation from the same bank in Oman using the name of the original remitter, but with instructions that the money be picked up in cash at the bank in Sarajevo? I'll see to it that we have someone inside the bank to tell us when the transfer comes through. Then we'll simply watch who collects it.'

There was some prevarication at the British Embassy in Masqat, but eventually $5,000 of British taxpayers' money was released and sent on its way by the bank in Oman. Twenty-four hours later, Dolph was on the line saying they had surveillance pictures of someone picking up the money. Dolph suggested that the look of surprise on the man's face meant one thing: he had been the one to send the first donation from Masqat and was therefore the primary financier.

Photographs of the helper were sent back to Laytham. A bank official remembered the man from a year before when he had changed a very large sum of Saudi riyals into the local currency and US dollars. Records showed that the man's name was Sa'id al-Azm. He had produced a Saudi passport and an Omani driving licence when setting up two business accounts. The driving licence meant he had been resident in Oman for some time. A search was ordered of the country's driver and vehicle licensing authority records. On the application form he gave his occupation as construction engineer and property developer. Further search of Oman's corporation registry yielded the fact that al-Azm was from a well-known professional family in Jeddah with business connections all over the Gulf.

Late that night, as Lyne and Herrick ate a meal in the Bunker canteen with the rest of Lyne's crew, Herrick suggested that al-Azm must have known suspect Four before they both ended up in Sarajevo.

'You got a point. The Parana suspects knew each other in Rome.'

'Right, maybe they attended the same Islamic college or worked together.'

'Everything says Four's got to be a Saudi, like al-Azm. We got pictures of both so why don't we start with those and get the Wallflowers to trawl through the picture agencies?'

It took just a day for the hunch to pay off. Sa'id al-Azm's professional life didn't merit a published photograph, but in a brief newspaper description of his work as project manager for a sewage works in Oman, it was mentioned that he had played for the Saudi national under-eighteen soccer side. Pictures of the side were sent to the Bunker, but Four was nowhere to be seen. Lyne wasn't about to give up.

'Maybe he made the local side with al-Azm.' A search of the newspaper libraries around the Gulf eventually produced pictures of the Jeddah touring team from 1984 and 1985. Al-Azm was seated in the front row holding the football. Standing in the back row was the man currently under observation in Sarajevo. His name was Abd al Aziz al Hafy. 'The servant of the Almighty,' said Lyne, translating the first part of the name. Then to anyone in earshot he announced, 'We've ID'd another wood pussy. He's in the cross hairs, brothers and sisters.'

A small celebration was held – champagne in throwaway cups and cheesecake bought from a pâtisserie near the US Embassy. Spelling and various American officials emailed their congratulations to Lyne. Vigo came over to them, made a courtly bow and said they were about to get a line into al-Azm's phone.

'With their usual lack of regard for our convenience,' said Vigo, 'it's quite possible that the suspects are passing messages by word of mouth – Chinese whispers from person to person. But somewhere along the line, someone has got to make a telephone call.'

We know that, thought Herrick rather testily. The satisfaction she got from the identification of Four had not done much to reduce her unease about RAPTOR, which seemed to her to be displaying the classic growth of bureaucracy. When later someone wandered over to ask Nathan Lyne whether they should mount an operation to get DNA samples from the suspects, she shot a look of cold fury at the man. 'Why the fuck would anyone want to know their DNA profiles? The only thing that matters is what these men are planning, not whether they drink *café macchiato* in the morning or have a predisposition to male pattern baldness.'

'I agree with Isis,' said Lyne, looking a little startled at her outburst. 'I think that's a really dumb idea.'

When the man had left, Lyne steered her away to a coffee machine. 'Something eating you, Isis? Maybe you need to go get some daylight. I know I feel like a goddam earthworm down here.'

'Yes, but that's not what's bothering me. This thing is too remote. We're no nearer to knowing what they're planning. We have no concept of their leadership, although that was what my people said they wanted when they told me about all this.'

'Hey, the whole point is to watch these guys at work. We're learning all the time. It's a long process and it may go on a year or more. That's what a good intelligence operation takes – sweat, frustration and hard labour. Who said it was going to be fun?'

'All that's true. But doesn't it strike you that in this microscopic observation we're missing some of the big things?'

'Like what?'

'Like what happened to Youssef Rahe, the MI6 agent who was found murdered in Lebanon. Like what happened to the twelfth man who got on the same flight as Rahe and is presumed to be responsible for his death. We don't *know* that, yet no one has bothered to find out where he went or who he was. We just assume he was the hit man and that he's disappeared into the sands of the Middle East. Why are we ignoring him?'

'You got a point about Rahe,' said Lyne. 'But the rest of what you say challenges the policy, the whole purpose of RAPTOR. You signed up for it.'

'Well, someone needs to challenge it. Remember, these men are masters at flying under the radar. What we have here is a fantastically complicated radar system designed to detect everything but the obvious.'

Lyne shook his head sympathetically but didn't agree. 'What do you want, Isis? Arrest the suspects and lose the chance to learn who's pulling their strings and how they receive money and instructions? What we're doing here is gathering life-saving intelligence that's going to be important for maybe the next five years. It's a real opportunity you created. As Walter says, it's your baby, Isis, for chrissake.'

She nodded. 'Yes, but we're missing something. I know it, but I can't tell you what it is.' She didn't like saying this. She knew that graft, logic and occasional inspiration solved problems in their world, not some kind of daft women's intuition.

'I like having you work with me,' said Lyne. 'You're solid talent right through. The real thing. But if you're going to buck against this, you may feel you're more comfortable quitting and going back to Vauxhall Cross.' Then he slapped his forehead. 'Hey, you know what, I have an idea for getting you out of here for a while but not losing you entirely.'

'What is it?'

'I'll tell you when I've talked to Jim Collins and *Lord* Vigo. Meantime, get your ass back to work.'

She returned to the desk, picked up the phone and dialled a number in Beirut. After a little while a familiar English voice answered. Sally Cawdor was placing her ineffably sunny nature at Herrick's disposal.

In the headquarters of Albanian State Security in Tirana, Khan heard the other prisoners being beaten and brutalised during the day, and at night the groans and terrified whispers between the cells. Yet the interrogators did not lay a hand on him and after a week he was beginning to recover some of his health. They fed him well, or at least regularly, with pasta and potatoes and chicken broth. On the third day they even called a doctor to stitch the lip split by Nemim's cane. The doctor smelled his breath and gave him antibiotics for the abscess. Throughout the visit the man did not say a word, but before leaving he touched Khan's shoulder lightly and gave him a strange look, as though measuring him in some way, gauging his character.

Part Two

10

Robert Harland inched upwards from his chair in the café on 31st Street and waited for the spasm to shoot from his lower back into his leg. He gritted his teeth as the pain reached a point behind his knee in a pure molten form. For a month now he had not been able to lie down, and had to sit perched on one buttock, holding his leg out at a particular angle. When he walked, he had first to stand, slowly stretching his frame, then move off with his right side leaning down and his head turned up to the left. The pain was unrelenting and lately, as he dragged himself between specialists, he'd begun to wonder if it would ever leave him.

He shuffled out of the way of the people on the sidewalk and reached a gingko tree where he fought for a space with a dog that scurried round him before squirting the other side of the trunk. He breathed in. Eva had once told him he could breathe into pain, but it didn't help. What did help was the neat whisky he had poured into the black coffee. It blunted his senses, and he resorted to it increasingly even though he had been warned not to mix it with the anti-inflammatory drugs, pain-killers and sleeping pills.

He started looking out for a cab to take him just six blocks to the Empire State building. A couple cruised by with their lights on but did not see him flap his arm wanly from the kerb. Finally a waiter came out of the café and asked if he could hail one for him, but Harland had changed his mind. New York cabs were as much of a problem for him as a convenience. The only way he could travel in one was by almost lying across the back seat, exposing his spine to the full force of the jolts as the cab surfed over the bumps and metal plates that lay in Manhattan's streets. That was his life today, a querulous, narrow existence filled with obstacles. The pain had come to occupy his whole being and it was now a matter of making small gestures of resistance. He decided to walk, whatever it damn well cost him, and moved off slowly, forcing himself to take notice of the early summer sun pouring into Park Avenue. He summoned Benjamin Jaidi to his thoughts.

The Secretary-General had called him at home that morning from a plane somewhere over North Africa and ordered him to phone Dr Sammi

745

Loz. With a thousand things on his mind and a Middle East crisis, he was apparently worrying about Harland's mysterious condition. True, the injury had prevented Harland from carrying out a mission on the West Bank in advance of Jaidi's arrival in the Middle East and he had been irritated. Still, it was thoughtful of him to have phoned and elbowed a space in Loz's schedule late that afternoon.

'The appointments with this man are like gold, you understand,' said Jaidi. 'He *will* cure you, I have no doubt of that. But in return I will expect you to look after my friend. I believe he may be about to enter a difficult period. This is the deal, Harland.'

It was typical of Jaidi to leave the conversation without specifying the doctor's difficulties or how Harland could be expected to help. But Harland had heard of Loz and dared to hope that, after the procession of chiropractors, nerve specialists and bone doctors, this man would do something for him.

He reached 5th Avenue and turned right towards the Empire State building. Now the sun was on his back and with the effort of walking like a clown he began to sweat profusely, something that Harland, once so fit and trim, loathed intensely. He paused and looked up at the building thrusting into the brilliant, almost white sky above Manhattan and remembered lines that Jaidi had pointed out to him. 'This riddle in steel and stone is at once the perfect target and the perfect demonstration of non-violence, of racial brotherhood, this lofty target scraping the skies and meeting the destroying planes halfway.'

Jaidi had said, looking out over the city from his suite in the UN tower, 'That was written in forty-eight by E.B. White, about the very building we're standing in now. "A single flight of planes no bigger than a wedge of geese can quickly end this island fantasy." A great artist must be prescient, don't you think, Harland? He must know things even though he doesn't understand where they come from. Troubled times, Harland. Troubled times.'

Harland reached the entrance where a line of doughty American tourists stretched round the corner into 34th Street, passed through security and took the elevator to the sixty-fourth floor. He was grateful to be in the cool and when he got out of the elevator, he rested a while, mopping his face and neck, regretting the whisky which he knew had caused the sweating fit and made him smell. He looked around. The corridor was quite silent, except for the gasp and whine of the elevators as they rose and plunged through the 1,200 odd feet of the Empire State. A door opened and a man in shirt-sleeves looked out and examined Harland pointedly before turning back inside. At the far end of the corridor another man in a suit and tie showed a close interest in him. Harland called out to ask where Dr Loz's office was. The man gestured with a turn of the head. 'Four down on the right,' he said and returned to his newspaper. As Harland crept along the wall, he passed a third man, sitting just inside an open door. This one was armed and wasn't bothering to hide it.

He pushed on the door that announced Dr Sammi Loz DO FAAO and found a slender man in a smoke-blue tunic buttoned to the neck, standing behind the reception desk. He moved out to greet him.

'You must be Robert Harland. Forgive me, I've sent my assistant off to organise the clinic at the hospital this evening.' He stood still for a moment, his eyes running over Harland. 'Yes, you *are* in a lot of pain.' Loz was in his mid-thirties, with a high forehead, wavy, well-groomed hair, a thin, slightly aquiline nose and a generous mouth that spread easily into a smile. Harland guessed he was Iranian or Armenian, though he spoke with an unimpeachable English accent and his voice was modulated with concern as his eyes made easy contact with Harland's. 'Yes, we're going to have to do something about this immediately. Come,' he said, gesturing to a room. 'Come in here and take the weight off your feet.'

Harland perched on a raised bed, now nauseous with the pain. Loz began to take down his medical history, but seeing that Harland could no longer really concentrate, helped him off with his trousers and shirt and told him to stand facing the wall. After examining him from behind for a minute or two, Loz moved round to his front and looked at his patient with a gaze directed about five inches to the right of him, in order, Harland assumed, to see his whole. He placed one hand on Harland's sternum and the other in the middle of his back and exerted a tiny amount of pressure for about five minutes. His hands began to dart around his torso, pausing lightly on his upper and middle chest, neck, spine and the top of his pelvis. He was like a Braille reader finding meaning in every bump and depression, and once or twice he paused and repeated the movement to make sure he had not misunderstood. Then his hands came to rest on the marks and scars on Harland's contorted body and he peered up into his face to seek confirmation of what he suspected. 'You've had a rough, tough old life, Mr Harland. The Secretary-General told me you were the only survivor of that plane crash eighteen months ago at La Guardia. I remember seeing your picture on the television news. That was something.'

Harland nodded.

'And these burn marks on your wrist and ankles, the scars on your back. These are older, aren't they? What caused them?'

Harland was embarrassed. He didn't like to use the word torture – it shocked people and tended to evoke a sympathy that he had no use for.

'It's a long story. I was held prisoner for a while back in the nineties.'

'I see,' said Loz gently. He told him to sit on the couch then lifted Harland's legs up so he was able to lie on his back.

'I don't think I can take much manipulation,' Harland said, at the same time noting that the pain had subsided a little.

'Nor do I,' said Loz. His hands moved to Harland's feet. He bent first one leg then the other, holding the kneecap in the palm of his hand.

'What are the men doing in the hallway?' Harland asked.

'That's a long story.' Loz's attention was elsewhere.

Harland's eyes came to rest on an Arabic inscription hung in a simple frame. 'What's it say?' he asked.

'Oh, that. It's a warning against pride and arrogance. It was written by a man named al-Jazir two hundred years after the Prophet died. It says, "A man who is noble does not pretend to be noble, any more than a man who is eloquent feigns eloquence. When a man exaggerates his qualities it is because of something lacking in himself; the bully gives himself airs because he is conscious of his weakness."'

'Very true,' commented Harland.

Loz had moved behind him and, after holding his head and working his neck very gently, slipped his hands down to the middle of his back, his fingers moving with the whole of Harland's weight pressing down on them. Although the pain still lurked beneath the surface, the heat had been taken out of it and for the first time in four weeks Harland felt free to think.

'The air crash,' said Loz suddenly. 'This has caused your pain. The trauma you experienced has come to the surface.'

'After all that time?'

'Yes. You've kept that shock at the centre. You are a very strong and controlled individual Mr Harland – impressively so. But it was going to happen some day. The body has to get rid of it.' He paused. 'And the other things in you. These too will have to come out.'

Harland ignored this. 'You can treat it then?'

'Oh yes, I *am* treating it. You will recover and you'll be able to sleep tonight without the use of alcohol.' He peered at him with an expression of deep understanding that unsettled Harland. 'We'll need to work on this over the next few months. It's a very serious matter. You will feel not quite yourself for twenty-four hours, as though you have a mild case of 'flu. Rest up and get as much sleep as you can.'

He continued working for another twenty minutes on the hips and pubic bone. Harland's eyes drifted to the slightly tinted glass of the window and the glistening silver helmet of the Chrysler building. 'The Empire State is an unusual place to have your practice,' he said.

'Yes, but I am disinclined to go to the Upper East Side where many of my patients are. It's an arid part of the city, don't you think? No heart. Too much money. Besides, I love this building. You know they began it just before the Crash, continued building it through the Depression and finished it forty-five days ahead of schedule. It's a lucky building with a strong personality, and not a little mystery.'

'A riddle of steel and concrete.'

'Ah, you've been talking to Benjamin Jaidi. He told me he had found that passage when I visited him the other day.'

He left Harland's side and went to a small glass and steel table to write something down. He returned and placed a note in Harland's hand. 'This is the time of our next appointment.'

Harland read it to himself. 'Sevastapol – 8.30 p.m. tomorrow. Table in the name of Keane.' He looked up at Loz, who had put his finger to his lips and was pointing to the ceiling with his other hand.

'Right, we will see each other in a week's time. But now I must go to the hospital. Rest here for ten minutes then turn off the lights and pull the door to. It will lock automatically.' He smiled and left Harland in the cool solitude of the room, watching the light slip across the buildings outside. He looked round the room again, noticing five battered postcards of the Empire State lined up along a shelf, copies of the Koran and the Bible and a fragment of stone, which looked like an ancient spearhead.

He left after about half an hour and went to the apartment in Brooklyn Heights, where he ordered in a Chinese meal and settled down with a book about Isaac Newton.

The Sevastapol was much more than a restaurant of the moment. The same writers, film and money people and city politicians had been haunting the same tables for decades. It was above fashion. Harland had been twice with Eva, who was fascinated by the place and its noisy owner, a Ukrainian named Limoshencko, a pet brigand of the downtown crowd.

Harland passed through the tables outside, consciously putting Eva from his mind, and asked for Mr Keane. He was pointed in the direction of a table that was obscured by the bar and by a tall young woman who was gesticulating in a manner designed for public consumption. Loz was seated with his hands folded on the table, looking up at her with an unwavering if rather formal politeness. He rose to greet Harland but did not introduce the woman, who then left rather resentfully.

'It's good to see you,' he said. 'You're looking a different man.'

'Thanks to you. I'm a bit fragile, but a lot better. Look, call me Robert or Bobby, please.'

'You know, I prefer Harland. It's a good name.' They sat down. 'It's a good dependable name.' He moved closer. 'I'm afraid we had to come here because the FBI couldn't get a table in a thousand years.'

'The men in the hallway were FBI?'

'Yes, they've been with me since the first postcard arrived. Did you look at them when I left?'

'The postcards of the Empire State? Of course not.'

'That's interesting, an investigator with principles.'

'I'm not an investigator, Dr Loz. I do research work for the UN. Most of my time is spent on clean water issues. It's pretty unexciting.'

'Jaidi told me you were due to go to the Middle East to talk to Hamas. That isn't just research, surely?'

Harland ignored the remark. 'He was rather oblique about you, Doctor. He said you were about to have some problems. I will certainly help if I can.'

Loz flashed a discreet, slightly awkward smile at him. 'You see them out there? The black van down the street by the mailbox? I know that vehicle as if it was my own. It's the FBI. They follow me everywhere. They're making my life very difficult indeed and I think it's quite possible that I will be arrested. I've seen a lawyer – a patient of mine – and he told me to be utterly open in all my dealings, but I couldn't be more open. I live a very simple and uncomplicated life. Apparently there's nothing I can do to fight this kind of harassment. America is no longer the land of the free, Mr Harland. People like me with Muslim backgrounds can disappear into jail and never be heard of again.'

'I think they'd have to have strong grounds for arresting someone like you. You're very well connected.'

'Oh believe me, that's not true. How many innocent people have they detained without charge or trial? Here in the United States of America people are disappearing as though it's a police state in *Latin* America. I love this country beyond any in the world. I believe in it. That's why I became a US citizen. I sometimes think I was born to be an American and to work in the Empire State building.' For a moment his eyes flared with hurt and indignation. The waiter who had been hovering to take their orders beat a retreat.

'When did this start?' asked Harland.

'When the first postcard arrived, at the end of last year. I guess some mailman with a keen eye thought it was odd for a postcard of the Empire State to be sent to the Empire State with a foreign postmark. They read my name and saw the signature Karim Khan and came up with a plot. Who knows what they think these days.'

'Who is Karim Khan?'

'A friend.'

'What was written on it?'

'In essence each one told me of my friend Karim's progress from Pakistan to the West. The first one was from Pakistan, then there was one from Mashhad, a town in Iran, another from Tehran, one from Diyarbakir in Turkey, and the last came from Albania.'

'But why pictures of the building? It does look odd. Is there any significance?

'No, I just kept a stack of cards of the building. I have done since I first visited New York in the eighties. And when Karim went off to Afghanistan I gave them to him with my address written on because I knew that while I might move apartment I would never move my practice.'

'Do the FBI know your friend was in Afghanistan?'

'Maybe. They have lists of these things. I am certain.'

'You're telling me he fought with the Taleban?'

'Yes, but he used a *nomme de guerre*. He had one before he left.'

'You must expect this kind of trouble. To all intents and purposes he may be regarded as a very likely enemy of the state.'

'No,' Loz said with finality. He smiled at Harland once, a brief piece of punctuation that closed the issue. He turned and ordered for them both – caviar, blinis and Kobi beef with spinach. 'Will you have some wine? I don't drink.'

Harland shook his head.

'Good, I'm glad to hear you're giving your system a rest.' He paused. 'What if I told you I was going to be arrested tonight?'

'I would be very surprised if you had advance notice of that.'

'It's a feeling. The pressure has been increasing over the last few days. I cannot be arrested and I cannot submit to confinement. I want your help to avoid it.'

'Tell me about your friend,' said Harland, noticing now that nearly every woman in the restaurant had either waved to or was stealing looks in Loz's direction.

'We were both sent to Westminster School in London to gain qualifications to go to college in England. Karim was from an affluent family in Lahore – very old, very pukka. I was brought up in Lebanon, though my father was Iranian; my mother had a Druze background. We were outsiders in an English public school so it was natural that we became friends, despite being unlike each other in practically every way. He was wilder, more gregarious, more daring and I suppose more fun. I think we relied on each other's strengths.'

'Tell me about these postcards.'

Loz took five postcards from his pocket and laid them out in their order of arrival. Harland examined the images then turned them over. On each there was a short message in an educated hand. The first said:

Greetings, my old friend. I am in Pakistan and hope very soon to be in London. I may need a little help from you. I have good news. I am returning to complete my medical studies, as you always said I should.

The next two were less upbeat and gave only details of where Khan was in Iran. The card from Turkey told how much of his money had been stolen.

He still had $400 that his mother had given him and he hoped to use this to get to London. But there were unspecified visa and passport problems.

Harland read them again. 'They seem harmless enough,' he said eventually. 'But these days intelligence services are likely to look at them with an eye for codes and hidden messages.'

Loz wasn't listening. 'Karim needs my help,' he said, looking straight past Harland into the mêlée of diners and table-hoppers. 'The last postcard, from Albania, was followed by this letter. I assume they read this as well, but there were no signs of the envelope having been opened.' He withdrew a single sheet of lined paper from his jacket. The letter was signed by a Mr Skender. It told of Karim Khan's arrest and imprisonment and his transfer to the state security centre in Tirana. The letter mentioned that Khan had made the local TV news in the context of a massacre in Macedonia.

'I know something about this incident,' said Harland. 'The UN has been asked to investigate by the Albanian minority in Macedonia.'

Loz turned to him. 'I had a friend go through the Balkan news websites – it's clear those men were murdered. They had come from Turkey. Karim must have been travelling with them.'

'Then why wasn't he killed?'

'Because he knows what to do in such situations.' He produced a printout of a web page from a Greek newspaper and pointed to a photograph of a bedraggled man, dwarfed between two policemen. 'That is Karim, though he is barely recognisable. You can see that he is very thin and has been hurt.' A troubled look swept his face and he reached for the bottle of water. Neither of them had eaten much of the first course, and when he had drained his glass he pushed his plate aside and waved to the waiter.

'I had the caption beneath the picture translated.' He handed Harland a piece of white card.

TERRORIST SNARED AFTER GUN BATTLE IN MACEDONIA.
Jasur al-Jahez, the man who escaped from Macedonian security forces in a raging gun battle has been found to be a Palestinian terrorist wanted in connection with outrages by the Israeli authorities and also by Syria, Egypt and Lebanon. Jasur al-Jahez, also known as The Electrician, was believed to have died of natural causes eighteen months ago and has not been heard of since. Israel, Syria and Egypt are now seeking his extradition.

Loz took back the card. 'This *is* Karim, but for reasons I cannot comprehend they believe he is Jasur. Jasur has killed many, many people. Apparently he split with Hamas in the early nineties and formed a group that assassinated moderate clerics and politicians all over the Middle East.'

'I have heard of him,' said Harland. 'Your friend is in a lot of trouble if they think he's Jasur.'

'Now you see why I cannot be arrested,' he said, placing his hand lightly on Harland's. 'I must help him.'

Whether or not something was transmitted in the touch Harland could not say, but he was aware that a part of him submitted very easily with the pressure of Loz's hands, and something made him try to resist. 'What can you do?'

'I don't know, but I must try. Now I think we should go. There's a letter on your desk from the Secretary-General. He wrote it before he left and asked me to let him know when it should be released to you. In that letter you will find his instructions.'

'Does he know about Khan?'

'Some of it, but he left before I discovered the business about the mistaken identity.'

'And this letter, what does it say?'

'I don't know.'

'Right, I'll pick it up tomorrow,' said Harland.

'Why not this evening? You are feeling better, are you not? We should go now. I have a small bag at the back of the restaurant and we will leave through the kitchens. It has been arranged. I will go first and wait for you at the rear entrance. The bill has already been settled.'

With this he got up. On his way to Sevastapol's kitchens he paused at two tables, shaking hands and saying hello. Harland noticed how he made contact with each person, drawing a palm across a shoulder, touching a bare forearm or clasping a hand for just a second or two longer than was usual. This casual laying on of hands over, he moved without haste to the kitchens and vanished through the swing doors.

Harland got up a little stiffly and walked through the kitchens to find Loz waiting with small black bag at the rear door. He worked the double lock, moved out into the warm evening and indicated to a car across the street. Just then a man hurried to them clutching one of his pockets.

'Mr Loz. Federal Bureau of Investigation. Agent Morris. I need you to come with me, sir.'

Harland stepped forward. 'I'm afraid that's not possible. This man is in my custody. I'm taking him to the headquarters of the United Nations under the explicit instructions of the Secretary-General.' He showed him the UN police badge that Jaidi had issued him during an internal investigation six months before.

'I'll check this out sir,' he said, pulling the microphone on his lapel towards his mouth.

'You do that Agent Morris,' Harland replied, knowing it would be a matter of seconds before his colleagues at the front of the restaurant came on the scene to seize Loz legitimately. 'But I have to take this man with me now. It's a matter of the greatest urgency.' The agent, who was saying something and pressing his hand against his ear at the same time, put himself between Harland and Loz. 'Back off, sir,' he said to Harland. 'This is a Federal matter.'

'Go to the car,' Harland told Loz.

'No, you stay right where you are, sir,' the FBI man replied, moving for his gun. Harland clamped his hand round the holster and moved his forearm up against the man's Adam's apple, forcing him back to Sevastapol's door. He held him there and wrenched the gun from its holster. 'This is one occasion the United Nations takes precedence over the United States – okay!' He ran over to the car and scrambled in, but as he reached round to pull the door closed he felt his back go, and fell in agony across the seat. 'Take us to the UN building,' he shouted to the driver.

The Ukrainian chauffeur supplied by Limoshencko warmed to the task of out-driving the FBI and shot up 6th, running lights on Houston and West Four, then crossed to the East Side along the top of Washington Square Park. In less than five minutes they were on 1st Avenue, speeding towards the sanctuary of the United Nations. No car followed.

11

'Harland, pick up! I know you've got that goddam back doctor with you.'
Harland recognised the voice of Special Agent Frank Ollins of the FBI.
Ollins had led the air crash investigation two years before. For a time they
had been uneasy allies during the investigation, but then Ollins had been
warned off by the Bureau.

Clutching his back, Harland moved to the phone. 'Hello, Frank. How
can I help you?'

'I guessed right,' said Frank.

'How'd you get my direct line – the switchboard isn't working this time
of night.'

'I got a phone directory for the UN, for chrissake. What's it to you?'

'Then do me a favour and look up the number of the Secretary-
General. Ask the duty officer what Mr Jaidi's instructions are concerning
Dr Loz. After that, find the number for Senator Howard Staple. You
know who he is, Frank? He's one of New York's two senators. Mr Staple
is a long-time patient and friend of Dr Loz's. You ask him whether he
thinks arresting an innocent American citizen on the grounds that he is a
Muslim is either fair or just, or indeed tactful at this point. You ask him,
Frank, then come back to me.'

'Look, we just want to talk to him.'

'Then book an appointment like everyone else. You know where to
find him. You know his schedule. Your men have got his office covered
twenty-four hours a day.'

'Why don't you just put him on the street now, Harland? We know
he's with you.'

'Good for you. But to answer your question, no, I'm not going to give
him to you.'

'For Christ's sake, Harland, you do realise you could be aiding a major
terrorist? We can file any number of charges for your treatment of Agent
Morris in the street this evening.'

'I don't think so, Ollins,' said Harland, laughing. 'You want me to have
a word with the fellows in the press department? By noon tomorrow I'll
have a story about the FBI harassing UN officials on every news service in

Europe and the Middle East. I take it you're aware of the situation in the Middle East, Frank? I know it's not your beat, but even you understand that the US is in a bind. What do you think the State Department is going to say to Justice and the director of the FBI when you try to arrest Dr Loz? You're out of your depth, Frank. Leave this man alone.'

'I hear you threatening me,' said Ollins calmly. 'And I'm sure you're acting with the best motives, but you don't want to be caught up in this, believe me. I'll be waiting outside.' There was a click as he hung up.

Harland turned to Loz, who seemed unfazed by what he'd heard. 'How's the back?' he asked. 'I'm afraid it's not going to get any better with me treating you on a desk. But what I did should work for a day or two. You want a glass of water? You should drink more water, you know.'

Harland replied that there was whisky in his assistant Marika's room – his whisky, but kept in her cabinet at her insistence. When Loz had gone into Marika's office, he stretched a little and moved to an armchair where he opened Benjamin Jaidi's letter.

My dear Harland,

If you are reading this, Sammi Loz has signalled that he is in need of our help. This should be offered unconditionally by you on my behalf, and you should regard all United Nations facilities and the influence of my office as being at your disposal. Your role will be simply to watch Dr Loz and watch over him. I stress the distinction between those roles, though he has performed numerous services for this office and I believe we owe it to him to help him through his present difficulties. I enclose a letter which states that you are working for me and directs anyone who challenges or questions you during the course of this assignment to my office. This, I hope, will be of some use to you, my dear Harland.

Yours with gratitude,

Benjamin Jaidi (signed in his absence)

He folded the two sheets of paper and placed them in his pocket. Loz returned with the whisky.

'You read the letter. I was right, wasn't I? Jaidi wants you to help me.' He handed the glass to Harland. 'What do we do now?'

'I'm thinking,' Harland replied. 'Perhaps you'd better tell me what you want, apart from avoiding arrest?'

'To go to Albania,' said Loz simply.

'Just like that? It's not Atlantic City you know.' He exhaled heavily and took a mouthful of whisky. 'If you turn up in Tirana waving a picture of your old school pal they're likely to put you straight in jail. And when it comes to prisons, I'd choose American over Albanian any day.'

'I have to go. You must understand that there's no other way.'

'Even if you get there, you have to realise your man will have been seen by the CIA. Despite all protestations to the contrary, the CIA and FBI *do* talk. When you show your face in Albania the CIA will tell the FBI and that is likely to confirm all the suspicions they have about you. You'll wind up in prison for a very long time. Much better to go to the FBI. Tell them the story of Khan and then go to Albania if you must.'

Loz was unmoved. 'That is not possible.'

'It's your only course.'

'And where will you be, Harland, if they lock me up? What will you do for your back? You have a very serious condition and I am confident that I'm one of the very few people who can treat it. The Secretary-General told me you had tried everything before coming to see me. Is that right?'

Harland shifted in the chair and drank some more whisky, wondering about the imperturbable man in front of him.

'I want to know more about you and Karim Khan – all the things you left out in the restaurant. If I think you're keeping anything from me, I'll put you back on American soil straight away.'

'What do you want to know?'

'Why you owe him.'

'He saved my life.'

Harland revolved his hand. 'More, Doctor, I need more.'

'In Bosnia he offered his life for mine.'

'When were you there?'

'Ninety-two to ninety-three. I had finished my course at Guy's, Karim had one year to go. We joined a convoy taking supplies from London to Sarajevo. We went for the adventure and we didn't imagine what we'd find when we got to Bosnia. The trucks never reached Sarajevo of course and most of the stuff was looted in Krajina, not far from the coast. But Karim and I managed to communicate with the peacekeepers and became involved.'

'You fought the Serbs?'

He lowered his gaze. 'We were Muslims. Although neither of us had attended a mosque for many years, we felt obligated to help our people. I was there for a short while; Karim remained until nineteen ninety-six.'

Loz took off his jacket and started unbuttoning his shirt. He slipped off the right side and turned to reveal a patch of mottled light skin on his back, matched by a similar, smaller patch on his front to the right of his diaphragm. 'These are the grafts I received after being wounded by a mortar shell.' He did up his shirt and put on his jacket, fastidiously nipping at his collar and sleeves. 'We were serving with the brigade in the north of the city. We were in a trench, very much like you have seen in pictures of the First World War, facing the Serb lines. Ahead of us was an outcrop of rock where the Serbs had a heavy machine gun and mortar. Snipers used the rock also. They could look down almost into our trench and we were losing a lot of men. The outcrop was about fifty yards from the Serb lines and we believed if we captured it we'd save many lives as well as improving our concentration of fire.' As Loz talked he moved his hands through the air and glanced up to give an idea of the angles of fire.

'We launched an attack but were beaten back. As we retreated across no man's land they got the mortar range right and I was hit in the back and the leg. I was lying out there all night. The Serbs didn't finish me off because they thought my cries would demoralise our lines.' He stopped and moved to perch on the side of Harland's desk. 'Karim got back safely. He could not stand to hear my pain. He shouted to the Serbs that they could have him in exchange for allowing me to be taken back to our lines. The Serbs agreed, although we knew they would try to trick us and kill Karim and his helpers, as well as me. The arrangement was that two of our men would accompany Karim to the spot where I was lying and bring me back. At the same time two of their men would walk out and take Karim. All six of us would be exposed and both sides knew their men could be killed instantly. It was all about timing.

'Karim reached me and walked on with his hands in the air to meet the two Serbs, leaving our two guys by me. As he left, the two men who had come to pick me up began to count the seconds away. One . . . two . . . three – very slow, like that. It looked to the Serbs like they had the advantage because they could get their men back to safety and pick the rest of us off. When Karim reached the Serbs they called out, and this big Algerian man, very strong in the legs, lifted me on his back and we set off to our trench with the other man counting out loud. They knew they had thirty seconds to get me back because Karim was counting also. As they reached thirty they lowered me into the trench. Then Karim put his plan into action.'

Loz stood up, put his hands behind his neck, then continued. 'He had strapped hand grenades under the hood of his jacket, attached by the pins, so when he pulled the grenades away, the pins came out. Remember, his arms were raised like this, so he was able to let them drop back behind his neck. Just as they reached the trench with me, he took hold of two hand grenades, slipped behind his escort and threw them in the direction of the Serb lines. He could throw a cricket ball a hundred and fifty yards and aim it like he was dropping a penny into a glass. Two more followed. By this time our side were firing to cover him, but the Serbs couldn't get a clean shot at him because their men were in the way. He had many more grenades in his pockets and a couple of handguns concealed in his waistband. He dealt with the Serb escort and then went on to take that rock outcrop by himself. God knows how many people he killed in those few minutes but it was certainly the bravest act any of us had seen. And it didn't end there. He took me to find treatment and waited until he knew I was going to be okay.'

During the telling of this story some of the polish had slipped from

Loz's manner and Harland sensed that he regretted his vehemence. Loz's eyes returned to his shoes and he smiled to himself.

Harland said nothing.

'You know, Karim was soft. He liked the easy life in London, *la dolce vita* – the women, the clubs, the alcohol, the restaurants. When he got to Bosnia he couldn't take the cold, the lack of sleep and the food. But instead of crawling back to London with his tail between his legs, he became a real soldier, one of the best men defending Sarajevo. He buckled down to it.'

'When did you last see him?'

'In London – 1997.'

'So by then you had moved to New York and set up your practice in the Empire State?'

'Yes.'

'But you weren't trained as an osteopath by then?'

'No, I took the premises while I was training.'

'Expensive.'

'Mr Harland, that's what I wanted. I was a rich young man. So was Karim. It wasn't a problem for me, you understand.' He paused. 'So, have you heard enough about us?'

He shook his head. 'I am not going on the run with you, Doctor. You're going to see the FBI and tell them what you told me. Straight. Explain who Karim is.'

'They'll put me in prison.'

'They won't be able to: Ollins will come in here and talk, then he will leave.'

The interview went on until dawn in Harland's office. Ollins insisted that Harland leave so he went off and found himself somewhere to stretch out. He was woken by the toe of Ollins' well-worn black brogue at six, but had to be helped up.

'You're too old for this shit, Harland,' said Ollins, without letting the slightest sympathy crack his face. 'Why don't you stick with the water sports in Dubai?'

'Water supply, Frank – drinking water for people who don't have it.'

'You know what, Harland? Your back quack doesn't ring true to me. Just because we can't lay a glove on him now doesn't mean we're going to quit trying.'

'But you got some of what you wanted?'

'Nowhere near.'

'Still, you have to agree you've had unobstructed access to someone in UN custody.'

Ollins levelled his gaze at him. 'I just want to know one thing. What are you and the Secretary-General going to do if this guy is a terrorist, as we believe he is? How are your boys in the *press department* going to spin that one? 'Jaidi Aide Gave Terrorist UN Haven.' Don't imagine Jaidi will stand by you for that. He'll stiff you, Harland, and then where will you go – a guy with a back problem who knows about water? Huh?'

'I'll get someone to show you from the premises, Special Agent,' said Harland.

When he returned to his office he found Loz gazing meditatively along the East River. 'What do you want me to do, Harland?' he asked.

'What did you tell Ollins?'

'Everything I told you.'

'Good, that should keep him quiet for a while. The canteen will open soon. You should go and have breakfast while I think and make some calls.'

As Loz wandered off, Harland received two calls in rapid succession, the first from an assistant Secretary-General who was with Jaidi in Cairo, wanting to know the situation. The second came from a man named Charlie Coulson, one of several MI6 officers attached to the British Mission to the UN. Coulson had somehow heard about the situation and tried to impress upon Harland the need to get Loz out of the UN as soon as possible.

'We don't want this to turn into a stand-off between the Americans and the UN with a Brit in the middle,' he said. There was something about the way he was speaking that made Harland think that there were others listening. 'Look, is there any chance of you leaving your chap and having a cup of coffee with me? There's a place called The Sutton Coffee House on First Avenue. I'll see you there in twenty. Your man's not going anywhere without you.'

Coulson was in a booth reading the *Financial Times*. He was exactly as Harland had guessed from his voice – a combination of military briskness and social ease. He was in his forties and wearing a dark blue suit, suede loafers and a spotted tie.

'We'd like to know what you're up to with this character,' he said, after the waitress had brought coffee.

'That's UN business, I'm afraid.'

'We think it goes beyond that,' said Coulson. 'We understand Secretary-General Jaidi is involved. That makes it very high profile. Tell me, what do you know about Loz?'

Harland didn't reply.

'For instance, did you know that before he started squiring half the available crumpet in New York, he fought in the Balkans and is very, very rich?'

'He doesn't make any secret of it.'

'Right,' said Coulson, looking slightly disappointed. 'But we think he's important and I know the Chief is most concerned.' This was a common enough ploy. The Chief wants this; the Chief thinks so and so; the Chief has placed the highest priority . . . It was all bullshit. When Harland was in the Service he used it often, implying to some greedy little defector that his case was under the constant scrutiny of the head of the British Secret Intelligence Service.

'I'm sure he is. Even in his final days at Vauxhall Cross, Sir Robin Teckman is watching developments in a thousand intelligence arenas with the keenest interest.'

'In this instance it happens to be true.' Coulson got up.

Two men had materialised by the booth. One of them was the unmistakably patrician figure of Sir Robin Teckman; the other was his bodyguard. Teckman placed a hand on Harland's shoulder. 'Don't get up, Bobby,' he said.

Harland couldn't help returning the smile. He had always liked and admired Teckman. 'What the hell are you doing here, Chief?'

'Oh, you know, routine stuff. But I must say it's very pleasant to be in New York at this time of year. The city gives one a spring in the step. I used to love it when I was doing my time at the UN.'

His guard dropped back to the bar and the three of them were left alone.

'We were talking about the situation at the UN,' said Coulson.

'I dare say,' said Teckman, fixing Harland with an interested gaze. 'Bit of a mess, is it Bobby?'

'I don't think so.'

'I'm glad you say that, because from the outside it looks rather as though it is. I mean, he can't live in your office for ever, can he?' He paused. 'I think we ought to be open with you. This man Loz interests us. We've been watching him, though not as intensely as your friends in the FBI.'

'Why?'

Teckman gave him the stonewall smile. 'Suffice it to say, we were never totally convinced by his story.'

'But why would you even be aware of his story?'

'We're always interested in the Secretary-General's friends. Loz came to our notice a year or so ago and we felt he was not quite twelve apples to the dozen. We want you to stick with him. Find out everything he knows.'

'I don't work for you,' said Harland testily.

'But how does this compromise your position, Bobby? You would simply be doing what Jaidi asked you and letting us know as you go along. And of course you will want to keep in touch with Dr Loz because of your back.' He let out a chuckle. 'I hear he's very good but I wonder whether he has done all he can for you. That would be one way of keeping your interest, wouldn't it?'

That thought had occurred to Harland as he had lain face down on his desk the previous evening. 'My impression is that Loz is far too sophisticated and too successful to be involved in any kind of terrorism,' he said defensively. 'He's got everything to lose.' He wondered how much they knew about Loz's friend Khan. Probably nothing if they hadn't already mentioned him.

'Sophistication doesn't rule out evil. But in substance I agree with you. Still . . .' He leaned across the table and lowered his voice. 'I believe he can lead us to something very important, and I want you to let him take you with him. You won't even have to tell us anything. Just be aware that we'll be behind you.'

'If you're so sure he's got something to hide, why aren't you working with the FBI? You share intelligence on all this. Why not now?'

'He's got something to tell; not something to hide. I'm certain they don't see the difference.' The Chief shook his head anxiously. 'It's become awfully complicated, this business we're in, hasn't it? Now, tell me how you are.'

Coulson got up and went to join Teckman's guard.

'Nothing much to say,' said Harland.

'Any news of her? I had heard things hadn't been easy.'

Harland didn't like to talk about Eva, because it was almost impossible to utter a coherent sentence about her disappearance, especially to Teckman, who had been privy to her work for British intelligence and knew their story. Harland had been away in Azerbaijan for a few days. On his return he found that Eva had cleared out some, but not all, of her things and resigned from her Wall Street job where she'd worked on an Eastern European investments desk. No note, no calls, not a single transaction on their joint account or on any of her credit cards. So he had gone to Karlsbad in the Czech Republic and searched for her. There was no trace. The large apartment where she had once lived with her mother had been re-let and there was no forwarding address. Eva Rath had disappeared again. No, things hadn't been easy.

'Bobby, we'd be more than happy to help on this. If there's anything you think we can do, you know you just have to say the word.'

'Thank you.'

'You think she's alive?'

'Yes.' Why not tell someone, he thought. Why not say what you actually think instead of this fucking secrecy? 'I believe . . . I believe she just decided it wasn't going to work, and rather than going through the distress of explaining, she just cut out. That's her.' Articulating it didn't make him feel better.

The Chief nodded. 'Well, I really am very sorry indeed. You deserve happiness more than most.' He paused. 'On this other business, I think you understand that I wouldn't ask you unless I thought it was of the utmost importance. It really is. All you have to do is keep tabs on this man and we'll follow along at a discreet distance.'

He nodded. He knew it would be more than that, but what the hell. It might pay to have some help on hand.

'And this meeting hasn't taken place. Even with our own people, you haven't seen me. I can't stress the importance of this too much.' He got up, gripped Harland's shoulder and squeezed it. 'Look after yourself old son, and get that back better.' Then he was gone, slipping across the stream of office workers into a black Lincoln.

Coulson's exfiltration skills were not required. When Harland took him to his office in the UN building, he found a note from Sammi Loz on his desk.

> I have discovered a way of leaving the building undetected. I shall be in the Byron hotel in Tirana in two days' time and will expect you there. Before flying, take a day's rest on your back and drink plenty of water.
> With warmest regards,
> Sammi Loz

'He won't get out of the country,' said Harland.

'I'm not so sure,' said Coulson. 'After all he's not on the watch lists and if he's managed to dodge the FBI outside the building, they'll assume he's still in here. They won't be looking for him at the airports yet.'

'That's true,' said Harland. 'Ollins must believe he's with me for as long as possible.'

'And when they eventually demand you give up the man in your office, you can shove a surprised British diplomat out into the sunshine. That is to say, yours truly.'

12

Herrick and Nathan Lyne took to having a drink together after a late shift, during which a kind of truce operated and they talked about anything but RAPTOR. One evening Lyne told her to hang around because a decision had been taken to arrest the suspect in Stuttgart the following morning at 1.30 a.m. local time. The man known as Furquan, the third member of the Parana group, had in fact turned out to be called Mohammed bin Khidir. His voice had been recorded while he was speaking on a payphone a few hundred yards from his apartment. By chance someone at GCHQ had compared this with samples in their archive and matched it with what was known as the Bramble video.

Lyne explained that Mrs Christa Bramble, a young widow from Woking in Surrey, had been visiting the ancient sites of Carthage in Tunisia. At one of the sites, she and her party came under attack from a group of seven men armed with machine guns. Twelve tourists were killed and twenty-one others, including Mrs Bramble, were injured. As she fell to the ground, she kept her finger on the record button of her video camera and captured some blurred scenes and – crucially – the sound of the terrorists shouting and talking. From these came three distinct voiceprints, one of which was that of bin Khidir. Enhancing techniques, applied by the FBI to the film, clinched the identification. One of the moving figures matched Furquan's height, weight and gait exactly, and that man they knew to be Mohammed bin Khidir.

Under the terms of RAPTOR, any of the suspects confirmed to have been involved in international terrorism had to be killed or taken off the street – as Lyne put it, 'stiffed or lifted'. The former seemed a great deal easier, but they knew that a professional killing would act like a bird scarer for the other ten suspects. So a plan was developed, in which bin Khidir would be kidnapped from his apartment in the Turkish district of Stuttgart, and taken to an airfield nearby.

Herrick and Lyne went to their desks and hooked up to the live feed from Stuttgart. There was a commentary of sorts from a van parked near bin Khidir's apartment and they caught the clipped sentences of the armed members of the snatch squad.

Lyne sat tensely. 'If this fucking thing goes wrong . . .' he said.

'I don't see why they're taking him,' Herrick said. 'We know they're all terrorists. Why's he any different?'

'They're the rules we're playing by.'

'I'm not sure there should be any rules,' she said.

'That's not a very smart thing to say.'

Her gaze drifted to the glass box, where the operation was being run. Everyone was there – Spelling, Vigo, Collins and the nameless head of the Special Collection Agency who had flown in from Washington DC in order to escort bin Khidir from Northolt back to an unknown destination outside the United States for interrogation.

They listened as the team gained entry into bin Khidir's apartment without difficulty. Bin Khidir and his flatmate were drugged before they even woke and he was bundled into an airline services truck and driven to a plane waiting at the airfield twenty miles away. The plane took off for Northolt, but over Luxembourg the pilot reported that bin Khidir had come round and was proving difficult to restrain, even though his hands were tied behind his back. He was lashing out with his feet and throwing himself around the fuselage.

Herrick picked up the summaries of Southern Group activity from that day and went to the control box. As she entered, Vigo nodded to her from the table where he sat watching Jim Collins.

'Tell them to give him another shot,' said Collins.

There was silence until the pilot said that 'the horse' – the plane was normally used for transporting racehorses – had gone to sleep of its own accord. Vigo looked straight at Herrick.

'I expect you understand what's happened, Isis.' Then, without waiting for her to answer, he turned back to Collins. 'You'd better tell them to turn the plane around.'

'Why, for chrissake?' Collins demanded.

'I think you'll find the horse has swallowed a cyanide capsule concealed in its teeth.'

Confirmation came in a matter of minutes. The crew had found a dribble of foam on bin Khidir's chin.

'I don't imagine there'll be many takers for mouth-to-mouth resuscitation,' said Vigo, without mirth. 'Tell me, Isis, what would you do now?' Spelling and the rest of them turned to her.

'I'd get him back to his own bed, if possible.'

'Which is exactly what we should do, gentlemen, though quite how they're going to get the body off the plane is another matter. The transport arrangements only worked *into* the airport. We have not allowed for the return journey.'

Herrick went to call up satellite maps of the airport on her screen, printed them off and returned to Vigo and Collins with her idea. Twenty-five minutes later the plane landed at the airport, the pilot having complained to the German air traffic control of two un-commanded aileron movements. As the de Havilland Dash taxied through the first light of dawn towards the end of the runway, a hatch in the belly of the aircraft opened and four members of the Special Collection Service, who had cut their way through the perimeter fence, sprang from the darkness to receive the body. Forty-five minutes later, they reported back to say bin Khidir was in bed and the other man was still out cold. Everything was as it should be in the apartment, and bin Khidir's helpers would assume that he had bitten through the capsule in his sleep. RAPTOR was safe.

'It will be interesting,' mused Vigo, 'to see if they report this to the authorities and risk the pathologist discovering the cause of death. My bet is they'll dispose of the body and get in touch with the man running things. That provides us with an unusual opportunity.'

Isis watched the glitter of Vigo's eyes fade as he became absorbed in his thoughts. Then his head turned slowly to the men from GCHQ and the National Security Agency. 'We should pay great attention to phone calls from Stuttgart over the next few hours, for we know they must deliver a message that their man is dead.'

Next morning, Herrick went back to her house. The isolation of the Bunker and its eerily regulated conditions – the fact that it was neither hot nor cold, humid nor dry, light nor dark – were getting to her. She and Lyne were getting on each other's nerves, which had as much to do with her bad temper as his unwavering faith in RAPTOR. She was still sure that RAPTOR was missing something in the flood of information, yet when challenged by Lyne found it difficult to be precise. At that point, he gave her a twenty-four-hour break. 'Take off, go to a hair stylist, see a movie, get laid,' he had said, without looking up from his screen.

Just one of those would be enough, she thought. She booked an appointment at the hair salon opposite Rahe's bookshop and submitted to the pleasure of a hair wash and head massage. As she had done a couple of weeks before, she moved to the seat that enabled her to watch the bookshop as her hair was being cut. This was how it started, she thought: an average-looking bloke, a bit on the chubby side, bustling from his bookstore to meet a cab and then a plane. She stared at the shop front, imagining him there in his ludicrous green jacket; Vigo's man rushing to a terrible death in his Sunday best.

She left the hairdresser and walked up and down the street, noticing a couple of *bureaux de change*, a printing shop and a Lebanese restaurant. Then she went into the Pan Arab Library – despite Rahe's absence, the bookstore was still open and doing a reasonable trade. She stopped at the cash desk, smiled pleasantly at the young woman, and asked if the store had a book called *The Balance of Power in the Jordanian Islamist*

Movements by Al-Gharaibeh, a title she remembered seeing on one of the Wallflowers' desks. The woman explained she was new and wasn't sure which section the book would be found in: she'd check the computer stock list. As her varnished nails skittered across the keyboard, Herrick's gaze came to rest on the smears of grime on the return key and space bar – grime accumulated in tens of thousands of keystrokes by Youssef Rahe. She realised suddenly that she had found what she was looking for.

'That's a Dell computer, isn't it?' said Herrick. 'I've had the exact same one for three years and it's never caused me any trouble.'

The woman looked at her oddly. 'Yes, it seems to be very reliable.'

'Can I look?' asked Herrick, leaning over and memorising the model number. The woman was still trying to find the book on the stock list. 'I can always come back later,' said Herrick. 'I've quite a number of purchases to make. Perhaps it would help if I brought a list this afternoon.'

The woman seemed relieved. Herrick left the shop and caught a cab to Notting Hill Gate where she began to search the second-hand shops. Very soon, she found a Dell for sale, slightly newer than the one in the bookstore, but with an identical keyboard. She examined the socket at the back of the computer and practised pressing the plug home. Then she negotiated with the youth behind the counter to buy the keyboard separately. Clutching her prize in an old supermarket bag, she walked a few doors along the street and entered a large bookshop. The back of a recently published book in the politics section called *Jihad* had an excellent bibliography, from which she took the titles of half a dozen obscure-sounding books on the Middle East.

This done, she returned to Rahe's bookshop with the list and the keyboard, but the obliging young assistant at the desk had been replaced by a rather stout and ill-tempered woman wearing a hijab to cover her hair and neck, who must have been Rahe's wife. She told Herrick to leave the list overnight and return to collect the books next day, then picked up the phone and began speaking. Herrick placed the list on her desk and moved to the door, taking from her pocket another piece of paper now nicely compressed into an oval pellet. As she reached the door, she again checked for an alarm, then wedged the pellet into the metal opening of the lock and slipped into the street.

She made her way to Westbourne Grove and took lunch in a brasserie – sea bass with half a bottle of Mersault – and read the *Guardian*, which had a detailed analysis of the Norquist shooting and raised the possibility of a stray police bullet. She was interrupted by a man who said she reminded him of an American film actress, whose name he couldn't quite recall. She tolerated him for a little while, admitting to herself that being complimented wasn't such a bad experience after nearly a fortnight in the Bunker. But at length, she made her excuses and went to a department store, buying a small plastic pill container, a make-up powder brush and a thin, very flexible metal spatula.

With these she went home to wait. In the hours that followed, she made some calls, took a nap and packed a fresh set of clothes for her return to the Bunker. At midnight, she drove her car to a road leading off Forsythe Street and parked opposite Rahe's bookshop. At 1.00 a.m. she left the car and crossed the road. There were still one or two people about, so as she approached the bookshop door she pulled out her own flat keys and lifted them as if to unlock it. At the same time, she shook the head of the spatula from her sleeve, raised it to the door-frame and worked it in at the point where the wad of paper had prevented the lock from sliding home. One firm push and the door opened.

She removed the keyboard from her bag and went round the desk to face the computer. As she stretched behind the box to remove the keyboard plug, she knocked the mouse. The computer whirred and the screen flashed on. Instinctively, she moved to block the light from the window, but as she did so, she noticed the aquarium screensaver appear and begin to animate. It was exactly as Dolph had described, but what interested her now was the noise coming from the hard drive. Behind the picture of the fish making their progress across the screen, something was going on. She changed the keyboards, knowing this would not affect the computer, and put Rahe's into her bag, never letting her eyes leave the screen. A few seconds later, she heard the modem dial out. Suddenly she was looking at a web page in Arabic. She read the words 'Ansar Allah' – helpers of God.

A noise came from the door. 'Is there a problem here, Miss?' A policeman was standing in the doorway with a flashlight.

'Oh, you gave me a shock, officer.'

'What are you doing here?' he said, moving from the door.

'Just changing the keyboard – I've had a nightmare trying to find the right one. Mrs Rahe wanted it here by morning.' She pointed to the ceiling. 'We'd better keep our voices down. I don't want to wake her.'

The policeman looked doubtfully at her. 'You work here? I've never seen you in the shop.'

'I read Arabic, so I look after the stock at the back and do the re-ordering from publishers in the Middle East. I'm part-time.'

'Let's have some light, shall we? Where's the switch?'

'By the door,' she said. 'But I'm going now.'

'It must be difficult to learn Arabic. What's that say there?' he asked, pointing to a card.

'This? It says the Pan Arab Library welcomes you. Our staff will be happy to offer every assistance in finding your purchases – Youssef Rahe.'

'Very impressive,' said the policeman. 'I don't know how you manage it.' His radio crackled with a voice and he turned down the volume. From upstairs, there was the sound of a light footfall.

'I'll just shut down the computer,' she said. 'They left it on.' She got up and moved around the desk. 'I must say it's very reassuring to see you, officer. You hear so much about there being no police on the beat.'

The policeman nodded. 'Would you mind if I took a few details from you, Miss? Just as a precaution.'

'Not in the least,' she said, leaning against the door and letting her forefinger remove the pellet of paper from the lock. 'My name is Celia Adams. I live at 340 Ladbroke Grove.' She smiled again, this time more coquettishly. 'You could give me a lift there.'

'Just a moment,' he said, writing in his notebook. 'Celia . . . Adams. Do you have some form of identification with you?'

'Yes, of course.' She made as if to look in her bag, but just then a voice called out from the back of the shop. She looked up to see the woman whom she'd spoken to on her second visit. 'My apologies, Mrs Rahe,' she said in Arabic. 'We have woken you up. This officer was worrying about your lock but I told him there was a knack to it.'

The woman stared at them uncomprehendingly. Herrick knew she had to make a run for it or be arrested. She stretched her hand to the door, flipped the latch upwards and jumped into the street, pulling the door shut behind her. She ran straight across Forsythe Street, dodging a bus, but did not immediately make for her car. Instead, she turned into another side street, glancing behind to see the policeman tearing towards his patrol car with his radio to his mouth. She was badly out of condition, so she took the first possible escape route, a short driveway leading to a high wooden gate. She scaled the gate and found herself in an untidy London garden. Thanking God there were no intruder lights, she negotiated a wall covered by a rambling rose, and lowered herself into the next garden. She was aware of the blue light flickering in the gap between the houses behind her, but kept going through several gardens until, eventually, she ended up in the street where her car was parked. Out of breath and feeling slightly silly but elated, she moved without haste to her car and drove off in the direction of Paddington.

Ten minutes later, she parked under a street light, placed the keyboard on her lap and unscrewed it with infinite care. She prised it apart and began to stroke the inside surfaces with the make-up brush, gathering the dust and strands of hair that had worked their way down through the keys, and sweeping it all into the pill container. She wasn't surprised at how much matter had accumulated in the keyboard, for she had once unscrewed her own to repair a jammed key and found a mass of hair and a couple of dead insects. After a few minutes of brushing, the bottom of the box was covered with a few millimetres of debris. She closed the box and placed it in an envelope that bore the address of an establishment in

South Parks Road, Oxford. This she fed into a nearby postbox, then drove home.

Next day, Isis got to the Bunker early and passed through the numerous security checks to find that her place at the archipelago of investigation desks was taken. Nathan Lyne saw her and rose. 'We have some business, you and I, in the conference room,' he said, jabbing his finger over her head.

Vigo and Spelling were ranged on one side of the table. Lyne took up a seat at the end, leaving her standing.

Spelling didn't look up. 'We understand you broke into Youssef Rahe's shop last night. Can you explain why?'

How did they know? Surely the bookshop couldn't still be under observation. 'I wanted to take a look at his computer,' she said. 'His role in all this still seems unclear.'

'Unclear?' said Spelling. 'In what way unclear?'

'It doesn't seem sensible to put all this effort into the eleven others without trying to work out what happened in Lebanon: why Rahe fell for it; who the other man on his flight was. We're missing something.'

The room was thick with pious male complacency. Spelling finally looked up, his reading glasses magnifying the anger in his expression. 'I specifically instructed you not to press your personal inquiries further, for the very good reason that if these people understand we know Rahe is dead, they're very likely to conclude their entire operation is compromised. I assumed you had grasped this elementary point and yet you go off on your own, break into the premises and provide the police and Mrs Rahe with a very good idea of what you look like. What if you had been apprehended and charged? How would you have explained your presence in the shop?'

'But I wasn't caught.'

'Don't be bloody stupid. I'm talking about the risk you took.'

Vigo shifted in his chair. 'We were extremely lucky,' he said. 'The local police were aware of our interest in the shop and alerted Special Branch about the break-in, so we were able to acquire the film from the security cameras outside the adjacent premises.' He slid a photograph across the table. She looked down and saw herself moving from the door with the plastic carrier bag in her arms.

'What was in the bag?' he asked, fixing her with utterly expressionless eyes.

'I took a keyboard. You know, to look as if I had some business being there . . .'

'A little amateurish for you, I would have thought,' said Vigo. 'What would anyone be doing mending a computer at that hour?'

'It nearly worked,' she said. 'If Mrs Rahe hadn't come down, I would have been okay.'

'That's beside the point,' said Spelling. 'Your actions threatened RAPTOR. It was exceptionally irresponsible of you.'

She held her temper and spoke deliberately. 'I concede that I may have been a bit rash. But I don't agree that my actions jeopardised anything.'

'I'm not going to argue with you,' Spelling shot back. 'Mr Collins and I believe you've forfeited our trust and therefore your place in RAPTOR.'

Lyne clenched his hands together and turned them out to click his knuckles. 'Look, gentlemen, we all agree this was very dumb of Isis, but in her defence I'd like to point out that she's easily one of the best investigators we have – you saw how quick she was the night before last. Hell, she really gets it. I'd hate to lose her.'

Herrick tipped her head in thanks.

'What were you hoping to find on the computer?' asked Vigo. 'You know we had all that covered. Did you imagine we had overlooked something?'

'To be honest, yes. I feel we're all missing something. I've told Nathan this, countless times.'

'I can vouch for that,' said Lyne. 'She's been a real pain in the ass.'

'And you think that because you spotted the switch at Heathrow, you have some superior insight into this operation?' said Vigo.

'Well, at least my *personal inquiries* achieved something on that occasion.'

'So you felt you had the right to go off piste again?' said Spelling.

'I suppose so, yes.'

'And did you see anything on the computer that interested you?' asked Vigo.

'As a matter of fact, yes, it was in sleep mode and when I touched the mouse it automatically logged on to an Islamist website. I didn't have time to read much, but it struck me as interesting that the messages were still coming through to a man they knew was dead. I wondered whether his wife had knowledge of the way the screensaver operated as a gateway. I wondered about the site I saw. The internet address showed it was based in Malaysia.'

'The screensaver – did you know about it before?'

'I made it my business to find out as much as I could about Youssef Rahe. I still feel he's important.'

'But where from?' demanded Vigo.

She returned his stare and gently shook her head. 'My sources,' she said defiantly. Damn Vigo: he'd still be selling second-hand books if it hadn't been for her. He owed his resurrection to her. She turned to Spelling, determined to get off the subject of the computer for good. 'I've done nothing wrong, and if you don't mind, I repeat that we are ignoring an essential part of this case. What happened to Youssef Rahe?'

Spelling rested his chin on his hands, then removed his glasses. 'That will be all,' he said.

Twenty minutes later the three men emerged, and Lyne came over to Herrick. 'You're off the team,' he said. 'They're sending you to Tirana. A suspect is being held there, and we think he's interesting.'

'Why me? We've got our own people at the British Embassy. Why can't they give him the once-over?'

'The resident officer is ill – cancer. His stand-in is too inexperienced and besides, he's not in on the big secret. Maybe the suspect has something to tell, and if he does, I want you to be there to hear it. There's a really good case for going. I was arguing for them to send you before you started burglarising bookstores. Hell, Isis, this is a reprieve. They want you back in a couple of weeks. Jim Collins thinks you're shit hot.'

'I wish you could persuade Spelling of that.'

'I think he's already there. But Christ, you're a fucking handful. You know that?'

She smiled sheepishly. 'By the way, thanks for sticking up for me in there. It's not everyone who would do that.'

'That's okay. You're flying out tomorrow morning to Zurich, then Mother Teresa airport, Tirana. Spelling says you'll have the usual diplomatic status, but they don't want you mixing too much at your own Embassy, so you're to stay at the Byron – it's Tirana's only good hotel. You'll see a lot of the guys at the US Embassy, but again, I don't have to tell you to stay off the subject of RAPTOR. Some of them may have got wind of it, because of the involvement of so many personnel, but you're Garbo – right?'

'Who am I reporting to?'

'Me – this is an officially sponsored RAPTOR tour. Just see the guy interviewed, turn in a report and bring your butt safely back here in a couple of weeks. It's a piece of cake. You'll probably end up with a beautiful tan.' He paused and placed his hand on her shoulder. 'But you be careful. There are some bad, bad people out there.'

'Then I'm going to need a story. That requires a little preparation. I don't know if I've got enough time. '

'You got all day. But make it better than the keyboard story. That was bush-league stuff, Isis – just terrible.'

She stayed for a further two hours to read the file on the Tirana detainee and draw some money – $7,000 in hundred-dollar bills – from a character who came from the US Embassy and stressed that every last cent was to be accounted for.

13

Around five-thirty in the afternoon, the public areas of the Hotel Byron in Tirana began to fill, mostly with Albanian gangsters who left their bodyguards out in the car park. They moved through the bar to a crescent-shaped area bordering the gardens, trailing an air of listless menace, and sank into the Lloyd loom chairs to drink, smoke without pause and fiddle with their cell phones. There were some foreigners too; insanely risk-averse businessmen, low-level diplomats and a few edgy American evangelists sipping soft drinks and wearing hiking gear, as if the mere fact of being in this godless, chaotic country required rugged clothing.

The tableau was not difficult to decode, and as Herrick waited on her second evening for Lance Gibbons, her contact from the local CIA station, she realised that more or less the same groups appeared and seemed to settle at regular tables. Bashkin, the driver who had attached himself to her at Mother Teresa International airport, told her the Albanian men were mostly engaged in drug trafficking, prostitution rackets and smuggling people, cigarettes and fuel.

Gibbons arrived late, a large, shambling man who quickly announced that he was a veteran of the war against al-Qaeda in Afghanistan, or the 'Big A' as he called it. After a couple of drinks, Isis brought up the purpose of her trip and asked when she could see the suspect.

'Look, that's going to be kinda difficult right now,' he said, toying with the scarf loosely hung round his neck. 'We have to tread carefully with the Albanians. He's their prisoner. We're just observing.'

Herrick gave him a sceptical look, pulled out her phone and dialled Nathan Lyne. 'I'm having some unexpected difficulty inspecting the goods,' she said to Lyne. 'I wonder if you could intervene with the local representative and tell him there'll be hell to pay if he doesn't cooperate. I'll put you onto him now.'

She handed the phone to Gibbons, who listened silently then said, 'You got to understand, Nathan, that these goods are not in our possession yet. They're still being held by the customs service.'

He hung up and handed the phone back. 'You know, that was real unfriendly of you.'

'I have to see this man quickly and report back to London. That's all there is to it.'

'You and your man Lyne don't cut any ice here. Here is dif–fer–ent. Period.' He sipped his drink then lit a cheroot. 'So, Isis Herrick, tell me about RAPTOR. What the fuck is going down? We hear something big's happening. All our guys pulled in from the field. Operations suspended without warning. What's the deal?'

She shrugged. 'That name doesn't mean anything to me, but if there is something going down, as you put it, you better be sure that I see this suspect. It comes from the top.'

He laughed. 'The top of what – my organisation? No way. The British Secret Intelligence Service? Hey, that would be something, wouldn't it? I'll stand to attention and drink to Her Majesty.'

'Where's he being held?' she asked.

'That's classified information.'

'The intelligence headquarters, the prison – where?'

He shook his head and stroked the three-day-old stubble on his chin.

'What's the problem with giving me access? If this man is talking, you must have transcripts.'

'Oh yeah, he's talking.'

'Then you'll get the transcripts to me?'

'I can't be certain of that.'

'I'm not fooling around,' she said icily. 'If I don't get your agreement this evening, I'll have Nathan Lyne call his friends in the State Department and Langley. By morning your communications centre will be jammed with cables. Give me what I want and I'll get out of your hair.'

'Don't misunderstand me, Isis. I'd like you *in* my hair. This town gets pretty tedious and you're definitely the best thing to happen to me all week, but this is real difficult. I don't see the Albanians letting you visit the suspect. Hell, you're a woman. You know what that means to these people, right?'

'Mr Gibbons . . .'

'Lance.'

'If you've heard that something unusual is going on,' she stopped while the waiter placed another drink in front of Gibbons, 'you should know that the authority behind it doesn't get any higher.'

Gibbons exhaled a low, sarcastic whistle. 'Hey, you already said that. Look, I'll see what I can do, okay? But you have to understand that this is not a Western jail and right here they don't have Western standards of prisoner care – you follow me?'

She nodded. 'I want the transcripts this evening.'

Gibbons shifted the small, black pack from his lap – the standard cover for an automatic weapon – shouldered it and rose from the chair. 'Maybe tomorrow,' he said, looking down at her.

'This evening,' she said.

'We're on Albanian time, Missie. Tomorrow.' He gave her a two-fingered salute and loped out of the hotel, beckoning to his driver on the way.

She had dinner and then went to her room to smoke a rare cigarette on the balcony overlooking the gardens. At ten-thirty her cell phone rang and she dived for her bag.

'Hello, darling. It's your father.'

'Dad, what are you doing?'

'Merely phoning my daughter to find out how she is and what she's up to. Can you speak?'

'Yes. Did you go on your trip to the West Highlands?'

'Yes, yes. Saw a lot and did a good bit of sea trout fishing.'

She was smiling to herself, swamped by a rush of affection for the old man. 'That's exactly what I'd like to be doing now,' she said, glancing around the bleak hotel room.

'Then we should take a trip together when you have some time off. I know how much you love being driven in the Armstrong.' He laughed. 'Look, I gather from friends that you're in Albania. The first thing to say about that is, be careful. They're a treacherous bunch. I was there at the end of the war when I was no longer needed in France and witnessed a very ugly side of them. Anyway, the reason I'm calling is that I have a message for you. It's from my old student.' She understood he meant Sir Robin Teckman. 'He wants to talk to you on a secure line. So you're booked to go and see our ambassador tomorrow.'

'Dad, why's he using you to talk to me?'

'No doubt you'll find out. He wants you there at eight-thirty sharp. You should go to Skenderbeg Street. Our Embassy is next door to the Egyptians'. Be discreet, Isis. If you have a driver, don't use him. Take a taxi. The student says the driver may be unreliable.'

Herrick found herself reluctant to let her father go and asked him a succession of questions about Hopelaw and its inhabitants, the tap-room gossip that she missed, about barns burning down, sheepdogs going wild, poachers being caught and people running off with each other. Her father, though elliptical about himself, was an acute observer of village life and she liked hearing him speak about it. At length, she said goodbye, re-lit her cigarette and began to read a book about Albania she'd picked up in the hotel shop.

Just as she thought of turning in, the room doorbell rang. She looked through the spy hole and saw Gibbons standing with his thumb hooked in his shirt pocket and another cheroot hanging from his lower lip.

'Hey there, Isis. Brought what you wanted,' he said when she opened the door. His eyes scanned the room. 'Any chance of a little of that Johnny Walker Black Label?'

She had bought the bottles as useful bribes. 'Help yourself, Mr Gibbons.'

'Lance,' he said. 'That stuff you have is from the first ten days. Most of what he's said is in there. You'll see that this character is quite fly. He's educated in Britain and speaks good English. He's not the usual Mujahadin type. He's sharp and kind of civilised. Tough too. He got over the border and managed to survive long enough to be taken by the police. We think there is something more to him. For one thing, he was carrying the documentation belonging to a man thought to be dead, name of Jasur Faisal, otherwise known as The Electrician or The Watchmaker – a wanted Hamas terrorist. Maybe you've heard of him? So you see he's a deal more interesting than the average holy warrior. We don't know what he's doing in Europe and why he's flat broke, but he's the kind of guy who could form the nucleus of a very big terrorist attack. We think one tough sonofabitch lies beneath the polite exterior.'

'And what happens now? They've had him for ten days. Can't be much more to get out of him.'

'You're wrong. There's a truckload of stuff he can tell us about. He's been ID'd by people in Camp X-Ray and elsewhere. Beyond that, we're not sure. He may have served in Chechnya.'

'But it's been established that he's a Pakistani national?'

'Who knows, Isis. The way he looks, he could be either Pakistani or Palestinian.'

'So what happens to him?'

'Anyone's guess.'

Herrick looked at the first few pages while Gibbons sipped and swilled the whisky round his mouth, making pain-pleasure grimaces.

'Well, thank you for bringing this round so quickly. I take it I can keep this?'

'For sure, but don't leave it lying around.'

'Is there much more?'

'Some,' he said, rolling the tumbler in his hands. 'But it's pretty much the same as what you got there. They're doing a slow job on the stuff they know he'll talk about. This is not a Defense Intelligence Agency operation – it's the Company. We're doing it thoroughly. The Pentagon knows shit.'

She moved to the door and opened it. Gibbons got up with a sigh. 'If you need anything or any company while you're here, this is my mobile number.'

'Thanks again,' she said.

'Hey, we're all on the same side in this thing.' He gave her another salute and went out.

'Exactly.' She closed the door behind him and returned to the chair on the balcony. For the first time that day, the air was fresh and cool. She looked across the gardens to the lights illuminating the Palace of Congress and noticed a swirl of bats feeding on the moths that had gathered beneath each lamp. Then she turned to the interview transcripts.

She rose early the next day and left the hotel by a side entrance, knowing that Bashkin would already be waiting for her at the front. She crossed the city's main boulevard and cut through the old politburo compound, passing Enver Hoxha's villa, built in a curiously open style and surrounded by gardens now partly taken over by a McDonald's restaurant. A little later she came across the diplomatic quarter, a haven of police patrols, well-barbered hedges and almost no traffic.

At the Embassy she pushed past a dozen locals, showed her passport and was led to a communications room in the basement, stuffed with equipment and a couple of large computers. The ambassador was drinking a cup of coffee and chatting to one of his staff.

'Ah, Miss Herrick, welcome, welcome. Take a pew. The line is all set up for you.' He left her alone with a copy of the *Spectator*.

When the call came through, Teckman was at his most distilled. He explained that he wanted her to make contact at the Byron with a former SIS officer named Harland, who at his request was escorting an osteopath named Sammi Loz, 'a rather unusual figure from New York high society', who he felt was interesting. She had heard of Harland, and knew he'd had something to do with the demise of Walter Vigo, but stopped herself from mentioning it. Instead she asked if he thought Karim Khan was important, or merely an excuse to get her out of the Bunker.

'Both, though they won't suspect that he is important. I think the fact the osteopath is interested seems to indicate something. Harland says that Loz owes Karim Khan for saving his life in Bosnia and feels obligated to try to free him. This is probably true, but there may be something else, and you and Harland are going to have to get it out of him, even if you have to mislead him about the possibility of achieving Khan's release. I should warn you that the Americans are already alert to Loz's possible significance but, like us, they don't know why he's important. Also, it's unlikely there has been much serious communication between the FBI, who have been watching him in New York, and the CIA in Albania. He's not on any watch list, and you know relations between everyone in Washington are at an all-time low.'

'What do I say to the Americans? They're being a bit tricky about access.'

'I'll see to it that you get in this afternoon. Present yourself at the US Embassy at three unless you hear from me.'

'And RAPTOR?'

'Just see Khan, do your stuff and send back a report to the Bunker. Believe me, they're very preoccupied with the other nine active suspects and it will only confuse things if you start kicking up in your usual way.' He paused and laughed quietly. 'So, no break-ins for the moment, Isis. Keep your powder dry and use those observant eyes of yours. I'm afraid I can't brief you more clearly than this, because things are very fluid: I'm relying on you and Harland to respond in a way that I know you're both capable of.' He gave her a number, then hung up, leaving her sitting in the cool of the communications room, wondering what the hell was going on. Her father had observed that the Chief might be waiting to make his move, but with only three or four weeks left of his tenure, it seemed a little late. Besides, everything he was interested in seemed way off the point.

She left the Embassy and walked out into the dust and noise of Rruga e Durresit, along which she had noticed some shops. She entered one of the boutiques, a sad little place with almost no stock, bought two brightly coloured T-shirts and a canvas shoulder bag she had seen some of the Tirana women carrying. In another, where there was more sense of actual commerce, she chose a belt and some jeans with studded seams. She moved on to a market and threaded her way into a rickety wood and tin structure pierced with shafts of light. Beyond the pyramids of vegetables and boxes of live chickens, she found a woman with a tray of cheap costume jewellery, and bought some imitation gold bangles and a necklace of white and black plastic beads. She turned to the adjacent stall, which was run by a young man with a wispy moustache, and bargained for a black fish-net shawl and a pair of high-heeled ankle-length boots with a cowboy fringe at the top. She placed all her purchases in a white supermarket bag, together with some fruit, and walked purposefully through the stall holders, who had now cottoned on to the presence of a foreigner and were plucking at her jacket.

By ten-thirty, she reached the hotel and, deciding that she would wait for Harland to contact her, went to the swimming pool with a couple of books and a newspaper.

When the doctor first came to Khan in the headquarters of SHISK, the Albanian intelligence service, and treated him for the abscess and broken lip, Khan assumed he was Albanian, but through the days of his interrogation he had learned that the man was Syrian. The SHISK interrogators referred to him as The Syrian or The Doctor, the latter always accompanied by a brief ironic smile that puzzled him. The Doctor also had a habit of making notes when Khan was answering a question. What did a doctor need to know about his past in Afghanistan? More unnerving was the way he interrupted proceedings by leaving his chair near the window and walking over to grasp one of Karim's arms or dig his thumbs into the tendons at the back of his leg. While the doctor went about his curious inspection, the two Albanian interrogators would sit back and light up; the Americans, of whom there were never fewer than three, stretched, rubbed their necks and murmured under their breath.

At first he was reassured by The Doctor's presence, thinking it would protect him from the treatment meted out to the other prisoners, but he gradually came to resent, then loathe the strange prodding and pinching that went on. Besides this, the expression in the man's face had hardened in blood-chilling appraisal. He wished fervently never to be left alone with this man.

The interrogations had followed the same pattern since the first days, when he had given them the outline of his story from Bosnia to Afghanistan. Their interest focused on the last four years. They took it for granted that he met and knew the leadership of the Taleban and al-Qaeda, although he told them over and over again that he was just a mountain commander and had little experience of the regime, and none of the terrorist training camps. But, prompted by the Americans, the Albanian intelligence officers went on asking: 'Where did you train? Who trained you? What methods were you taught – car bombs, sniper attacks, butane bombs, timing devices? What about dirty bombs?' Did he know of any radioactive material coming over the border from Turkmenistan, Uzbekistan or Tajikistan? He had admitted being in that area during the summer of 1999, they said, so he must have known of the shipments of strontium and caesium chloride. He insisted that he didn't know anything about these shipments, but would not have hesitated to tell them if he had known. He was numb with repetition, going over the details so often that the words lost meaning for him.

They showed him books of photographs, brought by the Americans in two metal cases. This was a welcome break in the routine. He used these to show that he wanted to cooperate, and for all of two days they went through the four or five hundred faces of men who were suspected of having trained in Afghanistan. He gave them names of about a dozen he had fought with, and pointed out that three of the men – a Saudi, a Yemeni and another Pakistani with a British passport – were dead. He had seen the young Yemeni killed in front of him by a Northern Alliance rocket, and he'd buried him with five others under a mound of rocks, the ground being too hard to dig.

The interrogators returned again and again to the al-Qaeda camps. Khan explained that he had gone already trained, battle-hardened from Bosnia. As far as tactics and weaponry went, he knew much more than any of the men he fought with, but he had absolutely no contact with the terrorist training camps. During the last two winters, he had been trapped at the front with no supplies, freezing his arse off, men dying of cold and illness all around him. They had radio contact with Kabul but nobody seemed to care about them. 'I was a soldier,' he concluded wearily. 'I was nothing to them, and the Arabs mostly kept to themselves.'

'But you were the big hero from Bosnia. You commanded Arabs in battle with the Northern Alliance and on the Tajik border,' said one of the interrogators.

'The Arabs without money stayed with us, yes. And they became good fighters. But the rich ones always bought their way back south. I saw them come and knew they would not last more than a few weeks. You may have heard of the different Arab words for them. *Tharwa* were the rich ones, *Thawra* were the revolutionaries. It is an old joke in Arabic – a pun, I believe.'

'Why didn't you leave earlier?' asked one of the Americans. 'You say you hated the Taleban and you had no respect for the Arabs, yet you stayed in Afghanistan longer than anyone we have interrogated. Why?'

'I was committed to the men I fought with. There were ten of us who'd been together since ninety-eight. We survived all the hardship together, the dangers and the crazy decisions that came from men in Kabul who didn't have to fight. We ate with each other, shared our possessions; we saved each other and buried our brothers. When you're out in the mountains like this for years, depending on one another, without supplies, you don't think about what is going on in the outside world. It's easy to become cut off . . .'

'Myopic,' offered another one of the Americans.

'Yes, myopic. I was guilty of that. Yes.'

'Horse-shit,' said a man named Milo Franc. He was leading the American team and was easily the most hostile. 'That's hypocritical horse-shit, Khan. You're a mercenary and you fought for a regime that executed women for reading school books!'

'I didn't support those things.'

'You enjoyed killing. That's the truth, isn't it? You're a professional killer. And when your people in Afghanistan were thrown out, you were ordered to the West to kill again.' He paused and lowered his voice. 'You left Afghanistan in December – is that right?'

Khan nodded, and stared at the patterns of chips in the wall paint. He knew every square inch of the room and was familiar with the routine noises coming from the street: the surges of traffic, the calls of vendors who appeared at exactly the same time every day, and the sound of students issuing from an academy up the road.

'So,' said Franc, hitching up his trousers. 'At the same moment the leadership disbanded all al-Qaeda fighters and told them to continue the struggle from their own countries, you get it into your head to return to London to complete your medical studies. You go over the border at Spin Boldak and dodge around until you make contact with your family in Lahore. You went through Quetta, travelled north to the tribal areas then doubled back westwards to Iran. We have the Inter-Services Intelligence Agency report, so we know all this. It just so happens that at *exactly* that moment, hundreds of al-Qaeda fighters took the same route from Mashhad or Zabol in Iran, two cities you admit visiting. And you're saying that all this is coincidence?'

'Yes, I wanted my old life back. I realised I'd made mistakes with my life. I wanted to go back ... to leave the killing and become a doctor.'

'That's crap. You were a lousy student and your professors in London – the ones that remember you – say you didn't give a shit about medicine. Screwing around and drinking, yes. Medicine, no. We checked with them. Your attendance record was terrible and you never turned in your term papers.'

Khan shook his head. 'I was a silly, misguided young man. I know that. But I have committed no crime.'

Franc looked at the two SHISK agents to see if they minded him continuing. One made an exaggerated flourish with his hand, as though to say 'be my guest'. Franc approached him and knelt down by the table so he was looking up into Khan's face.

'You see, Karim – or whatever the fuck your name is – you've had it good so far. Regular meals, a bed, treatment for your injuries. That's like three star service here. But it can all change. We can just leave you to these people. I guess you know what that means.' He turned and glanced at The Doctor over his shoulder and smiled with his harsh, grey eyes boring into Khan's face. 'This man is a real doctor. Like any real doctor he cures people and saves them,' he paused. 'That is, after he has hurt them so much that they want to die. But he doesn't let that happen. Oh, no. You see, he preserves the life of his subjects and then starts over with the pain. With your medical training, maybe you have an idea of what he can do. It's not just scalpels, draining the blood from your body; it's not electricity, or beating, or drowning. No, The Doctor is very scientific. He does things from the inside as well as the outside. He feeds you drugs, acid and every goddam shit you can imagine. The pain is total, you understand that, Khan. Total. He takes you to another place, a place that no man alive can imagine, because it's so terrifying, so relentless. He can keep you in that state for *years*. Imagine that, Khan. He's had a lot of practice because he worked for Saddam Hussein. He had so many people to experiment with there that he became the best in the business. No one has ever failed to tell him what he wants to hear.' He got up and raised his voice. 'And you know what, you little prick sonofabitch? We've got you an appointment with The Doctor. His time is booked for you, baby, and he's willing to start work whenever we give the word. So you better cooperate and answer our questions.'

Khan stared at the table and composed himself. 'I've told you everything I know,' he said. 'I have committed no crime. I fought a war as a foreign soldier in a foreign land, much like your people did in Vietnam.

781

We both found we'd made a bad mistake and I wish to repay my debt to humanity.'

'You're a terrorist. That's the difference, buddy.' Franc went over to his chair, picked up a folder and returned to the table. 'Now you know about The Doctor, let's see what you say about this.' He withdrew the two remaining postcards of the Empire State. 'Can you explain these cards, which were found in your possession?'

'Yes, they were given to me by a friend a long time ago to remind me to keep in touch. That's why he addressed them to himself.'

'Yes, Dr Sammi Loz. You studied together in London and then went to Bosnia, right?'

'Yes.'

'Why the Empire State? What's the significance?'

'My friend had a love of the building, an obsession with it, you might say. He said he would always work from the Empire State because of its spirit. He said it was a lucky building. He can tell you this. I'm certain he's still there.'

Franc gave him a sardonic smile. 'We were going to ask Dr Loz, but he went missing when federal agents approached him four days ago. He is currently being sought in the United States. When we find him we will of course ask him, but at the present time we're going to have to rely on you.' While Franc paused to consult some photostats, Khan absorbed the news that Sammi was a suspect too.

'These postcards are written in code, aren't they? Our analysis has shown they may include an attack date and target information.' He placed five photostats on the table. 'I want you to read them for us and explain the code.'

'I can read them, but there's no code.' He shook his head and looked down at the surface of the table, then picked up the photostats and read the first one. 'Greetings, my old friend. I am in Pakistan and hope very soon to be in London. I may need a little help from you. I have good news. I am returning to complete my medical studies, as you always said I should. With warmest wishes, Khan.' He stopped. 'That is all there is – there's no message.'

'You sent that from Quetta, Pakistan, where you got the passport doctored. Is that when you received your instructions? From the same people who gave you the name of the man who did the work on your documents?'

'No, I did everything I could to avoid those people in Quetta. My family told me the ISI were looking for me. I had to be very discreet.'

'So you managed to find the man who does work for al-Qaeda by yourself?'

'I didn't know he worked for them.'

'Continue,' said Franc.

He read the postcards and, when he had finished, slammed his hand on the table with frustration. 'These mean nothing, I tell you. Nothing.'

Unmoved, Franc produced a second set of copies and put one in front of him. In the first postcard sent from Quetta, Khan saw that the capital letters were ringed in red:

GrEetings, My old friend. I am in PakIstan and hope veRy soon to be in London. I may neEd a little help from you. I have good news. I am returning to complete my stuDIES, as you always said I should.

Karim looked up at him, mystified.

'Let me remind you about this,' said Franc. 'All the letters you made into capitals spell EMPIRE DIES.' He ran his finger along the message, stopping at each capital letter.

Khan shook his head incredulously. 'This is stupid. It is like a school kid's code. You think I wrote this to my friend? Honestly?'

'But you did. Take a look at the first one you sent from Iran. It's a little more complicated.'

He placed a grid of letters alongside a phrase from the postcard, which read, 'I want to hide in Lundun for all time. KariM.'

'This is the way you concluded your postcard from Iran. It's certainly an odd phrase, especially when you compare it to the rest of the postcard, which reads pretty naturally and is correctly spelt. So our analysts had a look at it and they came up with this.' He indicated the grid.

```
A   L   K   U   F
R   M   I   L   A
T   U   N   W   A
H   I   D   U   N
```

'What you wrote was a near anagram of a well-known Hadith, a saying of the prophet – 'Al kufr milatun wahidun' – meaning unbelief is one nation. It's a call to arms against the unbelievers.'

Khan stared at the letters. 'I don't understand.'

The American took a pencil and ticked off the letters that appeared in the Arabic phrase.

'But it doesn't work. There are too many letters in my postcard.'

'It's near enough. Why would anyone spell London like that? And again you use capital letters where they don't belong – the M in Karim is a capital. We're working on the next two cards but we think this is enough to put you and your friend Dr Loz in jail.' He paused. 'Unbelief is one nation. You people! What kind of shit fills your minds?'

'This is crazy.'

'All you have to do is tell me where the target information is hidden. I want the date and time of the attack and the names of your associates. What does the Empire State building have to do with all this? Is that your target? We need answers, Khan.' He was shouting now.

'There isn't a plot. I am innocent. I wasn't used to writing English – writing anything. The capital letters are a mistake and the codes you've found are coincidence. They don't exist.' He was sweating profusely, his throat parched with fear, and he had to hold his hands under the table to stop them shaking.

'Yeah, like the other coincidences in your story. Right now, we're all a little tired of listening to your crap so we're gonna leave you for a couple of hours with The Doctor. When we come back, we want answers.'

14

At two, Herrick walked from the pool with a bitter taste in her mouth, the result of inhaling Tirana's polluted air for most of the morning. She walked through the lobby to the elevator bank and pulled out a card which acted as both a lift and room key.

'May I?' said a voice at her shoulder. She was aware of a friendly, dark face and a wide smile.

'Thank you,' she said, and stepped back. He pressed three, and asked which floor she wanted. 'That's okay, my floor's after yours anyway,' she lied.

The doors closed.

'Would it interest you to know that I'm going to Robert Harland's room?'

'If I knew who he was, it might,' she said, looking away.

'Oh, I'm sorry. I understood you were a colleague of Mr Harland's. He told me to find you in the hotel.'

'And who are you?'

'Dr Sammi Loz. I'm afraid circumstances have forced me to go under another name while travelling. I am calling myself Charles Mansour, which I like even less than my own name.' Another smile.

She studied him in the mirror. He was wearing a linen jacket, dark blue, unstructured trousers and a white, probably silk, shirt, fastened at the neck. He was evidently rich and took care over his clothes. There was also self-assurance, vanity and deliberateness in his movements.

'Dr Loz, why didn't Mr Harland find me himself?' she asked.

The lift came to a stop and the doors opened.

'Because he is laid up with a bad back after three separate flights and since I am his doctor, I have ordered total rest. He's getting better gradually and should be on his feet tomorrow. The room's three twelve. I'll wait here if you would prefer it.'

'Thank you. I would.'

She knocked at the door and glanced back to the elevator where Loz stood with his arms folded.

The door opened and a tall, but stooped middle-aged man held out his hand and said hello. 'I'm sorry I had to get Loz to find you, but I'm pretty immobilised at the moment. Come in.' Robert Harland returned crookedly to his bed and lay down very slowly. 'I gather you were at the Embassy, so you know what I'm doing here.' He laughed grimly. 'Actually, I don't know what the hell I'm doing here, so I can't expect you to.'

'The Chief has got me in to see Karim Khan this afternoon. I'm due at the US Embassy at three. Perhaps we should talk after that?'

'I'd like you to talk to Loz first.' He frowned, more out of perplexity than pain, she thought. 'I'd like to know what you think of him. He got here under his own steam, with a fake passport. Teckman believes he knows something, but God knows what, which is why I'm sticking to him. Your brief, I gather, is to help me.' He stopped and felt the front of his pelvis. 'Look, I've been thinking it may be worth letting Khan understand that you're with Loz, but in a way the Albanians don't appreciate.'

'Why?'

'Because I want to know what his reaction is, though that's not what I've told Loz. Let's have a talk with him, shall we?'

She opened the door to find Loz waiting outside. He came in and Harland explained what he needed.

'I see,' he said. 'You're looking for some code word or phrase which Karim will recognise.' He leaned against the desk, placed one hand at his elbow and stroked his nose. 'You could ask him about The Poet.'

'Who the hell's the Poet?' said Harland rather bad temperedly from the bed.

'That's the point,' replied Loz. 'Nobody knows. The Poet was a commander in Bosnia, but none of us knew who he was or where he operated from. Karim did. It was The Poet who persuaded him to leave for Afghanistan in 1997. If you mention him, Karim will know you have spoken with me because only I could have told you that.'

'Fine,' she said, thinking that this was all pretty daft. 'I'd better go now.'

A couple of hours later, she drove with Gibbons and a guard from the US Embassy to an anonymous four-storey building with blinded windows. They passed through some blue metal gates into a large car park where there was an unusual sense of order, regimentation even. Several off-road vehicles were lined up and were being hosed down, and the yellowish run-off was being swept into a drain by a young man in army fatigues. Around the high wall surrounding the SHISK headquarters were coils of razor wire, cameras and movement sensors, all of which she assumed were bought by the American money that had poured into Tirana during the mid-nineties. About half a dozen armed guards were in the yard. Two at the entrance to the building came to attention, while a third inspected their IDs before leading them to the second floor and along a dark corridor. They were told to wait.

'The big man in there is Milo Franc,' said Gibbons out of the corner of his mouth. 'He'll do most of the talking, together with the SHISK officers. I guess I don't have to tell you that it's best if you keep your yap shut. They don't like having a woman here.'

Herrick said nothing.

Her first impression when they got into the interrogation room, was of a gang of schoolboys caught tormenting an animal. All but one looked at her with a slight awkwardness. That man, heavy-set with a thick, black goatee, did not look up from a bag of nuts. Khan sat shrunken at the table, bedraggled with sweat and clearly at the end of his tether. As the two SHISK officers turned to look her up and down, his eyes darted to hers with an expression of utter bewilderment. She saw immediately that his right cheek was affected by a tic, and once or twice he put his hand up to swat the movement.

Gibbons pointed to a chair along the wall, next to the three Americans. She glanced at the one who she guessed must be Franc, another man in his thirties with a clean-cut and well-policed parting, and a clerical type who had a sheaf of documents on his lap.

No explanation about her arrival was offered to Khan, but his attention now fixed on her and she realised he was looking for a sign that she could offer him a way out of that room. She removed her gaze to a point between the two Albanians at the table, but felt uncomfortable doing so. 'Please continue,' she said.

One of the Albanians leaned forward. He was a slender man, with a russet complexion and a high forehead. He spoke with a somewhat stilted American accent.

'We have some confusion here. You were carrying two documentations. One related to Karim Khan and the other to Jasur Faisal al-Saggib, known also as Jasur al-Jahez and Amir al-Shawa. You say you saw this man killed in Macedonia two weeks ago. But our American colleagues have asked the Macedonian authorities to look for the body of this man. They searched the area where the incident took place and found no dead body there.'

Khan looked perplexed, as if they had suddenly started talking about architecture or botany. 'The man died with me. He was not killed – I told you that. He died of a heart attack. Maybe he was suffering from asthma. I don't know.'

Herrick was surprised by his upper-middle-class English.

'But they could not find this man,' returned the interrogator. 'What is the proof he was with you in these times?'

Khan did not answer, but shook his head hopelessly.

'What is the proof that these documents are not yours?'

'The pictures are not of me. Anyone can see that. They belong to a man who doesn't look like me. He was an Arab.'

The interrogator examined a photocopy. 'This looks like you to me.' He showed it to his colleague, who nodded vigorously. Herrick glanced at the copy on the CIA officer's lap. There was no resemblance whatsoever to Khan. However, she took out her notebook and wrote down Faisal's name and the other aliases.

'But it is natural that you do not want to look like a member of Hamas. The man Faisal is wanted in Damascus, Cairo and Jerusalem. *Everyone* wants to speak with Mr Jasur Faisal because he is responsible for many explosions and killings. In Syria they want to see Mr Faisal for two murders. In Egypt, Mr Faisal assassinated a politician and a newspaper editor and was sentenced to death by the courts in Cairo. Maybe Jasur Faisal – The Electrician – is sitting here in this room with us. Maybe we have big shot terrorist here, right here in front of us, a real soldier of Islam?'

'Why are you asking me questions I can't answer? Proof that I am not Faisal lies in front of you, but when you say you do not believe this, how am I meant to answer you? It's the same with the postcards. There isn't a code in the postcards. You have found what you wanted to find and I am to be punished for this.' After this speech Khan hung his head. The sweat trickled down his cheek and collected in the stubble at his chin.

There was silence. Franc turned to her and gave her a big, fat wink.

'May I ask the suspect a question?' Herrick said to the room. Then looking directly at Khan she asked, 'Who are you?'

'I am Karim Khan.'

'And you haven't used any of these other names – Faisal and the rest?'

'No. I found the identity on the man I fled with in Macedonia.'

'Have you ever been known as The Electrician, or The Watchmaker, or The Poet, or any other name?' She said it lightly, as though the names had come to her randomly, but Khan raised his head and his eyes filled with recognition.

'No,' he said, 'but I once knew a man who was nicknamed The Poet – a long time ago, in Bosnia. My friend Dr Loz knew of him.' There was no doubt he understood what she was saying. They had made contact.

Franc turned to her. 'A moment outside, Ms Herrick.' He steered her to the door, beckoning Gibbons to go with them. In the corridor, he pushed her to the wall and leaned into her face with his arm resting beside her head. 'I don't know what the hell you're doing in there, but let me tell you that you're here on my sufferance and those remarks were unacceptable. This is front line procedure, Miss Herrick, an extremely delicate interrogation, the result of coordination between us and officers of the Albanian intelligence service. I can't allow you to butt in with any damned thought that comes into your head. You *copy*, Ms Herrick?'

She moved her face from the blast of his breath and remembered Nathan Lyne's approach. 'Mr Franc, I am here under a joint Anglo-American authority, the likes of which you cannot even dream, and I will behave in the way that I believe is appropriate to the operation. If you want to test this, why don't you call your station in London and speak to the Deputy Director of the CIA, Jim Collins?'

Franc took his arm from the wall. 'What was that crap in there about?'

'I wanted to know if he recognised the code name for a Bosnian commander. You saw how he reacted to it. That means he can't be Faisal, and that the story of the man dying in Macedonia is probably true.'

'That proves nothing,' said Gibbons.

'You really believe he's a member of Hamas?'

'We have to explore all the possibilities, Ms Herrick,' said Franc, 'and if I am going to let you back inside that room, I need a guarantee you won't interrupt again. Lives could depend on us finding out what this man was sent to do. We know from the codes he sent to his associate, Loz, that he is part of a plot to mount a major attack in the US.'

'So why are you asking him about Faisal?' asked Herrick innocently. 'You know he isn't Faisal – that's clear to me from the early transcripts. Why waste the time?'

'The fact that he was carrying papers belonging to a member of Hamas, the most feared terrorist group in the Middle East, means there may be a connection between al-Qaeda and Hamas. I don't have to explain how important that is.' Franc had become avuncular, telling the little girl from England about the realities of 'front line procedure'. A look in his eye spurred her to wonder exactly what was going on.

'Okay,' she said, apparently placated. 'Shall we go back inside? I haven't seen enough to write anything sensible yet. By the way, who's the man with the bag of nuts?'

'He's a doctor,' Gibbons drawled. 'He's looking after the welfare of the suspect.'

When she went in, The Doctor was perched on the interview table offering Khan a pistachio nut. Relief spread over Khan's face as he saw Isis and his eyes leapt in hope, but then The Doctor leaned across and said something to him. When she saw him again his expression was blank and compliant.

She took her place as the questions about Hamas resumed, most of which Khan refused to answer, at one stage saying that he might as well be questioned about Colombia. An hour passed and although the sun was sinking outside, the room remained stifling. Suddenly Isis jumped up and left the room, this time to the sniggers of the two Albanians and The Doctor. Franc followed her out looking angry.

'You're yanking my chain,' she said. 'You're not interested in Hamas. In fact, I think this whole session has been arranged for my benefit. You're taking the interrogation up a blind alley so I don't get anything.' She stopped and looked at his glistening, fleshy face. 'I'll let you into a secret, Mr Franc. I am not here on some kind of training programme. There are literally hundreds of CIA and SIS officers engaged in a secret operation in London and all over Europe – one vast intelligence operation. I am here as part of that. Do you understand? So let's forget this Hamas business. It's a load of shite, and you know it. When I go back in, you steer the questions to the matter in hand.'

For a moment Franc was taken aback by her vehemence, but then he stretched and wiped his forehead. 'You're quite a spitfire, Miss Herrick, I'll grant you that. But you got to understand that this is not my interrogation. The man is in Albanian custody! We are here as their guests, for chrissake.'

'I don't give a fuck,' she hissed. 'If you want me to keep you out of my report, you will go back to the line of questioning you were pursuing in the transcripts.' With this, she turned and walked into the room again.

Evidently much of their exchange had been overheard. The Albanians were barely able to contain themselves and the other two Americans were smirking. Amidst all this brutal jollity, Khan looked even more pathetic. Suddenly he rose from his chair, but the restraints on his feet held him and he lurched onto the table. 'They're torturing me,' he shouted. 'This man, they call him The Doctor, he is the torturer. Tell him to show you the plastic bag he suffocated me with.' One of the Albanians was now at Khan's side, forcing him down and trying to clamp his jaw shut, but Khan ducked from his grip and continued shouting. 'Everyone here is tortured and brutalised. Is that what you want? Is that the policy of the British and American governments? Get me out of here and I will tell you anything you want.' He was silenced by The Doctor, who had got behind him and slipped a large forearm around his neck, locking it into the crook of his other arm. Khan coughed and slumped to the chair, staring at Herrick.

'Stop that,' Herrick screamed. 'Stop that now.' But the Americans were already leading her from the room. 'My government does not condone this,' she said out in the corridor.

'Nobody gives a damn what the British government thinks,' said Franc, physically handing her to Gibbons. 'Get her out of here, Lance, and make sure she doesn't come tomorrow.' He turned and went back into the room.

As the door opened she caught a glimpse of Khan, the whites of his eyes shining in the shadow cast by The Doctor's form.

It was dusk outside. The clouds above were mottled with the last rays of the sun and in the east the mountains were brushed with a dirty pink. The noise of the hot, swarming capital came to Herrick's ears like a roar.

Gibbons pushed her into the Toyota and climbed into the driving seat. 'You have some fucking balls,' he said, starting the engine. 'This is the way it is, you know! The way it has to be with these people.'

'What? Torture?'

'Hell, that's not torture. He's been slapped around a little. That's all.' His lips pouted downwards with a kind of patronising disgust.

'Oh, for Christ's sake! The man is going to be tortured because you can't get the answers you want. Has it occurred to you that he doesn't have anything else to tell you?'

They went a few hundred yards, swerving to avoid the worst of the potholes and the kids running into the street with iced drinks and cigarettes. Then, in a quieter spot, Gibbons pulled up and swivelled round in his seat, one arm hooked around the steering wheel. 'I know this is tough, but it is the only way. We have a man who could be part of a plot to kill thousands of people. We have learned our lesson about these guys. We have to fight fire with fire and be every bit as ruthless and cruel as they are, because we're here in this shitty little country, charged by the American people to protect them – at the very least, to give them warnings of terrorist attacks. How the hell do you think we're going to do that? Huh? I mean, like we treat Khan nicely when al-Qaeda's going to blow up this fuel tanker or drop a truckload of nuclear waste in DC, so he tells us? Get real, Isis. We're in a different kind of war now. We got to respond with all available means and, hell, if that entails one of the murderous little bastards being hung from a beam for intensive questions, I for one don't give a shit. What matters is that we get the result and protect our people. It's the same with the British. You think the average Brit cares a damn what happens to some Paki terrorist thousands of miles away? Of course he doesn't. He wants you to go out and get the answers and prevent these people from destroying his liberty and way of life. That's your job. It's as simple as that, and if you don't have the stomach for it, you should find yourself another line of work. This is the way it is from here on in, Isis. A long, cruel war between civilisations.'

'Civilisation,' she said, without looking at him, 'is exactly what this is about. That's what we're fighting for, the standard that says torture is wrong. There is nothing more absolute than the absolute wrong of what you're doing to that man. Don't you see that?'

'Don't be so fucking pious. You think this is an exclusively American vice? Give me a break, Isis. You Brits have been torturing people all over the goddam empire for a couple of hundred years. Hey, you even used those methods on your own citizens in Northern Ireland – bags over the head, sleep privation, beatings. And as long as the people were safe, they didn't want to know about it.'

She exhaled heavily. 'Torture and internment didn't stop the IRA. In fact, there's a good argument that the Peace Process only happened once those things had been abandoned. I didn't say we were perfect, but I know that if we start pulling people's fingernails out now we lose a sense of what we're fighting for.'

'The moral high ground, et cetera, et cetera.' He lit a cheroot and blew a stream of smoke through the crack in the window. 'You know about the guy who planned to crash a dozen airliners into the Pacific? He was arrested in the Philippines and after *intensive interrogation* he told them what was going down, and the whole goddam cell was detained. Maybe they broke a few bones on the way, but what's that compared to the people they saved, the vast numbers of Americans who aren't grieving because some nut says their lives offend the Prophet's teaching? You know what? We should go further. Every time they attack us, we should go after them, take the fight to every goddam mosque, every meeting held by every crummy imam and ayatollah, and if they don't get the point with a few smarts, we'll show what a little instant sunshine can do. It's about power, and using that power to dissuade.' He swept his hand at the street and the teeming life ahead of them on the Boulevard of National Heroes. The evening *volta* had begun, a procession of people walking up and down in the dusk, admiring each other's babies in a formal ritual found all over southern Europe. It seemed to speak of an ordered civil society. 'The only reason I can park up and talk to you is because those people know this is a US Embassy car and inside there's a guy with Lieutenant-Colonel Uziel Gal's finest invention on his lap.' He touched the sub-machine gun through the knapsack. 'Otherwise they'd strip the car and take you away.'

'What happens if you torture that man and get the wrong answers? What if you're asking the wrong questions?'

He smiled. '*We* are not going to be hurting anyone. *We* don't have any control over what happens in the state prisons here. It's like Colombia's baby brother. Everyone's corrupt, the gangsters are running the politicians, the police, the judges – everything. They sell their neighbours' children into sex slavery and when the kids get pregnant the gangs take the baby and put it to work for a living in the arms of some beggar. America doesn't run Albania, Isis. We got a toehold in the heart of darkness, that's all, and we use it to try to protect our own people.' He paused. 'We should have a drink back at your hotel and talk some more about this. There're things you should understand.'

Her first instinct was to say no, but then she thought there was every possibility of Gibbons getting drunk and talking about Khan. Besides, she wanted to see Khan again and she would need Gibbons to get her in.

'Why not?' she said. 'Yeah, why not?'

They passed through the lobby, Herrick drawing sullen, hungry looks from the knot of bodyguards, and went to the bar where Gibbons ordered whisky and a Diet Coke which he drank separately, downing each in one before Herrick had touched her glass of Albanian white. Another full glass of whisky followed and they went to the terrace and sat down, where Herrick recognised a piece of Schubert playing in the background. One or two of the evangelists were still earnestly hunched over lemonades. How odd, she thought, that in one part of town Americans were standing by as a man was tortured, while in another they were preparing a mission to convert the faithless masses. She made the point less harshly to Gibbons.

'Before you get too self-righteous, remember the British in India – missionaries and massacres. The sub-continent was virtually enslaved to the British Raj.' He paused and made a conciliatory gesture. 'You're a good person, Isis. I know your type from college. You've got genuine, honest to God goodness at your centre and, like all those people I knew, you believe in the healing power of liberal argument.'

She smiled a little vulnerably. 'Well, you have to believe in something, Lance.'

'Maybe we do, but belief doesn't work here. You got to see this as a vacuum. Since the communists fell, every goddam religion and ideology has been trying to fill it. That's why there're Christian evangelists in the mountains with a Bible in one hand and a machine gun in the other, and why every kind of shady Muslim charity came here and started building mosques. But these people don't give a shit about either of them.' He drank the whisky, eyes patrolling the tables on the terrace. Then he clutched his belt. There was a faint buzz. 'Hey, that's my phone going. I better make the call.'

'That's fine. I have a couple of calls to make, too.'

'Don't you get lost,' he said, and vanished into the gardens in a conspicuously clandestine manner.

Herrick dialled Harland's mobile.

'Who's that with you?' he asked.

'Where are you?'

'It doesn't matter. Who is he?

'The guy from the US Embassy.'

'There are some developments,' he said. 'One, you can't use the phone in the hotel, but I imagine you already knew that. Two, my charge has gone missing. Probably nothing to worry about, but I need to find him. He said the consignment you inspected this afternoon is much more important than anyone imagined. In a conference call to head office from the Embassy he blurted this out and now the MD is really interested. They're getting back to me. Meantime, you're to find out everything you can. Any movement of the consignment from the warehouse and they want to know about it.'

'Just like that?'

''Fraid so.'

'I'll do my best, which in the circumstances won't be much. How's the back?'

'Comes and goes. Your man's returning to the table. I'd better hang up.'

Out of the corner of her eye, in the darkened part of the terrace, she saw Harland get up from a table and walk to the dining room door, which she knew could be used to bypass the terrace. He was no longer bent double, but he was moving stiffly.

Gibbons flopped down beside her again. 'Hell, I thought I had more whisky than that. Isis, you been sneaking my booze?' He ordered another. 'So where were we?'

'What's going to happen to Khan?' she asked.

'That's all you ever ask.'

'Well, we would like to talk to him in slightly less threatening circumstances. Maybe he would tell us more. '

'He'll tell us.'

'Then what will happen to him? Where will he be tried?'

'Who the hell cares?' He drank some more and looked at her with sudden sharp focus. 'Forget about Khan. We just had word from London. I guess they told Milo Franc that you were a royal pain in the arse. They sent you here to get you out of the way. He talked to Collins, then a guy named Vigo, and he said you had no authority whatsoever. The way you threw your weight around has made Franc awful pissed. He said to tell you that you should write your report and get the hell out of Tirana. He doesn't want to see you again.' He laughed. 'Hey, have another drink for chrissake, you're making me feel awkward.'

'Vigo spoke to Franc?'

'Yeh, Vigo, he knows a lot of our guys at Langley.'

'I'll take that drink,' she said, brightening. 'It's a relief not to have to go to that place. I don't know how you stand it.'

'Goes with the territory,' said Gibbons in a manly, stoic way.

They drank while Herrick listened to Gibbons' theories about the lack of car mechanics in Albania and the fact – according to him – that no one was able to read a map because the communists had banned them for forty years. She was amenable, smiled a lot, and was certainly guilty of implying that things might develop further that evening. But just past nine o'clock he leapt up and said. 'Got to leave you, Isis. Date at the Valleys of Fire.' He said it as if it was a film title.

'What's that?'

He looked down at her without a trace of humour. 'A place where questions are asked and answers are given. I'll check in tomorrow. Hey, why don't we do dinner at Juvenilja?'

He navigated a pretty straight course through the tables of Tirana's underworld and hopeful reformers, which she thought was due more to momentum than any residual balance.

15

Herrick left the terrace and went upstairs, trying Harland several times on the way, but his phone was either switched off or out of range. Once in her room she spread the contents of the plastic bag on the bed, and after trying various combinations, opted for jeans, red T-shirt and knitted shawl around her shoulders. She tied her hair back, put on some lipstick and blueish eyeshadow, then slipped along the corridor to the fire exit. Outside in the boulevard she merged with the *volta,* which was still in full flood, but quickly dumped the shawl behind a bush because she suddenly felt it made her look like a street walker. She was glad she'd chosen to wear her trainers instead of the fringed boots.

As she made her way across the broken pavement in badly lit side-streets, she realised that a woman equipped herself with one of two attitudes on the street in Tirana – a kind of brassy hauteur, or beaten-down, famished servitude. The former implied that you had protection, which was everything in a town full of northern immigrants who had brought with them the ancient clan code *Kanun of Lek Dukagjin* which she had been reading about that morning. The dishonouring of a woman associated with a powerful man – the very smallest slight – could result in death and endless vendetta. So she strutted her stuff until she reached the SHISK compound, where she became more discreet and circled the place, noting the infra-red camera and the number of cars parked in the street leading to the headquarters. In the back of her mind was her father's advice about getting to know somewhere before attempting any kind of surveillance, and she had to admit she was woefully unprepared. If Khan was suddenly moved, she would have no way of following. The area was several degrees more sinister at night. There was no street lighting and the little light that came from the headquarters and the bar directly across the road only served to hint at what lay in the shadows. She was aware of people watching her from the darker recesses where they'd put up for the night. When one of the city's regular blackouts came, casting the neighbourhood into total darkness, she fumbled in the canvas bag for her mobile and called Bashkin, knowing that he would still be loitering hopefully outside the main entrance of the Byron. He agreed to meet her outside a newly renovated Catholic church a couple of streets away and flash his lights twice. She hung up and was about to switch off her phone when it vibrated in her hand.

'Yes,' she said hurriedly.

'It's Dolph – Andy Dolph!'

'Can't talk now, Dolph. I'm really busy.'

'Okay. Quickly then, you've got a message from Beirut. Your friend has news for you. She said you'd need to know straight away.'

For a moment Herrick couldn't think what he was talking about. 'Oh yes. Where are you?'

'At your old desk to fill in for you. I'm sitting next to sweetie Lyne. You didn't tell me about him, Isis.'

'But he *is* sharp.'

'Oh yeah, he's good, but re–lent–less.'

'Look, I've got to go. We'll speak soon. And, Dolph – thanks for ringing.'

'Be safe.'

About ten minutes later, just as the lights came back on, a pair of identical white Landcruisers with US diplomatic plates appeared in the street, crashed over the potholes and pulled up to wait for the compound gates to open. Herrick turned on her phone and dialled Harland. This time he answered.

'There seems to be some movement and Gibbons mentioned he was going to the Valley of Fires, wherever that is. The people from the US Embassy are here. Two cars. Maybe something is happening.'

Harland thought for a moment. 'Have you got transport?'

'Yes, but I don't know how reliable he's going to be.' She gave him Bashkin's mobile number because her battery was low, then hung up and made her way to the Mercedes where Bashkin was sunk down in the driving seat, smoking. She tapped on the window and he let her in. 'What we do now?' he asked.

'We wait,' she said. 'We wait, Mr Bashkin.' To pass the time she told him about her father coming to Albania in the war and fighting with the partisans.

Inside the SHISK headquarters, Karim Khan heard the sound of several men walking along the corridor between the cells. One of the prisoners had suffered some kind of convulsion earlier and despite cries of help from the other men no one had come until it was too late. At least, that is what Khan concluded from the wailing in a language he could not understand. He wondered wretchedly what they would do with the body and whether the man's relations would be told.

For a few moments the lights were thrown on and there was the sound of men moving something. But instead of the footsteps dying, they approached his cell and keys were turned in the lock. Two men came in and dragged him from the iron bed. Another pulled his arms roughly behind his back and bound them with a plastic restraint. He was marched along the cell block, fearful eyes watching him from the cages nearest the door, and taken outside into the night where he was hooded and rolled into the back of a vehicle. Now he'd better make his peace with God, he said to himself. There had been many nights before now when he'd known he would never see daylight, but the dawn had always come and Karim Khan had somehow survived. But tonight he was certain that his life would end, and the knowledge brought him an odd solace. For him the struggle was over.

They watched as the gates were shut and then opened again. Herrick had been urging Bashkin to take the handbrake off and allow the Mercedes to creep forward but he insisted on keeping his distance. The SHISK were people you didn't mess with, he said. The mere fact of watching the headquarters was enough to land him in jail. When they glimpsed the figure being brought outside she leaned forward to the dashboard, wishing she had a pair of binoculars. The build of the man was about right and he was wearing a blue T-shirt, as Khan had been, but she didn't get a clear view of his face before he disappeared behind the vehicles. Seconds later the cars emerged from the compound and moved off down the street.

'We have to follow them,' said Herrick, stabbing at her phone to call Harland.

Bashkin shook his head. 'It's no possible.'

'Of course it's bloody well possible. How much do you want?'

'For this?' He looked extremely doubtful, as if no amount of money would compensate for the risk he was about to take. 'Two hundred dollars.'

'Done,' she said.

Unable to hide his astonishment, Bashkin started the car.

Herrick put the phone to her ear. Harland had already answered. 'There are two cars,' she said. 'I'm ninety per cent certain that they're moving Khan. I'll follow them. They're going towards Skenderbeg Square.'

'I'll join you. Keep in touch.'

They followed the cars for about five miles to the western fringes of the city. The evening was still warm and a lot of people were milling on the side of the road, buying watermelons and cold drinks from fridges hooked up to the public power supply. Bashkin slowed down several times, once for a dog-fight that spilled into both lanes of traffic and then for a broken-down truck. As a result, they lost the two Landcruisers, and when they eventually cleared Tirana's chaotic outskirts and hit the dual carriageway to Durrës she shouted for him to put his foot down. For once Bashkin did as he was told.

They shot past the new Coca-Cola plant and a detergent factory, both incongruously neat and well-lit, like giant pieces of Toytown, then realised they must have missed the Landcruisers on the turning to Krujë a few miles back. They turned round and took a much smaller road. It passed through several villages and began to climb into a forest of low pines. Bashkin explained that this had once been Enver Hoxha's private hunting ground and was now the place where they made charcoal. There were fires up here that burned night and day, he said. She asked to borrow his mobile, and after haggling over the price for a call, she phoned Harland for the final time and told him she had found the Valleys of Fire. This was where they must have brought Karim Khan, for what purpose she could not say. Harland seemed oddly unimpressed, but said he was on his way.

After rounding several more bends they came to a headland overlooking a bowl in the landscape. Along the far side were about ten furnaces gouged out of the bedrock. Each one had an opening about the size of a door and a little above this was a hole which let out viscous smoke and muddied light. Herrick climbed out of the car saying she'd pay Bashkin another hundred dollars to wait. She also told him to direct a tall Englishman who was about to arrive down into the valley.

She started down the slope, picking her way through the scrub, all the while glancing ahead of her and up to the road above. As she drew near to the point where the bushes had been cleared, she saw dozens of young men and small, emaciated boys scurrying between the furnaces and heaps of rubber tyres that were responsible for the poisonous air. Their skin and clothes were blackened and the sweat on their bodies gleamed in the light. She crouched down and watched for a few minutes, almost hypnotised by the sight of them rolling tyres up the incline, then heaving them into the furnaces. Occasionally, downdrafts from the mountains caused the fires to blow back without warning and those nearest the furnace doors had to jump for cover. She saw one of these tar-black creatures, no more than four foot six tall, use a long metal poker to vault out of the way with great agility. When he landed he performed a jig like a monkey-demon cavorting in the flames of hell.

Maybe it was the roar of the underground fires, or the idea that she was witnessing a spectacle brought to life from Hieronymous Bosch, that dulled her attention. Either way, she was utterly caught off guard when they seized her from behind, lifted her bodily onto the clear ground in front and began to frisk her. She managed a little yelp but otherwise put up no resistance.

There were three of them, all armed. She recognised one from the SHISK headquarters. He gestured to the other two to bring her a little way down the hill and they walked to a pile of wood. The two men holding her relaxed their grip, and one – covertly it seemed to her – slipped his hand down to feel her bottom. What did this mean? Did it presage gang rape, or was this man's interest something she could use? Could she snatch a gun and run for it?

'You do know I'm a British diplomat?' she said in a voice that sounded all too thin and powerless.

The SHISK guard laughed without turning towards her. He was searching the track below them, shielding his face from the heat of the fires. 'No Ingleesh diplomat,' he said, wagging his finger without looking at her. 'You Ingleesh spy. Missease Jeemes Bond.' All three laughed. At this point, the little man she had seen leaping from the flames came over with a seesaw walk, holding the metal pole over his shoulder like a javelin. He had a round, hairless face with elfin ears and eyes that were too close together. They knew his name – Ylli – and beckoned to him, although his strange looks clearly made them feel uncomfortable. Ylli put out a hand and was given a cigarette and some notes which he stuffed into his back pocket. Then he strutted around Herrick, making observations about her in the high, unbroken voice of a boy. Twice he tried to touch her but was shooed away by the guards. Then he withdrew and let himself down onto a pile of four tyres where he smoked with quick, childish puffs and made gestures that suggested he was sitting in the finest armchair ever made.

The little man heard the cars first, and scrambled up to balance on the tyres with prehensile bare feet and waved excitedly with the pole. The two Landcruisers, now joined by a Jeep and BMW sped up the remainder of the hill and tore past them about fifty yards away. Herrick strained forward but couldn't make out any of the passengers because they were thrown into silhouette by the light of the fires and a lot of dust had been kicked up by the lead vehicle. They reached the top of the bowl and stopped just beyond a layer of black fog, at which Ylli jumped down and scampered over to them. Several men got out and started making for the higher ground above the furnaces. They were dragging someone with them, the man in the blue T-shirt, who evidently had his hands tied behind his back and was offering no resistance whatsoever. Behind them came The Doctor, who struggled up the slope with Ylli bringing up the rear. Something passed between this group: it almost seemed as if they were trying to reason with the prisoner. But at length all but two stepped away. The man was marched forward and without further hesitation pushed into the flue opening. Ylli rushed up to the hole and could be seen thrusting and jabbing at the body with his pole. Then a couple of car tyres were thrown in. These instantly caught light and belched a column of smoke and sparks into the night. Without a second look, the party descended to the cars, drove back down towards them and pulled up. A man she hadn't seen before got out. He was in his late forties, dapperly dressed for the evening in a light sports jacket, a thin polo shirt and well-cut trousers. He took off the jacket, hung it round his shoulders and dusted off his hands with a quick slapping motion.

'It was your choice to be here tonight,' said the man. His English was perfect; the manner reminiscent of the polo ground. 'You were spying, and unpleasant things sometimes happen to spies, as you are no doubt aware.'

Herrick was almost too shocked to speak. 'Why did you kill him?' she said. 'And like that?'

'We have no use for a filthy terrorist. He would not answer our questions. We gave him his chance as you saw this afternoon. How many people have been burnt and mutilated by the actions of men like Khan? You ask yourself that before you judge us. We believe in decisive solutions here in Albania.'

'Burning people alive,' she said quietly, 'is not an option in any war.'

'You have a phrase in English, do you not, Miss Herrick?

If you can't stand the heat of the fire . . . well, I'm sure you know it.' He gave a little chuckle, took a small notebook from his pocket and held it up to the headlights of the leading car. 'Your address in London and your telephone number are written here, and that belonging to your father, an old war hero, I believe. He lives in Scotland in a place called Hopelaw – a pretty name – and he has a servant there named Mrs Mackenzie. You see, you are no mystery to me, Isis Herrick.'

She shook her head. 'Who are you?'

'I am Marenglen.' He paused and took a folded handkerchief from his trouser pocket and held it under his nose. 'You see, we Albanians have been locked up in this land for many years, so when the communists fell we acquired a taste for travel. Many Albanians have left and set up enterprises all over the world. In some cases, regrettably, these did not meet with the approval of the authorities. However, in London my countrymen encountered little opposition to their activities and they were able to establish themselves in many different fields of endeavour. You will be familiar, perhaps, with the way they have taken over certain businesses in Soho, but they also have many other tricks up their sleeves. One is contract killing.'

He returned the handkerchief to his pocket and snapped his fingers. The guard who had first apprehended her handed him a cigarette and lit it. 'So,' he let out smoke from the side of his mouth, 'allow Marenglen to tell you now that if you place so much as a word of what you have seen in your report to London, I will have you and your father and his loyal servant killed. Naturally, these contracts will be issued in the order that causes maximum pain. If, however, you feel you cannot guarantee your silence to me now, then I don't see why we shouldn't advance things a little. You have met Ylli. I believe Ylli is a virgin, at least with humans, although the same cannot be said for sheep and goats. We can leave you with Ylli, he can take his pleasure with you and then, well, you will disappear. I think you can imagine that this would not be a happy end.'

She nodded.

'So why don't you go back to the Byron and prepare to leave Albanian soil within, say, thirty-six hours. That should give you time to send a convincing report saying you were given access to the prisoner Khan and that he was in every respect unforthcoming and uncooperative. Oh yes, there is one other thing. Take Robert Harland with you. I don't see that there is any point in his staying on after you've left.' He smiled, not very pleasantly, and walked the few paces to the car.

The men holding her let go and jogged over to the cars. When one of the doors was opened she was sure she caught a glimpse of Gibbons. A few seconds later the convoy bumped off down the hill. She turned and made her way to Bashkin's Mercedes, sickened and choking on the smell of the Valleys of Fire.

16

One question stayed in Herrick's mind on the ride back to the hotel, and when she was sitting on the balcony of her room with a packet of crisps from the minibar she said it out loud. Why would the CIA and SHISK go to such lengths to question Khan about a planned terrorist attack, then kill him without getting an answer? Even if Khan had talked in the few hours between her leaving the headquarters and seeing him taken off, that would be no reason to kill him. Surely it would be the moment for the Americans to produce him to the world's media as evidence of another thwarted terrorist plot, a triumph of vigilance and interception to be shared with their Albanian friends. There was only one solution. Khan had not been killed.

She phoned Harland's room and then his mobile. There was no answer on either. She waited for half an hour, drinking a little of the whisky opened by Gibbons the night before, not really enjoying it, and gazing across the garden. Then she went to the bathroom and washed the smell of burnt rubber from her hair under the shower. This took only a few minutes and when she came out she saw that a note had been slipped under the door. 'Rooms and phones bugged. See you at Embassy soonest.'

She dried her hair, changed and was downstairs in less than five minutes. Bashkin was still out in the car park. 'What is this, a twenty-four-hour watch?' she asked him.

He looked at her a little ruefully. 'Mease Errique leave soon? Tomorrow Bashkin drive you to airport.'

'You know my plans before I do,' she said, climbing into the Mercedes. 'Perhaps you could tell me what you thought of what we saw up in the hills?'

'Bashkin see nothing. Bashkin asleeping.'

'Right,' she said, 'Bashkin asleeping. But not tired enough to go home after he's dropped me at the hotel. Who do you work for?'

'For you Mease Errique.'

'And for Mr Marenglen also, I shouldn't wonder,' she said. 'Drive me to the British Embassy, please.'

Harland was waiting for her just inside the Embassy gates with one of the Hereford-trained guards, who introduced himself as Steve Tyrrel.

'Where the fuck did you get to?' she said to Harland. 'I thought you were following me. Where were you?'

'We'll talk inside.' He gestured to a door where another armed man stood. 'We've got Loz here, but I haven't told him anything and I think we should keep it that way until we know what's going on. There's more to him than you could imagine.'

They found Sammi Loz seated nonchalantly in an outer office with a cup of tea and a copy of the day's *International Herald Tribune*, looking for all the world as though he was about to go out in Manhattan on a warm summer's evening. 'Reunions later,' said Harland roughly as Loz got up and made an elaborate fuss over Herrick.

As soon as the metal door of the communications room thudded behind them, Herrick gave Harland a brief account of what she had seen on the mountains. When she reached the end she said, 'This wasn't for real. I know that. Gibbons dropped the stuff about the Valleys of Fire like a pile of plates after he had spoken on the phone – obviously to Milo Franc. They wanted me to go up there and watch someone being thrown into the fire.' She stopped and looked around. 'I don't suppose you've got any food, have you?' Harland phoned Tyrrel and asked him to scratch something together.

'Where'd you get to?' she asked when he put the phone down.

Harland gave her an odd, crooked smile. Now that his back was on the mend the strain had left his face. 'I went with Steve Tyrrel. I didn't tell you because I think the Americans are listening to our mobiles. So I had to pretend that I was following you up there. Steve had a hunch they were taking Khan out of the country and he was exactly right. Khan was driven to the airport and put on a private jet. The plane is being tracked by GCHQ and our people on Cyprus. I have no word yet as to where it's headed but the Chief will be on as soon as he knows.'

'So that's more or less that,' said Herrick. 'We've lost our man and I can go home.'

'Better hear what the Chief says,' he said with another smile.

Khan had known nothing after being rolled into the back of the car because a needle was plunged into his buttock. When he began to recover consciousness on the plane, all he was aware of was a raging thirst. He had been given no water during the previous day and whatever drug they'd used to knock him out had heightened the need for liquid. This blocked out his fear at finding himself on a plane, still hooded and bound, but now also with his mouth taped over and his ankles tied together. After a little while he started to explore his surroundings by moving his legs. He touched what he assumed was the seat in front of him and then angled them into the aisle and started to kick out, making as much noise as he could behind the tape. Someone stirred in front of him and he heard Lance Gibbons' voice, then the big CIA man, Franc. He kicked some more and became aware of them consulting each other. 'Look,' said Gibbons. 'Langley says he might have a capsule in his teeth.'

'He would've used it by now,' growled Franc.

Khan had no idea what they were talking about and heaved his torso forward so he was almost out of the seat and in the aisle.

'Hey, hey, hold still there, buddy,' shouted Gibbons.

The hood was removed and Gibbons' face peered into his. Khan stared back, eyes popping and cheeks blown out.

Gibbons examined him in the dim light of the cabin, then pulled back the tape so it hung from the corner of his mouth. When he heard what Khan wanted he grunted and fetched a clear plastic beaker of water which he lifted to his lips. He replenished it twice from a bottle before Khan's thirst was slaked and he was able to croak thank you.

'Now I'm gonna put this tape back. There's no use you getting excited. We got a lot of flying time ahead of us and unless you want us to give you another one of those shots you'll take a nap.'

Khan saw that he was considering whether to replace the hood so shook his head vigorously. Gibbons hesitated, then folded the cloth and placed it on the headrest in front of him. Before returning to sprawl in his own seat he jabbed his finger in front of Khan's face and said, 'Now, sleep, buster.'

Khan wasn't reassured by the water. These tiny acts of kindness meant nothing and indeed they often seemed to foreshadow some new, unpleasant turn in his story. In all the thousands of miles he had travelled he realised he had met almost no one he could trust, except perhaps in the case of Mr Skender – the consumptive interpreter who had accepted his money and the postcard with a look of solemn obligation. He was sure that Skender had posted the message and that it had arrived in New York. Moreover he understood that the pretty young English diplomat was letting him know she had met Sammi when she mentioned The Poet. It wasn't just chance she used that name because he caught the look in her eye as she said it. And yet she couldn't have any idea what it meant. Loz must have told her to drop it into the conversation, knowing he would recognise it while she would remain utterly ignorant of its meaning. That was smart of Loz.

But just as there seemed to be hope it was snatched from him. He was almost certainly on his way to Camp X-Ray, which he knew would be impregnable to all Loz's money and cunning. He had heard enough about the place while travelling through Iran to know that no one left unless the Americans wanted it. What hope did a veteran of the jihad in Bosnia and Afghanistan have of persuading the interrogators that he was simply a soldier? He wriggled a little to ease the pain in his ribs where The Doctor had hit him. The discomfort reminded him that at least the Americans did not practise torture. They may have been prepared to leave the room while The Doctor suffocated him and pressed his thumbs into his eye sockets. But that wasn't the same as doing it themselves. He could at least survive at Camp X-Ray and soon they would understand that he was cooperating with them and represented no threat whatsoever. Yes, he would make them understand that.

Although the drug made his mind sluggish and he was desperate for sleep, he kept on returning to the young woman. He had forgotten what a Western woman could be like and she brought back memories of his time in London. This woman was poised, intelligent and brave. It had taken courage to shout out in his defence when they tried to stop him talking.

He managed to doze for half an hour or so but then woke to a new kind of light in the cabin. He looked to his left and saw dawn rising through the window, an orange light below the wing tip, graded through azure to a deep mauve in the stratosphere. He watched it for a while before realising with a sudden, sharp dread that the sun rising on the port side of the aeroplane could only mean one thing – they weren't headed west for the Caribbean and Camp X-Ray, but due south.

Harland and Herrick sent a long encrypted email to Vauxhall Cross about Khan being taken out of the country while the CIA and SHISK had set up a diversion in the mountains, then sat back to consume a meal of bananas, Marmite sandwiches, digestive biscuits and coffee, rustled up by Steve Tyrrel from the Embassy kitchen. Herrick found she couldn't eat enough.

At 3.00 a.m. the Chief came on the phone. The British listening station in Cyprus had picked up the unscheduled flight an hour before and noted that, having executed a wide circle over the Mediterranean, the jet turned east into Greek air space and then followed the commercial air corridor down the coast of the Mediterranean, skirting Turkey's southern flank, Lebanon and Palestine.

'They're going to Egypt,' said Herrick, leaning into the conference phone.

'It looks like that,' said the Chief.

'It fits with today's line of questioning,' she said. 'The only thing they wanted to demonstrate in front of me was that Khan was Jasur Faisal – the man whose papers he was carrying. Faisal is wanted all over the Middle East, and in Egypt for the murder of a newspaper editor.'

'Yes,' said the Chief quietly. 'It means of course that the Albanians wouldn't want to be answerable for the degree of torture they're planning. This has happened before, in 1998.' There was a long pause during which Harland and Herrick wondered if the line had dropped. 'It complicates things a great deal.' Another pause. 'Yes, what we shall want you to do for the moment is to have that serious talk with Loz, using the information I sent you earlier. See how he responds. I'll get back to you. Oh, by the way, we're going to change encryption on the next call.' He told Harland to enter a six-digit code into the computer through which the phone was routed, then hung up.

As Harland worked at the keyboard, Herrick asked, 'What did Loz say to you that made you and the Chief so interested?'

'He told me that Khan knows the identities of two terrorist leaders who were already talking about al-Qaeda activity in the mid-nineties. He and Khan talked to at least one of them when they last saw each other in ninety-seven.'

'But surely Loz is just trying to get us to spring his friend?' she said. 'He's bound to exaggerate the importance of Khan's information.'

'It's a tip that the Chief's not prepared to ignore. He has very good reasons to think Loz is telling the truth, but I don't know what they are.'

'But what's the point?' she asked. 'If Khan is in Cairo, we can forget it. The only thing the Egyptians are concerned with is what target he's planning to attack, who his contacts are, and where he was trained. They'll be asking the questions the Americans want answers to, but with a cattle prod. When he denies being involved in a specific plot they'll torture him to a point where he has to dream up some cock and bull story. Meanwhile they'll miss the really valuable information.'

'One of the minor problems with torture,' said Harland grimly. He picked up the phone and told Tyrrel to bring Loz in.

Loz's buoyant expression collapsed when they told him that Khan had been taken to Cairo. 'This is very, very bad news,' he said, shaking his head and working his hands.

'Well, we're still evaluating what this means,' said Harland, steering him to a chair away from the computers. 'But it doesn't look good, I grant you that.' He paused and rubbed his chin, as though wondering how to proceed, then he focused on Loz. 'Isis had an encounter with one of the nastier scumbags of our time tonight, a man called Marenglen who is head of the local secret service here. It's a curious name which I understand is made from the first three letters of Marx, Engels and Lenin – a name forged in desperate communist times when people needed to ingratiate themselves with the regime.' He stopped again. 'Interestingly, it's the same kind of formation as TriBeCa in New York, the Triangle Below Canal. But I probably can't tell you anything about TriBeCa, Doctor.' He let that hang in the stuffy atmosphere of the Communications room and looked down at Loz intently. Herrick wondered where the hell this was leading.

'This Marenglen,' continued Harland, 'was picked up when he came to the LSE in London on a scholarship in 1987, and he was trained by former colleagues who of course had no idea that communism was about to collapse in Albania. He was a good spot because he was exceptionally clever, and useful to us after Enver Hoxha's death, but Marenglen turned out to be a rotten apple, as bad a man as you could ever meet. There is literally no crime in Albania that Marenglen does not in some way supervise from the safety of his position. Coming in contact with this man is like handling a test tube of bubonic plague. I do not exaggerate.' Loz looked mystified. 'We are here because of you, Dr Loz, and because of your friend. Isis took a big risk this evening to see if she could help Khan and that's when she came across Marenglen. It could have ended very badly for her but she took that risk because of you and your friend. But you know something? We don't really have any idea about either you or Khan. So, I want you to help us. Tell us everything about you.'

'Absolutely,' said Loz, eagerly leaning forward, hands clasped around his knee. 'But what more do you want?'

'You should understand your position,' said Harland. 'You're in Albania illegally. You travelled here on a forged passport and have none of the correct visa requirements. Remember, this was Khan's only crime in Albania, and yet he was held and beaten up. If they find that his main contact is also here, they are very likely to do exactly the same to you. Who knows, you may even end up in the same Egyptian jail.'

'But your responsibility is to help me.' A fleeting, rather professional smile crossed his face. 'That's what the Secretary-General instructed you to do.'

Harland shook his head. 'Believe me, Doctor, what happens to you is entirely my choice now.'

'So what do you want me to tell you?'

'Ninety-seven. What were you doing in 1997?'

'I was in New York, studying osteopathy. You know that!' he smiled at Herrick as though Harland was now being quite impossible.

'And the real estate business? How did that fit into your life?'

Loz's gaze hardened. 'What do you mean?'

'We know all about that. We know that while you were studying, you were also investing large sums in Manhattan developments. I have a figure of sixty million dollars, but London believes the amount transferred to you through twenty accounts may be two or three times that figure. All of it was placed at your disposal to buy real estate in Manhattan – mostly in Chelsea and TriBeCa. TriBeCa was the big killing of your operation, wasn't it? You made a profit of 15.7 million dollars on one deal in the Triangle Below Canal. There were many others.' He stopped and examined his notes. 'You know how we began to trace them? We started by looking up the name of a company that let your premises in the Empire State building – and still does – the Twelver Real Estate Corporation. That name rang a few bells in London. Anyone who knows anything about Islam knows that the Shi'a sect is called in Arabic *Ithna Ashariya* – the Twelvers. The movement of money from the Shi'ite banks in Lebanon to New York had been noted between 1996 and 1999 and so had the name of the Twelver Real Estate Corp. What they didn't know was who was controlling the investments. A week ago, they began to dig again and found your signature on documents held by the City Authority in New York. Who were you investing the money for, Dr Loz?'

'Some former associates of my father.'

'And these people were connected with the Hizbollah organisation?'

'No. But I cannot say definitely, of course.'

'But you agree that the utmost was done to disguise the origin of this money before you invested it and, given your father's Shi'ite background, it is likely that it came from Hizbollah?'

'It's a possibility.'

'But more interesting is that you deceived almost everyone about the extent of your wealth and your real occupation.'

'But I *am* an osteopath.'

'Yes, you are, and a very good one. But you are also a property tycoon. You've made many millions of dollars for your partners *and* for yourself. A rough estimate puts your wealth at fifty million dollars – enough, as someone observed in London, to finance one hell of a terrorist operation. Enough money to buy as many sets of fake identity as you could need. That's why you found it so easy to leave the States and bribe your way through the Balkans.'

Loz sank into the chair. 'I had to leave the US, as you are very well aware. I spent what was necessary.'

'Yes, but what other back doctor has your sort of contacts – members of Bosnian crime fraternities outside Chicago, gun runners, people smugglers in Southern Bosnia and Montenegro? We've only just begun to research you, but it's already clear that you are seriously 'connected'. Your pose as a society figure in Manhattan is a carefully constructed cover.'

Loz shook his head. 'I *really* am an osteopath. That's what I do! It fulfils me in a way I cannot describe. Why else would I run free clinics every week in three New York hospitals? Yes, it is true I have made a lot of money, but I can arrange for you to talk to my lawyers and they will tell you that I have donated much of my fortune to charity. In other circumstances I would not mention this, but you should know that I have made grants and donations of nearly twenty million dollars in the last three years. This can all be confirmed in New York, by my lawyers, my accountant. Even the charities will tell you.'

'But you still have a tidy sum in the bank.'

Loz uncrossed his legs and threw his hands out hopelessly. 'Of course, but the money was gained honourably on the rising market of the late nineties. Would it be any different if I had invested in new technology and sold at the right moment? What's the problem with real estate?'

'The difference to us is that you were investing on behalf of a Middle Eastern terrorist organisation. Where the profits from those deals went is certainly interesting, and you will face questions on this when you return to the United States. That is a legitimate concern of the FBI and I will make sure Special Agent Ollins is fully briefed with the information we have. No one can protect you from that. But for the moment I want to know what occurred when you met Khan in London in 1997.' He raised a hand. 'Before you answer, be clear that I have the authority to turn you over to Marenglen if I'm not satisfied with what you say.'

He nodded. 'Look, there isn't a problem about this. Karim phoned me in New York and said he wanted my advice. He was like that. He relied on me, trusted my judgement.'

'And you agreed to go to London?'

'Yes, I flew the next day and we spent a couple of days together, seeing old haunts, talking about Bosnia. Eventually he got round to the subject of Afghanistan. He told me he had decided to join The Poet in Pakistan. As I explained this was our name for a man he had met in Bosnia whose real name we did not know. Anyway, Karim was offered a role in Afghanistan training fighters. That can mean a lot of things. Karim understood it to mean that he would be continuing the war against the oppressors of Islam on Afghanistan's northern borders, the republics of the former Soviet Union. But he was torn between Western and Muslim values and wanted the moral view of what he was going to do. He felt I would understand because I had suffered the same agonies of guilt in Bosnia. I told him that he should stay in London and return to medicine. But he was caught up with the idea of himself as this great adventurer, even though he knew the horrors of war and had seen the very worst things in Bosnia. We had an argument – a terrible argument – because I could not believe he was going to make this mistake. I was appalled, disappointed. I accused him of being addicted to killing and failing to face his responsibilities as a human being, a doctor and a good Muslim. For his part he said I was a coward and running away from my duties as a Muslim. We made it up the following day, which was when I gave him those postcards and some money.'

'How many postcards?'

'Oh, a handful. I can't remember.'

'And how much money?' asked Harland.

'I don't recall exactly – fifteen thousand dollars, something like that.'

'Did you hear from him again, apart from the postcards?'

'No.'

Herrick looked at Harland then asked, 'If you haven't changed your address in the last six or seven years, presumably your phone number hasn't changed either?'

'No, it's the same.'

'So why didn't he call you instead of sending these postcards? There was very little guarantee of them getting through to you. Why didn't he just pick up the phone and ask you to wire him some money?'

'I have wondered about that,' said Loz. 'Maybe he was worried about the calls being monitored.'

'Yes,' she said. 'But it still doesn't really make sense, unless of course he had to send those cards because of the coded messages in them.'

Harland stood up and let his right arm slide down his thigh.

'You shouldn't do that yet,' said Loz gently. 'In a week's time you can begin the exercises I showed you, but not yet.'

'Isis makes a good point,' said Harland, removing his hand and straightening.

'I agree,' said Loz, 'but I can't answer her question.'

'You must have some idea of The Poet's identity,' she said. 'There can't have been many Bosnian commanders that Khan was friendly with.'

'I believe he was originally a scholar . . . but I only inferred that from what Khan said.'

'Where was he from?' asked Herrick.

'The East, maybe Pakistan or Iran, but I do not know.'

'And you think this is the man that Khan can tell us about? What reason do you have for believing he's still alive?'

'Because he was very smart. Khan was in awe of him. He said he was the most civilised and dangerous man he had ever met. Those were the words he used – civilised and dangerous.'

Herrick took out a piece of paper and wrote 'Phone Dolph', then on a second line, 'Beirut'. She had suddenly had an idea.

'But all this is guesswork,' said Harland contemptuously. 'I need a lot more.'

'We really need to know everything that you know,' said Isis, leaning forward and looking into Loz's eyes. 'Trust us for Christ's sake. We've certainly earned that.'

Loz breathed in deeply, seemingly to savour the air. 'Eighteen months ago I was phoned by a man in New York. He was a foreigner, but well-spoken and educated. He said something like, 'I expect you have heard of me. I am The Poet.' I knew he must have been given my number by Khan, so I listened and he told me straight away that he wanted thirty thousand dollars. He said there was no question of my not giving it to him – he made it sound as if I owed him. In the background of what he was saying there was a threat and I understood that he would harm me if I didn't give him what he wanted. So I got the money together the next day, put it in a bag and began to walk to the agreed meeting place in

Union Square. He specified that I should walk, even though it was winter and there was a lot of snow on the ground. On the way, a homeless beggar came up to me asking for money. He wouldn't leave me alone and followed me down the street, then he grabbed hold of my arm and handed me a card which said, "The Poet thanks you for your donation." He reached out and took the bag from my hand.'

'You gave thirty thousand dollars to a New York beggar?' said Harland incredulously.

'Yes. When I got back to the building there was the same message on my answerphone. "The Poet thanks you for your donation."'

'You were had,' said Harland.

'I don't think so. Two days later I received an Arabic inscription in a frame. You remarked on it when I was treating you. If you remember, it says, "A man who is noble does not pretend to be noble, any more than a man who is eloquent feigns eloquence. When a man exaggerates his qualities, it is because of something lacking in himself. The bully gives himself airs because he is conscious of his weakness." Also in the package was this . . .' he opened his jacket, then handed Herrick a small black and white photograph wrapped in cellophane. It was of Karim Khan dressed in tribal costume and sporting a boldly patterned turban. 'This was proof that he was in touch with Khan and had seen him recently. I suppose it was also proof of his own identity.'

'Why didn't you show me this before?'

'Because you're of a sceptical disposition, Mr Harland. If you don't mind me saying, you're too nervous to believe.'

'I would have believed a bloody picture,' said Harland, holding it away from him.

'You need glasses,' said Loz.

Harland took no notice and put the photograph in his wallet. 'I'll keep this for the moment.'

'What did this man look like? ' asked Herrick.

'A homeless person,' he smiled. 'I'm being serious. He was covered in coats and wore a long beard. I couldn't see his face beneath it all and anyway he was a few inches shorter than I am. Maybe only five foot five or six.'

'So you're telling us you may have seen The Poet?'

'I have no doubt about that.'

'When was this?'

'The winter of 2000, just after the millennium celebrations.'

Harland walked to the door and opened it. 'Right, that will be all for the moment. We will talk later.'

When Loz had left he looked at Herrick and said, 'Well?'

'We either believe all of it or none of it. Either way, there's nothing we can do about Khan.'

Harland frowned. 'Does this overlap with anything you've been doing for RAPTOR?'

'No, but I would like to make a call on this phone if you wouldn't mind. I have a friend who may still be up.'

She got through to Dolph, whose brisk hello rang out on the conference speaker.

'Why're you up so late?' she asked.

'Waiting for you.'

'But what are you doing?'

'Turns out that the Americans are keen poker players. We've got two full tables on the go, playing for a monkey – that's five hundred nicker in your language, Isis.'

'Don't you sleep?'

'No one knows whether it's day or night down here. We're like beagles in a smoking lab, or labs in a smoking beagle. Whichever way you like it.'

'Are you drunk, Dolph?'

'No, merely rat-arsed.'

She was aware of Harland's disapproving gaze. 'Dolph, I need your help, so pull yourself together.'

'I love it when you're strict.'

'I want to know about Bosnia – the siege of Sarajevo.'

'Okay.'

'We're interested in a commander of Muslim soldiers. We have no name apart from The Poet, but this was not commonly used.'

'Well that narrows it down,' said Dolph, laughing.

'Come on Dolph. I haven't got time . . .'

'Well, there was Abu Abdel Aziz or Barbaros – the guy with the two-foot beard.'

'No, someone less obvious. Perhaps a scholar of some sort, but a good fighter.'

'So we're looking for a member of the Mujahideen Brigade that was disbanded after Dayton?'

'Maybe. We're right at the beginning with this one, so we're interested in anything.'

'I'll talk to some of the hacks who were there during the siege. They may have come across him. Any idea where this character came from?'

'Pakistan or Iran are possibilities.'

'Have you got a description? His age at the time?'

'No – we know he is about five foot five or six.'

'Don't burden me with detail, Isis,' he laughed. 'I'll call you if I get something. Where're you going to be?'

'On my cell phone.'

'Hey, Isis. You got to hear about Joe Lapping before you go.'

'Okay.' Herrick sat back smiling.

'So Lapping is left in Sarajevo instead of me. The French tumble him in precisely three and a half seconds and start making his life hell. Lapping can't move without one of the Frogs whispering 'Rozbeef spy' in his ears. He gets completely freaked, changes his address and then can't find his way home and has to put up with some aid worker while the apartment is found. Meanwhile the Frogs have moved every bird with a dodgy past into Lapping's place and opened it as a brothel.' Dolph broke off. She could hear him helpless with laughter and thumping something in the background. 'So when Lapping eventually gets home he's greeted by some lovely wearing the top of his Marks and Spencer pyjamas smoking a spliff, at which point the Frogs arrange for the place to be raided by the Bosnian vice squad.' He stopped again. Herrick glanced at Harland, who was smiling. 'You got to hand it to him,' continued Dolph, 'I mean there's never been anyone like Lapping in our business. He's classic.'

'Where's he now?'

'Still in Sarajevo. They're making new arrangements but there's no rush coz the suspect's gone to ground.' He paused. 'You know, Lapping could be really good on this. Seriously. He's a prize researcher, loves nothing better than sifting through dusty files in Serbo-Croat. That's like a threesome to Lapping. I can easily put him on to it through RAPTOR. Nobody will know.'

'Good.'

'And don't forget your friend in Beirut,' he said.

'I won't.'

The Chief did not phone until 6.30 a.m. local time. The plane carrying Khan had touched down at Cairo and been greeted by members of the local CIA station and the Egyptian intelligence service. As far as the local MI6 people could make out, he had been taken straight to police headquarters. There was some suggestion that he would make an appearance in court that day in connection with the slaying of the newspaper editor, but the Chief thought this unlikely because any lawyer appointed to Khan's defence would be able to demonstrate that he was not Jasur Faisal, and would move to have him released.

'Who else was on the plane?' asked Herrick.

'Two of the men from the Tirana station and the Syrian gentleman. He turns out to be Dr Ibrahim al Shuqairi, an extremely nasty piece of work. He has a Syrian passport but is from one of the Sunni tribes in Iraq. In any sane world he would be tried as a war criminal.'

'So, there's nothing we can do.'

The Chief mumbled, 'We'll see about that. Now, tell me, what did you make of Loz's answers?'

Harland and Herrick looked at each other. 'I'd say it's worth looking into the business of the Bosnian commander known as The Poet,' offered

Harland. 'It appears he was in New York in late 1999. But you know it may be all nonsense. There's nothing hard.'

The Chief digested this.

'We're working on the Bosnian angles,' said Herrick. 'Andy Dolph is going to ring some contacts.'

'Can he be discreet about this? He can't talk about it at RAPTOR.'

'There's no one more reliable,' said Herrick.

'Good. Right. Well, Isis, I think you'd better get back here. Harland, I wonder if you could help us to get Loz out. Nothing complicated. A boat ride to Italy. That's all. I'm putting the arrangements in place now. You'll get further instructions during the morning.'

Herrick noticed the expression in Harland's eyes had darkened a little.

'You do realise I'm not working for you, Chief,' he said.

'Of course, of course. Forgive me, Bobby. You know how grateful we are to you, I'm sure. I'm glad you've reminded me you're helping as an *irregular*. We're indebted to you. Oh, by the way, I have some movement on that trace we discussed in New York. I think it looks very promising.'

Harland said nothing.

'Eva – I think she's alive. Perhaps you would rather discuss it another time. We're likely to get some more.'

'Yes,' said Harland quietly. 'Yes, thank you. You understand I must consult with the Secretary-General about my movements. I have to answer to his brief.'

'Yes, you're quite right,' said the Chief emolliently. 'I just pray that you will be able to see your way to helping us on this one. Do you think there's any chance of Mr Jaidi letting you do your bit?'

'What is my bit?'

'We'll talk when you're in Italy. In the meantime, expect to be joined by several friends at the Embassy. They'll get Loz out. And Bobby, thank you again for all you're doing. I think you know how important this is.'

Isis watched his effortless manner sedate Harland. It occurred to her that he was susceptible only because there was some part of him that privately felt he still belonged in the Secret Intelligence Service, or at least was animated by the challenge and felt he could still rise to it better than most. In that way he was not unlike Munroe Herrick. She wondered about the woman mentioned by the Chief, and Harland's curiously subdued reaction. What the hell was that about?

He must do away with himself. That was his only thought as the plane touched down and sped along the runway to a desolate spot on the airbase where some vehicles waited. Gibbons cut the plastic restraints on his ankles and hooded him again. He avoided Khan's eyes and said nothing. Khan already knew he was to be tortured. During the last twenty minutes of the flight, as the light flooded the cabin, he had strained round to see who was behind him and caught sight of a powerful, fat leg jigging in the aisle. Then he heard the rustling of The Doctor's bag of nuts.

They hauled him from the seat and steered him towards the door, down the short flight of steps. Several men were shouting in Arabic and tugged at his arms, but Gibbons held on and guided him towards one of the vehicles where he was formally handed over. Beneath the hood Khan saw the shadows of the men and the outlines of the vehicles. The smell of the great city nearby came to his nostrils, a mixture of exhaust, wood smoke and shit. Gibbons said 'Welcome to Cairo, Mr Faisal.'

Someone spoke to him harshly in Arabic. When he didn't respond, he was hit in the small of the back with a rifle butt, and sank to his knees. He was picked up and the same phrase was repeated over and over. Gibbons shouted, 'Look, you fucking goons. His mouth is taped!' Someone took off the hood and ripped the tape back. He saw faces staring at him, men eager to hurt him. They spoke again, using the name Jasur Faisal, and although he understood better this time, Khan realised that it would be stupid to respond. Arabic was not his language; Faisal was not his name.

17

Speaking in a damp, official monotone, Vigo attempted to wind up the meeting with Herrick in the Bunker. He shifted in his chair and pushed her report on Karim Khan away from him as though confronted with a poor examination paper. 'And you're satisfied that Khan was the person executed on the hill?' His eyelids seemed heavy; his hands lay limp on the table.

She nodded. 'Yes. I observed him being loaded into the car by his Albanian guards at the SHISK headquarters. I noted his clothes and saw the same man taken from the same vehicle to the fire's edge. There's nothing more to say. They disposed of him.'

'Were any of our people there?' asked Nathan.

'No, just Albanians,' she replied. 'A man named Marenglen was in charge of the operation.' She stopped and looked at Vigo. How would Marenglen's tutor respond to that?

'We know of him,' said Vigo neutrally. 'And what was your impression of Khan? Did you believe he had any potential, or was he no more than what he claimed to be – a refugee, a disillusioned fighter?'

'As a veteran of the jihad in Bosnia and a field commander with years of experience in Afghanistan, he could have told us much that was useful, yes. But the constant threat of violence and the actual abuse during his interrogation were counter-productive. Aside from this, there was disagreement between the Albanian interrogators and the agency personnel, who seemed concerned only with proving that Khan was in fact the Hamas operative Jasur Faisal. It's clear to me that Khan's story about taking the identities from Faisal's body following the attack in Macedonia is true, but the presence of these papers was used to harass and intimidate him. Khan was guilty of no crime, whereas Faisal was wanted by several countries. And they wanted to pin Faisal's crimes on Khan.'

'Quite so,' said Vigo. 'Well, there's evidently nothing more we can do on this.'

She nodded.

'Now, as to your role here ...'

'I have a few questions about this,' said Lyne. 'It doesn't make sense. I looked at the transcripts and it's obvious that the questioning was unfocused, but what explains the change in direction when Isis went to the jail? You were having difficulty getting access, right? Then the moment you get in the room they start talking about Faisal. Why would they do that? And then why would they suddenly kill him? Whether they believed he was Faisal or Khan doesn't make any difference. He was still useful by any standards.' Herrick studied him. This was no play act. Lyne was genuinely puzzled, which meant he didn't know about Khan being flown to Egypt.

'In some respects it *is* regrettable,' conceded Vigo. 'But as you know, the American government has taken a firm line on terrorist suspects. They are to be eliminated . . .'

'Sure, if they're escaping through the desert like the al-Qaeda suspect in Yemen, but not if they are already in custody. I'm telling you, this doesn't make any sense, especially as our guys were involved in debriefing the suspect. They wouldn't let it happen like that.'

'I can only say what I saw,' said Herrick. 'I was certain it was him in that valley and my conversation with Marenglen confirmed it.' Vigo's eyes glittered with concentration. The Chief had taken pains to rehearse her and warned that if she appeared too credulous or too sceptical he would suspect she knew Khan was alive.

'But you, Isis,' said Lyne accusingly, 'the reigning queen of doubt, you know this doesn't add up.'

'Look, we weren't in charge of the operation. Your people were. There's a hell of a lot going on in Tirana that I couldn't find out because Lance Gibbons wouldn't tell me. You're in a much better position to discover why this happened. Call your friends at Langley.'

'I will do,' said Lyne.

Vigo's eyes moved from Lyne back to her with a slow, reptilian blink. 'In the meantime we must discuss whether you're willing to rejoin Nathan's team without indulging your wilder impulses. We just can't have that sort of behaviour, Isis. We must work together as a unit on this.'

'It's up to you,' she said. 'I apologised for the last incident and now I genuinely want to help with the ten remaining suspects.'

'Nine,' said Lyne. 'The Turkish guy in London is in a coma. Complications from surgery. He's not expected to recover.'

'Right,' said Vigo, evidently having made up his mind. 'You can start at the next shift in an hour's time. You better bring her up to date, Nathan.' He moved from the room with a slight limp on his left side.

Isis raised her eyebrows to Lyne.

'Gout,' said Lyne.

She smiled. 'Good.'

Lyne seemed to be weighing something in his mind. 'It's great to have you back, Isis. But I got to say I don't believe a word about Tirana, even though it's you telling me. What about the torture? Were our guys involved?'

'Not directly.'

'That's something, I suppose. I remember Lance Gibbons when I was in the DO. He was old school, crazy but brave as hell – and effective. He was captured in Kurdistan after the Iraqis penetrated one of the Kurdish groups up there in the mid-nineties. When he was being driven back to Baghdad he took out his guards with a concealed Beretta hidden on his ankle and then hiked back to Kurdistan and over the Turkish border through a fucking mine field. We need more people like him. I can't see him sitting in some fly-blown jail turning thumbscrews.'

'Can I ask you a question, Nathan?'

'Shoot.'

'What do *you* feel about the torture of terrorist suspects?'

'Depends on the circumstances. Clearly, if you know a man is in possession of vital information that may save thousands of lives, like the location of a dirty bomb or a suitcase full of smallpox, well, then I can see the argument that the harm done to one man, repellent though it is, may be excusable in the face of protecting thousands of innocent people. Eventually you have to do the math.'

'Even so, there's a moral problem, isn't there?' She was aware of herself sounding priggish.

'Yes, if you're dealing in absolute terms, I guess there is. But the war on terrorism is not about moral absolutes. This isn't a clash of moral systems of equivalent worth. The attacks on ordinary people aren't justifiable in either Islam or the Judaeo-Christian systems. What we are dealing with is a profound, undermining evil that threatens everyone, and I suppose it's understandable, if not forgivable, if the West tortures one or two men to save large numbers of people, some of whom may be Muslims.'

'But a line is being crossed. Once we condone it, we lose the thing we're fighting for.'

'I'm not persuaded of that. You could easily argue that killing someone is worse than torturing them. When those guys were targeted by a missile in the Yemeni desert, that was clearly extra-judicial killing and wrong by any moral standard. Yet almost no one objected because people saw it as the justifiable elimination of a threat. Why is torture any worse than that?'

Herrick thought for a moment. 'Because the slow and deliberate infliction of pain on any human being is in most instances worse than death. And then there's the question of whether it produces the information that you want, assuming you know the individual is in possession of that information in the first place.'

Lyne leaned back. 'Mostly I agree with you, Isis. A few years ago I wouldn't have condoned it in any circumstances. But say one of these guys we're watching is about to let loose a virus on the continent, a virus that might kill millions. No one could stand in the way of extracting the information by all available means. That's the nature of the inglorious, shitty war we're fighting. It's rough, but these guys chose it and now you and I are in the front line of the response. That's our job right now.' He put a pen to his lips and examined her, rocking silently in his seat. 'How badly was Khan tortured?'

'Not while I was there.'

'What would you say if I told you I believed he was still alive?' Lyne asked.

'The official version, the version that your people have decided will be the record, is in my report. By your people I mean the high command of RAPTOR – Vigo, Jim Collins, Spelling, the head of bloody MI5, God bless her. Who am I to doubt their wisdom?'

Lyne threw himself forward. 'You're shitting me. What do you know?'

'Nothing. I simply asked you about torture because all this took place with the CIA involved. I wanted to know what you thought about the issue.'

'No, you were sounding me out for another reason.'

'I thought you were sounding me out!'

'Either way, tell me what's up.'

'Honestly, Nathan, I think it would serve both our interests if you were to accept everything in my report and then forget about it.' She looked down.

'I hear you.' He raised his fingers in a boy scout salute. 'Don't tell. Don't ask.'

She smiled again. 'So what's been happening here?'

'It will be easier if we go out onto the floor,' he said, brightening. 'Andy Dolph is looking forward to seeing you. I think he carries quite a flame for you.'

They went together to Lyne's desk. On the way Herrick noticed new spaces had been opened in the short time she had been away, and there was a lot of new equipment manned by people she didn't recognise.

'Forget those guys,' said Lyne, gesturing in their direction. 'They can only talk number theory and they're losing their backsides in Dolph's poker school. One of them has been running a program based on the cards he draws, trying to figure out if he's cheating.'

'He is,' said Herrick.

Lyne also told her that 'Collection' had bugged all the apartments where the suspects were hiding. The live feeds from these could be seen on every computer hooked up to the RAPTOR circuit. The behaviour of the nine men – their toilet routines, exercise regimes, diet, reading patterns, religious observance and evidence of sexual frustration – was subject to minute scrutiny by behavioural psychologists.

'Did they find anything interesting?'

'Uh-uh.'

They arrived at Southern Group Three to find Dolph leaning back in his chair wearing a pair of lightly tinted sunglasses and a black trilby with a small rim.

'Hey, Isis, what's cooking?' he said, getting up and giving her a brief hug.

'Andy's won the Blues Brothers award for investigative excellence,' explained Lyne, 'which means he gets to wear John Belushi's hat until someone betters his achievement. The shades and ghetto-talk are optional.'

'How'd you win it, Dolph?' she asked.

'The Haj,' said Dolph, sitting down again. 'My man here will explain.'

Lyne grimaced. 'Andy did some research which tied all the suspects together. They basically all went on the Haj pilgrimage. Every single one of them arrived in Mecca on the fourth of February. They each went as one person and came away with a new identity.'

'A variation of the Heathrow switch,' she said.

'I told you she'd take credit for it,' said Dolph, raising his sunglasses to the rim of the hat.

'Okay then, tell me how it worked,' she asked, bowing in mock respect.

'How much do you know about the Haj?'

'A bit.'

Dolph put his feet on the desk. 'The Haj takes place every year for five or six days. Nearly one and a half million people from all over the world are issued with special visas by the Saudi Ministry for Religion. The pilgrim goes stripped of his worldly possessions, with nothing but a two-piece white cotton wrapping and a money-bag tied round his waist. The whole point is that you go as one person and return as another. "Re-chisel then your ancient frame and build up a new being," says a Pakistani poet. That sentence rang a bell with me and I realised the Haj was the perfect occasion for these guys to swap identities.' He stopped.

'That's the traditional break for applause,' said Lyne drily.

'I just knew that's what they had done. And after just forty-eight hours we found three had travelled to Mecca on the same day in the first week of February. The whole thing is so damned easy because the Saudi authorities insist that each pilgrim hands in his passport when he enters the country. They only give it back when he leaves. How much organisation would it take to do that switch? Answer, nil. By the way, all of them travelled in that period and acquired the identities they're currently using. They re-chiselled, Isis. And there are more. We think a total of seventeen men moved through Saudi Arabia during that week and came away as other people.'

She thought for a moment. 'But would they do this – sully the holiest pilgrimage of the year with a terrorist plot?'

'Of course they would. Anyway, I think it happened as they were leaving, after the visit to the holy sights was done and dusted.'

'You deserve the hat,' she said. 'But what would be the point of the second ID switch at Heathrow? If they'd already established a very efficient way of doing it on Arab soil why the hell would they risk everything by repeating the operation at Heathrow?'

'Aye, there's the rub,' said Dolph.

'So what's happening about this?'

Dolph looked pained. 'They put it on the back burner. They were interested, but the focus is on these nine men. We're going to hunt down the others at some later point.'

'Still, it was very smart of you.'

'That's what I keep saying,' Dolph exclaimed.

'I can vouch for that,' said Lyne.

Five minutes later, Herrick asked, 'You remember when the Stuttgart suspect killed himself and Walter Vigo ordered an intensive surveillance of calls from the Stuttgart helpers? He thought they would make contact with the leadership. Was a call traced?'

Before she had finished Dolph's eyes were revolving.

'Yep,' said Lyne absently, 'there was a trace to a satellite phone in the Middle East, but that's all I know. It's Umbra.'

'Umbra is NSA-speak for very restricted knowledge,' said Dolph.

'Right, so shut the fuck up,' said Lyne without smiling.

'Why's that so sensitive?' she asked. 'Anyway, where in the Middle East?'

'Search me,' said Dolph.

Lyne got up and made for the water machine shaking his head.

Herrick spent the next few hours doing what the Chief had instructed, roaming the system and reading anything that caught her eye. 'Go into the garden and pick what flowers you like,' he had said. 'Then come back to me.' She concentrated on the connections between the Lebanese-based terrorist group Hizbollah and the suspects who had visited the tri-border region in South America. It was a random thread, but she followed it because of Sammi Loz's background and her particular interest in Beirut.

When Lyne asked what she was doing, she told him she was familiarising herself with the new material and then added, 'You know, the suspects still seem like they're all half-asleep. Why haven't they been arrested?'

'Maybe they will be,' said Lyne wearily.

'When?' she demanded. 'When are they going to take these people into custody?'

Lyne revolved his chair and used his feet to wheel it round to her. 'You've been back precisely ten hours, Isis, and you already want access to the policy decisions. You understand the deal here. We gather the intelligence, okay? And the guys living up in the beautiful English summer get to make the policy, right? I don't see why you need to raise this again. If you want to decide policy, go see your Prime Minister. He and the President will decide when to take the suspects off the street. Not you, Isis. Not me.'

'But what kind of advice are they getting?'

'Twice daily assessments. The President and the Prime Minister value the information we're getting here. That's what we're told, and I believe it.'

'Nathan, I accept it's good material – really impressive in a way – but doesn't it strike you as odd that there's no movement, no sign of what they're planning, no hint of a target or of a battle formation? They're inert. '

'But this is exactly what they do. The key men always lie doggo before an attack, right up until the moment they're needed. In the files you've just read there are cross-references to the capture of a Spanish cell and their plans to drive a truck full of explosives and cyanide into the US Embassy in Paris. None of the principals cased the joint, none went anywhere near the target. That's the way they operate.'

'So if we already know their MO, why the hell are we studying it further?'

'You know, you're a very smart, very beautiful woman Isis. But you can't run the whole goddam programme.'

'You're beginning to sound like an old-fashioned male supremacist, Nathan.'

'That's not true. But you *are* becoming a royal pain in the ass.'

'Aha, the same phrase used to me by a member of the CIA in Tirana after a briefing from your Jim Collins. Were you in on that conversation, Nathan?'

'No, but I did overhear a little of what they said. Collins and Vigo were talking on the phone to Milos Franc. I heard that – yes.'

'Right. During that conversation, information about me – my address and my father's address – was released so that the Albanian Intelligence Service could threaten me.'

'I wasn't party to that,' said Lyne, looking her straight in the eye.

So Vigo was responsible, she thought. That was hardly surprising, but she was puzzled by his motive. 'Why do you think he would do that? It's not as though Karim Khan was remotely important to RAPTOR. Why would he go to the trouble of threatening me?'

'Has it occurred to you that he might just have wanted to scare you a little? Clearly you were causing trouble in Tirana. Maybe it's Vigo's way of warning you to toe the line.'

'By releasing my father's address, which is still classified information? That's a serious breach of security. Vigo is breaking the Official Secrets Act.'

'Look, Isis, my patience is kind of running out here. I saved your ass when you were in trouble with Vigo and Spelling over the break-in. Will you just give me a break and shut the fuck up? Okay, so you were threatened a little. So what? You're back here and now you're expected to work for a living.'

'You know I'm right, Nathan.'

'Right about what?'

'About RAPTOR. It's not working.'

'I'm not going to discuss it any longer. We both have work to do.' He pushed himself back to his screen.

Dolph had been watching the exchange. He got up and came over. 'Permission to give Herrick a jolly good spanking, sah.'

Lyne didn't smile.

'Failing that, perhaps we could go for a smoke up top?'

'Fine, I'll see you back here in half an hour.'

Herrick checked her watch. It was 4.20 a.m. Beirut was two hours ahead and she could just about get away with calling Sally Cawdor. She picked up her bag and followed Dolph to the elevator bank.

A minute or two later they walked out of the modest brick building which capped the Bunker and strolled a little way to the airfield, surrounded by the scent of mown grass mingled with dew. Dolph took out a pack of Marlboro and offered her one. She looked up with the first drag. 'No stars,' she said.

'Did you make the call to Beirut?' he said, flicking the match away.

'No, I will in a few minutes.'

'What are you up to, Isis?'

'Following my nose.'

'And what a nose. Tell me.'

'Not for the moment.'

'It's got something to do with you breaking into the bookshop?'

She shook her head.

'Why don't you just tell Dolph about it?'

'Because I can't,' she said.

'You think I'll tell Vigo?'

'You did work for him once.'

'That doesn't mean I'd grass you up, Isis.' He looked at her. 'You know, there's a really fascinating intelligence problem here. These guys are a mystery. They are not following any of the usual patterns. They're not making the connections with al-Qaeda, the Armed Islamic Group or any of the other groups – Salafist group for Call and Combat, for example. They're like a parallel group. There is no communication between the individual members. They're—'

'What about the money transfers from the Gulf, the network of helpers, the training in Afghanistan and the tri-border region? It looks pretty standard to me.'

'Yeah, but it's not. There's something else, isn't there?'

'That's what I've been saying. You're trying to draw me out by repeating my arguments to me. It's the oldest trick in the book, Dolph.'

A look of theatrical hurt passed across his face. 'Captious, that's the word for you. Even when someone agrees with you, you find a reason to doubt them.'

'I'm sorry,' she said distractedly. 'What about the foreign intelligence services? They must have got wind of RAPTOR by now.'

'Yeah, they have. In Hungary the local plods are showing interest in suspect Eight, the Yemeni, and the French are definitely on to the Saudi in Bosnia, though we don't believe they've sussed the operations in Toulouse and Paris. It's a matter of time though. In Germany the BND are showing interest in the late Mohammed bin Khidir, in particular his fake passport.'

'Time,' said Isis, screwing the butt of the cigarette into the ground with her toe. 'The whole thing is based on the assumption that we have time. Somewhere there's a clock ticking. We seem to have forgotten that.'

'Nathan hasn't. He wants to know when, where and how. He's just working within the system. He's a genuinely good guy.'

She nodded. 'Yeah, I know. Hang around, will you? I want to ask you about Lapping but I do need to make this call first.'

She walked off into the dark and dialled the Beirut number. A bleary male voice answered after half a dozen rings and she asked to speak to Sally Cawdor. Sally came on, also a little sleepy.

'It's me – Isis. I'm sorry to call so early but—'

'You picked your moment,' said Sally. 'We were up half the night trying to get me pregnant.' She paused and giggled. 'That's on a need to know basis.' In the background there was the sound of male complaint.

Isis smiled. Sally had been in the Service for four years before marrying a Lebanese businessman. Herrick had known her at Oxford but they were recruited independently. Sally was already in SIS when Isis joined.

'You know that problem I had . . . ?' started Isis.

'Yes.'

'Did you manage to do anything about it?'

'I emailed you and sent a message through Dolph to call me.'

'Sorry, I was out of the country.'

'I gained access – for which you owe me lunch – and managed to get a sample which I've sent to your home address.'

'You didn't! That's terrific. Thank you. Thank you. Thank you.'

'I know it's there because it was delivered by one of Rafi's couriers.'

'How the hell did you pull that off?'

'Rafi disapproves so I'll explain when I see you. I pray I got enough of what you want.'

Herrick thanked her profusely and said she'd let her know how things turned out.

'What was that about?' asked Dolph.

'Did Lapping find out anything in Sarajevo yesterday?' she asked.

'Not much, but I know he will.' Dolph had taken off the hat and was brushing his hair back.

He caught her look of appraisal. 'What're you thinking?'

'I was blank – sorry.'

'Well,' he said, replacing the hat so it was tipped forward over his brow. 'I did find something for you. There was a woman I knew, Hélène Guignal, a terrific looker. She spent most of the period from 1993 to 1995 in Sarajevo filing for Agence France Presse. For part of that period she had an affair with a man who was one of the defenders of Sarajevo. He was important, a kind of liaison between the Bosniaks and the foreign Muslims.'

'Has she got a photograph of him?'

'I didn't ask because she had no time to talk. I have tried to reach her but she's proving remarkably elusive.'

'Where does she live?'

'Brussels.'

She thanked him and gave him a peck on the cheek. Dawn was breaking and a thin layer of mist had settled over parts of the airfield.

'We need to get Joe Lapping onto this.'

'Yeah well, it's difficult because we've all got our hands full. I mean Lyne and the other guys never let up. We don't seem to be able to flit about the place like you, Isis.'

18

Three hours later a cab dropped her at the end of the one-way system on Gabriel Road, which was now decked out in the full municipal splendour of almond and cherry blossom. With her bag over her shoulder, she walked the remaining hundred yards to her house, telling herself that once she'd showered and had breakfast at the café round the corner she wouldn't feel so tired.

She reached her front door and lowered the bag to the ground to search for her house keys. As her hands moved from pocket to pocket, her eyes ran over the house and came to rest on an upstairs window where the curtains were drawn. She was sure they hadn't been left that way because when she was leaving for Tirana she had stood at the window watching for the cab. She put the key in one of the two locks and found it had already been turned; only the Yale lock was keeping the door shut. She placed her ear to the letter-box. The cool air from inside the house brushed her cheek like a breath. There was something wrong – a smell of someone, a sense of occupation.

She turned the Yale lock and slipped inside. There was a sound coming from upstairs: someone was moving about at leisure, unaware that she was in the house. She stepped back into the garden and dialled the emergency services on her mobile. The woman instructed her not to confront the intruder but to wait at a distance from the house, which was what she planned to do once she had retrieved a baseball bat she kept in her umbrella stand. She darted inside again, but as she seized the bat a dark shape appeared at the top of the stairs. She dived from the house, conscious only of the need for room to swing the bat. In almost no time at all, the man had rushed the stairs and taken hold of her, and was trying to drag her inside. She screamed and slipped from his grasp, then let the bat slide through her hands until she felt the knob at the top of the handle. She drew it back over her shoulder and brought it down against the side of the man's head, causing him to yell out. A second, much cleaner shot concentrated all her energy into the fat end of the bat and felled him, unconscious, into the path of another man who had come down the stairs. The obstruction gave her a fraction of a second to run through the gateway and dive behind the hedge, but in that moment she registered that the man had pulled a gun from his waistband. A bullet whistled through the hedge and tore into a car parked in the road, setting off its alarm. She spun round and ran a few yards down the street to shelter behind a van, hearing the screech of a police patrol car in the road. Two officers tumbled out just before bullets exploded in the bodywork and windscreen of their vehicle. A stocky man in trainers and an oversized leather blouson stepped into the road. The policemen had dropped behind the patrol car, but instead of running off, the gunman kept moving forward, taking aim and firing with cool deliberation. Herrick popped up and saw his close-cropped head through the front windscreen of the van and decided that unless she did something, he would kill the officers.

Crouching low, she hurtled along the gutter and rounded the front of the van. The man was obscured from her, but from the sound of two further deafening shots she judged he was only a matter of feet away. She moved a few paces, saw his back then lunged at him, leading with her left foot and bringing all her weight down with the blow. She connected squarely with the back of his neck and knocked him forwards. But the gun was still in his hand. She jumped to the right, knowing that she had just one chance, and struck him with all her might across the shoulder, aware of the tennis-serve grunt that escaped her lungs. The man was still on his feet, but the gun had flown from his hands and landed under the van. For a split second they looked at each other, then he scrambled away, his feet slipping momentarily on the snowfall of almond blossom, to flee down the centre of the road with his arms working double time like a character from a silent movie. Herrick crouched to retrieve the gun and without straightening, swung round and fired at the retreating figure. She missed, aimed again but didn't pull the trigger because one of the policemen yelled at her. 'Hey, Stop that. Put the gun down!' She stood up and handed it to him, and both officers set off after the man, but by now he was fifty yards away and opening a car door. In one movement he slid behind the wheel and started the car engine. Seconds later his car had vanished.

With a burst radiator and a flat, the police car was hardly in a state to pursue him. The officers radioed details of the fugitive and returned to examine the injured man, who had come round but was still lying on the ground in a daze. His head was bleeding copiously and Herrick went to fetch a cloth from her kitchen to stem the flow. She told the policemen that the incident should be regarded as a security matter and that she would need to make a call. They stood looking a little bemused as she phoned one of the Chief's assistants at Vauxhall Cross and asked him to get in touch with the local station.

The injured man struggled to a sitting position and began to curse and wail in a foreign language.

One of the officers knelt down beside him. 'What the hell's he speaking?'

'I think you'll find it's Albanian,' replied Herrick. She looked down at the stocky little man with russet-coloured skin and slightly protruding ears. He could be the Albanian interrogator's brother.

'With the way you must have hit him, miss, he's lucky to be alive.' He pressed the cloth to the gash on the side of the man's head. 'But by heck, I'm glad you dropped the other fellow. He meant business.'

The other officer looked at the gun and read the inscription on the side of the barrel. 'Desert Eagle fifty AE pistol – Israel Military Industries Limited.' He paused. 'You only have to see what it's done to the car to know you don't want to be in the way of that thing.'

People began to gather in the street and soon afterwards an ambulance and three other squad cars arrived. The man was taken away for treatment under guard while Herrick went inside with one of the two constables to find the house turned upside down. The policeman observed that burglars normally made a pile of the things they intended to steal, but in this case the obvious items of value – the TV set, jewellery, CD player, and odd bits of antique silver – had been left untouched.

'What would two Albanian villains be wanting to search your house for?'

'Your guess is as good as mine,' she said.

She made a statement, which he took down at laborious speed in his notebook, contriving to extend two or three minutes' action into a forty-minute feature. Herrick tidied and filled the drawers and cupboards while he spoke.

'What do you do for a living, Miss Herrick?' asked the constable finally.

'I'm civil service,' she replied. 'And I have a very important meeting in an hour.'

'We could give you a lift into town and I can fill the gaps in your statement while my colleague drives.'

'Fine, but I have to shower and eat and clear up a bit.' She thought for a second. 'It would make my life a lot easier if you would get me two bacon and egg sandwiches and a cup of coffee from the café on Rosetti Road, just round the corner.'

'Two!'

'Yes, two, unless you both want something, in which case I'll treat you.' She proffered a twenty-pound note. 'Really, it would be a big help.'

He examined her. 'Are you sure you're all right? Not suffering from shock or anything?'

'As a matter of fact, I'm feeling pretty damned good. It's not every day you get the chance to knock out a man with a baseball bat.'

He took the money and went to the door, just as the bell rang. Herrick looked round from the kitchen to see him open it to a man in a chauffeur's uniform.

'Yes?' she called out.

'Miss Herrick? A package from the Nabil Commercial Bank. You are expecting me. I have it for you, here.'

It was only when she took the fat brown envelope from him and recognised the handwriting on the address label that she realised this was the package Sally Cawdor had promised her.

It occurred to her that the contents of the package were the only thing that anyone could want from her. But why were two Albanian thugs looking for it? Some twenty minutes later as she sat at her kitchen table, working her way through the crusty bread bacon sandwiches, she began to put a theory together.

'Cunning is the dark sanctuary of incapacity,' said the Chief quietly. 'Are you familiar with that aphorism, Isis? It comes from the Earl of Chesterfield, who knew that cunning is a substitute for talent and originality. In this particular situation someone is being very cunning indeed, so perhaps it is simply a matter of looking around us and settling on the least talented.' She knew he was referring to Richard Spelling and Walter Vigo.

'Despite everything, I wonder if the business at my house is really a side issue, Sir Robin,' said Herrick, wanting to get off the subject of what the men were looking for and why they might have been sent by Vigo.

'If you really think that is the case,' he said, 'I am happy to leave it, at least for the moment.' He turned to the window with his glasses lodged in the corner of his mouth. 'Do you know how many people are under surveillance by the Security Services, Special Branch and us, Isis?' he asked suddenly.

'No.'

'About five hundred and fifty require close attention. And that's in this country alone. Outside, the number reaches into the thousands.' He paused and turned from the view. 'Yet the preponderance of our effort is deployed watching nine people.'

'I feel rather responsible for that. I'm—'

'You did your job. It is the reaction to the discoveries you made at Heathrow that is flawed, and I am more than responsible for that.'

'But the Prime Minister only has to say the word and we bring all the foreign intelligence services into the operation and immediately diminish the commitment as well as the exposure.'

He nodded slowly. He couldn't say it, but she understood that Spelling and Vigo had monopolised the advice going to the Prime Minister. 'Who knew that you would not be sleeping at the Bunker after your shift? You had your bag with you, so it was a fair assumption that you would be staying there.'

'Only Andy Dolph, I think.'

'So anyone else might imagine your house was free to be searched at leisure today?'

'I suppose so.'

'And you say they were definitely Albanians?'

'The second man wasn't apprehended, but the one in hospital is certainly Albanian.'

'Interesting,' said the Chief. 'But as you say, this is beside the point. I think we should move on to Karim Khan.'

He pressed a button on his desk and got up. 'I have made a lot of calls on your energy and I'm going to ask that you give a little more over the coming week. I hope that will be in order.'

He showed her to the door at the side of his office and they made their way to a room sealed off from the outside world, reputedly armoured and protected from every known surveillance device. They sat down at the table and the Chief looked expectantly at the door. After a few seconds it opened and Colin Guthrie, the head of the joint MI5 – MI6 anti-terrorist controllerate and his main aide, Gregor Laughland, came in. They were followed by Charles Harrison, head of Security and Public Affairs, his deputy Christine Selvey, Philip Sarre and three men she had not seen before. The group had a marked conspiratorial air about it and Herrick was intrigued that both Guthrie and Selvey were in attendance, since they had originally been supporters of RAPTOR. Perhaps they'd thrown their lot in with the Chief knowing they'd be thrown out under the new regime. More likely the Chief had encouraged them to attach themselves to RAPTOR to find out what was going on and report back to him.

The Chief began speaking in a quiet, uncertain tone that gave the impression he did not know quite what he was going to say. 'Time is short and I believe we have only a matter of days to act.' He gestured to the three strangers. 'These gentlemen are from a security firm that specialises in hostage negotiation. In a moment I will ask the firm's head of operations, whom I will call Colonel B, to speak about the plan he has been putting together for us in the twenty-four hours since we heard that Karim Khan had been flown for interrogation to Cairo. Colonel B's team will remain anonymous to all but myself and Colin Guthrie. It is Colonel B's condition that their involvement in this matter will not be referred to outside this room and so I stress to you all that the need for secrecy has never been more imperative.'

He stopped and looked round his staff, seeking a sign of consent in each person. Herrick understood that it was not simply for the consultant's peace of mind. The Chief was going beyond his powers as specified by the Foreign Office and Parliament. Despite the studied calm and modulation of his voice, this was a desperate last move and might very well also be Herrick's last work for the Service.

'Over the next few days,' he continued, 'we plan to remove Karim Khan from the custody of the local intelligence service and question him in the proper manner. It is my belief that this man possesses crucial information about future terrorist attacks in the West. In particular he can identify two, maybe even three, terrorist leaders who have so far escaped our attention. The first problem is that Mr Khan is being questioned simply as an operative who may, or may not, be involved in a particular attack. Mr Khan's knowledge is, I am certain, of a much more general and historic nature. He knows much, but is not in a position to appreciate what he knows, or how valuable it could be.

'The second problem is that our American friends are convinced Mr Khan knows things that are of immediate worth. They are therefore content to allow the Egyptians to torture him until he talks. Previously the Egyptians have been constrained by the requirement to produce foreign suspects in court, which entails exposure of their methods. But there will be no court case for Mr Khan because he is being held as Jasur Faisal and a sentence has already been passed on him, in his absence. So the Egyptians will have a free hand. Hence our need to move quickly.

'Now, we already have good information about where he is being held. Up until 6.00 a.m. today he was in a holding cell in police headquarters in central Cairo. At some stage he will be removed to a facility attached to a very secure prison on the southern outskirts of the city, at which point we may give up all hope of freeing him. According to our people, there are no signs of that yet. We have pulled out all the stops on this one and the sources of information are proving fast and responsive to our requests, so I am confident that at least in this regard we're not working in the dark.

'Before Colonel B outlines his thoughts, I want to say what happens after we have got Khan. The immediate aim will be to restore him to a condition where he is able to talk about what he knows. This will not be a simple matter. He is likely to be quite badly injured, to say nothing of the psychological trauma of torture. What I have in mind is this: we do not attempt to exfiltrate Khan immediately, but keep him in Egypt at the safe location being prepared at the moment by some unusual associates of ours. It is important that Khan sees some friendly faces – people he knows he can trust.

'His oldest friend, Sammi Loz, will be on hand. Loz is an excellent doctor and I am hoping we can rely on him to treat Khan. Also at this location will be Robert Harland who has been shadowing Loz, and Isis Herrick who saw Khan in custody in Tirana a couple of days ago. It will be Isis's job to question him, and since she has already attempted to intervene to prevent him being hurt, I believe he will be inclined to trust her. There will be backup but we will keep them out of sight. Once Khan has given us what we need, we will bring him to this country and provide safe asylum. Any questions?'

The only question in Herrick's mind was why the Chief believed Khan knew enough to risk mounting the operation, but no one asked a question and she decided to keep quiet. It was clear the members of SIS in the room had decided to pay him the supreme compliment of taking him on trust.

'I should point out that if any of you are caught in Egypt,' continued Teckman after a brief pause, 'Her Majesty's Government will deny all knowledge of you. However, I am satisfied that we stand a very good chance of success, and that even if we do not get Khan out, all of you will be able to disperse and leave the country without difficulty. The one problem is that our friends at the CIA will be in evidence. We should of course make every effort to avoid injuring these people. They may be misguided, but they are still our allies, and in the end I believe they will come to see the error of their ways in this matter.'

He handed over to Colonel B, a compact man in his mid-forties with sandy hair, a freckled tan and pale crow's feet at the corners of his eyes. The colonel stood and opened a laptop which sent a series of maps, diagrams and satellite photographs to a large screen at the end of the table. Over the next hour and a half, he roughed out several plans, each of which required intensive surveillance of the route between the police headquarters and the prison. Meeting places, covers and arrangements for communication between members of SIS and the snatch team were then settled.

After two hours, including a break for coffee and sandwiches, the colonel closed his laptop and looked around the room. 'Generally, I find in these operations that we have to be very light on our feet and willing to adapt to new circumstances. Everything we have sketched out may fall apart. Success *will* come, but only if we are prepared to change our plans at a moment's notice.' He shook the Chief's hand with military firmness and made for the door with his two silent lieutenants.

Before leaving, Teckman drew Herrick aside. 'A lot of this operation relies on your ability to gain the trust of Khan and Sammi Loz, but you will have to watch Loz like a hawk. Harland will be with you, armed. He is on his way to Egypt with Loz now.'

He reached over to a dark blue plastic box the size of a computer case. 'This is the medical equipment which Loz will need to treat Khan after his ordeal. It contains all the usual drugs – antibiotics, vitamins, anti-inflammatory drugs, painkillers, sleeping pills – and some unusual ones, together with bandages and syringes. Our people have tried to allow for the sorts of injuries Khan will have sustained at the hands of The Doctor. Loz will know what to do with them. If not, there are instructions for each. In the unlikely event of your being questioned by Egyptian customs, you will say this is the emergency pack for the elderly patient you and Christine Selvey are accompanying.'

'Which elderly patient?' she asked.

A flicker of a smile escaped the mouth that had been set in grim purpose for the past two hours. 'I'm afraid I haven't been entirely open with you, Isis, but there has been very little time. Your father has agreed to take part in the operation.'

'What! You can't be serious. He's in his eighties.'

'It's only a very minor capacity and I still have the highest regard for his abilities.' He put up a hand to silence her objection. 'Besides, what would be better cover than you and his devoted nurse travelling to see the Pyramids at Giza and Saqqara?'

'But it is such a liability. I can't think of a worse way of going about an operation.'

'Nonsense. The moment Khan is in our hands, your father will travel home with Christine Selvey, with whom, by the way, he gets on splendidly.'

'With Christine Selvey!'

'Security and Public Affairs are not all she knows. She gave up field-work a dozen years ago because there was no one to look after her ailing mother in the evening. She was an excellent operative. Quite superb.'

Herrick shook her head in disbelief. 'It's so bloody unorthodox, sending two related people on the same job.'

'The whole thing is bloody unorthodox, Isis.' He didn't smile. 'Now, all you have to concentrate on is getting Khan to a point where he can tell you what he knows. I believe you are right about Bosnia and I'm sure that line of inquiry will prove fruitful. In the meantime I will tell Spelling that you're doing some work for me.'

She wondered fleetingly whether to tell him about the package from Beirut that she had forwarded to the address in Oxford before getting to the office, then decided that there wouldn't be any point until she had got the results.

19

A large wheel was fitted into a wooden beam in the ceiling. Through it ran a dirty brown rope that had been stretched and pulled until it had the appearance of a rusty cable. One end of this hawser led through a pulley fixed on the stone floor, then to a two-handed winding mechanism, allowing the load to be lifted to the ceiling and held there by a ratchet. The other end was attached to a number of chains and manacles designed to be fastened round human limbs.

Though elementary, the capstan provided several options. A man could be hauled up by both arms, or just one; he could be suspended with one arm behind his back and bound to his leg; or he might be winched up by his neck only, so that for what seemed like many minutes he experienced the sensation of being garrotted. Usually, being hung by his arms for several hours was all any normal man needed to persuade him to talk.

The man in charge of the interrogation understood perfectly well that most people would talk when confronted with the prospect of this treatment, but in his trade there was a saying, which translates as 'squeezing the lemon dry'. It summarised the belief that when a man was broken he could always find something more to blurt out – the name of a street or a person, some old gossip about the activities of a neighbour. There is always another drop to coax from the crushed fruit. Even if the persistence of the interrogators produced stories and lies – for it was often the case that the man really had nothing more to tell the security forces – the process was still vindicated. The suspect was *talking*, wasn't he? And talk in all its forms – babbling, whispering, crying, pleading or cursing – is less threatening to the state than silence. Put simply, the information that came from a man experiencing such brutality was the operation's product and, like any diligent workforce, the men who stepped into this hellish place every day had standards of productivity, a yardstick by which they measured their output. The stories and lies were merely the husk of the operation, the off-cuts that would eventually be discarded after the creaking security apparatus had checked out the statement through its thousands of investigators and informers and established which parts were unlikely to be true. But even this might result in some innocent being lifted from the street and given similar treatment.

Karim Khan entered this brutal world at precisely 7.30 a.m. local time and was straight away hoisted by his arms so that his whole body was suspended four feet from the ground. The Doctor was in the cell with him but an Egyptian was in charge and gave the order for Khan's feet to be beaten by two men with long rubber truncheons. Khan cried out that he would tell them anything they wanted. They stopped and the Egyptian shouted questions at him in Arabic. Khan pleaded that he could only speak English. The men returned to beating him and soon the pain in his feet, together with that in his arms and shoulders, took hold of his mind, though he did experience a fleeting astonishment that strangers would take such care to hurt him. After several minutes they let him down to the ground with a bump so that the force of his weight shot through the injuries on his feet.

The Egyptian officer approached him and spoke in English. 'You will talk to us now.' He said it like a reprimand, as though Khan had been impossibly obstructive.

Khan nodded.

'And make full statement of your plans to make terrorist attacks.'

'I will do this.' Khan understood the pretence that he was Jasur Faisal had been dropped.

He was put on a tiny stool which required him to use his feet to balance, and the only way of doing this was to turn them in so that the outside of his soles rested on the floor. The Egyptian lit a cigarette and offered one to The Doctor, who shook his head, and then with fastidious care replaced the packet and lighter in the pocket of his jacket. With the cigarette in his mouth and one eye closed against the smoke, he put out a hand to one of the men who had been beating Khan and snapped his fingers for the truncheon. He slapped it gently into the palm of his left hand, then leaned forward and brought it down on Khan's collar-bone. Khan fell from the stool screaming and had to be lifted up and held straight by the two thugs.

'I was ... in Afghanistan,' he stammered. 'I was trained to use explosives. I was trained for political assassination and to eliminate large numbers of civilians. I know the plans. I know what they are going to do.' He threw these lines scattershot, hoping that one of them would interest them.

'We know all this. Where were you trained?'

'Khandahar ... for six months in 2000. I learned about political assassination. I know the plans to attack buildings in the West.'

'Which buildings?'

'Christian buildings, embassies and water supplies also.' This was remembered from one or two newspapers that Khan had read in Pakistan and Turkey.

'Which buildings?'

'A big church in England – London.'

'When are these attacks due to take place?'

'Soon – next month.'

'Next month? Then how were you expected to be in place? A man like you with no money walking through the mountains?'

'That was the plan, to enter Europe illegally. Then if I was caught, I would say that I was a man looking for work. That is all. They send you back to where you came from, but they don't put you in jail. They know terrorists have money and travel on planes, so they are watching the airports. But with all these men on the road they don't know who people are. It's much safer. I came with many other men. Many, many men. And I know who they are, where they went, what their plans are.'

The Eygptian turned to The Doctor, who shook his head. 'These are stories,' said the Egyptian.

Khan looked up at him. 'Ask yourself why you're questioning me. Ask yourself if I would lie about these things when I know what you can do to me.'

The officer threw the cigarette away into the gloom of the cell and returned the look. Khan noticed the whites of his eyes were muddied and that his skin, a degree or two darker than his own colour, was very thick and plump, as if blown up slightly from the inside. The Egyptian shook his head and without warning stepped behind and hit him several times. '*You* will answer my questions.'

'I am,' he cried out. 'I am trying.'

Khan now understood the game he had to play. The Egyptian must be seen to win. If he failed to make this happen The Doctor would take over, and this he had to avoid at all costs. So the Egyptian became a kind of ally. Khan had to work with him and make it look as though it was his skill that was persuading him to talk, and that there was no need of The Doctor's expertise. But this meant he would have to endure much more pain while letting the information out slowly.

He was terrified by this conclusion. He was taken up to the ceiling again and began to experience a quite new level of pain. He lost count of the times he passed out during these hours but the investment of pain seemed to be working. The gaps between the beatings grew longer and a man was summoned to write down what he said in English, which was a slow process because he had to stop and ask Khan how to spell certain words. This gave Khan time to collect his thoughts, however, and add convincing detail to the story of his training in an al-Qaeda camp. He found that the things he just made up out of desperation were the most readily accepted by the Egyptian.

Night came and the questions continued under a naked bulb. At some point in these hours, Khan's faith in humanity, more particularly his assumptions about his fellow men, slipped away. He had been changed, although his mind was in no state to hold such an idea or to know what it meant.

Herrick noticed that the prospect of the adventure in Egypt instantly took ten years off her father. His eyes shone with animation and he seemed to be moving less stiffly. Besides the essentials of the plan, he had mastered the hand-radios, the encryption phones and the topography of the district of Cairo where Khan was believed to be held. On the way to Heathrow he explained to Herrick and Christine Selvey that he'd spent two weeks in Cairo before leaving for Palestine in 1946, exploring the medieval quarter and the area around Khan al Khalili souk. He understood that little had changed.

They were booked, not into one of the modern hotels along the Nile, but the more central Devon Hotel that once acted as a kind of officers' mess for the British Army. Munroe had stayed there when the more exclusive Shepheard's had been full. He was astonished to find the same 1930s switchboard behind the front desk and the ancient lift that carried guests up to the rooms in a steel cage and stopped short of each floor by about a foot. He was even more taken by the scorched canvas which had once been a hunting scene and still hung in the dining room as a reminder of the anti-British riots that coincided with Nasser's coup in 1952. 'Of course they were right to kick us out,' he murmured. 'We had no business being here.'

'And what about now?' asked Herrick.

'That's another matter, as you well know, Isis.' He shook his head with affectionate despair. 'Anyway, we haven't time for this. We've got a rendezvous to make.'

They left Selvey at the hotel and caught a cab to the Sunset café, which was still nearly full even though it was well past midnight. They didn't know which member of the team to expect, just that someone would arrive with details of the next day.

When they had ordered tea and a hookah, Herrick said, 'You have to admit this is bloody weird, Dad.'

'I suppose it is,' he said. 'I was even less keen than you, but I believe the Chief needs our help, and you have to admit I'm an excellent cover.'

'But you're part of the operation, not just cover. That's what worries me. And what about the Chief? Even if we manage to pick up the package, this is bound to get out sooner or later.'

'I'm certain you're right. But he's not furthering his own interests. He's only trying to protect the Service from Vigo and Spelling.' He looked at her with a sudden, intense concern. 'The Chief told me what happened to you. He said it was almost certainly Vigo who'd put those two bloody Albanians on to you. You did well to fight them off. I'm impressed and immensely relieved.'

'That's what I mean. You shouldn't know about this stuff. How can I possibly be expected to work if I know you're being told about every minor danger? Anyway, they weren't after me. They were searching the place and I happened to turn up.'

'What were they looking for?'

'I don't know,' she said. It had now become almost a matter of faith that she told no one about the package from Beirut.

He smiled sceptically. 'But Vigo knew it was there.'

'Yes, that means he was listening to a phone conversation I had a few hours before with a friend. Though God knows why he would bother.'

'Come off it, Isis. You surely understand?'

'No.'

'He's jealous of your talent. You're a natural. The Chief never stops telling me how good you are. The idea that anyone could possess the sort of flair he once showed would certainly grate with him. Besides that, you're critical of his operation. He's bound to be put out.'

She shrugged and moved a little closer. 'What chance do you think we've got here?'

'Fifty-fifty. It relies on quick, accurate information and if we don't get that, we're jiggered.'

'Jiggered! Where did that word come from?' She looked at his eyes moving over the café's customers, discreetly noting who was showing an interest in them. 'Well, I suppose this is better than looking at snail shells through a magnifying glass.'

'Not a patch on it, but the change is certainly refreshing.'

They waited a further half hour gossiping about Hopelaw, and then a young man who had been browsing along a magazine stand twenty yards away came to sit at their table and ordered a pipe and coffee. He was pale and sickly looking with eyes set wide. Herrick noticed he moved awkwardly as though he had damaged his back or pelvis, and she asked him what was the matter.

'Big lorry jump on little car. Everyone dead except Mr Foyzi.'

'I'm glad you survived, Mr Foyzi,' she said.

'Yes, but treatment at hospital very, very expensive. Mr Foyzi needs money to make back straight. You want buy papyrus?' He handed Munroe Herrick a card. 'This address of best papyrus shop in all Cairo.' His arms danced in the air as he described the splendour and size of his brother's factory. 'Okay, you come. We have coffee and make party.'

'This sounds exactly what we want,' said Munroe. He handed the card to Isis. It read, 'Go with Foyzi – Harland.'

'What time should we come?'

'But of course now. There is not long distance to factory.'

They left money on the table and were ushered from the alley by Foyzi, who made a great show of leading his new and valued clients to the factory. They crossed at the intersection of two large streets then plunged into another alley. Either side of them rose elegant turn-of-the-century apartment blocks with balcony windows that jutted over their heads. They passed men labouring over tiny fires in dimly lit workshops and others loitering, picking at grilled corn cobs, smoking makeshift hookahs and offering advice from the street with the exaggerated movements of a mime troupe. No women were about and Herrick, dressed in jeans and a shirt, felt conspicuous, although Foyzi's presence seemed to reassure the men and they gave her barely a second glance. For fifteen minutes they dodged back and forth, moving through the dark maze of alleys until eventually they came to a courtyard where a man with welding equipment squatted by a car door. The sparks flew into the dark, illuminating three trees and washing lines that swayed in the warm breeze.

Foyzi stopped and beckoned them to the side of the courtyard. 'No speaks now,' he whispered, putting both hands to his lips, then turned to watch the entrance of the courtyard. A minute or two later the welder lifted his visor and snapped off the flame. The courtyard became utterly dark and silent. Foyzi guided them to an entrance, knocked on the door and spoke through a grille. Locks were turned heavily and bolts drawn back. Inside there were some candles in red glass pots and a figure wrapped in white cloth and a headdress who immediately slipped away into a recess. Without explanation, Foyzi hurried them along a corridor heavily scented with flowers and the smell of candle wax, then they burst into a brightly lit room with chandeliers and show cases full of bottles.

'Where the hell are we?' asked Herrick.

'A perfume factory, I think,' replied her father.

'Gentleman is correct, but we not stay here,' said Foyzi officiously. 'You buy lotus oil some other time, missus. We see your friends now in next store.'

A communicating door was opened and they were propelled into another cavernous space hung with carpets and huge brass lanterns. Foyzi took their arms and navigated them through the piles of rugs on the floor. When they reached a better-lit part of the shop, Herrick checked her father's face. He showed no signs of strain whatsoever.

'Isis, I will say this once,' he murmured as they approached a room where they heard voices. 'Do not fuss over me. I am perfectly all right.'

Inside, she saw Harland, Colonel B and, to her surprise, Colin Guthrie, who explained that it had been decided in London at the last moment that he would oversee the operation. Harland greeted them both with an enigmatic grin and said that Loz was already under guard at the place where they would take Khan. Foyzi sat down at one of the chairs and tipped a little liquid from a flask into a cup of coffee.

Guthrie unrolled a map on the table. 'Over the past twenty-four hours we have been observing the route taken from the police headquarters to the jail on the southern margins of the city. Without exception the trucks and cars making this journey have travelled along the streets marked in red. We have no reason to believe they will vary the routine for Khan. At the moment our sources say that the security people are exhausting their methods and are likely to hand over to The Doctor sometime tomorrow. That leaves us with very little time, yet also too much of it. While we have to be ready to go tomorrow we must also remember that it will be a considerable challenge to mount any kind of watch in an area which is at all times crawling with police and security personnel.'

Guthrie laid four A4 photographs on the table and joined them together to create a continuous picture of the street named Bur Said. He pointed to a three-storey stone Italianate building and a much larger and more modern office block, painted white and turquoise. 'The older building holds the courts. This is joined on the right to the police headquarters. At the back is the jail complex where Khan is being held. The truck carrying him will leave an entrance at the rear and take the crowded side-street to Bur Said. Beginning at this junction there is a run of shops, restaurants and cafés where The Doctor – Ibrahim al Shuqairi – has been observed talking to a CIA man whom Bobby Harland has identified in surveillance photographs as Lance Gibbons. He has been seen there four times in the last thirty-six hours and it is believed that he has been unofficially briefing the American on the progress of the interrogation. On the last occasion, earlier this evening, the couple appeared to have a falling out. We think Gibbons has failed to recommend that the responsibility for the interrogation should be given to The Doctor. Information from the police HQ, produced by Mr Foyzi this afternoon, would seem to confirm this. We know also that communications traffic from the US Embassy has featured the interrogation and its results. Unsurprisingly, Khan has admitted to being involved in a plot to blow up a number of churches and other prominent targets, but he has given them no definite date for an attack. Perhaps he senses that this is the one thing he still has to play with.'

Guthrie looked up from the pictures and moved a lamp to shine on them. 'This run of cafés is where you will be stationed, Isis. Your job will be to observe Gibbons and try to overhear what he says. We will have other people in the café, but you will be the person to signal the operation is on. Foyzi will be with you. The important point of course is that Gibbons and The Doctor both know you, which means you have to go well-disguised.'

Herrick nodded agreement that this would not present the slightest problem.

Guthrie turned to Munroe. 'The first part of your day will be spent in the newly restored Islamic Museum directly opposite the courts. This should not be arduous. The museum is air-conditioned and I believe possesses an unequalled collection of manuscripts and ornamental art. You will remain there with Selvey until such time as you receive a message. Then you will make your way out and look for a blue and white Peugeot with the words Zamalek Limousine printed on its side. You will be driven to this point here in the Northern Cemetery, about ten to fifteen minutes away, depending on the traffic. You will see that there are a number of right-angle bends there which require the truck to slow down to about ten miles an hour. It is here that the interception will take place. You will remain in the car until you hear from Philip Sarre and Gregor Laughland who will be positioned close by in the cemetery. One of them will radio you when they have visual contact. At this point, you will both get out and prepare to create the diversion we've already discussed. Once the wagon has stopped you will move as quickly as you can to the Peugeot and make your escape. It is likely to be hot so you will need to reserve all your energy for that walk, Munroe.'

Guthrie sat down. There was silence in the room for several seconds. This was the signal for Colonel B to speak.

'What you all need to know about the end of the operation is minimal,' he said. 'We will be in the area of the cemetery, but you won't see us before the truck arrives. We've spent most of the day recceing the area and in many respects have found it the perfect spot. There is very little traffic and the road there is poorly made. Our main object of course is to release Khan without loss of life, but there will be one or two bangs that will attract attention, so we'll be aiming to move out of the area with Khan very quickly.' He placed a packet of earplugs on the table and shoved them towards Munroe. 'These are for you and your colleague, sir. Once you've got the signal, be sure to ram them right in.'

'And me?' said Herrick. 'How do I hook up with you? Where's Harland going to be?'

'Harland is going to be with us, so we will need the medical kit you brought out from England.'

'Right, I can get that to you. But after the truck has passed what do I do? Follow it?'

'Exactly. We want you to watch for an escort. Generally these trucks travel alone, but given the interest in Khan there may well be a couple of cars following with some armed police. They shouldn't present too much of a problem, but we'll need a description of the vehicles and the number of men inside.'

'There's one thing I don't understand,' said Harland. 'Why does Isis have to hang around the café and then pursue the truck? Wouldn't it be a lot simpler to put Sarre or Laughland there to do the initial watch and have Isis tucked away in the cemetery ready to leave with me and Khan?'

Guthrie shook his head. 'No. For one thing Isis will be far less conspicuous. Two, she can dress in the traditional manner for an Egyptian woman and be to all intents and purposes unapproachable. Three, she has a rather special talent which I was reminded of only the other day by one of our colleagues in the Company.'

Munroe nodded and smiled. Harland looked mystified.

'She can lip-read English, and as long as she gets a good line of sight on Gibbons, we shouldn't have any problem finding out what's going on.'

'That's excellent,' said Foyzi in the perfect intonation of a middle-class Englishman.

Herrick and her father turned round to see him lying on a pile of rugs with his tea precariously balanced on his chest.

'Mr Foyzi is not what he appears to be,' said Guthrie. 'In fact Mr Foyzi is not even Egyptian.'

Foyzi gave him a demure nod.

'So between Isis and Foyzi we should be in business. Now communications. The first call will be made by Isis on her mobile phone. That will go to me in the control van, positioned halfway between the police HQ and the cemetery. Thereafter we should use the radios, earpieces and clip-on mikes which you all have. But chatter should be kept to a minimum. Specific details of the truck and any escort should be phoned to me and I'll pass them on in suitably obscure terms. Right, Foyzi will take you two back to the Devon and Harland can collect the medical bag. We should aim to be in place by 10.00 a.m. and let's hope we get a hint of movement sooner rather than later.' He gathered up the photos and map and stood up.

Later at the hotel Herrick told her father, 'This is just about the daftest plan I've heard. Practically everything can go wrong.'

'Well, there's an awful lot of room for manoeuvre. And that's no bad thing.'

'That doesn't make me feel any better.'

20

Khan knew neither night nor day. He was fed once with a plate of slop and given water, which the guards snatched away after he had drunk only a little. And he did not sleep. When the Egyptian and The Doctor were out of the cell he was let down to a sitting position on the floor with his arms still held above him by the rope. Except for an intermittent prickling sensation caused by the lack of circulation, he had lost the feeling in his hands. When he nodded off, or simply fainted during moments when the pain became extreme, the guards kicked him or banged the door with a truncheon.

Time had ceased to exist. Thoughts came in snatches of telegraphese. He knew he could not manipulate the situation to save himself from The Doctor because he had already begun to tell him what drugs he would use. He said they would paralyse him for hours, turn him mad, set rats loose in his mind, make his skin burn, cause his eyes to flinch at the light of a candle and give his body such discomfort he would neither be able to rest nor sleep.

Khan thought, I did this . . . I brought myself here . . . a journey of my devising . . . God have pity on me . . . The Prophet (peace be upon him) please stop these men . . . Stop these men, please . . . this is not your way . . . I beg you, stop these men . . . I am . . . I am hurting . . . I don't know myself . . . Let me die.

Prayers and self-recrimination circulated in his head for hours, or just seconds, he could not be certain. He had the strange idea that his mind was somehow becoming detached from his body, yet he knew this was not true because he had never been more aware of his physical self. They had locked his mind in a cage with a beast and the beast was his pain. Why? He had no answer to that question. The question no longer existed because there could not be an answer.

Perhaps he should have told the truth instead of all these fabrications about terrorist training and targets. But he *had* told them the truth. That's what he had done when he had first seen The Doctor, and it hadn't worked because the man had begun to hurt him.

It was cooler now and he guessed it was night. One of the two guards had propped himself against the door and hung his head in sleep. Khan's mind rambled and he thought of the now unbearable sweetness of his early life. Was it really his, or had he imagined it?

Then the cell door opened, sending the sleeping guard into the centre of the cell. When he recovered himself he struck Khan twice with his truncheon as though punishing him for a violation that had just taken place. In the light from the corridor, Khan glimpsed the guard's guilty, moronic face turn obsequiously to the Egyptian and The Doctor as they walked in. Then he caught sight of the trolley being wheeled behind them.

It was about the size of a cocktail trolley, although like everything in the prison it had been knocked together from scrap – an artless contraption with wires coiled on the top, a box and a wooden board on which there was a switch and a lever. One of the guards unravelled the flex and ran it to a power point outside the cell. The other uncoiled the wires lying on top. At the end of these were a couple of metal crocodile clamps such as might be used to charge a car battery.

The Doctor picked his teeth while the Egyptian bent down and dipped a rag in a pail of water, then handed it to the guard so it could be wrung out.

Herrick slipped out of the hotel early and went with Foyzi to buy a hijab, the head scarf that covers the hair, ears, shoulders and part of the face. Foyzi, himself wearing a long white jellaba and a red and white cloth on his head, assured her that once she was wearing a hijab, no one would look at her, particularly if they were together. She bought a black one with a severe cut.

Already the air was thick with pollution and the roads were teeming with every form of motor vehicle, hand-cart and wagon. They reached Bur Said by 9.00 a.m. and took a turn round the traffic system, cruising past the court and police buildings, then the museum where Munroe Herrick and Christine Selvey were to be kept on ice amongst the collections of incense burners and weaponry. They parked a little distance from the café near the police headquarters and waited for Gibbons to show. On the previous day one of Foyzi's men had observed him arrive at 10.30 a.m., but an hour and a half passed without sign of him. Guthrie called Herrick twice on the mobile to tell her to get out of the heat and into the café so she'd be sure to have a place by the time either of them arrived. She insisted that she must wait until she knew which table they were at.

The day dragged on, and although the density and noise of the traffic did not subside, there were fewer people walking on the streets. The women who had improvised a vegetable market on the other side of the road suddenly packed up and vanished in swirls of brightly patterned cloth. The men who had been listlessly hoeing and watering a narrow

845

flower border separating the two streams of traffic had sunk to their haunches in the shade of a tree to watch three hooded crows fight over the seepage from their hose.

Just past midday a hot wind blew up, whipping eddies of dust along the road and tearing at the flags outside the court. The crows took to the wing and flapped in the air above the traffic. Herrick and Foyzi slipped down in their seats and took sips from a bottle of mineral water. They moved the car several times to keep in the shade and at two o'clock saw a convoy of three police trucks making its way up the side street. The back of each vehicle was open, and as they swung into Bur Said, Herrick saw past the guards to the tiny steel cubicles which held the prisoners.

'They must roast in those things,' she said.

Foyzi nodded sadly then straightened in his seat. 'Here's the American. Look! Look! In the mirror!'

Herrick glanced in the right wing mirror and saw Gibbons stepping out of a taxi. She pulled down the sunshade to check the hijab and the Jackie O dark glasses and then plugged in her telephone earpiece and the microphone that ran up her right sleeve. He passed quite close to them and made straight for the café. After some indecision, he settled at an outside table in the breeze. They watched him while he ordered, then got out and walked together, rowing in Arabic about Foyzi's driving, and sat down just inside the door where there was both shade and a breeze. Foyzi had his back to Gibbons which meant that she could observe quite easily over his shoulder while talking. They ordered tea. Twenty minutes passed during which Gibbons made two short calls on his cell phone, allowing Herrick to test her skill on him. He was speaking to The Doctor, asking where the fuck he was. A few moments later she saw The Doctor lumbering up the side street in a pale green robe. He was with another Arab, a much smaller man who wore a jacket over his shoulders that flapped in the wind and revealed a pale blue lining. This man had a rather fussy manner and brushed the chair before sitting down with his back to Foyzi and Herrick, then plucked at the crease in his trousers. The Doctor let himself down heavily in profile to them and produced a bag of sunflower seeds which he proceeded to eat.

Once they'd given their orders, Gibbons leaned forward and began to speak. Herrick dialled Guthrie, raised her right hand to her face and murmured into her sleeve, looking away slightly but never letting her eyes move from Gibbons' lips. She gave Guthrie a verbatim account, only sometimes pausing to say which of the men he was addressing. 'What have you got for me?' Gibbons asked the Egyptian. He replied at great length. Gibbons examined him closely. 'Do you have definite dates? What about names? Did you get the names of his contacts?'

The man shook his head and The Doctor interrupted, slicing the air with his hand.

Gibbons ignored him. 'You say this was going to happen in Paris and London simultaneously. What about the States? Did you get anything about the postcards?' He nodded as the Egyptian replied. Again The Doctor interrupted, but Gibbons' eyes remained fixed on the other man. 'So he admits they were coded messages? Right, what about the Empire State? Is he saying the attacks will be coordinated in the States as well as Europe?' As they both attempted to answer, Gibbons began shaking his head. 'You guys gotta realise that's what we're all here for. We need to know. Right now, all I'm hearing is maybe this, maybe that, maybe now, maybe later. We have a ticking bomb here. My people need accurate information.' He stubbed his index finger on the surface of the table then slumped back in his chair and looked away in frustration. The Doctor also turned his gaze elsewhere, leaving the ball in the other man's court.

He made a long speech that seemed not to impress Gibbons, who ordered another drink and then dialled a number on his phone.

'No information ... no real details of the plan ... right ... okay ... sure ... I'll tell him ... that's right ... yeah, yeah. Leave it to me.' He lowered the phone and spoke to the Egyptian. 'Okay, so my people think we should pursue the second option. I'm sorry Mr Abdullah, but that's what they say. It's out of my hands. You got to see I'm in a bind here. We're very grateful for what you have already done and the US Embassy will make a formal recognition of your service to us with a letter of thanks. Here is something to be going on with. A kind of personal thanks.' He reached for the top pocket of the man's jacket and stuffed a roll of money into it.

Herrick now gave the first piece of commentary. 'He's paying off the Egyptian security officer. The interrogation is going to be handed over to The Doctor.'

'Tell Foyzi to activate his sources and find out when Khan's going to be transferred,' rasped Guthrie. 'We want to know which bloody vehicle he's in.'

Foyzi didn't need telling and gave Herrick a nod to say he understood.

Gibbons looked at his watch and said something she couldn't read, because he had raised a glass to his lips and held it there for some time without drinking. The Doctor felt in his robes for something and pulled out a set of black worry beads which he handled like a rosary, then repeatedly flipped over his index finger.

Gibbons lowered the glass and said, 'We need something tonight or tomorrow. The work has got to be finished by Monday.'

All this she communicated to Guthrie. Occasionally she heard him speaking on other lines to her father and Colonel B.

She hung up and started to speak to Foyzi in Arabic. Had he checked the car? Didn't he think he ought to be leaving? Foyzi allowed himself to smile at Herrick's portrayal of a nagging wife and made as though to grumble. He paid and left the café saying that he would see her in twenty minutes.

Herrick planned to return to the car the moment The Doctor left. From behind the sunglasses she looked ahead of her without acknowledging their presence or bothering to see what they were saying. Gibbons lit a cigarette and threw occasional interested glances in her direction, but she was certain he wouldn't recognise her and sat with what she hoped was the unapproachable poise of a young middle-class Arab woman.

After a desultory exchange The Doctor got up. Gibbons did not rise or offer a hand. Herrick thought she saw a fleeting look of distaste sweep across his expression. 'We'll speak soon.'

Herrick decided to leave, but just as she stood up, her phone began to vibrate. The momentary distraction meant that she did not pay attention to the wind, as the Arab women on the street do, and a gust took hold of the hijab, revealing her hair, neck and some of her face. She pulled it down swiftly and made for the car. As she opened the door she saw Gibbons rise, sling some money onto the table and start purposefully towards her. In a matter of seconds he had reached the car and shouted through the window. 'I'll be damned if that isn't Isis Herrick.' He bent down to her level. 'Shit! That *is* you, isn't it?'

She looked ahead of her without moving, realising that she couldn't just sit there – one call from Gibbons and the whole operation would be blown. She got out, pushed him away and shouted in Arabic to the passers-by that the American was bothering her.

'Well, what do you know,' he said, leering down at her. 'The cold-assed British spook has followed me all the way to Cairo for a little loving.' He felt in one of the pockets of his photographer's vest and pulled out a phone. She knocked it from his hands and spun round, cursing him in Arabic. The filthy American was making indecent suggestions – wouldn't someone help a virtuous woman?

Gibbons seemed to find this funny. 'Oh, you're good,' he said, unhurriedly bending down to retrieve his phone. 'You're very good, Isis. But I just gotta tell my people you've gatecrashed the donkey roast.' He stood up and placed a hand on her shoulder, dialling a number with the thumb of his other hand. Suddenly Foyzi appeared from nowhere and pulled Herrick away from him.

'Who's this? Omar Sharif?'

Foyzi smiled up at him. 'I have gun aimed at your heart, sir. Get into the car.'

'Yeah, and I'm King Farouk,' said Gibbons. 'Step aside, buster. This lady and I have business.'

Foyzi manoeuvred so he could show Gibbons the gun without displaying it to the rest of the street. 'I *will* kill you unless you get in the car, sir.'

'Okay,' said Gibbons, trying to maintain his dignity. 'So you're going to kidnap an American citizen. You can't get away with this, Isis – you and your little towel-head friend.'

'Such company we have to keep,' said Foyzi despairingly. He opened the back door and prodded Gibbons. 'Get in.'

Gibbons obeyed, but with a thunderous look that said he would soon have the upper hand. 'I'll see you on the fucking rack for this.'

She climbed behind the wheel. 'What now?'

'No problem,' said Foyzi, pointing ahead of them. 'No problem at all. Drive!'

She edged the Fiat into the traffic.

'Oh, I get it. You're going to try to spring Khan!' said Gibbons, laughing. 'Jesus, I'm gonna be ringside on fucking amateur night.'

'Last thing I heard, you said he was Faisal, not Khan,' said Isis over her shoulder.

'Right,' said Gibbons sourly.

They passed the police HQ and courts, then turned left to travel in the opposite direction. Foyzi wrested Gibbons' phone from him and crushed it underfoot on the floor of the car. Then he called someone on his own phone and spoke rapidly.

Gibbons talked over him, affecting not to mind the silencer lodged in his armpit. 'You understand what you're doing, Isis? You're interfering with the legitimate investigation of a terrorist suspect by the United States. If an attack should result from your actions you and your friend will be named as accessories. They'll come after you, wherever the fuck you are.'

'I understand just one thing about your activities,' she said calmly. 'You've instigated the torture of a man who hasn't been found guilty of a crime and—'

'That's the trouble with you fucking Europeans,' interrupted Gibbons. 'You want all the benefits of American power but you don't want to get your hands dirty.' He paused. 'Let me tell you, this is the big new game, and it's played with a whole new set of rules. Frankly, you don't cut it. You don't even come near. '

'There's nothing new about your *big new game*,' she said. 'You told me that yourself. You were right. Torture was used by the regimes in South America, all of them endorsed by the US government. Torture is actually a very old, very desperate game and it doesn't work. You don't get results by tearing a person's body apart.'

This gave Gibbons some pause. 'We're against the clock. There's no other way now.'

'There is,' said Isis. 'There always is.'

They were alongside the museum and Foyzi told her to drive two hundred yards further and take the first turning right. She negotiated a hand-cart loaded with crates of vegetables and swerved right into a shaded street where huge pieces of awning and cloth hung vertically from wires overhead. Foyzi was on the phone. They turned right again into a yard where there was a white Nissan van. Four men in jellabas rushed towards them. One opened the door on Gibbons' side and rammed a needle into his arm. Almost immediately the American's eyes closed and his body went slack. He was dragged from the car, carried off to the van and lifted into the back. Two of the men jumped in with him and the van moved off in a cloud of dust. Foyzi got out, ran round to take the wheel from Herrick and reversed out of the yard at a furious speed, span 180 degrees and rushed to rejoin Bur Said.

'Who were they?' shouted Herrick, thinking it was certainly fitting that Gibbons had now himself been drugged and driven off unconscious.

'My backup, my people,' he said.

'Who're your people?'

'Another time,' he replied, straining left and right to look for an opening in the traffic. 'The transport is about to leave the police building. We must get into position.'

'What will they do with Gibbons?'

'Take him somewhere and dump him. He'll be fine, but he won't remember who he is or where he is for a day or two.'

They found a way through the jam that brought them near to the café, and stopped alongside a line of minibuses disgorging passengers and admitting others with equal numbers of cumbersome packages. For a few minutes they waited in the sweltering heat. Foyzi's eyes darted between the screen of his mobile and the throng of people around the car. Then the phone beeped twice with a text message.

'It's coming,' he said. 'He's on the next truck.'

He nosed forward through the crowd and within a very short time they saw the truck moving out of the side street. It was accompanied by a car that had edged round the truck and was forging through the traffic with occasional blasts on its siren. Herrick relayed all this information to Guthrie. There were four policemen in the car, and two guards carrying automatics could be seen through the open back of the truck. She caught sight of The Doctor in the passenger seat of the truck. Khan had to be inside. Guthrie told her to use the radio from now on so that everyone could hear.

Foyzi worked the little Fiat into position, about three vehicles behind the truck, which was moving at about 15 mph. There was much competition among the other cars around them to fall into the truck's slipstream, but Foyzi held their place effortlessly.

They reached the Kahn al Khalili souk where the traffic became less responsive to the police siren, and they stopped for minutes at a time. Herrick used the fan fixed to the Fiat's dashboard to cool her face and glanced idly down the warren of passages into the souk. A further ten minutes passed. Then the traffic seemed suddenly to ease and the truck moved away at a speed of 40 mph. Foyzi dodged to keep in touch, but was forced to stop at some traffic lights where they knew the first lookout man was positioned. They heard his terse commentary over the radio and then shot off in pursuit of the truck, which to their relief followed the predicted route, turning left on a road called Salah Salem and then right into the cemetery. Herrick called out, 'Three minutes to landing. Repeat. ETA – three minutes.'

Harland had moved very little in the heat, but when he heard Herrick's voice he got out of the Isuzu and lifted his binoculars to the cemetery road. From his vantage point 150 yards away, he had seen the blue and white Peugeot stop some ten minutes before and Munroe Herrick leave the car with Selvey. Despite Munroe's reputation, Harland was extremely doubtful about allowing a man in his eighties to take part in the operation. However, he observed him now, moving without the slightest sign of age or heat fatigue. He was dressed in a light summer jacket and a broad-brimmed straw hat. Selvey was in a long floral skirt and a hat tied with a scarf under her chin. Together they looked as though they were about to attend the Chelsea Flower Show or a vicarage garden party.

Harland saw Munroe set up an easel in the shade of one of the monuments that bordered the road. Very soon he was sitting on a collapsible fishing stool, sketching the view that Harland had been staring at these past few hours – the parched sandstone necropolis and, beyond it, Cairo and the flood plain of the Nile in a dusty blue haze. It was a pity he'd never finish the picture.

In almost every respect the place was perfect for an ambush. The traffic was very light indeed. Just four cars had passed in the previous five minutes. The walls either side of the road were never less than ten feet high, so no one would be able to see what was going on when the police convoy was intercepted. And there would be very little danger from stray bullets. There were many open doorways into the cemetery either side of the road and the numerous smaller byways which criss-crossed the area. At two different points these held the vehicles that the snatch squad would use in their escape.

For a moment Harland's attention was caught by three or four black kites wheeling in the sky high above the cemetery. His concentration snapped back to earth and he moved the binoculars down the incline to settle on a group of barefoot children playing in the stretch about 200 yards from Munroe. He hoped they wouldn't get wind of the old man. If they were drawn to him for baksheesh it would badly complicate things. He swept the cemetery on the far side of the road, pausing to examine the figures moving between the memorials. One or two people were sleeping in the shade of the more elaborate tombs. He wasn't sure which of these belonged to Colonel B's squad of SAS veterans, but he knew they were there because of the radio checks every ten minutes.

He saw the police vehicles leave the main road and begin the steady climb towards Munroe. The car in front moved a little too quickly for the truck and twice had to slow down to wait.

Harland got back behind the wheel, started the engine and, leaving it in neutral, let the handbrake off so that the Isuzu began to creep down the narrow stony track to the cemetery road. If all went well, he would arrive behind the police truck, ready to receive Khan, Herrick and Foyzi. But the timing had to be just right.

The radio sprang to life. 'Final positions, please. Runway clear.' Then Sarre's voice could be heard counting away the distance – 'Five hundred yards and closing. Four hundred. Three-fifty.' When he reached two hundred, Munroe got up, felt in his pocket and handed something to Selvey. They were replacing their radio earpieces with earplugs.

Not far from them, a bundle of rags moved slightly – a beggar dozing in the dappled shade of a eucalyptus tree shifting something hidden in the sackcloth. Across the road a cart loaded with sugar cane seemed to move of its own accord. Harland could just make out two pairs of boots beneath it.

The police car showed round the first part of the Z bend and climbed the rutted stretch towards Munroe. Then came the truck, heeling as it took the potholes. Some way off, the little Fiat driven by Foyzi tore through the dust kicked up by the two bigger vehicles.

As Harland inched forward, his view of the road remained unimpaired. The whole plan began to unfold in front of him. Munroe was the first to move. He got up from his seat and managed to dislodge his hat, which rolled off across the road. This seemed to cause the old man some distress and he went in pursuit of it, holding his back and moving with great difficulty. He added further to the impression of frailty by waving a stick in the air and knocking over his easel. At this moment the police vehicle came round the bend and, without slowing down, drove between him and the hat. Munroe seemed to become disorientated in the cloud of dust, fell forwards and rolled onto his side. Harland prayed the driver of the truck would see him. He did brake, but only just in time, at which point several things happened. Smoke grenades went off in the road behind and in front of the two vehicles. The load of sugar cane erupted and three men wearing gas masks jumped into the road, shooting out the police car's tyres and radiator. The vehicle juddered to a halt with its blue light still flashing in vain. At this, another man sprang from an opening in the wall and propelled a small canister of knockout gas through the window. None of the four men had any time to react.

A second or two before, Munroe rolled over in the road and aimed a machine pistol with one hand at the truck's front tyres and engine. He was joined by Selvey, who raised her sidearm in a textbook two-handed aim. The rear tyres were cut to ribbons by two other men who had leapt from behind a wall, and for good measure they threw a stun-grenade in the general direction of the truck. The driver had been on the point of jumping down when it exploded and he fell to earth like a dead bird.

Harland plunged through the narrow opening, scraping the underside of his vehicle on a boulder, and landed in the road just behind the truck. He saw the Fiat parked with both its front doors open and Isis Herrick running up the road into the smoke. This was the very last thing she should have been doing because three policemen, who had been protected from the worst effects of the stun-grenade, had spilled from the open door at the back of the truck with their rifles. Harland had no choice but to steer the Isuzu into one and then slammed a second by opening his door while the vehicle was still moving. The third man had scuttled round the truck and was taking aim. Harland got out and sprinted to tackle him. The gun went off at the moment he collided with his upper thighs and sent him into the dirt. Harland was aware that his back wouldn't take the jolt but pushed the thought to the back of his mind. While Colonel B's men disarmed the three policemen, Harland picked himself up painfully and went to the front to find Isis bent over her father. He appeared to have sprained his right wrist but that was all. The Peugeot getaway car had already been summoned, and before long Munroe and Selvey were being rushed towards it through the smoke. Isis stood looking utterly stricken, but then her father bent down to pick up his hat and waved a cheery goodbye over his shoulder.

It was a bizarre sight, and no one was more astonished than The Doctor, who remained in the passenger seat of the truck as if he had suffered a seizure. Foyzi opened the door and pulled him down into the road at gunpoint uttering many imprecations under his breath, then took him by the scruff of the neck and marched him to the rear of the truck. Harland and Herrick followed.

They went through all the cells. Two men were released but neither bore the slightest resemblance to Khan and were told to make a run for it while they could.

'Maybe they've got him on another truck,' suggested Colonel B, wiping his face. 'Inform this cunt that you will shoot him if he doesn't tell us where Karim Khan is.'

Foyzi placed the silencer of his pistol against The Doctor's temple. After a moment of deliberation, The Doctor lifted his head and pointed inside the truck.

'There's a compartment in the floor,' shouted Isis. 'Look, there are two hinges.'

They wrenched the door up with crowbars. Beneath the steel plate

Khan was lying bound, gagged and blindfolded in a space not much larger than a coffin. His feet were a blackened mess and his groin was stained with blood and urine. The rest of his clothes were sodden. They lifted him from this hold with infinite care and moved him to the light. Herrick took off the blindfold and gag and told him he was in safe hands, but he seemed not to understand and moved his head rhythmically from side to side like a blind singer.

'For the love of God . . .' said one of Colonel B's men.

'No,' said Harland, remembering with an almost physical pain his own time at the hands of a torturer. He shook his head and turned to The Doctor ready to kill him.

The Colonel put up his arm. 'We'd better be about our business,' he said. 'Get Khan into Harland's vehicle and give him a shot of morphine.'

'What about this man?' Harland asked, pointing to The Doctor. 'He knows Isis. We can't leave him here.'

The Colonel nodded. 'I rather thought we'd take him with us.'

'And?' said Harland.

'Well, obviously we can't take him all the way home to Syria or Iraq, or wherever the devil he comes from, but we can certainly give him a ride to, say, the middle of the Sinai desert.'

Harland, Isis and Foyzi got in with Khan and made their way through the remainder of the smoke. Colonel B's men melted into the cemetery, two of them running The Doctor towards a container lorry waiting with its engine ticking over a little way off.

The radio came to life again. It was Guthrie. 'I'm sure you'll want to join me in thanking the Captain for a perfect landing. Local time is 4.25 p.m. The temperature is ninety-two degrees. Welcome to Cairo. Please remain seated until the aircraft has stopped moving.'

21

The island where they took Khan lay some two hundred miles south of Cairo, below a great bend in the Nile. Thirteen hours after leaving the cemetery they made a rendezvous with a boat named Lotus, hidden at the edge of a sugar plantation. Khan's stretcher was loaded across the bow and secured with ropes. The boatman pushed off into the current and, using only a long oar at the stern, steered them downstream towards the island. There was no man-made light to be seen for miles around and the moonless night had an infinite clarity. When the boat found a breeze in the centre of the river, Herrick peered down at Khan to see if he was cold. She watched his eyes open and then his entire face spread and relax. A curtain was being drawn back.

The Lotus glided silently towards a cleft on the island and the boatmen punted the last few yards to the bank with the oar. The shapes of several men appeared and moved down to the river's edge to catch the boat and lead it into a berth of ancient wooden piles. One man waded through the water holding up a white robe. It was Sammi Loz. He bent down, touched Khan's shoulder and said something. There was no response.

'How bad is he?' he asked Harland.

'Not good.'

The stretcher was borne up the bank by four men to a group of single-storey buildings arranged loosely around a courtyard and hidden from the river by a screen of vegetation. At the corner of the courtyard, light came from an open door, revealing a room with a faded mural of flowers and exotic birds, a low wooden bed, some chairs and a couple of oil lamps. They lifted Khan from the stretcher and laid him on the bed. He stirred and seemed to recognise Loz, then Herrick, but he plainly doubted what he was seeing and tried to reach out to touch Loz's face.

Loz told him to stay still, lifting Khan's head to give him some water and a sleeping pill. When Khan's eyes closed a few minutes later, Loz set about removing the rags from his friend's emaciated body with a pair of surgical scissors he'd found in the medical bag. He took each strip of cloth and dropped it neatly into a pile. Then he asked Foyzi to run a light over Khan very slowly so he could see the extent of his injuries. He stopped to look at the burns on his genitals where the electrodes had been applied. He sponged away the grime and blood and dabbed the livid red and black weals with anti-bacterial ointment. With Herrick's help he rolled Khan onto his side so that he could treat similar injuries on his back, buttocks and the inside of his thighs. Then he cleaned and dressed the chafe marks on his hands and ankles.

Khan's feet presented a greater problem. They were so swollen and bruised that it was hard to distinguish the toes from the rest of the foot. Loz suspected there might be one or two broken bones but said he wouldn't be able to tell until Khan had had an X-ray. There was little he could do, apart from giving him painkillers and arnica to help the bruising. He said that many weeks of physiotherapy lay ahead.

Throughout the hour he spent tending his friend, Loz paid as much attention to the general trauma as to the particular injuries, judging the position of his spine and shoulder blades now that he was in repose. He touched the back of his head, neck and pelvis lightly, gazing up to the flickering light on the ceiling to concentrate better on the distortions and misalignments that his fingers found. Occasionally he shook his head but said nothing. At length he asked Foyzi for a pen and paper, and made some notes on his lap.

Harland signalled to Herrick that he was going outside. She followed. They had agreed during the journey that one of them should always be with Khan and Loz to hear anything that passed between them, but Khan was obviously going to be out for some time and Foyzi was keeping a close eye on both of them.

They sat down on an open terrace a little distance away. For several minutes Harland stared down at the insects that had gathered round a light, then shook himself from his reverie and looked at her vacantly. 'Yes,' he said slowly. 'What we need is a drink and a smoke. I've got some whisky in my bag. Have you got any cigarettes?'

She shook her head.

'Damn.'

Foyzi came through the door and tossed him a packet of Camel Light. 'Compliments of the establishment,' he said, turning back to Loz.

'Who the hell is Foyzi?' asked Herrick quietly.

'He's in your business, actually – a freelance, as fly as you get. But he's reliable and loyal.'

'And all this?'

'He must have done a deal with the local Islamist nutters for the island. This area is crawling with them. They hide out in mountain caves either side of the Nile.'

'Where's he from?'

'He's Jordanian, based in Turkey. He had something to do with the Iraqi opposition but now works all over the Middle East. I came across him about a year ago when the UN needed a line to Hamas. Foyzi fixed a meeting in Lebanon.'

'And you trust him?'

'Yes, so does the Chief.'

They drank for a further fifteen minutes, then Harland looked at his watch and said they should call Teckman. He set up the satellite phone in a clear patch of ground nearby and plugged it into a laptop equipped with powerful encryption software. He dialled three times before getting through to one of the duty officers at Vauxhall Cross. There was a further delay while the office patched through the unscrambled call to the Chief. Harland passed the handset to Herrick. 'You're the secret servant round here,' he said. 'I'm just the help.'

The Chief came on. 'Your father is going to be fine – a suspected fracture in his wrist, that's all. They'll be back with us by midday today. What about our friends?'

'He's sedated, and the osteopath is doing a good job, as far as one can tell.'

'Well, we'll send reinforcements to you later. Two of your colleagues are nearby.' He paused. 'You've all done very well, but now comes the hard part. I need you to get as much as you can, as soon as possible. I know the fellow is in a bad way but you should make a start tomorrow. You can use the computer to send your reports. I'd prefer you do that than spend any time speaking on the phone. If you log on now, Harland will find a message.'

Harland was signalling that he wanted to talk to Teckman, but before she could tell the Chief, he had gone.

'What the bloody hell's he playing at?'

Herrick told him about the message. For the next ten minutes Harland struggled with the decryption program. Eventually she took over and retrieved the email.

'Good news, I hope?' she said.

He shook his head.

'Well?'

'It's nothing important.'

'Anything that comes through that computer is important. I need to know what it says.'

Harland lit another cigarette. 'This is personal. A deal which I don't propose to discuss with you.'

'If it has a bearing on this situation, I insist you do,' she snapped.

'It doesn't, except that I may have to leave the island over the next day and a half. This is your business now. I don't work for HMG. I've got another job to go to. And I *do* have to go – the Secretary-General is leaving for Syria and Jordan tomorrow. I must find a way of joining him.'

He paused and looked at her. 'You've got Foyzi. You won't have any problems.'

'Oh yeah, stuck on some bloody island in the middle of the Nile with a known Afghan veteran and a man who has direct links with Hizbollah. That's to say nothing of the minor interest the Egyptian government and the Americans have in finding Khan and apprehending those who freed him. And when you throw in the Islamic jihad skulking in the mountains, the whole thing is a mere picnic. You bloody well can't leave me here. I need you. Tell me why you're really going. It's not your job.'

Harland shook his head. 'Look, you knew I had a deal with the Chief. In return for helping to get Sammi Loz out of Albania and bringing him here, the Chief said he would find a friend of mine. And he has now given me the information. This is something I have to do.'

'Well, which is it? This friend or the job?'

'Both.'

She sighed heavily and swallowed the remainder of her whisky. 'I need sleep. I can't think about this any longer.'

They got up and went to Khan's room. Loz was sitting on a three-legged stool watching him sleep. He looked up.

'Thank you for rescuing my friend,' he said. 'You have undoubtedly saved his life.'

'We weren't doing it as a favour for you,' said Herrick.

'I know,' he replied, 'but you risked much. I am grateful to you both and so will Karim be when he's able to speak.'

'Which will be tomorrow. We need to talk to him as soon as he wakes in the morning.'

'That will be too soon,' said Loz evenly.

'Too bad,' she said.

'Perhaps you need some rest, Isis. You look tired.'

'Don't tell me what I need. Just make sure he's ready to speak to us by morning.'

Loz was taken aback. Even Harland was surprised by the sudden flare of temper.

She woke six hours later, and for a few minutes stared through an open door, astonished by the intense, green lushness that surrounded her. Apart from a few bird-calls there was a strikingly profound stillness, and she felt that only now had Cairo stopped ringing in her ears. She swung her legs from the bed and glimpsed a reed bank through the trees.

A few minutes later Harland called out from the courtyard and announced he was bringing her coffee. She drew over her the blue cloth that had served as a blanket during the night and said he could come in.

'Feeling better?' he said, as his head came round the door. He handed her a bowl of thick, black coffee, and held up a dark blue robe with a hood. 'It's been suggested by Foyzi that you might be prepared to wear this while you're here. He says you won't be so conspicuous to people passing in boats. If it makes you feel any better, they've found me one as well.'

'That's fine. Leave it over here,' she said.

He dropped it on the bed.

'What about Khan?'

'He's still asleep.'

'Something came to me in the night,' she said. 'I can't quite put my finger on it – a sense that we're looking at the wrong thing.'

'Maybe.' Harland's shrewd eyes narrowed. 'Let me know when you think of it. I'll go back to them now. One of us should be there when he wakes. Why don't you get something to eat from Foyzi and then relieve me in an hour or so?'

She put on the robe and trainers and walked around the building until she found Foyzi standing by a clay oven. With him was an old man in a brown skull cap and dirty shift who, on seeing her, whisked a roundel of unleavened bread from the fire. Foyzi cooled it by flipping it between his hands, then spun it through the air to her. He walked a little distance to a patch of bare earth and looked up at the smoke from the oven curling to the top of the trees.

'You should look around,' he said. 'It's quite a place. A piece of paradise.'

'You're moving better,' she said. 'You've lost your limp.'

'Oh yes, the doctor took a look at me last night and pressed a few buttons,' said Foyzi. 'He's got quite a touch.'

She nodded. '"Big lorry jump all over little car," I liked that. Were you actually hurt in an accident?'

'Yes, a long time ago in Manchester, England. I worked there for eighteen months. Four of those were spent in hospital with a broken hip bone.'

'What were you doing there?'

'This and that,' he replied.

She smiled at the evasion.

'Okay, I have a question for you,' he said suddenly in the manner of an eager college student. 'How did you learn to lip-read?'

She told him about catching meningitis when she was young, the deafness that followed and the operation to cure it a few years later.

'Only in English, not other languages?'

'Maybe I can lip-read as many languages as you can do accents, Foyzi,' she replied.

'Never,' he said.

A little later she took Foyzi's advice and began to look around. From the buildings clustered on the rock plateau in the south to the northern end, the island measured about three-quarters of a mile. At its widest point it was about five hundred yards. The banks were covered in dense shrubbery, but at the centre there were citrus groves, palms and several large dark green trees which bore fruit Herrick didn't recognise. There were also a few square fields cultivated with strips of lucerne, bananas, maize and flower crops, mostly roses and marigolds. Between these grazed tethered water buffalo, goats and a lone donkey.

There was very little noise as she walked – the rustle of a lizard over dead leaves, a bird call or the cough of buffalo – and because she barely glimpsed the river, the only sense she had of it was the smell of heated mud banks and an occasional distant whoosh caused by the current tugging at an obstacle on the bank. In a glade at the northern end she came across the old bread maker, who had made his way there along a more direct path, and was contemplating a wall constructed of drainage pipes and mortar. From the openings spilled swarms of bees that hung in the sun like skin pelts drying. He lifted the swarms with a stick, talking to them in a falsetto.

She made her way back and found a spot where she could see all the buildings and realised they had been designed to look like the blunt prow of a ship forging up the river. They were almost completely hidden from both banks of the Nile by vegetation, and even from where she stood they appeared deserted, a ruin from a colonial past.

She continued walking, deep in thought. She had never been so impressed by the beauty and stillness of a place, yet was aware of its dangerous isolation. The Chief had planned it this way, she was sure. He expected something to happen, some revelation to occur. And when it did, he wanted Loz and Khan away from the world and unable to communicate.

She went to Khan's room and saw that he was still asleep.

'I think you had better wake him,' she told Loz.

He shook his head. 'We've tried.'

She looked at Harland who nodded to agree with Loz. 'I want him conscious by midday,' she said, 'even if it means throwing water over him. Is that understood?'

'We will do our best,' said Loz.

'Just get him to the point where he can answer my questions,' she said, and turned on her heel. Harland followed, leaving Foyzi to watch them.

They walked to the most shaded part of the island in the east where a tree grew out into the river. Herrick perched on a low branch.

'So now you're going to tell me about this woman?'

He looked at her for a while, then shrugged. 'She left six weeks after nine-eleven,' he said. 'November first to be precise. Just vanished. No letter, message or phone call; no activity on her checking account; no record of her having left the United States or having bought a plane ticket in her own name. Nothing.'

'Had you been together long?'

'About a year. I fell for her nearly thirty years ago. That didn't work out, then we got together a couple of years back. It was after the business in the Balkans. You probably heard about it.'

'I know it did for Walter Vigo – at least temporarily. You had a son together?'

'Yep. When he died it was a very deep shock to her. She moved to be with me in New York but never settled down. She didn't know anyone there and turned in on herself. My job took me away. It was difficult.'

'And you tried to trace her?'

Harland nodded. 'She knew how to disappear. She did it once before when we were young.'

'Where is she?'

'In Tel Aviv.'

'She's Jewish?'

'Yep, though it was never particularly important to her, apart from the fact that her mother's family in Czechoslovakia was wiped out in the Holocaust. Her mother was the only one left.'

Herrick thought for a moment. 'Maybe she was reclaiming her Jewish ancestry. Trying to put herself in some kind of context.'

Harland nodded. 'Something like that.'

'How did they find her?'

'Spotted her at Heathrow, followed her and then traced her to Israel.'

She thought, he's holding something back. Either that, or there's something else he doesn't understand.

'So you'll try to see her?'

'Yes, I'll go directly from here. I've got work in Damascus anyway.'

'And you have to go now?'

'Yes.'

'Why?'

'Because I've got a bloody job to do.'

By the early afternoon the mercury in an old enamel thermometer in her room reached the 105-degree mark. Nothing moved. The leaves on the trees hung limp and the birds and insects had long ceased to make any sound. In search of some movement in the air, Herrick climbed to a covered turret and looked across the swathes of green either side of the river to the unforgiving mountains in the west and east. Harland spotted her and shouted up that Khan was awake. She rushed down the narrow stairway and went to the room with him.

'How are you?' she asked, approaching the bed.

'He's doing very well,' said Loz.

'That's good,' she said, smiling at Loz.

'I was just telling him that he must have lost forty pounds since I saw him last,' said Loz. 'I can't believe he's still alive.' There was certainly love in his eyes but also an expectant look.

'Have you explained that we have to ask him some questions?' she asked.

'It is too soon,' he replied. 'I don't think he has the strength.'

She crouched down so that she was at eye level with Khan. 'We know you've suffered terribly,' she said softly, 'but I was wondering if you wouldn't mind talking to us for a little while?'

He glanced at Loz. 'That will be all right,' he said. Again the perfect English she'd heard in Albania surprised her. 'I can try to help.'

She put the notepad and digital recorder down and touched his hand. 'I'm really sorry about this, Karim. The moment you feel too tired you must tell us.'

'It's okay,' he said. 'But there are some things that are . . . not very clear at the moment.'

'He's on very strong painkillers,' Loz interjected.

'Can I ask you about The Poet?'

'I've already told you about him,' said Loz.

'I know, but we really do need to find out more about him.' She turned to Khan. 'The Poet, who is he?'

'The Poet was a man in Bosnia. But this was only our name for him.'

'What was his real name?'

Khan shook his head helplessly.

'You know that a man calling himself The Poet went to see Dr Loz in New York to ask him for money? He mentioned your name and after Dr Loz had given him the money he gave him a photograph of you. Mr Harland has it here.' Harland delved into his shirt pocket and handed it to her. 'Is that you?'

'Yes, this is me . . . but I thought . . .' he looked towards Loz doubtfully. 'What?'

'I don't know . . . I'm confused.'

She waited. 'Who took the picture?'

'A man in Afghanistan. I don't know his name.'

'Did you give the picture away? How did it get into the hands of the man calling himself The Poet?'

He shook his head. 'I do not remember . . . I'm sorry.'

'That's all right. We'll come back to it when you've had a chance to think.' She paused and looked down at the recorder on the floor. 'You know why we're asking these questions, don't you? We believe that one of the men you knew in Bosnia is now a terrorist leader.'

He blinked slowly with a gentle nod.

'Are there any other individuals you remember from Bosnia – or from

Afghanistan, for that matter – who expressed the kind of views we associate with al-Qaeda or other extremist groups?'

'There were many in Afghanistan but I kept away from them. I was not interested in attacking the West.'

Loz nodded in agreement.

'But it must have been difficult not to be affected by the atmosphere. You are a Muslim and most of the people who came back from Afghanistan were very opposed to Western beliefs and lifestyle.'

'I believe in the teachings of the Prophet. I prayed to him when I was in prison . . . I prayed to Allah . . . in these last days I have prayed . . . and I was saved . . . but I have suffered moments of doubt. There was much cruelty in Afghanistan. Much violence. But I never hated the West.' This all came out very slowly. Quite suddenly his eyes closed and his forehead creased. Tears began to run down his cheeks.

Loz put a hand on his shoulder, but there was something in the gesture that made Herrick think Loz was content with the situation.

'Will you describe The Poet for me?' she asked when he had recovered.

'He was about five foot five or six . . . small build . . . He had dark hair, thinning at the front. His cheeks were sunken, which made him look older than he was, but this was because we had little food in Sarajevo. He went days without eating. I did not recognise him later . . .'

'Later? That was in Afghanistan,' said Herrick quickly. 'The Poet asked you to join him in Afghanistan in ninety-seven. And you saw him there. Is that right?'

Khan nodded. 'But he left.'

'Yes, we know he was in New York receiving money from your friend. And the only way he could do that was if you had given him Dr Loz's address and the picture of you to use as his *bona fides.*'

He nodded.

'Did you know he would use your picture in this way?'

'I do not remember.'

'But you must do. It was like the postcards you sent him recently. It was proof that you were still in the land of the living.'

Khan's brow furrowed. His eyes moved rapidly from her to Loz.

'It's okay, Karim,' said Loz.

She waited until his gaze returned to her. 'I would like to run a few names past you. They're men you may have come across while in Afghanistan.'

She went through a list of suspects. Some she had remembered from RAPTOR, others from the FBI watch list. She hoped the process had a ring of authenticity and thought she noticed a certain interest in Loz's eyes. Khan appeared to hesitate over one or two but was unable to say definitely whether he had met or seen any of the men. In any normal interrogation the failure of memory would have been unacceptable, but she let it pass and asked him instead to list the key men he'd met and describe them. He gave her a score of names, many half-remembered. Then she returned to ask him where he had last seen The Poet.

'It was in the south in the first three years. I stayed with him several times. He was with the men from the Taleban. The men who were giving us the crazy orders. He asked me to take the struggle to the West but I said no. After the second time he lost patience.'

'So he did try to recruit you as a terrorist?'

He nodded.

'With your background in London he must have thought you were an ideal candidate.' She wondered whether she was sailing too close to her actual target and before he had time to answer added, 'So when you refused, you helped him another way – by giving him the photograph and Dr Loz's address?'

'Yes ... I felt ...'

'You felt you had to compensate for not going along with his wishes?'

'Yes.'

She spent some time asking about his journey from Afghanistan to the West. 'There's something I don't understand,' she said. 'Why didn't you come back before the attacks in 2001? You say you were disenchanted with the Taleban and that you had seen too much bloodshed. The ambition to return to medicine must have developed in you before then. Why didn't you act on it? And why these postcards? Finding a phone to call Dr Loz was surely not beyond you – not in all that time.' She thought she was exerting just about the right degree of pressure, but then Khan looked around the room as though he suddenly didn't recognise anyone.

'That's enough,' said Loz. 'I think you are confusing him. You must remember what he's been through.'

'Yes, you're probably right. We'll take a break there and return to all this later.' She switched off the recorder and left the room. Harland followed her out while Foyzi made his presence felt by putting the chairs against the wall and lowering a canvas blind on a window that had suddenly been filled with sunlight.

'You know what you're doing?' he said when they reached the shade of a tree fifty yards away.

'I think so ... I hope so.'

'You don't seem to be getting much.'

'I don't expect to,' she said.

He wiped a trickle of sweat on his cheek with the back of his hand. 'Then what the hell are we doing here?'

'Well, as you're about to bugger off, I hardly think I need to answer to you. This is my operation and I'm going to run it the best way I can think of.' She paused. 'When are you leaving?'

'I'm waiting to hear from Foyzi, probably this evening. I would like to help. Really.'

'You can, by setting up the sat' phone. I need to send the recording I've just made plus an email.'

She went to the table where they had sat the night before and composed a message on the laptop.

At five the sun began its rapid descent into the western desert and the temperature eased a little. All around the riverbanks the steady call of frogs suddenly started up. Herrick moved from her room to the courtyard and came across Harland in a jellaba, getting his things together.

'Thanks for saying goodbye.'

'I was about to,' he said, and explained that he would try to catch the Luxor Cairo Express at a halt sixty miles away. If he waited until the following day for a train he'd fail to meet up with the Secretary-General in Tel Aviv on Thursday.

'I don't get it. If you're so bloody important to them why did they let you spend all this time with Loz?'

'I was no use with my back. I couldn't travel, let alone sit at a desk. Benjamin Jaidi put me in touch with Loz and things followed on from there.'

'It can't have been accident that gave you Loz's name.'

'Jaidi is also a patient so knew how good he was.'

'That I hadn't realised.'

'Whatever one's doubts about Sammi Loz, I have to admit he's a bloody good doctor. I'm pretty much all right now, even after the twinge in Cairo.'

She thought for a moment. 'And then as if divinely coordinated, just as you come under the care of Sammi Loz, the Chief pops up in New York and asks you to watch him. And what the fuck was Teckman doing in New York anyway? He doesn't travel abroad almost as a matter of policy.'

'He was there because of Norquist's death – a meeting.'

'Yes, the Norquist murder ... where this whole thing started.' She thought again. 'So both the Chief and the Secretary-General were steering you to Loz but without giving you their reasons. What was going on?' She started to pace up and down, then moved to the shade of a tree. 'I should have thought about this more seriously. What do they know? Why haven't they told us?'

'Look, I don't think Teckman or the FBI or the Secretary-General knew much. The information about Loz's property deals only came together when we were in Albania. And that's the most they've got.'

'Right. But they still must have suspected a connection between Loz and the assassination of Norquist.'

'And Khan?' he said.

'Khan? No, I don't think so.'

'You're very certain of that.'

'Yes, Khan is an innocent, in as much as any fighter with his kind of record can be innocent. The point of Karim Khan is that Sammi Loz loves him. You've seen the way he looks at Khan in there. Actually I find it quite moving to think he would cast everything to the wind because of this man. But that's the point, that's why we're here. It's Sammi Loz they're interested in.'

Harland's eyes had come to rest on a beetle doggedly making its way across the path. 'I see,' he said eventually. 'You think the Chief has put both of them on ice here, taken Sammi Loz out of circulation?'

She nodded impatiently. 'Sorry, have I been going a bit fast for you?'

He didn't smile.

'Tell me about Loz's life in New York,' she said. 'What kind of man are we dealing with here? I need to know more.'

'He's well-connected. He has beautiful consulting rooms in the Empire State building. He dines at the best places. Knows the best-looking women. A perfect life for a certain type of bachelor.'

'Any permanent girlfriend?'

'I would guess not. Why?'

'I'm wondering if that's his weakness. We know he's prepared to risk everything for Khan, so clearly he is a man who follows his emotions. To that extent, he's impulsive.'

'The one woman I saw him with in a restaurant was dismissed from his presence without much ceremony.' He stopped. 'You're not thinking you . . .'

'Jesus, no. He's attractive. Anyone can see that. But I'm hardly his type. Besides, I've always thought that seduction was overrated as an interrogation technique.'

Harland started to say something but decided against it.

'What?'

'Nothing . . . Look, I want you to be careful over the next few days.' He took her arm to move away from the buildings. The sun was plunging towards the mountains leaving the landscape bathed in a creamy apricot light. Through a gap in the trees she saw a pair of purple-green herons stalking the waters below. Beyond them a kingfisher hovered.

'Foyzi was right,' she said. 'It's extraordinary here. Almost too much to take in.'

'I mean it, Isis,' said Harland severely, pulling her round to face him. 'If for one moment Loz realises you're stalking him through your questioning of Khan, you'll be in trouble.'

'Foyzi's here,' she said. 'His men are all over the island, though one never sees them. And I've got one thing going for me: the fact that we went to so much trouble to spring Khan. No one could doubt the value we place on him, not when nearly a dozen people flew from Britain to free him. Not even Loz. That was brilliant of Teckman. I just wish he had told us, that's all.'

They walked back to the villa where Foyzi told them that the truck was already waiting on the east bank. Harland picked up his stuff and they walked down to the river's edge where he gave her an awkward kiss that missed her cheek and landed on the fabric of her hood. 'Foyzi, you look after her,' he called up the bank.

'What were you going to say back there?' she asked.

'That Teckman has left you on this island without the standard backup of a lot of puffing, red-faced SIS officers, for a reason.'

'Thanks,' she said. 'I'd got there.'

He produced a Walther P38 from his jellaba, together with half a dozen clips of ammunition, and offered them to her.

'I hardly know how to fire one of those things,' she said.

'You might as well take it. I'll have to dump it or give it away before I leave the country.'

'Right.' She took it and let it drop into the pocket of her robe.

'You've got my mobile number – it's good for anywhere. Call me.'

'What, for dinner?' she said sourly.

He shook his head with mild exasperation, wedged his bag in the bow of the little wooden skiff and clambered in, knocking his shin against the rowlock and swearing. Herrick smiled and began to climb the bank. She did not give the boat a second glance as it slipped downstream into the dusk.

22

She slept deeply that night and woke at six the next morning. After bread and coffee she went to Khan's room, taking her recorder and the notepad on which she had ordered a series of questions. Khan was propped up, smiling tentatively, as if a dream was about to come to an end. Beside him Loz worked in the morning light at a cane table, setting out the medicine and throwing solicitous glances in his friend's direction. Foyzi stood by the door and nodded to her as she came in.

'I must congratulate you on these supplies,' said Loz. 'I haven't wanted for anything yet, though we may need a little more of one or two drugs and I'm running low on the ointment. Any chance of a fresh delivery?'

'Maybe we can get something from Luxor,' she said pleasantly, sitting down on the opposite side of the bed from Loz. 'You're looking a lot better, Karim. You seem to have put on a little weight.'

'I hope so,' he said.

'We were just reminiscing about our life in London,' said Loz. 'We were trying to think of a restaurant we used to go to where there was a very pretty waitress that Karim took a fancy to. She was Polish. The food and service were atrocious but Karim insisted we had to eat there because of her. What was her *name*?'

Khan shook his head, unable to help.

'Katya!' said Loz triumphantly. 'That was it. She was a real beauty. She's probably two hundred pounds today, five children and a vodka habit.' He paused. 'The restaurant was in Camden High Street. We played snooker nearby, then went round to order just before the kitchen closed. You see, Karim wanted to walk her home at the end of the evening but after spending all that money we discovered she was having an affair with the owner.'

Karim was smiling, borne along with Loz's enthusiasm.

'Actually, I also wanted to talk about the past,' Isis said.

'If Karim feels strong enough,' said Loz.

'I'm sure the rest last night will have done him good. When you were on your way to Bosnia you travelled together, is that right? In a lorry?'

They both nodded.

'What date was this?'

'February 1993, I think,' said Loz.

'And you were prevented from going all the way to Sarajevo by Serb troops?'

'Actually the Croats,' said Loz.

'I'd prefer it if Khan answers,' she said, switching the recorder on and resting it against the chair leg.

'Yes, the Croats,' said Khan.

'So you made your way with UN vehicles into Sarajevo. What was the point of that?' She glanced at the recorder to check its light was pulsing in time with her speech.

'No, we got a lift in a plane. We took all the medicine we could carry.'

'Did you travel with any fellow medical students?'

'No.'

'So this expedition was your own idea?'

'Yes, we felt for our fellow Muslims. It was something we thought of together. I raised the money and we took two other people, one of whom could speak the language. But they both turned back with the truck.'

'So you got to Sarajevo and delivered your supplies. Then what?'

'We both worked in the hospitals. A lot of people were being injured by the snipers and in the daily bombardment. Thousands of people died in the siege.'

She nodded. She had the exact figure in her head – 10,500.

'How did you end up on the frontline?'

'It just happened. Sammi met someone who said they needed ammunition at the front. A big attack was expected. They asked us to help carry the boxes.'

'And ...'

'There was an attack going on as we arrived. Many of our men were being killed and they were over-running our lines. We picked up the guns of the dead and started firing. It was as simple as that.'

'As simple as that – from doctors to fighters in a few seconds?'

'Yes,' said Khan. ' But we still helped out as medics. We did both.'

Loz nodded approvingly.

'When did the incident take place when Sammi was injured?' Herrick said, raising her hand to stop Loz answering.

'Sometime in the winter of that year,' Khan replied.

'Of 1993?'

'Yes.'

'Where were you treated?' she asked Loz.

Loz replied that he was taken first to a hospital in Sarajevo and then to Germany. He recovered in London.

'Which hospital in London?'

A private one.

'Which?'

'King Edward's – this was for the skin grafts. They didn't do a very good job in Sarajevo.'

'But you, Karim, stayed on, for nearly two years. Why?'

'I was committed. I couldn't understand why Islam did not declare a proper jihad against the Serbs. To leave those people when they had so little help, no heavy guns, no fresh troops, would have been desertion.'

'So you were moved by very much the same emotions as The Poet. You were both men of peace who were turned into soldiers by the extreme conditions in Sarajevo. Tell me exactly where you met him.'

'On the front. He was just an ordinary soldier like me then.'

'Was that in the lines to the north of the city?'

He looked surprised. 'Yes – north-east actually.'

'Near where Sammi was wounded?' she said quickly.

'Exactly there. It was during that period.'

'At the same time?'

'No ...'

Loz got up and said, 'Karim, I think I need to change the position of your legs. The way you have them will do no good to your hip. I've told you about this before.' His tone was gently admonishing.

Herrick sat back as though she hadn't noticed the diversion. 'So you came across The Poet before Sammi was wounded?' she said.

'I don't remember now,' he said. He winced as Loz moved him.

'Maybe another painkiller,' said Loz, reaching for the table.

Khan shook his head. 'I'm okay.'

She waited.

'Yes it was sometime about then ... before or after, I'm not sure.'

'But it is perfectly possible that Sammi met The Poet during that time.' She paused and looked at Loz. 'Did you?'

'Yes,' said Loz, looking unsettled. 'I told you that we met him but I can't remember exactly when.' He got up again and started fussing over Khan's feet.

'I'm sorry, this is not going to work,' said Herrick. 'I think I'd prefer to talk to Karim alone.' Foyzi moved from the top of the bed and steered Loz from the room.

She smiled at Khan reassuringly. 'Sammi has told me about the brave way you saved him. I must say it's an extraordinary story. Was The Poet there to witness that?'

He shrugged helplessly.

'Let's say he was,' she said. 'What date was that – roughly?'

'It was winter – November 1993. I think.'

'Not after Christmas?'

'No, definitely not.'

'I just wanted to make sure, because we're looking for pictures taken by an English photographer at that time.'

Khan absorbed this.

'In fact, it would be helpful if you could identify as many people as you can when I eventually get the pictures.'

Khan grimaced.

'I'm sorry. You're in pain.'

'Yes, my feet hurt a little.' He stopped. 'Maybe Sammi could help with the pictures?'

'That's a good idea.'

Gradually she returned to the subject of the winter of 1993–94. She made notes, taking particular care over places, dates, weather conditions and names. Khan's memory was hazy, and it didn't work in a linear fashion, so building a chronology was difficult. He relived the terror of that winter in epic flashes – the din of bombardment from all directions; the incursions of the Serbs into the streets of Sarajevo, the danger from snipers and the hunger and cold. It was in the account of this time that he made several mistakes. She made a note of them, but her smile did not fade as he stumbled between what actually happened and what Loz had prepared him to say.

The air was oppressively heavy and with each blink his eyes stayed closed for seconds at a time. She rose and left the room, at which Loz returned with a slightly exaggerated look of concern.

She returned at four, sat down and placed the recorder in its usual position. Loz had straightened Khan on the bed and was holding his legs just above the ankle bone with his thumbs and forefingers. The rest of his fingers were splayed out so that they didn't touch the bruised flesh below the ankles. Then he lifted the legs, almost as if comparing their weight, and tugged each one gently. He moved to the knees and thighs with a gentle stroking motion, pulled up the shift and covered Khan's groin with a cloth.

She made to leave.

'Stay, I've already examined him there.'

His hands moved to the hips and he again seemed to weigh Khan's body. Then he went round to the side and slipped both hands under his back, working his fingers into place while looking away to the corner of the room. Herrick was struck by the concentration in his face.

'You see,' he said after a little while, 'by hanging him from the ceiling they stretched his body so everything went out of line. Apart from the damage this did to the muscles and ligaments, there are various skeletal problems. These will take longer to heal.'

'Have you treated this kind of injury before?'

'Yes, a young man – a New York cab driver from Cameroon. He had been tortured very badly three years before I saw him. The damage was hidden for most of the time, but came out at moments of stress. The man was mystified because the spasms seemed to be unconnected with the method of torture.' He paused. 'The body does not forget, you see.'

There were periods of inactivity over the next half-hour during which Loz's slender hands simply rested on Khan's chest, under his neck or at the back of his cranium. At other moments they became animated, brushing and pressing the skin and then once or twice flicking it with a screwing motion of the finger knuckles. The way he moved around Khan's bed was so precise and fluent that it had an almost hypnotic effect on her. When he had finished, it was clear Khan was having difficulty in keeping his eyes open.

Loz shook his head apologetically.

'That's okay,' she said. 'I want to talk to you anyway. We'll go under the trees.'

They walked out into a second perfect sunset.

'It's been interesting to hear about Bosnia,' she said conversationally. 'I'd forgotten about the brutality of it all.'

'People do,' he said.

'Of course, both sides did terrible things. People forget that too.' She was on more certain ground now.

'No, just one side.'

'There were Muslim war criminals too.'

'We were the defenders of Sarajevo,' he said, shaking his head. 'People were being killed every day by the snipers and artillery.'

'Even so, atrocities were also committed by the Bosniaks. Raiding parties on the Serb lines. Men were butchered and tortured.'

He continued to shake his head. 'You're mistaken.'

'It's true,' she said. 'The War Crimes Tribunal has the names.'

'Yes, but there were no indictments of Muslims. The only Muslims who appear at the tribunal are victims – women from the rape camps; men who saw their friends and family murdered.'

'But it did happen,' she said. 'We should always remember that Muslims are as capable of crime as Christians.'

'Not then,' he rounded on her, a startled look growing in his face. 'The market square bomb – what about that? What about those people?'

'I'm sorry,' she said. 'I don't recall . . .'

'These things are in the news for a few days and then forgotten, but for anyone who was there . . . One shell aimed into the central market place at midday. Seventy people killed. The carnage . . .'

'Yes of course, I remember. You mean, you saw that?'

'This is what I am saying.' The veins in his neck and in his forehead were bulging.

'That must have been terrible.' She knew the exact details of the massacre. The round had killed sixty-nine people and injured two hundred when it impacted on a plastic canopy just above the heads of hundreds of shoppers in the central market. More important to her was the date – Saturday February 5, 1994 – at least two months after Sammi Loz said he had been injured in another mortar attack and airlifted out of Bosnia to Germany and then London. How could he have made such an elementary mistake?

She nodded as though it was all coming back to her. 'There was some suggestion that mortar came from the Muslim side to gain sympathy from the world.'

'No, no. I was there! I was standing just a few streets away. The Serbs fired it from the hills above.'

'But you can't tell where a mortar comes from,' she said. 'It's lobbed up in the air with very little noise.'

'Listen! What Muslim would do this to his own people? Tell me that.' He was shaking. 'I was there. I saw it. Men and women blown to pieces – decapitated. Arms, legs everywhere.'

'I'm sorry . . . but that was the rumour at the time. I think our people in Sarajevo even investigated it.' She wasn't going to pursue the point because she'd got exactly the information she wanted: Loz was still in Sarajevo in 1994. And that meant his entire account of the last decade had to be called into question.

She wrote an email to Teckman at Vauxhall Cross with a series of terse requests, pretty certain it would end up with Andy Dolph. There was no need to outline her theory to him – he would get it straight away from the drift of her questions – she just prayed that he'd have the resources to follow up the idea. She stayed on line but nothing came, so she hung up and put the phone away, realising as she unplugged the leads that she had failed to send the latest recording of her interview with Khan. She'd left the damned recorder in with Khan and Loz.

She went again to the room and sat down beside Khan. Loz's composure had returned, but he was evidently worried about Khan, whom he was attempting to feed with small pieces of bread and goat's cheese. There were plates of tahini and sliced fruit on the bed, untouched. Khan's head moved from side to side, avoiding the food as a child would do. He wasn't hungry, he said, and there were pains in his chest and stomach. Loz explained this was indigestion and that he must eat if he was to build up his strength. The tussle went on until at length Loz set down the plate and turned to a bottle of vitamins. As he did so, Herrick's hand slipped down to the leg of the chair where the recorder was. She glanced down and noticed the flashing light that indicated that the memory was full.

'Look,' she said with a certain amount of irritation. 'I think we're probably done for the day. We need to have a good session tomorrow though. I'm going to eat now.'

'Thank you for being so understanding,' said Loz softly, without looking up.

Khan nodded goodnight.

She found Foyzi by the oven with the old man. A pile of flat breads was fast accumulating in a palm-leaf basket balanced on top of the oven.

'I'll be eating with my men,' said Foyzi, gesturing into the dark. 'There's food for you on the table. I won't be far away.' He adjusted the strap of a machine pistol over his shoulder, picked up a box of provisions, put the bread on top, then padded off into the dark, followed by the old man who was wheeling a container of water on a little carriage.

Isis set a lamp on the table and remembered the whisky, still lodged behind a stone on the ground. There were also some cigarettes there. She bent down, took one from the pack, lit up and tipped the chair so that she could rest her head against the wall and look at the necklace of stars strung across the tops of the trees.

A few moments later Loz appeared. 'Can I join you? Karim's asleep.' His tone was ingratiating.

'Yes, do. He didn't seem too good to me.'

'It's to be expected. He has got a slight intestinal reaction to the antibiotics. We have to remember what he's been through. It's not just the torture, but months of not eating or sleeping properly. But he will recover.'

'Thanks to you.'

'No,' he said, sitting down opposite her and placing his hands on the table. 'This is all due to you, Isis. You saved him and we are indebted to you.'

'Where will you go after this?'

'I've been thinking about it,' he said, surveying the food on the table. 'I have contacts and some money in Switzerland. I shall probably take Karim there, and after that ... well, we will have to see.'

Did he really believe they would let him slip away like that? 'I thought you would be tempted to disappear into South America for a year or two,' she said.

'I've never been, but I'm certain it wouldn't suit Khan.' He paused. 'And you?'

She pushed herself from the wall and stubbed out the cigarette on the ground. 'I'll go back to work in London.'

He massaged his neck and looked up at the sky. 'You know, in an odd way the time spent here has done me good. I may change my life after this.'

'You may be forced to,' she said sharply. 'The FBI want you in New

York and they expect you to explain about the money you sent to Lebanon.'

'I don't think so,' he said simply.

'Will you continue with your practice?'

'Who knows what happens. Did you have any idea a week ago that you would be on an island in the middle of the Nile with us?' He paused for an answer but got none. 'I read an article in the newspaper a few weeks back about a man who was driving along a road near his home in Connecticut. He had been to the local stores; the weather was fine; there was no traffic on the roads. As he reached the driveway of his home, a tree that had stood for hundreds of years suddenly fell down on his car and set it alight. His family and neighbours were unable to rescue him, and watched as he burned to death. In the newspaper, there were expressions of puzzlement from his family. Why should this good man – a loved and loving man – be taken in the prime of his life? Why? Who was behind it?'

'Do you believe in God, Dr Loz?'

'Yes, naturally.'

'How do you explain the wisdom of dropping a tree on an innocent man?'

'I don't need to. That's not for me to understand.'

'But you must try to fit it into your system of belief?'

He shook his head. 'I don't. And you, Isis, do you believe?'

'Maybe, but I don't think God intervenes in human affairs.'

'Why?'

'Compare the intricacy and scale of the universe,' she looked up at the sky, 'with the mess and pain of human life. There's no one running this thing except us, and we should take responsibility for it. When we do, things will improve.'

'That's an atheist speaking.'

'No, a rationalist.'

'Surely you believe in fate – destiny?'

She picked up some bread. 'They're words used to explain chance, luck, accident and coincidence. I don't believe in a pre-ordained life. No.'

He began eating also, smiling as though in possession of superior knowledge. 'With your name, Isis, you could have guessed that you would eventually end up here. That's fate.'

'Actually, I wasn't named after the Egyptian goddess,' she said. 'My name comes from the end and beginning of my mother's first two names – Alazais Isobel.'

'From two beautiful names comes one beautiful name – like a child.'

'Right,' said Herrick.

'But seriously, here you are on an island in the Nile. Did you know that

Isis's greatest temple is on the Nile, somewhere south of Luxor, and that she is associated with the river and the growing of corn?'

'Yes, I did,' she said without interest. 'How come you know so much about this?'

'I find Isis the most appealing of all the ancient deities because to begin with she used her magic to heal the sick. She brought her husband Osiris back to life, and nursed her son Horus. Also, she is made of contradictory passions: on the one hand she was ruthless and cunning; on the other, a loyal and devoted wife who went to the ends of the earth to find her husband's dead body. She is like all interesting people – a paradox. In her case, both deadly and caring.' With this he broke a piece of bread and scooped up some tahini.

'If anything, Dr Loz, the paradox is nearer to your character. I mean here you are healing your friend but in other lives you are, or have been, a soldier and fundraiser for a terrorist organisation. So perhaps the lesson is that we should never judge someone by one observation, but wait until the whole picture emerges from many observations, then decide which is the dominant trait.' She stopped. 'Would you like a drink?' she asked.

'I don't drink,' he said.

'Well, I'm going to have one.'

Loz wrinkled his nose.

'When I was at school,' she continued, 'I did read something about Isis, in particular about her relations with Ra, the sun god. Do you know about Ra, Sammi?'

He shook his head.

'Ra's might depended on his secret name, a name that only he knew. You see, the ancient Egyptians believed that if someone learned your secret name they gained power over you. Isis made a cobra from Ra's spittle, which had fallen to the ground on his journey across the sky. The cobra bit Ra and injected poison. Only when Ra told Isis his secret name did she agree to relieve his pain.'

'In other words, she tortured him. I told you she was ruthless.'

She smiled. 'I was wondering whether you had a secret name. Something that would give another person power over you if they knew it.'

'Why do you do this job? This spying.'

'It's very simple. I believe in the freedoms that we have in the West, and I am happy to work against those who want to destroy them.' She paused to sip the whisky she had mixed with a little mineral water. 'Also, I'm good at it,' she said, putting the glass down. 'Very good at it.'

His forehead puckered with disbelief. 'You want nothing else in your life?'

'You're making the assumption that I don't have anything else in my life.'

'You lack something,' he said, 'possibly love.'

'Oh, give me a break. Let me tell you I'm happy and utterly fulfilled in what I do.'

'No, I think not.'

'On what evidence?'

'Your body. The tension in your shoulders, the way you stand and move, the set of your mouth, the expression in your eyes. There are a hundred signs. You're a very attractive woman, but neither happy nor satisfied.'

'I guess that's the line you use on all the girls in New York,' she said.

'I'm serious,' he said. 'You should take more care of yourself, maybe visit an osteopath when you return to London.'

'There's nothing wrong with me.'

'Except your hip, which hurts when you get up in the morning, and your shoulders, which rise up during the day and cause you headaches, and perhaps a difficulty at night when you try to find a comfortable position for your neck on the pillow.' He sat back, satisfied. 'You could certainly use some help.'

She reached for a carrot and sliced it lengthways into strips.

'I would guess you've been very seriously ill at one time in your life. There seems to be some residue in your body of that sickness. When was that?'

'What is this – the osteopathic seduction?'

He shook his head. 'No, I am trained to observe people very closely. That's all. An artist's eyes do not stop noticing the shape of things or their colour when he leaves the studio. It's the same with me. When I saw you in Albania I noticed these things immediately.'

They sat in silence for a while, then she picked some fruit from the basket and got up from the bench. 'I have work to do now. I'll see you in the morning.'

23

Khan looked up into Loz's face when he returned from grinding the pills into a solution. He was glad Sammi had found something to ease the pain that was growing in his chest, to say nothing of the constant throb in his feet.

'No man has ever had a friend like you,' said Khan. 'I don't deserve you. I cannot believe my good fortune.'

'Don't tire yourself, old friend.'

'What's the matter with me, Sammi? Tell me. What is it? Why can't I keep my eyes open?'

'Because you have had years of ill treatment and hardship. You need rest. I will give you this shot, then you will feel much better tomorrow.'

'But you wanted to leave tonight.'

'That's okay. We can wait. The important thing is for you to get better. Then we'll talk about what we're going to do.'

While Loz wiped his arm and slapped it to bring up the vein, Khan's mind returned to the hillside in Macedonia and the wonder he'd experienced one morning as he watched the sun come over the hill and saw the light filtering through the trees. Now he could smell the dying embers of the fire, mingled with the rich, damp scents of the morning; taste the mint tea that the young Kurd had made him. The memory of those moments had been clouded by the terror that had followed less than half an hour later, but now he understood that the completeness he felt when walking down the track was something important. He should remember it.

'There was some kind of a bird there,' he said suddenly.

'A bird?' said Loz as he slipped the needle into Khan's vein. 'What kind of bird?'

'The smallest bird I have ever seen. It was almost round with a tail that stuck up. It had made its nest just where we camped. The fire was right below the vine where it lived ... it stayed there all night and the next morning it was still there to feed its young.'

Loz smiled down to him. 'And you liked this bird, Karim?'

He nodded. 'Yes, it seemed very brave and determined.'

'Like you.'

'No, like you, Sammi. You never give in.'

Loz sat down on the stool. 'Now, sleep, old friend. We need you to be strong in the morning.'

Khan nodded. There was much he wanted to say. He opened his mouth but then he felt his eyes close and could not bring to mind the words he needed.

Sammi seemed to read his mind and said it for him. 'There was never true love like this before. Never between a man and a woman; never between two men.' He picked up Khan's hand and clasped it in his, then bent and kissed him on the forehead.

Khan smiled and opened his eyes. The smooth plane of Sammi's forehead was broken with a single crease of anxiety, and there were tears running down his face. 'Thank you,' said Khan, and closed his eyes to a multitude of fleeting images: his mother opening her arms to him on a shady terrace; the mountains of the East and the dancing, spirited eyes of the fighters. *His* men, the men who'd fought with him and shared the hardship. *His* men.

Herrick climbed to the turret with her computer, satellite phone and digital recorder, and sat on the warm tiles to concentrate on the recording she'd inadvertently made. The machine had gone for a full two and a half hours before switching itself off. That time included the forty minutes she had spent watching Loz treat Khan, then a period during which Khan had been left alone while she and Loz talked outside, and finally about forty-five minutes of them alone together. She went through the recording, stopping at random, but found little of interest, so she copied it into the computer, encrypted it, then dispatched it to Vauxhall Cross. She would listen to it later when she was in the bath.

She logged off from the secure server and dialled Dolph's numbers one after the other, each time getting a message service. She decided to try him again in a couple of hours and left the computer and satellite dish on the ledge surrounding the turret, knowing they would be just as safe there as in her room. Then she descended to the courtyard, where she smoked a cigarette and thought about her strategy for the following day.

From somewhere on the other side of the building came the faint sound of music – strings overlaid with the chant of a male singer. Occasionally she heard snatches of the same voice as the previous night. Foyzi had told her it was the CD player of one of his men, a Sufi addicted to his sect's music. She listened until it stopped and silence fell on the island. Above her, the stars had been partly obscured by clouds moving from the north, which explained why the evening was still so stifling. She rose and took a few paces towards her room, then stopped in her tracks as she caught the sound of a motor some way off to the south. Her ears strained to the night, but she couldn't tell if it was coming from the sky or the river. After a few seconds it died away completely. She listened for a further five minutes but heard nothing more and reached the conclusion that it must have been a boat.

Sleep was impossible because of the heat. Besides, she could not stop thinking about Loz and Khan. She gathered up her sponge-bag, a set of earphones and the digital recorder, and went with a lamp to the bathhouse. It lay at the corner of the main building and was constructed from large granite blocks which even during the heat of the day retained a deathly chill. At the centre of the room was a square bath made out of porphyry, which in other circumstances might be mistaken for an ancient sarcophagus. She set down the lamp, but before plugging the waste pipe with a rag, she had to remove the insects and lizards that had accumulated in the bath, and kill a scorpion that scuttled into the light on the floor.

The water had a slight metallic odour, but she let herself down into it gratefully and found that she could lie almost fully stretched out. As the water rose, she noticed the light catch pieces of feldspar in the granite. She washed, then made a pillow for her head out of part of her robe and shifted the lamp so she could see the machine's display. Having forwarded the recording to the seventy-five-minute mark, she began to listen again.

There was nothing for the first fifteen minutes, apart from the even noise of Khan's breathing. Then she heard Loz come into the room. This must have been after he had lost his temper with her under the trees. Khan seemed to pick up on his mood and weakly asked what the matter was. No reply came, but then Loz moved close to him and began to whisper.

'We have to leave, Karim.'

Khan replied, 'Why?'

'Because we have to. This girl is not so stupid.'

Silence followed. Then Karim said, 'You go without me. I'll be all right here ... Does she know?'

'Know what?' His voice was far sharper than usual.

'That you were ...'

'No ... But now you are rested we must leave.'

'I cannot.'

'You must. We need to get away from here. It is too dangerous for us to remain. I have some help. You will be well cared for. A night's rest and you'll be fine, old friend.'

Both voices faded at that moment and for several minutes she listened to the muttering she had heard when she first sped through the tape before sending it to Vauxhall Cross. Then something suddenly occurred to her and she switched the machine off and sat up in the bath. 'Jesus wept, I'm an idiot,' she said aloud. She lay back again, this time not into the bunched material of her robe but into two hands which caught her head and then slipped to her neck. She looked up to see Loz.

'I don't think you're an idiot,' he said, relaxing his grip but not letting go.

'What the hell are you doing in here?' she demanded. 'Get the hell out.'

He drew back and studied her without saying anything.

'Get out!' she shouted.

'I have seldom seen such beauty in a woman – particularly in one who does not know it.' He moved from behind her, one hand still holding her neck so that it pressed against the side of the bath.

She struggled a little, but the pressure of his hand increased. 'Get out now.'

'But we need to talk. I wanted to thank you for what you have done for us.'

She covered herself with her hands as best she could.

'Don't do that,' he said playfully. 'If you could see yourself, you'd understand why I am lost for words.'

'But you're not lost for words.'

There was something different about his expression. The easy charm was there, but also an odd, embarrassed savagery. His face was streaked with sweat.

'I'm warning you. Please leave now.'

Loz pulled the robe from the end of the bath and felt the material. 'Ah yes, I thought you had something in here.' He pulled out and examined the pistol, then let go of her neck and drew back. 'I mean it, Isis, I'm awed by the sight of you. The way the light surrounds your body, yet does not reveal you completely.' He paused to contemplate her further. 'They say that each woman experiences a perfect twenty minutes during her lifetime when everything – her skin, hair, body, the expression in her eyes – is perfect. Have you heard of this?'

She said nothing.

'I believe I am witnessing that moment in your existence. You're truly radiant. I am overwhelmed.'

Herrick took stock. There was absolutely nothing she could do. The question was, what did he plan?

He smiled and moved to sit on the side of the bath. 'In my culture the use of water – the preparation and purification of the woman's body – is part of the act of love. Properly, there should be no division between the two.'

'In my culture you are committing a crime and behaving like an arsehole.'

'I mean you no harm. I took this away from you so that you didn't shoot me as we talked. That's all.' He pulled up his sleeve and slid his hand into the water, then ran it up and down the inside of her calf, stroking her other leg with the backs of his fingers. 'What were you listening to when I came in? Can I hear it too?'

'Please stop doing that.'

'What were you listening to?'

'One of the recordings I made of our conversations. You were there.'

'There's nothing to hear. We have done nothing. We are what we seem.'

'In which case you don't have anything to worry about. Would you please stop touching me?' She lifted his hand out of the water and placed it on the side of the bath. He dried it on his sleeve, then touched her face.

'Another place and another time, Isis, and we . . .'

'Give me my towel and my clothes, then leave!'

'We haven't had our talk,' he protested. His hand went to her face and played on her forehead and cheek, then slipped round to her neck. 'You know, this would be as great a pleasure for you as it would be for me.' His finger traced a line round the depression at the base of her throat. 'I could do so much for you.' He paused. 'After all, we may never see each other again and I for one would regret that we did not take the opportunity that has been given to us here.'

Herrick shifted her position in the bath and tried to read his expression in the light of the lamp. 'Look,' she said, her tone softening. 'You *are* an attractive man. Anyone can see that. And yes, in other circumstances I might be tempted. Even now I find myself drawn to you. But threatening me is no way to seduce me, and you *are* threatening me.'

'I am not,' he said with a note of injury.

'But you must see that to walk in here, take my gun and then use your advantage to touch me is very threatening behaviour.' She paused. 'Now, I am going to get out of this bath and I want you to hand me my clothes.' With this she stood up and faced him, without bothering to hide herself. He picked up the lamp and stood.

'Really, you're quite beautiful.'

'My towel,' she said, putting out her hand.

He did not move.

She lifted her foot to the flat rim of the bath.

'Stay,' he said. 'Stay there. I want to look.'

'For God's sake, give me my towel!'

Instead he reached out and touched her right breast, then moved to her left side. They looked at each other for a few seconds. She shook her head and removed his hand. 'No.'

'Let's start this scene again,' he said with a sudden boyish enthusiasm. 'Believe me, it will be worth it. This is how we will do it. I will come in again and you will be dressed, and then we will take our ease together.

You can drink a little of the whisky – but not too much – and we will talk.'

'Yes,' she said. 'But you will have to stop pointing that gun at me.' She stepped onto the damp floor and made for the towel herself, feeling ridiculous and very angry. As she bent down he seized her and held her in both arms so that the gun reached round to the back of her head. Then he placed his lips on her mouth and kissed her with incongruous tenderness. She did not return his kiss but pulled her head away and looked into his eyes.

'You're not going to do this. It's against everything you stand for. You render yourself a criminal in the eyes of God and a pathetic creep by the standards of the American society you profess to love.'

'No,' he said, in a tone that seemed to mock her unreasonable behaviour. 'This is what we both want. You do not understand yourself, Isis. I know this.' He bent down and kissed the top of her breast then moved to her neck with his lips. But he did not relax his grip on the gun.

'Stop,' she said, as his free hand began to explore her behind and the top of her leg. 'Why don't we talk for a while? That's what you said you wanted to do.' She shivered suddenly, knowing she would now have to scream or attempt to beat him off.

'Sure. Why not? We will talk. There's no hurry.'

'Then let me get my clothes,' she said. Without waiting for an answer she picked up the robe and put it on. Then she reached for the recorder, unplugged the earphones, and placed it in her pocket.

'What do you want to talk about?' he said indulgently.

'It was you who came to speak with me,' she said, 'but since you ask, I would like to talk more about your past.'

'You never give up,' he said.

She began to make for the door. 'Let's go and have that drink.'

'No,' he said sharply, then modified his tone. 'It's good in here. More romantic, don't you think?'

She turned. 'You said you wanted to thank me. That is exactly what you should be doing, instead of threatening me. You owe me. Without me, Karim would never have been freed. And now . . . well, this is a very strange way to show your gratitude.'

Loz thought about this. 'I am grateful to you. But you were doing it for your own ends as well. You wanted to know about Karim, just like the others did.'

'With good reason,' she said. 'We're fighting a war and Khan made some connections we're interested in.'

'Is this the way to fight your so-called war against terror? With torture, holding people without trial or legal representation, bombing innocent civilians? You know those people being held by the Americans? Nobody even knows their names.'

She shook her head. 'You know what I think about torture and that goes for the whole of the British government and scores of other countries in the West. Whatever the deficiencies of the war against al-Qaeda, it must be obvious that we did not start this thing.'

'But you did. Don't you see that?' Again the sudden flash of temper. 'Look at the conditions of the Middle East, the people in Palestine. Look at the poverty here in Egypt. Look at Africa. These people are suffering because of the West's greed and selfishness. No one can argue against this truth.'

'Look,' she replied quite calmly, 'we all understand that the West must help less wealthy nations and that we all have to do something about the social problems, but let me just remind you that in Arab countries torture is routine. Remember why the CIA brought Khan here – because he was being strung up to the roof of a prison cell by an Arab government. So don't give me a lot of bullshit about the mistreatment of suspects in the West. Torture and imprisonment without trial is the norm in your world.'

'You do not understand! You have not seen how our people suffered in Bosnia, in Palestine. Everywhere. That's what we are fighting for.'

'Fighting for, Dr Loz? Who are you fighting for? You're a US citizen and you enjoy all the delights and riches of the West, yet you say you're fighting. For whom? Against what?'

'No . . . I mean, the Arab peoples. This is what *they* are fighting for. They struggle for . . . justice.'

She exhaled heavily, realising that he was on the point of making an admission, and once he had there would be no turning back. He would have to kill her. At the moment there was still a residue of the urbane Manhattan doctor, the pretence of reason and consensus, but it had slipped twice already that day and she was certain he would not leave that room without getting what he wanted. 'Let's go and sit down outside,' she said quietly.

He shook his head.

'Look, it's you who needs to relax. You've barely had any sleep in the last three days.'

'I am fine,' he said. 'We will stay here.'

'Then let me get a cigarette.'

'No.' He raised the gun. 'Sit there.'

She wiped the edge of the bath with her towel and sat down.

'Let's not pretend any more,' she said. 'We're on different sides. You know what I do and I now have a pretty good idea of what you are. For example, I guessed you were injured in Afghanistan, not Bosnia, and that Karim Khan saved you there and took you to Pakistan to be treated. All along you have been worried not about Karim – poor, misguided Karim – but about what he might reveal. You knew you couldn't rely on him because, let's face it, he's really quite naïve, and the only reason he didn't tell them about you was because his interrogators didn't know precisely what questions to ask. Until you got the first postcard, you believed that the only man who could harm you was safely tucked away in Afghanistan, maybe even dead. Then the card came and you realised he was on the loose and – more dangerous to you and your organisation – untraceable in the shifting population of migrant workers coming from the East.'

Loz's eyes were utterly expressionless. 'Go on,' he said.

'Well, it's pretty simple really. The picture you had of Khan wasn't given to you by a homeless man in New York. You brought it back with you from Afghanistan. For some reason I recall that in 1998 all photography was banned by the Taleban except for official purposes. The portrait of Khan looks very much like the ones from the Taleban's records recently handed over by the Northern Alliance. So my guess is that you were in Afghanistan in 1998 or 1999 for a period of training and planning. And you managed to get a copy of one of those pictures. You were there. I'm right, aren't I?'

'You're forgetting that I'm a Shi'ite.' He said evenly. 'The people in Afghanistan were all Sunni Muslims, like Karim.'

'That's a detail. The point about your war is that it's not really about religious practice, despite all that bullshit about jihad; it's about the inequalities between the West and Islam. That's what you're fighting against, although the foot soldiers like Khan really have no notion of this. You don't believe it's a religious war any more than I do. It's about economics.'

'You're wrong,' he said.

'But look at your life in New York – the material wealth, the women, the fornication. What does the Koran say? "Approach not fornication; surely it is an indecency and evil as a way." But that is your way. Or is this just the sacrifice you've made to create a convincing cover? I think not. I think you genuinely bought all that stuff and you're such a fucking freak that you manage somehow to reconcile it with your other lives.'

He shrugged good-naturedly. 'You think I am a split personality, Isis.'

'Nothing so simple. You have compartments with communicating doors. Each side is conscious of the other and fully aware of what it is doing, but you can close the doors.'

'Maybe you see into me a little.'

'And The Poet?' she said rhetorically. 'The Poet doesn't exist, not in any relevant way today. But I do believe there's another man you have been protecting, an individual whom Khan knows but doesn't, *or didn't,* see the importance of. He gets it now because you have been schooling the answers he gives me.'

He shook his head. 'You won't be asking Karim any questions now.' He looked down. 'But since you have chosen to press the issue, which is certainly an unwise course for you, I can tell you that The Poet exists – it was the name we used in Bosnia when this individual, as you call him, refused to tell us his real name. This lasted a matter of days and when we learnt his real name we stopped calling him The Poet.'

'And this man is running your organisation – another Shi'ite perhaps?'

'I cannot answer you.'

'From Lebanon?'

He grinned. 'I can't tell you these things, Isis.'

'But you can. What good is it to me now? I know what you intend here. What is his name?'

He thought for a moment and smiled to himself. 'His name is John.'

'John?'

'Yes, John.' He laughed. 'Now, we do have some unfinished . . .' He looked down. A small green frog had hopped into a pool of light on the floor and remained there, blinking. This was the moment she had been readying herself for. She launched herself from the edge of the bath towards his stomach, but he had anticipated the move. He stepped out of the way, caught one of her arms and pulled her round like a rock'n'roll dancer into his chest. Then he lifted her with a strength that took her by surprise and placed her on the side of the bath, forcing her legs apart.

'No! Not like this,' she shouted out.

He stopped and held her by the shoulders. The gun was pointed at her right temple. 'Then you will behave.'

She shook her head, thinking only of how she could wrest the gun from him.

Then he did something odd. He stroked her face, brushing his hand across her lips and eyebrows. He considered her once more. 'You are a real beauty, Isis. You have a secret beauty. That's it – a secret beauty.' He pressed his mouth to hers hungrily and moved between her legs. 'You understand,' he said under his breath. 'I didn't want it this way. I wanted us to make love like equals.'

The gun had slipped down and now she was sure it must be pointing at the wall behind her. She put her arms around his neck. As she did so a triumphant smile flickered at the corners of his mouth and he kissed her neck.

'Tell me you want me,' he said.

'I want you,' she replied.

He was touching her breasts. She now felt such loathing for him that she was prepared to risk anything to stop him. The only way that presented itself to her was to use the purchase she now had on his shoulders to headbutt him. But she was slightly above him, and any blow would only connect with the top of his head. She had to get him to look up to her. 'I want you,' she said, smiling with as much acquiescence as she could muster and drawing back as though to see him clearly.

'I knew you desired me all along,' he said.

Then she hit him, not with her head, but with a chop of her hand at the carotid artery. He fell back but still managed to hold onto her with his left arm. And then she felt the incredible, athletic energy of him as he spun her round so that she was facing the bath, and forced her head down to within a few inches of the water. He was cursing, pulling her robe up and working her legs apart.

It was then that the first explosion occurred.

Herrick was thrown upwards and flipped over like a leaf so that she landed half in the bath, her body bent backwards. The blast seemed to have caused the room first to depressurise and then fill with a second deafening thunderclap. She knew nothing for several seconds, but then recovered enough to tell herself that she was still alive. She rolled into the bath and covered her head with her hands, concerning herself only with the masonry and timber falling from the roof. She had heard a cry from Loz at the moment of the explosion, but that was all.

A few seconds later there was another, equally demonic explosion, but this time another part of the area was hit and she was able to better comprehend what was happening. There were three distinct stages after the initial impact: a huge reverberation that must have been heard twenty miles away, a whoosh of air, and a short time afterwards, sounds of collapse and pulverisation.

She waited for a third blast, now convinced that the island was under bombardment from the bank of the river. But nothing came, and the only noise she could hear was a fire taking hold somewhere across the courtyard. She began to push upwards against a mass of debris that was trapping her in the bath. It was no good. For minutes on end she grappled with a beam and what seemed to be a large chunk of plaster attached to some stone, which lay across the top of the bath and gave her room to manoeuvre. All the time she could smell the fire taking hold. She lay back in the water, deciding that her best chance was to work at an opening she had found with her foot near the tap. This required her to bunch her legs to her chest and force herself forward in a somersault. It took many contortions and compressions of her frame before she managed it and then she was so out of breath that it was several minutes before she began working to enlarge the hole. At length she thrust her head and right shoulder through it and was able to start shifting larger pieces of stone and wood. A few minutes more and she was free, scrambling through the roof of the bath-house to see the damage in the light of two fires.

The first explosion had occurred in the rotunda and completely obliterated the structure, together with the stairway and the rooms either side. The second had hit the buildings on the far side of the courtyard. Where Harland and she had sat talking the first night, there was now a crater measuring thirty feet across. The wooden terrace and building had been atomised. She clambered down, cutting her foot on a piece of metal, and reached the ground. Two figures were running towards her from the north end of the island shouting her name. She sank to the ground, and before she knew what had happened, she was looking up into the anxious faces of Philip Sarre and Joe Lapping.

'Are you all right?' said Sarre.

'Yes . . . I think so. Where the fuck . . . did you?' she stopped, spat the dust from her mouth and wiped the blood and sweat from her face. Her eyes and hair were caked in a kind of clay. 'Where did you two come from?'

'We were over there,' said Lapping pointing to the east bank.

'Since yesterday. We were told to keep our heads down while you were getting so much from Sammi Loz.'

'But what the hell happened?'

Sarre shook his head. 'Joe'll explain – where are Loz and Khan?'

She pointed to the bath-house. 'Loz was in there with me. He must be dead. Khan might be alive. He's over there in the part that wasn't hit. I don't understand,' she stammered. 'What happened?'

'We think it was friendly fire,' said Lapping. 'It looks very much as though you were hit by a couple of Hellfire missiles delivered by a Predator. We heard it earlier and were halfway across the river when we saw the first strike.'

They heard Sarre shouting.

'Right, you stay here, old girl,' said Lapping. 'I'm just going to see what he wants. Be back in a tick.'

She looked up. Between the gaps in the smoke the cloud was beginning to clear, and one or two stars were showing again.

Part Three

24

As Harland moved towards Immigration at Beirut, acutely conscious that he would benefit from a shave, haircut and a new set of clothes, he noticed a group of three men standing a little way off from the visa counter. One nudged the other two to look in his direction.

Instead of making for the counter, he arrived in front of them and dropped his bag. 'Hello there,' he said pleasantly. 'Tell me, are you Syrian or Lebanese intelligence?'

The men shifted and pretended not to understand.

'I was hoping one of you could give me a ride into town.' He searched their faces expectantly. 'No takers? Oh well. Just in case you're wondering, I'm with the United Nations. Robert Harland, Special Adviser to Secretary-General Benjamin Jaidi.' He opened his passport and offered it to them. They looked the other way and began to walk off, one flicking worry beads, the other two finding the need to consult their cell phones.

He moved to the kiosk to pay his twenty-five dollars for the visa, then to the counter where his passport received a little stamp showing a sailing barque. Finally he passed through Immigration and Customs and made for the taxi rank, where a shabby Mercedes waited in the warm summer night.

Both Benjamin Jaidi and Sir Robin Teckman had told him to go to Beirut and, most importantly, it was the only place Eva Rath would agree to meet him when he phoned the number Teckman had given him. The reaction of his vanished partner had been surprising: she offered neither an expression of astonishment about his finding her, nor remorse for her disappearance, but simply forbade him to visit the apartment block in Shabazi Street, Tel Aviv, where she now lived with her mother. She had told him that Hanna Rath was now in her last weeks and she would not stand for Harland disturbing her peaceful end.

As the Mercedes bumped through the vast new developments in the central district that had risen on the ruins of Beirut's civil war, Harland found he was curiously at ease with the situation. The pain of her rejection of him had in the last week or so miraculously ebbed away. He was now concerned only with getting answers about her behaviour. Of course he now understood she must have left to look after her mother, who as one of the few Jewish survivors of the Holocaust in the Czech Republic, had presumably gone to Israel to die. But there were other aspects of Eva's departure which Teckman had told him about. SIS was certain that she was working for Mossad in a capacity requiring her to move between London, New York and Tel Aviv, possibly as a courier. Having been trained by StB, the security services in communist Czechoslovakia, then by the KGB spy school, Eva would have interested Mossad high command. Harland imagined she must have done a deal that allowed her mother to live the remainder of her days in Tel Aviv with medical assistance, in exchange for Eva's talents as a spy. It was unsurprising to him. If he'd been asked to describe the unseen parts of his lover, the first would be her need to deceive, the second was her habit of placing herself beyond control by vanishing, and the third was the unbreakable bond with her mother, Hanna. These were to a very large degree the drives of Eva Rath, although the things that had attracted him when he was barely twenty were her nimble intelligence and startling, intimate beauty.

Why hadn't she told him? Why not explain? She could never reasonably have doubted his devotion to her. It had spanned nearly three decades and, even in the long period when their son Tomas was growing up and he had no idea of his existence or where she was, he had still nursed his love for her.

But now, as he thought of her, he felt strangely unburdened. He was amused by things, which quite apart from anything else accounted for his twitting the graveyard shift of intelligence officers at the airport, usually an unwise move.

He arrived at the Playlands Hotel – specified by Eva and suggested by Teckman – and checked in. There were no messages for him and he tramped off to his bedroom in the southern wing of the hotel where he poured two miniatures from the fridge into a glass and took it into the shower. Fifteen minutes later he was standing on the balcony letting his hair dry in the sea breeze, when there was a knock at the door. He opened it to Eva, who stood in the corridor with a tight, drained smile. He instinctively bent down, took her by the shoulders and let his lips skate across each of her cheeks.

'You'd better come in,' he said.

She circled a finger in the air, which he took to mean that the room was probably bugged, and they walked through to the balcony.

'Where the hell did you go?' he said, unable to hide the anger of fifteen months. This was not how he'd planned it.

'Bobby, don't start . . .'

'Don't start! I thought you were dead. I searched everywhere. You just walked out with no explanation, no idea of the hurt you caused me or the effort I would put into finding you.'

'I knew you would eventually.'

'I didn't – Teckman did. You remember him?'

'Of course. I worked for them, like you, Bobby.'

He shook his head, wondering at his own earlier nonchalance about seeing her.

'Then why not tell me in the first place? You only had to explain about your mother. I'd have understood.' He examined her in the light from the illuminated swimming pool beneath them. Her hair was much shorter and as yet unflecked with grey. She was using less make-up than before and had put on a pound or two that showed in her cheeks. If anything, it made her look younger. 'You look good,' he said quietly. 'Really, a lot better than you did in New York.' He stopped, studied her, then exploded. 'Jesus ... are you incapable of understanding what I felt for you?'

'And you?' she asked, calmly turning towards the sea. 'Did it occur to you to ask what *I* was going through in New York?'

'But I did. I tried to talk about Tomas with you. You said so little that I thought you ... Look, I tried. You know that.'

'I knew no one. Only you. You were the one person who knew what I had been through. I had no other witness to my life in New York. Do you understand what I mean? No one who knew that I'd lost Tomas and what that meant to me.' She stopped. 'It was never going to work, Bobby. Never. We ... our love ...'

'Was overwhelmed by circumstances,' he said.

She grimaced. 'Yes, if you want to put it that way. But it was also destroyed by you, Bobby. You didn't know *how* to talk to me. Maybe that's because there was an inequality between us. I *lost* my son; you hardly knew yours. He was an acquaintance for a few weeks. That's all.' Her jaw clamped shut and her eyes welled with tears.

He touched her on the shoulder. 'It's okay,' he said.

'No it isn't!' she hissed, recoiling from him. 'That's the point. It's not okay. I'm not English. I have to be able to talk about this and be with someone who understands what his death means to me now – today. It doesn't go, you know. It doesn't just end like that.'

'I'm sorry,' he said, moved by the pain flaring in her eyes. 'I admit this is a failing of mine, but I wasn't responsible for his death. I did everything to try to save him.' He paused. 'And you know if you and your mother had not been so close to Viktor Lipnik, Tomas would never have seen the things he did in Bosnia. He wouldn't have been a danger to Lipnik. It was Viktor Lipnik – your lover – not I, who killed Tomas ...'

'Don't!' she said. A passionate hatred passed across her face. Without looking down, she felt for the arm of the metal chair and sat at the table.

'I'd like some vodka if you have some.' This was unlike her. He had only ever seen her drink wine. He went to the minibar, resolving to be calm.

When he returned with the drinks, he laid his hand on the table near hers. 'Eva, I'd have done anything to keep you with me. Anything. You knew how much I loved you. You should have helped me, shown me how to talk and listen to you.'

'You can't tell a man this. Either he knows or he doesn't know. You don't, Bobby. That's why I stopped loving you.' She paused to consider this. 'No, that's not true. I didn't stop loving you. There are many parts of you that are wonderful; it was just that my love for you was not deep enough to tolerate the way you were ignoring me.'

The self-evident truth of this stung Harland. That was exactly why she had left. She hadn't told him because she had been hurt and resented him.

'Christ, I'm sorry,' he said. 'Really, I don't know how to make it—'

'It's no use. You are what you are. I know why you're like this. You went through a lot when you were tortured, and with your cancer. That's why you're so bad at talking. You should have seen someone at the time. It's gone so deep.'

'I did. But that wasn't the reason I was so bad with you. I didn't know what to say. You erected a pretty impenetrable wall. You know that.'

'Yes,' she said, her head nodding in agreement. 'I know.'

They drank in silence, then he asked about her mother.

'She has cancer. It moves very slowly, but each day she is reduced in some way. The doctors are very good and we have two nurses who stay at the apartment, so I can leave when it's necessary. They have been good to . . .' She stopped when her voice cracked.

'It's very distressing – your only living relative.'

'I find that the strangest part,' she said, moving her head from side to side so that the sea breeze reached her neck.

Harland nodded. 'Well, you have my sympathy. I do understand what she means to you.'

She nodded thanks, lit a cigarette and looked at him more softly. 'Why are you in the Middle East?'

'Trying to hook up with Jaidi. They were due here yesterday but they aren't leaving Damascus until tomorrow.'

'Teckman called me before you. Did you know that?'

'So you wouldn't be caught on the hop,' he said. 'That was the right thing to do.'

'But this is not the first time you've been in the Middle East this year, is it? We heard that the UN talked to Hamas three months ago. Was that you?'

He shrugged. 'If I was talking to Hamas, I couldn't tell you about it, Eva.'

'I didn't say *talking* – present tense. I said *talked*.'

'My answer is the same.'

'I'll take it as a yes then.'

After that exchange he couldn't help but press her. 'They picked you up at Heathrow and followed you to the safe house in Kensington on the day Norquist was killed. They went over the security film for the day and found you.'

She didn't react to this but said, 'Look, if we're going to have this conversation, we should go down to the pool or the beach.'

They went down one floor, slipped through the fire exit and walked towards the beach where they removed their shoes and made for a line of parasols.

'You were waiting in line with Vice-Admiral Norquist at Immigration,' he started. 'He became suspicious after you dropped your stuff a couple of times. He knew you were trying to strike up a conversation with him and told our people to follow you.'

'Is that so?' she said indifferently.

'They realised your flight arrived several hours before his and that you only went to the Immigration desk when his flight from Reykjavik was disembarking. You were timing it. Were you going to trail him to the hotel? Pick him up ... that kind of thing?' No answer came. 'I guess Norquist was a big prize for you. To know what he was saying to the British government?'

'Teckman told you all this,' she said huskily and then cleared her throat. 'Are you still working for British Intelligence, Bobby?'

'Nope,' he said.

'They don't just give out information like that. What did you do for them?'

They were fencing again. He wondered how much this game had been part of their attraction. 'They owed me,' he said. 'They wanted me to keep an eye on someone and I did. In exchange I got your number.' He thought for a moment and decided to take a chance. 'A lot else went on at Heathrow that day.'

Her expression became animated.

'A dozen or more terrorist suspects passed through Terminal Three and exchanged identities at precisely the moment you arrived.'

She said nothing.

'What were you doing there?' he asked.

'It's complicated.'

'Surely you can answer that. It doesn't affect you or your security. Also it's important. There has to be a connection between the arrival of

Norquist at Heathrow and the identity switch of the terrorists. The current theory is that the Norquist killing was a diversion.'

'See! You're talking like you're still working for SIS.'

'That's because I can't avoid the conclusion that your movements that day could provide a clue. If you knew of Norquist's arrangements, it follows someone else could.'

She looked out into the dark towards the waterline, where the waves caught the light as they reared before breaking on the sand. 'Tell me more about the switch,' she said.

'No, you tell me something, Eva.'

'My name is Irina. It always has been.'

'You were Eva when I fell in love with you in Rome. You were Eva in New York.'

'But I *am* Irina,' she said with quiet defiance. 'That is my name, Bobby.'

'Look at us! We're still at it. Fencing with each other over some bloody secret. Why? Why're we still doing it?'

'Because that's our work. That's what we're good at.'

'Look, if there's anything you can tell me, please do. I'm instructed to tell you that you'll receive no hassle when you pass through London again on your regular trips. Everything will remain as it is.'

'There won't be any more.' The breeze lifted her hair at the front and for a moment he saw Tomas, standing in the cold outside his apartment in Brooklyn on that first night when he learned that he had a son.

He shook himself. 'How did you know when to follow Norquist?'

She said nothing.

'We know you were booked into the St James's Hotel, as Norquist was. We don't understand why you went to the safe house first, but we assume you were going to make your way to the hotel later, maybe make a pass at him?'

She shook her head despairingly.

'Well . . . what *was* the plan then? You do realise that SIS can blow your cover and render you useless to Mossad?'

'I need the money. I need their help in Tel Aviv. Don't threaten me. After all you have done . . . don't threaten me.'

'How did you know when to fly?' He demanded. 'Norquist's schedule was secret.'

She put her hand to her cheek. 'It was easy. Norquist started life as a naval helicopter pilot in Vietnam. His aircraft was hit and he crushed several vertebrae when it crash-landed. Every time Norquist was planning a long flight somewhere, he got treatment for his back problem in New York.'

Harland stiffened but said nothing about Sammi Loz. 'And?'

'We are interested in the man who treated him. It seems their relationship went beyond the normal doctor–patient thing. They did business together. That's all I can say without jeopardising my position. Please think of me and my mother.'

'What kind of business?'

'Some deals.'

'What deals? Stocks, restaurants, futures, real estate? What?'

She looked at him quizzically, then said, 'Real estate?'

'Why would you be interested in this?'

'Come on, you can't ask me that. Please.'

'Yes, I see.' He paused, several calculations going on in his mind at once. 'Information on high-ranking American officials is very useful to the Israeli government, but only if there is some impropriety that can be used against them, or even better, used to influence American policy in Israel's favour. So you were seeking evidence of this nature. But why in London?'

She shook her head. 'I can't tell you.'

Harland slapped his knee. 'Ah, I get it. You already had the evidence you needed and this meeting was part of a regular arrangement. He was working for you already. Was he telling you about American intelligence policy?'

She uncrossed her legs, leaned forward in the wicker chair and looked him in the eyes.

That was all he needed. 'Thank you.' He thought for a moment. 'We both know we're talking about the osteopath.'

Her gaze held his eyes.

'So let me suggest this. Not only was Norquist telling you about US intelligence planning, he was also keeping you informed about Sammi Loz, specifically the transactions in New York that enabled you to work out the money flow to Hizbollah. But of course it wasn't easy for Mossad to see Norquist, so your people had to fit into his arrangements. You never contacted him by phone or email; instead you popped up at some moment during his travels, to receive information and give instructions. Each time a different person would make contact, so Norquist's security wouldn't be suspicious. That explains why he didn't know who you were at Heathrow.'

She nodded, but by the way she looked at him he knew there was something more.

'What is it? What else?'

Again she shook her head. She was prepared to give a mute confirmation, but only if he reached the right solution without her aid.

'So let's think about this,' he said, wishing he had brought a couple of miniatures down to the beach. 'There was something unusual about the message you were going to give him that day. That would explain why you followed him from New York and waited before passing through Immigration with him. If it had been routine you would simply have bided your time until you saw him at the St James's Hotel. What was it? Did you have knowledge of the hit? Were you trying to warn him?'

Her eyes pulsed and he knew he was right. He was also momentarily aware that his attraction for her still moved deep in him. 'Does that mean you knew about the switch that was going on in Terminal Three?'

'No, we didn't. You have to tell me about that.'

He then proceeded to give her everything he had learned from Isis Herrick, aware that this was specifically against the instructions of Sir Robin Teckman. But he had no illusions that he was still being used by Teckman, and reasoned that he could consult his own judgement about what to tell her. She listened intently, memorising the salient details, logging and filing them away to be recalled in a matter of hours for the benefit of her controllers in Tel Aviv. After he finished, she asked him a series of penetrating questions about the tracking of the suspects, not all of which he could answer, but she nevertheless soon grasped the significance of the exclusive Anglo-American arrangements.

'Why is this? Why don't they use the other services in Europe?'

'Because they don't trust them.'

'But that is wrong. Only a few months ago the French told the British of some Algerian suspects. We help all the European agencies on Islamist terror cells, sharing information about the movements and backgrounds of suspects. This is the only way.'

'I'm sure there are many who agree with you, but I didn't design the policy.' He stopped and looked at her again. 'Has it occurred to you that this is the level we work best at – when we're discussing some fucking intelligence problem?'

'Yes,' she said, as though this had long been evident to her.

'Well,' he said with a bleak smile, 'let's think about the connection between Sammi Loz and the switch at Heathrow. How much notice did you have of Norquist travelling?'

'Eighteen hours.'

'And how did you know where he was going?'

'Other intelligence,' she said.

'Oh come on, Eva. What other intelligence?'

'I cannot say. Operational security.'

'Okay, okay,' he said, raising his hands in surrender. 'So when did you hear there was a threat to his life?'

'Just before I got on the plane at JFK. Our people had been monitoring a website. There was nothing definite, but we thought that Norquist was the likely target, and I was told to get to him as soon as possible at Heathrow and warn him.'

'Your service was ahead of everyone else on this. As far as I can gather, the British had very little notice of the threat.'

She shrugged.

'Right, so you did get to him at Heathrow. Did you warn him?'

'I was about to, but then I saw armed police waiting and I knew they must be there to protect him, so I thought it would be better to wait and talk to him about the other things later. I thought he was safe.'

'Is it the assumption of your service that Sammi Loz tipped off the would-be killers about Norquist's plans?'

'Yes.'

'Because?'

'We believed Loz knew or guessed that Norquist had been talking to us and had betrayed details of his dealings. Norquist was disposable.'

'I see. But if there's a connection between the switch and Norquist's death – and we should remember that was probably caused by a stray British bullet – it means that Loz must have had notice of Norquist's plans far in advance of you. A dozen or more men had to get tickets and time their arrival at Heathrow. That would need several days' prepara-tion. As soon as the operation had begun and all these suspects were in the air bound for London, someone leaked the fact that an American diplomat was about to be topped at Heathrow, on a website they knew was being monitored. Diversion strategy in place.'

'And because his plane was late, it worked even better than they had planned,' she said.

Harland leaned back in his chair and put his hands behind his head. 'That means Sammi Loz is the planner, or at least one of the planners. It's odd that Teckman hadn't sussed all this by now.'

'He couldn't, because he didn't know of the corrupt relationship between Admiral Norquist and Sammi Loz. Only we knew this.'

'Right, but he suspected something, because he asked me to watch Loz.' He paused. 'That's who I have been with.'

'With Loz!' She was shocked. 'Our people are looking for him all over. Where is he? You must tell me.'

'I can't.'

'You have to.'

'I can't, because you will wade in and others may be killed.'

'But he's in British hands?'

'Sort of.'

'I will have to tell my people that immediately. For God's sake, why didn't you say this before?'

'Operational security,' he said, grinning.

'Bullshit.'

'I needn't have told you at all, Eva.'

'But don't you see, we are working on this together now. There are things that only we can put together.'

'Naturally that idea pleases me, but forgive me if I have a jaundiced view of your motives, Eva. I know where your loyalties lie – with your mother and Mossad. I come pretty well down the list after those two.'

She lit a cigarette and blew a stream of smoke. 'I can't deny you're right. But this isn't a question of loyalty. This is about collaboration for a mutual benefit.'

'That sounds like a phrase from the communist era. Anyway, I'm out of this. I will tell Teckman what I've learned from you, but then I'm going to join the Secretary-General and go back to my work.'

'Talking to Hamas?'

'No, acting as a special adviser to Jaidi.'

'Who is another patient of Dr Loz's,' she said tartly. 'Does he receive home visits like Norquist did?'

'You *are* well informed,' said Harland. Then he told her about his own back problem and Sammi Loz's skills, neither of which seemed to interest her much.

'Will he be tried in Britain?' she asked suddenly.

'Probably.'

'But there is information that he has been arrested. Do the Americans know? They are looking for him too.'

'That's a rather sensitive point. I don't think anyone knows we've got him.'

She looked puzzled. 'How come?'

'He's not under formal arrest.'

'You mean you don't have him?'

'I'm not completely up to speed with the situation,' said Harland.

She pulled a cell phone from her shoulder bag and got up. 'I have to report on this. I am sorry, it is too important to wait.'

She went a little distance off into the sand and made her call. Harland's eyes flicked between her back and two men who had sat down in the shadows between the pool and the rear of the hotel's lobby. As he watched her he decided he still loved her, or rather needed her, but outweighing this was her propensity to hurt him, cut him out of her life. She had done it twice before and even if she came back when her mother passed on, there was no question in his mind that she would do it again. She was pathologically elusive.

When she returned he said, 'Were they pleased? Was it worth the trip?'

She nodded. 'Yes. Thank you for this, Bobby.'

'Well, at least you didn't have to sleep with me to get the information.'

'That's beneath you.'

Harland felt a guilty satisfaction that he could still hurt her. 'That's the old game, isn't it? That's what you were doing when we first met in Rome. The beautiful swallow from the East ensnaring all those tired officials and politicians.'

She gazed at him with the familiar look of defiance. 'Fuck you, Bobby.'

'Okay, okay. I'm sorry. But you should know how much I've missed you. Really, you should know that. I realise it's over but you bloody well could have told me why you were leaving, helped me understand.'

She lowered her eyes and drew a circle in the sand with her shoe. 'You're right. It was cruel of me. But I thought it was the best way.'

He glanced back to the hotel. 'You see we have company here. I saw them at the airport – Syrian or Lebanese footpads.'

'No, they're with me.'

'You travel with a bodyguard?'

'In Lebanon, yes. It's still a dangerous place. People go missing.'

'So you're not staying here?'

'No, I have to return. It is not easy to travel from here to Israel. I want to be back as early as I can for my mother's sake.'

'Right,' he said, getting up. 'So it's goodbye?'

'Yes.' She handed him a card. 'You may need to call me. This number will reach me wherever I am. I think we will need to be talking about this again.' Her flawless English was suddenly tinged with the Czech accent he once loved to hear.

'I'm not working that beat any more. I'm out of this business.'

'If you say so.' She held out her hand.

He took it, drew her to him and kissed her on the cheek. 'That's it then,' he said.

'We will talk. Sooner than you think.'

He let her go and she walked away towards the three men.

Harland took out his own cell phone and dialled the number on the card she had just given him. He saw her answer. 'You didn't take my mobile number,' he said, and gave it to her.

When she had disappeared into the hotel he made his own call – to Sir Robin Teckman.

25

Herrick arrived back in London from Africa with Philip Sarre and Joe Lapping three days after the attack. On the night the missiles struck, Sarre and Lapping took her to a desert airstrip about seventy miles from the island. Five hours later they were picked up by a Cessna Titan and flown to Khartoum, where Herrick was treated for her cuts and bruises. They remained there for nearly three days while their passports were equipped with registration stamps and visas to make it seem that they had been in Sudan for over a week. Then they took a flight to Frankfurt and finally one to Heathrow, landing at midday on Sunday. Herrick was never so pleased to see the orderly patchwork of Surrey and Kent appear through the plane window.

At home she listened to her messages, then took a pile of newspapers into the tiny south-facing garden with a jug of lime juice and returned calls to her father, Harland and Dolph. Munroe was overjoyed to hear she was back. He knew better than to ask what had happened after he left Cairo, and instead pressed her to make plans for a trip to the west of Scotland in late July. Neither Dolph nor Harland answered their phones. There was one other call, from a Dr Leonard Jay. She didn't recognise his name or the number he'd left, but called the cell phone anyway and left a message.

She browsed through the Sundays, trying to keep a sense of failure and deflation at bay. It was difficult. Karim Khan was dead. Sarre had seen a body in the burning ruins of the villa which was almost certainly Khan's. The body was quite cold and rigor mortis had already set in, which made them suspect that he had not been killed by the missile but had been dead for some time before the strike. There was only one conclusion. Sammi Loz had ended the life of his friend, either by suffocation or with an injection of a lethal combination of drugs from the medical kit.

Khan's death shocked Herrick, because she had calculated that one thing she could rely on was Loz's love for Khan. However vain and ruthless he appeared to her, this had seemed to be a constant in his life. But plainly he had decided to leave the island, and knew that he could neither take Khan with him nor risk leaving him to be questioned further.

But had Loz died after killing Khan? Sarre and Lapping spent as long as they dared in the ruins of the bath-house trying to see if anyone was still trapped below the rubble. Sarre emerged and offered the theory that only the rock-solid bath had saved Isis, and unless Loz had been in it with her he would certainly have perished beneath the tons of rubble. Herrick could not remember the slightest sound or movement to indicate that he had survived.

And the attack, coming out of the night with such demonic force. Why? The motives still baffled her, although she knew after receiving an oblique call from the Chief on Sarre's cell phone in Khartoum, that it had probably been her fault. The satellite phone she'd left plugged into the computer up in the turret had for some reason kept dialling out, dropping the connection and then dialling again. It seemed likely that the Americans, already monitoring the communications coming from the island, had picked up the endlessly repeated signal and used it as a homing device for the first missile. This meant the CIA was aware that Khan and Loz were on the island, which in turn meant that they had been decoding the traffic both ways. They must also have known that a British intelligence officer was responsible for sending those signals, but that consideration had been overridden by the need to eliminate Khan and maybe Loz too. At the back of her mind she wondered if the CIA station in Djibouti, which would have controlled the Predator, was in possession of entirely accurate information.

She lay dozing in the sun, running through it all and trying to focus on what was left in the ruins of the attack. Khan was gone. Loz was probably dead. However, she was still certain that a third person existed, a man whom both Khan and Loz had met in Bosnia and then subsequently in Afghanistan.

She picked up her cell phone and called Dolph again, who answered on the first ring.

'Welcome back, Isis,' he said, on hearing her voice. 'By Christ, we were all relieved when we heard you were okay.'

'Thanks,' she said. 'Look, I need to ask you something. A couple of weeks back you mentioned some photographs from Bosnia. You had an idea that there was a photographer on the front line where Loz and Khan were serving. Am I imagining it or did you actually say that? I was half-expecting you to send me some material by email.'

'That's right, but I never got hold of him.'

'Can you trace him and see if he is willing to empty his archives for us? Photographers keep everything, and he might just have what I'm looking for.'

'Sure.'

'And there was a French journalist who covered the siege of Sarajevo –

I think you said she now works for Nato. Can you get hold of her too? It's important.'

'I thought you were retired from this inquiry.'

'Not that I've heard.'

'Yeh, I can't imagine that Vigo and Spelling missed out on the full story of what happened. I mean, it doesn't look good for the people who went on the pyramids package tour.'

'Thanks for the encouragement. I was acting on the Chief's orders throughout. You know that.'

'The *former* Chief's orders. He's been airbrushed from the official history. He left on Friday, although he's not actually due to leave until Wednesday of this week.'

'Christ!'

'But I'll stand by you all the way.'

'Somehow that doesn't reassure me in the way it's meant to.'

'Seriously, Isis, you have my support, if it counts for anything. Look, I'd better go before you give me something else to do. We'll speak tomorrow when I know about the photographer and the French hackette.'

'Thanks Dolph, you're a good friend.'

The moment she hung up her phone rang again, and she answered to Harland, who asked, 'Can you do dinner tomorrow? I'll be at Brown's Hotel, Albermarle Street. We'll speak then.'

She managed to say yes before he hung up.

Monday morning came early with a summons from Vauxhall Cross. Spelling wanted to see her in the Chief's office no later than eight-thirty.

She took a cab into London. It was again a beautiful day, and as they drove through Kensington Gardens she suddenly felt a calm resignation about what was going to happen. If she was to be expelled from the Service under a cloud, so what? A summer in Scotland beckoned and then she'd find a job in the autumn and begin to lead a normal life, without having to allow for the possibility that every call she made was being listened to. There was nothing Vigo or Spelling or any of the other whey-faced bureaucrats could do to her, and she felt good about that.

As the taxi crept through the rush-hour traffic down Vauxhall Bridge Road towards SIS headquarters, her phone rang again.

'Hello, it's Leonard Jay.'

'Hello,' she said doubtfully.

'Dr Jay from Oxford!'

'Oh yes. Do you have any results for me?'

'Yes, that's what I'm ringing about,' he said huffily. 'I was concerned to get them to you as soon as possible since you did sign up for the priority service and we have already received payment. I would have sent them by post, but you specifically instructed us to convey the results of the analysis to you personally by phone.'

'Absolutely right. What are the results?'

'Well, it was difficult with the first sample because while there was a preponderance of material from one individual – ninety per cent of the scales of skin and the hairs came from that person – there were traces of other people too. So we made the assumption that it was this person who interested you and obtained a clear picture of his genetic profile.' He drew breath. 'Now the second sample, which reached us about ten days ago, was from one person. There was no contamination to contend with and we had—'

'And?' she said impatiently.

'To answer the question in your letter, these two samples are from different people.'

'Are you certain about that?'

'As certain as I can be about anything. We do a lot of forensic work, Ms Herrick, and we applied the same rigorous standards to your samples as we do to evidence for a criminal case. These are two different people. I am absolutely sure of it. I had a slight worry that sample B, that is the second one you sent me, might be matched against some of the minority material in the first sample. But we found B did not match any of the traces in A. There is no doubt about this.'

Herrick pressed a finger in her ear as the cab roared forward to make the lights on Vauxhall Bridge, and asked if the results could be couriered to London.

Dr Jay said that would be no problem.

'Is there anything else you can tell from either sample?' she asked.

'As a matter of fact there is. Both are male and both come from Mediterranean stock.'

'You can say that for certain?'

'Yes, recent advances mean we can show that on the Y chromosome of both men there is a common mutation present that originally appeared in the peoples of the Middle East. Indeed this marker has been very useful in the study of ancient migration patterns. There is still a distinction to be found in the character of the Y chromosome between the men of northern and southern Europe.'

'So you can assert that neither sample comes from, say Anglo-Saxon or Indian men.'

'Well, not categorically, but you might conclude that the two were from roughly similar genetic stock.'

'You might be able to say they were Arabs, for instance?'

'Yes, you could certainly argue that.'

The cab pulled up a little distance from the main entrance of SIS and Herrick asked the cab driver to wait while she finished her conversation.

'But to be sure,' she said, 'you would have to do the test again with new samples, is that right?'

'Oh, I don't think there's much point. As long as you are not proposing to take this to a court of law, I think we're on pretty safe ground.'

She gave him an address in central London used by SIS as a letter-box and then hung up.

The Chief's office had clearly suffered an unceremonious exorcism. Propped against the wall outside were Sir Robin Teckman's library of books about the Soviet Union and the Middle East, his family photographs and his collection of landscapes by Cavendish Morton. On the other side of the entrance was some rugby memorabilia that she recognised from Spelling's office, and a new widescreen TV.

After a few minutes in the corridor, Spelling's assistant told her to go in. Vigo and Spelling were sitting on one side of the maple veneer conference table that had also migrated from Spelling's office over the weekend. Vigo indicated that she should take a chair opposite them. Spelling did not look her way, but it was already plain to her that the battlefield general was glorying in his new power and the bold decisiveness that was expected of him.

'We haven't long,' he said, removing his glasses. 'I must be at Downing Street for a meeting of COBRA within the hour. Walter, where are the others?'

Herrick reflected that Teckman would never have announced he was going to Downing Street. She found herself idly wondering why COBRA – the Prime Minister's emergency committee, named after Cabinet Office Briefing Room A – had been convened.

'I believe they are on their way,' said Vigo. His eyes appeared more hooded than usual and the pallor and puffiness of his skin betrayed his long hours in the Bunker.

The others, it turned out, were the new head of Security and Public Affairs, Keith Manners, who had returned from the Joint Intelligence Committee, a man named Leppard, who was responsible for the 'deep background' briefings of the media, and a polished, dapper little fellow from the legal department, named Bishop. Finally came Harry Cecil, who had risen over the weekend on the thermals of sycophancy.

Isis was left with several seats empty either side of her, while the six men were ranged opposite, a seating plan eloquent of the trouble she was in. She noted too that she was unperturbed, crossed her legs and leaned back in the chair.

Spelling cleared his throat. 'Following a break-in at 119 Forsythe Street on the night of May twenty-four you were formally warned by Walter Vigo that your behaviour was not only illegal but a serious security risk. At that time Mr Vigo took pains to explain to you that anything which allowed Mrs Rahe to believe her husband was dead might in turn alert the suspects that we were aware of the Heathrow switch. Is this so?'

'I'm not sure what you're saying,' said Herrick coolly. 'If you're asking me whether I agree that it jeopardised security the answer is no. If you're asking whether Walter spoke to me, yes.'

'Don't play the dumb bunny with me, Ms Herrick,' said Spelling nastily.

'Okay, I agree that Walter did talk to me in the company of Nathan Lyne. But since Mr Lyne is not a member of this Service and nor was Mr Vigo at the time, I do not think that it can be classed as an official warning, not in the terms of current employment legislation at any rate.'

'It is not for you to question Mr Vigo's position with this office,' said Spelling.

'But I am right,' she said, 'and any lawyer would certainly back me on that, unless you can prove that Walter was re-employed by that date.'

Bishop from the legal department looked unsettled.

'Ten days ago,' continued Spelling, 'you were among a number of people from this office who became involved in an illegal operation in Cairo, during which you seized a known terrorist suspect by force from the custody of the Egyptian security services. By the extent of this operation and the measure of violence offered to the Egyptians, this action can only be classed as a very grave offence indeed. It was certainly an illegal one, both in terms of the remit granted to the Secret Intelligence Service by Parliament and in the context of Egyptian law.'

Herrick felt her temper rising and she cut in. 'Is that the same legal context that allows the Americans to export suspects to countries where torture is routine? Are the "extraordinary renditions" that emerge from these sessions part of the legal framework you refer to?'

'Torture is irrelevant to your behaviour,' said Spelling.

'As a matter of fact it is entirely relevant. Karim Khan produced a great deal more valuable intelligence when he was free of duress than he did when he was being threatened by the Albanian Intelligence Service and the CIA and then subsequently electrocuted, burned and hung from the ceiling by the Egyptians. That intelligence is still live and useful, particularly in regard to his association with Dr Sammi Loz.'

'Sammi Loz was a minor player,' said Vigo, shifting in his chair, 'and certainly not worth the grave risk you exposed this Service to both in Cairo and on the island.'

'So you were aware of the location,' said Herrick sharply. Vigo did not have time to reply before she set off again. 'Actually, Sammi Loz is, or was, a critical part of a network we are only just beginning to understand. The Americans have long appreciated this, even if their focus on Khan concealed that fact. I assume that my communications from the island were intercepted by them and that they are in possession of everything I got from my questioning of Loz and Khan. If Loz was worthless, why on earth would they aim two Hellfire missiles at the place they knew him to be staying? If they believed he was just a bit player, why would they have mounted a surveillance operation on his apartment and offices in New York?'

Spelling leaned forward over the desk. 'It is not for us to answer to you, Miss Herrick. And it's not for you to lecture us on spurious terrorist networks. It is simply our concern to process the disciplinary procedure against you as fast as possible. Believe me, you are in serious trouble.'

Harry Cecil, who had been making a note of the exchanges, licked his lips in anticipation of the kill.

'Really? I don't see that at all,' said Herrick. 'I was asked by the Chief to take part in an intelligence operation overseas. In case it escaped your notice, that is the job of this Service.'

'I will not have you tell me what our job is,' snapped Spelling.

'Nevertheless, I *am* going to tell you about this operation, the sole purpose of which was to wrest a valuable suspect from certain death, to say nothing of torture. It must be clear to you by now that the Chief's plan entailed reuniting two suspects in circumstances likely to induce them to betray their past and the associations they had in Bosnia and Afghanistan. This was beginning to work. It was an ingenious and thoroughly legitimate plan, and I am certain that anyone in the media would agree with that.'

'Let me just make this utterly clear,' said Spelling. 'You have signed the Official Secrets Act. Any notion you have of leaking the events of the last week will meet with the gravest possible response from this office.'

'I am sure of that, but you cannot deny that for me to have refused the Chief would have placed me in breach of both my contract of employment and my moral obligation to this country.'

'Nonsense,' said Vigo. 'You must have been aware that this was the desperate act of a man who wished to cling on to power in this office. In these circumstances, you would have been quite within your rights to refuse to join this adventure, at the very least to seek advice as to its wisdom.'

'Presumably you would have made yourself available for such a consultation?' she said, turning on Vigo. 'But with your record you can hardly blame me for not speaking to you.'

'That's enough!' said Spelling.

'Your relations with the arms dealer Viktor Lipnik,' she continued, 'and the circumstances of the attack on a plane carrying Robert Harland into Sarajevo are all well known in this Service. That's why you were forced out. And you're suggesting that I ask *you* about the *morality*, the *advisability* of an operation!'

Spelling had risen to his feet and placed both hands on the table. Cecil stopped writing and gaped at Herrick. 'The fact of the matter, Miss Herrick,' said Spelling, 'is that we no longer have need of your services. You will leave this building and hand in all your passes...'

'But I haven't finished,' she said. 'You see, I don't think you have the slightest idea what this lowlife has been up to.'

'Perhaps it would be better if I left,' growled Vigo.

Spelling shook his head irritably.

'You can stay or go,' said Herrick, relishing the dissolution of the panel facing her. 'But nothing will stop me saying what I know.'

Spelling cast around, then said, 'To put it in plain language, you are fired and you will remove yourself from this office forthwith. Do you understand that?'

'I will go once I have told you about Walter Vigo, the man in whom you place such misguided trust,' she said without a trace of emotion. 'In collaboration with the CIA station in Tirana and the head of the local intelligence service, Marenglen, Walter Vigo conspired to mislead me and this Service about the fate of Karim Khan when he was first held in Albania. His death was faked on a mountainside so I would not pursue what was a crucial inquiry about his connections in Bosnia and Afghanistan. Further to that, he arranged for my house to be broken into and searched while he believed me to be at RAPTOR's command centre in Northolt. Happily, the two Albanian criminals who were supplied by Marenglen did not find what they were looking for, which means I am now in a position to reveal the critical – some would say criminal – misjudgements made by Vigo in the course of Operation RAPTOR, which I emphasise came from my work at Heathrow during May.'

All six men were now standing. Spelling's face had drained. Harry Cecil and Leppard had moved round the table to take hold of her.

'Since you are no longer a member of this Service,' said Spelling, 'what you have to say is of no interest to us. You will now be escorted from the premises. Formal notice of termination will follow this day. In the meantime, I would remind you again of the very tough sanctions of the Official Secrets Act. If you choose to ignore them in the smallest way, we will come down on you so that you will live to regret it. That means certain prosecution and a custodial sentence. I trust I make myself clear. Now I have to leave.' With this, he stalked from the room. Vigo followed at a studiously sedate pace.

Cecil and Leppard waited for a few moments while the others filed out and then without speaking, steered her to the elevator bank. 'It's okay,' she said. 'I can find my own way out.' Nonetheless they went with her to the front desk and waited until she had retrieved her cell phone. As the security guard handed it to her it began to ring. She answered to Robin Teckman.

'They've just bloody well fired me,' she said. 'I'm being escorted from the building by that little twerp Cecil and Leppard.'

The Chief laughed. 'Really? Well, it happens to us all at some time or other. Now, pop yourself in a cab and come round to the Cabinet Offices. You'll find the entrance door a little way up from Downing Street. Present yourself there in forty-five minutes. There's a meeting I want you to be in on. Your name's on the door. Don't be early and don't be late.'

Herrick put the phone in her bag and with a broad grin said, 'Cecil, I wonder if you would be so kind as to get me a cab ... for Whitehall.'

26

Herrick presented the ID tag that Cecil and Leppard had failed to take from her and passed through the security gate of the Cabinet Office. She was met by a brisk young civil servant who introduced himself as Entwistle and asked whether it was her first time in COBRA. Only then did she understand she was to attend the same meeting as Spelling and Vigo.

'The Prime Minister is running a little late,' said Entwistle, 'so Sir Robin suggested we put you on ice for fifteen minutes or so in a room next door. Is that all right?'

'What's this about?' she asked.

'I think you're in a better position to say than I am,' he replied, pushing at a door and gesturing towards a stairway. He dropped her off in a small, windowless basement cell where there were old magazines and brochures issued by departments of state. He returned with some coffee brimming in a utility china cup. Herrick settled down to idle her way through the property ads in *Country Life* and briefly entertained a life in some distant shire with a couple of dogs and an undemanding man who cooked.

Forty minutes later Entwistle breezed in. 'Rightyho, you're on. When we go in, I will point out the seat you should take. The Prime Minister is opening the meeting with a brief preamble. If you're not sure what to do or say, just follow Sir Robin's lead. Okay?'

She shrugged hopelessly, unable to hazard what events had brought her from being fired an hour before to a meeting presided over by the Prime Minister. They moved along a carpeted corridor and came across a huddle of men and women, all in their early thirties, who Entwistle said were the staff of the Civil Contingencies Secretariat who would be swinging into action once the COBRA meeting was over. He reached a pair of doors, looked round and said, 'Okay?' again. She nodded.

He opened one of the two doors and she found herself propelled into a large white room with a low ceiling and somewhat harsh lighting. There were no pictures or other adornments. Seated at the centre of a long table was the Prime Minister with his shirt-sleeves rolled up, displaying a weekend tan. On his right was the Foreign Secretary, hunched over a pile of papers; on his left was the Home Secretary, who was the only one of the three to notice her entrance. Enwistle pointed to a seat two away from Sir Robin Teckman, four places from Richard Spelling and Walter Vigo, neither of whom acknowledged her. The remaining chairs were taken by the Director of the Security Services, Barbara Markham, members of the Joint Intelligence Committee and Ian Frayne, Intelligence Coordinator in the Cabinet Office, who had originally been head of Security and Public Affairs at Vauxhall Cross when Herrick was a trainee. He flashed her a welcoming nod.

'So I stress,' said the Prime Minister, 'I have not convened the Civil Emergencies Committee lightly. Overnight I have been given information which cast Operation RAPTOR in a very different light, and makes me doubt the value of the way it was set out in the wake of the assassination of Vice-Admiral Norquist. Clearly these faults must be rectified before I speak to the President this afternoon. I hesitate to call it a misjudgement until the internal inquiry has reported, but I do emphasise at the outset this morning that I am concerned that RAPTOR is being run without full recognition of the risks and dangers that we face at every hour of the day. We may have to consider that it is flawed in its very concept.'

There was a slight murmur around the room, a shuffling of papers, the almost perceptible adjustment of each person's position.

'Now, this committee's brief is not to take over the business of our Secret Intelligence Service, but I do intend to get to the bottom of what is happening and make my dispositions accordingly. I wonder if I could begin with you, Richard, as the Chief of SIS designate?'

Everyone noticed the stress on the last word. 'Well, Prime Minister.' Spelling's eyes swept confidently around the room, rallying support which, in the downward glances and blank expressions, was evidently less forthcoming than he had expected. 'I first of all want to draw the attention of the committee to the immensely detailed understanding we now have of the men who passed through Heathrow on May fourteen. There has never been an operation like this. This is the cutting edge of surveillance and both the United States and UK governments have benefited hugely from our ability to watch these men and monitor every move they make, at the same time as studying their backgrounds, psychological profiles, associates, support systems and financial backing. It is a triumph of modern intelligence gathering and it has greatly increased our knowledge of Islamist groups. Besides this, the risks of this *in vitro* experiment are minimal, because each man is covered by a squad of no less than six highly trained and armed personnel. The suspects are already virtually handcuffed.'

'That's very reassuring, Richard,' said the Prime Minister, with a slightly pained expression, 'but I've heard all this before. It seems to me and my two Cabinet colleagues that Sir Robin's new information does call RAPTOR into question, particularly the value of what one paper I have received from the Joint Intelligence Committee notes as its "unyielding and exclusive focus".'

'Yes,' he replied, 'but Prime Minister, these were the terms that our American partners insisted upon.'

The Prime Minister's gaze traversed the table and alighted on Teckman. 'Sir Robin, perhaps you would like to go over the material you brought to me on Friday evening?'

Teckman began to speak quietly, so that the people at the furthest extremes of the room had to lean forward to catch what he was saying. Herrick smiled to herself. This was always his method of drawing people towards his argument.

'While I don't want in any way to undervalue the efforts made by the men and women of RAPTOR, over the last forty-eight hours we have made certain discoveries about the nature of the terrorist threat to the West, the possibility of which has largely been neglected.' He stopped and glanced in Herrick's direction. 'Few of you will be aware that a key figure in this has been my colleague, Isis Herrick. She was first responsible for establishing what happened at Heathrow on May fourteen and subsequently worked with RAPTOR. Now she has brought crucial intelligence from Egypt. Even she is unaware of what she conveyed to us by satellite phone late last week.'

The faces around the table, including the Prime Minister's, began to examine her with interest. She acknowledged his compliment with a nod, inwardly wondering what on earth was in the recording that she had overlooked, then remembered that she had only managed to listen to a small portion of it. After that she had been fighting off Loz in the bathhouse.

'The part I am going to play you was of exceptionally poor quality and has been rescued by extensive work by GCHQ technicians.' He placed a briefcase on the table and unzipped it. Inside was a large tape player. 'Here we go,' he said, pressing the play button with the uncertainty of someone unused to electrical equipment.

There was a rustling noise, which Herrick recognised as coming from the dead leaves on a vine outside the window in Khan's room, followed by silence. You could hear a pin drop in the bomb-proof underground chamber, as the eyes of each person came to rest on the spools of the tape recorder.

Then came a voice – a whisper floating on the breeze that had now audibly taken hold of a cloth hung in front of the window, though only Herrick could possibly have seen this in her mind.

'She is a devil that girl – no?'

'That is Dr Sammi Loz,' said the Chief. 'The important part is coming up now.' He turned up the volume control.

'She thinks she is clever. And she is. She is catching us out all the time. You Karim, she plays with you. But we play with her also. We wait. And we let her think she is so fucking smart. Eleven days. That's all we have to wait for. *Inshallah*.'

There was silence, then a sigh from the bed. 'What are you doing, Sammi? What do you plan?'

'This is not for your ears, old friend. But it's good, very good. Months of planning and we have fooled them like children. *Al kufr milatun wahidun* – right, Karim?'

Teckman stopped the tape. 'That is an Arabic phrase which translates as 'unbelief is one nation'. It's a well-known Hadith among Islamist groups, and expresses the view that all non-Muslims are the enemy of Islam. They both knew this phrase. I understand from the Director of the CIA whom I spoke to last night, that one of the postcards sent by Khan to Sammi Loz at the Empire State building contains a crude rendering of the same phrase in code. However, I should stress that we do not believe Karim Khan knew of Loz's intentions and that the presence of this code is not significant. However, he did represent a considerable danger to Loz, which is why we believe Loz eventually had to kill him – hours before the strike. The clue to the nature of the threat comes now. Khan is speaking.'

He pressed the play button again and turned up the volume. The room was filled with a buzz of static and then the single word 'Yahya' was spoken by Khan.

It came again. 'Yah–ya.' Slow and deliberate.

Loz told Khan to be quiet. 'Not here,' he said sharply.

But Khan persisted. 'You follow Yahya too much, Sammi. Yahya is a bad person.'

'Please, old friend, I do not want to hear that name. Forget you ever knew it. If you don't, it will fall from your lips when you are with that woman and then we will be both be in trouble. She is communicating everything we say to her colleagues in London. Things move at lightning speed these days. You have forgotten because you have been away from the world for so long.'

Khan seemed to misunderstand him and asked groggily, 'Yahya in London? Is The Poet in London?'

'Forget The Poet,' said Loz. 'Forget Yahya. Forget these names. Okay?'

Teckman switched off the machine and put it away. Then the Prime Minister asked if there were any questions.

After a pause, Vigo coughed and said, 'I wonder if I might ask Sir Robin what relevance this has to RAPTOR. The recording is very impressive in its own way, but it does nothing to dissuade me of the value of our current operations.'

Teckman looked down the table and dispatched a parched smile in Vigo's direction. 'That's a very good question, Walter. Intelligence from Beirut over the weekend, provided by friends of ours, confirms that Sammi Loz, instead of being a peripheral interest, is right at the centre of this affair. There is a link between Loz and the suspects that you have under surveillance. Loz was connected to Vice-Admiral Norquist as a patient and a business partner. I am afraid to say that the latter association allowed the Admiral to be exploited by Loz and then subsequently by Mossad, who were aware of his dealings. I won't go into the whole story now. Suffice to say that Loz was in a position to know about the timing of Norquist's trip here and put into place a scheme to kill him. We have long been puzzled by the poor calibre of the men hired to kill Norquist. We know the bullet is likely to have come from one of our own people and not from the two tearaways who were killed on the motorway, but the fact remains that these men were tasked to kill him, or at least cause a substantial redeployment of security personnel in and around Heathrow.

'I have no doubt that Sammi Loz wanted Norquist dead. He must have known by then that Norquist was working for Mossad, and that information about Hizbollah was going straight to Tel Aviv. But I maintain that the primary objective was to create a strategic diversion. Incidentally, I note with interest that in the minutes of a meeting held five weeks ago at Vauxhall Cross, this was the exact phrase offered by Mr Vigo.'

He glanced at Vigo, who nodded vigorously.

'So what we have,' he continued, 'is a line which traces between Khan, Loz, Norquist and therefore the RAPTOR suspects. This clearly establishes the value of Isis Herrick's outstanding work in Albania and Cairo, and underscores the necessity of removing Karim Khan from the custody of the Egyptian Intelligence Service. Without taking Khan, we would not have been able to make these connections.'

Spelling leaned forward and caught the eye of the Prime Minister. 'But look, these men are all dead. Norquist, Khan and Loz are all dead. What we are left with are the RAPTOR suspects.'

'I agree that Khan is probably dead,' said the Chief. 'One of our men saw him, or a body on his bed. As to Loz, we cannot say. The ruins of the villa have now been searched thoroughly. We had very precise information from Isis about the location of Loz at the moment of impact and no body has been found there. So I am bound to conclude that one very cunning, wealthy and determined terrorist is on the loose. Maybe two, if we include the individual referred to as Yahya whom Loz is so obviously desperate to protect. For the record, I happen to think we have a problem, and that we have five days to find them.'

'But the evidence is so slight,' said Vigo.

'I am unpersuaded of that,' said the Prime Minister. 'How much of this do the Americans know?'

'A certain amount,' said Teckman, 'though I felt it wise to be circumspect about Norquist. There is no reason to trouble his family or his good memory.'

'Quite right,' said the Prime Minister. He looked around the table. 'Clearly radical adjustments are needed in the scope and direction of RAPTOR. What do your soundings in Washington recommend, Sir Robin?'

'Exactly what you suggest. I think it's fair to say that we have taken the Anglo-American experiment as far as we can. I don't doubt its usefulness in academic terms, but we now face a distinctly practical problem which I think must necessarily involve the BND in Germany, Mossad, and the Direction Générale de la Securité Extérieure, and the DST in France. Clearly the Italians, Spanish and Nordic services should also be involved.'

'But this means they will have the benefit of our knowledge,' said Spelling. The room noted the plangent tone in his voice and to a man and woman decided that he was not up to the job at this or any other time. 'We have to consider the history of security lapses in Europe,' he said.

'We *are* in Europe,' said the Prime Minister, and turned back to Teckman. 'Sir Robin, I should make it clear now that I want you to stay on at SIS at least until this operation is satisfactorily completed. I am very grateful for the efforts you and Miss Herrick have put into making sense of this over the last few weeks. Will you also convey my personal thanks to anyone else who was involved.' Teckman gave an oblique, patrician nod.

At this point, several things began to fall into place in Herrick's mind and without knowing what she was going to say, she began to speak. 'I'm sorry . . . but it just occurred to me who Yahya might be, sir. I mean, it's a long shot but, well, I think it's worth considering.'

The Prime Minister nodded. 'Yes . . . ?'

Her hand reached for a biscuit from the tray in the centre of the table, and she began to nibble unselfconsciously. 'I had some tests done . . . kind of out of hours, if you see what I mean. I took some material from the keyboard of a computer used by a man named Youssef Rahe. Rahe was involved in the switch, though he was our man – a contact made by Walter Vigo. Then Rahe disappeared in Lebanon and a body was found in a car – unrecognisable and badly burnt. I got a friend to obtain a sample from the corpse to see if the DNA matched the material that had fallen into the keyboard habitually used by Rahe – keyboards collect a lot of hair and skin, as you perhaps all know.' She paused, aware that most of her audience didn't know whether to be embarrassed or intrigued. 'I got the results this morning. There is no match between the two samples, which means that Rahe was not killed. Instead, I believe his place was taken by another man who we spotted passing through Terminal Three. He was tortured, executed and disguised as Rahe so that we would think our man had been discovered.' She stopped and nibbled some more. 'Sorry, am I making any sense?'

'Not to me,' said the Prime Minister, 'but please go on. I'm sure everyone else understands the significance of what you're saying.'

'Well, it just struck me that there was a connection between the eleven suspects and Rahe after his supposed death. When one of the men died – the Stuttgart suspect – all the telephone calls from the local group of helpers were monitored. There was one significant call and that went to Beirut, informing an unknown party that the man was dead. You see, a very strong argument can be made that Rahe was in on this from the beginning and was manipulating us. Would you mind if I asked Mr Vigo a question?'

Vigo's head turned to her and he blinked. 'I should remind you,' he said, 'that it was I who ordered those calls monitored from Stuttgart.'

'I know, but we all should have been thinking about Beirut. It should have set off some kind of alarm that Rahe had been taken from a hotel there. My question is this: where did we first learn about the website carrying the messages about future attacks? Was it through Youssef Rahe?'

'Yes, it was,' cut in Spelling, clearly having decided to jettison the co-architect of RAPTOR.

'So we have basically been sold a dummy by Rahe and Loz. I believe that we know who Yahya is. Yahya is Youssef Yamin Rahe. I have to ask you how you came in touch with him, because I believe he has been using his connection with us all the way along.'

Vigo shook his head. 'This is all guesswork. I am not going to answer these questions until there is some kind of evidence.'

'I think we shall have all the evidence you require,' she said. 'I just need that answer.'

'For God's sake answer her, Mr Vigo,' barked the Prime Minister.

'I met him through my book-dealing business.' He spoke as though drugged. 'Then I went to his shop in Bayswater. We talked and it was clear he might be able to help us.'

The room went silent again as Vigo slumped back in his chair, then in a lifeless voice asked the Prime Minister's permission to leave. The Prime Minister nodded. Vigo rose stiffly and limped from the room.

'Have you any more surprises for us, Miss Herrick?' the Prime Minister asked.

She shook her head.

'Sir Robin, does all this seem likely to you?' he asked.

'Yes,' he replied.

'Then it is clear that you must trace Youssef Rahe and Sammi Loz wherever they are, as a matter of urgency. You will, of course, have the complete backing of the Security Services, the police and the diplomatic service. What else do you propose?'

'The first thing is to get the eleven remaining suspects off the streets as fast as possible. I believe the BND and the French service may have already been alerted to some kind of operation. It was hopeless to expect us to be able to carry out this type of surveillance on their territory without them getting wind of it. We should make them party to everything we have learned, apologise and urge that these men be arrested.'

The Foreign Secretary stirred. 'On what charges?'

'Initially, on violation of immigration controls. We have the evidence on film that each man was carrying false passports. More serious charges may follow, but at least we'll know the Heathrow team is under lock and key.'

The Prime Minister whispered to the Foreign Secretary. Herrick could not help lip-reading what he said. 'Get that tosser of an ambassador in. Tell him the game's up and that I'll be speaking to the President this afternoon. Keep Norquist out of your talk. I'm going to need that as ammunition with the President. I'll want a note about that from Teckman.'

The Foreign Secretary got up and left. 'Right,' said the Prime Minister, also rising. 'The Civil Contingencies Committee will meet three times a day and liaise with the JIC staff. I expect constant progress updates for the next five days. Needless to say, there will be a media blackout on this. And that will last until I say otherwise. That's it. Let's get on with it.'

Only Herrick did not get up as she left. Instead, her hand darted forward to retrieve another biscuit.

27

The seascapes by Cavendish Morton, the photographs and the small bronze of a man fly-fishing were back in the Chief's office by lunchtime that Monday. Also returned to his complete control was the British end of RAPTOR, which took rather less time to effect than the hanging of his pictures. As he moved round his office, trying new positions for the canvasses, he dictated a memorandum that instructed RAPTOR to focus its efforts on preparing the foreign agencies for the arrest and charge of the suspects. The teams in the Bunker were instructed to concentrate their resources on predicting the exact location of every suspect over the next forty-eight hours, so that decisions could be taken about a coordinated action across Europe. At the same time, RAPTOR was tasked to provide evidence against the helper cells, the men and women who had smoothed the way for the suspects to merge into the life of cities all over Europe. Preliminary estimates suggested that in each case at least ten people might be arrested and charged with aiding and abetting a terrorist plot, although there was some doubt as to whether the evidence was strong enough to meet the requirements of more liberal regimes in Scandinavia. All governments were to be urged to use the Al Capone option: to seek convictions and custodial sentences for ordinary criminal matters such as theft, fraud and forgery, rather than for terrorism.

As British diplomats began to sound out and brief governments, they insisted that a news blackout was required until at least the end of the week, by which time the date mentioned by Loz in the recording would have been reached. In several conference calls, the Chief acknowledged that there were likely to be check-in systems designed to alert a central control figure of an arrest. The failure of one suspect to make regular contact might be enough to tip off the entire network. The reaction of most security services was still to press for arrest at the earliest possible date. The Chief also told them about Mohammed bin Khidir, the man apprehended in Stuttgart who had died when he bit into a cyanide capsule. The other suspects were likely to have been equipped with suicide pills in their teeth, so drugging them, perhaps by dart, would be a necessity rather than an option.

Herrick was present for most of these conversations and noticed once or twice a distinct lack of surprise in the voices of the various intelligence chiefs, especially from the French and Italians. Between calls she remarked as much to Teckman.

The Chief gave her an injured look and said, 'After the work you have done for us, you can pretty much write your own ticket, Isis, but I do urge you not to give voice to these unworthy suspicions.'

Of course, she thought, the crafty old buzzard had found a way of keeping his main European allies in the picture. For a moment she marvelled at the ferocious will that lay beneath the Chief's cheerful, gregarious presence.

One thing that remained held tightly to the chest of the British Secret Intelligence Service was the identity of Sammi Loz and Youssef Rahe, now in Teckman's mind established as Yahya or The Poet. The Chief considered issuing descriptions and backgrounds, but then decided not to risk either of the men hearing that they were still regarded as live threats. He saw to it that Sammi Loz's name lost the prominent place it had occupied on the FBI watch list for the last few weeks. Agents monitoring the empty consulting rooms in the Empire State withdrew.

In a gap between the Chief's calls and discussions, Herrick phoned Dolph on his mobile.

'Where are you, Dolphy?' she said.

'In the sticks, having coffee with Britain's premier war photographer. He's just agreed to download his entire Bosnian archive into my computer.'

'You should be here. Things are moving fast.'

'Yeah. I heard from Nathan Lyne. Look, I may have hit the jackpot with this stuff. I'm bringing it back.'

'Come to the office. There have been changes.'

'Yeah, Nathan told me that, too.'

'You don't seem surprised.'

'I'm not. They shouldn't have messed with you. Though I have to say I didn't fancy your chances yesterday.'

'You were right: they fired me.'

'Tossers. Now look, I'm kind of busy here. Why don't you call Hélène Guignal. She's the bird who was in Sarajevo. I think she's good. Really, I've got a feeling about her.'

She dialled Nato headquarters in Brussels five times before getting through to a colleague of Guignal's in the Press Office who said Hélène was on vacation. Pretending to be a spokesman from the Ministry of Defence who needed Guignal urgently, Herrick managed to extract a mobile number that would raise her on the island of Skiathos. She tried this, but the phone was turned off.

She returned to the Chief's office. Teckman looked distracted for a second, then leapt from his desk. 'Come with me.'

A Jaguar with outriders took them to Battersea Heliport, where Guthrie was already waiting with Barbara Markham and her deputy. The helicopter took less than ten minutes to touch down at Northolt, near to the Bunker's entrance.

'Do you know, I've never seen this operation,' he murmured to Herrick as they descended in the lift.

'You didn't need to,' she said.

'Perhaps if I had come here I would have seen what made you so annoyed,' he smiled.

When they had reached the Bunker, Teckman strode into the main space and nodded to the people he recognised. Nathan Lyne rose from his desk and came over to Herrick. 'So, Isis. I see no Vigo. I see Richard Spelling twisting slowly in the wind. And here you are with all the great panjandrums of the British security establishment. What the hell have you been up to?'

'Not much.'

He grinned. 'Just in case you're feeling bad about Walter . . .'

'I wasn't.'

'He knew you were on that island with those two men. Your communications traffic made that clear.'

'Did you know about it, Nathan?'

'Of course not. I had no idea where you were. Even Andy Dolph wouldn't tell me. But you're safe – that's what matters – and your stock's risen. Things have turned out well for you.'

'But we lost one of the suspects. This wasn't just any old suspect. He was really important. And we don't have much time.' She noticed that the Chief had sat down in front of one of the larger screens. 'Come and talk him through it all,' she said. 'He's going to need you over the next few days.'

The Chief shook his hand without rising. 'I've heard about you. I gather you were responsible for sending Isis to Albania, Mr Lyne. That was a very good decision. Now tell me what I'm looking at.'

Lyne pulled up a chair and went through the screens devoted to the nine remaining suspects. Most were live feeds from inside and around the apartments where they were living. Ramzi Zaman, the Moroccan, could be seen passing through the field of the camera, preparing a meal in his little kitchen in Toulouse. Lasenne Hadaya, the edgy Algerian, was seated on a couch, aimlessly throwing a ball into the air and catching it. In Budapest, Hadi Dahhak, a diminutive Yemeni with a hooked nose, was seen arguing with two men over a newspaper. Lyne said that all they ever talked about was football. He ran a piece of recent film which showed the Syrian suspect, Hafiz al Bakr, strolling in a park with one of his helpers.

The story was the same with the Saudis in Rome and Sarajevo, the Pakistani in Bradford, and the Egyptian in Stockholm. Each man was aimlessly frittering away his days. There were no breaks in the routine, no sense of imminent action, no sign of preparation. Lyne took the Chief through some of the background research but Herrick could tell he was losing interest, and he suddenly left Lyne's side and bounded up the stairs to the glass box where Spelling, Jim Collins and Colonel Plume of the National Security Agency were talking. A few minutes later he called for all the staff to assemble at the bottom of the stairs.

'We have a problem of interpretation, ladies and gentlemen, and I need your help on it. The men you have been watching over these last few weeks will in all probability be under lock and key within a very short time. We have other intelligence to indicate that there may be some kind of action by the end of the week, so obviously we can't allow these characters to be on the loose any longer. Before this happens, I want you to consider what their plan is. Why have they been put in place with such elaborate care? What is the meaning of it? I don't want proof, I want your thoughts, the wildest ideas that may have occurred to you over the last few weeks.'

Herrick looked around and saw a number of anxious expressions. This was something new to RAPTOR personnel.

'We are pursuing certain lines,' continued the Chief, 'which take the investigation further, but I do think we should try to work out what this is all about, don't you?'

There was an embarrassed silence and then Joe Lapping put up his arm.

'Yes, Mr Lapping,' said the Chief.

'Maybe it's about nothing,' said Lapping. Collins and Spelling looked up into the great black space above them.

'Perhaps you'd care to develop that idea,' said the Chief.

'I don't mean to take anything from Isis Herrick's achievement in spotting what was going on at Heathrow. I was there, and it was a really good piece of work. But maybe – just maybe – we were meant to see it. After all, we were led there by one of the suspects who hung around outside Terminal Three in a most public fashion. It was almost as if he was making sure we didn't miss him.'

Herrick realised he could be right. It was unlikely that Lapping would have heard about her testing Rahe's DNA against the corpse in Lebanon, so he wasn't falling behind the latest theory.

'But you are aware,' said the Chief, 'that the orthodox view on the events of that day portrays the assassination attempt on Vice-Admiral Norquist as a strategic diversion. What would be the point of such a strategy if the suspects were all part of some kind of hoax?'

Lapping cleared his throat. 'I haven't been involved much in the

922

operations down here, but always at the back of my mind it seemed that these men were acting like the Stepford Wives. They just drink coffee, read the papers, sleep, cook, do the shopping, watch TV, play soccer. They don't look as if they're going to do anything.'

'He may be right, sir,' Lyne chipped in. 'A double deception to draw our attention away from another action, or simply waste all our resources, is not out of the question. Al-Qaeda has vast resources, by our estimates three- to five-hundred-million-dollar revenues each year, mainly from Saudi princes and businessmen. A tiny fraction of this goes into terrorist actions. About ninety per cent is used in setting up networks and infrastructure. They could afford to string us along on an operation without having any material end in sight.'

'*The Subtle Ruse,*' said Lapping.

'And what's that?' asked the Chief. Every face turned to Lapping, who despite his confidence in matters of scholarship, was unused to public performance. Herrick saw his Adam's apple move up and down before he spoke.

'A book written a hundred years before Machiavelli by an anonymous Arab author – probably an Egyptian living in the time of the Grand Emir Sa'd al-Din Sunbul. It uses examples from Arab literature and seeks to edify the reader with stories of ruses, stratagems, guile and deceptions taken from different walks of life. In essence, it instructs you how to outwit your opponent and in turn be alert to his ploys.'

'I see. You're not suggesting this was directly taken from the book,' said the Chief, 'but you are saying . . .'

'That a man who had studied ancient Arab literature would know the book and have learned some of its lessons.'

Herrick remembered that Joe Lapping had been asked to research a man with a literary background who might have fought for the Bosniaks in the civil war. And Rahe, of course, spent most of his days in a bookshop. Certainly it was a suggestion that stood up to examination, but the more important idea was that Rahe had led them to Heathrow and hung about in front of various security cameras. She was appalled that she had not thought of it herself.

The Chief was nodding. 'That's an interesting theory. Anyone have any other ideas?'

There were a number of tentative suggestions which he dismissed politely, then in his most solicitous manner he told the assembled intelligence workers they'd done a fine job which would undoubtedly make the arrest of the men a lot simpler. When they began to disperse to their desks, still looking mystified, he told Lapping he would be required at Vauxhall Cross that afternoon and asked Lyne to be there on the following day. 'I'm sure you can be let off school this once,' he said with a wink to Lyne. 'You do speak Arabic, don't you?'

Lyne said yes, he did.

They arrived back at SIS headquarters just past 2.00 p.m. Herrick went straight to her desk and called the mobile number for Hélène Guignal. Mademoiselle Guignal answered drowsily. In the background Herrick heard the unmistakable sound of waves breaking and water running up a beach. She explained what she wanted, but Guignal said she was inclined to postpone the conversation until she was back at her desk in Brussels.

'Fine,' said Herrick. 'We can put a request through the Secretary-General of Nato for a formal interview on these matters by Nato security personnel. This is important and the United Kingdom *does* require your help.'

'Who are you?'

'It's enough that you know I am investigating an international terrorist cell and that I believe you hold information which may be useful, in fact, critical to my inquiries.'

The woman suddenly became cooperative.

'One of my colleagues says you knew some of the foreign Muslims who defended Sarajevo during the siege?'

'Yes, I lived with one. How can I help?'

'We're interested in two men, Sammi Loz and Karim Khan.'

'Ah yes, I knew them both, but not well. They were the medics, no? The ones that came out with supplies then stayed. Those guys?'

'Yes,' said Herrick. 'Would you mind telling me the name of the man who you lived with?'

'Hassan Simic. He was of mixed parentage but was brought up as a Muslim. He liaised with the foreign Muslims – the *jihadistes*. It was a tough job. They always wanted to do what they wanted to do. They kept themselves apart. They were not like the Bosnian Muslims.'

'Can I talk to Mr Simic?'

'He's dead. He died in ninety-five.'

'I'm sorry.'

'Don't apologise. He was born to die young. A very beautiful man but *un sauvage* – you know? If he had not been killed, he would have been taken to the Hague for war crimes.'

'How much did you see Khan and Loz?'

'I met them about four or five times. A few of the men used to come to our apartment when there were breaks in the fighting. I had food, you see. Not much, but more than they had. We made big pasta dinners. Karim was a favourite of mine. *Très charmant ... très sympathique.*'

'What about Loz?'

'*Un peu plus masqué, comprenez vous? Dissimulé.*'

'And you were working for press agencies then?'

'*Oui, l'Agence France Presse.*'

'The other men – the friends of Hassan. What were their names?'

There was a pause.

'Do you remember Yahya?' asked Herrick.

'Yahya? No, I do not remember this man. Who was Yahya? What did he look like?'

'He would have been in his late twenties, early thirties. A short man, of Algerian origin. We believe he was a very private man. Inconspicuous. He may have been some kind of scholar before he went to Bosnia. Perhaps he even studied in Sarajevo before the Islamic Institute was shelled. We are not sure.'

'And it is this man you are really interested in?'

'Yes, it is possible that he used the name Youssef. Karim and Sammi used to call him The Poet. That was their nickname for him before he became a friend of theirs.'

'Maybe . . . *Ah oui, oui, oui!* I know the man you mean, but his name is not Yahya. The man I think of was called Yaqub.'

'Yaqub?' said Herrick doubtfully. 'Are you sure?'

'*Oui, un autre prophète.*'

'How do you mean?'

'So, we have three names for this man and they are all the Arab names for prophets in the Bible.' Her tone was of someone being forced to talk to an idiot. 'Youssef – or Joseph, is the son of the Prophet Yaqub – or Jacob! And you mentioned Yahya, who is the Prophet John, son of the Prophet Zachariah. This is obvious. He is using *nommes de guerre* from the Bible. One day he must use the name Zachariah. That is logical. No?'

Herrick made a rapid note of this.

'And you know he was Algerian?'

'Yes, he comes from Oran. I know this because my father served in Algeria. I have been to Oran.'

'And this man was bookish and withdrawn, somebody who kept to himself?'

'He came to the apartment once with Hassan – never the others. He was a mystery to them. But he was polite and well-mannered. There is little else that I remember about him.'

Herrick hung up, thinking that it was a pity Hélène Guignal was not at her desk in Brussels to receive an emailed file of one of the images of Rahe at Heathrow. That way Herrick would be sure of an instant no or yes in her attempt to tie Rahe with Yahya or Yaqub. She got a picture out of the files nevertheless and put it in a plain white envelope, thinking it was bound to be useful over the next few days. Then, with her notes of the Guignal conversation, she went to find Dolph, who she heard had arrived back from Hertfordshire.

He was with Lapping and Sarre in one of the conference rooms near the Chief's office with his laptop fixed to a projector. They were sprawled about the room watching the photographer's archive of the Bosnian civil war; frame after frame of haggard faces staring from fox-holes and ruined buildings. There were men pleading for mercy, women dashing across the street, barefoot children wandering around in snowy craters and Serb gunners coolly observing their targets below.

'This is all stuff from ninety-three and ninety-four,' said Dolph, after he had given Isis a brief kiss and welcomed her back. 'He's organised it by date rather than subject. He spent the early winter of ninety-three on one of two fronts manned by the Mujahideen Brigade. So we should be nearly there.'

Herrick reminded herself that none of them knew Rahe was now a prime suspect. Lapping had got near the truth of the matter with his observations about Rahe's behaviour at the airport, but he hadn't gone the extra few yards to the logical conclusion. More important, they did not know there was now some urgency to find Yahya and Loz. The Chief had been most specific that she should not talk about this.

After forty-five minutes fruitlessly peering at all the group shots from the front, they came to the end of the relevant part of the archive.

'This photographer,' said Herrick, 'did he remember anyone like Khan or Loz?'

Dolph shook his head.

'Or anyone else significant?'

Dolph shook his head. 'I could do with a pint. What do you say we treat ourselves over the river, lads?'

Herrick asked if they had seen any groups of soldiers before she came into the room.

'A few.'

'I'd like to go back over those pictures.'

'Why?' asked Dolph a little truculently.

'Because *you* don't know what we're looking for.'

'We're looking for Khan and this guy Sammi Loz.'

'But none of you has seen them in the flesh and there may be someone else important in the photographs. This man was taking pictures throughout the crucial period.'

Dolph peered into his screen to locate the relevant files while Lapping went to get them all coffee.

At length Dolph found the photographs from mid-November 1993 showing a group of about a dozen men moving a burnt-out truck. The ground was covered with a light dusting of snow and the sky above was bright. Ice sparkled in the trees. Their faces were turned to the ground and in profile as they put their weight behind the truck. With the shadows playing across the snow, the energy expressed in the men's bodies and the interesting form of the wrecked vehicle, it was easy to see why the photographer's eye had been attracted to the scene, and why he'd kept his finger on the shutter button through eight frames. Dolph sped through the images, almost animating the sequence. At Herrick's insistence they went back over them again slowly. At the fourth image, she shouted. 'Stop there.' She went to the wall and pointed to a man's head which had lifted into the light and faced the camera. 'Can you enlarge it? Here, the area at the front of the car.'

Dolph highlighted the area with his mouse and made a couple of keystrokes. 'Who the fuck is that?' he asked as the picture sprang onto the wall.

'That,' she said, withdrawing the photograph from her envelope and slapping it against the wall, 'is Youssef Rahe, otherwise known as Yahya or Yaqub. Take a look for yourselves.'

Dolph got up and peered at the two pictures. It took him a few seconds to understand the significance of the match. 'Isis, you're a bloody marvel. He's the main man.' He thought for a moment. 'Everything that's happened this morning with Spelling and Vigo is because you knew that already. You were expecting to find Rahe here – or at least you were looking for him.'

She nodded.

'Fuck my Aunt Ethel's goat.'

They all approached the wall and made comparisons between the two pictures. 'And look here,' she said. 'The scrawny one with the beard. I'm pretty sure that's Sammi Loz.'

'If you say so,' said Dolph. ' Is Khan there too?'

She examined each face in turn. 'No.'

Dolph's shrewd eyes sought hers again. 'How did you find out about Rahe?'

'The bookstore,' said Sarre. 'You got something that night, didn't you?'

'Christ, you're a piece of work.' said Dolph. 'How long have you known?'

'Since this morning we have known that Rahe was not killed in Lebanon. The body belonged to someone else.' She explained about the samples she'd sent to the laboratory and the recording of Sammi Loz talking to Khan which gave her the name of Yahya.

'So all the crucial connections took place in Bosnia,' said Lapping.

'Yes, which is why we need to work out who these people are.' She jabbed her finger on the faces of the other men. 'We should get all the shots blown up, each face digitally enhanced.'

'But I can tell you now,' said Sarre, 'that none of these men came through Heathrow that day. I know their faces off by heart.'

'And that is rather the point,' said Lapping.

'Behold, ladies and gentleman,' said Dolph, 'the viscous matter that passes for Joe Lapping's brain is at last on stream.'

'But you didn't get there Dolphy,' returned Lapping. 'Isis left you in a cloud of dust.'

'Fuck you Joe, just because every hooker in Sarajevo tried on Mummy's Christmas pyjamas.'

'I hate to be a dampener,' said Herrick, unable to laugh, 'but we don't have time for this. We have to find out who these people are. If necessary, bring the photographer to London and fly that woman Guignal from Skiathos. We need all the help we can get. Anyone who was there – journalists, aid workers, soldiers. Get the Security Services to pull them in and give them a slide show. And we will need to compare these men with all the photographs we have on file.'

'What's the ticking clock?' asked Dolph.

'We don't know,' she said.

The three men exchanged looks, unnerved by the urgency in her voice and the undisguised command in her manner.

28

The operation to arrest the nine suspects would begin in the early hours of Wednesday morning, giving the security forces across Europe about thirty hours to prepare themselves. Vast amounts of surveillance detail, much of it merely proving minor crimes and association, was already hurtling from the Bunker to intelligence services in Paris, Rome, Copenhagen, Stockholm, Budapest and Sarajevo. With this went the names, addresses and photographs of the members of the helper cells. In its final hours, everything RAPTOR had hoarded and secreted was unloaded with abandon.

By the time Herrick went with Colin Guthrie to the Chief's office late on Monday afternoon, ninety-four people, including twenty-three female helpers, were on the arrest list. The Chief informed them that local agencies were gradually taking over the job of monitoring the suspects, though in some cases it was clear they were already familiar with the routines of the suspects as well as their Anglo-American watchers. The surveillance equipment installed by Collection and SIS was kept running so that each country could tap into the live feeds still flickering twenty-four hours a day deep underground at Northolt.

The US President and the British Prime Minister had been seized by an unusual spirit of international cooperation. RAPTOR would now be presented as an initial inquiry into what one diplomat termed the 'morphology of terrorist cells', an exercise whose purpose was to benefit all Western allies. To disguise the unwavering focus on the men who had passed through Heathrow, it was decided, principally by the French, British and American governments, that the dragnet should also include suspects who were not members of the Heathrow group. For this reason the Dutch, Belgian and Spanish governments were brought into the operation and asked to arrest people they had been observing independently of RAPTOR. The Spanish government which, with the French, had in the past mounted among the most successful operations against al-Qaeda and associated North African groups, said it would arrest three men living in La Rioja; the French opted for a man in Marseilles; the

929

Dutch and Belgians had any number of suspects who could be hauled in for questioning, if not actual arrest.

All hope of a publicity blackout had quickly been dropped. The number of people was far too large to contain the news, so it was decided they should make the most of the situation by issuing a joint statement by the Americans and major European governments about the unprecedented cooperation between intelligence services. The Russians were informed on the grounds that the Syrian suspect in Copenhagen, Hafiz al Bakr, had served in Chechnya and was connected with a group who had planned an attack against a Russian embassy.

'It's interesting how these things turn out,' said the Chief. 'You know, it's my firm belief that the idea of keeping this to ourselves was just as much ours as the Americans. A bit of sucking up.'

'Walter's bid to get back in the saddle,' said Guthrie.

'I suppose,' the Chief mused, without sign of malice. 'I must say he made a bit of a fool of himself with Youssef Rahe, given that he never acquired much from the man. Of course we'll need to debrief Vigo as soon as possible. Before we move on the bookshop.'

'You're going to search Rahe's shop?' asked Herrick.

'Yes, before the other arrests, sometime tomorrow evening. But I don't want the scene fouled up by a lot of heavy-handed Special Branch. I've arranged that you will go through the place the moment the police move in. But first I want you to see Vigo.'

'What about the photographs from Bosnia?'

'We'll hold off on that until tomorrow morning. For the moment it's enough that you've established Rahe was in Bosnia. We're ninety-nine per cent sure he is the man referred to as Yahya and you've got a picture of him from the period. That's not a bad day's work, Isis.'

She nodded, aware that the energy was suddenly draining from her.

The Chief noticed the expression in her eyes. 'I know you've had a time of it, but I need you for at least the next six days. Try to get some sleep before tomorrow. Don't spend more than an hour with Vigo.' He handed her an address in Holland Park. 'Take Harland with you. He knows how to handle the bugger.'

'Harland?'

'Yes, he should be at Brown's by now and I've asked him to help out.'

'Harland?' she said stupidly again. 'What's he doing here? I thought he was in the Middle East.'

'No, he's here.' The pale eyes narrowed slightly. 'You're not there to parry with Vigo. Just tell him we need a complete account of his relations with Rahe. If he proves difficult, mention that one way or another we will press for a prosecution.'

Normally Herrick would have relished the return match, but she left Vauxhall Cross without much enthusiasm and only when she found

Harland in a jaunty mood in the hotel bar did her spirits lift slightly. It had been a matter of days since she'd seen him climb into the little boat on the Nile, but it seemed like weeks, particularly as Harland appeared so different. She asked why he was looking so pleased with himself.

'I'm not,' he said, 'It's just that life seems suddenly full of possibility.'

'I know you were on the road to Damascus. Did you get God or something? What happened?'

'Nothing I'm going to tell you about, and you needn't look so bloody sour, Isis. Let's have a drink. You're looking a bit part-worn.'

He turned and ordered two Soho Cosmopolitans and just in case the man needed reminding, rattled through the ingredients. 'One measure of citron vodka, one measure of Stolichnaya oranj vodka, cointreau, cranberry juice, fresh lime juice and a twist of lemon. Plus two very cold glasses.'

They drank the cocktails with ceremony. When they'd finished, Harland said, 'And now for bloody Vigo.'

They took the Tube to Holland Park with perspiring office workers and walked up Holland Park Avenue. The evening was warm. Harland removed his jacket and hooked it over his shoulder with one finger. Herrick noticed how young he was looking, even though his hair seemed more grey than brown in the early evening sunlight.

They approached the impressive entrance to Vigo's double-fronted house. Harland pressed the bell for several seconds. The buzzer sounded and they were let in to find a nervous but perfectly attired middle-aged woman in the hallway.

'Davina, this is Isis Herrick,' said Harland. 'We've come to see Walter.'

'He's expecting you,' said Davina Vigo. 'He thought you might like drinks in the garden.'

Vigo was sitting in a slice of sunlight underneath the boughs of a spreading chestnut tree. He regarded them with a baleful look and limply gestured them to chairs. Herrick noticed that Davina remained standing in the French windows with her arms folded apprehensively. He offered them a Pimms cup which they both declined.

'Isis is here to ask you some questions.'

'And you Bobby, why are you here?'

'Because I am.'

'But . . . ?'

'But nothing, Walter. As far I'm concerned, you should be in jail. If you'd been prosecuted for the last business, none of this would have happened. You're within an inch of being arrested now, so . . .'

'On what grounds?'

'Aiding and abetting a burglary of Isis's house, for one thing. But that's only a start. They want your blood, Walter. What we need are straight answers to our questions and, more than that, we need you to volunteer everything in your mind, every tiny scrap of information, every faint suspicion that you possess about Youssef Rahe, also known as Yahya.'

Again the slow-motion blink. 'Yes, of course,' said Vigo. 'Where do you want to start?'

'How did you meet him?' asked Herrick.

'At a sale of early Arab manuscripts. Rahe was there to look at them before they went into private hands. I saw him at the preview. We talked.'

'Who made the first move?' asked Herrick.

'I forget.'

'In the light of what you know now, do you think you were targeted?' asked Herrick.

'Well, obviously,' he said disagreeably. 'But at the time I thought he might be useful in understanding the GIA – the Groupe Islamique Armé. The Islamists had taken their fight to France. We felt we were looking at the Islamic equivalent of the Cambodian massacre. He seemed to know quite a few people involved.'

'Sure he did,' said Herrick. 'He'd been in Bosnia with all of them.'

Vigo sighed. 'It's easy with hindsight to say that, but our job does involve taking calculated risks about people.'

'And as you got closer, he began to open up,' said Herrick, brushing the remark aside. 'Did he give you anything worthwhile?'

'Yes, there were names – names that were useful in the round-ups after September eleven.'

'And you plugged in and heard about the people passing through his shop, people asking for help in London. That sort of thing?'

'Yes, the information was always accurate.'

'How much checking of his background went on?'

'As much as was necessary. The story about his upbringing, his job, where he lived in Algiers, all that seemed to tally.' Vigo's manner was now markedly less cowed.

'And you got his brother and family out?' said Herrick. 'Where are they?'

'In England. They were granted asylum.'

'Did you meet the brother? Can you describe him? Where does he live?'

'In Bristol, under the name of Jamil Rahe. He's younger than his brother. Tall, a little overweight, an engineer by training.'

Herrick took out the envelope from a bag and dropped a selection of shots of Rahe and Sammi Loz in Bosnia into his lap. 'Is the man you know as Youssef Rahe here?' Harland looked at the picture but said nothing as he registered Sammi Loz.

Vigo pulled a pair of reading glasses from his shirt pocket and examined the picture a little wearily. 'Yes ... I see Rahe.'

'Anyone else?' said Herrick briskly.

He looked through the pictures and then handed them back, tapping the top image. 'That's the man I know as his brother – Jamil Rahe.'

Herrick glanced at the figure in a balaclava, pulled out her mobile and phoned Dolph, who said Jamil Rahe would be added to the arrest list.

'Let's wait,' she said. 'This may concern a murder charge, as well. He's important.'

She snapped the phone shut. 'A man of very similar appearance coordinated the switch at Heathrow, having come to an arrangement with a washroom attendant in Terminal Three named Ahmad Ahktar. Ahktar and his family died in a fire after the switch. The point is that we have witnesses who saw him watch the planes that day. Also, he appears to have shown interest when Norquist's escort left the airport.'

Vigo said nothing.

'About Youssef Rahe,' she said. 'In the last twelve months, what kind of information was he passing to you?'

'Much the same as before. Things he heard from the Arab community in Bayswater and Edgware Road areas. Useful material about mosques – who worshipped where, the financial support of certain charities, here and abroad. It all helped. Then he was approached by a group, mostly Saudi and Yemeni in origin.'

'And you encouraged him to be recruited?'

'Naturally. It seemed a very good opportunity.'

'When was this?'

'Summer of 2001.'

'And he told you about the website, the screensavers that contain a daily message?'

Vigo nodded. 'That's what you were looking at in the shop, I assume.'

'It would help if you'd just answer my questions,' she said. Vigo stared back at her and she became aware of something stir in the shadows of his personality.

'I wouldn't take that tone with me, if I were you.'

Harland got up and crouched by Vigo's chair. 'Walter, you should know that I'm here on the off-chance that I get to beat the living shit out of you. Otherwise I would not waste my time. Now, answer Isis's question, or by this time tomorrow you'll find yourself on remand in Wandsworth Prison.'

'The screensaver,' she said. 'You were monitoring the messages coming in each day?'

'You forget, I was no longer part of the Service by then.'

'So who was?'

'GCHQ and the Security Services.'

'But there was something different about the information on Norquist's travel arrangements?'

'I gather it was in a double encryption,' replied Vigo.

'We know the Israelis had access to this particular service,' said Harland. 'How long had it been going?'

Herrick wondered how the hell he knew that, but let Vigo answer.

'Two years or so. I'm not sure. You have to remember that once I had handed over Rahe to SIS, I had very little contact, although I did see him on the book-dealing circuit.'

'When the tip about Norquist came in, you were asked to check it?'

He nodded. 'Yes, I called him and he phoned me back on the day of the switch. Before he left for the airport.'

'Tell me about him,' said Herrick. 'What kind of man is Youssef Rahe?'

'Very able,' Vigo replied. 'A true scholar in his own field. A good father and husband too, I would guess. He has none of the obvious appearance of a fundamentalist. He goes to the mosque infrequently, doesn't pray five times a day, is relaxed and liberal in his attitudes.'

'Where do you think he went?' she asked.

'Beyond Beirut? Naturally, I have no idea.'

She sat back and laid her phone on the table deliberately. 'I'd like that drink now,' she said.

Vigo poured the Pimms, holding back the mint leaves and fruit in the jug with a silver spoon.

'What would you do if you were in our position?' she asked quietly. 'We have two or three main suspects who are rich and mobile. They plan months, maybe years ahead and have a very sophisticated understanding of the way we work. What would you do? Where would you go?'

'There are two options, clearly. You can make it very difficult for them to move by releasing their photographs and all the information you have on them. But that may not deter anything planned to happen this week. So I would be inclined to risk revealing nothing whatsoever and hope to trace them. Sammi Loz probably thinks we believe him dead, and neither Youssef or Jamil Rahe know you're onto them. So I would use that slight advantage.'

'How?'

He breathed deeply and looked away to a column of gnats dancing in the sunlight. A blackbird sang out some way off. 'Well, there's no obvious way. But if Youssef is unaware that we're onto him, Jamil also thinks he's safe. You say you believe Jamil is a major figure in the Heathrow plot. I suggest you find him and start by monitoring his phone. If an attack of some kind is expected, then Jamil will be part of it. From what you say, he's murdered before – his own people. Then there is the mosque. You say Jamil made contact with this attendant from Heathrow at the mosque. I take it you're referring to the Cable Road mosque in Belsize Park, the one attended by Youssef Rahe and which is now believed to be under the influence of Sheik Abu Muhsana?'

Herrick nodded.

Vigo talked on, unaffected by Harland's hostility, and began to adopt the professorial manner he had used with Southern Group Three back in the Bunker. At length, even Harland was listening with grudging nods. They discussed ways of prodding Jamil to make contact. He added that this should all happen before the raids on the continent, so that it appeared to come out of the blue, but would be sufficiently menacing for Jamil to break cover. 'These men are not without fear,' he said. 'As Seneca said, "Fear always recoils on those who seek to inspire it; no one who is feared is unafraid himself".'

'Let's keep to the point,' said Harland.

'I find Seneca is always to the point. It's a consolation that we experience nothing in the way of anger, failure, disappointment and sheer bad luck that has not been explored two thousand years ago.'

'I can see why you're reading him,' said Harland. 'I think it's highly unlikely the Chief will want anything more to do with you, other than arranging for you to be tried.'

'We shall see,' he said, studying Isis. 'After all, we've all been duped and made to look fools, have we not? Now, I know Bobby that you and I have never seen eye to eye; that we have a history, as my wife says. But I would suggest that we are the best people to be working on this. I know Youssef and Jamil Rahe, and you two both know Sammi Loz. We're the natural front line – the only front line. And with your contacts in Mossad, we should make an admirable team.'

Harland flinched enough for Herrick to notice. 'I agree with Harland,' she said. 'It's not going to happen.'

'Well, give it some thought overnight. If I don't hear from you or the Chief tomorrow I will understand.'

Herrick and Harland rose.

'And please, no more threats. You know as well as I do they can't put me on trial. Any more talk of this nature and I will make life extremely difficult for this government and several past governments. Tell Teckman that. He knows I mean it.'

'I suppose that's how you wrapped your coils around Spelling,' said Harland.

Vigo got up heavily and made towards a bed of hostas. 'I will expect to hear from you tomorrow.'

'One other thing,' Herrick called after him. 'I want you to admit that you had my house searched by Marenglen's men.'

Vigo stopped in his tracks. 'We wanted to know what you had got, Isis. We knew you weren't just looking at the computer. I think you'll find the Deputy Director was also aware of the need to find out. You could say it was an official operation.'

'What, with armed Albanian pimps?'

'Needs must,' said Vigo, turning back to his hostas.

29

They were in Holland Park Avenue again. Herrick snapped the phone shut after talking to one of the Chief's two assistants.

'He's going to call me later,' she said to Harland. 'They don't know when. Look, we don't want to be in a restaurant when he rings. Would you mind if I made dinner at my place? I've got a sort of garden – we can eat outside.'

Harland shrugged pleasantly and they went to a shop nearby to buy wine and some rump steak.

'Vigo is such a complete and utter bastard,' she said as they left the shop. 'I mean, what's his game? What does he want?'

'Influence,' said Harland, flagging down a cab. 'He likes pulling the strings without anyone seeing it's him. He likes the aura of power and he wants acceptance – the clubs, shooting parties, the best stretches on the Tweed; all that bollocks. In one way he's just an unrequited snob, both socially and intellectually.'

'But he is sharp,' she said, as they climbed into the cab.

'Oh yes, very, but somehow that makes him more disappointed. All that superior talent and where is he now? Desperate to have some minor role in the final stages of this operation.'

'You think Teckman will go for it?' she asked.

'Yes, he expected him to make the offer of help. He reads Vigo like a newspaper headline because Vigo wants everything that the Chief has acquired effortlessly. Teckman understands his longings.'

They were silent for the remainder of the journey and watched London slide by, bathed in a soft, crepuscular light.

When they arrived, Herrick went to change and put Harland to work on her terrace, clearing dead leaves and wiping down the chairs and table.

The garden was a triumph of neglect. Where a more careful gardener would have tidied and pruned and scraped away at the ground, Herrick had simply bought a collection of shrubs, vines and climbing roses one afternoon five years before, planted them and left them to their own devices, with the result that the roses had spread over the bushes and reached into two apple trees next door, closing off the garden to inspection from neighbouring houses.

Her attitude to cooking was similarly uncomplicated. As Harland drank a glass of wine outside, he watched her through the kitchen window as she threw together a salad, then briskly dealt with the steak and mushrooms. She had it all ready in under twenty minutes and brought it out to him.

'Have you heard from your father?' he asked.

'Yesterday. We're planning a trip when this is over.' She tore off the end of the baguette and began to work at the steak. 'Actually, I can hardly wait. You know they bloody well fired me this morning. I was pushed out of the building by a creature called Cecil.'

'But you were seen to be right – vindication is rare in your job.'

'I haven't even been officially reinstated yet.'

'How's his wrist?'

'Just sprained. He was lucky. It was his right hand, so he wouldn't have been able to paint and that would have killed him.'

'You're pretty close to the old man,' he said.

She picked up her glass and thought about it. 'Yes and no. Proximate in the sense that we have led our lives together without my mother for so long – yes; intimate in the sense that I know what's going on with him and he with me – no.'

'You rub along.'

She smelled the night air and said, 'God, I'm glad to be back,' then paused. 'These things are so bloody difficult to talk about, you know. People expect love to be one of a number of standard and recognisable varieties, but it isn't like that. The relationship – God, I hate the word – is as individual as the people, and that's all there is to it.'

'But you'll miss him.' He saw the look pass across her face and he wished he hadn't said it.

'Yep,' she said. 'He's exceptional, untrammelled. That's what I'll miss – the idea that there will be no one alive who is quite so independent and, well, strange.'

Harland remembered Eva looking after Hanna Rath in the Tel Aviv apartment, the protectiveness that had made her leave him.

'You want to talk about this personal stuff,' she continued, 'then tell me what happened in the Middle East and why you're so frisky suddenly?'

'I'm not.'

'Well, tell me how you knew the Israelis were deciphering the messages to Rahe from that website – the one that trumpeted Norquist's arrival in London. Who the hell told you about that? I mean, I've only known about Youssef Rahe since this morning, so how did you get onto this so quickly?' She fixed him with an acute look that let Harland know he couldn't be evasive.

He set down his knife and fork and told her about the strained meeting with Eva at the Playlands Hotel. Then about Sammi Loz's relationship with Norquist and Eva's appearance on the Heathrow security film. At one point during his account, Herrick darted to take one of the two remaining steaks and proceeded to consume it at a speed that temporarily put Harland off his stride. He shook his head in disbelief. 'Have the other one,' he said sarcastically. 'You obviously need it.' A very short time afterwards, her hand moved to the dish to take the third steak.

'So the upshot,' he continued, still shaking his head, 'is that Mossad were watching this thing very closely and were not surprised when Norquist was killed. They know about Sammi Loz, but they have no idea about Youssef and Jamil Rahe.'

'Which is the important one – Rahe or Loz?' she asked. 'Who gives the orders?'

'Youssef Rahe – everything points to it,' he said.

'But on the face of it you would say Loz. He's the one with all the money and he's got the better contacts both in New York and the Middle East, to say nothing of the Balkans.'

'So what? Rahe is better hidden. He's been the strategist all along.' He sighed. 'Look, Isis, I don't have the stamina to think about this any more.'

'There's something I don't get,' she said, sitting on the edge of her chair. 'Why are you still working for Teckman on this? Now that RAPTOR is winding up and Teckman has got his job back, we're hardly short of people. Why aren't you floating about with Benjamin Jaidi in the Middle East? I mean, I'm glad you're here and all that, but why? What are you doing?'

'Thanks,' he said, 'but I have to tell you you're becoming remorseless.' He reached over and touched her face, without thinking about it. For a second she looked startled, then let her head collapse into his hand and smiled with a mixture of shyness and devilment.

'What do you think about all this,' she asked. 'The clash of civilisations – Islam versus Christendom?'

'Christ, I don't bloody well know.'

'But don't you want to understand what we're in the middle of? How we got here?' she asked.

'All I know is that there are lunatics, envious of Western technology, resentful of Western wealth, who believe that the solution to humanity's problems is to drag us back into some barbaric state on the lines of the Taleban regime.'

'But you're not anti-Muslim?'

He shook his head. 'No, but I fail to see why Islam hasn't produced proper democracies. If people can begin to participate in democracies in South America there seems no reason why they shouldn't in the Arab countries.'

He noticed she was energised by the prospect of argument. She leaned forward, eyes suddenly glistening. 'And yet a democracy might produce a regime like the Taleban. The fact that people have the vote doesn't guarantee a social democratic system. So you could argue that it is the religion which is at fault, that it is inherently expansionist and intolerant. You could even say that the precepts of Islam are incompatible with democracy and *therefore* human rights, because only democracy can guarantee human rights.'

Harland hadn't seen this side of Isis Herrick before. He liked it, but felt that he was being sluggish. 'Then you make the fact of religious belief the belligerent act and that's very hard for a true democrat to accept.'

She smiled, her mind moving faster than she knew. 'But surely there's no difference between a person who holds doctrinaire political views, like the old style communist, and an Islamic fundamentalist. Their basic positions, whether involving a political creed or a religious one, are anti-democratic and so present a threat which all true democrats must oppose with equal force.'

'That's quite a right-wing stance, Isis. I assumed you were an out-and-out liberal.'

Suddenly the exhilaration in her eyes was tempered. She drank some wine and her gaze swivelled to the dark. 'I am a liberal, but when I was watching Sammi Loz the other night, I saw pure, visceral hatred in his face. He pays a lot of lipservice to Bosnia and the Palestinians, but I somehow didn't think that was his priority. There was an element of savagery which I simply can't contend with.'

He moved to touch her face again.

'In other circumstances, I would say this was rather romantic,' she said.

'Why, what's wrong with the circumstances?' His fingers splayed backwards into her hair.

'I'm sorry, it *is* romantic. Yes it is. To my amazement I find myself very happy to be with you here in my manky little garden. It's taken me by surprise, that's all.'

'Good,' said Harland, not really knowing what he intended. 'Your garden isn't manky, and you are exceptionally attractive – uniquely attractive, in my view – although it's clear you don't feel it.'

She stiffened in his hands. 'Don't say that. That's what Loz said to me.'

'I know . . . I know about what happened to you. Philip Sarre told the Chief.'

'How odd that he should tell you.'

'He was concerned.' He stopped. 'Anyway, you haven't said what's wrong with the circumstances.'

'It's just that I feel we ought to be doing something to work this thing out. Get Rahe. Find Loz. Look at Dolph's photographs . . . you know.'

'But you need rest.'

She put her lips to the palm of his hand for a second, then lifted her head. 'Why are you in London? Aren't you meant to be with Jaidi in the Middle East?'

'He's gone back to New York. Things didn't work out in Syria.'

'But that wasn't really my question. Why are you still working on this?'

Harland withdrew his hand, mild exasperation spreading across his face. 'I'm here partly because Teckman asked me to come. He thought he might need help persuading the powers that be that Norquist was in a tangle with Mossad and Loz.' He paused and picked up his glass. 'But the actual reason is that Jaidi and Teckman overlapped at Cambridge, something I only recently discovered. Teckman took pity on the little man from Zanzibar and introduced him to people, made his life bearable in the cold, damp fens. They have been friends on and off for thirty-five years and were especially close when Teckman was with the British mission to the UN and Jaidi was a minor official. At some stage in the last few months, Jaidi told Teckman about a character named Sammi Loz in New York. Teckman had probably already had him investigated or knew at least that he had shown up on their radar. So, in the wake of Norquist's death, Jaidi gets me an appointment. Then Teckman approaches me the day afterwards. They fixed it between them. Now that we know Loz was working for Hizbollah and has most likely set up a group with Youssef Rahe, clearly Jaidi wants to protect himself and the other well-known patients on Loz's books. You see, Jaidi has been recommending Loz to all manner of folk. Who knows, he may have been responsible for introducing Norquist to Loz and now suffers some kind of remorse. At any rate, you can see that with the Israelis sniffing around, everyone needs to be extremely careful. Information is power when it comes to Israeli foreign policy.' He stopped. 'That's why I'm here to see this thing through. And by the way, that was the reduced version of the story and I don't want to be cross-examined on it.'

'Okay, okay!' She held her hands up in surrender. 'But you have to admit it's interesting that there are so many parallels. These pairings across the Atlantic for instance – Jaidi and Teckman; Loz and Rahe . . .'

'You and me,' said Harland, grinning.

'That's not what I meant.'

He touched her lightly on her forearm and let his hand rest there.

'The question now is am I going to allow myself to be seduced by you?' She looked at him with an open expression that made him think she was considering it with the same fierce logic that she applied to everything else.

'I'm not necessarily seducing you,' he said. 'I'm more one for synchronised desire.'

'Really? That strikes me as an unworkable strategy. How do you know when you're synchronised?'

Now he was embarrassed. 'Believe me, I'm rather out of practice.'

'Why don't I make some coffee and you can try to remember what to do next.'

She divided the rest of the wine between them, then scooped up the dishes and went inside. He heard a clattering as everything was chucked into the dishwasher, then some music that was very familiar to him. 'What's that?' he called through the window. 'Where have I heard it before?'

Her head appeared in the window. 'It's Sufi music. You heard it on the island. When I was in Sudan I bought this in the market. It's wonderful, but I was worried it would seem silly and out of place in England.'

She reappeared a few minutes later with coffee. 'You know there's one thing I slightly resent about you and the Chief. Leaving me on that island with Khan and Loz. I was very exposed.'

Harland nodded. 'The Chief told me you had backup. By the time I left, Sarre and Lapping were within a few minutes' boat ride.'

'But I didn't know they were there and they couldn't know what was going on. What kind of backup is that?'

'I suppose he felt he had no option, because there were so few people at his disposal. But he was right in one way. You drew them out and got the crucial information about Yahya and the time frame we're working in.'

'Still, it was bloody irresponsible of him, don't you think?'

'Yes, but I'm afraid I was partly to blame. I insisted on leaving. I had to go.'

'Alpha shit,' she said matter-of-factly. 'Still, you pulled a rabbit out of your own hat, though it turns out to be a much smaller one than mine.' She smiled mischievously at him.

They were both aware that they were marking time, but Harland reckoned he had made one move and that it was now her turn. The music slipped into the night to entice the uncomprehending world of a London suburb, and they watched each other. Without warning, she moved from her chair to stand over him, then put her hands down to his jaw, cupped his face and bent down to kiss him.

'We don't have to go to bed,' she said. 'But I thought I'd let you know that we are synchronised.'

'Good,' he murmured as she kissed him again.

'But on the whole, I think I'd like to go to bed very soon – with you.'

'Yes,' said Harland. 'That seems a good idea.'

They left the table and went to her bedroom, which struck him as a remarkably private, perhaps even lonely, place. It was bare but comfortable, and on one side of the bed there was a stack of books and a picture of a small girl and a woman standing in the shade of a tamarisk tree. The woman looked remarkably like Isis, but he knew it must be her dead mother, and that the girl with her face creased with laughter was

Isis. He suddenly felt the scale of her loss all those years ago and turned to her and held her, partly because of this flash of understanding, but also because he was desperate now to end his own long, morose isolation, and prove to himself that he could love and listen as well as the next man. She wriggled free to undress, which she did with little fuss, then stood before him without the slightest embarrassment. Harland was aware of his inability to grasp the whole of her in his mind – to resolve the neat white figure in front of him with the turbulent, driven person he'd seen working in the field. She came to him, hung her arms round his neck and told him to take off his clothes. At length they fell to the bed and became lovers. Finally Isis grew silent and went to sleep in his arms. His eyes closed too, but less happily. In his mind were three words – victim, survivor, person; the three stages he had been told the torture victim must go through. Was he yet the person he had once been? Was this thing that had happened to him fourteen years ago in the cellar of the house in Prague still distorting him? He was now certain that was what his bad back had been all about; not Eva's disappearance, or the air crash.

As Sammi Loz had said, the body remembers. Old pain – that's what he had to ditch to become a person again. He looked down at Isis's face and remembered why he had first been drawn to her. It wasn't her looks, which in fact had taken him some time to get used to. It was her conviction that no matter what Khan had done or might be, his torture would be a crime.

Then he closed his eyes.

Some time later they were woken by the phone ringing. Harland heard her answer to the Chief. They were expected in the office at 6.30 a.m. the next day.

30

Early next morning a group of about thirty people assembled at Thames House. Herrick and the key members of the SIS team arrived shortly before Vigo entered the building. The Chief had evidently spoken with him overnight and agreed that the man Vigo had identified in the Bosnian photographs as Jamil Rahe was the only hope of tracing Youssef Rahe and Sammi Loz. Vigo was once again the architect of a plan, but now he had the support of the entire security establishment and, though looking drawn, somehow managed to present a picture of righteous self-possession.

Jamil Rahe had been traced to a maisonette in a quiet street in Bristol, and a surveillance team was already in place. At 8.15 a.m. a uniformed policeman and a member of the local Special Branch, posing as an immigration official from the Home Office, approached the building and rang the doorbell. The exchange with Jamil Rahe was relayed to Thames House from a microphone in the Special Branch officer's briefcase, and it was agreed that their manner was striking precisely the right balance between suspicion and reassurance. They explained that a form had been overlooked in the processing of Jamil Rahe's application for political asylum and that it must be completed that day to make everything legal. Across the street a cameraman, hidden in the back of a TV repair van, silently recorded the scene. The three men were still talking on the doorstep when the first images arrived through the secure internet server at Thames House. One glance showed that he was the man from the Bosnia photographs. These images were then forwarded by email to a laptop in the possession of Special Branch officers on the roof of Heathrow's Terminal Two.

At length, the big Algerian offered the two officers coffee while he filled in the form. They went in, and within a very short time the plain-clothes policeman had secreted a tiny transmitter in Rahe's home so that the sound coming to Thames House was of much better quality. Jamil said he was familiar with the form they'd brought and insisted that he had already filled in one like it. The officers apologised. While he sat at the table writing, they gently questioned him about the kind of welfare

943

benefits he had been claiming, his prospects of work and his wife's attendance at a language course. Once or twice Rahe's replies seemed rather too considered, particularly when one of the officers mentioned that with his brother Youssef in London things would not be as difficult for him as it was for other new immigrants. The fifteen minutes of talk and coffee passed off very amicably, yet by the time they left, saying that this would certainly be the last he saw of them, Jamil was plainly on his guard.

Five minutes later, the police at Heathrow contacted Thames House. Three plane-spotters had identified the Algerian definitely as the man who stood with them on the observation platform on May 14 and on several occasions before that. Jamil Rahe was now confirmed as a very significant element in the story, and not for the first time the Chief looked towards Herrick and winked his thanks. Now all they had to do was wait for Jamil to make contact with someone.

An hour passed, during which the Chief and Barbara Markham, the Director General of the Security Services, discussed the raid on Youssef Rahe's bookshop in Bayswater. The Security Services wanted to move on the premises immediately, but the Chief argued that they should wait for as long as possible, although plainly it had to be done by the time the arrests started across Europe the following morning. Eventually they compromised on 5.00 p.m. that afternoon, with the agreement that the staff of the Secret Intelligence Service would have the run of the place once it had been secured. The Chief returned to Vauxhall Cross, leaving Dolph and Herrick to watch as a stream of visitors looked over the shots from Bosnia. Journalists, diplomats, army officers and even the odd aid worker had been contacted the previous evening and asked as a matter of urgency to Thames House. They were all on time for the unusual invitation to coffee and croissants, but as each of them pored over the photographs laid out on a table and consulted a map where the photographs had been shot, it became clear that the remaining men would not be so easily identified. 'Well,' said Dolph as the last one left, 'we've still got the Guignal gal. Maybe Lapping should fly out to Skiathos with a disk. He might even lose his virginity.'

'It would be quicker to get her to an internet café and send them by email,' she said.

'You're not worried about security?' he asked.

'Damn security, and anyway we *do* need to speak to her about Jamil Rahe. She may remember him. Why don't you do that?'

Dolph's eyes flared. 'All of a sudden I'm your runner, Isis. Why the fuck don't you do it?'

'Sorry,' she said. 'We'll both talk to her, okay? It will be better.'

Dolph still looked put out. 'You're tired. You need to rest.'

'Yes,' she said, managing a grin. 'I'm sorry.'

'You've had a rough few weeks and sooner or later it's going to tell.'

'Lecture over?'

'I mean it,' he said, looking down at the photographs.

She *was* tired, damned tired. She thought of Harland in her kitchen that morning, sitting as though drugged, over a cup of coffee. They said little, but she had tried to let him know that she didn't regret sleeping with him. He was affectionate but also slightly remote, as though mentally drawing back to grasp the scale of something. Fine, she had thought, she'd wait, and if this turned out to be a one-night stand, all well and good. It had been very pleasant.

'Don't worry,' she had said, brushing her knuckles across the top of his hand as the cab pulled up at Brown's Hotel. 'There're no strings. I'm not like that.'

'I'm not *worried*, just astonished that it happened. More than that, I'm moved and extraordinarily grateful that you would favour my old bones.'

'Grateful is not a word that should ever be used in the context of sex.'

They smiled at each other and it was left at that, but as he reached for the handle of the cab door she noticed the haunted, puzzled look in his eyes. She clutched at his arm and immediately regretted it because it made her seem needy, when in fact she was just concerned for him.

'Are you okay?

He had replied with slight irritation, 'Yes, of course I'm okay.' Then he pulled free and got out of the cab.

It had been a very unsatisfactory parting and she wished she could put it right.

Dolph and Herrick had returned to Vauxhall Cross by 11.00 a.m. but it was not until 1.10 p.m. that they were told that Jamil Rahe had left his house with a sports bag over his shoulder and walked to the end of his road to catch a bus. A feed from Thames House was hooked up and they were able to hear Jamil's progress. The bus took him to the centre of Bristol, where he moved unhurriedly from store to store buying odd items – a pair of socks, a packet of soap and a school exercise book. At length he came to an electronics shop where he browsed through the display and then, as though on impulse, bought a pay-as-you-go cell phone. The phone stayed in the box and the watchers were fairly certain he wouldn't be able to use it straight away because it would require a period of charging. Rahe then whiled away time in a park, briefly visited a library and considered the programme of movies at a multiplex cinema. The consensus was that he had activated a pre-planned routine to make sure he wasn't being followed. Several times he went through 'dry cleaning' channels – an escalator in a shopping mall, an underpass and an alley, each of which allowed him to observe at leisure the people in his wake. The police response was briefly to implement a procedure known as cascade surveillance, which involved filling his path with watchers, like water falling over a boulder. But Rahe moved so slowly through the city centre that it soon became necessary to revert to traditional methods and just hang a little further back.

Herrick realised time was getting on. Even though the raid on the Pan Arab Library had now been put back to 6.00 p.m. she would need to leave Vauxhall Cross by 5.15 and it was now 3.30. She went and found Dolph and they tried for a fifth time to raise Hélène Guignal. She answered on the first ring, and in response to Herrick's question, told them that she had her laptop with her and could pick up her email. The Bosnia photographs were sent to her.

Ten minutes later she called them. Dolph put her on speaker.

'These pictures are *étonnant* – how do you say? Amazing. The whole group is here.'

'Which group? Do you remember their names?'

'The one standing in profile is Hassan, my boyfriend. And you have seen Yaqub and Sammi, yes?'

'That's Youssef Rahe, ' Herrick said to Dolph.

'Who else do you see?' he asked impatiently.

'Larry.'

'Larry? Which is Larry?'

'The man in the foreground. He is the American – a convert to Islam. *J'oublie son nomme islamique, mais Les Frères* – the Brothers – they called him Larry.'

'This group referred to themselves as the Brothers?' asked Dolph.

'Yes.'

'Right, the tall man by the tree. This man we now believe to be Algerian, like Yaqub. He is passing himself off as Yaqub's brother?'

'Please, I don't understand.'

'He is pretending to be Yaqub's brother?'

'*Non!* He is not his brother! But he is *Algérien,* yes.'

'His name?'

She hesitated. 'Rafik ... no, Rasim. That is it – Rasim.'

Dolph was scribbling a note to Herrick.

'Any other name for him?'

'No.'

'Do you know anyone else?'

'These are the only names. Some of the others I recognise but I did not know them well. I do not know their names.'

Dolph passed Herrick a note which said, 'THEY WERE ALL IN THE HAJ SWITCH.'

She wound up the conversation, saying that she or someone else would call that evening and that Guignal should keep her phone on. She also said Nato headquarters would be made aware of her help in this matter, a way of underlining what she had already told Guignal about not showing the pictures to anyone or speaking about them.

'We'll have to get someone to Guignal,' she said. 'We need to know everything she can remember about the Brothers.'

'There are so many fucking names in this thing,' said Dolph. 'As soon as we've nailed one group, up pops another with a fresh load of backgrounds and connections.'

'But we're peeling the onion.'

'Yeah, and I'm fucking sure that every one of them went to the Haj. Nathan Lyne wanted to keep on it, but Collins and the rest of them said we should focus on the suspects we knew about in Europe. They were going to come back to it. A bad mistake.'

'So what you're saying is that you agree with Lapping's theory about the Heathrow Group being a set of cardboard cut-outs. The Bosnia Group – the Brothers – are the core of the operation?'

'Fuck, I don't know. I guess we'll see tomorrow when they begin questioning the nine suspects. But think about it. Every year people are trampled to death on the pilgrimage. Twelve years ago 1,400 people were crushed in a pedestrian tunnel. The main problem was identifying the bodies because everyone is dressed the same and bits of ID get lost.'

A few minutes later, they went to report the conversation with Guignal to the Chief, and the information was relayed to the Joint Intelligence Committee. Sarre, not Lapping, was dispatched to Greece to interview Guignal and if necessary persuade her to return with him to London. The Chief was extremely keen that the pictures should not fall into the hands of the French DGSE, so the local MI in the Athens Embassy was sent on ahead to babysit her until Sarre arrived. Then Nathan Lyne was asked to focus all the resources he could muster at the Bunker on the Haj switch. There would be a joint CIA–SIS meeting at Vauxhall Cross that evening, at a time to be determined later.

In Bristol, Jamil Rahe was still aimlessly traipsing round the city centre. He certainly appeared cool, but a clue to his actual state of mind came when he called into a chemist and bought antacid tablets and a pack of double strength painkillers. Then he went to a coffee bar, took some of these with an espresso and settled by the window to watch the street. It was now believed that he was waiting for a check-in time or the right moment to use a dead-letter drop to make a contact somewhere in Bristol city centre.

By now it was 4.30 p.m. Herrick, Dolph and Lapping separately left Vauxhall Cross to go to Bayswater. Herrick had made an appointment in the hairdressing salon across the street from the Pan Arab Library, while Dolph and Lapping planned to install themselves in a betting shop fifty yards away. She had been told that Harland would also be there. On the way, he called her mobile to say he was already in position at a café named Paolo's down the street.

As she sat waiting for the hairdresser to finish his previous appointment, Herrick glanced up from her magazine. Everything was as normal. Rahe's disagreeable wife was sitting at the desk serving customers and working at the computer. The assistant whom Herrick had spoken to once could be seen darting between the shelves and a pile of books that had clearly just been delivered. The street itself was relatively free of traffic, though there were quite a few pedestrians about and a gas repair team was examining a hole in the pavement about thirty yards from the bookshop.

She received a hair wash then a head massage, which made her suddenly feel so drowsy that she had to ask the stylist for coffee. While a couple of centimetres were taken off her hair she watched the shop in the mirror. At about 5.30 she noticed the bookshop filling with an unusual number of customers. If these were members of the public it meant the raid might have to be delayed, but then it occurred to her that the book buyers were from the police and MI5 . It wasn't beyond either to raid the place early and take any evidence for themselves. Moreover, the Secret Intelligence Service had no rights in this domestic matter and agreements between chiefs tended to be ignored or bypassed by officers on the ground. She sent a text message to Dolph, asking him to have a look at the shop. A reply came. 'Just had 5–1 winner at Windsor.' A minute later she saw him pass the Pan Arab Library with Lapping in tow. Another text arrived – 'Nothing doing yet'. They headed back to the betting shop.

A few people left the bookshop, but one or two remained.

At 5.47 Herrick left the salon and took a stroll up to the café, where she spotted Harland with his head buried in the *Financial Times*. He did not look up, but signalled to her by waggling the fingers at the edge of his newspaper. It was 5.52. She walked back and noticed the gas workers ahead of her replace the manhole cover, pack away their gear into the back of the van and make a beeline for the shop. Then three unmarked police cars pulled up just before the shop. The raid was on.

She phoned Harland and hurried towards the entrance of the bookshop. Dolph and Lapping were already there and pressing their case to be admitted behind the police officers, apparently without success. When Herrick arrived, slightly out of breath, she was told by a thick-set Special Branch officer that he knew of no agreement that would allow SIS people to search the premises before it had been secured.

'Of course it's been secured,' said Herrick, pulling out her phone again. 'There're only a couple of women.' She used the speed-dial to call the Chief's office and walked a few paces away to explain the situation to his assistant. He told her to keep the line open while the problem was sorted out. Herrick went back to the policeman and said, 'Look, you do realise we're working for the Prime Minister's office? It's imperative that we have access to this building now.'

'I don't give a toss who you're working for,' replied the policeman.

Harland was behind her now and also began to argue with him. But at this moment one of the men inside the shop appeared to have been contacted and the policeman barring the door was told to stand aside.

Herrick's first thought on entering was that there were too many people there. Men were already rummaging around the shop, randomly picking books from shelves and searching the drawers of the desk. Rahe's wife and the shop assistant were seated on two chairs at the end of a run of bookshelves. Lamia Rahe, as they now knew her name to be, was looking at the ground, holding her head in her hands. The assistant's eyes oscillated wildly. No one seemed to have any idea what to do with them, and even Herrick didn't know whether they had an arrest warrant for Mrs Rahe. She went up to the officer in charge and was about to suggest clearing the shop when she realised that she was still holding an open line to Vauxhall Cross. She placed the phone to her ear. 'Christ, I'm sorry. Are you still there?'

'I gather you got in,' said the Chief's assistant. 'But while you're on, you might as well know that the man in Bristol appears to be about to make contact. He's just switched the SIM cards from the new phone to one he had in his pocket. We heard a few moments ago.'

Herrick hung up, and was about to ask the officer to stop the search, but at this moment she became aware of an insistent noise coming from the apartment above the shop. She noticed Lamia Rahe's head rise at the sound, but no one else seemed to have noticed. She found herself calling out to the room. 'Can everyone shut up for a moment.' She held up her hands and clapped rapidly. 'Please! Can you shut up!' The shop went silent and they all heard the sound of a mobile phone. Then it went dead.

'Have you searched upstairs yet?' she asked the policeman.

'There's no one there. We've checked.'

'No children?'

He shook his head.

'I'm certain that phone was silenced by someone. Didn't you hear the slight noise before it stopped ringing? And anyway, where the hell are the children? School finished at least two hours ago.'

Of course. There weren't any children. Suddenly she understood that they had been part of a cover.

Herrick was aware of Lamia Rahe's gaze coming to rest on her with an oddly thoughtful expression and knew she had recognised her from the night of the break-in.

She looked away. 'I think you should see who stopped it ringing.'

Then Lamia Rahe erupted from her chair, gesticulating and muttering in Arabic.

'Sit that woman down,' said the officer. But before anyone could take hold of her, she had produced a gun from her shirts and, still screaming, took aim in Herrick's direction. Herrick went blank, then at the precise moment the gun went off, something hit her like a train from behind. Next she was sprawling across a length of rope matting by the desk. Five or six shots were loosed off into the mêlée of men at the front of the shop. One of the policemen pulled a gun and fired a single round. Lamia Rahe sank to the ground, dead.

Herrick whipped her head round. Immediately in front of her was Harland, who had been hit in the back by a bullet meant for her. Beyond him lay Joe Lapping, who was writhing on the floor, clutching his right thigh, and Andy Dolph was on his back with blood all over his chest. For a moment she simply could not absorb what she was seeing. She scrambled over to them. Dolph was white but he grimaced a kind of smile and whispered an oath.

'Get help,' she shouted. 'Get an ambulance here.'

She cast around. The confusion was total. The shop assistant had dropped to the side of her dead boss and was shrieking and hammering on the floorboards with her fists. Two policemen were shouting into their radios and another three had taken off to the back of the shop to climb the stairs to the flat. There was a noise from above, something being moved across the floor, then a sash-cord window being flung upwards, but Herrick was unable to interpret these in any meaningful way. There were more shots, so rapid that it seemed like a machine gun was being fired. Something fell above them.

Somehow she got a grip on herself and, dimly remembering the first aid course she once attended during IONEC training, she began to conduct a hurried triage. Of the three, Harland was the best off. The bullet had sliced across his back like a sword stroke, giving him a gash of six to seven inches long on the left side. Dolph had been hit just below his collar-bone and there was a nasty exit wound in the middle of his shoulder blade. When she saw the massive amount of blood pouring from just below Lapping's groin on his right thigh, she knew she had to act.

'We can't wait,' she shouted. 'Let's get all of them to St Mary's right now. It's only minutes away.' The commanding officer agreed. St Mary's was alerted and two of the unmarked police cars moved to the front of the shop. Dolph was placed in the back seat of the first car, which tore off towards Paddington with a single blue light clamped haphazardly to its roof and a siren wailing. Lapping went in the second car, Harland having elected to wait for the ambulance. To show that he was going to be okay, he insisted on getting to his feet and then bent over so that a policeman could press a field dressing to the wound.

By now, the men who had gone up to the flat were spilling down the stairs. None was hurt, but they were evidently very shocked and couldn't answer Herrick's questions. She got up and physically accosted one of the men.

'What the hell happened?'

'Look for yourself,' said the young officer quietly.

Driven now by an insane need to complete what she had come for, she mounted the stairs to the flat and entered a kitchen. Sunlight streamed through a window. She passed through a living room at the front of the building and then turned left towards a bathroom and bedroom. It was here she found Youssef Rahe lying dead beneath an open window. Net curtains ballooned into the room. Beside him was a gun.

It was obvious what had happened. Having heard the shots from his wife's gun, Rahe had pushed at the door of a secret compartment built behind the headboard of the double bed, causing the bed to shift a few inches across the room. He had then attempted to escape through the window, but hearing the police already in the flat, had turned round to fire on them and been shot himself. There were four or five bullet wounds in his upper body and a number of holes around the walls and furnishings.

Herrick crouched down by the body to make sure it was Rahe. He had lost weight and grown a beard, and in his final expression there was a hardness and strain which was never evident in the film of him from Heathrow, but it was definitely the man she had thought of as a harmless little butterball. Two silver bangles on his left arm caught her attention, and then just beyond them, under the bed, the mobile phone. It must have flown from his pocket as he was hit by the hail of police bullets. She retrieved it and slipped it into her pocket, all the while looking at his face and half praying that his eyes would open and all the knowledge of what he had planned with his group would be restored. Already she understood that his death was a disaster.

She rose, stepped over the corpse and hefted the bed a little further into the room so she could get at the wall-hanging that disguised the entrance to the compartment. She lifted it and felt along the side of the entrance for possible booby traps. Satisfied that the entrance was clear, she reached inside and pulled at the cord switch. A single fluorescent strip flickered. She squeezed through the opening and immediately realised that the compartment had not just been taken from the bedroom, but ran the entire length of the flat, shaving space from three different rooms. At the far end there was another door which opened into the utility cupboard in the kitchen. Judging by the dusty impression of his hands around its edge, this was the preferred way in and out, even though it must have required Rahe to crouch down. She turned round. The compartment was oppressively narrow, measuring only four feet across, and was without natural light or ventilation. There was an air freshener at each end, yet there was still a marked staleness in the air, the odour of tedium and sweat. At the end nearest the street there was an old-fashioned army camp bed propped against the wall. Next to this was a rolled up prayer mat and some lifting weights.

Her eyes moved to a shelf where there was a cloth laid out with half an apple, an open packet of cheese crackers and a bottle of mineral water. Underneath she noticed a small red lightbulb. The wire from the socket ran down the wall and through the floor to the bookshop below. She guessed this was a warning light, operated from the cashier's desk. But there were no other power points – nowhere to plug in a computer or charge a phone.

She moved towards two wire coat hangers on a waste pipe that ran from the flats above. On one of these was an old brown suit jacket with biro stains in the lining. She felt the jacket with a clapping motion, then stopped, delved inside the pocket and withdrew a passport and a wallet. She was about to examine these when a man's voice called out from the bedroom. 'Don't shoot,' she shouted.

She left the foetid atmosphere to find four policemen in the room, two of them wearing body armour and carrying Heckler and Koch machine guns. One of them said, 'You have to leave the building now, Miss.'

'Of course,' she said. 'You know where to find me when you need a statement.'

'You can tell the officer downstairs,' came the reply.

In the event, she slipped away without being challenged and melted into the crowds that had gathered in the street to watch Harland being helped into an ambulance.

31

Herrick rushed to St Mary's Hospital but was told she would have to wait for news. After an hour, a woman in her thirties, still dressed for theatre, came to speak to her. Lapping's injury was far more dangerous than Dolph's because the bullet had grazed the femoral artery and he had been on the point of dying from blood loss when he was brought into casualty. He was now very weak, but out of danger. Dolph's injuries would take a lot longer to heal. The collar-bone had been shattered by the impact of the 9mm bullet and his shoulder blade would need further surgery. It would be three or four months before he was able to work again. Harland was also still under anaesthetic, having had an operation to repair the damage done to the muscle tissue and skin on his back. He wouldn't be fit to see anyone until the following day.

As the doctor spoke, she touched Herrick's shoulder. 'You know, you look pretty drained yourself. If you were involved in the shooting, you may experience some shock.'

She shook her head and said she had better be getting back to work. She left the hospital by the main entrance and walked through the courtyard. As she hit the street she saw a couple hurrying from a cab. They were unmistakably Dolph's parents. The man in his sixties moved with Dolph's heavy, rolling walk while the woman had his alert eyes. They looked modest people and somehow ashamed of the worry. Herrick turned to say something as they passed but suddenly couldn't find the words. She stopped in her tracks, realising she needed to sit down and collect herself, maybe have something to eat. Across the street there was a pub named the The Three Feathers, festooned with hanging baskets of petunias. She entered an almost empty lounge bar, where a barman and the few customers were glued to *Channel Four News*. A distant shot of the Pan Arab Library was being shown: police tape was stretched across the road, forensics were entering the building as plain-clothes officers left with boxes.

Herrick ordered a double whisky and a meat pie that was sitting unappetisingly in the display cabinet. She perched on a bar stool while the pie was microwaved and tried to get a hold of herself by concentrating on the pocket of anxiety lodged at the top of her diaphragm.

As the pie was presented to her on a paper plate, she heard a voice from her left. Walter Vigo stood with one hand on the bar. 'A bad business, Isis. Are they all right?' He attempted a sympathetic smile but produced only a leer.

She turned and examined him for a moment. 'No, they're bloody well not all right. Joe Lapping nearly died. What the fuck are you doing here anyway?' She cut into the pie. Vigo looked down at the flow of gravy with acute distaste.

'I was concerned to see how they were and spotted you crossing the road.'

'Right,' said Herrick, grimacing. 'What is it you really want?'

'A word – somewhere more private, perhaps.'

'I've got to go back to the office in a few minutes.'

'This can't wait,' he said.

'Then say it now.'

He waited for the barman to move away. 'I want to know what you found in the bookshop.'

'If I had found anything it would be none of your fucking business.'

Vigo's mouth pursed into a tight little hole. 'I need to know – lives may depend on it.'

She said nothing and continued eating the pie, noticing that the strange throbbing in her left arm had developed into an ache.

'It's important that I know. I gather there have been some useful discoveries in Bristol.'

'Then go to Bristol.'

'Look, Herrick. These are my people, Jamil and Youssef Rahe. They're my contacts. Where would we be if I hadn't made use of them?'

This amazed her. 'Well, three of my friends wouldn't be in hospital for a start. You were suckered. No one is going to see it any other way.'

'I don't care what they think about this. There may have been significant intelligence in that shop that only I am in a position to appreciate.'

She was struck by the plaintive note in his voice, and if she had been feeling less strange she would have thought about it more deeply. 'You forget, Walter, you're on the outside now. I can't talk to you about any of this.' She gestured to the TV set.

'Do you think I would bother to come here and talk to you if it wasn't important?'

Herrick shrugged. 'Frankly, I don't care what your interest is.'

'I am in touch with people who need this information and can make far better use of it than you. You have the opportunity to save lives.'

'Who?'

He shook his head.

She pulled out her phone and pressed the key to redial the Chief's office.

'What're you doing?' he snapped.

'If you want access to what I know, go through the Chief. You can talk to him now.'

Without a word, Vigo turned and made for the door. Herrick gave it a few seconds before hopping off the bar stool and rushing to the window. A new model Jaguar pulled out from the kerb with Vigo at the wheel. Then she put the phone to her ear and was about to speak to the Chief's assistant, but he interrupted her. 'You're needed here. Please return immediately.'

Herrick laid out the phone, wallet and US passport in front of the head of the MI5–MI6 controllerate, Colin Guthrie. He let out a low whistle. 'Where the hell have you been?'

'At the hospital.'

'And after that?'

'I needed some time, so I had a drink. Guess who I bumped into? Vigo. What the hell's he doing? He wanted to know what I had got from the bookshop.'

Guthrie thought for a moment. 'I imagine he's up to something in his capacity as head of Mercator. One always forgets that when Vigo was pushed out last time round he set himself up as a private intelligence agency. We thought it was pretty much dormant but perhaps we were wrong. Anyway, we've got a lot to get through so let's make a start.' He picked up a printout of an email. 'First, Jamil Rahe. He hasn't said a word since he was arrested, but a search of his house and a garage nearby produced a great deal – twenty passports, equipment to forge visas, blank credit cards, the records of 152 different credit cards, acquired by a skimming device, a telescope, airline schedules, a notebook logging arrival and departure times at Heathrow, computer records of payments to foreign banks, a mass of extremist literature and the usual bloody videos of Mujahadin victories in Chechnya et cetera.' His description tailed off as a dozen or so of Herrick's colleagues filed into his office.

He let the paper slip to the desk and gave them a brief update on the condition of the men in hospital, then divided the group into three teams to chase up leads provided by the items Herrick had taken from the bookshop. She was still feeling odd, but the tasks ahead moved the anxiety to the back of her mind and when Nathan Lyne appeared for a meeting on the Haj switch she began to feel better.

The passport she had found was held in the name of David Zachariah, a thirty-eight-year-old jeweller living in White Plains, New York. Herrick had opened it on the way to Vauxhall Cross and silently saluted Hélène

Guignal for predicting that the name Zachariah would appear somewhere in Rahe's portfolio of identities. While Rahe's replacement had been tortured and killed, Rahe had crossed the Syrian border. Fourteen days later he travelled as Zachariah to New York, with a stopover at Athens. He had stayed in the US until the previous weekend, then took an overnight flight back to Britain and landed at Gatwick Airport.

The wallet contained impressive confirmation of the existence of Zachariah. There were three different credit cards with billing addresses in White Plains, each of which was settled regularly by an account held at a bank in Manhattan, where all mail was delivered. Adding credibility to Zachariah's life were the business cards, a membership card of the American–Israeli Friendship Society, a US driver's licence, a dry-cleaning ticket in his name and various notes addressed to Zachariah. There was no such place as 1014 Jefferson Drive in White Plains, and no trace of Zachariah in any local records.

As crucial as the record of these recent trips was the evidence of his movements across Europe during the previous winter. Cross-referencing the point-of-entry stamps in its pages with payments made on his credit cards – acquired with his usual authority by Nathan Lyne – they produced dates for the purchases of airline and train tickets in Hungary, Germany, Italy, Denmark and Sweden, and for the payment of hotel bills. It was obvious that Youssef Rahe had used the Zachariah identity as a cover for his meetings with the helper cells all over Europe. This in itself would be useful evidence in subsequent prosecutions of members of the helper cells.

The credit cards had most recently been used in New York – again hotels and restaurants were in evidence. He also drew $8,800 in cash from his account at the Stuyvesant Empire Bank on 5th Avenue, leaving a balance of $22,000.57. Rahe was well-funded, but where from? The bank revealed that payments of $15,000 were made on the third of each month by a company named Grunveldt-Montrea, of Jersey City, New Jersey. No such company existed in the phone directory. Before leaving New York for London, Zachariah hired a car for a period of three days on one of the cards. Lyne put in a request to the FBI to see if any trace of his journey could be picked up by speeding or parking tickets, or even motel registers, because he had evidently not used his cards to buy gas. Herrick made a note, which ended with the word Canada and three question marks.

The cell phone produced less definite information, although it was now established that the call stifled by Youssef Rahe while he was hiding above the bookshop had come from his 'brother', Jamil. Police reported observing Jamil Rahe switch the SIM cards and dial a number at 6.15 p.m., presumably the agreed check-in time. When he failed to get an answer, he was seen to lower the phone and check the display with a look of puzzlement. At this point the police moved in and arrested him.

It was also clear that this particular phone of Youssef Rahe's was only used to receive calls. Several had been made to him in America over the first half of the year, but they weren't identified in the phone's memory and it would take time for the two or three phone companies likely to have handled them to search the records of millions of subscribers. Herrick was sure that elsewhere in the bookshop there would be other phones to investigate, and that in time much would be exhumed from the computer, although it was now being examined by the Security Services, who had proved resistant to suggestions that SIS should have access.

At 11.15 p.m. the Chief came in, looking grave. The news media had, it seemed, been well briefed by Special Branch about the involvement of SIS 'cowboys', to explain why two people were dead and a further three lay in hospital.

'We're bringing the arrests in Europe forward because the coverage may alert the suspects,' he said. 'However, Rahe's use of multiple identities may work to our advantage. It's likely the people he dealt with on the continent knew him only as Zachariah. They may not make the connection when they hear of the raid on the bookshop.'

He stopped and surveyed the drawn faces around the room. 'Look, I don't think there's much more you can do tonight. I'd rather have you all fresh for tomorrow than working through the night. There is very little we can do until these arrests have been made and we can begin to assess the information they produce.'

'There's a ticking bomb,' said Herrick. 'Loz said something would happen eleven days from last Wednesday night. That could be either Friday or Saturday, according to which day he was counting from.'

'We *think* there's a ticking bomb, which is not quite the same thing, is it? Youssef and Jamil Rahe are out of the picture; the nine suspects will be in the bag shortly; and the evidence is leaning towards Loz being killed on the island. We gather from Foyzi that four bodies were found, one very close to the spot where you say Loz was. Even with this unknown – and I am inclined to think that is *not* an unknown – the network you have done so much to expose, Isis, is dead.'

'But there are the other men in the photograph from Bosnia,' she said. 'We haven't got around to matching the faces with names from Dolph's research on the Haj switch.'

'All that's true. But go home now, then return as early as you like in the morning. By then the nine will be detained and we may know more.' He said goodnight and beckoned Herrick out into the corridor. 'Pace yourself, Isis. Get some sleep tonight. I mean it. You look bloody awful.'

She did not go straight home, but instead took a cab to Brown's Hotel, where she explained to an assistant manager what had happened to Robert Harland. After switching on the midnight news and checking with the hospital, he eventually agreed to let her into Harland's room. He watched as she gathered together some dark blue pyjamas, underpants, socks, shirt and a sponge-bag. She noticed a slim black phone book by the telephone and put it together with the clothes in a small overnight bag, then asked whether the manager would mind if she took a bunch of flowers that were on top of a bureau. He shook his head wearily and she wrapped them in a hotel laundry bag. Later, she dropped everything off at the hospital and talked to a nurse about her three friends. She heard that Harland's sister had been in touch and would be flying back from holiday.

It was 6.45 a.m. when she reached her floor next morning. Lyne was at her desk, using her computer. Nearby was Laughland who she assumed had been told to keep an eye on the CIA officer.

'What's going on?' she asked Lyne, dropping the bag.

He looked up. 'So much for *The Subtle Ruse*, Isis. These guys all meant business. Explosives, nerve agents. You name it, they got it.'

She moved to the coffee machine, thinking furiously. 'Do we know when they were going to attack?'

'No, I've only been here five minutes. I know no more than I've told you, but right now there's a briefing.' Laughland was already at the door agitating to leave.

By the time they reached the Chief's office the briefing was underway. There were about thirty people in the room. Herrick noticed several members of the Joint Intelligence Committee and one or two people from the COBRA meeting of two days before. The Chief was sitting in the window holding up his hand against the reflection of the sun, which bounced off a convoy of waste barges on the river below.

Guthrie was speaking. He paused for the three new arrivals to find a place to perch, then continued. 'The pattern was set by Fayzi al Haqq, the Pakistani national in Bradford. Al Haqq was armed, but was also in possession of a belt of Semtex. He was arrested before he could use either and is now in Leeds. He will be transferred to London later today. We believe he acquired these weapons only recently, and they must have been passed to him or were moved into his home right under the gaze of RAPTOR surveillance. Clearly the helper cells also served as armourers and scouts for the operation. The seven individuals that came in contact with al Haqq have all been arrested, together with a further six in London who were associated with the Turkish suspect, Mafouz Esmet. He is still in a coma.'

He drew breath and looked over his glasses. 'I am afraid that the surveillance not only missed the preparation that has been going on this past week, but it gave us no hint of the precise nature of these men's deadly intentions. So far it has been determined that three of them were in possession of nerve agents: Nassir Sharif in Stockholm, Lasenne Hadaya in Paris, and Ramzi Zaman in Toulouse, all had fifty millilitres of one of two different agents. Hadaya was equipped with GB – or Sarin – in an aerosol spray; the other two had VX, which is less volatile, but much more potent and long-lasting. We do not yet know how they intended to deploy these nerve agents, partly because all suspects are still suffering from the effects of the disabling darts or injections used to stop them biting into suicide pills. There is much work to be done on their targets and on the lines of supply. To this end, the helpers are being questioned exhaustively.

'So the theme emerging is one of random and varied suicide attacks. The Pakistani in Bradford was clearly going to blow himself up at some public target, as was Hadi Dahhak, the Yemeni suspect in Budapest. One of his helpers had the belt and another was discovered with a very recent batch of Czech Semtex – as you know, it's chemically dated. At some time in the near future these materials would have been brought together.

'But what of the other four men? What did they plan? All were detained last night, but no weapons or means of attack were found in any of the safe houses in Rome, Sarajevo or the two in Copenhagen. They are being taken apart piece by piece, as are the homes of helpers in each city, but nothing has been found. What we do know is that two of the men were planning to travel this coming Friday. The Saudi from Sarajevo had booked himself on a flight to Vienna and the Syrian in Copenhagen was due to go to Cologne. But we don't know why.' He paused, and let his gaze skate across the room.

Herrick rose so that Guthrie could see her. 'It's obvious that Sarajevo wouldn't be an ideal place for an attack because the population is Muslim.' She stopped, realising she was speaking too loudly. But then the sentence fled from her. She shook her head and waited as the words slowly came into focus. 'Sorry, it's a bit early for me. And . . . and . . . in Copenhagen they had doubled up. So maybe one was flying out to take the place of the man in Stuttgart who died.'

Guthrie gave her an odd look, and there were one or two concerned glances from around the room. Beside her, Lyne discreetly touched her elbow. Then she realised that the hand holding the empty coffee cup had been seized by a violent tremor. She sat down, placed the cup on the floor and gripped her wrist with her other hand.

The Chief cleared his throat. 'Yes, both those thoughts are probably right,' he said quietly. 'But it means they would have to be armed or equipped at their destinations and that seems to break with the pattern. My impression is that the organiser of this plan, likely to be the man we know as Youssef Rahe, took a view that the best way to achieve his ends was to put his chaps in place, then let the helpers service all their needs, including storage of the explosives and nerve agents. They minded each one, took all the burden until the moment arrived when he was required to kill himself. It's slightly different to the set-up of the earlier al-Qaeda cells where they lived together and each man had a defined role.'

The briefing went on for a further fifteen minutes. At the end, the Chief made a small speech about the success of the operation, again congratulating Herrick, Dolph, Sarre and Lapping for the work they had all done. But far from being triumphant about the arrests, Herrick left the room in a sombre mood, not helped by the return of the heaviness in her chest and the ache in her arm.

An hour later, just as she had recovered a little of herself and was able to focus on what Nathan Lyne was telling her about the Haj switch, she received a call from the Chief's office and was asked to hold. She waited, reading the conclusion of Dolph's brilliantly tight description of the switch, which gave the names of four more people who had not shown up in the Heathrow switch or on any watch list.

The Chief came on. 'Isis, I'm going to be direct about this. You're off the case. I believe you're suffering from exhaustion. Christine Selvey will be down in a few minutes. She is going to see to it that you get to a doctor in Upper Sloane Street.'

'But there's still work to do,' she said feebly.

'Not by you. You're prohibited from entering this building until I am satisfied you are fit for work. I don't expect to hear from you for at least two weeks. Is that understood? You have earned the rest. Now take it.'

Selvey was already at the door of her office as she put the phone down.

32

A young doctor at the private practice saw her quickly. He was short, with wiry black hair curling over a receding hairline and red blotches either side of his nose. Within a few minutes of Herrick describing her symptoms, he started nodding.

'You're suffering from an anxiety disorder,' he said. There was a slight hiss on the 's' in disorder.

'You mean panic attacks,' she said aggressively.

'Yes. I don't mean to be rude, but judging by your appearance, they're caused by all-round exhaustion – lack of sleep, poor diet, too many stimulants – and of course general pressure. Do you take any exercise?'

'No time.'

'You should make time, and you should certainly look into your diet and eating habits. Do you bolt your food? Eat irregularly? Sleep poorly?'

She nodded to all three.

'And you have a fair degree of unpredictable stress in your life? Do you ever relax?'

She shook her head. She knew this man was SIS-approved and must have seen the odd case of burnt-out spy before. Although the Service was notoriously bad at helping the casualties of the trade, it reacted quickly to any hint of psychological disrepair.

'So, how long is this going to last? What can you give me for it?' As she talked, the heaviness in her chest began to disappear and she breathed more easily.

'Nothing. As soon as you take some rest the symptoms will leave you but in future you'll have to learn to manage your stress levels. I suggest regular physical activity, maybe some abdominal breathing exercises. Perhaps you should consider yoga?'

'Yoga!' she said contemptuously.

He shrugged. 'Look, it's up to you. I can't give you a pill to affect the choices you make. You have an overactive fight and flight response. This releases your body's hormones to enable you to meet a dangerous situation, or flee from it. You're leading your life at such a pitch that your body is unable to distinguish between what is real danger and what is simply pressure. You're constantly on the alert, boiling over with unspent hormones. This is the first episode and there is very little to concern yourself about. It's an amber light, that's all. If I were you, I'd go home, have a sleep and then take some time off. If you don't accept this advice, you will eventually find yourself with more serious problems – possibly a nervous breakdown, alcohol dependency, that sort of thing. You have to look after yourself, you're getting on.'

'I'm in my early thirties!'

'As I said, getting on.'

'Do you have any advice for the short term?' she said sharply.

'If you experience the hyperventilation again, you can stop it by breathing into a paper bag to slow your intake of oxygen. But it's not ideal. It may not give the right impression.'

'I see that,' she said.

She left the surgery with Christine Selvey, whom she found sitting primly in the waiting room reading the *Economist*.

'Everything all right?' asked Selvey pointedly.

'Iron deficiency,' said Herrick. 'A few supplements and some rest and I'll be fine.'

'Good. Then we'll see you in a couple of weeks or so. I hope you don't mind me saying that the Chief was quite emphatic you take the time off.'

They parted, Selvey giving her a last matronly nod.

'Fuck it,' said Herrick, as she made her way up Sloane Street to find a cab.

When she reached home she had no difficulty in falling asleep. She woke at 2.00 p.m. feeling disorientated and vaguely guilty. How the hell was she meant to turn off just like that? She called her father, but found herself being evasive when he asked why she had so much time to talk. He was busy painting – the light was right, the tempera just mixed – and he would prefer to ring her later on. She read the paper and ate some salad with self-conscious restraint, then phoned St Mary's Hospital. Dolph and Lapping were still too poorly to receive visitors, but Harland was sitting up in his room. She asked them to tell him to expect her.

On the drive there, she stopped at Wild at Heart on Westbourne Grove and chose another bunch of flowers. As she waited for the credit card payment to go through, her eyes drifted to the couples sitting outside the cafés along the north side of the street, and she thought that the doctor was right. She really must find a way of taking more time off, having more fun.

It was 3.25 by the time she found Harland's room. He was sitting by an open window, in the shade of half-drawn curtains that lifted into the room on the breeze. One shoulder was bare, but the rest of his torso was wrapped in bandages. He sat forward so as not to risk his back coming in contact with the chair, and winced a greeting at her.

'What happened?' he snapped. 'Why were you out of the office? I phoned you. They said you were on holiday. What's going on, Isis?'

'I felt a little faint in the meeting this morning and suddenly I'm pegged as a borderline neurotic. I was given two weeks' gardening leave. More important, how are you?'

His eyes turned to the floor. 'Shitty. They won't give me any more painkillers.'

'Did you get the things I brought last night?' She was aware they were talking like a married couple, concern somehow metabolising into briskness and formality.

He nodded.

'Don't you have some painkillers in the sponge bag?'

'You're right.' He gestured to the bedside cabinet.

She gave him the bag and knelt down beside him, determined to end the difficulty. 'I don't know how to say this . . .'

'You don't have to. She wouldn't have hit you. I just put myself in the line of fire. Bloody stupid of me.'

She shook her head. 'That's not what the police say. They say you pushed me out of the way, and I know that to be the case. Please, I want to thank you . . . I mean, I *am* thanking you . . . I'm just not very good at putting it into words.'

'Isis, this doesn't suit you.' He smiled. 'Please get up and tell me what's going on. There are a few hints on the news, but they must be keeping most of it quiet.'

'They've arrested the lot of them, plus Rahe's associate in Bristol. But it was more serious than anyone suspected – nerve agents, suicide bombers. They still don't know what four of them were planning to do. That's as of this morning, when I was last in the loop.'

There was silence. Harland looked at the window. 'I've just had a call from Eva. She said she needed to see me in New York.'

'So it's back on – you and her?' asked Herrick.

'Don't be bloody stupid, Isis.' He paused. 'She told me there had been some activity on a website that had been dormant these past three weeks. It's an important site and before it went down they were gaining useful information from it.'

'You're talking about the thing on Rahe's computer. The encrypted messages in the screensaver?'

'No, this is something they kept to themselves.'

'By *they*, you mean *Ha Mossad Le Teum*,' she said.

'Yes, the dear old Institute for Coordination in Israel,' he said.

At this moment a nurse walked through the open door with Herrick's flowers in a vase. 'I hope you're telling Mr Harland that he's not allowed to use his mobile phone in here. Just because he's darling of the ward doesn't mean he can break all the rules.' She fussed over the flowers and bent down to look into Harland's face.

'I saw a doctor using one ten minutes ago,' he said.

'If you kept to the odd text message, no one would know.'

'I'll bear that in mind,' he said.

Harland swallowed a couple of pills with a gulp of water, then the nurse left with a friendly wink at Herrick.

'The *Institute* had been watching the activities of Sammi Loz for some while,' he said. 'And I know Eva well enough to be certain that she wouldn't leave her dying mother to go to New York unless it was absolutely essential. Second, if she called me about it, she probably needs help. And I'm not exactly in a position to give that help.'

'You say this website has been down for the last three weeks. You're thinking that was the time Loz was with us?'

He nodded.

'What did you tell her?'

'I said you would go, and that you would meet her in the breakfast room of the Algonquin tomorrow morning. That's why I was trying to call you, to tell you to get on a plane.'

'You said I would go to New York to see your ex-mistress! You must be suffering from shock.'

'Well,' he said, his eyes brimming with mischief, 'I imagined you might have thought you owed me. It was cheap of me, I know.'

'And you think what she's got to say is serious?'

'Yes. And I've been thinking about something else. Loz is utterly obsessed with the Empire State building. He goes on about it like it was his second love.'

'His first love being a contest between Khan and himself?'

'I'm serious, he's got a thing about it, and about the meaning of those tall buildings in New York. He picked up a quote from Benjamin Jaidi. After Loz mentioned it I got a copy of E.B. White's *Here is New York,* where it comes from.'

Herrick looked blank.

Harland turned to the window. ' "A single flight of planes no bigger than a wedge of geese can quickly end this island fantasy." '

'Well remembered,' she said.

'There's more. ' "This race – this race between the destroying planes and the struggling Parliament of Man – it sticks in all heads. The city at last perfectly illustrates the universal dilemma and the general solution; this riddle in steel and stone is at once the perfect target and the demonstration of non-violence, of racial brotherhood; this lofty target scraping the skies and meeting the destroying planes halfway, home of all people and all nations, capital of everything, housing the deliberations by which the planes are to be stayed and their errand forestalled." '

Herrick had sat down on the bed. 'That's some prescience. But surely it's about the United Nations building, not the Empire State?'

'True, but this has some meaning for him in a general sense. Look, I don't know if the little bastard is still alive. But if Eva called me, I know it's important. She's agreed to pass on everything she has to you. I told her you were trustworthy and that you were the most natural talent I'd seen since I met your father. That intrigued her.'

'Thanks. But you're forgetting I'm washed up. Besides, I am not that good. I've made a lot of mistakes over the last month.'

'Self pity doesn't suit you.' His tone softened. 'You're not yourself. Who would be, after finding a pair of armed thugs in their house, being on the end of a brace of missiles and watching their friends being shot up? The Chief is only concerned not to lose you. Let's face it, he took the right decision sending you home.' He paused. 'I think you should go to New York. It would be good for you. You can catch the last flight. It's always half-empty.'

'I've never been to New York.'

'Time to lose your virginity then. Hand me my bag.'

He took out the address book. 'That was very thoughtful of you,' he said, waving it at her. 'Look up the number for Frank Ollins. He's with the FBI – an awkward sod, but straight and reliable. He was in charge of the Sammi Loz inquiries.' She found the number and copied it down.

He asked her to get his wallet out of the bedside cabinet and then offered her ten hundred-dollar bills. 'You'll need it, and it will save you time. There's a flight at midnight.'

'I can't take it.'

'Why not? You're working for me now, you're my agent, and you're going to be dealing with Eva. That certainly requires payment of some kind.'

'That reminds me of something in Shakespeare. I forget where it's from. My father made me memorise it for obvious reasons. 'Friendship is constant in all other things, save in the office and affairs of love. Therefore all hearts in love use their own tongues. Let every eye negotiate for itself, and trust no agent.' ' She took the money and put it in her pocket. 'Don't trust me to say what you should be saying yourself.'

'Okay, okay. Now, go catch that plane. You have my mobile number and here's Eva's.' He pulled a card from his wallet and handed it to her. 'Stay in touch. If there's anything important I'll let the Chief know.'

She bent down, kissed his cheek and let her head hang by his so that she looked myopically into his eyes. 'Thanks,' she said. 'I do owe you.'

Then she straightened, a hand still lingering on his forearm. 'I'll call you first thing tomorrow.'

She walked from the room without a backward glance.

33

The last plane from Heathrow landed at JFK at 2.30 a.m. Herrick slept most of the way, having been given an upgrade by a kindly man on the check-in desk. By the time the cab dropped her at the Algonquin Hotel on 44th Street she was beginning to feel herself again. She slept a further six hours in her modest single room, then got up and hurried to the Rose Room to meet Eva Rath. She ate breakfast, read the *New York Times* and watched agitated New York professionals pick at bowls of fruit and granola. After forty-five minutes she dialled Harland in hospital.

'Your girlfriend's a no-show.'

'Wait a little longer. She may've been delayed.'

'She *did* know I was coming? I mean, you *are* certain you told her?'

'Have you tried the number I gave you?'

'I will. I hope she bloody well answers. Speak to you later.'

She signed the bill and went upstairs to make the call, and consider what she should do if Eva Rath didn't make an appearance. As she sat by a window looking out on an already steamy Midtown, her cell phone rang.

'Hey, Isis, it's Nathan. How're you doing?'

'Fine, really. Totally recovered. Just got up.'

'The big sleep. It's way past three.'

'How can I help you?' she said tartly.

'We know what the four other suspects were doing, or at least we think we do. A vial of mysterious fluid was found in a fridge in Copenhagen, and an empty one in Sarajevo. We think the four may have infected themselves with some kind of disease. None of them has track marks, so we believe they've inhaled it or simply administered it orally.'

'Has it been analysed?'

'The Danes think it's some kind of cold virus. That set off alarms because genetic engineers have used a modified adenovirus as a vehicle to carry messages into the body.'

'What?'

'Sorry, going too fast for you, Isis? Basically, the cold virus is killed by the immune system, leaving whatever is inside the virus to do its work.'

967

'Another virus?'

'Who knows? We don't really have a handle on that right now, but if these guys are using it we can assume they're treating it as a suicide bomb. So they're all in isolation until we know what the hell they're carrying.'

'And the people who arrested them, are they in quarantine?'

'Sure, all the members of the relevant helper cells, too. The apartments where they lived have been hosed down with every kind of anti-bacterial and anti-viral agent known to man.'

'Tell me about the Haj switch. How many men have you come up with?'

'It's still five, over and above those accounted for.'

'So how many in the picture from Bosnia?'

'Isis, should I be telling you this?'

'Whose desk are you sitting at, Nathan? I want everything you've got. How many people from Bosnia?'

'The French lady is here with Philip Sarre. I talked to her last night. She's hot stuff...'

'What about the photograph?'

'So, we've got the two Rahes and Sammi Loz. Plus there's the American named Larry. We think his second name is Langer, but we're not certain. There is one other in the photo, a Jordanian named Aziz Khalil. Hélène also remembered another man of unknown origin joined the group later. His name was Ajami, but he's not in the shot. She's given us a lot of general material on the Brothers. We're getting a picture of a very tight little group, a prototypical al-Qaeda cell, though the general feeling here is that we are not dealing with al-Qaeda *per se*, but an earlier formation. As you know, a few of these men trained in Afghanistan, but just as many holed up in the tri-border region in South America. North Africa is important and the crucial thing is that the three big civil wars – Lebanon, Bosnia and Algeria – have all contributed to the Brothers' membership. There's a lot of retributive energy in them. That's a strong theme.'

'Has the attack date let out by Sammi Loz been confirmed?'

'Shit, I was forgetting. Yeah, three of them have said it's tomorrow, beginning early in the morning with a suicide bombing of the conventional kind in Hungary.'

'And ending where? In America, later the same day?'

'No, we don't think so. There's been no indication of that.'

'Let's go back to the photo. We've got three faces – three members of the Brothers unaccounted for in the arrests – Larry Langer, Aziz Khalil and Ajami. Do they match with the Haj switch?'

'We think so. But it's difficult. Dolph did all the work on this. He's still in really poor shape.'

'But he hasn't got worse?'

'No, a lot of pain and some internal bleeding. They have it under control.'

She absorbed this. The image of Rahe's wife screaming like a banshee and Harland, Dolph and Lapping sprawling on the floor of Rahe's bookshop, filled her head.

'So, there are two more people in the Haj switch that we don't have pictures for, but have you got any names?'

'These guys change identities like T-shirts. We've got a couple of Arabic names – Latif Latiah, Abdel Fatah – but they don't show up on any watch list. We don't have a clue who they are, where they come from.'

'Are the Saudis helping?'

'Kind of, but there's a lot of resistance to the idea that the pilgrimage would be used in this way. The Saudi government put in security measures during the last Haj to stop any kind of demonstration by fanatics. They're saying the switch just didn't happen.'

'Right, they watched nearly three million people, all dressed identically in white, for a full five days and can definitely say what each one of them was doing?'

'Yeah, well . . .'

'There's a really good case for threatening to release Dolph's research on this. Has anyone thought of twisting their arm a bit?'

'We've already threatened. But they're not playing. Look, I've got to go.'

'Hold on, I have a couple more questions.'

At that moment a fire truck, horns blaring, passed along 44th Street under her window. Herrick blocked one ear.

'Holy shit!' said Lyne when the noise had died. 'That kind of proximity to a fire truck means you could only be in Manhattan. What the hell are you doing?'

She reached for the packet of Camels she'd bought at Heathrow and lit up. 'Okay, so I am in New York, but it's where I should be.'

'For chrissake Isis, you should be taking time out. You looked like shit yesterday.'

'Thanks, but to answer the question at the back of your suspicious corporate mind, I am perfectly okay, utterly sane. Besides, you've only to look at the evidence to see this is the place to be. We know Rahe was here as recently as last week; we know he hired a car for three days – what for? – and we know that this entire network has been funded by money made on the New York property market. Rahe had a whole different existence here as Zachariah. Besides these things, there's a website which was dormant during the period Loz was out of New York but has now started up again. What could be clearer?'

'Hold on there, gal. What website? What're you talking about?'

'Harland has a line in on Mossad – Eva, his ex. She was meant to meet me here with information about a site they've been monitoring. I suspect that is where the confirmation came from about the assassination attempt on Norquist, though I don't have any hard evidence.'

'You're losing me.'

'Sorry, *I'm* going too fast for *you*. Look, there were two sources of information on the Norquist hit. One came through the encrypted screensaver that we had access to through Rahe. The other one has never been explained properly, but I'd put money on it that this is where it came from.'

'That's all history. Do you know what the website is?'

'No idea. Bloody Eva didn't make the breakfast meeting.'

'So what are you going to do?'

'Phone her, then start looking into Rahe and Loz's lives here. You can help by getting the Chief to release to me all SIS research on the property dealings.'

'That means I have to tell him where you are.'

'But you were going to do that anyway.'

'Stop being such a ball-breaker. I am trying to help here.'

'Right, get me that stuff and send it to isish1232004 at Yahoo. Don't encrypt it. That's like a flag to the NSA, and anyway I don't have any of the programs on my personal laptop. Just serve it up as it comes.'

'Teckman is likely to want to put your people in New York onto this.'

'That's fine.' She stubbed the cigarette out. 'Now call me whenever you get something.'

She hung up. This was okay, she thought, she could do this. As long as she wasn't expected to go to meetings and watch the hours tick away, there wouldn't be a problem. She flipped open the phone again, dialled Eva's number and got the message service. 'I don't know where the hell you are,' she said. 'But I'm waiting at the Algonquin to meet you.' She left her own number and rang off.

She ordered coffee from room service and then started setting up her Apple laptop, fitting it with a US phone adapter. By the time the coffee arrived she had typed a list of what she needed to do, half-admitting to herself that she was shooting in the dark. The first item simply read Ollins. She dialled the number Harland had given her, and within a couple of rings an alert voice answered. 'Ollins here, please state your business.'

Herrick explained that Harland had told her to call.

'Yeah, I already heard from the sonofabitch. Last time I talked with Harland he was helping a fugitive from justice, as it happens, a man whom we knew to be a terrorist. I don't know how things are in your country, Ms Herrick, but in mine that's not a good place to start when you are asking a favour.'

She waited a moment before replying. 'Did Harland tell you he was in hospital with gunshot wounds? Did he tell you that he was shot by the wife of the suspect Youssef Rahe, Sammi Loz's principal European contact, who was in New York last week using the identity of David Zachariah?' She had guessed right. All this was new to Ollins. Now she had his attention.

'No, he didn't mention it. You say Youssef Rahe was here?'

'Right. He drew money and he used a rented car. We requested information from the FBI on this yesterday and got nothing. We really need to know where he went.'

She gave him the details of the car rental, then told him there were five other men thought to be part of the network in Europe. She could hear him making notes. 'Your people should know most of this. I know it's being shared.'

He grunted. Evidently it hadn't reached him. 'Okay, Ms Herrick, what do you need from me?'

'Two things. I want to go to the Stuyvesant Empire Bank on 5th Avenue and talk to them about the account David Zachariah used. I need you to be with me because otherwise I won't get access. Second, I want to get into Sammi Loz's rooms in the Empire State building.'

'You know Sammi Loz was one of the men killed in Egypt? There was a definite ID of his remains.'

'I was there, and I can tell you there was no proof.'

This seemed to impress Ollins and he gave another of his grunts. 'Look, about the bank, Ms Herrick. I can't make it until this afternoon. I'll meet you there at three-thirty, quarter of four. I'll call ahead. We'll see about the Empire State later.'

She gave her number and told him she was wearing a dark blue T-shirt and a beige linen jacket.

She left the hotel with a little tourist map and turned right to walk the hundred or so yards to 6th Avenue. On reaching Sixth she became aware of the enormous scale of Midtown, which she hadn't at all appreciated during the cab ride in from the airport during the middle of the night. Then the compressed, thunderstorm heat of Manhattan hit her. She walked south to Bryant Park, where she drew iced tea through a straw and tried Eva again but without success. Then she made her way along 42nd Street to 5th Avenue. Passing the New York Public Library she glanced up at the couples sitting on the steps, fanning themselves in the sluggish air like a theatre audience.

It took nearly an hour of tramping up and down 5th to locate the Stuyvesant Empire Bank, which turned out to be just half a dozen blocks from 34th Street. Its frontage was so nondescript that she passed it several times. All the while the Empire State building loomed imperious and Germanic in a strange apricot light that escaped from behind the massive cloud formations to the south and west.

Just six blocks away, she thought. Less than ten minutes' walk. Rahe must have visited the Empire State the previous week. This gave her an idea. She called Lyne from the street and asked him to send pictures of Rahe and the suspects in the Bosnia photograph to her email address. She also asked for a picture of Sammi Loz.

She began to retrace her steps to the hotel while going over the details of the pictures. Lyne tried to interrupt several times, eventually saying, 'Isis, you're not listening.'

'Sorry, go ahead.'

'We've got some good information on Larry Langer. He comes from a Connecticut family. They're rich people, originally in the garment industry, who moved out of New York. Langer was a delinquent kid – a real nut. Disappeared to Bosnia for five years and returned briefly to the States in ninety-nine after wandering the globe, saying he was a Muslim. That didn't please his family because they're Jewish. They haven't heard of him since. But they have reasonably fresh pictures, and these are being released worldwide tonight, together with the Bosnia photograph of Aziz Khalil. They didn't want to do it, but now they totally buy the idea that there may be five guys still out there.'

'Send one of Langer to me.'

'You got it.'

'What about Latif Latiah, Abdel Fatah and Ajami?'

'Nothing.'

'And you've circulated all the agencies with the information. What about Mossad?'

'I couldn't tell you about that. But I guess someone has talked to them.'

'So what are you doing now?'

'Nothing much. Waiting, I guess, and working through the night. Oh, I nearly forgot, I had a call from Dolph. He's doing fine now. So's Joe Lapping.'

Seeing the tourist map tucked under her arm, a beggar in ragged shorts and T-shirt had started to bother Herrick, singing her praises in extravagant terms. 'Honey, just let me drink your bathwater,' he shouted.

Herrick spun round. 'Will you fucking well leave me alone you creep.'

'I hear you're getting into the ways of the city,' said Lyne, when she returned the phone to her ear. It was then that her eyes caught sight of a familiar walk way off down 5th. A man holding some ice-cream cones, moving through the crowds just like Foyzi had in Cairo. Then he disappeared from sight.

'Are you there, Isis? What's up?'

'Nothing. I thought I saw someone I recognised.'

'Look, why don't you get a little rest? You're doing everything you can. Oh, one other thing. I told the Chief I heard from you.'

'I knew you would – you're a bloody boy scout...'

'He agreed I could send it, but he's awful sore you're not at home watering the roses, or whatever you English girls do when you're relaxing.'

'Leave it out, Nathan.'

'Well, it's good to have it official, anyway,' he said. 'Besides, you do need to rest. Go lie down for chrissakes, or you'll be thinking you know everyone in New York.'

She hung up and made her way back to the hotel, where she took a shower and lay naked in the cool sanctuary of her room for about an hour, getting up once to try Eva again and download her email.

She arrived at the bank at exactly 3.30 to find a dapper figure dressed in a black lightweight suit marching up and down the sidewalk, talking on his cell. She pulled her passport from her shoulder bag and put it under his nose. He nodded, but continued to speak. At length he hung up and put out his hand.

'Special Agent Ollins, pleased to meet you. Your guy, Youssef Rahe, made a trip up to the Canadian border last Wednesday. We got a payment at a gas station.'

'But we know he didn't use the Zachariah cards.'

'Exactly. He paid in the name of Youssef Rahe. Maybe he made a slip or something. Anyways, we can place him at a gas station outside Concord, New Hampshire, last Wednesday at 11 p.m. That's just eighty-five miles from the border. What do you think he was doing there?'

'Picking up someone.'

'Right. That's the only reason he would go up there. The attendant remembers him because of the Arabic name. He says the car was headed north and there was a passenger inside. Who might that be?'

She lifted her shoulders.

Ollins brushed the top of his close-cropped blond hair with the flat of his palm, apparently absorbing Herrick for the first time. 'Okay, let's see these people,' he said, jerking his thumb at the bank.

They were shown into a room, where three bank executives were nervously ranged along a table. Herrick withdrew her laptop from her bag and switched it on. 'Gentlemen,' said Ollins. 'We need your help, and fast. Miss Herrick is from England and she's working with us on a counter-terrorist operation. She has something to say to you and some questions to ask. We would appreciate it if you'd do everything in your power to help her.'

Ignoring the throbbing pain in her arm, Isis began to speak slowly, breathing as calmly as she could. 'You are aware that we've already made inquiries about account 312456787/2, held in the name of David Zachariah. And we're grateful for your service. First of all, I want you to confirm that the picture I am going to show you is of the man you knew as Zachariah.' She spun the laptop round on the table.

The three executives leaned forward, two of them reaching in their pockets for reading glasses. They exchanged looks, then one said, 'That is Mr Zachariah, yes.'

'Now I'm going to show you some of Mr Zachariah's associates.' She turned the laptop back to her and clicked on the icon for the Bosnia picture. 'This is not too clear, but I want you to look at it very carefully and see if you recognise anyone.'

Again they huddled round the laptop and squinted at the image. 'Maybe it would help if you emailed us this picture and we had it enlarged and printed out,' suggested one.

All this took five or six minutes and eventually a secretary appeared with the copies of the Bosnia photograph, as well as the new Langer picture, which Herrick intercepted and placed face down on the table. As they looked again, she ran through the names she had in her notepad – Larry Langer, Aziz Khalil, Ajami, Latif Latiah and Abdel Fatah.

'We believe all these men are still at large. We are particularly interested in Langer.' She turned over the study of Langer, a haunted-looking man in his thirties with sunken eyes and a beard, smiling ruefully at the camera. 'This man appears in the other picture before you.'

'Langer, Langer,' said one of the executives.

'His people were in the rag trade – the garment industry. It's close to here, isn't it?'

'Yes, we have had dealings with the family.' He swivelled to a terminal by the wall and turned it on. For some time he worked through the files. 'Yes,' he said, pushing himself back so the others could see. 'Lawrence Joseph Langer. Date of birth, 1969. He had a checking account with us for twelve years, though it was inactive for long periods.'

'Can you look up Zachariah's records and see if there are any transactions between the accounts?' asked Ollins.

'No problem,' said the man, printing off the file on Langer.

After a few moments he spoke again. 'It seems that Mr Langer was in receipt of money from Zachariah on several occasions. But more significant, perhaps, is that Mr Langer also provided a reference when Mr Zachariah set up his account here in the late nineties.'

Ollins had the printout of the Langer account on the table and was going over it with a pen in his hand. He ringed several items.

'Look at this,' he said, pointing Herrick to a line which read, 'Account holder's address: Room 6410,350 5th Avenue, New York, NY 10118 . . . Dr Loz's rooms.'

Over the next hour they turned up two more secrets from the records of Stuyvesant Empire. A search of the name Langer-Ajami produced a business account that had remained at the bank for just eighteen months before being transferred to Lebanon. This stirred the memory of one bank official, a solicitous man with silver hair and a gold pin that pinched his shirt collar together under the tie knot. He said he now remembered interviewing Langer about a carpet import business that was going to sell Turkish rugs and matting in outlets along the east coast.

Another suggestion from Herrick unearthed dealings between accounts held at a bank in Bayswater, London, in the name of the Yaqub Furnishing Company and Yaqub Employment Agency. Herrick explained that these were almost certainly Rahe's accounts. It was noted that for a period of two years, money had flowed from a real estate company called Drew Al Mahdi to the Yaqub concerns in England. Herrick pointed out that Al Mahdi roughly translated as 'rightly guided one' and that this was a phrase used by the Shi'ite community. The bankers all shrugged and said they weren't familiar with the different sects of Islam, or for that matter Arabic.

By five, Ollins had heard enough. 'You gentlemen will keep this bank open until we have been over every account here. Is that understood? Because what you have here is nothing less than the funding of a terrorist organisation with your bank at the centre.' He scooped up all the printouts and copies of photographs and asked for an envelope to put them in. Before leaving, Herrick emailed all the pictures to Ollins at his office so he would have them in electronic form when he returned.

Outside, Ollins made his dispositions on his cell phone, ordering three colleagues into the bank immediately and redeploying others in the Bureau's state headquarters down at Federal Plaza.

'You got to understand, this happened on my watch,' he said to Herrick with a pained expression. 'You know, we've been doing every goddam thing in this city – twenty-four-hour monitoring of suspects' phone calls, email and internet usage. We've monitored their credit card spending, their bank accounts. We pay attention to the people they talk to in the street, what newspapers they read, what their neighbours say. I'm telling you, there's nothing we haven't covered in the lives of hundreds of individuals. And then we miss this, for chrissake!'

'We did too,' Herrick managed to say, though she was now very short of breath. 'All the effort was concentrated in Europe.' All she could now think of was the sense of impending panic that had swamped her in the last few minutes of the meeting. 'Could we have a drink somewhere? I'm suffering a little from jet lag and a month or so of this bloody case.'

'I'm sorry, I don't have the time,' said Ollins automatically, then he seemed to notice something was wrong. 'Hey, sure I do. There's a bar a couple of blocks away. We'll get you something to drink. Maybe something to eat, too.' He took her elbow and led her downtown to O'Henry's Tavern on 38th Street. Above them the sky had darkened into a premature dusk and as they walked big drops of rain began to spatter the sidewalk. There was a pause followed by a sudden rattle of hail on car roofs. Herrick glanced up at the Empire State before they left 5th Avenue and saw lights beginning to dot its massive flanks.

In the bar, she put her hands over her mouth, trying to control the intake of oxygen.

Ollins looked at her, now genuinely concerned. 'I know what you got. I had it myself a couple of years back.' She looked at him doubtfully from behind her hands. 'You got a panic attack,' he said. 'You want to know a breathing exercise?' He didn't wait for an answer. 'Close your eyes. Shut off one nostril and breathe in on the count of four, hold it for twelve with both nostrils closed, then let it out on a count of eight through the nostril you closed at the beginning. Okay?'

She began the exercise forlornly while Ollins ordered a Scotch and a Diet Coke. When the drinks arrived she opened her eyes.

'Keep going,' he said, smiling. 'Do ten rounds. Then I'll let you talk.'

At length the symptoms began to disappear, although her arms felt weighed down and her legs were still like jelly. She took a sip of the Scotch, shook her head and slapped her cheeks.

'Listen,' said Ollins, 'I know what it's like. Our line of work, you never relax, you don't sleep nights, you eat shit and wind up a friggin' nutcase.'

She nodded as Ollins ran through the connections they had made. At length, she found the energy to press her case on the Empire State.

Ollins hesitated. 'Sure, why the hell not? What is it exactly you want to see? I mean, we've been over the place so many times I lost count, and when we heard Loz had died we sealed the place up.'

'You never know what's to be found. I've learnt that in this last month. Every wall has something behind it.'

The barman gave them an umbrella someone had left and they ran through the rain, hugging the buildings for shelter. The temperature had fallen dramatically and along the way there were still dirty drifts of hailstones. When they got to the Empire State Ollins pushed past the crowd of tourists lining up to ride eighty-six storeys to the observatory. A security guard intoned, 'Electric storm. Observation deck closed. Inside viewing area only!'

Inside the lobby, Ollins shook hands with the guards behind the desk and exchanged some words about a Mets signing that day. Then they took the elevator to the sixty-fourth floor. Ollins brushed his hair and flicked droplets of water from his clothes.

'I gotta tell you,' he said, 'I can only be ten to fifteen minutes maximum. I have to get back to the office for a meeting.'

She murmured her understanding and thanked him. The doors opened. Ollins turned left and hurried along a corridor on the north side of the building, the light fabric of his suit flapping as his legs worked. There was no one about, and she heard not so much as a voice or telephone bell from behind the doors they passed. 'Most of these offices are waiting to be leased,' he said, gesturing left and right with a flick of his hand. 'They're too big or too small or there's not enough light. Things are tight with the downturn. And this building always feels the draught first. You know it was built just after the crash?'

They came to a door with a plate that read Dr Sammi Loz DO FAAO. Ollins took out a pocket-knife from his belt and selected a small pair of pliers. He cut a wire loop that ran from the handle to a stud on the door jamb. From it hung a notice: FBI LINE – DO NOT CROSS. He turned two keys in the door, pushed and ushered her in. Herrick found herself in a cool, spotlessly clean waiting area with a couch, several chairs and a reception desk.

'What happened to his receptionist? Did you interview her?' she asked.

'Yes, but she wasn't any help.'

'Did she know anything about the other part of his life? The deals in TriBeCa done by the Twelver Real Estate Corporation, or for that matter Drew Al Mahdi?'

He shook his head. 'We didn't know about any of that when we talked to her, but my guess is she didn't. She's your normal single mother from the Bronx. Good-looking, but no college professor.'

'Can I talk to her?'

'Yeah. Maybe tomorrow.'

Herrick went through to the consulting rooms. She pushed at a bathroom door and changing room, both of which could be accessed from the reception area, and returned to the room where Loz obviously worked. There was an expensive chair and a maple veneer table, a light box, framed diagrams of human anatomy on the wall and plastic models of the different joints lined up on a shelf. A withered plant stood in the window and some bathroom scales nearby were covered in dust, but otherwise the place looked as if Loz had left half an hour before. She took her mobile from her bag and dialled Harland, ignoring the fact that it was past 11 p.m. in London.

'I am standing in Loz's consulting room,' she said without any preliminaries. 'Everything looks normal.'

'Describe it to me,' he said.

She went through everything she could see and ended by saying, 'There's nothing here. And by the way, Eva didn't appear or call.'

Harland cursed, but she couldn't hear him because Ollins was saying he really had to leave. 'Hold on a moment would you? Frank Ollins is here and would like a word.'

Ollins took the phone. 'I hear you got shot up, buddy. That explains why you sent a woman over to do your work. Get better. I want to see those wrists cuffed when you come back to New York.' He handed it back to her.

Harland said. 'The bed! Isis, you didn't mention the treatment bed in his room. There was a really sophisticated adjustable bed. Levers all over the place.'

'Well, there isn't one.'

'That's odd. There has to be.' said Harland. 'What about the Arabic inscription on the wall, the one that says something about a man who is noble doesn't pretend to be noble.'

'There's nothing of that sort, no.'

'This could be important,' said Harland. 'Find out if Ollins has removed anything and call me back.'

Ollins shook his head. 'There was nothing to take, Everything that was here *is* here.'

'What about the treatment bed in the consulting room?'

Ollins shrugged. 'I don't know about that but I can't delay my meeting because a goddam bed's missing.'

'And the computer, is that working? It might be worth going through it.'

'I have to go,' he said.

'But I can stay and bring the keys back to you later? Federal Plaza, right? Look, I have helped you, haven't I? I'm at the Algonquin. You have my number. I'm not going to steal anything.'

He thought for a moment. 'Okay, but have them back to me by morning. And call me on the cell when you leave this evening. I'll tell the guards in the lobby.'

With that he bade her goodbye and hurried through the door, letting it swing shut behind him.

Herrick walked to the window and looked down through the rain at the traffic crawling along 5th, aware of the unearthly solitude and detachment of the building. It rose above things, she thought, literally and metaphorically. She felt the weight of its presence.

Now utterly calm, she turned on the computer and for half an hour or so went through Loz's appointments diary, making notes. She spotted the initials RN, and concluded this was Ralph Norquist because of Loz's visit to RN on May 13. She also found BJ – Benjamin Jaidi.

There was still water in the cooler. She took a cup and wandered round the room gazing absently out of the window again. Her back was to the door when she heard a noise. She whipped round. The handle was moving. Then, improbably, someone knocked, and opened the door.

34

She knew instantly that the woman standing in the doorway was Eva Rath.

'Miss Herrick?'

'Why bother to ask? You know who I am. You've been following me all day.'

The woman gave her a formal smile and approached with her hand outstretched. Herrick declined to take it and instead lit a cigarette.

'Isn't there some kind of no-smoking policy in the building?' said Eva.

Herrick shrugged. 'What do you want? There's nothing to interest Mossad here. The FBI have been over this place a dozen times.'

'Then why are you here?'

Herrick thought for a moment. 'Because I'm interested to see where Loz worked. I want to know what this is about.'

'That is simple. It is about hatred and revenge.'

'Revenge for what, exactly?'

'The failure of the Muslim world – the failure to build a functioning state in Palestine, the failed jihad in Bosnia, the failure to retain Afghanistan, the defeat in Iraq. Take your pick. There's no shortage of causes. They have to assert themselves and terrorism is the only way they can do it.'

Herrick noticed that the trace of Eastern Europe in her voice clashed with her impeccable grasp of English idiom. 'Well, they might have had a better chance in Palestine if you hadn't wiped out all the moderate politicians.'

Eva smiled again. 'And the computer, what are you looking for?'

'The site you told Harland about on the phone. That's why I'm in New York.'

'It will not be on *this* computer,' she said imperiously.

'What exactly is the site? We're surely not still talking about the encrypted screensaver on Youssef Rahe's computer in London?'

'No, no. That was used to deceive you, although we didn't know that at the time either.'

'But it predicted the hit on Norquist?'

'Which was used to distract you.'

'Did the confirmation about the Norquist hit appear on this other site?'

'Yes.'

'Then who told us about it? We had two sources saying he was going to be hit.'

'It's simple. I told Walter Vigo by phone from Heathrow, while waiting for Admiral Norquist to arrive.'

'You *know* Walter Vigo?'

'Yes, I thought Harland must have told you our history. I helped him with a problem in the East some years ago. Vigo was my SIS handler.'

It was another story, an age ago, and anyway Vigo was finally out of the picture. Or was he? That clumsy approach in the bar a couple of days before came to Herrick's mind – the strange, almost plangent appeal, so completely out of character.

'And now he's working for you – right?' she said. 'The Mossad has contact with Vigo's company, Mercator? That's why he tried to get me to give him the stuff from the bookshop in London.' She slapped her forehead. 'Of course, Vigo had me followed from the bookshop and then you trail me around town here. You people are really plugged into this case, aren't you? Did you know about the suspects in Europe all along? Was Vigo keeping you in the loop the whole way through RAPTOR?'

Eva shrugged.

'So one way or another,' Herrick continued, 'it was the old alliance. America, Britain and Israel were working on RAPTOR even though the first two had no idea they were sharing with you people.'

'We don't have time for this,' said Eva.

'Let's get this straight,' Herrick said venomously. 'This is my investigation and I do have time for it.' She paused. 'As I understand it, the significant point about the website you've been monitoring is that it started up again after three weeks of inactivity?'

'Yes. That is true.'

'And you believe it's being run from New York?'

'But not from these rooms,' said Eva. She placed her shoulder bag on the reception desk and swept Herrick with a look of appraisal. 'Harland said you were the most natural talent he'd ever seen.'

Herrick ignored this. 'The site started up again last week when Rahe was here in New York. So he could well have had something to do with it?'

'Maybe,' she said.

'The trouble is that we've never worked out who was running this thing,' said Herrick. 'We thought it was Rahe, but if you look at the money trail it must have been Loz calling the shots.'

'Maybe both,' said Eva. 'Can I have one of your cigarettes?'

Isis handed her the crush-proof packet. Eva coaxed one out by tapping it on her palm and lit it with an oblong gold lighter. Then she walked to the window to look at the lightning illuminating the clouds on the northern horizon.

'Did you know this building is hit five hundred times a year by lightning?'

Herrick couldn't help but admire the woman's self-possession, the absence of the need to explain or to excuse herself. She returned to the computer. 'I guess that's why Loz liked it,' she said.

Eva turned. 'Outside the bank, you looked sick. What was the problem?'

'You were watching me then?'

'Of course.'

'Why? Why didn't you just make yourself known? You could have joined in at the bank.'

'I wanted to see what you would do.' She stopped and tipped her ash into the waste-paper basket. 'I admit . . . I was also interested in you. Are you Bobby's girlfriend?'

Herrick turned from the screen. 'I don't do this, okay?'

'So you are?'

Herrick shook her head. 'I'm really not going to talk about it.'

'But you were ill. There was something wrong. I saw you.'

'There was nothing wrong. I was tired. I needed to eat. I do now, in fact.'

Eva revolved her bracelet on her wrist. 'What are you doing? Let me see.' She came to stand at Herrick's shoulder. 'Let's look into the computer's history.'

She pulled the keyboard towards her and began to work, eyes flicking from her hands to the screen. Then she straightened and stood back, allowing Herrick to see a list of web addresses. There was almost nothing for the last six months, but in November and December of the previous year someone had visited the official UN website and sites concerned with Palestine, Bosnia, Afghanistan, Iraq and Lebanon. Herrick began to write down the pattern of research on a piece of Sammi Loz's headed notepaper. She scrolled down the list of sites visited in the last three years, noting down about twenty of them.

'Why're you taking these notes?' said Eva.

'Force of habit,' Isis replied. As she said it, her eyes drifted to the address printed at the bottom of the notepaper. She read it several times, then got up and walked to the door. 'This is 6420,' she called out. 'This office is 6420!'

'Yes,' said Eva. 'It's still listed in the lobby as Loz's place.'

'No, you don't understand! In the bank this afternoon there was a document in which the Empire State was given as the address of the account holder – an American named Larry Langer who was a member of the Rahe-Loz group in Bosnia – the Brothers. We assumed he'd given Loz's address for the account records. But he didn't. He gave 6410 – not 6420. That means they could have another space on this floor.'

'Well, let's go and take a look,' said Eva, picking up her bag.

The storm had moved closer and the windows and polished floors flickered with lightning. But in the corridor, as they checked the office numbers, there was only the sound of their footsteps and the feathery exhalation of the air-conditioning. As they rounded a bend into one of the main corridors on the northern side, the lift bell pinged and they heard the doors open. Both instinctively withdrew into the corridor they had just searched. Herrick noticed Eva's eyes, straining to interpret the new presence on the deserted sixty-fourth floor.

They waited. A pair of heavily booted feet were approaching them – the solid, purposeful walk of a man, but a man who didn't know the floor well. They heard him pause three times to look at the door numbers.

Eva peered round the corner. 'It's okay,' she whispered, 'I think he's a messenger looking for an office.' Then she called out. 'Can I help you?'

'No, I'm doing fine,' came the reply. Herrick didn't need to see the man to know who it was. He was just a few paces away now and there was nowhere she could possibly hide. She stepped out to join Eva.

The clothes were the same: a scarf was wound loosely round his neck; the faded khaki shirt looked in need of pressing and the blue jeans were sagging and creased. His only concession to the city was an unstructured dark blue jacket.

'This is Lance Gibbons of the CIA,' Herrick said in answer to an enquiring look in Eva's eyes. 'We met in Albania. Mr Gibbons is a great believer in the value of the 'extraordinary renditions' that come from torture victims.'

'Cut the crap, Isis. You know I was right about Khan.'

'It hardly matters now,' snapped Herrick. 'What are you doing here?'

'I'd ask you the same question, but I wouldn't get a straight answer,' said Gibbons.

'We were looking over Dr Loz's offices with the permission of the FBI,' said Eva coolly. 'Are you here for the same purpose?'

'Mam, last time I saw this piece of work,' he said, jabbing his finger an inch away from Herrick's chest, 'a fucking towel-head A-rab was about to stick a needle in my arm, which meant I didn't know shit from sawdust for three days and nights.'

'You deserved it,' said Herrick, moving off in the direction of the lifts. 'You didn't see what your friends had done to Khan. I did. It was disgusting.'

'So what *are* you doing here?' Eva asked Gibbons.

'Looking for someone.'

'Who?'

'None of your goddam business.'

'Maybe we can help each other,' said Eva. 'Which office do you want?'

Gibbons said he didn't have a number.

By now, Herrick was by a small corridor which ran from the main aisle to the south of the building. She looked up and saw a sign pointing to 6410.

'Got it,' she called out. At the far end they found the door. Herrick bent down and put her ear to it. There was no sound. Gibbons moved her aside with the back of his hand and put a card into the crack by the lock but after a minute of working had failed to open the door. He stepped back and hit the door twice with his boot just by the lock. There was still no joy. Then he moved to the other side of the corridor and prepared to launch himself at the door but was stopped in his tracks by a voice coming from the northern aisle.

'Hey, you there! What in hell's name d'you think you're doing?'

The silhouette of a uniformed guard had appeared against the pulses of lightning. Herrick saw the outline of the gun, then the silencer fitted to the end of its barrel. But it was the rolling, lopsided walk of the man approaching in the gloom that made her feel as though she was seeing a ghost, for the second time that day. Before she could see his face the man said, 'Big lorry jump all over little car.'

It was Foyzi.

Herrick struggled to understand what was going on, but Gibbons evidently had no such problem. 'This is the little cocksucker I've been tailing since Egypt.'

Foyzi's rubber-soled boots squeaked the final paces to the light, and his face came into view.

'I saw you in the street buying ice-creams,' she said stupidly.

Foyzi made a little bow to her. 'Tenacious as ever, Miss Herrick.' The New York accent had been dropped in favour of an almost Wodehousian English. 'I always find opening a door is more easily achieved with the appropriate keys, don't you?' He felt in the top pocket of his uniform. 'Here we are,' he said, flourishing them. 'Now, ladies, step aside and I will open the door for us all.' He waved the gun in a small arc in front of them.

'Mr Gibbons, perhaps you would like to lead the way.'

Inside Foyzi hit a switch and fluorescent light flickered behind five or six panels in the ceiling. They walked into an unfurnished, L-shaped space with a reception desk tucked into the angle. Everything but the steel-grey carpet was white. 'Welcome to sixty-four ten,' said Foyzi, prodding Gibbons in the back with the gun. 'If you would move to the furthest door, I'll introduce you to your hosts.' Then he seemed to change his mind. 'But of course, I'm forgetting the convention that CIA people never go anywhere without a gun.' He patted down Gibbons, conjured an automatic from the back of his waistband and put it in his pocket. 'How *did* security allow you into the building with *that*?' he said with distaste. 'And ladies, would you empty your purses over there.'

Herrick's Apple Powerbook slipped noiselessly onto the desk, but not her phone, which remained in her pocket. Foyzi murmured something and set it aside, then began to sift Eva's belongings, first examining her mobile phone, then a US passport and a piece of folded notepaper. He held it up to her.

'It's a medical prescription for my mother. She has cancer – her name is Rath.'

'In Hebrew,' said Foyzi, and placed the note in his top pocket.

He went to the door at the end, opened it and beckoned them to go through. Herrick saw a room mostly lit by candles. There was a smell of incense on the air and a faint sound of music – the Sufi chant Herrick had heard on the island.

Sammi Loz was bent at the centre of the room, working at his treatment. Karim Khan lay on the bed, wearing only a loin cloth.

Loz put his hand to his lips. 'We will speak quietly. Karim is asleep.' His hands returned to Khan's leg. 'We expected you two women, but not this person. Who is this, Foyzi?'

'The man who had Khan tortured,' said Foyzi. 'He followed me here.'

'That is interesting,' said Loz. He let Khan's foot down and stepped away from the bed. 'We found that it was best to travel with Karim sedated. It has certainly helped his recovery, but he will no doubt wake in a short while, and then I think it will be good for him to meet the man responsible for his torture. It will be a pleasing symmetry, for him to see his persecutor killed. Now tell me who this is,' he said, moving to Eva. 'A nice erect posture and a firm, well-exercised figure.'

Eva returned his look with an absolute lack of fear and said nothing. Herrick absorbed Loz. He had started a beard, which gave a pronounced hook to his chin and he seemed to be thinner. The wild look she had seen in his eyes on the island had been replaced with what she thought was a rather self-satisfied calm.

He waved a remote at the CD player to silence the music. 'Isis, who is this woman?'

'I don't know. She was trying to help me find this place. You should let her go. She has nothing to do with this.'

Foyzi handed him the passport and a piece of paper. Loz read out the name Raffaella Klein.

'She's an Israeli,' said Foyzi.

Loz dropped the passport and paper and brushed his hands on his white shift, then adjusted the little white hat that signified he had undertaken the pilgrimage to Mecca during Haj. 'She has everything to do with you, Isis. You see, we watch the comings and goings in my room.'

He pointed to a monitor sitting on a pile of telephone directories. The screen was divided between a view of the consulting room and one of the reception desks. They had watched everything for the last hour or so.

'I wish now that I had asked Foyzi to install microphones also. But then we didn't know we'd have such interesting visitors.' He looked at Herrick sharply. 'Why did you come here?'

'How did you get off the island?' she shot back.

Loz placed his palm in the air as if holding a serving plate. 'Foyzi helped us. I hired him on that last night on the island. British Intelligence was paying Mr Foyzi only a little money. I could pay a lot more. It's as simple as that. It was Foyzi who gave me the idea of placing the bodies of the men he lost to suggest that we had all perished in the missile attack. It worked well, did it not? And then we were able to travel to Morocco and to Canada with very little trouble.'

'To be picked up on the Canadian border by Youssef Rahe – the Poet?' said Herrick.

'Yahya. His name was Yahya al-Zaruhn. There was no one his equal. No one! And now he is dead, killed by British spies.'

'Police actually,' said Herrick. 'But let's not forget that Rahe had a man tortured and killed to make it look as though he had died. That's hardly heroic.'

'A traitor,' said Loz. 'A filthy Jewish spy.'

Herrick sensed Eva stiffen and realised that she must have known the man they were talking about. The Mossad had certainly been wired into the Rahe-Loz network from an early stage.

'Sit down,' he shrieked suddenly.

Foyzi waved the gun and they all sank to the floor. Herrick and Eva leaned against the wall while Gibbons sat upright with his legs crossed in front of him. Loz returned to Khan and began to stroke the backs of his legs. He seemed to have resolved to concentrate on the treatment, and for nearly an hour said nothing to them. Herrick let her eyes wander the room. Near the windows there was a bowl filled with candles, the flames shuddering in the draught from the window, and some dirty plates with the remains of a meal. Propped on the table was the Arabic inscription mentioned by Harland. There were also some books, a copy of the Koran and other texts. One, entitled *Hadith Literature and the Sayings of the Prophet*, was lodged in the seat of an elaborate new wheelchair that had evidently been purchased for Khan.

The three of them exchanged glances, but each time anything meaningful seemed to pass between them, Foyzi stirred himself from Herrick's computer and gestured at them with the gun. At length, Loz stretched upwards, cracked his knuckles and moved away from Khan's side towards the windows.

'How long are you going to keep us here?' asked Herrick.

'Not now, please,' he said. He seemed to be entranced by the passage of the storm, which had swept round to the south and was creating an astonishing display over the ocean.

Eventually, Herrick could stand it no longer and started to translate the framed inscription. ' "A man who is noble does not pretend to be noble, any more than an eloquent man feigns eloquence. When a man exaggerates his qualities it is because of something lacking in himself".' She paused. 'Why does that mean so much to you?'

Loz did not turn round. 'Because they were the first words spoken to me by Yahya, in the middle of a gunfight in Bosnia. Can you imagine that sort of presence of mind? Later, he gave me that to remind me of the friendship that was born in the moment all those years ago.'

'But what about the last part of the quote?' asked Herrick. She turned and read, ' "Pride is ugly. It is worse than cruelty, which is the worst of all sins." Hasn't it occurred to you that the action you and Yahya planned in Europe for tomorrow constituted the very worst kind of cruelty – the killing and maiming of innocent men and women. The suffering is almost too great to imagine.'

He got up slowly and straightened his robe. 'We are always like this,' he said to Foyzi, as though explaining an old and cranky friendship.

'Like what?' she said. 'Last time we laid eyes on each other you were trying to rape me. Tell Foyzi what you were doing in that bath-house when the missiles struck. I'm sure he has no idea you were attempting that.'

He moved across the room as quickly as a cat, seized her by the hair and banged her head rapidly against the wall five or six times. 'Dirty white bitch lies,' he said, still holding her hair. Suddenly Herrick was in the police interrogation room in Germany, where she was hurt in exactly the same way during the Intelligence Officers' training course. Later, she had decided that it was being screamed at that she couldn't stand, and so it was now.

Eva placed her hand on her shoulder and Gibbons threw her a look of sympathy. She prayed they realised she was pushing Loz for a reason.

'That hurt,' she said. 'Why do you take such pleasure in hurting women? Is it because you fear them?'

Loz returned to Khan. 'I do not, but sometimes it is necessary.'

'No, the truth is you're a psychopath who thinks that because you heal people you are morally excused when it comes to hurting and killing. I suppose it's a kind of God complex. The great Dr Loz dispensing kindness and random acts of cruelty and slaughter, with all the capricious will of God Almighty. I had heard of doctors playing God before, but I never dreamed I'd live to see one who actually thinks he's God.'

Loz's hands stopped moving and his gaze sought Foyzi's. 'Listen to that woman,' he said despairingly. 'It reminds you of every mother.' Foyzi nodded and opened Isis's Apple.

'Is that your problem?' she said. 'Is that why you're such a fucking psychological freak? A mother problem?'

His head turned to her and he lifted his upper lip to display a row of perfect white teeth, and picked at something in his mouth. 'I have none of those problems. I am merely doing what must be done.'

'But you're not – all the men have been caught. Hadi Dahhak, Nasir Sharif, Ajami, Abdel Fatah, Lasenne Hadaya, Latif Latiah.' She included names of people they knew had been to the Haj but had not been arrested. 'Those men who were going to spread disease, and murder with explosives and poison, they're all in jail.'

'She's clever, no?' Loz said to Foyzi. 'She thinks we do not know which ones are still at liberty. She thinks she can trick us. She is in love with trickery, this girl. But she doesn't know how many soldiers we have in the field. She has no idea, which is why she comes snooping in the Empire State building. She comes to my building and pokes around with her friends.'

Foyzi nodded and walked over to the bed with the open laptop. Herrick caught a glimpse of the Bosnia picture.

'This is very impressive,' said Loz. 'Where did you get this from?'

'A British photographer.'

'Yahya . . . Larry . . . myself. The Brothers. I must certainly have a copy.'

'You can get one in the papers tomorrow.'

He nodded, lost in the memory invoked by the photograph. Gibbons glanced at Herrick and raised his eyebrows.

'We all look so young,' continued Loz. 'A decade adds much care to a man's face.' He looked down. Khan had begun to stir. He had moved his feet, and Herrick could see they were still swollen. 'We have visitors, old friend, and they have brought us a gift which reminds us who we really are and what we stand for. Sit up and see what she has found for us. Providence has blessed us at an important moment.'

Khan pushed himself up on one arm. When he saw Isis he showed signs of recognition and, to her astonishment, a hint of a smile played at the corner of his mouth.

At that moment there was a thunderclap right above the building. The lights dimmed, the glass in the windows rattled and Herrick felt a tremor shoot down the wall. The next time it happened she was sure Gibbons would try to make a move. She had felt him flinch and get ready, but then restrain himself.

Khan lay back on the bed. Loz took the computer to the window and began to read the emails she had received from Nathan Lyne that day. Herrick understood they would delineate exactly what SIS didn't know about the Brothers, and cursed herself for breaking the most basic security rule. When he had finished, he examined the prescription found by Foyzi in Eva's things.

'Again Providence has smiled on us,' Loz said to the room. 'We have an English spy, an American spy and, if I am not mistaken, an Israeli spy at our mercy. Perhaps we should kill each one as a symbolic sacrifice to Islam and put it on the internet. That would be a fine conclusion to the life of the website, a finale to beat. Foyzi, do you think you can find a webcam at this time of night?'

Foyzi nodded obligingly, but Loz's eyes had gone to Khan, who was shaking his head.

'You think that's such a bad idea, Karim? But of course, I didn't tell you who this American is. This is the man who had you tortured. Don't you recognise the American pig?'

Khan raised his head and nodded. 'Yes, he was in Albania. It is the same man. But he also gave me water. And he was not the one to torture me. It was the Arabs.'

Loz shouted and jerked the gun at Gibbons. 'Stand up. I shall kill him now. Or do you want to do it?'

Again Khan demurred.

'Why do you see everything in these terms?' pleaded Herrick. 'Arabs against Jews; Americans against Arabs. Karim just said it. It was Arabs who were prepared to torture a fellow Muslim, and worse, they did it for money.'

The intervention had worked. Loz walked off, and Gibbons let himself down on the floor again. Herrick understood why he took the risk of doing so without asking.

'Look at the United Nations.' Loz was evidently pointing to the UN building over on the East Side, although none of them could see it. 'The people in that building are responsible for the death of Muslims everywhere – in Bosnia, Afghanistan, Palestine and Iraq. That building is the source of the evil because it is run by the Americans, the Jews and the British. You three are the United Nations. Not us. You. So you are our enemy.'

'Does your plan include an attack on the UN?' asked Herrick.

Loz flashed her an appreciative smile. 'You're very smart, Isis. I told you that we were made for each other.'

She nodded. 'I should have guessed why you made so much of your contact with Benjamin Jaidi. You were staring your enemy in the eyes. What's that quote about the riddle of steel and stone?'

Loz held his head back and stared at the rain. 'It goes like this. "This riddle of steel and stone is at once the perfect target and the perfect demonstration of non-violence, of racial brotherhood, this lofty target scraping the skies and meeting the planes halfway, home of all people and all nations, capital of everything, housing the deliberations by which the planes are to be stayed and their errands forestalled." Secretary General Jaidi likes that quotation but *not* for the reason I do. If you think about it, there is not one true statement in that quotation. It is all lies. Racial brotherhood ... try being an Arab or an African. Home of all people and all nations ... capital of everything ... None of it is true. The only time the deliberations stopped the planes flying was in Bosnia when Muslims were being killed by Serbs as the West stood by. That's when the United Nations stands back.'

'Actually, I agree with most of what you say,' said Herrick.

'That's because you are an intelligent woman,' said Loz. 'And you understand in your heart that that place cannot go on. Things must be changed from the outside. It is full of corruption. It is owned by you and the Jews and the Americans. You run it as though it is your back yard. How many times do you think the Americans have vetoed Security Council resolutions against Israel?'

Herrick shrugged and said she didn't know.

'Of course you do not because you do not notice these things. But we Arabs count. The answer is thirty-four times in the last three decades. What chance do the Palestinians have with that record?'

'Are you using planes?' she said calmly.

'We are soldiers, we fight on the ground.'

'So guns and explosives – bombs?'

'No, Isis, I do not tell you. You will see soon enough. You will see everything from here, and you will hear about the other things we plan. Patience, little girl.'

Harland had used up most of his illicit supply of painkillers and was now feeling distinctly seedy. His sister Harriet was keeping him company through his sleepless nights by reading to him from the diary of Samuel Pepys, which she insisted had the right combination of titillation and longueurs. She'd told him she would leave as soon as he dropped off, but that didn't look like happening soon because Harland couldn't get used to the sensation of sleeping on his front, especially now the painkillers had upset his stomach.

'Hold on one moment,' he said to Harriet.

She smiled radiantly. 'What, darling?'

'I think I should check on someone. Haven't heard from her since this afternoon.' He eased himself from the bed, swung his legs to the floor, then groped for the phone secreted in his sponge-bag. He dialled Herrick and waited. The phone rang ten times before she answered.

'How are you?' he asked.

'Fine,' she replied.

'What are you doing?'

'Staring at the rain. There's a big storm here.'

'Are you okay?'

'Sure. I had a nice glass of wine with Ollins in the bar. He's a real charmer. Now I'm back in the hotel room with a bottle of red and a book. It's great. I couldn't be happier, nor more relaxed.'

'Isis, are you all right?'

'Sure, I'm just a bit sleepy. Early start tomorrow. Got to hang up now.'

'Isis? Isis?'

She had gone.

'Something's wrong,' he said, looking at Harriet. 'I mean, this is a woman who makes you look straight-laced and dowdy. She is utterly driven. Doesn't sleep until she's attacked a problem a thousand different ways. I've never seen anyone like her before – not in my former line of work, anyway.'

'You sound smitten,' said Harriet.

Harland brushed this aside. 'The point is that everything she said was untrue. For instance, she said she had been to a bar with Ollins. She said he was charming. Whatever his merits, Special Agent Ollins is not charming. In the circumstances, it is utterly unlike her to curl up with a book and a bottle of red wine. So it follows that when she said she couldn't be happier or more relaxed she meant she was exactly the opposite. She has to be in some kind of trouble.'

Harriet saw he was serious. 'What're you going to do?'

'I'll phone Teckman, then try Ollins.'

Standing in the centre of the room, Herrick lowered the phone and deliberately pressed the button to end the call that Loz, with some pleasure, had insisted she take while he pressed Foyzi's gun to her neck.

'That was good, Isis. You're quite the actress.' Loz laid an arm across her shoulder and gave the gun back to Foyzi. 'Another time and another place, we would have been a sublime match. As the Prophet said, "to taste each other's little honey." '

She looked into his eyes and saw an oscillation in his pupils and what she decided was a profound and insane puzzlement. 'Do you know what you're doing? I mean, do you have any real understanding of other people's pain?'

'Of course I do. Look at Karim. I have done everything that a man could do for his friend. I have cleaned and mended his body, lavished my skill on his injuries. That is an understanding of pain and it is proof of the debt I owed him.'

'What makes Karim different from the people you're going to kill tomorrow? When Langer explodes his bomb or Ajami spreads the poison that infects the bodies of children and pregnant women, or Aziz Khalil coughs out his germs, they will in all probability kill people who have a much greater capacity for good than you, Karim or I have. Why is Karim to be saved and those people destroyed?'

Loz looked mildly unsettled. 'I do not have to answer to you.'

'But you do,' she said vehemently, chopping the air with one hand. The other slipped the open phone into her pocket. 'I was the one who saved Karim Khan, not you. I risked my career to stop this man being tortured. If you don't believe me, ask Gibbons. He knows what I did. He knows I risked my father's life to free Khan and place him in your hands.' Her hand went to her pocket and pressed a button at the right-hand corner of the keypad. 'You owe me an explanation and you have a duty to yourself to reconcile these things in your head – hatred and love of humanity. Because the love you profess for Karim and Yahya is mere egotism unless you recognise that the part of them you love is the human part, the thing we all have in common.'

Loz wagged his finger. 'If I spent any time with you I would go mad from these arguments of yours.'

'It is not me that drives you mad,' she said sadly, 'it is reason.' She stopped and, raising her voice, asked, 'What good do you think will come of blowing up the UN building tomorrow? What do Langer and Khalil and Ajami and Latiah and Fatah think they're doing? Sure, they're going to kill an awful lot of people at the UN, but what good will that do? The world will look at Islam and say Muslims cannot be trusted. You will achieve nothing but the exclusion and revilement of your own people.'

Foyzi had moved round Herrick as she was speaking. Without warning, his hand dived into her pocket and pulled out the cell phone. He showed it to Loz and pointed at the number displayed on the screen. Loz looked at her furiously, took the phone and threw it against the floor, where Foyzi crushed it under his boot. Then Loz whistled round and caught her on the side of her face with the flat of his hand. Again and again he hit her until she crumpled to the floor. Finally he took the automatic from Foyzi and beat the back of her head and neck with it.

Harland had picked up the phone on the first ring and immediately signalled to Harriet to give him a pen and paper. Then, as he listened, he wrote the number of a direct line in Vauxhall Cross and frantically whirled his index finger in the air to tell her to dial it on the hospital phone.

Harriet's call was answered and she nodded to her brother. Cupping his hand over his phone, he hissed, 'Tell them Herrick is with Loz in New York. Tell them he's alive. She's left the phone on so I can hear.'

Instead of relaying this information immediately, Harriet said to the operator, 'Put me through to Sir Robin Teckman and tell him to hold for a very important call from Robert Harland. Say those exact words to him. Mr Harland will be with you shortly. This is a matter of national security.'

Harland's hand moved across the paper and he managed to write 'UN – tomorrow – bomb (?) Langer, Khalil, Ajami, Latiah.' He missed the last name and waited. But suddenly the line seemed to be overwhelmed by static, and then she was gone. He gave the cell phone to Harriet and took the hospital phone from her lap. 'See if you can hear any more . . . Hello? Hello?'

'Yes,' said the duty officer at Vauxhall Cross.

'I need to speak to the Chief.'

'I'm afraid that's not possible.'

'This is a national security emergency. Get me Sir Robin. Tell him it's Robert Harland.' He gave an old identification code that he remembered from fourteen years before.

'Just putting you through.'

After a couple of minutes the Chief came on the line. 'Bobby, what can I do for you?'

'Herrick's in New York. She's with Loz. He's alive. She kept her phone on and I heard a conversation that seemed to suggest they're going to blow up the UN tomorrow.'

'Where is she exactly?'

'I've no idea. But I just had a very odd, coded conversation with her when I called her a few minutes ago. I believe she saw a friend of mine from the FBI named Ollins, who was investigating the Loz case. She had a drink with him, so I would imagine he knows where she was going after that.'

'Then get on to your friend.'

'I tried after talking to her. His phone is off and I don't have his home number.'

'Then ring the bloody FBI in New York.'

'Yes.'

'I'll send someone round to St Mary's to be with you in case you get another call. Let me know what Ollins says and I'll start cranking up things our end. If you need to call me again, tell the operator you're ringing on a Code Orange matter. They won't mess about if you say that.' He hung up.

Harland called international directory inquiries on Harriet's cell phone, got the number of the FBI in Manhattan, and found an equally unhelpful operator on the other side of the Atlantic. 'This is very important,' he said. 'My name is Robert Harland. I am ringing from Secret Intelligence Service headquarters in London and I need you to trace Special Agent Ollins and get him to the phone. Do you understand?'

'I am sorry, sir,' said the woman at the other end. 'I cannot do that at this time.'

'What's your name?'

'I am not at liberty to tell you, sir.'

'Let me just say this to you then. Ollins is in possession of information that may avert a terrorist attack in New York tomorrow. He may not know what he has. If you wish to keep your job beyond tomorrow afternoon, I suggest you get the Special Agent to the phone. I'll wait here until you do that.'

The line went dead for what seemed a period of endless deliberation. Eventually a man's voice came on the phone. 'With whom am I speaking?' he asked.

Harland gave his name. 'I need to speak to Special Agent Ollins on a very important matter. The British government will be in touch with the US government in the next hour, but if you get Ollins for me we might just be able to short-circuit the system and avert disaster. It's up to you. I hope for everyone's sake you make the right decision.'

From the floor, Herrick could see Eva's face, but not Gibbons'. She briefly wondered why neither had attempted to help her, but then reflected that they were both professionals and were likely to be playing a longer game, keeping themselves in reserve.

She raised her head slowly, giving the impression that she was more stunned than she actually was, and indicated to Foyzi that she would like to return to her place against the wall. Foyzi waved the gun with irritation. She crawled towards Eva and Gibbons and pushed herself up alongside them. Eva darted her a look that said, 'wait'; Gibbons stared unblinkingly ahead.

Something had come to pass while she had been collapsed on the floor, too shocked and beaten to have taken much in. Loz had wheeled the bed next to the window, and was engaged in a heated exchange with Khan, although none of them could hear what was being said. Each time Khan spoke he lifted his head from the bed, the muscles in his neck strained, and his wiry legs twitched towards the floor. He was trying to get up to confront Loz on equal terms, but Loz wouldn't let him, and interrupted by pressing down on his chest, leaning into his face to rebuke him.

Herrick slid down the wall a fraction so she could see Khan's mouth under Loz's elbow. When his head popped up again she had no difficulty in lip-reading what he said. 'I don't question your judgement, Sammi. But it was wrong to hit her. You have too much violence in you and I . . .'

He was again forced down, and this time Loz's hand moved nearer his neck.

Eva spoke very quietly to Foyzi. 'My people know of you. You're a freelance. You're not committed to this madness. My government will pay you five times what he has given you.'

He shook his head. 'A deal is a deal.'

'It wasn't on the island,' Herrick snapped.

Loz turned with one hand still restraining Khan. 'Shoot them if they talk. Shoot them . . .'

The rest of the sentence was obliterated by a crack of lightning overhead. The Empire State was tapping the storm and drawing its power to earth. The lights flickered again and then went out completely. Gibbons hurled himself at Foyzi. Eva went to the right, rolling and springing to her feet like a gymnast to deliver several ferocious kicks to Foyzi's upper body, just as he loosed off three rapid close-range shots at Gibbons. The gun dropped from his hand with the final kick. Herrick dived for it and came to her feet, aiming at Loz, who had not moved from his position near the window. She glanced left and right. Gibbons was hit; Foyzi lay dead from stab wounds from a knife still in Gibbons' hand.

Nathan Lyne ran panting to Harland's room after being driven across London in an unmarked Special Branch police car that topped 100 mph on the flat of Park Lane.

Harland had put the phone down on Ollins a few minutes before. 'She's in the Empire State,' he said, turning to his address book. 'The FBI man left her in Loz's old office. She's there by herself. I'm calling a friend who was due to meet her.'

Nathan took the hospital phone and spoke on the open line to Vauxhall Cross. 'You got all that?' he said. 'What floor?'

'Sixty-fourth,' said Harland, hearing the first rings on Eva's phone.

Eva heard her phone ringing out in reception and prayed it would be her headquarters in Tel Aviv. She ran out and picked it up, together with the gun that Foyzi had taken from Gibbons.

'Yes?' she barked, turning back to the room.

'It's Bobby. Where are you?'

'The Empire State.'

'Isis kept her phone on. We heard something. Is Loz alive? What the hell's happening?'

Eva went back into the room, where Herrick was on one knee beside Gibbons. 'It's okay,' she said between breaths, 'we disarmed them. Your friend is here. She's got Loz and Khan covered.'

Harland began to speak, but Eva lowered the phone because Gibbons was saying something. His voice was a whisper. 'If you say where we are, every fucking jackass cop will be here. We don't have time for that. We don't know what these men have planned. We can't let them be arrested.'

'You're losing blood,' said Herrick. 'You need to get to a hospital.'

'Forget that,' said Gibbons. 'Just get these bastards talking.'

Harland told Lyne what he'd just heard on Eva's phone. 'They're with another man – an American. They seemed to have overpowered Loz. This man has been hit, I think. He's insisting they don't get help until they've found out what Loz was planning.'

Lyne frowned. 'What the heck are they doing?' He stopped and met Harland's eyes, then spoke to Vauxhall Cross. 'The situation is under control. Tell the FBI to hold off. This is very important.'

Eva put her phone on the table, went over to Loz and placed Gibbons's gun at his temple. At the same moment, Herrick seized the end of the bed and wheeled it away from them.

The two women said nothing to each other. The situation was beyond words.

Herrick looked down into Khan's eyes and murmured, 'I'm sorry. I have to do this.' Without thinking any more, she raised Foyzi's gun, and brought the silencer and barrel down on Khan's still-bloated right foot. He shrieked. She looked up at Loz. 'Tell us the plan. Tell us where your men are. How many of them?'

Loz shook his head in disbelief. 'You cannot do this.'

'Hurt him again,' said Gibbons from the floor.

Herrick aimed and struck again. Although she pulled the blow at the last moment, the scream lasted much longer and died only when Khan had run out of breath. She paused. Her hand slipped to Khan's side and momentarily snatched at his hand and squeezed it. The pressure was returned.

Now Eva worked on Loz. 'We've only just started. We will cause your friend unimaginable pain. Are there five men or more? Where are they? Stop his suffering.'

Loz hung his head and then shook it.

Eva nodded at Herrick, who hit Khan again.

Gibbons had dragged himself from the floor. Holding his stomach with both hands, he lurched to where the food and the candles were by the window, picked up a plastic bag, then made his way to Herrick and handed it to her. Then he threw himself across Khan's body, pinning him to the bed. Herrick looked down at Khan and wrapped the bag over his head.

'No!' shouted Loz. 'I will tell you.'

Eva stepped back and reached for the phone. 'Can you hear this, Bobby?'

Harland told her he could.

'Tell us what the plan is. Then we'll let your friend breathe.'

'There are six,' mumbled Loz. 'Three in New York. Two in London. One in Holland.'

Eva repeated this to the phone.

Khan's legs were trembling and jerking in the air, as though he was suffering a seizure.

'Let him breathe,' pleaded Loz.

'What's your plan?' Eva screamed. 'What's your goddam plan?' She hit him on the ear with the gun.

He shook his head again.

Herrick was now aware of Gibbons whispering to her. He was pointing to the TV monitor on the floor. 'The cops are in the other room,' he hissed. She glanced down and saw the figures darting across both halves of the split screen. She held the bag tighter round Khan's head. His right hand weakly tore at Gibbons's back. The other flailed in the air near Herrick. His legs stopped moving.

Eva stepped back from Loz. 'Tell us and you'll save him.'

'They are martyrs. Martyrs with explosive. You understand! Martyrs! You cannot stop martyrs who give their lives to the struggle!'

'Suicide bombers with Semtex, men spreading disease and toxic agents?'

He did nothing and she repeated the question, screaming in his ear. He nodded. 'Yes.'

'When're they going to attack?'

'They have passes for two o'clock.'

'American or European time?'

Khan had now stopped moving completely.

'Please! Let him breathe!' Eva signalled to Herrick, who pulled the bag from Khan's head.

'American time – after the other attacks.'

'There aren't going to be any other attacks. Who are these men?'

'You know some of their names,' said Loz. 'I will tell you everything if you let Khan live.'

He gave them the names, haltingly, as if he couldn't quite remember, but soon they had six names, only three of which Herrick recognised. He repeated them slowly again while Eva held the phone to his mouth. Langer, Khalil, Al-Ayssid, Ajami Hossein, Mahmud Buktar and Iliyas Shar. One American, three Arabs and two Pakistanis. He told them the men's details. Their phone numbers and addresses were on a laptop by the table, which none of them had noticed before. Everything was there, including his last message to the martyrs.

Herrick looked down at her victim and nodded to him. Only she and Khan knew that she'd punctured the bag with her fingernails before wrapping it around his head. Despite the ferocious assault on his feet, he had gone along with her and play-acted his suffocation. She bent down, stroked his hair and kissed him on the forehead. Her other hand went to Gibbons' shoulder.

Loz saw all this. He looked perplexed for a moment, then seemed to understand. 'The goddess Isis used the essence of Ra to defeat him,' he said. 'That is what you did to me. You used my essence – my love for Karim – to defeat me.'

Herrick heard this but was too concerned about Gibbons' condition to reply. She tore to the reception area and bellowed into the corridor. Within seconds, the place filled with members of the SWAT team they'd seen on the CCTV. They pressed field dressings to Gibbons' wounds and then four of them picked him up and rushed to the elevator bank. Ollins, who had come in behind the men, crouched down by Loz.

'How much information have you got from him?' he asked Eva quietly.

'He's told us there are six men, three to attack the UN building here, two in London and one in Holland.'

'Where in London? The UN offices?'

Loz's eyes had come to rest on the patterned rug a few feet away. 'This has been my prayer mat since I was a small boy. It has been with me all these years.' He smiled to himself. 'It's the only thing I have left.'

'Forget the self-pitying shit,' said Ollins. He took hold of Loz's jaw and banged his head upwards against the wall. 'Where in London? Where in Holland? How are they going to make these attacks at the United Nations?'

'He can't speak if you're going to hold him like that,' said Eva.

Ollins let go and Herrick took over. 'You've got men at the Hague. Is that right? The War Crimes court, the Chemical Weapons Inspectorate – which part of the UN in Holland?'

'You will not find these men.' Loz worked his jaw from side to side as though recovering from Ollins' assault, paused and turned to Herrick, his eyes locking onto hers with the strange, wild look she had seen on the island. He bit into something, winced and opened his mouth to reveal foaming saliva. Herrick grabbed his shoulders, more out of desperation than any hope of saving him. Then, with only the smallest convulsion, the cyanide capsule silently took his life. His head lolled sideways and a little stream of dribble ran from his mouth onto his chest.

Ollins swore and thumped the floor. Herrick sat back, shocked.

'Is he gone?' They turned to see Khan, his head raised from the bed. 'Is he dead?'

'Yes,' said Eva.

Khan's head sank back.

'He killed himself because of the failure,' said Eva. 'He killed himself because he'd told us everything.'

'What makes you so damned certain?' asked Ollins.

'Because this man lived to outwit people. Once he knew he was beaten there was no point in living. If anything was still going to happen, he surely would have waited until at least the end of tomorrow to see the realisation of his plans.'

Herrick stood up and looked over to Khan. 'Are there any more surprises for us, Karim?'

'Yes,' he said at length. 'The man called Langer.'

'Larry Langer?'

'Yes. Langer is waiting to kill the Secretary General. Jaidi got him a job at Sammi's request six months ago. He has a pass that allows him anywhere in the building. He is waiting there now for Jaidi to meet the Israeli Ambassador to the United Nations for breakfast in his office.' He stopped and looked up at Herrick. 'If you bring me that computer, I will show you the other plans.' His hand flopped out towards the laptop. 'You see, Sammi told me everything because he trusted me. But you saved me, Isis Herrick, and now I will help you.'

Twenty-one days after that night in the Empire State building, Isis sat down for dinner with her father and Harland – effectively three generations of British Intelligence officers, as Munroe pointed out – at a pub in the Western Highlands. There were still several hours of daylight left, but they'd been forced to abandon fishing on the loch nearby because clouds of midges had risen when the wind dropped, making it impossible for them to concentrate. She glanced at Harland's face, already covered with tiny red blotches from midge bites, but he still looked jubilant. An hour before, he had caught his first sea trout from the old wooden rowing boat they were using. It was a big specimen, weighing just under five pounds, which had snatched at the fly as he dragged it across a ripple on the water, then fought for its life for a full twenty minutes before being landed.

They had said little to each other during the day and now there was silence between them. Without warning, her father rose to his feet in the empty dining room and held his tumbler of whisky up to her and then to Harland.

'This is to you two,' he said. 'And to the most remarkable intelligence operation of the last two decades.'

Harland smiled and, when Munroe sat down, raised his own glass to Isis. 'It was your success.'

She couldn't agree with them. She shook her head and stared down at the table mat.

'What is it?' her father asked. 'Come along, spit it out.'

'I hurt Khan ... real pain ... deliberately inflicted to get the information. That's torture, whichever way you look at it.'

'Yes, but even Khan understood why you had to do it,' Harland told her. 'Without it, those men would have caused havoc with their bombs and poisons and diseases. It was an operational necessity. You took the only course open to you in the circumstances. I know. I heard it all through Eva's phone.'

'Yes, but I did it without thinking. That's how these things happen – you slip into them without realising the threshold you've crossed. I'm no different from The Doctor, or Gibbons for that matter.'

'That's the world we live in,' said Munroe gently.

'But it shouldn't be,' she replied, turning to her father. 'If we are to stand for anything, we have to preserve our standards and morals whatever the price. The only way we can argue for our system and beliefs is if we are utterly rigorous with ourselves as well as other people. We have to make sacrifices not to become like the other side.'

Her father looked at Harland, who spoke. 'It's a matter of weighing the lesser of two evils. You were there and you had to make a decision. Besides, Khan went along with it. As a result he will soon be a free man, and can rebuild his life. That's all you need to take from this.'

'The question is, would I have done it anyway – without his cooperation?' She paused and put her hand up to her father who was about to interrupt. 'And the answer is yes, I would.'

Munroe tapped his daughter on the hand. 'Enough of this,' he said. 'Now, let's think about what we're going to order so we can get back on the water as soon as possible. The conditions are perfect and there's a bit of a breeze coming up.'

Herrick looked out over the slate grey loch but her mind was still in the Empire State.